W9-AKY-621

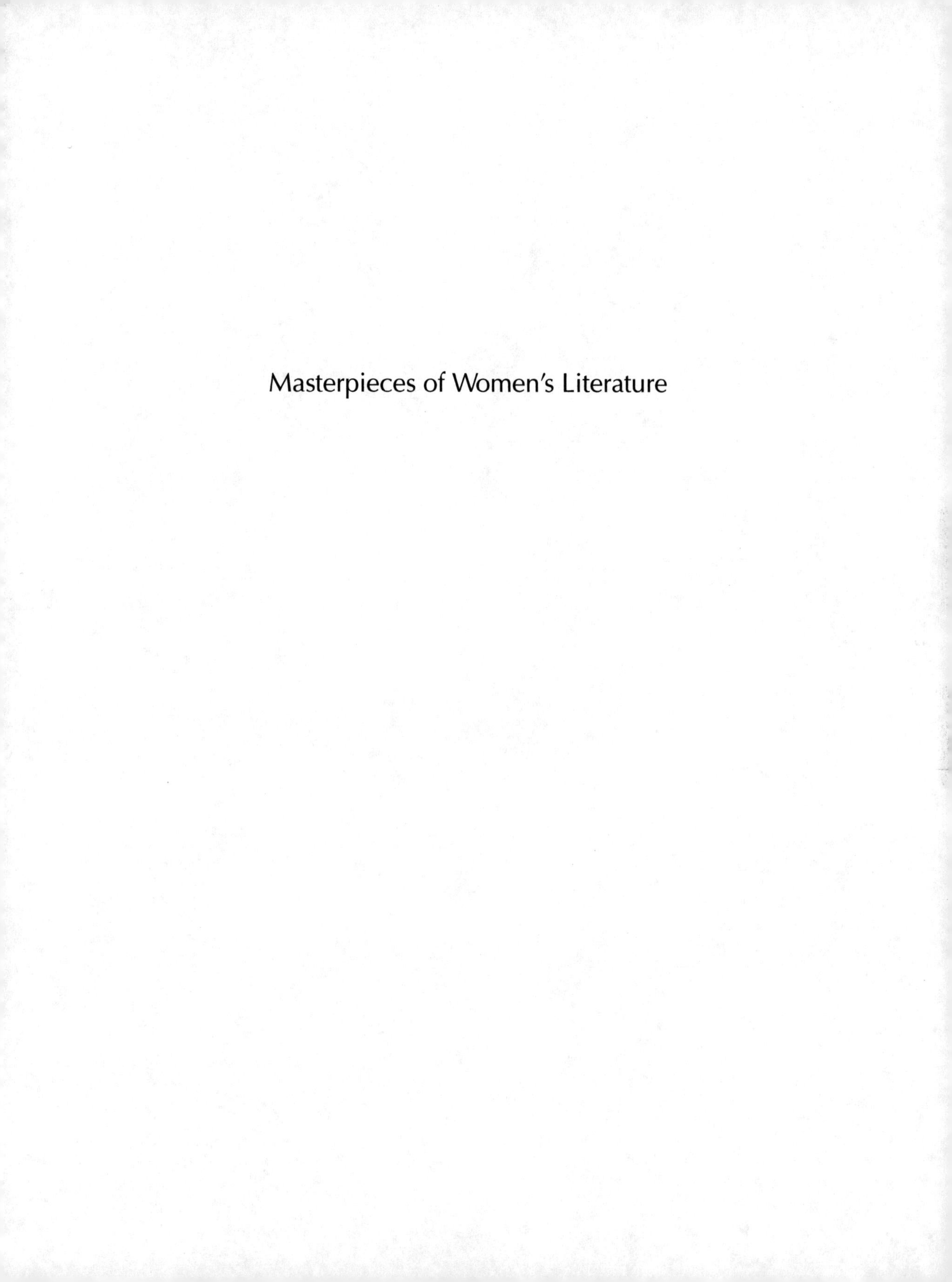

Masterpieces of Women's Literature

Masterpieces of Women's Literature

Edited by
Frank N. Magill

HarperCollins*Publishers*

 For information address HarperCollins Publishers, Inc., 10 East 53rd Street, New York, NY 10022.

FIRST EDITION

Library of Congress Cataloging-in-Publication Data is available

ISBN 0-06-270138-X

96 97 98 99 00 01 RRD 10 9 8 7 6 5 4 3 2 1

Preface

Masterpieces of Women's Literature is a companion volume to *Masterpieces of World Literature* (1989), *Masterpieces of African-American Literature* (1992), *Masterpieces of American Literature* (1993), and *Masterpieces of Latino Literature* (1994). This latest volume serves as a response to the growing field of women's studies and the reevaluation of the relationship between women and writing. This collection of essays emphasizes women's history and experience, feminist theory, and women's issues as it examines some of the most important works of fiction and nonfiction authored by women. The scope is broad—from ancient Greece to the late twentieth century, and from fourteen countries. In choosing works to be analyzed in this volume, an attempt was made to cover a relatively broad spectrum of women's literature by genre and by race, nationality, ethnicity, sexual orientation, and time period. As a result, the rich tradition of literature by women writers is displayed. The ideas of such influential women as Virginia Woolf, Simone de Beauvoir, Adrienne Rich, Toni Morrison, Sylvia Plath, Christa Wolf, Maya Angelou, Gertrude Stein, Colette, Margaret Mead, Wendy Wasserstein, Bell Hooks, Maxine Hong Kingston, Sor Juana Inés de la Cruz, Anne Frank, Leslie Marmon Silko, Joan Didion, Gloria Steinem, and Anaïs Nin can be found.

Masterpieces of Women's Literature contains 175 standardized articles. Of these essays, 76 examine works of nonfiction: autobiographies, diaries, memoirs, essay collections, history and current affairs, literary criticism, and social criticism, including such classic feminist tracts as Mary Wollstonecraft's *A Vindication of the Rights of Woman* (1792) and Betty Friedan's *The Feminine Mystique* (1963). The women's movement can be traced from Christine de Pizan's *The Book of the City of Ladies: A Fifteenth-Century Defense of Women*, to the *History of Woman Suffrage* (1881-1922) compiled by Susan B. Anthony and her colleagues, to such modern texts as Susan Faludi's *Backlash: The Undeclared War Against American Women* (1991). In addition, the trend toward revisionism in literary criticism, views of both male and female sexuality, and theology can be seen in Sandra M. Gilbert and Susan Gubar's *The Madwoman in the Attic* (1979), Susan Griffin's *Pornography and Silence* (1981), and Mary Daly's *Beyond God the Father: Toward a Philosophy of Women's Liberation* (1973), respectively. Essays on an equally broad range of fiction make up the other 99 articles: novels, novellas, poetry collections, plays, and short-story collections—most chosen because they address feminism or women's issues directly, some selected so that important authors would be represented. Articles analyze the poetry of Sappho and Emily Dickinson, the short fiction in Angela Carter's *The Bloody Chamber and Other Stories* (1979), and such plays as Lillian Hellman's *The Children's Hour* (1934) and Ntozake Shange's *for colored girls who have considered suicide* (1976). The novels covered include *The Yellow Wallpaper* (1892), by Charlotte Perkins Gilman; *The Awakening* (1899), by Kate Chopin; *Their Eyes Were Watching God* (1937), by Zora Neale Hurston; *Wide Sargasso Sea* (1966), by Jean Rhys; *Fear of Flying* (1973), by Erica Jong; *The Color Purple* (1982), by Alice Walker; and *The Handmaid's Tale* (1986), by Margaret Atwood.

The articles in this volume in the *Masterpieces* series are organized in an easy-access format with helpful ready-reference features. Each article begins with carefully checked reference data: the author's name and vital dates, the type of work such as short stories or literary criticism, and the original date of publication (including the foreign-language title and publication date where applicable). The essays analyzing history texts, memoirs, diaries, and autobiographies—works in which the lives of real people and events are presented—offer information concerning time period and location and a list and brief description of the principal personages of the text. Essays that examine novels and plays provide a genre category, identify the time period and setting of the plot, and then list and briefly describe the work's principal characters. The articles on plays also give the year and location of the first production. All essays then offer four sections of text: "Form and Content," "Analysis," "Context," and "Sources for Further Study." The first section serves as an overview of the subject of the work, while "Analysis" delves into the themes and ideas that each author is examining. The section entitled "Context" seeks to take a broader view in relation to women's literature. This section examines the influence of the work on other women writers and on literature as a whole, any controversy that arose from its publication, or the message the author attempts to convey through her female characters or through a discussion of her own experiences. This viewpoint often reveals the connections between the diverse works covered here and allows readers to follow the neverending quest of women to speak and live freely. A secondary bibliography furthers this purpose by offering a list of additional sources.

At the end of this volume, readers can find both an author index and a title index to aid them in locating particular works of interest.

Each of the essays in this volume is signed by the author. We would like to acknowledge the many fine academicians and other writers who contributed essays to this collection.

Frank N. Magill

Contents

CONTENTS

CONTENTS

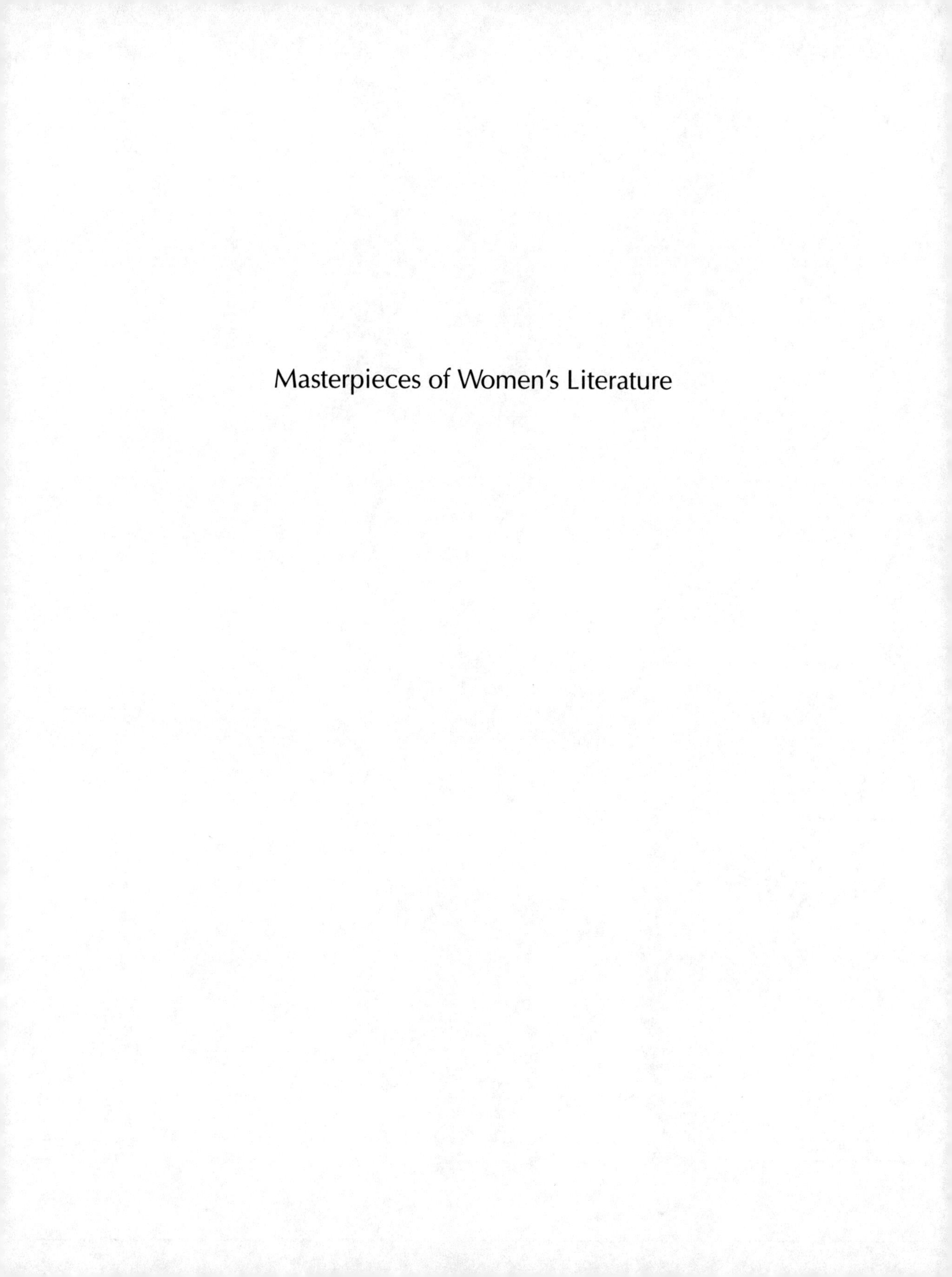

Masterpieces of Women's Literature

ADAM BEDE

Author: George Eliot (Mary Ann Evans, 1819-1880)
Type of work: Novel
Type of plot: Social realism
Time of plot: 1799-1801 and 1807
Locale: The fictional towns of Loamshire and Stonyshire, near the Staffordshire-Derbyshire border in rural England
First published: 1859

Principal characters:

Adam Bede, a carpenter in love with Hetty

Hetty Sorrel, an attractive but shallow and narcissistic orphan living with her aunt and uncle

Arthur Donnithorne, the heir to the Donnithorne estate, who seduces Hetty

Dinah Morris, a Methodist preacher from Stonyshire

The Reverend Adolphus Irwine, the Rector of Broxton and Vicar of Hayslope

Bartle Massey, a schoolmaster who counsels Adam

Seth Bede, Adam's compassionate, dreamy Methodist brother

Rachel and **Martin Poyser,** Hetty's aunt and uncle

Form and Content

Elaborated from a prison confession recounted by George Eliot's aunt, *Adam Bede* began as a fourth story for *Scenes of Clerical Life*, but it grew to a densely realized novel of rural, semifeudal English life. For an audience conditioned to accept class subjugation and a double standard in sexual conduct, Eliot dramatized the sufferings of a dependent class when the economically powerful behave irresponsibly, emphasizing particularly the traumatic isolation of a young farm woman seduced by a wealthy "gentleman."

Chapter 17, often cited as Eliot's artistic creed, argues that realism is necessary to moral art because the idealized, and therefore false, characterizations in contemporary fiction wrongly directed readers' sympathies, thereby denying sympathy to people who actually existed and also denying the proper cultivation of the moral sentiments expressed to readers. Eliot saw this cultivation as the true objective of art. She revolutionized characterization in fiction by her realistic psychological analysis and motivation, asking readers to "tolerate, pity, and love" their imperfect fellow mortals, including the oft-misrepresented laboring classes. Such direct address to readers was quite within the fictional conventions of Eliot's time. Indeed, the moral perspective of her male narrator, whether tender, wise, or ironic, organizes and carries forward the plot quite as much as action and dialogue.

The story, developed chronologically, begins on June 18, 1799, in a rural workshop where carpenters exchange homely comments on humanity's religious duty. Adam Bede, the foreman, introduces part of the theme: A man does as much good by building something that his wife needs and living productively as by ostentatious worship. His brother Seth leaves to hear the visiting preacher Dinah Morris, and, in chapter 3, the narrator broadens the theme: Morality based on human sympathy, such as that felt by Dinah and Seth, radiates through a community more effectively than abstract doctrine voiced by unreal characters. Speaking in the rural dialects that she knew, Eliot's characters dramatize the interpersonal dynamic that she hoped would replace religious debates in fiction.

Scenes alternate between the Hall farm, the Bedes' cottage, the rectory and Donnithorne estate, the school and church, and the outdoors, developing the characters and their milieus. Adam's growth begins when he discovers that his father drowned in a brook and, regretting his harsh judgment of his father's excessive drinking, he pities weakness. Hoping that the beautiful Hetty Sorrel will come to love him, he works hard to earn the financial base needed for him to marry. Hetty, however, has succumbed to Arthur Donnithorne's temptations. The heir to the estate meets her secretly in the woods near his hunting lodge, determining several times to break off the affair, which is forbidden by class boundaries as well as sexual mores. He is unable to sustain his resolve, however, despite nonspecific cautions uttered by the unknowing Adam and the Reverend Adolphus Irwine. In August, striding through the woods that Arthur has appointed him to manage, hopeful because of his improved financial position, and thinking well of both Hetty and Arthur, Adam comes upon the lovers kissing. Hetty flees and Arthur pretends innocence, but Adam calls him a "scoundrel," fights him, and forces him to write to Hetty disclaiming any meaningful attachment. In November, the resigned Hetty accepts Adam's proposal, and a March wedding is planned.

Then in February, pretending a visit to Dinah, Hetty goes to Windsor to find Arthur, but learns that his regiment has left for Ireland. Hints about her figure reveal that pregnancy has caused Hetty's journey, and the pitying narrator leaves her returning in despair. Back in Hayslope, just as Hetty is missed, word arrives that she is imprisoned in Stoniton for infanticide and will not speak. Witnesses at her trial provide missing details that establish guilt, and she is sentenced to be hanged, with the narrator emphasizing Adam's suffering and grief. Then Dinah arrives and awakens Hetty from terrified paralysis; she confesses to having abandoned, not murdered, her child. Just as she is to be hanged, Arthur gallops up with a commutation of the sentence to deportation. Arthur joins the army to prevent Adam and the Poysers from departing rather than continuing to work for him. Eighteen months later, a softened Adam marries Dinah, and the epilogue shows their loving family six years afterward. An ill Arthur has returned home to improve his health, but Hetty has died.

Analysis

The narrative voice, the drama, Adam's growth, and Dinah's loving presence structure the dominant spirit of *Adam Bede* as sympathetic relation, "our best insight and our best love." Repeatedly, characters are made realistic by the narrator's passionate reminders that when counselors fail to reach those they would save from disaster, when young people determine their own downfall, when young men in love misread the feelings of the loved one, when mothers are fearfully possessive toward their sons—when struggling mortals fall short of perfection—such everyday conditions prove the very humanity that should call forth "fellow-feeling."

Eliot's technique includes dramatizing the realities of class distinctions in mass gatherings and small groups, showing individuals defined by work relationship or its absence. A tone of reverence suffuses the products and the process of human labor. Scenes alternate between the indoors (the workshop, the Bede home, the rectory, the Hall farm) and the outdoors (the green, the woods, the churchyard, the orchard and garden) picturing the full range of a community. Characters are further developed by contrasts, such as Adam and Seth, Adam and Arthur, Dinah and Hetty, and Dinah and the Reverend Irwine. Ironies abound: Adam has been wrathful toward his derelict father just before finding him drowned; he is cheerfully hopeful about Hetty just before he sees her kissing Arthur; unknowingly, he voices confidence in Arthur's conscience and desire to do right; as Arthur is rationalizing away his earlier resolve to confess, the Reverend Irwine believes that his character will safeguard him from temptation with Hetty; Arthur is unable to understand the just-published poem "The Rime of the Ancient Mariner," a tale of wanton destruction leading to guilt followed by ongoing penance.

The story opens with the metaphor of a mirror reflecting reality, as preserved in the narrator's Wordsworthian memory. Hetty's mirror, however, reflects not reality but the fantasies that she spins as she admires her alluring face and neck, just as Arthur's mirror reflects his self-deluded fantasies. Dinah chooses to look not at a mirror but through a window; her prospect lies outward in community, not inward in fantasy-driven isolation. Adam's vision of the future is based on work and his belief that a man should leave the world a better place than he found it. Arthur pictures his future self receiving love for his generosity.

Eliot's theme of sympathy secularizes religious imagery. Seeing the wretched Hetty on trial, Adam remembers her under the apple boughs in the garden. The schoolmaster Bartle Massey reenacts the Last Supper as he brings bread and wine to Adam in an upper room while Dinah watches with Hetty. Adam's growth to a new power of loving is described as baptism and rebirth. Thus does Eliot embody her themes realistically in her characters, their speech, their action, and the consequences that they suffer or enjoy.

Context

Recognition of Eliot's feminist concerns has come less readily than for some nineteenth century novelists, partly because the perspective of the male narrator in her early works has been read as Eliot's perspective. In general it is, but the narrator's specifically male attitudes insist on emphasizing the suffering of men, Adam and Arthur, when the woman is the real victim. Eliot introduced this masculine voice that diminishes the significance of women in *Scenes of Clerical Life*, telling women's stories behind the appearance of men's. *Adam Bede* is Eliot's only complete novel to use this male voice before the author's true identity became known. It is consistent with her irony that the masculine narrator delineates realistically the nineteenth century world of men going on with their lives as the woman is punished and fades away.

Such fiction is a disappointment to feminist readers who hope to see heroines rising to new heights despite obstacles imposed by a patriarchal culture. Yet Eliot's literary aesthetic defined such a pattern of writing as idealized, as based on the author's sentimentalized fantasy, and therefore misleading. She knew well a woman's struggle to survive economically and to fulfill her creative potential, and she was committed to fiction based on the new concept from the French known as realism. Her achievement lies in having heightened readers' sympathetic awareness of the plight of working-class women—and of the men who supported or suffered with them—caused by culturally established gender stereotypes and limitations. Many contemporary readers were moved by Hetty's story.

Dinah also reveals Eliot's feminist concerns. She is ridiculed by some for preaching, but the Reverend Irwine finds Dinah a remarkable person. She succeeds in breaking Hetty's silence when others have failed, and she proves a more worthy wife to Adam than Hetty would have been. She must submit to the Methodist Conference's ban on women preaching, faulted by Seth's male view, but she embodies most fully Eliot's theme that it is feelings, not "notions," that hold a community together and give individuals the strength to bear their burdens.

Other elements point to the author's concerns for women. Rachel Poyser's having "her say" to the old Squire may be an object lesson to the too-outspoken, but her spirit, incisive wit and metaphor, and excellent home management also argue strongly against the stereotype of female docile passivity. Dependent older women—Lydia Donnithorne, Mrs. Irwine and her daughters, Lisbeth Bede—remind readers that male inheritance lines and economic control can limit men as well as humiliate women. Hetty's anger toward Arthur, and Adam's insistence that Arthur be punished as well and suffer equally with Hetty are more effective arguments against the double standard than later treatises proved to be. The unrelenting delineation of Hetty's childish, uncomprehending despair and terrified denial personalize the "fallen woman" cliché. Finally, the brilliant stroke of capturing woman-hating and woman-denigrating in Bartle Massey's comical diatribes against his dog Vixen, the woman in his life, ridicule such attitudes even as they amuse the reader.

Adam Bede was her last work before George Eliot was identified as Mary Ann Evans. Fiction by other women had received only reluctant praise, but this novel was deemed "first-rate" by a reviewer for *The (London) Times* who thought the author male. Since critics could not retract praise already published, perhaps the book's major impact was in proving that a woman's art could be just as admired as a man's if she could write anonymously and circumvent gender prejudice.

Sources for Further Study

Barrett, Dorothea. *Vocation and Desire: George Eliot's Heroines*. New York: Routledge, 1989. This book offers helpful insights concerning conflicts between women's desires for creative fulfillment and culturally defined gender limitations.

Beer, Gillian. *George Eliot*. Bloomington: Indiana University Press, 1986. Reappraises Eliot's struggle toward self-definition as a woman and an artist. Includes historical background, a bibliography, and an index.

Brady, Kristin. *George Eliot*. New York: St. Martin's Press, 1992. Summarizes contemporary reactions to Eliot and explains the historical gender assumptions that Eliot both worked within and tried to reform.

Haight, Gordon. *George Eliot: A Biography*. New York: Oxford University Press, 1968. This book offers the essential factual base for studying Eliot and her work.

______________, ed. *The George Eliot Letters*. 9 vols. New Haven, Conn.: Yale University Press, 1954-

1978. These volumes offer the best source for Eliot's own voice—candid toward those whom she trusted and distant, circumlocutious, or self-protective toward those whom she did not. Haight's notes and commentary are indispensable.

Hardy, Barbara. *Critical Essays on George Eliot*. New York: Barnes & Noble Books, 1970. This collection by a pioneer in Eliot studies helped interest critics in feminist analyses of her work.

Marshall, Joanna Barszewska. "Shades of Innocence and Sympathy: The Intricate Narrative Syntax of Gossip, Metaphor, and Intimacy in Eliot's Treatment of Hetty Sorrel." In *Dorothea's Window: The Individual and Community in George Eliot*, edited by Patricia Gately, Dennis Leavens, and Cole Woodcox. Kirksville, Mo.: Thomas Jefferson Press, 1994. Analyzing Eliot's narrative art, this article supports the argument that her treatment of Hetty is more sympathetic than many critics have recognized.

Pinney, Thomas, ed. *Essays of George Eliot*. New York: Columbia University Press, 1963. These selected essays represent some of Eliot's ideas about religion, education, the role of women, and standards for judging literary art that appear most frequently in her fiction.

Showalter, Elaine. *A Literature of Their Own: British Women Novelists from Bronte to Lessing*. Princeton, N.J.: Princeton University Press, 1977. This study relates women writers to one another and suggests ways to place Eliot's work in a continuity of similar attempts.

Uglow, Jennifer. *George Eliot*. New York: Pantheon Books, 1987. This critical biography examines in detail the interworkings between Eliot's life and her art, offering thoughtful analyses of her fiction in the context of Victorian feminism. Includes a chronology, a bibliography, photographs, and an index.

Carolyn F. Dickinson

ADAM, EVE, AND THE SERPENT

Author: Elaine Hiesey Pagels (1943-   )
Type of work: Literary criticism
First published: 1988

Form and Content

Elaine Pagels' work *Adam, Eve, and the Serpent* revisits and revises a number of her previous scholarly articles to make them more accessible for general readers. The six chapters trace varying and often clashing interpretations of the Creation accounts of Genesis during the first four centuries of Christianity. These interpretations, which culminated in the fifth century with the triumph of Augustine's writings on Original Sin, indicated that early Christianity was not monolithic, but included a range of remarkably diverse viewpoints that deny the existence of an early age of purer, simpler Christianity. Within this context, Pagels analyzes how early Christian interpretations of the Creation story, particularly those related to Eve's role in Paradise, established traditions that would define attitudes toward marriage, sexuality, and women for the next millennium and a half.

Beginning with ancient attitudes toward sexuality and moving chronologically through the struggles of the early Christians in the Roman Empire, Pagels' analysis of Christian ascetic movements and shifting imperial politics shows how interpretations of the Creation stories came to establish a particular view of humanity's fallen state and the role of woman in leading humanity astray. Because of Eve's corrupting function, the Christian Fathers ordained man to be the master of woman, and they condemned woman's sexuality. Pagels concludes by looking at how Augustine, whose arguments came to dominate Christian thinking after the fifth century, sealed this process. Augustine's pessimistic views of sexuality and human nature, based on the idea that Original Sin visited a ritual sin on all humanity thereafter, eventually colored all of Western society.

Predominantly a work of intellectual history, Pagels' book intricately traces how ideas about sexuality and moral equality arose. It focuses on the works of early Christian writers—both those who produced the gospels and later commentators who expounded on what the Scriptures had to say about marriage, family, procreation, and celibacy. Each chapter of the book analyzes a particular question or controversy sparked by the interpretations of the Creation story, and then resolves how and why Christian leaders adopted particular resolutions to those controversies. Furthermore, Pagels speculates on the impact of Judeo-Christian attitudes toward sexuality and human nature. The connections that she makes between history and the ideas that illuminate it create a cohesive work, both in form and in content.

Brief in its presentation, this book is broad in scope. Pagels' research into the development of the early Christian church ranges from Jewish traditions to Gnostic writings and orthodox thought. One area in particular on which the author draws is her familiarity with the texts from the Nag Hammadi Library, which were brought to light in 1945; they serve as a valuable reflection of the diversity of thought about women and sexuality in Christianity's beginnings. These Gnostic writings represent a group that resisted orthodox views of Eve's influence on the Fall of Man, which is why the church soon branded them as heretical. Although many of the texts presented in the book contain complicated reasoning, throughout her work Pagels maintains her goal of making them understandable to the general reader. Twenty pages of notes further illuminate her research.

Analysis

Using historical means to explore the origins of Christianity, Pagels argues that Christian views of freedom changed as Christianity moved from being a persecuted movement to being the official religion of the emperors. Inherent in these views of freedom were attitudes toward women and sexuality that emerged from varying interpretations of the Creation accounts in Genesis. Repeatedly throughout the book, Pagels emphasizes how the story of Adam and Eve came to be the justification for moralists to explicate their own situations and establish their own beliefs. For example, in chapter 1, she demonstrates how second century writers transformed the Genesis story into one of moral freedom and moral responsibility. This view placed new strictures on marriage by promoting celibacy as a higher form of Christian life and by instructing those who did marry to subordinate their desires of the flesh and reserve sex for procreation only. These views came primarily from writers who perceived celibacy as the "better" form of Christian life, a life that would separate new converts from the bonds of family pressures and social obligations and tie them instead to their "brothers and sisters in Christ." Stories of martyrs, such as the young wife and mother Perpetua, who defied her father's pleas to renounce her religion and return to her loving family, spread across the empire and emphasized the message that Christianity was a route to freedom.

The main way to achieve this freedom soon came to be a renunciation of the world to take up a life of poverty and celibacy. Pagels argues against those who see the Christian ascetic life as a demonstration of hatred of the flesh. There were, she admits, some interpretations of Adam and Eve that marked the flesh as sinful and evil: The fourth century ascetic Jerome, for example, even switched the verse order of Genesis to show that marriage followed sin and therefore encapsulated evil. Pagels contends, however, that celibacy in the third and fourth centuries often marked freedom for the individuals who pursued an ascetic life—freedom to overcome sexual passion and the world's restrictions. To demonstrate this point, she analyzes the anonymous fourth century biography of Melania the Younger, a wealthy matron who persuaded her husband to agree to a life of celibacy. With the emperor's help, she and her husband maintained control of their wealth and used it as they traveled through Africa, Egypt, and the Holy Land, founding and directing monasteries. This life allowed Melania more freedom than other married women: She retained her wealth, traveled freely, and directed her own spiritual pursuits as well as those of others in the monasteries that she established.

Despite such accounts, most Christian writers of the third and fourth centuries continued to draw their perceptions of women from their moral interpretations of Genesis. Tertullian, a second century convert, used the third chapter of Genesis to warn his Christian sisters that God's sentence against Eve lived on in them. The Christian church's standard view was that women, as co-conspirators with Eve, therefore were consigned to being lower elements in God's creation. Whereas Adam represented reason and the mind, Eve embodied passion and physicality. No wonder the Gnostics were declared heretical when they suggested that Eve represented a spirit presence that awakened Adam's mind to his spiritual nature, bringing about a marriage that created a harmonious union in the soul. The orthodox church would not accept an Eve who was an awakening spirit rather than the cause of sin. Pagels further asserts that the burgeoning institutional church feared the Gnostics' denial of the community ethics being imposed on all believers.

Finally, Pagels resolves the question of how Augustine's interpretation of Original Sin came to dominate Christendom. Against those who would say that Augustinian theology won the day because of its deeper truths, she contends that Augustine's interpretation of Adam and Eve's sin as the paradigm for the ordering of human society meshed with the requirements of an authoritarian state. Augustine argued that Eve's sin had led to a universal and irrevocable fall for the whole human race. No longer could humans control their passions or even govern themselves, and certainly they had brought upon humanity the unnatural evils of pain, suffering, and death. Original Sin, therefore, made both secular and ecclesiastical governments necessary. Augustine's elucidation of why humans needed governance came at a crucial time in history and provided a palatable rationale for an alliance of church leaders and emperors.

Context

Pagels' work represents the expanding influence of feminist scholars on the study of early Christianity. While the general impetus for this movement comes primarily from the perception that the Old and New Testaments treat women inequitably, Pagels elucidates even further the unfair views of women that emerged when initial Christian interpreters used the Scriptures as the basis for adopting attitudes toward sexuality and succeeded in creating a template that continues to govern individuals and society. Detractors warn that she reads her own personal agenda into the texts she scrutinizes, thus allowing that agenda to drive her scholarship. Still, Pagels remains one of the foremost authorities on Gnostic writings and has staked out her position as an authority on their powerful feminine imagery and ideology. In *Adam, Eve, and the Serpent*, she uses that knowledge to bring about a clearer understanding of Christianity's burgeoning attitudes toward women.

She joins a prestigious group of women—among them Phyllis Trible, Carol Meyers, and Francis Schüssler Fiorenza—who are reinterpreting how and why the Bible and its explicators justified the subordination of women. They are pioneers who, despite engendering much criticism, have opened new doors, asked pointed questions, and reminded their readers of the role that human minds had on shaping and sculpting religious attitudes toward women and humanity in general.

Elaine Pagels is also the author of *The Johannine Gospel in Gnostic Exegesis: Heracleon's Commentary by John* (1973); *The Gnostic Paul: Gnostic Exegesis of the Pauline Letters* (1975); *The Gnostic Gospels* (1979), which won the National Book Critics Circle Award and the National Book Award in 1980; and *Nag Hammadi Codices XI, XII, XIII* (1990), a translation of Gnostic writings. She was awarded a MacArthur Prize Fellowship in 1981.

Sources for Further Study

Brown, Peter. *Augustine of Hippo*. Berkeley: University of California Press, 1967. Brown's work, hailed as a definitive biography, provides a scholarly and thorough account of Augustine's life and writings. He focuses on how Augustine's inner transformations led him to precipitate changes in the world around him. Augustine's explications of the Genesis story and Original Sin are well detailed, but Brown does not emphasize their impact on women as Pagels does.

____________. *The Body and Society: Men, Women, and Sexual Renunciation in Early Christianity*. New York: Columbia University Press, 1988. A broad study of the patriarchal control of reproduction from the time of Christ to Augustine's fifth century restatement of the idea of self-control as the necessary restraint on sexual intercourse. Brown's strict analysis precludes any speculation about women's experiences since he focuses solely on male attitudes toward the body.

Clark, Elizabeth. *Women in the Early Church*. Wilmington, Del.: Michael Glazier, 1983. Clark presents an anthology of translated excerpts from many of the writers and texts to which Pagels refers. An extensive introduction provides an overview of the role of women in early Christianity, and explanatory notes precede each section.

Grant, Robert M. *Early Christianity and Society: Seven Studies*. San Francisco: Harper & Row, 1977. In opposition to Pagels, who finds early Christianity's preoccupation with sexuality and marriage as a striving to be different from paganism, Grant, in these independent studies previously presented as lectures, documents the social, political, economic, and cultural parallels of pagans and Christians. This general study serves best as background material.

Kraemer, Ross Shepard. *Her Share of the Blessings: Women's Religions Among Pagans, Jews, and Christians in the Greco-Roman World*. New York: Oxford University Press, 1992. A volume intended to accompany *Maenads, Martyrs, Matrons, Monastics: A Sourcebook on Women's Religions in the Greco-Roman World* (1988), Kraemer's English translation of hard-to-find primary materials dealing with women's religious beliefs and observances. This work provides a survey of the period from the fourth century B.C.E. to the fourth century C.E. and is an excellent source for basic information. Theoretically, Kraemer's stand is that women could achieve autonomy in religion only by repudiating their bodies and, thus, denying their sexual and reproductive capabilities.

Meyers, Carol. *Discovering Eve: Ancient Israelite Women in Context*. New York: Oxford University Press, 1988. A book that draws on biblical sources, archaeology, and social anthropology. One chapter illuminates the "Genesis Paradigms for Female Roles." Meyers' study provides a much-needed basis for understanding the Judaic background to early Christian views of Eve's role in the Creation story.

Marylou Ruud

AGAINST OUR WILL: Men, Women, and Rape

Author: Susan Brownmiller (1935-)
Type of work: Social criticism
First published: 1975

Form and Content

Susan Brownmiller was one of the first politically active feminists in New York City during the 1960's. Her interest in women's rights surfaced in much of her work as a free-lance journalist, and an article that she wrote about Shirley Chisholm, the first African American congresswoman, developed into a biography for young readers. In 1971, Brownmiller helped to organize a "Speak-Out on Rape," and in the process she realized that she had material for a book. She submitted an outline of her idea to Simon & Schuster and began researching the subject of rape. After four years of research and writing, she published *Against Our Will: Men, Women, and Rape*.

Against Our Will explores the history of rape, exploding the myths that, according to the author, influence one's perspective on the act. She traces the political use of rape in war from biblical times through the Vietnam War, explains the origins of American rape laws, and examines the subjects of interracial rape, homosexual rape, and child molestation. Brownmiller asserts that rape is a conscious process of intimidation by which all men keep all women in a state of fear. Supporting her thesis with facts taken from her extensive research in history, literature, sociology, law, psychoanalysis, mythology, and criminology, Brownmiller argues that rape is not a sexual act but an act of power based on an anatomical fact; it is the result of early man's realization that women could be subjected to a thoroughly detestable physical conquest from which there could be no retaliation in kind.

Against Our Will was serialized in four magazines and became a best-seller and a Book-of-the-Month-Club selection, and its nationwide tour made Brownmiller a celebrity. Her appearance on the cover of *Time* magazine on January 5, 1976, as one of the twelve Women of the Year for 1975 and on television talk shows as a frequent guest confirmed the timeliness of her book. Since Brownmiller's analysis of rape presented a new and controversial viewpoint on an already provocative subject, *Against Our Will* was received with mixed and at times passionate reviews, some of which were critical of Brownmiller's research methods and conclusions.

Analysis

Brownmiller's analysis of rape opens with a speculative historical survey of the origins of laws prohibiting rape, beginning in biblical times. Because of the inescapable differences in the construction of human sexual organs, human males are natural predators and human females natural prey. Brownmiller speculates that female fear of an open season of rape, rather than a natural inclination toward monogamy, motherhood, or love, was the single most important factor in woman's dependence on man for protective mating. The price of woman's protection by man against man was the imposition of rules relating to her chastity and to monogamy. A crime committed against her body became a crime against male property. Concepts of hierarchy, slavery, and private property, Brownmiller argues, depended upon the initial subjugation of woman.

Subsequent concepts of rape and its punishment in early English law reflect lawmakers' confusion as to whether rape was a crime against a woman's body or a crime against the male estate. In thirteenth century English law, the principle of statutory rape—felonious carnal knowledge of a child in which her consent is immaterial—first made its appearance.

The next chapter, and the longest in the book, studies the incidence and motivations for rape during war. Rape has accompanied wars of religion as well as wars of revolution, although by the twentieth century rape had been outlawed as a criminal act under the international rules of war. The American Uniform Code of Military Justice punishes rape by death or imprisonment, yet it persists. Among the ancient Greeks, rape was socially acceptable behavior well within the rules of warfare, an act without stigma for the warrior. Not until 1385 was rape prohibited in the conduct of soldiers. Although officially frowned upon, rape remains a hallmark of success in battle. Throughout the ages, triumph over women by rape became a way to measure victory, a part of a soldier's masculinity and success, and a reward for services rendered.

An aggressor nation rarely admits to rape; documentation of rape in warfare is something the other side collects and publicizes once defeat becomes a fact. Men of a conquered nation traditionally view the rape of their women as the ultimate humiliation, as part of the enemy's conscious efforts to destroy them. Rape by a conquering soldier destroys all remaining illusions of power and property for men of the defeated side. Brownmiller studies the occurrence of rape in World War I, World War II, Bangladesh, and Vietnam.

The chapter "Riots, Pogroms, and Revolutions" examines rape during the American Revolution, the pogroms in Russia and the Ukraine, the Mormon persecutions in the American West, mob violence and rape directed against African Americans by the Ku Klux Klan, and rape in Africa during the 1960's.

"Two Studies in American History," the fifth chapter, analyzes rape on the frontier, where the rape of American Indian women was not thought of as significant. Interestingly, in the captivity narratives of white women held prisoner by American Indian tribes, rape was a rare occurrence, for reasons that are still poorly understood. The second half of this chapter analyzes the rape of black women by white men as an institutional crime associated with slavery, part of the white man's subjugation of a people for economic and psychological gain. Since the slaveholding class created the language and wrote the laws pertaining to slavery, legally the concept of raping a slave simply did not exist.

"The Police-Blotter Rapist" examines the statistical profile of the rapist and finds the largest concentration of offenders to be in the sixteen- to twenty-four-year-old age range. According to the Federal Bureau of Investigation, forcible rape is one of the most underreported crimes, primarily because of fear or embarrassment on the part of the victim. Consulting authorities, Brownmiller finds that articles on rape in psychology journals are almost nonexistent. She argues against Freudian assumptions that see rape as a thwarted urge directed against the mother, or as an expression of natural male urges toward dominance and aggression. Instead, she agrees with studies that see rape as rooted in a subculture of violence and peer group displays of machismo. A woman is perceived by the rapist as both hated person and desired property. Hostility against her and possession of her may be simultaneous motivations for the rapist. Rape is an act against person and property in one violent crime. In group rape, the male ideology is most evident. Male bonding in the act of group rape stems from distrust of and contempt for women. The chapter concludes with analysis of the rarer, but still real, phenomenon of rape-murder.

The seventh chapter, "A Question of Race," examines interracial rape. African American men historically have received the stiffest penalties for raping white women and the mildest sentences for raping African American women. Throughout much of the South's slaveholding history, a death sentence awaited the slave found guilty of interracial rape. Famous Southern rape cases, including the Scottsboro, McGee, and Till cases, illustrate the racism underlying rape charges when the accused is a black man. Brownmiller concludes this chapter with an analysis of the revolutionary ideology that embraces rape as a defensible act in the writings of militants Franz Fanon and Eldridge Cleaver.

"Power: Institution and Authority" studies homosexual rape in prison settings as an acting out of power roles within an all-male, authoritarian environment in which the younger, weaker inmate is forced to play the role that in the outside world is assigned to women. Prison rape is a product of the violent subculture's definition of masculinity through physical triumph. Brownmiller then turns her attention to police rape, an abuse of power committed by those whose job is to control such abuses of power. Her chapter on rape by an authority figure then turns to the sexual abuse of children.

"Victims: The Setting" argues that women are, in a sense, trained to be rape victims. The word itself acknowledges a woman's special victim status. The male myths of rape that emphasize a woman's complicity in her attack or that argue for woman's innate masochism, as Freudian psychoanalysis does, are revealed. Again, the distortions of popular culture, including newspaper accounts of rape, are analyzed as they influence and often misrepresent an act that is always a terrible ordeal for the woman who experiences it.

The final chapter "Women Fight Back" argues a feminist perspective on rape that includes an antipornography position since pornography, to many feminists, encourages and validates male domination and control in sexual relations. Pornography, like rape, is a male invention, designed to dehumanize women and to reduce the female to an object of sexual access. According to Brownmiller, to free society of rape, it is necessary to free it of distorting, antiwoman propaganda.

Context

Against Our Will was an important work in the history of women's issues for its impact in the press and as a best-seller. It sparked public debate on the problem of rape and the male ideology of domination that Brownmiller argues surrounds the act. The book was of value to feminism for the research that the author marshalled in making her claims about women's victimization and for the support that it gave to feminists who were convinced of vital causal connections between pornography and violence against women. For many readers, Brownmiller's work forced them to make connections about social problems that had been too long evaded, and it changed the way that many felt about a subject that had been too long taken for granted—relations between the sexes. *Against Our Will* was listed among the outstanding books of the year by *The New York Times Book Review* in 1975.

Brownmiller's next book, *Femininity* (1984), is less confrontational in tone than *Against Our Will*, but it still provoked mixed reactions. *Femininity* examines the ideal qualities—both physical and emotional—that are generally considered feminine and the lengths to which women go to conform to those ideals. Brownmiller's work *Waverly Place* (1989) is a fictionalized account of a New York attorney and his lover who were accused during the late 1980's of beating to death their illegally adopted daughter; a feminist understanding of battery and abuse informs the author's treatment of the case.

Sources for Further Study

Groth, A. Nicholas. *Men Who Rape: The Psychology of the Offender*. New York: Plenum Press, 1979. This book examines the psychological and emotional factors that predispose a man to react to situational and life events with sexual violence. Provides a framework for understanding the developmental histories, the lifestyles, and the motivations of men who rape.

Nass, Deanna R., ed. *The Rape Victim*. Dubuque, Iowa: Kendall/Hunt, 1977. A collection of articles focused on the problems faced by the rape victim and articles dealing with the therapeutic response to this trauma. The psychological pain experienced by the rape victim arises not only from the event itself but also from societal factors that intensify her suffering.

Sanday, Peggy Reeves. *Fraternity Gang Rape: Sex, Brotherhood, and Privilege on Campus*. New York: New York University Press, 1990. A study of sexual practices on college campuses that explores the role played by pornography, male bonding, degrading jokes, and ritual dances in the gang rape of women at fraternity parties.

Walker, Marcia J., and Stanley L. Brodsky, eds. *Sexual Assault: The Victim and the Rapist*. Lexington, Mass.: Lexington Books, 1976. A collection of articles assessing rape and the criminal justice system, the impact of rape at different stages in the victim's life cycle, rape at work, medical treatment for the victim, the history of the women's movement in changing attitudes and laws, myths and realities about the rapist in treatment, and rape and race.

Warshaw, Robin. *I Never Called It Rape*. New York: Harper & Row, 1988. This book combines survey results and scholarly perspectives with first-person accounts to explain what date rape is, how it happens, and how it has remained a hidden crime for so long. Warshaw explores the magnitude of the problem, the attitudes of men who rape women they know, and the devastating aftereffects.

Roberta M. Hooks

AIN'T I A WOMAN: black women and feminism

Author: Bell Hooks (Gloria Watkins, 1952-)
Type of work: Social criticism
First published: 1981

Form and Content

Emerging out of Bell Hooks's frustration with the failure of the black liberation movement and the women's liberation movement to include the concerns of black women, *Ain't I a Woman: black women and feminism* traces the oppressive forces of racism and sexism as they affect black women in the United States. It argues that race and sex are intertwined aspects of identity and cannot be understood apart from each other. Written from a feminist perspective, the book examines the impact of sexism on black women during slavery, the devaluation of black womanhood, sexism among black men, racism among white women, and black women's involvement with feminism. In so doing, it attempts to move beyond racist and sexist assumptions regarding black women and to further the dialogue about and understanding of their experience. Finally, as it shows the deep interconnections between sex and race, the work places black women's struggle for liberation in the context of a larger movement for the liberation of all people.

Ain't I a Woman is structured as a critique of the dominant misconceptions, myths, and stereotypes regarding black women that white society has developed and fostered and that many black women have been socialized to accept. Beginning with the passage from Africa and slave life, the book describes the brutal methods slavers used to break black women's will—methods that included rape, whipping, and branding—thereby establishing the origins of the devaluation of black womanhood. It continues with the horrible treatment of black women slaves, illustrating how household labor was not necessarily less degrading than field labor: Black women slaves in the household were under constant surveillance, at the mercy of the whims of their mistresses and the lust of their masters.

Looking at the repercussions of slavery, Hooks discusses the racist mythology which depicted all black women as sexually loose and the stereotypes of Aunt Jemimas, Sapphires, and Amazons. She attacks the mistaken notion of matriarchy in the black family, reminding the reader that black women had none of the power commonly associated with matriarchs. She addresses the problems of the job market, explaining that although many black men have remained unemployed, refusing low-status jobs was deemed acceptable for them. In contrast, black women often had to sacrifice their personal dignity, all the while encountering condemnation for their efforts.

In addition to her historical account and her confrontation of stereotypes, Hooks examines the sexist exclusion of black women by Black Power advocates and the racist exclusion of black women by feminists. She shows how various civil rights advocates and Nation of Islam supporters emphasized the authority of the black man. Further, she documents how white feminists have been reluctant to heed the concerns of black women. For example, despite the claims of some white feminists that the women's liberation movement has a long antiracist tradition, Hooks points out that white women in the nineteenth century tended to be antislavery but not antiracist. Indeed, part of the efforts of white women in the abolition movement were motivated by the desire to keep white men away from black women. Furthermore, many white suffragettes argued that white women should be granted the right to vote on the grounds that it would help maintain white supremacy.

Yet, Hooks reminds those in both the Civil Rights and the women's movements that neither racism nor sexism can be overcome through separatism. Real change requires that people confront those attitudes within themselves and then find ways to work together for social transformation. She concludes with a view of feminism as neither a struggle to end male chauvinism nor a movement for equal rights. Instead, it is a commitment to ending domination on a variety of levels, including sex, race, and class.

Ain't I a Woman is an inspired and angry work. Having grown up in the segregated South, Hooks wrote it while working as an operator for the telephone company and sought directly to meet the needs of the other black women with whom she worked. Her goal was to write a book that would both improve their lives and make other people aware of the hardships of being black and female. Thus emerging from pain and rage, the book exposes the strengths and sufferings of black women. Indeed, Hooks's ability to engage the reader comes as much from her disturbing content as from her passionate tone. As it argues for the connection between racist and sexist oppression, *Ain't I a Woman* challenges its readers to pursue a collective and multi-dimensional approach to liberation.

Analysis

Ain't I a Woman analyzes how racist and sexist oppression have prevented a positive valuation of black womanhood. As it does so, it critically engages a variety of authors and assumptions, indicating their racist and sexist blind spots. A major theme of the book is how a preoccupation with black male masculinity has hidden and distorted the experiences of black women, leading to mistaken assumptions regarding "strong black women" whose dignity rests on their capacity to cope with and endure oppression and degradation. These assumptions, Hooks argues, have led to the erasure of black women's identity. The term "women" tends to refer primarily to white women; the term "black" or "Negro" tends to refer primarily to black men.

Hooks develops her argument by confronting the widely held view that the predominant damage caused by slavery was the demasculinization of the black male. She shows how, in fact, white patriarchy enabled African males to maintain a semblance of their societally given masculine role; they performed only "masculine" tasks and were encouraged to adopt traditional sex roles in the slave subculture. In contrast, many African women were assigned heavy labor. They were usually bred like cattle. Furthermore, those who worked as "house slaves" were often raped by their owners and brutalized by the owners' wives. To this extent, they came to be seen as the "other," the opposite of the real lady as idealized by the "cult of true womanhood." This patriarchal value system held that women were delicate, chaste, and feminine. Since black women were hardworking, sexually available, and "nonfeminine," they did not count as women at all. Thus, Hooks points out that far from demasculinizing black men, the experience of slavery masculinized black women.

Hooks also shows the continuation of the devaluation of black womanhood after slavery, taking white feminists to task for ignoring the sexist oppression of black women after manumission. For example, she criticizes Susan Brownmiller's *Against Our Will: Men, Women, and Rape* (1975), arguing that Brownmiller fails to acknowledge that the rape of black women has never received the same sort of attention as the rape of white women. Hooks explains that because of the slave system, which led to the designation of black women as sexually depraved, immoral, and loose, black women have been seen by the white public as sexually permissive and eager for sexual assault. Black women have been viewed as incapable of being raped.

To demonstrate the racist ideology that has made the term "women" synonymous with "white women," Hooks raises arguments against white feminists who have been unwilling to distinguish among varying types and degrees of oppression and discrimination. She points out that white women in the women's movement wanted to project an image of themselves as victims in order to gain entry to the job market. This image clashed, however, with black women's experiences as employees, as the maids and housekeepers of white women's children. Moreover, it ignored the fact that many lower-class women and women of color had to work, that not working was the privilege of middle-class white women. In this respect, Hooks offers a strong critique of Betty Friedan's *The Feminine Mystique* (1963), showing how it made the white middle-class "housewife" into a victim while ignoring the exploitation of poor black and non-black women in the American economy.

Although much of Hooks's argument exposing the impact of the slave system on understandings of black womanhood focuses on the racism of white feminists, she does not ignore the way in which many black women have themselves internalized racism and sexism. She explains that when confronted with racism in the women's movement, a number of black women responded by forming separate black feminist groups. While she perhaps underestimates the positive role of these groups in facilitating exchanges among black women and giving them a sense of community and purpose, she convincingly details many of the negative repercussions of separatism. First, segregated groups perpetuated the very racism that they were designed to attack, leading to the even greater polarization of the women's movement. Second, they failed to provide a critical assessment of the movement and a notion of feminism untainted by racism. Third, they forfeited the opportunity for coalition-building, enabling white women to continue to think of race and sex as unconnected. Thus, Hooks concludes that separatism serves primarily the interests of white men, pitting women against women and allowing white men to establish the meaning of liberation and freedom, success and opportunity.

Hooks teaches that as long as liberation means having the same power that white men have, white and black women will remain at odds with one another. This power is inherently divisive, denying the connections among people and creating a world of oppression and opposition. Yet once women cease to accept the idea of divisiveness and break through the myths, stereotypes, and assumptions that deny their commonality, they can grasp the connections between race and sex and begin forging a new sisterhood. This sisterhood will be one of accountability, whereby women take responsibility for ending division and oppression and recognizing the dignity and diversity of all people.

Context

Ain't I a Woman played a major role in changing the direction of feminism in the 1980's. Writers such as Michele Wallace, in *Black Macho and the Myth of the Superwoman* (1979), and Angela Davis, in *Women, Race, and Class* (1981), had begun criticizing the preoccupation with black male masculinity and discussing the concerns and experiences of black women. By directing many of her remarks to white feminists and adopting an explicit feminist perspective, Hooks challenged white feminists to attend to the diversity of women in whose name they speak and write. Because of Hooks's impact, feminists are more attuned to the differences of race and class, the importance of coalition-building, and the need for inclusion.

Furthermore, a number of feminists have drawn from the arguments that Hooks develops in this and other books. They have incorporated the idea of "speaking from the margins," or using one's oppressed or excluded status as a position from which to critique dominant practices and ideologies; employed her concept of a "self in relation," a nonindividualist notion of the person that attends to the importance of relationships; and abandoned the "woman as victim" mentality characteristic of some types of consciousness-raising. Other works by Hooks include *Feminist Theory from Margin to Center* (1984), *Talking Back: thinking feminist, thinking black* (1988), and *Yearning: race, gender, and cultural politics* (1990).

Sources for Further Study

Collins, Patricia Hill. *Black Feminist Thought: Knowledge, Consciousness, and the Politics of Empowerment*. Boston: Unwin Hyman, 1990. A critical, interdisciplinary overview of prominent black women thinkers, including Hooks. Synthesizes the contributions of black feminism as it argues for dialogue, accountability, and empowerment. The extensive bibliography is especially helpful.

Lerner, Gerda, ed. *Black Women in White America: A Documentary History*. New York: Vintage Books, 1973. A collection of documents, reports, diary entries, and speeches relating to the experiences of black women in America. Both Lerner's introduction and her extensive bibliographical notes make this an invaluable research source.

Mohanty, Chandra Talpade, Ann Russo, and Lourdes Torres, eds. *Third World Women and the Politics of Feminism*. Bloomington: Indiana University Press, 1991. A collection which builds from Hooks's insights into the interlocking systems of domination—race, sex, and class. Representative of one of the important directions of feminist theory in the 1990's.

Moraga, Cherríe, and Gloria Anzaldúa, eds. *This Bridge Called My Back: Writings by Radical Women of Color*. New York: Kitchen Table, Women of Color Press, 1981. One of the first major collections of writings by women of color, this work contributed to the redirection of feminism in the 1980's.

Smith, Barbara, ed. *Home Girls: A Black Feminist Anthology*. New York: Kitchen Table, Women of Color Press, 1983. A collection of some of the important contributions of black women to feminist writing.

Jodi Dean

ALONE OF ALL HER SEX: The Myth and the Cult of the Virgin Mary

Author: Marina Warner (1946-   )
Type of work: Social criticism
First published: 1976

Form and Content

In the culture of Western Christianity, the Virgin Mary has symbolized the ideal of female virtue. *Alone of All Her Sex: The Myth and the Cult of the Virgin Mary* examines different facets of Mary's persona to see how her myth and cult developed from the origins of Christianity to the present. Warner's interest in the myth of the Virgin arose from her experiences of parochial education whose rituals of devotion to Mary were designed to foster ideas of sexual purity and chastity in young women. By studying the ways in which the Virgin's myth was constructed, Marina Warner demonstrates how her exalted position undermines female worth and dignity.

The organization of the book is based on the major roles that the Virgin Mary assumed as her cult developed. The five sections look at her status as virgin, queen, bride, mother, and intercessor. To an extent, this sequence represents the chronological development of the Virgin's cult in Western Christianity. The issue of Mary's virginity concerned the early Church. The queen and bride were prominent concepts in feudal society of the twelfth and thirteenth centuries. In the Late Middle Ages, the focus shifted to the Virgin's life experiences as a mother, although with the Counter-Reformation's promotion of the Immaculate Conception, her maternal qualities waned. Finally, because the Virgin has always been called upon as intercessor, the last section provides an opportunity to study rituals connected with her cult.

Alone of All Her Sex can be read on two levels. On the one hand, the book is a work of historical research that provides a comprehensive documentation of the myth and cult of the Virgin. Warner utilizes an interdisciplinary approach that considers evidence from theological writings, anthropology, the sociology of religion, and art history. On the other hand, Warner subjects this extensive and varied material to critical analysis to expose the underlying negative or misogynistic attitudes toward women that are inherent in the myths surrounding the Virgin and the devotional practices associated with her cult. The book's feminist message is interwoven within the body of material that she has assembled and presented in elegant and often evocative prose. Its persuasive power comes from the scope of the documentation and from the author's balanced and rational tone.

Analysis

The essence of the Virgin Mary as the ideal woman is her virginity. This concept, according to Warner, controls the structure of the Virgin's myth and therefore provides a justification for the association of sex with sinfulness and for making women, with their reproductive processes, a continual reminder of this state of sin.

Accordingly, the first section examines how the Church and popular belief conspired to inculcate and reinforce the belief in Mary's virginity. Warner's discussion of this issue provides a good example of how she argues her thesis. She thoroughly analyzes the basic textual sources about Mary in biblical Scripture and in Apocrypha. In both cases, she demonstrates that there is little evidence for Mary's virginity in general or for a virgin birth in particular. Only strained interpretations and mistranslations by early Christian theologians or popular literary invention in the Apocrypha provide textual basis for Mary as virgin. The heritage of antiquity added support for virgin birth through mythology and Aristotelian philosophy, which accorded the female only a subordinate physical place in conception and birth. Finally, the early Church Fathers added the crucial moral dimension by emphasizing sexuality as the Original Sin which led to death and by advocating virginity and asceticism as the ideal state in which a Christian should live. Thus while Mary's virginity became essential to the idea of Christ's divinity through his human incarnation, the exceptional status of the virgin birth reinforced the concept of women's role in the sexual corruption of humanity.

A consequence of the belief in Mary's virginity was the question of what happened to her body after death. Did her complete and unique purity absolve her from mortal decay? Warner takes up this problem in the second section on the Virgin Mary as queen. She first considers the doctrine of the Assumption. She recounts the theological sources and visual iconography that amplified the idea that although Mary died, her incorrupt body was assumed into heaven. By her position as Mother of God and the special privilege of her assumption, she became the Queen of Heaven. The power elites of the medieval period drew on her regal status to reinforce their hegemony. In this guise, she became particularly associated with the sacerdotal power of the Church in the papacy and with the secular power of medieval courts. This aspect of the Virgin Mary, however, only created a wider gap between the actual inferior position of women and the unattainable ideal of this virgin queen.

Bridal images associated with Mary are closely related to her status as Queen of Heaven. In the third section, Warner considers Mary as bride and object of amorous devotion. The primary source of the Virgin as bride is the Song of Songs, the Old Testament poem of intensely beautiful and passionate love imagery. The Church chose to interpret this language allegorically by making Christ the lover and merging the Church (*ecclesia* is feminine in Latin) with the Virgin to become his bride. The height of this nuptial theology in the sermons of Saint Bernard coincided in the twelfth century with the development of the vernacular secular love poetry of the troubadour. When the lyric verses began to focus on an ideal of the courtly lady's love as pure and unobtainable, the Church was able to transfer this affective sentiment to the idealized virginity of the courtly Virgin Mary. These attitudes continued to reinforce the gulf between the real emotions expressed in human sexuality and the idealized, chaste love that Mary represented. Again, the affection directed toward the Virgin heightened the contrast with the reality of submissiveness and inferiority of women.

Although the Virgin Mary was accorded her central position in Christian belief because she was the Mother of God, her maternal qualities were not given prominence until the later Middle Ages. In the fourth section, Warner looks at the association of motherhood with the Virgin. Inspired in part by the Franciscans, who promoted empathetic imitation of Christ as a vehicle of popular piety, two maternal aspects of Mary were emphasized. First, she became the Madonna of Humility, who often knelt before her infant son and whose milk not only nursed the infant Christ but also served as a symbol of love, wisdom, and healing. Second, she was the sorrowing mother, *Mater dolorosa*, through whose deep grief the passion of Christ could be experienced. Both aspects of the maternal Virgin defined characteristic female virtues of docility, sweetness, humility, and ultimately submissiveness and dependence on men.

This section also discusses one particular theological dogma, the Immaculate Conception, which asserts that Mary was not only a virgin but was conceived, born, and lived without the stigma of Original Sin. As "the most perfect created being after Jesus Christ," she became even more remote from the actual experience of women. Out of this distance created by the Virgin's idealization arose antitypes represented by Eve and Mary Magdalene of women who sinned primarily through their abuse of sexual relations but who could undergo penance and redemption. Their human shortcomings, however, strengthened the misogynist association of the female gender with sin.

The aspect of the Virgin Mary's cult that has been most enduring concerns her activity as intercessor, the subject of Warner's fifth section. She examines the acts of devotion directed toward Mary's power of intercession by praying to her through relics, icons, the rosary, and at special shrines. People implore the Virgin's intercession for healing, for fertility, for defense in time of war, and especially for remission of suffering after death. Warner explains and probes these rituals without being judgmental about an individual's faith or belief. She does point out, however, that even as intercessor, the Virgin's position as a woman is defined only in relation to a man since she cannot act alone but rather through the mercy of her son, Jesus Christ.

The epilogue brings together the primary paradox that is present in all facets of the Virgin's cult. On the one hand, she is unique. She was immaculately conceived without Original Sin; childbirth and motherhood did not violate her virginity. On the other hand, her character is put forth as an ideal model for women to follow in her humility, sweetness, and purity. Understanding the historical basis for the duality inherent in the Virgin Mary's myth enables women to retain an appreciation of the aesthetics of its imagery without being bound by its moral import.

Context

In some ways, *Alone of All Her Sex* stands somewhat alone in its reception. Although it contains a feminist message, it is not a work that easily fits into a particular genre. In terms of historical scholarship, it is one of the most complete investigations of the broad ramifications of the Virgin's cult. Historians of medieval studies and religion, however, have not pursued its method or insights fully since it is often regarded as "popular history." Feminist religious studies have considered the impact of Mariology, but the extensive information and documentation in Warner's book mutes its message. Warner's historical approach, utilizing literary, artistic, and anthropological evidence, provides an interesting and compelling way to expose myths about women. For both its method and message, *Alone of All Her Sex* deserves to be more fully integrated into the literature of women's studies and issues.

Marina Warner has written several other books, including *Joan of Arc: The Image of Female Heroism* (1981) and *Monuments and Maidens: The Allegory of the Female Form* (1985), that deal with different aspects of the historical and aesthetic portrayal of women.

Sources for Further Study

Bynum, Caroline Walker. *Fragmentation and Redemption: Essays on Gender and the Human Body in Medieval Religion*. New York: Zone Books, 1991. A collection of essays that examines aspects of attitudes toward the body and gender in religious thought and practice, especially in the late medieval period. Several ideas that Warner discusses—such as gender reversal applied to priests and monks, the importance of the physical body in female devotion, and the symbolism of the Virgin's milk—are placed in the context of medieval religious practices.

Coakley, Sarah. "Mariology and 'Romantic Feminism': A Critique." In *Women's Voices: Essays in Contemporary Feminist Theology*, edited by Teresa Elwes. London: Marshall Pickering, 1992. This essay categorizes several contemporary discussions of Mariology according to type of feminism. Warner's book is discussed as an example of deconstructionist Mariology.

Daly, Mary. *Beyond God the Father: Toward a Philosophy of Women's Liberation*. Boston: Beacon Press, 1973. One of several works by Daly that explore the sexist implications inherent in the Christian religion, with proposals for ways that women can liberate themselves from these concepts. The problems with Mary as a feminine role model are discussed, with the author's objections similar to those raised by Warner.

Gold, Penny Schine. *The Lady and the Virgin: Image, Attitude, and Experience in Twelfth-Century France*. Chicago: University of Chicago Press, 1985. A look at the varied attitudes toward women in twelfth century France. One of the major sections deals with the iconography of the Virgin Mary at a key period in the development of Mariology in Western culture.

McLaughlin, Eleanor Commo. "Equality of Souls, Inequality of Sexes: Woman in Medieval Theology." In *Religion and Sexism: Images of Woman in the Jewish and Christian Traditions*, edited by Rosemary Radford Ruether. New York: Simon & Schuster, 1974. This essay places attitudes toward the Virgin within the broader context of attitudes toward women and sexuality in medieval theology.

Ranke-Heinemann, Uta. *Eunuchs for the Kingdom of Heaven: Women, Sexuality, and the Catholic Church*. Translated by Peter Heinegg. New York: Doubleday, 1990. This book surveys the theological attitudes toward women and issues of sexuality in Christianity from antiquity to the present. Against this broad background, Ranke-Heinemann includes a section on Mariology.

Ruether, Rosemary Radford. *New Woman, New Earth: Sexist Ideologies and Human Liberation*. New York: Seabury Press, 1975. These essays cover a broad range of feminist issues. One of the three sections deals with sexism in religion and contains an essay on the way in which Mariology reinforces sexist messages.

Karen Gould

AN AMERICAN CHILDHOOD

Author: Annie Dillard (1945-)
Type of work: Autobiography
Time of work: The 1950's
Locale: Pittsburgh
First published: 1987

Principal personages:

Annie Dillard, an essayist, poet, and teacher who records her childhood in Pittsburgh

Frank Doak, Annie's father, who quits his job to follow his dream of riverboating down to New Orleans

Pam Lambert Doak, Annie's mother, an irreverent, energetic social liberal

Form and Content

Writing about childhood and consciousness, Annie Dillard reveals in *An American Childhood* a pattern to her early life that clearly formed her as a writer. Growing up the eldest of three girls with loving, indulgent parents in comfortable, postwar Pittsburgh, she perceives herself as being able to feel alive from the inside, a quality she learned to recognize by vast amounts of reading. While those around her believed in Pittsburgh society, Dillard found alternative worlds through long hours spent reading all sorts of books. *An American Childhood* begins with small adventures in her early childhood, culminating in major teenage rebellions that leave even her understanding parents bewildered and distraught. All through her narrative, Dillard equates this feeling of distinctiveness with "waking up."

Childhood is when one first notices that one is alive, suggests Dillard. Therefore, she writes about the self-consciousness of children, using herself as an example. She equates her skills at classifying the elements from nature (such as butterflies), acquired as a youth, with the skills required of her as an autobiographer—analyzing and classifying the experiences from her past. Although she has claimed that she learned a good many things about herself and her family in writing the book, she put none of it in because she is not the subject. *An American Childhood* is not a book about how Dillard became who she is. She crafted the memories deliberately *as* a book. The origins of her writer's life result from this pattern of interest in the inner life set against the outer world, concretely set for her in Pittsburgh.

Dillard views her early life much in the way she views the natural world: as elements coming alive right before her eyes. Calling on an activity-filled background, from drawing to the study of plants, rocks, and insects, she records a life rich with experience. Her approach to life is as organic and self-conscious as each individual narrative, with an emphasis on the convergence of past and present selves. Each section is an individual memoir about one element of her intellectual history, providing an ontology but also recording her interest in the natural world. These narratives are carefully selected to show the pattern of development, not only of events but of insight as well, over those ten or eleven years of her childhood. Her diction and syntax often reflect the transfiguration of these events from the material world into the visionary.

Beginning with a prologue which is both a narrative of Pittsburgh's history and a memoir of her father, *An American Childhood* follows a roughly chronological order of events. Dillard's observations alternate between deeply meditative moments of self-discovery and warmly drawn portraits of family members, mostly her mother and father. The epilogue returns to the dichotomy between inner life and outer world first suggested by the prologue, being at once a meditation on the dreaminess of place and an intimate portrait of her father, taking the reader up to the present moment of writing this book. With her form (a dreamlike landscape) and her tone (ironic and detached), Dillard creates a memoir of her girlhood which through its metaphysical prose shows mystery and contradiction to be a part of every aspect of life. She "wakes up" and finds herself in a place that already existed; it remains a mystery that this world went on without her.

Analysis

In keeping with the spirit of "waking-up" that Dillard sees as essential to coming alive, *An American Childhood* analyzes how that "waking-up" begins and functions. The author's discussion of Pittsburgh, for example, notes the city's own consciousness from an unruly preindustrial dreamscape into an industrialized urban landscape. Similarly, her father "wakes up" one day to fulfill his dream of leaving Pittsburgh. Like Dillard, her father is deeply moved by books; after years of reading Mark Twain's *Life on the Mississippi* (1883), he leaves his young wife and three daughters to cruise downriver to New Orleans. Dillard presents the act as a natural adventure for her father to undertake; she is marked for good by his adventure, and because of it she will see her own, slower and less deliberate departure as equally appropriate.

Dillard's coming awake was a gradual discovery of her own recklessness. She asks, "Was everything beautiful so bold?" answering "yes" by building up narratives laced with a reckless and disturbingly bold beauty. One scene finds her family staring in awe at little Jo Ann Sheehy skating on the frozen street one icy winter night. "Here were beauty and mystery outside the house," writes Dillard, "and peace and safety within." Because her parents did not disapprove of such a scene, the young Dillard not only is captivated by the beauty of recklessness but also sees its value. That was the originating moment for her own unstoppable boldness.

The slight adventures Dillard recounts are for her as exemplary of freedom as Saint Augustine's stolen pears were for him. Even at age five, she learns how to enter the imaginative inner world of fiction deliberately or the outer world of reason at whim. At seven, Dillard roams the neighborhood freely, arming herself with memorized street names and phone numbers. She describes an incident in which a driver whose car she and some friends have pelted with snowballs in turn chases them across the neighborhood backyards until, finally, exhilarated by the hunt, Dillard believes she could now die happy.

Eventually, Dillard's joy in the beauty of recklessness develops into an overriding search for information about the dangerous and volatile world that she inhabits. She becomes a bookish child, and her frequent trips to the Homewood branch of Pittsburgh's Carnegie Library throw her into the "passive abyss of reading" while raising her from the stupor of childhood. Dillard is still seeking freedom but now within books, which make her delirious but reverential. Reading broadly, she eventually becomes immersed in *The Field Book of Ponds and Streams*. She lovingly studies every part of its surface and pores over its contents; the book shocks her with the revelation of strange worlds. One world, certainly, was that of ponds and streams, but she is more shocked by what the book suggested: Its full lending card indicated that many other readers joined in her fascination with pond life.

Even more noteworthy was the revelation of her own world: Most of the other readers of this book were African Americans, people who lived in the poverty-stricken area of Pittsburgh in which the library was located. She thought that such people had neither microscopes nor money nor time to study plankton, making their avid reading of this book all the more surprising. It was a revelation of social injustice. Moreover, she denies that the book was authored by a woman—although her name is clearly stated on the title page—imagining from the authority of the voice and freedom of its subject that its author had to be a man. Although she does not dwell on such insights, her attitude toward the discovery of social and gender inequality suggests that these issues are central to her own intellectual and moral education.

She discovers boys, too, as a curious naturalist might: She wakes one day and notices them at dancing school, a place centrally significant in her social milieu. Her attitude toward them is endearing; the boys are "cute," their rituals together novel and attractive. At age ten, they already seem to her as larger than life. Even at fifteen, they seem like "walking gods who conferred divine power with their least glances." The distinction she sees between the sexes is that while the boys were becoming responsible members of their world, learning self-control and real information about the world outside, girls "had failed to develop any selves worth controlling," and were instead "vigilantes of the trivial." While the tone here is as factually distant as when she is cataloging her rock collection or listing the books she has read, the diction suggests a bitterness over an inequity that she could only articulate from the distance of adulthood. In the middle of it, she is as certain of her own negligibility as a girl as were the boys whom she believed always shared that view.

Dillard's adolescence is feverish. Her "girlish" lack of self-control rockets into no control at all, exasperating her parents, her teacher, and to a lesser extent, her own self. Because she feels her "self" so keenly, she disproves her theory that girls do not develop selves. While other girls may have failed to notice the world outside, Dillard brought home every scrap and ounce of it, cataloged and ordered it, examined it critically and enthusiastically, and eventually transfigured it into her own self. The melancholy for the past she reveals at the end of her narrative indicates that life has not been without struggles for her, but she nevertheless finds the current view fine.

Context

Annie Dillard won the Pulitzer Prize at age thirty for her first prose book, *Pilgrim at Tinker Creek* (1974). Her autobiographical work *An American Childhood* observes one woman's life with the same priorities of the natural scientist as the earlier book. Although such writers as Charlotte Perkins Gilman, Virginia Woolf, Anaïs Nin, and Maxine Hong Kingston had previously written autobiographical works chronicling their lives as women writers, Dillard's work was widely praised as an "American" childhood—an inward and intellectual history, not specifically an American woman's intellectual history. Dillard suggests that in examining the small but powerful dramas of one's childhood, one finds those moments of self-awareness without regard to gender.

Her dissatisfaction with the inequities, the unquestioned codes of her social landscape forced her—as a highly conscious, well-read, spirited young woman—to leave her childhood landscape behind. While other people saw in her "rough edges" that needed smoothing, she wanted a can opener to cut herself a hole in the world's surface and exit through it. Dillard's work does have its detractors in those who argue that she cares more about the intellectual life than the physical or bodily life of a woman, or that in her drive to establish her childhood as American she glosses over the physical distinctiveness of female development. Other critics point out that as a study of the childhood of a natural scientist, *An American Childhood* sorts, catalogs, and examines the author's life in the most appropriate way.

Sources for Further Study

Clark, Suzanne. "Annie Dillard: The Woman in Nature and the Subject of Nonfiction." In *Literary Nonfiction: Theory, Criticism, Pedagogy*, edited by Chris Anderson. Carbondale: Southern Illinois University Press, 1989. Clark's analysis probes Dillard's prose style in order to question how one knows that this is "woman's" writing.

Gunn, Janet Varner. "A Politics of Experience: Leila Khaled's *My People Shall Live: The Autobiography of a Revolutionary*." In *De/Colonizing the Subject: The Politics of Gender in Women's Autobiography*, edited by Sidonie Smith and Julia Watson. Minneapolis: University of Minnesota Press, 1992. A somewhat advanced study, this essay is nevertheless useful for providing a comparison to Dillard's focus on the significance of landscape to memory.

Johnson, Sandra Humble. *The Space Between: Literary Epiphany in the Work of Annie Dillard*. Kent, Ohio: Kent State University Press, 1992. A study of literary epiphany, this work examines all Annie Dillard's writing as a "perusal of illumination." Includes a secondary bibliography and a thorough index.

Scheick, William. "Annie Dillard: Narrative Fringe." In *Contemporary American Women Writers: Narrative Strategies*, edited by Catherine Rainwater and William Scheick. Lexington: University Press of Kentucky, 1985. This essay discusses Dillard's narrative technique as a metaphysical concept.

Smith, Linda L. *Annie Dillard*. New York: Twayne, 1991. This biographical work sums up Dillard's career and anticipates its future direction.

Holli G. Levitsky

ANGELA DAVIS: An Autobiography

Author: Angela Davis (1944-)
Type of work: Autobiography
Time of work: The 1950's to the 1970's
Locale: Birmingham, Alabama; New York City; Helsinki, Finland; Frankfurt, Germany; and Marin County, California
First published: 1974

Principal personage:

Angela Davis, a socialist and civil rights activist

Form and Content

Angela Davis, a socialist scholar and longtime activist for African American liberation, wrote *Angela Davis: An Autobiography* shortly after her acquittal on charges related to a 1970 Marin County, California, prison revolt. Davis had also been actively involved in the American Communist Party, the Black Panther Party, and the Soledad Brothers Defense Committee, an organization working to defend prison activist George Jackson and others against politically motivated murder charges related to another prison revolt. In principle opposed to "individual-focused" interpretations of history, Davis offers her autobiography not as a "personal" story but as a political autobiography of the time and the movements with which she was involved. In the process, she provides readers with significant insight into the complexity of her experience as an African American socialist during the intense period of black liberation politics in the 1960's and 1970's. Throughout the autobiography, Davis keeps a primary focus on the larger political, racial, and social issues of the day. She intertwines her own accounts of political work and prison experience with the lives of other women and men of the time who were working for revolutionary change in American society.

In a section entitled "Nets," Davis opens the book with an account of her flight to avoid arrest following the Marin County revolt. She is eventually captured by police in New York City, and much of this opening section consists of her account of her incarceration in the New York Women's House of Detention. She describes conditions for the women prisoners there, condemning the inhumane treatment of mentally ill women and speaking forcefully of the unnecessary dehumanization of the inmates, a disproportionate number of whom are poor, African American, or Puerto Rican. She describes her own jail experience in relation to these other women, presenting much of her experience in explicitly political terms: "I fought the tendency to individualize my predicament." Given her overall purpose in the book, it is not surprising to find the autobiography beginning on such a clearly political note.

In the next section of the book, "Rocks," Davis recounts her childhood in Birmingham, Alabama. She tells of racist attacks against black middle-class families as neighborhoods slowly integrate, and again uses the events of her childhood to emphasize her growing awareness of racial and economic injustice in American society. When she later goes away to high school in New York City, she encounters the world of socialist economic and political philosophy through her readings and her emerging friendships with the offspring of New York leftist intellectuals.

"Waters," part 3, takes Davis to Brandeis University for her early college years and increasing involvement in socialist- and communist-affiliated activities, such as the 1962 Eighth World Festival for Youth and Students, held in Helsinki, Finland. Davis focuses on these years as a way to chart her increased exposure to an international framework for understanding American politics. After spending part of her undergraduate years at the Sorbonne in Paris, Davis later begins graduate study in Frankfurt, Germany. It is here that she realizes a tension between her desire to maintain a broad socialist focus and her frustration at being away from the United States during the years of the Civil Rights movement and the evolving Black Liberation movement. In 1967, propelled by a growing need to express her commitment to black liberation politics directly, Davis returned to the United States.

These opening sections allow Davis to set the necessary political and intellectual context for the rest of the narrative sections, entitled "Flames," "Walls," and "Bridges," in which she explains in much more detail the series of events and political involvements that lead to her eventual arrest.

Analysis

Angela Davis: An Autobiography is consistently and overtly political and analytical, not highly personal or confessional. In fact, Davis repeatedly describes her own efforts to pull all of her immediate personal experience into a broader political context, thus keeping her readers focused on her overarching socialist critique of American culture. In this sense, the book reads primarily as an extended critique of American class, race, and gender politics, then secondarily as an account of one woman's life. Davis suggests that the two are interrelated. Her tone and structuring of the narrative suggest clearly, however, that she prioritizes the significance of the political above that of the personal.

Several key issues emerge as central to Davis' portrayal of her simultaneous involvements in the emerging Black Liberation movement and in the evolving politics of the socialist Left, including her membership in the Communist Party.

One theme running as an undercurrent throughout the book is the tension between political priorities as they were defined by the racially integrated Left, including the Communist Party, and political priorities as they were defined by the Black Liberation movement, including the Black Panther Party. Davis was originally drawn to the Los Angeles based Black Panther Political Party (BPPP) in 1968, while she was still deciding whether to join the Communist Party. Later that year, the BPPP transformed itself into a branch of the Student Nonviolent Coordinating Committee (SNCC) after a conflict erupted with the Oakland-based Black Panther Party for Self-Defense (BPP). As Davis discovered, her own socialist priorities were often in conflict with the SNCC national leadership at the time. After her close friend Communist Party member Franklin Alexander was expelled from the SNCC in what Davis perceived as an anticommunist purge, Davis left the SNCC and later in 1968 joined the Communist Party through the Che Lumumba club, a Los Angeles black "cell" (small section) of the Party. Although Davis later also joined the Black Panther Party for Self-Defense, partly because she believed they were more sympathetic to Marxist ideas, she often recounts tensions between her socialism and some aspects of cultural and political black nationalism, especially regarding issues of class and black separatism.

Central to Davis' socialist analysis is the linking of race, class, and gender. Because she believes that these three realms of experience are inextricably linked, she is reluctant to embrace a black nationalism that excludes explicit consideration of class or gender. As a result, during the 1960's (and later), Davis often found herself at odds with black cultural nationalists who advocated absolute separatism from whites, including poor whites and committed socialists. While Davis also argued a strong indictment against white racism, her experience in the integrated Left led her to accept the strategic legitimacy of multiracial coalition work, especially relating to class issues and prison reform. Many black nationalists objected to this position on the grounds that the so-called integrated Left was, in fact, white-dominated, and thus not fully trustworthy when it came to the goals of black liberation. This debate, so clearly outlined by Davis and exemplified by her own strong identification with both socialism and black liberation, remains a central debate for African American socialists.

Davis also speaks bluntly of the sexism that existed within the Black Liberation movement, particularly the resistance that she encountered when she assumed leadership roles in relation to men. Time and again she faced what she labels as sexist resistance and criticism from men in the BPPP, SNCC, and the BPP. At one point in the narrative, she claims to be tired of "men who measured their sexual height by women's intellectual genuflection." Davis and many other African American feminists have identified such sexism as a major obstacle hindering the effectiveness of both individuals and organizations during this period. Davis' critique in her autobiography is one of the earlier literary and public political confrontations of the problem.

One of the most interesting and central themes of *Angela Davis: An Autobiography* is the reality of jail experience in relation to the symbolic political significance of jail for the prisoners' rights movement. Davis herself uses the terms "jail" and "prison" as a metaphor for political oppression generally. Yet she also graphically reveals the dehumanizing reality of prison for herself and others, especially for those who because of their race and poverty end up in prison for years after convictions on relatively minor charges. The book deals centrally with Davis' work for prisoners' rights and with her deep personal and political commitment to George Jackson and the Soledad Brothers. She chronicles the intense and sometimes lethal police harassment of black liberation activists of the period. In addition, Davis details her own incarceration in New York and California, focusing on the special oppression of women in prison. Throughout the narrative, Davis develops her own experience as an African American political prisoner as paradigmatic of political prisoners more generally. For Davis, incarceration must be analyzed politically at the outset as a mechanism for state control and political coercion. Her own experience illustrates the vulnerability of American citizens to legal persecution because of their political views. Davis uses her personal story to pose this broader political indictment of American society.

It is in posing these radical critiques of American culture that Davis writes a revolutionary, rather than "reform," analysis for creating economic and racial justice. She also shows, through descriptions of her education abroad and her trip to socialist Cuba, that she positions herself and American socialism within an international socialist movement.

Context

Angela Davis: An Autobiography both continues and alters the autobiographical tradition in African American women's writing. By using the story of her life as a framework for social analysis, Davis follows in the literary footsteps of such noted American authors as Harriet A. Jacobs (*Incidents in the Life of a Slave Girl*, 1861), Ida B. Wells-Barnett (*Crusade for Justice: The Autobiography of Ida B. Wells*, 1970), Zora Neale Hurston (*Dust Tracks on a Road*, 1942), and Maya Angelou (*I Know Why the Caged Bird Sings*, 1970, followed by other autobiographical volumes). Additionally, Davis' autobiography offers an interesting contrast and important opportunity for comparative reading with other autobiographies by African American women dealing with the politics of the Black Liberation movement and the Civil Rights movement of the 1950's, 1960's, and 1970's. For example, Anne Moody's *Coming of Age in Mississippi* (1968) and Elaine Brown's *A Taste of Power: A Black Woman's Story* (1992) both offer differing perspectives on the same period. Together with Davis and many other African American writers (both women and men), these sources give an increasingly full and complex view of this critical era in African American and American history.

Unlike most other women writers in African American culture, however, Davis takes an explicitly socialist approach to her analysis of women's experience. Davis' longtime participation in the American Communist Party reflects her emphasis on understanding broader economic structures, a step that she believes is necessary for understanding the true nature of pervasive racial oppression and widespread sexism in American society. Davis' membership in the Party sets her apart theoretically and tactically from mainstream or "reform" feminism and at times puts her in tension with black nationalist and separatist feminists, as well as middle-class "integrationists" who argue for fuller black participation in an otherwise accepted American economic culture. Davis is explicit in her analysis of the special oppression facing African American women: Her book *Women, Race, and Class* (1981) focuses primarily on racism and sexism as central forces in the history of black women. As always, however, Davis links this oppression to class oppression in general, and she argues for multiracial coalitions of both women and men as a fundamental requirement for making revolutionary social change.

Davis' persistent and very public socialism, combined with her ongoing participation in black liberation politics, has made her a highly visible and controversial activist and scholar. Anticommunist sentiment has a long history in American society, both among intellectuals and in popular culture. Despite broad cultural pressure against her views, Davis has maintained a firm public commitment to the Communist Party, to the liberation of African American people, and to revolutionary economic and social change. She thus occupies an important place along the broad spectrum of American political philosophy.

Sources for Further Study

Braxton, Joanne M. *Black Women Writing Autobiography*. Philadelphia: Temple University Press, 1989. This excellent volume offers literary and historical context for reading Davis' book in the tradition of African

American women's autobiography. Does not address Davis specifically, but provides important background and interesting essays on Harriet Jacobs, Ida B. Wells-Barnett, Era Bell Thompson, Zora Neale Hurston, and others.

Brisbane, Robert H. *Black Activism: Racial Revolution in the United States, 1954-1970*. Valley Forge, Pa.: Judson Press, 1974. Gives a political analysis and historical overview of the Black Liberation movement, including full chapters on the Black Panther Party, Black Nationalism, and "Black Literature and the Black Revolution." Important for more fully understanding the context of Angela Davis' political work. Contains a very good bibliography of less well known sources for the period.

Davis, Angela Y. *Women, Race, and Class*. New York: Random House, 1981. A focused historical study of the significance of race, class, and gender in the history of American culture. Provides good insight into Davis' broader and evolving political analysis.

Gates, Henry Louis, Jr., ed. *Reading Black, Reading Feminist*. New York: Meridian Books, 1990. An extensive anthology of African American feminist theory, both literary and political. An important source for understanding Angela Davis in the broader context of contemporary theorists. Offers a range of perspectives.

Jones, Jacqueline. *Labor of Love, Labor of Sorrow: Black Women, Work, and the Family from Slavery to the Present*. New York: Vintage Books, 1986. An excellent analytical history of the experience of African American women. Provides an extended economic and social analysis. An excellent bibliography is included.

Sharon Carson

ANYWHERE BUT HERE

Author: Mona Simpson (1957-)
Type of work: Novel
Type of plot: Domestic realism
Time of plot: The 1930's to the 1970's
Locale: Bay City, Wisconsin, to Hollywood, California
First published: 1986

Principal characters:

Ann August, the daughter of Adele August who recalls the tensions in her relationship with her mother

Adele August, a woman in search of a glamorous identity for both herself and Ann

Carol, Adele's down-to-earth sister

Lillian, Adele and Carol's mother

Form and Content

Anywhere but Here presents the ordinariness and the extraordinariness of the lives of four women in nine alternating, nonchronological sections that detail their hopes and fears over several decades, from Lillian in the 1930's to Carol and Adele in the 1940's and 1950's to Ann in the 1970's. Ann is the book's most frequent narrator, arguably its protagonist, and the focus of the book revolves around her often stormy relationship with her mother, Adele.

The book begins with a crystallized moment of the tension between mother and daughter as Ann, not yet in her teens, reflects on a recurrent pattern of events that take place as she and her mother cross the western United States in her stepfather's car. Repeatedly after a fight, Adele stops the car and makes Ann get out, as if abandoning her for good. Then, as soon as Ann is out of sight in her rearview mirror, Adele turns around and comes back for her.

This ritual of abandonment and reconciliation acts as a foil to Adele's abandonment of her home and family, which Adele repeatedly justifies as necessary to Ann's "progress." Freeing herself from her mother's manipulations, Ann brings these repeated highway abandonings to a halt when she takes matters into her own hands, leaving the spot where her mother left her to call her grandmother in Wisconsin. Unable to ask Lillian to send for her, she at least proves to Adele that she can survive without her if necessary.

Adele is obsessed with making Ann a child star, thereby avoiding, she thinks, the humdrum monotony of life in Wisconsin. To make her dream come true, Adele uses people, steals credit cards and her second husband's car, wanders from job to job in California, and forces Ann to live in hovels in order to maintain an official residence in Beverly Hills. Through Ann's narration, and finally through her mother's, readers observe Ann watching and learning from her mother, adopting her mother's resentments as well as her capacity to survive.

While Adele and Ann struggle to lead the ideal glamorous life, Lillian and Carol wade through the hardships of their own lives. Lillian, who like Adele only narrates one chapter, describes her relationships with her daughters. A revealing overlap between Lillian's narration and Carol's revolves around Carol's decision to join the WACs in World War II. Carol remembers her mother calling her at work and asking her what she has done this time, yet Lillian, concerned about her daughter's welfare, remembers asking Carol, "What in heavens did you do?" This subtle difference in perspective points to how tensions are created between mothers and daughters, providing insight into Adele's eventual concerns over Ann's aloof, disdainful behavior as a young woman.

Just as Lillian realizes the weaknesses in her ability to mother her two daughters, having given more to Adele than to Carol, Adele eventually admits that she was a controlling mother. She retains her elitist attitude, however, insisting that her daughter has grown up away from the working-class background in which she herself was reared in Wisconsin. Because Ann has succeeded in becoming at least a minor television personality, Adele revels in her triumph. Throughout the book, Adele has been the possessive mother, repeatedly proclaiming that Ann is her child, her property, to do with as she sees fit. She convinces herself, in the end, that everything she did was for the right reasons and brought about the right results.

Analysis

Mimicking the traditional *Bildungsroman*, in which a young man must leave home to find his own identity, *Anywhere but Here* focuses on this theme in a parallel examination of Adele's escape from small-town, midwestern living in Bay City, Wisconsin, and Ann's eventual escape from her mother's manipulative way of living vicariously through her daughter. Yet the book is remarkably more substantial than this simple theme because Mona Simpson provides her readers with a perspective parallel to the traditional American leave-home-to-find-success ideal—that of Lillian and Carol, who stay in Bay City to live out their lives, lives that are no less intricate or successful than those of Adele and Ann.

By combining these parallel views of escaping from home and remaining there, Simpson emphasizes the familial ties that bind human beings, especially those of mother-daughter relationships. Even though Adele moves half a continent away from home, the life that she lived in Bay City remains the marker she uses to measure the success of her life—the further she manages to remove herself from what she sees as working-class conditions, the more successful she feels. Simpson manages to point out the fact that Adele's ideals are very similar to those of millions of other Americans who see life as a quest for the American Dream—a dream that changes, notably, with each generation, as seen in the differences between the dreams of Lillian, Carol, Adele, and Ann.

Lillian, like Carol, expresses the importance of family several times in her narrative, remarking about the closeness of her mother's sisters and the intense affection, which was an almost incestuous one like Adele and Ann's relationship, between her mother and her brother, Milton. Lillian, advanced in years when she speaks to Ann, relates several instances of how she or other family members took the rest of their family for granted, such as the time her husband died and Adele would not come home from college. Yet Lillian, like the other three women in the novel, was never very close to her own mother.

The near incestuousness in the mother-child relationships causes tensions within both the mothers and the children. Lillian suspects that Milton leaves home because of the one time when they kiss more as man and woman than as son and mother. Adele seems oblivious to Ann's disgust toward her desire to touch parts of her daughter's body any time she wants. For Adele, this form of incest reveals in a dramatic way her belief that Ann is her property, to do with as she pleases. The undesired sexual contact with her mother makes Ann want to have the same control over others, going so far as to make neighborhood children lie on the bathroom floor while she fondles and photographs them. While both Adele and Ann want to control people with their sexuality, Lillian regrets her actions with Milton because of the distance it created between them.

Carol, a teenager during the Great Depression, merely seems to have wanted something different in her life. After having had a fairly adventurous life in Europe with the WACs and her secret marriage, she willingly settled down to life in Bay City, rearing a family of her own while maintaining a close relationship (in proximity although not in affection) with her own mother, Lillian.

It is Adele who is constantly dissatisfied. Even though Lillian notes that Adele was born in 1929 and was a Depression child, Adele remembers none of the consequences of poverty because her parents had enough money to meet her needs and desires, including sending her to college for bachelor's and master's degrees. Never having known real want, Adele thinks nothing of scraping by for short periods of time until something better comes along, when she risks everything to grab at the mythical brass ring.

Ann, modeling her behavior and attitudes toward people after her mother, uses people for her own, unexpressed needs. While she constantly remarks about her mother's aberrant behavior, she continues to reluctantly do what her mother wants her to do, while rebelling in small ways such as by not shaving her legs. Such rebellion is her attempt to create her own niche in life and to make clear her independence from her mother.

Tied closely to the women's search for their own dreams is the characters' preoccupation with a sense of place—a sense of belonging somewhere, as is hinted at by the novel's title. Ann, the child moved about against her will, especially seems conscious of tying events to specific places, but all the women comment on the importance of places in their lives. Notably, the most exciting things happen away from home, such as Carol's time in the WACs, but the most frightening things happen at or near home, such as the death of Carol's son Benny.

Ultimately, *Anywhere but Here* is about abandoning ideals that no longer fit and finding solace in ones that people create themselves, no matter how artificial or forced, in a place they can call their own. Sometimes this creation of dreams is damaging to others, but more often than not it scars the disillusioned dreamer. Through the lens of these mother-daughter relationships, Simpson shows how daughters, no matter how hard they fight it, come away with something of their mothers in them.

Context

Because of the success of her first novel, *Anywhere but Here*, Simpson was heralded by many as a pioneering domestic writer in the tradition of Anne Tyler and Alice Munro. She was one of the first of many women writers, such as Amy Tan and Louise Erdrich, who would utilize multiple narrators and circular narratives as a major method of conveying stories. Such intertwined tales, once considered separate stories, are now considered by many critics as a relatively new genre called the short-story cycle, a genre clarified by Sherwood Anderson's *Winesburg, Ohio* (1919). Many argue, however, that such works are still novels.

Anywhere but Here noticeably excludes the voices of men, focusing on women's perspectives to provide multigenerational points of view rare in most literary works, although often utilized in romance novels. This ambiguous tie between what has often been considered "higher" forms of literature and the traditionally female-dominated field of the romance novel has created concerns among some scholars that women's writing is still not being taken seriously by literary scholars. Of special concern and debate are works of fiction that rely heavily on common, name-brand items to create the milieu, or the overall environmental setting, of the work. Simpson's heavy use of such description has been the most dominant negative criticism about the novel. While not heavily written about in scholarly circles, *Anywhere but Here* demonstrates that contemporary women's writing is strengthening. Women such as Simpson, who has been called both a poet and a novelist because of the rich details and the strength of characterization inherent in *Anywhere but Here*, dare to experiment, altering perceptions both about women writers and about the nature of fiction writing.

Mona Simpson wrote a sequel to *Anywhere but Here* entitled *The Lost Father* (1991). She was awarded the Whiting Writers' Award and a National Endowment for the Arts grant, both in 1986. In 1988, she received the John Simon Guggenheim Memorial Foundation fellowship and a Hodder fellowship. She has had numerous short stories anthologized, such as in the *Pushcart Prize: Best of the Small Presses XI* and in the *Best American Short Stories of 1986*, and published in literary magazines, such as the *Iowa Review*, the *Paris Review*, and *Ploughshares*.

Sources for Further Study

Beevor, Antony. "Heading West." *Times Literary Supplement*, June 26, 1987, p. 698. A review of the novel which discusses how the specific social and economic time periods depicted influence the women's lives and personalities.

Heller, Dana A. "Shifting Gears: Transmission and Flight in Mona Simpson's *Anywhere but Here*." *The University of Hartford Studies in Literature: A Journal of Interdisciplinary Criticism* 21 (1989): 37-44. This essay examines the nature of change in the lives of the characters in *Anywhere but Here*.

Kakutani, Michiko. Review of *Anywhere but Here*. *The New York Times*, December 24, 1986, p. C16. This review analyzes the effectiveness of Simpson's characterization of Adele and Ann, as well as the effectiveness of Lillian and Carol's intertwining narratives. Takes an important look at how the American family structure influences the effect of the novel.

Morse, Deborah Denenholz. "The Difficult Journey Home: Mona Simpson's *Anywhere but Here*." In *Mother Puzzles: Daughters and Mothers in Contemporary American Literature*, edited by Mickey Pearlman. New York: Greenwood Press, 1989. This essay draws attention to ideas about home in mother-daughter relationships as they apply to the novel.

Shreiber, Le Anne. "In Thrall to a Lethal Mother."

The New York Times Book Review, January 11, 1987, p. 7. Examines the love-hate relationship between Ann and Adele, astutely observing that Adele is a character who creates awe and exasperation in both Ann and Simpson's readers.

Stone, Laurie. "Motherhood Is Powerful." *The Village Voice* 32, no. 5 (February 3, 1987): 47. Examines Ann and Adele's relationship, points out Simpson's use of the traditional American road story, and admires Simpson's way of making the reader listen.

Ruth J. Heflin

ARCHETYPAL PATTERNS IN WOMEN'S FICTION

Author: Annis Pratt (1937-)
Type of work: Literary criticism
First published: 1981

Form and Content

Convinced that women's fiction over the past three hundred years has formed a body of work with a continuity of themes and issues, Annis Pratt undertook an investigation into what specifically ties women's fiction together. She based her research on the Jungian notion of archetypes. Psychologist Carl Jung had suggested that throughout history humans have been heir to unconscious, primordial images that exist across cultures and across time, which he named archetypes. Pratt set out to look for what archetypal images underlie women's fiction, and whether these are the same images found in men's fiction.

What she found was that although women writers share thematic patterns with male writers, they also have a thread of their own, expressing a peculiarly feminine body of concerns and issues. Examining a large number of women's fictional writings, Pratt found that they seem to divide into several categories archetypally. Further, she discovered that when women write about the same archetypal themes as men, they look at the images from a different point of view.

An example is the mythical image Pratt chose for the frontispiece of her own book, that of the Greek nymph Daphne turning into a tree rather than be raped by the god Apollo. Noting that this same image would be evaluated differently by individuals and cultural groups with varying points of view, she gives some examples. Medieval Christians would focus on Daphne's purity for going to such lengths to maintain her virginity, or they would blame her for tempting Apollo in the first place. A modern, chauvinistic man might cheer Apollo on and advise Daphne to relax and enjoy the experience. Most women authors, Pratt notes, tend to interpret situations embodying this archetype with empathy for the victim and anger at the assault.

Given that archetypes do show up in literature and that interpretations of them vary depending on the author and the culture, the interpretations of women authors tend to be based on women's life experiences. Women's experience is based on the common experiences of humankind and on the stumbling blocks put in their way as they try to live in a patriarchal culture that thwarts their full development as human beings.

Pratt thus sees four primary themes in women's fiction: the young woman resisting the restrictions and constrictions that the patriarchal society would place on her; the mature woman struggling within the roles of wife and mother as defined by her culture; the issues and consequences around choosing one's own relationships; and the older woman who is finally relatively free from the expectations of society and can do as she likes. In all cases, Pratt senses a tension between the societal norms that the authors accept, at least to some degree, and the yearning for full development and individuation that would transcend these restrictions.

Analysis

Noting that a common literary theme is the youthful quest for self and identity, Pratt shows how women writers tend to portray this quest. Because for women the urge for self-development includes the opposite pressure to narrow oneself down into the roles and behaviors considered appropriate for womanhood, women writers tend to handle this theme differently than do men writers.

The desire for self-fulfillment, Pratt says, is often embodied in a love of nature, which she identifies with the archetype of the "green world." The quest often includes the terrible choice between real self-fulfillment, on the one hand, and human love and relationship, on the other. For women, this is presented as an "either/or" situation.

One example from a popular novel of the nineteenth century is Louisa May Alcott's *Little Women* (1868, 1869), in which Jo, the one of the four daughters who has the most difficulty growing up, struggles mightily against the proscriptions of women's lives. She wants to follow her own interests, have adventures, and look as she wishes, but she is counseled to turn up her hair, wear long gowns, and act like a young lady.

Once women are enclosed in the domestic bonds of patriarchal marriage, other themes come to the fore. Pratt identifies two categories of fiction in this section: novels of marriage and novels of social protest. An example of the first is Jane Austen's *Pride and Prejudice* (1813), in which the concept of a practical and financially secure marriage as woman's best choice is satirized. Themes prevalent in this first type include the struggle with marriage as social enclosure which narrows women's boundaries, women's complicity in the choice for marriage and enclosure, the insanity that is portrayed as the result of rebellion against the strictures of marriage, and fantasies about equal marriages. The novel of social protest involves its author in a search for the reasons behind society's problems. In this case, she looks beyond the marriage itself into the social structures that surround it. This can involve interest in Christianity, socialism, and communism as social movements that should improve society's lot. What the authors often find, according to Pratt, is that regardless of the social system envisioned, women's lives are still constricted by patriarchy.

Next Pratt takes up fiction that deals with true eroticism for women. She finds that one characteristic identifying women's successful search for real eroticism is that it involves transcending gender norms and taking on a sense of androgyny. In this section, Pratt looks at fiction that deals with authentic relationships between women and men, between women and women, and finally, lives of chosen solitude.

About fiction dealing with authentic love and passion between women and men, Pratt points out that the woman is always punished for her eroticism. Married women, she submits, are expected not only to be monogamous but also to be essentially eunuchs; that is, they are not to enjoy their sexuality. Women who make their erotic choices, or even enjoy their eroticism, are punished by tragic outcomes. In the occasional story in which the woman is uncritically allowed to make such choices, the authors are punished. An example is Charlotte Brontë, who was severely criticized after the publication of *Jane Eyre* (1847) simply because she allowed Jane to declare her love and affection for Rochester.

In novels of relationships between women, whether based on sexuality or simply close friendship, the women are treated either as marking time until marriage or as somehow silly and worthy of mockery. If serious about their female relationships, naturally, the women are punished.

The final chapter in this section addresses fiction about single women, who may be portrayed as odd, strange, and perhaps ugly, or even as witches. Such portrayals exist because of society's fear of unattached women who control their own lives. Some novels accept these portrayals; others go beyond them and create women who, despite society's disapproval, live fulfilled and happy lives alone. This concept of positive solitude is a regular theme of May Sarton's books, explored in her stories and also in depth as it relates to her own life in her autobiographical *Journal of a Solitude* (1973).

In Pratt's final section, she analyzes stories about women who, after struggling with the restrictive roles of patriarchy, move beyond the roles and into themselves, usually toward the ends of their lives, in a process of rebirth. In this process, the heroines return to the "green world," finding their values within themselves and in nature.

Although much of the book's content deals with the concept of recurring themes in women's fiction, the idea of archetypes on which Pratt believes these themes are based is brought together in her summation, in which she notes the five primary archetypes found in women's fiction: the green-world epiphany (finding oneself in nature), the green-world lover (the encounter with a woman's authentic erotic yearnings), the rape trauma, enclosure, and rebirth.

Context

While Annis Pratt accepts in her book the reality of Jungian archetypes, attempting to use this concept as a framework for understanding women's fiction, it is possible to find value in *Archetypal Patterns in Women's Fiction* without any reference to Jungian theory. What Pratt analyzes is the themes of women's fiction, which is a valid and helpful approach with or without the Jungian underpinnings.

The advantage of the archetypal framework is that Pratt is able to see how women authors have taken archetypal patterns used by men and transformed them into completely different themes based on women's experiences of their own development within their restrictive patriarchal roles. She finds that, in reflecting the stages of women's lives under patriarchal structures, women's fiction can be grouped under three life-stages and a fourth category which might be called authentic relationship. This category is an androgynous lifestyle which is usually punished regardless of the life stage of the woman living it, but which can also serve as a model of female possibility.

What Pratt's analysis does is to take the body of women's fiction over the past three hundred years, sort it out, and group it together in such a way that it provides an illustrative pattern of the lives of Western women under patriarchy. The reader learns of the pain of choosing to follow prescribed roles that require giving up the developmental freedom and authentic eros of the green world. The reader learns of the paradoxes and sacrifices of women enclosed within marriage and family. The reader learns of the consequences of the chosen relationship, whether it be heterosexual, woman-to-woman, or the relationship of the woman in solitude to herself. Finally, the reader learns of the freedom many women finally find at the end of their lives to pursue their own destiny. In essence, Pratt's analysis is a picture of the three life-stages of the ancient goddess, as distorted by patriarchy: the maiden, the mother, and the crone.

Pratt's book is also a history of women in patriarchy. Although patriarchal structures go back much further than the three hundred years in her analysis, the images and issues that she presents and the stories that she discusses create a portrait of women's lives over this time period.

Sources for Further Study

Alcott, Louisa May. *Little Women*. 1869. Reprint. New York: Grosset & Dunlap, 1947. This popular novel of the Civil War period chronicles the lives of a mother and her four daughters, each with a distinct personality and approach to life. Pratt suggests that the character of Jo fits into the theme of the young woman struggling between authentic development and submission to patriarchal restriction.

Austen, Jane. *Pride and Prejudice*. 1813. Reprint. New York: Macmillan, 1962. A popular nineteenth century novel about two young women in England and the choices they make from within the range allowed for women of their time. Pratt describes this book as an example of novels of marriage.

Brontë, Charlotte. *Jane Eyre*. 1847. Reprint. London: Longmans, Green, 1959. The story of a young orphan growing up in nineteenth century rural England and of the hurdles that she had to overcome, including the struggle to fulfill her love for her employer, Rochester. Pratt uses this book as an example of the disapproval given to females who declare their love, or to authors who allow them to do so unpunished.

Harding, M. Esther. *Woman's Mysteries Ancient and Modern*. New York: Harper & Row, 1971. Discussed extensively by Pratt in her opening explanation of archetypes, this work takes the Jungian archetypal framework and applies it to women's use of the archetypes, particularly in the realm of spirituality and mythology.

Jung, Carl G. *Archetypes and the Collective Unconscious*. Translated by R. F. C. Hull. Princeton, N.J.: Princeton University Press, 1969. Jung's theory of archetypes, which are present across cultures and across history in what he calls the collective unconscious, is the basis for Pratt's study. This work by Jung will explain further what these concepts mean.

Sarton, May. *Journal of a Solitude*. New York: W. W. Norton, 1973. This autobiographical journal takes the reader through a year in the author's life. Past midlife, she reflects on the importance of solitude while at the same time juggling the demands of friendships, her love relationships, and her writing.

Eleanor B. Amico

ARIEL

Author: Sylvia Plath (1932-1963)
Type of work: Poetry
First published: 1965

Form and Content

Ariel, Sylvia Plath's most celebrated book of poetry, is credited as the first collection of poems in which Plath finds her unique voice. The forty-three poems are bound together by an overwhelming sense of urgency and common themes. Some scholars consider Plath to be one of the few poets to address the traditional female world without being trite, obvious, or unimportant. Even those who discount the content of her work as self-indulgent praise her marvelous use of language, her mastery of rhythm and use of sound, and her unusual sense of metaphor—in short, her poetic craft.

Ariel was compiled posthumously by Plath's estranged husband, the English poet Ted Hughes. Most of the poems were written in the final five months of Plath's life, sometimes at the rate of several each day, a frenzy of productivity reflected in the furious pace of the poems. According to Hughes, around Christmas of 1962 Plath selected the poems for *Ariel*, ordering them in a binder beginning with "Morning Song" and ending with "Wintering," so that the work opened and closed with the words "Love" and "spring," respectively. Hughes omitted twelve of the intended works in the published edition—primarily the ones that dealt with her anger about his extramarital affair. These poems were published later.

While Plath's earlier poetry is controlled, showing a development of technical mastery, in *Ariel* she releases a torrent of extreme violence and passion. In "Daddy," probably her best-known poem, the speaker confronts the fury that she feels toward her father, who died when she was ten. "Daddy" is written as a child's poem, a nursery rhyme which uses playful words, rhyme, and repetition, all of which contrast sharply with the poem's content. The sing-song cadence and use of the affectionate term "Daddy" convey the feelings of a grown woman who longs for her dead father. She expresses the desire to reunite with him, which is possible only in death. At the same time, "Daddy" is a violent poem: The speaker vehemently hates her father and accuses him of heinous crimes.

This combination of opposing form and content is an example of Plath's unusual talent for connecting, even fusing, disparate realities. In *Ariel*, she frequently presents different landscapes in the same world, fluidly moving from one image to another. For example, in "Cut," the speaker of the poem slices the tip of her finger as she chops onions. The cut is first a hinge, then a hat, then a scalped pilgrim. The blood turns into soldiers, placing her in a world of war and violence, saboteurs, kamikaze missions, and the Ku Klux Klan. Each image flows to the next naturally, quickly moving far away from the woman preparing a meal in her home.

Also remarkable is Plath's fusion of reality and dream worlds. In "Fever 103°," the speaker combines her feverish hallucinatory state with a lucid one. She travels to the gates of hell and finally sheds her old self, as sullied clothes; in so doing, she is reborn and reaches paradise. Nightmarish images of hell, of Hiroshima, and becoming her own thermometer intersect a very real world of sickness—traveling to and from the bathroom and recognizing get-well flowers and loving caretakers.

Plath has been called a landscape poet, but she distinguishes herself from the tradition by emphasizing her internal or emotional "landscape." In "Tulips," a woman is convalescing and resents the vivid presence of bright red tulips, which draw her back to life. Plath immediately breaks from the landscape of the hospital room; her white surroundings transport the reader to a winter scene (where she is "snowed in"), then to the seashore (the nurses are sea gulls), then to a brook (her body is a pebble and the nurses smoothing waters). Throughout her poems, Plath creates a landscape of the self, the world where her emotions live. She constructs a world ravaged by battling emotions: love and hate, desire to live and hope for death, emotional strength and despair.

The title poem is a masterful work in which Plath incorporates her major themes and exercises her remarkable use of metaphor. The poem opens with the speaker galloping on her wild horse, Ariel, toward her own death. There is no hesitation, no turning back. The meaning and the event of the poem are seamlessly joined. The poet, the horse, and the rider all become one. The poem climaxes as she rides into the morning sun, symbolizing a new day, and for the protagonist, a new life. The name

Ariel denotes both a horse that Plath rode in England and the airy servant spirit in William Shakespeare's *The Tempest* (pr. 1611, pb. 1623). These references also reflect on the poet—a woman controlled by her surroundings yet extraordinarily powerful in her art. One can see Plath as the racehorse, running to finish her collection of poems before the end of her life.

Analysis

Much of Plath's earlier work is seen as influenced by or derivative of other writers. In *Ariel*, however, Plath speaks with her unique voice. Plath's poetry deals with life and death from her own, female perspective. Her expression is honest and full of raw emotion, which, when combined with her extraordinary poetic talent, makes her work powerful. She tantalizes readers, taking them with her to the edge of death, unsure whether she will simply state what she sees or jump into the abyss.

Plath is often categorized as a confessional poet as she draws on intimate details of her life for subject matter. Many readers find it difficult to read Plath's poems without her suicide in mind. The experience of the "I" of "Lady Lazarus," a poem about a thirty-year-old woman who tries to kill herself every ten years, is glaringly personal. The speaker refers to a public, theatrical death that mirrors Plath's own.

Ariel, however, goes far beyond biography. First of all, it contains monologues by characters who are not necessarily Plath. More important, it presents concerns of mythic proportion. Plath said that her poems originated from events that affected her emotionally, but that she believed in controlling and manipulating those experiences to make them relevant to larger issues, such as the Holocaust or Hiroshima. For example, "Lady Lazarus" is not merely a poem about suicide attempts, nor does the woman simply die and disappear. Rather, she is reborn, emerging like a phoenix from her own ashes. The central theme of the collection is ritualistic death and rebirth, with numerous subthemes including the struggle to find true identity (the search for the real self and the killing of the false one), the destruction of a tainted experience and regeneration of a pure one, and the innocence of childhood and the evils of the adult world.

Plath draws on her life in her poetry. For example, her father died unexpectedly when she was eight years old. Further, she had attempted suicide. Plath chooses a presentation, however, that alters the actual facts of her life to achieve greater effect. The father in "Daddy" died when his daughter was ten, not eight, which makes the daughter's suicide attempt at twenty more symbolic, implying a pattern to death. Similarly, in "Lady Lazarus," the voice of the poem is a victim of the Holocaust and also attempts suicide every ten years. Very different women in very different circumstances, the protagonists of these two poems are sharing a mythic reality.

Plath presents contrasting images or feeling about the same events. In "Daddy," the daughter longs for her father and simultaneously wishes to destroy him. In "Fever 103°," the heat is evil and destructive (in the forms of hell and the atom bomb), yet it purifies the protagonist. In "Death & Co.," Plath paints two contrasting faces of death, the condor and the kindly old man, reflecting her fear and fascination with death, respectively. Instead of contradicting one another, Plath's opposites coexist.

Plath varies her structure, line length, stanza length, rhythms, sounds, and vocabulary to inform the reader of emotional content and underlying meanings. Structure and sense work together powerfully in her poems. While presenting emotionally charged themes and powerful images, she is reputed for her ability to use colloquial American speech. Yet Plath's writing is not simplistic; her use of language is brilliant.

Many of the poems express the need of the speaker to rid herself of the men in her life. Lady Lazarus eats men. In "Wintering," "winter is for women." The daughter in "Daddy" symbolically kills men, rejecting the false self that she has become: a timid, frightened woman living in the male-dominated shadow of evil. Unburdened by male forces, Plath's females can be reborn into a powerful true self—one that is pure, innocent, untouched, and full of all the possibilities of a newborn baby, an image Plath often uses.

Context

Sylvia Plath is one of the most widely read poets of her time, and many poems from *Ariel* have become part of the poetic cannon. *Ariel* has been placed among the best-selling poetry collections of the twentieth century;

it sold more than 500,000 copies in its first twenty years in publication. Few scholars have been able to discuss Plath's body of work without addressing the facts of her life and death, either interpreting her poems using the knowledge of her history or arguing that her personal life should be ignored in scholarly study. It is difficult, however, not to discuss Plath's history, as the poet, herself, has become a mythic figure. Her suicide often is viewed romantically giving credibility and authenticity to her artistic expression.

In *Ariel*, as in much of Plath's work, a female voice presents a woman's perspective. Her poems draw from traditional female roles, responsibilities, or concerns, such as cooking, childbearing, and mothering. Growing up in the 1950's, Plath battled against the roles that she felt compelled to play: the perfect daughter, the perfect poet, the perfect wife, the perfect mother. She expresses her feelings of being stifled by society's more in "A Birthday Present": "When I am quiet at my cooking. . ./ Measuring the flour, cutting off the surplus,/ adhering to rules, to rules, to rules." Her protagonist asks for death as her gift, the only thing that can free her from these social constraints. Fettered by obligations, some of Plath's female protagonists kill their male influences in order to live again; these women must become vicious in order to save themselves from brutish men.

Though her most famous poems deal with the more common poetic issues of isolation, suffering, and death, Plath wrote more poems centering on the subject of motherhood than on any other. In *Ariel*, this is reflected in works such as "Balloons," where a mother describes balloons and her son's act of popping one, and "Edge," a portrait of a dead woman with her two dead children. Further, Plath uses birth (and rebirth) as a symbol of innocence, purity, and new life throughout her poetry. Her protagonists do not actually wish to die, but instead to be reborn. In creating, or "birthing," these poems, Plath achieves a kind of rebirth, in the living legacy of her art.

Plath communicated the duplicity of nature, expressed the contradictions presented her by the expectations of the middle-class nuclear family, and reflected a growing feeling of female resistance to available models. She was preoccupied with death, yet ironically she was able to capture the vibrancy of domestic life. The women's movement created a political language for her frustrations with juggling expectations and desires. Plath seems to commend herself in "Lady Lazarus" when the speaker says, "Dying/ Is an art, like everything else,/ I do it exceptionally well." Here, Plath recognizes her own talent with a confident voice. Despite her successes, however, she decided that living was too difficult.

Sources for Further Study

Alexander, Paul. *Rough Magic: A Biography of Sylvia Plath*. New York: Viking, 1991. Drawing upon extensive research and exclusive interviews, this biography includes a chapter entitled "Edge" dealing with the last period of Plath's life when she wrote most of the *Ariel* poems. Contains a section of photographs, notes, and an index.

Barnard, Caroline King. *Sylvia Plath*. Boston: Twayne, 1978. Barnard begins with a chronology, followed by a review of Plath's history. She then studies Plath's texts closely, dividing the work into periods of development. Includes notes and references, a selected bibliography, and an index.

Ehrenpreis, Irvin. "The Other Sylvia Plath." *The New York Review of Books* 29, no. 1 (February 4, 1982): 22-24. In his essay, Ehrenpreis studies *The Collected Poems*, including some of the poems from *Ariel*.

Kroll, Judith. *Chapters in a Mythology: The Poetry of Sylvia Plath*. New York: Harper & Row, 1976. Kroll convincingly argues that Plath's poetry deals with a mythic reality.

Lane, Gary, ed. *Sylvia Plath: New Views on the Poetry*. Baltimore: The Johns Hopkins University Press, 1979. Carole Ferrier's chapter "The Beekeeper's Apprentice" discusses how Plath was a product of the 1950's and was expressing frustrations with societal expectations and her own desires.

Newman, Charles H., ed. *The Art of Sylvia Plath: A Symposium*. London: Faber & Faber, 1970. This informative book contains criticism and articles discussing Plath's work from different perspectives, including intellectual, cultural, analytical, and biographical. Contains reviews, essays on specific works, an appendix of lesser-known or "indicative" writing (including drafts of one poem from the handwritten first draft to the final version and pen drawings). Newman includes a helpful table of contents which summarizes each section.

Rosenblatt, Jon. *Sylvia Plath: The Poetry of Initiation*. Chapel Hill: University of North Carolina Press, 1979. Rosenblatt concentrates on Plath's poetry as literary work, emphasizing its ritualistic patterns, rather than discussing her personal history. Includes notes, a bibliography, and an index.

Stevenson, Anne. *Bitter Fame: A Life of Sylvia Plath*. Boston: Houghton Mifflin, 1989. In addition to published works, this biography uses information from interviews and unpublished sources (as a result of the cooperation of Plath's sister-in-law, Olwyn Hughes). Includes a photograph section, sources and notes, an index, and three memoirs.

Wagner-Martin, Linda. *Sylvia Plath: A Biography*. New York: St. Martin's Press, 1987. This biography breaks Plath's life into sections (childhood, adolescence, Bradford High School, and so on), one of which is "The Ariel Poems." Complete with notes on sources, major sources and acknowledgments, and an index.

Ursula Burton

AN AUTOBIOGRAPHY

Author: Janet Frame (1924-)
Type of work: Autobiography
Time of work: 1924 to the 1960's
Locale: New Zealand, England, and Spain
First published: 1991 (*To the Is-Land*, 1982; *An Angel at My Table*, 1984; *The Envoy from Mirror City*, 1985)

Principal personages:

Janet Frame, a New Zealand writer who overcame poverty, a troubled family life, and mental illness
George Samuel Frame, Janet's father
Lottie Godfrey Frame, Janet's mother
Frank Sargeson, a writer who supports Janet's work and provides her with a temporary home
Myrtle Frame, Janet's older sister, who drowns
Robert "Bruddie" Frame, Janet's only brother, who suffers from epilepsy
Isabel Frame, Janet's younger sister, who also drowns as a young woman
June Frame, Janet's youngest sister

Form and Content

An Autobiography is New Zealand author Janet Frame's three-volume examination of her life from her birth through the early years of her career as a writer. The volumes were published separately over a four-year period, and each one deals with a distinct phase of Frame's life. The first volume, *To the Is-Land*, looks at the years of her childhood until her departure from home for teachers college. The second, *An Angel at My Table*, deals with her training as a teacher, her nervous breakdown and the years of hospitalization that followed, and her gradual emergence as a promising young writer. The final volume, *The Envoy from Mirror City*, tells of her travels to England and Spain, her first experiences with love, her growing success as a writer, and her eventual return to New Zealand.

Frame's life story is a compelling one, marked by poverty, hardship, illness, and her long struggle to come to terms with herself and her need for self-expression through writing. The early years of her childhood are among the book's happiest. With the arrival of the Great Depression in the 1930's, however, the mood of family life gradually changes as the pressures facing her father sometimes bring out a difficult, even cruel, side to his character. The situation is exacerbated by the onset of her brother's epilepsy. As her family's internal structure begins to fray, Janet also faces problems at school, where, although she is an excellent student, she remains an outsider. Her sister Myrtle's death by drowning is a devastating blow for the family, yet Frame continues to excel academically and, inspired by her love of literature, begins to write poetry.

In the book's second volume, Frame leaves her family for the first time to attend teaching college, although she continues to dream of becoming a writer. Painfully shy, she has difficulty making friends and is also ill at ease with the aunt and uncle with whom she lives. After completing her training, she finishes a year as a probationary teacher but flees the classroom on the day she is to be observed by the school inspector. The action puts an end to her future as a teacher and marks the beginning of her long slide into emotional despair. An unsuccessful suicide attempt leads to her hospitalization in a mental institution, where Frame is misdiagnosed as schizophrenic and left largely untreated in conditions that serve only to worsen her emotional state. Her twenties, which are also marked by the deaths of her mother and her sister Isabel, are divided between long stays in institutions and brief periods spent working at low-paying, menial jobs. She continues her writing, however, and receives a literary prize while still hospitalized that eventually leads to her friendship with fellow writer Frank Sargeson. Sargeson offers her a place to live and write upon her release, and at his urging, she also applies for and receives a government travel grant.

In the book's third volume, Frame lives for a time in England and in Spain in an attempt to "broaden her experience." Still shy and unsure of herself, she has her first experience with love with an American she meets in Ibiza, Spain. The affair ends unhappily, and Frame suffers a miscarriage before drifting into a second relationship, which she breaks off to return to England. There she begins an extensive course of psychotherapy and devotes herself to her writing, publishing several novels and stories. Her father's death leads her to return to New Zealand, where she decides she will remain, exploring the country of her birth for its literary potential.

Analysis

Janet's Frame's moving, skillfully told autobiography reflects both her abilities as a writer and the talent for introspection that her often difficult life has taught her. Far from being merely a factual retelling of the events of her life, the book is instead an illuminating look at the forces that shaped her particular experience of the world and a thoughtful study of how that experience has affected her work as a writer.

In the book's first volume, *To the Is-Land*, Frame creates a vivid portrait of her early family life. Her mother, Lottie, emerges as a cheerful, loving woman who instills in her children her own love of poetry and literature. The responsibilities of caring for a husband and five children prevent her from pursuing her early attempts at writing poetry for a local newspaper, but Frame recalls her mother's ability to invest even commonplace objects with a sense of wonder that captivated her children. Frame's father, George, although more reserved than his wife, seems at first an amiable and engaging man, singing for his family and playing the bagpipes. When financial worries and his son's illness arise, however, George Frame gradually grows bitter and distant, and his daughter conveys the family's growing alienation in sharply remembered detail.

Frame also succeeds in re-creating her early sense of the world from a child's point of view: the songs and sights and stories that caught her young imagination, the fear and excitement of moving to a new home, her belief that the song "God Save Our Gracious Tin" (as she then pronounced it) referred to her only toy, a silver kerosene tin. The unhappiness of her first years at school—where she was an outsider, the child of a poor family, often unwashed and wearing the same dress for days at a time—is captured with painful accuracy, as is her later blossoming as a scholar and her grateful embrace of the realm of literature and imagination as a refuge from the harshness of her daily life.

The book's second volume, *An Angel at My Table*, explores Frame's tentative steps into the world beyond the scope of her childhood experience. In the shy, awkward student at Dunedin Training College, preparing for a career as a teacher although her cherished desire is to write, one can see the first signs of the crippling emotional problems that will later overwhelm her. Her eventual breakdown—largely the result of her extreme isolation and timidity—and hospitalization lead to the misdiagnosis that will haunt Frame for years to come. The label of schizophrenia colors her relationship with her family, with society as a whole, and, perhaps most important, with herself. Yet throughout this difficult period, she continues to write despite the belief of those around her that her dream of a writing career represents a denial of reality. With the gradual establishment of her literary reputation and her friendship with Frank Sargeson, Frame begins the slow process of pulling herself free of her recurring mental collapses and beginning her life as a full-time writer. The period spent in Sargeson's spare cottage is recalled by Frame as a crucial turning point in her life, a generous and lifesaving gesture from a fellow writer.

With a Literary Fund travel grant, Frame leaves New Zealand in search of experience abroad in the book's third volume, *The Envoy from Mirror City*. It is during this period in her life that Frame begins to come to terms with herself. This gradual process of self-acceptance involves both extensive psychiatric help from British doctors, who recognize and correct the earlier misdiagnosis of schizophrenia, and Frame's own realization that the label of mental illness has become a crutch for her, a disability behind which she can hide. Although she remains painfully shy, she has a love affair while living in Spain, attempting to hide her inexperience from her lover. She also comes to accept the necessity of expressing herself through her writing and organizing her life in a way that will make that possible. The volume's title refers to Frame's metaphor for creativity and imagination, which she terms a "Mirror City," reflecting the outer world through the filter of her own experiences and perceptions. The envoy is both Frame herself and what might be termed the poetic muse, that inexplicable connection that exists between the writer and the realm of inspiration. At the book's close, Frame has returned to New Zealand and her literary roots, seeking untapped sources of material for her work. As she explains her decision: "Europe was so much on the map of the imagination. . . . Living in New Zealand, would be for me, like living in an age of mythmakers . . . to be a mapmaker for those who will follow nourished by this generation's layers of the dead."

Context

An Autobiography is a powerful account of one woman's difficult journey from childhood through a painful adolescence and young adulthood to her gradual emergence as a writer. Frame's book is a testament to the determination to write that somehow survived her devastating years of hospitalization and personal tragedy, and her story is an illuminating look at a writer's development. Frame's growth as a writer is chronicled throughout the book, beginning with her first improvised story as a small child. She discusses both the joy and the salvation that she found in writing and the difficult and day-to-day tedium of sitting alone in a room with only her typewriter for company; one of the book's most important contributions is the success with which it conveys a sense of the writer's life.

Beautifully written itself, the book is also a celebration of the writers whose work inspired and influenced Frame. She quotes frequently from poems that were important to her throughout the various stages of her life and describes the chords that they struck in her own experience. Frame's love of literature is a sustaining force in her troubled life, and her own need to write is both a lifesaving means of self-expression and a longing to become a part of the creative realm that has played such a crucial role in her own development. Her autobiography explores the link between the artist and the world of art that has preceded her; for Frame, this connection also prompted a desire to live and work in New Zealand, where the lack of an extensive literary tradition casts her in the role of a writer who will help shape that tradition.

Several of Frame's novels deal with mental illness and patients in psychiatric hospitals, and her autobiography provides the personal background for these works. Indeed, she does not present a detailed description of her hospitalization as a result of her feeling that she has covered this ground sufficiently in her fiction. *An Autobiography* is therefore an intrinsic part of her body of work, supplying a context within which her fiction may be viewed.

The book was also the inspiration for New Zealand director Jane Campion's film *An Angel at My Table* (1991), which, although it takes its title from the central section, covers all three volumes of the autobiography. Frame's wish, upon her return to New Zealand at the book's close, to become one of her country's "mythmakers" has had repercussions that she could not then have imagined: Her work and her life itself have touched her fellow artists and have found an audience throughout the world.

Sources for Further Study

Frame, Janet. *The Carpathians*. New York: George Braziller, 1988. In this novel, a woman from New York moves to a small New Zealand town. This meditative exploration of inner and outer worlds received the 1989 Commonwealth Writers Prize.

______________. *Faces in the Water*. New York: George Braziller, 1961. Frame's fictional portrait of a woman's hospitalization in a mental institution draws on her own experiences. Its heroine, Istina Mavet, undergoes the trauma of mental illness amid New Zealand's then-primitive approach to treatment.

______________. *Living in the Maniototo*. New York: George Braziller, 1979. A strange, comic story centering on a woman with multiple identities, among them a writer and a ventriloquist. The novel is an exploration of the creative process.

______________. *Owls Do Cry*. New York: George Braziller, 1960. Frame's first novel draws heavily on her own New Zealand childhood and family life. The book helped to establish her literary reputation.

______________. *A State of Siege*. New York: George Braziller, 1966. This novel offers a perceptive, thought-provoking examination of the psyche of a woman who, freed from difficult responsibilities, retreats to an idyllic island.

Janet Lorenz

THE AUTOBIOGRAPHY OF ALICE B. TOKLAS

Author: Gertrude Stein (1874-1946)
Type of work: Autobiography
Time of work: The first three decades of the twentieth century
Locale: Paris
First published: 1933

Principal personages:

Gertrude Stein, an experimental American writer who lived most of her life in Paris

Leo Stein, Gertrude's brother, with whom she first lived in Paris

Alice B. Toklas, Stein's faithful companion for nearly four decades

Pablo Picasso, a Postimpressionist Spanish painter living in Paris and a close friend of Stein and Toklas

Henri Matisse, a French painter whose work Gertrude and Leo Stein collected

Ernest Hemingway, an American novelist and Stein's estranged friend, who was influenced stylistically by Stein

Sherwood Anderson, an American novelist and a frequent visitor in the Stein-Toklas household

Thorton Wilder, an American novelist and playwright

F. Scott Fitzgerald, an American novelist and an attendee of the Stein-Toklas Saturday salons

Form and Content

For years, Gertrude Stein nagged Alice B. Toklas, her lifelong companion, to write her autobiography. When Toklas did not, Stein did it for her. The format of *The Autobiography of Alice B. Toklas* is deceptively simple. Its seven chapters—ranging in length from the three pages of chapter 1, "Before I Came to Paris," to the forty-nine pages of chapter 6, "The War" (World War I), or the fifty-nine pages of chapter 7, "After the War: 1919-1932"—detail the artistic development of Gertrude Stein and only incidentally the life of Alice B. Toklas.

When Toklas arrived in Paris in 1907, Stein, with an A.B. from Radcliffe College and a few courses short of a medical degree from The Johns Hopkins University, was already established there, as was her brother Leo. Toklas, spending her first day in Paris after her arrival from San Francisco, met Gertrude Stein and lived with her for the next thirty-nine years. The autobiography tells of how, when Toklas found herself in the presence of genius, little bells went off in her head. This happened only three times in her life, but the loudest ringing occurred on the day that she met Gertrude.

Stein's mother died in 1888, her father in 1891. Leo and Gertrude attended Harvard and Radcliffe, respectively, traveling frequently in Europe on their small but sufficient inheritance. Leo, an artist, had relocated in Florence, Italy, in 1901. The next year, he moved to Paris. (*The Autobiography of Alice B. Toklas* details Leo's life and Gertrude's background, as well as Alice's.) In 1901, abandoning medical school with the excuse that she was thoroughly bored, Gertrude joined Leo in Europe. Today she would be called a dropout. In her day, however, it was rare for women to attend medical school, so her not finishing, if regrettable, surprised no one.

In *The Autobiography of Alice B. Toklas*, Stein chronicles the involvement that she and Toklas had with the artistic community that flourished in and around Paris between 1910 and 1930. Toklas fed the artists and entertained their wives while Stein picked the men's brains. When the Stein trust fund occasionally yielded more than anticipated, Gertrude and Leo spent the surplus on paintings. When she died in 1946, Stein owned more than a hundred paintings by the most important painters of her time: Pablo Picasso, Henri Matisse, Paul Cézanne, Juan Gris, Marcel Duchamp, and other legendary artists. Stein entertained these artists at the salons that she and Toklas held every Saturday at 27 rue de Fleurus, where she and Toklas lived until 1937. Stein also posed for such artists as Picasso and the sculptor Jo Davidson.

Following World War I, young Americans flocked to Paris, members of what Stein named "the lost generation." The brightest and best of them sought out Gertrude

Stein. Ernest Hemingway, Ford Maddox Ford, Sherwood Anderson, F. Scott Fitzgerald, Thornton Wilder: All of them found their way to 27 rue de Fleurus, where they found intellectual exhilaration. All owe a debt to Stein, who directly affected their writing. *The Autobiography of Alice B. Toklas*, Stein's first commercially successful book, presents in detail a record of the Stein-Toklas household from 1907 to the mid-1930's.

Analysis

The longest chapter in *The Autobiography of Alice B. Toklas* covers the fourteen years from the end of World War I to 1932, the years during which talented Americans swarmed into Paris. Stein wrote the book in six weeks during 1932, modeling it loosely on Daniel Defoe's *Robinson Crusoe* (1719). It is significant that Stein devotes three pages to Toklas' background but twenty-two to her own and to her move from the United States to Paris. Obviously, despite its whimsical title, *The Autobiography of Alice B. Toklas* is Gertrude Stein's autobiography, fancifully presented.

The writing style in this book is unique. In previous works, Stein had used her combined psychological and medical training to observe closely how people actually speak and to represent that speech as accurately as she could. In *Three Lives* (1910), she recorded precisely if often monotonously the actual speech cadences of three domestics: Lena and Anna, German immigrants, and Melanctha, a serving girl, the first African American protagonist seriously presented by a white American writer. The speech of these three women involves endless repetition and circularity. Although they sometimes talk drivel, Stein presents them with respect. In *The Autobiography of Alice B. Toklas*, Stein is still experimenting with a style that bewildered her earlier readers but that has delighted many later ones. She allows thoughts to flow as they do in the unconscious mind. She uses punctuation sparingly. Her sentences often ramble in Stein's attempt to depict how the unconscious mind processes thought. Stein's deviations from the mechanical and grammatical norms to which most writers adhere alarmed early publishers, who refused to publish her writing. Stein herself financed the printing of some of her early work, although Harcourt, Brace and Company published *The Autobiography of Alice B. Toklas*, which was commercially successful.

One can analyze this book in terms of its structure, its use of language, its social commentary (particularly its revelations about more than three decades of artists and writers), and an experimental approach which shocked many readers and still startles the uninitiated. In the first place, novices might ask how an author dares to write the autobiography of another person. The inherent contradiction in doing so is obvious, but it is also indicative of the outrageous way in which Stein uses contradiction and of her marked ability to find the truths inherent in it. Stein knew what she was about artistically. She was never swayed by the demands of publishers and readers who failed to appreciate her heterodox manner of representing her unique vision of life and society.

Stein's writing will annoy readers who value linear thinking. Those, however, who enjoy divergent thinking, who revel in the wordplay of Lewis Carroll or J. R. R. Tolkein, will delight in Stein's inventions. In this autobiography, probably the most linear of all of her writing, Stein shows rather than discusses how women can compete in the world of men.

The Autobiography of Alice B. Toklas evoked considerable interest when parts of it appeared in *The New Yorker*. Behavioral psychologist B. F. Skinner in 1934 published "Has Gertrude Stein a Secret?" in the *Atlantic Monthly*, contending that Stein's early work in psychology in Harvard's laboratories motivated her writing directly, pointing out striking similarities between it and the automatic writing that these experiments produced.

One of Stein's most quoted lines is, "Rose is a rose is a rose is a rose." This is not a simple line. It represents Stein's essentialism, but it also poses the question, by not beginning the line with an indefinite article, of whether "Rose" is a flower, a color, or a person. Such is the enigmatic quality that pervades much of Stein's writing and that makes a book such as *The Autobiography of Alice B. Toklas* yield more to readers on second, third, or fourth readings than on the first one.

Context

The Autobiography of Alice B. Toklas—indeed, Stein's work in general—demonstrates that women have minds and are quite capable of functioning as independently as men. On an artistic and philosophical level,

Stein identified more easily with men than she did with women.

Just as Stein was ahead of her time in entering medical school at an age when most American women of her class were settling into marriages that would make them second-class citizens, mere appendages of husbands who were deemed the important members of society, Stein was striking out courageously in new directions. Stein, nevertheless, needed Alice B. Toklas, who was to their enduring relationship what conventional, middle-class wives were to conventional marriages.

One of Toklas' chief functions through the years of her relationship with Stein was to protect her from boring people, to occupy the wives of the interesting male artists and writers who clustered around her fascinating, brilliant mate. The autobiography makes clear that Stein did not appreciate artists' wives.

Toklas was far from a silent partner in the relationship, but she acceded—publicly, at least—to Stein's wishes. Toklas had a fine mind and a strong sense of herself. Her devotion to Stein was absolute. Toklas could be petty and jealous. She vetoed some of Stein's friendships—most notably her friendship with Ernest Hemingway, perhaps because she sensed Hemingway's wish to seduce Stein. Behind the scenes, Toklas was a force to be reckoned with.

In *The Autobiography of Alice B. Toklas*, Stein is assertive, artistically intractable, and single-mindedly certain of her artistic aims. Her boredom with the wives of the celebrities she attracted suggests that she did not value their intellects, but her aversion to wives was probably much more complicated than this: It likely had much to do with Toklas' jealousy and with Stein's desire to keep peace in her household.

Sources for Further Study

Bloom, Harold, ed. *Gertrude Stein*. New York: Chelsea House, 1986. Part of the Modern Critical Views Series, this volume contains fifteen essays on Stein, a chronology, and a bibliography. The selection is astute, and, although there is no specific essay on *The Autobiography of Alice B. Toklas*, there are frequent passing references to it.

Bridgman, Richard. *Gertrude Stein in Pieces*. New York: Oxford University Press, 1970. Bridgman offers one of the fullest analyses of the overall structure and style of Stein's writing. The book is carefully conceived and clearly presented.

Hemingway, Ernest. *A Moveable Feast*. New York: Random House, 1961. Hemingway gives his side of the story about his relationship with Gertrude Stein and about its fracture. His view is biased but fascinating. An interesting supplement to *The Autobiography of Alice B. Toklas*.

Hobhouse, Janet. *Everyone Who Was Anybody: A Biography of Gertrude Stein*. New York: G.P. Putnam's Sons, 1975. Offers a helpful catalog of the significant people who frequented 27 rue de Fleurus and of both Stein's and Toklas' opinions of them. Well illustrated.

Mellow, James R. *Charmed Circle: Gertrude Stein and Company*. New York: Praeger, 1974. This book, rich with illustrations, captures the vibrant spirit of the exciting circle of painters, sculptors, writers, and fascinating passersby that came within the Stein-Toklas social orbit before and after World War I.

Souhami, Diana. *Gertrude and Alice*. London: Pandora, 1991. The most thorough account of Gertrude Stein's long lesbian relationship with Alice B. Toklas, this book shows how strong Toklas was and how she dominated many aspects of her forty-year association with Stein.

Sprigge, Elizabeth. *Gertrude Stein: Her Life and Work*. New York: Harper Brothers, 1957. Like James R. Mellow's book (above), this well-written biography is replete with excellent illustrations. Along with Mellow's biography, it remains among the most valuable resources for Stein scholars and enthusiasts.

R. Baird Shuman

THE AWAKENING

Author: Kate Chopin (1851-1904)
Type of work: Novel
Type of plot: Domestic realism
Time of plot: The late nineteenth century
Locale: New Orleans and its vicinity
First published: 1899

Principal characters:

Edna Pontellier, a sensitive woman who marries into Creole society and falls passionately in love with Robert Lebrun

Leonce Pontellier, Edna's husband

Adele Ratignolle, a young and beautiful married woman who is Edna's friend and confidante

Robert Lebrun, a handsome, emotional man who likes to flirt with married women

Alcee Arobin, a young man of fashion who serves as a substitute for Lebrun in Edna's life

Form and Content

The Awakening deals with the sexual awakening of a woman who has led the conventional life of an upper-middle-class wife and mother until the age of twenty-eight, then finds herself feeling so frustrated and suffocated that she is willing to defy the conventions of Louisiana Creole society to gain spiritual independence. She gradually abandons housekeeping, social visits, entertaining at home, and all the duties of a woman of her station. Defiantly, she begins to lead a bohemian lifestyle and to exercise freedom of choice in matters of sex.

The novel is divided into thirty-nine short chapters, each consisting of a single significant scene. Most of the story is told through the viewpoint of Edna Pontellier, an exceptionally sensitive and observant woman who can see into the characters of other people. The scenes not only present the various characters' personalities but also paint a picture of homes, furnishings, clothing, servants, entertainment, and other aspects of life in the late nineteenth century.

The first scenes take place at a summer resort on Grand Isle near New Orleans. City dwellers come to escape the city heat, but even on the island the subtropical heat and humidity are oppressive. The women and children remain on Grand Isle throughout the summer, while most of the men come over only on weekends and return to the city to conduct business.

A few younger men have no pressing business matters to which to attend. These bachelors amuse themselves by flirting blatantly with the married women. This behavior is tolerated in Creole society because the code of sexual morality is so strict that it is taken for granted that the relationships will remain platonic. Edna Pontellier, who is the most attractive woman on the island, is courted by the handsome young Robert Lebrun with the benign approval of Edna's husband. A combination of factors, however, turns their affair from a game into something more complex and potentially disastrous.

Once Edna falls in love with Robert, she experiences an adverse reaction to her husband. She realizes that she has never truly loved him and can barely stand to continue having intimate marital relations with him. Edna's character transformation is described in detail; it is also dramatized through Edna's overt behavior.

In one nighttime scene, Leonce keeps calling to his wife to come to bed. It was impossible for authors in Kate Chopin's day to discuss sex in explicit terms; however, Edna's repeated refusals to her husband's entreaties make it clear what is happening. She knows that he wants to have sexual intercourse and, for the first time in their marriage, she is refusing to allow herself to be used.

Robert is in love with Edna but not so deeply that he is willing to make any extraordinary sacrifices. Instead, he goes to Mexico to pursue a lucrative business opportunity. Robert steadfastly avoids communicating with her by mail because he realizes that such correspondence would exceed the bounds of social propriety.

Edna accepts the advances of another young man, Alcee Arobin, although she senses that he is only intoxicated by her beauty and does not understand her as a fellow human being. Here again, the author is unable to describe how far their relationship goes, but she provides strong suggestions that Edna and Alcee become illicit lovers.

By this time, Edna finds her husband so repulsive that she insists on moving out of their home and setting up her own household, providing her with better opportunities to see Arobin. She is becoming a successful artist, and her sketches and paintings are bringing in enough money to allow her to declare her independence.

When Robert returns, Edna finds that she is even more in love with him and that Arobin means little more to her than her own husband. Robert still loves her but lacks her courage and contempt for public opinion. At the last moment, when she is prepared to run away with him, she finds a note stating that he cannot bring himself to violate her marital bonds and to disgrace himself in Creole society. Edna's disappointing experiences with her husband, Arobin, and Lebrun have plunged her into a state of depression. Feeling that life is no longer worth living, she takes off all of her clothes and swims out into the ocean until she becomes exhausted and drowns.

Analysis

Edna Pontellier's "awakening" is a complex physical and psychological phenomenon with many different causes and many different results. Chopin describes this awakening by remaining steadfastly in Edna's point of view throughout the novel, so that the reader sees people and things from the perspective of a woman whose eyes have been opened for the first time in her life to the cold, hard truths about human existence.

The author also uses symbolism as a traditional poetic means of suggesting what is going on inside the heroine. As a result of her awakening, Edna becomes more susceptible to the beauty around her—the sea, the sky, the flowers, and the romantic music of the late nineteenth century.

The author does not attempt to interpret any of the other characters' thoughts and motivations but freely enters into Edna's mind to describe it in detail. Edna is unable to find anyone in her environment who truly understands her, and so she is extremely limited in her ability to discuss her thoughts and feelings through dialogue. The characters indulge in considerable conversation but seldom express their true thoughts or feelings—either because they do not understand themselves or because they are unwilling, in this repressive society, to say what they really think. Edna is the only major character in the novel who is truly awakened to what she describes as "life's delirium"; the others appear to be content to remain in a dream world.

Edna's awakening is an ongoing process which does not really end until she dies. It actually begins before she falls in love with Robert Lebrun. Its cause is somewhat ambiguous and has been debated by numerous critics. She is twenty-eight years old and becoming psychologically mature. The hot, humid weather on Grand Isle has a stimulating effect on her sexuality. She has learned to swim for the first time in her life and is sexually aroused by swimming in the warm Caribbean. Her husband is away most of the time, either in the city on business or fraternizing with his male cronies; this gives her more freedom than she has enjoyed since her wedding. Edna feels like an outsider in his exotic Creole society. The attentions of Robert Lebrun arouse exciting new thoughts and feelings; they also make her husband seem more alien and unattractive. She is beginning to realize that she married an older man for money, social position, and security and not for love.

Furthermore, Edna has an exceptionally bold and inquiring mind. She never attends church or discusses religious matters. She has unconsciously adopted the existentialist position that there is no afterlife in which people are rewarded or punished for good or bad behavior; whatever they experience in the way of love, happiness, or self-actualization, must be achieved in their one brief lifetime.

Edna's awakening also has complex outcomes. She is awakened to her own strong sexuality; to the repressed condition of women; to the degradation of being used as a sexual object; to the mystery of life; to the beauty of nature; to the hypocrisy of her society; to the insincerity, timidity, and selfishness of many males; to the fact that marriage and motherhood are an insufficient career for some women; to her own talents as an artist; and to her ability to become self-supporting rather than a glorified house servant. Sexually, she awakens to the fact of her existence as a unique human being who has an innate right to develop to her fullest potential.

Kate Chopin's favorite author was Guy de Maupassant (1850-1893), and she published many translations of his short stories. The story that made the deepest impression on her was "Solitude" (1893), in which the melancholy French genius wrote: "Whatever we may do or attempt, despite the embrace and transports of love, the hunger of the lips, we are always alone." The realization of the essential isolation of every human being is the final stage of Edna's awakening. It is this realization that drives her to suicide.

Context

Kate Chopin's *The Awakening* has become one of the classics of feminist literature because of its theme of sexual awakening and a woman's right to freedom of choice in matters of love. Feminists believe that the sexual repression of women, which is still common throughout the world, is a necessary precondition of the political repression and economic exploitation of women that are also still found on every continent of the globe. Feminists believe that until women have control of their own bodies, they cannot hope to have control of their own lives.

Chopin was ahead of her time. Her novel *The Awakening* met with critical abuse and public denunciation. A reviewer writing for the magazine *Public Opinion* in 1899 stated that he was "well satisfied" with Edna's suicide because she deserved to die for her immoral behavior. Chopin never wrote another novel and gradually gave up writing altogether. During the early part of the twentieth century, she had become virtually forgotten. Then the very qualities that had caused her to be condemned as an evil influence brought her to the attention of a few critics who saw that Chopin had created a minor masterpiece of feminist literature.

Currently, *The Awakening* is enjoying great popularity and is available in many different editions. The rediscovery of this novel has revived interest in Chopin's other writings. Several biographies have been published, along with a number of full-length critical studies. *The Awakening* is assigned as required reading in many women's studies and literature courses. Because of the renewed interest in her groundbreaking novel, Chopin is also being read in translation in many foreign countries, including France and Japan. She is one of the few writers to have had the good fortune to be figuratively brought back from the dead, and her work is exerting a considerable influence on women's literature and feminism in general.

Sources for Further Study

Bloom, Harold, ed. *Kate Chopin*. New York: Chelsea House, 1987. A collection of ten critical essays on Chopin's works, with considerable discussion of *The Awakening*. The editor's introduction contains a comparison of *The Awakening* with the poetry of Walt Whitman.

Bonner, Thomas, Jr. *The Kate Chopin Companion: With Chopin's Translations from French Fiction*. New York: Greenwood Press, 1988. An attractive and useful volume consisting mainly of a dictionary of characters, places, titles, terms, and people from the life and work of Chopin. Most of the translations are of stories by Guy de Maupassant, including "Solitude," which is essential reading for anyone wishing to understand Chopin's psychological outlook.

Ewell, Barbara C. *Kate Chopin*. New York: Frederick Ungar, 1986. A biography of Chopin which surveys her writings in their entirety. Ewell emphasizes that *The Awakening* is Chopin's best-known and most important creation but represents only a portion of her total achievement as a writer. This excellent study also contains a chronology, a bibliography, and endnotes.

Martin, Wendy, ed. *New Essays on "The Awakening."* Cambridge, England: Cambridge University Press, 1988. A collection of four essays about Chopin's novel with a lengthy introduction by the editor, who provides an overview of Chopin's life and work. Each essay offers a distinct point of view; together they are intended to represent the best contemporary ideas about *The Awakening* by the so-called New Critics.

Seyersted, Per. *Kate Chopin: A Critical Biography*. Baton Rouge: Louisiana State University Press, 1969. Reprint. New York: Octagon Books, 1980. An excellent biography by an authority on the author who served as editor of *The Complete Works of Kate Chopin*, published by Louisiana State University Press in 1970. Seyersted was influential in bringing Chopin back into the literary spotlight as a feminist writer of the first rank.

Toth, Emily. *Kate Chopin*. New York: William Morrow, 1990. An exhaustively researched book regarded by many critics as the definitive biography of Chopin. Toth identifies real-life models for Chopin's literary characters. Many photographs are included.

Bill Delaney

BACKLASH: The Undeclared War Against American Women

Author: Susan Faludi
Type of work: Social criticism
First published: 1991

Form and Content

Susan Faludi's landmark feminist work, *Backlash: The Undeclared War Against American Women*, was published just after the close of the 1980's, a decade during which, the author posits, efforts were made to undermine the gains made by women during the 1970's. Faludi examines several areas of popular culture and documents the dramatic shift that occurred in the presentation of issues dealing with women and the women's liberation movement. She then traces this shift in attitude to those individuals and institutions that she believes helped to shape the change, either through blatant opposition or through revisions in their earlier positions. Her final chapters examine the results of the backlash in women's lives—physically, psychologically, and economically.

Faludi's book rejects the idea that women's gains within society have been so substantial that there is little or no need for a continuing women's movement. Drawing on information from studies by the U.S. Bureau of the Census and several published reports on women's economic status, she questions this assumption of equality attained, noting that women represent two-thirds of all poor adults, earn far less than men—in the case of 80 percent of all full-time working women, under $20,000 a year—and make up only a tiny percentage of the executives and corporate officers of the Fortune 500 companies. She goes on to suggest that women are, in fact, in danger of losing the advances that they have achieved because of the efforts of those individuals—primarily men—who are unhappy or uncomfortable with recent social and economic changes.

Backlash is broken down into four sections: "Myths and Flashback," "The Backlash in Popular Culture," "Origins of a Reaction: Backlash Movers, Shakers, and Thinkers," and "Backlashings: The Effects on Women's Minds, Jobs, and Bodies." The first of these sections discusses several stories related to women that received considerable attention during the 1980's, including a study popularized by a well-known *Newsweek* cover article claiming that single women over the age of thirty-five had an extremely small chance of marrying. Similar studies regarding pregnancy, day care, divorce, and professional women abandoning careers for home and family are also investigated and analyzed. The results that Faludi obtains lead her to state that no evidence supports many of these stories, and that there has been an unacknowledged desire on the part of the media to promote them regardless of their accuracy. After describing other periods of backlash in American history, Faludi moves on to an examination of popular culture and its portrayal of women and women's issues. She finds increasingly negative images of single and professional women in the media, in films, and on television, and she profiles such successful films as *Fatal Attraction* (1987) and *Baby Boom* (1987) to support her case. Trends on television toward shows featuring traditional housewives or single fathers abandoned by selfish working wives are also explored, as well as the difficulties faced by *Cagney and Lacey* in its attempts to offer positive portrayals of two working women. The fashion industry also comes under scrutiny, as does the increasing dissatisfaction expressed by women regarding their appearance in the wake of media emphasis on plastic surgery.

In the book's third section, Faludi traces the roots of the backlash to several sources, including the so-called New Right in politics and religion as she chronicles the development of an orchestrated campaign against the women's movement by fundamentalist Christian ministers. She also looks at the problems facing women attempting to advance in politics, devoting a segment of the section to the 1984 presidential campaign, which featured Geraldine Ferraro as the first female vice presidential nominee. The section concludes with profiles of several people whose writing Faludi feels has contributed to the backlash, including Allan Bloom, Robert Bly, and feminist leader Betty Friedan. The book's final section examines what Faludi believes are efforts to undermine women psychologically, as well as the results that the backlash has had on working women and on the area of reproductive rights.

Analysis

Backlash appeared on the scene at a time when America's attention had been dramatically refocused on women's issues by Anita Hill's accusations of sexual harassment against Supreme Court Justice nominee Clarence Thomas. Political analysts would later point to a direct correlation between the anger many women felt over the results of the hearings—and Thomas' subsequent confirmation—and the increase in the number of women elected to Congress the following fall. Although *Backlash* had already gone to print at the time of the hearings and the controversial case is not included in Faludi's analysis, the book's reception is inextricably linked to the events unfolding at the time of its publication.

Whether one sided with Thomas or with Hill, the focus of all discussions relating to the case was women in the workplace and the sometimes complicated male/female dynamic that can underlie and inform working relationships. *Backlash*, with its strongly pro-feminist position, offered a larger context within which to view the events of the hearings. It also provided welcome documentation for those who had long questioned the stability of women's advances, as well as a thought-provoking overview of the shift in attitude toward working women.

Faludi's central premise, simply stated, is that feminists and the women's liberation movement have become popular scapegoats for those who oppose their goals. She quotes several studies in which women repeatedly point to their jobs as a primary source of security and self-esteem, juxtaposing them with articles in national magazines blaming the women's movement for the problems facing modern women. Faludi's approach is to trace these articles to their sources and examine the methodology used to obtain their conclusions. In every case, she maintains that she could find no hard evidence to support either the claims of disillusionment on the part of working women or the dire warnings of "spinsterhood," childlessness, and imminent psychological collapse.

In perhaps the best-known case that she examines, Faludi challenges the 1986 study on the likelihood of single women over the age of thirty-five ever marrying. This study, quoted out of context before it was completed, received such attention in the media that it quickly became a part of popular folklore, with *Newsweek*'s claim that single women were likelier to end up as victims of terrorists than get married becoming a catchphrase. What Faludi finds when she examines the study is statistical work based on questionable methodology drawn from an off year in the U.S. census statistics. In consultation with a demographer and a statistician from the Bureau of the Census, Faludi reports that, computed correctly, the figures are quite different from those reported in the study.

Faludi uses this same method of examination in her study of film and television and the role that they have played in the backlash. Her look at the box-office hit *Fatal Attraction* turns up the revealing fact that James Dearden, the author of the screenplay, originally intended for the audience to sympathize with the single woman in the story. His plan to make a film about the need for a married man who has an affair to face up to the consequences of his actions was quickly altered by the film's director, Adrian Lyne. The final film shows a sympathetic married man who is stalked by a deranged career woman who threatens his wife and child.

Faludi's list of those whom she believes to be leading or contributing significantly to the backlash includes several intriguing entries. Allan Bloom and his book *The Closing of the American Mind* (1987) are called into question for blaming feminism for the decline in American educational standards. One-time male feminist writer Warren Farrell is criticized for reversing his position in what Faludi suggests is an attempt to remain in the limelight. "Men's movement" leader Robert Bly, the author of the best-selling *Iron John: A Book About Men* (1990), is profiled during an encounter at a weekend seminar, and the picture that emerges is not a flattering one. Neofeminism also comes under scrutiny in her assessment of think-tank expert Sylvia Ann Hewlett, as does postfeminist revisionism in her essay on feminist author Betty Friedan.

Faludi's principal concern throughout the book is women themselves, and in *Backlash*'s final section she looks at the effect that the backlash has had on their lives. The section examines aspects of modern culture, from self-help books to radio talk shows, in its appraisal of what Faludi describes as an effort to lay blame for women's frustrations at their own psychological doorstep. She also points out substantial discrepancies between media claims of achieved economic equality and statistics that indicate the reverse. The book's final chapter takes on the explosive subject of reproductive rights, a central focus in any discussion of women's issues, with a critical look at the anti-abortion movement and profiles of several women whose lives have been profoundly affected by interference with their reproductive choices.

Context

Backlash created a stir and provoked sharp discussion at the time of its publication. Like such earlier landmark feminist works as Friedan's *The Feminist Mystique* (1963) and Germaine Greer's *The Female Eunuch* (1970), the book quickly left the ranks of little-known theoretical literature and entered the realm of feminist writing familiar at least by name to the public at large. Reviews of *Backlash* and articles sparked by it appeared in mainstream magazines and newspapers, and Susan Faludi became a frequent interview subject as well as a favorite representative of the feminist point of view on television news shows and programs relating to women's issues.

The book's most important impact was the dialogue that it began on the issues discussed. Whether one agrees or disagrees with Faludi's conclusions at its close, *Backlash* succeeds in calling many unexamined assumptions about the trends in women's lives into question. For those in agreement, the book provides a staggering amount of information in support of feminist positions; those who disagree do so after giving time and thought to women's issues. The book's provocative assertion that powerful sectors of society are hostile to the advancement of women and are in fact engaged in an insidious attempt to undermine them made the book a subject of controversy. Faludi's detractors questioned or denied her assertions, while her supporters applauded her documentation of what they saw as a growing trend in American society. Some critics of the book believed that not all Faludi's targets were entirely deserving of her criticism, with her section on Friedan receiving considerable attention. For those who agreed with the book's premise, however, and welcomed its outspoken refusal to accept public perceptions at face value, *Backlash* was an immediate source of information and, at times, ammunition in the "undeclared war against women."

Sources for Further Study

Beauvoir, Simone de. *The Second Sex*. New York: Alfred A. Knopf, 1953. One of the earliest works of modern feminist literature, French writer Beauvoir's look at the secondary status of women enjoyed renewed popularity during the women's movement.

Fraser, Antonia. *The Weaker Vessel*. New York: Alfred A. Knopf, 1984. An intriguing perspective on women's issues is offered by Fraser's examination of women's lives in the seventeenth century. A surprisingly diverse collection of portraits emerges.

French, Marilyn. *The War Against Women*. New York: Summit Books, 1992. This book offers a historical examination of women's repression. French explores, from a feminist perspective, the traditional treatment of women socially, politically, economically, and culturally.

Friedan, Betty. *It Changed My Life*. New York: W. W. Norton, 1985. This collection of Friedan's writings over three decades provides an overview of the evolution of feminism from the perspective of the woman sometimes referred to as the "mother" of women's liberation.

Kauffman, Linda S., ed. *American Feminist Thought at Century's End: A Reader*. Cambridge, Mass.: Basil Blackwell, 1993. As its title suggests, the book contains a collection of recent writings by feminist leaders and scholars. Its topics range from political activism to women's sexuality.

Wolf, Naomi. *The Beauty Myth: How Images of Beauty Are Used Against Women*. New York: William Morrow, 1991. This best-selling book examines the ways in which modern society and popular culture put pressure on women to conform to an unattainable standard of beauty.

Janet Lorenz

THE BEAN TREES

Author: Barbara Kingsolver (1955-)
Type of work: Novel
Type of plot: Social realism
Time of plot: The late 1980's
Locale: Tuscon, Arizona
First published: 1988

Principal characters:

Taylor Greer, the protagonist and narrator, who adopts Turtle, an abandoned American Indian child

Lou Ann Ruiz, a woman who becomes the roommate of Taylor and Turtle in Arizona

Mattie, the widowed proprietor of Jesus Is Lord Used Tires

Estevan, a refugee from Guatemala living in Tucson with his wife

Esperanza, Estevan's wife

Turtle Greer, Taylor's adopted American Indian daughter

Virgie Mae Parsons, an elderly woman who lives next door to Taylor and Lou Ann

Edna Poppy, Virgie Mae Parsons' housemate, who is elderly and blind

Alice Jean Stamper Greer, Taylor's mother

Form and Content

The Bean Trees interweaves the stories of several women, all living in Tucson, Arizona, who create successful and fulfilling lives for themselves without male partners. Although these main characters are all white, working-class women, they interact with a larger, more diverse Tucson community of Hispanics, American Indians, Central American refugees, and Chinese immigrants. Political and social issues such as the treatment of illegal aliens and the struggles of single working mothers inform the novel's plot and its characters' actions, but the narrative never becomes solely ideological in its focus. Rather, it shows the everyday difficulties and triumphs of women who succeed by working together to overcome the challenges facing them.

The majority of the novel is told from the point of view of Taylor Greer, one of the many outsiders in the novel who comes to Tucson accidentally. Although Taylor arrives in Arizona with little money and no friends, she soon becomes part of a community of mutually supportive people, most of whom are women. Taylor moves in with Lou Ann Ruiz, another single mother struggling to make ends meet, and the two share the rent, child care, and other domestic responsibilities. Their neighbors, Virgie Mae Parsons and Edna Poppy, are two elderly women who live together and take care of each other, as well as helping Taylor and Lou Ann. Mattie, the successful owner of Jesus Is Lord Used Tires and a committed political activist, is widowed but has created a wide network of friends and volunteers in the sanctuary movement for Central American refugees. Next door to Mattie's tire shop is Lee Sing's market, which is run by a Chinese woman who cares for her "ancient" mother; they provide yet another example of an intergenerational women's community. Family is both biological and socially constructed; Taylor's and Lou Ann's mothers are both featured, as is Lou Ann's mother-in-law.

When Taylor gets a job working for Mattie at the tire store, she also becomes involved in the sanctuary movement. Taylor becomes especially close to Estevan and Esperanza, learning firsthand from Estevan about the horrors of Guatemala's repressive government. At first naïve about the political situations of Central American countries, Taylor soon becomes a participant in the sanctuary movement, proving her commitment by transporting Estevan and Esperanza (an illegal action) to a safe house in Oklahoma at the close of the novel.

Taylor's primary attachment in the novel is to Turtle, a child whom she initially knows as little about as she does the role of mother. Completely unprepared for motherhood, Taylor learns from Lou Ann and Mattie—

and by trial and error—how to take care of Turtle, who becomes so important to Taylor that she legally adopts her. Taylor is only one of several mothers in the novel. Lou Ann, although overprotective and constantly worrying, is also a very caring mother to her son, Dwayne Ray, and a second parent to Turtle as well. In fact, Turtle has so many women taking care of her that she calls them all by their names and "ma"—for example, "Ma Woo-Ahn" for Lou Ann and "Ma Poppy" for Edna Poppy. Knowing that Estevan and Esperanza lost their daughter makes Taylor even more thankful for Turtle, who in turn becomes a surrogate child for the couple. The novel ends with Taylor taking Estevan and Esperanza to their new life in Oklahoma, where she also formally adopts Turtle. The two will return to Tucson and to their "family" there, now also a legal family themselves.

Analysis

The novel's title refers to the name that Turtle uses for wisteria: Their seed pods resemble beans. When Turtle finally begins to talk, she does so in a vocabulary rich with vegetable and other plant names. Organic metaphors can be found throughout the book. For example, a large, unstructured garden behind Mattie's tire shop spills over into Lee Sing's yard—just as the characters form friendships without regard for artificially constructed boundaries. Relationships grow naturally out of mutual needs and interests. The final chapter, "Rhizobia," refers to microscopic organisms that aid in fertilizing wisteria; as Taylor explains it to Turtle, "There's a whole invisible system for helping out the plant. . . . It's just the same as with people"—on their own, wisteria vines "would just barely get by," but "put them together" with rhizobia (or their friends) and "they make miracles." Mutual support and interdependence allow all the characters to flourish in ways that they could not on their own.

With the exception of the second and fourth chapters, which are told in a third-person omniscient point of view and focus on Lou Ann Ruiz before she meets Taylor, the novel is told from Taylor's first-person point of view. Taylor is thus both outsider and central focus; as a transplanted Kentuckian living in Tucson, she meets people different from any she knew back home. As a working-class mother in a community of other working-class women, however, she shares their concerns and their struggles.

Taylor's first-person narration is one of the many examples of the novel's focus on language: Her Southern idioms seem "poetic" to Estevan, while his precise and grammatically perfect English seems beautiful and formal to Taylor. The early chapters have titles that seem at first nonsensical—"New Year's Pig," "Jesus Is Lord Used Tires," "Tug Fork Water"—but whose meanings are revealed in the chapters themselves. Because these examples occur at the beginning of the book, they signal Taylor's initial confusion with being in this new part of the country, having a suddenly acquired child, and not being able to "speak the language" of either motherhood or the Southwest. Many characters speak Spanish; Estevan and Esperanza use it as a lingua franca, for their native languages are two different Mayan dialects. Lou Ann Ruiz's in-laws all speak Spanish, and her mother-in-law speaks no English, just as Lou Ann does not speak Spanish. Turtle creates a language of her own, based largely on vegetable names; this combination of two of the novel's central motifs, organic growth and language, points to the importance of both communication and community.

Issues of community and interconnectedness figure prominently throughout the novel. Turtle, an American Indian, looks a lot like Ismene, the daughter of Estevan and Esperanza who is taken from them. Lou Ann's relatives, the Central American refugees, and the Hispanic community in general appear at first strange and foreign to the Kentuckians Lou Ann and Taylor, but they soon become family, both literally and figuratively. When Taylor, Turtle, Estevan, and Esperanza travel to Oklahoma, Taylor—ever on the lookout for those who might try to arrest and deport the refugees, who do not have identification papers—is comforted by the fact that Estevan and Esperanza look "Indian." Even though they are Mayan and not Oklahoma Cherokee, their physical likeness to the resident American Indians makes them less anomalous than Taylor in this environment.

More broadly construed, issues of race figure in subtle ways. All the characters can be seen as outsiders or foreigners, but the real focus here is on their common humanity: how their race and nationality are one characteristic of their personalities, but not the defining one. Moreover, the characters continually break stereotypes: Estevan, the Guatemalan refugee, speaks perfect and precise English; even though he washes dishes now, he was a respected teacher in his native country. Edna Poppy, who seems at first fastidious and confused to Taylor and Lou Ann, is actually blind—something these younger women do not discover until weeks after meeting her.

Many women in the novel take charge of their lives without the aid of male partners: Mattie creates a successful business after her husband's death; Taylor, reared without a father, sees no need for a father for Turtle or husband for herself; and Lou Ann manages to support herself and her son after her husband leaves them. In fact, the one main female character in the novel who is married, Esperanza, is suicidal and depressed—clearly, because of the torture she suffered in Guatemala, and not because she is married—but the implication here is that women with husbands fare no better than those without them. The relationship between Virgie Mae and Edna, while not overtly lesbian, shows that two older women can care about and for each other deeply, without suffering any social stigmatization.

Context

The Bean Trees was Barbara Kingsolver's first novel, but the themes on which she focuses—single motherhood, working women, United States policies in Central America and toward its refugees, American Indian communities—recur in her subsequent novels *Animal Dreams* (1990) and *Pigs in Heaven* (1993); the latter is a sequel to *The Bean Trees* and details Taylor's interaction with the Cherokee Nation, which views her adoption of Turtle as illegal. Kingsolver's concern for ordinary people—not celebrities, but real people performing acts of everyday heroism—informs all of her writings; her nonfiction work *Holding the Line* (1989) deals with women's roles in a copper mining strike in Clifton, Arizona.

Kingsolver fits into the tradition of Southern writers; she has noted that Eudora Welty, Carson McCullers, and Flannery O'Connor were authors whom she enjoyed reading as a child; later influences include Doris Lessing, Ursula K. Le Guin, and William Faulkner. In her focus on the lives of working-class people and relationships, her novels resemble those of Bobbie Ann Mason, but Kingsolver's settings are in the Southwest, not the Southeast.

The Bean Trees is one of many recent novels which detail female friendships and the powerful bonds between and among women; Lessing's *The Golden Notebook* (1962), Marilyn French's *The Women's Room* (1977), and Alice Adams' *Superior Women* (1984) are a few early examples of this kind of fiction. Kingsolver's work can be seen as different from these other novels, however, in its focus on working-class, non-college-educated women and in its inclusion of a racially diverse cast of characters.

The Bean Trees has been considered an autobiographical work; like Taylor, Kingsolver was born and reared in Kentucky and moved to Arizona as a young adult. Likewise, Taylor's political involvement with the sanctuary movement parallels Kingsolver's own commitment to aiding Central American refugees. Kingsolver wrote the novel while pregnant with her first child and suffering from acute insomnia; before *The Bean Trees*, she had written mostly technical, scientific pieces and political pamphlets.

In its lyrical style and the unique voice of its narrator, in its complex interweaving of several plot lines and many different kinds of characters, *The Bean Trees* succeeds as a novel that incorporates political activism with social realism into a work of fiction populated with ordinary, likable characters performing extraordinary acts.

Sources for Further Study

Butler, Jack. "She Hung the Moon and Plugged in All the Stars." *The New York Times Book Review*, April 10, 1988, P. 15. In this review of *The Bean Trees*, Butler praises Kingsolver's realism and her poetic style, even though he finds some of the characters too good to be true and some aspects of the plot too contrived.

FitzGerald, Karen. "A Major New Talent." *MS.* 16 (April, 1988): 28. In this very positive review of *The Bean Trees*, FitzGerald focuses on the portrayal of women's friendships in the novel, as well as on its political themes.

Randall, Margaret. "Human Comedy." *Women's Review of Books 5* (May, 1988): 1. Randall's review of The Bean Trees offers great praise for the novel. She frames the discussion of her review around the issue of invasion: both in terms of Turtle's sexual abuse (the invasion of a child's body) and the invasion of Central America by United States forces.

See, Lisa. "Barbara Kingsolver." *Publishers Weekly* 237 (August 31, 1990): 46-47. See conducted interviews with Barbara Kingsolver, and this article provides very useful background and biographical information. She also covers some of Kingsolver's other work, including *Holding the Line* (1989), *Homeland and Other Stories* (1989), and *Animal Dreams* (1990).

Ann A. Merrill

THE BELL JAR

Author: Sylvia Plath (1932-1963)
Type of work: Novel
Type of plot: Psychological realism
Time of plot: 1952
Locale: New York City and Boston
First published: 1963

Principal characters:

Esther Greenwood, a gifted college student who suffers from anxiety and depression

Mrs. Greenwood, Esther's mother, a widow who works hard to support herself and her daughter

Buddy Willard, a medical student with whom Esther has a relationship

Joan Gilling, a fellow patient at Esther's mental institution

Dr. Nolan, Esther's psychiatrist

Philomena Guinea, a rich benefactor who pays for Esther's tuition and for her care at a private mental facility

Form and Content

From the first page of *The Bell Jar*, with Esther Greenwood describing a day in New York City during the summer of 1952, when she is a guest-editor of *Mademoiselle* magazine, author Sylvia Plath vividly re-creates the perspective of a depressed, highly intelligent, sensitive young woman who feels herself losing contact with reality. This oppressively introspective atmosphere is relieved, however, by Esther's sardonic and incisive insights into life's unfairness and the often-amusing accounts of her own gauche experiences.

Esther has spent her adult life up to this summer between her junior and senior years of college in intellectual study and competition at a prestigious university. Although the round of parties, plays, and professional writing opportunities working for the magazine seems to mark another success in her life, instead she is experiencing a feeling of frustration and failure as she faces the choices of life beyond college.

Torn between her personal needs and society's expectations, Esther is assessing her past life, especially the value of studying for academic awards, her present desire for personal fulfillment as a woman, and her need to choose a professional career for the future that will both support her financially and fulfill her aesthetically. Her inability to find solutions that will include all of her needs is driving her into a reclusive mental state. Before she leaves New York City at the end of the month, she goes to the rooftop of the hotel where she is staying and symbolically discards all of her newly bought, expensive clothes. Esther has officially begun her retreat from life.

Esther's hostility toward men constitutes a major part of her mental instability. That hostility partly arises from society's expectation that a woman must be attractive to men. For example, Esther finds that Buddy Willard's invitation to attend the junior prom at Yale University with him immediately gives her status in the eyes of her classmates, even the seniors. Buddy's mother expresses another subordinate role for women: They should support their husbands' careers. Esther retorts, "The last thing I wanted was infinite security and to be the place an arrow shoots off from. I wanted . . . to shoot off in all directions myself, like the colored arrows from a Fourth of July rocket." Esther recognizes that her experience with Buddy typifies her experiences with all men: Each one looked like a "flawless man off in the distance, but as soon as he moved closer I immediately saw he wouldn't do at all." Esther also has a problem with society's double standard for men and women. "I couldn't stand the idea of a woman having to have a single pure life and a man being able to have a double life, one pure and one not." She becomes obsessive about losing her virginity without the fear of pregnancy.

After Esther's attempted suicide, she is taken to an expensive private sanatorium, paid for by her college sponsor, Philomena Guinea. Esther finally trusts her new psychiatrist, Dr. Nolan, a woman, because she takes Esther's fears and anxieties seriously and does not condemn Esther for her feelings, such as her hatred of her mother, that are socially unacceptable. After her treatment at the sanatorium, Esther, wearing a diaphragm, has sexual relations with a stranger. For the first time, she feels that her gender is not a liability.

The conclusion of this journal of mental illness is expressed in very tentative terms. After successful shock treatments, Esther feels that the "bell jar" separating her from normal interaction with others has been raised a few feet. She has no guarantee, however, that it will not descend again.

Analysis

Plath's central intention in *The Bell Jar* seems to be to depict the harrowing reality of a worsening mental condition when the person is beginning to lose contact with the world around her. One impressive technique is the distorted descriptions of everyday life. For example, her new and expensive clothes are hanging "limp as fish" in her closest; German words are "dense, black, barbed-wire letters"; and to describe the clothes of Hilda, a fellow guest-editor, "fashion blurbs, silver and full of nothing, set up their fishy bubbles in my brain." As Esther returns home after her month in New York City, the phrases indicating distortions give way to distorted descriptions of entire landscapes and incidents.

The theme of appearance versus reality is important in *The Bell Jar* in several ways. Externally, Esther Greenwood seems to enjoy a very successful life: She is a scholarship recipient at a prestigious school, a published poet, and the winner of a month in New York as the guest-editor of a magazine. Internally, she questions her identity, believes that she cannot continue to be successful, finds herself socially awkward, and feels herself to be sexually unfulfilled. Existentially, she challenges the meaning of the successes that she has attained.

The ironic tone of the narrator is one of the principal literary devices used to create the bifurcated vision of a highly intelligent young writer who sees both the conventional façade and the reality behind it. One example of such duplicity is the luncheon for the guest-editors given by *Lady Day* magazine. Although the kitchens gleam with spotless stainless steel counters and ranges, the crab meat gives them food poisoning. On another occasion, Esther observes Dr. Gordon, her first psychiatrist, carefully creating a physical and psychic space between himself and his patients. The problem is that this ironic perception creates the divisiveness within Esther. She wishes she could be like fellow guest-editors Betsy and Doreen, who commit themselves totally to the view of life in which they believe.

Some female characters are used as alter egos. Of the young women who are also guest-editors during the summer in New York, Esther believes that two of them represent two divisive parts of herself. Betsy, from Kansas, is like the part of Esther that has conformed almost obsessively with the norms of society. Doreen, on the other hand, is Esther's shadow side: the urges she has not expressed but would like to. Esther alternates in loyalty from one to the other but feels torn between the two.

Esther's treatment at the sanatorium is paralleled with that of another student from her college, Joan Gilling. Esther has been unable to find a man who can measure up to her expectations, but she is still shocked to discover that Joan is a lesbian. Just when Joan seems to be recovering and is therefore allowed more periods of time outside the sanatorium, she commits suicide. Attending Joan's funeral, instead of being drawn to suicide, Esther finds herself opting for life.

Since Plath was a poet, it is not surprising that she used many thematic images in *The Bell Jar*. Several images continue the theme of depression. The fetus of a dead baby in a jar suggests the unfulfilled life; yet Esther, when she is skiing down a slope for the first time, wants to return to the womb, apparently as a refuge to avoid decision-making. Later, she recalls a dream of a fig tree containing figs that represent all the choices life holds out to her; the only condition, however, is that she must make one choice. Since Esther wants all of them, she is unable to choose, and all the ripe figs turn black and die.

The major symbol is expressed in the title. As Esther feels herself retreating from life, she compares her isolation to being under a glass bell jar: She is unable to make contact with the world around her that she can see through the glass. Although the electroconvulsive therapy that she is given has lifted the bell jar, she sees it as temporarily suspended, ready to drop down and enclose her again.

Context

The Bell Jar was first published in England in 1963 under the name of Victoria Lucas; it was published in the United States eight years later. It is one of the early novels to handle self-consciously three of the major concerns in the women's movement: a woman's place in society, the development of her creative ability, and the place of femininity in the life of an artist. The fact that the novel was published after the author's suicide heightened the implicit message: There are few role models in society for the creative woman.

Sidonie Smith, in *A Poetics of Women's Autobiography: Marginality and the Fictions of Self-Realization* (1987), emphasizes the choice women writers have to make between social ostracism and developing a voice of their own. In *The Madwoman in the Attic: The Woman Writer and the Nineteenth-Century Literary Imagination* (1979), Sandra M. Gilbert and Susan Gubar state the conflict clearly: "For a woman-artist is, after all, a woman—that is her 'problem'— and if she denies her own gender, she inevitably confronts an identity crisis as severe as the anxiety of authorship she is trying to surmount."

George Stade, in his essay "Womanist Fiction and Male Characters" (1985), believes Plath to be the first of a line of female authors in whose work "the rejection of men in all their ways is at last explicit." Not one of the males in *The Bell Jar*—Buddy Willard, Marco, Mr. Manzi, Dr. Gordon—meets Esther's standards for men.

Other works offer female protagonists who succumb to at least temporary madness because they cannot find a place for themselves in the image of a woman proposed by contemporary society: *Play It as It Lays* (1970), by Joan Didion; *Surfacing* (1972), by Margaret Atwood; and *The Four-Gated City* (1969), by Doris Lessing. Lessing's Kate Brown in *The Summer Before the Dark* (1973) suffers a very brief breakdown in London before she is able to separate her own identity from society's images of wife, mother, and career woman.

Since *The Bell Jar* is Plath's only prose work to reach publication, comparison with her poetry seems inevitable. Her reputation as a poet rests on the posthumous volumes *Ariel* (1965), *Winter Trees* (1971), and *Crossing the Water* (1971). The poem "Daddy," from *Ariel*, uses some of the phrases found in the novel. Since Plath was proofreading *The Bell Jar* when she was writing "Daddy," the similarity of phrases found in both is not surprising, nor is the love and hatred expressed by the daughter in the poem who tries to find the father who died when she was ten, "the last time she was really happy." The poem "Lady Lazarus," as the title indicates, deals with recurring attempts to commit suicide; several of its lines may seem thematically familiar to the reader of *The Bell Jar*.

Sources for Further Study

Alexander, Paul, ed. *Ariel Ascending: Writings About Sylvia Plath*. New York: Harper & Row, 1985. The essays in this volume concentrate on Plath as a craftsman. The two essays "Esther Came Back Like a Retreaded Tire," by Robert Scholes, and "Victoria Lucas and Elly Higginbottom," by Vance Bourjaily, offer interpretations dealing solely with *The Bell Jar*.

Axelrod, Steven Gould. *Sylvia Plath: The Wound and the Cure of Words*. Baltimore: The Johns Hopkins University Press, 1990. In the preface, the author describes his work as "a biography of the imagination." The index indicates several references to *The Bell Jar*. The chapter "A Woman Famous Among Women," proposing Virginia Woolf's influence on Plath, offers an interesting contrast and comparison between Clarissa Dalloway, from Woolf's 1925 novel *Mrs. Dalloway*, and Esther Greenwood. A portrait of Plath and an extensive bibliography are provided.

Bundtzen, Lynda K. *Plath's Incarnations: Women and the Creative Process*. Ann Arbor: University of Michigan Press, 1983. Combines psychological and feminist criticism in a critical biography. Bundtzen traces Plath's personal development as an artist and relates that development to the image of women in society and the world of art. The index provides topical guidance for information on *The Bell Jar*, and the chapter "*The Bell Jar*: The Past as Allegory" offers an interpretation of the novel as feminist allegory. A bibliography is included.

Kroll, Judith. *Chapters in a Mythology: The Poetry of Sylvia Plath*. New York: Harper & Row, 1976. The index contains many extended references to *The Bell Jar*. A chronology is included.

MacPherson, Pat. *Reflecting on The Bell Jar*. New York: Routledge, 1991. This study stresses the social context of *The Bell Jar*. The "Cold War Paranoia," the repressive atmosphere of the 1950's introduced in the novel by the execution of Julius and Ethyl Rosenberg, affects the protagonist personally. Some specific social topics include life in the suburbs, hatred of one's mother expressed in contemporary films, and homosexuality. The bibliography contains relevant sociological and political entries.

Newman, Charles, ed. *The Art of Sylvia Plath: A Symposium.* Bloomington: Indiana University Press, 1970. A collection of essays mainly discussing Plath's poetry. Mary Ellmann, in "*The Bell Jar*—An American Girlhood," sees the work as a "poet's novel" and proceeds to discuss it in terms of images and brief moments of pain. Contains a brief annotated bibliography for *The Bell Jar* ending with 1966. Pen drawings by Plath are included.

Wagner, Linda W., ed. *Sylvia Plath: The Critical Heritage*. New York: Routledge, 1988. The select bibliography identifies two extended bibliographies, one containing all periodical publications. Offers mostly reviews of Plath's work as it was published, including ten reviews and essays on *The Bell Jar*.

Agnes A. Shields

BELOVED

Author: Toni Morrison (Chloe Anthony Wofford, 1931-)
Type of work: Novel
Type of plot: Historical realism
Time of plot: The late nineteenth century
Locale: Kentucky and Ohio
First published: 1987

Principal characters:

Sethe, a former slave woman who killed one of her children eighteen years ago when she was almost captured as a fugitive

Beloved, the ghost of Sethe's baby, who appears as a young woman calling herself by the only word carved on her tombstone

Denver, Sethe's youngest child

Paul D, a former slave who comes to Cincinnati looking for Sethe

Baby Suggs, Sethe's mother-in-law, whose freedom was bought by her son, Halle

Form and Content

Beloved portrays the life of a former slave after the Civil War who is haunted by the horrors of her past. The stories told by the characters in the novel describe the dehumanization that results from slavery and eventually reveal Sethe's dark secret: her murder of her baby daughter eighteen years ago, when Sethe was caught following an escape attempt. Sethe killed her baby so that the child would not have to live as a slave, without dignity and in a world where her body would be used for a master's pleasure and for the reproduction of his "property." Beloved, the spirit of Sethe's dead baby, returns as a woman of twenty to the house where Sethe and her daughter Denver live. Taking her name from the word on her tombstone, Beloved demands compensation from Sethe for her missing childhood.

The novel begins with visits from Paul D, one of the former slaves at Sweet Home in Kentucky, and from Beloved. Urged to tell stories, Sethe recalls memories of the past that she has long buried. She was owned by a humane master at Sweet Home, where she married Halle and gave birth to three children. After the master's death, a new master, Schoolteacher, tried to dehumanize his slaves, which led to their escape attempt. While the other slaves failed in their attempt, Sethe sent her children ahead to the North.

Unable to find her husband, Sethe, pregnant and barefoot, succeeded in arriving in Cincinnati, where her mother-in-law Baby Suggs waited with the children. On the way, Sethe gave birth to Denver in a boat on a river with the help of a white woman. Before she left Sweet Home, she was whipped by her master. Upon her arrival in Cincinnati, Baby Suggs attended to the tree-shaped scar on Sethe's back and nursed her back to health. A month later, when the master came to capture her and her children, Sethe instinctively tried to kill her children, cutting her baby's throat with a handsaw and almost dashing out Denver's brains before she was stopped.

After eighteen years of alienation from her community, Sethe now rejoices with Paul D's visit. Soon after, she enjoys her reunion with Beloved. Yet the appearance of this young woman is an ominous one: Baby Suggs soon dies in distrust of God, Sethe's two sons run away from home, and Paul D leaves upon learning of the murder and being made unwelcome by Beloved. In addition, Beloved's demands eventually exhaust Sethe. Denver soon recognizes Beloved as the ghost that has been seen in the house and believes that she is her dead sister.

Although Denver enjoys Beloved's company, she ventures into the outside world when Sethe's exhaustion becomes unbearable—a world from which she has been isolated by her mother's actions. She asks neighbors for food and work, which they provide for her. Soon the women in the community gather to exorcise the ghost from Sethe's house. Confronted by a chorus of thirty singing women, Beloved vanishes. Paul D comes back to see Sethe and tries to inspire in her a will to live and an ability to realize her own worth.

Analysis

Toni Morrison's central intention in writing an individual history of a former slave is to reclaim the unrecognized past and to furnish these records to future generations, ensuring that the horrors of slavery will not be repeated. *Beloved* is based on an actual incident that occurred in 1856 when a fugitive slave woman killed her child when they were caught. Reconstructing this incident, Morrison tries to understand the intention of the mother's action. The novel focuses on a protagonist who kills her child and alienates herself from her world, and it shows how the memory of the past can haunt the present.

The novel reveals that Sethe's act of murder is rooted in a motherhood crippled by slavery, thus illuminating slavery's inhumanity. In slavery, the basic value of a woman is her role in the reproduction of her master's commodities, as well as in his sexual pleasure. In these circumstances, mothers are neither nurturers nor protectors of their children. Baby Suggs remembers little of her seven children who were sold away; Ella, another slave, refuses to nurse her baby born from forced sex with her master.

Like many of the others, Sethe does not enjoy motherhood, either as a child or as a mother herself. As a baby, she is nursed with milk not from her mother but from another slave with the little milk left after she nurses white babies. When Sethe is still small, her mother tries to run away, leaving her behind. Later when she is a mother, Sethe is violated and has her milk stolen by Schoolteacher's nephews. Such symbolic acts break the nurturing tie of mothers and children. Beloved mirrors Sethe's longing for her own mother. Through her, Sethe sees herself as the daughter she might have been if her mother had been with her. It is not only Beloved but also Sethe who wants both compensation and explanation for the absence of a nurturing mother.

Through the narratives told by the characters, it is shown that Sethe's intention in killing her daughter was to provide her with the ultimate protection from slavery's agony. In order to compensate for the absence of motherhood in slavery, Sethe becomes an overly powerful nurturer and protector. Whether her action is right or wrong, in putting her daughter's life to an end she remains a protector of the dead child. Her action reclaims the rights of deprived mothers and of all humans in slavery. The ironic nature of her action emphasizes the tragedy of the slavery system.

In the novel, the recovery of an individual's history parallels that of all slaves. Sethe and Beloved, both abandoned children who cry out for the missing ties with their mothers, represent all slave mothers and children. They also signify the longing of many African Americans for the missing ties with their cultural heritage in Africa. While Sethe's experiences mirror the suffering of the "sixty million and more" slaves to whom Morrison dedicates this novel, Beloved represents those who are not even counted in the official numbers in slavery. Beloved's life is not recognized; she does not even have a name. Her thirst for recognition and for her mother's love suggest the necessity of recognizing forgotten people. By giving a body and a voice to the spirit of Sethe's dead daughter, Morrison recognizes and recovers the forgotten people in the history of slavery.

Written in the African American storytelling tradition, *Beloved* is full of metaphors and symbols that suggest slavery, such as water. The initial separation of the African slaves from their homeland took place in the Middle Passage across the Atlantic Ocean, and the Ohio River often separated slaves from successful fugitives. In the novel, Denver's birth is in a river, and Beloved first rises from a river and drinks much water upon appearing. The image of a ghost also suggests the situation of slaves, who possess nothing, not even their own bodies. Furthermore, it symbolizes the African American reality that has been treated as nonexistent from the perspective of the dominant society. In narrating her characters' histories, Morrison frequently uses exact figures concerning length of time and number of people. This approach provides a contrast to the official written documents, which record the history of slavery in vague numbers.

Context

Beloved provides a feminist's perspective on historical writing. As such, it challenges the accepted content and narrative mode of historical documents. Morrison shines a light on those who have been silenced and marginalized by history. She chooses to focus on a slave woman's act of murder as a historical incident to be narrated, and she recounts it through a tradition of storytelling which is the principal literary form in African

American culture. Morrison's achievement in *Beloved* is having contributed to the recording of an important part of American history from the viewpoint of the oppressed.

Morrison is primarily concerned with the psychological trauma that social conditions create by showing how the protagonist's alienation and despair result from her experience in slavery. One of the social conditions that Morrison reveals is that only white males such as Schoolteacher have the authority to record history and determine literary tradition. She also provides evidence of African American women's double suppression because of their gender and race. These concerns are still the central problems of many women's lives in the author's contemporary society.

The reality of such problems is not foreign to Morrison, who has faced some obstacles as an African American woman writer. Despite its high literary quality, achieved through a unique narrative style and the use of symbolism and poetic imagery, *Beloved* was overlooked by two major literary prizes, the National Book Award and the National Book Critics Circle Award. These oversights brought controversy, and many African American writers and critics demanded recognition of Morrison's achievement in *Beloved*. Eventually, the novel was awarded the Pulitzer Prize in fiction. Moreover, Morrison won international recognition when she received the 1993 Nobel Prize in Literature; she is the eighth woman and the first black woman to win the prize.

Sources for Further Study

Anderson, Linda, ed. *Plotting Change: Contemporary Women's Fiction*. London: Edward Arnold, 1990. Offers feminist criticism on the novels of Morrison and other women authors whose writing questions traditional modes of thought. The first part of the essay on *Beloved* examines historical novels by women, and the latter part analyzes the work and provides commentary on Morrison's reinterpretation of historical writing.

Horvitz, Deborah. "Nameless Ghosts: Possession and Dispossession in *Beloved*." *Studies in American Fiction* 17, no. 2 (Fall, 1989): 157-167. This critical essay discusses the overall work, focusing on elements of memory and history, and presents a thorough analysis of the characterizations of Sethe and Beloved.

Pearlman, Mickey, ed. *Mother Puzzles: Daughters and Mothers in Contemporary American Literature*. New York: Greenwood Press, 1989. Essays on the writings of Morrison and other women writers that examine the physical and psychological absence of mothers. The chapter on *Beloved* provides a critical interpretation of the theme of love in the novel.

Rainwater, Catherine, and William J. Scheick, eds. *Contemporary American Women Writers: Narrative Strategies*. Lexington: University Press of Kentucky, 1985. A compilation of critical essays on Morrison and other contemporary women authors. The chapter that focuses on Morrison thoroughly analyzes her narrative technique in her first four novels. Although written before *Beloved* was published, this critical essay presents useful insights into Morrison's major themes and into the different narrative techniques that she employs in each novel.

Spillers, Hortense J., ed. *Comparative American Identities: Race, Sex, and Nationality in the Modern Text*. New York: Routledge, 1991. A compilation of essays on the writing of Morrison and other contemporary authors. The essay on *Beloved* examines the novel in the context of contemporary historical theory and provides an insightful examination of the relationship between history and fiction.

Yasuko Akiyama

BETSEY BROWN

Author: Ntozake Shange (Paulette Williams, 1948-)
Type of work: Novel
Type of plot: Domestic realism
Time of plot: 1959
Locale: St. Louis, Missouri
First published: 1985

Principal characters:

Betsey Brown, a thirteen-year-old from an African American middle-class family who struggles with adolescence
Greer Brown, Betsey's father, a physician
Jane Brown, Betsey's mother, a social worker
Vida Murray, Betsey's grandmother, who lives with the family
Mrs. Maureen, the owner of a beauty parlor
Carrie, the housekeeper

Form and Content

Betsey Brown tells the story of one thirteen-year-old African American girl's struggles with adolescence. Although the issues of growing up would resonate for any young girl, Ntozake Shange wrote the novel specifically to provide reading matter for adolescent black girls—the literature that she could not find in her own youth. Betsey Brown is the oldest of five unruly children in a middle-class family. Like all adolescent girls, she feels estranged from her family: They do not understand or appreciate her. Jane, Betsey's mother, wants her to start acting like a young lady, to stop climbing trees, to be careful around boys, to take more responsibility for her siblings and young cousin, and to have refined tastes. Betsey's father, Greer, wants her to grow up to lead her people to freedom. He teaches the children about black history and culture, beating on his conga drum, chanting, and taking the children to march in demonstrations. Betsey's only release from the pressures put upon her is to get away by herself, up her special tree or on one of the house's many porches. When she is alone, watching the sunrise, Betsey is at peace.

The story moves forward in a straightforward chronological manner, and it is firmly rooted in its specific time and place. In 1959, St. Louis took its first steps toward integrating the public schools, and the Brown children are among that first cadre of children bused to formerly all-white schools. Greer has tried to prepare the children for this event by giving them a firm sense of self and of heritage. He is eager for his children to enter the fray, even as Jane fears it.

When her teacher requires each student to recite a poem, Betsey chooses one by the African American poet Paul Laurence Dunbar, one of her father's favorites, and is ridiculed by the teacher. The white students do not seem very different from the children in her own neighborhood, but neither group knows how to cross the invisible barriers that divide them. Betsey cannot help wondering what the point of integration is, why she must ride three busses to learn the same things as before.

Feeling that everyone wants her to be something different, Betsey decides to run away. Her plan is to work in Mrs. Maureen's beauty parlor and eventually elope with Eugene, her thirteen-year-old boyfriend. When she learns that Mrs. Maureen makes most of her money running a brothel, Betsey has to give up her childish notions about adults and love; she is on her way to becoming a woman.

Back home, things are strained between Greer and Jane. Overwhelmed by her career as a social worker and her responsibilities at home, Jane is tired and bored. She wants to rediscover the exciting woman she was when Greer courted her, yet she fears allowing her middle-class values to slip. She too runs away, and she is gone for months.

During her absence, Greer hires Carrie to run the household and manage the children. She teaches them manners; shows them how to sew, cook, and clean; and gradually brings order to the house. Carrie is an important older friend to Betsey, and she shows Betsey how to have pride and confidence in herself, to accept feelings of love, and to make decisions by herself and for herself. When Jane returns, Betsey has more understanding of her position in the family, and she is ready to stand beside Jane as a woman.

Analysis

Shange's intention in writing *Betsey Brown* was to provide a look at the adolescence of one black girl. In her own youth, Shange reports, she could find no books to help her sort out her own life: Books about young women were written by whites for whites, and most books by African Americans were by and about men. *Betsey Brown* presents Betsey's struggles with gentle humor and love; for this book, Shange puts aside her own rage at sexism and racism to present a more reassuring view. The reader knows from the beginning that things will come out right in the end.

That is not to say that Shange does not take Betsey's worries seriously. In one gentle, comic scene, Betsey and her girlfriends retreat to Susan Linda's bedroom to compare their developing breasts. Susan Linda is worried because one of her nipples is larger than the other. When they begin to touch them, and even to count their pubic hairs (Betsey has five), one of the girls runs away, fearing the wrath of God. Shange presents the girls' reflections and comments in a serious, straightforward manner; there is no hint of her laughing at the girls. She knows that for girls (and her young readers) the issues are important, even though an older reader may smile at their innocence and ignorance.

Interestingly, Shange does not take the opportunity presented here to educate her young readers. She does not allow her narrator to comment on the relative sizes of women's nipples, to reassure Susan Linda—and an inquiring young reader—that the supposed deformity is not a problem. Instead, she simply presents the scene as it happened, with no adults there to whisk worries away. Readers are meant to relate to the character of Betsey Brown, not to learn anatomy from her. By the end of the novel, however, the young reader will understand that growing up happens on its own, and that knowledge and power are handed down from older women. If the reader has questions about her body, she may be ready to ask them.

A central issue of the novel is the importance of passing down information and understanding, especially about heritage. Greer wakes his children every morning with a conga drum and chanting, and then leads them through a quiz on black history. All the children can recite poetry by Paul Laurence Dunbar and Countée Cullen; they know the music of Dizzy Gillespie, Chuck Berry, and Duke Ellington. Betsey herself has been rocked to sleep by W. E. B. Du Bois, and she once tried to sneak into a Tina Turner concert.

As much as Jane loves and admires Greer, she fears that this cultural exposure will limit her children instead of expanding their horizons. She would like the children to grow up with nice middle-class manners and tastes, and she is afraid that they will be in real danger if they become too involved in the civil rights struggle. It is not until Jane can reembrace her heritage and the need for involvement that she can really be a part of the family. While she is absent, Carrie takes her place and teaches Betsey and the other children how to combine the dreams of both parents. She shows them the importance of standing up for themselves and honoring their culture and history, and she also teaches them to be well-mannered and self-sufficient.

The story unfolds chronologically, in short scenes full of dialogue and internal monologue. The language is simple and poetic, reflecting Shange's enormous talents as playwright and poet. Shange has a strong ear for language and speech; each character has a distinct voice. Even the narrator's voice is rich with character. From the opening chapter's fourth sentence—"She'd shake Sharon or Margot outta they beds and run to the back porch . . ."—the novel captures the sounds of African American speech. Descriptive words used in the novel, like "Negro," "niggah," and "colored," place the story firmly in its time and place. It is important to note that Shange does not use apostrophes when she writes "outta they beds" or "he'd fix em." The word "outta" is not a derivative that needs the apology of apostrophes; it is a word in the language that these characters speak.

Context

Like other novels by African American women writers of the late twentieth century, *Betsey Brown* is concerned with how a young black girl can find her way through a world filled with meddling parents, racist whites, and ever-expanding dreams. Unlike Toni Morrison's *The Bluest Eye* (1970) and Alice Walker's *The Color Purple* (1982), however, *Betsey Brown* gives an important look at the black middle class. Betsey lives in a large comfortable home with two loving parents. Whatever difficulties Betsey faces with growing up, and with growing up in a society struggling through integration, she is free to think about them and work through them, unhindered by hunger, crime, or violence. This setting allows Shange to focus on Betsey's inner world, because her outer world is relatively safe.

Betsey Brown is also different from many other late twentieth century novels about adolescent girls in its depictions of men. Betsey's father is kind, if somewhat detached; her boyfriend, Eugene, is nearly as innocent as she is; her brothers and cousin are wild but sweet children; and Mr. Jeff the gardener nurtures Carrie and his flowers. Shange is a committed feminist. Some of her other work, most notably the play *for colored girls who have considered suicide/ when the rainbow is enuf* (1976), have drawn charges that she presents unfairly negative male characters (charges that she disputes). In this novel, men are incidental or benign. Shange chooses instead to focus on the power that women draw from one another, the wisdom that they hand down to one another. In Betsey's world, sisterhood is powerful.

Shange has said repeatedly that she thinks of herself as a poet first and a playwright second. *Betsey Brown* received generally favorable reviews, but it has attracted scant serious critical analysis. Shange wrote the novel for an adolescent audience, and it is among those readers where the impact of the novel has been most strongly felt. To give young African American girls a novel about girls like them was Shange's purpose, and *Betsey Brown* is found on secondary school suggested reading lists across the United States.

It is interesting to note that Shange continued to work with the idea of *Betsey Brown* long after its publication. A rhythm and blues musical based on the novel has been produced in different versions beginning in 1989. These versions have adapted the story for an adult audience.

Sources for Further Study

Lester, Neal A. "Shange's Men: *for colored girls* Revisited, and Movement Beyond." *African American Review* 26, no. 2 (Summer, 1992): 319-328. Although this article deals specifically with Shange's play, it offers useful insights that refute charges frequently made against Shange that her black male characters are stereotypical and negative.

Shange, Ntozake. "At the Heart of Shange's Feminism: An Interview." Interview by Neal A. Lester. *Black American Literature Forum* 24, no. 4. (Winter, 1990): 717-730. Describes the dynamics of Shange's feminism, and her desire to write books for black adolescent girls. Also offers insights on pornography, sexuality, and the role men would play in Shange's ideal world of gender equality.

______________. "Interview with Ntozake Shange." Interview by Brenda Lyons. *Massachusetts Review* 28, no. 4 (Winter, 1987): 687-696. Of available commentary by Shange about *Betsey Brown*, this is the most extensive in print. Discusses Shange's intended audience—adolescents of color—and describes Shange's own youth.

______________. "An Interview with Ntozake Shange." Interview by Neal A. Lester. *Studies in American Drama, 1945-Present* 5 (1990): 42-66. This interview covers Shange's writing process and political intentions. Readers of *Betsey Brown* will be particularly interested in the discussion of the functions of language in her work and of how language reveals character. Includes a photograph of Shange.

______________. *See No Evil: Prefaces, Reviews, and Essays, 1974-1983*. San Francisco: Momo's Press, 1984. Although this book was published before *Betsey Brown*, it gives useful insights into Shange's artistic vision and the racial and gender politics that inform her writing. Illustrated.

Tate, Claudia, ed. *Black Women Writers at Work*. New York: Continuum, 1983. A collection of interviews conducted by Tate with several writers. The chapter on Shange includes an important discussion of Shange's inability to find suitable reading material as an adolescent girl and her wish to provide for future girls like her. This desire directly leads, a few years after this interview, to *Betsey Brown*. The chapter begins with a brief biography.

Cynthia A. Bily

BEYOND GOD THE FATHER: Toward a Philosophy of Women's Liberation

Author: Mary Daly
Type of work: Social criticism
First published: 1973

Form and Content

Mary Daly, professor of theology and philosophy, was motivated by anger at what she and other feminists call the patriarchal oppression of women, reinforced by the Judeo-Christian tradition that views God as male and thus denies women their humanity and spirituality. (The word "patriarchy" comes from the Greek meaning "rule of the father" and refers to a system of unequal social, economic, and sexual relations which creates and reinforces men's authority and power over women.) Daly hoped that her radical approach to theology and philosophy in *Beyond God the Father: Toward a Philosophy of Women's Liberation* would make a difference by inspiring women with the courage of "Be-ing," her verb describing "an Other way of understanding ultimate/intimate reality." In a sequel to her work *The Church and the Second Sex* (1968), Daly here introduces her departure from "reformist" feminism (that which tries to work within a patriarchal system such as the Christian church) to a "post-Christian radical feminism" (that which calls for the destruction of the male power structure in its spiritual institutions).

Daly acknowledges her debt to twentieth century British writer Virginia Woolf, whose essays in *A Room of One's Own* (1929) and *Three Guineas* (1938) have inspired countless feminists. Woolf was one of the first to analyze British society as a patriarchy and the first to introduce the idea of woman used as a scapegoat for all humankind's ills. These concepts are keys to Daly's thought as well.

Daly uses references to books and journal articles as the basis for her discussion of the "sexual caste" system that she believes exploits women. Her purpose is to examine the potential of a woman's revolution to "generate human becoming"—that is, to allow the freedom of human consciousness to flourish in women by cutting away at the value system and naming power of patriarchal society. Women would be enabled to become what psychologist Abraham Maslow, in *Toward a Psychology of Being* (1962), calls "self-actualizing" persons, those who display boldness, courage, freedom, spontaneity, perspicuity, integration, and self-acceptance.

Throughout her discussion, Daly makes reference to ancient and modern theologians, philosophers, psychologists, political activists, and anthropologists in support of her attempt to create a feminist philosophy to enlighten as well as enliven the feminist debate with traditional religious thinkers, especially Christian theologians. Her sources range from the antifeminist writings of the Bible, Greek philosopher Aristotle, Catholic saint Thomas Aquinas, theologian Paul Tillich, and comparative religionist Mircea Eliade to such feminist writers as Simone de Beauvoir, Kate Millet, Rosemary Radford Ruether, Elizabeth Gould Davis, H. R. Hays, Janice Raymond, and Robin Morgan. Each chapter begins with quotes from feminist thinkers whose words underscore the major import of Daly's work. She also quotes such men as the early Church founder Tertullian to show the extent of the misogyny that Daly perceives in much traditional theology. Christianity in particular holds women responsible for the Fall of Man, which therefore necessitated Christ's sacrificial crucifixion. *Beyond God the Father*, thus, is a pioneering work of radical feminist theology. Every chapter is energetic, fluid, and provocative, as Daly steers the reader through the roots of antifeminism and toward a reassessment of traditional assumptions about women as humans, thinkers, moralists, and souls.

Daly issues a denunciation of the false polarities of the "masculine" image of hyper-rationality and the "feminine" image of hyper-emotionality in order to suggest that these extremes are artificially created by men to maintain their power structure. Daly analyzes the ways in which Western civilization's images of God have fostered the oppression of women, as when theologians claim that women's subordination to men is "God's will," or that God by definition is male and therefore women cannot participate fully in worship. She also reexamines the myth of the Fall (when Adam and Eve disobeyed God, bringing sin into the world) and the ways in which the belief that women created Original Sin is destructive to women's sense of self-worth and autonomy, as well as a time-honored excuse for patriarchal society to abuse women and other minorities. Daly thus calls for a new sisterhood which would reject the myth of male superiority and instead celebrate woman's unique, loving spirit freed from spiritual bonding to a male icon.

Analysis

In *Beyond God the Father*, Mary Daly traces a "spiraling journey" of discovery to enable women to change their "conception/perception of god from the 'supreme being' to Be-ing," that is, from a male, patriarchal God to a nonsexist verb that shows life and spirituality as continually evolving processes. Daly urges women to live "on the boundary"—outside of patriarchal institutions such as Christianity—so that women can rediscover their own potency, creativity, and potential for metamorphosis. Daly claims that the sexual caste system and the totally masculine symbolism of Christianity reinforce and justify the oppression of women. Too many people trivialize this problem by suggesting that war, racism, and poverty are more important; they may deny women's oppression by claiming that "in Christ there is neither male nor female."

In "After the Death of God the Father," Daly argues that patriarchy takes advantage of a false polarity between the "masculine" image of reason, objectivity, and aggression versus the implied "feminine" image of emotion, passivity, and self-sacrifice in order to argue for male superiority. The identification that occurs between men and God, who is always referred to as a "He," leads many theologians and philosophers to assume that God has ordered women's subordination and exploitation. This belief and the language of faith ("Our Father") force women to remain outsiders, strangers, the Other—not male, thus not God-like, thus not true persons. To establish the nature of the struggle facing women, Daly dismisses male myths of separation and return and of conflict and vindication, instead urging women to embrace the myth of integrity and transformation that leads to independent spiritual rebirth. She further seeks to dethrone false deities that excuse or justify oppression or that reward believers after death, requiring passive acceptance.

In "Exorcising Evil from Eve: The Fall into Freedom," Daly radically redefines the Fall and Original Sin in terms of the false naming of Eve (and therefore of all women) as the source of evil, the lie that allows religion to serve as "patriarchy's prostitute." This destructive belief blames women for their own oppression, leading to guilt, hopelessness, fear of disapproval, fear of success, and emotional dependence. Daly assesses the "scapegoat syndrome" that punishes women for prostitution, but not their male customers, and that persecutes and tortures women who challenge the patriarchal system.

Daly explores the extent to which "Christolatry," the idolatrous worship of Christ as uniquely male, has confirmed a sexual hierarchy that dehumanizes women and denies them full participation in worship. She also dismisses "Mariolatry," the idealization of Mary, the mother of Jesus, by the Catholic church; it makes women feel inferior by portraying Mary as a passive receptacle of God's, and therefore man's, plans.

In "Transvaluation of Values: The End of Phallic Morality," the author castigates what she calls the hypocrisy of traditional morality, which claims to honor selflessness and sacrificial love but which rewards men for being selfish and ignoble. Daly argues that men control discussions of rape and abortion while practicing worldwide rape and genocide, biblical stories praise men who sacrifice their virgin daughters, and the "sexual revolution" abuses women by leaving them "no freedom to refuse to be defined by sex." Daly wants to end sexist labeling and to harness the "energy of psychically androgynous women" to create a "Holy Trinity" of Power, Justice, and Love.

In "The Bonds of Freedom: Sisterhood as Antichurch," Daly rejects the patriarchal world, Church, and Christ—the "big lie"—and seeks a bonding of women as sisters, an essential act of survival. She dismisses a "feminist liturgy" (a prescribed ritual for public worship which would focus on feminist views) because it would, she says, simply reinforce the status quo, the myth of patriarchy. Daly also contends that Joan of Arc, who was burned at the stake for heresy as a witch but later made a Catholic saint, might have been a worshipper of the Dianic cult, called the Old Religion. This fear of women as challengers of patriarchy is evident throughout Christendom.

Finally, Daly describes an "exodus community" of women in "Sisterhood as Cosmic Covenant," as women agree to leave the church spiritually as well as physically and to listen to "true"—that is, feminist—prophets. "The Final Cause: The Cause of Causes" concludes Daly's treatise by rejecting "the static, timeless being" of the patriarchal Heavenly Father (a person) and identifying instead "with Be-ing in which we participate actively" in a leap beyond the male-controlled religion (a verb). No longer, she says, will women be forced to be "magnifying mirrors" for men.

Context

Daly's visionary work is a cornerstone of radical feminist philosophies, some of which demand separation from patriarchal rule. According to Daly, *Beyond God the Father* was written in an atmosphere of what Linda Barufaldi describes as "communal inspiration," a representation of Daly's new word "Be-Friending" introduced in *Pure Lust: Elemental Feminist Philosophy* (1984). Be-Friending means "the creation of a context/atmosphere in which leaps of Metamorphosis can take place." In her "Original Reintroduction" to the 1985 reissue of *Beyond God the Father*, Daly compares herself and other feminists to Cassandra, the true prophetess in Greek mythology who was never believed. Too often, life in the 1980's was disheartening for Daly, who deplored the escalation of rape, spouse battering, pornography, poverty, and the sexual and incestuous abuse of females.

Although reviewed well by feminists, *Beyond God the Father* had little impact on the patriarchal institutions that Daly denounces. Yet it was a necessary second step on her "spiraling journey" into radical feminism, opening the way for *Pure Lust* and *Gyn/Ecology: the Metaethics of Radical Feminism* (1978), in which Daly rejects Christian theology. *Gyn/Ecology* examines evidence of the worldwide physical oppression of women, using examples of Indian *suttee* (the practice of forcing wives to throw themselves on their husbands' funeral pyres), Chinese footbinding, African genital mutilation, European witch-burning, and American gynecology. Her tone moves from severe anger in *Gyn/Ecology* to comedy in *Pure Lust*, as she delights in women's sensuality and sexuality. She also addresses critics of her separatism and her focus on European and American white women's oppression by revealing the commons threads of oppressive experience shared with women of color.

In these works, Daly revels in her newfound ability to change women's perceptions of life by introducing words viewed from a unique, feminist, woman-centered perspective. The effect is to free women from the "false naming" of patriarchal institutions and to regain a sense of female potency and wisdom. In doing so, she reclaims the "Metaphoric force," stolen under "phallocratic rule," of such terms as "Spinster, Webster, Weird, Hag, Witch, Sibyl, Muse, and many Others, as well as Goddess." A study of the original meanings of these words reveals good, positive, descriptive words for wise women. These terms are used in a derogatory sense by male-dominated society to deny women their abilities and goodness, according to Daly.

In all of her works, Daly hopes to return women to their rightful place "outside," beyond patriarchy to "Wanderlusting and Wonderlusting," "Be-Longing, Be-Friending, Be-Witching," and regaining "the Courage to Be, the Courage to See, the Courage to Sin" ("sin" is from the Latin *est*, "to be"). She calls for women to be "Wicked" (from "wiccen," or witches): "As Websters, Wicked Wiccen Women unwind the bindings of mummified/numbified words."

The responses to Daly's works have ranged from the view that her arguments are disappointing and unconvincing to the view that her arguments are compelling, generally to those women who have experienced male domination on the woman-identified community envisioned by Daly.

Sources for Further Study

Bal, Mieke. *Lethal Love: Feminist Literary Readings of Biblical Love Stories*. Bloomington: Indiana University Press, 1987. Using tools from language study and psychoanalysis, Bal examines five familiar love stories, from Adam and Eve to David and Bathsheba, to suggest powerful and exciting new meanings that enable readers to focus on the true import of these tales.

Chernin, Kim. *Reinventing Eve: Modern Woman in Search of Herself*. New York: Times Books, 1987. A reexamination of Eve as the first rebel challenging the subjugation of women. Delves into religion, psychology, mythology, and literature in a search for the Goddess Myth to free modern women.

De Beauvoir, Simone. *The Second Sex*. Translated and edited by H. M. Parshley. New York: Alfred A. Knopf, 1953. Written by the woman who developed the philosophy of existentialism (which deals with humanity's essence and the nature of freedom and choice), this work represents her attempt to reveal the way in which women are abused by a male culture that defines them as "the other"—not male, and therefore less than human. Her analysis of myth and literature has influenced many other writers.

Gornick, Vivian, and Barbara K. Moran, eds. *Women in Sexist Society: Studies in Power and Powerlessness*. New York: Basic Books, 1971. A groundbreaking collection of essays that argue passionately about beauty, love, marriage, and the socialization and images of women, as well as social issues of race, work, gender, and radicalism. Contributors include psychologists and sociologists, college professors, writers, and editors. The book has been praised for its well-reasoned and research-supported attack on the antifeminist culture that stratifies people by class, race, and sex.

Larrington, Carolyne, ed. *The Feminist Companion to Mythology*. London: Pandora Press, 1992. Using the work of feminist anthropologists, literary historians, and other experts, Larrington takes a fresh look at myths of the Near East, Europe, Asia, Oceania, and America with a focus on difference, variety, and uniqueness that distinguishes this work from other discussions of "The Goddess." A comprehensive guide with illustrations, cross-references by theme and name, and extensive bibliographies.

Stone, Merlin. *When God Was a Woman*. New York: Dial Press, 1976. Using archeological documentation, Stone analyzes the Goddess Myth, which predates patriarchal cults by centuries. This is an intriguing and controversial look at Near and Middle East worship of Astarte, Isis, and Ishtar and a reinterpretation of the Adam, Eve, and serpent legend.

Linda L. Labin

BLOOD, BREAD, AND POETRY: Selected Prose, 1979-1985

Author: Adrienne Rich (1929-)
Type of work: Essays
First published: 1986

Form and Content

Blood, Bread, and Poetry collects fifteen essays by noted American poet, lesbian, and feminist Adrienne Rich, some of which were first presented as lectures or speeches. The essays are arranged in chronological order of composition, from 1979 to 1985. The anthology revolves around the central thematic issues of contemporary feminism, articulating a range of subtopics, particularly women's history, women and literature, and academic women's studies. In a clear and accessible voice, Rich addresses subjects pertinent to understanding not only the development of feminist studies but also a feminist point-of-view on the position of women during the Reagan Administration. The essays often adopt a lively hortatory tone, alternating with thoughtful, thought-provoking inquiry.

Several essays discuss important but underappreciated figures in women's literature. "The Problem of Lorraine Hansberry" (1979) identifies the late African American playwright as an astute feminist who wrote of women's issues and ideas well before the women's liberation movement of the late 1960's. In 1957, Hansberry began an essay on Simone de Beauvoir's *Le Deuxième Sexe* (1949; *The Second Sex*, 1953) and corresponded to *The Ladder*, an early lesbian periodical, about the "hetero-social" pressures that lesbians face. Rich tells poignantly of how Hansberry's papers and dramatic corpus have been manipulated by her former husband, Robert Nemiroff. Rich suggests that Hansberry's female voice has been at least partially diluted through male mediation of her texts.

Similarly, in "The Eye of the Outsider: Elizabeth Bishop's *Complete Poems, 1927-1979*" (1983), Rich describes Bishop's work as incompletely appreciated by the literary establishment that canonized it, and she considers exemplary poems in terms of Bishop's "outsiderhood." She concludes that "Bishop was critically and consciously trying to explore marginality, power and powerlessness." The 1984 title essay, "Blood, Bread, and Poetry: The Location of the Poet," contextualizes Rich's concern over how women writers are situated and studied in the academy—or how they are not. Typically autobiographical and personal, the essay describes Rich's life progress as an academic and canonical poet; she brilliantly exposes how women's writing often employs sociopolitical critique which the academy chooses to ignore, leading to minimal female representation in literary curricula. The essay calls for greater attention to women's (political) art in a world where most illiterates are women.

In fact, women's social history, personal and collective, plays some part in nearly every essay, but it is central to the opening work, "What Does a Woman Need to Know?" (1979); Rich asserts that "what a woman must know" is the history of women, no matter how elusive or hidden. Women's history has grown more accessible since 1979, but the need for young women to comprehend how women's place in society has developed is no less crucial. "Resisting Amnesia: History and Personal Life" (1983) explores the problem; Rich recalls Susan B. Anthony's abolition work and remarks on the American notion "that one can be socially 'twice born,'" a function of U.S. immigrants' hyphenated relation to the "original" Anglo-Saxon establishment.

Making pointed connections between women's history and African American history in the Americas, Rich suggests that, although "to the victor go the spoils of history," subaltern histories permit members of social "minority" groups a vital sense of continuity and the foundation for future struggles. In "Split at the Root: An Essay on Jewish Identity" (1982), Rich analyzes her personal history as an example of multiple subaltern histories. Her relatively privileged life—as a middle-class, white, educated, Southern, "once-married" lesbian—specifies secular Jewish experience in America. She seeks connection, comprehension of her family's historical culture, and discovers a connectedness among all "minority" groups in their mutual oppressions.

Of the several essays focused on problems within academic women's studies, "Compulsory Heterosexuality and Lesbian Existence" (1980) is exemplary. Certainly the best known of Rich's essays, it forwards an incisive and influential lesbian-feminist analysis of the social construction of heterosexual praxis, enforced on females virtually from birth. Rich describes women's sexual-affectional experiences as points on a continuum delimited by the extremes of exclusive lesbian behavior and exclusive heterosexual behavior, mediated by a range of less-exclusive practices. By placing all women's sexual-affectional praxes on a single continuum which incorporates woman-to-woman "homosocial" but nonsexual relations, Rich revolutionized lesbian theory.

In "Compulsory Heterosexuality and Lesbian Existence," and indeed in every essay, Rich speaks strongly for women's solidarity, for a feminist sensibility that both interrogates and wields power, in the academy and in the world. Throughout *Blood, Bread, and Poetry*, the feminist strands of history, multiple cultural viewpoints, and political self-awareness are intricately interwoven with literary and academic concerns to form a readable text that truly embodies the feminist principle that "the personal is political."

Analysis

Adrienne Rich's first essay collection, *On Lies, Secrets, and Silence: Selected Prose, 1966-1978* (1979), bracketed the first decade of the "second wave" of the twentieth century U.S. women's movement. The work may be characterized by the title of its foreword: "On History, Illiteracy, Passivity, Violence, and Women's Culture." *Blood, Bread, and Poetry: Selected Prose, 1979-1985* continues Rich's examination of these issues. The two titles indicate Rich's sense of chronological continuity, not least in the scrupulous dating of each collection and of individual essays, which enhances their value as historical documents.

More pertinently, the titles of the collections qualify perceived periods during the feminist struggle. The feminist movement of the 1960's and 1970's arose from a female condition of social oppression based quite literally in lies perpetrated by fathers, secrets passed between mothers and daughters for generations, and an all-pervasive silence where women's voices might have been but were not. Virginia Woolf's *A Room of One's Own* (1929) and Joanna Russ's *How to Suppress Women's Writings* (1983) have notably addressed women's textual silencing. By 1986, however, when Rich published *Blood, Bread, and Poetry*, the feminist focus had shifted somewhat from an analysis of negative social conditions to a celebration of women's collective strengths. Ultimately, if patriarchal oppression can be defined by its "lies, secrets, and silence," then the feminist revolution could surely be defined by its three essential qualities, "blood, bread, and poetry." Rich's public voice helped to create the change.

The feminist movement addressed by *Blood, Bread, and Poetry* had changed in ways that the essays themselves acknowledge, though sometimes only implicitly. By the mid-1980's, the work of "women's liberation" no longer took place primarily in kitchens and borrowed office spaces; rather, 1980's feminism was located largely in universities and such groups as the National Organization of Women. Rich had cautioned faculty about "Taking Women Students Seriously" in 1978; by 1981, she could address the National Women's Studies Association on the possibilities for radical "Disobedience and Women's Studies." Yet in 1984, Rich observed the insidious persistence of lesbians' "Invisibility in Academe" (and in feminist organizations), just as women of color have been marginalized in academe and in the feminist movement.

While her first collection contained many academic-oriented essays in women's literary studies, such as on Emily Dickinson, Rich takes a popular, sociohistorical approach in *Blood, Bread, and Poetry*. This substantive shift reflects Rich's own career: Not simply a poet and academic, she had become a feminist leader. The essays therefore evidence her concern for broader issues. Collectively, the essays clarify integral interrelationships between a woman's personal experience and the historical situation of all women as a class; they pinpoint the interrelatedness of multiple oppressions. For example, Rich often tackles the oppression of women of color as a personal and a political issue; in a sense, she has used her privilege as a white person to raise others' consciousness.

Nevertheless, one detects a certain leveling of multicultural experience in Rich's essays; she dwells more on the apparent similarities between whites and "other," marginalized women (for example, African Americans and Nicaraguan Sandinistas) than on specific aspects of marginalized groups' actual experiences. Her approach to the secular experiences of American Jewish women is more informed. Still, Rich was discussing racial and intercultural issues at a time when most "mainstream" feminists were unrelentingly white, middle-class, educated, and excruciatingly "color-blind" out of ignorance, anxiety, or both.

Partly through *Blood, Bread, and Poetry*, Rich shows herself as a major theorist of women's studies, articulating in plain language the value of women's texts and the impact of women's history on the interpretation of contemporary women's lives, showing how the patriarchy oppresses all women regardless of race and culture.

Context

Each essay in *Blood, Bread, and Poetry* has value, as feminist discourse and as historical documentation of feminist concerns between 1979 and 1985; however, "Compulsory Heterosexuality and Lesbian Existence" can be singled out as the most significant essay in the collection, perhaps even the most important of all Rich's writings. Rich radically recontextualized women's social, affectional, and sexual relations—with men and with other women. Rich exposes the social origins of patriarchal heterosexuality: Not "natural," inevitable, or essential, the pervasive tool of women's compulsory subjugation is constructed by the lifelong "education" of individual women to support men through sexual and affectional servitude.

Yet the idea of "compulsory heterosexuality" disguises the essay's even more radical contribution: This essay first framed a theoretical construction of "lesbian existence," when published in *Signs* magazine in 1980. Rich moved beyond the "Woman-Identified Woman" of the Radicalesbians Manifesto (1970) that fostered often-celibate "political lesbianism." Rich considers diverse lesbian praxes as a viable aspect of female-female relations, pointing out the paranoid erasure of lesbians from male-organized "reality." Based on material lesbian experience, rather than on male, patriarchal psychoanalytic categorization of lesbianism as abnormal and pathological, Rich's "lesbian continuum" posits an inclusive paradigm for women's sexual-affectional experiences. This idea has profoundly influenced subsequent lesbian theory.

Rich's concepts were considered controversial, not least because she perceives some women as "lesbian" even when not self-identified as lesbian. Some lesbian thinkers have rejected Rich's lesbian-heterosexual continuum as essentialistic; such critiques bespeak the political and theoretical concerns of their authors, not the insignificance of Rich's work. For example, in her acclaimed work *Gender Trouble: Feminism and the Subversion of Identity* (1990), Judith Butler refers to the lesbian continuum as "a hegemonic discursive/epistemic model of gender intelligibility." Butler disavows the lesbian continuum because it relies on two stable, binarily opposed sexual categories and two stable genders, all actually unstable and artificial; yet, she acknowledges Rich's influence. Diana Fuss critiques the lesbian continuum partly for its sociopolitical tendency to align lesbians and heterosexual women together against the patriarchy, instead of aligning lesbians and gay men against "the institution of compulsory heterosexuality."

Yet no lesbian theorist can ignore the importance of Rich's lesbian continuum, for this concept transformed the discourse of lesbianism from sociopolitical rhetoric to high theory. Rich gave lesbian discourse an academic credibility which has burgeoned into the discipline of lesbian and gay studies. More important, as an open lesbian herself, Rich has made readers aware of lesbianism as a part of real women's experience. By putting "the big issues" of feminism in terms with which individual women can identify, Rich's *Blood, Bread, and Poetry* has earned a lasting place in feminist literature and in "women's knowledge."

Sources for Further Study

Allen, Jeffner, ed. *Lesbian Philosophies and Cultures*. Albany: State University of New York Press, 1990. The essays collected here, many by well-respected lesbian scholars, make substantial contributions to lesbian/feminist studies, following Rich's lead.

Benstock, Shari, ed. *Feminist Issues in Literary Scholarship*. Bloomington: Indiana University Press, 1987. Essays in this well-known anthology extend the ideas considered in *Blood, Bread, and Poetry*. Elizabeth Fox-Genovese, Judith Louder Newton, and Hortense Spillers address women's history and literature, including that of African Americans; others address feminist poetics and criticism.

Freedman, Estelle B., et al., eds. *The Lesbian Issue: Essays from "Signs."* Chicago: University of Chicago Press, 1985. This book reprints selected *Signs* articles from 1982 to 1984, including Stanford Friedman on Rich and responsory dialogue with Rich.

Frye, Marilyn. *Willful Virgin: Essays in Feminism, 1976-1992*. Freedom, Calif.: Crossing Press, 1992. Partly contemporaneous to *Blood, Bread, and Poetry*, Frye's essays on feminism, women's studies, and lesbianism permit informative comparison to Rich's topically similar views.

Montefiore, Jan. *Feminism and Poetry: Language, Experience, Identity in Women's Writing*. New York: Pandora, 1987. Focusing on poetry, Montefiore also discusses Rich as an essayist, relating her works to those of other contemporary feminist thinkers and poets.

Phelan, Shane. *Identity Politics: Lesbian Feminism and the Limits of Community*. Philadelphia: Temple University Press, 1989. This comprehensible theoretical text describes the relationships between lesbians and the feminist community, and between lesbians and the gay community. Lends historical perspective to several Rich essays.

Russ, Joanna. *How to Suppress Women's Writing*. Austin: University of Texas Press, 1983. This elemental feminist work incisively analyzes the many ways in which women's writings have historically been dismissed, censored, and derogated, with references to Rich's texts.

Penelope J. Engelbrecht

THE BLOODY CHAMBER AND OTHER STORIES

Author: Angela Carter (1940-1992)
Type of work: Short stories
First published: 1979

Form and Content

In her fiction, Angela Carter combines elements of surrealism, myth, and eroticism with feminist and political observations. Her work is distinguished by its display of unrestrained imagination, colorful imagery, and sensuous prose. Although alternately praised and faulted for her extravagant gothic approach, Carter is highly regarded as a writer of unique and imaginative fiction.

The Bloody Chamber and Other Stories contains thematically linked stories, many derived from fables and fairy tales. In this collection, Carter is both an analyst of fairy tales and their cultural implications and an improviser, using the tales as a base for imaginative speculation. To supply the missing erotic quality at the narrative level is one of her objectives. Each of the ten stories in this collection has a starting point in a fairy tale or legend, but from this point it expands into an elaborate, fanciful sexual allegory. The substance of the old tales can accommodate fresh varieties of meaning and reverberation, and although the imagery remains traditional, its range of associations is easily extended. In the tales of Charles Perrault, Hans Christian Andersen, and the Brothers Grimm, the fundamental emotions of fear, relief, horror, and triumph are unambiguous, but the pattern of events is often more complex than it appears. The story of Little Red Riding Hood, for example, raises interesting questions about exactly what is embodied in whom, and in "The Werewolf" and "The Company of Wolves," Carter draws out with impressive economy two alternative strands of meaning: Only the sturdy figure of the child remains constant. Wise and armed only with her father's hunting knife and her own integrity, she stands up to confront whatever is coming to her. In both cases, she is the wolfsbane.

The first and longest story in the collection, from which it takes its title, exemplifies Carter's method. An innocent young music student is brought as the Marquis' fourth bride to his remote castle on the Breton coast, a collector's item to be ranged alongside his priceless jewels and his library of rare and pornographic books and to be enjoyed between business trips to New York. It is not simply the bride's curiosity that opens the door to the horrors of the bloody chamber. It is the positive desire to be corrupted even while being repulsed by the evidence of corruption, which is underlined by the voluptuousness of the description of the heavily scented lilies and the smell of Russian leather.

"The Tiger's Bride," a version of "Beauty and the Beast," achieves its effect by a reversal of the story's usual conclusion. Stripping away all of the artificialities of his human mask—his hereditary palace, his treasure chest, his Benvenuto Cellini salt cellars—the Beast reveals the flesh and sinew of his true nature, pacing backward and forward on rank, wet straw. He is joined there by Beauty.

"The Lady of the House of Love" recasts the tale of Sleeping Beauty. The queen of the vampires sits in her decaying ancestral castle in her bridal gown, her beauty is unchanged by time, playing her tarot cards and cursing the destiny that forces her to consume her unusual diet. Onto this stage bicycles a young English officer. His is the kiss that releases her to death: The rose that she bequeaths him becomes a generation's blood that will soak the battlefields of World War I. In such ways, Carter works on the reader's imagination, undermining and reshaping its fictive models.

Analysis

Carter rewrites the legend of Bluebeard in "The Bloody Chamber," making it her tour de force in this collection. The confessional voice of the tale is that of experience, the girl-bride recalling her initiation into the adult world. Carter's story and all the earlier versions of the Bluebeard legend are about women's masochistic complicity in male sexual aggression.

"The Bloody Chamber" uses all the images and

trappings of the gothic romance: the remote castle, the virgin at the mercy of the tormented hero-villain, the enclosed spaces, hidden atrocities, women masochistically eager for the corruption of sexuality. The pervading themes of pornography are there as well: domination, control, humiliation, possession through murder, all perpetrated on willing, eager victims. Carter's tale carefully creates the classical pornographic model of sexuality, which has a definite meaning and endorses a particular kind of fantasy—that of male sexual tyranny within a marriage that is grossly unequal. The child-bride is responsive to her husband's desire and ready to be "impaled" among the lilies of death, while his face has a promise of debauchery and a rare talent for corruption. Carter creates a sexual model that endorses the natural and normal sadism of the male, complemented by the normal and natural masochism of the female. The husband of "The Bloody Chamber" is a connoisseur, a collector of pornography. When the child-bride peers at the titles in his bookcase—*The Initiation*, *The Key to the Mysteries*, *The Secret of Pandora's Box*—she finds the texts for the knowledge she later reads in blood, a guide to her fate. These titles are made real in her husband's collection of murdered wives when she finally does penetrate the secrets of the bloody chamber.

Yet Carter has created two other figures in her rewriting of the tale whose actions and presence alter the terms of the unequal conflict between husband and wife. One of the child-bride's rescuers is the blind piano tuner, Jean-Yves, who loves the child-bride not for her beauty, but for her gift of music. Only with the blind man who humbly serves her music can Carter envision a marriage of equality for the Marquis' bride. The real savior of the child-bride, however, is a figure who seldom if ever appears in fairy tales: the mother as traveling heroine, who arrives to shoot the Marquis just as he is about to decapitate her daughter. Here Carter is transforming the sexual politics of fairy tales in significant ways: The mother of Bluebeard's bride never deserts her child. She has the wisdom to give her child the freedom demanded by sexual maturity, the freedom denied to Sleeping Beauty by her royal parents when they try to protect her from the fairy's curse that her hand shall be pierced by a spindle. The mother arrives in "The Bloody Chamber," however, with melodramatic timeliness as Carter demonstrates the tenacity of the mother-daughter bond. Her tale carries an uncompromisingly feminist message, for the women's revolution would seal up all the doors of all the bloody chambers forever.

"The Courtship of Mr. Lyon" is an updated version of Beauty and the Beast complete with telephones and motor cars. The essence of the fairy tale, however, remains unchanged, with Beauty's sweetness, virtue, and love for the troubled Beast effecting his transformation into a man. The conclusion of the tale focuses on the married domestic bliss of Mr. and Mrs. Lyon walking in the garden in a drift of fallen petals. "The Tiger's Bride" reimagines the transformation at the end of "Beauty and the Beast" so that Beauty is the one transformed out of her humanity into a state identical to that of the Beast. In the beginning of the story, the female narrator is mystified by the Beast's otherness, his difference from herself. Yet this difference is held in tension by Beauty's awareness that both she and the Beast are distinct from men like Beauty's father, a compulsive gambler who has lost his daughter to the Beast in a game of cards. Beauty's fear of the Beast gradually changes as he is revealed more fully to her and as she is known by him. "The Tiger's Bride" is about how a relationship between two characters, strange to each other and uncertain about their own roles and identities, shapes their mutual experiences of fear and desire.

When Beauty's father gambles and loses his daughter at cards, the Beast takes her to his palace. She is told that the Beast wishes to see her naked. Afterward, she will be returned to her father. Beauty understands the Beast's desire to be pornographic. She resists this demand until they go horseback riding together, and the Beast reveals himself to her without his mask and clothes. In a moment of reciprocity, Beauty reveals herself partially naked to the Beast. Without her garments, Beauty suffers pain in revealing herself, both physically and spiritually, in a new, tentative relationship that she is beginning to trust. Beauty does not perceive the Beast's gaze as indifferent or voyeuristic when she exposes herself. Instead, she experiences liberty after their encounter of mutual exposure. In the conclusion of the tale, the Beast purrs and licks Beauty until she is metamorphosed into a tiger-beast. The strangeness of one for the other and their ambivalent roles and identities have prepared Beauty and the Beast for a new relationship that is not one of devourment. It has opened Beauty, in particular, to new terms of a relationship that allow her to live without an oppressive, socialized appearance. Equally, the Beast has come to be accepted without a man's mask, without a false appearance.

The rest of the tales in *The Bloody Chamber and Other Stories* retell the stories of Snow White, Sleeping Beauty, Puss-in-Boots, and Little Red Riding Hood with Carter's characteristic emphasis on gothic sensuousness and on making apparent the sexuality latent in the original fairy tales.

Context

By retelling traditional fairy-tale plots with a heightened interest in their erotic subtexts, and with an emphasis on female narrators, Angela Carter reclaims a traditionally conservative literary genre for the female reader. The clearly feminist resolution of "The Bloody Chamber," with the narrator's mother speeding to her daughter's rescue, pistol in hand and ready to fire, adds a new dimension to the familiar fairy-tale genre. Richly inventive, the stories in the collection exude an aura of the forbidden as they place in the foreground female responses to fear and desire, an area of response frequently ignored in fairy tales and folktales. Her colorful imagery and sensuous prose have the power to cause readers to think again, and deeply, about the mythic sources of common cultural icons and to plunge them into speculation about aspects of animal and human nature.

The stories here anticipate Carter's macabre inventiveness in *Black Venus* (1985), where Charles Baudelaire's mistress, Edgar Allan Poe and his mother, and alleged ax-murderer Lizzie Borden make their fantastic appearances.

Sources for Further Study

Carter, Angela. Interview by Kerryn Goldsworthy. *Meanjin* 44, no. 1 (March, 1985): 4-13. Carter surveys the progress of her career, books which have been influential on her development, the role of the writer in society, and forms and genres that lend themselves to women's writing.

______________, ed. *The Old Wives' Fairy Tale Book.* New York: Pantheon Books, 1990. This collection gathers together less well known fairy tales and folktales from the English-speaking world. What is distinctive here is Carter's insistence that all the tales have female protagonists and that one section of the anthology be devoted to "Clever Women, Resourceful Girls, and Desperate Stratagems."

______________. *The Sadeian Woman.* New York: Pantheon Books, 1978. This book examines the relationship of sexuality to power. Using the extreme perceptions of the French revolutionary the Marquis de Sade as a point of departure for her own controversial insights, Carter demonstrates that sexuality is constructed not from gender, but from relations of power and politics.

Duncker, Patricia. "Re-Imagining the Fairy Tales: Angela Carter's Bloody Chambers." *Literature and History* 10, no. 1 (Spring, 1984): 3-14. This article examines the eroticism of the tales in *The Bloody Chamber and Other Stories* and argues that Carter is following a pornographic model in which women's sensuality is simply a response to male arousal. Claims that Carter has no conception of women's sexuality as autonomous desire.

Fowl, Melinda G. "Angela Carter's *The Bloody Chamber* Revisited." *Critical Survey* 3, no. 1 (1991): 71-79. A study of Carter's treatment of the foreign, or "the other," in "The Tiger's Bride" and "The Lady of the House of Love." Exploring the dynamics of self and other in these tales allows Carter to probe issues of identity and difference, gender relationships, and paradoxical longings for independence and mutuality in a relationship.

Roberta M. Hooks

BLOOMING: A Small-Town Girlhood

Author: Susan Allen Toth (1940-)
Type of work: Memoir
Time of work: The 1950's and the 1970's
Locale: Ames, Iowa, and Minneapolis, Minnesota
First published: 1981

Principal personages:

Susan Allen, a younger version of the author

Jennifer Toth, Susan's daughter, a young child

Form and Content

In *Blooming: A Small-Town Girlhood*, Susan Allen Toth recalls her experiences as a young girl in Ames, Iowa, in the 1950's. She describes the pleasures and trials of growing up female in a small community during a time when gender roles were clearly defined. Each chapter explores one facet of everyday life as Toth recounts experiences from her junior high and high school years. By beginning each chapter with an incident in her life in the 1970's as a single mother, teaching college English courses, Toth compares her own girlhood with that of her daughter and considers how her earlier experiences have affected her adult life.

Beginning with a chapter called "Nothing Happened," Toth suggests that despite its limitations, small-town life offered rich opportunities for a young girl to develop intellectually and personally. After describing a conversation that she had as an adult with other women who insisted that growing up in a small Midwestern town was "hell," Toth acknowledges that her life was not exciting and that Ames did not offer all the cultural or intellectual resources that she later found in college and in cities. She insists, however, that her world was a "garden" that nurtured her into adulthood with a strong sense of safety and community.

The book examines the central experiences of Toth's life, which, as the first chapter suggests, were neither unusual nor particularly exciting. In Toth's telling, however, these experiences are shown to be both important and interesting. She describes the town's climate as generally peaceful, with only a few divorces and one murder to interrupt the flow of daily life. Yet she admits that the town probably was more divided than she recognized as a teenager. She was more aware, she reports, of divisions between Catholics and Protestants than between whites and blacks, but looking back she acknowledges that racial prejudice and other divisions may have existed.

After describing the community, Toth moves on to reminisce about her relationships with both boys and girls, suggesting that while having a boyfriend was nice, having a circle of girlfriends was essential. With her boyfriends, she did little except drive around town, but she spent most of her time as a teenager with other girls, talking, seeing films, or shopping. She writes about the importance of science in Ames, a college town with strong schools of engineering, industrial science, and agriculture, and her sense that science was both fascinating and mysterious. She never really understood the subject, and she looked to male scientists (including her husband Lawrence, years later) to explain it to her. For Toth, books were always more attractive, and she tells about her love and reverence for the local library, where she spent many hours as a child and teenager. Although the local librarian had hoped that Toth would join the ranks of student library assistants, Toth worked instead doing housecleaning and detasseling corn. She also describes how she spent her teenage summers writing and filling in for vacationing page editors at the local newspaper, an experience she calls "Preparation for Life." She also devotes several chapters to descriptions of celebrations, including slumber parties, holiday dinners, and summer vacation trips to a rustic lakefront cabin owned by her grandfather. Finally, she tells of her experiences outside of Ames, including school trips, shopping expeditions to Des Moines, and her eventual departure for Smith College, about which she writes in *Ivy Days: Making My Way Out East* (1984), the second volume of her memoirs.

In the opening sections of her chapters, Toth suggests comparisons between life in the 1970's and life in the

1950's. As she describes conversations with her daughter, Jennifer, Toth asks questions about the meaning of her own experiences as a girl and the values and ideas that she brings to her adult life. What does a mother want for her daughter? Why are women friends so important to a woman's life? What is the relationship between one's past and one's present? These sections also answer a common reader's question: What happened next? In the opening of each chapter, Toth offers the reader glimpses into her later life as well as reflections back on her past.

Analysis

Given Toth's argument that growing up in a small town in the 1950's could be pleasant and fulfilling, *Blooming* appropriately uses a balanced, lighthearted tone. Toth often pokes fun at herself, but she also has great sympathy for her community and the younger version of herself. She offers detailed descriptions of 1950's material culture, and her stories and reflections bring to life the texture of everyday life in a small midwestern town during the decade.

Beneath this often-humorous storytelling, however, *Blooming* also provides a useful analysis of how gender marked the lives of girls in the 1950's. She reveals some of the strongly defined gender expectations in Ames, such as the notion that males would be inclined to science and females to literature, but she also shows her own faith in these visions of gender difference. While the adult narrator looks back critically at the sometimes clear divisions between male and female behavior, Toth also shows how her younger self found guidance and fulfillment in those divisions. In a humorous but also critical passage, for example, she describes the pleasure and agony of classic rituals such as preparing for and attending high-school dances. For girls, such rituals offered the first chance to wear stockings and lipstick, two signs of adult femininity that Toth remembers with both nostalgia and disdain. This ironic stance allows her to demonstrate both how traditional gender expectations could place limits on a young girl during her coming-of-age and how she might find such ideas about masculinity and femininity attractive.

One attractive aspect of being female was the essential link that shared gender identity created among Toth and other members of her community, both peers and adults. In the chapter "Girlfriends," Toth emphasizes the supportive camaraderie girls provided for one another, though she also recognizes the underlying competition over who would be whose "best friend." Having a circle of close friends was essential, she says, but such relationships were fraught with conflict as well. The competition, according to Toth, was not over boys but among girls competing for one another's attention and devotion.

Toth suggests that relationships between young girls and adult women were also important. In describing the many hours that she spent in the library, her summer vacations with her mother and sister, and shopping trips with a friend and their mothers, Toth emphasizes the importance of female role models and her sense of growing up in a mostly female world. She notes especially how her mother, the head librarian, and the women with whom she worked in her various jobs offered her models of women as workers, as well as models for her appearance and behavior. In her chapter-opening descriptions of conversations with her daughter, Toth makes her awareness of the importance of women as role models even more apparent as she considers what kind of model she will provide for her own daughter. Her descriptions of her girlfriends and women role models all focus on the supportive aspects of women's culture. *Blooming* offers a mostly positive vision of what life was like for girls in the 1950's, although it does not ignore the power of traditional ideas about gender to mold the thinking and behavior of teenage girls.

Toth's representation of gender difference is not, however, based on an assumption that women might be better or more important than men, even though they were more central to her experiences. Men were pleasant enough, she suggests, and some were quite valuable as friends, boyfriends, and coworkers. Nevertheless, in young Susan Allen's experience, men and women were clearly different. They were boyfriends (not best friends), scientists (not librarians), the newspaper editor who gruffly helped her learn to be a journalist, and her formally distant grandfather. She does not criticize men or the cultural ideas about gender that created and enforced such gender differences. Rather, her stories explore the differences between women and men as if they were natural and mostly unproblematic. Her book does not, then, offer an especially critical analysis of the meaning and practice of gender difference in the 1950's. It does offer detailed, interesting descriptions of how she experienced growing up female during that period, with all of its contradictions.

Context

The structure of *Blooming* makes it more of a memoir than an autobiography, but like many of the women's autobiographies written and studied in recent years, it provides a previously unrecognized female perspective on everyday life. Toth takes her own experiences seriously, and her sympathetic, ironic voice suggests that experiences that appear simple and unimportant on the surface may be central to a woman's life. Indeed, in *Blooming* as in other women's autobiographical writing, daily life and ordinary women move from the neglected margins to center stage. In this book, the common experiences of white, middle-class, midwestern women and girls become the key to understanding what it means to be female in the 1950's and beyond.

While *Blooming* has not received much critical attention from critics in women's literature or women's studies programs, the book represents an unusual example within the growing field of women's writing about their own lives. Although other writers, such as Nancy Mairs and Patricia Hampl, have written memoirs that reflect on the experiences of growing up female, Toth's books, both *Blooming* and *Ivy Days*, offer unusually positive, sympathetic visions of women's lives. Instead of focusing on the limitations of gender or on the struggles of understanding oneself, but without ignoring the pain and self-doubt of adolescence or the impact of gender on her experiences, Toth emphasizes the sweetness and security of small-town life.

Toth continued writing about her own life in *Ivy Days*, which describes her experiences at Smith College; *How to Prepare for Your High School Reunion* (1988), in which she comments on life in middle age; and *Reading Rooms* (1980), a book that collects Toth's and other readers' feelings about reading.

Sources for Further Study

Barbre, Joy Webster, et al., eds. *Interpreting Women's Lives: Feminist Theory and Personal Narratives*. Bloomington: Indiana University Press, 1989. The essays in this collection, which grew out of a national conference, examine the context, forms, and use of voice in women's personal narratives. None addresses Toth specifically, but they provide helpful background material.

Benstock, Shari, ed. *The Private Self: Theory and Practice of Women's Autobiographical Writings*. Chapel Hill: University of North Carolina Press, 1988. In this essay collection, a number of feminist critics examine theories of autobiography and analyze central examples of women's use of the genre in the nineteenth and twentieth centuries. While none of the articles addresses Toth's work in particular, the approaches included here offer valuable models for critical analysis of Toth's memoir.

Heilbrun, Carolyn. *Writing a Woman's Life*. New York: W. W. Norton, 1988. Heilbrun writes critically about how traditional accounts of women's lives have represented women as passive, rather than active, and she argues for closer readings of women's life stories. This book is useful for its analytical approach to women's autobiographical writing.

Lochner, Frances C., ed. *Contemporary Authors*. Vol. 105. Detroit: Gale Research, 1982. This reference entry offers a brief biography of Toth, a useful listing of her publications, and a short comment from the author on her goals in writing.

Sherry Lee Linkon

THE BLUEST EYE

Author: Toni Morrison (Chloe Anthony Wofford, 1931-)
Type of work: Novel
Type of plot: Psychological realism
Time of plot: The early 1940's
Locale: Lorain, Ohio
First published: 1970

Principal characters:

Claudia MacTeer, the narrator, the nine-year-old daughter of poor African American parents
Frieda MacTeer, Claudia's ten-year-old sister
Pecola Breedlove, an eleven-year-old African American girl who becomes obsessed with blue eyes
Pauline Williams Breedlove, Pecola's mother, who is called Mrs. Breedlove by everyone, including her children and her husband
Charles (Cholly) Breedlove, Pecola's father, who rapes her while in a drunken state
Elihue Micah Whitcomb, called Soaphead Church, a "Reader, Adviser, and Interpreter of Dreams" who molests little girls
Maureen Peal, a half-white girl with "sloe green eyes"

Form and Content

The Bluest Eye tells the story of Pecola Breedlove, a young African American girl immersed in poverty and made "ugly" by the American culture of the early 1940's that defines beauty in terms of such actors as Greta Garbo, Ginger Rogers, and Shirley Temple. Her mother beats and abuses her, and her father rapes and abandons her. Toni Morrison introduces the novel with a two-page parody of the Dick-and-Jane reader; the monotonous sentences of the reader repeat with increasing speed until the words run together. The parody is followed by a one-page interior monologue from the main narrator, Claudia MacTeer, who sets the scene for the four sections that make up the rest of the novel: "Autumn," "Winter," "Spring," and "Summer." The subsections are introduced by run-together lines from the Dick-and-Jane parody.

"Autumn" begins with Claudia MacTeer's bleak sketch of her own home and impoverishment and moves toward Pecola's brief stay with Claudia's family after Cholly, Pecola's father, burns the Breedlove home. While staying with the MacTeers, Pecola begins to menstruate and learns that she can now have a baby if some man loves her. "Autumn" ends with a sketch of three misanthropic "whores" who, unsentimentally, provide Pecola with the little warmth that she experiences.

"Winter," a shorter section of the novel, begins by sketching the face of Claudia and Frieda's father and then sketching his nakedness, which the daughters see accidentally. Because Mr. MacTeer's nakedness is nonthreatening, it leaves Claudia and Frieda more astonished than offended. In contrast, the section ends with Pecola's misery in the home of Louis and Geraldine, elitist African Americans who regard people such as Pecola as trash. Pecola has been lured into the home by their mean son, Junior, who promises to give Pecola a kitten. Once there, Junior, who is jealous of his mother's blue-eyed, black cat, throws the cat in Pecola's face and locks her in the room. When Junior discovers that Pecola likes the cat, he hurls the cat against the wall, leaving it unconscious when Geraldine arrives home. Junior blames the cat's near-death on Pecola, and Geraldine, enraged by Pecola's impoverished ugliness, calls Pecola a "black bitch" and tells her to get out.

"Spring," comprising almost a third of the novel, begins with Claudia's father beating up Mr. Henry, their roomer, for fondling Frieda, another scene contrasting the father-daughter relationship in the Breedlove family. Most of "Spring," however, focuses on flashbacks to the earlier lives of Mrs. Breedlove and Cholly. In Mrs. Breedlove's narration, she traces the loss of her romantic illusion and recollects the details of making love with Cholly in their youth. Her section ends shortly after her recollection of an orgasm. In Cholly Breedlove's narrative, Morrison avoids interior monologue but uses an external first-person perspective to reclaim Cholly's history in Georgia as an infant abandoned by his insane mother and reared by his Great Aunt Jimmy. Though Cholly's story includes his marriage to Mrs. Breedlove, the final sexual image refers not to her but to his rape of their daughter.

"Spring" concludes with the pregnant Pecola seeking out Soaphead Church to petition him for blue eyes. Soaphead affirms Pecola's desire to have blue eyes so that she will no longer be ugly. As Pecola's rite of passage, Soaphead tricks her into poisoning his landlady's dog, an animal that offends Soaphead's sensibilities. Concluding "Spring," Soaphead writes a letter to God on Pecola's behalf and then sleeps dreamlessly while Pecola drifts into madness and his landlady finds her poisoned dog.

"Summer," the shortest section of *The Bluest Eye*, is narrated by Claudia. She and her sister try to sell marigold seeds to earn a bicycle, and as they listen to neighborhood gossip, they piece together Pecola's story. Pecola is pregnant with Cholly's child. Cholly has fled. Mrs. Breedlove has beaten Pecola. Claudia and Frieda are disillusioned that no one wants the baby to live. As a petition for Pecola and the baby's life, Claudia and Frieda bury the money for the bicycle and plant the marigolds. Yet the marigolds do not grow. Claudia speculates that maybe she planted the seeds too deep but that maybe "the entire country was hostile to marigolds that year."

The final scenes focus on Pecola's madness and on her obsession with having the bluest eyes. Claudia, as narrator, reveals that the baby is dead; that Pecola's brother, Sammy, left town; that Cholly died in a workhouse; and that Mrs. Breedlove still does housework. Claudia realizes that Pecola's beauty was turned ugly by society and that "[l]ove is never any better than the lover." Claudia ends with the lament "it's much, much, much too late."

Analysis

In *The Bluest Eye*, Morrison works with many themes, among them impoverishment, destructive mythologies, gender relations, and loss of innocence. Impoverishment is clearly tied not only to cultural and racial identities but also to familial values. Mrs. Breedlove works for more than one white family, but she respects only the Fishers, who satisfy her lifelong need for order; ironically, the order that she respects strips her of her marital status (as Mrs. Breedlove) and even of her Christian name, Pauline. She becomes "Polly," the "ideal servant." Impoverishment becomes more than a racial issue, however, as Morrison explores the differences among African American families. Only partly a racial issue, the contrast between the comfortable life of the half-white Maureen Peal, who is "rich" by Claudia MacTeer's standards, is juxtaposed against the lives of Frieda and Claudia, whose mother bitterly laments the three quarts of milk that Pecola drinks and Claudia's illness because such economic losses represent a hardship for the MacTeers.

Finally, there are the Breedloves, whose "blackness," poverty, and familial values make them ugly. Geraldine, an African American woman groomed for property and family status, explains to her son the difference between "colored people" and "niggers." When Geraldine finds Pecola trapped in the living room by Junior, she has her chance to demonstrate this distinction. Deceived by Junior's lies, contemptuous of Pecola's ugliness and filthiness, Geraldine calls Pecola a "black bitch"—slurring Pecola's racial and feminine identity—and throws her out. Morrison's authorial voice addresses these indignities and demonstrates that in a racist and impoverished culture, beauty and ugliness can be reversed. It is Claudia who sees that Pecola has been stripped of her beauty, but the reader sees clearly the ugliness of Geraldine and Junior, the insensitivity of Maureen Peal, and the unquestioned entitlement of the Fishers.

Morrison also addresses many destructive American mythologies, perhaps most powerfully the romantic mythology and the beauty mythology alluded to in her title *The Bluest Eye*. Mrs. Breedlove is destroyed, in part, by the romantic myth. As a young girl, she dreams of a "Presence" that will show up and know what to do. Cholly Breedlove, who accepts her and even makes her feel special about her crippled foot, plays a part in this mythology. They marry, and Cholly surprises her by being happy that she is pregnant. During her pregnancy, she goes to motion pictures, where she succumbs to her earlier romantic ideas and learns the American ideal of beauty as she watches Clark Gable and Jean Harlow. In the novel, Morrison says of the American ideas of romantic love and physical beauty that they are "[p]robably the most destructive ideas in the history of human thought." These are the myths embedded in the Dick-and-Jane parodies that introduce subsections, and not surprisingly, Pecola Breedlove, like her mother, accepts the myths of romantic love and blue-eyed beauty. Pecola's obsession with blue eyes begins with the Shirley Temple cup in which Frieda MacTeer brings her milk, and the obsession finally consumes Pecola in her madness, when she believes that she has attained the bluest eyes. Morrison's characters demonstrate that such ideals cannot withstand the realities of human relationships.

In part as a result of the poverty and ugliness and the resulting disillusionment, gender relations fare poorly in *The Bluest Eye*. The central male, Cholly Breedlove, cannot imagine being content with one women for his entire life. He finds his solace in drinking, womanizing, and finally raping his daughter. The other men and boys in *The Bluest Eye* also offer little of the ideal. Mr. Henry, the MacTeers' roomer, is run off for molesting Frieda. Soaphead Church, who also molests little girls, says of the men and women in his family, "Our manhood was defined by acquisitions. Our womanhood by acquiescence." Even Junior and the other boys on the playground torment the luckless Pecola. Claudia and Frieda's father provides a contrast of sorts to the other male characters, but he remains more an idea than a real human being.

Morrison's women and girls are complex and varied. Some are types, such as Geraldine, the women of the church, and Maureen Peal. Others, such as Mrs. Breedlove and Pecola, are culturally impoverished by false values. Still others, such as Cholly's Great Aunt Jimmy, are strong and decisive. Some are challenges to types, such as the three merry and misanthropic "whores": Miss China, Miss Poland, and Miss Marie. These women pursue their pleasures without guilt, apology, or introspection. They do not question their value or their beauty. They find a kind of freedom in being outsiders in their culture. Unlike the women in Soaphead's family, they acquire; they do not acquiesce. Loss of innocence does not concern them. Morrison says of them: "They were whores in whores' clothing, whores who had never been young and had no word for innocence."

Innocence, however, concerns Claudia. In her introductory monologue, she says, "Cholly Breedlove is dead; our innocence too." Again, in her conclusion, she speaks metaphorically of "searching the garbage" for the "thing we assassinated." She recognizes that the loss of innocence lies in the wrongness of acquiescing to the destruction of another, and she laments that the wrong cannot be undone.

Particularly characteristic of Morrison's style are interior monologues and complex ideas embodied in common objects and in people. Through the interior monologues, Morrison uses the layout of the novel itself to convey part of the content. "Autumn," "Winter," and "Summer" begin with ragged right margins, indicating interior monologue, and end with justified right margins, indicating external narrative. "Spring" moves between ragged and justified margins, using the ragged right margins for Mrs. Breedlove's interior monologues.

Complex ideas are woven into the very fabric of the objects in the novel. For example, embedded in "Autumn" is a sketch of the sofa in the Breedlove home; it is an irritating piece of furniture, torn by the delivery drivers. The Breedloves detest the sofa, even as they have to make time payments on it. It becomes the idea of the ugliness of the family, and it is, in fact, the place where Pecola is raped by her father a second time. Likewise, the marigolds that will not grow become, for Claudia and Frieda, the idea of barrenness and loss. Claudia speculates that the earth itself may be the problem. Similarly, Morrison's people act as ideas. Geraldine becomes the idea of a sort of class brutality. Pecola becomes the idea of madness, caused by the myth of blue-eyed beauty. Shirley Temple becomes the idea, a sort of mythology, of blue eyes.

Context

Toni Morrison, the 1993 recipient of the Nobel Prize in Literature, is best known for her novels and literary criticism. *The Bluest Eye*, Morrison's first novel, was followed by *Sula* (1973), *Song of Solomon* (1977), *Tar Baby* (1981), *Beloved* (1987), and *Jazz* (1992). Morrison won the National Book Critics Circle Award for *Song of Solomon*, and she won the Pulitzer Prize in fiction for *Beloved*. Best known of Morrison's critical writing is *Playing in the Dark: Whiteness and the Literary Imagination* (1992).

According to an interview with Morrison, *The Bluest Eye* began as a short story for a writer's group. It was written during a time of loneliness, following her divorce, when she was parenting her two preschool-age sons. In the interview, Morrison talks about her interest in focusing her novels on friendships between women, as she does in *Sula*. Morrison rejects the notion that friendships between women are "subordinate" to other "roles they're playing."

Reviews of *The Bluest Eye* were mostly favorable, though the work was somewhat overlooked until Morrison's other novels began to form a body of work. Many critics then looked at *The Bluest Eye* as background for Morrison's later explorations of racial, gender, and cultural issues. For example, Sula, the central character in Morrison's second novel, is unconventional and unbound by social codes, and Jade, the fashion model in *Tar Baby*, rejects the romantic myth. Increasingly, Morrison's women seek freedom and autonomy. Like Claudia MacTeer in *The Bluest Eye*, they reject romantic myths, beauty myths, and roles of acquiescence. Yet *The Bluest Eye* is more than groundwork for Morrison's later novels: It deserves to be read for itself.

Sources for Further Study

Harris, Trudier. *Fiction and Folklore: The Novels of Toni Morrison*. Knoxville: University of Tennessee Press, 1991. Focusing on five novels by Morrison, Harris' book contains an introduction, an index, and comprehensive notes. A full section of the book discusses *The Bluest Eye*.

Holloway, Karla F. C., and Stephanie A. Demetrakopoulos. *New Dimensions of Spirituality: A Biracial and Bicultural Reading of the Novels of Toni Morrison*. New York: Greenwood Press, 1987. Each section of the book contains an article by Holloway and one by Demetrakopoulos. Particularly useful are the introduction, the two final analytical chapters, and the two essays on *The Bluest Eye*.

McKay, Nellie Y., comp. *Critical Essays on Toni Morrison*. Boston: G. K. Hall, 1988. A collection of reviews with and essays about Morrison and her fiction, McKay's book contains an introduction and a section focused specifically on *The Bluest Eye*.

Morrison, Toni. *Playing in the Dark: Whiteness and the Literary Imagination*. Cambridge, Massachusetts: Harvard University Press, 1992. A collection of Morrison's literary criticism, *Playing in the Dark* focuses primarily on racial issues and their influence on the literary imagination.

Tate, Claudia, ed. *Black Women Writers at Work*. New York: Continuum, 1983. This collection of interviews explores the creative processes of fourteen black women writers. The book contains a useful introduction.

Carol Franks

BONE

Author: Fae Myenne Ng (1956-)
Type of work: Novel
Type of plot: Domestic realism
Time of plot: The 1960's to the 1980's
Locale: San Francisco's Chinatown
First published: 1993

Principal characters:

Leila "Lei" Fu Louie, a community relations specialist for a public school
Dulcie "Mah" Leong, Lei's mother, who owns a children's clothing store
Leon Leong, Lei's stepfather, a retired seaman
Nina Leong, Lei's half sister who rebels against the traditional demands placed upon her
Ona Leong, Lei's half sister who has recently committed suicide
Mason Louie, Lei's husband, a car mechanic

Form and Content

The children of immigrants have often been called upon to translate for their parents. Their ability to switch from the language of their parents to the language of their birthplace makes them the bridge between the customs of the old world and the expectations and demands of the new. Not only are these children faced with a generation gap, but also they must cope with a cultural gap. This enormous responsibility can become an overwhelming burden. Fae Myenne Ng's first novel, *Bone*, confronts and explores this responsibility and burden. Ng, who grew up in San Francisco, is herself the daughter of Chinese immigrants and in an interview explained the title of her novel: "Bone is what lasts. And I wanted to honor the quality of endurance in the immigrant spirit."

Bone relates the story of the Leong family, which has recently suffered the death by suicide of the "Middle Girl," Ona. Ona committed suicide by jumping off one of Chinatown's housing projects. She left no note, and although the police reported that she was on downers, there was no apparent cause for the suicide.

The novel is narrated by "The First Girl," Leila Fu Louie, Ona's half sister and the eldest daughter in the Leong family. Lei's attempts to come to terms with her sister's death, and thereby her own life, lead her to muse about incidents from their childhood and the everyday circumstances of the present. The story unfolds in a series of stories that move from the present into the past. As the book opens, Lei has just returned from New York and must tell her mother that she married Mason Louie while there. The conversation jumps between languages:

> I went up to Mah and started out in Chinese, "I want to tell you something."
>
> Mah looked up, wide-eyed, expectant.
>
> I switched to English, "Time was right, so Mason and I just went to City Hall. We got married there.... In New York.... Nina was my witness."
>
> Mah grunted, a huumph sound that came out like a curse. My translation was: Disgust, anger. There's power behind her sounds. Over the years I've listened and rendered her Chinese grunts into English words.

Lei's attempt at accommodation by approaching her mother in Chinese falls away in the American reality of her deed; she must speak in English. Her mother counters in her ancient language, one that goes back to primitive grunts, to express her displeasure and provoke guilt in her daughter. Not only does Mah have a Chinese vocabulary on which to draw, but she can invoke the universal language of motherhood as well. Lei survives the encounter because she chooses not to retaliate against her mother by reminding her of her own failed marriages; instead, she reaches across the divide of affection by shifting the focus to Mason.

"You don't like Mason, is that it?"

"Mason," Mah spoke his name soft, "I love."

For love she used a Chinese word: to embrace, to hug.

I stepped around the boxes, opened my arms and hugged Mah.

Although Lei must continually face the chasm between her parents' expectations and her own reality, her ability to build a bridge of translation is grounded in her strong need and appreciation for the family.

Her youngest sister, Nina, the "End Girl," refuses to shoulder this burden of translation. Her rebellion has caused her to move to New York, far away from San Francisco's Chinatown where her parents live. Although she returns for Ona's funeral and later tries to alleviate her mother's grief by taking her on a trip back to China, she declares her independence by refusing to lie in order to appease her parents. She bluntly announces to them that she has had an abortion.

Yet it is the permanent, self-imposed silence of Ona that is at the center of the novel. Ona, the middle child, is caught in the middle; she learned too well how to keep secrets.

Analysis

Fae Myenne Ng does not seek to solve the mystery of Ona's death in this novel—it is a mystery that is unsolvable. Rather, through the narrative voice of Lei, she explores the languages and silences of love, grief, assimilation, avoidance, anger, guilt, and finally acceptance.

The novel begins with the language of gossip: "We heard things. 'A failed family. That Dulcie Fu. And you know which one: bald Leon. Nothing but daughters.' " Whispers are heard behind children's backs—a failed family because there were no sons, because Dulcie had left her first husband, because Dulcie and Leon fought and Leon had moved out, because Nina had moved to New York, because Ona had committed suicide, because Lei had moved in with Mason Louie and then married him in New York without the benefit of the traditional banquet.

Gossip gives way to lies when Lei begins to work through her relationship with Leon. Leon needs a steady source of income to pay his rent at the resident hotel into which he has moved after Ona's suicide. When Lei finally persuades him he can still earn some money while collecting Social Security, he agrees to apply for his benefits. Lei accompanies him to the Social Security office, where she and the interviewer try to sort through the morass of aliases and multiple birthdates that Leon has claimed over the years. These are the lies that Leon had used to survive and to support his family in a society which patronized him and devalued his masculinity.

The Social Security interviewer sends them home to find proper documentation. What Lei finds is a suitcase full of papers, neatly sorted by year and bundled by decade: a history of rejections, letters from Mah when he had shipped out, photographs, newspaper clippings, receipts of money sent to China, official documents that contradicted one another, and finally the needed certificate of identification and entry into the country. The contents of the suitcase attest a life created by papers—writing that is at once sacred and duplicitous, a testimony to the difficulties of sustaining an existence in an alien society. Lei realizes that Leon Leong had to imagine himself into being: "I'm the stepdaughter of a paper son and I've inherited this whole suitcase of lies. All of it is mine. All I have is those memories, and I want to remember them all."

These threads of affection and memories, spun of gossip and lies, draw Lei and the reader into the fabric of the family's life that was rent by Ona's suicide. Everyone in the family longs for escape: Leon from the humiliations of failure, Mah from loneliness, and the daughters from the expectations and needs of their parents. They long to escape from the boundaries of Chinatown, from their own lives. The children are drawn away by fast cars, drugs, casual sex, and the world of American youth, but each is bound more or less tightly by complexities of loving and living in the ambiguous reality of two languages. Lei, the translator from one language to another, finally succeeds in moving across town, but even as she leaves, she realizes the truth of what Leon once told her: "The heart never travels."

Bone is eloquently understated. Ng explores how the force of words—whether in English or Chinese, whether spoken or left unsaid—determines the course of lives. Perhaps it is the words not said that haunt the book most tellingly. Was there a conversation, a secret revealed, a word said that might have saved Ona? What does one do with those secrets, those unspoken promises that are the bones of every family?

Context

Fae Myenne Ng's *Bone* continues in a tradition of Asian American novels and memoirs by women that includes Maxine Hong Kingston's *The Woman Warrior: A Girlhood Among Ghosts* (1976), Amy Tan's *The Joy Luck Club* (1989), and Cynthia Kadohata's *The Floating World* (1989). These works, of necessity, mediate between demands of gender and ethnicity. Asian American writers first gained prominence in the mainstream of American literature in the 1970's. Writing from a strongly patriarchal cultural heritage, Asian American women novelists have had to create new strategies and invent new plots in order to express the paradox of resistance to and affirmation of that cultural heritage.

One of the strategies employed to lessen the masculinist impact has been the diminishment of the power of the father within the family structure. Fathers are often absent, whether through death or abandonment or from the necessity of employment, as with Leon in *Bone*. Also, as immigrants, the fathers have been disempowered by their lack of status and success in the new country. The task for the daughters of such fathers is to make some kind of accommodation in their lives in contemporary American society for the traditions and histories of their families.

Each of the three daughters in the Leong family approaches this accommodation in her own way: Ona jumps out a window, Nina carves out a life for herself as far away from the family as she can travel, and Lei moves across town, although retaining her memories and connections. Ng's novel lacks the bitterness or accusatory tone of some feminist fictions. Her characters struggle with frustration, discrimination, poverty, and tragedy, but Lei, as narrator, affirms the fragile and tenuous ties between parents and children and between men and women.

Bone is a journey into a territory that is at once the common heritage of all non-native Americans and the particular traditions of Chinese immigrants. The path to assimilation into American society is one fraught with contradictions and ambivalence about what to preserve and what to discard. Ng provides a few answers, simply revealing one family's experience.

Sources for Further Study

Lim, Shirley Geok-lin. "Assaying the Gold: Or, Contesting the Ground of Asian American Literature." *New Literary History* 24, no. 1 (Winter, 1993): 147-165. Traces the image of "the dream of the gold mountain"—from the early twentieth century writings at Angel Island, the immigrant's port-of-entry, to contemporary authors' preoccupations with paradoxes of promise and imprisonment, assimilation, and ethnic identification. Lim's analysis does not include Ng's work, but her discussion of mainstream Asian American authors who have reached success by mediating between non-Asian American readers and their own ethnic identities, includes much that would also pertain to a study of *Bone*.

______________. "Feminist and Ethnic Literary Theories in Asian American Literature." *Feminist Studies* 19, no. 3 (Fall, 1993): 571-595. Although this essay was written before the publication of Ng's novel, it delineates feminist issues in writings by Asian American women that help to illuminate similar issues in *Bone*. Lim focuses on how the literature reflects the oppositional demands of ethnic and gender identity. Claims that Asian American women have had to invent new plots, in which patriarchal power is diminished by the disempowerment of the father-figure, in order to reclaim their "mother/other" origin.

Miller, Heather Ross. "America the Big Lie, the Quintessential." *Southern Review* 29, no. 2 (April, 1993): 420-430. A review of five books of fiction, including *Bone*. Miller focuses on how the American Dream is supposed to be achieved by the adherence to a strong work ethic. Although these authors reveal the corruption of the innocent that such a belief engenders, their fictions recall a history of suffering transformed into life and hope.

Ng, Fae Myenne. "False Gold: My Father's American Journey." *New Republic* 209 (July 19, 1993): 12-13. Ng discusses her father's immigration to America. He was of the generation that took the sacrificial role to venture forth, and now at the end of this life he is bitter and believes that he has had no luck. Although she does not draw direct parallels between her father and the character of Leon Leong in *Bone*, they share similar antecedents—both are "paper sons" and both have been disappointed in their "Golden Venture" to the Beautiful Country.

Stephenson, Heather. "Out of the Kitchen and Traveling On: New Fiction by Asian Women." *New England Review* 16, no. 1 (Winter, 1994): 169-176. In this comparison of Banana Yoshimoto's *Kitchen*, Duong Thu Hong's *Paradise of the Blind*, and Fae Myenne Ng's *Bone*, Stephenson discusses how each author uses the language of food, kitchens, and ritual offerings to integrate family histories into current lives.

Tannenbaum, Amy. "Getting to the Marrow." *New York* 26, no. 4 (January 25, 1993): 26. A brief profile of and interview with Fae Myenne Ng in which she describes her childhood in San Francisco when she helped her mother in a sewing sweatshop. She sees herself as a traveler, an itinerant who, like the oldtimers, makes a home wherever she is.

Jane Anderson Jones

BONJOUR TRISTESSE

Author: Françoise Sagan (Françoise Quoirez, 1935-)
Type of work: Novel
Type of plot: Psychological realism
Time of plot: One summer and early fall in the 1950's
Locale: The French Riviera and Paris
First published: 1954 (English translation, 1955)

Principal characters:

Cécile, a seventeen-year-old girl spending the summer in the south of France with her father and his mistress
Raymond, Cécile's father, a forty-year-old widower
Elsa Mackenbourg, Raymond's mistress
Anne Larsen, one of the closest friends of Cécile's mother, who reared the girl
Cyril, a twenty-six-year-old law student who falls in love with Cécile

Form and Content

The title *Bonjour Tristesse* (hello sadness) is a quote from a poem by Paul Éluard that opens the novel and sets the tone for the bittersweet narrative to come. The narrator, Cécile, seems older than her years, unable to concentrate on activities, such as schoolwork, that are alien to the sophisticated high society to which she already belongs. At the beginning of her story, she identifies strongly with her father, Raymond, sharing his love of beauty and pleasure, but also acutely aware of the superficiality and transience of the world of the idle rich in which both of them live.

The narrator's dilemma is acutely defined by the two older women in the novel: Elsa, an unreflective sybarite whose life is given meaning by sports cars and nightclubs; and Anne, her dark, serious, and contemplative counterpart, whose very presence seems to call into judgment the lives of the other characters.

After Anne arrives at the Riviera summer house where Cécile, Raymond, and Elsa are vacationing, the relationship between Cécile and Anne quickly becomes complex. Anne seems to bring out the worst in Cécile, who never misses an opportunity to play the disrespectful adolescent rebel in the older woman's presence.

It becomes apparent, however, that her provocations are really a symptom both of her admiration for Anne's aloof superiority and of her growing jealousy. There is something possessive about Cécile's affection for her father. The frivolous affairs between Raymond and women such as Elsa do not excessively arouse this jealousy, but when Anne enters the scene and it becomes evident that Raymond is genuinely falling in love, the ugly side of Cécile's character reveals itself. One of the complexities of the novel is that the reader never knows whether Cécile is simply jealous of Anne or whether she is angry at Raymond for having betrayed their philosophy of uncommitted pleasure-seeking by falling in love.

When Anne and Raymond decide to marry, after having abandoned Elsa and Cécile in a nightclub so that the newly formed couple could spend the night together, Anne begins to fill the role of mother. In particular, she forbids Cécile's ever seeing her lover Cyril again and tells her to concentrate on preparing for her exams instead. Furious at what she considers an intolerable invasion of her freedom, and intent on destroying the relationship between Anne and her father, Cécile manages to have Elsa and Cyril play the role of lovers, convincing Elsa that in this way she will win back Raymond. Cécile succeeds in making her father jealous, to the point where he makes a secret rendezvous with Elsa. Anne accidentally sees the two of them together and flees from the house in her car, while Cécile finally realizes the damage she may have caused by her Machiavellian schemes.

Cécile and her father are in the process of writing a letter of apology to Anne when the telephone rings: Anne has died in an accident on a particularly treacherous road along the Mediterranean coast. Hospital workers believe that it was no more than an accident, while Cécile and

Raymond are left with the feeling that they may have caused Anne's suicide. In the final chapter the two are back in Paris, where they slowly resume the life of leisure and irresponsibility that had been interrupted by the events of the summer. Yet Cécile cannot suppress her guilt concerning Anne's death, and there is a strong suggestion that her life will never be as it was before.

Analysis

When *Bonjour Tristesse* first appeared, Françoise Sagan was only nineteen. Her remarkable achievement in producing a stylistically masterful novel at such a young age accounts to a large degree for the worldwide celebrity that immediately ensued. Sagan, whose pen name was borrowed from a character in Marcel Proust's *À la recherche du temps perdu* (1913-1922; *Remembrance of Things Past*, 1922-1931, 1981), was romanticized by the public, which saw the novel as an allegory of adolescent alienation and identified the author with her tragic heroine. Sagan tried to live up to the image she had created, using literature to achieve the kind of celebrity later associated with Elvis Presley and Andy Warhol. As such, she remains an important figure who bridges the gap between high and popular culture and whose status as a media icon has at times overshadowed her accomplishments as an author, playwright, and filmmaker.

The tragedies of Sagan's own life, such as a near-fatal accident in her Aston Martin in 1957, her history of alcoholism and addiction during the 1960's and 1970's, and her physical collapse while accompanying French president François Mitterrand on a trip to South America in 1985, have dominated tabloid headlines in France and around the world. Her love of fast cars is in itself famous, and she has used the image of driving at the limit of control as a metaphor for life. She became addicted to painkillers during the recovery from her car accident, an experience that she recounts in *Toxique* (1964), a powerful text on the psychological effects of drugs.

Sagan has always been aware of the dangers associated with wealth and glamour, and she even addressed those dangers prophetically in her first novel. The manner in which the frivolous, pleasure-seeking world of her characters tends ineluctably toward tragedy and emptiness is a remarkably clear-sighted commentary on the mechanism of popular culture to which *Bonjour Tristesse* belongs. The novel is a best-seller that manifests literary ambition and philosophical overtones, yet it is a best-seller all the same. If Sagan had deliberately set out to write the book that would bring her the greatest amount of fame in the shortest amount of time, she need not have done anything differently.

In the light of the sensationalism that accompanied the novel's release, it is ironic that much of its early fame (or infamy) was partly the result of misinterpretation: It was widely assumed that Cécile represented a new, amoral generation that echoed, though in a more superficial mode, the atheism and pessimism of the existentialist movement. That early response, while contributing to the novel's popularity, failed to take into account two important elements: first, that Cécile learns her nihilistic attitude from her elders, especially her father; second, the fact that the entire novel is written as a confession, as a purging of guilt, and not as the proud manifesto of a new amorality. As time passed, the scandalous reputation of Sagan and her work subsided, and appreciation of her talent became more subtle; the artificial public image that it created, however, continued with little change.

People were perhaps not too far off the mark, on the other hand, when they saw a connection between *Bonjour Tristesse* and the existentialist movement which by that time had become a solidly entrenched fashion in the Saint-Germain-des-Prés neighborhood of Paris. In 1980, Sagan kept Jean-Paul Sartre company during the last days of his life, after having published an open letter in which she declared her admiration for him and his influence on her career. Since this is one of the few examples of Sagan's claiming any kind of intellectual heritage, it needs to be studied carefully. Certainly, *Bonjour Tristesse* is not far from being an existentialist novel. Centering as it does on the irremediable consequences of one's actions, it is a kind of moral parable in the spirit of many of the fictional works of Sartre and Albert Camus. Sagan was steeped in the spirit of French cultural life of the early 1950's, and the impact of that particular time reverberates throughout her work. For some time, the roots of her novelistic sensibility in the period of her own early adulthood made people think of her work as outdated, but that judgment, like many others made over the years, is gradually losing credibility.

Context

According to Judith Graves Miller, the foremost expert on Sagan in the United States, Sagan's commitment to feminist issues accurately reflects her degree of political engagement in general: She often speaks out on an issue and then distances herself from the debate rather than remain associated with it for an extended period. Her most visible participation in the feminist movement occurred in 1971, when she signed the Manifesto of the 343, a famous document signed by women, many of them well known in French society, claiming to have undergone abortions; by doing so, they placed themselves in danger of immediate arrest and imprisonment. This very effective protest drew national attention to the issue and was one of the factors leading to the legalization of abortion in France.

Although Sagan herself has shown limited, though genuine, interest in feminist issues, her work has much to offer to the field of feminist literary criticism. *Bonjour Tristesse* first of all gave voice to the alienation of postwar youth; had Cécile been a young man instead of a woman, however, the novel undoubtedly would not have had the impact that it did. Cécile's sexual sophistication and worldliness, the loss of her virginity (which she celebrates), and her powerful manipulation of the adult world that surrounds her were, for contemporary readers, nothing short of shocking. The well-known Catholic novelist François Mauriac wrote an editorial in the conservative newspaper *Le Figaro* in which he argued that the novel should not have received the Prix des Critiques for 1954; while he admitted that it was an admirable work from a literary standpoint, he wrote that the moral bankruptcy it betrayed was symptomatic of all that had to be resisted in French culture and society. Mauriac's reaction was typical of much of the artistic and political establishment of the time. According to Miller, such reactions as Mauriac's are common whenever a threatening new voice, especially a feminine one, is heard. Sagan's enduring contribution to women's literature can be said to lie in the initial transgression of societal norms by her heroine, Cécile, who set the pattern for many of the characters in Sagan's later works.

On the other hand, some criticize Sagan for the same reasons that certain other female writers, such as Colette, have been criticized. By concentrating on the traditional feminine sources of power, the argument goes—that is, primarily the power to arouse desire and curiosity in men—Sagan perpetuates conventional gender roles instead of redefining them. As with Colette, however, there is much more to Sagan's characters than the stock figure of the vamp; she explores the intricacies of male-female relationships in a manner that cannot be reduced to stereotypes. In particular, her powerful female characters, in that they display a rebellious attitude toward many social conventions, cannot easily be categorized as mere slaves to the game of seduction. Now that Sagan criticism based on an informed and sophisticated feminist perspective is appearing, a certain reevaluation of her situation in contemporary women's literature is at hand.

Sources for Further Study

Cismaru, Alfred. "Françoise Sagan: The Superficial Classic." *World Literature Today* 67 (Spring, 1993): 291-295. A critique of Sagan's concept of freedom, this article tries to find the reason for Sagan's obsession with worldliness and frivolity. Cismaru speculates that the source of much of Sagan's inspiration is her own repressive, petit-bourgeois background.

Miller, Judith Graves. *Françoise Sagan*. Boston: Twayne, 1988. The first full-length critical study of Sagan in English, and an excellent one. Miller examines the phenomenon of Sagan as a public figure and analyzes her works partly as attempts to blur the boundary separating fiction and autobiography. Includes a useful chronology and a selected bibliography.

Poirot-Delpech, Bertrand. *Bonjour Sagan*. Paris: Herscher, 1985. Although published in French, this book is a fascinating Sagan iconography, with photographs and other documents from all periods of her life. Even an English-speaking reader will appreciate those aspects of Sagan's much-publicized private life that are copiously displayed in these pages.

Updike, John. "Books." *The New Yorker* 50 (August 12, 1974): 95-98. Updike devotes the regular book review column of *The New Yorker* in this issue to Sagan, on the occasion of the publication in English of *Scars on the Soul*. It is a useful insight into the appreciation of one of America's foremost novelists for Sagan's work, especially as Updike's own fiction displays some degree of affinity with hers.

M. Martin Guiney

THE BOOK OF MARGERY KEMPE

Author: Margery Burnham Kempe (c. 1373-c. 1438)
Type of work: Autobiography
Time of work: The fifteenth century
Locale: England and Jerusalem
First published: Written 1436, published 1936

Principal personages:

Margery Kempe, a woman who relates her mystical relationship with Christ and the Virgin Mary

John Kempe, Margery's husband, a burgess in the town of Lynn in eastern England

Form and Content

The Book of Margery Kempe, the first known autobiography in English, is the account of a fifteenth century mystic. Unlike most medieval mystics—persons who enjoyed an intimate rapport with God—Kempe was neither a recluse nor a member of a religious order, but rather the wife of a town burgess and the mother of fourteen children.

Although she worried that her wifehood made her less pleasing to God than if she had been a virgin, Christ assured her through her meditations that He loved married women too and that her reward in Heaven would be equal to that of the virgin martyrs and holy, celibate widows. This assurance, to which Kempe makes repeated reference, offset the prevalent medieval opinion that only those women who were physically chaste could attain a high degree of spirituality.

While the chronology of Kempe's religious experience is somewhat ambiguous, her book centers around the key events that shaped her life: her conversion from worldliness to a close communion with Christ; her vow of marital chastity; her voyages to the Holy Land and elsewhere; and her fits of loud weeping. After she had been married for several years, Kempe suddenly heard melodious sounds and leapt from her bed, exclaiming, "It is full merry in heaven!" From that time on, she abandoned her preoccupations with beauty and material success, turning her thoughts to Christ. At the approximate age of forty, she exacted from her husband a promise of chastity, for, despite her sensual nature and Christ's assurance that He loved wives, she felt that intercourse and childbirth decreased her potential for spiritual growth. As a token of her chastity, she began dressing in white, which evoked the criticism of others, as did her eventual separation from her spouse.

During her pilgrimage to the Holy Land, Kempe suffered further ostracism for her tears, her unofficial preaching, and her admonitions to those who swore or behaved in an irreverent manner. Moreover, on her return to England, she was cross-examined by several prelates who suspected her of being a Lollard, or follower of the religious reformer John Wycliff.

It was in Jerusalem that Kempe experienced her first bout of boisterous weeping and sobbing, accompanied by writhing on the ground. These fits, provoked primarily by meditations on the Passion, continued for more than ten years and were beyond her control. Inevitably, Kempe's bizarre behavior made her unwelcome in public places and aroused the suspicion of many that she was either ill or possessed by a demon. On the other hand, there were people in Lynn and elsewhere who regarded her tears as blessings from God, not only abiding her exhibitions but also protecting her from critics, succoring her with food and ale from their tables, and asking her to pray for them.

Since Kempe was illiterate, she narrated her experiences to an anonymous man from Germany. Unfortunately, the man died in a short time, and a priest of Kempe's acquaintance undertook the project. The first amanuensis' usage of both English and German was so poor, however, and his letters so faultily formed, that the priest was initially unable to read his manuscript. Nevertheless, he returned to the task after several years, and thanks to Kempe's prayers, found the writing legible and intelligible.

During the fifteenth century, *The Book of Margery Kempe* was maintained at a Carthusian monastery at

Mount Grace. By the eighteenth century, it had found its way into the library of an English family, where it was rediscovered and identified by a descendant, Colonel William Butler-Bowdon, in 1934.

Analysis

Written in Middle English, in the dialect of the East Midlands, *The Book of Margery Kempe* typifies the style of medieval prose. Like many authors of her time, Kempe was humble and self-effacing, referring to herself as "this creature." Furthermore, the sentence structure employed by her amanuensis is similar to that found in other writings of the fifteenth century. Virtually all the sentences are simple or compound, often beginning with "and" or "then," thereby producing an effect which may seem monotonous to twentieth century readers.

Its style notwithstanding, the work portrays Kempe in the context of her time and offers rich examples of medieval thinking and faith. Although the intimacy of her dialogues with Christ and the Virgin Mary was extraordinary, her basic ability to conceive of the supernatural in concrete terms was not. Since the twelfth century, Christians had been steeped in the devotional tradition of affective piety (so named by later scholars for its appeal to the affections, or emotions), the purpose of which was to incite feelings of love and pity toward Christ. Initiated by the Cistercian monks, affective piety emphasized Christ's humanity, stressing His physical suffering throughout the Passion and the inevitable grief of Mary. During the following centuries, the Franciscans carried on the tradition through their sermons and lyrics. By graphically describing Christ's pain, the monks made their audiences feel that they were there with Him at the Crucifixion. Thus, Kempe's participation in the life and suffering of Christ differed only in degree from that of other devout Christians. Although she acknowledged that Christ and Mary appeared to her "ghostly sight" and spoke to her "in her mind," she considered these apparitions and conversations as real and substantial as those she encountered in the earthly realm.

The Book of Margery Kempe also bears witness to the prevalence of unquestioning faith in the supernatural, particularly in the convictions of Kempe's neighbors that her tears and swooning came either from God or from a demon. In another example, Kempe recounts a fire that broke out in the center of Lynn. Fearing for the safety of the people, the pastor of Saint Margaret's Church carried the tabernacle containing the Eucharist to the scene of the conflagration and prayed as the flames began to spread. Followed by his parishioners, he proceeded back to the church, where the congregation importuned God to send either rain or snow to extinguish the blaze. According to Kempe, it was the prayers of the faithful, including herself, which brought about a snowfall. Not once did anyone take control by trying to extinguish the fire; the townspeople were convinced that their lives depended solely upon the will of God and that only petitions could sway that will.

In the beginning of her narrative, Kempe refers to God's turning things upside down: "health into sickness, prosperity into adversity, worship into reproof, love into hate." Although *The Book of Margery Kempe* is loosely structured, a careful reading reveals a turnabout in Kempe herself. During her young and middle adulthood, she was protected and nurtured by others; in her later years, however, she herself became a nurturer. She tells, for example, of calming a woman maddened by the ravages of childbirth, much as her pastor had once attempted to console her after the birth of her first child. Kempe also relates that her encounters with Christ decreased in frequency or intensity when she was occupied in caring for sick folk. One of these ill persons was her husband: At the approximate age of sixty, he fell down a flight of stairs, sustaining a head injury which rendered him senile and incontinent. Following the advice of Christ, Margery returned to her spouse, assuming the role of his nursemaid rather than that of his vulnerable and protected wife. Finally, the abbess of a convent often asked Kempe, who had once sought counsel, to counsel the nuns.

Kempe's ability to nurture others seems to correspond to her changing image of the Virgin Mary. As a relatively young woman, she envisioned the mother of God as a child whom she tended from birth; as a young mother whom she assisted in childbirth; and as a sorrowing mother with whom she stood at the Crucifixion. As Kempe grew older, however, Mary came to her spiritual vision in a more parental guise. In one meditation, she promised to be a good mother, and in another, she counseled Kempe to forgo her accustomed weekly fast, as she needed physical nourishment to carry on her spiritual life. Thus, as Kempe received succor through her meditations (perhaps in compensation for the lack of succor in the concrete world), she seems to have become more capable of offering comfort and nurture to those around her.

Context

Kempe's conflicts over the worthiness of her marital status and her desire for chastity undoubtedly arose from a long-lived consensus, originating in the fourth century, that in the eyes of God, virgins and celibate widows were closer to sanctity than were wives. One of the sources supporting this stance in the Middle Ages was *Hali Meidenhad*, an early thirteenth century treatise for young women. The author claims that in heaven, wives will have their reward "thirty fold"; widows, "fifty fold"; and virgins, "one hundred fold." The opinion was still flourishing more than two centuries later, when Geoffrey Chaucer's Wife of Bath challenged the Catholic church's lauding of virginity, arguing in favor of Christian women who embraced marriage and the sexuality that accompanied it. Although Kempe could not have read either piece of literature, she could hardly have escaped their import: that wives were more remote from God than their chaste sisters—especially since this conviction was frequently voiced in church pulpits.

Despite Kempe's negative self-assessment, others apparently did not view her wifehood as an obstacle to spirituality. The abbess was a case in point. Presumably a virgin or widow, she nevertheless revered the mysticism of Kempe—who was a wife and mother, her chaste marriage notwithstanding—and valued her counsel to the nuns. Moreover, a priest in Lynn read to Kempe from Scripture and the writings of the church fathers; in this way, he acknowledged not only her spiritual understanding but also her intelligence, contradicting the conventional opinion of the clergy that women—particularly those who had succumbed to the lures of marriage and maternity—were limited in mental acumen.

While there is no direct correlation between the production of Kempe's narrative and later literature, some scholars view her work as a forerunner of religious writing by women. Furthermore, the combination of her mysticism and marital status seems to foreshadow a new attitude which had its inception in the sixteenth century: that marriage and motherhood, rather than chastity and seclusion, were the means by which women could achieve sanctity. This attitude was promulgated especially through the teachings of Martin Luther and the writings of such Catholic humanists as Thomas More, Erasmus, and Francis de Sales.

Sources for Further Study

Atkinson, Clarissa W. *Mystic and Pilgrim: The Book and the World of Margery Kempe*. Ithaca, N.Y.: Cornell University Press, 1983. Kempe is compared to other female mystics, especially Saints Brigitta and Dorthea. Atkinson also provides background material on affective piety and the religious education of medieval women.

______________. *The Oldest Vocation: Christian Motherhood in the Middle Ages*. Ithaca, N.Y.: Cornell University Press, 1991. Examines the status of maternity from early Christianity to the late twentieth century, along with nuances in the concept of "mother." Atkinson classifies Kempe among the Christian mothers whose prayers wrought the salvation of their children and calls attention to the Virgin Mary's position as the perfect mother of the Middle Ages—a position which may have influenced Kempe's image of Mary as a nurturer.

Cockayne, Oswald, ed. *Hali Meidenhad*. New York: Greenwood Press, 1969. An anonymous Middle English treatise with a modern translation. Written for young women, it attempts to promote virginity by detailing the hardships and sordidness of marriage, childbirth, and child rearing. Although it was composed in the early thirteenth century, *Hali Meidenhad* had a significant hold on the thinking of the later Middle Ages, convincing some married women, such as Kempe, that they were "unfit" for a spiritual life.

Glasscoe, Marion. *English Medieval Mystics: Games of Faith*. London: Longman, 1993. Compares Kempe to other mystics, both English and continental, and discusses her life within the context of fifteenth century urban society. Glasscoe also explicates particular passages from *The Book of Margery Kempe*.

______________, ed. *The Medieval Mystical Tradition in England*. Cambridge, England: D. S. Brewer, 1984. A collection of essays on various English medieval mystics, including Richard Rolle, Walter Hilton, Julian of Norwich, and Margery Kempe. The selection on Kempe provides an overview of affective piety, while another discusses the medieval mentality and its fusing of "inner" and "outer" realities.

Rebecca Stingley Hinton

A BOOK OF SHOWINGS

Author: Julian of Norwich (1342-after 1416)
Type of work: Essays
First published: Written, c. 1393; published, 1670

Form and Content

Written by Dame Julian of Norwich, a fourteenth century anchoress or religious recluse, *A Book of Showings* (also known as *Revelations of Divine Love*) is the record of sixteen visions that came to Julian during a nearly fatal illness in May, 1373. While no original fourteenth century manuscripts survive, four later, complete copies still exist. One is shorter than the rest and may be based on Julian's original record of her experience. The other three, from the sixteenth and seventeenth centuries, preserve a longer version that reflects Julian's fifteen to twenty years of meditation on the visions; this is the version usually read today. The overall theme, as suggested by the alternate title, is the love of God shown in Creation, in Jesus Christ, and in the life of the believer. Although Julian is not the only female religious mystic of the Middle Ages, she is unique in style and in her exposition of the feminine aspects of God.

After a brief outline of the book, Julian explains how the visions came to her on May 8, 1373; she was thirty-one years old. She views the illness that brought her near death and the visions that came when everyone, including Julian herself, had given her up for dead as the answer to her prayers to understand Christ's suffering on the cross, to suffer physically for God's sake, and to experience sincere repentance, compassion, and a desire to know God.

The first twelve revelations deal with the love of God revealed in Christ's suffering and death on the cross. Julian finds herself present at these events, and she seems to feel Christ's physical pain as well as inexplicable spiritual joy. She explains the spiritual significance of Christ's crown of thorns, whipping, and crucifixion, as well as the suffering of his mother, Mary. She is shown that the world was made by an all-powerful, all-wise, and all-loving God who works in and through every occurrence.

The thirteenth revelation deals with the nature of sin and the power of God's mercy and love to forgive sin and transform it into joy. Julian's understanding is that those chosen for salvation retain "a godly will that has never consented to sin" even if they have committed sins. The fourteenth vision deals with prayer, by which God enables the soul to commune with God, and with the nature of God's love, which Julian understands as the essence of God's nature, which is absolutely incompatible with anger. In this revelation, Julian receives an understanding of the Trinity as father God, mother Christ, and love and goodness in the Holy Spirit. The fifteenth revelation is concerned with the nature of Heaven, which will compensate for and erase all suffering experienced on Earth. The final, sixteenth vision shows Julian the soul's value in God's sight. The account of the visions is followed by a series of further meditations on the whole experience.

Analysis

Although divine love is the overarching theme of Julian's visions, two other, related issues dealt with in *A Book of Showings* are the problem of sin and suffering and the nature of prayer. In addition, the nature of mystical experience itself is considered, as Julian attempts to explain to her readers the physical, intellectual, and spiritual means by which she perceived certain elements of the visions. Most critics accept Julian's visions as genuine spiritual experiences, rather than attributing them to physical or mental conditions.

Julian perceives God's love as the force that holds the universe together. Julian's God is not at all a God of wrath or condemnation; some have interpreted this theology as leaning toward universalism, the belief that all humanity will ultimately be saved, as opposed to the doctrine that some will reject salvation and be punished eternally in Hell. Others point out that Julian never explicitly states a universalistic view, but she does state that "though the revelation was one of goodness, with very little reference to evil, I was not drawn thereby from any article of the Faith in which Holy Church teaches me to believe." Nevertheless, in her visions she is repeatedly told that "Everything is going to be all right."

Julian understands sin as both real and unreal. It has a real effect on human lives and spirits (that is, pain or suffering) and is the cause of Christ's sacrificial death—the focus of twelve of the sixteen visions. At the same time, sin is unreal in that ultimately it has no existence without God's permission. Julian sees God's love as nullifying the spiritual damage caused by sin, using suffering to draw people closer to God, and turning sin's suffering into heavenly bliss. According to Julian, Christians may sin, but they need never fear for their ultimate salvation, an idea resembling John Calvin's doctrines of predestination and election.

Another main theme of *A Book of Showings* is the nature of prayer, especially contemplative prayer, which draws the believer to a deeper understanding of and oneness with God. Although Julian acknowledges the value of petitionary prayers and is assured that God answers all prayers, contemplative prayer strengthens her spiritually and aids her in dark times.

Julian's meditations on Christ as mother are unique in medieval mysticism, though the concept itself appears in early church writings. Although Julian acknowledges the role of the Virgin Mary as a spiritual mother, in *A Book of Showings* the motherhood of Christ far surpasses Mary's role. Some critics dismiss Julian's idea of feminine aspects of God as merely her personal view; others argue that Julian is part of a long tradition in the Christian church. For Julian, the image of Christ as mother is integral with the nature of God as Trinity—Father, Son, and Holy Spirit. Although the Son is masculine, his motherhood is manifested in his primary functions of mercy and pity for humankind on earth. Christ gives birth, spiritually, to the believer and nurtures the believer through the sacrament of the Eucharist. Julian describes God the Father as responsible for the creation of humanity, and God the Spirit deals, naturally, with spiritual things, including the state of the soul after death. All three functions are inextricably interwoven and are echoed in Julian's exposition of human nature as a kind of lesser Trinity. This Trinitarian emphasis makes Julian's teaching on the motherhood of Christ different from earlier writings.

Julian's style has been praised for its simplicity, even as she attempts to convey the extremely complex doctrines encompassed by her visions. Her vividly detailed descriptions appeal to the reader's visual imagination. Her down-to-earth figures of speech compare various elements of the visions to common foods, clothing, household items, and elements of nature. Whether her rhetoric is influenced by her gender, she seems to be trying to put spiritual things into terms that anyone, male or female, could understand. She frequently speaks of God's "homely" interaction with her and all believers—that is, intimate, familiar, or homelike.

Context

A contemporary of Geoffrey Chaucer and William Langland, Julian was apparently well known locally as a holy woman and spiritual counselor during her lifetime, as shown by bequests to her in several wills of that time and by a visit with her recorded by another English mystic, Margery Kempe, in the autobiography *The Book of Margery Kempe* (wr. 1436). From the few surviving manuscripts, however, it seems that *A Book of Showings* was not widely read, perhaps because the theological views of women were not highly valued, with few exceptions. Julian herself acknowledged that some readers would question the validity of her revelations because of her sex. Julian's visions were preserved by exiled English Benedictine nuns in France, whose chaplain produced the first printed edition in 1670. Julian is cited as an influence on Florence Nightingale, the nineteenth century pioneer in nursing. Late twentieth century writers Annie Dillard and Mary Gordon have also been influenced by *The Book of Showings*.

Interest in Julian's visions began to revive at the beginning of the twentieth century when Grace Warrack translated the long text from Middle English in 1901. T. S. Eliot's *Four Quartets* (1943) shows the influence of Julian's mysticism, especially in "Little Gidding." The first critical edition of *A Book of Showings*, by Anna Maria Reynolds, appeared in 1956. In 1973, the Anglican church celebrated the six-hundredth anniversary of the visions, and interest in Julian and her work has continued to grow since then, with numerous scholarly studies and translations into several languages. Although Julian has never been canonized, May 8 (the date of Julian's revelations) is now officially part of the Anglican church calendar.

Julian has been recognized as an outstanding theologian by many authorities, including Thomas Merton, and she has obviously influenced both men and women. In the mid-1980's, Julian's work came to the attention of feminist theologians, interested in a woman who is the author of a generally recognized masterpiece of spiritual mysticism and who develops a unique interpretation of feminine aspects of God in her vision of Christ as mother. While critics of the first half of the twentieth century tended to dismiss Julian's idea of feminine aspects of God as merely her personal view or purely metaphorical, later critics demonstrated that Julian is part of a long biblical and theological tradition. Studies of Julian and her work contribute to the ongoing critical exploration of how women's approaches to literature and theology differ from men's.

Sources for Further Study

Beer, Frances. *Women and Mystical Experience in the Middle Ages*. Woodbridge, Suffolk, England: Boydell Press, 1992. Beer summarizes and explicates *A Book of Showings*, focusing on Julian's visions of the Crucifixion and Christ's suffering as parallel to human suffering, which is intended to draw people to God. The author clearly admires Julian as a person and as a spiritual authority.

Bradley, Ritamary. "Julian of Norwich: Writer and Mystic." In *An Introduction to the Medieval Mystics of Europe*, edited by Paul E. Szarmach. Albany: State University of New York Press, 1984. Bradley analyzes Julian's style and use of figurative language, and she outlines what she considers to be the key features of Julian's theology: the nature of the Trinity and of God's transforming love. Discussions of Julian's place in the Christian mystical tradition and of her modern influence are particularly helpful.

Coleman, T. W. *English Mystics of the Fourteenth Century*. Westport, Conn.: Greenwood Press, 1971. In his chapter on Julian, Coleman gives detailed biographical background and resists the supernatural nature of the visions, citing several expert opinions to suggest that they may be attributed to Julian's physical and mental state at the time.

Heimmel, Jennifer P. *"God Is Our Mother": Julian of Norwich and the Medieval Image of Christian Feminine Divinity.* Salzburg, Austria: Inst. für Anglistik und Amerikanistik, University of Salzburg, 1982. An in-depth study of the history of the title theme, which Heimmel contends reaches its greatest depth in *A Book of Showings*. Includes a bibliography.

Jones, Catherine. "The English Mystic: Julian of Norwich." In *Medieval Women Writers*, edited by Katharina M. Wilson. Athens: University of Georgia Press, 1984. Jones examines Julian's background and sources for *A Book of Showings* and considers her place in medieval and modern spirituality. She compares Julian's innovative rhetorical and stylistic techniques to Chaucer's and shows how Julian's development of the idea of God as mother is unlike any previous or contemporary treatment. Parallel excerpts from the short and long versions of the text are included, along with a bibliography.

Julian of Norwich. *Revelations of Divine Love*. Translated by Clifton Wolters. 1966. New York: Penguin Books, 1982. The standard modern English translation of Julian's work. In his generally helpful introduction, Wolters argues that Julian's vision of Christ as mother is her own, idiosyncratic concept.

____________. *Showings*. Translated by Edmund Colledge and James Walsh. New York: Paulist Press, 1978. This translation includes both short and long versions, with a comprehensive bibliography.

Llewelyn, Robert, ed. *Julian: Woman of Our Day*. London: Darton, Longman & Todd, 1985. This collection of essays, many devotional in nature, is united by the idea that parallels between the fourteenth and twentieth centuries make Julian's spiritual insights especially applicable today. Includes a brief bibliography.

Nuth, Joan M. *Wisdom's Daughter: The Theology of Julian of Norwich*. New York: Crossroad, 1991. An excellent, comprehensive study of Julian's work from a feminist theological viewpoint. With an extensive bibliography and an index.

Elizabeth L. Rambo

THE BOOK OF THE CITY OF LADIES: A Fifteenth-Century Defense of Women

Author: Christine de Pizan (c. 1365-c. 1430)
Type of work: Social criticism
First published: *Le Livre de la cité des dames*, written 1405, published 1982 (English translation, 1521)

Form and Content

Written in 1405 by the daughter of an Italian astrologer attached to the court of France, *The Book of the City of Ladies: A Fifteenth-Century Defense of Women* is Christine de Pizan's retelling of universal history from a feminist as well as a late medieval perspective. The work is an extensive, three-part prose allegory developed in accordance with established conventions of classical rhetoric—a form considered by Christine's contemporaries to be accessible only to formally educated male writers.

The three sections of the book are clearly delineated by such phrases as "Here begins the book second part" and "Here begins the book third part." In part 1 Christine, alone in her study and saddened by the many disparaging remarks against women that she has found in her reading, is visited by three ladies: Reason, Rectitude, and Justice. Each of these allegorical figures becomes the respective narrator of a section of the book.

Reassured by Lady Reason that these negative concepts of women are in direct contradiction to the truth, Christine is charged with the task of building a fortified city for all good ladies. Using the medieval practice of offering exempla, Reason recounts stories of renowned female military leaders such as the Amazons, a community of women warriors of considerable physical strength. A second group of illustrations presents women of great mental prowess. The stories are encapsulations of narratives drawn primarily from Boccaccio's collection of tales about famous women, *De mulieribus claris*, and serve as the stones with which to construct the foundation and walls of the allegorical city.

In the second part, Christine begins to build the houses of her city and to populate them with women whose virtues and special powers have gained them wide recognition: prophets (Greek, Roman, and biblical), daughters who exhibited prodigious filial devotion, and wives who demonstrated extraordinary love for their husbands—even husbands much older than themselves. Narrated by Lady Rectitude, or "Right Behavior," with interjections and questions from Christine, these examples refute the common misogynist notions that women are inconstant in love, cannot keep secrets, are incapable of giving good advice, only contribute to the ills of humankind, are naturally greedy, and want to be raped. This portion of the text closes with an invitation from Christine addressed to all women of virtue—past, present, and future—to rejoice for the establishment of their "honorable lodging."

The third division of the allegory introduces the women who are given the residences of honor in the City of Ladies: The Virgin Mary is named queen, and her entourage is composed of Mary Magdalene, female saints and martyrs, women who witnessed the martyrdom of their children, and other saintly women. These stories are narrated by Lady Justice, who then gives the city to "all honorable ladies who love glory, virtue and praise" as a refuge and defense against their enemies. A long segment is devoted to Saint Catherine and is followed by an interruption in the allegory as the author steps out of her literary persona and addresses an intimate prayer to her patron saint. The book concludes with an admonition to all women to be all the more virtuous and humble, to be wary of deception, to be well-informed, and to flee "foolish love," which can only cause physical and spiritual harm.

Analysis

Inspired by the reading of Saint Augustine's *De civitate Dei* (413-426; *City of God*) and the building of new city walls around Paris, Christine framed her defense of women in allegorical architecture. Although her city may be figurative, Christine made the women populating it very real. Even goddesses and mythological personages such as Ceres, Medea, and Minerva are depicted as mortal women whose great virtues and benefits to humanity earned them their titles. To lend further credence to her characters, Christine, in conversation with the narrator, often interjects brief mention of contemporary women or women of the recent past such as the wife of the military commander in chief Bertrand du Guesclin or Valentina Visconti, the wife of the duke of Orléans—real people familiar to her readers.

In the three divisions of the book one can discern three levels of defense. The physical level, in part 1, states that women can have physical and mental powers equal to those of men: Menalippe and Hippolyta unhorsed the great Greek warriors Hercules and Theseus, and Minerva invented a numerical system and mathematics, wool-carding and the art of weaving, and the first musical instruments. The moral level, in part 2, states that women have natural gifts that often enable them to predict the future (such as the biblical prophetesses of the Old and New Testaments and the sibyls) and can love both parents and spouse to a greater degree than men: A certain Roman woman breast-fed her own imprisoned mother, and Argia turned over rotting corpses on the battlefield desperately searching for the body of her slain husband, Polyneices. The spiritual level, in part 3, states that women are capable of such religious devotion that they can endure the most horrible tortures: Saint Catherine continued to sing praises to God when plunged headlong into boiling oil.

From these stories and dialogues between Christine and the three allegorical ladies emerge certain themes central to the author's purpose. Foremost among these is the education of women. Lady Reason states unequivocally that "if it were customary to send daughters to school like sons, and if they were then taught the natural sciences, they would learn as thoroughly and understand the subtleties of all the arts and sciences as well as sons." In portraying illustrious women, Christine is careful to specify those women who have "learnedness in letters." To the capacity for learning Christine adds every woman's "natural sense" or "prudence," that is, her common sense and cleverness that enable her to outwit men. For Christine, this gift is used to good ends, as demonstrated by Ops, the queen of Crete, who used her wits to save her sons, and the Lombard women, who foiled their would-be rapists by putting putrid chicken meat on their own breasts.

Another predominant motif is the necessity for women to keep their behavior above reproach. Caveats are issued throughout the work warning women against extramarital or premarital sexual intercourse, which Christine calls "foolish love." Even though some of her exemplary tales concern adulterers and fornicators, Christine is careful to caution her readers and to point out the tragic outcome of this comportment. She clearly believes that women engaging in such conduct have been beguiled by deceptive men who, "just as one lays traps for wild animals," have forced them to act contrary to their basically chaste natures.

Although the author's tone is serious and her sentence structure often long and convoluted, there is a lightness of style that pervades the work as a result of her attention to interesting details. When speaking of Drypetina, the daughter of Mithridates, Christine mentions the fact that she had an extra row of teeth and then comments, "what a monstrosity!" Many of these aside remarks concern word origins. She explains that the word "Amazons" means "breastless ones," for these warriors cut off their left breasts in order to facilitate the use of their shields. One learns that Queen Artemisia built a spectacular monument to her deceased husband, Mausolus—thus the genesis of the term "mausoleum." Christine enjoys puns and clever phrases, such as her comment on the Lombard women, with the malodorous meat on their breasts: "But this stink made them quite fragrant indeed!"

Throughout the work, Christine demonstrates the broad scope of her erudition. Her literary references include classical Greek and Roman writers, such as Aristotle and Cicero; great vernacular works of Old French literature, such as the Tristan legend and *Le Roman de la rose* (*The Romance of the Rose*); other venerable European writers of the medieval period, such as Dante and Petrarch; and the Bible. She even recommends manuscripts to readers who may wish to know more on a particular subject and frequently documents her sources within the text. As the future author of a manual of instruction for knights, Christine evidences her knowledge of the tactics of war and rivals the great *chansons de gestes* in her vivid and bloody battle descriptions.

Context

Christine de Pizan is a seminal figure in feminist studies. Considered by many to be the earliest professional woman writer, she was also the first to write a book for women about women. In *The Book of the City of Ladies*, she addresses problems which are still of primary concern today: the belittlement of women, defamation of the gender, discrimination, brutality, and rape. In the arguments of Lady Reason, she seeks not only to destroy established misogynist notions but also to allow women to look into Reason's allegorical "mirror" in order to see a true image of themselves—in every way the equal of men.

Until the recent reinterpretation of Christine's works, *The Book of the City of Ladies* was considered a mere translation or, at best, a gloss of Boccaccio. Researchers now see the book as a clever reworking of Boccaccio's own material for the purpose of invalidating the negative concept of women implicit in it, a literary technique that reappears in the seventeenth century with Blaise Pascal's refutation of casuistry in *Provinciales* (1656-1657). For such critics as Earl Jeffrey Richards and Maureen Quilligan, the book indicates Christine's involvement in the Quarrel of the Rose, a debate originating with Jean de Meun's misogynistic remarks in his continuation of Guillaume de Lorris' thirteenth century epic, *The Romance of the Rose*. Critics Eleni Stecopolous and Karl Uitti see the process as "positive mythic restoration."

The works of Christine de Pizan are now part of the standard canon of French literature, women's literature, and women's studies programs. Because *The Book of the City of Ladies* was first published in English, her impact as a feminist has been greatest on the English-speaking world. Although there are detractors who criticize her for advising women to be humble and wives to remain subject to their husbands, her admirers continue to accrue. There is now a Christine de Pizan Society, which regularly publishes a newsletter and boasts an international membership.

Sources for Further Study

Curnow, Maureen Cheney. " 'La Pioche d'Inquisition': Legal-Judicial Content and Style in Christine de Pizan's *Livre de la cité des dames*." In *Reinterpreting Christine de Pizan*, edited by Earl Jeffrey Richards et al. Athens: University of Georgia Press, 1992. Curnow finds much evidence that the author's fourteen-year involvement in legal battles exposed her to a lexicon and style of argument which served her well in *The Book of the City of Ladies*.

Kellogg, Judith L. "*Le Livre de la cité des dames*: Feminist Myth and Community." *Essays in Arts and Sciences* 18 (May, 1989): 1-15. In this essay, which details Christine's reworking of examples borrowed from Boccaccio, *The Book of the City of Ladies* is presented as a feminist revision of the mythographic tradition—the Christian allegorization of history and myth.

Quilligan, Maureen. *The Allegory of Female Authority: Christine de Pizan's "Cité des dames."* Ithaca, N.Y.: Cornell University Press, 1991. Drawing on her extensive research in the field of medieval allegory, Quilligan goes through each part of the book offering an in-depth commentary which often suggests Christine's purpose in choosing certain tales to include in the work, indicates sociopolitical views intimated in the text, and expresses Christine's ideas in terms of modern psychology. The author includes a defense of Christine against present-day detractor Sheila Delany and a discussion of *Le Livre des trois vertus* (1406; *The Book of the Three Virtues*), also known as *The Treasure of the City of Ladies*, Christine's sequel to *The Book of the City of Ladies*.

Willard, Charity Cannon. *Christine de Pizan: Her Life and Works*. New York: Persea Books, 1984. An extensive biography that contains thorough summaries of her works and documents Christine's long and ardent involvement in the Quarrel of the Rose. The chapter entitled "A Feminine Utopia" examines the contents of *The Book of the City of Ladies*, its sources and its relationship to the corpus of Christine's works. Numerous manuscript illuminations are reproduced in black and white.

______________. "The Franco-Italian Professional Writer Christine de Pizan." In *Medieval Women Writers*, edited by Katharina M. Wilson. Athens: University of Georgia Press, 1984. A concise introduction to the life and works of Christine, this essay by one of the leading authorities on Christine de Pizan contains a brief summary and evaluation of the contents of *The Book of the City of Ladies*, twelve pages of abstracts from the 1982 English translation by Earl Jeffrey Richards, elucidating notes, and a substantial bibliography.

Judith L. Barban

THE BRIDE

Author: Bapsi Sidhwa (1938-   )
Type of work: Novel
Type of plot: Domestic realism
Time of plot: 1920-1960
Locale: Pakistan
First published: 1983

Principal characters:

Qasim, a tribal Kohistani from the Himalayan mountains
Zaitoon, his adopted daughter
Nikka, his friend, a businessman and political operative in the newly established country of Pakistan
Carol, an American married to a Pakistani
Sakhi, Zaitoon's tribal husband

Form and Content

A title such as *The Bride* at first might suggest a happy story, but it soon becomes evident that it contains an ironic twist. The novel opens with the wedding of the central character, Qasim, and an account of his and his bride's shared humiliation on their wedding night. He is only ten, and his father has married him to a woman twice his age. The novel records with swift movement his maturation, the developing relationship between husband and wife in spite of their age difference, the deaths of his wife and children, his move from the Himalayan mountains to the Punjabi plains, and his life as a bank guard in that unfamiliar territory. Then what little security Qasim has found during his four years in the Punjab vanishes when independence comes to India and the subcontinent is divided into India and Pakistan. After murdering a man who has humiliated him, Qasim decides to flee India and take his chances in Pakistan; he boards a train loaded with refugees bound for Lahore, one of the major cities given to the newly created nation.

At the border, a group of marauding Sikhs attacks the overcrowded train and murders most of the refugees. Qasim manages to escape, and in the chaos he rescues a young girl whose parents have been slaughtered. With the help of Nikka and Miriam, a couple he meets in a refugee camp, he settles in Lahore and rears the child, whom he has named Zaitoon for his dead daughter. Mothered by Miriam—who has not borne children and thus is something of an outcast—Zaitoon rehearses the role for which she is destined: to become a bride. As well as receiving instruction from Miriam, Zaitoon spends much of her time in various zenannas—women's quarters—where "the benign squalor" draws her, "as it did all its inmates, into the mindless, velvet vortex of the womb." Some zenannas are inhabited by brides who have entered plural marriages. Bound by tradition, all the women acquiesce to their own subjugation, and Zaitoon learns this lesson well.

The scene shifts to another bride, an American woman named Carol who has married a Pakistani man in the United States and then moved home with him. Unaccustomed to the subordinate role of women at all levels of Asian society, Carol rebels against the restrictions, against her husband's jealousy and suspicions, and against the sexual repression that hinders free exchange between men and women. Carol is in turn flattered, fascinated, and revolted by the sexual innuendos constantly directed toward her by Pakistani men.

A meeting between the two unlikely brides, Zaitoon and Carol, occurs when Qasim promises his sixteen-year-old adopted daughter to a tribal man. Father and daughter travel from the bustling city of Lahore to the sparsely populated Himalayas, where the marriage is to take place, and spend a night at the government house that Carol and her husband are visiting. When the two women meet, even with backgrounds so contradictory, they feel a kinship as brides in a land where women are considered chattel no matter what their social status may be.

Once Zaitoon has been married and left by Qasim in the primitive mountain village, the young bride soon realizes the absurdity of her romantic illusions about marriage. Unaccustomed to so harsh a life, Zaitoon rebels, and her husband Sakhi, goaded on by the other men, sets out to tame her. In constant fear of his beatings and his sexual force, she runs away from the village and spends days lost in the mountains as she searches for the government house where she can find refuge. Zaitoon does reach safety after experiencing terrible physical privation and rape. Even though she is rescued, she remains a marked woman who can never return home, for she has failed as "the bride." Moreover, she has been raped and will always bear the stigma of this physical violation.

Thus the simple title of this novel lies heavy with irony. To be "the bride" in a patriarchal society that demeans women translates into bondage—sometimes subtle, other times total.

Analysis

In an interview, Bapsi Sidhwa insisted that she was not writing "overtly feminist literature" in *The Bride*; she went on to explain that she wanted the ideas to be embedded in the novel itself and added that she has little use for "didactic fiction." In this book she succeeds in avoiding didacticism and integrating theme with the essential ingredients of plot, character, and setting. The novel is constructed with admirable economy as it unfolds a complex story, introduces and develops numerous characters, and creates settings both exotic and realistic.

Because Sidhwa was writing in English about a non-Western society, she needed to forge new methods of storytelling. First, the story had to appeal to Asian readers of English familiar with the world she was re-creating. Second, the narrative needed to be clear and meaningful to the English-language reader abroad, who might be altogether unfamiliar with Pakistani history and traditions. She could not appear to be condescending to either group of readers by explaining too much, nor could she withhold details from her international audience. *The Bride*, Sidhwa's first novel but the second to be published, had a good reception in Europe and the United States as well as in Pakistan and India.

Perhaps that acceptance has been attributable in large part to the simplicity of the prose and the force of the action. A prime example of these qualities is the few pages that cover the violence accompanying the partition of India and the subsequent creation of Pakistan. At the outset Sidhwa explains how the partition tragedy came about:

> The earth is not easy to carve up. India required a deft and sensitive surgeon, but the British, steeped in domestic preoccupation, hastily and carelessly butchered it. They were not deliberately mischievous—only cruelly negligent! A million Indians died.

This spare unfolding of events continues throughout in a manner just as vivid as the account of the senseless bloodshed that dominated partition; for example, Zaitoon's struggle in the mountains is told with a similar narrative force.

The settings, whether the crowded streets of Lahore or the grandeur of the Himalayas, spring to life. The colors, the odors, the shapes, the movement are captured in a word or phrase that suggests more than what appears on the page. For example, when Qasim visits the part of Lahore given over to brothels, the prose conjures up a rich, variegated scene: "the narrow lanes streaming with men, and the tall rickety buildings leaning towards each other . . . the heady smell of perfume, the tinkle of payals on dancers' ankles, the chhum-chhum of feminine feet dancing." Equally well realized later in the novel is the stark landscape of the mountains:

> More and more the Indus cast its spell over her. . . . The strangely luminous air burnished her vision: the colours around her deepened and intensified. They became three dimensional. Were she to reach out, she felt she could touch the darkness in the granite, hold the air in her hands and stain her fingers in the jewelled colours of the river.

While *The Bride* has much to say about a patriarchal culture where women have little control over their fates, it does so without forsaking the demands of storytelling. Sidhwa has succeeded in embedding ideas within a novel that is breathtaking in its action, engaging in its characterization, and exotic in its rendering of place.

Context

There is no tradition of women's literature in Pakistan; in fact, the country has no tradition of English-language literature. Sidhwa can only be considered a pioneer in both areas. Whether *The Bride* has had any dramatic impact on the treatment of women in Pakistan remains doubtful, for it is altogether possible that each bride represented in the novel still exists, whether in the zenanna, in the mountains, or in the drawing rooms of wealthy, Westernized Pakistanis. Perhaps, though, a woman—Western or Asian—reading the novel might realize at last that she need not acquiesce, that she need not accept her victimization.

Sidhwa's work was somewhat slow to establish itself internationally. Once *The Bride* has been fully discovered abroad, however, it will certainly find a place in women's literature. In the 1990's, plans by the Ivory-Merchant company to film the novel seemed likely to win for it a wider readership.

Sidhwa based *The Bride* on an actual story she had heard about a Punjabi girl like Zaitoon who had entered into an arranged marriage with a Himalayan tribal man, attempted to escape, and after fourteen days of wandering in the mountains was found by her husband; he cut off her head and threw her body into the river. That Sidhwa allows her heroine to escape is significant. By altering the original story, Sidhwa sends the message to women that they must rebel no matter the consequences. Further, through the voice of the American bride she denies the male excuse expressed by Carol's husband that women "ask for it": "Women the world over, through the ages," Carol thinks with sarcastic disgust, "asked to be murdered, raped, exploited, enslaved, to get importunately impregnated, beaten-up, bullied and disinherited. It was an immutable law of nature."

Sidhwa herself exemplifies the rebellion against this false "immutable law." After a sheltered childhood in a wealthy Pakistani home, she entered an arranged marriage at age nineteen, soon became the mother of three children, and succumbed to the demands of her role as wife of a successful businessman. Like Zaitoon, she escaped, in her case by writing fiction, secretly at first lest she be thought pretentious by her family and friends. After a long struggle to get published and recognized, her work—four novels in all—at last began to gain attention both in Asia and abroad. In 1991, *Cracking India* (1991) won the Liberatur Prize, a German award presented annually to a non-European woman writer. In 1994, she received one of nine Writers' Awards of $105,000 given by the Lila Wallace-Reader's Digest Fund. Sidhwa became an American citizen in 1992.

Certainly Sidhwa's stories, always about women who dare to go beyond the limits set for them, along with her own story, can only raise the awareness of women—and of men as well. Although the men in her novels may often be weak, unreasonable, and cruel, Sidhwa sees them caught in the webs of another so-called immutable law that needs to be reversed. They, too, must rebel against the role in which tradition has placed them. In Sidhwa's view, only when this dual rebellion takes place will the story of "the bride" be a happy one.

Sources for Further Study

Afzal-Khan, Fawzia. "Bapsi Sidhwa." In *International Literature in English*, edited by Robert L. Ross. New York: Garland, 1991. Provides a detailed biography of Sidhwa. Focuses on *The Bride* and *Cracking India* (referred to by its original title, *Ice-Candy-Man*). The writer takes a feminist view and through a detailed discussion of the two novels concludes that they both stress the "anti-victim stance that Sidhwa advocates for women."

Collins, Larry, and Dominique Lapierre. *Freedom at Midnight*. New York: Simon & Schuster, 1975. Presents a clear, readable, and detailed account of the events leading to the 1947 partition of India and its aftermath. Excellent background reading for *The Bride*.

Jussawalla, Feroza, ed. "Bapsi Sidhwa." In *Interviews with Writers of the Post-colonial World*. Jackson: University Press of Mississippi, 1992. In this interview, Sidhwa recalls her life in Pakistan, including her partition experiences during childhood. Discusses the subordinate place of women in Pakistan and the way those conditions influence her fiction, which she does not see as "overtly feminist." Talks about the role a postcolonial novelist plays in the international literary picture.

Ross, Robert L. "Revisiting Partition." *The World & I* 7 (June, 1992): 369-375. Focuses on *Cracking India*, but also looks at Sidhwa's work in general. Provides historical background material on the partition of India; examines the narrative voice of Lenny and the role of Ice-Candy-Man; and discusses the novel's adept use of history.

Robert L. Ross

BROWN GIRL, BROWNSTONES

Author: Paule Marshall (1929-)
Type of work: Novel
Type of plot: *Bildungsroman*
Time of plot: During and shortly after World War II
Locale: Brooklyn, New York
First published: 1959

Principal characters:

Selina Boyce, the daughter of Barbadian immigrants
Silla Boyce, Selina's mother
Deighton Boyce, Selina's father

Form and Content

The first full-length American novel to offer an in-depth treatment of a black girl growing up, *Brown Girl, Brownstones* describes the coming-of-age of Selina Boyce, the daughter of Barbadian immigrants living in Brooklyn, New York. Beginning when she is ten, the novel traces the various influences that affect her development until she reaches college age. As she struggles with warfare between her parents, her sexual awakening, racism, and the development of her own values, Selina's is a painful coming-of-age. Yet she seems strong and resolute at the novel's end.

The novel is divided into four parts. The first, "A Long Day and a Long Night," introduces the various characters as they go about their business in a Brooklyn neighborhood on a single day. The second part, "Pastorale," is a lyrical evocation of two girls' friendship and Selina's despair at the physical prospect of growing up. Part 3, "The War," occurs simultaneously with World War II but centers on the warfare between Selina's parents over Barbadian land willed to Deighton. Silla wants to sell it and "buy house"—a New York brownstone—while Deighton wishes to return to Barbados. The fourth part is entitled "Selina" and treats Selina as a young woman finally come of age, challenging her mother and community, having her first love affair, attending college, and being wounded by racism.

Besides being the first American novel to treat a black girl's coming-of-age, *Brown Girl, Brownstones* is also the first to explore fully a black mother-daughter relationship. Silla and Selina have a relationship deeply complicated by the warfare between the determined Silla and Deighton, Selina's beloved but weak-willed father. Through much of the book, Selina hates her mother, for she ruthlessly cheats Deighton out of his inheritance and then, after he regains it and squanders it, causes him to be deported. Silla also speaks contemptuously of Selina's older friends, Miss Thompson and Suggie Skeete.

Yet even as Selina seems to reject her mother, she begins to act like her. When her older lover Clive, whose weak will and artistic temperament are reminiscent of Selina's father, finds it difficult to detach himself from his mother to attend to Selina's needs, Selina rejects him as decisively as Silla would have. She shows an equal amount of resolve when she rejects the community of materialists in the Barbadian Homeowners Association and when she decides, at the end of the novel, to return to Barbados. Although these latter two actions may represent an effort to follow her father's wishes, her capacity for resolve derives entirely from her mother.

Analysis

Literary critic Barbara Christian argues that a major theme of Paule Marshall's fiction is the black woman's search for wholeness. In *Brown Girl, Brownstones*, Selina tries to integrate a number of confusing and even contradictory elements into her life as she grows into adulthood. She must come to terms with her gender, race, community, and individual relationships. Even the brooding, ghost-haunted brownstones themselves influence her life. In forging her own identity, she tries to reconcile the conflicting viewpoints of her parents and to incorporate elements of the lives of other women of whom her mother disapproves, such as Suggie Skeete and Miss Thompson. She find that each of these persons has experiences that have value.

Christian also calls Marshall a relentless analyst of character. The thoroughness of her analyses makes for well-rounded and memorable characters. For example, the young Selina's salient characteristic is her openness to others' influence. Even after she tries to shut out certain persons, such as her mother and the members of the Homeowners Association, she realizes that she has not done them justice, for she carries their values with her. When she determines to gain vengeance on her mother and the Barbadian community for her father's defeat and death, Selina is displaying both her father's disarming charm and her mother's strength of will.

In Silla and Deighton, Marshall creates fully developed characters whose mixture of flaws and virtues gives them complexity and credibility. Critic Mary Helen Washington calls Silla a pioneer ruthlessly cutting a path in the American wilderness for her children. Concerned with survival, she cannot afford to tolerate her husband's weakness. Deighton, on the other hand, seems bewildered by the new land and does not have the strength of character to make an impression on it.

Marshall derives symbols that characterize this feuding couple from the everyday details of their lives. For example, Silla is pictured making coconut bread in the kitchen, suggesting that she is a provider for her family and maintainer of Bajan customs. Selina also sees her at work among the noisy and dangerous machines in the war factory and notes that the formidable force of her character alone enables her to manage the job. Deighton, on the other hand, is surrounded throughout the novel with inconsequentials: books on accounting that he only half-reads, a trumpet that he only half-practices. In the climactic moment of the third book, when he returns home after having spent all nine hundred dollars from the sale of his land, he unveils a brand-new three-hundred-dollar golden trumpet, which, among the other frivolous gifts he has bought, symbolizes his glittering and inconsequential life. The enraged Silla, who had hoped to put the money into a home of their own, smashes the trumpet on the floor, and its crumpled remains represent Deighton's defeated manhood.

Marshall skillfully weaves these dramas of character into a cultural fabric unique to the community of which she writes. For example, she devotes a chapter to a Bajan wedding in which Deighton is shunned by the community for his improvidence. The Bajans dance with their backs to him. This community pressure helps to defeat him and to lead him into total dependence, symbolized by his eventual conversion to Father Peace's religion. Drawing on an actual historical figure from Harlem, Father Divine, Marshall pictures a religion that offers salvation at the expense of autonomy and independence. Father Peace offers a "heaven" that rewards Deighton's tendency toward weakness by making him totally dependent.

One of the pleasures of this novel is its skilled use of the Bajan dialect and generally brilliant rendering of oral language, particularly in Silla's incisive assessments of other characters. She says of Deighton, "You was always looking for something big and praying hard not to find it." She remarks on her daughter's strong will, "You's too own-way. You's too womanish!" Marshall has said in an interview that, as a girl, she was awed and sometimes frightened by the powerful language of the women who used to come to her mother's kitchen. Clearly this memory informs the chapter in which Silla ominously vows before her female friends to sell Deighton's land so that she can join the rest of the community in purchasing a home of her own: "Be-Jesus-Christ, I gon do that for him then. Even if I got to see my soul fall howling into hell I gon do it."

Context

In a society that paid little attention to the welfare of young women of color, *Brown Girl, Brownstones* provided a much-needed contribution. Like many other works of women's literature, it was not properly appreciated when it was first published, but it has grown in influence and importance as the study of women has developed. Adopted and reissued by the Feminist Press, the novel now must be regarded as one of the masterpieces of coming-of-age literature.

That Paule Marshall had no precedent for such a novel makes her achievement all the more remarkable. She eagerly read Gwendolyn Brooks's *Maud Martha* (1953), which was the first book to describe a black woman's consciousness, but she had no model for a book about a black girl's interior life. Moreover, she could find few literary models of a strong woman character like Silla Boyce. In an interview Marshall attests the importance of creating such characters: "Traditionally in most fiction men are the wheelers and dealers. They are the ones in whom power is invested. I wanted to turn that around. I wanted women to be the centers of power." Thus *Brown Girl, Brownstones* is one of the pioneering works of black women's fiction.

Sources for Further Study

Christian, Barbara. "Paule Marshall." In *African American Writers*, edited by Lea Baechler and A. Walton Litz. New York: Charles Scribner's Sons, 1991. Argues that the novel represents the search for wholeness of a black woman of the diaspora. Analyzes the novel's four sections and the meaning of its title; also identifies Thomas Mann, Joseph Conrad, Ralph Ellison, and James Baldwin as influences.

____________. "Paule Marshall: A Literary Biography." In *Black Feminist Criticism: Perspectives on Black Women Writers*. New York: Pergamon Press, 1985. Contains biographical information, a list of Marshall's publications, a bibliography of secondary sources about her, and a good analysis of *Brown Girl, Brownstones*. The same essay appears in *Dictionary of Literary Biography: Afro-American Fiction Writers After 1955*, edited by Thadious Davis and Trudier Harris (Detroit: Gale Research Press, 1984).

Christol, Helene. "Paule Marshall's Women in *Brown Girl, Brownstones*." In *Women and War: The Changing Status of American Women from the 1930s to the 1950s*, edited by Maria Diedrich and Dorothea Fischer-Hornung. New York: Berg, 1990. Treats Silla and her work in the war factory as representative of an important historical event that permanently changed women's roles in American society.

Deniston, Dorothy. "Paule Marshall." In *American Women Writers*, edited by Lina Mainiero. Vol. 3. New York: Frederick Ungar, 1979-1982. This brief biographical sketch provides a birthdate, listing of marriages, and given name, as well as a bibliography.

Eko, Ebele. "Beyond the Myth of Confrontation: A Comparative Study of African and African-American Female Protagonists." *Ariel: A Review of International English Literature* 17 (October, 1986): 139-152. Compares the treatment of black mother-daughter relationships in Gloria Naylor, Bessie Head, Ama Ata Aidoo, and Marshall's *Brown Girl, Brownstones*.

Evans, Mari, ed. *Black Women Writers (1950-1980): A Critical Evaluation*. Garden City, N.Y.: Anchor Doubleday, 1984. Contains two essays on Marshall's fiction. "The Closing of the Circle: Movement from Division to Wholeness in Paule Marshall's Fiction," by Eugenia Collier, treats several works, including *Brown Girl, Brownstones*, which she describes as dealing with the divided psychology of the oppressed and the necessity of achieving wholeness through identification with one's own community. "And Called Every Generation Blessed: Theme, Setting, and Ritual in the Works of Paule Marshall," by John McCluskey, Jr., argues that the novel is more than a sociological commentary and that its aesthetic beauty should be appreciated.

Kubitschek, Missy Dehn. "Paule Marshall's Women on Quest." *Black American Literature Forum* 21 (Spring/Summer, 1987): 43-60. Analyzing three Marshall books, including *Brown Girl, Brownstones*, the author explores the mythic heroic quest and how women's literature adds to the heroic paradigm the important element of female mentoring.

Marshall, Paule. "Shaping the World of My Art." *New Letters* 40 (Autumn, 1973): 97-112. In this interview, Marshall describes the power of women's words that she heard in her mother's kitchen and her view that they embodied true art, which is inseparable from life.

Willis, Susan. "Describing Arcs of Recovery: Paule Marshall's Relationship to Afro-American Culture." In *Specifying: Black Women Writing the American Experience*. Madison: University of Wisconsin Press, 1987. Analyzing images from the novel, Willis stresses Marshall's talent in showing individuals who articulate the complexities of the community. In Selina's neighborhood, this means the difficulty of being part of two different worlds at once: Barbadian and American.

William L. Howard

CALM DOWN MOTHER

Author: Megan Terry (1932-)
Type of work: Drama
Type of plot: Feminist
Time of plot: The 1960's
Locale: Various settings, such as a delicatessen, a nursing home, and an apartment
First produced: March, 1965, at the Sheridan Square Playhouse, New York
First published: 1966

Principal characters:

Woman One, Margaret Fuller, a delicatessen clerk, a New York career woman, a nursing-home resident, a call girl, and a member of a mother-daughter trio
Woman Two, a nineteen-year-old girl, a New York career woman, an elderly woman in a nursing home, a call girl, and a member of a mother-daughter trio
Woman Three, a delicatessen clerk, a call girl, and a member of a mother-daughter trio

Form and Content

Calm Down Mother is a one-act transformational play that dramatizes the limitations imposed on women both by society and by other women, as well as women's dawning recognition of the root causes of those limitations. Organized loosely in scenes that transform—at times abruptly, sometimes with the help of bridging commentary or ritual chant—into other scenes in other locales, the play depicts vignettes of women's daily lives and shows how interactions between women are structured by their familial or societal relationships, economic status, ages, professions or occupations, and above all, gender. Megan Terry has said that she wrote the play because at the time of its creation she could find no good roles for women in current stage offerings.

Structured into eight scenes, the play has only one set, described in the stage directions as "An open stage. Four chairs are in View." This minimal staging, a characteristic of much of Terry's work, allows the actors to create various social and cultural milieus through their use of movement, posture, and voice and through their ability to transform themselves from identity to identity. The nearly bare stage also forces the audience to participate actively in the creation of the illusion onstage.

The play opens as the lights come up slowly during the taped recitation of a brief speech about the prehistorical evolution of one-celled creatures into the first plant, and the further splitting of that plant into two parts, one of which "stretches toward the sun." Three women, clustered together to resemble a plant, are revealed on stage. As the speech ends, Woman One comes forward to introduce herself as Margaret Fuller, a woman who knows that she is strong because "my father addressed me not as a plaything, but as a living mind." She announces her acceptance of the universe as her home, and Woman Two and Woman Three chant their concurrence with her decision. The scenes that follow outline the boundaries—boundaries of age, class, race, mortality, sexuality, and gender stereotyping—that define a woman's universe.

A scene in a delicatessen dramatizes a woman's grief over her diminished attractiveness as a result of hair loss after surgery. The women's loud lamentation at the end of the scene metamorphoses into rage that drives Woman One to scream "I want to hit!" as she drives her fist into the palm of her other hand. Woman Three's brief monologue about the "pitiful few facts" of a woman's life leads to a scene in a New York flat where two young women's pleasure in the new apartment is destroyed when one of the women gives in to hysteria under the burden of having, yet again, to be the "old bulwark of the family" when trouble strikes. A brief interlude about girlhood as "a green time" introduces Woman One and Woman Two as two elderly women in a nursing home. As the women talk about how "the days go by and the days go by and the days go by," they are rudely interrupted by a nurse who—treating them like children—insists that they eat their cereal. Abruptly, the old women become a subway door that opens and closes repeatedly as they chant, until finally Woman Three breaks through the "doors" to reveal a completely different world.

The new scene situates the three women, transformed now into call girls, in an apartment that they share uneasily. They are connected only by their profession and by their thrall to a pimp named Ricky, to whom they owe rent, the cost of police bribes, and a hefty proportion of their earnings. The women argue, taking turns siding with each other against the third. A brief connecting chant changes the scene into a tenement kitchen in which a mother and her two daughters discuss menstruation, pregnancy, and contraception until the mother suddenly becomes aware that one daughter is sexually active although unmarried—at which point the mother orders her daughter out of the house. The play ends as the three actresses, now simply unnamed women, enact a ritual that questions whether a woman should be content with an identity solely as childbearer, proud of her unique and gender-specific reproductive capability.

Analysis

As she does in so much of her work, in *Calm Down Mother* Megan Terry examines women's roles both within and without the family structure, depicting the tensions as well as the bonds that exist between women in various situations. The play is set in the present, in the immediacy of women's lives, in the day-to-day tasks and experiences that circumscribe a woman's universe.

The play's key scenes develop out of one another, drifting from one to the next in a movement that grows out of the opening scene in which the three characters are bonded together in a human representation of primitive plant life at the bottom of some primordial swamp. From the initial portrayal of woman at the moment of creation with all the universe before her, the action moves through successive scenes, dramatizing the societal expectations that continue subtly to oppress women: the cultural insistence on beauty as the most desirable female trait; the taboo on visible female anger; the valorization of a woman who, at the expense of her own happiness, puts everyone else's needs first; the expectation that women should grow old quietly; the prevalent image of woman as plaything; and the universal view of woman as reproductive machine. The last scene suggests that from the cultural point of view, women cannot seize the universe because their role is passive and maternal rather than active and societal.

At the heart of the play is Terry's feminism of inclusion. Her three characters portray the rich variety of American women: senior citizens and teenagers, career women and prostitutes, mothers and daughters, friends and colleagues, allies and competitors. These women experience the range of emotions from elation to anger, apathy to celebration, envy to love. Terry's women are acquiescent, defiant, self-righteous, forgiving, practical, romantic, and above all, human. They are all Everywoman. Not one is "a furry animal plaything"; each one wants, in her own way, to be accepted as "a living loving blinding mind."

The one-act play is an unforgiving dramatic genre for the less-than-gifted playwright, but in Terry's skillful hands, the form becomes both entertainment and forum. Deftly and with considerable humor, she appropriates the techniques of both film and theater in the service of transformational drama. Transitions between scenes are reminiscent of fades, dissolves, and jump cuts on the motion-picture screen. Even the voiceover with which the play opens is reminiscent of a cinematic device often employed to provide historical or background information. Terry also plays on the audience's peculiar relationship with a theatrical production—the fact that audiences are aware of the dual identities of the actors who are, simultaneously, performers and dramatic characters. Thus she forces the audience to participate imaginatively in the transformations on stage, in the performers' frequent transitions from one role to another, in the creating and undermining of stereotypes and prescribed roles.

Context

Well received by critics when the Open Theatre premiered it in 1965 at the Sheridan Square Playhouse on a double bill with *Keep Tightly Closed in a Cool Dry Place*, *Calm Down Mother* has become one of Terry's most popular and most frequently anthologized plays. Like her other transformational plays, including *Comings and Goings* (1966) and *Viet Rock* (1966), it constructs a constantly changing series of stage realities, challenging both performers and audience to rethink cultural assumptions about gendered behaviors.

Leading drama scholar Helene Keyssar has referred to Megan Terry as the mother of American feminist theater, an identification whose truth is demonstrably evident in the body of dramatic work that she produced from the 1960's to the 1990's. Repeatedly, she has dramatized women's issues: gender stereotyping, reproduction, patriarchal language, woman as victim, woman as hero, competition and sisterhood, the bonds and separations between mothers and daughters, and the perils of male-female relationships. Her treatment of these themes is part of her continuing focus on the societal forces that define women, the cultural icons that provide women with negative self-images, and the political barriers that prevent someone from discovering who they are and what they can be.

More important to the development of feminist drama, however, is Terry's considerable contribution (widely acknowledged by theater historians) to the creation of transformation drama. It is this genre—a product both of the theatrical ferment of the 1960's and of Terry's own creative experimentation—that has done the most toward breaking down the gender stereotyping so prevalent on the American stage until the middle of the twentieth century. Transformational drama frees performers from the baggage of acceptable images and cultural models, allowing them to explore different characters, different theatrical styles, and new forms of interaction—all within the same play. The implications of such freedom have proved significant for women writers who struggled for a time to create a form of theater that would lend itself to the portrayal of women whose very lives were a multiplicity of roles, a panoply of selves. With transformational drama, women playwrights can simultaneously dramatize women's split identities and suggest new and integrated ways of living female.

Calm Down Mother displays many of the characteristics that would later become commonplace in feminist drama. The play explores and dramatizes women's internal states of being, showing women to themselves by valuing women's experience through its depiction of commonplace activities and images—furnishing an apartment, washing dishes, applying makeup. Terry uses negative images in positive ways, creating accurate characterizations to shatter female stereotypes and dismantle female myths. Seemingly meek elderly ladies harbor regret for the end of their fertility; one of the call girls defiantly conceals some of the tips from her pimp because she dares to dream about taking a vacation out of New Jersey. These personal rebellions are minor, but they signal the strength of inner identities all but obliterated by culturally constructed images. When feminist theaters flowered in the late 1960's and early 1970's, many of the plays that they produced were (like *Calm Down Mother* and Terry's other transformational dramas) collagelike, multilayered constructions that used poetry, ritual, and lyrical language to portray the reality of women's lives.

Terry, meanwhile, although not abandoning the early forms of transformational drama, has forged ahead to create two other distinct bodies of work: role-model plays, which showcase admirable women such as Simone Weil and Mother Jones as appropriate strong female icons; and political and public service drama, focusing on such issues as teenage alcoholism, dysfunctional families, and domestic violence. These new issues can still be identified as women's concerns, but where Terry's earlier work focused on the personal, her later work addresses public and community affairs from the woman's point of view.

Sources for Further Study

Betsko, Kathleen, and Rachel Koenig, eds. *Interviews with Contemporary Women Playwrights*. New York: Beech Tree Books, 1987. This valuable book includes an interview in which Megan Terry comments on the influences on her work, the sources of her themes and ideas, and her working habits. She also discusses her work in the context of the development of American theater since the 1960's, focusing on her association with the Open Theatre and later the Omaha Magic Theatre.

Chinoy, Helen Krich, and Linda Walsh Jenkins. *Women in American Theatre*. New York: Crown, 1981. A collection of essays, interviews, reflections, and reminiscences about and by notable American dramatists, actresses, directors, and other theater professionals. Of special interest is Dinah Leavitt's interview with Megan Terry—an interview in which Terry speaks of her desire to explore in her work what it means to be a woman in American society.

Hart, Lynda, ed. *Making a Spectacle: Feminist Essays on Contemporary Women's Theatre*. Ann Arbor: University of Michigan Press, 1989. Included in this collection of essays is Jan Breslauer and Helene Keyssar's "Making Magic Public: Megan Terry's Traveling Family Circus." Although the essay does not focus specifically on *Calm Down Mother*, it is valuable reading for its discussion of Terry's work as feminist drama. The rest of the collection is significant because it provides a theatrical context for Terry's work and for her contribution to American drama.

Keyssar, Helene. *Feminist Theatre*. New York: Grove Press, 1985. An extremely important study of the beginnings and development of feminist theater. Especially significant to the student of Megan Terry's plays is Keyssar's description of Terry as the mother of American feminist theater, and the subsequent discussion of Terry's contributions to the dramatization of women's issues and concerns on the American stage.

Savran, David, ed. *In Their Own Words: Contemporary American Playwrights*. New York: Theatre Communications Group, 1988. Savran's collection of interviews includes a conversation with Megan Terry in which the playwright names the plays and playwrights that have influenced her style and describes the emotions in which she finds ideas for her work. She discusses her own plays and her work with the Omaha Magic Theatre, and she speculates about the future of American drama.

Schlueter, June. "Megan Terry's Transformational Drama: *Keep Tightly Closed in a Cool Dry Place* and the Possibilities of Self." In *Modern American Drama: The Female Canon*. Rutherford, N.J.: Fairleigh Dickinson University Press, 1990. Although this essay focuses on a play other than *Calm Down Mother*, Schlueter's discussion of transformational drama as a genre is important for its illumination of Terry's technique in *Calm Down Mother*.

E. D. Huntley

CASSANDRA: A Novel and Four Essays

Author: Christa Wolf (1929-)
Type of work: Novel and essays
Type of plot: Social criticism
Time of plot: The Trojan War (around 1200 B.C.)
Locale: Troy, ancient Mycenae, East Germany, and modern Greece
First published: *Kassandra* and *Voraussetzungen einer Erzählung: "Kassandra,"* 1983 (English translation, 1984)

Principal characters:

Cassandra, the princess of Troy, whose prophetic visions come not from the gods but from astutely observing her society

Aeneas, the son of Anchises, who opposes the insanity of the war

Anchises, the wise old man of Troy

Priam and **Hecuba,** the king and queen of Troy

Arisbe, Troy's wise old woman, who introduces Cassandra to a society of women who worship the goddess Cybele rather than the male gods

Achilles, instead of the hero of classical tradition, a cowardly, sadistic beast who derives sexual pleasure from murder and desecration

Agamemnon, the victorious commander of the invading Greek fleet

Christa Wolf, the author, who enters the novel in its first and last paragraph

Form and Content

In 1982, East German author Christa Wolf agreed to deliver a series of lectures on poetics at Frankfurt University. She surprised her audience by presenting not the expected scholarly analysis of poetics, but rather a series of four talks including two "Travel Reports," "A Work Diary," and a "Letter," which explain how she became interested in the figure of Cassandra. Her fifth "lecture" was the narrative *Cassandra* itself. This refusal to play by the expected academic rules shows Wolf's attempt to break the boundaries of literary genres and to incorporate more intimate and personal, first-person literary forms into the canon of high literature.

The first four lectures, entitled *Voraussetzungen einer Erzählung: "Kassandra"* (conditions of a narrative), and the novel *Cassandra* were published as a single volume in East Germany. In West Germany, the narrative and essays were sold separately. Jan van Heurck's 1984 English version rejoins them under the title *Cassandra: A Novel and Four Essays* but ironically places the "Voraussetzungen" (conditions or "presuppositions") after the narrative.

Wolf's novel revises the story of Troy as told from the point of view of the ignored seer, Cassandra. Like Euripides in his play *The Trojan Women* (415 B.C.), Wolf narrates from the perspective of the vanquished survivors of war. The novel begins with Cassandra in Mycenae at the gates of Agamemnon's fortress. Cassandra's interior monologue as she awaits her death takes her back in memory to Troy.

Cassandra remembers peaceful scenes of the pregnant Queen Hecuba discussing Troy's administration with her attentive husband, King Priam. These scenes give Cassandra a glimpse of society at a moment of balance between matriarchy and patriarchy. In the early days of Troy, there is no conflict between politics and family, no social wall between men and women. This fleeting moment of political and gender balance attracts Wolf. She is looking not for a moment of nostalgia but for a model of a different kind of social arrangement.

Cassandra recalls the destruction of that delicate balance. Hecuba's close ties to Priam and to political power disintegrate during the war, and she is finally barred from the political conference chamber. Matriarchal vision and patriarchal political power are pitted against each other—and patriarchy eventually wins.

The war also perverts the Trojans in other ways. An effective propaganda machine (familiar to twentieth century readers) changes attitudes, moralities, and even vocabulary in order to fuel the war. Wolf's antiwar message is evident in her portrayal of the real reasons for war. Rejecting the Trojan War as a battle over the beauty of Helen of Troy, Wolf depicts the war's economic underpinnings. She also lays bare the lies that use women such as Helen as scapegoats. Cassandra learns that Helen is not in Troy; Cassandra's brother Paris lost Helen to the king of Egypt when returning home. Paralleling Stesichorus' alternative tradition of Helen being in Egypt rather than in Troy, Wolf implies that the war is fought for a phantom Helen. She goes one step further, however, than the ancient tradition. Wolf's ruling family knows that neither Helen nor her phantom is in Troy. They fight for a bald-faced lie that they themselves sustain. Clearly, male egotism, and not female beauty, breeds the conflict.

The "heroic tradition" rapidly degenerates into bestial cruelty as Wolf indicts the major heroes of the Trojan War. She reduces the archetypal military hero, Achilles, to a sadistic coward who must literally be dragged into the war by the scruff of his neck. The most disgusting of his breed, Achilles becomes in Wolf's text the sexually obsessed brute whose first "heroic" action is the perverse slaughter of Cassandra's defenseless brother Troilus in a temple. Surrounded by the threat of total destruction and war in her own life, Wolf uses these earlier warriors and war images to warn her contemporaries.

The remainder of Cassandra's reminiscences trace the degeneration of the government and people of Troy. The narrative ends as Cassandra recalls her rejections of Aeneas' offer of salvation and a new life. She knows that Aeneas will be swept into a new heroic tradition. The reader is aware that the history of Rome bears out her fears. Cassandra goes to her death partly as a refusal to participate any longer in such a degraded "heroic" world.

Cassandra also recollects, however, a moment of hope for peace and community during the war. An alternative society of outcasts forms around the benevolent figures of Aeneas' father, Anchises, and the wise woman Arisbe. This society, composed largely of women, cuts across class and national boundaries. Its members offer one another the human nurturing missing from Troy. Aeneas takes this society with him when he flees. A brief utopian moment in the text, this little band will nevertheless be entrapped in the bellicose currents of history once they found the new community that will become the Roman Empire.

Wolf's novel makes both psychological and political use of earlier epics and dramas, which she weaves into a modern novel of impressive force and subtlety. By giving Cassandra a voice that can finally be heard in the twentieth century, Wolf resituates women as subjects in a history and community in which they were too often objects.

Analysis

In the first four of her Frankfurt Lectures on Poetics, which make up the essays of the volume, Wolf places herself as the central subject. In the essays, Wolf reflects on her 1980 trip to Greece during which she explored materials for *Cassandra*, as well as on contemporary events such as the attempt on U.S. president Ronald Reagan's life. She examines the historical Cassandra and conditions for the woman writer (or speaker) of the past and present. Wolf recounts simultaneously visiting Greece and reading Aeschylus' trilogy *Oresteia* (458 B.C.), which helped trigger her writing of *Cassandra*. Wolf adds her own experiences to those of the Greeks, Americans, and Germans whom she meets in her travels to form a body of communal memories that make up the text as a whole. Wolf refuses to be bound by any genre definition, which contributes to her revision of the tradition.

Part of Wolf's reconsideration of literary tradition focuses on the position of women. She asks, "To what extent is there really such a thing as 'women's writing'?" Wolf's four essays and her narrative help to answer this question. She provides an explicit response in her third essay, in which she suggests that there is "women's writing"

> to the extent that women, for historical and biological reasons, experience a different reality than men and express it. To the extent that women belong not to the rulers but to the ruled, and have done so for centuries. . . . To the extent that they stop wearing themselves out trying to integrate themselves into the prevailing delusional system. To the extent that, writing and living, they aim at autonomy.

Although Wolf investigates the dehumanization of modern and classical humanity in toto, she also focuses on those subjects who have been most excluded from history and buried in art objects—women. In addition to the general alienation of modern culture, women experience a secondary alienation within the culture. They find themselves silenced or missing from the historical record. This deletion necessitates a female revision of literary history and of the figure of Cassandra. Cassandra is mentioned only twice in Homer's *Iliad* (sixth century B.C.); she gains a literary voice in Aeschylus' *Oresteia* and Euripides' *The Trojan Women* only after the war ends. The bulk of Wolf's text focuses on Cassandra's actions during those war years. Wolf restores Cassandra as a speaking—and protesting—subject where she is often only an object.

A strongly antiwar text, Wolf's novel and essays investigate the roots of the military tradition in Western culture by taking a new look at "heroes" such as Achilles from the point of view of a woman on the losing side rather than of a man on the winning side. Her essays discuss modern wars in Vietnam and Latin America, as well as the threat of nuclear annihilation in Europe in the early 1980's, while her novel investigates the obliteration of the people and culture of Troy in 1200 B.C. The parallels between these two historical periods reinforce her antiwar message.

Wolf is intent on giving voice to the different reality experienced by women, in seeing the world anew through a woman's eyes. The figure of Cassandra, the prophetess whom no one believes, parallels the position of many women writers in Wolf's own time. Her novel attempts to create a second narrative tradition that runs parallel and in opposition to the "heroic" narrative tradition of the epic. Wolf undercuts the roots of the Western heroic tradition by depicting it as a sham created by propaganda to save the "honor" of those involved. She opposes to it a glimpse of a different society dedicated to life rather than to killing. Wolf is too much a realist to imply that this utopian society will be easily achieved—or even that it is recorded anywhere in the historical record. Such a society can, however, be envisioned by a woman writer (or narrator) who is willing to question the very premises underlying the patriarchal tradition.

Context

Christa Wolf seeks to remake thousands of years of literary tradition, to displace the hero from its center and to make a place for women in it. She clearly attempts to return women to the position of subjects rather than objects, to make them tellers, singers, and seers again rather than characters in a male plot. She is faced, however, with the problem that people do not live in a world that is whole and balanced between men and women; patriarchy has dominated for thousands of years and defined narrative in its wake. If Wolf is to narrate at all, she must do so within a tradition determined by patriarchy. She cannot rewrite the patriarchal myths without invoking and inscribing them anew in Western culture. This painful irony is the recurrent and unavoidable problem of all women "re-visionists." Wolf counters, however, by demystifying myth, laying bare its rationalizing pragmatism. She does not want simply to inscribe new female myths; she wants reasonableness to replace the need for myth entirely. Ironically, Cassandra's "madness" is the constant insistence on truth and reason.

Writing in the former German Democratic Republic (East Germany), where 90 percent of the female population was in the workforce, Wolf displays a wider range of active female roles than patriarchy has traditionally suggested. Her women participate in political and religious power, as well as fulfilling the more traditional role assignments of mothers or exploited sex objects. Wolf, in espousing the need for "women's writing" and criticizing the male literary tradition, also questions both East Germany's claim of sexual equality and the whole Western literary establishment. Her writing is thus subversive in both commmunist and capitalist contexts.

Wolf suggests within her text an alternative social possibility in the community of women devoted to the mother goddess Cybele. Wolf is careful, however, not to provide an easy Utopia. While her alternative society is attractive, history tells that it will eventually be swallowed up in the next major military patriarchy—Rome. Relentlessly honest, Wolf does not give her characters all the necessary knowledge or answers. Questions of future solutions and lasting alternatives to the unacceptable social and political structures depicted in the text are reserved for the reader's reflection.

Wolf's Cassandra stands out as a woman who is not only able but also willing to see political realities and to voice her knowledge. This voice carries to the listener/reader the problems of political and sexual power, as well as women's place in the patriarchal tradition. Yet Wolf does not simply repeat the tradition; she challenges its rules and underpinnings. She reasserts the female and the undifferentiated male/female whole that has been suppressed. Wolf and her Cassandra provide the type of re-vision of history that Adrienne Rich and many contemporary feminist theorists suggest.

Sources for Further Study

Fries, Marilyn Sibley, ed. *Responses to Christa Wolf: Critical Essays*. Detroit: Wayne State University Press, 1989. A collection of essays by twenty-one critics covering many of Wolf's texts from a variety of critical perspectives. Not only includes essays from a feminist perspective but also gives some idea of the varieties of literary methodologies applied to Wolf's work. Contains an index and an extensive bibliography.

Herrmann, Anne. *The Dialogic and Difference: An/Other Woman in Virginia Woolf and Christa Wolf.* New York: Columbia University Press, 1989. Insightful feminist analysis of the construction of the female subject in the works of Virginia Woolf and Christa Wolf. An index and a bibliography including many references to feminist theory are provided.

Kuhn, Anna K. *Christa Wolf's Utopian Vision: From Marxism to Feminism.* New York: Cambridge University Press, 1988. An insightful analysis of Wolf's development from her early works to *Storfall* (1987; *Accident*, 1989). Kuhn traces Wolf's movement from a reliance on Marxism as an ideology to a later development of a more feminist position. Includes an index and an extensive bibliography of primary and secondary works.

Wolf, Christa. *The Author's Dimension: Selected Essays*. Edited by Alexander Stephan. Translated by Jan van Heurck. New York: Farrar, Straus and Giroux, 1993. A collection of essays by Wolf on a wide variety of political and literary topics. Provides useful insights into the author and her attitudes toward literature and politics. Includes an introduction by Grace Paley.

__________. *The Fourth Dimension: Interviews with Christa Wolf.* Translated by Hilary Pilkington. New York: Verso, 1988. A collection of interviews with Wolf. Very useful for understanding Wolf's process of composition, as well as her political concerns. A short bibliography of primary works is included. Contains an introduction by Karin McPherson.

Kathleen L. Komar

CECILIA: Or, Memoirs of an Heiress

Author: Fanny Burney (1752-1840)
Type of work: Novel
Type of plot: Satire
Time of plot: Christmas, 1778, to May, 1780
Locale: London
First published: 1782

Principal characters:

Miss Cecilia Beverley, the sole heir to her family fortune if she retains her surname when she marries

Mortimer Delvile, the young man whom Cecilia eventually marries

Mr. Harrel, one of Cecilia's guardians and her indulgent host in London

Mr. Briggs, one of Cecilia's guardians, who, despite his wealth, lives a miserly existence

Mr. Compton Delvile, one of Cecilia's guardians and the father of Mortimer

Mrs. Augusta Delvile, the wife of Mr. Delvile and the mother of Mortimer

Mr. Monckton, a young married man from Suffolk, who has designs to marry Cecilia when his wife dies

Form and Content

Fanny Burney is one of the few women novelists whose reputation as an important figure in the development of the novel has been traditionally acknowledged. Writing in formats developed by dominant novelists Samuel Richardson and Henry Fielding, Burney is also often singled out as a major influence on Jane Austen, whose classic work *Pride and Prejudice* (1813) borrows many elements, including the title itself, from *Cecilia: Or, Memoirs of an Heiress*, Burney's second novel.

Focusing on the issues of romantic love and the use and abuse of money, Burney's narrative moves chronologically through a seventeen-month period surrounding Cecilia's inheritance of a family fortune, provided she abides by the restriction that she not surrender her surname if she marries. This stipulation, which is first mentioned casually, will turn out to be the pivotal issue of Cecilia's future happiness. The novel opens with Cecilia's farewells to her friends in her quiet, rural hometown of Bury in Suffolk before she moves to London, where she will reside with one of her three guardians, Mr. Harrel, until she reaches the age of twenty-one. Although she is clearly out of place in London society, Cecilia is levelheaded, gracious, and confident, and she astutely discerns that her enthusiastic reception has more to do with her inheritance than any genuine fondness for her personally. She is at first amused by the egocentric, frivolous, shallow manner of the people she meets. When the flighty Miss Larolles intently recalls the fortunate circumstance of obtaining a last-minute invitation to a party only when a friend became ill and was unable to attend, Cecilia laughs at the irony. Later, however, Cecilia learns that such insensitivity has its serious side and potentially tragic consequences, as in the case of the Hill family, ill and starving because Mr. Harrel refuses to pay Mr. Hill for work done months ago. Cecilia's attempt to persuade Mr. Harrel to pay his workers are the first of many frustrations in dealing with the callous, cruel insensitivity of many members of the privileged classes. Her generosity in helping this family and others, which ironically contributes to the depletion of her fortune and to her own destitution, gives her a sense of purpose in life.

The superficial, vain judgments of people in regard to status become painfully and more personally evident to Cecilia when she falls in love with young Mortimer Delvile, whose family coldly rejects her as an appropriate bride because of her inferior social standing and because they are not willing for Mortimer to give up their family surname. After many tragedies and much suffering, including a period in which Cecilia is first penniless and then driven temporarily insane, the marriage is sanctioned and the family united. Although the costs have been exceedingly high, Cecilia observes and accepts the reality that life will always be imperfect, that good people can have serious flaws, and that love has its qualifications.

Analysis

After the stunning success of her first novel, *Evelina: Or, The History of a Young Lady's Entrance into the World* (1778), which she wrote in secret, Fanny Burney was in the unfamiliar position of being commissioned to write a novel. Many critics and historians have speculated that the strong influence of two men—Burney's father, Dr. Charles Burney, and her mentor, Samuel "Daddy" Crisp—in addition to these circumstances, accounts for the more self-conscious, less spontaneous, and darker view that is characteristic of this and later works. In *Cecilia*, which shares certain elements of plot and themes with its predecessor, Burney's objective is to expose the hypocrisy and materialism of upper-class London society. Abandoning the epistolary form used in that first novel that was so popular in the eighteenth century, Burney presents a third-person, omniscient narrative which covers diverse personal viewpoints and various social boundaries.

Originally published in five volumes, *Cecilia* is considerably longer than *Evelina*, permitting Burney to introduce a greater abundance—some consider it an excess—of diverse, eccentric characters, who are intricately woven into various related subplots. Although there is considerable disagreement in the assessment of *Cecilia*, most agree that the second novel is weaker, more loosely constructed, more contrived, and less natural than *Evelina*. Although *Cecilia*'s basic plot and primary theme are similar, the second novel clearly presents a darker view of life, with the expected happy ending somewhat tempered by the preceding events. Burney herself responded to this objection from some of her closest friends, insisting that *Cecilia* presents a more realistic view of life's compromises.

The omniscient point of view, though it offers Burney considerable flexibility, seems inconsistently applied, withholding information and not allowing the reader to draw inferences on the basis of the action and dialogue. A common complaint about *Cecilia* is the highly artificial, melodramatic dialogue between major characters in some of the novel's most crucial scenes. The language, even in highly emotional passages, is often stilted, overly formal, and distracting.

Ironically, it is also the language of some of Burney's characters, most notably Mr. Briggs, that has inspired some praise of Burney for her innovative attempt to distinguish between characters' speech patterns as they reflect personalities.

Another troublesome aspect of *Cecilia* is its heavy reliance on coincidence to generate plot. Mortimer and Cecilia seem almost fated to encounter each other at times and places that seem to confirm damaging misconceptions. The main story depends on these mistakes about character and presumptions about alliances in order to support its theme of pride and prejudice. Although coincidence is a characteristic plot device of eighteenth century novels, some readers find that *Cecilia* contains a superfluous number of incidents which lack credibility.

The two major themes of the novel revolve around the love story between Cecilia and Mortimer and the issue of her money. The various subplots also employ these two themes, love and money, by complex and sometimes coincidental parallels in the lives of some of the minor characters who come into Cecilia's life. The novel is laden with irony, and the greatest irony and source of conflict is that Cecilia must give up one to have the other, that she is forced to choose between her love for Mortimer and her desire to gain her inheritance. The destructive potential of money is demonstrated at its worst in the story of Mr. and Mrs. Harrel, who continue to spend lavishly without having the funds to support their lifestyle. Even when the creditors come to take possession of the house, the couple insist on going out for the evening to squelch rumors of their bankruptcy. Ultimately, this recklessness leads to Mr. Harrel's suicide, but the couple's financial irresponsibility has also ruined a number of other lives, including Cecilia's, in the process.

The superficial value placed on wealth and status is reflected in the story of the Belfields, a working-class family with aspirations. Mrs. Belfield has showered all of her attention on her son, seeing that he is educated and encouraged to seek the company of the wealthy. She not only neglects her other children but also convinces them that they are socially inferior. Her daughter, Henrietta, probably the most noble character in the entire novel, never questions her supposed inadequacy. The striking difference between the devoted Henrietta and the insensitive Mr. Delvile best demonstrate to Cecilia that power and wealth have little, if anything, to do with character.

Context

Fanny Burney has long been acknowledged as an important literary figure in the history and development of the English novel, although only in the last half of the twentieth century have critics begun to subject her work to intense and in-depth analysis. Both *Evelina* and *Cecilia* were enormously popular, as were her later works, and Burney was one of the first women to make a living as a writer. Yet, as a woman in the eighteenth century, Burney felt compelled to conceal her writing until after the success of *Evelina*.

Cecilia presents an atypical eighteenth century heroine who is intelligent, who cherishes independence, and who is emotionally stronger than her mate. The novel offers a rare, perhaps visionary insight into the psychology of women, as it examines the tension between women's dual desires for love and an independent sense of purpose in life. The critical evaluation that Burney's novels decline after *Evelina* is often based in large part on the detection of an increasingly dark view in subsequent works. Others argue that this changing perspective reflects an increasingly mature vision of the world. As satire, *Cecilia* demonstrates that even when a woman has the desire, the capability, and the financial resources to be independent, society tends to disallow such freedom.

Feminist critics have proposed that Cecilia's episode of madness might ironically be a sign of her rationality, as it is the only reasonable response to her frustration and powerlessness in the society that Burney satirizes. The violence that is an ever-present factor in *Cecilia* further suggests that rather than looking back to discover Burney's literary debts to established, male novelists such as Fielding and Richardson, scholars should look ahead to trace Burney's contributions to the gothic emphasis in late eighteenth century fiction, a genre dominated by women.

Sources for Further Study

Adelstein, Michael. *Fanny Burney*. New York: Twayne, 1968. This study incorporates biographical and historical elements with a sound, comprehensive analysis of Burney's works. In his examination of *Cecilia*, Adelstein focuses on the theme of prudence in regard to money. A selected bibliography and an index are included.

Cutting-Gray, Joanne. *Woman as "Nobody" and the Novels of Fanny Burney*. Gainesville: University Press of Florida, 1992. Cutting-Gray detects significance in Burney's writing to "Nobody" in her diary and argues that the recurring theme of namelessness in Burney's work reflects the identity problems of eighteenth century women. Contains informative notes, a bibliography, and an index.

Daugherty, Tracy Edgar. *Narrative Techniques in the Novels of Fanny Burney*. New York: Peter Lang, 1989. A reexamination of the technical aspects of Burney's novels in the light of modern narrative theory. Daugherty considers point of view, plot, tempo, and characterization. He also evaluates Burney's novels within a broad context and objectively outlines the weaknesses as well as the strengths of *Cecilia*. A bibliography and an index are provided.

Devlin, David Douglas. *The Novels and Journals of Fanny Burney*. London: Macmillan, 1987. Devlin attributes the influence of the French Revolution to the darker view evident in Burney's later works and rejects the critical consensus that the quality of her work declined after the first two novels.

Doody, Margaret Anne. *Frances Burney: The Life in the Works*. New Brunswick, N.J.: Rutgers University Press, 1988. Biographies of Burney abound, but this recent volume acknowledges studies of Burney which shed new light on her writing, producing a more accurate and a less sentimental critical biography. Includes extensive notes useful for bibliographic information, as well as a family tree of the Burney family.

Epstein, Julia. *The Iron Pen: Frances Burney and the Politics of Women's Writing*. Madison: University of Wisconsin Press, 1989. Epstein's objective is to point out an overlooked theme in Burney's writing: the tension between the public, proper lady and the private, angry writer. The prominence of violence in the novels prefigures the direction of the novel toward the gothic, a genre dominated by women. Extensive notes and a selected but lengthy bibliography are included.

Rogers, Katharine M. *Frances Burney: The World of "Female Difficulties."* New York: Harvester Wheatsheaf, 1990. Tracing the increasing political emphasis in Burney's novels, Rogers argues that Burney's greatest contribution to the development of the novel is her insightful rendering of the psychological problems of women.

Straub, Kristina. *Divided Fictions: Fanny Burney and Feminine Strategy*. Lexington: University Press of Kentucky, 1987. Straub studies the tension of women's issues in Burney's time, arguing that what have previously been viewed as flaws in Burney's fiction expose criteria that may not be appropriate for women writers; indeed, these very elements might provide even greater insights. Contains notes and an index.

White, Eugene. *Fanny Burney, Novelist: A Study in Technique: "Evelina," "Cecilia," "Camilla," "The Wanderer."* Hamden, Conn.: Shoe String Press, 1960. Studying the technical aspects of plot, characterization, manner of presentation, and style, White demonstrates how Burney made use of contemporary techniques and also made contributions that shaped the direction of the novel. Suggests that Burney is a more sophisticated craftsperson than has been acknowledged.

Lou Thompson

CENTURY OF STRUGGLE: The Woman's Rights Movement in the United States

Author: Eleanor Flexner (1908-)
Type of work: History
Time of work: The early nineteenth century to 1920
Locale: The United States
First published: 1959

Principal personages:

Emma Willard, the founder of Troy Female Seminary
Mary Lyon, the founder of Mount Holyoke College
Sarah and **Angelina Grimké,** sisters and abolitionists
Lucy Stone, an orator for abolitionism and women's rights
Lucretia Mott, an organizer of the Seneca Falls Convention in 1848
Elizabeth Cady Stanton, another organizer of the Seneca Falls Convention
Susan B. Anthony, chief organizer of women's rights movement
Carrie Chapman Catt, a women's suffrage advocate
Harriet Stanton Blatch, a militant suffrage leader
Alice Paul, another militant suffrage leader

Form and Content

Eleanor Flexner's *Century of Struggle: The Woman's Rights Movement in the United States* covers the period from the early nineteenth century to the adoption of the Nineteenth Amendment to the Constitution in 1920, which gave women the right to vote. Published in 1959, it was one of the first histories of the women's rights campaign and explored the question facing women, and the nation, in the nineteenth century and since: whether the Jeffersonian ideal that "all men are created equal" applied to whites males only or encompassed all people, regardless of race or sex.

Century of Struggle is organized chronologically. Although Flexner briefly discusses the Colonial and Revolutionary periods, the story proper begins in the early nineteenth century with the movement to provide an advanced education for women. Emma Hart Willard's Troy Female Seminary opened in 1821 in New York City. The first college that offered education to women and men equally was Oberlin College in Ohio, and Mount Holyoke, the oldest women's college in the United States, opened its doors in 1837. After the Civil War, the new land-grant colleges were more supportive of women, and at the same time new women's colleges were founded, such as Smith, Wellesley, Vassar, and Bryn Mawr colleges.

The antislavery movement drew many women, both black and white, into the campaign to free African Americans from bondage. Some women saw their status as similar to slaves. The abolitionist Sarah Grimké argued for women's equality, stating that "I ask no favors for my sex. . . . All I ask of our brethren is that they will take their feet from off our necks." Lucy Stone also found it impossible to separate abolition from women's rights, and when she married Henry Blackwell in 1855, they publicly objected to a legal system which perpetuated women's inferior status.

The major watershed of the women's rights movement before the Civil War took place at Seneca Falls, New York, in 1848. Organized by Lucretia Mott and Elizabeth Cady Stanton, the meeting attracted about three hundred persons, both men and women. At the conclusion, a Declaration of Principles was agreed to, a brilliant paraphrase of the Declaration of Independence of 1776: "We hold these truths to be self-evident: that all men and women are created equal." The most controversial issue was Stanton's proposal that the focus of the movement's attention should be obtaining the vote, because many believed that legal equality and educational and professional opportunities were more important issues.

During the Civil War, the National Woman's Loyal League, under the leadership of Stanton and Susan B.

Anthony, supported the war as an abolitionist crusade. There was great disappointment and anger, however, when the Fourteenth Amendment to the Constitution gave citizenship only to men. In 1869, Stanton and Anthony formed the National Woman Suffrage Association. A few months later, the more conservative American Woman Suffrage Association was founded, avoiding questions of divorce or organizing working women and advocating that women's suffrage be brought about on a state-by-state basis. Anthony's National Woman Suffrage Association, however, argued for a federal amendment, first introduced in Congress in 1878. Known as the "Anthony Amendment," it was reintroduced many times over the next forty years.

The late nineteenth century was an era of organization and reform, attracting many mainly middle-class women. The Young Women's Christian Association (YWCA), the American Association of University Women, the General Federation of Women's Clubs, the National Association of Colored Women, and the Women's Christian Temperance Union achieved prominence. Working-class women occasionally gained positions of leadership in labor unions, but this was unusual. Most women worked in piecework or unskilled trades and were largely ignored by the major labor organizations. There were strikes, especially in the garment trades, and the Women's Trade Union League was formed in 1903. With notable exceptions, however, the middle-class leaders of the suffrage movement distanced themselves from working-class issues. In 1890, the two major suffrage organizations merged, forming the National American Woman Suffrage Association. Stanton was the first president, followed by Anthony, and then, after her death in 1906, by Carrie Chapman Catt and Anna Howard Shaw, but the impetus for a federal suffrage amendment waned.

Toward the end of Theodore Roosevelt's presidency, the suffrage movement made new progress, partially inspired by the radical approach of Great Britain's suffragette movement. Roosevelt, running on a third-party ticket in 1912, supported women's suffrage but lost to Woodrow Wilson. In 1914, the "Anthony Amendment" came to a vote in Congress but was narrowly defeated. Wilson finally committed himself in January, 1918. The amendment passed the House, but the Senate failed to approve it. After the new Congress convened in 1919, the House repassed the amendment, 304 to 89, and in June the Senate concurred. The Nineteenth Amendment was finally ratified by the required number of states in August, 1920. Twenty-six million women had the vote.

Analysis

Century of Struggle is one of the seminal works about the history of women in the United States, and one of the author's major strengths is her clear, concise, and straightforward narrative style. Beginning with an introduction in the Colonial and Revolutionary eras with such figures as Anne Hutchinson, Mercy Otis Warren, and Abigail Adams, Flexner populates her story with hundreds of women from the early nineteenth century to 1920, detailing their efforts and accomplishments. Some of her many characters were relatively well known when the work was published—for example, Lucretia Mott, Elizabeth Cady Stanton, and Susan B. Anthony—but many figures were not. Augusta Lewis, the first president of the Women's Typographical Union No. 1, was hardly a household name, and Ida B. Wells and Josephine St. Pierre Ruffin, African American activists for both racial and gender rights, were likewise excluded from books on American history. Their stories and many others are successfully re-created by Flexner out of the past.

In *Century of Struggle*, Flexner attempted two major goals that were not necessarily compatible. First, she tried to be as inclusive as possible in her history of American women. Educators, abolitionists, nurses, doctors, lawyers, writers, editors, labor activists, community leaders, the middle classes, the working classes, women of European background, and African Americans occupy her pages. Given the magnitude of her task, Flexner succeeded brilliantly. She has a talent for brief descriptions and apt phrases and quotations. Her organizational abilities and her clear narrative style save *Century of Struggle* from becoming simply the recitation of one woman and her accomplishments after another, and in spite of the number of figures discussed, the women invariably retain their individuality in the reader's memory.

Her second goal was to chronicle the campaign for women's suffrage, which is a somewhat narrower subject. Yet the final several years of the suffrage campaign take up approximately one-third of *Century of Struggle*. In her concentration upon this goal, everything else—the education of women and their advancement in the professions, labor, and community involvement—becomes somewhat ancillary to the struggle to gain the vote. The background is handled well: The reader is made aware of the societal changes that occurred from the rural and small-town lifestyle of most people in the early nineteenth century to the industrial, urbanized, and bureaucratic society that had emerged by the twentieth century. Still, there is a danger that all the names and events might overwhelm the reader.

In her recitation of the suffrage struggle, Flexner nicely sorts out the various characters and organizations. Anthony is a key figure, but Flexner also admires Carrie Chapman Catt for her consummate organizing skills, which finally ensured the adoption of the Nineteenth Amendment. The work relates some of the activities of the more radical suffrage campaigners, such as Alice Paul and Harriet Stanton Blatch, but there is little doubt as to Flexner's belief that it was not radical confrontation but superb organization that finally resulted in victory in 1920. Although one reviewer complained about the absence of men in Flexner's history of the women's suffrage movement and suggested that she was too sympathetic to her women characters, *Century of Struggle*, an explicit criticism of the failure of historians to tell the history of women, is itself a product of its own times, reflecting the organizational and political assumptions of the Eisenhower years instead of the radical movements of the 1960's. Later, in the 1970's, when questioned about her own ideology, Flexner described herself not as a radical feminist but as a moderate, desiring specifically equal pay and equal opportunities for women.

Context

Flexner's *Century of Struggle* was one of the first scholarly histories of the women's movement since the six-volume *History of Woman Suffrage* (1881-1922), and that earlier work was, as one scholar noted, unreadable. When Flexner's volume was published in 1959, there were few other studies that told of the challenges that women had faced in achieving recognition, if not parity, in American society. As the author noted in her introduction, as early as 1928 Arthur M. Schlesinger, Sr., had complained that histories of the United States ignored the story of women and their fight for rights, and little had changed by the late 1950's.

As a work of academic history, *Century of Struggle* did not have the obvious revolutionary impact of other contemporary works about women, such as Simone de Beauvoir's *Le Deuxième sexe* (1949; *The Second Sex*, 1953) and Betty Friedan's *The Feminine Mystique* (1963). Nevertheless it was a milestone, coming as it did at the end of the complacency of the 1950's and the beginning of the upheavals of the 1960's. More than filling a gap, Flexner's work became the standard text in the numerous courses in women's history that came into being in the 1960's and 1970's. More than any other single volume, *Century of Struggle* educated a generation of students about the women who had fought for increased opportunities and legal rights in the hundred years before the adoption of the Nineteenth Amendment.

In time, however, *Century of Struggle* was superseded by more recent works with new approaches and philosophies, as well as new information. The Great Depression, World War II, the Civil Rights movement of the 1960's, and the feminist movement of the 1970's made Flexner's study, ending as it did in 1920, no longer sufficient to be the standard text in women's history classes. Nevertheless, if not the last word (or even the latest word), *Century of Struggle* will stand as an enduring landmark in the story of women in the United States.

Sources for Further Study

Blumberg, Dorothy Rose. Review of *Century of Struggle*. *Science and Society* 25 (Winter, 1961): 90-92. Blumberg admires Flexner's scholarship in re-creating the past from obscure archival records but wishes that she had placed more emphasis on the role of women in the socialist movement.

Dearing, Mary R. Review of *Century of Struggle*. *The American Historical Review* 65 (April, 1960): 620-621. Dearing, in the premier journal for American historians, reviews Flexner's volume and praises its comprehensiveness and objectivity. The reviewer particularly liked the book's organization and the many biographical sketches.

Degler, Carl N. Review of *Century of Struggle*. *Mississippi Valley History Review* 46 (March, 1960): 733-734. Degler, one of the history profession's most eminent scholars, reviewed *Century of Struggle* for this major journal of American history, praising it as readable, balanced, and comprehensive. He noted, however, Flexner's lack of interest in the ideology of her characters.

Evans, Sara M. *Born for Liberty*. New York: Free Press, 1989. One of the more recent histories of American women which has replaced Flexner's *Century of Struggle* in women's studies courses. Written from a feminist perspective, it carries the history of women through the 1980's.

Flexner, Eleanor. *Mary Wollstonecraft*. New York: Coward, McCann & Geoghegan, 1972. In this prize-winning biography, Flexner tells the story of England's Mary Wollstonecraft, author of *A Vindication of the Rights of Woman* (1792) and an inspiration to later generations of women.

Eugene Larson

THE CHILDREN'S HOUR

Author: Lillian Hellman (1906-1984)
Type of work: Drama
Type of plot: Problem play
Time of plot: The 1930's
Locale: New England
First produced: 1934, at Maxine Elliot's Theatre, New York City
First published: 1934

Principal characters:

Karen Wright, a partner and teacher at the Wright-Dobie private boarding school for girls
Martha Dobie, Karen's partner and fellow teacher
Joseph Cardin, Karen's financé and a physician, the nephew of Amelia Tilford
Mary Tilford, the fourteen-year-old granddaughter and ward of Amelia Tilford and a student at the Wright-Dobie school
Lily Mortar, Martha's aunt, a teaching assistant at the school
Amelia Tilford, a wealthy widow and a leader in the local community

Form and Content

Lillian Hellman structures *The Children's Hour* into three acts. The first act presents events on an April day at the Wright-Dobie boarding school for girls. Fourteen-year-old Mary arrives late for her class with Lily, a teaching assistant, and lies about the reason for her absence. In reality, she was finishing *Mademoiselle de Maupin* (1835), by Théophile Gautier, a novel that includes scenes of homosexuality. Karen, one of the owners of the school, later catches Mary in this lie, and a struggle develops over whether Mary will admit it. Mary fakes a heart attack to prove her absence legitimate, and Karen's fiancé, Dr. Joe Cardin, is called to look at her. Joe's arrival brings out the discomfort of Martha, the school's other owner and Lily's niece, with his impending marriage to Karen. Lily's clumsiness in dealing with Mary and the other girls leads Karen to suggest that they send her to London. Lily has talked often of her wish to go, and Karen believes they can afford to keep her there. Lily focuses on their wish to be rid of her, ignoring the better of their intentions, and blurts out her belief that Martha is doomed to unhappiness when Karen marries because of her "unnatural" love for Karen. Genuine privacy being almost impossible in the farmhouse school, the girls observe and hear some of what goes on between the adults. Mary later coerces this information out of the other girls and then decides that she will leave the school to avoid punishment.

The two scenes of act 2 are set at the home of Amelia Tilford, a society matron who is Joe's aunt and Mary's grandmother. In the first, runaway Mary looks for a way to avoid returning to school. Eventually, she hits upon a story that her grandmother simply must believe, that Karen and Martha are lesbian lovers. Amelia then telephones the parents of the other students. In the second scene, Joe, Karen, and Martha demand an explanation and then a retraction of the lesbianism charge. Meanwhile, Mary, by threatening to report a petty theft, forces Rosalie Wells, a fellow student spending the night at Mrs. Tilford's, to support her story. Certain that Mary could not have made up this charge, Amelia refuses to retract it, and the teachers promise a libel suit.

The third act takes place in November, more than a week after Karen, Martha, and Joe have lost their suit against Amelia. Ostracized and ridiculed in their community, the teachers cannot bring themselves to go outside their now-empty school. Joe has remained loyal, but he cannot help his suspicions. He would like for all three of them to start a new life in Vienna, but Karen believes that this is impossible and sends him away to think for a few days about whether they should end the engagement. Martha tells Karen that she now believes she really does love Karen sexually, and Karen, attempting to deny any such feelings, makes it clear that her love for Martha is not sexual. Ruined, isolated, and despairing, Martha shoots herself. Then the deeply repentant Amelia arrives, having discovered Mary's lie, to learn that she cannot undo the damage.

Analysis

Hellman found the story upon which she based this play in a nineteenth century criminal case recounted in *Bad Companions* (1931), by William Roughead. In that story, two women who headed a boarding school in Scotland were falsely accused of lesbianism by a student in 1810. Though Hellman's source also emphasizes the theme of lesbianism and the problems of defining and controlling female sexuality, Hellman herself, in talking about the play, tended to deemphasize the lesbian theme. She spoke of it as a play about good and evil, about class power, and about scandal-mongering. The theme of scandal-mongering, or the "big lie," came to seem more important when the play was revived in New York in 1952, shortly after Hellman's appearance before the House Un-American Activities Committee, where she refused to name acquaintances who might have been connected with suspected communist organizations. She managed, however, to avoid the fate of her lover, Dashiell Hammett, who was imprisoned in 1951 for contempt of Congress when he refused to give names.

To later scholars, the play's sexual themes seem central because the outcome turns on an accusation of lesbianism. The power of this accusation depends upon silence not merely about lesbianism, but about female sexuality as a whole. No one in the play can say the word "lesbian," not only because New York playgoers were queasy about the subject in the 1930's but also because to the characters the very idea is an unspeakable horror. When Joe questions Mary about her story, Amelia is most horrified at the prospect that he will make Mary name what she claims to have seen. All the characters believe lesbianism to be so defiling and corrupting that the very charge proves guilt and, that if the young girls hear of it, they themselves are liable to be infected. Even Joe's love for Karen cannot prevent his suspecting her. Once Mary has accused the teachers of lesbianism, a specter looms behind the action. This specter may be understood in part as the assumed instability of female sexuality, an instability that requires the most rigid social control.

In this school for adolescent girls, sexuality is not spoken of. The girls know that they must satisfy their curiosity about sex by secret and forbidden means. Mary is the most sophisticated in the group because she has actually finished the Gautier novel, and even she knows so little about sex that she merely stumbles upon the correct formula to transfix her grandmother by replaying and amplifying the themes that get the strongest reaction. Adults are not supposed to talk to girls about sex, and girls are not supposed to know about it. Inevitably, girls learn about it in forbidden and unreliable ways; they come intuitively to understand that their knowledge must remain secret and that it can be powerful.

In act 2, scene 2, Hellman shows the power of silence about female sexuality and lesbianism when Martha, Karen, and Joe confront Amelia and Mary. Although the audience knows that Amelia is being deceived and can easily see the clumsiness of Mary's moves, still Amelia must decide whom to believe in the absence of completely reliable evidence. Should she believe the three professionals, with their established reputations, or the unreliable young girl who has claimed to see what Amelia believes no young girl could even imagine had she not actually seen it? Amelia may believe that lesbianism is "catching," or she may simply believe that girls should not know there is such a thing, but in either case the very possibility that Karen and Martha are lesbians poses a danger too great to risk trusting them to teach girls. Whatever the specific danger that she has in mind, Amelia is concerned about maintaining the silence about female sexuality.

The reasons that this silence is so important are many and complicated. Women's sexuality in the culture of this play is unknown, a blank filled with possibilities, like Mary's whispering to Amelia. As a result, a woman's sexuality seems to need tight control; otherwise, there is no telling what she will do. In the decades preceding this play's appearance, for example, there was considerable public debate over whether women should have legal access to birth control information. Would women marry and have children if they could choose when to become pregnant? Would they remain in their marriages if they chose not to have children? The possible answers to such questions seemed to threaten the foundations of social order. Hence the necessity for rigid social control, and the vicious circle is completed when the primary means of social control becomes the very silence that ensures ignorance about female sexuality.

This sketch of part of the ideological background of the play helps to make clear why the themes of lesbianism and female sexuality are central. All the action and the tragedy of the play come out of the characters' virtually unquestioned assumptions about these themes. Amelia cannot keep from believing the accusation, and even Joe's love for Karen cannot weather it. Martha struggles with her own feelings in silence and denial, and when she admits them, she is only able to see herself as a kind of disease. Karen can only deny Martha's feelings. No one has a constructive way to deal with lesbianism, in part because all are ignorant about women's sexuality and in part because no one speaks of such feelings and issues in public discourse.

Context

The Children's Hour was the first and most successful of Hellman's produced plays, with a long first run of 691 performances. The play received mixed reviews, was banned in several cities, and was passed over for a Pulitzer Prize, though later critics tend to agree that it was the best American play of 1934. Nevertheless, the play earned Hellman a small fortune and led to a well-paid screenwriting position with Samuel Goldwyn, where she quickly achieved further success with her screenplay for *Dark Angel* (1935). In 1936, she wrote her own well-received screenplay of *The Children's Hour*, called *These Three*, taking out the lesbianism and substituting a love triangle, and ending the story with Karen joining Joe in Vienna after misunderstandings are cleared up. This early work established Hellman as the foremost of a small group of American women dramatists that included the older Susan Glaspell, along with Zoë Akins and Rose Franken.

During most of Hellman's lifetime, *The Children's Hour* remained important mainly as a good play by a woman, and it helped to sustain her reputation as a writer, activist, and social critic. During the years when the shadow of the House Committee on Un-American Activities lay over artistic life in the United States, the play in revival joined similar works, such as Arthur Miller's *The Crucible* (1953), that commented on the power of ideologically motivated lies to distort social order and destroy dissent. In later years, the play became increasingly important for its presentation of sexual themes, such as the social control of female sexuality and the silence about and repression of lesbianism.

Hellman used the sexual themes as key parts of the social order out of which the play emerges, but there is little direct exploration of those themes in the play, suggesting that Hellman's own feelings about lesbianism were quite complicated. Nevertheless, her portrait of the restraints and silences, the terrors and compulsions surrounding the lesbian theme rings true and thereby helps to open up the fruitful and more complex exploration of this subject that has followed.

Sources for Further Study

Estrin, Mark. *Critical Essays on Lillian Hellman*. Boston: G. K. Hall, 1989. Following an extensive introductory overview of Hellman's writings and their reception are selections of essays on the plays, the memoirs, and Hellman's persona.

Falk, Doris. *Lillian Hellman*. New York: Frederick Ungar, 1978. A biographical study that includes summaries of Hellman's works and information about the composition, production, and reception of her plays.

Lederer, Katherine. *Lillian Hellman*. Boston: Twayne, 1979. This critical examination of Hellman's works includes a good discussion of her sources for *The Children's Hour*, as well as a biographical chronology and sketch and an annotated bibliography.

Moody, Richard. *Lillian Hellman: Playwright*. New York: Pegasus, 1972. This early biography includes information about the composition and two main New York productions of *The Children's Hour* and stills from several productions.

Rollyson, Carl. *Lillian Hellman: Her Legend and Her Legacy*. New York: St. Martin's Press, 1988. This literary biography offers a full account of the complex and elusive playwright. *The Children's Hour* receives extensive treatment. Contains many photographs of Hellman and her associates.

Wright, William. *Lillian Hellman: The Image, the Woman*. New York: Simon & Schuster, 1986. This readable popular biography is less concerned with analysis of her work than with a detailed narrative of Hellman's life. Contains an interesting selection of photographs.

Terry Heller

CLOUD NINE

Author: Caryl Churchill (1938-)
Type of work: Drama
Type of plot: Comedy
Time of plot: Victorian times and 1979
Locale: A British colony in Africa and London
First produced: 1979, at Dartington College of Arts, England
First published: 1979

Principal characters:

Clive, a stereotypical patriarch
Betty, his wife, played by a man in act 1
Joshua, Clive's black servant, played by a white actor
Edward, Clive and Betty's homosexual son, played by a woman in act 1
Victoria, Clive and Betty's lesbian daughter, who is played by a dummy in act 1 and is the central character in act 2
Ellen, Edward's governess, who is in love with Betty
Harry Bagley, an explorer who has sexual relationships with Edward and Joshua
Mrs. Saunders, a widow who has an affair with Clive
Martin, Victoria's husband
Lin, Victoria's friend and lover, a lesbian who left an abusive husband
Cathy, Lin's five-year-old daughter, played by a man
Gerry, Edward's lover

Form and Content

The central focus of *Cloud Nine* is sexual politics, an admittedly general topic that Caryl Churchill suggested to a Joint Stock Theater Group workshop, which became the inspiration for her play. The work is divided into two very different acts. The first is set in Africa in Victorian times, with the patriarch Clive trying to maintain control of his section of the British Empire and of his family, the members of which demonstrate difficulty staying within the boundaries of accepted gender roles. Clive introduces them: himself as father to both the African natives and his family; his wife, Betty, whose aim is to be what Clive wants in a wife; their servant, Joshua, who lives only for his white master; and their son, Edward, who confesses that he finds it difficult to be what his father wants him to be. The marginalization of women is clear when Clive declares that his daughter (literally a doll), his mother-in-law, and the governess do not need to speak.

With the arrival of the explorer Harry Bagley and the widow Mrs. Saunders, the sexual games begin, with Harry romancing Betty and then taking Joshua to the barn. Clive disappears under Mrs. Saunders' skirt for a farcical sexual encounter interrupted when the others arrive for the Christmas picnic. Betty tries to convince Harry to take her away, but he says that he needs her where she is. Harry and Edward reveal a sexual encounter together that Harry insists was a sin. Ellen confesses her love to an uncomprehending Betty.

The games are interrupted by a native uprising, and the women, in a darkened room, discuss the men's flogging of servants. Mrs. Saunders is critical, arguing that the only way out is to leave the colony. Edward returns to the women's circle and is punished by Betty for playing with Victoria's doll. He confesses to Clive that he also said he hated his father and did not want to be like him. He is forgiven because of his brave confession, then stands up to Joshua when he insults Betty.

In rapid succession, Edward confronts Harry, Ellen again confesses her love to a still-mystified Betty, and Harry mistakes Clive's glorifying of male friendship for a homosexual overture. Shocked, Clive insists that Harry get married in order to save himself. Mrs. Saunders, refusing Harry's proposal, brings news that Joshua's mother and father were killed by whites. Joshua responds that Clive is his mother and his father, but when Joshua informs Clive of Ellen's overtures to Betty, Clive orders him out of his sight. As Clive proposes a toast to the hastily arranged marriage between Ellen and Harry, Joshua approaches with a gun to shoot Clive. Edward sees him but merely covers his ears.

Act 2 opens in 1979 in a London park, but the characters are only twenty-five years older. This act is primarily realistic. Lin, a divorced lesbian mother, and Victoria watch their children at a playground. Edward, now openly homosexual, brings Betty, who is leaving Clive and thinking about getting a job, to visit. Her change leads the others to consider their own relationships. Lin and Victoria begin an affair. Victoria considers a job in Manchester, wishing that her husband, Martin, could be a wife and follow her. Edward loses his lover Gerry, and Lin learns that her soldier brother has been killed in Northern Ireland. Victoria, Edward, and Lin get drunk and try a ceremony to call up the goddess. Instead, the ghost of Lin's brother comes, not to impart wisdom but for sex. Victoria, Edward, and Lin decide to live together, with Edward doing the housework and the women working. In a long monologue, Betty discusses the joys of masturbation and coming into her own. The play ends with characters still trying to renegotiate roles and relationships, as Betty rejects Clive and embraces Betty from act 1.

Analysis

In *Cloud Nine*, Churchill carefully examines the effect of rigid gender roles learned by both men and women in Western society. The difficulty that people can have in learning these roles is evident in the experiences of the three children in the play. To dramatize her point, Churchill has the young Edward played by a woman, Cathy played by a man, and the child Victoria represented in the first act by a dummy or doll.

Edward demonstrates the most difficulty adjusting to the male role. He has an affinity for dolls and necklaces, and he is unable to perform well in the male arena, whether he is playing ball or watching servants begin flogged. He nevertheless internalizes these rigid gender roles, for even in the second act, when he is openly homosexual, he wants to be the "perfect wife" and turn his lover, Gerry, into the "perfect husband." Following the attempt to call up the goddess, he lives with Victoria and Lin. Here he learns to stretch the prescribed roles; even though he is doing the housework, he tells Gerry that he no longer thinks in terms of the wifely role.

Cathy, the modern child, should be freer than the Victorian Edward. She is being reared by her mother, a lesbian who dislikes men and encourages Cathy's free expression, even when it includes an affinity for guns. Yet Cathy is not immune to peer pressure, and she insists on wearing dresses to school after she is called a boy.

Restrictive gender roles continue to be trouble for adults. Betty, who appears to be the perfect wife, longs to betray her husband and family by running off with the dashing explorer. Maud, her mother, still serves as an enforcer of what is proper, reminding her daughter of her duty. Betty does not escape until she leaves Clive in act 2 for her own journey of self-discovery, including sexual experimentation. When she talks about the joys of masturbation, she finally rejects the control of her mother and Clive and is able to accept herself. This acceptance is dramatized by the embrace shared by the Betty from act 1 (played by a man) and the Betty from act 2 at the end of the play.

Homosexuality complicates the already difficult task of dealing with prescribed gender roles. Harry Bagley is a man in conflict, viewing his homosexuality as a sin and trying to project the image of the virile man that society expects him to be. Out of his self-hatred, he engages in sexual relations with two powerless males—Edward and Joshua—and accepts marriage to Ellen as the proper solution for him. Ellen seems more positive about her homosexual desires, but as a lesbian in Victorian times, she is invisible. She accepts marriage reluctantly—not out of a sense of sin, as Harry does, but out of a sense of having no other real alternatives.

The absurdity of sexual politics, which causes people to limit themselves in terms of relationships and sexual pleasure, is amply illustrated in the first act of *Cloud Nine*. With the exception of Edward, the characters are two-dimensional and elicit little sympathy. The game of hide-and-seek is a metaphor for the lives of these adults, who are without exception hiding from the reality of their lives—and attempting to hide from one another as well.

In choosing a colonial setting for the first act, Churchill was influenced by French playwright Jean Genet, a homosexual who saw a parallel between colonial oppression and sexual oppression. This is illustrated in the position of Joshua, who is totally alienated from his own culture and thus his own identity. He is abused sexually by Harry and used by Clive in the role of a eunuch, spying on others' escapades and informing the master.

His impotence evidently extends to his inability to use his gun effectively, for Clive survives for act 2.

Though Churchill does not answer all the questions raised in the play, she clearly favors an openness in defining sexual roles and sexual relationships. The focus on Betty at the end of the play suggests the need for self-acceptance as the key. Betty is at a point where she can see possibilities in her future. The restriction of high ideals belongs to the rigid Clive; in this play, being on cloud nine means confusing your life, turning things upside down, choosing to explore and to accept freedom and possibility.

Context

In *Cloud Nine*, Churchill focuses on an important feminist topic—sexual politics. She views the subject from a wide range of points of view and with humor and sensitivity. Expanding the feminist concern that restrictive gender roles rob women of power, she includes homosexuals and those oppressed by colonialism, connecting their powerlessness to the "feminization" of women. This approach is consistent with Churchill's socialist feminism, for certainly colonialism is the most ruthless extension of capitalism. Churchill allows patriarchy and capitalism to dominate the first act of *Cloud Nine*, primarily through the character of Clive, but the second act belongs to Victoria and Betty, both of whom are stretching the boundaries of their sex-related roles.

Churchill breaks important ground in several areas. She deals with gay and feminist politics and the relationship between them. She presents a socialist feminist's perspective of the sexual revolution of the 1970's. She goes beyond viewing sexuality as an area of oppression to see it as a place where, with some effort, gains can be made. Yet the play has been criticized by a number of reviewers, including some feminists, for its failure to arrive at a solution for the problems that it delineates. The second act has been seen as devoid of struggle. It may be, however, that these critics are looking for the same sort of "right" answer hoped for by men such as Clive.

What Churchill has offered in this play is a series of portraits of women—and others—struggling with prescribed roles, looking for ways out, and finally committing themselves to a continued search, based on self-acceptance and an openness to myriad possibilities, as opposed to a right answer. As Churchill herself has said, "Playwrights don't give answers, they ask questions." Churchill's contribution, in this play as in others, is to ask questions that challenge assumptions and to leave her audiences and critics with vivid stage pictures that present strong images of those questions.

Sources for Further Study

Betsko, Kathleen, and Rachel Koenig, eds. *Interviews with Contemporary Women Playwrights*. New York: Beech Tree Books, 1987. In an interview, Churchill discusses the necessity of feminism being connected to socialist goals and decries feminism tied to "getting ahead," or to capitalist goals. She also discusses the differences between the London and New York productions of *Cloud Nine*.

Churchill, Caryl. "A Fair Cop." Interview by Lynne Truss. *Plays and Players*, no. 364 (January, 1984): 8-10. Churchill discusses the doubling of roles and the effect of the changed ending in the New York production of *Cloud Nine*.

Cousin, Geraldine. *Churchill: The Playwright*. London: Methuen Drama, 1989. This book contains information on Churchill's use of the workshop process, as well as analyses of her plays and a summary chapter that connects themes shared by the plays. A section of *Cloud Nine* discusses Churchill's workshop with the Joint Stock Theatre Group and analyzes the play's structure.

Fitzsimmons, Linda. *File of Churchill*. London: Methuen Drama, 1989. A comprehensive list of plays, including unperformed ones. Features a selection of reviews and Churchill's comments on her work, including a letter that Churchill wrote to a director in rehearsal for the play. The letter focuses on character analysis and on how the characters should be played.

Kritzer, Amelia Howe. *The Plays of Caryl Churchill: Theatre of Empowerment*. New York: St. Martin's Press, 1991. Written from a feminist perspective, this book opens with an overview of theories of drama and theater and of feminist and socialist criticism in relation to Churchill's drama. The chapter entitled "Sex and Gender" includes an extensive analysis of *Clound Nine*.

Randall, Phyllis R., ed. *Caryl Churchill: A Casebook*. New York: Garland, 1988. This casebook features a variety of essays and an annotated bibliography. " 'The Work of Culture': *Cloud Nine* and Sex/Gender Theory" discusses the play in the contexts of both feminist and gay politics and writing.

Thomas, Jane. "The Plays of Caryl Churchill: Essays in Refusal." In *The Death of the Playwright?*, edited by Adrian Page. New York: St. Martin's Press, 1992. This essay analyzes *Cloud Nine* and *Top Girls* (1982) in light of Churchill's acknowledged reading of Michel Foucault's *Surveiller et punir: Naissance de la prison* (1975; *Discipline and Punish: The Birth of the Prison*, 1977).

Elsie Galbreath Haley

THE COLOR PURPLE

Author: Alice Walker (1944-)
Type of work: Novel
Type of plot: Social realism
Time of plot: The first half of the twentieth century
Locale: Rural Georgia and Africa
First published: 1982

Principal characters:

Celie, the central character
Nettie, Celie's younger sister
Shug Avery, a blues singer and the mistress of Albert, Celie's husband
Albert, Celie's husband
Harpo, Albert's oldest child
Sofia, the strong, independent woman who marries Harpo
Mary Agnes (Squeak), Harpo's woman after Sofia leaves him
Alphonso, Celie's abusive stepfather, whom she mistakenly believes to be her real father
Samuel, a preacher and missionary to Africa
Corrine, a missionary and Samuel's devoted wife
Olivia and **Adam,** Celie's children
Tashi, a young Olinkan woman who is a dear friend of Olivia and Adam
Reynolds and **Miss Millie,** the mayor and his wife
Eleanor Jane, the mayor's daughter

Form and Content

The Color Purple is a series of seventy short letters; the first fifty-one are from Celie to God. Celie's stepfather, Alphonso, rapes her repeatedly when she is so young that she does not even realize what is happening to her. She does not know that she is pregnant until her first baby is born. Alphonso steals it, as well as a second baby, and threatens her not to tell anybody but God what he has been doing to her; he says that if she tells, it will kill her mother. Celie pours out her confusion and pain in her letters to God. Her mother dies anyway, and Alphonso immediately marries again. Celie, who dropped out of school when she became pregnant, is virtually alone and has neither the strength nor the will to fight for herself.

Alphonso "gives" Celie to Albert, who had asked to marry Celie's younger sister Nettie. Albert, whom Celie refers to as "Mr.——" through most of the book, abuses Celie even though she has sex with him, cares for his three children, cleans his house, and works in the field. Celie invites Nettie to live with them to save her from Alphonso's sexual advances. When Nettie refuses sex to Albert, however, he sends her away and hides all of her letters to Celie. Meanwhile, Albert continues his long-time relationship with blues singer Shug Avery. Everyone in the community knows of their relationship, which Albert does nothing to hide.

When Shug is suffering from "that nasty woman's disease," Albert brings her home for Celie to nurse back to health. Celie, who has always been fascinated by Shug's photograph and her scandalous reputation, bathes her, feeds her, combs her hair, and learns to love her. At first, Shug is hateful to Celie, ridiculing her weakness and her inability to stand up to Albert. She then begins to feel close to Celie, learns to respect her, sings to her, composes a song for her, helps her find the letters from Nettie that Albert has hidden, and teaches her to respect herself and to assert her own independence. When Celie realizes that Albert has kept Nettie's letters from her, she wants to kill him. Shug instead encourages Celie to become more independent, using her artistic talent as a seamstress to make and sell pants.

Harpo, Albert's oldest son, and his strong and determined wife, Sofia, also encourage Celie and in various ways help her to learn to assert herself. She is also greatly empowered by finding Nettie's letters and learning that both Nettie and Celie's own children are alive and well in Africa. She also learns that Alphonso is not her real father; her children are not the products of incest, as she had believed.

By the fifty-sixth letter, Celie is writing to Nettie instead of to God, since she is not sure if she believes in God anymore. Shug has taught her to know and to appreciate her own body and to enjoy sexual pleasure. Shug has listened to Celie recount the story of the brutal abuse that she suffered as a child, while Celie has also listened to the story of Shug's past, including the circumstances of her relationship with Albert. Much to Albert's surprise, Shug starts sleeping with Celie instead of him. By the sixtieth letter, Celie is living with Shug in Memphis, has become a successful businesswoman, and for the first time has enough self-respect and dignity to sign her own name to her letters.

When Alphonso dies, Celie inherits the farm, to her surprise and pleasure, and is able to provide a home for herself and Shug and to prepare a place for Nettie and her children when they return from Africa. In the last letter—which Celie begins "Dear God. Dear stars, dear trees, dear sky, dear peoples. Dear Everything. Dear God"—she describes the happy reunion, after thirty years, with her beloved sister Nettie and the children who were stolen from her.

Twenty-two of the letters in *The Color Purple* are from Nettie to Celie, telling of her life with the missionaries Samuel and Corrine, who have taken in Celie's children as their own. She finds both of them to be very kind, loving, and well educated. In her letters to Celie, Nettie shares her trips and her adventures in New York City, London, and Africa. In Africa, among the Olinkan people, Nettie finds the same reluctance to educate women, to accept new ideas, and to change traditional behavior that she had experienced in Georgia. Nettie's spiritual growth and increase in self-respect and self-confidence are in many ways parallel to Celie's. After Corrine's death, Nettie and Samuel discover that they love each other and marry so that they can work together more effectively to serve the needs of the African people. Samuel stops preaching the American religion and begins to minister to the sick and care for the children.

Olivia and Adam, Celie's children, have matured into beautiful, thoughtful adults; both of them love Tashi, a young Olinkan woman who returns to Georgia as Adam's wife after having undergone the female initiation ceremonies of her own people. Adam demonstrates his love and support of Tashi by having the traditional scarring done to his face just before the wedding.

Harpo and Sofia are part of the family celebration at the end of the story. Sofia left Harpo because he tried to dominate her; she was then thrown in jail for refusing to work for the mayor's wife. While Sofia served her sentence, Harpo and his new woman, Mary Agnes (or "Squeak"), take care of Sofia's children. Later Sofia and Harpo, both more mature, are happily reunited.

Analysis

The Color Purple is most clearly about the transforming power of love; Celie, Shug, and many of the other characters grow and change after being loved and learning to love in return. After Celie has left Albert, he is loved and cared for by his son Harpo. Albert reflects on the way in which he has treated Celie and the lessons that he has learned from watching Celie and Shug together; he becomes more thoughtful and considerate as a result. Albert and Celie become friends in the end and sit on the porch together smoking pipes and talking; when Nettie and the children return, Celie introduces Albert, along with Shug, as "her people."

Albert lets Celie teach him to sew and helps her to make the clothes that she sells; he is no longer afraid that he will lose his masculinity. Harpo has also learned to accept his "feminine" traits and is content to stay home and take care of the house and the children while Sofia manages Celie's store. Sofia learns to control her desire to dominate everyone and everything and is able to accept help not only from Harpo but also from the mayor's daughter, Eleanor Jane, who assists Harpo in taking care of the children. Along with Celie, both Sofia and Mary Agnes teach powerful lessons in forgiveness. As these women grow in their ability to love and accept themselves and others, they also learn to forgive themselves and others.

In teaching Celie to love, Shug has helped Celie not only to understand and accept her own individuality but also to broaden her conception of spiritual truth beyond that of the old, white-bearded, blue-eyed God that she has imagined and the narrow conception of the Bible as having been written by white people for white people. Shug's conception of spiritual truth includes a God who is neither man nor woman, neither black nor white, but is in every living thing and in every human being. Shug's God also appreciates sexuality and wants people to enjoy themselves. In faraway Africa, Nettie realizes that her traditional picture of Jesus is out of place in her hut in the Olinkan village, and she realizes that the roofleaf which protects the Olinkans is in a sense God to them. Both Celie and Nettie learn that God is not found in church, where people come to share God rather than to find him. An important part of spiritual growth for each individual is developing a unique, personally appropriate image of God, as well as unique, personally appropriate relationships. More spiritual sharing and loving kindness is shown in the juke joint that Harpo opens than in the local church. In the juke joint, Shug sings the song she had written for Celie, and Celie feels appreciated and special. On the other hand, at church Shug has been judged, condemned, and ridiculed.

Another equally important theme deals with the destructive effect of keeping a secret when telling the simple truth could save untold amounts of pain and suffering. Corinne finally learns that Nettie is Adam and Olivia's aunt rather than their mother, as she had long assumed. She had already decided that Samuel was their father, as no one told her that Samuel had taken the children from Alphonso. Because she was not given an honest explanation, Corinne endured years of painful suspicion about Samuel and Nettie. Moreover, if Celie had realized that her real father was lynched by white people because of his success in managing his store and that Alphonso was her and Nettie's stepfather, she would not have had to cope with the thought of incest.

Context

The powerful Pulitzer Prize-winning novel is in the tradition of *Their Eyes Were Watching God* (1937), by Zora Neale Hurston, and deals with many issues dealt with in the novels of Toni Morrison and other outstanding African American women writers.

In the opening pages of the novel, Alice Walker invokes "the Spirit" to assist her in the writing of the book; at the end, she refers to herself as A. W., "author and medium." In speaking of writing the novel, she frequently refers to the fact that she is simply telling Celie's story for her in Celie's own words. This approach to character explains the harsh language and the vividly graphic words Celie uses to describe the brutal treatment that she received and her attitudes toward it; it is important for Celie as well as for other young women to tell their own stories as they recall their experiences. As Celie's world expands and she begins to heal, her language becomes more "pleasant" and is easier to read. Women need to learn to love and accept themselves and their histories and to have the courage to write their lives in their own words.

Another important message to women in *The Color Purple* is the importance of women's supporting one another and encouraging one another in the expression of their unique talents. Sofia and Celie make a quilt together, and even Shug allows Celie to teach her to quilt; quilting symbolizes their solidarity and strong mutual support. Mary Agnes supports and helps Sofia even though Sofia literally knocked Mary Agnes' teeth out when she first saw her with Harpo. Sofia finally accepts Eleanor Jane's assistance even though she is white and a member of the family that has treated her so terribly. Corrine finally forgives Nettie for "looking like" Adam and Olivia and for loving them and Samuel so much when she realizes the truth about Nettie not being their mother. Olivia and Tashi are bound by the same love and mutual devotion that Shug and Celie share, and they show the sisterly loyalty that Celie and Nettie feel. Women love and support other women in this novel.

Sources for Further Study

Buncombe, Marie H. "Androgyny as Metaphor in Alice Walker's Novels." *College Language Association Journal* 30, no. 4 (June, 1987): 419-427. Offers a helpful look at the treatment of sex roles in *The Color Purple* in comparison to Walker's other novels.

Christian, Barbara. "Alice Walker: The Black Woman Artist as Wayward." In *Black Women Writers (1950-1980): A Critical Evaluation*, edited by Mari Evans. Garden City, N.Y.: Anchor Press-Doubleday, 1983. This essay focuses on the strength of Celie as an African American woman who liberates herself through her sister's strength and wisdom.

Harris, Trudier. "From Victimization to Free Enterprise: Alice Walker's *The Color Purple*." *Studies in American Fiction* 14, no. 1 (Spring, 1986): 1-17. This article looks at Celie's survival as a victimized African American woman.

Parker-Smith, Bettye J. "Alice Walker's Women: In

Search of Some Peace of Mind." In *Black Women Writers (1950-1980): A Critical Evaluation*, edited by Mari Evans. Garden City, N.Y.: Anchor Press-Doubleday, 1983. Celie affirms herself and finds the strength that she needs by discovering that God is within, that God is herself.

Proudfit, Charles L. "Celie's Search for Identity: A Psychoanalytic Developmental Reading of Alice Walker's *The Color Purple*." *Contemporary Literature* 32, no. 1 (Spring, 1991): 12-37. Proudfit offers a good example of a psychoanalytic approach to the development of Celie's self-concept.

Tavormina, M. Teresa. "Dressing the Spirit: Clothworking and Language in *The Color Purple*." *Journal of Narrative Technique* 16, no. 3 (Fall, 1986): 220-230. A study of language in relationship to sewing and quilting as they relate to the development of the self.

Walker, Alice. *In Search of Our Mothers' Gardens: Womanist Prose*. San Diego: Harcourt Brace Jovanovich, 1983.

————. *Living by the Word: Selected Writings, 1973-87*. San Diego: Harcourt Brace Jovanovich, 1988. These essays provide an opportunity to get to know Alice Walker as a person. The earlier volume provides numerous insights into the writing of *The Color Purple*, the latter on Walker's reactions to its reception.

Constance M. Fulmer

THE COLOSSUS AND OTHER POEMS

Author: Sylvia Plath
Type of work: Poetry
First published: 1960

Form and Content

The poems of Sylvia Plath's *The Colossus and Other Poems* are metrically free but stanzaically strict; only rarely does the poet choose the foot over the syllable. That the poems are nevertheless very rhythmic is attributable less to an adroit syllabic measure than to felicitous aural features such as internal rhyme and alliteration. If Plath's line was only modestly fresh in 1960, her marriage of sound and sense in poetic diction was dramatically innovative and became a hallmark even of her most mature period. The free line is, however, joined almost invariably to patterned stanzas that repeat themselves precisely within poems. Tercets, quatrains, and quintains predominate. Pervasively, however, the free rhythms of the verse soften the rigid impression made by the formality of the stanzas. Such an effect underlies "Aftermath," within which the separation of the octave and sestet and the nine-syllable line mask the fact that the poem is an Italian sonnet. The play of these apparently oppositional choices created the blend of tradition and reformation that Plath desired for her first collection of lyrics.

The imagery and metaphors of the poems convey relentlessly the inner emotional life of the persona. Indeed, there is but one voice behind these poems. It may be called "confessional," a word too often applied to Plath's verse, but it must be understood as less singular and female than modernly nihilistic in a fashion beyond gender characterization. Images derive from the family, art, nature, and a mental hospital, though with this last source they are incidental, giving the sense of a psychiatric ward without naming or picturing it. Metaphor controls every poem and is usually employed to render the similarities between the nonhuman world, on the one hand, and the state of the persona's nihilistic consciousness, on the other. The series of landscapes presented by the poems, at once imagistic and metaphorical, expresses an unalleviated despair concerning the world's death-driven modus operandi, the universe's blank indifference, and most important, the speaker's anxiety about the hope of a fruitful self-identity.

These poems stand at the end of the high modern period of literature and look back to both romanticism and Symbolism in their conceptions of voice, expressive figuration, and depersonalized confession. They have much of the technical mastery and subterranean imagery of the poetry of Theodore Roethke, but they harken back to more colloquial phrasing (despite their often erudite diction) and they discover no relief from darkness.

Analysis

The past for Plath is a province of ghosts who offer nothing but their abiding absence of life as a tool for the management of existence. In "The Beekeeper's Daughter" and the title poem, the father's bequest to her is "the winter of [his] year" and "fluted bones . . . littered/ In their old anarchy to the horizon-line," respectively. It is no better when she turns to the larger family or even to humankind's prehistoric forebears. This is the menacing point of "All the Dead Dears," wherein the "long gone darlings"—constituted equally by the relic "lady" in an archaeological museum and one's own female progenitors, who always reappear at family affairs via photograph and anecdote—come only to "Reach hag hands to haul me in." It is a point made summarily in "The Ghost's Leavetaking." To see the dead properly is to see oneself with them, in each next second of one's life. They steal the impulse to live or to fashion a self engaged by being rather than atrophied by extinction. Plath's speaker has taken to heart the paradox that at the moment of conception, a life is borne forward by death. This is much more a matter of feeling than of disinterested observation, and it is what makes voice and emotion the substance of these poems, over which a pall of self-doubt and despondency is brilliantly cast.

Like Alfred, Lord Tennyson's, Plath's natural world is "red in tooth and claw." In the second section of "Two

Views of a Cadaver Room," a poem clearly imitative of W. H. Auden's "Musée des Beaux Arts," the speaker dissects the painting *The Triumph of Death*, calling it a "panorama of smoke and slaughter" to which a pair of young Flemish lovers are oblivious, though "not for long." Within it, desolation is "stalled," for both the couple and a "foolish, delicate" country, but "only in paint." More often, however, Plath conveys mortality in terms of grinding obliteration and an absence of light. Again, this view involves projecting a doom-filled mind onto only those facts of nature that bespeak an incessant withering of vitality.

"Suicide off Egg Rock" builds on the essential irony that a great rock, long likened to an egg (a basic life symbol), sits not upon a fecund sea but upon a "blue wastage." The surf of this "wastage" laps interminably at this egg of rock. Stone is literally and figuratively at the core of this collection, but its durability is rendered as merely another impermanence. The persona's father is a Colossus of Rhodes, broken to bits and strewn over a landscape, inclining to the dust of Percy Bysshe Shelley's Ozymandias, who turned to grit and merged with the desert when faced with the winds of time. Thus it is that in "The Beekeeper's Daughter," with her heart under the foot of that father, the speaker counts herself the "sister of a stone." The relic lady of "All the Dead Dears" is no mere museum piece: Lying dead forever, she is transmuted to "kin" and suited out with a "granite grin." As relics, this kin and the mouse and shrew that had gnawed her anklebone simply prove that the very stars are "grinding. . ./ Our own grist down to its bony face."

The dark becomes, then, the persona's appropriate abode. Having spied two dead moles "out of the dark's ragbag," she employs their fate as a reminder that as the veteran of wars revisits the battlefield nightly in dreams, so she must "enter . . . the pelt of the mole," moving in the deep darkness of a native and lonely habitat. It is the place for a life of ungratified appetite and a place to realize that "what happens between us" (from reader to spouse) occurs without light, vanishing as perpetually and erosively as "each breath." The desultory lesson of the bedroom is that there is no life with another, only shared dissociation.

Context

The reader interested in the feminist character of this collection should remember that it was written in 1960 by a young poet who, like Adrienne Rich, assumed a standard that had been set by men, not women. Only "Spinster," "Strumpet Song," and "I Want, I Want" approach that indirect but seminal judgment of male dominion and the female disavowal of it which undergirds Rich's very early and masterful poem "Aunt Jennifer's Tigers." While it is probably true that Plath always had her female nature in mind when writing, this viewpoint is clearly much less manifest in *The Colossus and Other Poems* than in *The Bell Jar* (1963) and *Ariel* (1965). There are two principal reasons for this fact. The first is that the basic nihilistic viewpoint of these poems gains its power and authenticity precisely from not being rooted in gender. Plath's generalized voice of despair has to meet the standards not of a revolutionary woman but of an illusionless human. This is the reason that the poems elaborate primarily the misery found not in the relations of men and women but rather in the natural, often fatal struggles of nonhuman beings, even moles.

In these poems, Plath is out to meet a test of disillusioned observation established by all the great modern deconstructors of a benignly and purposefully governed universe. Her success in the enterprise, both spiritually and aesthetically, demonstrated a talent in need of no special, patriarchal approval. Here was a brilliant young poet, not a brilliant young female poet. The figures within the poems who most embody and convey the fully realized implications of this unremitting challenge to the idea of a purposeful existence are the man in black (in the poem of the same title) and the male protagonist of "Suicide off Egg Rock." While it is Plath herself who is projected as persona onto these male figures, she has carefully made that persona a hyperconscious but genderless witness for the case of the pure dominion of death.

Even when turning to the title poem, one notices no significant attention to the person's being a daughter of the patriarchal colossus; that role will be explored in "Daddy," the much-evolved offspring of this poem. Here one senses only an angry and disconsolate child, whose remarks about the monstrous father could as easily be a son's as a daughter's. Given Plath's tense willingness in the 1950's to both conform and rebel, she seems to have chosen to position the most important utterances of these poems outside the arena of sexual politics and inside the broadly human one of existential absurdity and failed self-identity. Plath would not have found offensive the identification of her persona as a lost Everyman, whose nihilist voice is the modern extension of Shelley's "legislative" one. The other side of this coin—and here one can locate the second reason for the minimally feminist orientation of the volume—is that Plath simply was not yet prepared to muster and declare her anger as a woman, anger that would go a considerable way toward the creation of a plausible identity. When the voice in these poems is either manifestly female or nearly so, as in the three poems mentioned above and in "The Beekeeper's Daughter," it is only fetally as challenging of patriarchy as the voice of the more mature "Daddy" and "Lady Lazarus." It does not matter if that later voice is riddled with doubt—it is a voice more willing to do battle even if the victory should prove Pyrrhic. That voice is, however, certainly shaping itself here.

While the woman's resolve in "The Spinster" is clearly understood as a coolly rationalized rejection of eros, the poem, at the edges of its satire, envisions the male as an unwarranted and impossible savior. Yet Plath is so subtly attuned even here to that other more broadly existential function of her work that the male's frailty is not seen by the woman directly but only after she has assimilated the "birds' . . . babel" and the "leaves' litter." Though there is a direct attack on Otto Plath, her father and an entomologist, in "The Beekeeper's Daughter," there is none upon men as a class, despite Plath's having made many remarks to those who knew her in the late 1950's about the weakness and folly of the male. It may be that the closest she was able to come to this task was in "I Want, I Want," but the "inveterate patriarch" of the poem—understood as the creator of wasp, wolf, shark, and gannet's beak—is the Western deity, God, and not the literal male as "fascist" (to use the term of severest judgment in "Daddy"). There can be no mistaking, however, that these lyrics were auguries of more severe judgments to come.

Sources for Further Study

Butscher, Edward. *Sylvia Plath: Method and Madness*. New York: Seabury Press, 1976. This biography closely links the stages of Plath's life to a chronological assessment of the poems. The poet's "madness" or obsession is seen to be ordered by the "method" of her aesthetic practice via the agency of the artistic ego. Butscher offers much about which to argue.

King, P. R. "Sylvia Plath." In *Nine Contemporary Poets*. London: Methuen, 1979. An exceptional introduction to Plath's work, including a section on *The Colossus and Other Poems* which argues that the collection displays a "deep dread of experience" and that Plath intended the argument of the poems' speaker to be general, not unique to herself or to some rarefied type.

Kroll, Judith. *Chapters in a Mythology: The Poetry of Sylvia Plath*. New York: Harper & Row, 1976. An indispensable study of all the poetry in light of Robert Graves's myth of the white goddess and Plath's adaptation of her life's material to it. No book so thoroughly, and rightly, dispenses with the spurious ideas of the "confessional" in Plath's practice. The treatment of the series "Poem for a Birthday" helps to fix the relation of this collection to *Ariel*.

McNeil, Helen. "Sylvia Plath." In *Voices and Visions*, edited by Helen Vendler. New York: Random House, 1987. This volume is the companion piece to a Public Broadcasting System television series on American poetry. It is a fine critical starting point for the serious reader. McNeil looks at the poems mainly in terms of how they negotiate the simultaneous and antithetical claims of repression and declaration that seemed to press so heavily upon Plath.

David M. Heaton

COMMUNITIES OF WOMEN: An Idea in Fiction

Author: Nina Auerbach (1943-   )
Type of work: Literary criticism
First published: 1978

Form and Content

Communities of Women: An Idea in Fiction traces the presence and development of the idea of communities of women in nineteenth and twentieth century novels by both men and women writers in England and America in order to trace the expansion of women's freedom in literature, if not in life. In her search for these communities, Nina Auerbach employs provocative and original pairings and readings of texts and authors, ranging from Jane Austen and Louisa May Alcott to Henry James and George Gissing.

Auerbach notes that while initiation into society through brotherhood is a highly prized tradition, belonging to a sisterhood usually means exclusion from society. She argues that communities of women, however, exert a "subtle, unexpected power" throughout history, and it is the presence and power of women's associations which she analyzes in the novels. These communities are self-generative and empower women by allowing them alternative patterns of conduct beyond those of wife, daughter, and mother. Because the presence of communities of women is often veiled and subtle, however, their power is not obvious and their definition is not fixed; their nature, then, will differ from text to text and from century to century. As she identifies communities of women within the novels she analyzes, Auerbach argues that communities of women gain in strength and importance from the nineteenth to the twentieth centuries.

In the introduction of the text, the author discusses the nature and origin of women's, as distinguished from men's, communities and the different reactions to associations of women in England and America. In subsequent chapters, her readings of the texts locate the communities she finds in history: In *Pride and Prejudice* (1813) and *Little Women* (1868-1869), women wait for history because they cannot enter it; in *Cranford* (1851-1853) and *Villette* (1853), women's communities denounce history and devise alternative forms of power; in *The Bostonians* (1884-1885) and *The Odd Women* (1893), women appropriate and redeem history; and in *The Prime of Miss Jean Brodie* (1961), women pass from history into myth.

Communities of Women is a scholarly but highly readable work. Auerbach has read widely, and this text demonstrates her ability to make connections between literature and society from antiquity to the present. *Communities of Women* seeks to define a tradition throughout history of woman's power in literature. Auerbach locates this tradition not only in fiction by women but also in novels by male writers. The work itself is indebted to the presence and power of such communities; the author asserts that her personal and professional associations with women provided her with both spiritual and intellectual support while she was writing the book.

Analysis

The introduction to *Communities of Women* examines essential differences between communities of men and communities of women. Auerbach uses examples of women in classical literature to show the traditional vulnerability of sisterhood to the male hero and to reveal the mutilation, both social and physical, which is associated with isolated groups of women. Yet, these marginalized groups also possess power. The Muses' control of immortality, for example, attests women's exclusion from, yet centrality to, civilization.

The power of communities of women is not obvious because the classical image of mutilation associated with women who exist without men persists throughout history. Male and female communities differ in terms of authority, which is granted to male communities outwardly by the realities of the world or inwardly by the nature of man's own power. Female communities, on the other hand, must create their own authority; their goal is partially to gain a sense of self. Both male and female communities are united by a code, but the male code is overtly articulated and inspirational, while the code within the groups of women is private and subversive.

Auerbach argues that the controversy aroused by the idea of strong communities of women is proof of the importance of that idea and traces contemporary ideas about women's groups to nineteenth century perceptions of sisterhood in England and America. In England, attitudes toward groups of women were situated in traditional gender role stereotypes; they assumed that such communities were based on women's shared sense of suffering or saw them as a solution for the problem of increasing numbers of single women that occurred toward the end of the century. The idea of powerful communities of women, reinforced by the strong Victorian feminist movement toward the end of the century, became a source of fear, driving some women to isolate themselves in order to claim power or to gain validity for groups of women through professionalization.

In America, women's communities posed less of a threat but were still seen as unnatural and undesirable. Consequently, these differing attitudes in England and America led to different results in the formation and perception of women's groups. In England, the thrust was practical and resulted in such specifically historical events as the founding of Queens College, which would train women professionally. In America, the thrust was spiritual and transhistorical, giving rise to a powerful sense of community which, however, was never translated into action. In *Communities of Women*, Auerbach seeks to discover why and how women form communities by analyzing pairs of seemingly dissimilar texts. Auerbach argues that these disparities can be accounted for by the lack of both a shared cultural sense of womanhood and a shared sense of an audience.

Both Jane Austen's *Pride and Prejudice* and Louisa May Alcott's *Little Women* show women moving from the protection of the mother to the protection of the father. Both families are matriarchies in which it is the business of the mother to find husbands for the daughters, and both novels are less about being girls than about women finding a place in an adult world. The novels differ, however, in their sense of completeness with respect to sisterhood. In *Pride and Prejudice*, domesticity and sisterhood assert themselves only through the presence of men. The value of the home rests in leaving it; this situation reflects the economic and legal invisibility of women in a household without a male heir. In *Little Women*, the household world is visible and complete in and of itself; the women reach out to include men in their circle. In both communities, however, women are educated only to wait; they cannot enter history because of their gender.

Elizabeth Gaskell's *Cranford* and Charlotte Brontë's *Villette* represent an advance in the importance of women's communities as both novels subvert and triumph over external truth. In these works, the boundaries of the family disappear as women move out of the family into communities that are either native and friendly or foreign and strange. The isolation and solitude of Cranford allow the women within it to sustain a sense of their own importance. Men are superfluous to this community, but Cranford is able to generate them when they are needed and dispose of them when they are not. Consequently, rather than being victims of the patriarchal system, the women of Cranford triumph over patriarchy by absorbing it. *Villette* is a world of women outside the family in which the maternal and the administrative are mutually exclusive. Its atmosphere of suspicion and intrigue is much different from the nurturing Cranford; in *Villette*, domesticity is waived in favor of power. The novel explores roles of women other than the traditional ones; as such, it is the story of Lucy Snowe's initiation into "the art of ruling."

Auerbach examines late nineteenth century reflections of communities of women in two novels by male authors. In Henry James's *The Bostonians* and George Gissing's *The Odd Women*, history and communities of women merge as women prepare themselves for both spiritual control and service. In *The Bostonians*, Auerbach interprets James's vision of a community of women as an abstract but a triumphant one which, through the friendship of Olive Chancellor and Verena Tarrant, supersedes class differences. George Gissing's *The Odd Women*, on the other hand, historicizes the problem of the "spinster" by associating single women with a deteriorating class. Therefore, his emphasis is economic and social rather than historical. In both of these novels, sisterhood has the potential for political and social change, options which are generally open to men. Auerbach argues that because of gender roles which allow men more freedom than women, only male writers could envision such potential.

Communities of Women concludes with an analysis of contemporary fiction, particularly Muriel Sparks's *The Prime of Miss Jean Brodie*. Contemporary communities of women are characterized by turbulence, disappearance of the family, isolation, and the repudiation, yet embodiment, of male violence. Therefore, Auerbach argues, communities of women have come full circle in that they appropriate male mythology to their own world and become merged with history. This total merging of womanhood with the culture causes women to lose their identity as individuals, but Auerbach sees this changing as women become more assured of their own powers.

Context

Communities of Women represents several significant changes in the direction of feminist criticism. First, Auerbach's emphasis on the importance of women's bonds makes women's friendships visible and meaningful at the same time that it validates the importance of the idea of friendships between members of the same sex, male or female. Second, the author's location of these communities of women within specific historical contexts represents a movement away from the ahistorical nature of some feminist literary criticism. As she fixes the texts within their historical and social framework, Auerbach also points to a tradition of women's relationships rooted in, but with the ability to transcend, their particular historical contexts and argues for the power of such relationships.

Communities of Women is also innovative in Auerbach's ability to locate the friendships and communities she evaluates within fiction written by male authors, rather than working solely within a female literary tradition. This breadth of scope is an important movement away from more traditional feminist studies which locate women's power within literature by women and associate male literature with women's victimization.

In order to develop her historical and literary analysis of female friendship, Auerbach gives highly original readings of texts which are not traditionally thought to deal with communities of women or communities of powerful women. *Villette*, for example, is generally read as a woman's escape from community, and James and Gissing are thought to be, at best, ambivalent about women's power. One might argue that Auerbach's assertion that the concept of a community of women defies a fixed definition gives her broad powers of interpretation, but *Communities of Women* is representative of the author's wide range of reading and her ability to synthesize that reading with original and sometimes provocative interpretations of the literature.

Sources for Further Study

Auerbach, Nina. *Romantic Imprisonment: Women and Other Glorified Outcasts*. New York: Columbia University Press, 1986. This work is representative of Auerbach's independent readings of nineteenth and early twentieth century fiction in which she refuses to isolate women from their culture. Includes essays on Jane Austen, as well as Charles Dickens, Robert Browning, and Lewis Carroll.

Gilbert, Sandra M., and Susan Gubar. *The Madwoman in the Attic: The Woman Writer and the Nineteenth-Century Literary Imagination*. New Haven, Conn.: Yale University Press, 1979. This wide-ranging and groundbreaking work examines the responses of nineteenth century women writers to the male-dominated literary tradition in England. While the readings of the texts are provocative, like Auerbach's, and emphasize the idea of a community of women writers, the emphasis is on women's victimization rather than on power.

Newton, Judith Lowder. *Women, Power, and Subversion: Social Strategies in British Fiction, 1778-1860*. Athens: University of Georgia Press, 1981. This study combines Marxist criticism and feminist analysis of British fiction by women to argue that the novels discussed demonstrate women's challenge to the ideology of women's power as defined by self-sacrifice and influence.

Rich, Adrienne. "When We Dead Awaken: Writing as Re-Vision." In *On Lies, Secrets, and Silence: Selected Prose 1966-1978*. New York: W. W. Norton, 1979. In this essay from her book, Rich argues for the critical necessity for women to reject traditional notions of gender in order to become artists. She uses her own poetry to show how her changing sense of self influenced the development of her art.

Showalter, Elaine. *A Literature of Their Own: British Women Novelists from Brontë to Lessing*. Princeton, N.J.: Princeton University Press, 1977. This text analyzes the idea of a women's tradition in British fiction. Showalter uses a social and literary approach as she compares women novelists to their female contemporaries in order to trace the complexity of women's literary relationships.

Karen Volland Waters

THE COMPANY OF WOMEN

Author: Mary Gordon (1949-   )
Type of work: Novel
Type of plot: Social realism
Time of plot: 1963-1977
Locale: Orano, New York City, and Brooklyn, New York
First published: 1980

Principal characters:

Felicitas Maria Taylor, the young protagonist, who is supported by Father Cyprian, her mother, and four other women

Father Cyprian Leonard, an archconservative priest

Charlotte Taylor, Felicitas' mother

Elizabeth McCullough, the genteel, otherworldly friend of Charlotte

Clare Leary, a wealthy businesswoman

Mary Rose, an usher at a Broadway motion-picture theater

Muriel Fisher, the outsider within the group of women

Robert Cavendish, Felicitas' handsome political science professor and her first lover

Leo Byrne, a quiet, steady hardware store employee whom Felicitas marries

Form and Content

The Company of Women is set in the 1960's and 1970's, when institutions, traditional authorities, and mores were under attack. Initially removed from such inquiry, the novel's plot, like that of Mary Gordon's first novel, *Final Payments* (1975), evolves through a pattern of "closed world," "opened world," and "redefined world." The three-part story, organized around 1963, 1969-1970, and 1977, spans fourteen years in the lives of Felicitas Maria Taylor (from ages fourteen to twenty-eight); a group of five working women including Felicitas' mother, Charlotte; and an ultratraditionalist priest, Father Cyprian Leonard. In the early 1930's, losses brought these single women to Cyprian and one another. During subsequent decades, the friends share unwavering parochial trust in Cyprian's advice. The women and Cyprian place their hopes for the future on young Felicitas. Even though her virgin martyr's name suggests "some hope for ordinary human happiness," there is little that is typical about Felicitas' youth and the radical love and expectations that surround her. She will not find an easy route to ordinary joys and to her adult life as a woman who, in Gordon's words, will no longer "suddenly buckle to the authority of a male mentor, whether it's a priest or professor or a lover."

The story begins in 1963 in western New York, where young Felicitas, her mother, Clare, Elizabeth, Mary Rose, and Muriel gather for their annual August retreat with their mentor. Father Cyprian, whose orthodoxy has reduced his career to the group, takes comfort only in his surrogate daughter Felicitas; she, in turn, adores him and feels closest to the center of God when she is with Cyprian at Mass or in his pickup truck. Despite her mother's and others' occasional private worries, Felicitas is being groomed in Latin, logic, and theology for a future without a man, marriage, or motherhood; Cyprian wants no "womanish" life for her. When Cyprian has a car wreck and Felicitas is hospitalized, their closeness intensifies.

By 1969, however, their relationship has ruptured. Twenty-year-old Felicitas, about to transfer to Columbia University, visits his hometown briefly. Her opposition to the Vietnam War triggers another argument with Cyprian, who has a heart attack. Vowing to change her life, Felicitas leaves, exhausted with their expectations, Cyprian's rages, and the women's propping up of his ego. At Columbia, she falls in love with her professor Robert Cavendish, who pursues, seduces, and adds her to his apartment-commune of sexual and political groupies. Felicitas is back inside a circle of women (one with a young child), devoted to a man who sets their lives' patterns. Attempting to win Robert's waning approval, she sleeps with a student named Richard. Pregnant, she flees an illegal abortion clinic, Robert's circle, and her studies and returns home.

The story's 1977 conclusion shifts to Orano and seven first-person monologues. Only Mary Rose, with a new life outside the circle, does not speak. Charlotte, now starting her own insurance agency, and Elizabeth retired from their jobs to bring Felicitas to Orano before the birth of Felicitas' daughter, Linda, in late 1970. Clare, who built a home for these four next to Cyprian's house, is planning to retire nearby. The seriously ill Cyprian is humbled by the joy that Felicitas, Linda, and the others bring to his life. Muriel remains jealous, but she delights in Linda. Sustained by their reprioritized acceptance, Felicitas emerges from trauma to create a life for herself and Linda—a life that does not rely on male authority for its particular power, one that carefully integrates friendships, chores, plans, intelligence, fears, and mysteries. Felicitas admits to herself now that she will wait for God to come to her. Yet she does not wait to claim "ordinary human happiness" for herself and Linda. Felicitas quietly assumes leadership of the aging group, completes her education, and decides to marry Leo Byrne. When young Linda—who has persuaded Cyprian to pray that she can be a priest—closes the story, her observations confirm how felicitous a woman's gifts can be to a daughter. Linda is in good company.

Analysis

One of Gordon's central preoccupations is to examine women's unquestioning abdication of responsibility to male authority: father figures, priests, lovers, or professors and the male-dominated institutions that each represents. Certainly, Gordon affirms that Father Cyprian has given the five adult women assistance and comfort since the early 1930's, when each was attempting to cope with traumas such as the death of a husband, father, or child; brutal or abandoned marriages; the sole care of aging parents; and various disappointments. Moreover, his mentorship nurtures their remarkable spiritual devotion, which was already becoming an anomaly for their generation. Gordon shows, however, that it is through these women's unquestioning surrender of their and young Felicitas' spiritual, intellectual, emotional, and social lives to Cyprian that very real damage occurs.

While each of the five adult women confesses—sometimes to herself, sometimes to Cyprian—a candid rebellion against his pronouncements, none acts against his advice. For example, Charlotte, who grew up in a large, lively family, knows that she is not providing a normal childhood for Felicitas; however, she entrusts her daughter's development to Cyprian's charge, a trust that no one really questions. They also do not question projecting their hopes on the young girl. When Felicitas attempts to establish a life for herself, the radical damage created by the group's unchecked adoration and trust is obvious. Felicitas' eventual re-creation of a more holistic life for herself and her child demonstrates the necessity and difficulty of such a task for any contemporary woman. At the same time, however, Gordon extends her commentary on authority by showing (through Cyprian, in particular, and Robert, to a lesser degree) that men's unquestioning presumptions of authority and/or adherence to authoritative structures invariably restrict their own lives.

Gordon's exploration of authority can be viewed as a part of her more fundamental preoccupation with systems and standards. According to the novelist, she uses Catholicism as a metaphor for "high esthetic standards and a closed (enclosed) social system" that allows her to explore a wider visionary world as well as "a fiercely limited terrain." Her characters occasionally articulate Gordon's interest; in *The Company of Women*, for example, Charlotte muses: "They were connected to something, they stood for something. . . . When all of them came together, they were something." The more urbane Clare, on the other hand, recognizes that all the others in the group center their professional and private lives so completely on the Catholic church that they "lived in a virginity far more radical than their intact physical states"—a virginity of standards within an enclosed system of faith and devotion that isolates them, as a sort of remnant, from the questions, events, and changes of the 1960's and 1970's. Young Felicitas absorbs the group's radical devotion and high standards with a singleminded relish that isolates her, in turn.

The cloistered nature of this circle of seven, however, masks its own contradiction. For throughout the novel, Gordon sets into motion a less apparent countersystem—one which Cyprian does not recognize or appreciate until the end of the novel and one which the adult Felicitas will explore as she restructures a life for herself, her daughter, and the aging group. This counterpoint is based on several of the older women's capabilities for friendship, problem-solving, business transactions, humaneness, humor, cultural passions, and daily celebrations of life and love. It is a countersystem that has developed alongside that represented by Cyprian and the women. Still, its distinctiveness is its inclusive impulse that counteracts the exclusiveness of "radical virginities" of minds, bodies, spirits, and lives. When one begins to trace these contradictory impulses throughout *The Company of Women*, one is better equipped to appreciate Gordon's working title for the novel: *Fields of Force*. The plural "fields" seems to be an important clue, since a "field of force" is a particular space in which the force produced by a single, invisible, powerful agent (such as electricity) operates. Thus, Gordon's final title for the novel suggests that the women's countersystem—particularly that fashioned by Felicitas—points to the novel's search for wholeness, what novelist and critic Margaret Drabble describes as Gordon's "reaching for . . . a way of connecting the different passages of existence."

Context

The Company of Women and Gordon's other novels raise important, disturbing questions about the difficulties that women face in their decisions about sexuality, marriage, motherhood, careers, and most important, personhood. Gordon introduces such questions in tandem with equally important questions about the moral and spiritual dimensions of contemporary women's lives. Her linked inquiry tests imposed and self-inflicted boundaries at the same time that it explores collisions of transcendent visions of life, such as those of feminism and Catholicism. While her double inquiry remains focused on women, Gordon's questions are clearly intended for men as well; no male character in her novels demonstrates this more thoroughly than Gordon's remarkable character Father Cyprian, whose life continues to be as complex a yearning for and struggle with boundaries as that of Felicitas. Gordon's comprehensive intention for this novel is one that a *Los Angeles Times Book Review* critic, for example, recognizes in a review of *The Company of Women*: "Mary Gordon is on the verge of moving into the company of writers such as William Golding, Bernard Malamud, Walker Percy and Samuel Beckett—the foremost moral novelists of our day."

Such critiques that attempt to place Gordon in various novelistic traditions continue to be revised as Gordon's prize-winning work evolves. Irrespective of categories, assessments of *The Company of Women* must take into account revelations by the novel's highly intelligent and spiritual female protagonist, Felicitas. As a child, she admits to herself that she does not mean the prayer "*Domine, non sum dignus*" (Lord, I am not worthy); she sees herself worthy enough, her soul important enough, to "take God in." She also is capable, for example, of ridiculing Cyprian's disapproval of Jane Austen's novels, which Elizabeth and Felicitas adore. As she whispers to Elizabeth, "He doesn't know everything. He's not God." Still, Felicitas and Elizabeth, wary of displeasing Cyprian, whisper, and Felicitas' sense of self-worth—which equals Cyprian's—will prove to be as dysfunctional as her mentor's. Seeking independence, Felicitas subordinates herself to another man who, with his selfishness, archliberalism, and female coterie, is a secular mirror image of Cyprian's stance. Still, Felicitas' traumas result as much from the older adults' unquestioning, radical nurture of her dysfunctional sense of specialness as they do from her and the older women's unquestioning capitulations to male authority. The unquestioning and radical components remain the novel's most singular warnings. The challenge, as the adult Felicitas recognizes, is in finding healthy ways to put all of life together, to discover and encourage a robust, well-integrated sense of self that can declare "*Sum dignum*"—I am worthy—in the midst of life.

Sources for Further Study

Bauman, Paul. "A Search for the 'Unfettered Self': Mary Gordon on Life and Literature." *Commonwealth* 118 (May 17, 1991): 327. Offers brief but highly useful comments.

Gordon, Mary. "Radical Damage: An Interview with Mary Gordon." Interview by M. Deiter Keyishian. *The Literary Review* 32 (Fall, 1988): 69-82. Includes Gordon's specific comments on the characters Cyprian and Felicitas.

______________. "A Talk with Mary Gordon." Interview by Le Anne Schreiber. *New York Times Book Review*, February 1, 1981, 26-28. A particularly important interview in which Gordon addresses the major themes of *The Company of Women*.

Kessler-Harris, Alice, and William McBrien, eds. *Faith of a (Woman) Writer*. New York: Greenwood Press, 1988. Susan Ward's chapter, "In Search of 'Ordinary Human Happiness': Rebellion and Affirmation in Mary Gordon's Novels," is a thoughtful, interesting study of the heroines of Gordon's first two novels.

Pearlman, Mickey, ed. *American Women Writing Fiction: Memory, Identity, Family, Space*. Lexington: University Press of Kentucky, 1989. An interesting collection of essays, each followed by bibliographies. While John W. Mahon's essay on Gordon focuses on her third novel, it comments briefly on *The Company of Women*. His bibliographies—writings by and about Gordon—follow.

Seabury, Marcia Bundy. "Of Belief and Unbelief: The Novels of Mary Gordon." *Christianity and Literature* 40, no 1 (Autumn, 1990): 37-55. Seabury's analysis of the female protagonists in Gordon's first four novels and her critiques of other scholars' analyses are insightful.

Zinsser, William, ed. *Spiritual Quests: The Art and Craft of Religious Writing*. Boston: Houghton Mifflin, 1988. Includes Gordon's significant lecture "Getting Here from There: A Writer's Reflections on a Religious Past."

Alma Bennett

THE COMPLETE POEMS OF EMILY DICKINSON

Author: Emily Dickinson (1830-1886)
Type of work: Poetry
First published: 1960

Form and Content

Seventy-four years after Emily Dickinson's death, all of her existing poems were gathered into the single volume *The Complete Poems of Emily Dickinson*, a text that represents one woman's rebellion against her patriarchal society's institutions and literary conventions. After the poet's death on May 15, 1886, her sister Lavinia began the customary burning of the deceased's papers but stopped when she discovered the locked wooden box that contained the forty handmade volumes of Dickinson's poems, fifteen sets of unbound volumes, and hundreds of loose rough-draft poems. Thus began the disclosure of what is now commonly known as the most fantastic instance of self-publication in literary history, a career that extended from about 1858 until the early 1870's.

Immediately after discovering the volumes, Lavinia began her attempts to get them published. First, she took some of the volumes to her sister-in-law Susan Dickinson, who apparently proceeded to study them methodically. Two years later, Lavinia decided she was moving too slowly. It is significant that, at a time when women held little power, Lavinia turned for help to still another woman, her brother's lover Mable Loomis Todd, who was responsible for the first editions of Dickinson's poems. By turning to Todd, the somewhat reclusive Lavinia placed herself between two formidable forces; as a result, first there was a fissure in Lavinia and Susan's already strained relationship, then another between Lavinia and Todd. Dickinson's poems were scattered between the Todd and Dickinson residences, and the manuscripts remained so divided until 1950, when ownership of Dickinson's literary estate was transferred to Harvard University.

The Complete Poems of Emily Dickinson, edited by Thomas H. Johnson, is a condensed reading version of the three-volume variorum text published by Harvard University Press in 1955, which brought together all the poems from the editions published by Todd and Thomas W. Higginson (a longtime friend of Dickinson persuaded by Todd to coedit) and by the daughters of Todd and Susan. For ease of reading, the shortened edition makes no distinctions between volume, set, and workshop poems, and unlike the variorum text, it excludes almost all variants. Like the three-volume edition, *The Complete Poems of Emily Dickinson* makes use of handwriting analyses in order to present the poems in chronological order. This edition, which prints with each poem both the approximate composition date and the first publication date, presents Dickinson's canon as extending from the single poem written in 1850 to the two poems written in the year of the poet's death. Since Dickinson herself did not title her poems (except for a handful included in letters), Johnson has headed each of the 1,775 poems with a number for ease of reference.

Johnson's edition was groundbreaking. Before he collected and initiated the handwriting analysis, scholars hoping to study Dickinson's poems had to rely on separate editions of undated texts (since Dickinson herself did not date her poems). Johnson's dating, however, is in no way absolute. Also, Dickinson's incorporation of variant word choices, her several multiple drafts, her use of dashes (sometimes slanted up, sometimes down, sometimes long, sometimes short), and even her placement of words on a page complicate any editor's task. Most especially, her handwriting is at times extremely difficult to read. *The Complete Poems of Emily Dickinson* is the definitive edition, but it is not a perfect text.

Analysis

Emily Dickinson had the extraordinary ability to convey in her poetry her experience of reality. For her, there were both surfaces and evasive underlying meanings. Unlike her contemporaries, she refused to provide definite readings of life's surfaces, and her ambivalent, contradictory, and at times baffling poems reveal this rebellion against doctrinaire certainty, this willingness to reside in indeterminacy.

Confused by such indeterminate verses and concerned about public reaction, Dickinson's first editors conventionalized her poems. They smoothed her syntax, her rhythms, and her rhymes, they altered word choices they believed to be eccentric, and they arranged her challenging poems in categories with interpretive headings such as "Love," "Death," and "Nature." Although done with the best of intentions, these editorial decisions "robbed" (a term Dickinson herself once used under similar circumstances) the poet's lines of much of what makes them powerful and difficult.

In her elliptical, intensely compressed verses (usually four-line stanzas averaging twenty lines), Dickinson omitted conjunctions, used imperfect rhymes, tossed aside agreement between nouns and verbs, created her own adverbs when there were none that fit her needs, and incorporated the subjunctive tense seemingly at will. Especially upsetting to Higginson, Dickinson ignored rules governing article usage, as in her use of the indefinite article in the line "I wish I were a Hay."

In setting her thoughts to rhythm, Dickinson did turn to the conventional meters of popular nineteenth century hymns (the hymn meter of alternating lines of iambic tetrameter and iambic trimeter), but in order to achieve meaning she often incorporated this meter with a twist, such as the addition of an occasional one- or two-stress line. Her "Wild Nights—Wild Nights!" is metrically provocative and startling, terms a contemporary also used when describing Dickinson's piano improvisations. In tone, Dickinson is at one moment intimate and the next stark, at one moment appropriating the voice of a child and the next that of a queen. Whatever voice she appropriates, though, the idiom, with its complexity of syntax and richness of music, is uniquely her own.

Todd and Higginson were too prescriptive in selecting headings for Dickinson's poems. Though certain themes are indeed recurrent, Dickinson's exploration defies the simplistic interpretations that these headings imply, and her overall canon defies compartmentalization. Dickinson followed no school of thought. She easily moved from the realism of "A narrow Fellow in the Grass" to the metaphysics of "I died for Beauty—but was scarce," and poems such as "Sweet Mountains—Ye tell Me no lie—" are not just nature poems but transformations, the creating of a more woman-centered religion that incorporates a reverence for the things of the earth. Though she also created poems about love, Dickinson wrote not the sentimental love poems of her contemporaries but hauntingly erotic and complex explorations, incorporating imagery rich in male and female symbolism. Her religious poetry reveals her unwillingness to accept carte blanche either the patriarchal God of her Puritan forebears or the more maternal version contemporary poets depicted. With her usual mixture of tones, she demands that her Heavenly Father ("Papa above!") "Regard a Mouse." Equally complex, her plumbing of psychological states, physical pain, and death is both unnervingly honest and imagistically descriptive. Poems such as "Crisis is a Hair," "I heard a Fly buzz—when I died—," and "I felt a Cleaving in my Mind" stay with a reader long after the poems are read.

Dickinson's manuscripts, with their many variants, show how much she loved to play with the multiplicity of language. As feminist scholars have pointed out, Dickinson's awareness of connotative meaning transforms "She rose to His Requirement—dropt" from a poem that seems to accept patriarchal conventions into a subversive text that applauds female creativity. Scholars who stress these subversive qualities note that this poet appropriated conventional language, images, and themes and twisted them, disrupting their usual meaning. Because the appropriateness of language, images, and themes was established and governed by a patriarchal society, these scholars define Dickinson's rebellion as being against male authority in general.

Other scholars view Dickinson's poetry not so much as subversive texts as texts that are able to conform to conventional dictates while at the same time rebelling against them. Instead of focusing on Dickinson's duplicity, they place attention on the duality of her language. For them, for example, "The Drop, that wrestles in the Sea—" depicts both male power and female challenge. To see the dualism in Dickinson's poetry, then, is to recognize the situation of women in nineteenth century America. Legally and physically, women were a powerless and oppressed minority in a patriarchal capitalistic system; yet because they were excluded from the marketplace, they were viewed by men as the morally superior sex.

Whether read as duplicitous or dualistic, Dickinson's complex poems certainly reflect the uncomfortable position in which she as a nineteenth century American woman poet found herself. By remembering the times in which this poet created, readers can come a little closer to seeing the extent of her poetic rebellion in creating a language of her own.

Context

When Dickinson was writing, she had few women role models. There were poets such as Elizabeth Barrett Browning whom she admired greatly, but there was no one—female or male—using language the way she was in her volumes. In midcentury America, the most popular lyrics of the day were the conventional and sentimental verses composed by Henry Wadsworth Longfellow, James Russell Lowell, and John Greenleaf Whittier (the "Fireside Poets") and their female counterparts, such as Lydia Huntley Sigourney. In a way, Higginson was correct when in 1862 he deemed her poetry conventionally unpublishable. Dickinson herself had seen what would happen to her unique style when editors, without her permission or knowledge, conventionalized her lines. So her volumes waited, secreted in the bureau drawer.

It is significant that Lavinia, the woman who had protected Dickinson's need for solitude, was the determined force in bringing Dickinson's poetry to a late nineteenth century audience then ripe for change. Furthermore, two generations of women were her first editors (and biographers), thus initiating the scholarly recognition and popularity of Dickinson's poetry. The first collection, *Poems* (1890), went through seven printings in one year, and the 1891 *Poems: Second Series* went through five printings in two years. By the third edition, *Poems: Third Series* (1894), Dickinson was known internationally. Today she is widely accepted as the greatest woman poet. Clearly, Emily Dickinson is a significant literary and cultural force.

Though they were conventionalized, the poetry of those first editions anticipated the verses of the modernists, and leading figures of that movement, such as Hart Crane and William Carlos Williams, pointed to Dickinson's role in poetry's revolution. Certainly, her unconventional grammar, punctuation, and word choices opened up language, making way for the experimentations of the modernists. Another poet who has been very much affected by Dickinson—her poetry and her life—is Adrienne Rich. Sitting in the Dickinson homestead in the 1970's, Rich could not help but marvel at Dickinson's formidable strategy in surviving as a poet and at her absolute rule over her household, society's social conventions, and the language strictures of the time. In the solitude she demanded, Dickinson pursued her self-publishing with total control. She was not a suffragist. As she herself explained, she followed no doctrines. To the patriarchal times in which she lived and to the literary conventions handed her by tradition, however, Dickinson turned her back. She was America's first self-reliant woman poet.

Sources for Further Study

Duchac, Joseph. *The Poems of Emily Dickinson: An Annotated Guide to Commentary in English, 1978-1989*. New York: Macmillan, 1993. This bibliography is organized by poem and is an easy and helpful reference tool for those wanting information on specific poems.

Ferlazzo, Paul. *Emily Dickinson*. Boston: Twayne, 1976. Written specifically for those new to Dickinson, this easy-to-understand text is a good introduction to Dickinson's poetry and life.

Juhasz, Suzanne, ed. *Feminist Critics Read Emily Dickinson*. Bloomington: Indiana University Press, 1983. This collection of essays by some of the most respected Dickinson scholars is prefaced with a piece by Juhasz giving a brief history of feminist interpretations of Dickinson's poetry. Thus it is a good source for students interested in recent criticism.

Rosenbaum, S. P., ed. *Concordance to the Poems of Emily Dickinson*. Ithaca, N.Y.: Cornell University Press, 1964. This one-volume text indexes each word in Dickinson's poetry and is therefore especially helpful when one is studying particular images or subjects.

Wolff, Cynthia Griffin. *Emily Dickinson*. New York: Alfred A. Knopf, 1986. This critical biography makes use of past biographies and is much more manageable and accessible than they are. Also, the bibliography is extensive and the index helpful.

Anna Dunlap

THE COUNTRY GIRLS TRILOGY

Author: Edna O'Brien (1930-)
Type of work: Novels
Type of plot: *Bildungsroman*
Time of plot: The 1930's to the 1960's
Locale: The west of Ireland, Dublin, and London
First published: 1986 (*The Country Girls*, 1960; *The Lonely Girl*, 1962; *Girls in Their Married Bliss*, 1964; *Epilogue*, 1986)

Principal characters:

Caithleen (Kate) Brady, one of the narrators of the novel, a woman who is vulnerable to the attentions of older men

Baba (Bridget) Brennan, Kate's irrepressible school chum and alter ego, and the other narrator of the novel

Form and Content

From the beginning of her writing career with *The Country Girls*, Edna O'Brien served notice there was a new voice, and a woman's voice at that, on the literary scene. In a 1984 interview in the *Paris Review*, O'Brien claimed that women are "fundamentally, biologically, and therefore psychologically different" from men. Women writers are better at expressing emotions and "plumbing the depths," she said, and admitted to not being "the darling of the feminists," who consider her too preoccupied with "old fashioned themes like love and longing." Love and the pursuit of love are certainly dominant themes in her work. That O'Brien's almost exclusively female narrators define their chances of happiness in relation to finding a man, function in a political vacuum, and indeed are rarely equipped by any professional training to operate outside the traditional dependent *Kinder, Kirche, Küche* (children, church, kitchen) relationship is at the root of this antagonism felt by those speaking for women's liberation.

Caithleen (Kate) Brady's first-person narrative begins in a realistically detailed, evocative first page, with its shock to the senses of the cold linoleum on bare feet (her bedroom slippers are, on her mother's orders, to be saved for visits from uncles and aunts). O'Brien quickly establishes what will be recurrent themes in her fiction—the dysfunctional family, with the drunken and brutal father and the long-suffering and overprotective mother, and the protagonist's search for happiness—set against the splendidly realized world of Catholic Ireland in the 1940's and 1950's. It is a world divided into warring camps (male and female, church and laity, country and town) where the hopes of Kate, a romantic, are doomed to failure. Her alter ego is the ebullient realist and her lifelong friend, Baba. The girls spend their midteen years boarding at a strict convent school, with its lingering smell of boiled cabbage. Baba eventually stages their expulsion for writing a "dirty" note that she has composed.

In their late teens, joyously, the two of them come to Dublin. Baba takes a business course; Kate works as a grocer's assistant until she can take the civil service examinations. Loneliness, however, follows them: Baba contracts tuberculosis; Kate's male caller, "Mr. Gentleman" (Jacques de Maurier), whom she had first met in the west, disappoints her. He is the first in a long line of rotters whom O'Brien's heroines encounter: the ugly father and Eugene Gaillard in this trilogy, Herod in *Casualties of Peace* (1966), Dr. Flaggler in *Night* (1972), and many others. In O'Brien's fiction, such unsavory types far outnumber the few good men with decent inclinations, such as Hickey in the trilogy and Auro in *Casualties of Peace*.

The Lonely Girl continues the girls' Dublin saga. Baba is healthy again, but this is largely Kate's story; she is again the narrator. O'Brien involves her romantically with Eugene Gaillard, whose face reminds her of a saint's and who is about the same height as her father. He is a cultivated snob, often cold to her, in bed and in the salon, as he begins the education of his still-naïve, prudish "student." At the novel's conclusion, Kate, wild and feeling debased "because of some damned man," is learning and changing. She is, as she says, finding her feet, "and when I am able to talk I imagine that I won't be alone." Still seeking their connection, she and Baba sail for England. They effect their escape, physically at least, from the constraints of their home environment. O'Brien's humor, and her ear for the best of overheard conversational exchanges, is a saving grace in an otherwise grim situation. "I've a pump in the yard, a bull, and a brother a priest" is the blandishment, easily rejected by Kate, that the reader hears from one of her rural suitors.

Girls in Their Married Bliss, with its ironic title, follows the story of the two women, now in London, two years later. For the first time, Baba assumes the first-person narration. She alternates with an omniscient voice distancing both O'Brien and the reader from the character of Kate. The two women, now about twenty-five-years old, have not left all of their Irishness behind with their sojourn in England. There is a splendid, Celtic rush to Baba's style. Kate too has her share of one-liners, word associations, zany metaphors, and epigrams. "Self interest," she observes, "was a common crime."

In these early novels, as she shows her heroines learning and developing, O'Brien is polishing and improving her writing skills. In *Girls in Their Married Bliss*, the topic is still the search for a loving connection, though here the reader is involved in observing the psychologically realistic and precisely drawn breakup of Kate's marriage to Gaillard. His initials, Grace Eckley notes in her 1974 study *Edna O'Brien*, are those of O'Brien's former husband, Ernest Gebler.

People, in the context of women's roles in society, often rub exquisitely on one another's nerves; in the smaller context of bedroom politics, it is noted, "Men are pure fools." Marriage, at least for the reasons that Kate and Baba enter it in this saga, is not the solution to the quest for female happiness. Baba makes a calculated move for comfort; Kate sees that her interest in men is generated solely by her own needs. They have both matured to the point that they no longer believe in romantic plans. Beginning with the 1967 Penguin revision of *Girls in Their Married Bliss*, the pessimistic tone deepens when Kate has herself sterilized. Divorced, and with the custody of her son lost, she will not make the same mistake again.

In a one-volume reissue of the complete trilogy in 1986, a short *Epilogue*, a monologue delivered by Baba, resolves what might have been regarded previously as a complete personality split between the two women. The ebullient Baba brings readers up to date on past events. The despairing Kate is dead; she drowned, perhaps committing suicide.

This resolution of the twin-heroines in favor of "Baba" in O'Brien's fiction is, however, not final. In *The High Road* (1988), readers are thrown back once again into the narration of a "Kate" figure. Here again is a London-Irish woman who has gone abroad to try to forget a failed love affair in the company of the jet-setters on the Mediterranean. Here is an environment and a social milieu with which O'Brien is much less successful than she is with Ireland and the Irish, whose particularity and universality she feels and captures much more deftly and convincingly.

Analysis

O'Brien's central theme in *The Country Girls Trilogy* is the pursuit of happiness through a loving relationship. That her two central characters are female may win her an audience with some women, but the notion, particularly in Kate's case, that loneliness and despair can only be combatted through a dependent relationship with a man is not acceptable to many.

Baba's objectivity about herself, on the other hand, is more stimulating. Despising "Mavourneen mush," she has no time for whining self-pity; normally clear-eyed, she takes the party with her wherever she goes. "Self-emulation" to the bitter end is her verdict on her friend Kate. What does this malapropism mean? Kate certainly tries to "emulate" many romantic heroines, from Cinderella to her dream mother; "immolation" of self is the result. Baba, for her part, is not given to that kind of fantasy. She is a survivor, a pragmatist, and one who loves her friend, surely rebutting critic Anatole Broyard's suggestion that O'Brien's women cannot get along in life.

To open the trilogy at any of O'Brien's Irish scenes, or any scene in which Baba is onstage, is to be swept away by the fascination of the minutiae of living, superbly observed and articulated, and to enter a fully realized and complex world. The cast of neatly sketched supporting characters is impressively large. Tom (the Ferret) Duggan, of indeterminate age, is one such village "character" who inhabits the world of the girls' years in the west of Ireland. His erratic services as driver (he has only one hand) allow Kate to escape from her father and give him a chance to propose himself as a husband: "What more could a woman want?"

Yet it is through Baba—who came to her, O'Brien writes, through impatience with her own character—that the trilogy finally triumphs. This character, redolent of Geoffrey Chaucer's Wife of Bath and of James Joyce's Molly Bloom, is for critic Mary Jo Salter a large part of the reason that the reader comes away from the trilogy "feeling at least a little glad." For her part, O'Brien is on record admiring the work of her fellow Irish novelist Joyce, and she has indeed written about him enthusiastically in her biography *James and Nora* (1981) and elsewhere.

Context

O'Brien's fictions as a whole fit very uneasily into the history of positive images of women in literature. The trilogy is representative of the problem: Kate is an all-too-typical O'Brien, romantic heroine who defines her chances of life and happiness in relation to her capacity to find a man. She is not equipped with skills to make it on her own, however, and her choice in men inevitably dooms her to failure: If the men with whom Kate associates are not already married, they are otherwise users and abusers of women. As a counterbalance to this syndrome, and in large part the strength of this trilogy, O'Brien gives the reader Baba. She also has no particular job skills, but such is her vigor and iconoclastic approach to life that she is triumphant; it is a pleasure to be in her challenging, abrasive company, living as she does at the top of her voice.

A positive role such as Baba plays in the trilogy is best exemplified elsewhere in O'Brien's work by the Molly Bloom-like Mary Hooligan of *Night.* Such healthy affirmation of female gusto, of joy in life and living, of seizing the day, is, however, the rare exception rather than the rule in O'Brien's fiction. More typical is the whining, romantic loser of the Kate type rendered again, with no name at all, in *A Pagan Place* (1970)—O'Brien's favorite among her works. This choice of a passive-reactive heroine, rather than the active Baba prototype who seizes her opportunities with some flair, continues to preoccupy O'Brien in *Time and Tide* (1992), in which the protagonist, Nell, is inconsolable, but is again able to do little more with life than "bear it."

O'Brien's convent-bred upbringing in the 1940's and 1950's in Ireland may well contribute to her doing better with negative portraits of her leading women. Against other forms of repression—whether in sexual, family, community, or religious forms—she is much more successful; witness the troubles that she had with the Irish censorship board.

Sources for Further Study

Broyard, Anatole. "The Rotten Luck of Kate and Baba." *The New York Times Book Review*, May 11, 1986, 12. O'Brien is the subject of little scholarly attention; with the exception of Grace Eckley's work (below), she is the subject of no book-length study. This one-page, hostile review of the trilogy finds both women antipathetic and in their "furious passivity" a "powerful [negative] argument for feminism."

Eckley, Grace. *Edna O'Brien*. Lewisburg, Pa.: Bucknell University Press, 1974. This work is an excellent, though brief, sympathetic study. It needs to be updated, however, in its primary and secondary materials.

O'Brien, Edna. "The Art of Fiction: Edna O'Brien." Interview by Shusha Guppy. *Paris Review* 26 (Summer, 1984): 22-50. A lengthy and comprehensive interview including O'Brien's views of women writers and her own place in the literary continuum.

__________. "A Conversation with Edna O'Brien." Interview by Philip Roth. *The New York Times Book Review*, November 18, 1984, 38-40. A perceptive, restrained, and generally sympathetic interview. Elicits revealing personal avowals from O'Brien: "The man still has the greater authority and the greater autonomy."

__________. "Why Irish Heroines Don't Have to Be Good Anymore." *The New York Times Book Review*, May 11, 1986, 13. In a one-page article, O'Brien comments on her choice to let the "asperity" of Baba finish the trilogy—"lyricism had to go."

Salter, Mary Jo. "Exiles from Romance." *The New Republic* 194 (June 30, 1986): 36-38. Salter finds the first part of the trilogy best, but she comes away even from the final "soap opera" feeling "at least a little glad."

Archibald E. Irwin

THE COUNTRY OF THE POINTED FIRS

Author: Sarah Orne Jewett (1849-1909)
Type of work: Novel
Type of plot: Domestic realism
Time of plot: The late nineteenth century
Locale: The Maine coastal village of Dunnet Landing
First published: 1896

Principal characters:

The boarder, a woman writer from Boston who comes to Dunnet Landing to find peace and solitude for her work

Mrs. Almira Todd, the town herbalist and the narrator's guide to Dunnet Landing

Mrs. Abby Martin, a woman who fantasizes that she is the twin sister of Queen Victoria

William Blackett, a fisherman who courts Esther Hight

Esther Hight, a shepherdess and William's lover

Elijah Tilley, a fisherman who has devoted his life to the memory of his dead wife

Captain Littlepage, an old sea captain

Form and Content

In *The Country of the Pointed Firs*, Sarah Orne Jewett weaves together several sketches and tales that show the New England character. Taken together, the stories form a portrait of New England life in the late nineteenth century. Individually, each chapter can stand alone as a character sketch or short story.

The novel opens with the arrival of the boarder, a woman writer, in June and closes in the fall, when she leaves Dunnet Landing. The rustic locale is described in the realistic detail of the local color school of American literature. For example, Jewett's descriptions of scenes are sprinkled with names of flowers, such as portulaca, pennyroyal, elecampane, lobelia, and tansy.

The life of Dunnet Landing stands in contrast to the life of the outside world. This Maine coastal village is populated with older characters—unmarried women, widows, farmers, and former sea captains. These people live ordinary, simple lives. The men and young couples have left the community, and those who stayed behind reminisce about the past, when the shipping industry was flourishing. The sketches reveal the personal stories of the inhabitants left behind. As Mrs. Almira Todd guides the boarder through the village, the reader meets these villagers and hears their stories.

One day when the boarder is working on her book, Captain Littlepage stops to visit with her. He talks to her about his love of books and his experiences as a sea captain. He then relates a strange tale told to him by a sailor who had been at the North Pole and seen "human-shaped creatures of fog and cobweb." Littlepage believes that these shadowy creatures were waiting for their passage from this world to the next.

When Mrs. Fosdick pays a visit to Mrs. Todd, the two women spend their time reminiscing and telling the boarder about the townspeople. One evening, Mrs. Todd tells the story of her cousin, "Poor Joanna," whose man left her for another woman. Unable to bear the pain, Joanna left Dunnet Landing to live in isolation on a small island. Although passing fishermen left provisions for her, they respected her privacy and never visited her. Joanna never returned to civilization, choosing to live out her days on the island. Late in August, Mrs. Todd and the boarder attend the Bowden family reunion, where the boarder meets members of the community in one of its rare social gatherings. This reunion shows the importance of continuity in the life of the village and provides the boarder with an opportunity to interact with the local people and to participate in their customs.

Later in the summer, the boarder pays a visit to Elijah Tilley's cottage. The old fisherman tells the boarder about his wife and their life together. When his wife died, leaving him alone, Tilley consoled himself by working to keep the house in the same condition it was in when "Poor Dear" was alive. An atmosphere of melancholy and nostalgia pervades the cottage, but the old fisherman seems content to live among the things that he and his wife had shared.

In "The Queen's Twin," a sketch that was written as a sequel and added later, Abby Martin builds a fantasy world around her imagined bond with Queen Victoria. She was born on the same day as the queen, and she too married a man named Albert. As she talks to Mrs. Todd and the boarder, Mrs. Martin shows how she has spent her life collecting pictures and facts about the queen and tells them that she even named her children after the queen's children. She dreams of a day when she will actually meet Queen Victoria. Near the end of the summer, fisherman William Blackett finally marries shepherdess Esther Hight after a forty-year courtship. Esther had been supporting her paralyzed mother, and when her mother died, the couple decided to marry. This quaint relationship points to the scarcity of young people, children, or conventional couples in the world of Dunnet Landing.

These anecdotes, incidents, and scenes make up the novel. There is no single, strong narrative, but a series of sketches that show the life of Dunnet Landing. As the boarder led readers into this world when she arrived at Dunnet Landing, she leads them out again as the novel ends, when she leaves the village to return to her life in the outside world.

Analysis

Jewett, as a creator of regional fiction, focused on the life of New England towns that no longer exist. In *The Country of the Pointed Firs*, a masterpiece of the local color school of American literature, she shows the sociological and historical aspects of a New England fishing village. The provincial life of the inner world of such coastal villages contrasts with the bustling, prosperous outside world from which the summer visitors come for a time and into which some of the inhabitants escape. Jewett realizes that the changes brought about by industrialization are inevitable, but she laments the loss of the New England village, with its unique customs and independent individuals. In her description of Dunnet Landing, Jewett seeks to re-create the world that she knew so well.

The personal sketches point to Jewett's concern for the survival of the community. She writes about simple country people and dwells on the commonplaces of life—visits to neighbors, family reunions, and tea parties. Jewett uses accurate dialect to create believable characters who speak the native idiom of the region. The rustic locale, scenes from the domestic life of New England, eccentric characters, and local customs provide the subject matter for Jewett's sketches of New England life. With the passage of time and the loss of the shipping industry, this Maine coastal village has lost its vitality; Jewett's characters can only reminisce about life as it used to be. She describes a type of life that she knew was ending. By providing a clear description of Dunnet Landing and its people, she has captured and preserved this part of American life and history for future generations.

The specific personal histories of the people of Dunnet Landing also emphasize that a way of life, once robust and healthy, is dwindling and fading. There are few young people or children, and almost no young men or couples. Rather, the reader is introduced to eccentric older people such as Abby Martin or heartbroken people such as Joanna and Elijah Tilley. Most of the men have moved out into the world and left the women, particularly the older women, behind.

While Jewett wants to depict the charm of this coastal village, she does not hesitate to compare its past and the present. The once-thrilling community is now dying out. The lifeless provincial isolation of the village stands in contrast to the busy, vibrant days when the shipping business was at its peak. Mrs. Todd's garden, alive with herbs of many varieties, is the one aspect of the community that retains its vitality.

Context

Jewett's greatest contribution of American literature is her portrayal of a way of life in New England coastal villages that has since disappeared. In the preface to *The Best Stories of Sarah Orne Jewett* (1925), Willa Cather makes this claim: "If I were asked to name three American books which have the possibility of a long, long, life, I would say at once, *The Scarlet Letter*, *Huckleberry Finn*, and *The Country of the Pointed Firs*. I can think of no others that confront time and change so serenely." Though others may argue with Cather's choices, Jewett was in the forefront of local color writers of the nineteenth century, and *The Country of the Pointed Firs* is widely accepted as her masterpiece.

Jewett is often categorized as a local color writer known for her realistic portrayal of a particular region. Women dominate the local color school of American literature. Such writers as Mary Wilkins Freeman, Harriet Beecher Stowe, and Rose Terry Cooke were contemporaries of Jewett, who was especially influenced by Stowe's *Pearl of Orr's Island* (1862), a pioneering work of the local color school. According to Josephine Donovan, "The New England women created a counter world of their own, a rural realm that existed on the margins of patriarchal society, a world that nourished strong, free women." As a local color writer, Jewett provides a clear picture of a New England coastal town during the last half of the nineteenth century. She goes beyond the description of a particular place in a particular time, however, to portray the lives and strengths of women who lived in those villages, and in so doing, validates those lives. By reading *The Country of the Pointed Firs*, one can gain an understanding of what life was like for women in the nineteenth century.

Jewett is especially fond of older women. In the preface to *The Best Short Stories of Sarah Orne Jewett*, Cather remembers, "She once laughingly told me that her head was full of dear old houses and dear old women, and that when an old house and an old woman came together in her brain with a click, she knew that a story was under way." In *The Country of the Pointed Firs*, Jewett presents older women characters in a way that allows the reader to see their strengths. These older women are reservoirs of knowledge of the past, and Jewett's own longing for the past shows itself in her characters. One sees the beauty of old age in the description of Abby Martin, the queen's twin: "She was a beautiful old woman, with clear eyes and a lovely quietness and genuineness of manner."

Jewett recognizes and appreciates women's work as she focuses on domestic traditions. Mrs. Todd admires her eighty-six-year-old mother, who turned the carpet as she cleaned her house. Abby Martin believes that Queen Victoria must be a "beautiful housekeeper." The sketches are full of the feminine rituals of tea parties, neighborly visits, confidential talks, and reminiscing. The bonds between women—mothers, daughters, cousins, and friends—are strong and enduring.

Sources for Further Study

Cary, Richard, ed. *Appreciation of Sarah Orne Jewett: Twenty-nine Essays*. Waterville, Maine: Colby College Press, 1973. Six of the twenty-nine essays included in this collection deal specifically with *The Country of the Pointed Firs*. Looking at the novel from a historical and sociological perspective, Warner Berthoff argues in "The Art of Sarah Orne Jewett's *Pointed Firs*" that the main story of the book is "the economic disintegration of the coastal towns, the withering away of the enterprise that gave them life." In "An Interpretation of *Pointed Firs*," Francis Fike looks at the major unifying themes of the book.

______________. *Sarah Orne Jewett*. New Haven, Conn.: College and University Press, 1962. The first part of the book contains a chronology of the major events in Jewett's life and a brief biography. Cary provides a summary and evaluation of *The Country of the Pointed Firs*.

Cather, Willa. Preface to *The Best Stories of Sarah Orne Jewett*. 1925. Reprint. Gloucester, Mass.: Peter Smith, 1965. Cather praises Jewett's work for its ability to present sketches of character and scenes in such a way that "they are not stories at all, but life itself."

______________. *Not Under Forty*. New York: Alfred A. Knopf, 1936. In the chapter on Jewett, Cather discusses the design and beauty of the novel: "The *Pointed Firs* sketches are living things caught in the open, with light and freedom and airspaces about them. They melt into the land and the life of the land . . ."

Donovan, Josephine. *New England Local Color Tradition*. New York: Frederick Ungar, 1983. Donovan argues that Jewett was more than simply a local color writer, that she provided examples of strong, independent women and, in doing so, offers a glimpse of what life was like for nineteenth century women.

Sherman, Sarah Way. *Sarah Orne Jewett, an American Persephone*. Hanover, N.H.: University Press of New England, 1989. Sherman treats the subject of the relationships between the women in Jewett's works. She uses the mother-daughter myth of Demeter and Persephone as a vehicle for exploring the relationships between mothers and daughters. In her discussion of *The Country of the Pointed Firs*, Sherman looks at the bonds between mothers, daughters, cousins, and friends.

Judith Barton Williamson

THE CREATION OF FEMINIST CONSCIOUSNESS

Author: Gerda Lerner (1920-)
Type of work: Social criticism
First published: 1993

Form and Content

With *The Creation of Feminist Consciousness: From the Middle Ages to Eighteen-Seventy*, Gerda Lerner has completed her two-volume magnum opus, *Women and History*, which she began with *The Creation of Patriarchy* (1986). Ranging over the whole of Western history from prehistory to the late nineteenth century, Lerner has theorized how and why the system of patriarchy originated (in the first volume) and the long process by which women began to "think their way out" of that systematic subordination (in the second volume). Unlike many historians, Lerner is undaunted by the task of working in so many areas—sources in medieval Latin, Middle English, and Old High German; meditations of medieval mystics and Reformation visionaries; Jewish Romantic poetry; and medieval drama. This view enables Lerner to speculate and generalize about women in history over varied epochs and cultures.

Lerner's book is courageous not only because she covers such a long period of time but also because she considers so many whose work has already been the subject of much historical and literary analysis—from medieval writers Christine de Pizan and Hildegard of Bingen to poet Emily Dickinson. Additionally, she challenges traditional assumptions about women's intellectual prowess. Lerner is not cowed by the task, simply noting that women have not been system-builders in the past because they lacked access to education and their own history. Her own background as a short fiction and screenplay writer (in New York in the 1940's before she returned to academe) undoubtedly helps with her exegesis of poets and dramatists and with her translations of such German women poets as Anna Louisa Karsch (1722-1791).

Lerner rigorously examines her disparate sources to help answer her central question: How and when did feminist consciousness develop? Feminist consciousness, according to Lerner, is a five-step process:

> (1) the awareness of women that they belong to a subordinate group and that, as members of such a group, they have suffered wrongs; (2) the recognition that their condition of subordination is not natural, but societally determined; (3) the development of a sense of sisterhood; (4) the autonomous definition by women of their goals and strategies for changing their condition; and (5) the development of an alternate vision of the future.

This process could only come to fruition once there was the possibility of autonomous women's organizations and a knowledge of women's history—such that women could build on what had been done by women before them instead of just arguing with the ideas of the men before them.

Analysis

Lerner points out how, time after time, perceptive women discovered important arguments to combat women's supposed inferiority, and yet had not known or used the work of their predecessors a generation or several hundred years before their time. This is particularly true of feminist interpretations of biblical passages. Even more critical is the fact that a woman thinker did not have the encouragement and mentoring of her foremothers, but believed that she was the only woman attempting to tackle the problem. Even into the twentieth century, Virginia Woolf in *A Room of One's Own* (1929) and Simone de Beauvoir in *Le Deuxième sexe* (1949; *The Second Sex*, 1953) made erroneous assumptions about women writers and women's history because they simply did not have access to their own history. Lerner's great insight here is that women's subordination cannot be changed as long as history is obscured. For women, this long denial process of more than three thousand years has been devastating.

Reviewing the patriarchal assumptions that she had analyzed at length in the first volume, Lerner uses ancient philosopher Aristotle's *Politics* and the modern debate over the U.S. Constitution to show how such assumptions continued to deny women membership in the polity. Both Aristotle and the framers of the Constitution debated the rights of slaves but not of women. The notion of women's rights lingered below the threshold of the conceivable. Men had the power to define, and women were not a part of the discussion.

Lerner analyzes women's struggle for education ("The Educational Disadvantaging of Women"); the importance of mysticism, biblical criticism, and religious thought for women's autonomous being; how the concept of motherhood gave women authority; the uses of female creativity; the beginnings of female spaces and networks; and the development of women's history. Two generalizations are made about women's education: Women were almost always less well educated than their brothers, and any education was a privilege of class. When education became institutionalized (instead of being handled by the family and apprenticeships), then the disparity between male and female education became obvious. Women were not prepared for university education by being taught Latin and Greek, unless they were of nobility and in line for rule. Nevertheless, there were islands of possibility for some women to be well educated at different times in history: the double monasteries and nunneries (presided over by an abbess) of the Middle Ages, the lay women's religious communities in the cities of Holland and the Rhineland in the twelfth century, some Renaissance courts in Italy and France, and centers of the Protestant Reformation. Still, Lerner estimates that there had been fewer than three hundred "learned women" in all of Western Europe up to the year 1700. A daughter had a better chance if there were no sons in the family, if her family were noble or wealthy, and if her father cared about women's education.

Fully a third of the book is taken up with discussion of the importance of religion in women's quest for autonomy. The mode of mystical revelation has been essential for women. Christianity believes that the Holy Spirit is no respecter of persons and that neither class nor gender is of qualifying importance. A sudden revelation of knowledge can come to anyone, and the "way of the mystics" is honored in church tradition. This kind of revelation is particularly available to women. While only 20 percent of all saints are female (according to one study), a much larger proportion (40 to 52 percent) of saints known for mystical visions and contemplation were women.

Lerner carefully analyzes Hildegard of Bingen and her works, including her visions, letters, sermons, biographies, biblical commentary, and medical texts. Lerner believes that Hildegard is the first woman who derived her authority from God and convinced others (both in her own time and in subsequent centuries) that she had this authority. Her visions are the basis for her remarkable public role as abbess of the Rupertsberg convent. In this capacity, she became a spiritual authority to whom people wrote for advice and answers to religious questions. She also traveled, visited, and preached to emperors and popes, as well as to common people. Her "sapiental theology" (divine wisdom) and her use of female symbolism and iconography derived from her visions, are truly unique. Eve, for example, is not shown as a person but is depicted as a seashell filled with stars.

Other sections discuss Margery Kempe, mystic and pilgrim, the writer of the first autobiography in English; the Cathar and Beguine religious communities of the late medieval period, which gave women leadership roles; women in the left-wing sects of the Protestant Reformation, such as German Pietist Anna Vetter, who prophesies redemption through the female, or Quaker Margaret Fell, or "Mother" Ann Lee, the founder of the Shakers. In the nineteenth century, a number of African American women became known for their mystical visions, preaching, and evangelistic fervor. A luminous example is Rebecca Jackson, who founded a Shaker community for black women in Philadelphia. The rare Jewish women mystics (since women are specifically prohibited from these religious leadership roles in orthodox Judaism) are also examined here.

Women had to find some way of authorizing themselves to speak and write in the public world, some way of overcoming the assumption that their sex automatically excluded them. Lerner examines the history of three modes of self-authorization: through mystical experience (using the example of Hildegard of Bingen), through the experience of motherhood, and through independent creativity, especially poetry (using an extended discussion of Emily Dickinson).

Lerner ends with two chapters designed to counterbalance the weight of the earlier negative stories. She chronicles women's support groups from the medieval religious communities through the salons and "bluestockings" of the eighteenth century, and completes the section with an analysis of the German Romantic women, especially Bettina Brantano von Arnim. The last chapter reiterates Lerner's belief that only with the development of women's history and an active women's movement have women been able to advance beyond the repetition of individuals working in a vacuum.

Context

Gerda Lerner could be called the mother of modern women's history. Her books—beginning with her biography, *The Grimké Sisters from South Carolina* (1967) and especially with *The Majority Finds Its Past* (1979)—have nourished a whole generation of women's history scholars, helping them to ask new questions and use new sources in order to restore women to history, to find the great women of history, and more important, to put women at the center of their analysis. Lerner insists that historians see with both eyes (traditional and nontraditional views of history) in order to correct for historical blind spots, gaining peripheral vision and depth perception. Recalling the seventeenth century astronomer Galileo's whispered "And still, it moves" after his forced retraction of the heliocentric view of the universe, Lerner concludes: "Once the basic fallacy of patriarchal thought—the assumption that a half of humankind can adequately represent the whole—has been exposed and explained, it can no more be undone than was the insight that the earth is round, not flat."

Far-reaching and well-written, *The Creation of Feminist Consciousness* is an excellent general text for the nonspecialist in women's history. The bibliography, arranged topically, chronologically, and by individual, is especially useful. Lerner has managed to negotiate the inevitable trade-off a scholar must make between the narration of a galvanizing story and the necessary scholarly evidence. In telling these stories and in arguing that women must have both knowledge of their own history and a viable collective movement in order to come to feminist consciousness, Lerner creates a believable alternative to patriarchal history.

Sources for Further Study

Anderson, Bonnie S., and Judith P. Zinsser. *A History of Their Own: Women in Europe from Prehistory to the Present*. 2 vols. New York: Harper & Row, 1988. A narrative history of women which reconceptualizes history, dividing eras from the standpoint of women, not on the basis of kings and wars. Very much influenced by Lerner's early work.

Gill, Katherine. "Why Women Have No Usable Past." *The New York Times Book Review* 98 (May 2, 1993): 7, 12. A favorable review of the book by a medieval religious scholar.

Lerner, Gerda. *The Majority Finds Its Past*. New York: Oxford University Press, 1979. Lerner's first theoretical work on women's history, including essays written over the ten years preceding the research and writing of *The Creation of Patriarchy* and *The Creation of Feminist Consciousness*.

Offen, Karen, et al., eds. *Writing Women's History: International Perspectives*. Bloomington: Indiana University Press, 1991. An indispensable collection of articles on the state of women's history in nineteen different countries, as well as theoretical and methodological essays on issues in women's history. Nearly every author cites Gerda Lerner. Contains very useful bibliographies.

Scott, Joan Wallach. "Gender: A Useful Category of Historical Analysis." In *Gender and the Politics of History*. New York: Columbia University Press, 1988. An influential article, tracing the ways gender has been used in historical analysis and Scott's view that the concept of gender must signify power relationships.

Margaret McFadden

THE CREATION OF PATRIARCHY

Author: Gerda Lerner (1920-)
Type of work: Social criticism
First published: 1986

Form and Content

The Creation of Patriarchy, the first book of the two-volume work *Women and History*, begins with Gerda Lerner's conviction that patriarchal systems are historical, that they emerge from historical processes and therefore can be ended by historical processes. If one does not understand patriarchy's historicity, one may be tempted to see it as natural, a product of human biology or psychology and perhaps ordained by God. In fact, these very views of patriarchy have dominated Western culture for more than two thousand years. Lerner's book traces the emergence in the ancient Near East and classical Greece both of patriarchal social systems and of the structures of ideas that led most women and men to accept them as immutable.

Patriarchy, as Lerner defines it, is more than the sexual asymmetry of many tribal societies in which the tasks assigned to women are different from those given to men. It is a system which has institutionalized men's dominance over women and children, both in the family and in the larger society. In a patriarchal society, legal systems give men power within families, and organizational systems deny women access to power in the society's important institutions. The term does not imply that women in patriarchal societies are completely without rights, power, or resources. Lerner leads the reader through the steps, however, by which women in the ancient world came to live in cultures which strictly regulated their sexuality, subjected them to the rule of husbands, and severely limited the powers which they once had shared with men or to which they had held privileged access.

Lerner's model of this transformation sketches the interplay of economic and political forces with ideas about gender as human societies shifted from relatively egalitarian hunter-gatherer tribes to early agricultural societies and, later, to the archaic states in Mesopotamia between the fourth and the second millennia B.C. She devotes half her book to Mesopotamia, exploring the connections between developing class structures, military elites, and increasing limitations on women. Some especially illuminating features of her argument are her insistence on the relationship between slavery and men's domination of women, and her attention to the development of the distinction—central to women's acquiescence in patriarchy—between "respectable" and "non-respectable" women. Finally, in a richly detailed sequence of chapters, she describes the pattern (repeated in many ancient societies) in which venerated mother goddesses were replaced by powerful male gods, and she then connects this with the Hebrew development of monotheism. The Hebrews' "symbolic devaluing of women in relation to the divine," she contends, "becomes one of the founding metaphors of Western civilization." For the second founding metaphor, she turns to classical Greece and the context its culture provides for the philosopher Aristotle's assumption that women are "incomplete and damaged human beings, of an entirely different order than men."

Lerner takes on a vast stretch of human history, one about which our information, especially concerning women, is often frustratingly sketchy. Moreover, this project moves her far from the field to which she devoted much of her career: the creation of feminist perspectives on U.S. history. Nevertheless, Lerner's scholarly habits of mind enable her to keep a firm grip on her questions and hypotheses, while maintaining a cautious open-mindedness and carefully noting the cases in which she and others are speculating and those in which evidence is well established. She organizes her book with "propositions" central to each chapter, and she moves back and forth between detailed explorations of evidence of various sorts—including such literary texts as the Sumerian epic *Gilgamesh* (third millennium B.C.), Homer's *Iliad* and *Odyssey* (eighth century B.C.), and Aeschylus' *Oresteia* (458 B.C.)—and systematic statements of her argument.

Analysis

A major strength of *The Creation of Patriarchy* is Lerner's insistence on avoiding explanations based on a single cause. There was no single "overthrow event" back in the dim prehistorical mists in which men seized control of a matriarchal culture. In fact, Lerner sees some contemporary feminists' quest for an original matriarchy as a step away from historical understanding.

The establishment of slavery in ancient societies is one of Lerner's central examples of a complex change in human relations. She suggests that the institutionalization of slavery requires a crucial human innovation: the possibility of thinking of the group to be dominated as somehow entirely different, other than human. Slavery was possible, Lerner thinks, because, before its invention, men had already experienced the subordination of women of their own group. In early agricultural societies, an increased need for labor had made women's reproductive capacities a commodity which was exchanged or acquired to strengthen families. The practice of the exchange of women meant that men had rights over women that women did not have over men and that women had less autonomy than men. Historians have known that the majority of those first enslaved were women—in warfare, for long periods, enemy men were commonly killed, while women and children were brought into the households of the victors. Lerner asks why this happened and points to the victors' power to control female captives who could be attached to them by rape and pregnancy, who would want to protect their children, and who could have no hope of rescue because their male kin were dead. The ownership of enslaved women and their children may have been the earliest form of private property. Furthermore, just as the idea of women's "difference" had been a starting point for the concept of "slave," so images of slavery reflected back on the definition of "woman."

Economic and political factors interacted with gender relations, then, in the development of militarism, in the practice of turning captives into slaves, and ultimately in the institutionalization of slavery and the establishment of structured classes. All these changes increased male dominance in the public life of archaic states while weakening the kinship and communal structures which could protect and empower women. The "mixture of paternalism and unquestioned authority" which came to characterize the archaic state was mirrored by the patriarchal family, at the same time that the state, in early law codes giving fathers unlimited authority over children and regulating women's sexual behavior far more strictly than men's, recognized its dependence on the functioning of the family.

A long-lasting source of power for ancient women was the religious structures which grew out of early humans' awe for female reproductive powers. The capstone of Lerner's analysis of the relation between the growth of patriarchy and men's increasing control of women's sexuality is her synthesis of research on changes in cosmogonies, which first gave consorts to mother goddesses, then displaced these goddesses as rulers of pantheons by male wind and thunder gods, then finally, in Hebrew monotheism, eliminated them altogether. These changes began in conjunction with the assumption of power by male military leaders, and the mother goddess's replacement by a dominant male god typically occurred after the establishment of an imperialistic kingship. Nevertheless, despite economic and sexual subordination, women's religious power continued for centuries. They could be priestesses, seers, and healers, mediators between humans and gods; the female power to give life continued to be worshipped by men and women in the form of such goddesses as Isis, Ashtoreth, and Venus.

A decisive historical turn, then, was taken as Jewish monotheism, in transforming earlier Near Eastern cultural themes, attacked cults of fertility goddesses. Genesis reverses the life-giving process to make Eve come from Adam's body, negates Earth goddess powers with the creation of humanity by the breath of a sky-god, makes creation an abstract and male-dominated process by giving Adam the power of naming, and, in the stories of God's convenants with the Hebrew people, makes it clear that the convenants are primarily with men who are marked by circumcision and to whose progeny God's promise is given. When the Hebrews' distancing of women from God is joined by Aristotle's view of women as incomplete and lacking autonomy, one can see "at the very foundations of the symbol system of Western civilization" constructs which presented the subordination of women to be natural and, hence, nearly invisible.

Context

The Creation of Patriarchy won the Joan Kelly Prize of the American Historical Association for the best work on women's history in 1986. Reviewers praised the fearlessness and systematic thought underlying its presentation of almost twenty-six hundred years of human history. A survey of such scope necessarily simplifies the causes involved, but Lerner goes far in suggesting the complex and subtle nature of her material and the uncertainty of modern conclusions about ancient societies. To her exploration of the processes by which men's collective dominance of women was built into social systems and systems of religion and philosophy, Lerner brings a contemporary feminist's questions about the interaction of class and race domination with gender relationships. While to some, the persistence of patriarchal domination through many social and cultural formations might bring a conviction of patriarchy's timelessness, Lerner gives students of early history a provocative framework for future investigation of its gradual construction. She also reinforces the conviction that with understanding and a will to change, transformations away from patriarchy are possible.

Lerner says she commenced her study with two questions. The first asked what definitions and concepts can enable one to explain and interpret the particular relationships of women to the making of history. The second explored the explanation for the long delay in women's arrival at an articulated consciousness of and resistance to their subordination, the explanation for their participation in the upholding and transmitting of patriarchy, and the reason for their marginalization in recorded history. Though *The Creation of Patriarchy* begins to answer the second question, it concentrates on the first. Lerner completed her project—whose overall title is *Women and History*—with *The Creation of Feminist Consciousness: From the Middle Ages to Eighteen-Seventy* (1993). These two follow six books on U.S. women's history: *The Grimké Sisters from South Carolina: Pioneers for Woman's Rights and Abolition* (1967), *The Woman in American History* (1971), *Black Women in White America: A Documentary History* (1972), *The Female Experience: An American Documentary* (1977), *The Majority Finds Its Past: Placing Women in History* (1979), and *Teaching Women's History* (1981).

Sources for Further Study

Anderson, Bonnie S., and Judith P. Zinsser. *A History of Their Own: Women in Europe from Prehistory to the Present*. 2 vols. New York: Harper & Row, 1988. Opening chapters discuss the origins of attitudes toward women and traditions subordinating and empowering women. Later chapters give useful attention to the role of class differences in women's experiences, from peasant field workers to mistresses of salons. Volume 2 ends with a history of European feminism. Extensive bibliography.

Eisler, Riane. *The Chalice and the Blade: Our History, Our Future*. Cambridge, Mass.: Harper & Row, 1987. Less scholarly and more polemical than *The Creation of Patriarchy*, this work examines the pattern of early European and Near Eastern history as one in which peaceful, goddess-worshipping "chalice" cultures were defeated by invading militaristic and patriarchal Indo-European groups, "blade" cultures, and connects the contrasts between the two to decisions facing humanity today. Looks more briefly than Lerner does at the ancient Near East; also touches on prehistoric Europe, Minoan Crete, and early Christianity. Maps, chronological tables.

Pantel, Pauline Schmitt, ed. *From Ancient Goddesses to Christian Saints*. Translated by Arthur Goldhammer. Vol. 1 in *A History of Women in the West*, edited by George Duby and Michelle Perrot. Cambridge, Mass.: The Belknap Press of Harvard University Press, 1992. First volume of a series about women's history, originating with Italian scholars and including a number of essays related to Lerner's themes—goddesses, Greek culture, and the myth of matriarchy. Bibliography.

Richlin, Amy. "The Ethnographer's Dilemma and the Dream of a Lost Golden Age." In *Feminist Theory and the Classics*, edited by Nancy Sorkin Rabinowitz and Amy Richlin. New York: Routledge, 1993. Discusses the aims and theoretical approaches of feminist work on ancient history, including Lerner's work. Bibliography.

Scott, Joan Wallach. *Gender and the Politics of History*. New York: Columbia University Press, 1988. Introductory essays, "Women's History" and "Gender: A Useful Category of Historical Analysis," are highly regarded and frequently cited explorations of issues facing historians who attempt a feminist rewriting of history. One of Scott's points in the second essay, written before Lerner's book appeared, is that theories of patriarchy fail to show what gender inequality has to do with other inequalities; *The Creation of Patriarchy* addresses this very question.

Anne B. Howells

CRIMES OF THE HEART

Author: Beth Henley (1952-   )
Type of work: Drama
Type of plot: Comedy
Time of plot: The 1970's
Locale: Hazlehurst, Mississippi
First produced: February, 1979, at Actors Theatre, Louisville, Kentucky
First published: 1981

Principal characters:

Babe Botrelle, the youngest MaGrath sister, modeled on the mythic Southern belle
Lenny MaGrath, the oldest sister, the stereotypic "good girl"
Meg MaGrath, the middle sister, a conventional "bad girl"
Chick Boyle, the sisters' superficial cousin

Form and Content

Crimes of the Heart focuses on the reunion of the three MaGrath sisters at a critical time: The youngest sister, Babe, has shot her husband, Zackery, and their grandfather is hospitalized because of a stroke. Divided into three acts, the play traces the emotional rebirth of the sisters as they move from a feeling of isolation and abandonment to a renewed sense of community and support. As children, they were deserted first by their father and later by their mother: Their father physically left the family when Babe was an infant, and their mother subsequently committed suicide. The legacy of the parents' betrayal is the daughters' repression of emotion and their dysfunctional relationships with men. Babe marries an abusive bigot whom she winds up shooting, Meg deserts her lover Doc Porter before he can desert her, and Lenny fashions a makeshift relationship with their grandfather. During the play, the sisters discover hope and nurturance in their love and concern for one another.

The first act opens on Lenny, sitting alone in the kitchen trying to celebrate her thirtieth birthday by sticking a candle into a cookie. She is interrupted by Chick, who comes on the pretense of picking up a pair of pantyhose. Her real interest, however, is to gossip about Babe and to belittle Meg and her mother. Meg returns home from California, and Babe is released from jail. Meg tells Babe about her failed singing career (she has lost her voice), and Babe tells Meg about Lenny's fling with a Memphis man named Charlie Hill. Yet the focus of the act is Babe's attempted murder of her husband, a wealthy lawyer who is interested in politics. Though Babe frequently says that she shot him because she did not like his looks, she finally admits that he abused her physically and emotionally and brutalized her boyfriend, fifteen-year-old African American Willie Jay.

The second act concentrates on Meg, who appears as an outsider in a culture that values women for the appearance of sexual purity. She is their grandfather's favorite, however, causing Lenny to resent her. The tension builds between these two sisters. First, Lenny is bothered by Meg's lying about her singing career and then by her snitching a bite from each piece of Lenny's candy. Finally, Meg leaves with Doc Porter, who is now married with two children, for a moonlight ride and upsets the sisters' plan to play cards together. The act ends with two disruptive events: Babe's lawyer, Barnette Lloyd, discloses that her husband has photographs of Babe and Willie Jay together, and the grandfather has another stroke.

The third act focuses on the positive insights reached by each of the sisters. After going out with Doc Porter, Meg returns home singing happily. She knows that he is not romantically interested in her, yet she still is jubilant because she can care for someone else, an awareness that causes her to rediscover her singing voice. Babe comes to terms with her mother's suicide and why she hanged the cat with her. After two failed attempts at suicide herself, Babe realizes that her mother did not want to be alone. Meg assures Babe that, unlike their mother, the

MaGrath sisters will never be alone since they have one another. Lenny grows more self-confident and asserts her independence by chasing Chick out of the kitchen with a broom and then calling her Memphis boyfriend. The play finishes in a celebratory note as Meg and Babe watch Lenny blow out the candles on an enormous birthday cake, which they eat together.

Analysis

Beth Henley's central theme in *Crimes of the Heart* is betrayal, particularly that of a fierce and rigid, life-denying patriarchy associated with the South. The three sisters around whom the play revolves have been abandoned by their father, an act which subsequently leads to their mother's suicide. This concern with the father's betrayal suggests the larger issue of how the South historically has victimized all but white, Anglo-Saxon males of "sound" mind and social connections.

Henley creates a female-centered drama with a community largely defined by women. The play is confined to one indoor set—the kitchen, traditionally the heart of the home and the province of women, where men are conventionally seen and treated as interlopers and intruders upon female space. Doc Porter, Meg's old boyfriend, and Barnette Lloyd, Babe's young lawyer, are the only male characters seen on stage, though the looming presences of the sisters' father and grandfather and of Babe's husband, Zackery Botrelle, are felt throughout the play. Unlike these patriarchal figures, Porter and Lloyd are not part of the good-old-boy culture; they too are outsiders. They are nurturers, supporting women rather than abusing them.

The central relationships in the play are those shared by the sisters, but each of them must come to terms with self vis-à-vis a male. The playwright is realistic; she does not imagine a world exclusive of men. Instead, she presents a world where the old dies into the new, where not only Meg but also Babe and Lenny must find potential for a positive male-female relationship based on compatibility, equality, and warmth. Before finding this possible kinship, however, each sister must grapple with her own demons.

Henley draws on stereotypic images of women, especially those associated with the South, in order to undercut and reshape them. Babe recalls the dominant ladylike image engendered by the Southern belle myth of the virginal white goddess. Henley describes Babe as having "an angelic face and fierce volatile eyes." The ambivalence in Henley's description implies the ambivalence in the ladylike myth. Babe MaGrath, like Scarlett O'Hara, is anything but a submissive, asexual, porcelain doll. She is a survivor. She violates the patriarchal code in two very distinct ways: She has an affair with an African American boy, and she shoots her well-established husband. Both acts of passion—one for intimacy and the other for freedom—are her ways of beginning to understand who she is apart from an effacing and abusive patriarchy.

In her treatment of Lenny, the playwright draws on the image of the sexually repressed "spinster," traditionally a negative model in Southern literature. She tends to her grandfather, wearing her dead grandmother's gloves and hat and sleeping in the kitchen to be closer to him. Lenny discovers her own identity, however, as she asserts herself against Chick and calls her former boyfriend.

Meg is the traditional bad girl who refuses to abide by a sexual double standard. She is also the most blatantly self-destructive of the sisters: She smokes too much, drinks too much, and constantly flirts with danger. Their father's desertion and their mother's suicide are the catalysts for Meg's attempt to anesthetize herself against feeling and suffering by staring at pictures of grotesquely diseased people. Henley suggests that Meg's collapse in California results from her denial of emotion. When she breaks down, she tries to cram all of her valuables into the March of Dimes collection box.

The title *Crimes of the Heart* invites several interpretations. There are definite crimes according to the law, such as Zackery's abuse of Babe and Babe's shooting of Zackery. Yet the majority of crimes suggested by the title are those of passion committed against the self and against others. Misplaced anger, fear, jealousy, and revenge are the key passions, all of which are a response to the father's initial betrayal and desertion.

Central to the sisters' crimes of the heart are the repression and displacement of emotion, as they frequently mistake heartache for hunger pains. They consume food to deaden the feeling of abandonment and isolation, behavior that their grandfather encourages. Because the sisters are accustomed to masking their pain with food, they have difficulty identifying what they truly feel. After Babe shoots Zackery, she makes a big pitcher of fresh lemonade with excessive amounts of sugar and does the same thing after telling Meg about the shooting. Meg constantly eats, ransacking Lenny's candy for nuts. When Lenny gets upset, it is evident that she really is upset about Meg's leaving their card game, hence deserting Babe and Lenny to be with Doc Porter.

The play can be read as a celebration of familial bonding and the past, but it is a past which is revised and reconstructed. The final scene with the sisters celebrating Lenny's birthday together clearly contrasts with the opening scene, where Lenny tries to celebrate alone. The movement from isolation to connectedness, from Lenny's mock celebration to the sisters' real celebration, indicates that the emergent MaGraths do not betray one another. This is a new community based on consideration and support, though such nurturance may be temporary.

Context

In 1980, Henley's *Crimes of the Heart* became the first drama to win the Pulitzer Prize before its Broadway debut, also marking the first time in twenty-two years that a woman had won the prize for drama. Acknowledgment of the play also included a Guggenheim Award from *Newsday*, a New York Drama Critics Circle Award, and a Tony nomination. In addition to receiving critical acclaim, the play was well received by theatergoers and was turned into an equally popular film in 1986, for which Henley wrote the screenplay.

Crimes of the Heart is distinctively Southern in its focus on place, community, humor, violence, and the past. Yet Henley's perspective, like that of her contemporaries Alice Walker, Maya Angelou, and Rita Mae Brown, is from the view of the historically betrayed female. Considering the father's betrayal as emblematic of how the traditional family and community at large have failed women especially, it is necessary to Henley's revision of community in the play that the sisters come to terms with the past. Part of that understanding involves seeing the potential for a reciprocal relationship with men.

An element of that male-dominated past with which they must struggle is the very real presence of the grandfather, who does not abandon them physically like their father. Seemingly, the situation is quite the reverse: The grandfather provides a home for them. Yet he imposes his desires upon them, effacing theirs. When Lenny says that he only "wanted what was best" for them, Meg responds, "Sometimes I wonder what we wanted." Her response suggests the crucial point from which a new community emerges—not from a prescribed code of behavior, but from the needs and desires of the individual members.

Henley's play clearly grows out of a Southern literary tradition characterized by a fascination with how communal ties and a sense of the past shape character, how laughter alleviates suffering. Distinguishing her treatment in *Crimes of the Heart* is that she presents a new vision of community, one based on tolerance and acceptance. Without sacrificing or rejecting her literary legacy, she reshapes it to create space for the female voice. Her next two plays, *The Miss Firecracker Contest* (1980) and *The Wake of Jamey Foster* (1982), also centered on women protagonists who discover their strength and integrity while coming to terms with the past, but the community that emerges is not as tolerant and accepting as that in *Crimes of the Heart*. The characters remain largely isolated and abandoned in a world ultimately defined by a standard that excludes the personal needs of diverse members.

Sources for Further Study

Gwin, Minrose C. "Sweeping the Kitchen: Revelation and Revolution in Contemporary Southern Women's Writing." *Southern Quarterly* 30 (Winter/Spring, 1992): 54-62. Gwin argues that the play's narrative dismantles patriarchal power and replaces it with maternal strength. She convincingly shows that the kitchen of the grandfather's house becomes the space of empowerment for the sisters as they share joy and pain.

Haedicke, Janet V. "A Population (and Theater) at Risk: Battered Women in Henley's *Crimes of the Heart* and Shepard's *A Lie of the Mind*." *Modern Drama* 36 (March, 1993): 83-95. Haedicke rereads Henley as a reactionary, upholding traditional male-female relationships based on a male hierarchy. Argues that Henley trivializes violence against women in the family, hence reaffirming female victimization.

Harbin, Billy J. "Familial Bonds in the Plays of Beth Henley." *Southern Quarterly* 25 (Spring, 1987): 81-94.

Harbin studies Henley's treatment of family, community, and their disintegration. He concludes that the sisters, through their endurance of pain and suffering, move toward a renewed sense of familial trust and unity.

Hargrove, Nancy D. "The Tragicomic Vision of Beth Henley's Drama." *Southern Quarterly* 22 (Summer, 1984): 54-70. Noting that Henley's plays are essentially serious though presented in a comic mode, Hargrove discusses the negative themes, such as physical and emotional death, associated with Henley's bleak view of human life. Hargrove decides, however, that this tragic vision is relieved by the sisters' affection and solidarity.

Kachur, Barbara. "Women Playwrights on Broadway: Henley, Howe, Norman, and Wasserstein." In *Contemporary American Theatre*, edited by Bruce King. London: Macmillan, 1991. Kachur examines how Henley underscores the relationship between death and comedy, generating laughter in the face of existential madness. Kachur argues that the playwright raises women above the domestic sphere, making them models of strength and integrity.

Laughlin, Karen L. "Criminality, Desire, and Community: A Feminist Approach to Beth Henley's *Crimes of the Heart*." *Women and Performance: A Journal of Feminist Theory* 3 (1986): 35-51. Laughlin examines the play against feminist theories on criminality and desire in order to determine whether the experience of the MaGrath sisters reflects female experience generally. She persuasively shows that the sisters are oppressed by a patriarchal structure and that their choices are based on those of their grandfather.

Shepard, Alan Clarke. "Aborted Rage in Beth Henley's Women." *Modern Drama* 36 (March, 1993): 96-108. Shepard explores how the fantasies of murder in Henley's plays are strategies for coping with emotional and physical abuse while repressing rage. Shepard concludes that the sisters try to repair and preserve their lives within the seriously flawed, patriarchal system that they have inherited.

Chella Courington

A DIARY FROM DIXIE

Author: Mary Boykin Chesnut (1823-1886)
Type of work: Diary
Time of work: 1861-1865
Locale: Montgomery, Alabama; Richmond, Virginia; and Charleston and Camden, South Carolina
First published: 1905

Principal personages:

Mary Chesnut, a highly educated observer of Civil War events and people

James Chesnut, Jr., Mary's husband, a wealthy and influential Southern planter, senator, and general

Jefferson Davis, the president of the Confederacy and a close friend of the Chesnuts

Abraham Lincoln, the president of the United States during the war years, who is mentioned frequently in the diary

Sarah Buchanan ("Buck") Preston, a beautiful young friend of Mary who had a romance with Confederate General John Bell Hood

Form and Content

Mary Chesnut kept her journal from early in 1861, just before the Civil War began, to shortly after the end of the war, in 1865. Her commentary on the conversations and events of her day reveals a keen awareness of the oppression to which women—black or white, slave or free—were subjected during that period. While she would not consider herself a feminist, her diary reveals sensibilities and concerns that place her far ahead of her time and led to problems in the publication of her work after her death.

Chesnut's diary is also important as a historical document. Since she and her husband were socially prominent and he was a major figure in the war itself, everyone who was important in the war was dramatized in her pages. Because of the Chesnuts' position, they were always at the scene of major events—in Montgomery, Alabama, for the formation of the Confederacy and later in Richmond, Virginia, its second capital; in Charleston, South Carolina, for the firing on Fort Sumter, which began the hostilities of the war; in various towns and cities near the path of Union General William Tecumseh Sherman's march to the sea, often just escaping capture; and after the end of the war, back at their plantation near Camden, South Carolina. After the South's defeat, the Chesnuts experienced the terrors and privations of the war's aftermath: poverty, raids, destruction, and at times near starvation.

Yet it would be misleading to think that one can learn from the diary only about major events of the war. Mary Chesnut was interested in and cared about everything. She wrote about the slaves on the plantation with the same attention to the individual that she gave to major social, political, and military figures, so that the reader learns much about slavery and the pain of her position as a slaveowner morally opposed to the institution of slavery. An avid lover of literature, Mary Chesnut read, and commented astutely upon in the diary, almost every major English, American, and French writer of her time, and she personally knew important Southern writers, such as William Gilmore Simms and Paul Hamilton Hayne. She was passionately interested in the lives of women of all ranks of society, from the African American slave women, to the white Sandhill women (normally the sort called "poor white trash" in the South) who begged food from her family, to the women of the first families in Southern society. She considered the lives of women of every station to be a form of slavery in a male-dominated culture, and she wrote about them all, leaving a document just as important to the understanding of women's history as it is to the knowledge of a watershed political and military crisis.

The diary has a complicated publication history. The journals were written in the 1860's, but Chesnut revised them extensively in the 1880's, hoping to see them published. Severe ill health caused her to give up the work, however, and she bequeathed the journals to a young relative, Isabella Martin. Fearing that their frankness made them unsuitable for publication, Martin did little with them for some time. Fortunately, in 1904, Martin met Myrta Lockett Avary, a scholarly young Southern woman, and together they brought out the journals in 1905, both in serial publication and in book form, under the title *A Diary from Dixie*. They included less than half of the original work, and they revised freely in a mistaken attempt to "improve" on Chesnut's writing. In 1949, Ben Ames Williams, a descendant of Mary Chesnut, brought out another edition of *A Diary from Dixie*. Though considerably longer than the 1905 version, Williams' edition also improvises freely; he even added whole sentences of his own. According to Elisabeth Muhlenfeld, Chesnut's best biographer, neither Martin and Avary nor Williams acknowledged that their versions were greatly altered from the original. The diary finally found, nearly a century after Chesnut's own revised version, an editor who was faithful to her text. The distinguished historian C. Vann Woodward, working from all of Chesnut's versions, brought out in 1982 a definitive, faithful, and complete version of the diary; it won the 1982 Pulitzer Prize in history. Noting that Mary Chesnut herself did not like the term "Dixie" and never used it, Woodward gave the diary a new title—*Mary Chesnut's Civil War*.

Analysis

It comes as no surprise to a reader of Jane Austen that Mary Chesnut was also an Austen reader. It shows in three primary ways: the humor blended with seriousness, the novelistic tendencies of the diary, and the commitment to the lives and problems of women. Even in the darkest days of the war, Mary wrote in the diary, "I laugh aloud." She was determined to show no one, not even her husband, how grim her fears and forecasts for the future were. Like Austen, Chesnut also loved novels; perhaps her favorite was William Makepeace Thackeray's *Vanity Fair* (1847-1848), for it showed, as she was attempting to do, all levels of society, both moments of nobility and episodes of ridiculous behavior. She also saw life and society as a Vanity Fair.

Indeed, the novelistic aspect of the diary has been often remarked upon, most notably by Edmund Wilson, the eminent literary critic, who observed that Chesnut establishes, "as a novelist does, an atmosphere, an emotional tone." Wilson especially draws attention to the story of Sarah Buchanan "Buck" Preston and General John Bell Hood, whose on-again, off-again romance lends suspense to the pages and whose final failure to marry serves as a metaphor for the end of the war and the decline of the South.

Chesnut's inclination toward novels actually led her to attempt the writing of fiction in between the writing of the journals in the 1860's and the major revision of the 1880's. Her first novel, *The Captain and the Colonel*, takes place in wartime and draws upon her family and friends for the characters. She spent much time revising her work, trying to improve on the plot, character development, and dialogue. Her second fictional attempt was *Two Years of My Life*, also drawing on her own life, including her romance with her husband, James Chesnut, Jr. Neither novel was ever published, but surviving chapters suggest, according to Woodward, that these serious efforts at the writing of novels influenced and helped to shape the major revision of the diary in the 1880's.

Context

Chesnut was passionate about the plight of women, seeing all women, even the wealthiest, as slaves to men. Though she was very fond of her husband and of other male family members and friends, she was appalled at much male behavior and often exclaims against it in the diary. One of the horrors that most disgusted her was the practice (of which her husband was apparently not guilty) of white men raping slave women and keeping them and their children in the household. She draws a vivid comparison between women condemned as prostitutes and men whose households are shamelessly peopled with their unwilling mates and children. She felt sorry for all the women involved—both for the men's wives and daughters and for the African American women—and for the children.

She also was shocked at the silence of women, except on the topics considered to be appropriate to them—social events, finery, the duties of the household. The much-praised softness of the voices of women she believed to be the result of this suppression: "So we whimper and whine, do we? Always we speak in a deprecating voice, do we? And sigh gently at the end of every sentence—why? . . . Do you wonder that we are afraid to raise our voices above a mendicant's moan?" Along with this repression, Chesnut noted a contradictory impulse of men to blame the women they had rendered powerless: Her own husband "cannot forbear the gratification of taunting me with his *ruin*, for which I am no more responsible than the man in the moon. But it is the habit of all men to fancy that in some inscrutable way their wives are the cause of all evil in their lives."

It is both appropriate and ironic that Chesnut's diary was almost lost to history when the woman she trusted to be her editor long resisted publication because of Chesnut's indelicacy. Isabella Martin thought that she was protecting her relative's memory. This sentiment gives the reader some idea of the suppression of women's voices that Mary Chesnut never accepted. One can be very glad that she did not, for she speaks as a woman and to women, and to men, in a voice that all people need to hear.

Sources for Further Study

Aaron, Daniel. *The Unwritten War: American Writers and the Civil War*. New York: Alfred A. Knopf, 1973. A brief but perceptive discussion of Mary Chesnut and her diary. Particularly valuable is the examination of specific characters and groups of characters.

Freeman, Douglas Southall. *The South to Posterity: An Introduction to the Writing of Confederate History*. Port Washington, N.Y.: Kennikat Press, 1964. Calling the diary "a remarkable human document," Freeman offers passages from Chesnut's character sketches.

Martin, Isabella D., and Myrta Lockett Avary. Introduction to *A Diary from Dixie, as Written by Mary Boykin Chesnut, Wife of James Chesnut, Jr., United States Senator from South Carolina, 1859-1861, and Afterward an Aide to Jefferson Davis and a Brigadier General in the Confederate Army*, by Mary Chesnut. Edited by Isabella D. Martin and Myrta Lockett Avary. New York: Peter Smith, 1929. Chiefly interesting for Martin's explanation of why she delayed publication of the diary for so long.

Muhlenfeld, Elisabeth. *Mary Boykin Chesnut: A Biography*. Baton Rouge: Louisiana State University Press, 1981. The longest and best biography of Chesnut, it contains an overview of the diary and its publication history and seven chapters divided by milestones in Chesnut's life. The study is based on Muhlenfeld's 1978 University of South Carolina Ph.D. dissertation, "Mary Boykin Chesnut: the Writer and Her Work," which also includes Chesnut's memoir on her sister Kate and an essay on James Chesnut, Jr., Mary's husband.

Williams, Ben Ames. *House Divided*. Boston: Houghton, Mifflin, 1947. A Civil War novel by Mary Chesnut's descendant who published the second major edition of the diary. Draws heavily on *A Diary from Dixie*, and one of the characters is modeled on Mary Chesnut herself.

Wilson, Edmund. *Patriotic Gore: Studies in the Literature of the American Civil War*. New York: Oxford University Press, 1962. Of the writings on Mary Chesnut, this work makes strongest case for the diary's literary qualities. Wilson calls it "an extraordinary document—in its informal department, a masterpiece."

Woodward, C. Vann. Introduction to *Mary Chesnut's Civil War*, by Mary Chesnut. Edited by C. Vann Woodward. New Haven, Conn.: Yale University Press, 1981. The best overall introduction to Chesnut's life and work.

June M. Frazer

THE DIARY OF A YOUNG GIRL

Author: Anne Frank (1929-1945)
Type of work: Diary
Time of work: 1942-1944
Locale: Amsterdam, The Netherlands
First published: *Het Achterhuis*, 1947 (English translation, 1952)

Principal personages:

Anne Frank, a German Jew in hiding with her family in war-torn Amsterdam

Otto Frank, Anne's father, a businessman

Edith Höllander Frank, Anne's mother and Otto's wife

Margot Betti Frank, Anne's sister, who is three and one half years older than Anne

Mr. and **Mrs. Van Daan,** Jewish business associates of Otto Frank, also hiding from the Gestapo

Peter Van Daan, the Van Daans' fifteen-year-old son

Albert Düssel, a middle-aged dentist who is hiding with the Franks

Form and Content

On June 12, 1942, Anne Frank celebrated her thirteenth birthday. Of the gifts that she received, the one that she liked best was a clothbound diary. Anne and her family lived in Nazi-occupied Amsterdam, and the net of genocide was closing inexorably around them. A few weeks after Anne's birthday, her sister, Margot, was ordered to report to the reception center for a concentration camp.

The family, driven to desperate measures, foresaw their future. They had prepared a space above Otto Frank's warehouse and office at 263 Prinsengracht, where they planned to hide, aided by loyal Dutch friends. They entered their loft through a door hidden by a bookcase made in anticipation of this eventuality.

The family went into hiding in July, 1942. Anne's diary, first published in its totality in 1989, reveals that the Frank family had planned to disappear on July 16, but that the situation in The Netherlands became so threatening for Jews that on July 9 they left their apartment and began their twenty-five-month exile at 263 Prinsengracht. In the full version of Anne's diary, the resettlement of the Frank family, related in some detail, is accompanied by a detailed description of the rooms where the Franks and four other Jews—the Van Daan family (in real life, the Van Pels family) and Dr. Düssel—lived.

The diary, written chronologically with occasional additions and revisions made within some of the entries, exists in two versions because Anne recopied the original. Also, as she ran out of space, she wrote entries, always dated, on loose sheets of paper. Otto Frank's former employees gathered these materials immediately after the Nazis arrested and removed the eight people hiding in the loft, leaving these papers behind.

The Diary of a Young Girl is one of the most important documents about Adolf Hitler's attempts to destroy a major part of Europe. Anne Frank did not set out to create a public document. Rather, on an almost daily basis, she related what life was like for her and the seven people sharing the small space in the loft. A toilet unthinkingly flushed, a water faucet turned on, a laugh, a cough, or a song might call attention to the presumably unoccupied space above the warehouse. Even though the windows were painted blue against air raids, light from the rooms of this hiding place might escape through a chip in the paint and be noticed.

Obviously, none of the eight people in hiding dared ever venture into the street. Their only respite was brief weekend excursions into the warehouse when it was officially closed, but even those outings jeopardized their security. Given such confinement, the tempers of the eight people sequestered in the loft sometimes flared. They had no respite from one another and little privacy. The specter of arrest and deportation always loomed over them.

Despite this situation, the Franks did what they could to live as normally as possible. Otto educated his daughters and Peter Van Daan. Anne and Margot helped their mother bake cakes and cookies when they got some butter at Christmas. Anne Frank was unfailingly optimistic despite occasional bouts of moodiness. Her sense of humor never left her, nor did her hope for the future.

Analysis

Young children often have imaginary friends. As they mature, they replace these spectral companions with real playmates. Anne Frank, after she followed her family into hiding, never enjoyed this luxury. Her diary became her friend, her retreat from a microcosm imposed upon her and the seven other Jews imprisoned in the loft because of Hitler's master plan of genocide against Jews and other groups. Even before the Franks entered the loft, Anne had named her diary "Kitty." The day that she received the diary, she wrote that she expected great support from it because she would use it to confide things that she had never been able to tell anyone she had known.

As the diary begins, the young girl writes about herself more than about others, but her scope broadens. As the diary continues, the reader encounters a bright, vibrant adolescent growing into womanhood; in the face of what eventually happens to Anne, the coming-of-age takes on an almost mocking tone for the reader.

Few can read this diary as Anne Frank wrote it. She, unlike her readers, was innocent of the outcome of her family's twenty-five-month exile. Her last entry, an introspective, self-analytical assessment, is dated August 1, 1944. The dreaded *Grüne Polizei* made its raid on the Franks' loft on August 4. By the end of the following March, all of the Franks except Otto were dead. Margot succumbed to typhus at the Bergen-Belsen concentration camp, probably in early March, 1945. The same illness killed Anne a week or two later.

No matter how much detachment readers bring to *The Diary of a Young Girl*, any reading of it is inevitably overshadowed by the specter of death that hung over Jews in Hitler's Germany and the satellites that it occupied. The book and the subsequent film and stage versions tweak the consciences of those exposed to the story.

Writing with no audience in mind, Anne Frank achieved a voice at once authentic and extraordinarily touching. In the pages of her diary, one is privy to the deepest thoughts of a young girl growing up. Readers are struck by how rapidly Anne Frank matures emotionally and intellectually, having maturity thrust upon her because she has nothing except her imagination to divert her. Introspection becomes her favorite pastime, self-analysis her perpetual game. In a situation in which privacy was impossible, Anne retreated to the privacy of her diary and there made tentative sallies into the young womanhood that most girls of her age make by associating with friends, playing games, seeing films, and dating. These normal outlets were foreclosed, forcing Anne to invent her own.

Given the Frank family's future and the final outcome of their exile, one discovers ironies in Anne's diary that are simultaneously chilling and ingratiating. For example, in her entry for December 24, 1943, Anne writes of news that Mrs. Kleiman, one of her family's Dutch protectors, brings about her daughter, Jopie, also an adolescent. Anne is jealous at hearing how Jopie plays hooky from school, has friends, and belongs to clubs. In this same entry, however, she acknowledges how much luckier she is than many Jewish children of her age.

According to survivors, Anne Frank was a conciliator even during her final months in the concentration camp. Within the confines of exiles' meager space, Anne becomes Peter Van Daan's confidante. Peter's parents frequently argue, which upsets their son. In her entries of March 4 and 6, 1944, Anne speaks warmly about Peter and insightfully of her concerns about his parents. She wonders whether he will fall in love with her; her exuberance in telling Kitty about him suggests that Anne has a heavy crush on this only boy in her sphere. In subsequent weeks, Peter and Anne become closer still and engage in the teenage flirtations expected of young people.

The Van Daans' cat, Mouchi, enters exile with them, giving them another small mouth to feed but providing them with some diversion. One soon realizes, however, that is it dangerous for the exiles to keep Mouchi: Once when Mouchi relieves itself in a pile of shavings rather than in its litter box, its urine drips through the ceiling of the old building and into a bag of potatoes stored below. No great harm is done, but had the drip been into the warehouse rather than into another part of the loft, everyone's safety would have been compromised.

Writers create microcosms within which to unfold their stories. Anne Frank's microcosm was almost as confined as the one that Jean-Paul Sartre created for his play *Huis-clos* (1944; *No Exit*, 1946), but Anne did not manufacture the microcosm that was her world for more than two years.

Context

Anne Frank's diary is a chronicle of a young girl growing to womanhood. At a time when she should have been exploring her world, Anne, an optimistic, bright, gregarious adolescent, was confined with seven other people to a small, enclosed space. Sounds, light through the painted window, or any small miscue put everyone in this hiding place at risk. The concerns of this young girl focused on a society that arbitrarily singled out specific groups of people and marked them for annihilation. The organized madness that marked more than a decade of Hitler's rule in Germany blurred the lines that usually define human morality. Under Hitler, wrong equaled right, despotism equaled patriotism.

In such a climate, the thirteen-year-old Anne began a diary that suggests extraordinary writing skills in a young woman coping with a hopeless situation by thinking and writing her way around it. Although she cannot be called a feminist writer, Anne Frank stands as a beacon to all people, especially to writers. The diary contains little rancor, because Anne believed that she would prevail in the end. Although she died, she was correct in her assumption: In the end, she has prevailed through her words. Her most lasting monument is the diary that she left behind. Translated into more than forty languages and transformed into drama, it has perhaps made those who have been exposed to it less willing to subscribe to the kind of despotism that marked the era in which Anne Frank grew to womanhood.

Sources for Further Study

Berryman, John. *The Freedom of the Poet.* New York: Farrar, Straus & Giroux, 1976. Berryman's essay "The Development of Anne Frank" reads the diary as an important document about a girl's maturation into an adult. Berryman draws heavily upon specific examples from the diary, sometimes interpreting them in Freudian terms.

Bettelheim, Bruno. *Surviving and Other Essays.* New York: Alfred A. Knopf, 1979. In his essay "The Ignored Lesson of Anne Frank," this noted child psychologist and concentration camp survivor criticizes Otto Frank for not fleeing Holland when he could and for trying to sustain some semblance of normal life for his exiled family. Bettelheim suggests that, once in their situation, the Franks might have armed themselves and had a shoot-out when the *Grüne Polizei* arrested them.

Ehrenburg, Ill'ia. *Chekhov, Stendhal, and Other Essays.* New York: Alfred A. Knopf, 1963. Ehrenburg's chapter "Anne Frank's Diary" deals feelingly with Anne's recollection of her school days and with the personal contradictions that one expects to find in a girl at the formative stage Anne was in when she went into hiding.

Frank, Anne. *The Diary of Anne Frank: The Critical Edition.* Edited by David Barnouw and Gerrold van der Stroom. Translated by Arnold J. Pomerans and B. M. Mooyaart-Doubleday. New York: Doubleday, 1989. The most important piece of Anne Frank scholarship. Besides offering detailed chapters about the Franks' background and their arrest and subsequent detention, it provides the only complete version of the diary in its various forms. Indispensable for those seriously interested in Anne Frank research.

Morton, Frederic. "Her Literary Legacy." *The New York Times Book Review*, September 20, 1959, 22. In this review of *The Works of Anne Frank*, Morton attempts an objective assessment of her writing. He concludes that none of it has the power and literary strength of the diary, her best-known book.

R. Baird Shuman

THE DOLLMAKER

Author: Harriette Simpson Arnow (1908-1986)
Type of work: Novel
Type of plot: Social criticism
Time of plot: The 1940's, during World War II
Locale: The Appalachian area of Kentucky and Detroit, Michigan
First published: 1954

Principal characters:

Gertie Nevels, a strong woman, both physically and intellectually, who must move her family when her husband decides to take a factory job in Detroit

Clovis Nevels, Gertie's husband

Reuben, Gertie and Clovis' son who returns to Kentucky by himself

Cassie, Gertie and Clovis' daughter who is killed by a train

Form and Content

Harriette Simpson Arnow's *The Dollmaker* is a story of the displacement of a Kentucky hill family by the promise of a better life in the industrial, World War II North. Upon learning that he will not be called up for immediate military service, Clovis Nevels decides, without consulting his wife, Gertie, to seek employment in Detroit. When he finds a job, Clovis sends for his family and settles them in Merrie Hill Alley, a ghetto of transplanted industrial workers and their families.

Arnow opens *The Dollmaker* by introducing the reader to Gertie, the work's large, rawboned protagonist. In the opening section, Gertie Nevels is riding alone on a mule with only a baby held securely in her arms as a companion. This surreal scene soon assumes meaning when Gertie flags down a car occupied by an Army officer and his driver and forces them to take her and her child into town. The desperate nature of Gertie's trip becomes apparent when Arnow discloses that Gertie's child has typhoid and will surely die if medical attention is not soon forthcoming. The strength of Gertie's convictions and the delicacy in her large hands is demonstrated when, with only a pocket knife, a hairpin, and a poplar twig at her disposal, she performs a tracheotomy on her infant son Amos as the car speeds toward town.

For the next eight chapters, Arnow paints a naturalistic portrait of the Kentucky mountain world into which Gertie has been thrust, a world of hardships and unrecognized dreams. One dream, however, keeps Gertie going: She wants to own a small piece of land to which she and her family can belong. She saves a few cents here and there toward the day that she will be able to buy the land. When her brother Henley is killed in the war, Gertie learns that he has left her nearly three hundred dollars of his "cattle money." With her newfound wealth, Gertie moves toward making her dream a reality. She buys a piece of land known as the Tipton place from her uncle and begins making her new purchase conform to her expectations.

Gertie's dream is thwarted and the degree of the actual control she has over her life becomes clear, however, when Clovis sends word that he wants Gertie and his children to join him in Detroit. Instead of supporting Gertie in her quest for a personal identity, Gertie's mother and uncle insist that she take back the money she gave her uncle for the farm and use it for the move to Detroit. Receiving no encouragement, except for passive acceptance from her reclusive father, Gertie gives in to the pressure.

Gertie's dilemma introduces the theme of the mother-child rift that will appear again in the conflict between Gertie and Reuben. Gertie's mother condemns Gertie for her sinful ways of playing cards and dancing, pleasures that she enjoyed with her father and brother. The unrelenting, fundamentalist concept of condemnation is apparent when Gertie's mother declares that Henley was killed as a punishment for his sinful ways. Gertie refuses to accept this judgment and instead finds her spirituality in a transcendental relationship with the land on which she lives, leading to her need to own land of her own.

Arnow recounts Gertie's move to and residence in Merrie Hill. Removed from their familiar surroundings and extended family, Gertie and Clovis' immediate family begins to polarize and disintegrate. On one side is Clovis and several children who find adventure and a new identity in their new home. Each of them loses any emotional connection with the lives they had left behind; their speech takes on new connotations, and their attitudes come into line with their new cosmopolitan surroundings. In contrast, Gertie, Reuben, and Cassie refuse total immersion into the Promised Land of Detroit. Gertie and Cassie try to create worlds of their own, while Reuben gives up on his family and returns to Kentucky.

The move to Detroit offers Clovis more than simply a job: He finds a brotherhood based upon antimanagement sentiments and total disdain for the factory owner. Just as when he decided to move his family to Detroit, Clovis couches no interference with his union leanings. When Gertie questions the actions committed in the name of the union, he insists that she does not understand what is happening.

Detroit continues to destroy the things near and dear to Gertie. She loses the children most akin to her in spirit. Although she understands his reasons for leaving, Gertie is deeply hurt when Reuben blames her for the family's removal from their home in Kentucky. It is Cassie's death, however, that is most painful for Gertie. To reinforce the effect of Cassie's death, Arnow creates an emotionally draining scene in which Cassie not only is killed but also is mutilated as her mother watches. The reader experiences the accident almost in slow motion. Each wound suffered by Cassie is witnessed by her mother and Arnow's readers.

Although it is not as traumatic as Cassie's death scene, Arnow creates another highly emotional scene in which Gertie demolishes her prized piece of cherry wood that she had preserved so long for her proposed carving of Christ. Her destruction of the piece of wood demonstrates her understanding that she will never be able to create an appropriate face for her statue. When Gertie strikes the cherry wood with the ax, she finally realizes that her ability to create as she wishes is gone.

Gertie Nevels' resolution to her situation contrasts the situation in which she found herself at the opening of the novel. With baby Amos in her arms, Gertie had begun a quest to protect and deliver her family. In the end, she realizes that she and her family have been caught up in the vast sea of humanity being pushed by the ever-increasing needs of World War II. Like Gertie's, most individuals' needs were subordinated by the needs of the larger social structure of the country and the world.

Analysis

Arnow's intention in *The Dollmaker* is to show how an individual's dreams and aspirations can be ignored and how those of a woman often take a backseat to the wishes of her husband. The realism of Arnow's work is built upon a series of motifs, the most dominant of which are the quest and the Earth Mother. Such recurring concepts provide the novel's artistic and structural foundation.

In the classical sense, Gertie Nevels' story is the story of a quest—in her case, the quest for an identity. To be herself, Gertie knows that she must have an identity other than that of the wife of Clovis Nevels or the mother of Reuben and Cassie Nevels. All of Gertie's life is spent in this quest. By scrimping and saving every spare cent that comes her way, Gertie takes the first step toward achieving an identity—owning a piece of land to call her own. When she receives money upon the death of her brother, Gertie's dream is at hand. The time that she spends readying the Tipton place for habitation is the first real example of Gertie's ability to create a world of her own. As is the case in classical quest stories, however, obstacles are thrown in Gertie's way. Gertie's husband accepts a job in a factory in Detroit and demands that his family join him, negating Gertie's dreams. Her mother and uncle stand staunchly against her and demand that she give in to the wishes of her husband.

Arnow complicates Gertie's underlying quest by having her serve as an Earth Mother figure with a need to create. As with her ownership of the land, Gertie's need to create is thwarted by social conditions and demands. The act of wood carving that gives Gertie so many hours of pleasure and hope is transformed into an impersonal, mass-production of ornaments and tidbits to be bartered and sold to supplement Clovis' meager salary. The soul is taken out of Gertie's work, much as it is from her, a reality that Arnow illustrates when Gertie destroys the cherry wood.

Context

The Dollmaker made both a popular and critical splash when it appeared in 1954. The reading public rushed to read of the struggles of Gertie Nevels, and the critical establishment placed its stamp of approval on the novel when it came in second to William Faulkner's *A Fable* for the 1955 National Book Award. *The Dollmaker* differs from other American migration novels, such as John Steinbeck's *The Grapes of Wrath* (1939) and James Still's *River of Earth* (1940), by centering its plot and theme upon how such a forced move affected a woman.

Arnow's intention is to show the second-class status in which many American women found themselves during the first half of the twentieth century. By drawing specific attention to the trials and tribulations of Gertie Nevels, Arnow intensifies her message regarding the greater scope of the work. She depicts a family which belittles the needs and dreams of a female member, much as society as a whole belittled the needs and dreams of the working class.

Arnow's novel enters the canon of women's literature alongside other works that show the indifference of society to its population as a whole through the treatment of women. One can discern parallels between *The Dollmaker* and Rebecca Harding Davis' *Life in the Iron Mills: Or, The Korl Woman* (1861), Kate Chopin's *The Awakening* (1899), and Willa Cather's *My Ántonia* (1918) because they all depict the secondary roles that women's dreams often play in society.

Sources for Further Study

Baer, Barbara L. "Harriette Arnow's Chronicles of Destruction." *The Nation* 222 (January 31, 1976): 117-120. Baer shows how Arnow's *The Dollmaker* is an intricate part of what is considered her "Kentucky trilogy." Argues that although *The Dollmaker* can be read from the feminist view, it is an excellent example of a work which documents the initiation of American society into the modern, industrial age.

Cunningham, Rodger. " 'Adjustments and What It Means': The Tragedy of Space in The Dollmaker." In *The Poetics of Appalachian Space*, edited by Parks Lanier, Jr. Knoxville: University of Tennessee Press, 1991. This article approaches Arnow's novel from a different perspective. Cunningham discusses how the novel is the story of an individual seeking space of her own but tragically finding her dream destroyed at every turn.

Eckley, Wilton. *Harriette Arnow.* New York: Twayne, 1974. This book-length study of Arnow's works offers an excellent appraisal of her canon through the completion of *The Weedkiller's Daughter* (1970). Three particular chapters should be of interest to anyone delving into the significance of *The Dollmaker*. Chapter 1 is a biographical sketch which illuminates some of the major events in Arnow's life. Chapter 5 is an analysis of *The Dollmaker*. Chapter 8 gives an overview of Arnow's career and makes some suggestions as to where her career might lead.

Gower, Herschel. "Regions and Rebels." In *The History of Southern Literature*, edited by Louis D. Rubin, Jr., et al. Baton Rouge: Louisiana State University Press, 1985. This article places Arnow in the context of the Southern writers of the late nineteenth and early twentieth centuries who provided a depiction of common folk, as opposed to earlier writers who recalled the good old days of the plantation South.

Oates, Joyce Carol. "On Harriette Arnow's *The Dollmaker*." Afterword to *The Dollmaker*. New York: Avon Books, 1972. In her commentary, Oates presents two dominant factors to be considered when reading *The Dollmaker*. First, the Nevels family's story represents humanity as a whole, caught in a neverending cycle of beginnings and endings. Second, Oates sees the work as representative of American literary naturalism in which the individual is controlled by social forces, most specifically economic forces.

Thomas B. Frazier

DUST TRACKS ON A ROAD

Author: Zora Neale Hurston (1891-1960)
Type of work: Autobiography
Time of work: The late nineteenth century to 1940
Locale: Florida, New York, and California
First published: 1942

Principal personages:

Zora Neale Hurston, the author, who tells her story from her birth in Eatonville, Florida, to her middle years in California

John Hurston, Hurston's father, the mayor of Eatonville and a pastor of the Macedonian Baptist Church

Lucy Potts Hurston, Hurston's mother, who died when Hurston was nine years old

Albert W. Price III, Hurston's lover and the man who inspired her 1937 novel *Their Eyes Were Watching God*

Form and Content

Zora Neale Hurston's life has been surrounded by questions and controversy. Although *Dust Tracks on a Road* is Hurston's official autobiography, many of these questions, especially about her adult life, are not answered in this work. While parts of Hurston's personality and life will always remain elusive, she has selected certain experiences and images that appear repeatedly in her novels and nonfictional works, most notably in her anthropological work *Mules and Men* (1935) and in her most famous novel, *Their Eyes Were Watching God* (1937). These experiences and perceptions, many of them written in African American dialect, reappear in *Dust Tracks on a Road*, her last fully completed work, and disclose much of her personality. Hurston thus reveals much more of herself than she probably intended. While her narration is written in an informal, conversational style, her point of view is definitely feminist—or, according to fellow African American writer Alice Walker, "womanist." The womanist stance in Hurston's works became an inspiration and a model for a new generation of African American women writers in the last quarter of the twentieth century.

Dust Tracks on a Road begins with the courtship and marriage of Hurston's parents and ends with Hurston's move to California in 1940. Her mother, Lucy Potts, was reared in Georgia but left for Florida when she married a penniless "over-the-creek" black man who was not acceptable to her family. Hurston's father built a home in the town of Eatonville, Florida, and soon became its mayor and the minister of the Macedonian Baptist Church. Hurston was thus born in the all-black town of Eatonville in 1891. Although she was somewhat late in learning to walk, her audacious personality emerged when she finally started. She claims that once she began walking, she simply could not stop. Her feet "took to wandering," she had an urge to go places, and her spirit moved to the horizon. Her life was dramatically changed by the death of her mother when Hurston was only nine years old; she considered this event to be a turning point in her life. The loss of a possible matriarchal world and the consequences of that loss reverberate throughout Hurston's writings.

Hurston's determination to succeed, to become educated, and to write also echoes throughout her account. In the second half of her autobiography, Hurston writes of research, love, religion, her books, and her race. She details her struggle for an education and names the people who helped her attain one. She describes her role in the Harlem Renaissance and how and why she wrote her novels, stories, and anthropological works. Her autobiography is the account of a writer's life. The obstacles that she faced would have been insurmountable for a less determined, less talented writer because Hurston lived and wrote as a woman in a male-dominated society and as a black in a racist world.

Although Hurston wanted to speak her mind, her publishers and the white reading public limited how freely she could speak in print. Critic Claudine Raynaud states that Hurston's self-consciousness about her white audience led her to create another voice. For example, she does not give the name of her first husband in her autobiography, nor does she mention that she married Albert W. Price III. Despite the significant difference in age between Hurston and Price, Hurston instead credits the demands made by her career for the demise of their relationship. Price once told her that his wife would not work, and he deeply resented her commitment to intellectual pursuits. Even though Hurston is silent about many aspects of her life and is somewhat ambivalent about the society in which she lived, her autobiographical work is a tribute to her womanist artistry.

Analysis

In her introduction to the 1991 edition of *Dust Tracks on a Road*, noted poet and author Maya Angelou states, "It is difficult, if not impossible to find and touch the real Zora Neale Hurston." Hurston's autobiography certainly reveals many gaps and silences that raise many questions about her life. According to critic Henry Louis Gates, Jr., Hurston's narrative has two voices that call attention to the simultaneous existence of two fragmented cultures in the United States—modern American culture and African American culture. The narrative voice of *Dust Tracks on a Road* at one moment is speaking as one formally educated in the Western European tradition and at the next moment is speaking in African American dialect from the store's porch in Eatonville, Florida.

The tension between these cultures and voices accounts for several of the seeming contradictions in Hurston's narrative. For example, Hurston relates the story of the elderly white man who helped bring her into the world and who later became her friend. This "gray-haired white man" told her never to lie, that only "niggers lie and lie." Hurston claims she understood that her white friend was speaking not of race but of class; however, she later states that her favorite pastime was listening to the "lyin' " sessions that took place on the porch of the local store, and that "anyone whose mouth was cut sideways" was given to lying. In such instances, Hurston's voice reflects the double consciousness of which W. E. B. Du Bois spoke, a sense of standing outside oneself and viewing oneself with the consciousness of the oppressor. Gates suggests that the "real" Zora Neale Hurston can be found in the silences between these two voices, that she is both and neither. Hurston speaks of standing outside her culture as an observer at an early age. She states that she felt a "terrible aloneness" because she was in a "world of vanished communion" with her people.

As an African American feminist, Hurston's voice reflects not only the tension of a black in a nonblack world but also the tension of a woman in a male-dominated society. The reader senses not a double, but a triple consciousness in Hurston's account of the lyin' sessions on the porch at the store. While Hurston states that she loved to listen to the stories that were "passed through" the men's mouths on the porch, the purpose of many of the stories were to elevate men at the expense of women. The porch tales reinforced feelings of male superiority while insisting on female inferiority and submission. The mostly male sessions were punctuated with comments such as "Ada Dell is ruint, you know!", or a tale was told that ended with the comparison of a woman to "an old tin can out of the trash pile." Hurston's criticism of the "porch talkers" was personal. It was, to some extent, the reflection of her relationship with her own father. She states that her father was used to being "a hero" on the store porch and in church, and therefore was angry when his intelligence was challenged at home. The real Hurston stood alone, outside the role that society had created for her as a woman.

Hurston's voice, or voices, can be located in the tensions created by the intersection of race and gender and in the creative linguistic practices that characterize her autobiography. The images and metaphors that occur repeatedly in her text are a careful "naming" of her emotions, a common practice in African American culture. In the account of her mother's death, Hurston personifies Death as a strange being with "huge square toes" who lives in a secret place in her yard. Although Death is polite to Lucy Potts Hurston, he has a weapon in his hand. In all Hurston's personifications of Death, he carries a weapon, a symbol of ultimate victory or defeat.

Hurston is also concerned with the subjects of God and religion. She discusses her father's role as minister, describes the church services she attended as a child, and then explains why she sees religion in more universal terms. She tells her readers that she has made peace "with the universe" as she found it. Peace with the universe was necessary for Hurston because, perhaps more than any other writer of her era, she spoke from the periphery of both her own community and the larger society in which she lived in order to address the tensions created by the intersection of race and gender.

Context

Despite physical and financial hardships, Hurston wrote and researched for thirty years. In that time, she published four novels; two books of folklore; numerous stories, articles, and plays; and her autobiography, *Dust Tracks on a Road*. Her works went out of print and remained almost forgotten until Alice Walker discovered her autobiographical narratives, placed a marker on her forgotten grave, and excavated her buried life. Since then, Hurston's work has been read and reinterpreted by a new generation of readers and literary critics. *Dust Tracks on a Road* is one of the important literary narratives that constitute Hurston's autobiography. Hurston's autobiography has had a tremendous impact on African American feminist theory.

In all Hurston's literary works, her nonfiction as well as her fiction, she presents the same personality in the same language. She also presents the same issues. In *Dust Tracks on a Road*, Hurston calls attention to the male practice of objectifying women. Her depiction of porch tales or "lyin' " sessions carries a double message. While Hurston applauds the creative aspect of the "John de Conquer" and mule stories, she also criticizes the community that allowed males to set the boundaries of discourse. She informs her reader that women only "visited" the store's porch to "have it proven" that their husbands were good providers. Hurston, on the other hand, disrupted the boundaries of male-generated discourse and spoke out against the objectification of women. Hurston's free spirit and audacity have inspired a generation of African American women writers, including Walker, Gayl Jones, Toni Morrison, Toni Cade Bambara, and Terry McMillan.

Sources for Further Study

Awkward, Michael. *Inspiriting Influences: Tradition, Revision, and Afro-American Women's Novels*. New York: Columbia University Press, 1989. In this intertextual analysis of four novels in the African American women's tradition, Awkward connects Hurston's *Their Eyes Were Watching God* to novels by Toni Morrison, Gloria Naylor, and Alice Walker. He demonstrates that each of these women have "blackened" their works in various ways by reflecting the African American culture.

Gates, Henry Louis, Jr. *The Signifying Monkey: A Theory of African-American Literary Criticism*. New York: Oxford University Press, 1988. Gates's essays focus on the narrative strategies of African American writers. The chapter on Hurston discusses her use of the "Speakerly Text," or the African American oral tradition.

Hemenway, Robert E. *Zora Neale Hurston: A Literary Biography*. Urbana: University of Illinois Press, 1977. In this historical analysis of Hurston's life and writing, the chapter on *Dust Tracks on a Road* describes Hurston's struggle to write her official autobiography. Hemenway also details the final tragic decade of Hurston's life.

Howard, Lillie P. *Zora Neale Hurston*. Boston: Twayne, 1980. This literary biography provides a critical analysis of Hurston's life and times and of her works. The first three chapters are devoted to her life, while the remaining chapters analyze her four novels.

Russell, Sandi. *Render Me My Song: African American Women Writers from Slavery to the Present*. New York: St. Martin's Press, 1990. Among the concise accounts of the lives of African American women writers in this volume is an overview of the life and major works of Hurston.

Showalter, Elaine, Lea Baechler, and A. Walton Litz, eds. *Modern American Women Writers*. New York: Charles Scribner's Sons, 1991. A collection of essays that covers a wide range of women writers. Includes essays on Maya Angelou, Gwendolyn Brooks, Toni Morrison, and Zora Neale Hurston. Craig Werner's essay is an updated overview of Hurston's novels and most of her shorter works from an Afrocentric perspective.

Weixlmann, Joe, and Houston A. Baker, eds. *Studies in Black American Literature*. Vol. 3. Greenwood, Fla.: Penkeville, 1988. Two essays in this collection focus on Hurston and her literary works. Claudine Raynaud's essay, "Autobiography as 'Lying' Session," analyzes Hurston's autobiography and the criticism that surrounds it.

Yvonne Johnson

THE EDIBLE WOMAN

Author: Margaret Atwood (1939-   )
Type of work: Novel
Type of plot: Satire
Time of plot: The mid-twentieth century
Locale: A major city in Canada, probably Toronto
First published: 1969

Principal characters:

Marian MacAlpin, a researcher for a product test-marketing firm
Ainsley Tewce, her roommate and mirror opposite
Peter, her conservative fiancé
Duncan, her lover, the antithesis of Peter
Clara Bates, her old college chum
Len Slank, a college friend who becomes the sperm donor for Ainsley's child
Trevor and **Fish,** Duncan's roommates
The lady down stairs, Marian and Ainsley's priggish landlady

Form and Content

The Edible Woman, the debut work of fiction by noted Canadian poet Margaret Atwood, is a forerunner of much of the feminist literature that would follow the theme of woman in search of individual identity and worthwhile meaning in her life. The work is divided into three distinct sections, separated by the literary device of alternating narrative point of view. Although the narrator does not change, the voice changes as her perspective of herself alters. Section 1 employs first-person, though unreliable, narration, in section 2 the narrator refers to herself in third person as she essentially loses touch with who she is, and the third section returns to first person as the narrator reclaims her identity. At the time of its release, the novel was a fresh approach to the presentation of women characters in fiction, an almost surreal type of feminist black humor.

Although the story is set within the time frame of the free-love 1960's, when women were beginning to discover themselves as individuals, the protagonist, Marian MacAlpin, seems wedged in by the values and myths of the generation that preceded her. Consequently, it is her adopted belief that in order for a woman, even an educated woman, to attain full identity, she must be defined by association with a successful man. In acquiescence to this code, Marian becomes involved with and subsequently engaged to Peter, an attractive young up-and-comer who expects her to act and react only in prescribed, predictable, and, above all, sensible ways.

The metamorphosis of Marian begins one evening when she has too much to drink at a dinner party and begins to realize that she is essentially disappearing as an individual. To illustrate this point, she first crawls under a bed, mentally escaping the others in attendance; then, when discovered, she physically runs away. Peter pursues and reclaims her. Titillated by her behavior, he proposes marriage. Atwood employs a trite but effective conceit as, at Marian's moment of acceptance, lightning flashes, permanently etching her reflection in his eyes.

Because the impending marriage also implies subsequent childbearing, Marian is surrounded by signs of fecundity; almost every female character in the novel is either already a mother, expecting a child, or plotting to become impregnated. It is no accident that the novel opens at the beginning of Labor Day weekend and that Marian refers to herself as a rabbit—not based on her desire for fertility but because of her basic vulnerability.

At a second party, an engagement party of sorts hosted by Peter, Marian begins to feel trapped and equates Peter with a carnivorous hunter destined to capture and to consume his prey. Yet subjected to his constant scrutiny of her behavior, Marian attempts to suppress these negative warnings from her subconscious and to return to "normality." The feelings persist, however, and begin to manifest themselves in different ways: first in her affair with Duncan, an Ichabod Crane-shaped graduate student in English literature, whom she meets while conducting a meaningless consumer survey for the marketing firm where she works, and later in her body's refusal to accept certain foods. Beginning as an aversion to eggs (an obvious fertility symbol) and to meat (the trophy of the hunter), the block is eventually generalized to other foods and culminates in her not eating at all, even though the majority of scenes are set in restaurants or kitchens and much of the action involves ingestion. At this point in the novel, Marian's only means of control is over what she will or will not eat; she descends into an anorexic claustrophobia, afraid of losing her shape, of spreading out—in essence of losing herself. Eventually, as she rejects sustenance completely, Marian realizes that she equates herself with food, that she is being consumed, gnawed away by those persons making demands on her life, and that she must eat or be eaten.

Accepting her own complicity in being a victim by allowing others to dictate her actions, Marian, ceremoniously and appropriately, bakes a sponge cake shaped like a woman and dressed as she was dressed for the party at Peter's. She offers the cake to Peter as a surrogate for herself, a variation of ritualistic cannibalism. When he refuses the offer and subsequently walks out, Marian realizes that she is free, and with Duncan's assistance, she consumes most of the cake, thus ending her anorexia. The irony is that even though the conclusion contains a certain element of optimism because Marian has indeed freed herself from victimization, she is right back where she started, a circular wanderer locked into an inconsequential existence.

Analysis

Through Marian MacAlpin's rather pathetic attempt at becoming an independent woman, the author illustrates the prevalent feminist view of a male-dominated world in which woman is relegated to the role of victim. Although Marian is certainly no archetypal hero in the strictest sense of the term, she nevertheless manages to break away from the constraints of her prudish background and attains an element of optimistic freedom. To convey her message, Margaret Atwood employs various devices of alternating narration, literary allusion, and extended metaphor.

By dividing the book into three sections and switching narrative perspective, Atwood demonstrates her narrator's loss of control. The novel begins and ends in first person; however, the crucial middle section of the work features third-person narration. It does not use an objective third-person narrator; instead it depicts the protagonist referring to herself as "Marian" instead of "I." This approach to narration is more disconcerting than merely switching from one narrator to another because the reader sees the narrator lose touch with herself and fade into the story. On the other hand, this switch allows the narrator more objectivity, as she is now permitted microscopic observance of her own behavior while staying removed from it. From a feminist perspective, this narrative style allows the reader to view the protagonist as both subject and object, and it is the creation of the cake icon that unites the two. As soon as Marian severs the cake's head from the body, the work returns to first-person narration.

Literary allusion is a major factor in *The Edible Woman*, not only within the work but the work itself. The novel has been compared repeatedly to *Alice's Adventures in Wonderland* (1865) and uses much of the same imagery: getting small, getting large, the rabbit, spiritual guides, the "Eat Me" cakes, and the frequent references to food and eating. The conclusions of the works also are similar: When Alice awakes from her dream, her life is just as it was before, unchanged by her circular fantasy wanderings.

Additional allusions exist throughout the work, presented both blatantly and under disguise. Duncan and his roommates are graduate students in English, and much of their discussion revolves quite naturally around literature. The most intriguing of the minor characters is Fish (aptly named for his predilection of "fishing" for interpretation), who is constructing a term paper on the "womb symbols in Beatrix Potter," initiating extended discussions on *Through the Looking Glass* (1872) and seeking the literary theme of Woman with a capitalized W in various works.

Other references, though present, are more obscure. One of the more veiled allusions comes when Marian enters Duncan's apartment for the first time and is told that each occupant has his own chair—Mama Bear (Trevor, who has obvious feminine/homosexual characteristics), Papa Bear (Fish, who represents authority), and Baby Bear (Duncan, for whom the others function as surrogate parents). Another less obvious allusion is incorporated in the pumpkin imagery surrounding the idea of pregnancy; Peter comes to symbolize the nursery rhyme character of "pumpkin eater," and Marian begins to suspect Duncan as he devours pumpkin seeds.

Extended metaphors and repeated images also control the flow of the novel. Food and sex are inextricably linked in the novel, as they are in life. Food is to the individual what sex is to the species; it becomes a means of self-reproduction and its absence a means of self-annihilation. The creatures one eats must be weaker than one is oneself; therefore, if a human or a character is weak, she is edible and thus powerless. Through a refusal to eat or to be eaten, Marian MacAlpin is empowered and becomes somehow more human. By using extended metaphors related to food, hunting, and consumption, Atwood reinforces this point.

Other extended metaphors in the work deal with reproduction. Marian essentially reproduces herself and can make from the raw clay of her rebirth whatever she chooses. Her interior dream-monologue and her exterior life unite in the concluding third section of the novel, and although her life is basically unchanged, the opportunity for change has come into existence. She, like Alice, has regained time in which to devise a plan for her life according to her own criteria.

In addition to having technical flair, Margaret Atwood is masterful at characterization. Although other characters are presented through the myopic vision of the protagonist, they are credible, if a touch stereotypical. Atwood uses little exposition, allowing the secondary characters to develop through the piling up of details and through dialogue and interaction, thus illustrating their motivation more objectively than through the mere observations of an unreliable first-person narrator.

Context

Although *The Edible Woman* was poorly received in initial reviews, it has come to be considered one of the first heraldings of women's right to independence. The book was not released until 1969, after a delay of five years, and despite the fact that the women's movement had made significant strides during the 1960's, an independent woman was not yet a totally acceptable ideal at that time. Additionally, and regardless of the fact that ritualistic cannibalism has been a theme in the world's literary canon since its conception, some critics were offended by the approach in Atwood's work, chiding her for moral irresponsibility when discussing birth and emotions in such tones.

Near the end of the work, Duncan, as alter ego to the protagonist, points out, as they sit on the edge of an empty pit, that Marian's life is her "own personal cul-de-sac," that she invented it and she would have to find her own way out.

Although Marian MacAlpin has been little changed by the unfolding events in her life, she nevertheless becomes more human as she retreats slightly from her dead-end destination and becomes a hero of sorts in accepting her own complicity in her victimization, thus serving as a positive role model for future authors and readers alike. One reviewer missed this point, however, and complained that the novel was wasted paper, peopled with insignificant characters. Although the work is open-ended, one is left with the faint hope that Marian will escape her "abnormal normality" and become a beacon of hope for others trapped in their own constrictive relationships.

Sources for Further Study

Grace, Sherrill E., and Lorraine Weir, eds. *Margaret Atwood: Language, Text, and System.* Vancouver: University of British Columbia Press, 1983. A compilation of critical essays written about Margaret Atwood and her work. One piece discusses Atwood's transition from poetry to fiction; another is a feminist reading of her poetry. The longest entries discuss the novel *Surfacing* in relation to syntax and theme, particularly related to Amerindian influences and shamanism.

Nicholson, Mervyn. "Food and Power: Homer, Carroll, Atwood, and Others." *Mosaic* 20 (Summer, 1987): 37-55. This essay discusses the uses of ritualistic cannibalism for effect throughout literature. Although the majority of the text is devoted to Homer, there are many references to Atwood as well as comparisons to Lewis Carroll.

Peel, Ellen. "Subject, Object, and the Alternation of First- and Third-Person Narration in Novels by Alther, Atwood, and Drabble: Toward a Theory of Feminist Aesthetics." *Critique* 30 (Winter, 1989): 107-121. An in-depth discussion of the narrative technique of alternating first-and third-person accounts to illustrate a change in the narrator. The author attempts to correlate this style to feminist perspective as a means of reinforcing feminist themes.

Rosenberg, Jerome H. *Margaret Atwood.* Boston: Twayne, 1984. A critical overview of Atwood's fictional canon that addresses each novel in encapsulated format, discussing themes, symbols, imagery, and narrative techniques. An extensive bibliography is included.

Joyce Duncan

EMMA

Author: Jane Austen (1775-1817)
Type of work: Novel
Type of plot: Romance
Time of plot: The early nineteenth century
Locale: Highbury, a village in southern England
First published: 1815

Principal characters:

Emma Woodhouse, a high-spirited, bright young woman who is also spoiled
Mr. Woodhouse, Emma's father, a widower
Miss Taylor, Emma's governess
Mr. Knightley, a thirty-eight-year-old bachelor neighbor of the Woodhouses
Harriet Smith, Emma's new friend and protegée, an orphan
Mr. Weston, a widower who marries Miss Taylor
Frank Churchill, Mr. Weston's son
Jane Fairfax, a poor, beautiful, and genteel young lady
Isabella and **John Knightley,** a married couple, Emma's older sister and Mr. Knightley's younger brother
Mr. and **Mrs. Elton,** the minister of Highbury and his new wife
Robert Martin, a hardworking and sensible young farmer

Form and Content

Emma, a romantic comedy of manners, paints a sparkling and amusing picture of genteel village life in Great Britain during the brief Regency period preceding the Victorian period. Marriage and social position are the primary focus of this work as the women characters, faithful to the social dynamics of the time, seek financial and social security through advantageous marriages. Of the many genteel women in the novel, only Emma can choose to stay single without serious financial and social sacrifice. The other unmarried women of the story are either prospective brides or the "unfortunate" ones, such as Jane Fairfax's aunt Miss Bates, obliged to earn a living looking after others and receiving pity or indifference from most of their neighbors. Though the picture of village life drawn by Jane Austen is filled with humorous scenes and characters, the underlying grim reality of unmarried women's lives is a sobering one.

Emma clearly understands that marriage is the only answer to her new friend Harriet Smith's uncertain social position and undecided future. Emma quickly dismisses Harriet's eager suitor Robert Martin as unacceptable because he lacks sufficient social position to be worthy of her friend; he is merely a hardworking, modest farmer. When Mr. Knightley, Emma's brother-in-law, points out that Emma has grand plans for a young woman lacking virtually any social position, and in fact one who could be a member of a disreputable family, Emma strongly objects to his negative comment, countering that her protegée can as likely be a romantic heroine, a lost heiress of a noble family. She later learns from Mr. Knightley that Harriet is the illegitimate daughter of a prosperous businessman, not a lost heiress.

Each suitor whom the matchmaking Emma considers for Harriet proves to be unsatisfactory and to have matchmaking plans of his own. The handsome village minister, Mr. Elton, coldly refuses to consider the match, for Harriet is unworthy of his social position; to Emma's amazement, he declares himself interested in and worthy of her own hand. Frank Churchill, a very charming and eligible bachelor who soon appears in Highbury to visit his father, is far too independent and much too preoccupied with his own affairs to fall for Emma's romantic scheme of marrying him to the docile Harriet; in fact, at times he seems to intimate to Emma that he would propose to her instead, but he never does so. Later he reveals his long-standing secret engagement to beautiful but poor Jane Fairfax. Finally, Mr. Knightley seems to be a possible husband for her compliant friend, for he does admire Harriet. At this point in Emma's matchmaking efforts, she realizes that Mr. Knightley is not for anyone but herself and that, unexpectedly, she is ready for marriage.

In each case, Emma herself has been an obstacle to her plans for her protegée's happiness. She is humbled by her inept handling of Harriet's marriage prospects and withdraws from her friend. With Mr. Knightley's help, the abandoned Harriet finally does become engaged to her long-suffering admirer Robert Martin.

This theme of marriage and social position is treated not only in the main plot of Emma's elaborate designs to marry off Harriet but in three romantic subplots as well. The already-married couple of Miss Taylor and Mr. Weston gradually settle into happy domestic life and announce that they expect a child of their own. Next, the unexpected marriage of Mr. Elton to his unknown bride, Arabella Hawkins, brings social conflict to Highbury as the new Mrs. Elton jealously and arrogantly challenges Emma's role as social leader of the village. Third, the melodramatic secret engagement of Frank Churchill and the destitute Jane Fairfax shows the desperate means that lovers used to stay together despite financial problems and parental disapproval. Finally, the novel ends with a flurry of weddings, those of the three couples created in the story but not yet married: Harriet Smith and Robert Martin, Emma Woodhouse and Mr. Knightley, and Jane Fairfax and Frank Churchill. Through marriages, these young women find their social identities and positions.

Analysis

Jane Austen dedicated *Emma* to the Prince Regent, as an expression of her appreciation for his compliments and encouragement. It is a romantic comedy of manners that treats the middle-class values of marriage and family and hardly goes beyond the concerns of three or four families of an English country village.

Yet these commonplace themes are presented with such skill and depth to make *Emma* a popular novel among readers, from its time of publication to today. Its themes are the favorite ones of Jane Austen, the unmarried daughter of an Angelican minister in rural southwest England. Some may say that marriage and family concerns are all that she knew, living her entire life among a large, close family of well-educated, well-read parents; six siblings; and many nieces, nephews, cousins, aunts, and uncles. Certainly she accurately describes the small-town values, aspirations, behaviors, and concerns common to her age and social class.

Austen, however, also touches on universal human themes relevant to other times and places. Among these themes are the transition of young adults from parental authority to independence, the managing of conflicts between parents and adult children, the wise choice of marriage partners, and the overcoming of psychological obstacles to realizing love and marital happiness.

Emma centers on the interests and concerns of handsome, clever, and rich Emma Woodhouse, who faces all these issues as she separates from her nurturing governess (a substitute for her long-dead mother), fails to guide a needy friend toward happiness and security, and ultimately opposes her devoted father by choosing to marry rather than remain single in order to care for him. Other characters face difficult trials of love and friendship as well: Harriet Smith chooses her humble husband in spite of her friend and mentor's strong disapproval; Frank Churchill chooses a destitute wife whom his aunt will never accept; and Jane Fairfax enters a forbidden secret engagement with a capricious young man who refuses to acknowledge their relationship publicly. All these characters face choices of love and loyalty that test their strength of purpose and wisdom.

The story's point of view allows readers to see events and situations through the eyes of the manipulative but well-meaning Emma. They know that she sometimes feels disappointed in herself and that she suffers guilt for her cruel words and thoughtless actions. They share her sympathetic view of the people of Highbury and so also tend to excuse her conceited and foolish mistakes, hoping that she corrects her self-absorbed views and stops seeking power over those weaker than herself or expecting continual admiration from her friends.

Austen deftly captures the pain and poignancy of these characters' difficulties in the minor events of the story: a broken boot lace, the emerging message of a parlour word game of anagrams, a love letter hidden and secretly read, a mysterious gift of an expensive piano, a gallant rescue from a band of curious gypsies, an afternoon picnic in the country, a cruel snub at the town ball. In these small events, hearts are revealed and their messages both understood and misunderstood by those most interested. These difficulties are the stuff of tragedy as well as comedy. Austen allows her lovers' difficulties to be conquered, after they suffer in embarrassing and comic situations.

Readers may ask whether these characters' romantic successes do, in fact, bring them their expected happiness. This important question is not so easily answered in the novel. In many ways, the major romantic couples are comically mismatched: high-spirited, imaginative Emma with proper, fatherly Mr. Knightley; flighty Frank Churchill with melancholy, delicate Jane Fairfax; hard-working, sensible Robert Martin with vacuous, silly Harriet. Rather than bringing out the best in each other, these partners may bring out the worst, as newlyweds Mr. and Mrs. Elton certainly do. Austen grants these couples their heart's desire, but she may be laughing at them as she does so.

Context

Emma, considered one of Jane Austen's finest works, was received with considerable praise and public interest. Even the great novelist of that time, Sir Walter Scott, admired her work for its artistry and elegance. Austen's novels followed and improved on a tradition begun by the popular writer Fanny Burney (1752-1840), the author of *Evelina* (1778). This genre of social comedy novel presented women's stories more naturally than other English novels had. Unlike the popular fantasies of exotic places and melodramatic events, such as the gothic thriller *The Mysteries of Udolpho* (1794), by Ann Radcliffe, *Emma* is a comic story of rather ordinary events in a typical English village. The characters could be found around many card tables in country houses of those days.

Though the domestic events in novels such as *Emma* may seem ordinary or even trivial to modern readers, Austen and others were attempting to present a clear and fair picture of the very restricted domestic world women lived in at that time. Women in these novels seem preoccupied with making advantageous marriages simply because marriage was the sole respectable occupation available to well-bred women. Some readers may also criticize *Emma* for its excessive emphasis on marriage as a calculated means to acquire money and materialistic possessions—houses, land, servants. In truth, these possessions often ruled the marital choices that women made as they considered their life's prospects. For women to make marital choices without considering such material advantages meant risking hardship, poverty, and even death to themselves and their children. Alternatives to marriage were to remain unmarried, like Miss Bates, dependent on relatives' generosity, or to enter domestic service as an upper servant, a housekeeper, lady's maid, or governess, as Jane Fairfax was destined to become. Those who entered domestic service became independent of their families' incomes but lost their social positions in exchange for security and the tiny income earned.

Because a prosperous marriage was an eligible woman's best economic choice, entertaining novels treating this choice and its alternatives in entertaining and thoughtful ways became popular reading for women. Austen's novels presented these issues in humorous and lively ways, using dialogue brilliantly to draw out the comic aspects of well-known character types and devising clever plots to point out absurdities in courtship and marriage situations. Her gentle humor and insight into human motivations are subtle, sometimes leaving readers to wonder what she thought of the events and people portrayed in her novels.

Sources for Further Study

Austen, Jane. *Emma: An Authoritative Text, Backgrounds, Reviews, and Criticism*. Edited by Stephen M. Parrish. New York: W. W. Norton, 1972. An excellent beginning for the student first reading *Emma*, this collection brings together the definitive text, the background materials that Austen may have used, and important critical articles. A selected bibliography is included.

Burrows, J. F. *Jane Austen's "Emma."* Sydney: Sydney University Press, 1968. A detailed study of the novel considering important critical interpretations and the use of language and comic style. A selected bibliography is included.

Lascelles, Mary. *Jane Austen and Her Art*. London: Oxford University Press, 1963. A classic study of Austen's life and fiction, with emphasis on how she developed her literary taste and style. Refers to specific novels to show her evolving art and her mastery of the novel form.

Monaghan, David. *Jane Austen: Structure and Social Vision*. New York: Barnes & Noble Books, 1980. This critical work examines the moral ideas presented in Austen's novels and considers their sources in the traditional social values and the new individualistic ethics of her time.

Sherry, Norman. *Jane Austen*. New York: ARCO, 1969. A general introduction to Austen's works, this critical review offers a balanced approach to her work, covering background, themes, characterization, and style.

Watt, Ian, ed. *Jane Austen: A Collection of Critical Essays*. Englewood Cliffs, N.J.: Prentice Hall, 1963. A collection of critical, interpretive essays on Austen and her works, focusing on her style and themes with reference to broader human values and conditions.

Patricia H. Fulbright

EVELINA: Or, The History of a Young Lady's Entrance into the World

Author: Fanny Burney (1752-1840)
Type of work: Novel
Type of plot: Social realism
Time of plot: The 1770's
Locale: London, England
First published: 1778

Principal characters:

Evelina Anville, the young ward of the Reverend Mr. Villars

The Reverend Mr. Villars, the kindly and benevolent clergyman who rears Evelina

Lord Orville, the wealthy and powerful nobleman who falls in love with her

Sir Clement Willoughby, an upper-class gentleman whose intentions toward the beautiful Evelina are anything but honorable

Madame Duval, Evelina's French grandmother

Lady Howard, a country gentlewoman and close friend to Mr. Villars and Evelina

Mrs. Mirvan, the daughter of Lady Howard and a lifelong friend of Evelina

Captain Mirvan, the husband of Mrs. Mirvan

Mr. Macartney, a melancholy and mysterious young man

Form and Content

As its subtitle accurately indicates, Fanny Burney's *Evelina* recounts the story of a young woman's "entrance into the world." "The world" is a particularly rich and meaningful term in Burney's formulation, implying not only the world of London society, ranging from a modest silversmith's shop to the grand pleasure garden of Vauxhall, but also the entire world of adult experience—in particular love, courtship, and marriage. Burney's youthful and vivacious heroine also finds herself continually and uncomfortably caught between worlds: between the safe world of her childhood and the often-threatening "adult" world, between the country world with its fairly simple code of behavior and the city world with its bewilderingly complicated set of behavioral codes and social rituals.

Burney's novel opens in Evelina's sixteenth year. The kindly Reverend Mr. Villars has been the only parent Evelina has ever known, and her entire life has been spent in the safety and seclusion of a country existence, with Lady Howard and her family her only contacts to the "outside" world. Though she is the daughter of a wealthy baronet, Evelina's future prospects (which for women in the eighteenth century almost always depended upon marriage) are severely limited by what amounts to orphan status: Her father refuses to recognize her as his daughter and heir, and she is thus left with only the modest dowry that Mr. Villars can provide her.

Evelina's journey to London occurs as a result of Lady Howard's intercession. She worries that Evelina's narrow country life will eventually lead her to imagine London life as far more exciting and glamorous than it really is, and she manages to convince Mr. Villars that several months in the city will allow Evelina to return more comfortably to her place in the country. Thus Evelina finds herself in London in the company of Lady Howard's daughter, Mrs. Mirvan, and her granddaughter Maria.

Evelina's stay in London is marked by a series of social misadventures, most of them the result of her inexperience. Soon after she arrives, for example, Evelina attends a private ball at which she attracts the unwanted attention of a foppish young man named Lovel, who asks her to dance. Comically repulsed by Lovel's absurd appearance and manner, Evelina refuses him, though shortly thereafter she accepts the invitation of a handsome man about the same age as Lovel. This second young man proves to be Lord Orville, and Evelina is at once struck by his intelligence and good manners. She is startled, however, by the ensuing commotion, for she has been unaware that an "unwritten rule" of social decorum prohibits young ladies from dancing with one man after refusing another. Later, during an outing to Marybone Gardens, Evelina is separated from her friends and finds herself in the company of two prostitutes—without recognizing them as prostitutes or realizing how others will interpret the situation. Such episodes underscore Evelina's innocence and vulnerability, while also suggesting that there is something fundamentally wrong with a society that can neither accommodate the innocent nor offer sympathetic protection to the vulnerable.

Many of Evelina's misadventures bring her into contact with Lord Orville and the unctuous Sir Clement Willoughby. No two characters could be more different, although Evelina's inexperience blinds her for a time to Sir Clement's true motive in pursuing her: seduction. Evelina's gradual education in the ways of the world, involving encounters with nearly all the ranks of London society, allow her time and again to measure the conduct of other characters by the high standard set by Lord Orville. Burney certainly suggests something important about her heroine's intrinsic worth by placing her so high in Lord Orville's esteem.

The novel's major subplot involves Madame Duval, Evelina's French grandmother, who comes to England for the express purpose of gaining control of her granddaughter and pursuing Evelina's legal claims as the daughter of Sir John Belmont. With these aims in mind, the offensive Madame Duval forces herself into Evelina's life. For a time Evelina is compelled to live with Madame Duval and to bear the company of Madame Duval's crass London relations, the Branghtons. Though Evelina is ultimately able to free herself from her grandmother, it is only after a considerable amount of unpleasantness, much of it the result of a series of increasingly vicious tricks played on Madame Duval by Captain Mirvan.

Evelina's story ends in fairy-tale fashion: She meets and wins over Sir John Belmont, who immediately acknowledges her as his daughter and heir; she discovers a half brother she never knew existed; and, having become a titled lady, she marries Lord Orville.

Analysis

Like many other English novels of the eighteenth century, *Evelina* provides a keen and detailed examination of English society, in this case the wonderfully rich social world of London. What sets *Evelina* apart from the works of Burney's male contemporaries, however, and in the process gives the novel its peculiar charm and power, is the narrative perspective created by Evelina herself. Reared in virtual seclusion by a country clergyman determined to protect her, Evelina finds herself totally unprepared to maneuver smoothly through the complex maze of London society. Yet it is precisely Evelina's naïveté and inexperience that enable Burney to point out the relative emptiness and artificiality of much that her heroine sees, and thus to imbue the narrative with both wit and satiric bite.

Burney's first work, written when the author was in her early twenties, is an epistolary novel—that is, it consists entirely of a series of letters exchanged by several of the major characters over a period of some eight months. Most of the letters are from Evelina's pen, and nearly all of these are directly addressed to Mr. Villars. In adopting the epistolary method, Burney followed the example of Samuel Richardson, author of *Pamela: Or, Virtue Rewarded* (1740) and *Clarissa: Or The History of a Young Lady* (1747-1748) and one of the eighteenth century's greatest novelists. More important, though, the epistolary method allows Burney direct access to Evelina's thoughts and feelings—even more so, perhaps, than a conventional first-person narration. The letter is a more immediate and intimate form, particularly when it is written to a figure such as Mr. Villars, who combines in himself the offices of mentor, guide, and friend and thus encourages freedom of expression. Because Evelina is able to express herself openly and candidly, her narrative rings true psychologically.

While it might not be entirely fair to call *Evelina* a social satire, the novel has an undeniable satiric dimension, especially in its first half, when Evelina provides detailed reports of—and occasionally pointed commentary on—her social misadventures. Because she is writing "privately," to her beloved mentor, Evelina is relatively free to criticize the characters and social practices she encounters in London. By a neat trick, Burney is thus able to do publicly what would not otherwise be entirely "proper" for a female author in the eighteenth century to do: criticize the male establishment with its double standard and oppressive codes of behavior and hold up to laughter the vain and pompous antics of Londoners.

Further facilitating Burney's satire is her heroine's "natural" goodness, which often stands in stark contrast to the obviously unnatural (insincere and artificial) behavior of such characters as Lovel and Sir Clement

Willoughby. Because readers' sympathies lie clearly with Evelina, they tend to judge Lovel's foppishness and Sir Clement's duplicity even more harshly than does Evelina.

What complicates and to an appreciable degree undermines Burney's satire is her novel's romantic core: However much one may want to see *Evelina* as a sustained satiric attack on the male establishment, one simply cannot ignore the many romantic elements. The plot itself and many of the characters come straight out of the fairy-tale tradition: Evelina is an eighteenth century Cinderella waiting to be swept off her feet by Prince Charming; she is the princess-in-disguise bedeviled by a wicked old witch and searching for her true father, who turns out, naturally, to be a great and powerful king. Unfortunately, satire and romance are finally not compatible forms, and the lively satiric energy that animates the first half of Evelina's narrative dissipates under the demands of a traditional happy ending in which Evelina finds herself socially and emotionally redefined in traditional male terms: one man's daughter, another man's wife.

Context

The eighteenth century has traditionally been seen as the period during which the novel began a long process of development and refinement which eventually made it the dominant literary form in the Anglo-American world. For many years the history of the novel's "rise" to dominance was told in exclusively male terms: it was the story of several eighteenth century men (Daniel Defoe, Samuel Richardson, Henry Fielding, Tobias Smollett, Laurence Sterne) who experimented with and, in some cases, brought to perfection this new art form. These were the great "fathers" of the novel, and whenever their story was told, it was told in such a way that the influence of women on the process was minimized if not ignored or flatly denied.

Yet eighteenth century women were experimenting with the new form as well. In fact, by the end of the century many more novels were being written by women than by men. If none of these novels can legitimately be said to equal Fielding's *Tom Jones* (1749) or Richardson's *Clarissa*, it in no way diminishes the contributions of these "mothers" of the novel, who typically had much greater difficulties to overcome than their male contemporaries.

A more truthful history of the novel must recognize the accomplishments and contributions of these women. Like other women novelists, Fanny Burney wrote at a time when writing itself, as a public profession, was seen as an exclusively male domain. Women, quite simply, were not supposed to write, much less publish, novels. Women who did write were either shunned by their male peers or, perhaps worse, treated condescendingly, as pets. Yet in *Evelina* Burney managed to overcome the odds and write a novel that was admired by male and female readers alike, even though it cast a critical eye on many of the social practices of her day, particularly those that contributed to the oppression of women.

Sources for Further Study

Doody, Margaret Anne. *Frances Burney: The Life in the Works*. New Brunswick, N.J.: Rutgers University Press, 1988. The best biography, with an extensive discussion of Burney's work.

Newton, Judith Lowder. *Women, Power, and Subversion: Social Strategies in British Fiction, 1778-1860*. Athens: University of Georgia Press, 1981. Newton devotes an entire chapter to *Evelina*, finding in Burney's novel an unresolved conflict between Burney's desire for artistic freedom and the demands of patriarchal authority.

Simons, Judy. "Fanny Burney: The Tactics of Subversion." In *Living by the Pen: Early British Women Writers*, edited by Dale Spender. New York: Teachers College Press, 1992. A useful, brief introduction to Burney and her work. The anthology as a whole provides an excellent survey of women writers in the eighteenth century.

Spencer, Jane. *The Rise of the Woman Novelist: From Aphra Behn to Jane Austen*. New York: Basil Blackwell, 1986. A compelling study of the emergence of the woman writer in England in the period from the late seventeenth to the early nineteenth centuries.

Spender, Dale. *Mothers of the Novel: One Hundred Good Women Writers Before Jane Austen*. London: Pandora, 1986. Spender's purpose in this important treatment of women writers from the seventeenth and eighteenth centuries is to challenge and ultimately to overthrow the traditional view that the novel was "fathered" by a handful of male writers. She devotes a chapter to Burney and her contemporary Maria Edgeworth.

Straub, Kristina. *Divided Fictions: Fanny Burney and Feminine Strategy*. Lexington: University Press of Kentucky, 1987. Straub's is probably the best sustained critical examination of Fanny Burney's work. The chapters on *Evelina* are excellent.

Todd, Janet. *The Sign of Angellica: Women, Writing, and Fiction, 1660-1800*. New York: Columbia University Press, 1989. Another important study chronicling the emergence of the woman writer in England. The final chapter is on Burney.

Michael Stuprich

EVERYTHING THAT RISES MUST CONVERGE

Author: Flannery O'Connor (1925-1964)
Type of work: Short stories
First published: 1965

Form and Content

Everything That Rises Must Converge is a gathering of Flannery O'Connor's short stories written between 1956 and 1964 which had not been previously published in book form. It includes the title story and eight others. The story "Everything That Rises Must Converge" is one of O'Connor's best, and it remains one of her most often anthologized stories. The title is a quotation from Catholic theologian Pierre Teilhard de Chardin, who imagined an "omega point" at which the "rising" or evolving human being would meet God. By analogy, people of the lower classes who "rise" socially must inevitably "meet" with the higher. To Mrs. Chestny in the story, Southern blacks "should rise, yes, but on their own side of the fence." Her liberal son Julian tries to "teach her a lesson" about her prejudice, but it becomes clear that his overtures to a black man on the bus are motivated by scorn for his mother, not genuine sympathy.

Mrs. Chestny's striving to set herself above and apart from perceived inferiors is a common trait in O'Connor's characters, seen also in the protagonist of "Greenleaf," Mrs. May. Mrs. May looks down on the family of her farmhand, Mr. Greenleaf, even though the Greenleaf boys have done more to better themselves than have her own two boys. The characteristic O'Connor shock ending comes when Mrs. May, frustrated by Greenleaf's reluctance to remove a "scrub" bull that has wandered into her herd, tries to do so herself and is fatally gored.

In the third story, "A View of the Woods," the aptly named Mr. Fortune, another O'Connor protagonist who sets himself above others, sells the front lawn with its "View of the Woods" from under his son-in-law Pitts, whom he thinks unworthy of his daughter. The sale alienates the only family member for whom Fortune retains any feeling, his nine-year-old granddaughter, Mary Fortune Pitts. The child attacks him in the woods; he smashes her head on a rock, but the ordeal strains his weak heart. The clash seems fatal to both.

The protagonist of "The Enduring Chill," Asbury Fox, is much like Julian of the title story. He fancies himself an artist, a writer, beyond the narrow rural Southern sensibilities of his domineering mother. Having "escaped" to New York, he becomes ill and returns home, ostensibly to die. It turns out, however, that the very act of defiance he thought would liberate him—drinking unpasteurized milk against his mother's orders—has given him ungulant fever, and that it is not fatal.

The conflict with the mother in "The Comforts of Home" is almost the inverse of that in the previous story. Here it is the son, Thomas, who clings to "virtue," though his idea of virtue is static, passive. His mother offends his sense of virtue by taking in a nymphomaniac; in trying to drive her away, he accidentally shoots his mother. A more peculiar sense of virtue divides Mr. and Mrs. Parker in "Parker's Back": Parker feels oppressed by his wife's violent Christian denunciation of any kind of "idolatry." He tries to appease her by having a Byzantine mosaic of Christ reproduced in a tattoo on his back; this she sees as the worst kind of idolatry, and she hits his back with a broom until it bleeds.

In two stories the filial conflict is modulated by a surrogate. In "The Lame Shall Enter First," Sheppard ignores his son in order to lavish attention on a juvenile delinquent he hopes to "save." In "Revelation," the protagonist, Mrs. Turpin, has no children, but she talks in a doctor's waiting room with a "stylish lady" while the woman's daughter scowls at Mrs. Turpin's self-righteous philosophy, obviously a mirror image of her mother's. When she has had enough of their talk, it is Mrs. Turpin, not her own mother, whom the girl attacks without warning, hitting her with a book and choking her.

In "Judgement Day," the conflict becomes father-daughter, as the elderly Tanner is taken against his will when his daughter moves to New York. When Tanner treats a Northern black man with the easy, condescending familiarity he knew in Georgia, the stranger turns on him and beats him.

Though they all differ in details of plot and characterization, each story ends with a characteristic shock, combining violence with the possibility of revelation for the point-of-view character.

Analysis

At the heart of all of Flannery O'Connor's fiction is the theme of the surprising action of God's grace in a world that seems oblivious to it. The invisible action of this grace moves through each story, becoming visible at a key point in the action (usually the very end), though sometimes to the reader only. These moments of epiphany, or "revelation," to use the title of one of these stories, redeem the otherwise dark and sordid vision O'Connor offers of the fallen world. "Grotesque" is the term critics most often use for this vision, though O'Connor repudiated the word.

One of the devices O'Connor uses to effect the reader's participation in each epiphany is the subversion of the story's point of view. She chooses as her protagonist a character whose point of view is furthest from that of the story. After building sympathy for the point-of-view character, she then allows an action (usually violent) to upset the status quo, revealing the weakness of that point of view. In the title story, for example, the reader takes part in Julian's condemnation of his mother's prejudices, but when his own prejudices lead to her collapse from a stroke, he reveals not only his prejudices but also his need for her. In "Revelation," Mrs. Turpin's neat hierarchy of classes of people is disturbed by violence when she is attacked by someone she had pegged as on the bottom rung; the story ends with her vision of the lower classes entering Heaven before her.

Another favorite characterization technique of O'Connor is her flair for exotic names of the type critic Franklin P. Adams called "aptronyms," names that are appropriate descriptions of the characters who hold them. "Turpin" suggests "turpitude," or moral baseness, an ironic name for a woman who scorns the baseness of others; it comes from the Latin *turpis*, meaning "ugly," and the girl who attacks Mrs. Turpin had been categorized by her as "the ugly girl." Another ironic aptronym is "Sheppard" in "The Lame Shall Enter First"; he thinks himself a good shepherd to the delinquent boys he counsels yet has only empty social psychology to offer them. Mr. Fortune is the wealthiest character in "A View of the Woods" and sees the woods only as potential wealth. His opposite is the lowly Pitts. "May" and "Greenleaf" suggest the generative nature of spring, as does the bull that threatens to "spoil" Mrs. May's herd.

Though her fiction is universal, a striking feature of all O'Connor's stories is her regionalism—like "grotesque," a term she rejected. Every story evokes the American South of the middle twentieth century in its setting, dialogue, and ethos. The only story in *Everything That Rises Must Converge* not set in the Deep South, "Judgement Day," is filled with the protagonist's yearning to return there, and so much of it consists of flashbacks to and dreams about Georgia that the New York setting seems unreal. O'Connor's dialogue captures the nuances of Southern American speech not by the absurd misspellings that Northern writers sometimes overuse to suggest it (though she uses them sometimes, and always effectively; oddly enough, she used dialect spelling more in her private letters than in her fiction). More important, O'Connor reproduces the sound of conversation, of small talk woven almost entirely of clichés (a trait certainly not limited to Southern speech).

One of the most important observations on O'Connor's characterization was made not by literary critics but by her neighbors and relatives, who asked why her stories never seemed to have any likable people. Critics make a similar charge in another way when they see her flawed characters as the end product of a Jansenist or pseudo-Calvinist belief in the total depravity of human nature, totally given to the World, the Flesh, and the Devil. Yet O'Connor's church does not hold such a doctrine, and neither did she.

As her friend Robert Fitzgerald pointed out in his introduction to *Everything That Rises Must Converge*, there is much evidence of beauty in the world in O'Connor's fiction, and fellow fiction writer Joyce Carol Oates points out that the physical is the way to the spiritual for O'Connor's characters. O'Connor presents characters distorted by sin, as she believes all people to be, but she also offers avenues of repentance and redemption.

A criticism that follows from the deliberate distortion with which O'Connor painted her characters is that they are not as fully rounded as those of her contemporary writers. O'Connor has been accused of producing caricatures, cartoons instead of people—an interesting charge, since her ambition in high school and college was to be a cartoonist rather than a writer. Yet caricature itself can be an art, and the harsh outlines of personality can be more effective, more shocking, in O'Connor's fiction than more subtly drawn and rounded characters. The fact that the shock involved in her characterizations is often the shock of recognition may be proof that they are closer to reality than they first seem.

Context

Though labeled a Southern Catholic female writer, Flannery O'Connor did not consider herself a female writer or a regional writer; the only issues that her fiction dealt with were spiritual issues transcending both gender and geography. Nevertheless, her female characters often reveal the effects of social attitudes toward women that help shape them. Two character types in particular, the domineering mother and the artistic or scholarly daughter, appear frequently.

The unnamed "ugly girl" who becomes the object of Mrs. Turpin's pity in "Revelation" illustrates a destructive societal norm for young women, both in personal appearance and in intelligence. Mrs. Turpin assumes that the girl deserves her pity because she is overweight, unattractive, and blighted by acne. Worse—or perhaps the two are causally related—she is an intellectual, buried in a book with the ironic title *Human Development*. Her mother, with Mrs. Turpin's tacit assent, lectures in vain that the girl could compensate for external "ugliness" by a cheerful disposition.

A similar character in "The Enduring Chill," Mary George Fox, is scorned by the one character who should most sympathize with her, her brother Asbury. Both aspire to artistic, or at least intellectual, escape from the limits imposed by their society, but Asbury is unable to see his sister as anything but "husband-bait." "Asbury said she posed as an intellectual," readers are told, "but that her I.Q. couldn't be over seventy-five, that all she was really interested in was getting a man but that no sensible man would finish a first look at her." Mary George rises as high as a woman with intellectual ambition can in her world by becoming the principal of the county elementary school.

Intelligence and artistic development are feared by the mothers in O'Connor's fiction—such things are bad enough in sons, but they are nearly fatal in daughters. O'Connor must have encountered this attitude among her neighbors and family, though there is no evidence that her mother shared it. Her conviction as a college senior that she would be a writer and her leaving the South for the Iowa Writer's Workshop (and much worse, a year writing in New York City and Connecticut)—all of this cut against the domestic expectations that Milledgeville, Georgia, must have had for its young ladies. Yet O'Connor never scorned those expectations, and her neighbors, despite some discomfort at the nature of her characters, expressed pride in having a writer of note in their midst.

Sources for Further Study

Asals, Frederick. *Flannery O'Connor: The Imagination of Extremity*. Athens: University of Georgia Press, 1982. By dropping the prejudicial term "grotesque" in favor of "extremity," this full-length study of O'Connor's work is able to study a distinctive quality of O'Connor's literary imagination without distortion.

Brinkmeyer, Robert H. *The Art and Vision of Flannery O'Connor*. Baton Rouge: Louisiana State University Press, 1989. A fine general study of O'Connor's work, this book is sometimes limited by its reliance on Russian critic Mikhail M. Bakhtin's theory of "dialogism."

Hendin, Josephine. *The World of Flannery O'Connor*. Bloomington: Indiana University Press, 1970. One of the first major studies to suggest a disparity between O'Connor's theology and her fiction, Hendin's book asserts that O'Connor's fiction has it source in rage, not Catholic orthodoxy.

Oates, Joyce Carol. "The Visionary Art of Flannery O'Connor." *Southern Humanities Review* 7 (1973): 235-246. Though brief, this article focuses exclusively on *Everything That Rises Must Converge*, which Oates calls O'Connor's greatest book. As a fellow fiction writer, Oates offers insights that other critics who are only critics might miss.

O'Connor, Flannery. *The Habit of Being*. Edited by Sally Fitzgerald. New York: Farrar, Straus & Giroux, 1979. This collection of O'Connor's letters to friends, family, editors, and fellow writers is valuable not only for biographical background to the stories but also for the author's analyses of many of the stories in *Everything That Rises Must Converge*.

Ragen, Brian Abel. *A Wreck on the Road to Damascus: Innocence, Guilt, and Conversion in Flannery O'Connor*. Chicago: Loyola University Press, 1989. This critical study of religious motifs in O'Connor's fiction explores the psychology of her characters. Its discussion of the stories in *Everything That Rises Must Converge* focuses on the moments of "revelation" in nearly every story.

John R. Holmes

EXCELLENT WOMEN

Author: Barbara Pym (1913-1980)
Type of work: Novel
Type of plot: Satire
Time of plot: The 1940's
Locale: London, England
First published: 1952

Principal characters:

Mildred Lathbury, an unmarried woman who lives in a flat near her parish church

Helena and **Rockingham "Rocky" Napier,** the married couple who move into the flat below Mildred's

Julian and **Winifred Malory,** the rector of St. Mary's parish and his unmarried sister

Allegra Gray, a clergyman's widow who becomes engaged to Julian

Everard Bone, a prim, self-centered anthropologist

Dora and **William Caldicote,** sister and brother

Form and Content

The plot of *Excellent Women* centers on Mildred Lathbury, her thoughts about the other characters in the novel and her actions toward them. She injects herself into the lives of a young couple, Helena and Rockingham Napier. He is something of a low-grade ladies man, and she is an anthropologist. Mildred befriends them as a couple and individually. Their marital difficulties generate varied expressions of concern from Mildred. Father Julian Malory and his unmarried sister, Winifred, are another pair of characters. St. Mary's is Mildred's church, and Julian and Winifred are significant friends to Mildred; however, she still has the capacity for ironical remarks about them. It is Julian's engagement to the widow Allegra Gray that creates the biggest concern in this comic novel of manners. An egotistical anthropologist, Everard Bone, "courts" Mildred but in a disjointed and inconsistent manner; his is a very satisfied existence. Dora and William Caldicote, brother and sister, are the last major characters in the novel. Dora's friendship with Mildred has an off-putting quality, and William is only interested in his own feelings and experiences.

The men in this novel are not attractive or strong. They are indecisive, lacking in some moral quality. They are not evil; they are simply ineffectual. The women, on the other hand, are "excellent." Except for Allegra, the husband-seeking widow, they all have qualities that contribute to their enduring strength, allowing them to carry on from where life has deposited them.

In this first-person narrative, Mildred tells of her relationship with the Napiers and the Malorys. Her story reveals much about them, but more important, the reader discovers more about Mildred and her concept of excellent women. In an economy of words, Barbara Pym reveals Mildred as a fascinating character who is both amusing and sad. Pym is a comic writer, with a sharp eye and sharper words for her world of excellent women; she also describes a world of quiet sorrow and stoic suffering, relieved by a strong element of hope for a better tomorrow.

"Excellent women" is a code word that defines Mildred and the other women of St. Mary's parish. They are unmarried by choice or because of circumstances beyond their control. It is by Pym's literary artistry of indirection, understatement, and social reserve that she develops her theme of excellent women. How Mildred fits into that category provides a reflective pause for the reader. Helena tells Mildred about her marriage to Rocky; such concerns about marriage, marital prospects, and the general qualities of men form the basic structure of the novel.

For example, when Dora and Mildred attend a school reunion, their talk is speculation about who is married and what social type the husband is. The speculation is witty, but a melancholy element is also present. This tension between the comic and the pathetic allows Pym, through her main character, to present the reader with this state of affairs: "It was not the excellent women who got married but people like Allegra Gray, who was no good at sewing, and Helena Napier, who left all the washing up." Mildred is hurt by being passed over, but she carries on with a bittersweet regard for her place in life.

This concern about marriage, husbands, and wives provides the major dramatic thrust of the novel. When Mildred and Everard Bone are discussing Helena, who has left Rocky, the concept of excellent women is dealt with in an ironic manner: Unmarried ladies achieve a state of excellence because nothing can be done about them except to respect and esteem them on the proper occasions.

Pym's use of the term "excellent women" has a religious aspect as well, such as when Father Malory announces his engagement to Mrs. Gray to the excellent women connected to the church. Because Mildred is a clergyman's daughter and active in the affairs of St. Mary's, she reflects on the Church of England's norms and on the Roman Catholic church. The text suggests that Mildred and other excellent women are almost de facto nuns. Yet Mildred also has a strong social sense and knowledge that help her as an excellent woman.

Analysis

In a particular manner, *Excellent Women* is a typical Barbara Pym novel. Such an observation is not a damning one, indicating banality, but a celebration of her literary skills. Pym generally writes about a small range of social classes and types, and yet her skill in this novel and other writings reveal a wide universe of insight. Her heroine, Mildred, observes the social situation, making judgments and offering solutions when asked (and sometimes when she is not asked). The result is a person whose basic humanity readers can recognize, but whom they might pass by in real life and never understand.

Excellent Women is a middle-class English novel. The action is never violent, never untoward, but its quiet voice does not mask the deeply felt sentiments of Mildred Lathbury. Her narration has the perfect moral pitch and crystalline discriminations befitting her education (she is well read) and her life experiences. From Mildred's perspective, the reader can explore the underlying loneliness of life, the absence of self-pity, scrupulousness in one's relations with others, and the small, blameless comforts that one has in life. Rich with psychological insights, Mildred has the ability to understand people's weaknesses and to forgive them, because she is honest about her thoughts and their behaviors.

Two scenes illuminate the tone and texture of this novel. The first is when Mildred is having her annual luncheon with William Caldicote, the brother of Mildred's friend Dora. The origins of this ritual date from the time that Dora, and perhaps William, thought something might come of it. Mildred observes, however, that "as the years had passed our relationship had settled into a comfortable dull thing." The conversation turns to friends, marriage, and life generally, and Mildred rejects the idea that she might marry Julian Malory, the rector of St. Mary's. Mildred switches easily from describing a social situation to how she feels about it.

The second scene also indicates Mildred's moral or ethical code. Her text directly offers an immediate insight for the reader. The rector's sister, Winifred, has come for tea. She believes that she will lose her home when Julian and Mrs. Gray marry. Mrs. Gray has informed Winifred that this possibility is actually a certainty. Although upset, Winifred calmly asks Mildred if she might move into Mildred's flat. The following excerpt reveals Pym at her artistic best.

> For a moment I was too taken aback to say anything and I knew that I must think carefully before I answered. Easy excuses, such as the difficulty of finding a whole pair of clean sheets that didn't need mending, would not do here. I had to ask myself why it was that the thought of Winifred, of whom I was really very fond, sharing my home with me filled me with sinking apprehension. Perhaps it was because I realised that if I once took her in it would probably be for ever. There could be no casting her off if my own circumstances should happen to change, if, for example, I ever thought of getting married myself. And at the idea of getting married myself I began to laugh, for it really did seem a little fantastic.

This key passage reveals the essence of Mildred's narrative, her world, her ideas, and her feelings.

Context

Excellent Women is not, in a strict sense, a feminist novel. Pym's work is not driven by ideology and politics. Rather, her subjects and ironic style can be traced to Jane Austen—a worthy tradition, indeed, in the history of the

British novel. To appreciate Pym's art, her biography is instructive. Hers was a middle-class background. She started writing when she was sixteen. Pym graduated from the University of Oxford, and all of her life she read widely. She lived at home after graduation but moved to London just before the start of World War II in 1939. She had traveled much in Europe. During the war, she joined the WRNS, a women's military support group, that did varied tasks on the home front. After the war, she worked for the International African Institute, where she became a student of anthropology. Writing constantly, she published six novels from 1950 to 1961. Then, in a bizarre turn of events worthy of a Pym novel, by the 1960's publishers were rejecting her manuscripts; apparently, her material had become "dated." Her life was then bounded by English literature, the Anglican church, and her work at the institute. She continued to write, however, and as a result of praise from Philip Larkin and Lord David Cecil, her novel *Quartet in Autumn* was published in 1977; three other novels followed. She was shortlisted for the Booker Prize, the highest literary award in English letters. Pym died in 1980.

Pym's literary landscape, like Austen's, is small but deep with insight. Her subject is men and women and their experiences with one another. Often the men are dull-witted and vague about the consequences of their actions. Pym forgives them and the women involved by stressing the common humanity of all and by giving emphasis to the comic side of the human condition. She explores the lives of ordinary people who, upon closer examination, are not ordinary at all. Isolated by choice or by circumstance from the ideological wars of the women's liberation movement that was so strong in the United States and England, Pym produced a remarkable series of novels, such as *Excellent Women*, and unforgettable people, such as Mildred Lathbury, an excellent woman.

Sources for Further Study

Cotsell, Michael. *Barbara Pym*. New York: St. Martin's Press, 1989. This brief but heavily factual biography is well researched. With a select bibliography, Cotsell ties the particulars of Pym's life to her novels. He believes that, unable to identify with or accept the England of the 1960's, Pym made a pained comedy out of her newfound incongruity.

Holt, Hazel. *A Lot to Ask: A Life of Barbara Pym*. London: Macmillan, 1990. Written by Pym's friend and literary executor. Holt had also worked with Pym at the International African Institute for nearly twenty-five years. Holt provides a warm portrait of a woman who was given to romantic fancies and yet who had the capacity for critical self-examination, as demonstrated by the character of Mildred. The text is based on the Pym papers at the Bodleian Library at Oxford. Quoting generously from the Pym archives, Holt brings forth a delightful, complex person for the reader. Photographs are included.

Liddell, Robert. *A Mind at Ease: Barbara Pym and Her Novels*. London: Peter Owen, 1989. Focusing on the novels that Liddell believes sustain Pym's popular reputation, he speculates about Pym's vast popularity since her "comeback" in 1977 and about the ironies of literary fashion. This brief book is divided into three parts: the early years, the canon, and the later years.

Pym, Barbara. *Civil to Strangers and Other Writings*. Edited by Hazel Holt. New York: E. P. Dutton, 1987. Contains a previously unpublished novel and short stories; its key worth is "Finding a Voice: A Radio Talk." Transmitted on April 4, 1978, it is an honest judgment by Pym of her life and work. She names her literary models and describes her general outlook on life. An excellent introduction to Pym's world.

———. *A Very Private Eye: An Autobiography in Diaries and Letters*. Edited by Hazel Holt and Hilary Pym. New York: E. P. Dutton, 1984. The editors are Pym's literary executor and sister. Drawing on the vast correspondence and other writings, they have fashioned a most informative autobiography. Pym's writings are organized around the sections "Oxford," "The War," and "The Novelist." A must for understanding Pym's life and her art and how she looked at both with an ironic and compassionate gaze. Contains illustrations, a publishing history, and an index/glossary.

Rossen, Janice. *The World of Barbara Pym*. New York: St. Martin's Press, 1987. This book deals with England as it is perceived and re-created in Pym's novels. Seven chapters explore Pym as writer: "A Style of One's Own," "Love in the Great Libraries," "Spinsterhood," "High Church Comedy," "Anthropology," "The Artist as Observer," and "*A Few Green Leaves* as Apologia." Argues that Pym's subjects are downtrodden, mild women who exemplify excellence on an uncommon level.

Donald K. Pickens

FEAR OF FLYING

Author: Erica Jong (1942-   )
Type of work: Novel
Type of plot: Social realism
Time of plot: The early 1970's
Locale: New York City, Vienna, and other parts of Europe
First published: 1973

Principal characters:

Isadora Wing, a twenty-nine-year-old poet torn between the need for security and a supportive husband and the desire for freedom, adventure, and sexual exploration

Bennett Wing, Isadora's husband, a Freudian psychoanalyst who is silent and withdrawn

Adrian Goodlove, a British Laingian psychiatrist whom Isadora meets in Vienna

Judith Stoloff White, also known as Jude, Isadora's mother

Form and Content

Fear of Flying is the story of the self-discovery of a twenty-nine-year-old woman who seeks new freedom and a new way of being in the age of women's liberation. As the story opens, Isadora is on a plane in flight to Vienna, accompanying her psychoanalyst husband Bennett Wing to a congress of psychoanalysts. Literally afraid of flying, Isadora believes that only her concentration keeps the plane aloft. Her fear of flying also has important metaphorical significance, however, indicating her fear of independence, of following her spirit of adventurousness. Sharing her flight are a number of psychoanalysts, some of whom have treated her—for the most part incompetently, usually by telling her that she should accept being a woman. The novel follows Isadora's adventures in Vienna and later in Europe, and alternates her account of these events with flashbacks that tell of her early life in New York City.

At the conference in Vienna, Isadora meets Adrian Goodlove and is immediately strongly attracted to him. He urges her to leave her husband behind in Vienna and join him on a trip across Europe. Pulled in two directions, Isadora agonizes over the choice between Bennett, who represents safety and the predictable, and Adrian, who represents the spontaneity and excitement that is lacking from her marriage. Adrian promises to teach her not to be afraid of what is inside her, and the two embark on what is supposed to be a completely spontaneous adventure, a series of purely existential moments. What ensues is a disappointing odyssey from one grubby campsite to another, with Adrian alternately lecturing Isadora on the need to go down into herself to salvage her own life and attempting to make love to her—with disappointing results, since he is usually impotent.

In a series of flashbacks, Isadora tells of growing up female in the United States. She has been reared in a secular Jewish family which celebrates the "winter solstice" with a Christmas tree. The most powerful influence on Isadora is her mother, a talented woman who has turned her frustrated creativity to bringing up four daughters. Highly original in her manner of dress and insisting that she values uniqueness above all, Jude has the effect of cramping Isadora's search for creativity and originality.

Isadora became a feminist at thirteen when a boy from Horace Mann school asked her if she was planning to be a secretary. In college, she met her first husband, Brian Stollerman, who delighted her with his brilliant talk. She married him after graduation, but he soon had a mental breakdown—insisting that he was Jesus Christ and could walk on water in Central Park Lake—and was institutionalized. Isadora then married Bennett, who seemed eminently safe after Brian. With Bennett, she went to live in Heidelberg, Germany, when he was drafted during the Vietnam War.

As Isadora and Adrian reach France in the present of the novel, he tells her that he will leave her in Paris because he has a date to meet his wife and children. Isadora is furious, but she has already become disillusioned with him and goes to a hotel on her own. There she reads through her notebooks and diary and comes to the conclusion that she herself must be the source of the meaning in her life. She then goes to London, where she thinks that Bennett may have gone, and the novel ends with Isadora in the bathtub in his hotel room, waiting for his arrival but determined to be her own person and not to "grovel."

Analysis

In *Fear of Flying*, Erica Jong presents the journey of a woman who moves from dependence on men to reliance on herself for feelings of accomplishment and self-worth. Isadora embodies the new female consciousness of the early days of feminism, or women's liberation, as it was then called. Isadora is in touch with her own sexual nature. She makes no secret about the fact that she is strongly attracted to men and strongly aroused by sex. She is candid about her own sexual past, detailing the sexual history of her youth: her first "phallos," encountered at thirteen with her first boyfriend; the affairs that she had in Europe after her first marriage broke up, and her use of masturbation. She discloses her sexual fantasies, especially that of the ultimate sexual experience: It must be both spontaneous and momentary, and the two parties must not get to know each other well. It is clear that such an experience is completely a fantasy, but it is a fantasy born of the frustrations of marriage (as that institution has evolved in a patriarchal society) and the result of the ideology of romantic love of twentieth century America. Isadora longs for a fulfilling marriage such as she imagines that of novelist Virginia Woolf and her husband, Leonard, to have been. Bennett's only response to her wish for a closer relationship is to send her to an analyst.

Having grown up female in the United States has encumbered Isadora with considerable emotional and psychological baggage. Like other young women, Isadora has been bombarded with commercial messages that articulate the ideology that if one perfects oneself by following all the advice of the cosmetic advertisements, one will be rewarded with total romantic fulfillment. Isadora's marriage, however, has become predictable and her lovemaking with Bennett a matter of routine ("as bland as Velveeta cheese").

Isadora cannot imagine herself without a man, even though she has other aspirations that have nothing to do with men. When she is with a man, she has a tendency to act the toady. Men make her turn soft and mushy, but she knows that feeling to be the enemy. Isadora has what she calls a "hunger thump": a powerful desire to get the most out of life. Nevertheless, she has found no way to reconcile her sexual needs with her intellectual ones.

One feature of the novel that shocked Jong's contemporaries when it first appeared is Jong's raunchy vocabulary—especially in view of the fact that Jong is a woman writer and her narrator-protagonist is a woman. Jong used this vocabulary in order to underline her assertion that women, far from being pure Victorian lilies, have sexual natures similar to men's. It is also possible that Jong was parodying the male sexual language used by the tough or realistic male novelists of the time, such as Norman Mailer and Henry Miller.

The comedic nature of Jong's text is important. Isadora describes much of her past in a slapstick vein, from her first fumbling attempts at sex at thirteen to the sexual adventures of the European trip that she took with her friend Pia. On this trip, she and Pia collected men like sex objects and often laughed uproariously over their sexual encounters. The comedy of Isadora's early family life and the tendencies of her mother and sisters to be rendered as caricatures also contribute to the comic tone. Isadora's sister, Randy, is exaggeratedly fecund (with nine children) and something of a harridan in her attacks on the childless Isadora, whom she insists has made the wrong choices in life. Isadora mocks herself, such as her timidity and her propensity to behave like a woman conditioned by advertising and ideology, but she also satirizes various aspects of late twentieth century life, such as the Madison Avenue influence and the behavior and attitudes of psychoanalysts. The latter are mocked through their strange-sounding (and suggestive) Germanic names, such as Dr. Schrift (as in "short shrift"); their accents; and their habit of simply reinforcing society's dictums about women in their diagnoses and treatment. The comic possibilities of German life are also exploited in the sections of the novel set in Germany. Germans are satirized for being overly concerned about their physical well-being, for being outwardly concerned about cleanliness while being secret slobs, and—on a potentially more serious note—for denying or avoiding their Nazi past.

An important part of the novel is Isadora's discovery in Germany of her own Jewishness. Isadora had been critical of the provincialism of Jews she had known in her youth—and she certainly exploited their comic possibilities—but in Germany she undertakes a serious quest for her heritage. She comes to understand the horrors of Jewish persecution and her own connection with a rich past.

Isadora's discovery of her Jewishness complements her growth in self-direction and self-understanding. She has always been gifted and intelligent, and she has always valued creativity and intellectual and educational achievement. As the novel winds to a close, she takes command of her own life. It becomes increasingly clear that no man will alone be able to provide the fulfillment that she seeks (though she will always, one understands, be a woman who is strongly affected by sexual chemistry). Adrian, who seemed to offer the perfect sexual experience, is, like all fantasies, disappointing in reality. Although he claims that he wants to help her center herself and direct her life more firmly, he is quick to abandon her when it suits his convenience. Isadora finds herself by seeking meaning in her identity as a writer and by turning inward to realize her own strength.

Context

When *Fear of Flying* appeared in 1973, it was immediately seized on by both men and women as representing the new feminist consciousness of women's liberation. The reviews indicated that some readers were shocked by the candidly sexual language and by the novel's protagonist, who insists on describing sexual fantasies and sexual experience from a women's point of view and who does not apologize for an insistence on her right to sexual pleasure. On the other hand, feminist reviewers represented many women readers in applauding a fictional heroine who was creative and intellectual but also highly sexual.

Men also welcomed the novel, indicating that they learned much about women's sexual feelings from the book. The ultimate message in the novel about female sexuality is that it is not so different from male sexuality. The novel's impact is suggested by the fact that it was a best-seller, with three million copies sold in the first year.

Many women related to Isadora's difficult struggle to stand on her own. For many years, women had been conditioned to defer to men and to value their roles as sweethearts and wives above all others. Isadora is like the typical woman in that she had a tendency to fawn over men, but she is also an accomplished and creative person in her own right—a poet—and her identity as an individual and a writer becomes increasingly important to her in the course of the novel. Isadora also recounts her search for female artistic role models. She says that, lacking such models, she had to learn about women from D. H. Lawrence, a twentieth century British novelist who wrote about female sexuality. *Fear of Flying* made an important statement about women's newly discovered desire for female role models and literary "foremothers."

Sources for Further Study

Reardon, Joan. "*Fear of Flying*: Developing the Feminist Novel." *International Journal of Women's Studies* 1 (May/June, 1978): 306-320. Reardon analyzes *Fear of Flying* as an education novel, finding in Isadora's journey parallels to the journeys of Alice in Wonderland and Dante. She calls attention to Jong's utilization of images of menstruation (including basing the whole novel on one twenty-eight-day cycle) to signify Isadora's journey into her own womanhood.

Suleiman, Susan. "(Re)Writing the Body: The Politics and Poetics of Female Eroticism." In *The Female Body in Western Culture*. Cambridge, Mass.: Harvard University Press, 1986. Suleiman sees Jong's novel as a milestone in "sexual poetics" and calls attention to the self-irony in the work and the parodic nature of the obscene language.

Updike, John. "Jong Love." In *Picked-up Pieces*. New York: Alfred A. Knopf, 1975. Updike's rave review, reprinted from *The New Yorker*, compares Jong to Geoffrey Chaucer's Wife of Bath. He argues that Jong has invented a new form of female prose and praises her comic gift. The review gave a boost to the novel's reputation and was often quoted by subsequent writers.

Charlotte Templin

THE FEMALE EUNUCH

Author: Germaine Greer (1939-)
Type of work: Social criticism
First published: 1970

Form and Content

The Female Eunuch, by Germaine Greer, is remarkable both for its style and for its substance. Stylistically, it presents a nonstop journey of blistering eloquence, as Greer scores point after point against what she sees as the wrongheaded ways that people think about sexuality, love, the family, politics, and society in general. The relatively loose organization of the book gives Greer free rein to search out and destroy myths which promote oppression and unhappiness for women and men alike. Interspersed with Greer's own prose are boxed quotes from numerous authors, past and present, who—sometimes foolishly, sometimes wisely—have approached the book's subject matter (sex and gender) in a revealing way. These quotes are not always clearly related to the main text, but they are always provocative and entertaining, which is also true for the book as a whole. Substantively, the book addresses the issues of female sexuality and gender equality in an original and profound way, one which, joined with its provocative style, struck a chord with many women and more than a few men. The book also aroused stern opposition from inside and outside the women's liberation movement.

As the book's title indicates, Greer's central thesis is that, in numerous ways, western culture castrates women (this castration is literal in the case of clitorectomies, formerly a way of controlling female masturbation), thoroughly repressing their natural sexuality and replacing it with the myth of passivity. Women are reduced either to idealized eunuchs—morally pure, odorless, pert, and attractive—or, if they reject their asexual designation, witches and whores. Either way, women's lives, liberty, and pursuit of happiness are seriously proscribed. Moreover, this oppression of women does not profit men, at least not in the long run. Men are sexually overburdened, weighed down by overbearing mothers and frustrated by the psychological hobbling of their mates.

In fleshing out her argument, Greer ultimately takes aim at gender role models, marriage (and monogamous relations in general), the family, and even romantic love. Capitalist politics also do not escape unscathed. By the time the book is finished, most of the established social institutions of Western society (circa 1970) have been discarded by Greer as unnatural, counterproductive, and just plain wrong. She even takes a number of potshots at the women's liberation movement.

According to Greer, boys and girls share much more in the way of a common nature than is usually admitted. This includes, for females as well as males, the potential for a fully active libido and active careers outside the home. Conventional socialization, however, suppresses female sexuality as well as female ambition. Instead, women are geared to seek romantic, monogamous love. This love is supposed to end in marriage, a joyful life devoted to rearing children, and happiness ever after. These prizes are all counterfeit, according to Greer. Romantic love is a fictional concept which has never really existed and never will, monogamy is unnaturally confining, marriage is a trap for both partners, and the modern nuclear family is a disaster for parents and children alike. Yet these myths are perpetuated, partly because they serve to buttress the foundations of the political and economic order, which, according to Greer, also runs counter to human nature.

Greer's fellow feminists also receive explicit and implicit criticism, though Greer definitely sees herself as a part of the women's movement. Moderate feminists such as Betty Friedan are criticized for not penetrating deeply enough into the problem and therefore advocating cosmetic remedies that leave essential institutions such as marriage and the family intact. Various sorts of radical feminists are taken to task for their excessive academicism, reductionism (this is true for Marxist feminists, especially), identification of liberation with lesbianism, rejection of the biological relationship between men and women, and flirtation with revolutionary violence. Implicit in this analysis is an overall criticism of contemporary feminists for allowing their movement to be weakened by fragmentation and the quest for liberation to degenerate into a war against men. For Greer, the enemy is not men, since the social manners and mores which oppress women are promoted by men and women alike. (In addition, Greer remains a proponent of healthy heterosexual relationships.)

Greer closes her book with a call for revolution, as opposed to mere radical reaction or reformism. She makes it clear, however, that this revolution is to be one of consciousness rather than physical violence. After all, when the enemy is *us*, at whom do we point our guns?

Analysis

The Female Eunuch deftly combines the depth and challenge of serious scholarship with the accessibility (and entertainment) of journalism. This reflects Greer's background as doctor and professor of English literature, on the one hand, and as an "underground" writer and television personality (in Great Britain, where she emigrated after growing up in Australia), on the other. Classifying the nature of Greer's feminism, however, raises difficulties. In some ways deeply radical, yet also rejecting certain radical solutions and approaches, Greer seems to occupy an ideological slot all her own, a situation which probably does not displease her in the least.

Greer might be categorized as a radical feminist because she rejects basic institutions such as marriage and the family and because she calls for revolutionary change. For Greer, reformism and moderation become essentially conservative in nature. Yet Greer also rejects many popular tenets of radical feminism. She believes that men are also victimized by modern institutions and therefore not to be understood merely as oppressors. She embraces biology, including sexuality, and eschews the kind of unremittingly dense scholarly approach of many radical feminists.

According to French scholar Ginette Castro, Greer may be classified as an advocate of androgyny. This means that Greer believes in the essential identity of nature shared by females and males. It also means that Greer envisions the full sharing by females and males in a liberated lifestyle featuring new forms of solidarity (for example, new forms of extended family and communal living), increased opportunities for creativity, guilt-free sexual pleasure, and perhaps even realistic forms of love (as opposed to romantic love, which is possessive and narcissistic). On the other hand, any category which lumps Greer together with Mary Daly, who has a distinctly religious perspective, may be of limited utility.

In the years after *The Female Eunuch* was published, Greer made no notable effort to clarify her exact place in the women's movement or to elaborate and refine her theory. She remained active as a writer, lecturer, and quasi-celebrity, but she seemed to take pleasure in remaining a free-spirited, freelance critic rather than achieving a more advanced theoretical synthesis. Indeed, this inclination is reflected in the book itself. *The Female Eunuch* has an ad hoc, hastily constructed—perhaps improvised quality. Its coherence and force come from the consistent, gut-level convictions of its author rather than from scholarship or theoretical sophistication.

Context

The Female Eunuch had an immediate impact on the reading public, becoming a best-seller despite its publisher's initial hesitancy to put large quantities of the book in print. This surprising marketability, in turn, increased publishers' interest in other feminist authors, many of whom rode Greer's coattails to commercial success and, most important, a broader audience. *The Female Eunuch* also has displayed a certain amount of lasting power.

In addition, Greer herself became a widely exposed spokeswoman for women's liberation. She was the first of the contemporary feminists to become a media star, more than holding her own with various television interviewers and discussion panelists. Tall, articulate, and unremittingly provocative, Greer made an impressive role model for young and not-so-young women working toward greater independence and a stronger personal identity. Both Greer and her book made significant contributions to the "sexual revolution" of the late 1960's and early 1970's, helping to legitimize female sexuality as well as a more free orientation toward sexual activity for both men and women.

On the other hand, Greer's influence on feminist thought pales beside that of figures such as Betty Friedan, Kate Millett, Shulamith Firestone, and Mary Daly. While Greer is occasionally quoted and her books have been avidly reviewed in periodicals, she really has been channeled into the role of entertainer and pop-culture commentator, while the women mentioned above have made a sustained effort to develop and adapt their theories to changing conditions. In particular, Greer has never refined her concept of "revolution." While she calls for radical change, she has never offered a tangible description of how change may be brought about, how long such change will take, and what its costs will be. This, doubtlessly, has reduced her impact on movement intellectuals and, ultimately, on the women's movement itself.

Greer's own view on the impact of *The Female Eunuch* may be found in her foreword to the book's 1991 edition. She is not optimistic, pointing out that, though appearances may have been to the contrary, things had not changed very much in the more than twenty years since the book's original publication. Obviously, the revolution in consciousness Greer advocated is not making the headway for which she hoped. Indeed, society had complemented the illusions of romantic love, marriage, and family with that of a revolution which, in reality, has changed little or nothing in essential human relationships. Yet Greer makes no attempt to update or refine her theories. Instead, she offers her brief lamentations and offers the book in its 1970 form. She seems unwilling to consider the possibility of a positive correlation between the book's disappointing impact on everyday behavior and its lack of theoretical specificity and rigor.

Sources for Further Study

Castro, Ginette. *American Feminism: A Contemporary History*. Translated by Elizabeth Loverde-Bagwell. New York: New York University Press, 1990. This book provides an eminently accessible introduction to the range and varieties of contemporary American feminism. Chapter 5, in which Greer is treated as an advocate of feminist androgyny, is especially relevant.

Coole, Diana. *Women in Political Theory: From Ancient Misogyny to Contemporary Feminism*. 2d ed. New York: Harvester Wheatsheaf, 1993. Though this book does not include Greer's book in its bibliography, it helps to put her work in perspective both by placing contemporary feminism into the context of Western political thought and by showing the incredible range, depth, and complexity of feminist political ideas.

Greer, Germaine. *Daddy, We Hardly Knew You*. New York: Viking Penguin, 1989. An investigation into the life of her father after he died in 1983, this book sheds light on Greer's skeptical attitude toward the idealized nuclear family.

———. *The Madwoman's Underclothes: Essays and Occasional Writings* 1968-85. London: Picador, 1986. This highly diverse collection illustrates Greer's pungent, eclectic—critics might say ad hoc and undisciplined—brand of commentary. Topics range from an analysis of Jimi Hendrix's tragic demise to Greer's dealings with self-proclaimed critic of feminism Norman Mailer to her brief association with *Suck* (a pornographic newspaper that she helped to found).

Mailer, Norman. *The Prisoner of Sex*. Boston: Little, Brown, 1971. Mailer's swipe at feminism. Greer, however, is treated rather favorably, a fact that neither she nor other feminists appreciated. Greer later appeared in a televised debate with Mailer, describing the experience in an essay entitled "My Mailer Problem." The essay is included in *The Madwoman's Underclothes* (listed above).

Ira Smolensky
Marjorie Smolensky

THE FEMININE MYSTIQUE

Author: Betty Friedan (1921-)
Type of work: Social criticism
First published: 1963

Form and Content

The Feminine Mystique is a classic of the early years of the late twentieth century's feminist movement. Its title is also the term coined by Betty Friedan to define the post-World War II image of women, which suggested that all women should find their female fulfillment as happy, contented housewives and in their families and homes.

In a 1957 survey of her Smith College classmates from fifteen years earlier, Friedan notices a real clash between the educations women were receiving and the ways they were expected to live out the rest of their lives. Having attempted to live up to this feminine ideal herself and experienced at first hand the vague sense of unease, boredom, and frustration many women felt in that narrow role, Friedan, a free-lance magazine writer at the time, tried to publish her findings in several women's magazines, including *McCall's*, *Ladies Home Journal*, and *Redbook*. Yet her conclusion that the problem was not the education women received but the circumscribed roles those educated women were asked to play afterward was too radical and threatening for these magazines, and Friedan realized that to get her ideas into print she would have to write a book. This book became *The Feminine Mystique*.

With driving passion, Friedan systematically analyzes her topic. She begins by describing "the problem that has no name," the boredom, frustration, and lack of fulfillment felt by women trying to live up to the feminine mystique of the 1950's. Most of the remainder of the book is an analysis of the forces that underlay the mystique: where it came from in the first place and why, ideologies used to bolster it, and how it was reinforced and presented to the postwar world as normal.

In the process she discusses Sigmund Freud, the founder of psychoanalytic theory, who believed that ambitious women were driven by envy of the male penis and whose ideas were very popular during this time; Margaret Mead, an anthropologist who herself had led an unconventional life chronicling great varieties of cultural systems, but who could be read in women's magazines advising women to fulfill their functions in the home; these women's magazines themselves, which Friedan identifies as the primary popularizers of the feminine mystique; and other forces of the post-World War II American worldview.

She then moves on to analyze the damage the feminine mystique does, not only to the women themselves but also to their husbands and children. Departing from the then-popular notion that the problem is women's inability to adjust and fit into their natural roles, Friedan argues for the radical idea that it is the role that is wrong. The feminine mystique is itself the problem. The book finishes, appropriately, with suggestions for how women can escape the trap of the mystique.

Analysis

Women's magazines, Friedan suggests, were one of the primary popularizers of the feminine mystique, encouraging women to focus on home and family to the exclusion of anything else. She describes in detail articles, stories, and whole issues whose primary message was that women who aspired to any interest beyond the home were unhappy, unfulfilled, and abnormal.

She goes on to analyze the genesis of the mystique in postwar values, as a way for war-weary Americans, frightened of the changes in the modern world, to hide in an idealized notion of a safe home complete with happy housewife and contented children. She also notes that a fear of "masculinized" women helped drive the development and popularity of the feminine mystique. The gains in women's rights and freedoms as a result of the feminist movement of the nineteenth century were threatening to U.S. society as a whole, and during the 1950's the feminists of earlier days were portrayed as ridiculous characters who had simply been unable to attain love and feminine fulfillment. Friedan commits an entire chapter to explaining what these feminist pioneers really did and who they were.

Further chapters focus on popular ideas and belief systems that bolstered the feminine mystique, and each is exploded in the analysis. For example, Freud's concept that women are driven by penis envy was used as justification for mocking the ideas and work of feminists, since they could be dismissed as maladjusted women who had not resolved their penis envy. Friedan counters the popular dependence on Freudian ideas by delving into the forces that motivated Freud himself and pointing to his distorted experiences with the women in his life.

Women, Friedan says, were offered a choice: either succeed in a "masculine" career and be celibate and sexless, or be a housewife and mother, a truly feminine woman, and experience the love of husband and family. It is one or the other. Given that kind of choice, she points out, many women chose the latter.

Yet why would women accept such a choice? Friedan suggests that there were several factors, including the effect of the war years with the fears and loneliness engendered by that experience, the job discrimination women experienced after the war as they were fired to make way for returning veterans, and a fear made popular during this time that women were harming their children by a loss of femininity and by working outside the home. The feminine mystique was a boon to one arena of American society, the world of commercial interests. Friedan devotes a chapter to the importance of consumerism to women whose lives centered on home and family. Products and advertising were geared to the woman in the home, who was encouraged to buy as never before.

Nevertheless, the feminine mystique backfired in many ways, Friedan argues. Men became resentful of overly dependent wives—women who, having no lives and interests of their own, clung to their husbands. Children whose mothers were encouraged to concentrate on them as the primary products of their lifework grew up soft, dependent, and incapable of building their own meaningful lives. Women themselves forfeited any self-identity and could define themselves only as their husbands' wives and their children's mothers.

Friedan concludes her dense, passionate, and provocative essay with a chapter urging women to look beyond their homes and the feminine mystique, to educate themselves and look for dreams of their own. She suggests ways for the women of her day to begin to break out of the trap foisted upon them by the popular culture of the postwar world and to find themselves as human beings.

Context

This was a book that had to be written. Chafing under a limited vision of what they could and should be, American middle-class women were bound to explode in frustration. Friedan's book named the unnamed source of their dissatisfaction, analyzed it, and made sense of where it came from, identifying it as a social phenomenon rather than a manifestation of natural womanhood. This analysis gave them a glimpse of a way out, providing the vehicle they needed.

Thousands of women saw themselves in the pages of this book. The phenomenon named by Friedan was real; it was a social force that arose, as she says, both out of the experiences of World War II and out of fears of the gains women had been making since the feminist movement of the nineteenth century. Any perusal of the women's magazines of the 1950's, which can now be found in antique shops and flea markets, shows that Friedan was right about the propaganda these magazines were publishing.

Friedan's naming of the problem helped women struggling under the feminine mystique to see that their problems were not uniquely their own, were not caused by their own inadequacies, but were the result of an ideology that simply did not fit the realities of most women's lives. The corsets of the nineteenth century distorted the body shapes of the women who wore them, harming them in the process, and the feminine mystique was a social corset that distorted and harmed the lives and identities of the women of the 1950's who tried to "wear" it.

Yet like the corset of the nineteenth century, which only wealthy women could afford to wear, the feminine mystique, while proposed as the model for all American women, was in reality something to which only middle- and upper-class women could aspire. Many women were not trapped in their homes, for their families' economic survival required that they leave home every day to go to work. It fell to another feminist, the African American Bell Hooks, in *Feminist Theory from Margin to Center* (1984), to point out that Friedan, while seeming to speak for all women in *The Feminine Mystique*, was really speaking only for those primarily white, college-educated, middle-class women who had the economic luxury of aspiring to the feminine mystique.

Hooks's critique is an important corrective to the picture painted by Friedan. The fact remains, however, that for the thousands of women who did find themselves trapped in the mythology of the feminine mystique of the 1950's, Betty Friedan's book was galvanizing and revolutionary. This book, and the effect it had on the women who read it, was one of the factors leading to the feminist movement that began in the late 1960's.

Sources for Further Study

Blau, Justine. *Betty Friedan*. New York: Chelsea House, 1990. Part of the American Women of Achievement series, this book is intended for grades five and up. Yet far more than an interesting storybook about Betty Friedan, this volume goes into depth both on Friedan's life and on the feminist movement she helped spark. It also includes several pages on *The Feminine Mystique*—its writing, its content, and responses to it.

Chafe, William H. *The Paradox of Change: American Women in the Twentieth Century*. New York: Oxford University Press, 1991. Includes a brief but helpful discussion of *The Feminine Mystique* which not only deals with its effect on American women but also notes the reasons that Friedan's approach has been criticized by other feminists.

Cohen, Marcia. *The Sisterhood: The True Story of the Women Who Changed the World*. New York: Simon & Schuster, 1988. This book combines biographical material on a number of feminist activists of the late twentieth century. There are several chapters on Betty Friedan, including an entire chapter on *The Feminine Mystique*.

Ferree, Myra Marx, and Beth B. Hess. *Controversy and Coalition: The New Feminist Movement*. Boston: Twayne, 1985. This history of the late twentieth century feminist movement incorporates a brief but cogent description of *The Feminine Mystique*, including its effects and its weaknesses. It also helps the reader get a grasp of this feminist movement as a whole.

Friedan, Betty. *It Changed My Life: Writings on the Women's Movement*. New York: Random House, 1976. Perhaps the most autobiographical of Friedan's books, this one documents her activism in the women's movement she helped found, showing the reader what occurred in Friedan's life and work in the thirteen years after *The Feminine Mystique* was published.

Henry, Sondra, and Emily Taitz. *Betty Friedan: Fighter for Women's Rights*. Hillside, N.J.: Enslow, 1990. Part of the Contemporary Women series, this book is intended for grades six and up. It also, however, is a detailed account of Friedan's life, including several references and valuable material on *The Feminine Mystique* and responses to the book.

Hooks, Bell. *Feminist Theory from Margin to Center*. Boston: South End Press, 1984. This volume on black women and feminism begins with a scathing critique of *The Feminine Mystique* as a racist, classist book that, while claiming to speak for all women, ignores the reality of many women's lives.

Eleanor B. Amico

FEMININE PSYCHOLOGY

Author: Karen Horney (1885-1952)
Type of work: Essays
First published: 1967

Form and Content

A collection of fifteen essays written by Karen Horney between 1922 and 1936, *Feminine Psychology* presents groundbreaking material for the study of women as intellectual entities in their own right, rather than theories based on women's supposed disappointment in not being born male. Initially intended as refutations of much of Sigmund Freud's theoretical construction for psychoanalysis, the essays included are representative of Horney's early work and teaching in the area of psychotherapy. The volume is not a comprehensive compilation of all of her essays written during this time period or on this subject. Rather, it is meant to encompass the breadth of Horney's ideas. The book was edited by Harold Kelman, a disciple of Horney and one of the psychoanalysts who, with her, founded the Association for the Advancement of Psychoanalysis and later became its president.

The essays in *Feminine Psychology* follow a roughly chronological order ("roughly" because dates of presentation and dates of publication often overlap). They span a period of Horney's life which included the collapse of her marriage and her emigration with the youngest of her three daughters to the United States. These personal upheavals are reflected in such essays as "The Problems of Marriage," "Maternal Conflicts," and "The Distrust Between the Sexes."

Most of the essays included in this work were presented as scholarly papers at meetings of various medical and psychoanalytical societies. This fact is often highlighted by specific comments on the work and theories of other analysts, especially Freud, but also including Karl Abraham (Horney's own first analyst), Melanie Klein (who analyzed all of Horney's daughters), Helene Deutsch, Sandor Rado, and others. The first paper in the book, "On the Genesis of the Castration Complex in Women," was a direct dissent from Abraham's espousement and extension of Freud's theory of penis envy, the contention that women suffer from the childhood realization that they lack penises and are therefore defective. While Horney's paper was only a mild dissent and reflected the fact that she still adhered to most Freudian psychoanalytic theory, it set the stage for her subsequent development of a coherent doctrine on feminine sexuality and psychology.

Prior to Horney's work, psychoanalysis had been limited almost completely to the male point of view. It was exceedingly rare for women to attend medical school (Horney was one of the first women in Germany to do so), so virtually all analysts were male. Although many of the patients were female, their neuroses were interpreted from the generalization of the experiences of men and boys. *Feminine Psychology* presents Horney's pioneering work which not only brought to analysis a feminine perspective for the first time but also reevaluated existing Freudian views in light of this perspective. In the 1932 essay "The Dread of Women," Horney proposes that the development of the concept of penis envy was a manifestation of men's fear and envy of women's ability to bear children. "The Problem of Feminine Masochism," presented in 1933, was a criticism of both the theory and the methodology of Rado's and Deutsch's statements that masochism in women is both universal and a result, once again, of penis envy.

Other essays include Horney's assessments of the genesis of female physiological problems ("Premenstrual Tension," "Psychogenic Factors in Functional Female Disorders") and sexual dysfunction ("Inhibited Femininity," "The Denial of the Vagina"), as well as the previously mentioned essays on the problems of courtship, marriage, and motherhood.

Analysis

Taken together, the essays in *Feminine Psychology* present the basis of a philosophy of psychotherapy that Horney continued to develop throughout her life. Horney was primarily a therapist and teacher rather than a theoretician. The findings in her writings are based on her work with patients and her own experience, not on other analysts' studies.

The essays here can be grouped into a few broad categories (with considerable overlap). The essays on the castration complex and its origins have already been discussed briefly. The concept of the vagina as a wound left after castration predominated in much of the work of Freud and his followers. Horney took issue with this, arguing that this image of being genitally wounded was instead an identification with the mother as having been damaged by sexual violation. Horney acknowledged that penis envy existed, but she believed that it was caused by girls' envy of boys' ability to see and touch their genitals and to urinate standing up, rather than to some feeling in girls that they were defective through some fault of their own. She also maintained her conviction that, rather than being a minor consideration, as Freud had supposed, male envy of women's ability to become mothers was of enormous import in male society's domination of women.

Horney used these basic ideas as jumping-off points for her other essays. She pursued related concerns in her writings on marriage and motherhood, including "The Problem of the Monogamous Ideal" (1928), "The Distrust Between the Sexes" (1931), "The Problem of Marriage" (1932), and "Maternal Conflicts" (1933). Horney asserted that marital problems often occur because of disappointment and guilt from early identification with the mother's sexual role in marriage and from a corresponding desire to engage in intercourse with the father. She believed that the husband's residual attitudes toward his mother and the unconscious demands of each partner on the other because of unfulfilled Oedipal desires from childhood give rise to inevitable conflicts in marriage. These demands and desires bring "a perilously heavy load of unconscious wishes" to the marriage, often leading husband or wife to seek fulfillment in sexual relationships outside the marriage.

Horney used her theories on the castration complex to explain phenomena associated with female development and dysfunction. In "The Flight from Womanhood" (1926) and "The Denial of the Vagina" (1933), Horney contends that sexual dysfunction in later life and "immature" feelings of pleasure upon stimulation of the clitoris (this was considered dysfunction if it persisted in adulthood, for only vaginal sensations were deemed to be "mature") are caused by childhood fears of vaginal injury. The young girl's Oedipal desire is coupled with both the instinctual realization that her father's penis would be far too large and the guilt from the incest taboo, and these combine to cause the child to deny the existence of her vagina. This can lead to frigidity later in life, as well as masochistic tendencies or homosexuality.

Horney also believed that many feminine psychological problems manifest themselves physically. In "Premenstrual Tension" (1931), she wrote that when she learns of such tension in a patient she looks for "conflicts involving the wish for a child." She expanded on this theme in "Psychogenic Factors in Functional Feminine Disorders" (1933) and "Personality Changes in Female Adolescents" (1935).

Throughout all of Horney's writing, and more specifically in some, runs the theme of the individuality and worth of women. Horney was possibly the first psychoanalyst to incorporate the sociology of the time in her theories; she used male dominance in society as evidence to support her ideas. Her assertion that the "patriarchal ideal of womanhood" is determined by cultural factors, as opposed to being a biological imperative, was a major step away from prevalent theories of her day. Two of her later essays in *Feminine Psychology*, "The Overvaluation of Love" (1934) and "The Neurotic Need for Love" (1937), focus on societal expectation for women to "have a man" and link this with the fear of being "abnormal" if one does not achieve this or the fear of dependency if one does. These papers also propose a predominant force in women's lives previously unrecognized: intense competition with other women. Horney's emphasis on the interweaving of biological and psychosocial factors in the psychology of women can be seen most clearly in these writings.

Context

Feminine Psychology was not published until twenty-five years after Horney's death. During her lifetime, her work, like the women of whom she wrote, was devalued and dismissed. In her later years, her work became increasingly controversial, to the point that the New York Psychoanalytic Society split between the traditional Freudians and the disciples of Horney. This led to the establishment of the Association for the Advancement of Psychoanalysis.

Out of the bitterness that arose from this split, the New York Psychoanalytic Society launched a campaign to discredit Horney's work—a campaign that proved to have substantial influence for many years.

In 1967, however, Horney's colleague and friend Harold Kelman compiled the collection of essays that became *Feminine Psychology*. Leaders of the nascent feminist movement, hailed Horney's work as a confirmation and vindication of their cause. Indeed, Horney's attention to the consequences of sexual inequality in society put her ahead of her time. Her celebration of individuality validated the feminist position on the intrinsic worth of every woman. Her praise for the wonders of motherhood helped to establish the societal value of women. Her constant refusal to bow to the pressures of a male-dominated profession and world continue to be an example to respect and emulate.

This is not to say that Horney's work is now universally accepted, even among feminists. She was not herself a feminist in the modern sense of the word, and some of her claims, such as the innate wish of every woman to be raped, are extreme enough that some critics want to discard all of her work. She was a product of her culture, just as she states the ideal of womanhood to be. Yet increasingly, even those who originally repudiated her work have come to acknowledge its insight. It is indisputable that Karen Horney and her work in feminine psychology provided the impetus for a movement in psychotherapy away from the patriarchal "father figures" of analysis to a more respectful treatment of women, both in analysis and in the greater society.

Later works of Horney include *The Neurotic Personality of Our Time* (1937), *New Ways in Psychoanalysis* (1939), *Self Analysis* (1942), *Our Inner Conflicts: A Constructive Theory of Neurosis* (1945), *Are You Considering Psychoanalysis?* (1946), and *Neurosis and Human Growth* (1950), as well as numerous articles in *The American Journal of Psychoanalysis* and other scholarly publications.

Sources for Further Study

Chodorow, Nancy J. *Feminism and Psychoanalytic Theory*. New Haven, Conn.: Yale University Press, 1989. A highly acclaimed collection of essays that trace a history of the development of a feminist view of psychoanalysis, crediting Horney as the first to challenge the Freudian theory. Indexed.

Horney, Karen. *The Adolescent Diaries of Karen Horney*. New York: Basic Books, 1980. The diaries themselves are interesting, covering Horney's life from the age of thirteen through her first year in medical school. More useful in many ways, however, is the introduction written by Horney's daughter Marianne.

Quinn, Susan. *A Mind of Her Own: The Life of Karen Horney*. New York: Summit Books, 1987. A clearly written biography, this work does not say much about Horney's influence after her death but does provide a very complete analysis of the forces at work in her life. Extensive notes, a bibliographic essay on each chapter, a chronological list of Horney's writings, and a thirteen-page index are included.

Rubins, Jack L. *Karen Horney: Gentle Rebel of Psychoanalysis*. New York: Dial Press, 1978. A sympathetic analysis of Horney's life and work. A chapter on Horney's views of feminine psychology connects her writings to key factors in her life and career. Contains notes, a bibliography, and an index.

Sayers, Janet. *Mothers of Psychoanalysis*. New York: W. W. Norton, 1991. A good introduction to Horney's work, the volume comprises four essays on female psychoanalysts: Deutsch, Klein, Anna Freud, and Horney. Rather scathing on some of Horney's beliefs, it provides a short, objective overview of her achievements. Features extensive notes and an excellent index, plus six pages of bibliography.

Westkott, Marcia. *The Feminist Legacy of Karen Horney*. New Haven, Conn.: Yale University Press, 1986. As this work presents a theory of women's personality development in terms of the feminist perspective, it brings together all of Horney's writing to assess her influence on the women's movement. It emphasizes the concept of feminine alienation and explores cultural influences that encourage character traits commonly associated with women, especially nurturing inclinations. Includes a twenty-one-page bibliography and an index.

Margaret Hawthorne

FEMINISM WITHOUT ILLUSIONS: A Critique of Individualism

Author: Elizabeth Fox-Genovese (1941-)
Type of work: Social criticism
First published: 1991

Form and Content

Feminism Without Illusions: A Critique of Individualism is a work of history and social criticism, and as such it covers a wide range of opinion and a number of topics. There are nine chapters: The first four explore feminism and political life, and the next five deal with feminism and the intellectual life, particularly the issue of an academic canon. Elizabeth Fox-Genovese's thesis is that a paradoxical relationship exists between feminism and individualism. The relationship is complex: One of the origins of individualism was the market revolution of the eighteenth century, and modern feminism developed during that same period. Feminism also claims rights and citizenship for an entire group—women. The author discusses feminism as the claim to equal rights in its autonomous expression and downgrades the notion of domestic feminism, a choice which weakens her presentation. A reform Marxist, Fox-Genovese treats political ideas seriously, but her primary concern is with the social and philosophical consequences of feminism.

Chapter 1, "Beyond Sisterhood," explores the eternal issue of class, education, and life experiences among all kinds of women. The historic issue is between community and society, drawing on the famous distinction created by the German sociologist Ferdinand Tönnies. Fox-Genovese recognizes that feminist agitation and reform had a kinder impact on American life. This observation carries the narrative into the next chapter, "Women and Community." Aside from her thesis dealing with individualism's inadequacy, this chapter offers little insight.

The next two chapters, "From Feminist Theory to Feminist Politics" and "Pornography and Individual Rights," provide the heart of Fox-Genovese's thesis. Citing a wide group of writers and theorists, she reveals some fascinating issues and policies as feminism emerged as a presence in modern American life. This movement has, she observes, provided paradox. For example, the feminist policy regarding abolition was grounded in individualism, but the comparative worth argument regarding equal pay for equal work is really a collectivist concept. As a result, government and the rise of the modern welfare state have a curious position in her text. Government is very important; it carries out the electoral mandates of the people in tempering the abuses of the market.

"Individualism and Women's History" and "The Struggle for a Feminist History" outline the driving force in women's lives. Since 1865, the market has embraced all aspects of American life. Public or private, society or self, the market bends all things to its will. Only women, using Fox-Genovese's theory of feminism, can withstand such institutional and historical challenges. Both chapters are solid summaries of the history of feminist scholarship. The author recognizes that diversity is a vital part of women's history; however, the ideal of a common culture prevents all culture from becoming mere personal experience. Her measured judgments of what constitutes the private and public aspects of women's lives enhance the value of *Feminism Without Illusions*.

Although Fox-Genovese does not cite the four standard positions dealing with gender equality, they are noted here to aid in understanding the long-standing debate in this academic field. The four major interpretations are innatism, environmental feminism, superior feminism and differential egalitarianism. The first concept argues that the gender difference is eternal. The second postulates that social conditioning can overcome any difference in male-female relationships. The third argument simply notes that despite the oppression of history, women are superior to men, particularly regarding morality. Differential egalitarianism recognizes the difference between the sexes but contests that it is not sufficient for any claim of dominance. The resulting issue is the difference between male and female, but the significance of the concept, according to Fox-Genovese, is how it changes over time.

After exploring the implications of these four positions, Fox-Genovese turns to her autobiography in the last three chapters and the afterword and uses herself as an example of differential egalitarianism. A rich and varied bibliography completes the book.

Analysis

The subtitle of this work is critical to Fox-Genovese's thesis. She recognizes that feminism and individualism came into the world of ideas at the same time, supporting each other. Taking a historicist argument, she claims that rights grow out of the group experience, out of history, and that rights for an individual do not exist outside or prior to the larger collectivism, the state or society. As a historical concept, individualism came into existence with the creation of the modern middle class in its institutional setting, the market. As she states, "Individualism, carried on the rising tide of capitalism, transformed community into a fiction that has largely benefited men by easing their transition into that rootless, atomized world that conservatives have so long prophesied and decried."

Writing with respect to Marxism, Fox-Genovese accepts that her radical critique has a conservative consequence. Despite the violent nature of capitalism regarding social relationships, women have the power to maintain community against the fragmenting force of the market. Generally her analysis is in a critical, nonidealist mode. Psychological analysis is a very small part of the text. At least once, however, she uses the current fashion of psychological analysis, as shown in her following statement: "Anger lies at the heart of the matter, for without anger there is no feminist consciousness at all." Unfortunately such a sentiment is out of place in her generally effective narrative and analysis. It is a generalization with an inadequate historic reference. Fox-Genovese's reliance on such an argument is rare. Her usual presentation is more measured, with proper citations to the vast literature regarding feminism and individualism. History is her strong suit, not psychological assumptions. She knows that the French Revolution and the writings of Mary Wollstonecraft opened the way for modern feminism. This book is best when it maintains its historical character.

Her concern with individualism extends to the issue of the academic canon. The idea of such a canon is basic to the argument that there is a tradition, a continuity, to history and education and that a list of basic texts is essential to the fulfillment of the ideals of Western thought. Fox-Genovese is of two minds on this matter. First, she recognizes that time changes events and texts and that nothing is constant. She notes that it is the very canon, with its assumed male tyranny, that provided the intellectual means for feminist liberation. Yet she also realizes that male oppression occurs but that it is not the systematic and automatic creature that radical liberationists have assumed. She recognizes that women's writings are an important part of the canon, particularly since the Enlightenment and the birth of modern feminism.

Fox-Genovese's biggest foe in this book, although it is not directly named, is intellectual laziness. While she does not label this premise, she does note that all political images are connected to power via biology. The assumption in society is that whatever exists does so as a natural, given part of the cultural world. A second theme runs through her text: The early beginnings of female liberation actually gave birth to male liberation. Therefore, men have once again achieved more freedom of action and being than women in the name of individualism, which brings the reader to her primary theme. It is little wonder that anger forms a basis for the history of feminism. Ideals are historically difficult to maintain in such personal and public contexts.

Fox-Genovese's final evaluation is a common feature of this book: Despite an often radical rhetoric, her final judgment is measured and quite conservative. What saves this book is history. Fox-Genovese has too much intellectual respect for the past to engage in questionable arguments. She is a committed feminist; her autobiography reveals a dedicated worker in the ideological vineyard of feminism. Intellectual feelings and beliefs, however, can take one only so far. History provides the reality check for Fox-Genovese.

Context

Elizabeth Fox-Genovese is a major historian whose writings have much importance. This is particularly true abut *Feminism Without Illusions*. Basing her arguments on wide reading and deep questions, Fox-Genovese can question certain aspects of the historical development of feminism because she is an insider. Her academic achievements cannot be challenged.

Her book also is an excellent summary of feminist scholarship which suggests future issues and concerns in the field. The field of women's history has grown and changed since the 1960's, and this book is especially vital in discussing those changes. The text is a close discussion of varied writers in the field. The result is a handy index to many of the standard arguments and concerns in the area of women's history.

Sources for Further Study

Degler, Carl N. *At Odds: Women and the Family in America from the Revolution to the Present*. New York: Oxford University Press, 1980. Degler argues that women's history has an articulate, dedicated group (women) supporting the further development of women's history but that no sizable academic or political element speaks for the family. Because of this, its history does not have the appeal of women's history, although most people spend the majority of their lives within the institution of marriage. The result is an uneven scholarly development of the discipline and de facto emphasis on what Fox-Genovese would label individualism.

Okin, Susan M. *Women in Western Political Thought*. Princeton, N.J.: Princeton University Press, 1979. This book provides scope to understanding how, in Western societies, the male image became the natural in politics, beginning with the ancient Greeks. Plato's concept of "forms" helped to shape this basic assumption, and habit, tradition, and language continued the practice. The early association of the private with the female and the public with the male resulted in segregation.

Pickens, Donald K. "Domestic Feminism and the Structure of American History." *Contemporary Philosophy* 12 (November, 1989): 14-22. Grounded in existing literature, this article argues that the ideal of America is a middle-class utopia and, as a result of this structure, that feminism became two expressions: autonomous and domestic. Autonomous feminism appeals to liberationist sentiment and domestic feminism to the progressive creed of reform.

Smith, Daniel Scott. "Family Limitation, Sexual Control, and Domestic Feminism in Victorian America." In *Clio's Consciousness Raised*, edited by Mary Hartman and Lois Banner. New York: Harper & Row, 1974. Smith's article outlines in an effective way how domestic feminism shaped the major thrust of progressive reform. Because many women wanted to defend their homes from the historical challenges of the market, they turned to the state as a means to that end. The resulting welfare state demonstrated that American women often used assumed-radical means for assumed-conservative ends.

Wolgast, Elizabeth H. *Equality and the Rights of Women*. Ithaca, N.Y.: Cornell University Press, 1980. Wolgast's work is based on a conviction that men and women are different. She anticipated Fox-Genovese's position regarding justice, which demands that women and men be treated differently in some very important areas (for example, only women can give birth to babies).

Woloch, Nancy. *Women and the American Experience*. 2d ed. New York: McGraw-Hill, 1994. Well written and with a strong bibliography, this textbook provides a crucial guide to the historical and emotional issues that have constituted women's history. Woloch's book offers scope and a wide coverage of topics, making it a fine background volume.

Donald K. Pickens

FIFTH CHINESE DAUGHTER

Author: Jade Snow Wong (1922-   )
Type of work: Autobiography
Time of work: The 1930's and 1940's
Locale: California
First published: 1950

Principal personages:

Jade Snow Wong, a second-generation Chinese American who feels constrained by her culture

Mr. Wong, her father, who follows the Chinese way but rejects the subjection of women

Mrs. Wong, her hardworking, upright mother, who acquiesces in male dominance

Jade Precious Stone, her beautiful younger sister, who is her parents' pet

Joe, a high school chum who encourages Jade Snow to go to college

Form and Content

Jade Snow Wong's *Fifth Chinese Daughter* is an autobiographical account, though it is written in the third person, of a Chinese American girl's growing up in California in the 1930's and 1940's. Like many coming-of-age stories, this one concentrates on how the subject chooses a career, establishes viable relations with her parents, and develops a life philosophy adequate to both her ancestry and the new situation she faces. Ironically, though much of the conflict in the book is generated by Jade's struggle to break with the role of obedient Chinese daughter—a role that her father most demands that she play—ultimately Jade's desire to be an independent woman is rooted in her father's advanced views on women, which had already separated him from his own generation.

Wong's work differs from those of later Chinese American women writers in centering the protagonist's desire for more autonomy in the Chinese milieu rather than in a conflict between Asian and American environments. For example, in *The Kitchen God's Wife* (1991), by Amy Tan, the daughter's distance from her mother is based in the fact that her mother grew up in China and she grew up in California, so they "necessarily" have opposed views on interfamilial relations. Wong, on the other hand, shows that her independent streak was formed before she was even exposed to American life.

Although she does go to American schools, until she enters college Wong's life focuses on Chinatown: her father's clothing factory, the church, and the Chinese night school. The contrast between her father's intolerance for any injustices in the running of business or in any of the Chinese community organizations of which he is a director—a righteousness so rigid that it alienates him from his peers—and his tolerance for the injustices that Wong detects in her household's arrangements provides the occasion for her first protests against women's subservient position in traditional Chinese society. She applies her father's formulas for judging public life to her private family circle and ends by protesting the inequalities on which this circle is founded.

The first part of the book charts Wong's rise to a consciousness that she is her own person and must set her own goals. The second part concerns how she gradually finds and defines what her goals are as she moves out from Chinatown into the wider American world. As she goes to junior college and then, based on her high scholastic achievements, to a prestigious women's college, she discovers what her aptitudes and preferences are. Then, working in the shipyards as a secretary and researcher during the building boom brought on by World War II, she learns how to work with Americans, handle business affairs, and organize and carry out complex plans. All of this culminates in her opening her own ceramics shop, where she manufactures and has success in selling the wares she makes; thus she establishes her independence by doing what fulfills her.

Analysis

Fifth Chinese Daughter is about a path breaker. Though Jade Wong is modest, reserved, and not openly assertive, she works diligently to become an independent person. In the period immediately after World War II, when American women were being discouraged from embarking on careers—since, it was said, they would be taking jobs from the returning soldiers—the author, a Chinese American, dares to break not only with American stereotypes of females, but even with the more confining traditions of Oriental culture.

The book, then, answers the question of how a girl from a tradition that consistently downplays female worth can grow up to be a self-assured, free woman. It posits that she can do so by drawing on male role models and by choosing to follow the more enlightened strands within Chinese customs. All of this is done privately, in adolescence, and later the elements she will take from Western culture will merely supplement beliefs drawn from her Chinese roots.

Though Jade Wong feels compassion for her mother, it is by her father that she will be most molded. Like him, she will become a businessperson. He runs a garment factory, and she will make and sell pottery. Like him, she will be outraged by and speak out against injustice. In a key first moment of combativeness, when still in elementary school, she talks back to a teacher who intends to whip her for passing notes: "I am no more guilty than the girl who passed it to me. . . . If you whip me, you should also have here all the girls from my row. . . . And I won't hold out my hand until I see theirs out also!"

Moreover, Jade Wong follows her father in believing that women should not be as debased as they have been in Asian tradition. Though Mr. Wong cannot share his daughter's idea that a woman has the right to choose a career over a marriage, he elected to relocate his family to the United States because he was disgusted by the degraded status of women in China. Thus Jade Wong is not discovering feminism for herself so much as furthering the protofeminist views already held by her father.

Wong's independence is nourished not only by her father's opinions but also by certain strands in Chinese life that are contradictory (and so spur questions) or that can be employed to validate an excelling female. Chinese family life revolves around complexly calculated patterns of deference, with each position having particular ranked dues and duties. Thus, for example, an older sister cannot be called by name by a younger sister or brother (this would be inappropriate), but the opposite does not apply. This system would probably have made for docility in the Wong household if it had been applied equitably. Yet Jade Snow's younger sister Jade Precious Stone, because she is both sickly and outstandingly pretty, manages to avoid most of her requisite chores, which further burdens Jade Snow. Seeing the violation in roles, Jade Snow questions other elements of the setup, such as the special favor shown to her younger brother compared to the little attention paid to the family's daughters.

Chinese tradition emphasizes education, and though study was long considered a masculine preserve, Mr. Wong breaks with custom by insisting that his daughters get the best possible training. Jade Wong seizes on this area as the one in which she can prove herself. She reaps many academic honors. Her successes in scholarship embolden her to set out on an independent path.

Her fundamental development of an independent character takes place in the Chinese community, but as she matures and moves into the wider American world, she finds articulated the feminist feelings that had been the basis of her decisions, and she is helped in realizing her hopes by meeting fellow students who want to be social workers, not homemakers. These women show her that her long-desired goal of living independently is not as aberrant as it seems to other Chinese.

The book is not a simple tale in which an immigrant woman breaks with the patriarchal traditions of the Old World after being exposed to the more relaxed relations between the sexes in the New World. It is a more complex presentation in which the American milieu facilitates an immigrant's daughter's drawing on positive models and particular streams within her own Asian culture. She ends up endorsing strands of individualism to be found in both the East and the West. Her autobiography is written in a style that combines both the self-assertion of the United States (one wants to tell one's story) with the proper dignity and egolessness that constitute the ideal of Chinese civilized living (one's story is told in third person).

Context

Wong came of age at a time when women were playing an increasing part in economic life. With the United States' entrance into World War II, there was a new demand for production, particularly of military supplies, at the same time that there was a drain on the male employment pool, since men went into the armed services in droves. Women obtained work in all fields of heavy industry and earned the respect that went with such employment. Further, and even more important for understanding Wong, China was an ally of the United States in the war, and Chinese citizens were viewed as members of a loyal minority who were contributing in their own way to American life.

Because of this situation, Wong's autobiography had much more impact on race relations than on women's issues. In fact, the book was popular with the U.S. government because it described no instances of racial prejudice (except for a racial taunt hurled in grammar school). Eager to disseminate this picture of America as a land of ethnic harmony, the State Department had the book translated into a number of Asian languages and sponsored Wong on a speaking tour of the Far East.

Later Asian American critics have looked askance at Wong's rosy portrayal of Chinatown life. Wong, they point out, never discusses such things as the United States' exclusionary immigration policies. Elaine Kim makes this charge in *Asian-American Literature* (1982), as well as pointing out that Wong makes Chinese life seem quaint. Other critics, notably the Chinese American playwright Frank Chin, have lambasted Wong for being a man-hating ultrafeminist. Chin traces a genealogy leading from *Fifth Chinese Daughter* to Maxine Hong Kingston's *The Woman Warrior* (1977) and Amy Tan's *The Joy Luck Club* (1989), and he claims that all these writers give heroic portraits of women while picturing Chinese men as weak, ineffectual patsies.

One does not have to accept Chin's opinions to agree that there is a line connecting Wong's book to the novels of later Asian American writers. Although Kingston and Tan focus on mother-daughter relations while Wong is concerned with the father-daughter dyad, the three agree that growing up Chinese American demand the creative integration of aspects of the Eastern and Western worlds. All have independent women as protagonists, women who reject but then come to a reconciliation with their parents' lives. Finally, in the books mentioned, all locate womanly individualism in a strain of Chinese culture, not in Western feminist notions. Kingston draws on Chinese mythology to develop the image of a female swordswoman, while Tan customarily makes the Chinese mothers, not the Americanized daughters, the stronger, more active women.

Unfortunately, critics have said that Wong's later prose work, *No Chinese Stranger* (1975), lacks the unity and emotional force of her first tale. This book tells the story of her life from the 1950's to the 1970's.

Sources for Further Study

Chin, Frank. "Come All Ye Asian-American Masters of the Real and the Fake." In *The Big Aiiieeeee!: An Anthology of Chinese American and Japanese American Literature*, edited by Jeffery Paul Chan et al. New York: Meridian, 1991. Chin argues that Wong breaks with proper Chinese literature in two ways: She chooses Christian Chinese as models rather than Chinese who remain with their ancestral religion, and she portrays Chinese men as either lifeless or inconsequential.

Kim, Elaine. *Asian American Literature: An Introduction to the Writings and Their Social Context*. Philadelphia: Temple University Press, 1982. Kim finds Wong's very reticence about certain aspects of Chinese life admirable. Wong does not play up the Christianity or Americanization of her heroine. Kim does find the protagonists of *Fifth Chinese Daughter* manipulative, for by the end she is acting "Chinese" for Caucasians and "Caucasian" for Chinese.

Kingston, Maxine Hong. *The Woman Warrior: Memoirs of a Girlhood Among Ghosts*. New York: Vintage Books, 1977. Kingston's heroine follows a similar route to independence as Wong's, by going back to Chinese tradition; however, Kingston does everything in a grander way. The Chinese woman's traditional subservience is denounced more militantly, and the cultural values embraced by the heroine are more playfully distorted than in Wong's book.

Lowe, Pardee. *Father and Glorious Descendant*. Boston: Little, Brown, 1943. This was the first full-length second-generation Chinese memoir published in the United States, preceding Wong's by seven years. The book is considered more Americanized than Wong's, exhibiting Asians as quaint exotics and more blatantly extolling American values.

Tan, Amy. *The Kitchen God's Wife*. New York: Putnam, 1991. Tan's book is not so much about a daughter combining Chinese and American tradition—the daughter is too Americanized for that—but about her coming to appreciate her mother's experience. In appreciating it, she comes to value some of the same things in Chinese culture that Wong does.

James Feast

FOR COLORED GIRLS WHO HAVE CONSIDERED SUICIDE/ WHEN THE RAINBOW IS ENUF

Author: Ntozake Shange (Paulette Williams, 1948-)
Type of work: Drama
Type of plot: Feminist
Time of plot: The 1960's to the 1970's
Locale: Inner-city America
First produced: 1976, at the New Federal Theatre, New York City, New York
First published: 1977

Principal characters:

Lady in Red, one of the seven nameless characters; she enumerates the many methods she has used to get a man to love her

Lady in Blue, a victim of emotional and physical abuse who speaks of the myriad excuses black men contrive for inexcusable behavior

Lady in Orange, who turns to music to cure her pain

Lady in Purple, who chooses as a companion someone she knows cannot comprehend her, as a means of avoiding hurt

Lady in Green, who squanders her love on an indifferent man

Lady in Brown, who pays the choreopoem's only positive tribute to a black man

Lady in Yellow, the character who summarizes the predicament of black women

Form and Content

Ntozake Shange's "choreopoem" *for colored girls who have considered suicide/ when the rainbow is enuf* is a dramatic spectacle structured around a series of poetic monologues and dialogues which examine the complex experiences of black women in American society. At its core lies a mission to give voice to the voiceless and to articulate the pains and triumphs of black women through poetry, song, and dance. Shange's feminist text presents the pains of a sexist environment and posits liberation through the creation of a female collective voice. The poems are read by seven women, each wearing a dress that is one of the colors of the rainbow—blue, green, orange, purple, red, or yellow—plus brown. Alone, the women appear vulnerable and victimized, but collectively, as a choric voice, they gain strength and find the ability to discover a certain divinity and dignity in themselves.

The piece looks at several experiences of women, ranging from the confessions of a young woman about her first sexual encounter to the vivid and evocative description of a woman's loss of her two children to the insane pathologies of her boyfriend. In between are stories about women who try to escape the squalor of their existence through dreams of being other than themselves (of being Latina instead of black) and through escape in fantasy. Confessions are important in this work, and the women are candid and explicit in their descriptions of abortion, date rape, and assault and abuse by men. The actors dramatize each story through the use of dance and stylized movement.

A stripper who dances for money in wrestling tents discovers that her way of escape from her squalid existence can only be through a fantasy of being an African goddess, an Egyptian icon whose dignity Shange celebrates. Her striptease act metamorphoses into the mystic dance of the Egyptian goddess Sechita. She makes the point that the stripper still possesses the capacity for dignity and beauty. Shange repeats this pattern in a later piece in which a woman declares to the world that someone has stolen her "stuff." Her stuff constitutes everything that belongs to her as a woman, as a black person, as a human being. Her music, her dance, her language, her sexuality, and her capacity to love are all stolen from her by an individual who happens to be male. She expresses the loss in a language and style that is blues-like in its capacity for humor and self-reflective satire.

The women are sexually expressive and identify a

close link between who they are and how they define their sexuality. They seek to demand sexual gratification despite the negative associations that may come with that demand and appear to have come to a cynical understanding of the deceit and hypocrisy of their male lovers. Yet the women remain committed to the dream of a genuine sexual and emotional relationship with a man. The collective thinking described here effectively pulls the women together.

At the end of the piece, however, Shange posits that any attempt by women to rely on men for security and a sense of self must be futile and misguided. The climactic story of Crystal and Beau Willie emphasizes this point. Beau Willie, a sympathetically drawn Vietnam veteran hooked on alcohol and drugs, manages to persuade Crystal to drop her guard even though she knows that he is inclined to abuse her and to act out his destructive selfishness. He grabs hold of their children, dangles them out a fifth-story window, and then drops them when she is slow in responding to his proposal of marriage. This act constitutes a powerful dramatic moment from which Shange must derive the potential for hope and possibility.

The women discover hope in a religious ritual in which they declare that they have found divinity in themselves, in their femininity, and in their collective strength. Shange not only offers a detailed examination of the lives of several women but also crystallizes, in the process, her singular vision and imagination through the infusion of her creative intelligence into the structure and form of the piece.

Analysis

The most consistent criticism leveled at Shange's play has come from those who have accused her of portraying black men in a very negative light. Her critics argue that in her attempt to articulate a feminist viewpoint, she attacks the black male as being void of anything positive to contribute to the life of the black woman. Such criticism is misdirected. Shange's play succeeds because of its relentlessly honest look at the pain of being a black woman in white society. Rather than creating a discourse that posits white oppression as the core reason for black suffering, Shange instead focuses on the black experience and tries to allow black women to talk about their most intimate secrets. Most of the women in the play share a view that positive male-female relationships are a desirable dream. (Shange's later lesbian politics do not emerge in this work, as she posits heterosexuality as a norm.) Also, Shange grants the black male a certain dignity in her narrative about the Haitian leader Toussaint L'Overture, who becomes actualized in the young boy Toussaint Jones. This incarnation has deep symbolic importance, because it suggests that the black woman can find a heroic figure even within her limited existence in working-class America.

There is little question, however, that Shange seeks to challenge the patriarchal worldview that has prevented the black woman from having her own stories told in American literature. The play evolved out of a need to join the growing voices of Third World women who sought, in the early 1970's, to express the visions and aspirations of women of color. It also attempted to present a distinctively black interpretation of the "white feminist movement" in a manner that demonstrated that the women's movement was not necessarily articulating the needs and expectations of black women. Shange's care for detail in her depiction of the black working-class experience points to this fact explicitly. Her characters are not middle-class, privileged women seeking to gain an upper hand in the patriarchal world order, but working women who have discovered a need to share secrets and truths about how they have survived for so many years.

The very "blackness" of the work, evident in the use of black music, Afrocentric dance, and a distinctly Afrocentric narrative style, situates the piece squarely as a work that locates its ethos in African American culture. The art of storytelling and the carefully constructed, nonlinear pattern of echoes and resonance become metaphorical expressions of the African American experience. Consequently, the feminist content of the work is defined in terms of this experience. Ritual, as a means to arrive at spiritual awakening and truth, becomes central to the work, and the impact of the call-response and chant oratorical patterns (common to Afrocentric folk patterns) on the ultimate vision of triumph and possibility at the end of the work illustrates Shange's commitment to an Afrocentric vision in her articulation of her feminist perspective.

This distinct perspective is most apparent, however, in her use (or misuse) of language. In the drama, Shange literally usurps Prospero's language and makes it her own as a weapon to challenge the norms perpetuated by Prospero. As a feminist Caliban, Shange uses a lexical system that is primarily aural in its adherence to tonality and rhythm. She remains unrestrained by imposed conventions and generates a work that shifts from the transcendence of symbolism and metaphor (as she demonstrates in "sechita"), to stark and minimalist realism (as she demonstrates in "a nite with beau willie brown"), to the raw and explicit language of the street (as she shows in the sequence "somebody almost walked off with alla my stuff"). Related to this use of language is her consistent articulation of the need for black artists to use Afrocentric artistic forms to express their own ideas. The narrative that looks at Toussaint L'Overture expresses well the need for blacks to reclaim important historical figures that have been erased from their psyche for centuries. She repeats this statement in her description of Sechita, the goddess figure.

Shange's work succeeds as well as it does because she does not remain locked in lofty generalizations and polemics. Her characters are grounded in everyday reality. One woman complains about her fear of being mugged in the streets of New York, while another weeps alone at night after empty sex with yet another lover in San Francisco. Similarly, three women try to find some dignity after recognizing that they are victims of one man's duplicity. The women humorously, but with startling candor and accuracy, list some of the excuses that they have received from men who have in some way abused or hurt them. Shange demonstrates the feminist adage "the political is personal" in a most compelling manner in this play.

For colored girls who have considered suicide must be experienced as a series of related vignettes with a central dramatic rhythm that explodes in the final few movements. This intelligence about what works dramatically, even when significant experimentation and a certain degree of didacticism is taking place, makes Shange's work a monumental achievement in American theater.

Context

Ntozake Shange, whose work is frequently anthologized, remains one of the foremost American dramatists. Her piece *for colored girls who have considered suicide* constitutes one of the more important dramatic works written by an African American author in the late twentieth century. The play, commonly regarded as an articulation of feminist ideology from the perspective of a black woman, had an impressive and critically successful run on Broadway in the mid-1970's and has been produced all over the world.

Shange's achievement lies in her ability to demonstrate that the suffering of women can cross ethnic and racial lines. By reaching for elemental truths in the experiences of black women, Shange's characters demand that audiences pay keen attention to the exposition of issues such as date rape, abortion, spousal abuse, poverty, prostitution, goddess worship, and female sexual liberation and aggression. The work gives credence to the idea that a black woman's voice has full validity in the women's movement.

Shange's play posits a poetics of dramatic presentation that explores experimentation with form and content to create a structure that reflects the thematic intent of the piece. The choric patterns are central to the work and become metaphorical expressions of the need for women to find a collective voice in whatever they do. The dance, music, mime, and storytelling represent the common features of black culture and American women's culture. Shange harnesses these forms and generates a play that defies easy definitions and classifications. As a feminist piece, it can be appropriated as a forthright articulation of the need of a movement of women to work against a strongly patriarchal world order. More critically, however, she opens the eyes of white feminists to the complexity of the movement because she opens their eyes to the world of black feminists. She simultaneously challenges both the assumptions of white racist society (which includes white feminists) and those of the patriarchal social structure (which includes black men).

Sources for Further Study

DeShazer, Mary K. "Rejecting Necrophilia: Ntozake Shange and the Warrior Re-Visioned." In *Making a Spectacle*, edited by Lynda Hart. Ann Arbor: University of Michigan, 1989. DeShazer presents Shange as a warrior-woman, reinventing the term "warrior" from a feminist perspective. A good study of the feminist politics in Shange's plays.

Geis, Deborah R. "Distraught Laughter: Monologue

in Ntozake Shange's Theater Pieces." In *Feminine Focus*, edited by Enoch Brater. Oxford, England: Oxford University Press, 1989. Geis argues that Shange's use of monologues and other dramatic devices is tied directly to her quest to create a distinctly Afrocentric dramaturgy. Geis posits that Shange's success in this regard is elemental to her stature as a dominant innovator in modern theater.

Keyssar, Helene. *The Curtain and the Veil: Strategies in Black Drama*. New York: Burt Franklin, 1982. Keyssar explores with authority the dynamics of ritual and ideology in African American drama. Her discussion on Shange's work provides useful insight into the organic relationship between form and content in Shange's feminist aesthetic.

_____________. "Rites and Responsibilities: The Drama of Black American Women." In *Feminine Focus*, edited by Enoch Brater. Oxford, England: Oxford University Press, 1989. Keyssar tackles the problematic issue of "double-voicedness" in the plays of African American women. Her commentary on Shange illustrates the complex challenges inherent in Shange's works that seek to speak both to feminist issues and issues of race. A useful contextualization of Shange's work with the plays of other important African American women playwrights.

Mitchell, Carolyn. " 'A Laying on of Hands': Transcending the City in Ntozake Shange's *for colored girls. . . .*" In *Women Writers and the City*, edited by Susan Merrill Squier. Knoxville: University of Tennessee Press, 1984. Mitchell's analysis of Shange's play explores the spiritual and political implications of cleansing and healing in the work.

Shange, Ntozake. "Ntozake Shange: An Interview." Interview by Edward K. Brown II. *Poets and Writers* 21, no. 3 (1993): 38-47. In this candid interview, Shange forthrightly addresses some of the criticism that she received for her portrayal of African American men. She is characteristically outspoken and articulate about her mission as a writer, which she sees as speaking the truth about sexism and racism in society. A useful introduction to the polemic and intelligence of Shange.

Wilkerson, Margaret B. "Music as Metaphor: New Plays of Black Women." In *Making a Spectacle*, edited by Lynda Hart. Ann Arbor: University of Michigan Press, 1989. Wilkerson's study of music in Black women's drama devoted some attention to Shange's use of music as political statement.

Kwame S. N. Dawes

THE FORCED MARRIAGE: Or, The Jealous Bridegroom

Author: Aphra Behn (1640-1689)
Type of work: Drama
Type of plot: Romantic
Time of plot: The seventeenth century
Locale: France
First produced: 1670, at Duke's Theater, Lincoln's Inn Fields, London, England
First published: 1671

Principal characters:

The King, a wise and just ruler
Prince Philander, the King's son, one of the heroes of the play
Alcippus, the second hero of the play, a young soldier who is promoted to the rank of general
Erminia, the daughter of the old general Orgilius
Galatea, the daughter of the King and the sister of Philander
Orgilius, the old general, who is willing to resign his place in favor of the young Alcippus
Alcander, a friend of Prince Philander
Olinda, maid of honor to Princess Galatea
Pisaro, a friend of young General Alcippus
Labree and **Cleontius,** the men servants
Isillia and **Lisette,** the women domestics

Form and Content

The Forced Marriage: Or, The Jealous Bridegroom, although seemingly conventional in structure and subject matter, offers a perspective that is different from that of other plays of the period. In contrast to the usual pairing off of young couples according to the dictates of their parents, this play explores the freedom of choice that the two heroines have dared to demand. Princess Galatea wants the young General Alcippus, who is not her social equal, for her husband; Prince Philander hopes to make Erminia, who is also not of his class, his bride. Both women believe that they have the right to pick their mates—just as much right as men have. Thus, while the play uses mistaken identities, misinterpretations of motives, misreadings of situations, and all the devices dear to such plots, Aphra Behn succeeds in putting a novel idea before her audience. Furthermore, in her prologue she alerts everyone in the theater to the fact that they are witnesses to a rare event: A woman has dared to write a play.

At the opening, the King announces his gratitude both to his son, Philander, and to his favorite, Alcippus, for their bravery in battle. To show how devoted the two young men are, they deliver speeches in which each praises the other for being more responsible for the victory. When the King offers to make Alcippus his new general, the young man first declines the honor, feeling embarrassed because he is in the presence of the old general, Orgilius. The latter cedes his position willingly, however, and so the audience is introduced to a group of well-intentioned, heroic, and reasonable men who respect one another and, while appreciating their own worth, are not conceited. This pleasant atmosphere is soon dissipated when the King inquires of Alcippus how he may reward him further, and his new general asks for the hand of the old general's daughter, Erminia, a request that both the father and the King are happy to grant. In separate asides to the audience, Erminia and Philander declare their horror at the news.

After everyone leaves except for Alcander and Pisaro, the friends respectively of Philander and Alcippus, the two discuss Erminia and her seeming treachery, as if to suggest that she had encouraged Alcippus to ask for her hand and basely deserted the prince. In short, she is held responsible for a political decision to dispose of her future without once being asked for her own feelings in the matter. Later, Erminia meets Princess Galatea, and the two women share their grief: Each loves a man that neither can hope to marry. Their dialogue, for all its "soap-opera" quality, is an honest exploration of a woman's dilemma when she is forbidden to follow her own heart. Their predicament has indeed made them sisters. Both understand, however, that they cannot challenge the decrees of the King, and Behn gives them strong speeches lamenting their powerlessness. When Erminia appeals to her father, he is angry with her because she dared to fall in love with the prince without asking permission. Reminded of her duty, Erminia submits.

Meanwhile, the two rivals, having discovered that they love the same woman, threaten each other with swords. When the princess hears that her brother, the prince, wished to take the life of Alcippus, she is devastated; at this point the brother realizes that she is in love with his enemy. Despite the intricacies of the plot, some relief is in the offing. Erminia says that she will marry Alcippus but will never share his bed—a promise that relieves both the prince, who loves her, and his sister, who loves Erminia's intended.

Alcippus, however, has no intention of permitting such an arrangement; he has become jealous of the prince and does not trust his bride. He pretends to depart on a mission but plans to return and spy on his wife. Meanwhile, the prince has begged to see Erminia. As is usual in such plays, his presence is discovered by the angry husband, who unexpectedly makes his reappearance. After a fair amount of harsh words and some swordplay, the King intervenes and the truth is revealed: Erminia has never ceased to love the prince and, despite the wedding ceremony, has remained chaste and faithful to him. Alcippus, finally moved by such devotion and flattered that the princess has been in love with him all the time, resigns Erminia to the prince and proposes to the princess. With the blessing of the King and the old general, Erminia's father, the play comes to a joyful end.

Analysis

Because *The Forced Marriage* was Aphra Behn's first play, she modeled it largely on the accepted romantic tragicomedies with which the audiences were familiar. Such plays contained standard prologues and high-flown speeches assigned to the chief characters. Yet even in Behn's earliest effort, she diverged from the mainstream.

Generally, the prologue, a device that could be traced back to Roman comedy, served to tell the audience what to expect from the play, providing a theme, a moral, or even a capsule version of the plot. Behn introduces a male actor who not only announces that the author is a woman but also maintains that with this play women are going to use their wit as a weapon. Then a female actor joins him to suggest that women will be the victors in the contest between the sexes, because their beauty will benefit from their wit. Furthermore, by proving that they are more than merely decorative, women will be able, when they are old, to retrieve "the wandering heart."

Then Behn inserts a bit of autobiography that must have been well known but that she showed great daring in mentioning. She had been married to a Dutch merchant who left her penniless at his death. Before turning to writing to support herself, she had been briefly employed by the British government as a secret agent: Her knowledge of Holland was useful to her own country, then engaged in rivalry with the Dutch. In her prologue she touches upon her past activities by mentioning the word "spy." She warns that spies have been planted all over the theater—but only to discover how the audience has received the play. The prologue concludes with the assertion that its only aim is to prove constancy in love, adding that "when we have it too/ We'll sacrifice it all to pleasure you." It is an artful hint that while fidelity is to be admired, sex might be more fun. Although a certain amount of license was permitted women in elegant society, it was not considered proper for them to utter such sentiments.

Within the play itself, the characters boast no special individuality; they are very much prisoners of the tragicomic style. Yet Behn endows her women with attributes not usually found in the heroines of the day. They weep copiously, to be sure, for such was the fashion, but they also try to find a solution to their problem instead of simply wringing their hands and waiting for men to rescue them. They understand the necessity of submitting to the authority of a king or a father, but they also rebel against the situation. Moreover, whereas men are quick to express their anger and even quicker to draw their weapons, the women are far more willing to conciliate, to compromise, to seek some measure of justice. Erminia and Galatea are reasonable; it is the men who display emotion in a crisis. Behn, in short, reversed the universal, still-accepted theory that women rely only on their feelings and men on their intellect.

In other plays of the time it was taken for granted that marriages were to be arranged between men and women who were social equals. Yet Behn gives her audience not one but two couples who not only challenge the class code but also are successful in defying it. The old general, shocked that his daughter Erminia has so far forgotten herself, her position, and her father's orders that she has dared to fall in love with a prince, finally realizes that love may be more important than custom. The King, expecting his daughter Galatea to make a royal match, is equally reconciled to this new order. There were few playwrights in her day who dealt with this subject as effectively as Behn.

The question of form was also of concern to her. After William Shakespeare had perfected the use of blank verse in iambic pentameter, it became the preferred mode of expression until the theaters were closed in 1642 by order of the Puritan dictatorship. When the Stuart kings were restored to the throne and the theaters were reopened in 1660, the new dramatists, now dazzled by all that was French—the manners, the clothes, the fashions—succumbed as well to the French style of writing poetry. They adopted the Alexandrine, a longer meter than the pentameter, and the couplet rhyme scheme, which was favored over the simple rhythms of blank verse. The precision of the French language is perfectly attuned to the couplet, but English, with its looser structure and wider range of vocabulary, seems confined by such devices. In England, a literary battle raged between these poetic forms. Behn, who had a talent for turning out witty couplets, also had a good ear that prevented her from discarding the sonority of blank verse. Her solution was to employ both types of poetry in *The Forced Marriage*, not always to its best advantage, yet indicating that she had given some thought to the matter. In 1675, five years after she wrote this play, John Dryden, the most distinguished poet, dramatist, and essayist of his day, published his manifesto in the preface to his tragedy *All for Love*: Henceforth, blank verse must be considered more suitable for tragedy than the couplet.

Context

When *The Forced Marriage* was produced in 1670, England had changed considerably from what it had been ten years before. The austerity of Puritan rule had given way to the excesses of the Restoration; even the theater had changed. Formerly only boys and men had been members of theater companies, but now women were admitted to the stage and brought a new realism to their roles. There was greater freedom in discussing sex, and a number of popular plays on the subject drew large audiences. Yet while critics on the whole enjoyed such comedies written by men, they disapproved of Aphra Behn for making use of the same material because she was a woman. After her death, poet laureate Alexander Pope complained that she was always getting her characters into bed (she had deserted romantic tragedy for comedy, to which she was more suited and which gave her greater latitude); he failed to mention the fact that male playwrights were equally busy doing the same thing.

The success of *The Forced Marriage*, which enjoyed a run of six days—a near-record for the time—encouraged Behn to continue to write. Tired of the attacks on her plays, she defended herself eloquently against the charge of vulgarity, asking why men were permitted and women forbidden freedom of expression. In the preface to a later and better play, *The Lucky Change* (1686), she wrote:

> All I ask is the privilege for my masculine part—the poet in me (if any such you will allow me)—to tread in those successful paths my predecessors have so long thrived in. . . . If I must not, because of my sex, have this freedom, but that you will usurp all to yourselves, I lay down my quill, and you shall hear no more of me, no not so much as to make comparisons, because I will be kinder to my brothers of the pen than they have been to a defenceless woman.

Behn did not lay down her quill, however, but went on to produce eighteen plays and many novels. The most famous of them, *Oroonoko* (1688), has been compared to Harriet Beecher Stowe's *Uncle Tom's Cabin* (1852) in its plea for racial justice. In addition, she was the author of a number of poems and translations and was the first Englishwoman to earn her living by her writing. She also took an important part in the casting of her plays. For *The Forced Marriage* she engaged a nineteen-year-old college student eager to become an actor and gave him the role of the King. He suffered such stage fright on opening night that he forgot all of his lines; only Behn's quick action in finding a substitute at the last minute saved the play from disaster. The young man, Thomas Otway, went on to become a famous playwright and always defended the reputation of the woman who had given him his first chance.

Despite what might be called today her feminist point of view, Behn exerted no influence on later writers, because the kind of comedy at which she and her fellow playwrights were adept was going out of fashion. Its frankness and sophistication alienated a more idealistic audience; Restoration comedy sank into disfavor and did not enjoy a revival until the beginning of the twentieth century. Even then, while William Wycherley, author of *The Country Wife* (1675), and William Congreve, author of *The Way of the World* (1700), were rediscovered and fittingly applauded, Behn languished in obscurity, her name still tarnished by the accusation of coarseness. Yet thanks to recent scholarship, she too has been rediscovered. The gross unfairness of the judgments against her have been exposed, and several of her plays, notably *The Lucky Chance* and *The Rover* (1677), have been performed in London to great acclaim. Both her art and her life seem very modern despite a distance of more than three hundred years.

Sources for Further Study

Bevis, Richard. *English Drama: Restoration and Eighteenth Century, 1660-1789*. London: Longman, 1988. A survey of the major writers of the period. Provides a discussion of Behn's strengths and weaknesses as a writer, with the greatest attention paid to her comedies. She is given high marks for the way she handles dramatic intrigues; the author notes that even if her plots are sometimes silly, she carries them along by the sheer vivacity of her style.

Carlson, Susan. *Women and Comedy*. Ann Arbor: University of Michigan Press, 1991. The author explores the connection between women and domestic comedy. She contrasts the male writers of comedy, who give their heroines only limited freedom, and shows how women writers such as Behn create unorthodox, liberated types.

Duffy, Maureen. *The Passionate Shepherdess*. London: Jonathan Cape, 1977. The author, a leading Behn scholar, has unearthed new information about Behn's early life. In addition to supplying the reader with a full biography, she devotes a large part of the book to assessing Behn's place in the Restoration theater. This is one of the most valuable sources on Behn, supplying helpful notes to each chapter, a comprehensive bibliography, and a number of illustrations of Behn and her circle.

Sackville-West, Victoria. *Aphra Behn*. New York: Russell & Russell, 1970. One of England's most eminent writers discusses the life and accomplishments of a woman she believed to have been misunderstood and underrated in her day and for long afterward, a person of whom "one cannot take leave without respect."

Summers, Montague. Introduction to *The Works of Aphra Behn*. 6 vols. New York: B. Blom, 1967. Aside from the monumental task of rescuing Behn's works for publication, since she had been out of print for many years, Summers contributed a valuable essay on her life and letters in his introduction to volume 1. He successfully refuted attacks on Behn's ability and talent and was mainly responsible for engaging Sackville-West's interest in Behn. All subsequent scholars have made this collection the foundation of their studies.

Mildred C. Kuner

FRANKENSTEIN

Author: Mary Wollstonecraft Shelley (1797-1851)
Type of work: Novel
Type of plot: Horror
Time of plot: The late 1700's
Locale: Principally Geneva, Switzerland; also the Arctic Ocean, the Hebrides, and elsewhere in Western Europe and Britain
First published: 1818

Principal characters:

Robert Walton, a traveler who describes his encounter with Victor Frankenstein

Victor Frankenstein, a scientist who succeeded in creating a living being from the fragments of dead bodies

The monster, Victor Frankenstein's creation

Elizabeth, Victor's adopted sister and eventual betrothed

Form and Content

Frankenstein is, in many ways, a tale of mixed identities. Thus it seems somehow fitting that tradition has always linked the name of Frankenstein with a monstrous being rather than with the mad scientist who created him. Yet in Mary Wollstonecraft Shelley's novel, the original version of this popular story, Frankenstein is that scientist, and only on a symbolic level does the reader confuse him with his horrible creation. This is not the only pair of linked identities in the novel. The monster, as he is called here, serves as a kind of alter ego to each of the novel's main characters—and even, finally, to its author. Shelley seems to sympathize more fully with the monster than with any other character.

Shelley structures the story like a Russian nesting doll: It is really a story within a story within a story. Robert Walton opens the tale, writing letters home to his sister as he embarks on a fantastic voyage of Arctic exploration. He hungers for a friend, a like-minded companion. Then, in his fourth letter, he describes how he has found a man out wandering on the ice, weak from exposure and malnourishment, and taken him into his ship. He sees in him the potential friend for whom he has longed. The man is Victor Frankenstein, and Walton lets him speak.

Victor recounts the story of his life, starting with his privileged childhood in Geneva, Switzerland. From an early age, he was obsessed with creating life. All science was, to him, the body of knowledge that gave human beings godlike powers. The intensity with which he pursued his studies made it nearly impossible for him to maintain closeness to his family and friends. His dear friend Henry Clerval did not see the danger in his studies. Elizabeth, his sister by informal adoption and eventually his betrothed, saw that his work was driving him to poor health and estranging him from his family, but she was powerless to bring him home.

After years of nearly frenzied study, Victor was ready. Robbing body parts from graves, he constructed a monstrous form. Finally, one stormy October night, he brought it to life. Yet when he saw his creature reaching out toward him, trying to smile, Victor rushed from the building, unable to take on the creature as his own charge. By the time he returned to his rooms the next day, accompanied by Clerval, the monster was gone. Victor became feverish, and Clerval nursed him back to health over some months.

When Victor returned home to his family and to Elizabeth, he was greeted by news that brought his feelings of dread into painful focus: His younger brother William had been found murdered. Authorities had arrested Justine Moritz, a beloved and trusted young servant, on circumstantial evidence. Victor, walking mournfully on Mont Blanc one stormy night, saw the monster's form suddenly illuminated by a flash of lightning on a far peak, and he understood: The monster had killed his brother. Later, in agony, he watched as Justine was convicted and executed for the crime. Another stormy night in the mountains, the monster approached Victor closely enough for them to converse and begged him to hear his story. Victor agreed.

At this point, the monster becomes the narrator, as the reader hears how he told his own, very different life story. He told of eking out a miserable existence, of terrifying everyone who saw him, and of learning to hide, watch, and listen. He told of finding a kind of shed attached to a hut occupied by a family; from them, listening through the cracks in the wall, he learned to speak and to read. He told of reading John Milton's *Paradise Lost* and other books, and of coming to understand the intense pain of his solitude. Finally, he asked Victor to create a partner for him and promised to leave him alone forever if he would.

Victor agreed to create a mate for the monster but found himself unable to follow through with it. For the rest of the novel, he tells how he and the monster engaged in a deadly cat-and-mouse game. First the monster killed Clerval. Then Victor believed that the monster was hunting him but learned on his wedding night that he was to suffer rather than die: The monster killed his beloved Elizabeth on the bridal bed. Victor then pursued him to the Arctic wasteland in which Walton has found him.

As Victor finishes his tale, he warns Walton to learn from his example—and then he dies. At that moment, the monster enters, mourns the loss of his creator, and announces his own imminent suicide by self-immolation. He then vanishes into the darkness.

Analysis

Any interpretation of Shelley's novel must come to terms with the central relationship between Victor and his creature. When one reads the monster's story in his own words, it is impossible not to feel sympathy for him. As a result, Victor must share some of the blame for the monster's violent acts. How much? How much other blame is to be uncovered in this novel that is so full of pain and death? Why, too, in this novel written by a woman are the female characters flat and uniformly blameless? The question Shelley's contemporaries asked was, as she put it, "How I, then a young girl, came to think of, and to dilate upon, so very hideous an idea?" Taken together, these questions seem to ask: What is this young woman writer saying about the masculine culture of her day?

Interpretations of the novel have seen considerable cultural criticism implicit in it. It has been read as a critique of modern science, for example. In this interpretation, Victor represents the tendency of science to divorce itself from ethics. As a scientist, Victor does not consider the consequences of his research, and he does not take responsibility for them when they are tragic. What is more, this lapse in Victor's judgment arises in part from his absence from home, both literally and figuratively: In order to do his work, he must cut himself off from other human beings. Other interpretations of Victor have emerged. It has been argued that he represents the Byronic hero, the Faustian quality of the male Romantic poet. Shelley quotes often in the novel from the poetry of Samuel Taylor Coleridge, William Wordsworth, and Percy Bysshe Shelley, and the poems help to express Victor's (and Walton's) sense of isolation and the haunted, feverish energy that dooms them.

Other interpretations of Victor and his monster have focused on the scenario of bringing life into the world. Readers note that Mary Shelley had given birth to a baby who died the year before she began *Frankenstein*, that she gave birth to a son six months before she began the novel, and that another child was born only three months after she finished it. Thus there were concrete reasons that her mind might have been full of thoughts about childbearing and parents' responsibilities. Still, readers have differed in the connections they have drawn between Victor's monstrous creation and Shelley's own childbirths. Some have seen parallels and insisted that for Shelley childbirth must have seemed in some ways a hideous process. Others have instead drawn a contrast between "natural" birth, the domain of the woman, and the "unnatural" creation that Victor undertakes and for which he is aptly punished. Still others have instead drawn connections between the creation of the monster and the writing of a book—a metaphor Shelley herself implies in her introduction.

Another fruitful parallel that can be drawn between the novel and Shelley's life has to do with her apparent sympathy for the monster. Just as the monster gathered his education by eavesdropping in silence, as a kind of outlaw student, so Shelley describes herself as having listened silently to the many conversations about science and poetry taking place among Percy Shelley, her husband, the poet George Gordon, Lord Byron, and their male friends. As a woman writer in the company of men, she may well have felt herself to be monstrous—not visibly, perhaps, but deeply. In this interpretation, the monster represents all that the woman writer must repress. The creature's murders enact violent urges, then, that symbolically vent private rage. This may help explain both the flatness of the female characters and the powerful sympathy readers feel for the monster.

It may also explain the potent afterlife of the monster, as he has survived in version after version of the story in popular culture. Until the revival of scholarly interest in the novel during the 1970's, Frankenstein was probably more strongly associated with the horror film than with Shelley's book. That seems appropriate for a work that, in its own day, was written in a little-respected popular genre: the gothic novel. Many elements of the gothic novel are present: hauntings and graveyards, murders and picturesque Continental settings, innocent young women who are victims. Yet Shelley did not simply write a formula gothic. The scientist and his creature, and the complex narrative structure with all of its interconnections, are strictly her own. In this novel, she at once comments on the gothic and raises it a notch in complexity.

Context

The revival of scholarly interest in *Frankenstein* has directly paralleled the emergence and development of feminist literary scholarship. On the one hand, Shelley's novel has perhaps been an obvious subject of study for those who investigate the separate tradition of literature by women. On the other hand, *Frankenstein* anticipated and provided many of the concerns that feminist scholars would have. It expresses the rage and pain felt by those who are left out, who are not allowed a full place in their own culture.

Mary Shelley tells the reader that she felt some pressure to be a writer: Both her parents, Mary Wollstonecraft and William Godwin, were celebrated writers, and it was expected that she would continue the tradition. Yet her introduction is full of apologies for her work, and one sees everywhere the marks of difficulties she had being taken seriously. Not the least of these is the preface that was written by Percy Shelley in her voice, in which he acknowledges that the "humble novelist" needs to explain why she might aspire to the heights of great poetry. *Frankenstein* represents, symbolically, both some of the pressures on a woman writer and her critique of the culture that has created her but sees her as its "monster."

The female characters in Shelley's novel do not offer any kind of model response to the failures enacted by the males. Only in the novel's symbolic vocabulary, in its acts of violence and its sympathies for the most hideous of creatures, do readers find a program for change. This work by a woman in a "feminine" genre—the gothic novel—is complex enough to provide generations of readers and scholars with puzzles to unravel. On the whole, it is not Mary Shelley's prose that readers have admired; in any case, scholars are not sure how much of it is hers and how much Percy Shelley's, since he went over it and rewrote many of its sentences. The power of this novel lies in its plot and in its central characters, the monster and his creator. Here is Pygmalion with a vengeance—and written by a woman.

Sources for Further Study

Gilbert, Sandra M., and Susan Gubar. *The Madwoman in the Attic: The Woman Writer and the Nineteenth-Century Literary Imagination*. New Haven, Conn.: Yale University Press, 1979. An important early study that emphasizes Shelley's response, as a woman writer, to John Milton.

Homans, Margaret. *Bearing the Word: Language and Female Experience in Nineteenth-Century Women's Writing*. Chicago: University of Chicago Press, 1986. Discusses *Frankenstein* as a central feminine text in its century.

Levine, George, and U. C. Knoepflmacher. *The Endurance of Frankenstein*. Berkeley: University of California Press, 1979. The essays in this groundbreaking collection helped to return *Frankenstein* to prominence as a novel, and they still seem fresh.

Mellor, Anne K. *Mary Shelley: Her Life, Her Fiction, Her Monsters*. New York: Routledge, 1988. A treatment of *Frankenstein* and of Shelley's other works in the context of her life.

Poovey, Mary. *The Proper Lady and the Woman Writer: Ideology as Style in the Works of Mary Wollstonecraft, Mary Shelley, and Jane Austen*. Chicago: University of Chicago Press, 1984. Analyzes Shelley's works in the context of the pressures experienced by women writers in the nineteenth century.

Shelley, Mary. *Frankenstein*. Edited by Johann Smith. Boston: St. Martin's Press, 1992. This edition contains five essays exemplifying different approaches to the novel and a good bibliography.

Sarah Webster Goodwin

FROM REVERENCE TO RAPE: The Treatment of Women in the Movies

Author: Molly Haskell
Type of work: Social criticism
First published: 1974

Form and Content

In *From Reverence to Rape: The Treatment of Women in the Movies*, feminist Molly Haskell, drawing on her experience as film critic for the *Village Voice*, traces the depiction of women in films from the 1920's to the 1970's. The first chapter, "The Big Lie," provides an overview of the book and establishes Haskell's recurring theme: Women are the pawns of a male- dominated motion-picture industry and are used in films to perpetuate images of female inferiority, serving as scapegoats for men's problems and as vessels for the projection of male fantasy. Further, women are degraded and denigrated in such stereotypes as virgins, whores, sex objects, Earth Mothers, and dumb blondes because males, in a constant state of insecurity and anxiety, need to assert their superiority and independence. Haskell contends that some heroic directors and actresses have managed to subvert these proclivities, but these images come from the past. Her analysis of women's roles in a historical context reveals a steady deterioration of positive images, culminating in the most demeaning portrayals in the films of the 1970's, when this work was written.

The remaining chapters are organized in a roughly chronological pattern, examining the ways in which these themes are played out or subverted in five eras: the 1920's, 1930's, 1940's, 1950's, and in "The Last Decade," the 1960's and 1970's. Although the chapters focus on the idiosyncrasies of the films in each decade, Haskell compares and contrasts them with films of the other eras. In addition, Haskell addresses the political and social concerns of women, placing their portrayals in a historical context. Two chapters, "The Woman's Film" and "The Europeans," digress from the chronological structure of the book, but Haskell employs a similar method to clarify and amplify her themes.

The tone of the work is both personal and scholarly. The writing is lively and witty, calling on a variety of sources: Haskell's own extensive knowledge of film; exhaustive examples of stars, studios, and directors; film commentators; psychologists Sigmund Freud and Carl Jung; and French feminist Simone de Beauvoir. Although Haskell defines herself as "film critic first and feminist second," *From Reverence to Rape* is clearly a diatribe against the inequities of women's status and what she sees as the distorted and contradictory images that create and/or promulgate a culture of misogyny. On the other hand, Haskell lavishly praises directors, films, and stars that subvert the system by transcending stereotypes.

Although Haskell occasionally relies on mainstream film critics as sources to support her ideas, in general she berates them for their indifference or naïveté about women's film roles. In contrast, she uses her own extensive background as critic to articulate feminist concerns heretofore ignored in film criticism. As such, *From Reverence to Rape* is a pioneering work, constituting an important contribution to feminist theory.

Analysis

Implicit in *From Reverence to Rape* is a belief that the director creates the film and shapes the images. Particularly powerful are the "auteurs," or great directors, whose work is easily identifiable because of recurring themes and/or idiosyncratic visual markers. The controlling nature of the director's work is inherently masculine, and when the films are merely extensions of a patriarchal mentality, they victimize both genders, according to Haskell. When they shape a different vision, however, films are at their best. Directors such as D. W. Griffith in the 1920's, for example, tended to select leading ladies with strong personalities, and stars such as Theda Bara, Gloria Swanson, and Lillian Gish were allowed to modify these archetypes, enriching the roles with subtlety and complexities. In the 1930's, Hollywood imported European director Ernst Lubitsch, who showed assertive women in as much control as men. Howard Hawks and George Cukor, whose works spanned the 1930's and 1940's, emphasized themes of mutuality, portraying the exchange of gender roles and traits as beneficial to both men and women. Haskell maintains that even in the declining years of the 1950's, directors such as Douglas Sirk, Otto Preminger, and, in their later films, John Ford and Billy Wilder created classic films that broke through stereotypes and gave women an interior life. Haskell perceives these directors as having a passion and affection for women that allows them to create images outside their male egos.

In contrast, directors of the 1970's view women as "satellites" to themselves and project all their own fears and adolescent traits of vanity and narcissism onto their female characters, resulting in the real and metaphorical "rape" in Haskell's title. European auteurs, in their view of woman as mysterious "other," project similar images: Jean Luc Godard's love-hate relationship, Francois Truffaut's self-destructive women, Ingmar Bergman's pedestal. Yet the Europeans, too, have exemplary exceptions: Roberto Rosselini and Michaelangelo Antonioni's sensitivity to women's issues, Bernardo Bertolucci's understanding of women's erotic fantasies, and in the 1920's, Carl Dreyer's feeling for the plight of women.

Haskell associates the decline of positive images with the collapse of the studio system in the 1960's. In prior decades, studios promoted a mystical relationship between star and public. Glamorous stars achieved a larger-than-life image. Great actresses such as Gloria Swanson and Lillian Gish in the 1920's and Greta Garbo, Bette Davis, and Joan Crawford in the 1930's and 1940's had a presence that transcended stereotypes, rising above the material and projecting images of power on the screen. Both male and female in her sexuality and eternal in her beauty, a sex goddess was the "object of women's admiration and men's desire." According to Haskell, actresses in the 1970's were placed in roles of marginality, all packaged in one bland, youthful image. Before the Movie Production Code of 1934, all women, not simply goddesses, were permitted a healthy sexuality. Designed to repress overt sexuality, particularly in women, this code effectively undermined "sensualists without guilt"—such actresses as Jean Harlow, Mae West, and Marlene Dietrich. In fact, Haskell believes that the code was a direct response to West's uninhibited expression of uncensored sexual desire. Postcode films sanctified marriages and clearly delineated who was a virgin and who was a whore.

Yet even postcode 1930's films had certain redeeming features. Because they were forced out of the boudoir, some women were admitted in limited ways to the man's world of work. The "superwoman" was a hyperactive working woman such as Katharine Hepburn, who brought an intelligence and presence to her roles. Superwomen prevailed into the 1940's until post-World War II pressures forced them back into the home, where they were likely to become "super females." Flirtatious, duplicitous, and competitive with other women, they were a contrast to the solidarity of women in the "backstage" and "gold digger" genres of the 1930's. Post-World War II paranoia produced the treacherous women of *film noir*, whose tendency toward mayhem and murder created a particularly vicious stereotype.

In the 1950's, the number of parts for women had declined to an all-time low, and the "working girl" tended to be the "actress," with all her negative permutations: fearful of aging, viciously ambitious, vain, phony. Marilyn Monroe, in her personification of images of women in that era, was sex object and "nincompoop"; her only true work was to cater to men's needs. Forced to remain childlike, she sacrificed her own desire to attain the dubious love and approval of the male. In contrast, Haskell sees Doris Day, one of the bright spots in a dismal era, as closer to the real American woman in her "working girl" comedies, with an intuitive sense of identity and wholeness.

Haskell discusses the way in which Hollywood's disregard for the whole woman manifested itself in a fetishism of female body parts: Busby Berkeley's ironic abstractions in the 1930's, in which he choreographed women's faces, arms, and legs to create a whole, appealed to men and women alike. This style evolved, however, into Betty Grable's legs in the 1940's, Monroe's breasts in the 1950's, and in the 1960's and 1970's, soulless prostitutes and "sexploited" victims.

The differences between "men's movies" and "the woman's film" exemplify some of the most important ideas in *From Reverence to Rape*. Women's films flourished in the 1930's and 1940's, foundered in the 1950's, and, replaced by television soap operas, barely survived the 1960's and 1970's. Women and their gender-specific dilemmas, their interior lives—the moral constraints of marriage or society, victimization, sacrifice, motherhood—were central to the films. At their best and at their worst, these motion pictures were important because they were expressions of women's desire, unlike most films. Haskell takes the position that even those women's films that appear on the surface to serve male needs contain enough contradictions to satisfy a woman's view. Male films, on the other hand, are clear manifestations of misogyny. Haskell analyzes Westerns, gangster films, war films—in short, a whole series of "male melodramas" that marginalize or exclude women. She associates this exclusion with an adolescent fantasy of male camaraderie and virility that does not really exist. She also suggests, however, that this type of film—so alarmingly present in the late 1960's and 1970's—functioned as a backlash to the escalating women's liberation movement. *From Reverence to Rape* ends by invoking the return of the charismatic women and directors of Hollywood and charging women with the difficult task of resisting the current trends and fighting the backlash.

Context

From Reverence to Rape was published at a time when the treatment of women in films, especially in a historical context, was virtually ignored by mainstream film critics. As such, Haskell produced an important work in film criticism. Her book has been widely praised for its timeliness and was cited at the time of publication as a valuable contribution to understanding tension between the sexes in real life as well as in films. Readers sympathetic to her views extolled the scholarship and expansiveness of the work. Yet *From Reverence to Rape* had its detractors, who believed that Haskell focuses only on major stars and ignores character actresses and grade "B" films. Others, in contrast to those who found the prose witty and readable, criticized the writing as impenetrable and the structure as convoluted. Some took a more balanced view, commending the intelligence and perceptiveness of the work on the one hand while criticizing its emotionality on the other.

The early 1970's produced two other books on the same subject: Marjorie Rosen's *Popcorn Venus: Women, Movies, and the American Dream* (1973) and Joan Mellen's *Women and Their Sexuality in the New Films* (1973); comparisons were inevitable. Many reviews incorporated all three books in one critique, comparing and contrasting strengths and weaknesses. In general, Haskell's work was considered superior overall to the other two texts. Regardless of its reception at the time, *From Reverence to Rape* is a seminal work, and few of the many studies that followed in subsequent years fail to reference it.

Sources for Further Study

Baker, Joyce M. *Images of Women in Film: The War Years, 1941-1945*. Ann Arbor, Mich.: UMI Research Press, 1980. Criticizes both Haskell's and Marjorie Rosen's works as superficial, while nevertheless noting their importance in "pressing for a broader dialogue." Discusses B-films and specific issues portrayed in films, such as the education of women, women in the military, and women as patriots.

Basinger, Jeanine. *A Woman's View: How Hollywood Spoke to Women, 1930-1960*. New York: Alfred A. Knopf, 1993. At more than five hundred pages, this work analyzes hundreds of films from a feminist perspective. Includes relatively unknown but politically significant films.

Erens, Patricia, ed. *Sexual Stratagems: The World of Women in Film*. New York: Horizon Press, 1979. Anthologizes a number of writers, including Haskell and Marjorie Rosen. Discusses images of women and compares male and female directors.

Fischer, Lucy. *Shot/Countershot: Film Tradition and Women's Cinema*. Princeton, N.J.: Princeton University Press, 1989. A comprehensive and scholarly work which incorporates new feminist criticism. In keeping with its academic perspective, an appendix is included which suggests teaching models.

Higashi, Sumiko. *Virgins, Vamps, and Flappers: The American Silent Movie Heroine*. St. Albans, Vt.: Eden Press Women's Publications, 1978. An interesting commentary analyzing the role of women in films of the 1920's. Contains photographs and a filmography.

Kay, Karyn, and Gerald Peary, eds. *Women and the Cinema: A Critical Anthology*. New York: E. P. Dutton, 1977. Includes two essays by Haskell and a number of other scholarly works in a similar vein.

Kuhn, Annette, ed. *Women in Film: An International Guide*. New York: Fawcett Columbine, 1991. An encyclopedia devoted to the contributions of women to films, both mainstream and independent. Hundreds of cross-references are included.

Stoddard, Karen. *Saints and Shrews: Women and Aging in Popular Film*. Westport, Conn.: Greenwood Press, 1983. Stoddard claims that Marjorie Rosen "manipulates facts to fit theory" and that Molly Haskell oversimplifies. Stoddard offers many scholarly notes and draws from a variety of academic sources to make her point.

Williams, Carol Traynor. *The Dream Beside Me: The Movies and Children of the Forties*. Madison, N.J.: Fairleigh Dickinson University Press, 1980. Williams discusses the effects of films of the 1940's, including B-films, on women of her generation. Cites Haskell frequently—sometimes agreeing, sometimes disagreeing. Contains an extensive bibliography and an appendix by subject.

Susan Chainey

GIFT FROM THE SEA

Author: Anne Morrow Lindbergh (1906-   )
Type of work: Essays
First published: 1955

Form and Content

While spending a week alone on the island of Captiva, Florida, Anne Morrow Lindbergh wrote *Gift from the Sea*, a collection of eight short essays inspired by the ebb and tide of the ocean. Each meditative piece focuses on a particular seashell, which Lindbergh uses to symbolize various perspectives on modern life. *Gift from the Sea* was on the best-seller list for more than six months, and it is still shared among women of all ages.

To become aware of inner rhythms, one must let today's tides erase yesterday's scribblings. With a mind free of responsibilities and time schedules, one is ready to receive the gift from the sea. Lindbergh uses these thoughts to introduce her collection of meditative essays. During her walks along the beach, she finds various shells; each unique design symbolizes different aspects of life, love, relationships, and identity.

The first shell is a channeled whelk, which is simple and bare. She realizes that her life is not simple since she has a husband, five children, and a home which require her attention. Her background, education, and conscience also contribute to the roles that she believes she must carry out in life. In satisfying external forces, she feels that she has lost a personal core, an individuality that lets her be herself. She wants to give to the world as a woman, an artist, and a citizen. Only when she has found her own means of giving will she feel an inward harmony that will be translated into an outward harmony. With a simple, unitary purpose that gives her direction, she will not feel fragmented by the multiplicity of life. She concentrates on removing the distractions that are inherent in her life and on replacing those tensions with a balanced core of inner peace.

The next shell is the moon shell whose spiral forms a solitary eye. To Lindbergh, this symbolizes that all people are alone. She claims, however, that people have forgotten how to be alone because they clutter their lives with constant music, chatter, and companionships. She encourages individuals to relearn how to be by themselves. When alone, people can get to know themselves, and in knowing themselves as individuals, they will be more willing to accept the individuality in others. Lindbergh goes on to explain that time alone is essential for women to replenish their wellspring of giving. She explains that women are forever nurturing children, men, and society. Time alone brings the quiet necessary to recharge resources. She addresses women who believe that their gifts are not needed by their families and society. To feel of value, women must turn inward. Time alone also brings out the creative life that resides within each individual and that may be expressed physically, intellectually, or artistically. She suggests that women do not need to compete with men in outside activities, that they need to develop their own inner springs.

Another shell is the delicate double-sunrise shell, which seems to wear a self-enclosed perfection. This beauty is used by Lindbergh to symbolize the early stages of relationships. She claims that the original pattern of ecstasy, that for which people hunger nostalgically, can never be held in an unchanging state. Life becomes too complicated and changes continuously, and so the love within that life must also change. She concludes that the ecstasy of early relationships is valid, but that validity is not dependent on continuity. Instead, it is one period in the ever-evolving spectrum of love.

Observing an oyster shell, Lindbergh sees a functional shell filled with many irregularities. She relates this to marriage after years have spread the relationship in many directions. Interdependencies and shared experiences are the bonds that keep the relationship together. She suggests that in middle age, people must begin shedding shells: "the shell of ambition, the shell of material accumulations and possessions, the shell of the ego." Then, they can become completely themselves by pursuing those intellectual, cultural, and spiritual activities that were set aside in their efforts to become worthy in society.

From the argonauta, Lindbergh meditates on the growth of relationships. Each partner must be given the space to grow in his or her respective direction. The distance that results must not frighten the partners because each is still strongly rooted in the marriage and in the family. The two separate worlds that result provide more to share with each other. She suggests that a couple should not look back to capture the ecstasy of the early relationship, nor should they look forward trying to define the future. Instead, they must be poised in the present, flowing with each day's tides. The couple must accept the ebb and flow of love, which is constantly in motion.

After greedily collecting shells, Lindbergh begins to realize that in the clutter of multiplicity, the beauty of individual shells is unappreciated. She realizes that in life people let too many activities, people, and possessions distract them from appreciating the significance of each. Only in simplicity can people retain a true awareness of life.

As Lindbergh departs from her week-long vacation, she reflects on what she has learned. She realizes that the "inter-relatedness of the world links us constantly with more people than our hearts can hold." She also reflects on America's appetite for the future, which results in rushing past the present. She concludes that people must make time for solitude, accept intermittency, and seek simplicity.

Analysis

During the 1950's, women's roles as housewives and mothers brought about some restless feelings. Women began to search for answers to ease their unhappiness. Lindbergh's book offered possible avenues for spiritual replenishment by suggesting that women simplify their lives. She wrote that technology, rapid changes, and the fast pace of modern life had cluttered women's lives. She suggested that women make time in their days to be alone, away from responsibilities, in order to nurture their spirituality.

In *Gift from the Sea*, Lindbergh discusses relationships between women and men. She encourages women to pursue personal growth and to accept growth in their mates. Although some distances may result from each spouse growing in different directions, Lindbergh concludes that the distances are not to be feared. The growth in relationships is like the growth of branches on a tree: each reaches in ever-broadening directions, but the trunk still remains stable in the ground.

Lindbergh also offers perspectives on love. She writes that love cannot be viewed as a permanent emotional condition that is without movement and change. Instead, love is constantly alive and altering in expression and feeling. By allowing for the fluidity of love brought about by growth, relationships are made stronger. Love must be given the freedom of ebb and flow.

As family members grow and begin to take independent paths, a mother's role is often left in limbo. Lindbergh addresses this issue and that of becoming middle-aged. Besides simplifying life in regard to time schedules, acquaintances, and space, women need to pursue activities that let them continue to give with purpose. For Lindbergh, this need is met by finding a solitary place where she can write, where she can forget herself, her companions, and the future. She suggests that women find their own creative activities to escape briefly the routines and responsibilities that surround them.

In solitude, women can nurture their inner lives, that aspect that is so often lost as one nourishes husband and family. In this way, women can find a sense of dignity as individuals, rather than letting themselves be standardized in thought and action. Lindbergh encourages women to nurture themselves as well as their families by finding a balance that allows for physical, intellectual, and spiritual development. Simplicity of time and space provides the environment in which such development can take place.

Context

Anne Morrow Lindbergh did not set out to write a book for women; she was writing meditations to resolve conflicts in her own life. Her friends persuaded her to put the essays into a book because all women could relate to her experiences. *Gift from the Sea* was published eight years before *The Feminine Mystique* (1963), the groundbreaking feminist work by Betty Friedan.

In *Gift from the Sea* Lindbergh does not ask women to abandon home life in order to pursue careers. As her several collections of diaries and letters reveal, especially the book *The Flower and the Nettle: Diaries and Letters of Anne Morrow Lindbergh, 1936-1939* (1976), Lindbergh devoted her life to her children and to her husband. Nevertheless, she also searched for time alone each day to write. Her lifelong practice of writing in every spare moment led her to Captiva and to write the meditations for *Gift from the Sea*.

Lindbergh did not encourage women to go out into the business world to seek meaning for their lives or to feel productive in society. Instead, Lindbergh encouraged them to find strength and meaning by turning inward, by nurturing their spirituality, and by expressing themselves creatively. Competing with men was not the answer that she offered; rather, simplifying life and nurturing the spirit would allow women to be the hub of a wheel around which the world turned. Without their inner strength, the wheel that represented all the lives that women touched would weaken. By finding and maintaining a balance of self—physically, intellectually, and artistically—women manage the distractions that occur in their everyday lives. They can utilize their inner strength to balance family life and social responsibilities.

Lindbergh acknowledged that life was stressful for women because of the constant demands to meet time schedules, to socialize with increasingly larger numbers of acquaintances brought about by mobility, and to maintain the numerous possessions resulting from industrialization. A woman's world was cluttered and could only be simplified by conscientious effort. Because it addresses the need for women to deal with the chaos of too many possessions, too many activities, and too many people, *Gift from the Sea* was popular when it was first released and remains so. Lindbergh's book offers encouragement to those women who want to be the hub of the wheel around which home life revolves. Lindbergh reveres the roles of mothers and wives without condemning those who choose professional roles. She presents a path by which those women choosing traditional roles can find self-worth and social meaning.

Sources for Further Study

Herrmann, Dorothy. *Anne Morrow Lindbergh: A Gift for Life*. New York: Ticknor & Fields, 1992. This candid biography focuses on Anne as an individual rather than as Charles Lindbergh's wife. Includes a bibliography of Anne's works, fine chapter notes, and an excellent bibliography for the study of Charles and Anne Morrow Lindbergh.

Lindbergh, Anne Morrow. *Dearly Beloved: A Theme and Variations*. New York: Harcourt, Brace & World, 1962. This book, like *Gift from the Sea*, was written during a dissatisfied period in Lindbergh's marriage. Using fiction rather then the nonfiction of *Gift from the Sea*, Lindbergh explores various conflicts in marriage, particularly the inadequacy of communication. Nevertheless, she firmly supports marriage for its sense of community.

____________. *The Flower and the Nettle: Diaries and Letters of Anne Morrow Lindbergh, 1936-1939*. New York: Harcourt Brace Jovanovich, 1976. A collection of diary entries and letters that are valuable in understanding Lindbergh's view of women's roles.

____________. *War Within and Without: Diaries and Letters of Anne Morrow Lindbergh, 1939-1944*. New York: Harcourt Brace Jovanovich, 1980. This final volume of Lindbergh's diary entries and letters covers the years of World War II. Anne discusses the Lindberghs' response to the accusations that Charles was a "traitor." She comments on the American attitude that raises individuals to hero status and then knocks them down by contempt and ostracism. She also reveals her personal struggles as she reconciles her devotion for her husband and their differing views about war.

Saint-Exupéry, Antoine de. *Wind, Sand and Stars*. Translated by Lewis Galantière. New York: Reynal and Hitchcock, 1939. This work was greatly admired by Lindbergh, who wrote a glowing review of it for the *Saturday Review of Literature*. Saint-Exupéry is often quoted in Lindbergh's writing because he was an aviator like herself and a writer who shared her perspective on the need for inner spirituality.

Linda J. Meyers

GIGI

Author: Colette (Sidonie-Gabrielle Colette, 1873-1954)
Type of work: Novella
Type of plot: Fairy tale
Time of plot: 1899
Locale: Paris, France
First published: 1944 (English translation, 1952)

Principal characters:

Gigi, a fifteen-year-old schoolgirl reared by a family of aging courtesans to become a wealthy man's mistress

Gaston ("Tonton") Lachaille, the heir to a sugar fortune and a man of the world who falls in love with Gigi

Madame Alvarez, Gigi's grandmother, a former courtesan

Aunt Alicia, the matriarch of the family

Andrée Alvarez, Gigi's mother, a singer in the chorus of the Paris Opera who never married Gigi's father

Form and Content

Gigi is Colette's fairy tale of a young girl who grows up and marries her Prince Charming. Like the stereotypical fairy-tale princess, Gigi becomes the wife of a "prince" at the end of the story and will presumably live happily ever after; unlike the pristine storybook characters, Gigi is surrounded by sexual innuendo of which she is highly conscious. Indeed, she becomes the recipient of an indecent proposal herself before she takes control, shifting the balance of power away from others and into her own hands.

It is no surprise that *Gigi* has translated so well to the stage and screen. The novella is composed largely of dialogue revealing the interaction between people rather than the private thoughts and interior journey that usually constitute the focus of the novel. Because of this, Colette's novella is sometimes called superficial; however, the conversations not only explore social customs and values but also reveal how off-center the customs and practices of this particular family of courtesans are. These women speak their minds to one another. They talk honestly and without euphemism so that the reader is able to become part of a web of relationships that centers on planning the future of Gigi.

As a family friend, called Tonton ("uncle") by Gigi, Gaston Lachaille is charmed and amused by Gigi, who speaks without guile. It is through their repartee that he becomes enamored of her; it is what he does not say to Gigi that prompts her to refuse his offer to install her as his mistress in a fine home where he will take care of her. Finally, when she discloses to him that she would rather be miserable with him than without him—and he knows that she speaks from a pure heart—his own jaded persona melts away (his "silence seemed to embarrass her") and he asks for Gigi's hand in marriage. She accepts because he tells her that he loves her: "Oh!" she cried, "you never told me that."

The descriptive paragraphs do not attempt to penetrate the interior meanderings of the characters and, in fact, deal mostly with the outward appearances that reveal the personal quirks and tastes of these people who exist within a world of ritual, rigid rules, and planned reactions. Gigi's hair must be curled only at the ends, for ringlets all around would be too flashy. Madame Alvarez sleeps on a divan in the dining-sitting room waiting for her daughter to come home from the opera every night. Lachaille's preposterously lavish parties are dutifully given in order to satisfy what is expected of him, yet he is too often bored at his own soirées. Character transformations are clearly drawn using subtle changes of so-called outward demeanor that Colette reveals to the reader through her prose. At the beginning of the story, Gigi is a dishevelled and energetic schoolgirl dressed in childish clothing. Later, she is a well-dressed young woman asking for headache medicine. Gaston, who is the picture of perfection and pride in all his finery, must humble himself to Gigi in order to gain her hand in marriage. There are no superfluous moments in *Gigi*. Every detail serves to reinforce the notion of the fairy tale and to deflate it at the same time. Gigi begins as no beauty. She does not live in a castle, but she will. She begins the story an ordinary girl and by the end of the story becomes an extraordinary woman.

Analysis

When Colette wrote her captivating fairy tale *Gigi*, she was nearly seventy years old. It was 1944, and Europe had been conquered and destroyed by Hitler's Nazis. Colette's own husband, Maurice Goudeket, a Jew, had been arrested and sent to a prison camp in 1941. By the time that Colette published *Gigi*, both the author and the reader were in great need of a lovely story that took them to another place and time. The world of Gigi takes one back to the *belle époque* of Paris, when the world was optimistic and fun—a "once upon a time" for people surrounded by devastation.

Colette's attention to the small pleasures of daily French life—a warm cup of tea, a hearty plate of cassoulet—are intended to feed the reader's spirit at a time when food was hard to come by. Little candies and the gentle tug of a bead-embroidered bellpull are tiny memories that ring and echo in the memories of the Frenchmen during their most trying times. The fact that Colette chose sugar as the commodity controlled by the Lachaille family is indicative of her wish to spin her fairy tale with sweetness and light.

So many of the luxuries adored by the French are focused on in *Gigi* as symbols of the beauty and elegance that once surrounded them. Gaston brings Madame Alvarez bottles of champagne and *pâté de foie gras*. When Gigi is fitted for her feminine clothing, the seven and a half yards of rustling fabric, the wide flounced skirt of blue and white silk, recall the crisp, outdoor Impressionist paintings that captured only a moment before the subject moved on. Time moves on, warns Colette, and although the past seems even more desirable when the present cannot be endured, there must always be hope for a brighter future. Aunt Alicia, still living in the past, is described as having "fastidious taste." Elegance never goes out of style, good taste is timeless, and barbarians cannot remove beauty from the world. Aunt Alicia's apartment sparkles and shimmers: her tea set, the silver walls, her jewels, the knife blade one uses to cut lobster. It is a haven that is both luxurious and safe—the bed is covered in chinchilla, the rosary with seed pearls, the floor with Persian rugs.

Tantamount is the beauty of womanhood. Lest the gray world of 1944 plague men with grim, dull uniforms and plainly dressed women, Colette writes of a time when a woman was admired for "the turn of a wrist like a swan's neck, the tiny ear, the profile revealing a delicious kinship between the heart-shaped mouth and the wide-cut eyelids with their long lashes." Although the war that was being fought gave Colette and her countrymen some of their saddest moments, *Gigi* is, after all, a celebration of the triumph of woman. The fact that a young schoolgirl is about to begin a wonderful future is Colette's offering of hope to her reader. The future, for Gigi, will be a better one than anyone had dreamed for her.

Colette's novella, like the stories she had been writing for the French newspapers during the war, is about the world of women. Gigi is reared by women, is surrounded by female schoolmates, and has virtually no contact with men other than with "Tonton" Gaston. It is a feminine world that Colette has created choosing her symbols of nourishment and objets d'art about the home, portraying the inner sanctums where women have control. Once, when Gaston is visiting, Gigi's mother, Andrée, appears in dressing gown and curlers. Madame Alvarez comments: "It's plain that there's no man here for you to bother about, my child! A man in the house soon cures a woman of traipsing about in dressing-gown and slippers."

Man is a foreign intruder that one must work tirelessly to please and go to great extremes to suffer for. Aunt Alicia's discipline and beauty regimes are imparted to Gigi as essential to enhancing her face and figure. Although she is well past her prime, Aunt Alicia still retains these little tricks as if she were expecting a new lover at any moment. Liane d'Exelman, Gaston's girlfriend, attempts suicide when he discovers her with another lover. According to fashion, consuming an astonishingly painful overdose of laudanum is expected of the courtesan, and, in fact, she attempts suicide with predictability: "She has only one idea in her heart, that woman, but she sticks to it," remarks Andrée. Andrée is the only one of the four women who steps outside this female world to work at the opera. She has very little regard for men and, unlike her mother and aunt, does not view men as providers and rescuers. Her opinions, however, are not imparted to Gigi because, as a self-absorbed "artiste," she relinquishes her daughter's education to the older courtesans, whose lessons are decidedly of a sexual nature.

Context

Gigi is not a fairy tale for children. It is a book about the potency of women's sexuality and is replete with sexual metaphor. The matriarchal fortress serves to protect Gigi's virginity: "Don't get to know the families of your school friends, especially not the fathers who wait at the gates to fetch their daughters home from school." When Gaston innocently offers to take Gigi skating, Madame Alvarez forbids it, explaining that Gigi will be perceived by society to have been compromised. Gigi is told to "keep your knees close to each other, and lean both of them together," but she complains that it is too uncomfortable and that she would rather have her skirts lengthened because "with my skirts too short, I have to keep thinking of my you-know-what." Madame Alvarez explains that if Gigi's skirts were longer people would perceive her to be older and that would ruin her mother's career. In other words, her mother is still singing in the chorus not because of her great talent but because she is believed to be sexually vital. Although Gigi is still a virgin, she playfully asks Gaston to bring her "an eau-de-nil Persephone corset with rococo roses embroidered on the garters." Gigi, who was expected to be virginal nevertheless, was reared to be acutely aware of her sexuality. As Madame Alvarez instructed her, "You can, at a pinch, leave the face till the morning, when traveling or pressed for time. For a woman, attention to the lower parts is the first law of self-respect." A classmate of Gigi's is given a solitaire by a baron. Her grandmother immediately understands what this implies and forbids Gigi to remain her friend. Gigi has been made to know that the sexual power of women can be their most important asset. She considers falling into the trap set by the generations of women in her family but is saved from having to repeat history when Gaston asks her to marry him. At once, she has also saved her family and becomes their new matriarch, their heroine. Her potential for self-fulfillment becomes the happy ending.

Sources for Further Study

Cotrell, Robert D. *Colette*. New York: Frederick Ungar, 1974. Contrell provides a thorough biography of Colette and undertakes the task of applying her life to her various works. He also studies the symbols and tendencies prevalent in these works.

Lottman, Herbert. *Colette*. Boston: Little, Brown, 1991. Lottman's biography is an informative account of Colette's rise to fame and her life among the international set. Contains rare photographs of Colette's family.

Richardson, Joanna. *Colette*. New York: Franklin Watts, 1984. A comprehensive and well-researched book that studies the life and work of Colette in a most factual and methodical way.

Stewart, Joan Hinde. *Colette*. Boston: Twayne, 1983. Stewart sees Colette's theme as the shift of power away from men to women. *Gigi* is about a young woman who creates a new world where love is important, destroying an old order where sexuality was a commercial commodity.

Ward Jouve, Nicole. *Colette*. Bloomington: Indiana University Press, 1987. Ward Jouve discusses the theories of psychiatrist Sigmund Freud in relation to Colette's female characters and looks at the writer's singular contribution to the small list of women writers who, she claims, are neglected in school curricula.

Susan Nagel

GOBLIN MARKET AND OTHER POEMS

Author: Christina Rossetti (1830-1894)
Type of work: Poetry
First published: 1862

Form and Content

Goblin Market and Other Poems was the first book of poetry that Christina Rossetti published, although her grandfather had privately printed a collection of her juvenilia when she was seventeen. Despite its appearance at the beginning of her literary career, *Goblin Market and Other Poems* contains some of her finest and most enduring writing: the title poem, "Goblin Market," still her best-known work: "Up-Hill," "After Death," "Remember," "The Three Enemies," "A Better Resurrection," "An Apple Gathering," "Advent," "The Convent Threshold," "Dead Before Death," "A Triad," "Winter: My Secret," and "No, Thank You, John," among others. Though Rossetti would continue writing for another thirty years, no later poems surpassed these.

"Goblin Market," her most anthologized and discussed poem, is also, at 567 lines, one of her longest. A narrative poem (a rarity for Rossetti), it tells the story of two sisters, Laura and Lizzie, and their close brush with a sinister group of goblin merchants. The first of the twenty-nine irregular stanzas simply records the cries of the goblin men for someone to buy their magical fruits. In the following stanzas, Laura and Lizzie listen to the tantalizing cries; Lizzie warns Laura not to succumb to temptation, reminding her of the fate of their friend Jeanie who, after tasting the goblin fruit, wasted away with premature age and died. Laura ignores the warning, and, though she has no money, buys the enchanted fruit with a lock of her golden hair.

The fruit delights Laura, but leaves her wanting more, which she cannot have since she can no longer see or hear the goblins. Her addiction becomes her obsession, and she pines away for the fruit, not eating or sleeping and, like Jeanie, dwindling and turning gray. The only antidote is a second taste of the fruit, which the goblins withhold from their victims. When Lizzie realizes that her sister is dying, she goes to the goblins, whom she can still see and hear, and offers to buy their fruit. When they realize that her intention is not to partake of the fruit herself but to take it to the ailing Laura, the goblins try to force-feed her. Wearing down the goblin men with heroic resistance, Lizzie returns to Laura—not having tasted the fruit, but having its juice and pulp smeared all over her face by the struggle. When Laura kisses her sister, she tastes the juice, which removes the curse of the goblin fruit and restores Laura's youth and health. The final stanza is an epilogue in which the sisters, now married and with children of their own, use the story of the goblin market as an object lesson to their children of the salvific virtue of sisterhood.

Many of the shorter lyrics in *Goblin Market and Other Poems* demonstrate Christina Rossetti's characteristic and almost obsessive preoccupation with death as a release. Four Petrarchan sonnets in the collection treat the theme of love and death in four different ways. One, "After Death," surveys a deathbed scene from the point of view of a recently deceased maiden who triumphs in finally having captured the attention of a young man whom she had loved in vain. In another sonnet, "Remember," the young woman is alive but anticipates her death, urging her young man to remember her, but only if the memories will not make him sad. "Remember" utilizes the Petrarchan sonnet form to advantage, using the break between the octave (the first eight lines) and the sestet (the final six) to contrast the admonition to remember with the plea not to be sad.

A third sonnet, "Dead Before Death," laments the contrast between what one expects of life (and death) and what one gets. Unlike the other two sonnets, "Dead Before Death" makes no overt mention of romance, but the image of a fallen blossom which bears no fruit seems to refer to a love that could have been, the possibility of which is forestalled by death, who shuts the door. The octave begins the lament, while the sestet forms a kind of dirge in which the word "lost" is repeated six times. A fourth sonnet, "A Triad," looks at three women whose failed pursuits of love end in death: the first, a wanton whose indulgence in a sensual love brings her only shame; the second, a wife whose marriage is proper but "soulless"; the third, an unmarried woman who dies yearning for love. The octave describes the three women, while the sestet tells the results of their loves, all negative.

Analysis

The poetry of *Goblin Market and Other Poems* was immediately recognized as a significant contribution to English literature, and it set the tone for Christina Rossetti's later writing: Her metrical inventiveness, as well as her themes of death, ascetic renunciation, and thwarted love, were established here.

The theme of renunciation is central to the title poem "Goblin Market," and critics Sandra M. Gilbert and Susan Gubar have identified it as a key aspect of all Rossetti's writing. Though not overtly Christian or devotional as her later poetry, "Goblin Market" seems at first to express a traditional Christian attitude of renunciation of the sensual, of the flesh. Yet many critics have noted an ambiguity in the way in which sensuality, represented by the goblin fruit, is depicted in the poem. Laura's devouring of the fruit, paralleled later by her equally sensuous sucking of the juices off her sister's face, is described in a lushness of physical imagery unusual in Christina Rossetti's poetry (though typical of the verse of her brother, Dante Gabriel Rossetti).

The overt moral on the value of sisterhood, found in the final six lines of "Goblin Market," is often disparaged as an afterthought, unrelated to the rest of the poem, which is about renunciation. A close study of Lizzie's sacrifice for her sister, however, reveals that the themes of renunciation and sisterhood are related. Lizzie's resistance to the charms of the goblin fruit is merely temperance in the first scene, but when she seeks the goblin merchants after Laura's illness, her resistance takes on a heroic, sacrificial quality. Lizzie's Christlike self-giving defines sisterhood and makes her even more Christlike as Laura's savior, resurrecting her from the death-in-life caused by the evil fruit—a parallel to the Eden story.

A few critics have been tempted to discover an autobiographical element in "Goblin Market," which leads to a general question of how subjective a reader should consider Rossetti's poetry to be. Christina dedicated the poem to her sister Maria Rossetti, and her brother William speculated that Lizzie represented Maria and that the poem referred to some specific incident of "spiritual backsliding" on Christina's part, of which he was unaware. Violet Hunt picked up the hint in her study *The Wife of Rossetti: Her Life and Death* (1932) imagining that Maria had saved Christina from eloping with James Collinson, whose proposal Christina had refused nine years earlier and who had married another. Lona Mosk Packer's 1963 biography *Christina Rossetti* painted the same scenario, but with another married man, William Bell Scott. With nothing but circumstantial evidence for such speculation, most critics prefer to limit the interpretation of "Goblin Market" to its imagery and form.

The meter of "Goblin Market" is much freer than that of most poetry of the mid-nineteenth century, which led to much criticism by her contemporaries. The first review of *Goblin Market and Other Poems*, in the April 26, 1862, issue of *The Athenaeum* (where much of Christina Rossetti's early verse had been published), praised the volume generally, yet lamented its "discords" and "harshness." The leading critic of the day, John Ruskin, made the same criticism in reading the work in manuscript, judging that no one would publish them because of their metrical irregularity. Yet Rossetti rightly trusted her ear rather than the metronome that her critics demanded, and by the twentieth century "Goblin Market" was recognized as a precursor of the metrically freer verse of modern poetry.

The theme of unsatisfied love in "The Triad" and the modulation of the fruit imagery from Genesis in "Goblin Market" are combined in one of Rossetti's finest lyrics, "An Apple Gathering." Actually a dramatic monologue, the poem is a young woman's lament for tasting love too early, and thereby losing her beau, "Willie." In the first stanza, she tells of plucking apple blossoms, so that when she returns to her tree at harvest time there is no fruit. In subsequent stanzas, she is teased by the sight of other young women who return with baskets full of apples. Here, as in "Goblin Market," Rossetti has altered slightly the traditional sexual connotation of the Edenic fruit image. The speaker's act of plucking the blossom before it could become fruit is an act of renunciation similar to Lizzie's in "Goblin Market." Instead of winning her Willie's love, however, it drives him to seek out "plump Gertrude" who passes the speaker arm in arm with Willie, her basket full of apples.

Critics have noticed, and sometimes lamented, the prevalence of the idea of death as a release from the oppressions of the world in Christina Rossetti's poetry. The reviewer for *The Athenaeum* mentioned above faulted her for overusing a melancholy tone. The frequency of the theme of death as release was ascribed simply to pious morbidity until 1980, when Jerome J. McGann noted its debt to an obscure Anabaptist doctrine of "Soul Sleep," the belief that the souls of the saved remained in a trance from the time of their deaths until Judgment Day. This explains the peculiarly static image of death as a bed in "Up-Hill" and of the newly dead speaker of "When I Am Dead" simply "dreaming through the twilight."

Context

Gilbert and Gubar have argued that the act of renunciation that forms the core of "Goblin Market" was emblematic not only for Christina Rossetti but for all women writers of the nineteenth century as well. To become a poet, Rossetti's life and poetry seem to imply, a woman must isolate herself. She must become that peculiarly nineteenth century phenomenon which the novelist George Gissing called the "Odd Woman," who refuses marriage in order to devote herself to her art, as if the two were at odds.

Whether Rossetti's refusal of three marriage proposals (two from one suitor, in 1848 and 1850, and one from another in 1866) was related to her writing, the picture of a young woman letting go of a young man who wants her is seen in many of the lyrics of *Goblin Market and Other Poems*—particularly "No, Thank You, John," which, as the title suggests, is the voice of a woman declining a marriage proposal. In "After Death," a dead woman smiles at the pity of the young man she is leaving behind, with perhaps an ironic double meaning in the closing line, "he still is warm tho' I am cold." While there are also painful images of unrequited love in this collection, there are just as many of love purposefully renounced.

Rossetti's tribute to sisterhood in the last six lines of "Goblin Market" can be seen in the context of this renunciation. Sisterhood is defined as a sort of self-giving in a fairy-tale world safe from the taint of men. As Gilbert and Gubar have pointed out, the only male figures in the poem are the hurtful and animal-like goblins. The counterpart to the divine "sister" is the diabolical "brother," as the goblins are twice described with negative adjectives: "brother with queer brother" and "brother with sly brother." The poem ends with marriages for Laura and Lizzie, but their husbands are not even mentioned; there are "children," but we are not told if any of them are sons.

Christina Rossetti was one of the first female poets about whom critics argued over the sexist term "poetess." In 1891, Richard Le Gallienne agreed that "Miss Rossetti is the greatest English poet among women," but that gender distinction "in questions of art" is a false one, "a distinction which has given us the foolish word 'poetess.' " In 1897, Arthur Symons, himself a leading poet who recognized Rossetti's superiority, used the offensive term, but only by way of saying that she rises above categories: "she takes rank among poets rather than among poetesses."

Sources for Further Study

Battiscombe, Georgina. *Christina Rossetti*. London: Longmans, Green, 1965. A handy starting point for studying Rossetti, this brief booklet offers a summary assessment of her literary accomplishment, as well as critical comments on a few selected poems.

Bellas, Ralph A. *Christina Rossetti*. Boston: Twayne, 1977. Following the format of the Twayne English Authors series, this volume opens with a biography, then discusses Rossetti's works chronologically. The first part of chapter 3 is a discussion of *Goblin Market and Other Poems*, including a summary of criticism to date.

Bowra, C. M. "Christina Rossetti." In *The Romantic Imagination*. New York: Oxford University Press, 1949. An illuminating study of Rossetti's poetry, but dominated by Bowra's thesis that Rossetti was torn between being "the woman and the saint" and that her devotional verse is inconsistent with the rest of her writing.

McGann, Jerome J. "Christina Rossetti's Poetry." In *Cannons*, edited by Robert von Hallberg. Chicago: University of Chicago Press, 1984. After a thorough and valuable summary of Rossetti's poetic technique, McGann demonstrates that technique in Rossetti's most famous (and, he argues, most typical) poem, "Goblin Market."

Packer, Lona Mosk. *Christina Rossetti*. Berkeley: University of California Press, 1963. An exhaustive biography of Rossetti, this book also offers occasional literary comments where helpful. Its publication caused a little stir by Packer's assertion that Rossetti's love poetry was inspired, not by her two suitors, as previously assumed, but by William Bell Scott. Packer implies that Bell's love for another woman was an immediate influence on *Goblin Market and Other Poems*.

Woolf, Virginia. "I Am Christina Rossetti." In *Second Common Reader*. New York: Harcourt Brace, 1932. One of the earliest feminist studies of Rossetti by a leading twentieth century literary figure, this essay summarizes a 1930 biography, but warns the reader that biographies can distort. Tending toward the fanciful rather than the scholarly, Woolf's essay is an antidote to the overanalysis of Rossetti's work found elsewhere.

John R. Holmes

THE GOLDEN NOTEBOOK

Author: Doris Lessing (1919-)
Type of work: Novel
Type of plot: Social criticism
Time of plot: The 1940's to the 1950's
Locale: London, England
First published: 1962

Principal characters:

Anna Wulf, a novelist experiencing writer's block who begins to write notebooks to figure out her life
Molly Jacobs, Anna's friend, a marginally successful actress rearing a teenage son alone
Richard Portmain, Molly's former husband, an extremely successful businessman
Tommy Jacobs, Molly and Richard's son
Marion Jacobs, Richard's present wife, an alcoholic who rebels against him
Ella, a character in the Yellow Notebook who is a double for Anna, but without her political consciousness
Saul Green, Anna's American lover

Form and Content

The Golden Notebook is divided into six sections that interlock and interact with one another to form a complex meaning. The first section, called "Free Women," is a conventional novel telling the story of Anna Wulf's and Molly Jacobs' lives in 1957 London. Anna and Molly are old friends who come together to talk about their experiences with men, politics, and life as "free women," women who are not living with a man. Anna is becoming bored with their talks and begins to suspect that their complaints about how they are treated by men contribute in some way to the continuation of these types of relationships. She wishes "to be done with it all, finished with the men vs. women business." Indeed, this is what she accomplishes by the end of the book.

In "Free Women," Molly's son, Tommy, goes through an identity crisis. His business tycoon father, Richard, offers him a job which he scorns as morally corrupt, but neither can he embrace his mother's socialism. He attempts suicide, is blinded, and then takes on Marion, Richard's alcoholic wife, as a protégé. Marion eventually leaves Richard and opens a dress shop. Molly marries a progressive businessman, Tommy follows in his father's footsteps, and Anna explores the meaning of life in her notebooks, then has a breakdown in her relationship with Saul Green. At the end of the novel, she goes to work as a marriage counselor with a man with whom she has worked at a magazine.

Every section of "Free Women" is followed by entries from each of Anna Wulf's notebooks. The Black Notebook deals with money, specifically with the royalties from her first novel, *Frontiers of War*; the notebook examines the part of her life about which the novel is written and later critical responses to the book. Anna and her group of communist intellectuals are in Rhodesia during World War II, and they spend their weekends at a resort hotel in the veld. One of Anna's friends becomes involved with an African woman who is the wife of the hotel cook, creating a scandal. The second focus of this section is how critics and producers try to manipulate her novel to serve their own political agendas.

The Red Notebook is an examination of Anna's relationship to the British Communist Party. In this section, she joins the Party, works for it for a while, and then eventually leaves. Anna's concern is with her relationship to political rhetoric, dogma, and slogans, how they function to control her thinking processes and sense of identity. The Yellow Notebook is a sort of novel, *The Shadow of the Third*, narrated by Ella, who is a shadow of Anna minus her political awareness. In this notebook, Ella explores her obsessive relationship with Paul, a married man with whom she has an affair. When Paul predictably leaves her, Ella tries to find out why she is so controlled by her need to be with a man, how the rhetoric of male-female relationships shapes her thinking and identity. In her attempt to escape this social conditioning, Ella begins to realize that a profound connection exists between reality and story. She writes a series of plot summaries of possible love relationships at the end of the Yellow Notebook that Anna reenacts with her lover, Saul, at the end of the novel. It is this reenactment which allows Anna to break free from her social conditioning as a woman.

The Blue Notebook is Anna's attempt to write a diary, a true account of her life with no political or sexual dogma, prearranged phrases, or plots intervening. Eventually in this notebook, words lose their meaning and Anna dissolves into a breakdown. The Golden Notebook is an account of how Anna comes through her breakdown into a new identity.

Analysis

The structure of *The Golden Notebook* is perhaps its most important feature and the most overlooked aspect of the novel when it was first released. Critics immediately pronounced the novel to be simply about the "sex war," a notion which provoked Lessing into adding a preface directing the reader's attention to the shape of the novel and the theme of "breakdown" which is reflected in the shape. Anna Wulf cannot write about her world as a whole, because it no longer fits together for her, so she breaks it down into parts in hopes that she can discover an underlying meaning which will bring a new order. Anna understands that she is herself internally divided when she examines the discrepancies in her belief system or sense of self and her actual behavior. By allowing herself to move into these contradictions and to live them rather than suppress them, Anna is eventually able to break through into a new paradigm.

A large part of this novel considers the function of language as ideology, and therefore a way to stop or to control the thinking process. Each section adds to this theme in its own way. The Black Notebook interrogates literature, the relationship between Anna's memories and the novel that she wrote out of them, and how literature is co-opted by cultural ideology. The Red Notebook separates out and examines the ideology of political life. Anna discovers how she is manipulated, how her identity is shaped, by the surrounding cultural belief systems. She knows that the Communist Party has become corrupt, that members (including herself) will say one thing when alone or with one another and adopt or be taken over by another "viewpoint" while functioning in an official Party capacity. Yet this does not stop Anna from participating in all this activity even while she is ironically aware of its irrationality. The Red Notebook ends with clippings and a story about a man whose whole life was built on the delusion that the Russians would one day send for him to set the history of the Party straight.

The Yellow Notebook separates out sexual politics and examines the "woman in love" figure who emerges in the psyche of Ella. She is dismayed at her own conventional responses to her lover and realizes that she cannot stop herself from acting out cultural ideas and formulas. Paul, however, is as internally divided as Ella is, and he acts the parts of the irresponsible husband and the jealous lover seemingly against his will as well. Both genders are permeated by social ideology. Ella escapes these social formulas by writing out plot summaries in which she discovers preplanned scenarios encapsulated in her head, thus purging herself of their influence.

In the Blue Notebook, Anna experiences "the thinning of language against the density of our experience." Language becomes inadequate to reflect reality. Try as she might, she cannot stop social ideology from contaminating her attempts to capture "pure reality" in her diary. Anna comes to understand slogans and ideology as substitutes for self-knowledge and independent action. The notebook ends with the purchase of the Golden Notebook, which contains the dreams that bring Anna out of the group of the cultural image of woman and the mind-containing slogans of politics and psychoanalysis.

Anna escapes the disintegration of her personality, which is intricately related to the social disintegration around her, by playing out all the possibilities of the male-female role with Saul Green, a man whose personality is as fractured as Paul's. By exploring each other's psychosis, by having both sides of the formula of gender available, Anna and Saul are able to break through their entrapment in the ideology of male-female relationships. Anna discovers in this process that individual consciousness is not isolated and discrete, as society would have her believe, but that consciousness is connected to culture and to other humans in a much more intimate way.

The "Free Women" section stands in ironic juxtaposition to the rich complexity of the journals. Lessing believed that the shape of the book would "make its own comment about the conventional novel," which would amount to "how little I have caught of all that complexity." The reader understands that this conventional novel fails because the surrounding source material of the notebooks is much richer, more complex, and interesting, but Anna Wulf has succeeded in creating a new definition of the nature of human consciousness and identity.

Context

The Golden Notebook was hailed as a feminist manifesto of sorts when it was first published, but Lessing was as dismayed by this simplistic reception of the novel as she was by the equally simplistic reaction against women speaking their minds that followed. Lessing makes it clear in her preface that, while she supports the aims of the women's movement, she is interested in a larger, although related, issue: the disintegration of Western society. She took the centrality of women's consciousness and problems for granted when she wrote the novel: "Some books are not read in the right way because they have skipped a stage of opinion, assume a crystallisation of information in society which has not yet taken place."

Yet this novel is important to women's literature. In writing this book, Lessing was interested in capturing the cultural milieu of mid-twentieth century Great Britain and, in so doing, chooses a female narrator. Not only is Anna Wulf the narrator, but also her life and problems, the very structure of her psyche, serve as the vehicle for exploring Western culture at this point in time. For a woman's consciousness to serve as the center of a work of such scope was unusual even by the 1960's, although Lessing's Children of Violence series revolves around a similar female character.

The Golden Notebook expressed many women's experiences in print for the first time. The novel explores issues of intimate relationships, sexuality, and identity which had not previously been discussed in such detail or from a woman's perspective. Yet the novel does not stop there: It takes women's concerns and relates them to other issues. For example, Saul Green's continual barrage of "I, I, I, I" is likened to the rapid fire of a machine gun, and Anna and Saul's battle is considered part of "the logic of war." Lessing anticipates feminist writings of the 1970's and 1980's which explore the connections between the suppression of women and imperialism and the exploitation of the environment.

This novel also challenges Western culture's epistemology, the way in which it has defined human consciousness and the nature of reality. Anna Wulf breaks through into a new sanity by realizing that the divisions she tried to enforce in her notebooks are false—that she is not a discrete entity separate from all other people and events, but that her consciousness is part of everything and everyone around her. Western science established itself by suppressing the older European beliefs that humans were connected to nature, that knowledge came through bodily connection and intuitive insights, then spread the new worldview through several centuries of imperialism. Lessing challenges this worldview through a woman's insights about the nature of her own mind.

Sources for Further Study

Greene, Gayle. *Changing the Story: Feminist Fiction and the Tradition.* Bloomington: Indiana University Press, 1991. Feminist criticism of Lessing, among other writers. Examines how language plays an important role in *The Golden Notebook.*

Hite, Molly. *The Other Side of the Story: Structures and Strategies of Contemporary Feminist Narrative.* Ithaca, N.Y.: Cornell University Press, 1989. This work of feminist criticism offers a thorough discussion of Lessing's experiments with form.

Kaplan, Carey, and Ellen Cronan Rose, eds. *Approaches to Teaching Lessing's "The Golden Notebook."* New York: Modern Language Association, 1989. An excellent look at *The Golden Notebook*, with helpful applications of contemporary feminist theory.

Pickering, Jean. *Understanding Doris Lessing.* Columbia: University of South Carolina Press, 1990. Excellent summaries of the novels with helpful commentary.

Pratt, Annis, and L. S. Dembo, eds. *Doris Lessing: Critical Studies.* Madison: University of Wisconsin Press, 1974. A collection of essays on Lessing's work, containing an excellent interview with Lessing conducted by Florence Howe and some early feminist criticism.

Rubenstein, Roberta. *The Novelistic Vision of Doris Lessing: Breaking the Forms of Consciousness.* Urbana: University of Illinois Press, 1979. This book gives special attention to Lessing's focus on human consciousness, what the theme means in her work and how she challenges the limits of consciousness in her prose.

Sprague, Claire, and Virginia Tiger, eds. *Critical Essays on Doris Lessing*. Boston: G. K. Hall, 1986. A collection of insightful essays on Lessing's work.

Theresa L. Crater

GONE WITH THE WIND

Author: Margaret Mitchell (1900-1949)
Type of work: Novel
Type of plot: Romance
Time of plot: The Civil War and Reconstruction
Locale: Georgia
First published: 1936

Principal characters:

Scarlett O'Hara, the spoiled, self-centered daughter of a wealthy Georgia plantation owner

Rhett Butler, a Southern aristocrat by birth and upbringing who scorns the idealism and hot-headedness that plunges the South into the Civil War

Ashley Wilkes, Scarlett's great love, the representation of an aristocratic Southern idealism whose day is past

Melanie Wilkes, Ashley's cousin and his wife, the supreme representative of ideal Southern womanhood

Frank Kennedy, a fussy bachelor and the second husband to Scarlett

Form and Content

Gone with the Wind is a historical romance that uses Scarlett O'Hara as the symbol for Reconstruction in the South. Like Atlanta, which sheds its image of Southern gentility after the Civil War, Scarlett is allowed to break away from the conventionalities of proper Southern womanhood. The exigencies of war, its devastation and defeat, enable Scarlett to adopt behavior more suited to her energy and character as she struggles to support her family, to restore the plantation Tara to productivity, and later to become a commercially successful businesswoman in Atlanta, operating a general store, a lumberyard, and a mill.

Scarlett is motivated by her need to survive and to care for an extended family, which includes Ashley and Melanie Wilkes, their child, and the loyal family slaves. Only Scarlett has the determination, courage, and practicality—perhaps even the stubbornness—to accept the challenge of survival in the radically changed post-Civil War world. Her second and third marriages, to Frank Kennedy and Rhett Butler, are marriages of expedience, both for commercial gain.

Scarlett lacks both analytical and sensitivity skills, replacing them with her determined will to act. Thus, as she faces death, starvation, rape, exhaustion, loss of her beloved mother, and fear of losing Tara, as she acknowledges the commodification of sex and marriage disguised as romance by her culture and barters her body for tax money, she is forced to face the worst. Yet the novel is also about heroic growth to maturity for Scarlett. As she develops a sense of security about her survival, she begins to develop those qualities of sensitivity and concern for others that complete such maturity.

Intertwined with Scarlett's story of growth to heroic selfhood is a typical woman's romance tale. Rhett Butler, who moves in and out of Scarlett's life, plays the typical scoundrel hero so popular in this kind of fiction. He perceives Scarlett as a brave but naïve woman-child whom he can rescue and indulge after they are married. The romance formula is undermined, however, when Rhett neglects to come to Scarlett's rescue on several occasions, forcing her to develop the self-confidence and courage that he later rejects. Thus, Scarlett is empowered by the failure of both romantic heroes—Rhett and the ineffectual Ashley. Also at odds with the romance novel formula are Scarlett's three marriages, all occurring during the time that she is in love with a fourth man whom she no longer desires by the end of the novel. Also, when she finally "comes to realize" her love for Rhett, a central aspect of the formula, he no longer desires her. There is no happy ending or reconciliation of lovers; rather, Rhett walks out the door into a fog of confusion.

Gone with the Wind is also a story about land and agriculture. When she realizes that her mother has died, Scarlett's need to find comfort and security either on her mother's or Mammy's bosom is replaced by the stability and meaning that she finds in the red earth of Tara. It is farming about which Scarlett cares most, although her insistence on keeping Tara and restoring it to some degree of productivity requires her to leave it to marry Frank Kennedy. At the unhappy ending, Scarlett decides to return home to Tara and to its beloved earth in order to restore her sense of hope and of purpose.

Analysis

While it seems that Margaret Mitchell intended to create a formula-driven historical romance novel that celebrates the glory of war even in retreat, *Gone with the Wind* can also be understood as a kind of female *Bildungsroman*, a story of the growth to maturity that is traditional in Western literature that is generally reserved for male characters. Rhett Butler remains the stereotypical buccaneer throughout, but Scarlett begins as a spoiled adolescent flirt and becomes a sensitive, unselfish woman by the novel's end. Unfortunately, this process is slowed by Scarlett's very real fears of starvation and by her insecurity.

Mitchell portrays this process of development by sending Scarlett on a series of journeys which function as learning experiences for her, a typical part of the *Bildungsroman*. For example, returning home to Tara from a besieged Atlanta with Melanie, two children, and the maid Prissy, Scarlett realizes that she must be a survivor if her whole family is to survive. Her second journey is from Tara to a rebuilding Atlanta, wearing a dress made from green velvet drapes. In spite of the religious training that she received from her mother, Scarlett is willing to do anything to save Tara, including selling herself to Rhett as a mistress or, when that does not work, to Frank Kennedy, her sister's fiancé, in marriage. Scarlett's third journey is through human misery as she endures her father's death, the scandal over her most innocent hug from Ashley, her pregnancy and miscarriage, Rhett's rejection, her daughter Bonnie's death, and finally, Melanie's death. At this point, she realizes that financial security is not enough, but rather that compassion, community, and an understanding of reality are vital to her growth. Thus, her fourth journey is home to Rhett, as she is finally aware of how he also has been suffering. When Rhett rejects her, she prepares for a fifth journey—home to Tara to make a plan for her life.

In *Gone with the Wind*, Mitchell depicts several Southern female stereotypes—especially that of the helpless, passive, and sometimes silly woman, such as Scarlett's sisters and Ashley's sister, India Wilkes—and then undermines them by delimiting their roles. In Scarlett, she has created the stereotypical romance heroine who escapes the limits of her role and, in fact, is forced to expand her possibilities. Scarlett becomes the shrewdest businessperson among her old friends, and she has learned how to manipulate her feminine role to get what she needs for survival. Melanie Wilkes, who seems to typify the frail, passive, ideal woman, actually has a tough, pragmatic interior.

While Melanie lives within conventions, she sees beyond their limits. Thus she alone supports Scarlett through every contingency, however painful and difficult, including death, murder, and scandal. Against a background of conventional expectations for female behavior, Mitchell has set two women, seemingly complete opposites linked by courage, endurance, and pragmatism, into a bond of loyalty and support. The enduring and unexpected friendship between Scarlett and Melanie subverts the patriarchal expectation that women will compete with other women for men, who are perceived as prizes. Scarlett resists Melanie's friendship at first because she was taught that women were weak and inadequate people with whom to make alliances. Soon, however, Scarlett perceives Melanie as armed with a sword so that she can act as Scarlett's loyal and passionate protector.

On the other hand, Mitchell critiques male romance roles and the sentimental longing for the old Southern plantation days by creating Ashley Wilkes, whose character, even in the beginning of the novel, seems limp and washed out. Ashley is brave enough as a soldier, but he has no real place either in the practical farm world to which he returns or in the world of commercialism that follows the war. Rhett's sense of dangerous mystery as a stock figure of melodrama is exposed by Scarlett's movement from being the central romantic heroine to being a person in a state of development. An understanding, compassionate adult cannot also be a childlike pet, to be protected and spoiled as Rhett has spoiled Bonnie. Rhett would prefer to spoil Scarlett rather than to accept her as an adult.

Mitchell warns that when independence is forced on women, they cannot readily be returned to a passive dependence, which she illustrates through both Scarlett and Melanie, as well as through Scarlett's mother, the figure of responsibility at Tara. The one-dimensional Rhett Butler ends his opportunistic adventurings by desiring a return to his genteel Charleston origins. In the end, Rhett gives up his role of romantic pirate to take on Ashley's role of perfect knight, while Ashley becomes only a burden inherited from Melanie by Scarlett.

Context

Margaret Mitchell worked steadily on *Gone with the Wind* for four years, from 1926 to 1929, but it was not published until 1936, receiving a Pulitzer Prize in 1937. It is an antiwar novel that depicts the devastation of war not only as it affects an entire region but also as it specifically affects the land and women's lives, forcing them into independence, poverty, and/or loneliness.

Like other Southern women writers, Mitchell identifies the Southern lady either with ideal passivity, selflessness, and exquisite moral virtue or with feminine beauty and flirtatiousness, at the same time that her main female character struggles against these limitations to become a person. Issues of women's work, independence, and need for wholeness, rather than role-playing, are typical issues faced by these writers, including Mitchell.

Mitchell raises two key feminist issues, but she leaves them for her readers to resolve. One occurs when the drunken Rhett carries Scarlett up the stairs to their bedroom. Many feminist critics condemn this as a rape scene which, therefore, may be used to romanticize rape, denying its pain and dehumanization in real life. The second issue revolves around the final scene in which Rhett rejects Scarlett's newly realized love for him and leaves her. Is Rhett Butler worthy of the person Scarlett is in the process of becoming? Can a strong male hero accept a strong female counterpart? These questions are made more problematic by the popular film version of *Gone with the Wind*, which came out in 1939. Although the film does a credible job of depicting Scarlett as a survivor in the period during and immediately after the Civil War, it does not allow her the growth that Mitchell has created for her in the novel.

Gone with the Wind also exists within a tradition of women's rural literature, which includes such novels as *So Big* (1924), by Edna Ferber; *Barren Ground* (1925), by Ellen Glasgow; and Willa Cather's *O Pioneers!* (1913) and *My Ántonia* (1918). These novels depict women as intelligent and capable farmers. In *Gone with the Wind*, Scarlett is primarily a farmer who must leave the farm in order to support it. Like Scarlett, these female farmers value the land that they successfully cultivate. It becomes more than a means to success, but a transcendent force that sustains them spiritually as well as economically.

A problem in *Gone with the Wind* that is unresolved by Mitchell is a racism inherent in her glorification of antebellum plantation life as an idyllic setting with happy slaves and bountiful land. Furthermore, her portrayals of Mammy, Prissy, and Big Sam all represent stereotypes developed to justify slavery and the plantation system as a benevolent institution. Unfortunately, Mitchell fails to provide any kind of serious critique of a plantation life that is based on slavery, although she readily undercuts many other aspects of Southern life, especially the limitations of women's lives.

Sources for Further Study

Edwards, Anne. *Road to Tara: The Life of Margaret Mitchell.* New Haven, Conn.: Ticknor & Fields, 1983. A biography of Mitchell which describes her as a mixture, like Scarlett, of Southern belle and emancipated woman, both conventional and rebellious.

Egenreither, Ann E. "Scarlett O'Hara: A Paradox in Pantalettes." In *Heroines of Popular Culture*, edited by Pat Browne. Bowling Green, Ohio: Bowling Green State University Popular Press, 1987. Places Scarlett O'Hara in the context of popular culture heroines while describing her resistance to such limits.

Harwell, Richard, ed. *"Gone with the Wind" as Book and Film.* Columbia: University of South Carolina Press, 1983. A series of essays from both scholars and the popular press that review the traditions of Southern and Civil War novels, Margaret Mitchell as person and writer, the novel and its characters, and *Gone with the Wind* as a film event.

Jones, Anne Goodwyn. *Tomorrow Is Another Day: The Woman Writer in the South.* Baton Rouge: Louisiana State University Press, 1981. Jones describes the influences from Mitchell's life that forged her sometimes contradictory positions regarding the roles of the traditional Southern man, the ideal Southern woman, the courageous woman, and the rebel.

Pyron, Darden Asbury, ed. *Recasting "Gone with the*

Wind" in American Culture. Miami: University Presses of Florida, 1983. A collection of essays by various authors that explore *Gone with the Wind* from a critical perspective, as art, and in terms of its historical location.

Taylor, Helen. *Scarlett's Women: "Gone with the Wind" and its Female Fans*. New Brunswick, N.J.: Rutgers University Press, 1989. A collection of women readers' responses to survey questions about the novel and Scarlett, reflecting the basis for their constant popularity. Includes analyses of theme, character, biography, politics, and film and literary history.

Janet M. LaBrie

THE GROUP

Author: Mary McCarthy (1912-1989)
Type of work: Novel
Type of plot: Social criticism
Time of plot: 1933-1940
Locale: New York City
First published: 1963

Principal characters:

Catherine Leiland Strong Petersen (Kay), the leading figure in a group of young women who graduate from Vassar College in 1933

Polly Andrews Ridgeley, the only member of Kay's group who required scholarship money

Elizabeth MacAusland (Libby), a successful literary agent

Helena Davison, a wealthy young woman

Dottie Renfrew Latham, a social worker in a Boston settlement house

Elinor Eastlake (Lakey), an art historian

Mary Prothero Beauchamp (Pokey), the wealthiest member of the group, who had to be coached in order to pass her exams

Priss Hartshorn Crockett, an economics major who takes a job with the National Recovery Administration

Norine Schmittlapp Blake Rogers, a classmate of the group who has an affair with Kay's husband

Harald Petersen, a playwright and director who marries and is later divorced by Kay

Gus LeRoy, an editor who has an affair with Polly

Putnam Blake, a politically active young man who is the first of Norine's two husbands

Mrs. Davison, Helena's self-educated and widely read mother

Mr. Andrews, Polly's eccentric father, who comes to live with her

Form and Content

The Group traces the lives of nine members of Vassar College's class of 1933 (eight of whom compose "the group"), from Kay's marriage shortly after their graduation until the day of her funeral. In a loosely woven narrative, Mary McCarthy documents the personal growth of each character and explores the ways in which their education had an effect upon their lives. Though McCarthy described *The Group* as illustrating the failure of America's "faith in progress," the novel should not be dismissed as mere satire. Far more than McCarthy's other works of fiction, *The Group* displays sympathy for its central characters at the same time that it dissects their values. It is thus as a chronicle of the beliefs shared by a class of educated and privileged young women that *The Group* makes its greatest contribution.

The novel is arranged chronologically in fifteen chapters, each of which is centered upon an incident in the life of one of the group's members. For this reason, the group itself rather than any individual serves as the novel's protagonist. Kay and Harald's wedding, for example, provides the author with an opportunity to demonstrate the personalities of all of her central characters. Kay herself appears adventurous and daring by inviting no parents to her wedding. Pokey displays her superficiality by speaking disdainfully of Harald's shoes. Lakey's angry reply to Pokey's remark reveals the contempt that she has even for other members of the group. Dottie, the most devout and traditional of the central characters, becomes uneasy at the unconventional nature of the ceremony.

Only in the first and last chapters of the novel do most members of the group appear together. In the intervening chapters, McCarthy shifts from character to character, focusing upon representative events in their lives. Two days after Kay's wedding, Dottie loses her virginity to Dick Brown, a young painter whom she had met at Kay's reception. Although she had been extremely conservative while in college, Dottie had been intrigued by the prospect of an illicit affair and agreed to Dick's suggestion that she be fitted for a diaphragm. One night, when Dick fails to meet her for a rendezvous, Dottie leaves the diaphragm under a park bench and returns to Boston.

The Group also explores the sexual awakening of its other major characters. Norine begins her affair with Harald when Putnam, her first husband, proves to be impotent. Libby fends off the advances of Nils Aslund, a Norwegian baron who manages a ski run. Polly has a lengthy affair with Gus LeRoy, Libby's former boss. Lakey returns from Europe with a lesbian lover. The explicit sexuality of *The Group* helped to make it the most widely read of all McCarthy's works, but it also suggests that *The Group* is largely a coming-of-age novel exploring the maturation of its group protagonist. The loss of virginity experienced by each of the book's central characters parallels the loss of innocence that the group itself faces after leaving Vassar and confronting the disappointments of the real world.

When the group reconvenes seven years later for Kay's funeral, each of them still possesses the traits delineated in the opening chapter. Yet each of them has also matured by having dealt in some way with a loss. Polly recovers from her affair with Gus and marries a young psychiatrist. Lakey has grown to accept her sexual identity. Norine emerges from an unsatisfying first marriage to a happy second relationship. Only Kay, the leader of the group and the first to marry, proves to be destroyed by the world that she encountered after college. McCarthy intentionally leaves unanswered the question of whether Kay's death was an accident or resulted from suicide.

Analysis

The Group documents, in a nearly journalistic fashion, the development of its nine central characters during their first years after college. The members of the group indulge in considerable experimentation, both political and sexual, throughout this entire period. Reacting against the conservative values of their parents, one character after another becomes attracted to left-wing causes. Several individuals are fascinated with Joseph Stalin's trials of other Bolshevik leaders from 1936 to 1938. Sympathies with trade unionists, socialists, Trotskyites, and Stalinists emerge, only to be set aside later for more conventional values. Characters thus appear to be trying on political causes like garments, attempting to find one that fits the person each has become.

Sexual experimentation is another means by which members of the group seek to find their identities. A number of the novel's major characters have affairs. Others go through successive marriages looking for the right partner. In the end, most of the characters' sexual roles are as ephemeral as their political affiliations. They experiment sexually because this gives them one more opportunity to rebel against the values of their parents and to discover something of their own identities.

The amount of detail that McCarthy has devoted to the group's political and sexual adventures serves two purposes. First, it reinforces the novel's role as a social commentary. Dottie's loss of virginity and her visit to an early birth control clinic are described in elaborate detail. In a similar way, the views of the Stalinists and the Trotskyites are explored at some length. This amount of detail helps the reader to enter into the minds of McCarthy's characters and to share the experiences of their social class. Second, the author's analytical style parallels the approach to life that her characters absorbed during their college education at Vassar. Members of the group have learned to distance their emotions from a situation, to gather relevant details, and to make judgments based upon the best information available. McCarthy's journalistic style thus applies this same approach to a study of her central characters.

Of special concern to the author are the ways in which this type of education either prepared or failed to prepare the group for the world awaiting it after graduation. Throughout the novel, there are repeated references to individual teachers and courses taken by the group at Vassar. Two of these instructors, "old Miss Washburn" and Hallie Flanagan, stand in opposition to each other. Miss Washburn, who taught a course in animal behavior, represents the rational side of the group's education. She is a teacher who had "left her brain to Science in her will," and she is frequently cited as a model of the modern analytical approach. Miss Flanagan, an influential instructor of dramatic production, represents the emotional aspect of the students' experience at Vassar. She fostered their ability to deal with their own emotions and cultivated their aesthetic sense. Appropriately, it is Kay, who has difficulty reconciling these two sides of her character, who was influenced most strongly by both of these teachers. Her fatal fall (or jump) occurs, appropriately, from the twentieth floor of the Vassar Club, suggesting the destructive role that her education has played in her life.

Context

As a social commentary, *The Group* documents in elaborate detail the minutiae that filled many women's lives during the years between the two world wars. Enthusiastic plans for social work, agricultural school, and politics gradually give way to discussions of babies, toilet training, birth control, and dress patterns. To a certain extent, this is part of the characters' process of growing up. The group learns to reconcile its ambitions and cultural interests with the more mundane aspects of domestic life. Nevertheless, the novel also suggests that the restrictions of the traditional roles assigned to women prove to be more daunting than the characters initially believed. By the end of the novel, Kay is dead, Lakey has abandoned all pretense at conformity, and the other characters have settled for being far more similar to their parents than they once had wished.

McCarthy's depictions of male characters are generally unflattering. Harald is the one individual in the entire novel who shows no sign of maturity. Probably the most unappealing of all McCarthy's characters, his last appearance in the novel occurs as he tries to find a ride to New York City, away from the cemetery where Kay is about to be buried. Gus LeRoy, Libby's former boss and Polly's lover, "was ordinary. That was what was the matter with him." Mr. Andrews, one of the most engaging male characters in the work, is eccentric and probably insane. His continued spending after the family is impoverished by the stockmarket crash of 1929 nearly ruins Polly financially.

Therefore, members of the group face the double burden of limited opportunities and of men who make their lives all but unbearable. For this reason, nearly all the novel's central characters fail in some way. Kay has a nervous breakdown and may well have taken her own life. Dottie abandons her career as a social worker and her dreams of romance, settling for bourgeois respectability in Arizona. Priss becomes a reluctant subject in the behaviorist experiments adopted by her husband. Only Lakey, who turns her back on men entirely, fulfills her dream of European travel and study of art history. The portrait that McCarthy paints is thus a highly pessimistic one.

The Group has always enjoyed more success with the public than with its critics. Some readers have been attracted to the novel for its detailed descriptions of sexual seduction. Others have seen parallels between their own lives and the incidents described in the novel. The work's failure to characterize each of its nine central figures with equal clarity and its inability to suggest solutions to the problems that it addresses, however, have limited its impact upon women's literature.

Sources for Further Study

Auchincloss, Louis. "Mary McCarthy." In *Pioneers and Caretakers*. Minneapolis: University of Minnesota Press, 1965. Auchincloss criticizes *The Group* as an entertaining but disappointing book. He does not regard the central characters as sufficiently interesting or distinct from any other group of young adults.

Grumbach, Doris. *The Company She Kept*. New York: Coward-McCann, 1967. A biography of Mary McCarthy that contains some insightful literary analysis. Grumbach sees *The Group* as a "profoundly feminine" novel but argues that none of the characters matures through her experiences.

McKenzie, Barbara. *Mary McCarthy*. New York: Twayne, 1967. In this biographical and literary analysis, McKenzie interprets *The Group* as a social satire. Kay is presented as the one character who develops sufficiently to face her own failure.

Mailer, Norman. "The Case Against McCarthy." In *Cannibals and Christians*. New York: Dial Press, 1966. Mailer criticizes McCarthy for "not reaching far enough" in *The Group*. He sees the novel's main characters as largely identical and as anachronistic in their espousal of 1950's values during the 1930's.

Stock, Irvin. *Mary McCarthy*. Minneapolis: University of Minnesota Press, 1968. A concise and readable discussion of McCarthy's fiction. Stock considers *The Group* "not particularly successful" as a novel, but he refutes the view that its nine central characters are indistinguishable.

Jeffrey L. Buller

THE HANDMAID'S TALE

Author: Margaret Atwood (1939-   )
Type of work: Novel
Type of plot: Fable
Time of plot: The future
Locale: Cambridge, Massachusetts
First published: 1985

Principal characters:

Offred, following the revolution that established the Republic of Gilead, a Handmaid, (surrogate mother) in the home of the Commander

The Commander (Fred), a member of the administrative elite of Gilead and Offred's master

Moira, a friend of Offred, who refuses to become a Handmaid but instead is forced to work in a brothel

Serena Joy, the Commander's wife, a former television evangelist

Nick, the Commander's chauffeur and Offred's paid lover

Ofglen, a Handmaid who is a member of the underground

Form and Content

Margaret Atwood's *The Handmaid's Tale* takes place in the United States at the turn of the twenty-first century. A revolution sponsored by fundamentalist leaders has produced a monolithic theocracy called the Republic of Gilead. Although inspired by divine power, the administrators of Gilead rely on human control to implement their religion-based policies. Overt military control is conducted through a series of agents—such as Commanders, Eyes, and Guardians—who use electronic devices, blockades, and spies to maintain surveillance over the population. Those who are not members of the Gilead forces become servants, a role reserved almost exclusively for women.

Women, who the revolution was supposedly fought in part to protect, are relegated to serving in eight narrowly defined categories easily identified by the color of their prescribed wardrobe. The blue-clad wives of the Commanders are the most visible of all the women in Gilead. They are to preside over the Commanders' homes, create beautiful gardens, and attend social functions, which include public hangings and ritual beatings of men who break the Gilead rules. The green-clad Marthas are responsible for cooking and keeping the house clean. Econowives, women married to midlevel members of the Gilead administration, wear multicolored uniforms to designate their mixed functions as housewife, cook, maid, and mother. A small number of women wear black, widows whose life is ill-defined in Gilead; as a result, they are rarely seen. Two other groups of women are not seen in Gilead: the gray-clad Unwomen, those who refused to cooperate with the system and have been sent to work in the Colonies (where environmental pollution will soon kill them), and the women who work in the underground brothel, where the Commanders go for pleasures that are officially restricted by the republic. The remaining two categories of women rival the wives in importance. The Aunts, wearing Nazi-brown dresses, train the other group to become surrogate mothers. Because of the environmental pollution, the loss of life during the revolutionary fighting, and the age of some of the wives, sterility has become Gilead's most visible problem. The solution to this problem is the procurement of fertile women who will bear children for the Commanders, the red-clad Handmaids.

The Handmaid is limited to offering her body as a vessel for procreation during bizarre bedroom encounters with the Commander and his wife. Lying fully clothed in her red habit between the open thighs of the wife, the Handmaid receives the Commander, who is also clothed except for an open zipper. No communication between the Commander and the Handmaid is allowed. The sexual encounter becomes both asexual and pornographic at the same time.

The desire for a child consumes Serena Joy, the wife of one Commander, to such an extent that she accepts the private nighttime meetings of her husband and the Handmaid Offred in the hope that this might lead to a pregnancy. These private encounters allow both the Commander and Offred to assume more human qualities than either is allowed by the republic. Both at first relish the intellectual cat-and-mouse game that develops between them. Offred continues the game because the Commander provides items that she otherwise would never have, such as magazines, alcohol, and special soaps. The Commander pursues the game in the hope of creating a sexual intimacy that is not permitted during the procreation ritual. The game does not produce the desired result, however, for either the Commander or Serena Joy: Offred does not become pregnant. Desperate to produce a child for her house and bask in the rewards of Gilead's society, Serena Joy secretly employs the Commander's chauffeur, Nick, to have sex with Offred. At first hesitant, Nick and Offred discover a sexuality with each other that the republic forbids. Thus, even when the private meetings are ended by Serena Joy, Offred continues to sneak to Nick's room when possible. At about the same time, the Commander takes Offred for a nighttime excursion to an underground brothel. Once there, Offred is reunited with her college friend Moira, a rebel. Although glad to see her, Offred is dismayed that Moira is a prostitute. Moira explains that the decision was either to die in the poisonous Colonies or to remain alive and endure—to perhaps escape, as she has done twice before.

Moira's courage, Offred's revulsion to the brothel, and her exploitation by another woman, Serena Joy, lead to Offred's decision to attempt escape. Befriended by another Handmaid, Ofglen, who has contacts with the underground, and assisted by Nick, Offred escapes and attempts to reach Canada. During her trip north, she discovers a tape recorder and tells the Handmaid's tale.

Analysis

The Handmaid's Tale is a political fable whose purpose is to act as a cautionary tale for women. Dedicated to Perry Miller, the foremost authority on the Puritans and their influence in American history, and to Mary Webster, an ancestor of the Atwood family hanged as a witch in Connecticut, the catalyst for Atwood's concern was the self-proclaimed triumph of the religious fundamentalists in elections held in the early 1980's. Like the Puritans of Colonial America, who hoped to create the model city upon the hill, the religious right hoped to create a moral, utopian society where their interpretation of the Bible prescribed the proper behavior and societal roles for men and women. Atwood uses science fiction to extend the logical outcome of such a society if the fundamentalists held power; a woman must conform or be declared a threat, a witch.

The concept of the Handmaid is based upon the biblical story of Rachel and Jacob: "Behold my maid Bilhah, go into her; and she shall bear upon my knees, that I may also have children by her" (Genesis 30: 1-3). Thus the Handmaid's sole function in the Republic of Gilead is as a procreation device for the Commander and his sterile wife. The individual autonomy of the Handmaid is stripped away, beginning with her name. The Handmaids are provided new names that reflect their subservient status, patronymics: names composed of the possessive preposition and the Commander's first name, such as Ofglen, Ofwarren, or the central character in the novel, Offred.

Clothed in long red gowns, their faces hidden from view by veils and wimples, the Handmaids resemble a religious sect who have just emerged from a convent. Their daily rituals resemble the rules of a strict medieval order. Cloistered in a bedroom within the Commander's house, the Handmaid is not permitted any reading or writing materials, nor are objects that might assist suicide permitted. To suppress her identity further, not even a mirror is allowed in the room. Thus like a cloistered nun whose sole daily function is reflection and preparation for her relationship with God, the Handmaid is limited to one function, procreation, in order to ensure the future of the republic.

Despite the religious trappings of the Republic of Gilead, the purpose of the new order is not to protect women but to suppress them. Thus, Atwood's depiction of Serena Joy is a warning to the women supporters of the religious right that they must be careful what they wish for, for they might one day get it. Serena Joy, once a woman of some independence and social importance as a television evangelist, has been reduced to being an extension of someone else. She is the Commander's wife, and her world is his house and her roles as wife and mother. Unable to perform the latter role, Serena Joy must bear the presence of the Handmaid and the ugliness of sex between her husband and this stranger who is a constant reminder that she is now wife in name only.

Atwood's tale also acts as a cautionary note for men who might support the phallocentric Republic of Gilead. Just as women are reduced to limited role-playing, so too are the men. The full range of human sexuality becomes limited to the asexual procreation process—no joy, only duty. The pressure on men to be all things—father, husband, leader, and provider—creates an anxiety between Serena Joy and the Commander that makes their marriage a legal relationship but not a human one. The only interesting relationship that exists for the Commander is the one he establishes with Offred. The relationship is not equal, however, and thus not fulfilling for either participant. Each uses the other: The Commander hopes for an intimate sexual relationship, while Offred receives material items otherwise denied her. The unequal relationship is doomed when Offred, a slave, is reminded of her identity as the Commander's property when she is put on display at the underground brothel.

One woman in the novel remains admirable from the opening pages. Offred's old college friend, Moira, fights against the republic during the revolution, refuses to cooperate with the republic after its triumph, and even in captivity retains a personal identity by reversing the goal of her capturers and using her sex as a means to empower herself. Regardless of her situation, she maintains a level of integrity and becomes a catalyst for Offred's decision to chance escape.

The narrative force of the novel is the transformation of Offred from victim to hero, from passive to active. Throughout the novel, Offred reminds the reader that she is recording her Handmaid's tale in order to warn others that they must always be attentive and must realize that a time will come when they must act. As she declares in her tape recorder, "I intend to last."

Context

When it was first published, *The Handmaid's Tale* was immediately compared to the appearance almost forty years before of George Orwell's *Nineteen Eighty-Four* (1949). Both novels suggest that to create a world of perfect order and stability would require that the imperfections of human beings be brought under control. The future societies of both novels ban writing, the written word being a weapon feared by those in charge. Both worlds restrict relationships, reducing them to sterile, superficial role-playing. Violence as a method of control and citizen participation in that violence appear in both novels. Yet Winston Smith, the main character in *Nineteen Eighty-Four*, is a man and has at least a marginal sense of independence and identity. Offred in *The Handmaid's Tale* is a woman who has no independence and has been stripped of all identity.

Because of this difference, Atwood's novel is closer in relationship to the words spoken by the cofounder of the modern women's movement, Elizabeth Cady Stanton. At the end of the nineteenth century, Stanton was asked to speak on behalf of women's rights in the nation's capital. Her speech, quickly reprinted and published in newspapers throughout the United States, was about the "solitude of self." An appraisal of the forty years that had just passed and a speculation on the future, Stanton's address was a sober reminder that regardless of the success of the movement, women must realize that they are individuals first and that each must encounter the world alone. She implied that no utopia was imminent—nor should it be, because women are individuals and a collective success approved by all was neither possible nor, in the long run, desirable. The solitude of self was the acknowledgment of personal responsibility and the courage to endure—the qualities possessed by Moira and admired by Offred, and the reason that Atwood's character records *The Handmaid's Tale*.

Sources for Further Study

Grace, Sherrill E., and Lorraine Weir, eds. *Margaret Atwood: Language, Text, and System*. Vancouver: University of British Columbia Press, 1983. Includes nine essays examining Atwood's literary "system" and her development of style and subject matter up to the publication of *The Handmaid's Tale*.

Kostash, Myrna, et al. *Her Own Woman: Profiles of Ten Canadian Women*. Toronto: Macmillan of Canada, 1975. Contains a biographical essay by Valerie Miner, "Atwood in Metamorphosis: An Authentic Canadian Fairy Tale," that examines the evolution and maturation of Atwood's writing.

McCombs, Judith, ed. *Critical Essays on Margaret Atwood*. Boston: G. K. Hall, 1988. The best edition of criticism on Atwood. Contains thirty-two essays, arranged in the chronological order of her publications. The monograph contains an excellent analysis of *The Handmaid's Tale*.

Rigney, Barbara Hill. *Margaret Atwood*. Totowa, N.J.: Barnes & Noble Books, 1987. An analysis of Atwood as poet, novelist, and political commentator, all from a feminist perspective. Includes a useful bibliography.

Rosenberg, Jerome H. *Margaret Atwood*. Boston: Twayne, 1984. A concise literary biography of the Canadian novelist and poet that provides a useful introduction to her works.

David O'Donald Cullen

HEAT AND DUST

Author: Ruth Prawer Jhabvala (1927-)
Type of work: Novel
Type of plot: Romance
Time of plot: The 1920's and the 1970's
Locale: Satipur, India
First published: 1975

Principal characters:

Olivia Rivers, a beautiful, sensitive young English woman in 1920's India

Douglas Rivers, Olivia's husband, the Assistant Collector of Satipur

The Nawab, the ruler of the princely state of Khatm, who has an affair with Olivia

Harry, the Nawab's English house-guest

The narrator, a young Englishwoman in the 1970's who is drawn to India by her fascination with Olivia's letters

Inder Lal, the narrator's landlord, a simple Indian clerk who is seduced by her

Chid, a confused English boy searching for salvation among the Hindu swamis

Form and Content

Heat and Dust is the story of two English women who traveled to India, about fifty years apart in time, and recorded their experiences there in letters and journals. The stylistic arrangement of two parallel stories is creatively handled by means of excerpts from the narrator's journal interspersed with the details that she provides from the letters of the now-dead Olivia that she has in her possession. The reader needs to be alert to the constant shifts between the two tales as they trace fairly similar developments in the lives of the two women. The major historical difference that they encounter is that while Olivia came to India during a time when it was still a part of the British Empire, the narrator finds herself in a free country; the passage of time also means that there has been some progress in the way in which women are able to conduct their lives. The novel is focused on the lives of the two women and the decisions that they make fifty years apart: Though there are ironic similarities in the way in which their lives progress in India, their attitudes and actions are completely different in terms of personality. Through these differences, the author is able to convey the changes that have come about in women's lives through the years.

Olivia Rivers is bored and unhappy as the wife of a British colonial administrator in Satipur, India, and though she loves and adores her handsome husband, Douglas, she is moody and irritable until she meets the Nawab, a minor Indian prince of a neighboring state, and his English house-guest, Harry. The Nawab and Harry begin to provide the regular company and entertainment that Olivia craves, and though her husband and his friends disapprove of her friendship with a man of whom they are suspicious, she continues to see the Nawab, often without Douglas' knowledge. Aware that she is stepping in too deep, Olivia nevertheless seems powerless to stop her growing fascination with the handsome and unpredictable Nawab, until their closeness is sexually consummated. Meanwhile, Olivia and Douglas had been hoping to start a family, and when she finds herself pregnant, each man believes that he is the father (Douglas is unaware of her intimate relationship with the Nawab). Olivia, particularly upset when she learns from Harry that the Nawab is jubilant at the prospect of humiliating the British crowd when she gives birth to his child, arranges for an abortion; in the scandal that follows, she chooses to leave Douglas and go to the Nawab, who sets her up in her own house in the hills. She spends the rest of her days quietly, never leaving India, even after the death of the Nawab. Her only legacy is her letters, left with her sister Marcia.

These letters come into the hands of the narrator, who is Douglas' grandchild by his second marriage. She is inspired to trace Olivia's story in India more than half a century after it began in Satipur. The plain and unmarried narrator takes up residence in a house owned by Inder Lal, a simple Indian clerk with a life full of petty problems, and she keeps a journal of her life as she visits the buildings and places described in Olivia's letters and attempts to piece together the story of her life. Like Olivia, she ends up with two men in her life, the British boy Chid and her Indian landlord; unlike Olivia, however, she is married to neither and, in the progressive times in which she lives, is able to carry on her liaisons without scandal and without making any of them permanent. When she discovers herself to be pregnant, she decides to keep the child without informing the father, Inder Lal, and moves into the mountains where Olivia lived out her life. There she awaits the new phase in her own story.

Analysis

Ruth Prawer Jhabvala's central intention is to provide a voice for women, especially in the story of Olivia, which is chronologically earlier in time. A character such as Olivia is historically accurate, but very little is known about the thoughts of such people because they were never given a hearing. She is representative of the many English women who accompanied their husbands to India during the rule of the British Empire there and spent years in the country without ever recording or letting others know of their experiences or impressions; their lives were controlled by their husbands and the rest of the British community in India.

In fact, in *Heat and Dust*, Jhabvala is seen as rewriting the stories of such women in many colonial novels of the early twentieth century in which their opinions were not adequately voiced, the most well known of them being the English writer E. M. Forster's *A Passage to India* (1924). Even though Olivia's story, too, is regarded as a scandal by her own generation and is hushed up, the reappearance of her detailed letters to her sister makes it possible for the narrator to track down her life in India two generations later and to offer the reader her side of the tale. By cleverly juxtaposing her own experiences in India with those of Olivia, the narrator is also able to provide a sense of how women's lives changed all over the world in the course of the twentieth century.

Jhabvala, in both Olivia's and the narrator's stories, presents a range of strong women characters, against whom the men appear weak and ineffectual. Olivia must deal with the Begum, the Nawab's mother, who is a powerful matriarch in the palace. The narrator is befriended by Inder Lal's mother, who runs his household, as well as by Maji, an old woman of the town who is said to have supernatural powers. In contrast, all the men—Douglas, the Nawab, Harry, Inder Lal, and Chid—despite being the main political and social players, seem to lack strength, an indication perhaps that had women always been accorded the positions they deserved, all stories in history would have been different.

While the concept of a novel in the form of letters or journals is not original, Jhabvala's chosen form, excerpts from the narrator's journal interspersed with recollections from Olivia's letters, provides a new and interesting way of reading about two parallel lives lived many decades apart in the same Indian town.

Context

In the late twentieth century, the suppression of the woman's voice in history was given much attention. Jhabvala's *Heat and Dust* confronts the issue directly by telling the story of a woman who lived an unusually interesting existence in the early part of the century but was considered an embarrassment to her society because she did not live by the norms; by providing a voice for her through the interest of another woman, two generations later, Jhabvala seems to indicate not only that times have improved for women but also that only women can be relied upon to provide a fair hearing for other women; it is the duty of later generations of women to unearth the hidden lives of their forgotten female ancestors.

Besides providing a social commentary by two women living in times that are chronologically distant, *Heat and Dust*, one of Jhabvala's few historically based novels, offers a candid view of the life of a British colonial woman in India. It is a view that is rarely available in historical records or literary expositions of the time, despite the fact that there are hints in them of incidents and activities that make Olivia's fictional story believable.

Winner of the 1975 Booker Prize for fiction, *Heat and Dust* can be read in counterpoint to prior colonial novels based in India in which the woman is never given a strong voice. At the same time, it is a modern update on Olivia's story because the narrator's life and activities in India provide a glimpse of historical changes that have allowed women to make independent decisions about their own lives, without necessarily being criticized and ostracized by society.

Sources for Further Study

Crane, Ralph J., ed. *Passages to Ruth Prawer Jhabvala*. New Delhi: Sterling, 1991. Contains ten previously unpublished essays that cover her novels and her short stories and delineate useful connections with other writers, such as E. M. Forster and Saul Bellow. Crane's essay "A Forsterian Connection: Ruth Prawer Jhabvala and *A Passage to India*" expounds on the important influence of the Forster novel on Jhabvala's work.

____________. *Ruth Prawer Jhabvala*. New York: Twayne, 1992. One of the most comprehensive and useful critical appraisals of Jhabvala. Crane's analysis provides biographical details; readings of her work through the early, middle, and later Indian novels; analyses of the short stories and the American novels; and a commentary on the reception of her work by literary critics. Crane offers a time line of Jhabvala's life and work and a good bibliography for interested scholars.

Gooneratne, Yasmine. *Silence, Exile, and Cunning: The Fiction of Ruth Prawer Jhabvala*. New Delhi: Orient Longman, 1983. Building on work published in a number of earlier articles, Gooneratne has compiled an excellent, in-depth study of Jhabvala's fiction and her extensive work in writing for films.

Jha, Rekha. *The Novels of Kamala Markandaya and Ruth Jhabvala*. New Delhi: Prestige Books, 1990. Jha takes a thematic approach in considering the works of two major Indian women novelists in tandem; in her reading of Jhabvala's work, she concentrates on the novels up to *Heat and Dust*, which is the writer's last fully Indian work of fiction, and provides a useful analysis of her major themes.

Jhabvala, Ruth Prawer. "The Artistry of Ruth Prawer Jhabvala." Interview by Bernard Weintraub. *The New York Times Magazine*, September 11, 1983. Jhabvala speaks frankly about her early life and her career as a writer in this indispensable interview/profile.

Shahane, Vasant A. *Ruth Prawer Jhabvala*. New Delhi: Arnold-Heinemann, 1976. May be used as an introduction to Jhabvala's fiction up to *Heat and Dust*; a number of chapters have since been reprinted in journals and collections of essays.

Sucher Laurie. *The Fiction of Ruth Prawer Jhabvala: The Politics of Passion*. Basingstoke, England: Macmillan, 1989. Along with Ralph Crane's full-length study (above), an invaluable contribution to Jhabvala criticism that provides a feminist perspective to her work. Sucher discusses four of the novels (including *Heat and Dust*) and some related short stories in detail. She gives the reader a comprehensive overview of the passions of Jhabvala by tracing her quest for love and beauty in her fiction. Includes a selected bibliography.

Brinda Bose

THE HEIDI CHRONICLES

Author: Wendy Wasserstein (1950-   )
Type of work: Drama
Type of plot: Feminist
Time of plot: 1965-1989
Locale: Largely New York City, with several scenes set in Chicago; Manchester, New Hampshire; and Ann Arbor, Michigan
First produced: 1988, at Playwrights Horizons, New York City, New York
First published: 1989

Principal characters:

Heidi Holland, a professor of art history at Columbia University

Scoop Rosenbaum, Heidi's friend and sometime lover, who founds *Boomer* magazine

Susan Johnston, Heidi's high school friend, who becomes a legal clerk at the Supreme Court, a member of a women's health and legal collective, and an executive vice president for a television production company

Peter Patrone, a gay pediatrician who is one of Heidi's closest friends

Form and Content

The story of *The Heidi Chronicles* is told through a series of vignettes that extend from a high school dance in 1965 to Heidi's near future in 1989 (Wendy Wasserstein completed the play in 1988), when Heidi is a successful professor of art history at Columbia University. Throughout the play's thirteen scenes, the audience witnesses Heidi's development from an ordinary schoolgirl through her increasing dissatisfaction with her life before she finally develops greater acceptance of her career, her goals, and herself. The play also explores Heidi's evolving relationships with Susan, Peter, and Scoop, the three friends with whom she shares many of her most important moments.

While Scoop is always Heidi's friend, he is also occasionally her lover. She meets him in New Hampshire at an event supporting Eugene McCarthy's campaign for president. Heidi finds herself both attracted to and repulsed by Scoop's overwhelming confidence. His readiness to be judgmental exasperates Heidi, though she envies his self-assurance and the faith that he has in his own opinions. Unwilling to make a commitment to Heidi, Scoop ultimately marries Lisa, an illustrator of children's books who readily places Scoop's needs ahead of her own. By the end of the play, however, Scoop has grown as a human being. He sells his magazine, demonstrates concern for his children's future, and considers running for public office.

Peter functions in the play largely as an antithesis to Scoop. When he first meets Heidi in 1965, they form a close friendship through their youthful cynicism and the contempt that they display for conventions. Heidi comes to believe that, although she is strongly attracted to Scoop, Peter is the man with whom she has the most in common. On August 9, 1974, the date of Richard Nixon's resignation from the presidency, Peter reveals to Heidi that he is gay. From that time on, their friendship deepens as they share with each other the details of their romantic and personal relationships. On Christmas Eve of 1987, Heidi gives up her plans to accept a job at Carleton College, in Minnesota, so that she can remain near Peter, whom she has come to regard as a member of her own family.

Of all the characters in *The Heidi Chronicles*, Susan undergoes the most transformation. At the beginning of the play, she is a date-conscious teenager who cannot comprehend Heidi's indifference to the boys they meet at a dance. Throughout the 1970's and early 1980's, Susan experiments with several feminist causes. She is an active member of the Huron Street Ann Arbor Consciousness Raising Rap Group, considers founding a journal devoted to women's legal issues, and moves to Montana, where she joins a feminist health and legal collective. By the end of the play, however, Susan's shallowness has reemerged. She abandons her ideals and devotes her life to producing mindless situation comedies for television. With great insensitivity, Susan ignores Heidi's unhappiness and abruptly switches the topic to her plan for developing a comedy about women artists in Houston. One of the final references to Susan in the play occurs when Peter announces that she has contributed part of the profits from this television series to his hospital for children with AIDS: Susan's concern for others has degenerated to writing checks for popular causes.

Analysis

The Heidi Chronicles is Wendy Wasserstein's semi-autobiographical play about life from the mid-1960's through the late 1980's. Although few of the incidents in the play have exact parallels in Wasserstein's life, Heidi serves as the author's witness to the confusion, frustration, and sense of disappointment that many young women felt during this period. It is not coincidence that the name "Heidi Holland" reflects the alliteration of Wasserstein's own name. Moreover, she also shares the name of the title character in the children's novel *Heidis Lehr und Wanderjahre* (1880; *Heidi*, 1884) by Johanna Spyri, about an energetic young girl who lives in the Swiss Alps. This character displays a mixture of youthful enthusiasm and maturity. While growing up, she helps the other characters deal with the problems that they encounter in their own lives. So, to a large extent, does the character of Heidi in Wasserstein's play.

This connection between Wasserstein's Heidi and the title character of Spyri's novel is reinforced during a climactic scene in the play when Peter wonders, "Did you know that the first section [of *Heidi*] is Heidi's year of travel and learning, and the second is where Heidi uses what she knows? How will you use what you know, Heidi?" Built upon this same structure, the first act of *The Heidi Chronicles* takes place in numerous locations as it follows Heidi's period of travel and learning. The second act, set solely in New York City, illustrates Heidi beginning to use what she knows and gradually coming to terms with herself and her own identity.

One of the most important lessons that Heidi must learn in *The Heidi Chronicles* is how to balance her career with her need to serve others and find meaning in her own life. This, in fact, is the goal that all the characters in the play are trying to attain. Peter becomes a successful pediatrician who develops a special ward for children with HIV infections. Scoop ultimately realizes the importance both of his children's future and of the political dreams he once had as a young man. Heidi finds a way of reconciling her need to love others with her desire to become a respected author and professor at Columbia University. In the final scene of the play, it is revealed that Peter has helped Heidi adopt a young daughter. Wasserstein indicates that this daughter, Judy, represents Heidi's hope for the future.

Other characters in the play fail to achieve Heidi's degree of balance. Susan, for example, tends to be motivated by whatever happens to be fashionable at the moment. During the mid-1960's, she is almost the stereotype of the teenaged baby-boomer. Her interests do not extend beyond dating, boys, and being popular. During the 1970's, Susan seems to have developed substantially and even appears to be more committed to feminist causes than Heidi herself, but this change of character is only a phase. During the economically aggressive 1980's, Susan forsakes both her feminist ideals and her friends, settling for financial success in the television industry. The picture of Susan that emerges is of a shallow individual who reflects the ideas of others rather than developing her own.

In a similar fashion, Jill, one of the members of the Huron Street Ann Arbor Consciousness Raising Rap Group, also fails to achieve the balance sought by the central characters. Though she speaks of her unhappiness in allowing everyone else to "lean on perfect Jill" while forgetting to take care of herself, Jill continues to demonstrate this fault. She nurtures the members of the discussion group as she had once nurtured her husband and children, always putting the needs of others ahead of her own. Lisa, too, prefers to serve Scoop and advance his career rather than satisfying her own needs. Her frustration with, and at times blindness to, Scoop's infidelity should prompt her either to leave home or to confront him with the situation. Lisa's habitual role of subservience to Scoop, however, prevents her from giving serious consideration to either of these options.

Of all the play's female characters, Heidi achieves the greatest balance between satisfying her own needs and meeting those of others. Nevertheless, Heidi still sees the final liberation of women as something that can be achieved only in the future. In 1986, she speaks to students of the girls' high school that she herself had attended and complains of feeling "stranded" as a woman. She had thought that "we were all in this together," and she is disappointed when other women fail to act this way. Even in the final scene of the play, she hopes that her daughter will "never think she's worthless unless [some man] lets her have it all. And maybe, just maybe, things will be a little better." For the moment, however, that hope has not yet been fulfilled.

Context

The Heidi Chronicles examines the frustration and disappointment that many women felt as they examined their opportunities and relationships throughout the 1970's and 1980's. The play explores these problems, however, without developing a tone of rancor toward men. Even Scoop, the one character whose cockiness and self-interest make him almost a villain for most of the play, is allowed to grow as a human being by the end of the drama. Fran, the character who is most bitter toward men and who blames them for most of the problems in the world, is a comic figure. Wasserstein's point is that women should regard men as sources of neither their self-worth nor their problems. If women hope to achieve balance in their lives, they must take charge of their own lives, realize that they are "all in this together," and create a future that will be more satisfying both for their daughters and themselves.

The importance of *The Heidi Chronicles* is that it expresses these ideas in a form that is palatable to a large popular audience. Rather than speaking of women's issues only to women, Wasserstein creates a work that entertains audiences of both genders. By including references to popular music, current events, and fashions that many viewers will remember from their own youth, Wasserstein presents characters with whom it is easy to identify. Because of its widespread appeal, *The Heidi Chronicles* won not only the 1989 Susan Smith Black Prize for the best play by a woman playwright but also the Pulitzer Prize for drama, the New York Drama Critics Award, and a Tony Award for the best play of 1989. Its success transcended boundaries of gender and allowed men and women alike to reflect upon the shared experiences of their young adulthood.

Perhaps for this reason, feminist reactions toward *The Heidi Chronicles* tended to be largely negative. Many critics did not regard Wasserstein as going far enough in explaining Heidi's unhappiness. A number of these authors also thought that the play dealt far too much with Heidi's romantic relationships and not enough with her work or her friendships with other women. The result, several critics have noted, is that Heidi gives lip service to feminist values but still appears to be dominated by the male characters in the play.

Sources for Further Study

Austin, Gayle. Review of *The Heidi Chronicles*. *Theatre Journal* 42 (1990): 107-108. Austin regards the play as simplistic and insufficiently feminist. She notes that Heidi is always depicted as deriving her happiness from the traditional roles of mother or lover and rarely from her work.

Hornsby, Richard. "Interracial Casting." *Hudson Review* 42 (1989): 464-465. In a scathing analysis of *The Heidi Chronicles*, Hornsby views the play's plot as aimless, its ideas as trite, and its characters as stereotypes. The critic attributes the play's popularity to "trendiness" and the fact that its author is a woman.

Keyssar, Helene. "Drama and the Dialogic Imagination." *Modern Drama* 34 (1991): 88-106. Keyssar regards *The Heidi Chronicles* as a failure since it depicts its title character only in reaction to an essentially male-dominated world, not in revolution against it. The author views few of the central characters as changing over the course of time.

Rose, Phyllis J. "Dear Heidi: An Open Letter to Dr. Holland." *American Theatre* 6, no. 7 (October, 1989): 26-29, 114-116. Rose argues that all art is political: It either supports or attacks the existing power structure. For this reason, she criticizes *The Heidi Chronicles* as focusing upon Heidi's relationship with men rather than the role that art or work plays in her life.

Weales, Gerald. "American Theater Watch, 1988-1989." *Georgia Review* 43 (1989): 573-575. The author questions why single parenthood seems to "fill the vacuum" in Heidi's life. Weales notes that Wasserstein lampoons most of the idealistic impulses of the 1960's and 1970's.

Jeffrey L. Buller

HERLAND

Author: Charlotte Perkins Gilman (1860-1935)
Type of work: Novel
Type of plot: Social criticism
Time of plot: 1914-1915
Locale: Herland, a remote and uncharted country populated entirely by women
First published: 1915 (serial), 1979 (book)

Principal characters:

Vandyke (Van) Jennings, a sociologist who is observant, thoughtful, and introspective
Terry Nicholson, a wealthy explorer, pilot, and chauvinist
Jeff Margrave, a physician, botanist, and gentleman who worships women sentimentally and uncritically
Ellador, a young woman of Herland who marries Van and prepares to accompany him on a reconnaissance of the outside world
Alima, a strong young woman who marries Terry but rejects him when he tries to subdue her physically
Celis, an artistic young woman who falls in love with Jeff, marries him, and becomes pregnant
Somel, Van's tutor
Moadine, Terry's tutor
Zava, Jeff's tutor

Form and Content

Herland is the first half of a witty, sociologically astute critique of life in the United States. This story concentrates ostensibly on three men—Van, Jeff, and Terry—who discover a small, uncharted country called Herland which, by force of an unusual accident of nature, has been governed and populated for two thousand years solely by women. Biological reproduction occurs miraculously by parthenogenesis (that is, without insemination). Charlotte Perkins Gilman exploits this contrived situation in order to contrast and compare the social features of a hypothetical woman-centered society to the harsh realities and crushing inequalities of everyday life found pervasively in male-dominated societies. The cohesive theme and primary purpose of *Herland* is the exposition of Gilman's interconnected ideas about economics, education, clothing, prisons, parenting, male-female relationships, human evolution, and social organization generally. In *With Her in Ourland*, the neglected sequel to *Herland* published in 1916, Gilman presents the second half of the Herland chronicle, dissects the patriarchal and technological madness of World War I, and points constructively to an alternative future based on the pragmatic application of feminist values. *Herland* is not fundamentally a utopian novel; rather, it is a lucid, persuasive analysis of modern life as Gilman saw it.

Gilman frames *Herland* as a series of narrative reminiscences told by Van, one of three male explorers who trek to Herland. Van recounts his easy capture, humane imprisonment, and gentle indoctrination to the language, culture, and history of Herland's all-female society. Van's detailed memoir includes recitations of the lessons taught to him and his male colleagues by three middle-aged female tutors, his firsthand observations and personal reflections, and the results of his supplemental readings form Herland's libraries. The effect is sometimes didactic. Readers learn many gazetteer-type facts: For example, Herland is ten to twelve thousand square miles in area, has a population of three million women, and supports a highly efficient, scientifically balanced agricultural economy based on tree culture. Van describes Herland as a pacific, highly evolved, and rationally ordered society molded by women who, beyond all else, value the happiness and welfare of their parthenogenically created children.

Gilman enlivens *Herland*'s didactic formula by having Van report verbatim several of his conversations (and those of his male companions) with Ellador and other Herland women. These frequently amusing and sometimes painfully ironic dialogues provide a point of direct contact where the men of Ourland and the women of Herland discover one another, argue, fall in love, and—

in Terry's case—temporarily shatter the equality and powerful maternal calm of Herland. Unlike Terry, who never comprehends his chauvinism and its inherent destructiveness, Van finds his social consciousness raised through his discussions with Ellador. He is increasingly embarrassed by the massive shortcomings of the male-dominated culture that he represents.

The arrangement and style of *Herland* result in part from its publishing history. Gilman, unable to interest established publishing houses in her work, originally self-published the twelve brief chapters that comprise *Herland* as monthly installments in her feminist magazine, *The Forerunner*. The frequent restatement of central themes from chapter to chapter reflects Gilman's practical need to remind her readers of key elements in the story left unattended during the month-long intervals between issues of *The Forerunner*. *Herland* sparkles most brightly from within the pages of *The Forerunner* where, in many well-stocked libraries, *Herland* can still be read serially in context and in concert with Gilman's essays, poetry, and other major serialized fiction and nonfiction projects published during the brief but extraordinary life of *The Forerunner* from 1910 to 1916.

Analysis

By Gilman's own estimate, her novels failed as literary experiments. As a pedagogical device, however, *Herland* is an engaging, persuasive, and highly effective effort. The novel's light, patient, sympathetic voice is a worked example of the tolerant, noncoercive instructional mode employed by Herland's exemplary tutors: Somel, Moadine, and Zava. Sociological instruction through fiction is one of Gilman's literary strengths, and it is difficult to find a more straightforward instance of this genre than Gilman's own *First Class in Sociology* (1897-1898), a short novel of hypothetical classroom dialogue serialized in the *American Fabian*. Sociological instruction via fiction is a powerful educational tool used by several women sociologists: Examples include Harriet Martineau's *Illustrations of Political Economy* (1832-1834), Mari Sandoz's *Capital City* (1939), and Agnes Riedmann's *The Discovery of Adamsville* (1977). Judged pedagogically as a work that entertains and provokes while also teaching complex and sophisticated ideas, *Herland* is a superb sociological accomplishment.

The socially problematic issues that Gilman outlines in *Herland* echo the theoretical proposals of Lester F. Ward (1841-1913), a major American sociologist who admired Gilman and vice versa. Ward's concept of gynecocentric (that is woman-centered) social theory reinforces Gilman's strong belief in the fundamental rationality of women's values and social contributions. Gilman developed this perspective at length in her nonfiction works. *Herland* reflects, in greatly simplified form, sociological ideas comprehensively examined in Gilman's *Women and Economics* (1898), *Concerning Children* (1900), *The Home: Its Work and Influence* (1903), *Human Work* (1904), and the novel *The Man-Made World* (1911).

The overarching theme in *Herland* is that from women's roles and values as mothers springs a fundamentally important social current that society ignores at its collective peril. Mothering, in this view, is a social activity in which all members of society engage together. A social mother, Gilman maintained, is concerned with not only the welfare of her own children but also the support, happiness, and prosperity of all children. If the world were run from the point of view of social mothering, it would, presumably, evidence many of the positive social attributes of *Herland*: a healthy and well-educated populace, humane prisons, efficient use of resources, and so forth.

The premise that women's values provide an excellent basis for society was not unique to Gilman. Several prominent women sociologists, including American Nobel laureate Jane Addams (1860-1935), were feminist pragmatists who subscribed to a range of views similar to Gilman's. A brief and important precursor to *Herland* is Addams' witty and biting 1913 essay "If Men Were Seeking the Franchise," which was published in *Jane Addams: A Centennial Reader* (1960). Addams, who was a friend and colleague of Gilman, describes a hypothetical society of men and women (otherwise similar in situation to *Herland*) in which women dominate the populace and have the political power to deny men the right to vote. Addams whimsically concludes that men, much like the men who venture to *Herland*, cannot safely be allowed to share in government until they abandon their selfish and destructive ideas.

Gilman's personal perspective as a mother is revealed in her autobiography, *The Living of Charlotte Perkins Gilman* (1935). Gilman's decision after a much-publicized divorce to give custody of her daughter, Katherine, to her former husband, Charles W. Stetson, is a consequential example of Gilman's idea that children should be reared by the one who is best at parenting—and that this individual is not necessarily the biological mother. The cooperative, mothering attributes of the society sketched in *Herland* no doubt comprise the kind of social situation that Gilman wished for her own daughter.

Context

The initial influence of *Herland* was restricted primarily to regular readers of *The Forerunner*, in which *Herland* was serialized in 1915. By extending reduced-price subscriptions of *The Forerunner* to participants, Gilman tried to encourage the formation of "Gilman Circles" in which the contents of her magazines, including *Herland*, were to be discussed by women in small, face-to-face groups. Poor sales, however, caused the demise of *The Forerunner* and the collapse of Gilman Circles. Overall, *The Forerunner* reached few readers, and thus *Herland* had minor social or literary force. From 1916 to 1979, the novel remained buried in the pages of Gilman's defunct magazine.

The impact of *Herland* increased dramatically when its chapters were collated and republished together in book form by Pantheon Books in 1979. *Herland*, forty-four years after Gilman's death and sixty-four years after the serialized first publication, reached a new feminist audience. The republication of *Herland* was promoted as the recovery of "a lost feminist utopian novel," and the work quickly attracted attention from feminists in the growing women's studies movement.

Yet, radically abstracted from the serial context of *The Forerunner* and divorced from *Herland*'s concluding sequel, the 1979 edition of *Herland* had a perplexing impact on the women's movement. Gilman was championed in some quarters as advocating the establishment and superiority of women-only communities of the type outlined in *Herland*, and the book version became a popular rallying point for radical separatists within the women's movement. That result, paradoxically, is opposite to Gilman's clearly expressed view that the future of the world depends crucially on the enlightened cooperation of men and women, mothers and fathers, laboring together side by side.

Other feminists, criticizing the 1979 book-length edition of *Herland*, find it sometimes naïve, ethnocentric, masculinist, and even racist. Superficial readings of Gilman's enthusiastic embrace of evolutionary principles and her complex ideas relating to race improvement brand Gilman in some quarters as politically incorrect. Such criticisms, however, often neglect the intellectual context in which *Herland* was originally published and ignore the precise ways in which Gilman defined her terms and offered cooperative solutions to many social problems. Gilman never intended the satirical, fictional romps that comprise *Herland* and *With Her in Ourland* to be definitive or comprehensive statements on the complicated moral and philosophical issues that she discussed at length in *The Forerunner* and elsewhere.

The potential impact of *Herland* on women's issues today remains largely unfulfilled. Whereas the work has become justifiably a recognized classic in women's literature, separatist politics and postmodern critiques deflect serious discussion of Gilman's insightful analyses of oppressive patriarchal social systems, as well as her dedication to constructive human advancement. When *Herland* is conjoined to *With Her in Ourland* and carefully studied in the context of *The Forerunner* and Gilman's nonfiction books, the progressive feminist ideas reflected in *Herland* may someday have the cooperative, forward-looking social impact that Gilman so ardently intended.

Sources for Further Study

Allen, Polly Wynn. *Building Domestic Liberty: Charlotte Perkins Gilman's Architectural Feminism*. Amherst: University of Massachusetts Press, 1988. An outstanding analysis of Gilman's interrelated ideas about homes, communities, and the social arrangement of the built environment.

Deegan, Mary Jo. *Jane Addams and the Men of the Chicago School, 1892-1918*. New Brunswick, N.J.: Transaction Books, 1988. This monograph is the major study of the Chicago women's sociological network, centered at Hull House, in which Gilman participated. Deegan's work is indispensable for untangling many of the relevant intellectual currents that defined Gilman's era, especially the concept of "cultural feminism."

Hill, Mary A. *Charlotte Perkins Gilman: The Making of a Radical Feminist, 1860-1896*. Philadelphia: Temple

University Press, 1980. A major biography of Gilman and the one to which students should turn first. Hill presents an astute and well-documented account of Gilman's early life and the origins of her ideas.

Karpinski, Joanne B., ed. *Critical Essays on Charlotte Perkins Gilman*. New York: G. K. Hall, 1992. An ambitious compendium of wide-ranging contemporary, reprinted, and original literary essays and critical assessments. Although somewhat technical, Lois Magner's study carefully explores Gilman's ideas on evolution and social Darwinism.

Keith, Bruce. "Charlotte Perkins Gilman (Stetson)." In *Women in Sociology*, edited by Mary Jo Deegan. New York: Greenwood Press, 1991. Presents a useful and straightforward overview of Gilman's work, writings, and stature as a sociologist. Keith includes a bibliography of Gilman's major works and a list of critical sources.

Lane, Ann J. *To Herland and Beyond: The Life and Work of Charlotte Perkins Gilman*. New York: Pantheon, 1990. This popular biography interprets Gilman primarily from a psychological perspective (an orientation that Gilman rejected) and stresses Gilman's family and interpersonal relationships. Unfortunately, Lane gives short shrift to major social issues and the intellectual milieu in which Gilman labored.

Meyering, Sheryl L., ed. *Charlotte Perkins Gilman: The Woman and Her Work*. Ann Arbor, Mich.: UMI Research Press, 1989. This compendium offers fourteen frequently referenced critical essays, three of which focus on *Herland*.

Scharnhorst, Gary. *Charlotte Perkins Gilman: A Bibliography*. Metuchen, N.J.: Scarecrow Press, 1985. This reference is indispensable for serious students. Scharnhorst lists 2,173 of Gilman's writings, including many found only in obscure magazines. This useful book also includes a compilation of published criticism, biographical materials, and relevant manuscript collections.

Michael R. Hill

HISTORY OF WOMAN SUFFRAGE

Authors: Susan B. Anthony (1820-1906), Matilda Joslyn Gage (1826-1898), Ida Husted Harper (1851-1931), and Elizabeth Cady Stanton (1815-1902)
Type of work: History
Time of work: The late eighteenth century to 1920
Locale: The United States and Great Britain
First published: 1881-1922

Principal personages:

Mary Wollstonecraft, an eighteenth century British feminist and author
Harriet Martineau, a British novelist and economist
Lucretia Mott, an important American social reformer
Sarah and **Angelina Grimké,** American sisters who worked for the abolition movement
Margaret Fuller, an influential advocate for women's rights in the United States
Carrie Chapman Catt, one of the women responsible for the passage of the Nineteenth Amendment granting women's suffrage
Francis Wright, an American women's rights activist
Lydia Child, an American women's rights activist

Form and Content

History of Woman Suffrage, a chronological narrative with documents, comprises six volumes averaging one thousand pages apiece. The broad purpose of this massive work was to lend intellectual and moral support to feminists, male and female, in their struggles between 1881 and 1920 to extend the franchise to women. Universal white manhood suffrage had all but been accomplished by the mid-1840's, an area in which Americans then led the world. In 1870, as a part of post-Civil War Reconstruction, ratification of the Fifteenth Amendment prohibited denial of the vote because of race, color, or previous condition of servitude; thus the franchise was extended to African American males, including those who had been freed from slavery by the Thirteenth Amendment in 1865.

The great discontinuity in such extensions of the franchise in the extension of democracy was the general preclusion of voting by women. Despite the fact that in some locales a few women had participated in voting during Colonial days and a few subsequently enjoyed voting rights during the first half of the nineteenth century, though still only locally, these were insignificant exceptions to the prevailing practices of a male-dominated society. Whatever the opinions the majority of women may have held regarding the value of the franchise during the eighteenth and nineteenth centuries—and these are unknown—many thousands of educated and articulate women certainly considered their denial of the vote a rank injustice. Abigail Adams had reminded her husband, John, of that fact during the drafting of the Constitution, and others like her had gained notoriety during each of the nation's nineteenth and early twentieth century cycles of reform. For example, the principal authors-editors of *History of Woman Suffrage*, Elizabeth Cady Stanton and Susan B. Anthony, had organized and led the famous gathering of feminists at Seneca Falls, New York, in 1848. Another author- editor, Matilda Joslyn Gage, had been an active participant in the agitations following it from the 1850's into the 1900's. Each advocated a wide range of women's rights, chief among them the right to the vote.

Not until 1879, late in their long careers as feminist reformers, did Stanton and Anthony decide to compile *History of Woman Suffrage*. Division between the American Woman Suffrage Association (AWSA), headed by Lucy Stone, and their own National Woman Suffrage Association (NWSA) lent impetus to the project. They sought primarily to establish the greater significance of their association, to emphasize the priority of suffrage reform over other feminist objectives, to provide subsequent generations of suffragists with documentation of their movement, and not least to make it more difficult for male historians (there were scarcely any other kind) to overlook their lifetime of struggle for all forms of feminine equality.

History of Woman Suffrage, was an intensely collaborative effort. To further their work, the principal authors-editors lived together for months at a time. Anthony, who for years had been collecting documents, continued to do so, while Stanton assumed general responsibility for writing most of the connective narrative passages. The somewhat younger Gage wrote three chapters of volume 1. Both Stanton and Anthony labored in unison over the tedious editing required for the three initial volumes, while Ida Husted Harper supervised the latter three. Overall, the work includes references to and excerpts from newspapers, journals, and speeches and the writings of scores of outstanding feminists and female suffragists, as well as contributions by some of their male colleagues. There are reminiscences, notably by Stanton and Anthony; detailed reports of suffragists' efforts in many states, along with the legislative results thereof; records and proceedings of state and national woman suffrage conventions; documentation on the complex political and gender divisions over suffrage during Reconstruction; and accounts of the activities of woman suffrage organizations and the actions of state legislatures that led to the drafting and ratification of the Nineteenth Amendment in 1920, granting women the vote.

Analysis

With their suffrage proposals triumphant in only four western states when they died, Stanton, Anthony, and Gage nevertheless suffused the first three volumes of their history with their ebullience, with their unswerving belief in the justice of their cause, and with their informed high purpose, producing an élan that marked subsequent volumes as well. While they were confident of their own high principles, their advocacy of woman suffrage, as the work amply documents, was plagued nevertheless by the criticisms and indifference of society at large, crippled by personal animosities and organizational frictions among suffragists, and wracked by conflicts between suffragist priorities and those of other feminists and reformers. Yet despite the density and tedium of some of its inclusions, the tome of *History of Woman Suffrage* conveys frank good sense, as if with distant vision the suffragists had assumed the stance of future generations asking why, given the obvious justice of universalizing the vote for women, its attainment required so many years of struggle.

History of Woman Suffrage is more than a painstaking assemblage of speeches, journal excerpts, documents, legislative activities, and organizational vicissitudes. The first volumes, chiefly the handiwork of Stanton and Anthony, which they completed in 1886, are thus rich in historical context designed to deepen the suffragist movement's self-awareness. To this end, volume 1 traces the origins of suffrage reform within broader ranges of feminist reformism, discernible by the late eighteenth century and reaching an early pinnacle at the Women's Rights Convention assembled in Seneca Falls on July 19, 1848. During these years, as part of the expansive democratic sentiments that were affecting much of American society—most apparently during the presidency of Andrew Jackson—women's rights advocates promulgated a comprehensive challenge to traditional and predominantly male social values. In their thrust toward winning equality, they demanded legal reevaluations of marriage, divorce, and birth control, as well as reassessments of property rights for women. They were a principal force behind temperance movements and a vigorous adjunct to the increasingly vocal and influential antislavery movements of the 1850's. Within this wide spectrum, the demands for suffrage advanced by women such as Stanton, Anthony, Gage, and others became the key to achieving most other feminist objectives.

Because the authors-editors of *History of Woman Suffrage* recognized their own place within this environment of general reform, they were mindful of the importance of other feminist leaders whose principal goals did not center on the suffrage issue. For this reason, Stanton and Anthony respected, by inclusion, references to the writings and speeches of the great British feminists Mary Wollstonecraft and Harriet Martineau, as well as foremost Americans such as Lucretia Mott, Sarah and Angelina Grimké, Margaret Fuller, Francis Wright, Lydia Child, and Carrie Chapman Catt. They also addressed the concerns of dozens of other figures less familiar to later generations, such as Martha C. Wright, Eliza W. Farnham, Mariana W. Johnson, Harriot K. Hunt, Lydia Fowles, Pauline Wright-Davis, Ann Preston, and Mrs. Collins, who was also credited with being the founder of the first women's suffrage society. (The American Woman Suffrage Association is mentioned in the work, but Lucy Stone, the leader of these rival suffragists, refused to contribute).

The first volume is the record of a movement growing in confidence and influence, one supported on principle by a number of prominent male reformers, most of them leading abolitionists. This confident note continues into the early pages of the second volume, which cites women's contributions to the antislavery cause and their Civil War efforts; their subsequent support of the Thirteenth, Fourteenth, and Fifteenth Amendments to the Constitution; and the convening of the first postwar woman suffrage convention. Yet the suffrage movement, the history notes, fell upon hard times during Reconstruction (1867-1877). When erstwhile abolitionists and male legislators confronted what they perceived as a political choice between winning extensions of civil rights, including voting rights to African Americans (meaning at the time African American males) or universalizing the vote for women, they chose to back extensions of freedoms to black males and virtually abandoned the cause of woman suffrage.

Volumes 3 through 6, therefore, survey what were predominantly the campaigns of the National American Woman Suffrage Association (an organization created by the merger of the NWSA and the AWSA) in key states and localities, the strategies formulated in annual conventions, and legislative losses and gains year by year until the ratification of the Nineteenth Amendment in 1920.

Context

By the close of the twentieth century, *History of Woman Suffrage* was judged by male and feminist historians alike to be a major source for the study of nineteenth century women's rights movements, as well as an important source for the study of the lives and views of Stanton and Anthony. Accordingly, it was reprinted in 1970 by Source Book Press, while Mari Jo and Paul Buhle condensed and edited *The Concise History of Woman Suffrage: Selections from the Classic Work of Stanton, Anthony, Gage, and Harper*, published by the University of Illinois Press in 1978. Though the original work was never intended for general readers, later perceptions of its importance fully justified the efforts of Stanton and Anthony in launching this multivolume work and overseeing much of it to fruition. Judged within the context of its times—that is, the years from 1881 to 1922—*History of Woman Suffrage* may rank as the principal, if not the sole, scholarly contribution to literature concerning the struggle for women's rights in the United States.

History of Woman Suffrage is regarded as a monument in particular to the steadfastness and perseverance of Stanton and Anthony. In a social and political environment that was almost continuously hostile to their aspirations and objectives, they not only invested the six volumes with their emotional and intellectual substance but also drew heavily upon their own financial resources to bring them to publication. It was a feat accomplished amid extremely busy individual, familial, and public lives.

Sources for Further Study

Banner, Lois W. *Elizabeth Cady Stanton*. Boston: Little, Brown, 1980. A useful portrait of Stanton intended for nonspecialist readers. Banner focuses on Stanton's radicalism in the context of her times and the interplay of her conservative origins and radical bent upon her personality. Contains brief chapter essays on sources and an inadequate index.

Barry, Kathleen. *Susan B. Anthony: A Biography of a Singular Feminist*. New York: New York University Press, 1988. An excellent, enjoyable study which concentrates, as might be expected, on Anthony's character development, rather than on *History of Woman Suffrage*. Offers many splendid photographs, chapter notes, and an extensive bibliography.

Dubois, Ellen Carol. *Feminism and Suffrage*. Ithaca, N.Y.: Cornell University Press, 1978. A clearly written, scholarly study of the independent women's movement in the United States from Seneca Falls (1848) through the early years of Reconstruction (1869). Excellent for its examination of the political complexities and divisions over suffrage and other women's rights. A bibliography and an index are included.

Griffith, Elisabeth. *In Her Own Right: The Life of Elizabeth Cady Stanton*. New York: Oxford University Press, 1984. A vigorous, scholarly study that treats the full range of Stanton's feminist activities and places her powerful advocacy of woman suffrage in an appropriate context. An important work since Stanton was widely recognized as the principal leader and chief advocate of women's rights during the nineteenth century. Excellent photographs, appendices, notes to pages, and a valuable index are provided.

Kraditor, Aileen. *The Ideas of the Woman Suffrage Movement, 1899-1920.* New York: Columbia University Press, 1965. An outstanding study which carefully traces its subject and important personalities through the ratification of the Nineteenth Amendment in 1920. When supplemented by Ellen Carol Dubois' study (above) and by perusal of *History of Woman Suffrage* itself, Kraditor's work completes a continuous history of woman suffrage. Contains a bibliography and an index.

Clifton K. Yearley

HOLY FEAST AND HOLY FAST

Author: Caroline Walker Bynum (1941-)
Type of work: Social criticism
First published: 1987

Form and Content

Focusing on the lives of several hundred Christian women in Europe between 1200 and 1500 who were noted for their religious devotion, *Holy Feast and Holy Fast: The Religious Significance of Food to Medieval Women* is a groundbreaking exploration of their lives. These women's religious practices centered on the Eucharist: a rite of communion by which, in partaking of bread and wine, they received into their bodies the body and blood of Christ in all of its redemptive power. According to author Caroline Walker Bynum, in their elaboration of Eucharistic practices these women created distinct forms of spirituality with deep personal meaning and broad cultural influence.

Bynum's portrait of the lives of medieval holy women, marking a clear departure from previous studies of their lives, has inspired broad reassessments among historians about women of that era. Before Bynum, scholars who studied medieval women focused on their marginalization in society. While Bynum grants that women were subjugated, she argues forcefully that, generating their own distinct spirituality, numbers of women in the late Middle Ages exercised considerable power in relation to families, church authorities, and communities.

Bynum locates women's power in a piety centered on food: food from their tables that sustained the poor, food from their bodies (milk or other fluids) that healed others, and food of the Eucharist that united them with God. She establishes the variety of religious roles available to medieval women, outlines the significance of food practices to these roles, and demonstrates that, although food was featured in the religious life of all medieval Christians, it figured most prominently and distinctively in the lives of holy women. Refusing standard interpretations of medieval women's lives, Bynum summons a wealth of evidence to secure her larger claim: Medieval holy women employed resources available to them—especially food—to soar in triumph above the "tidy, moderate, decent, second-rate place" that society had intended for women.

Bynum's account is notable for its subject—the religious lives of medieval women—and also for its form: gender-sensitive historical analysis. Bynum's compelling study of medieval life establishes that the previously documented marginalization of women was produced, in part, by modes of inquiry hitherto favored by historians. Because scholars used tools of inquiry that did not permit a sophisticated grasp of gender in medieval society, they overlooked or misconstrued important facets of that society. The lives of holy women were misunderstood, as were the religious practices and social interactions of men and women in the larger society. By contrast, Bynum's tools of inquiry, fashioned expressly for the exploration of gender, not only bring women into focus but also illuminate a medieval world that is different from the one that scholars had observed previously. Thus, Bynum's work marks a turning point inn historical research for what she says about women's lives and for the means that she employs to build her case: a gender-sensitive mode of historical analysis that reshapes not only what is known about medieval women but also what is known in general about the Middle Ages.

Analysis

According to Bynum, food and food metaphors were featured prominently in thirteenth and fourteenth century Europe. Food divided rich from poor and informed a key cultural ethic: Overeating was a mark of privilege, and sharing food with the hungry was a primary symbol of benevolence. Food also had religious significance. Christians believed that those who luxuriated in food paid the penalty for the sin of gluttonly; those who renounced food through regular fasting obtained salvation. Moreover, in late medieval piety, Christians linked salvation with the individual reception of God in the Eucharist, which they described by appeal to graphic metaphors of nourishment. Tasting the broken body of Christ in the Eucharist, Christians became one with the suffering flesh crucified on the cross and obtained their salvation.

Notable among those for whom the Eucharist was central to faith were women who, in saintly asceticism, deliberately abstained from all food but God's food: the Eucharist. Hagiographic records which Bynum examines indicate that, although women were only 18 percent of those canonized as saints between 1000 and 1700, they comprised 23 percent of those who died from asceticism and 53 percent of those for whom illness was central to their sanctity. Moreover, the majority of Eucharistic visions and miracles were attributed to women: Of the twenty types identified by Bynum, only two were performed exclusively by men and those were linked to consecration of the Eucharist, which was a male prerogative in any case. Eight other types of miracles featured women primarily, and four were associated exclusively with women's spirituality.

Because hagiography is not entirely reliable in the reconstruction of history, Bynum supplements her argument with evidence drawn from the lives of religious men. Acknowledging that food asceticism and Eucharistic devotion can be located in the vitae of men, Bynum shows also that, in contrast to the holy women of the late medieval age, food in all of its miraculous and mystical powers was not at the center of men's religious lives.

Tracing further the special significance of food asceticism for holy women, Bynum observes its association with practical dualism: Some women, ascribing a negative value to their bodies and to nature, did cease to eat in order to discipline and defeat bodies that they perceived as sinful. Distancing herself, however, from historians who had claimed previously that dualism played a prominent role in medieval women's lives, authorizing and sustaining their subjugation, Bynum demonstrates that fasting by holy women was a "flight not so much from as into physicality." Believing that God saves the world through the physical, human agony of the crucified Christ, these women viscerally embodied that theology: In their Eucharistic piety, these holy women incorporated as their own the suffering body of Christ and became the tormented flesh that saved. Subsequently, their bodies bore stigmata (bodily wounds like those of Christ) or produced fluids (like the blood of Christ) that healed others.

Moreover, citing the larger social significance of holy women's embrace of fasting, Bynum observes that, far from constraining women's lives, asceticism empowered women. Holy women could use their ascetic behaviors to manipulate parents into acceding to their wishes not to marry. Were they to vomit up the Host, testifying that it had not been consecrated and was yet human food, they could successfully challenge the authority and integrity of the priest who had offered it. More than one priest was run out of town, condemned in his sin by the testimony of holy women. Throughout Europe, many persons were drawn to the charismatic authority of women who saved others through the powerful example of their own suffering and their gift of healing. Escaping subjugation, these women were able to maneuver beyond societal limits in fulfillment of spiritual visions that also granted them significant social power.

Although Bynum's scholarly erudition is above reproach, some critics of her work have challenged her conclusions. That asceticism brought much physical pain to holy women, sometimes culminating in their deaths from self-starvation, has led some persons to qualify Bynum's assertion that holy women were personally and socially empowered by their religious practices. Nevertheless, few historians would subscribe today to a model of medieval religious life that would bypass Bynum's work, for the larger cultural context that she has so brilliantly illuminated is now viewed as a necessary point of departure for the study of asceticism and other aspects of medieval religious life.

Context

Bynum uses gender in *Holy Feast and Holy Fast* as a basic grid on which to lay out her research findings and deploys food, with all of its mystical and sacred potential, as a unifying theme on that grid. As a result, she brings the lives of late medieval women to visibility in ways that have required historians to recast their presentation of religious and cultural life in the late Middle Ages. Although the increased attention given by historians of the Middle Ages to issues of gender cannot be traced solely to Bynum's influence, she has played and continues to play a central role in these ongoing developments. That so many new assessments of medieval asceticism and/or the lives of medieval women bear the mark of her influence confirms that Bynum, more than other historians, is responsible for breaking the mold in which previous scholarship about women and the society of late medieval Christendom was produced.

Bynum's influence on the way in which gender is examined in the fields of history, literature, and the academic study of religion also has exceeded the boundaries of her own specialization in the late Middle Ages. That *Holy Feast and Holy Fast* has been received so positively in academic circles as a work of exceptional scholarship has energized an entire generation of women scholars who, conducting research on gender in a variety of fields in the wake of Bynum's intellectual achievements, have found that their efforts are taken more seriously by their colleagues. Because Bynum blazed such a broad trail with this work, the road traveled since by women scholars who study gender has been less rocky: They have consolidated earlier gains in scholarship on gender and have forged ahead in new directions, often using Bynum as a model for their own explorations of gender.

Sources for Further Study

Bell, Rudolph. *Holy Anorexia*. Chicago: University of Chicago Press, 1985. Using autobiographies, letters, confessors' testimonies, and canonization records, Bell examines the lives of more than 250 Italian holy women for signs of anorexia. He argues that these women, like some modern teenagers who engage in self-starvation, fasted as part of a larger struggle for liberation from a patriarchal family and society. Bell's quantitative data (enhanced by helpful charts) augments Bynum's research; however, Bynum's cultural analysis of the significance of food for medieval women is richer and more nuanced than Bell's, which focuses primarily on the psychology of women's fasting.

Bynum, Caroline Walker. *Fragmentation and Redemption: Essays on Gender and the Human Body in Medieval Religion*. New York: Zone Books, 1991. Written before and, in some cases, after *Holy Feast and Holy Fast*, these essays clarify the major themes of that larger work. Confirming Bynum's status as a preeminent historian of the late Middle Ages are her reflections on theological debates concerning the resurrection of the body.

_____________. *Jesus as Mother: Studies in the Spirituality of the High Middle Ages*. Berkeley: University of California Press, 1982. These early essays established Bynum's profile as an historian. Attentive to lay spirituality, Bynum explores religion in its social context without abandoning the ecclesiastical focus favored previously by historians. Already present are sustained reflections on gender that will distinguish Bynum's later work.

Catherine of Siena. *The Letters of St. Catherine of Siena*. Translated by Suzanne Noffke. Binghamton: Center for Medieval and Early Renaissance Studies, State University of New York at Binghamton, 1988. The first English translation of the entire corpus of Catherine's letters and a vital record of a woman whose role in medieval Catholicism was most significant. The centrality of fasting and Eucharistic piety in Catherine's life and her persistent appeal to metaphors of food and maternal nourishment in her letters establish Catherine as a key figure in Bynum's work.

Hadewijch. *The Complete Works*. Translated by Columba Hart. New York: Paulist Press, 1980. In poems, letters, and recorded visions written between 1220 and 1240, this Flemish poet and mystic employs images of hunger and food as principal metaphors in describing her relationship to God. Her prose illuminates and provides compelling support for pivotal claims made by Bynum in *Holy Feast and Holy Fast*.

Weinstein, Donald, and Rudolph M. Bell. *Saints and Society: The Two Worlds of Western Christendom, 1000-1700*. Chicago: University of Chicago Press, 1982. The major secondary source influencing Bynum's own book and a groundbreaking contribution to a social history of medieval Christendom. Demonstrates that explorations of the lives of saints illuminate the society in which they lived, even as an examination of that society enhances knowledge of holy men and women in that age.

Martha J. Reineke

THE HOME-MAKER

Author: Dorothy Canfield Fisher (1879-1958)
Type of work: Novel
Type of plot: Domestic realism
Time of plot: The 1920's
Locale: A town in the Midwestern United States
First published: 1924

Principal characters:

Evangeline (Eva) Knapp, an organized and energetic woman frustrated with housekeeping
Lester Knapp, her husband, a sensitive and poetic man unhappy with his job as an accountant
Helen, the eldest of the Knapp children, who is like her father
Henry, the middle child, who is small and sickly
Stephen, the Knapp's rebellious five-year-old, who is Eva's favorite
Jerome Willing, the owner of Willing's Emporium and the employer of first Lester and then Eva
Nell Willing, Jerome's wife and the advertising director for Willing's Emporium

Form and Content

The Home-Maker, by Dorothy Canfield Fisher (who published her fiction under her maiden name, Dorothy Canfield, and her nonfiction under her married name), explores the problems implicit in ascribing roles to individuals based on their gender, rather than on their specific talents, abilities, and desires. The turning point of the novel occurs when Lester Knapp loses his job in the accounting office at Willing's Emporium. Devastated by this development, Lester contemplates suicide, but he must make his death look like an accident if Eva and the children are to receive any insurance money. He sees his chance when his neighbor's roof catches fire. He slips and falls trying to put the fire out, but he does not die; instead, he is paralyzed and confined to a wheelchair.

The task of supporting the family now falls on Eva's shoulders, and she asks Jerome Willing to hire her. Although Eva keeps repeating to herself and members of her community the aphorism that a woman's first duty is to her home and her family, Eva loves her new job, which calls on her aesthetic abilities in working with fabric. Eva begins as a stock clerk in the ladies' cloak and suits department and quickly moves up to saleswoman. She takes great pleasure in knowing her stock and helping her customers find the clothes that will best suit them at a price they can afford.

Meanwhile, Lester runs the household, learning how to cook and devising creative ways to clean. Most of all, he devotes his time to getting to know his children. Because Lester has a greater imagination and a deeper perception than Eva, he is able to understand his children in a way that Eva never could. With her penchant for organization and love of detail, Eva is the perfect candidate for running a department, a fact that Jerome Willing soon realizes. Lester's imagination and his love for thought and storytelling suit him better for rearing children; he ignores the dusting and sweeping to talk to his children, to learn what kind of minds and hearts they have. They flourish under this kind of attention.

If socially prescribed gender roles are not flexible enough to allow house husbands and working women, individuals suffer. By the time that Lester unexpectedly regains the use of his legs, Eva is making more money than Lester ever did, and the children's physical ailments have disappeared; indeed, the children are much healthier physically, emotionally, and intellectually under Lester's patient care. It is clear, however, that if Lester is able to walk again, society deems that he must go back to work because he is a man; Eva must go back to what for her is the prison of home because she is a woman. The novel ends with Lester's decision that he will forgo the use of his legs so that the true homemaker can stay at home. His decision is a secret kept by Eva, Lester's doctor, and a relative, Aunt Mattie, who each agree, privately that it must be concealed from their community. It is clear that maintaining this secret life is the only way that the Knapp family can be socially acceptable.

Analysis

After *The Home-Maker* was published, Fisher was disconcerted that many reviewers interpreted it as, in her words, a "whoop for women's rights"; her intention, she said, was to depict the rights of children. Fisher does spend much detail on the learning processes of the Knapp children, especially Stephen. For example, when Lester becomes concerned about Stephen's seemingly unmanageable temper, he devises a plan to harness the energy that Stephen expends in being angry. He gives him an eggbeater and challenges him to figure out how it works. Fisher devotes several pages to the description of Stephen's initial frustration with the tool and his eventual mastery of it. She demonstrates how the frustrations of a "problem child" can be alleviated by a creative, caring parent.

Yet, in devoting a fictional project to the subject of homemaking, traditionally women's work, Fisher is certainly writing about women's rights. When Aunt Mattie visits Lester at home and is dismayed to find him cooking and darning socks, he says to her, "Do you know what you are saying to me, Mattie Farnham? You are telling me that you really think that home-making is a poor, mean, cheap job beneath the dignity of anybody who can do anything else." He realizes that women's work in the home is never accorded the worth or respect that it deserves, largely because profit, at least in terms of monetary gain, is not involved. By making Lester her spokesperson, Fisher emphasizes the fact that home-making should be everyone's job; she corrects the platitude "A woman's place is in the home" by showing that both men and women have places there.

Fisher also criticizes a burgeoning American consumerism through Lester, who finds Jerome Willing's tactics in drawing customers to his store morally reprehensible. This critique is countered, however, by the fact that both Willing and Eva find meaningful work in the department store. Thus, Fisher emphasizes the fact that all individuals should have the opportunity to find the work that sustains them.

The unsatisfactory resolution of the novel—Lester is metaphorically castrated, and there is no suggestion that he will be able to find satisfying work outside of the home to complement his work inside it—demonstrates that society should be more tolerant of individual needs and less rigid in inflicting work styles on people. In a perfect world, it would be acceptable for Lester to stay at home because he is the best caretaker for his children, not because he is crippled and unfit for anything else.

One can, in fact, interpret *The Home-Maker* as a novel about men's, women's, and children's rights. Fisher's shifting point of view is quite democratic, divided between all of her principal characters and a few minor ones. As a result, one can see the cost to each individual, and the community, when Lester and Eva Knapp are each prevented from doing the work for which they are best suited. Fisher was a pioneer in using this method; Virginia Woolf, James Joyce, William Faulkner, and others were experimenting with it at this time as well.

Unlike Fisher's other novels, where the spirit of place is painstakingly described, the environment in *The Home-Maker* is fairly generic. There is no description of landscape at all; the town atmosphere is provided by the glimpses one gets into the minds of various townspeople. This is also a democratic move on Fisher's part because her implication is that Lester and Eva's situation can occur in any home, anywhere in the United States. Indeed, the novel is almost claustrophobic in its confinement to the minds of the characters and the inside of a limited number of buildings: the Knapp home; the Willing home; Willing's Emporium, which has as its motto the "home-like store"; the rectory of the church and the church itself as a spiritual home; and Aunt Mattie's home. This confinement reflects Fisher's belief that all the truly important developments in life—the building of self-esteem, the feeling of self-worth, the ability to love and be loved—happen at home and in its immediate environs.

In her fiction, Fisher is devoted to chronicling the aesthetic details of everyday life, such as the episode with the eggbeater. Art, according to Fisher, not only resides in art galleries and concert halls but also encompasses the creative solutions with which people correct problems of everyday living; Lester makes an art of being a father. This aesthetic determines Fisher's agenda in writing fiction. As she writes in her prologue to *A Harvest of Stories* (1956):

> no novel . . . is worth the reading unless it grapples with some problem of living. Beauty of description, a stirring plot, the right word in the right place . . . all these are excellent. But without that fundamental drive, they are only words—words—words.

Context

Fisher's themes remain constant in all of her work. First, she broadens the definition of the *Künstlerroman*, or the artist's coming-of-age plot, to include the domestic coming-of-age of her male and female characters. Second, she reimagines men's roles in the home, her male characters having, and needing, a significant place there. Third, she presents complex portraits of the minds and hearts of modern women who are struggling with the redefinition of self that resulted from the social evolution of the "new woman"—that is, women who, at the beginning of the twentieth century, pursued the same freedom and opportunity that was granted to men. Fisher's agenda is to show men who need home lives and women who need work lives in order to be fulfilled as human beings; she believed that neither men nor women could be totally satisfied with roles that were defined by gender.

The Home-Maker occupies a unique place in Fisher's canon; her sixth novel, it is the only one in which she imagines a total role reversal: a female provider and a male homemaker. It can be read as part of a continuing tradition of stories and novels by women that depict the limitations of gender roles and the psychological and emotional costs of such limits. Examples of this tradition include *The Story of Avis* (1877), by Elizabeth Stuart Phelps; *A Country Doctor* (1884), by Sarah Orne Jewett; *A New England Nun and Other Stories* (1891), by Mary E. Wilkins Freeman; *The Awakening* (1899), by Kate Chopin; *The House of Mirth* (1905), by Edith Wharton; *A Woman of Genius* (1912), by Mary Austin; and *The Song of the Lark* (1915), by Willa Cather.

Fisher's fiction differs from these other works because she takes into consideration the fact that men, too, are damaged by lives that have limits, lives that only include work outside the home. Her concern is always to present a balance for both men and women that includes fulfilling work in the public sphere and a supportive and satisfying home life in the private sphere. The fact that *The Home-Maker* was one of the ten best-selling novels of 1924 shows that achieving this balance was important in many American lives at the time; the reprinting of the novel in 1982, as well as the increasing attention to and reevaluation of Fisher's work, undoubtedly shows that it still is.

Sources for Further Study

Fisher, Dorothy Canfield. *Keeping Fires Night and Day: Selected Letters of Dorothy Canfield Fisher*. Edited by Mark Madigan. Columbia: University of Missouri Press, 1993. Fisher's lively personal voice is present in this excellent collection. In his introduction, Madigan provides a detailed chronology of Fisher's life and an examination of her friendship with Willa Cather. A thorough bibliography and an annotated list of Fisher's correspondents are included.

Madigan, Mark. "Profile: Dorothy Canfield Fisher." *Legacy: A Journal of American Women Writers* 9, no. 1 (1992): 49-58. A narrative chronology of Fisher's life and work. Madigan also discusses three of her novels as particularly worthy of critical attention: *The Brimming Cup* (1919), *The Home-Maker*, and *Her Son's Wife* (1926).

Rubin, Joan Shelley. *The Making of Middle Brow Culture*. Chapel Hill: University of North Carolina Press, 1992. This well-researched study profiles the five people who made up the first Board of Selection for the Book-of-the-Month Club, a job that Fisher held for twenty-five years.

Washington, Ida. *Dorothy Canfield Fisher: A Biography*. Shelburne, Vt.: New England Press, 1982. The first critical biography to be published about Fisher, this book gives an overview of Fisher's prolific career. Also includes valuable information about Fisher's family and a good analysis of how Fisher drew on their varying influences in shaping her career. A good starting point for learning more about Fisher in general.

Yates, Elizabeth. *The Lady From Vermont*. Brattleboro, Vt.: Stephen Greene Press, 1971. First published in 1958 as *Pebble in a Pool*, Yates's book is a general biography of Fisher.

Anne M. Downey

HOUSE OF INCEST

Author: Anaïs Nin (1903-1977)
Type of work: Novella
Type of plot: Allegory
Time of plot: No particular time
Locale: No particular place
First published: 1936

Principal characters:

The narrator, a woman who introduces the reader to the other characters and to the House of Incest

Sabina, the narrator's lover and her complementary missing half

Jeanne, a crippled figure tortured by her love for her brother

The paralytic, a writer pained by the failure of language to record the complexity of his inner life

The modern Christ, an empath so sensitive to other people that he has essentially been flayed alive

The dancer, a woman who lost her arms by clutching too firmly everything she loved

Form and Content

House of Incest (first published as *The House of Incest* in 1936) is a difficult work to categorize or summarize. In reality, it is a prose poem with a breathtaking series of images and themes. Its characters and plot—if there really is one—remain deeply veiled. Overall, the atmosphere is distinctly dreamlike.

The book is prefaced by a brief statement and a somewhat longer fable, both of which indicate the work's deep psychological roots. The first section of the main text describes the narrator's previous idealized existence in a world of water—Atlantide. It ends with the narrator cast ashore like the skeleton of a wrecked ship. The second section opens with the narrator gazing at Sabina as she approaches in the haunting twilight. The narrator describes Sabina's appearance and personality, her compulsive lying and yet also her primitive vigor. "There is no mockery between women," the narrator states. It is clear that she is in love with Sabina. She also points out the fact that the women share an identity, that they are each other's missing halves: "YOU ARE THE WOMAN I AM," states the narrator. She closes with a passage about her own tormented inner fragmentation into many selves. Obstinate images and cracked mirrors surround her as she searches unsuccessfully for Sabina's face in a crowd. The brief third section presents more images, with the narrator "enmeshed" in her own lies.

The fourth section of the novella introduces the paradoxical Jeanne, who is oddly elegant yet also hampered by a withered leg. Jeanne is in love with her brother, married to a husband who does not understand her, and fixated on her own image in the mirror. In what appears to be a dialogue with the narrator, Jeanne describes her own fragmentation and concludes with the revelation that her love for her brother can never be realized.

In the fifth section, the narrator is finally led into the House of Incest by a mysterious "she." (Or is "she" the previous narrator and the new narrator a new character?) The house is described as having a room that could not be found. The narrator stumbles from room to room. In one, she sees the biblical figure Lot with his hand on his daughter's breast. From the city in flames behind them come the cries of incestuous lovers—fathers and daughters, brothers and sisters, mothers and sons. The narrator moves on to a forest of decapitated trees and then to a room of white plaster as the section comes to an end.

In the sixth section, Jeanne is looking through all the rooms for her brother. She begs for help. Coming to the conclusion that she loves nothing except the absence of pain, she stands for many years and dies. (Her crippled leg had previously kept her from escaping life.) Upon dying, she finds her brother asleep among some paintings. He says that he has been admiring her portrait, hoping that she would die so that she would never change. The two bow, but not to each other, according to the narrator. In truth, they bow only to their own likenesses in the other. They wish each other a good night.

In the seventh and last section, the narrator walks into her book to seek peace, is cut by sharp glass, and discovers that lies create solitude. She then returns from the book to the paralytic's room. The paralytic stares at blank sheets of paper. He writes nothing because to capture the truth he would have to write many different pages simultaneously; the whole truth defies language and defies self-awareness. The paralytic bows to the narrator, Sabina, and Jeanne, introducing them to the modern Christ. The modern Christ's painful sensitivity—"Do you know what it is like to be touched by a human being!"—is envied by the paralytic, whose nerves have been deadened. Together, the group long for escape from the House of Incest, where they can only love themselves in the other—that is, where they can engage only in narcissistic love. They are afraid, however, of the tunnel which leads away from the house to "daylight." They turn to see the dancer, whose arms had been forfeited because she clutched too firmly at the things she loved. Now her arms have been returned. Opening them in a Christlike invitation and embrace, she dances toward the daylight.

Analysis

Just as it is difficult to categorize and summarize, *House of Incest* is not easily interpreted. Indeed, it is not clear that Anaïs Nin wished to reveal her intentions clearly. She openly resisted fellow author Henry Miller's suggestion that she provide more clues for the reader. Perhaps she thought that analytic language could not capture poetic truths effectively, or that the absence of an authoritative interpretation would leave readers free to respond from the heart, just as her book was written from the heart. Perhaps Nin's high regard for surrealism led her to believe that reality is too multifaceted and perspectives too diverse for a work of complexity and depth to yield itself to a single interpretation.

Nevertheless, *House of Incest* has been subjected to intense interpretation from a number of perspectives. One likely approach, in the light of Nin's exhaustive diary, is to look at the work as autobiographical in nature. There is some basis for this approach. *House of Incest* was written at a time when Nin was engaged in a torrid and somewhat tortured love affair with both Henry Miller and his wife June, to whom Sabina bears a definite resemblance. *Henry and June* (1986), Nin's account of this relationship, repeatedly comes back to the theme of incest, with Nin's older lovers serving as father surrogates. More to the point, Nin had an incestuous relationship with her father just before *House of Incest* was published and is alleged to have been a childhood victim of incest at her father's hands. The House of Incest itself bears some resemblance to the home that Nin shared with her husband in Louveciennes—it, too, seemed to have a missing room. Finally, the dreamlike qualities of the book as well as its deep psychological probing of the subconscious bring to mind Nin's fascination with psychoanalysis at the time the book was written. Consistent with this approach is the prominence of lies and self-fragmentation (possibly the bitter fruits of incest in thought or deed) as themes in the work.

On the other hand, Nin denied any simple linear relationship between her life and fiction. Furthermore, there are many images in *House of Incest* that seem to defy biographical parallels. This is not to say that reading Nin's nonfiction of the period casts no light on the novella: The nonfiction does make the book's landscape more familiar. Yet it does not seem to explain all or even most of the book's many mysteries. A recommended strategy for unraveling *House of Incest* would be to read the book on its own terms if possible before putting it into a biographical context. Certainly, the book lends itself to being reread; indeed, Nin appears to have designed the work so that multiple readings are a requirement.

Despite Nin's persistent interest in the theme of incest, *House of Incest* is often interpreted as dealing primarily with narcissism, a vain self-love indicated by the conspicuous presence of mirrors throughout the text. According to this interpretation, incest in this case refers to the sterility of having a love affair with one's self as reflected in someone similar—another woman in the case of the narrator and Sabina, one's sibling in the case of Jeanne and her brother. The point is to escape this narcissism by truly loving another person, not one's self through another person. This is the "daylight" toward which the dancer is moving at the novella's conclusion. This theme hearkens back to the eighteenth century philosopher Jean-Jacques Rousseau's distinction between natural and vain self-love in his critique of modernity in the *Discours sur l'origine et les fondements de l'inégalité parmi les hommes* (1755; *A Discourse upon the Origin and Foundation of the Inequality Among Mankind*, 1761).

No matter what theme one ascribes to *House of Incest*, one thing that must be noted is the incredible richness of the book's language. Though stylistically unique among Nin's works, the novella resembles her other work—and Henry Miller's as well—in its seemingly limitless mastery over the English language. Each paragraph contains at least one pure reading delight, and there is an almost unending abundance of memorable images, described with exquisite precision and power. Even as one struggles, perhaps in futility, to find the meaning of *House of Incest*, the work's beauty remains transcendent and completely undeniable.

Context

The impact of *House of Incest* has been felt in two waves. It was her diary rather than any of her fiction that firmly established Nin's reputation as a writer, and only her volumes of erotica *Delta Venus* (1969) and *Little Birds* (1979) have achieved best-selling status. Yet *House of Incest*, which Nin essentially published herself in 1936, played a key role in her career by helping her to build a small but loyal following and laying the groundwork for her later fictional works and subsequent experiments by other authors, especially women writers. As such, the novella deserves credit for helping to inspire—along with works by authors such as Djuna Barnes—a proliferation of literature marked by striking candor, penetrating psychological realism, experimental forms of narrative, and unorthodox styles. In short, even had Nin's diary never been published, *House of Incest* would have made its mark on literature despite what would have been a tiny readership.

With the publication of the diary beginning in 1966, Nin's readership and influence were greatly magnified. She became a major literary figure almost immediately. She also became a hot political property. Her liberated views toward female sexuality were seen as an effective antidote to the quickly unraveling double standard then current in society. Her work also fit in with the increasing desire to explore reverently the unique attributes of women, which for many promised liberation not only for women but for men as well. Finally, Nin's willingness to pursue her unorthodox writing career and lifestyle rather than conform to accepted norms brought a kind of personal admiration or aura. Nin presented an example of a woman triumphing on her own terms in a male-dominated world. Along the way, as Kate Millett pointed out in *Sexual Politics* (1970), Nin had even elicited words of praise and awe from the dreaded Henry Miller, disdained by feminists for his reputed ruthlessness toward women.

House of Incest also had political and social implications for feminists. The structure and behavior of family life was being examined in unprecedentedly critical ways during the late 1960's, with the incidence of incest being alleged to be far more common than anyone had been willing to admit previously. For this reason, the book has struck a particularly relevant chord, despite its resistance to any clear interpretation with regard to this issue.

Sources for Further Study

Evans, Oliver. *Anaïs Nin*. Carbondale: Southern Illinois University Press, 1968. One of the earliest critical studies of Nin's work. Evans, a Nin enthusiast since the mid-1940's who was personally acquainted with the author, provides detailed analysis of each of her fictional works, including *House of Incest*.

Fitch, Noel Riley. *Anaïs: The Erotic Life of Anaïs Nin*. Boston: Little, Brown, 1993. Fitch offers a thorough account of Nin's life and writing, showing the complex way in which the two were entwined. Special attention is paid to the relationship between Nin and her father, which Fitch believes to have been incestuous. Well referenced, with an excellent bibliography and index.

Franklin, Benjamin V., and Duane Schneider. *Anaïs Nin: An Introduction*. Athens: Ohio University Press, 1979. Provides a basic biography and assessment of Nin's work. Franklin and Schneider believe *House of Incest* to be Nin's finest work of fiction.

Harms, Valerie, ed. *Celebration! With Anaïs Nin*. Riverside, Conn.: Magic Circle Press, 1973. Proceedings from an informal weekend conference involving Nin, various acquaintances, and a variety of fans, all of whom discuss her life and work.

Knapp, Bettina. *Anaïs Nin*. New York: Frederick Ungar, 1978. Provides a sympathetic introduction to and chronology of Nin's life and work. Knapp devotes a chapter to *House of Incest*, linking it to Nin's experience with psychoanalysis.

Nin, Anaïs. *Henry and June: From the Unexpurgated Diary of Anaïs Nin*. San Diego: Harcourt Brace

Jovanovich, 1986. Drawn form Nin's "unexpurgated" diary (earlier versions were edited severely for popular consumption out of consideration for Nin's husband, among others), this volume chronicles Nin's love affairs with Henry and June Miller and was written at about the same time as *House of Incest*. The prominent themes are those of incest, narcissism, psychoanalysis, and dreams.

______________. *Incest—from a Journal of Love: The Unexpurgated Diary of Anaïs Nin, 1932-1934*. New York: Harcourt Brace Jovanovich, 1991. As with *Henry and June*, this volume was extracted from Nin's diary after having originally been heavily edited for publication. Details Nin's relationship with her father when they were reunited just after her thirtieth birthday.

Spencer, Sharon. *Collage of Dreams: The Writing of Anaïs Nin*. Chicago: Swallow Press, 1977. Spencer treats the full range of Nin's work available to her, likening it to the compositions of surrealistic art. Original and accessible.

Ira Smolensky
Marjorie Smolensky

THE HOUSE OF MIRTH

Author: Edith Wharton (1862-1937)
Type of work: Novel
Type of plot: Social realism
Time of plot: The late nineteenth century
Locale: New York City, upper Hudson estates, and Monte Carlo
First published: 1905

Principal characters:

Lily Bart, an unmarried New York socialite in need of a husband
Lawrence Selden, a lawyer and a friend of Lily
Simon Rosedale, a wealthy Jewish capitalist and social climber
Mrs. Peniston, Lily's wealthy but stuffy aunt
Gus Trenor, a wealthy capitalist married to Judy Trenor, who has adopted Lily socially
Mrs. Haffen, an impoverished charwoman
Gerty Farish, Selden's cousin, a poor but respectable philanthropist
Bertha Dorset, Carry Fisher, Mattie Gormer, and **Norma Hatch,** four women of compromised reputations whose parties Lily attends

Form and Content

The House of Mirth is a work of social realism that criticizes a very specific world—that of wealthy, nineteenth century New York society—yet it is also much more than that. It is a moral fable with timeless insight into the problem of finding and keeping clarity of vision in a corrupt culture. The novel also reflects aspects of the feminine experience that are common, in one form or another, to modern Western culture. Lily Bart's moral failures are those of the world in which she lives. Edith Wharton leaves little doubt about her condemnation of that world. She does, however, leave some doubt about her protagonist.

From the very start, Lily both attracts and repels the reader. Her keen sense of independence, her astuteness about what motivates other people, her desire to rise above the petty concerns of those around her—all make her seem like a sound heroine. Yet repeatedly, Lily Bart disappoints the reader by making foolish choices that she seems not to have thought through. She cannot bear to plunge into the values of her social world, blinding herself to their stupidity, but she also fails to pull away from them altogether.

The reason for that failure is basic: money. Having grown up with luxury, with no real sense of how to manage money but a clear sense of how much power comes with having it, Lily wants badly to have a large fortune at her disposal. She has always been led to believe that her beauty alone will suffice to secure her the right marriage proposal, that she need only play the game right. Repeatedly, one finds Lily on the brink of receiving a proposal; each time, she dodges it by committing some minor indiscretion that makes the match impossible. As the indiscretions add up, it becomes increasingly difficult for her to be marketed by her friends. They begin to seek distance from their somewhat tainted acquaintance.

Lily's downward spiral is already hinted at in the novel's first scene, when she unwisely yields to the impulse to take tea in Lawrence Selden's flat. It is a typical move: Morally sound, like all of her indiscretions, it nevertheless breaks the rules of behavior for unmarried women in her set. It also gives two other characters some power over her reputation. A much more far-reaching indiscretion is the acceptance of a loan—disguised as a return on an investment—from Gus Trenor, her friend's husband. This move not only costs her the friendship of her primary protector on the marriage market but also results in the complete (and unjust) destruction of her reputation once it has become known.

Only after Trenor has tried to impose himself on her in the most alarming way does Lily turn to Simon Rosedale, the wealthy Jewish businessman who has long eyed her as a woman who might be the perfect wife to ensure his success in her social set. By this time, however, even Rosedale will not have her. Disinherited by her aunt, penniless, and denounced publicly by Bertha Dorset in most damaging (but again unjust) terms, she struggles to maintain herself as something of a social guide and parasite with a series of unappealing women. Eventually, she leaves that sorry business to try to support herself by working for a milliner.

Near the end of the novel, Lawrence Selden finds her in abject poverty and determines to try to help her. He comes too late: Before he returns to her rooms, she has taken an overdose of chloroform perhaps intentionally. Her death, readers realize, was already implicit in the novel's very first scene. At Selden's flat, Lily has both resisted playing by the rules and failed to find an effective substitute for them. There too, Selden appears to offer a tantalizing, real alternative to the vacuous bridge games of Bellomont, but he seems to fall just short. There, she is seen by the charwoman, who will be something of an emblem of her downfall: all the beautiful gowns and mansions of New York cannot protect her from the basic lowness, mean-spiritedness, and moral bankruptcy of most human beings around her.

Analysis

The House of Mirth is written in third-person narration, largely but not exclusively from Lily Bart's point of view. The narrator has a quick sense of irony, and irony pervades the work, both in its language and in the dramatic juxtapositions of its episodes. For example, the novel opens in New York's Grand Central Station, with Lawrence Selden catching a glimpse of Lily. The narrator notes, "It was characteristic of her that she always roused speculation." Wharton is playing ironically with all the meanings of the word "speculation." Selden, like the reader, is speculating about what Lily Bart's presence means at this moment. He is also, like the other men in the novel, speculating about her value and considering an investment. In a world in which money has such supreme importance, the concept of speculation introduces the range or ironies that the novel repeatedly brings into play.

The final irony may be that readers remain speculative about Lily Bart. The distant, sometimes witty narrator withholds clear judgment. Much of the critical response to the novel has focused on this question. How much is Lily to blame for her downfall? Is she a moral failure or a tragic heroine? Until her final weeks, she is consistently unable to choose between an immoral life of wealth and a rebellious life of morality and intellect, and the waffling costs her everything. Yet there is also some grandeur in her rise to moral superiority as she straightens out her affairs before her death, and critics have sometimes complained that the novel becomes positively sentimental in its closing pages.

One senses, however, that Lily is not fully to blame even for her worst lapses in vision: The choices available to her, as a woman, are few, and the chances to see beyond her world are nonexistent. As a woman in a rarified subculture, she has no opportunity to experience other ways of life and of thinking. Her failures, then, are also the failures of her culture.

It is a culture of speculation, in which money determines value and morality is confined to appearances. Wharton's scathing critique of this social world did not make her well-loved in it, and it should not be surprising that after this novel's immense success she chose to leave New York to live in Europe. Scarcely any character comes out looking good in the moneyed circles of the Trenors, the Dorsets, and the Gryces. Perhaps the one exception is Carry Fisher, a young mother twice divorced who supports herself by helping the nouveaux riches to master the nuances of the elite's social behavior. Some readers have wondered how she has been able to maintain some integrity, when every other character in the novel seems to have been warped by the culture's excessive emphasis on money and appearances. It is a culture in which nearly all live beyond their means and are badly behaved behind closed doors. Reputations rise and fall like (and with) fortunes. Speculation is the apt metaphor for this social world.

Even Lawrence Selden, whom many readers find to be a compelling figure, has major flaws. Recent critics have seen his flaws more clearly, in general, than earlier ones. Wharton's narrator describes him as a "reflective" man, and he seems generally more cultivated and less superficial than the other men in his world.

He has distinctly chosen to stay outside the money game (and the marriage game), preferring his independence on all counts. Yet he also allows his view of Lily to be colored in crucial ways by the questionable values of the culture that he pretends to disdain. At a crucial moment in the plot, he yields to the general suspicions about her reputation and avoids her in a cowardly way. At moments when he might intervene, he fails to, right up to the end. When he finally does arrive on the morning that she has died, the ironies do not end.

Some readers have found that moment to be genuinely tragic, his sentiment for her sincere. Others have thought that on some level he prefers her dead, her beauty a kind of frozen icon, rather than have to engage in life with her and in all the challenges that such a life might represent. In either case, Selden does fail to provide a model for any proper response to the difficulties posed by Lily Bart. He remains a speculator, most aloof and disengaged.

It is precisely that stance of disengagement that the novel seems most incisively to criticize. The world of Lily Bart is a world in which all relationships appear to be transactions, in which as little emotional capital is spent as possible. Most recent critics note at least in passing that this novel's metaphorical language is the language of the marketplace. From the moment in which Selden notes that Lily Bart's beauty must be a real asset to the many relationships in which it becomes clear that running accounts are kept of every debt and gesture, the novel reveals a world in which value is almost never intrinsic. The characters show almost no moral sense; social position is purely a matter of effective manipulation of assets. Lily Bart seeks to rebel against that marketplace—ironically, by scrupulously paying back her debts. As one critic has claimed, that is the least effective form of rebellion, because it is swallowed up in the very marketplace that it seeks to replace. Lily Bart's life and death ultimately appear to have no meaning for her world. Their sense can only be measured in their larger impact on the world beyond the novel.

Context

The House of Mirth was an immediate success when it was published in 1905. It remained on the best-seller list for four months, and its sales became the basis for Edith Wharton's independent fortune. Readers immediately recognized the novel's attack on Old New York. Although some believed that the critique was unjust, more were concerned, ultimately, with its aptness as a subject for art. Despite its commercial triumph, the novel was not viewed as a real aesthetic success. Wharton was viewed as a poor imitation of Henry James, despite all the ways in which she deliberately distances herself from his art. She was also criticized for adopting too high a moral tone and for killing her heroine unnecessarily—two contradictory criticisms, it must be admitted.

Not until after her death in 1937 was Wharton's body of work, and especially *The House of Mirth*, taken seriously as the complex work of art and meditation on modern values most consider it today. It can be seen now as a kind of early feminist response to both James and Gustave Flaubert, whose *Madame Bovary* (1857) it resembles in certain ways. *The House of Mirth* represents most astutely and sympathetically the dilemmas of a woman living in a culture that does not permit her to work and that views her body and her sexuality as her most important capital.

Sources for Further Study

Goodman, Susan. *Edith Wharton's Women: Friends and Rivals*. Hanover, N.H.: University Press of New England, 1990. A study that moves back and forth between Wharton's relationships in life and her fictional characters.

Lauer, Kristin O., and Margaret P. Murray. *Edith Wharton: An Annotated Secondary Bibliography*. New York: Garland, 1990. A useful, extensive, and annotated bibliography of the criticism of Wharton's fiction.

Nevius, Blake. *Edith Wharton: A Study of Her Fiction*. Berkeley: University of California Press, 1953. A landmark study that is still highly regarded. The first book-length study to treat Wharton as a major author.

Wharton, Edith. *The House of Mirth*. Edited by Elizabeth Ammons. New York: W. W. Norton, 1990. This critical edition reprints some key essays about the novel and includes a full text.

______________. *The House of Mirth*. Edited by Shari Benstock. Boston: St. Martin's Press, 1994. This edition offers five essays exemplifying different approaches to the novel, along with introductory essays by the editor, and a useful bibliography.

Sarah Webster Goodwin

HOUSEKEEPING

Author: Marilynne Robinson (1944-)
Type of work: Novel
Type of plot: Allegory
Time of plot: The late 1950's to the early 1960's
Locale: Fingerbone, Idaho
First published: 1980

Principal characters:

Ruth Stone, an awkward adolescent in search of her identity

Lucille Stone, Ruth's younger sister, who wants a conventional lifestyle

Sylvie Foster Fisher, Ruth and Lucille's mysterious aunt, who comes to take care of them

Sylvia Foster, the grandmother of Ruth and Lucille and the mother of Sylvie and Helen

Helen Foster Stone, the mother of Ruth and Lucille and Sylvie's sister

Lily and **Nona Foster,** sisters-in-law to Sylvia Foster

Miss Royce, the home economics teacher who eventually takes in Lucille

Form and Content

Narrated in the first person by Ruth Stone, *Housekeeping* examines a world of female relationships and experience. The sisters, mothers, aunts, and other relatives in the novel form a web of female kinship played out against the tensions of poetic vagrancy and stalwart rootedness. Set in the isolated town of Fingerbone, Idaho, *Housekeeping* reconsiders what it means to inhabit that traditional female space, the home. The book begins with Ruth's description of how her family ended up in the mountains of Idaho.

Edmund Foster, Ruth's maternal grandfather, arrived in Fingerbone, a frustrated artist who saw the world in his own way. Although he is never alive in the book, through the house he built, the objects and art that furnish it, even the decision to locate in Fingerbone, Edmund Foster and his choices conspire to define the physical and emotional space of the women in the novel. While working for the railroad, Edmund disappears with an entire train full of passengers in a spectacular derailment into the icy waters of the lake near Fingerbone. His widow, Sylvia, is left with her three daughters in the small town. For five years after Edmund's death, Sylvia and her daughters Molly, Helen, and Sylvie have lives of self-enclosed contentment. Masculine encroachment, however, claims the young women, one by one—Molly heeding a call from Jesus, Helen marrying Reginald Stone, and Sylvie leaving to visit her married sister and returning only once to her mother's home to marry Mr. Fisher in the garden. Left alone, Sylvia Foster realizes that she had not taught her daughters to be kind to her.

After her marriage fails, Helen returns with her daughters, Ruth and Lucille, to Sylvia's house in Fingerbone. Without explanation, Helen leaves the girls with Sylvia and drives the car that she borrowed from a friend in Seattle into the lake that claimed her father. Stunned by this event, Sylvia nevertheless manages to provide a good home for her granddaughters for the next five years. When Sylvia dies, her unmarried sisters-in-law, Lily and Nona Foster, come to care for the girls, but they are ill-prepared for parenting and constantly fearful of imagined disasters. By the end of the first two chapters, all biological mothers are dead and all fathers are absent. Sylvie, contacted by letter, arrives to care for Ruth and Lucille and free the unhappy Foster sisters. Sylvie, who has been living as a vagrant, is poised to take up both housekeeping and mothering.

Sylvie's notions about homemaking are unconventional, and after the girls discover that their aunt can add little to their store of information about their mother, Ruth and Lucille themselves begin a slow drift away from the society of Fingerbone. Frightened at the direction that their lives seem to be taking, Lucille attempts various schemes—such as dressmaking—to get back to a more mainstream lifestyle. Sylvie continues to inhabit her own world, occasionally including Ruth in some of her ventures, and the two grow closer. As Ruth and Sylvie become more alike, Lucille becomes determined to reenter what she considers the "real world." After several attempts to include Ruth in her plans, Lucille finally gives up and parts from her sister, though not without reluctance. Lucille cannot and will not live in Sylvie's dreams, and she moves in with her home economics teacher, Miss Royce.

After Lucille leaves, Sylvie takes Ruth on a journey onto the islands in the lake outside Fingerbone. Stealing a leaky rowboat, the two row over to a mysterious valley of abandoned and decaying houses, where Sylvie proposes they "watch for the children." Sylvie suddenly leaves Ruth in the cool, misty valley in a test or initiation into the world of transience to which Sylvie wishes to return. Left alone to muse over the unfamiliar landscape and her own losses, Ruth comes to terms somewhat with the loss of her mother, Helen. Cradled in the folds of the long coat that Sylvie wears, Ruth is reborn as a child of her mysteriously returned aunt.

The two return to Fingerbone by boat and freight train, where they are spotted by several townspeople. As a result, the sheriff comes to the house—the only living male to breach their space—to warn Sylvie that she cannot continue to care for Ruth in such a haphazard manner. Sylvie tries to conform to the notions of the town and its church women, but she is not able to persuade them of any change in her ability to "keep house." Thus, Ruth and Sylvie abandon housekeeping and any notion of permanence by setting fire to the house and fleeing Fingerbone by crossing the train trestle spanning the lake. The book ends with Ruth imaging Lucille in Boston waiting for them and the others who will not come and who are known only by their absence.

Analysis

Marilynne Robinson's lyrical first novel is concerned with mothering, female space, and cultural myths concerning mothering and family. The book suggests that in rejecting conventional norms of "housekeeping," women might gain autonomy, by embracing the transience of persons, events, and even memory rather than futile attempts at permanence. These themes are underscored by Robinson's major metaphor, water.

Water in its many forms flows throughout the work. The lake, for example, is the repository of the town's major event—the derailment of the Fireball—and of several Foster family members, including Edmund, Helen, and supposedly, Sylvie and Ruth. Like memory, the lake swallows up whole that which enters it, and surprising artifacts emerge—such as the suitcase, the seat cushion, and the cabbage—as the only tangible evidence of an event such as the derailment. Also, like memory, the boundaries of the lake are unreliable. Every spring, parts of the lake long forgotten rise up from the earth and flood Fingerbone, including the Fosters' orchard and house. Water inhabits the house and takes it over. Sylvie and Ruth row across the water to "watch for children" and, at the end of the novel, must cross the bridge over the lake to escape the confines of Fingerbone. Water appears in the forms of snow, ice, rain, mist, and frost throughout *Housekeeping*.

The Foster family home is another important element in the book. Its location on the edge of a town that itself is at the edge of a lake follows the Foster family tradition of being on the edge or fringe of things. Also, being close to the edge of town makes the house easier for Sylvie and Ruth to abandon. The presence of light and dark both within and without the house is noteworthy, as are the windows of the house. Ruth "spends too much time looking out of windows," which can be either mirrors or barriers to the world of possibilities. When Sylvie does attempt to "keep house," she does so by opening doors and windows to let the air in, and it does not occur to Sylvie to close either, so much of the outdoors comes indoors. When the house burns and Ruth and Sylvie escape across the bridge, the windows shatter with loud retorts. Lucille, who turns on the lights in the darkened house, also abandons "keeping house" in the sense that she leaves the Foster home. She moves in with her home economics teacher, however, and presumably will be adequately trained in the proper ways to keep house and shut windows at appropriate times.

The importance of names is constant throughout the novel. Ruth and Lucille are cared for by a series of "Foster" mothers until they are able to act on their own (Lucille to leave for a conventional life and Ruth to drift). Sylvie's married last name is Fisher, suggesting her connections to water, drifting, and perhaps Christ (in that she redeems Ruth). Helen, whose name suggests the mythical Helen of Troy, marries Reginald Stone, and like a stone, sinks to the bottom of the lake. Ruth's name—which she announces with a Melvillian directness ("My name is Ruth") in the first sentence of the book—has obvious biblical implications, while Lucille's name is never shortened. The name Sylvia brings to mind both a "sylph," a slender, graceful young woman, and "sylvan," one who frequents groves or woods. Even the name of the town, Fingerbone, has implications suggesting its insignificance and something perhaps not worth keeping.

Context

In *Housekeeping*, Robinson's protagonists Sylvie and Ruth abandon ownership of one of the objects most closely associated with defining women—the home. Instead of a traditional, functional nuclear family, Robinson presents readers with a family made only of women. Through death, fear, choice, or fate, these women are quite ready either to walk from or at least (even if only for a short while, as in the case of Lucille) to consider rethinking the whole project of "keeping" house. Transience, usually associated with male protagonists, is introduced as a possibility. Ideas about mothering and nurturing are also reexamined in *Housekeeping*.

For example, the woman who is a childless drifter—Sylvie—is the one most able to "mother" Ruth and Lucille while maintaining a somewhat autonomous existence herself. Judged by conventional middle-class American expectations, however, Sylvie is viewed as a failure at mothering. The women from the town and church visiting with casseroles and inquiries are appalled by what they find to be Sylvie's mode of acceptable housekeeping. The women call in the authorities in the form of the local sheriff who offers to take Ruth home with him. She refuses, and that night, with Sylvie, burns the house down, aunt and niece almost as one in their actions and intent.

It is when their Adamless Eden is invaded that the pretense of housekeeping, with all of its layers of meaning, totally falls apart. Robinson's point seems to be that women are certainly capable of making and inhabiting their own niches which do not have to be part of the patriarchal structure and that women are capable of walking away and abandoning that which has imprisoned them. Unlike previous female protagonists, Sylvie and Ruth do not suffer the traditional literary endings of marriage, madness, or death. Instead, like Mark Twain's Huck and Jim, they "light out for the territory." The choice is not without danger, but it is preferable to the slow suffocation offered by maintaining the fictions of housekeeping. As portrayed by Robinson, transience by choice is a poetic and viable alternative.

Winner of the Ernest Hemingway Foundation award for best first novel and the Richard and Hinda Rosenthal Award from the American Academy of Arts and Letters, *Housekeeping* also received nominations for the Pen/Faulkner fiction award and for a Pulitzer Prize. Robinson's evocative prose and persistent yet gentle characters combine to question the value of an enterprise supposedly entrenched within the cultural myths surrounding women.

Sources for Further Study

Aldrich, Marcia. "The Poetics of Transience: Marilynne Robinson's *Housekeeping*." *Essays in Literature* 5, no. 16 (Spring, 1989): 127-140. An in-depth discussion of the meaning of transience in relation to female choices and as a specifically female experience. This article also discusses mother-daughter relationships in *Housekeeping*.

Booth, Allyson. "To Capture Absent Bodies: Marilynne Robinson's *Housekeeping*." *Essays in Literature* 5, no. 19 (Fall, 1992): 279-290. A provocative study of how metaphors of the body inform the novel. Includes a worthwhile discussion of some of the images and symbols in the book, such as the dresser painted by Edmund and other objects.

Champagne, Rosaria. "Women's History and *Housekeeping*: Memory, Representation, and Reinscription." *Women's Studies* 20, no. 3/4 (1992): 321-329. This essay considers how memory functions in the novel, as well as examining competing definitions as to what "good" housekeeping is within the parameters of the work.

Foster, Thomas. "History, Critical Theory, and Women's Social Practices: Women's Time and *Housekeeping*." *Signs* 14, no. 11 (1988): 73-99. Applies theories of deconstruction to *Housekeeping*. Also considers issues of how historical approaches to the public and private spheres of women and their roles are useful in thinking about the novel.

Meese, Elizabeth A. *Crossing the Double Cross: The Practice of Feminist Criticism*. Chapel Hill: University of North Carolina Press, 1986. An excellent study of feminist criticism, lucid and well written. Includes an informative chapter on *Housekeeping* that views the novel as "A World of Women."

Saltzman, Arthur M. *The Novel in the Balance*. Columbia: University of South Carolina Press, 1993. A useful and in-depth look at several modern novels, including *Housekeeping*. Offers the interesting juxtaposition of *Housekeeping* with John Hawkes's *Second Skin* (1964), Hawkes being one of Robinson's early mentors.

Virginia Dumont-Poston

HOW TO SUPPRESS WOMEN'S WRITING

Author: Joanna Russ (1937-)
Type of work: Literary criticism
First published: 1983

Form and Content

In this witty analysis of the critical reception of women's literature, Nebula Award-winning science-fiction writer Joanna Russ explores the social connections of literature and art from a feminist perspective. Russ stresses that her discussion is not a history of oppression; rather, it is an investigation of the ways in which women's writing has been suppressed, discouraged, and marginalized.

How to Suppress Women's Writing traces patterns in the suppression of women's writing, mostly by male critics, drawing on examples from high culture of the eighteenth through twentieth centuries in Europe and the United States. Russ uses the examples of such diverse literary figures as the Countess of Winchelsea, Aphra Behn, Emily and Charlotte Brontë, George Sand, Emily Dickinson, and Anne Sexton to show how societal conditions and expectations are brought to bear on the work of women writers. Russ also provides illustrations of artists and musicians to support her argument.

In her analysis of women's literary marginalization, Russ draws heavily on the work of other feminist critics, especially Ellen Moers, Elaine Showalter, and Virginia Woolf. The text begins with a prologue in which Russ uses her science-fiction background to create an alien society in order to draw a parallel with the earthly conditions about which she is concerned. Each succeeding chapter addresses one of the patterns of marginalization that Russ has identified, explaining how the pattern works to suppress women's creativity and giving many examples, both historical and contemporary, to support her argument. Chapters at the end of the text address literary women's response to their suppression (including Russ's own); a call for a redefinition of cultural aesthetics, which would move culture away from the center toward the margin; and the voices of women of color, who are often excluded from the literary canon.

Analysis

While admitting that women have not been subject to formal prohibitions against writing, as were black slaves in America, Russ nevertheless asserts that the informal prohibitions of poverty, lack of leisure, lack of education, and "climate of expectation"—the belief in traditional gender roles, which placed women in the home—were instrumental in preventing women from writing. Many women, particularly in the nineteenth century, were financially dependent on their families or their husbands; their household duties as either daughters or wives left them little if any time to write; and if they still expressed a willingness to create literature, the pressure of gender roles was brought to bear upon them—artistic creativity was a masculine ability not to be attempted by women.

Most of the text, however, is devoted to an identification and analysis of the practice of what Russ calls "bad faith," a term borrowed from philosopher Jean-Paul Sartre. One displays bad faith by perpetuating the status quo in order to maintain discrimination. Women who insist on writing despite informal prohibitions are met with one or more of the following patterns of bad faith: denial of agency, pollution of agency, double standard of content, false categorizing, isolation, and anomalousness.

Denial of agency is used to refute a particular woman's claim of authorship by asserting that the work in question was written by a man, that the text wrote itself, that the "masculine" part of the woman did the writing, or that the woman writer is "more than a woman." Mary Shelley, for example, is denied authorship of *Frankenstein* (1818) by a male critic who asserts that she was simply a repository of ideas that were circulating "in the air around her." Similarly, critics generally agree that Emily Brontë lost control of *Wuthering Heights* (1847) and wrote an entirely different novel than she had intended (that is, a "good" one).

Pollution of agency calls into play traditional gender

roles; a woman who writes is unfeminine, ridiculous, or immoral. *Jane Eyre* (1847), published pseudonymously by Charlotte Brontë, was judged by critics to be a masterpiece if written by a man, degrading if written by a woman. Russ contends that the designation of much twentieth century poetry by women as confessional, or highly personal and therefore shameful, is a contemporary version of the nineteenth century charge of impropriety against women writers.

The double standard of content privileges male experience over female experience and renders women's lives and experience invisible. Russ points out that critical assessment of *Wuthering Heights* changed from positive to negative after Emily Brontë's authorship (and gender) became known, and in *A Room of One's Own* (1929), Virginia Woolf notes that books which deal with war are judged to be more important than books about domestic life.

False categorizing occurs when women's artistic and literary contributions are subsumed under or eclipsed by men's. For example, the composer Gustav Mahler forbade his wife to write music even though she had been a composer before their marriage. Also included under the pattern of false categorizing is the renaming of women's literature so as to exclude it from serious critical consideration. Thus, Willa Cather and Kate Chopin are called "regionalists" in order to emphasize the limited scope of their works, or writing by women is rendered inferior because it does not occur in acceptable or "literary" genres, such as novels or poetry, but in "inferior" forms, such as letters or diaries. False categorization also includes the marginalization of women authors through biographical readings of their works in which traditional women's roles are assigned to them; these roles then become the lens through which their works are read. Elizabeth Barrett Browning, for example, becomes the Wife (therefore her political and feminist poems are ignored in favor of her love poetry) and Emily Dickinson is the madcap/sad spinster.

If a woman is admitted to the literary canon, Russ argues that she is subject to isolation, the pattern by which only one of her works is recognized and her others are ignored. The work that is chosen for inclusion is generally one which supports stereotypical notions of women's artistic abilities. Therefore, Browning's *Sonnets from the Portuguese* (1850) (her love poems) are frequently anthologized; *Aurora Leigh* (1856) (her feminist "epic novel") is not. Isolation also occurs when the work of a woman writer is "recategorized" and then marginalized. Woolf, for example, is frequently criticized for her elitist attitudes when, in fact, her essays were depoliticized by her husband after her death.

When a woman writer is admitted to the literary canon, she also suffers from what Russ calls anomalousness. The relatively low percentage of women writers included in literary anthologies (the average is 7 percent) obscures the notion of a tradition of women writers and strengthens the assumption that women do not belong in the male literary tradition. Anomalousness is also used to justify an individual woman's personal eccentricity. Dickinson, for example, is treated as an isolated spinster whose talent "came from nowhere and bore no relation to anything." Russ declares anomalousness to be the most powerful means of marginalizing women, for if the literary canon were opened to include a tradition of women writers, the possibility of other marginalized groups would also have to be entertained, and aesthetic standards would have to be revised.

The remaining chapters of *How to Suppress Women's Writing* discuss the effects of these patterns of bad faith on women writers and potential women writers. The resulting marginalization of women and their texts deprives women writers of a sense of a woman's tradition in literature; it deprives them of models, so that each new generation of women writers must invent its own tradition and find its own models.

Women respond to the challenges presented by these patterns of marginalization in several ways: They do not write; they agree that women writers are inferior to male writers; they deny that they are women; they assert that they are not "ordinary" women; they become angry; or they shift their focus to "woman centeredness," or a concern with other women. The work of feminist literary critics has led to the questioning of an absolute set of aesthetic values. Russ's solution to the problem is to propose aesthetic criteria that allow many centers of value, each based on historical fact. Therefore, in formulating a more inclusive set of aesthetic standards, one must move away from the center.

How to Suppress Women's Writing concludes with the author's confession of her own difficulties in visualizing the margin. She relates her reassessment of the work of Zora Neale Hurston and other black women writers, which she had always considered to be "different" and therefore not "literary," and concludes the text with excerpts from writing by women of color, including Audre Lorde, Rosario Morales, Maxine Hong Kingston, and June Jordan.

Context

The humor in *How to Suppress Women's Writing* makes the text amusing and easy to read (the title itself makes the text sound like a handbook for insecure male critics), but Russ's humorous tone throughout masks her serious intent. Like many feminists, Russ uses humor to cushion the impact of her sharp social criticism. This is a scholarly text—each chapter contains a minimum of fifteen footnotes—but its contribution to the field of feminist criticism is not so much in the research, which is largely derivative, but in Russ's ability to relate the social and material conditions under which women live to the art that they create. Thus, *How to Suppress Women's Writing* represents an important movement in feminist literary criticism away from a preoccupation with images of women in literature toward a broader consideration of the impact of society on the production of art. The text tends to emphasize the victimization of women writers over their obvious successes in circumventing suppression, but the reader gains important insight into the ways in which the institutionalization of gender bias can influence what literature is read, how literature is read, and what constitutes the meaning of "literature" and "author."

How to Suppress Women's Writing is also important for its insistence on an alternative, more inclusive definition of culture which would include literature and art judged by standards other than the traditional Western, white, middle-class, and male orientation.

Sources for Further Study

Gilbert, Sandra M., and Susan Gubar. *The Madwoman in the Attic: The Woman Writer and the Nineteenth-Century Literary Imagination*. New Haven, Conn.: Yale University Press, 1979. This wide-ranging and groundbreaking work examines the responses of nineteenth century writers to the male-dominated literary tradition in England. Psychologically rather than socially oriented, this text traces a female tradition in literature.

Poovey, Mary. *Uneven Developments: The Ideological Work of Gender in Mid-Victorian England*. Chicago: University of Chicago Press, 1988. Poovey's work is a sophisticated extension of the social perspective used by Russ. In it, she argues that nineteenth century representations of gender were sites of struggle for power and authority between the genders and reads such texts as Charles Dickens' *David Copperfield* (1849-1850) and *Jane Eyre* from this position.

Showalter, Elaine. *A Literature of Their Own: British Women Novelists from Brontë to Lessing*. Princeton, N.J.: Princeton University Press, 1977. A text from which Russ derives much of the support for her study, this book is one of the first analyses of a woman's tradition in literature. Like Russ, Showalter uses a social and literary approach as she compares women novelists to their female contemporaries in order to trace the complexity of women's literary relationships.

Spender, Dale, ed. *Living by the Pen: Early British Women Writers*. New York: Teachers College Press, 1992. This collection of essays traces the literary heritage of early British women writers in order to distinguish that tradition from the male tradition. Includes essays on the women themselves, the topics on which they wrote, and their achievements as artists.

Todd, Janet. *Feminist Literary History*. New York: Routledge, 1988. In this introduction to feminist literary theory, Todd seeks to defend the early sociohistoric enterprise of American feminist criticism, of which Russ's text is an example. She refutes the claim of French feminists that this criticism is historically naïve and, while admitting its limitations, attempts to place it within a larger context of feminist literary criticism.

Karen Volland Waters

THE HUNGRY SELF: Women, Eating, and Identity

Author: Kim Chernin (1940-)
Type of work: Social criticism
First published: 1985

Form and Content

Emerging from the intersection of female identity and the prevalence of eating disorders among American women, *The Hungry Self: Women, Eating, and Identity* asks why so many women have a troubled relationship with food. In answering this question, Kim Chernin draws upon her work counseling women suffering from bulimia and anorexia. She argues that underlying women's obsession with food are the basic components of a rite of passage, the elements of a transition from one stage of life to the next. The problem of food thus becomes its failure as such a rite, its inability to enable women to move from one stage of life to another.

Throughout the book, Chernin recounts the stories that women have told her about the place of food in their lives. These are stories of obsession, descriptions of the compulsion to exercise, to ingest huge quantities of food and then vomit, and to allow calorie-counting to disrupt normal activities and behavior. Furthermore, as Chernin delves more deeply into women's stories, she explains how the problem of food cloaks a more fundamental problem of identity. Her thesis is that at a time when women are encouraged to forgo traditional feminine pursuits, eating disorders appear as sites for the struggle over the meaning and validity of female identity. In other words, an eating disorder signifies an identity crisis.

For example, some women develop eating disorders when turning to a new career after having spent a number of years mothering and caring for husbands and children. Others, generally younger and preprofessional, the first generation of women socialized to expect career and educational opportunities, take on the styles and manners of the group in power—men. These young women seek to rid themselves of the flesh that makes them feminine and often adopt the men's-wear look encouraged by the media. Both groups, the older as well as the younger women, are conflicted about their identities as women.

At the heart of this conflict, Chernin argues, is the relationship between mothers and daughters. Extending Betty Friedan's discussion in *The Feminine Mystique* (1963), she observes the change in the societal understanding of motherhood in America in the middle of the twentieth century. Whereas previous generations of women could find fulfillment in carrying out their natural duties to be good wives and mothers, once the "naturalness" of these roles came under scrutiny, a number of women could no longer see their self-sacrifice as serving a larger purpose or order. Once motherhood became a choice, the only reason to devote oneself to mothering was personal fulfillment.

Unfortunately, many women did not find the day-in, day-out work of housekeeping and child rearing especially fulfilling. Consequently, these women communicated this dissatisfaction to their daughters. As daughters have grown into adulthood, moreover, many of them have been reluctant to accept the opportunities and advantages denied to their mothers. Eating disorders emerge, in part, out of this sense of guilt. Feeling as if their mothers' lives were "shrunken," "impoverished," or "depleted," daughters act out these sufferings upon their own bodies, symbolically playing out the mother-daughter bond so as to save the mother.

This "playing out" tends to take on the character of a rite of passage. Analogizing the behavior of contemporary American girls with the tribal rituals described by Mircea Eliade in *Rites and Symbols of Initiation: The Mysteries of Birth and Rebirth* (1958), Chernin convincingly describes the retreat to infancy, separation, and dietary prohibitions common among female adolescents as aspects of a transition from one stage of life to another. She provides a stark and often shocking discussion of the social aspects of bingeing and purging on college campuses: Some girls, perhaps athletes or sorority members, engage in collective eating sprees; once they have eaten more than they can possibly hold, they may take turns vomiting or all purge themselves together. As they transform the traditional elements of ritual into an obsessive ritualization involving food and the body, eating disorders take on the functions of a rite of passage. Food becomes the vehicle for the daughter's separation from her mother: The daughter both takes control of what she eats and bonds with the girls around her through food rituals. Additionally, the preoccupation of food reconnects the daughter to her mother: Like her mother, the daughter, too, is engaging in food preparation.

Chernin concludes that women need to develop new rituals. As women take on different cultural roles, they have to find new, more authentic modes of transformation. She suggests that, in part, the new type of transition will require a revaluation of the work of mothers and a renewed investment of meaning in the rituals of food preparation that embody appreciation and forgiveness rather than obsession and guilt.

Analysis

In writing *The Hungry Self*, Chernin claims for eating the same sort of significance that Sigmund Freud and other psychoanalysts have found in sexuality. Like sexuality, eating is both a fundamental aspect of human existence and an activity with deeply symbolic meaning. Thus, just as Freud's work considers neurosis in the light of infantile memories and the cultural import of ancient and mythic rites and rituals, so does *The Hungry Self* analyze anorexia and bulimia with regard to early childhood experiences and tribal initiatory practices signifying the passage into adulthood. By linking the particular psychological experiences of individual women with larger societal issues involving the acceptance and inclusion of women as full participants in society, Chernin is able to provide a rich analysis of the epidemic of eating disorders disabling so many contemporary women.

Chernin describes the societal dimensions of eating disorders in stark terms. Using various studies from 1982, she estimates the number of girls and women suffering from anorexia and bulimia to range from one in a hundred between the ages of sixteen and eighteen and one in five college-age women. Given the vast number of women suffering from an obsession with food, weight, and body image, Chernin argues for the necessity of looking beyond each individual story to discover the larger social causes for this epidemic. Beginning in the 1970's and 1980's, women have been given more options, and pressures, than ever before: They are now able to move from the home into society at large. Yet many still find themselves feeling empty and confused, unsure of who they are and unable to turn to their mothers as role models in this new world. Thus, Chernin claims that women's eating disorders are not simply personal dilemmas, but a larger societal problem occasioned by women's ability to take on the rights and prerogatives of men.

Chernin neither belittles this advancement nor urges a return to traditional domesticity. Rather, she reads the messages of media and culture as signaling to women the need to be like men if they are to succeed in the workplace. Accordingly, the tight, muscular masculine body is more valued than the fleshy, maternal curves of feminine bodies. Not surprisingly, then, many young women attempt to rid themselves of the flesh that signifies their womanliness in an effort to measure up in this male-centered world. In yet another twist, however, the media also glorifies a particular image of femininity. In the bedroom, women are instructed to be sensual and seductive, garbing themselves in lingerie that reveals large breasts and lean, flat stomachs. The tension between the two messages traps women, giving them conflicting models of female identity.

Turning to the psychological level, a shift that some critics have found in need of further explication, Chernin locates even deeper sources for the epidemic of eating disorders in the relationship between mothers and daughters. Drawing from the work of the psychoanalyst Melanie Klein, Chernin explains the way in which infants experience both intense rage toward and a fierce attachment to their mothers. On the one hand, the mother is the source of food, whether from the breast or from the bottle. On the other hand, the child's sucking may take on a violent character, a way of expressing and acting out frustration and aggression. No matter how angry the infant becomes, the mother remains whole and comforting. As the child develops and begins to separate from the mother, however, her failings may seem to be the result of the infant's rage. For example, the child being weaned may come away with the impression of having sucked the mother dry, depleting her. The mother is no longer magically all-protective, but a human woman harassed by the inconveniences and inequities of daily life. The child thus finds that her own development required the diminishment of her mother.

Although boys also experience oral aggression toward their mothers, they do not develop the same debilitating sense of guilt that later plagues so many girls. Chernin explains this difference with reference to the gendered nature of child-rearing practices. From an early age, boys are taught that they are like their fathers and that, as men, they will have the same freedoms and opportunities. In contrast, girls are offered an ideal of self-sacrifice. Reared to identify with their mothers, they are given to expect that they, too, will become mothers and hence must forfeit any plans of their own for the sake of marriage and family. Thus, when as adolescents girls are told that they need not make the same sacrifices as their mothers, they face a complex developmental problem. Should they choose an independent path of their own, they reenact the separation and depletion of the mother of infancy. Should they accept the maternal role, they make of themselves the food sacrifice their mothers were to them.

While the psychoanalytic dimensions of Chernin's discussion are not always convincing, her ability to link eating disorders with deeper societal and psychological issues provides an innovative way of considering anorexia and bulimia. Once these terrible disorders are exposed as aspects of an identity crisis experienced by many women, although in perhaps less damaging ways, it becomes possible to think more clearly about the way in which feminine identity develops now and the way it might emerge in the future.

Context

Kim Chernin's *The Hungry Self* is an important contribution to the understanding of the developmental issues particular to female identity. Perhaps more important, it is a shocking exposé of the horrors of eating disorders, both as aspects of a widespread phenomenon in American society and as deeply personal obsessions with food and weight. As one of the earliest nontechnical, book-length studies of anorexia and bulimia, it affected the way in which many women think about their own relationship to their bodies. Whereas previous feminist analyses of development had stressed sexuality, Chernin reminds her readers that while many contemporary women are comfortable expressing and acting upon their sexual desire, the vast majority of women experience deep guilt and ambivalence with regard to food. Eating is the new sin, the taboo to be secretly enjoyed and later absolved through penitential rituals. *The Hungry Self* further develops arguments and ideas Chernin raised in her book *The Obsession: Reflections on the Tyranny of Slenderness* (1981).

Sources for Further Study

Bordo, Susan. *Unbearable Weight: Feminism, Western Culture, and the Body.* Berkeley: University of California Press, 1993. A collection of critical essays exploring problems of the body for women. Includes discussions of anorexia, slenderness, and body image with reference to and elaboration on Chernin's work.

Brumberg, Joan Jacobs. *Fasting Girls: The Emergence of Anorexia Nervosa as a Modern Disease.* Cambridge, Mass.: Harvard University Press, 1988. An account of the scope and dimensions of anorexia, with attention to the historical context of the disease.

Bynum, Caroline Walker. *Holy Feast and Holy Fast: The Religious Significance of Food to Medieval Women.* Berkeley: University of California Press, 1987. An important discussion of fasting and other food rituals for medieval women. Contains an index and extensive notes.

Spitzack, Carole. *Confessing Excess: Women and the Politics of Body Reduction.* Albany: State University of New York Press, 1990. An analysis of contemporary dieting and weight loss literature which draws upon Chernin's work.

Wolf, Naomi. *The Beauty Myth.* London: Chatto & Windus, 1990. A general discussion of the media images of an ideal femininity. Draws upon Chernin's discussion of eating disorders and body image, providing later statistical data confirming the epidemic proportions of these problems. Includes a helpful bibliography.

Jodi Dean

I KNOW WHY THE CAGED BIRD SINGS

Author: Maya Angelou (Marguerite Johnson, 1928-   )
Type of work: Autobiography
Time of work: 1931-1945
Locale: Stamps, Arkansas; St. Louis, Missouri; and Los Angeles and San Francisco, California
First published: 1970

Principal personages:

Maya Angelou, a poet and author who recounts her life from ages three to sixteen years
Bailey Johnson, Jr., Angelou's older brother and closest childhood friend
Mrs. Annie Henderson, called Momma, their paternal grandmother
Mrs. Bertha Flowers, a teacher who inspires Angelou to read poetry
Uncle Willie, their father's crippled brother
Mrs. Vivian Baxter, Maya and Bailey's mother
Bailey Johnson, Sr., Maya and Bailey's father
Grandmother Baxter, Maya and Bailey's maternal grandmother
Mr. Freeman, Vivian Baxter's boyfriend, who rapes Angelou
Daddy Clidell, Maya's stepfather

Form and Content

Maya Angelou's autobiography *I Know Why the Caged Bird Sings* tells her story: that of a Southern black girl moved from place to place, along with her brother Bailey, after their parents' divorce. The book is divided into thirty-six chapters and begins with a vignette, a sketch of the young Maya trying unsuccessfully to recite an Easter poem in church. She cannot remember the words. "Peeing and crying" in fear, she flees the church and concludes, "If growing up is painful for the Southern Black girl, being aware of her displacement is the rust on the razor that threatens the throat. It is an unnecessary insult." With this cultural setting, Angelou shifts to Long Beach, California, in 1931, where Maya and Bailey Johnson, Jr., ages three and four, are being sent by train to the home of their paternal grandmother, Mrs. Annie Henderson (called Momma), in Stamps, Arkansas. From there, the chapters are arranged chronologically and geographically, following Angelou's youth to the age of sixteen and the displacements of the children—to Stamps, to St. Louis, back to Stamps, to Los Angeles, and finally, to San Francisco. Along with the geographical displacements are familial displacements, as Angelou lives with her parents, with Momma and Uncle Willie, with her mother and Mr. Freeman, with Grandmother Baxter, with her father and his girlfriend, and with her mother and stepfather, Daddy Clidell.

Angelou wrote *I Know Why the Caged Bird Sings* after several requests from Random House publishers. Though it is an autobiography, it is also an exploration of survival. In a 1983 interview, Angelou says,

> When I wrote *I Know Why the Caged Bird Sings*, I wasn't thinking so much about my own life and identity. I was thinking about a particular time in which I lived and the influences of that time on a number of people. I kept thinking, what about that time? What were the people around young Maya doing? I used the central figure—myself—as a focus to show how one person can make it through those times.

Angelou talks about her survival as a black Southern girl in a society that devalues her beauty, talent, and ambition.

She contends that all of her work is "about survival." The sketches in *I Know Why the Caged Bird Sings* support her contention. Although parts of the book are humorous, such as the revival scene in chapter 6, when Sister Monroe knocks out Reverend Thomas' false teeth, many of the sketches deal with painful struggles for survival, such as the encounter between Momma and the racist white dentist who will not treat Angelou and the rape of the eight-year-old Maya.

In 1979, when Angelou was adapting *I Know Why*

the Caged Bird Sings for film, she became keenly aware of the story line. She described it as "very delicate." It is the story of surviving both racism and childhood, and it culminates in a scene of the sixteen-year-old Angelou, having recently been graduated from high school, lying in bed and snuggling close to her three-week-old son, the result of a brief and loveless encounter with a teenage boy. Angelou's second autobiographical novel, *Gather Together in My Name* (1974), takes the story from there.

Analysis

I Know Why the Caged Bird Sings, its title taken from Paul Laurence Dunbar's poem "Sympathy," is an autobiographical story of survival. The vignettes, held together by time, place, and narrator, are joyous, angry, fearful, and desperate, but not bitter.

One of the most desperate and fearful events in the book is the account of Mr. Freeman raping the eight-year-old Maya. Angelou's candid narrative explores her childhood desire to be loved and her pain and horror at the psychological and physical violation of the rape. Mr. Freeman threatens to kill Bailey if Maya tells what she and Mr. Freeman did. By using the words "what we did," Mr. Freeman makes her feel responsible for his actions. When Bailey realizes that Mr. Freeman has somehow hurt his sister, he convinces her that Mr. Freeman, who has moved out of the house, can no longer hurt them. Trusting Bailey's judgment, she tells him about the rape. Angelou is hospitalized, Mr. Freeman is arrested, and the family comes to her aid. Bailey sits by her hospital bed and cries, her mother brings flowers and candy, Grandmother Baxter brings fruit, and her uncles clump around her bed and snort "like wild horses." After Mr. Freeman is sentenced to "one year and one day," his lawyer gets him released. Later he is "found dead on the lot behind the slaughterhouse," where his body has been dumped; he appears to have been kicked to death. Angelou, feeling responsible for Mr. Freeman's death, remains a mute until she is thirteen years old.

Angelou is often asked why she put the rape scene in *I Know Why the Caged Bird Sings*. In a 1983 interview, she said that she "wanted people to see that the man was not totally an ogre. The hard thing about writing or directing or producing is to make sure one doesn't make the negative person totally negative. I try to tell the truth and preserve it in all artistic forms." Angelou's profile of Mr. Freeman is, in fact, complex. Angelou also candidly explores, through this rape, the feelings of guilt in victims. In a 1987 interview, she said that guilt is still part of the victim's burden. Referring to child rape, she concluded that "the victim, especially if you are a member of a depressed class or gender or sex, is loaded with the guilt for that action against herself or himself." Nowhere else in *I Know Why the Caged Bird Sings* do the fear and desperation in survival surface more painfully. Nevertheless, Angelou consistently rejects bitterness as a response to pain, fear, and despair. She maintains that bitterness destroys the bitter person but has no effect on the object of the bitterness.

Connected to the theme of survival are flights from danger and searches for sanctuary. Ironically, the opening vignette shows Angelou fleeing the church, a traditional sanctuary, and seeking safety at home, where she knows that a beating awaits her. Again, when the teenage Maya flees her father's violent girlfriend, she seeks safety in the streets. An implied theme is that church and home, traditional sanctuaries, can fail and that survival depends on individual strength. In her journey to adulthood, Angelou comes to realize that her survival rests on believing in her own value, regardless of the low value that her culture places on her race and gender.

Context

In a 1973 interview, Maya Angelou was referred to as a Renaissance woman. The term is apt: She is an author of nonfiction, drama, and poetry; a stage and screen performer; a nightclub singer; a dancer; a producer; an editor; a television host of documentaries and educational films; a university teacher; and a social and political activist. Surviving her childhood rape, institutionalized racism, a teenage pregnancy, and, later, prostitution, Angelou emerged as a voice in American literature and politics.

In addition to her many honorary degrees, Angelou has received numerous other awards. In 1954 and 1955, Angelou, participating in *Porgy and Bess*, was sponsored by the United States Department of State to tour twenty-two countries. In 1959 and 1960, Angelou was appointed Northern Coordinator for the Southern Christian Leadership Conference. In 1970, *I Know Why the Caged Bird Sings* was nominated for a National Book Award. In 1972, Angelou became the first black woman to have an original script produced, and the same year, she received a Pulitzer Prize nomination for her poetry collection *Just Give Me a Cool Drink of Water 'fore I Diiie* (1971). She received a Tony nomination in 1973. In 1975, President Gerald R. Ford appointed her to the American Revolution Bicentennial Council. Angelou was named Woman of the Year in 1976 by the *Ladies' Home Journal*. In 1977, she was named by President Jimmy Carter to the National Commission on the Observance of International Women's Year. Also in 1977, she received another Tony nomination, and she received the Golden Eagle award from the Public Broadcasting System for her documentary series *Afro-American in the Arts*. In 1982, she received a lifetime appointment as Reynold's Professor of American Studies at Wake Forest University in Winston-Salem, North Carolina. (This appointment, which lets her teach any subject in the humanities, is usually for two to five years. In an interview, Angelou remarked that her lifetime appointment "didn't sit well with some of the white male professors.") In 1984 and 1985, Angelou was appointed by Governor James B. Hunt to the Board of the North Carolina Arts Council. In 1992, Angelou accepted an invitation from President Bill Clinton to compose and read a poem at his inauguration.

Through these experiences, Angelou has continually reexamined her views, discarding those that she no longer accepts. For example, in her early years as a writer, Angelou called herself a "womanist" rather than a "feminist," because she believed that feminists lacked humor. In contrast, in 1986, when an interviewer asked Angelou if she were a feminist, Angelou responded, "I am a feminist. I've been a female for a long time now. I'd be stupid not to be on my own side." When the interviewer commented that she had not always held this opinion, Angelou admitted that her views had changed. Nevertheless, Angelou often contrasts black women's issues and white women's issues, believing that their positions in history and culture make their views different. In *I Know Why the Caged Bird Sings*, Angelou describes several black women: Momma, her mother, Grandmother Baxter, and Mrs. Bertha Flowers. It is not until her later books, such as *The Heart of a Woman* (1981), however, that Angelou begins to explore the significance of womanhood in general.

Sources for Further Study

Angelou, Maya. *Conversations with Maya Angelou*. Edited by Jeffrey M. Elliot. Jackson: University Press of Mississippi, 1989. An excellent collection of interviews with Angelou, arranged chronologically from 1971 to 1988. Contains a useful introduction, a chronology, and an index, as well as photographs of Angelou.

____________. *Gather Together in My Name*. New York: Random House, 1974. This book, a combination of fiction and nonfiction, begins with a dedication both to Angelou's "blood brother" Bailey and to a group of "real brothers." A continuation of *I Know Why the Caged Bird Sings*, it explores Angelou's struggles as a single parent and provider.

____________. *The Heart of a Woman*. New York: Random House, 1981. This autobiography, which begins with a dedication to a group of women that Angelou calls "Sister/friends," covers Angelou's early mature years as a writer. In it, she explores her creativity and her success.

____________. *Singin' and Swingin' and Gettin' Merry Like Christmas*. New York: Random House, 1976. The autobiography covers the time of Angelou's stage debut through her international tour with *Porgy and Bess*.

Tate, Claudia, ed. *Black Women Writers at Work*. New York: Continuum, 1983. A collection of fourteen interviews with black women writers, this book focuses on creative processes. Though it lacks an index, the book offers a useful introduction, and each interview is preceded by a brief biographical sketch of the writer. The interview with Angelou includes some of her views on both women's and racial issues.

Carol Franks

IMMACULATE DECEPTION: A New Look at Women and Childbirth in America

Author: Suzanne Arms (1944-   )
Type of work: Social criticism
First published: 1975

Form and Content

Suzanne Arms, a photojournalist and mother, was motivated by her own sour experience with hospital obstetrics to research the American birth experience. She interviewed and photographed not only credentialed experts—midwives, nurses, and doctors—but also experiential experts—mothers. Based on these interviews and her research into the literature of giving birth, she wrote *Immaculate Deception: A New Look at Women and Childbirth in America.* She presents a well-constructed argument against routing all births through the hospital, an institution designed to intervene in pathological conditions. Arms's primary insight is that most births are normal births; that is, they are not pathological at all. The appropriate response to the healthy birth is watchful, unhurried support, not intervention. The appropriate source of this support is the patient and experienced midwife, not the highly paid medical doctor. In the hospital, with its predisposition to discern pathology, normal variations in labor are extremely likely to be labeled abnormal, which starts the laboring woman on a merry-go-round of intervention. Each obstetrical interference causes harm that requires another interference, until the woman loses all control of her own labor.

In *Immaculate Deception*, Arms interweaves several different types of presentation. Scores of photographs present the visual reality of the world that she describes in the text: harsh institutional labor and delivery rooms, masked doctors looming over trays of metal instruments or proudly presenting babies as if they had produced them themselves, the calm faces of midwives, the frightened eyes of young mothers, and one straining female hand, locked in a heavy leather handcuff. The photographs are generally small, literally "marginal" to the text, but they are nevertheless crucial to conveying on an emotional level the argument that Arms builds so solidly on an intellectual level.

Arms quotes many mothers, briefly or at length, on their experiences with hospital childbirth. With their birth stories, she also includes the words of American midwives, nurses, and doctors, as well as the bemused comments of foreign birth attendants, who often seem faintly puzzled as to why anyone would behave as Americans do toward birth. She not only presents the words of proponents of rehumanizing birth but also quotes from the doctors who frankly argue that modern women are unable to give birth safely without the assistance of their guardian angels, aggressive obstetricians. Arms supplies many facts and figures, with clear documentation of her sources. In tabular form, she presents statistical evidence, such as infant mortality rates that show the United States trailing behind many less wealthy nations. Arms's multifaceted presentation leaves her reader with a sense of the sturdiness of her position.

Analysis

Immaculate Deception situates contemporary childbirth in a broad historical context. In tribal agrarian cultures, Arms suggests, childbirth was not necessarily a fearful experience for women, because they lived face to face with all the processes of natural life. Birth, death, and reproduction had not yet become clandestine. Because childbirth was so mysterious to men, however, societies in which men were not allowed to witness the miracle often saw the development of peculiar male fantasies about its nature. Men's ambivalent fear and wonder thus led to attempts to gain control over the creative powers of women. Perhaps the most notorious of these is the curse in Genesis 3:16, where Eve is cursed to suffer in bringing forth children. This began the long trajectory of the Judeo-Christian self-fulfilling expectation of pain in childbirth.

With Christianity vanished any empiricism that the Greco-Roman tradition had brought to medicine. Pain became a matter of divine will or diabolic action, so that male religious authority moved in on childbirth. Midwives were identified with witches, with lethal results. Male barber-surgeons began to perform crude obstetrics. The Catholic church gathered sick and dying people, together with laboring women, into the early Christian hospitals, which became centers of massive dissemination of infectious diseases, especially childbed fever. The death rate in these "charity" hospitals was staggering; the possibility of labor and delivery in one of these virtual charnel houses greatly added to women's fear of childbirth. Into this atmosphere of helpless (and quite reasonable) terror came the invention of the forceps in 1588. This seemingly magical device, the nature of which was long kept a close secret by the men who invented and used it, finally seemed to consolidate the shift in the meaning of birth from "something a woman can give to a child" to "something a man can do for a woman." Then in the mid-1800's came obstetrical anesthesia which, by rendering them unconscious, completed women's surrender of the birth experience into the hands of male experts.

Arms's rich historical perspective contributes to another of the chief strengths of *Immaculate Deception*: its careful logical presentation of linked cause-and-effect sequences. For example, when male convenience dictated that a woman should labor flat on her back on a bed or a table, this diminished the effectiveness of her contractions (which are meant to work in the direction of the pull of gravity). Because of this, men devised metal implements for pulling the baby out of her, which made birth more painful and dangerous. Men then created anesthetic agents to relieve her pain and anxiety, but these further decreased the efficiency of labor and endangered her baby. This required further intervention, such as the medical stimulation of labor. Artificially stimulated labor is even more painful than natural labor, so even more pain-killing drugs are called for. Drugging the laboring woman, besides slowing labor and depressing the newborn, also takes away her ability to use conscious self-control and cooperate with the process. She ends up unconscious or strapped down to a table so that she will not hurt herself, which further retards labor. So it goes, with each medical interference taking the mother and child further away from the normal birth that would have been their due if patience and trust in nature's way reigned over childbirth.

Because she explicitly highlights such interlocking factors, Arms succeeds in showing birth not as an isolated event, but as a vortex of many of the streams that flow together in a woman's life: her taking or relinquishing responsibility, her connectedness or alienation from her body, her trust or fear of her own nature. The focus on chain reactions of intervention also tends to minimize blaming. Although Arms unapologetically opposes the practices of the obstetrical establishment, her understanding grasp of cause-and-effect relationships results in a text that is not adversarial, contentious, or aggressive. Instead, she simply shows how and why counterproductive obstetrical measures came to exist. She places responsibility on both the deceptive medical industry in control of birth and on the women who passively allow themselves to be so deceived and controlled.

Context

After many decades of scanty discussion of American birth customs, the mid-1970's saw an abrupt crescendo of public debate. Contributing to this sudden interest was the popular experiential psychology movement of the late 1960's and early 1970's. Many of the schools of thought within that movement (such as transactional analysis, Gestalt therapy, and primal therapy) placed considerable importance on the psychological aftermath of early childhood trauma. It was perhaps only natural that the earliest childhood trauma, birth itself, should finally receive some attention. In addition, the liberalization of sexual behavior of the same period led, as day follows night, to an interest in reclaiming that common accompaniment of sex, the birth of a child.

The year 1975 was a milestone in the reevaluation of technologized obstetrics. By a miracle of synchronicity, this year saw the publication of *Immaculate Deception*, Frederick Leboyer's *Birth Without Violence*, and Ina May Gaskin's *Spiritual Midwifery*. In addition to these soon-to-be classics, such lesser-known works as Doris Haire's *The Cultural Warping of Childbirth* (1972) and William Woolfolk and Joanna Woolfolk's *The Great American Birth Rite* (1975) also appeared. Even in the midst of this sudden abundance of material, *Immaculate Deception* stood out. Its fine balance of photojournalism, polished prose, sound research, careful logic, and emotional impact earned it generally good reviews. Poet Adrienne Rich compared it favorably to Leboyer's work.

Arms and her contemporaries left the American birth

scene changed. By the very diversity of their approaches—the melodramatic prose of Leboyer, the hippie mysticism of Gaskin, and the good sense of Arms—they managed to establish beyond reasonable argument that American hospital obstetrical practices were damaging mothers and babies. Because of their attempts to demystify and reclaim birth, the intellectual landscape around reproduction shifted significantly. American women gained greater choice in how they can bring children into the world. Anesthetized, high-tech deliveries still occur, but the mother who wants a home birth, a birthing center, or rooming-in in a hospital can find these options if she takes the trouble to look. Breast-feeding is no longer considered odd and eccentric. Midwifery has gained public, if not legal, acceptance. Unfortunately, this progress in the United States has not halted the profit-oriented export of technologized birth fads to other countries. In the rush to Americanize, "progress" often comes to mean imitating the mistakes of the United States.

Sources for Further Study

Behuniak-Long, Susan. "Bibliographic Essay: Feminism and Reproduction." *Choice* 29 (October, 1991): 243-251. Lists and briefly describes scores of books that engage issues of reproductive technology from a feminist viewpoint.

Dwinell, Jane. *Birth Stories: Mystery, Power, and Creation*. Westport, Conn.: Bergin & Garvey, 1992. A midwife's casebook containing the stories of twenty-one specific births in American hospitals, homes, and birthing centers. Each is accompanied by discussion of the general issues of women's health care and spirituality that it exemplifies.

Ehrenreich, Barbara, and Deirdre English. *For Her Own Good: 150 Years of the Experts' Advice to Women*. New York: Anchor Books, 1989. Examines not only the victory of the obstetrical establishment but also the ascendancy of the other psychomedical experts who assumed power over women's lives: scientists, doctors, psychotherapists, home economists, and child-rearing specialists.

Gaskin, Ina May. *Spiritual Midwifery*. Rev. ed. Summertown, Tenn.: Book Publishing Company, 1978. This midwifery handbook and compilation of birth stories became one of the primers for the revolution against technologized hospital birth. It blends mysticism and practicality in a way that became typical of the resurgent midwifery movement.

Haire, Doris. *The Cultural Warping of Childbirth*. Hillside, N.J.: International Childbirth Education Association, 1972. This slender pamphlet is one of the sources to which Arms often refers in *Immaculate Deception*. Haire lists thirty hospital practices that tend to turn birth from a normal into a pathological process. Haire's well-documented appeals are based less on emotions and more on cognitive reasoning.

Leboyer, Frederick. *Birth Without Violence*. New York: Alfred A. Knopf, 1975. Uses highly emotional photography and rhapsodic prose to advocate gentle handling of the infant immediately after birth. Although this French obstetrician's method is decidedly doctor-centered, his focus on the experience of birth by the newborn was revolutionary in its time.

Mitford, Jessica. *The American Way of Birth*. New York: E. P. Dutton, 1992. Perhaps the most direct descendant of *Immaculate Deception*, this highly readable work surveys the history of power-hungry and profit-hungry male annexation of the traditional female territory of birth.

Rich, Adrienne. *Of Woman Born: Motherhood as Experience and Institution*. New York: W. W. Norton, 1976. Combining both historical-social and personal material, this in-depth analysis of the female nurturing role considers motherhood both as the self-defined potential relationship of each woman with children and her own powers of reproduction and as a socially defined institution directed toward keeping women under the control of men.

__________. "The Theft of Childbirth." *New York Review of Books* 22 (October 2, 1975): 25-30. A sensitive and sensible review which contrasts *Immaculate Deception* and *Birth Without Violence*. Also includes a concise review of the history of male intervention in normal childbirth, from the invention of the forceps and the first uses of obstetrical anesthesia, and gives a briefer treatment to some of the same concepts that are detailed in *Of Woman Born*.

Donna Glee Williams

IN SEARCH OF OUR MOTHERS' GARDENS: Womanist Prose

Author: Alice Walker (1944-)
Type of work: Essays
First published: 1983

Form and Content

The essay collection *In Search of Our Mothers' Gardens: Womanist Prose* gathers nonfiction that Alice Walker, a novelist, short-story writer, and poet, wrote between 1966 and 1982. It includes book reviews published in scholarly journals and popular magazines, transcripts of addresses to groups and institutions, and articles for *Ms.* magazine. The earliest selection is the essay "The Civil Rights Movement: What Good Was It?" which won Walker a prize in the annual *American Scholar* contest when she was twenty-three. Among the latest is "Writing *The Color Purple*," which sketches how Walker wrote the novel that won her the Pulitzer Prize for fiction.

The title of the book is taken from the title of the major essay, a classic and groundbreaking discussion of the black woman writer's struggle for freedom of self-expression and her search for the roots of her creativity. The front matter includes a definition of "womanist" as a black feminist that distinguishes "womanist" from "feminist" as purple is distinguished from lavender. The publication acknowledgments at the back of the book provide detailed information on the original publication and presentation of the articles and speeches.

The thirty-six selections, ranging from three to twenty-nine pages, are arranged in four parts, each of which is loosely organized around several themes. A principal theme of part 1 is the artist's need for models, which Walker explores by discussing models important to her own development as a writer. Part 2 centers on the formative influence that Martin Luther King, Jr., and the Civil Rights movement of the 1960's had on Walker. These selections, such as a review of Langston Hughes's most radical verse, reveal Walker's recognition of the relationship between struggle and social change, her commitment to the struggle, and her recognition of the dignity of poor and oppressed persons. Part 3 begins with the title essay, "In Search of Our Mothers' Gardens." It also includes an interview in which Walker discusses a painful period while she was in college. Contemplating suicide, she wrote the collection of poems later published under the title *Once* (1968). Part 4, the smallest section, addresses such issues as the danger of nuclear weapons and the Middle Eastern conflict. It concludes with a moving explanation of the dedication of the book to her daughter Rebecca and a joyous celebration of life. The publication acknowledgments provide detailed bibliographic data on the selections.

The style of the selections is personal and down-to-earth. A principal method is flowing from experience to insight, telling the story of an experience and reflecting on the meaning and value of that experience. The tone is honest, straightforward, and human, by turns serious and playful. The prevailing theme is a vision of what makes for the flourishing of human beings: the freedom of all persons to be themselves, to decide for themselves, to be respected, and to respect others. What emerges from the selections is a portrait of a woman who is aware, intelligent, searching, committed to seeing life as it is, and working to make it richer for the community of creatures who inhabit the planet.

Analysis

The book opens with the article "Saving the Life That Is Your Own: The Importance of Models in the Artist's Life." This text of a speech Walker gave to the Modern Language Association in San Francisco in 1975 sets the personal tone and direction for part 1. Walker asserts the importance of writers—especially those outside the mainstream of the literary tradition, writing not what others want but what they themselves want to read. In doing so, they not only set the direction of vision but also follow it. This integrity of purpose puts it in the power of the black woman artist to save lives and makes it her business to do so because she knows that the life she saves is her own.

Several of the other selections in part 1 explore the

lives, work, and significance of several of Walker's literary models, especially Zora Neale Hurston, Flannery O'Connor, Virginia Woolf, Jean Toomer, and Rebecca Jackson. Wanting to write an authentic story drawing on black witchcraft, Walker undertook research into black folklore. She discovered that most research in this field had been published by white anthropologists, but in a footnote she discovered the work of Hurston. She found Hurston's *Mules and Men* (1935) the "perfect book," because of its "racial health," its depiction of black persons as "complete, complex, *undiminished* human beings." Recognizing Hurston as one of the "most significant unread authors in America," Walker visited Eatonville, Florida, Hurston's birthplace. Learning that Hurston had died in a home for the indigent and had been buried in an unmarked grave, Walker bought a tombstone to mark the gravesite. Walker recognizes the role this painful pilgrimage played in her own development as a black woman writer.

Walker, the daughter of Georgia sharecroppers, also made a pilgrimage to her own birthplace, Eatonton, Georgia, and to the home of another of her models, Flannery O'Connor. The daughter of Irish Catholic landowners, O'Connor lived in Milledgeville, Georgia, just down the road from Eatonton. Walker was drawn to compare herself with O'Connor, who is for her the first great writer of the South.

Part 2 opens with "The Civil Rights Movement: What Good Was It?," which Walker wrote at twenty-three. Her first published essay, it won the annual *American Scholar* essay contest. It sets the focus for the following selections: Dr. Martin Luther King, Jr., and the Civil Rights movement of the 1960's. King's heroism and the ideals of the movement stirred Walker to new life and to a commitment to work for social justice, for all oppressed peoples, especially African Americans.

As Walker began to realize the inadequacies in her education, she set about discovering and reading the black authors whose works had never been introduced to her. She began to see herself as a revolutionary artist. While her art might change nothing, she saw it as a way to preserve for the future the extraordinary lives of persons neglected by politics and economics.

In the extensive essay "My Father's Country Is the Poor," Walker reflects on her experiences in Cuba during a visit there during the Cuban Revolution. She was impressed by the compassion, intelligence, and work that the Cubans brought against all that oppressed them.

In part 3, Walker explores in depth the question of her roots as an artist in the lead essay, "In Search of Our Mothers' Gardens." Focusing on her feminine inheritance, she traces the images of black women in literature, such as the women in *Cane* (1923), the novel written by the Southern black male writer Jean Toomer, and the few women such as Phillis Wheatley, a slave in the 1700's, who were able to express themselves in poetry. The major contribution of this essay is its exploration of the legacy of creativity that slave women and black women after them passed on subtly and subversively to their daughters. Looked upon as mules of the world, denied the channels of creativity open to others, these black women expressed their creativity in gardens, cooking, and quilts. For Walker, the unique, imaginative, and spiritually powerful quilt made of rags and now preserved in the Smithsonian Institution in Washington, D.C., is a symbol of this legacy and a model for the exercise of her own craft as a writer.

Part 4, the smallest section of the book, includes reflections on having a child and writing the novel *The Color Purple* (1982). A principal theme of these selections is carried in the title of one selection, a speech Walker gave at an antinuclear rally: "Only Justice Can Stop a Curse."

Context

Alice Walker is one of the most prominent figures in the development of black women's literature in the United States. Winner of the Pulitzer Prize for fiction and the American Book Award in 1983 for her novel *The Color Purple*, Walker came to popular attention with the film version of the novel in 1985. Recognizing her own debt to the work of Zora Neale Hurston, folklorist and novelist of the early part of the twentieth century, she played a major role in rescuing Hurston's work from obscurity and expanding its audience. The essays, interviews, and book reviews in this collection reveal some of the persons, events, and experiences that Walker believes helped to create the person she is and the work she has done.

This collection demonstrates that Walker speaks out, often eloquently and passionately, against racism, classism, sexism, homophobia, and despoliation of the environment. Finding the term "civil rights" colorless and limited, she openly supports the movement toward human liberation: the right and need for all individuals to express themselves freely within the context of the earth community. Some critics find fault, however, with Walker's commitment to feminism and her portrayal of African American men.

This work is one of the first collections that emerged in the 1980's to express the struggle of African American women to define themselves in a society often indifferent and hostile to them and to see their experience recognized for its value in understanding the world. The collection reveals the process of self-discovery and self-development in which Walker has been engaged, some of the origins and changes in her thought, and the ideas that kindle her energy. Her search for understanding the significance of her mother's garden helps to unearth the tradition for contemporary black women writers that enables their efforts to claim their lives, assert their value, and articulate their meaning. It also contributes to an understanding of the nature of the artistry of black women writers. Among Walker's other works are the collection of poetry *Revolutionary Petunias and Other Poems* (1973), a collection of short stories about black women entitled *In Love and Trouble: Stories of Black Women* (1973), and the novels *The Third Life of Grange Copeland* (1970), *Meridian* (1976), and *The Temple of My Familiar* (1989).

Sources for Further Study

Blackburn, Regina. "In Search of the Black Female Self: African-American Women's Autobiographies and Ethnicity." In *Women's Autobiography: Essays in Criticism*, edited by Estelle C. Jelinek. Bloomington: Indiana University Press, 1980. Blackburn explores the themes occurring in the writings of black women: identity, pride, self-hatred and doubt, and the "double jeopardy" of being both black and female.

Christian, Barbara. *Black Feminist Criticism: Perspectives on Black Women Writers*. New York: Pergamon Press, 1985. A collection of a noted black feminist literary critic's previously published essays and lectures on contemporary black women writers and some of the issues and questions their work raises.

Evans, Mari, ed. *Black Women Writers (1950-1980): A Critical Evaluation*. Garden City, N.Y.: Anchor Press/Doubleday, 1984. This lengthy volume includes reflections of fifteen significant black women writing between 1950 and 1980 and critical essays examining their work, as well as brief biographies and selected bibliographies.

Gates, Henry Louis, Jr., ed. *Reading Black, Reading Feminist: A Critical Anthology*. New York: Meridian Books, 1990. Gates, a scholar in African American Studies, has collected a wide range of studies by and about some of the leading black feminist writers and critics whose shared structures and themes unify their works into a literary tradition.

McDowell, Deborah E. "New Directions for Black Feminist Criticism." In *The New Feminist Criticism: Essays on Women, Literature, and Theory*, edited by Elaine Showalter. New York: Pantheon, 1985. Recognizing the exclusion of black women writers by both white feminist and black male critics, McDowell points out some weaknesses of black feminist criticism.

Pryse, Marjorie, and Hortense J. Spillers, eds. *Conjuring: Black Women, Fiction, and Literary Tradition*. Bloomington: Indiana University Press, 1985. These articles raise questions about individual writers and their works, as well as their collective significance toward the goal of writing a literary history of black women novelists.

Smith, Barbara. "Toward a Black Feminist Criticism." In *The New Feminist Criticism: Essays on Women, Literature, and Theory*, edited by Elaine Showalter. New York: Pantheon, 1985. In one of the first essays distinguishing the writing of black women from that of white women, Smith also protests the exclusion of black women writers, especially lesbian writers, from the literary tradition.

Walker, Melissa. *Down from the Mountaintop: Black Women's Novels in the Wake of the Civil Rights Movement, 1966-1989*. New Haven, Conn.: Yale University Press, 1991. Walker demonstrates how eighteen novels by black women relate both to the Civil Rights movement and to the historical conditions that brought about its rise and decline.

Christian Koontz

INDIANA

Author: George Sand (Amandine-Aurore-Lucile Dupin, Baronne Dudevant, 1804-1876)
Type of work: Novel
Type of plot: Psychological realism
Time of plot: The early eighteenth century
Locale: France
First published: 1832 (English translation, 1833)

Principal characters:

Indiana, a beautiful, melancholy young woman
Noun, Indiana's maid
Colonel Delmare, Indiana's husband, an elderly retired soldier
Sir Ralph Brown, Indiana's cousin
Raymon de Ramière, the lover of first Noun and later Indiana

Form and Content

Indiana is devoted to exploring women's position in society, the marital relationship, and the family and to condemning the laws that govern women's existence. The book begins on a rainy autumn evening in Brie, when Colonel Delmare, hunting charcoal poachers, shoots Raymon de Ramière. Raymon, brought into the house and revived, claims that he slipped over the wall to examine the machinery in Delmare's factory, but he has actually come to meet Noun, Delmare's maid.

When Raymon wearies of Noun, he re-encounters Indiana, the colonel's young wife, at a party in Paris and is struck by her beauty and delicacy. He woos her ardently, and Indiana begins to reciprocate his passion. A letter from Noun announcing her pregnancy forces Raymon to meet her at the Delmare estate. Sensing that her lover's interest has waned, Noun prepares a seductive nest in Indiana's own boudoir. Her tears and pleas persuade Raymon to make love to her—although, drunk, he imagines that she is Indiana.

Raymon tells Noun that he will not marry her, although he offers her a substantial settlement. Indiana returns unexpectedly, and Noun, panic-stricken, hides Raymon behind a curtain. Indiana discovers Raymon, who covers himself by claiming that his love for her has brought him there. Indignant, Indiana orders him away and reproaches Noun for aiding him. Although she says nothing, Noun realizes that Raymon loves Indiana. The equally unexpected return of Sir Ralph Brown, Indiana's devoted cousin, forces Raymon to flee. The following day, Indiana discovers the body of Noun, whose despair has led her to drown herself.

Two months later, Colonel Delmare invites Raymon to inspect his factory. Indiana avoids Raymon, but eventually they are thrown together and her love for him revives. Ralph tries to separate them but is unable, resigning himself to keeping the affair from Delmare. When Delmare breaks his leg, Raymon visits him daily in order to see Indiana, and he and Ralph, although forced to appear friends, develop a strong antipathy for each other. Delmare leaves on a business trip, and Ralph sets up a vigilant watch over Indiana and tries to warn her by revealing the cause of Noun's suicide. When Raymon comes to her that night, she questions him. As he is admitting his culpability in Noun's death, Ralph slips a note under the door alerting them to Delmare's return.

When Delmare plans to retire to Île Bourbon, Indiana declares her willingness to abandon him, and Raymon's ardor cools. Indiana runs away from Delmare and comes to Raymon, who reproaches her and tries to send her away, saying that it would be dishonorable to accept her sacrifice. She replies that since she has not spent the night beneath her husband's roof, she is already disgraced in the eyes of society. Raymon forces Indiana from the house. Leaving, the distraught Indiana throws herself in the river, seeking to follow Noun's example. Ralph rescues her and brings her home. Her husband demands to know where she spent the night, but she refuses to tell him. Delmare and Indiana leave for Bourbon, accompanied by Ralph.

Raymon falls ill and begins to regret Indiana's loss, imagining her nursing him. On a whim, he writes her a letter urging her to leave her husband and come to him, but he then forgets about the letter. Meanwhile, Delmare reads Indiana's journal and discovers her affair. He attacks her and subsequently suffers a stroke. When Raymon's letter arrives, Indiana finds a ship going to France and bribes the captain in order to arrange passage. Meanwhile, Raymon courts and wins Laure de Nangy, a wealthy heiress. Upon Indiana's arrival, she is met by the sardonic Laure, who sees in the confrontation a chance to forever gain the upper hand over her new husband. Raymon puts Indiana in a carriage for Paris, where she finds Ralph, who brings news of her husband's death. Ralph reveals his love for Indiana, and the two resolve to commit suicide. They do so, but in the contradictory final chapter, the reader discovers the two living in solitude on Bourbon.

Analysis

Indiana deals with the freedom of the individual; in it, George Sand tries to do away with romantic notions of choice and to present humans made thoroughly miserable by the structures and imposed silences of society. She observed in the preface to the 1832 edition that "the being who tries to free himself from his lawful curb is represented as very wretched indeed, and the heart that rebels against the decrees of its destiny in sore distress." Throughout the novel, an atmosphere of gloom and melancholy prevail, while physical love is presented as a hallucinatory delusion. Indiana and Ralph, the most sympathetic characters, are shown as passive beings driven almost mad by the pressures of society, while the guileless Noun is impelled to kill herself from similar pressures.

Speech is the way in which these characters attempt to declare their autonomy; throughout the work, characters engage in lengthy monologues or equally lengthy letters, which Sand reproduces in full. Ralph, inarticulate at the beginning of *Indiana*, is by the end able to utter the prolonged statement which preludes his and Indiana's suicide attempt; Indiana, silent and dreamy, pens lengthy missives to Raymon and finally silences him with her eloquence. It is their final breaking through to articulation which allows them to remain unsilenced by the attempted suicide and to emerge in the final chapter as beings who speak directly with the narrator for the first time. Those movements toward eloquence reflect a similar movement in the author; Sand repeatedly emphasized that *Indiana*'s writing was a process of inspired rush, of finding and claiming her authorial voice. Certainly, the publication of *Indiana* moved Sand from anonymity to literary celebrity.

It is not only the characters of Ralph and Indiana who speak. Delmare employs the diction of a soldier from the onset, but he accompanies it with actions designed to silence those around him, such as shooting Raymon or killing Indiana's dog. Raymon himself is a creature, it seems, purely of words. His words allow him to win Indiana, while his letters rekindle their love every time that she tries to repudiate him; in fact, his letter leads Indiana to the final desperate act of fleeing Bourbon and coming to him. Both these characters employ a speech recognized and validated by society—the language of warfare, politics, or seduction by men. Sand stresses that both characters, whom the reader comes to see as despicable, are working within society's rules and are defined by society as good and valued individuals, despite any feelings that the reader might possess to the contrary.

The ending is ambiguous. Although Indiana and Ralph have survived, they live in a state of exile, which seems to indicate that an ideal relationship between a woman and a man can exist only outside society, and their relationship can also be read as an incestuous one. This ambiguity is troublesome when one reads the work as the story of the individual's development. Indiana does learn to look beyond the narratives presented to her by society, such as the idea that she, like Sleeping Beauty, will be awakened and brought to psychological fruition by a Prince Charming such as Raymon. Yet the story that becomes her life is one of isolation and a hermit's existence, which admittedly seems preferable to the claustrophobic scene that opens the novel.

At the same time, the ending returns the reader to the beginning of the story when the narrator's relationship to the story is explained: He is simply retelling the story told to him by Ralph at the end of the book, which implies that the individual's struggle for autonomy will never achieve resolution.

Context

Indiana, one of Sand's earliest novels, is a strongly feminist work which analyses the restrictions that a patriarchal society places on women, and it explores the individual's options in trying either to obey or to circumvent those restrictions. The device of using a narrator marked as male who is strongly sympathetic to a female character demonstrates the move toward androgyny that permeates Sand's work. *Indiana* was originally assumed by critics to have been written by a man with the assistance or input of a woman; when it became known that the author was female, she was hailed as an extraordinary being. The book was affirmed one of the most important works of the year; Honoré de Balzac called it "delightfully conceived" and asserted that its success was inevitable.

The book is, to some extent, autobiographical, but the reader who focuses only on this aspect will lose much in doing so. The text represents an attempt to reclaim the novel—a form becoming at that time increasingly respectable and hence increasingly masculine—for women. The protagonist is presented as a being as sensitive and introspective as any male character of the time. Indiana's impassioned speeches condemning the system of power that has brought her to an oppressive marriage were cited as examples of Sand's interest in women's rights, and certainly an assertion of those rights was a major theme throughout her writings. Sand points out repeatedly that Delmare, who abuses his wife and condemns her to stultification and isolation, is considered by society a "good" man and that, in fact, he is only obeying society's rules. Simultaneously, the characters of Noun and Indiana show that the two roles traditionally assigned women, either the chaste upper-class angel or the sexually active lower-class servant, are equally fraught with difficulty and frustration.

Women's studies scholars have revived interest in George Sand: Her work was largely ignored at the beginning of the twentieth century, and it was not until feminist scholars began to explore women's writing that interest in her substantial body of work revived.

Sources for Further Study

Cate, Curtis. *George Sand: A Biography*. Boston: Houghton Mifflin, 1975. This biography of Sand may help readers understand parallels between the subject matter of *Indiana* and her own life. Also provides an account of how *Indiana* was received.

Crecelius, Kathryn J. *Family Romances: George Sand's Early Novels*. Bloomington: Indiana University Press, 1987. An interesting and invaluable work, this text limits itself to Sand's works published between 1827 and 1837. Looks at the ways in which her early novels employ and alter conventional forms, and spends considerable attention examining how Sand describes women's psychological development in terms of a female Oedipal structure.

Datlof, Natalie, Jeanne Fuchs, and David A. Powell, eds. *The World of George Sand*. New York: Greenwood Press, 1991. Contains papers presented at the Seventh International George Sand Conference at Hofstra University in 1986. A number of articles are useful to *Indiana* scholars, such as Marilyn Yalom's "George Sand's Poetics of Autobiography" and Margaret E. Ward and Karen Storz's "Fanny Lewald and George Sand: *Eine Lebensfrage* and *Indiana*."

Moers, Ellen. *Literary Women*. London: Women's Press, 1978. This overview of women's literature devotes considerable space to George Sand, exploring motivations for and themes in her works.

Naginski, Isabelle Hoog. *George Sand: Writing for Her Life*. New Brunswick, N.J.: Rutgers University Press, 1991. This book avoids the biographical approach common to Sand criticism. Identifies four specific periods of Sand's writing and examines each, focusing on common themes.

Powell, David A., ed. *George Sand Today: Proceedings of the Eighth International George Sand Conference—Tours 1989*. Lanham, Md.: University Press of America, 1992. Contains essays in French and English. Of particular interest are Tamara Alvarez-Detrell's "A Room of Her Own: The Role of the *lieux* from Aurore to *Indiana*" and "The Politics of George Sand's Pastoral Novels," by Marylou Gramm.

Thomson, Patricia. *George Sand and the Victorians: Her Influence and Reputation in Nineteenth-Century England*. New York: Columbia University Press, 1977. While not focusing on *Indiana*, this work provides an excellent overview of the reception given Sand's work in England and underscores many of the gender-related issues raised by reviewers and critics.

Catherine Francis

INTERCOURSE

Author: Andrea Dworkin (1946-)
Type of work: Social criticism
First published: 1987

Form and Content

In *Intercourse,* Andrea Dworkin attributes women's societal subordination to their becoming a colonized people through the act which intimately connects them to their oppressor—sexual intercourse. She asks if since women have no physical privacy—that is, they must be entered for intercourse—can they truly be free? Her answer is no.

In the first section, "Intercourse in a Man-made World," Dworkin discusses the portrayal of intercourse and sexuality in works of five male authors: Leo Tolstoy, explaining how his writings reflect repulsion at being sexual; Kōbō Abe, whose images of intercourse invoke the sense of going beneath the skin, sometimes through its removal; Tennessee Williams, who connects sexual expression in females with a negative stigma; James Baldwin, who illustrates the pain which must be experienced for two people to commune with each other sexually; and Isaac Bashevis Singer, who provides an example which Dworkin uses to suggest that, for women, intercourse is destructive and requires being possessed. Attitudes and behaviors depicted in the fiction are treated as reflecting real-world attitudes toward the sexuality of women.

In part 2 of the text, Dworkin examines "The Female Condition" first through changing views of virginity, as evidenced in the lives of Joan of Arc and the fictional characters of Madame Bovary and Dracula's female victims, and then through woman's agreement or collaboration in being "occupied" by man.

In part 3, "Power, Status, and Hate," Dworkin examines religious and secular laws that limit men's behavior in intercourse and encourage men to experience erotic feeling through violating laws. Here she looks at images which connect woman with filth and death (using comments by psychoanalyst Sigmund Freud), as well as at sexual violence perpetuated against women in Nazi concentration camps and other settings.

Dworkin carefully scrutinizes what men say, think, and do regarding female sexuality and speaks the truth as she sees it; namely, that the social subordination of women is perpetuated through the sexual domination of women, and that the difference between men's behavior toward women in the matrimonial bed from that evidenced in sadistic torture is one of degree, not of kind.

Prior to the publication of *Intercourse*, Dworkin had written extensively on the topic of woman-hating and violence against women. Her book *Pornography: Men Possessing Women* (1981) is a starting point for most feminist discussions of the subject, whether or not individuals agree with her conclusions. With Catherine MacKinnon, Dworkin authored a description of pornography as violating the civil rights of women in 1983, later published as *Pornography and Civil Rights: A New Day for Women's Equality* (1988). *Intercourse* represents an attempt by Dworkin to broaden the discussion, which has focused on violent pornography, to include popular works deemed acceptable and even celebrated literature. It is interesting that *Intercourse* was published the same year as Dworkin's first novel, *Ice and Fire* (1987), a work in which sex within marriage is the most violent form that the female protagonist experiences. Her novel, like *Intercourse*, was greeted by a few supportive and many strongly negative reviews.

Dworkin's tone has been referred to as elegant, passionate, profound, shocking, and even comic at times; others describe it as crass, self-absorbed haranguing and as rhetoric stuck in the 1960's. *Intercourse,* which includes a thirty-five-page bibliography, twelve pages of notes, and a ten-page index, draws the reader into exploring the real-life sex lives and attitudes of men and their portrayal and treatment of women and women's sexual behavior.

Analysis

Dworkin opens the discussion with "Intercourse in a Man-made World," examining men's repulsion at sex with women. Using Leo Tolstoy's short novel *Kreutserova sonata* (1890; *The Kreutzer Sonata*, 1891), she contrasts the male protagonist's killing of his wife with Tolstoy's behavior. The man in the novel kills his wife not only by stabbing her but also by having intercourse with her, resulting in many pregnancies which drain her youth and energy. Tolstoy uses his wife for sexual release for which he in turn "blames and hates" her; she gives birth to thirteen children. Dworkin uses Tolstoy to argue that celibacy would help establish equality between the sexes.

In "Skinless," Dworkin examines novels by Kōbō Abe, including *Suna no onne* (1962; *The Woman in the Dunes*, 1964) and *Tanin no kao* (1964; *The Face of Another*, 1966). The metaphor for sexual intercourse that Dworkin draws from these works is the need for people to touch, not merely skin to skin but with that below the skin as well. She describes the difficulties that Abe's male characters have in achieving this touch without violence.

In Tennessee Williams' plays, Dworkin explores the stigma for women attached to intercourse and sexual desire. In *The Rose Tattoo* (1951), a wife is mystically marked by her husband's tattoo when she becomes pregnant. Stanley Kowalski's animalistic rape of Blanche in *A Streetcar Named Desire* (1947) drives her insane and destroys her relationship with her sister Stella, Stanley's wife. In *Summer and Smoke* (1947), Alma loses her aspirations for the ethereal communion of souls and ends her life addicted to pills and meaningless sex with strangers.

In "Communion," Dworkin uses James Baldwin to support the need to examine whether sex is good. Baldwin's male characters in *Giovanni's Room* (1956) and other works want to experience "not doing it, but being the beloved." In attempting to attain this state, they cause their sexual partners and themselves great pain; by the time that they are ready, they have destroyed those whom they desire.

Through *Sotan in Goray* (1935; *Satan in Goray*, 1955), by Isaac Bashevis Singer, Dworkin illustrates that sex to a woman means being taken over (possessed), and to a man means conquering (possessing). The female protagonist is possessed: by her father; by an uncle who wants to marry her; by a husband who possesses many wives, shaming each because of his impotency; by a lover who forces her husband to divorce her and then marries her himself; and lastly by the devil. As a result of the last possession, she dies. All these possessions are sanctioned by rules of the community that protect male power.

Throughout part 1, Dworkin draws primarily from fictional representations of sexuality. Some object that while writers of fiction mine the societal psyche for material, it is fiction, not reality. Others support Dworkin's mixing of the real and unreal, citing a tradition from Plato to Jean-Jacques Rousseau "that condemns representation as dangerous and corruptive."

In part 2, "The Female Condition," Dworkin explores virginity, with Joan of Arc exemplifying the power that a woman can obtain if she is celibate and if she rejects female trappings. Flouting tradition, however, causes Joan's downfall; she burns because she defies the male power. Returning to fiction, Madame Bovary, the title character in Gustave Flaubert's 1857 novel, is a woman who has an extramarital affair in which she begins to enjoy sex. The affair and her enjoyment violate social restrictions on women's sexuality, and Madame Bovary is ruined. In Bram Stoker's *Dracula* (1897), virgins Lucy and Mina, unlike heaven-protected Joan of Arc, draw evil to them. They couple passionately with Dracula with the "place of sex moved to the throat." To regain purity, Lucy is mutilated by men who wanted to marry her, and Mina's demon lover is killed. Dworkin sees in *Dracula* inspiration for pornographic "snuff" films in which women are taped being tortured and murdered.

"Occupation/Collaboration" has been cited to suggest Dworkin believes that women's subordination is "natural." Man must enter woman if the human race is to continue; hence, woman, according to Dworkin, is doomed to "have a lesser privacy, a lesser integrity of the body." Furthermore, a woman initiates her own degradation by allowing her own colonization and experiencing pleasure in her own inferiority. Dworkin argues that individual men and women cannot escape negative societal expectations of women's subordination and men's domination and that intercourse can never be an equal, loving event. Some cite Dworkin's experiences with men, some extremely abusive, as reason for her analysis. Others attribute it to her being a radical feminist lesbian. Still others claim that Dworkin receives negative reviews because she dares to ask forbidden questions about the nature of intercourse.

In part 3, "Power, Status, and Hate," Dworkin explores how law, both religious and secular, has defined acceptable sexuality. Here it becomes clear that Dworkin believes women's inferiority is a social construct, as she says that "Laws create and maintain male dominance." These same laws also create excitement for men in violating women sexually.

In "Dirt/Death," Dworkin ventures into attitudes toward and treatment of women by professors of gynecology, in concentration camps and prisons, and in comments by philosopher Friedrich Nietzsche and Freud. Sex is dirty because it is with women whose bodies produce slime and filth; female circumcision cleans women who "carry death between (their) legs."

Context

In *Intercourse*, Andrea Dworkin has added a new dimension to the pornography debate, showing how much mainstream literature (in addition to so-called actual pornographic literature) includes themes expressing men's perception that women's sexuality exists to be controlled and punished, often violently.

Dworkin believes as Baldwin does that, "It is really quite impossible to be affirmative about anything which one refuses to question." Hence, addressing sex-role conditioning, Dworkin has posed a previously unasked question; namely, whether sex is an inherently intrusive act perpetuated on women by men and whether as such it stands in the way of truly equal and loving relationships between women and men.

Some reviewers have referred to Dworkin's language as filthy, not reprintable, and mimicking the very pornographic speech that she would see eliminated. Others have reacted to it as powerful and lyrical. Response to *Intercourse* has been overwhelmingly negative, in part because of Dworkin's language usage and tone and in part because of her ideas, which have not been popular among women and which have made some men too angry to consider the work rationally. After such a negative reception, it is interesting to note that references to *Intercourse* are almost nonexistent in many late 1980's and early 1990's publications that cite other works by Dworkin, such as *Right-Wing Women* (1983), *Letters from a War Zone* (1988), and *Pornography: Men Possessing Women*. References to *Intercourse* do appear in discussions on changing views of masculinity, much of it written by men. While references to *Intercourse* may not occur directly in feminist conversations on female subordination, male domination, popular literature, sex-role conditioning, and pornography, the questions that Dworkin has asked will remain an undercurrent in these discussions.

Sources for Further Study

Assiter, Alison. *Pornography, Feminism, and the Individual*. London: Pluto Press, 1989. Assiter dedicates two chapters to examining works by Dworkin, *Pornography: Men Possessing Women* and *Intercourse*. She argues that Dworkin's rhetoric is impressive but that her theories are flawed, mainly because they rely on individual action for change and deny the need for collective responsibility.

Booker, M. Keith. *Literature and Domination: Sex, Knowledge, and Power in Modern Fiction*. Gainesville: University Press of Florida, 1993. This text is for those well versed in literary criticism. Issues of domination are examined in works including Vladimir Nabokov's *Lolita* (1955). Types of domination range from female-male relations to class relations.

Brittan, Arthur. *Masculinity and Power*. New York: Basil Blackwell, 1989. Although making no reference to *Intercourse*, Brittan does mention two of Dworkin's earlier works. This feminist author explores connections between masculinity and social and political power, what men could do about imbalances, and why they do so little.

Ferguson, Ann. *Blood at the Root: Motherhood, Sexuality, and Male Dominance*. London: Pandora, 1989. In this text, the author's theory "weaves together . . . key insights of radical feminism, Marxism and Freudianism while avoiding some . . . problems." Ferguson devotes six pages to an analysis of the Dworkin/MacKinnon antipornography ordinance, passed in Minneapolis and later ruled unconstitutional by the U.S. Supreme Court.

Rosen, David. *The Changing Fictions of Masculinity*. Urbana: University of Illinois Press, 1993. Like Dworkin, Rosen examines literature for what it can "tell about men." Using an "Anglo-American feminist perspective," he explores works from English literature, including *Beowulf*, William Shakespeare's *Hamlet, Prince of Denmark* (1600-1601), John Milton's *Paradise Lost* (1667, 1674), and Charles Dickens' *Hard Times* (1854), garnering stereotypes about masculinity in general rather than in female-male relationships.

Russell, Diana E. H., ed. *Making Violence Sexy: Feminist Views on Pornography*. New York: Teachers College Press, 1993. In this collection, many articles refer to Dworkin's work on pornography. Some reactions are negative; most, however, are extremely positive. Although *Intercourse* is never referred to, here is a largely appreciative audience for Dworkin's ideas about pornography. Contains an extensive bibliography of feminist works.

Segal, Lynne. *Slow Motion: Changing Masculinities, Changing Men*. New Brunswick, N.J.: Rutgers University Press, 1990. The author explores "masculinities" in the hope that understanding differences between men will assist in the "struggle for change" in male behavior toward women and one another with reference to women's liberation and gay liberation. Segal refers to Dworkin and other radical feminists and finds their work lacking because of its emphasis on sexual power and the penis as the basis of male dominance.

Su A. Cutler

JANE EYRE

Author: Charlotte Brontë (1816-1855)
Type of work: Novel
Type of plot: *Bildungsroman*
Time of plot: The nineteenth century
Locale: England
First published: 1847

Principal characters:

Jane Eyre, an independent, spirited woman
Edward Fairfax Rochester, the master of Thornfield Hall and Jane's primary love interest
Bertha Mason Rochester, Edward's wife, who has become insane
St. John Rivers, Jane's cousin, a minister
Sarah Reed, Jane's cruel aunt, who reared her until she was ten
Helen Burns, Jane's friend at Lowood, a school for poor orphaned girls

Form and Content

Charlotte Brontë's *Jane Eyre* traces the personal development of a young woman who must struggle to maintain a separate identity and independence in the suffocating pressures of her culture. She grapples with the societal expectations of her gender, which frequently conflict with her intuitive sense of self. Each setting and situation that Jane encounters denotes a phase in her personal progress, teaching her and preparing her for the next experience.

The linear organization of Jane's maturation process is attributable to the viewpoint of the narrator. The narrator is not the child, teenager, or young woman that Jane is during the course of the narrative, but the adult wife and mother who is recounting her story. With hindsight and from a mature perspective, Jane can recognize the pivotal, shaping events of her life. She takes account of her life, selecting events so that a pattern of personal development becomes apparent, what all people do in making sense of their past. The reader also senses Brontë's voice. Although the novel is not an autobiography, it contains autobiographical elements—Brontë's experience at the Clergy Daughter's School is similar to Jane's years at Lowood, for example. Certainly Brontë draws from her own experience as a maturing young woman in describing the life of Jane Eyre.

Each setting indicates a stage of growth for Jane. Under the cruel treatment of her aunt, Sarah Reed, at Gateshead Hall, Jane learns as a child to rely on her own inner strength. The strong self-reliance that she develops as a protective mechanism in this brutal environment sustains her throughout her life. At Lowood, Jane finds sincere friendship in Helen Burns and a compassionate mother-figure in Maria Temple. Jane learns from Helen's religious stoicism, but realizes that she is too much in need of human companionship to accept such a solitary existence completely. When Miss Temple leaves to get married, Jane believes that she also must leave, having matured enough to break free from this surrogate mother.

As governess in Thornfield Hall, Jane finds in Edward Fairfax Rochester a kindred spirit equal to her in passion and strong individualism, but also suffering from a faltering sense of identity in regard to what he is and what is expected of him. Bertha, Rochester's insane wife, who lives in the attic, haunts them both as a symbol of their still-unresolved identities. They cannot truly be united until each has worked out these inner problems.

Jane finally finds real family support with her three cousins at Moor House. She attains self-confidence from her success with the school and financial independence from her uncle's inheritance. From her unemotional relationship with her cousin St. John Rivers, a zealous minister, she realizes that she needs a passionate love, and her inner standard of religious morals are further solidified in contrast to his frigid piety.

Jane Eyre contains gothic, Romantic, and Victorian elements. Elements of these styles do not simply exist for their own sake, but underscore the major theme of Jane's personal progress. The gothic and Romantic elements—Bertha's ghostlike haunting, Thornfield's dark and castlelike image, the spiritual connection between Rochester and Jane, nature's sympathetic response to Jane's emotions with storms and sunshine—are symbolic of Jane's dark struggles with her identity and her romantic tendency to follow her intuition. The Victorian emphasis on realism, on domestic concerns of marriage and family, and the reconciliation of feeling with reason also pervade the novel.

Analysis

Belonging to a family is a major theme in *Jane Eyre*. Family was extremely important to a woman in the Victorian period. It provided emotional and financial support to her as a child and an unmarried woman. Later, it defined her as a wife and mother. As an orphan, however, Jane is cast into a Victorian domestic wilderness, without a mother to prepare her for her proper place in society and without a father to care for her until her husband can replace him.

The absence of family creates a mixed effect in Jane. Her painful solitude spurs her to spend much of her young life in search of a family. Many of the characters serve as symbolic mothers for Jane. The harsh mothering of her aunt, Mrs. Reed, causes Jane to suffer, forcing her to withdraw into a lonely shell for protection. Miss Temple at Lowood is Jane's first positive mother figure, showing compassion and caring and leading her on the path to self-fulfillment by encouraging her studies in French and literature.

The novel's structure buttresses the theme of Jane's search for a family. Beginning with the false, hurtful family of Mrs. Reed and her spoiled children, Jane encounters increasingly more rewarding versions of family coinciding with her personal maturation. At Lowood, Helen Burns and Miss Temple are a caring sister and mother. At Thornfield, Jane becomes a pseudo-mother to the sweet Adele and Mrs. Fairfax is a comforting mother-figure, but Jane is not yet able to be Rochester's wife.

At Moor House, she encounters an even stronger sense of familial belonging with St. John, Diana, and Mary Rivers, her cousins. She lovingly prepares the house for their Christmas reunion and shares her inheritance with them. Therefore, the strange coincidence of Jane ending up on the doorstep of Moor House should not be seen as a rupture in realism, but a thematic device. She rejects St. John's proposal of an authoritative, loveless marriage as a warped confusion of brother, husband, and father roles. Finally, Jane returns to a more enlightened Rochester to start a true family.

Jane's lack of family also has instilled in her a strong sense of self-reliance and independence. Even as a child in Sarah Reed's house, Jane recognizes the essential injustice of her predicament. She rejects the qualitative judgments that society makes on the basis of class and recognizes her cousins for the shallow, self-indulgent children that they are. Her personal standard of ethics tells her that Reed's children are not her superiors. She also balks at Mr. Brocklehurst's estimation of her as dishonest, recognizing his hypocrisy in demanding that his pupils live humbly and poorly, while his wife and daughters are bedecked in plumes and furs. Jane seems most humiliated and angered when her integrity is in question.

Jane's self-reliance and personal ethics allow her to recognize the unfairness of many societal conventions. She is belittled and ignored as a "mere governess" by Rochester's upper-class guests, but she recognizes them as arrogant and self-centered. Although she ranks far below Rochester in social rank and wealth, a profound impediment to a marriage in the Victorian era, she feels equal to him in soul, understanding his true nature. Jane finds his courting of the frivolous Blanche Ingram for her political and social connections disturbing because she knows that she herself is more his intellectual and spiritual equal.

Rochester's courtship of Blanche is particularly ironic in the light of his marriage to the insane Bertha, who he was tricked into marrying for the sake of monetary and political gain. It is significant that the primary symbol of hypocritical societal propriety, Thornfield Hall, in which Rochester lives a sham life of decorum, must be destroyed by fire before he and Jane can live together happily and truthfully.

The most convincing evidence of Jane's strength and independence, however, is her narrative voice. From the very beginning of the novel, the reader is struck by the sense of confidence and control in the narrative voice. Brontë cleverly manipulates reader response through the compelling voice of Jane. At times, one is brought close to the narrator in an intimate relationship in which Jane makes the reader a confidant, revealing inner feelings and weaknesses. Yet she never allows herself complete vulnerability as a narrator. Often Jane addresses readers directly, never letting them forget that she is aware of their presence. Readers are not eavesdroppers as in a third-person narrative, but invited guests of Jane, who is in complete control of the narrative. She creates suspense by withholding information from readers, such as the identity of Rochester when he is disguised as an old gypsy, playing with them to heighten their interest. Jane's voice is so commanding that her reliability and sincerity do not come into doubt.

Context

Published in 1847, *Jane Eyre* was a popular success. Although many women writers were read by the Victorian public, true literary respectability required a masculine name; hence Brontë used the pseudonym "Currer Bell." The popularity of this intelligent novel should force one to reconsider the often belittled and maligned tastes of the largely female reading public of the period. One can imagine that the novel appealed to women then, and today, because it reflects the frustratingly limiting condition of women in the nineteenth century. Although the novel's end suggests a typically Victorian domestic solution to Jane's problems—the reconciliation of Jane and Rochester—this conclusion does not assuage the more pervasive difficulties that Jane encounters in defining her identity as a woman within nineteenth century constraints. Modern readers appreciate Jane's strength and independence and her admirable struggle to live with integrity within a culture stifling for women.

For example, Jane's job as a governess exemplifies only one confusing female role in the 1800's. Women had very few alternatives for survival. If not supported by a father or a husband, an educated, middle-class woman likely was forced to become a governess, a position of lifelong servitude and repression of personal desires. As a woman who possesses the education, tastes, and behaviors of upper-class decorum so that she can teach them to her charges, the governess was frustrated to be treated as simply another household servant. Much of Jane's confusion about her identity at Thornfield stems from her contradictory role as governess.

Marriage, however, was no saving grace. Jane expresses the very modern fear, practically unheard of in the nineteenth century, of losing her identity in marriage. She resists compromising her identity and denigrating herself in conforming to Rochester's idea of a wife. In her wedding dress, she does not recognize herself before the mirror, nor can she write "Mrs. Rochester" on her luggage. As St. John's wife, she fears she would be "always restrained, and always checked—forced to keep the fire of my nature continually low." When Rochester is maimed and socially ruined, essentially bringing his physical strength and social position equal to that of Jane, the threat of domination no longer exists. Jane announces her decision in the powerful, self-asserting words of the final chapter: "Reader, I married him."

Sources for Further Study

Blom, Margaret Howard. *Charlotte Brontë.* Boston: Twayne, 1977. This introductory work asserts that *Jane Eyre* reflects Brontë's own contradictory struggle to be both independent and controlled by a man. Using biographical information as a springboard for analysis, the work examines Brontë's novels in separate chapters, including notes, an index, and a bibliography.

Gilbert, Sandra M., and Susan Gubar. *The Madwoman in the Attic: The Woman Writer and the Nineteenth-Century Literary Imagination.* New Haven, Conn.: Yale University Press, 1979. This feminist work examines recurrent themes in the works of major nineteenth century female writers. Interprets *Jane Eyre* as a progress novel tracing Jane's maturation, emphasizing the complex meaning of Bertha. Although 700 pages long, the book's extensive index and chapters divided by writer and work make it convenient for research.

King, Jeannette. *"Jane Eyre."* Philadelphia: Open University Press, 1986. An effective introduction to *Jane Eyre*, the book is arranged by literary elements with chapter headings such as "Characterization," "Language," and "Structure and Theme." Based on a tutorial approach in which readers are asked to reread certain chapters before reading discussion portions carefully examining the passages.

Macpherson, Pat. *Reflecting on "Jane Eyre."* London: Routledge, 1989. The author's conversational style and humor make this an entertaining work of criticism. Offers extensive character examinations of Jane, Bertha, and St. John and suggests that Brontë is practicing biting social criticism behind the disarming disguise of feminine confession.

Nestor, Pauline. *Charlotte Brontë's "Jane Eyre."* New York: St. Martin's Press, 1992. Arguing that Jane does not control her own actions, this work of new feminist criticism rejects previous estimations of Jane as a feminist hero. Offers interesting analyses of the themes of motherhood, sexuality, and identity and surveys the work's historical background and criticism. Includes an index, notes, and a bibliography.

Pinion, F. B. *A Brontë Companion*. New York: Barnes & Noble Books, 1975. A good reference work on all the Brontës, including biographical material, chapter-length analyses of their novels, a section on characters and places, an index, an annotated bibliography, and illustrations.

Heidi Kelchner

THE JOY LUCK CLUB

Author: Amy Tan (1952-)
Type of work: Novel
Type of plot: Psychological realism
Time of plot: The 1910's, the 1940's, the 1960's, and the 1980's
Locale: San Francisco and China
First published: 1989

Principal characters:

Suyuan Woo, the founder of the Joy Luck Club, who dies two months before the book opens

Jing-mei (June) Woo, Suyuan's daughter, who learns that she has two half sisters in China

Lindo Jong, Suyuan's competitive and critical best friend

Waverly Jong, Lindo's daughter, a divorced woman with a five-year-old daughter

An-mei Hsu, a member of the club whose mother brought disgrace on herself in China and poisoned herself

Rose Hsu Jordan, the third of An-mei's seven children, whose husband, Ted Jordan, wants a divorce

Ying-ying St. Clair, the wife of an American man who calls her "Betty"

Lena St. Clair, Ying-ying's daughter, who is unhappy in her marriage to the self-centered and success-oriented Harold Livotny

Form and Content

Amy Tan's *The Joy Luck Club* is a narrative mosaic made up of the lives of four Chinese women and their Chinese American daughters. Because of its structure, the book can only loosely be called a novel. It is composed of sixteen stories and four vignettes, but like many novels, it has central characters who develop through the course of the plot. The daughters struggle with the complexities of modern life, including identity crises and troubled relationships, while the mothers reflect on past actions that were dictated by culture and circumstance. The lives of the older women are bound together through their similar situations as immigrants and their monthly mah-jongg games at Joy Luck Club meetings.

Each of the stories is a first-person narration by one of the Joy Luck Club's three mothers or four daughters. Each narrator tells two stories about her own life, except for Jing-mei (June) Woo, who stands in for her deceased mother, telling a total of four stories. The tales are arranged in four groups, with a vignette preceding each group. The first group is told by mothers (plus June), the second and third groups by daughters, and the fourth by mothers. Jing-mei's final story, in which she learns her mother's history, concludes the book.

Since *The Joy Luck Club* is concerned with the relation of the present to the past, many stories take place in more than one time period. For example, in the last group of stories, the mothers begin their narration in the present time of the 1980's but then recall incidents that occurred when they were girls or young women: An-mei's mother's death, Ying-ying's first marriage, and Lindo's immigration to the United States. The narratives of the daughters are set in the 1960's, the time of their youth, or in the 1980's, with flashbacks to various earlier times. The first group of daughters' stories focuses on significant childhood experiences, while their second stories explore issues that they are experiencing as adults.

The daughters' tales are all set in the San Francisco Bay area, whereas the mothers' stories span two countries, China and the United States. Both rural and urban scenes in prewar China are depicted, and details related to festivals, customs, dress, housing, and food provide a rich backdrop to the central events in the narratives. June's final story, "A Pair of Tickets," takes her to a more modern China, where she finds Western capitalistic influences making inroads after nearly forty years of Communist Party rule.

The book examines a number of sociological issues from a woman's perspective: the death of parents, husbands, and children; marriage, adultery, and divorce; childbirth and abortion; and aging. The exploration, however, is often indirect. Situations are presented and later their consequences are shown. For example, Ying-ying's guilt over the death of her first child haunts a later pregnancy, and her daughter Lena's bulimic episode as an adolescent affects her eating habits as an adult. Exotic touches are added to the book's realistic rendering of emotions and incidents by means of references to Chinese folklore and superstition. Tan balances Eastern and Western points of view in her portrayal of the significant events of life.

Analysis

At first glance, *The Joy Luck Club* may seem randomly structured, but in actuality the book's organization is complex. Tan's use of multiple narrators and connecting vignettes shows the influence of writers such as William Faulkner and Louise Erdrich, but the narrative scheme is also patterned after the game of mah-jongg. Each family is represented once in every group of stories, just as each family is represented at the mah-jongg table at the Joy Luck Club. In mah-jongg, after each of the four players has started a round, a series is complete and the players change positions round the table. Likewise, the order of narrators changes after each group of stories. The first storyteller in the book is June. This corresponds to the position that she assumes at the mah-jongg table, the East wind, which always starts the game.

The stories in *The Joy Luck Club* are structurally self-contained. Built around a central incident or conflict, each one can be read without reference to the other stories. Yet there are numerous links among the stories that give unity to the book as a whole. Characters appear in one another's narratives, as when the Jongs eat Chinese New Year's dinner with the Woos in June's story "Best Quality." A recurring motif throughout the work is misunderstanding caused by cultural differences. All the mothers are perplexed by their American-born daughters, as are the daughters by their Chinese-born mothers. A more subtle device occurs in the third and fourth sections of the book. Each of the daughters' stories in the third group mentions the narrator's mother in the first sentence. Likewise, each of the mothers' stories in the fourth group begins with a reference to the narrator's daughter. The effect is not only to create unity within each group but also to suggest a close tie between the pairs of mothers and daughters. What one thinks, says, and does is important to the other, even in relationships where conflict is pronounced, as with Lindo and Waverly.

The short vignettes between groups of stories are an important structural feature as well. They are narrated by an omniscient voice, and their fablelike quality derives from their depiction of universal situations, such as a child challenging her mother's warnings against danger and a grandmother musing aloud to her infant granddaughter. The vignettes introduce important thematic concerns, such as preserving hope in the face of loss and passing on one's cultural legacy.

The quest for personal identity is the central theme in *The Joy Luck Club*. The death of Suyuan Woo causes Jing-mei to realize that she knew very little about her mother's life, and in her stories she ponders the meaning of her own life. Her discovery that she has two half sisters in China prompts her to take her cultural heritage seriously for the first time in her life. Rose, Lena, and Waverly are also engaged in various stages of the quest for selfhood. Rose and Lena are both learning to think and act independently of their husbands, and Waverly is discovering that her mother is not an adversary that she must outsmart. The author depicts the mothers as having resources that the daughters lack. Suyuan, An-mei, and Lindo were all severely tested by circumstances when they were young and found the strength to survive cruelty and hardship. Although Ying-ying lost her inner drive for many years, her daughter's unhappy marriage inspires her to try to regain her true nature in order to show Lena how to survive.

Context

The Joy Luck Club highlights the influence of culture on gender roles. The Chinese mothers in the book, all born in the 1910's, grew up in a hierarchical society in which a woman's worth was measured by her husband's status and his family's wealth. When they were young, the women were taught to repress their own desires so that they would learn to preserve the family honor and obey their husbands. The difficulties in marriage encountered by Lindo and Ying-ying as well as by An-mei's mother emphasize how few options were open to women in a tightly structured society in which their economic security and social standing were completely dependent on men.

Consequently, when the mothers immigrate to the United States, they want their daughters to retain their Chinese character but take advantage of the more flexible roles offered to women by American culture. The postwar daughters, however, are overwhelmed by having too many choices available. They struggle to balance multiple roles as career women, wives or girlfriends, and daughters. The materialistic focus of American culture makes it difficult for the daughters to internalize their mothers' values, particularly the self-sacrifice, determination, and family integrity that traditional Chinese culture stresses.

In addition to gender roles, mother-daughter relationships are an important focus of the book. Mothers are shown to have profound influence over their daughters' development, yet their influence is constrained by the surrounding culture. As girls, the Chinese women wanted to be like their mothers, whereas the American-born daughters are estranged from their mothers. This contrast is consistent with a difference between cultures: Americans expect their children to rebel against parental authority, while the Chinese promote obedience and conformity. The daughters in *The Joy Luck Club* think that their mothers are odd because they speak broken English and miss the subtleties of American culture pertaining to dress and social behavior. They also tend to see their mothers as pushy. Waverly and June rebel against their mothers' expectations without understanding that Lindo and Suyuan are trying to give their daughters the opportunities that they never had themselves. As adults, Waverly and June struggle with the conflicting desires of pleasing their mothers and developing their own individuality. Because they perceive their mothers' guidance as criticism, they are slow to understand the depth of their mothers' love and sacrifice for them.

Despite such generational and cultural gaps, the author suggests that daughters resemble their mothers in character as well as in appearance. Waverly possesses Lindo's shrewdness, and Rose shares An-mei's passivity in the face of suffering. By developing four central mother-daughter relationships rather than only one, Tan reveals that the factors which shape family resemblance, both negative and positive, are varied and complex.

Sources for Further Study

Chan, Jeffery Paul, Frank Chin, Lawson Fusao Inada, and Shawn H. Wong. "An Introduction to Chinese-American and Japanese-American Literatures." In *Three American Literatures*, edited by Houston A. Baker, Jr. New York: Modern Language Association of America, 1982. Arguing from the viewpoint that white supremacist thinking controls American culture, the authors detail the origins of a distinctly Asian American literature, a category not readily recognized by critics. The stereotype of the Asian American "dual personality" is rejected.

Fong, S. L. M. "Assimilation and Changing Social Roles of Chinese Americans." *Journal of Social Issues* 29, no. 2 (1973): 115-127. Examines the influence of acculturation and assimilation on traditional Chinese family structure and Chinese social hierarchy. Conflicts over parental authority and changes in sex roles and attitudes toward dating are discussed.

Kim, Elaine H. "Asian American Writers: A Bibliographical Review." *American Studies International* 22, no. 2 (1984): 41-78. Provides a useful overview of various types of Asian American writing and its special concerns, such as the Vietnam War and gender issues, and discusses problems in the criticism of Asian American literature. A bibliography of primary works is included.

____________. " 'Such Opposite Creatures': Men and Women in Asian-American Literature." *Michigan Quarterly Review* 29, no. 1 (Winter, 1990): 68-93. The author briefly discusses mother-daughter relations in *The Joy Luck Club* in her examination of the different ways in which Asian American men and women portray gender and ethnicity in their writing.

____________. *With Silk Wings*. San Francisco: Asian Women United of California, 1983. Following twelve profiles and forty short autobiographical sketches of Asian American women, this well-illustrated book provides the social and historical background of various groups of Asian women immigrants to the United States.

Tan, Amy. Interview by Barbara Somogyi and David Stanton. *Poets & Writers* 19, no. 5 (September 1, 1991): 24-32. In an informative interview, Tan talks about the origins of *The Joy Luck Club*, its autobiographical elements, and its portrayal of mother-daughter issues.

Patricia L. Watson

THE LAIS OF MARIE DE FRANCE

Author: Marie de France (c. 1150-c. 1215)
Type of work: Poetry
First published: *Lais*, c. 1167 (English translation, 1911)

Form and Content

Marie de France is the earliest French woman poet whose name is known today. Her major work, *The Lais of Marie de France*, consists of twelve poems that range in length from 118 to 1,184 lines. Although these poems were composed over a number of years, Marie decided at some point to collect the *lais* into a single book. She added a fifty-six-line prologue dedicating the volume to a "noble king" whom she never names. For more than a century, scholars have attempted to determine this king's identity—and even the land that he ruled—but the matter remains a mystery. One leading possibility is that Marie's "noble king" was Henry II, the English ruler who came to the throne in 1154. Like Marie, Henry was of French descent but lived in England, where a large number of the *Lais* were set.

The word *lai* (plural *lais*) that Marie adopts for her poems is a French borrowing of the Provençal term for "ballad." Originally, *lais* were short, lyric poems sung to the accompaniment of a stringed instrument. By Marie's time, however, the term *lais* had expanded to include nonmusical poems intended to be read, either privately or as part of a court entertainment. In Marie's *Lais*, references to such figures as the Roman poet Ovid, the medieval grammarian Priscian, and the legendary Babylonian queen Semiramis make it clear that these works were intended for a highly educated audience. Marie herself appears to have been quite learned. She knew both Latin and English and attained a wide reputation for her poetry during her own lifetime.

The Lais of Marie de France were written in Old French with rhyming couplets of eight-syllable lines. Each of the poems presents a romantic crisis that leads the central characters to an adventure. Some stories, such as "Equitan," attempt to teach a moral lesson; most are pure entertainment. A few of the *lais*, including "Chaitivel" and "The Two Lovers," end tragically. Most of the poems, however, represent love as ultimately triumphant over obstacles arising during the course of the story.

Analysis

The Lais of Marie de France are important both as folklore and as literature. As Marie herself says at several points, most of her stories originated in the oral legends of the Bretons. As a result, poems such as "Lanval" contain many plot elements found in oral traditions all over the world. Like Elsa in the Germanic legend of Lohengrin or Psyche in the Greco-Roman legend of Cupid and Psyche, the hero Lanval temporarily loses his beloved by breaking his promise. Like Potifar's wife in the Old Testament or Anubis' wife in the Egyptian tale of Anubis and Bata, Guinevere falsely claims that a man molested her when he had actually refused her advances. In "Eliduc," the king of England's daughter is restored to life in a manner almost identical to that by which both the healer Asclepius and the seer Polyeidus were said to have revived Minos' son Glaucus in Greek mythology.

By recording the legends of the Bretons, Marie preserved these tales at a time when oral traditions throughout Europe were being obliterated by a rapidly expanding literary culture. Even as Marie was preserving these stories, however, she was also reshaping them, giving them a distinctly literary form. She added geographical names and a touch of the archaism that she found in such chronicles as Geoffrey of Monmouth's *Historia Regum Britanniae* (c. 1135; *History of the Kings of Britain*) and Geoffrey's Gaimar's *Estoire des Engleis* (c. 1150; *History of the English*). In "Chevrefoil," she adapted the familiar legend of Tristan, the same story that would later be treated by such authors as Béroul (c. 1200) and Gottfried von Strassburg (c. 1210).

Like Chrétien de Troyes in the late twelfth century and the other writers of medieval romance, Marie combined supernatural elements with heroic exploits. Her character Guigemar, like Galahad and Parzifal before him, boards an enchanted ship that carries him to a distant land. Bisclavret is transformed into a werewolf, and Yonec's father becomes a hawk. The hero of "The Two Lovers" uses a magic potion that greatly increases his strength. In addition to these supernatural details, Marie also borrowed a number of unrealistic situations from the romantic tradition. In many of her stories, her hero and heroine fall in love without ever having met: The mere report that a woman is beautiful or that a man is noble is enough to stimulate the deepest affections. Spouses, parents, and other impediments to the marriage of the central characters conveniently die or vanish from the story at the appropriate moment so that the lovers may be united.

Beneath this layer of fantasy and wish fulfillment, however, Marie's poems reflect many values that would have been familiar to her aristocratic audience. Nearly all Marie's heroes are either kings or noblemen. Nearly all of her heroines are kings' daughters or ladies of the court. In every case, the characters adhere to the complex set of social conventions that came to be known as *courtoisie* (courtesy). Medieval authors represented courtesy through such traits as generosity, fidelity, valor, and romantic love. Discourtesy is usually introduced by Marie only to be punished quickly and severely. Equitan, for example, is killed by the same plan that he had intended for his steward. Bisclavret's wife and her lover are banished because they have plotted against the hero. Guigemar kills Meriaduc for the discourtesy that he displayed to the hero's beloved. Situations such as these helped to reinforce the values of Marie's aristocratic audience and encouraged readers to identify with the noble figures depicted in her poems.

While the central characters of Marie's *Lais* thus generally follow the code of behavior known as courtly love, this does not mean that they are constrained by every precept of that code. For example, lovers are occasionally unfaithful or even treacherous. Eliduc, although married, takes a lover when he is sent into exile. The heroine of "Chaitivel" has four lovers, all of whom she loves equally. Moreover, the knights in Marie's poems rarely suffer the prolonged period of "languishing" that was common in courtly romances. The female figures in *Lais* are neither as disdainful as the heroines of many romances nor pure, unattainable women such as Beatrice in the *La divina commedia* (c. 1320; *The Divine Comedy*) of Dante Alighieri (1265-1321). To the contrary, Marie's heroines are usually amorous women who succumb to their lovers shortly after their first meeting. In part, this departure from the romantic tradition is attributable to the short length of the *lai*, which did not permit Marie to describe long periods of unfulfilled passion. In part, too, it was attributable to the age in which Marie was writing, a time when all the conventions of courtly love had not yet been firmly established.

One of the most important values shared by Marie's original audience was the view expressed in "Equitan" that honorable love can exist only between social equals. While it is true that Marie continues this discussion by saying that a man who is poor and honorable is of far greater worth than a king who is discourteous, strict social boundaries still separated the two classes. Humble individuals, Marie notes, will come to disaster if they search for love above their station. In fact, all the central characters in Marie's poems are aristocrats. Unlike such literary forms as the *fabliau*, the *lai* was a type of poem written *about* the nobility *for* the nobility. It dealt with characters who had sufficient wealth and leisure to devote to such activities as falconry, tournaments, courtship, and listening to ballads.

The values of Marie's social class also help to explain her emphasis upon male characters, often at the expense of women. Since Marie herself was a woman author, the reader might expect the heroines of her stories to be prominent. In fact, this rarely occurs. While most of Marie's heroes have names, most of her female characters are referred to only by their titles. In "Guigemar," the hero concludes (incorrectly) that a woman whom he sees cannot really be his beloved since "all women look rather the same." In "Eliduc," the hero's wife humbly retires to a convent so that her husband will be able to marry his lover. These situations reflect the conventions of the literary genre that Marie had adopted and the aristocratic values of the late twelfth century. There is no way of knowing whether they also reflect the feelings of the author herself. Nevertheless, it should be noted that Marie gives roughly the same attention to the romantic plights of her male and female characters. She portrays women as highly creative, even as the guiding forces in several stories. In "The Two Lovers," for example, it is the female character who suggests that the hero travel to Salerno to acquire the magic potion. In "Milun," a noblewoman rather than the hero develops the plan by which her pregnancy is kept a secret.

Context

Marie de France was a pioneer in women's literature not because she limited herself to issues of concern to women but because she achieved prominence in a genre that would long remain dominated by men. Throughout the entire Middle Ages, Marie was the only woman author of romantic tales to achieve a status equal to that of Chrétien de Troyes, Guillaume de Lorris, Jean (Clopinel) de Meung, Gottfried von Strassburg, and Wolfram von Eschenbach.

As a result of both the conventions of medieval romance and the culture of her time, Marie often gave more attention to the male characters in her poems than to the female characters. With the exception of Le Fresne ("Ash Tree") and La Codre ("Hazel Tree"), whose names are central to the plot of the story, few women in Marie's *Lais* are even named. Most women simply have titles, such as "Meriaduc's sister" and "Eliduc's wife," that define their position in terms of their male relatives. Even Guinevere, who appears as a minor character in "Lanval," is called simply "the queen." Nevertheless, Marie's success in her genre prepared the way for such later women authors as Marguerite de Navarre (1492-1549), whose *Heptaméron* was based upon the structure of the *Decameron* (1348-1353; English translation, 1702), by Giovanni Boccaccio (1313-1375). Moreover, Marie's aristocratic and intellectual poetry anticipated the later works of such authors as Anna, Comtesse de Noailles (1876-1933) and Catherine Pozzi (1882-1934).

Sources for Further Study

Burgess, Glyn Sheridan. "Chivalry and Prowess in the *Lais* of Marie de France." *French Studies* 37 (April, 1983): 129-142. Burgess argues that the *Lais* are primarily an upper-class phenomenon presenting twelfth century knights in the context of their social superiors. This article also studies the vocabulary that Marie adopts for various courtly virtues.

______________. *"The Lais of Marie de France": Text and Context.* Athens: University of Georgia Press, 1987. The best general analysis of the *Lais*, this work deals with such matters as chronology, chivalry, character analysis, vocabulary, and the status of women in the poems. Includes an extensive bibliography.

Damon, S. Foster. "Marie de France: Psychologist of Courtly Love." *Publications of the Modern Language Association* 44 (1929): 968-996. This article argues that, since Marie was writing before the "laws" of courtly love were established, she was freer than later authors to develop the actions of her characters. Also includes a useful chart analyzing the hero, heroine, and villain of each *lai*, as well as the solutions to the romantic crises of the poems.

Jackson, W. T. H. "The Arthuricity of Marie de France." *Romanic Review* 70 (1979): 1-18. Jackson suggests that Marie's purpose was to question the assumptions of the courtly romance. As a result, she created almost a parody of that genre.

Mickel, Emanuel J. *Marie de France*. New York: Twayne, 1974. Intended for the general reader, this is a good introduction to many aspects of the *Lais*. Contains a discussion of Marie's possible identity, the sources of her works, a historical background, and a concise discussion of each poem.

Jeffrey L. Buller

THE LEFT HAND OF DARKNESS

Author: Ursula K. Le Guin (1929-)
Type of work: Novel
Type of plot: Science fiction
Time of plot: The future
Locale: The imaginary planet of Gethen, also called "Winter"
First published: 1969

Principal characters:

Genly Ai, a young man from Earth who has come to Gethen as the envoy of a benign interplanetary league

Therem Harth rem ir Estraven, the Lord of Estre in Kerm and Ai's ally

Argaven XV, the mad king of Karhide

Tibe, Argaven's cousin, who gains power in the court and causes Estraven's exile from Karhide

Faxe the Weaver, an Indweller at Otherhord Fastness and a member of the Handdarata

Foreth rem ir Osboth, Estraven's former lover, or "kemmering"

Obsle and **Yegey,** two of the thirty-three Commensals who rule the nation of Orgoreyn

Commissioner Shusgis, a politician in Mishnory, the capital of Orgoreyn

Esvans Harth rem ir Estraven, the Lord of Estre, Estraven's father

Arek Harth rem ir Estraven, Estraven's brother, who vowed kemmering with Therem

Sorve Harth rem ir Estraven, the heir of Estre and the son of Arek and Therem

Form and Content

The Left Hand of Darkness is one of several novels describing the results of experiments carried out on other planets by beings from the planet Hain. On Gethen, the Hainish established a race of ambisexual humans. Gethenians are usually androgynous and asexual; once a month, however, they enter a state called "kemmer." During this period sexuality predominates over everything else. In kemmer, Gethenians develop male or female characteristics, but their specific gender is completely arbitrary and may vary from one cycle to another.

The novel takes place thousands of years later, when Genly Ai comes to this ambisexual world as an envoy from the Ekumen. Gethen has evolved into a complex society, shaped not by gender differences but by the alternation of frigidity and sexual activity; it has also developed two national superpowers (Karhide, a monarchy, and Orgoreyn, a communist state) and two principal religions (the Handdara and the Yomesh). *The Left Hand of Darkness* traces Ai's adventures on this planet in the course of fulfilling his mission. He gradually convinces the Gethenians—in particular, Estraven—that his stories of other worlds are true. Equally important, he himself comes to understand Gethen.

The novel begins in Ehrenrang, Karhide's capital, where Estraven has arranged Ai's audience with the king. Ai does not trust Estraven, however, and he is scarcely surprised when Estraven tells him that he can no longer represent Ai's interests to the king. The following morning, however, Estraven is gone, banished from Karhide on pain of death; the king condemns him as a traitor and shows no interest in the Ekumen. Despondent, Ai decides to leave Ehrenrang.

He goes to eastern Karhide to learn more of the country and to learn the answer to a question. In eastern Karhide are the Fastnesses, retreats for practitioners of the Handdara. Like Taoism, this religion advocates living in the moment as a meaningful response to the one certain fact known by every person: He or she will die. In order to demonstrate the uselessness of all other knowledge, the Handdarata perform a ritual in which a "weaver" foretells the answer to a stranger's question. Handdarata legends confirm both the answers' accuracy and the questions' essential irrelevance. Nevertheless, Ai asks this question: Will Gethen join the Ekumen within five years? Hours later, he receives his answer: yes.

When Ai arrives in Orgoreyn, he finds Estraven already there, garnering support for Ai's cause among the ruling Commensals. Yet Ai still does not trust him, even though Estraven's kemmering, Foreth, begged him to assist Estraven in his exile. To Ai, Estraven's presence in Orgoreyn merely confirms his treachery and his political expediency. Ai therefore ignores Estraven's warning that his life is in danger. The next morning, he is arrested and sent to a work farm—where he almost dies, but for Estraven's brilliant rescue.

By crossing the dangerous Gobrin Ice, Estraven and Ai hope to return to Karhide, where Ai's mission may fare better now. On this journey, they risk starvation, injury, and death—and become true friends. Ai teaches Estraven a form of telepathy that precludes misunderstanding; they call each other by their first names; and, when they reach Karhide, Estraven skis directly toward the border guards' guns—a sacrifice that facilitates the political success of Ai's mission in Karhide.

Karhide does join the Ekumen, confirming the Foretellers' answer to Ai's question. Yet as Ai journeys to Estre to tell Estraven's father of his son's death, he realizes that question's irrelevance to what he has learned on Gethen. At Estre he meets Estraven's son Sorve, who asks a better question in the book's final sentence. Rather than assuming a yes or no answer, Sorve begins a dialogue: "Will you tell us about the other worlds out among the stars—the other kinds of men, the other lives?"

Analysis

In form as well as content, Ursula K. Le Guin's novel emphasizes that the whole is greater than the sum of its parts. Ai's mission asks the Gethenians to look beyond their personal interests, to join in solidarity with other lives and other worlds. Estraven is the only Gethenian capable of such large-mindedness, and even so, Ai initially thinks him disloyal or unpatriotic, because he does not care whether Karhide or Orgoreyn is the first to join the Ekumen. By the end of the novel, however, Ai understands the selflessness of Estraven's motives. He tells Argaven XV that Estraven had served neither Karhide nor its king, but the same master that he himself served. When the king asks suspiciously whether that master is the Ekumen, Ai answers that it is humankind. Similarly, *The Left Hand of Darkness* asks readers to look beyond gender roles and sexual identities, and to focus instead on the common humanity that all people share.

The novel's title emphasizes this theme. "Light is the left hand of darkness/ and darkness the right hand of light," according to a poem of the Handdarata that Estraven recites to Ai as they cross the Gobrin Ice. The novel consistently acknowledges dualities such as light and dark, left and right, but emphasizes that they are complementary rather than opposed. Together, they make up something greater than either alone, as the poem's ending suggests:

> Two are one, life and death, lying
> together like lovers in kemmer,
> like hands joined together,
> like the end and the way.

It is fitting that a sacred poem from an imaginary religion, which one character recites to another, should gloss the title of *The Left Hand of Darkness*. The novel is filled with embedded texts that add depth and verisimilitude to the story. Chapters that develop the plot alternate with others that feature Karhide folk tales, Handdarata or Yomeshta writings, Orgota creation myths, or the field notes of the first Ekumenical investigator on Gethen. Each interlude provides a mythic, religious, or anthropological context for an episode in the novel's plot; it also generates suspense, since the reader is anxious to return to the main story line. Most important, these fragments of other writings serve as complements to the story of Ai and Estraven.

In chapter 6, Le Guin's narrative strategy becomes more complicated. Up to this point, the chapters developing the main story line are narrated in the first person by Ai. Now they are narrated alternately by Ai and Estraven, as each describes his own adventures in Orgoreyn; later, the two take turns describing their shared adventures on the Gobrin Ice. The reader gradually understands that Ai, the novel's frame narrator, believed that he could most accurately describe his experiences by including other voices and other texts in his report to the Ekumen. As he explains on the novel's first page, "I'll make my report as if I told a story. . . . The story is not all mine, nor told by me alone." The novel's narration thus reiterates the theme that the whole is greater than the sum of its parts.

Context

The Left Hand of Darkness can be compared to other works of fantasy or science fiction that concentrate on gender. Charlotte Perkins Gilman's separatist feminist novel *Herland* (1915; 1979) imagines an entire society of women. Herland—whose architecture, economy, industry, and religion is described in considerable detail—is a land of peace, harmony, and creativity. So, at first, is the society of hermaphrodites that Theodore Sturgeon describes in his classic science-fiction novel *Venus Plus X* (1965); Sturgeon's novel darkly suggests, however, that such utopias can only be attained by means of genetic engineering. Doris Lessing's science-fiction novel *The Marriages Between Zones Three, Four, and Five* (1980) suggests the difficulty and necessity of leaving behind separatist models of men's and women's "zones."

Because science fiction facilitates imagining alternatives to contemporary society, many feminists choose this genre to express their ideas. Yet *The Left Hand of Darkness*—which won both Hugo and Nebula Awards for best science-fiction novel of 1969—stands out among other works, for both the originality of its conception and the care with which it is worked out. The novel was a "thought-experiment," as Le Guin explains in her introduction, in which she tried to imagine a world without gender. Le Guin's solution to this problem—making the Gethenians utterly androgynous and asexual, except in kemmer—also enabled her to imagine a world in which sexuality is separate from daily life. On Gethen, no one is limited by predetermined gender roles; which partner bears children, for example, is a matter of chance. On Gethen, war and rape do not exist. Yet cruelty, violence, and injustice still flourish there—along with kindness, compassion, and pursuit of truth. Significantly, this planet of androgynes is neither a utopia nor a dystopia. Indeed, *The Left Hand of Darkness* resists such dualistic thinking. Le Guin's novel forgoes separatist feminism in order to establish common humanity beyond assigned gender roles.

The Left Hand of Darkness is not without flaws. Early critics claimed that the Gethenians' ambisexuality was a gimmick and was unimportant to the plot; however, careful reading shows that this is not the case. Other critics have claimed, more convincingly, that the novel is not truly feminist, because it emphasizes a masculine perspective rather than a feminine or androgynous one. It is true that *The Left Hand of Darkness* tends to express its humanist vision in terms of men and masters. In her essay "Is Gender Necessary?" Le Guin admits that her consistent use of male pronouns fails to convey the Gethenians' androgyny.

Le Guin's essay also makes clear, however, that she considers *The Left Hand of Darkness* an ongoing experiment to be completed in the minds of individual readers. In this sense, the novel is certainly successful: Critics continue to debate its merits in the contexts of feminist theory, male feminism, and gay and lesbian studies. Ultimately, however, *The Left Hand of Darkness* is a feminist novel because it challenges readers to transcend gender and discover a common humanity shared by both men and women.

Sources for Further Study

Barrow, Craig, and Diana Barrow. "*The Left Hand of Darkness*: Feminism for Men." *Mosaic* 20, no. 1 (Winter, 1987): 83-96. This insightful essay suggests that Le Guin's feminist novel was specifically intended for male readers.

Bloom, Harold, ed. *Ursula K. Le Guin*. New York: Chelsea House, 1986. A collection of chronologically ordered and previously published essays tracing the general critical reception of Le Guin's work.

————. *Ursula K. Le Guin's "The Left Hand of Darkness."* New York: Chelsea House, 1987. This useful collection contains nine previously published essays, arranged in chronological order, which examine the novel in various contexts: archetypal narrative patterns, social criticism, feminism, and speech-act theory. Martin Bickman's essay on the novel's unity persuasively counters earlier charges that the Gethenians' ambisexuality is irrelevant to the plot.

Cummins, Elizabeth. *Understanding Ursula K. Le Guin*. Columbia: University of South Carolina Press, 1990. The third chapter of this book compares *The Left Hand of Darkness* to Le Guin's other novels about the results of Hainish experiments. Good annotated bibliography.

Frazer, Patricia. "Again, *The Left Hand of Darkness*: Androgyny or Homophobia?" In *The Erotic Universe: Sexuality and Fantastic Literature*, edited by Donald Palumbo. New York: Greenwood Press, 1986. Frazer's essay discusses issues of sexuality—rather than gender—in the novel. The collection features an excellent annotated bibliography on sexuality in science fiction.

Le Guin, Ursula K. "Is Gender Necessary?" In *The Language of the Night: Essays on Fantasy and Science Fiction*, edited by Susan Wood. New York: G. P. Putnam's Sons, 1979. In this important essay, Le Guin critiques her own novel as a feminist experiment—not wholly successful—in which she tried to discover the essence of humanity by eliminating gender.

Rhodes, Jewell Parker. "Ursula Le Guin's *The Left Hand of Darkness*: Androgyny and the Feminist Utopia." In *Women and Utopia: Critical Interpretations*, edited by Marleen Barr and Nicholas D. Smith. Lanham, Md.: University Press of America, 1983. This essay argues that the novel's exploration of androgyny is undermined by Le Guin's own patriarchal bias.

Spivack, Charlotte. *Ursula K. Le Guin*. Boston: Twayne, 1984. A good overall introduction to Le Guin's work in fiction and other genres.

Susan Elizabeth Sweeney

LIFE IN THE IRON MILLS: Or, The Korl Woman

Author: Rebecca Harding Davis (1831-1910)
Type of work: Novella
Type of plot: Social realism
Time of plot: The mid-nineteenth century
Locale: An industrial town in the United States
First published: 1861

Principal characters:

The narrator, an unnamed individual of unspecified gender, a member of the privileged class

Hugh Wolfe, a nineteen-year-old iron mill worker

Deborah, Hugh's cousin, a cotton mill worker who loves Hugh

Janey, a Irish girl who is the focus of Hugh's dreams

Young Kirby, the son of the man who owns the iron mill

Mitchell, young Kirby's brother-in-law, a wealthy dilettante

May, a friend of young Kirby

Form and Content

Life in the Iron Mills: Or, The Korl Woman is a long-neglected literary classic, written by a woman who in a number of her works rejected the sentimental stance that was expected from her gender and class in favor of uncompromising realism. By focusing on one tragic episode, Rebecca Harding Davis exposes the hypocrisy of a society which pretends to offer opportunities to all but in actuality exploits and oppresses the many in order to preserve the privileges of the few.

In early 1861, when Davis submitted *Life in the Iron Mills* to the *Atlantic*, she was uncertain whether to call her work a short story or an article. Although the editors who accepted it chose to classify it as a story, twentieth century critics have been unhappy with that designation. Davis' biographer Jane Atteridge Rose gives a plausible explanation for their reactions: She suggests that the work is so dense with symbolism and significance that it seems longer than the typical short story. In her edited collection *Life in the Iron Mills and Other Stories*, Tillie Olsen italicizes the title work, arguing that it has the "weight" of a novella. In contrast, she classifies as short stories both "The Wife's Story," which is very nearly as long as *Life in the Iron Mills*, and the briefer "Anne."

There is ample justification for looking at *Life in the Iron Mills* as a novella. In form, it is complex. The central plot is framed and punctuated by the comments of a narrator, who, by describing past events that he or she could not have witnessed, takes on the function of an omniscient author. Moreover, instead of concentrating on one protagonist, as she does in "The Wife's Story" and "Anne," in *Life in the Iron Mills* Davis gives equal importance to two characters, Hugh Wolfe and his cousin Deborah. Their function is also complex. Though they are individualized, they also represent, separately, their respective genders and, jointly, an entire social class.

The plot itself is simple. In an introduction, the narrator proposes to tell about events that occurred thirty years before, most of them during a single night. After a twelve-hour workday in a cotton mill, Deborah prepares some food and takes it to her cousin Hugh Wolfe at the iron mill where he works. After she has delivered his supper, she lies down in a warm area of the mill to rest for a while before returning home. When young Kirby, the mill owner's son, arrives with the mill overseer and some prominent friends, they hardly notice Deborah. They do notice, however, the carving of a woman which Hugh has made out of ore refuse, or korl. They first compliment him on his talent, then callously refuse to help him develop it. Desperate to help the man she loves, Deborah steals a pocketbook from Mitchell, young Kirby's brother-in-law, which she later gives to Hugh. Although he knows that he should return it, he cannot force himself to do so.

The story now moves forward a month. One of the men who had spoken to Hugh that night, Dr. May, reads his wife the newspaper report of Hugh's sentence.

Quickly the scene shifts. In jail, Hugh says goodbye to Deborah, cuts his wrists, and bleeds to death. Hearing about the tragedy, a Quaker woman comes to the jail and befriends Deborah. After she emerges from prison, Deborah is taken to a Quaker settlement in the mountains, where she regains her health and gains religious faith.

At the end of the novel, the narrator returns to the present and to his or her library. There, behind a curtain, stands the statue of the korl woman, who represents all the agony and the yearning of the helpless poor. Sometimes, however, when the narrator draws aside the curtain just before sunrise, the korl woman seems to gesture toward the coming dawn.

Analysis

In the initial pages of *Life in the Iron Mills*, Rebecca Harding Davis asserts that her work is intended not only to expose the evils of industrial society but also to promise a better future. Her hope for change is based not on the good will of the ruling classes, which she reveals as empty posturing, but on the human aspirations of the downtrodden, which their exploiters have not been able to eliminate.

The industrial overlords have chosen to insulate themselves from any appeal to sympathy or call for justice by believing that society consists of two worlds: their own, which is inhabited by "civilized" people, and another world filled with vicious creatures who can hardly be classified as human. The upper-class characters who visit the mill voice this attitude in rational, persuasive terms. Davis' method of proving how wrong they are is to show her readers the truth before they are presented with the falsehood.

Thus she begins the novel by proving that the mill workers do not in fact dwell in a separate world. In long descriptive passages, she shows that the smoke from the mills permeates the entire town, that the polluted river flows out of the mill town into distant fields and gardens. At this point, the narrator abandons a vantage point at the window, which has kept him or her both detached from the workers and above them, in order to negate the second part of the argument. No one can enter the Wolfe household and look into the hearts of its inhabitants, as the omniscient author now does, and still contend that mill workers are less than human.

Both Hugh Wolfe and Deborah are sensitive, virtuous individuals. Deborah is kind to Hugh's aged father; she shares her food with young Janey, who has fled to the Wolfes for refuge; and even though she is exhausted after a twelve-hour day in a cotton mill, she ventures out nightly to take Hugh his supper. Admittedly, in all of her actions Deborah is motivated less by her conscience than by her love for Hugh. For that reason, she does not hesitate to steal the money. Yet Deborah does nothing for herself. Realizing that Hugh does not love her, she is willing to see him marry Janey; all she wants in life is for him to be happy.

It is suggested that Hugh's temperate conduct, which sets him apart from the men who work beside him, may be the result of his schooling. His generosity cannot have been learned, however, nor can his passion for creation, which drives him to transform refuse into beauty. As for Hugh's honesty, one wonders whether young Kirby is ever tormented by his conscience when he does for profit what Hugh does out of desperation.

Yet, even though she is sympathetic with the mill workers, Davis is too much of a realist to show them as totally good or the upper classes as totally evil. For every Hugh or Deborah, she indicates, there are dozens of workers who live in degradation and vice. Similarly, while she has no time for the heartless young Kirby, the self-centered Mitchell, or the hypocritical Dr. May, the author does admit the existence of such upper-class people as the sympathetic narrator, who hopes to effect social reform by influencing public opinion, and the Quaker woman, who takes direct action to help at least one of the victims of industrialism.

Through her extensive use of symbolism, Davis defines not the workers but their environment as being inhuman. Even the river that passes through the mill town is enslaved, she says, as the workers are: Bound to their jobs until they die, they are in essence slaves. They are also tormented souls. Young Kirby admits that his mill resembles Dante's Hell; however, he indicates that because they are "bad" and "desperate," the workers deserve to be there.

By the time that she shows Dr. May pontificating at his breakfast table while Hugh is deciding to kill himself, Davis has proven that nineteenth century industrial society is based on the callous exploitation of one set of human beings by another. Less clear, however, is exactly what she sees as grounds for hope. It has been argued that the social reform that is so clearly needed may come through the narrator or through the establishment of communal groups such as that in which Deborah ends her life. What is not so obvious, however, is how Davis' ending offers hope to artists such as herself. Hugh has been denied help and destroyed, and the only remaining evidence of his genius has become a mere conversation piece in a private apartment. The ambivalence of Davis' conclusion may well reflect her uncertainty about her own future in art.

Context

In *Life in the Iron Mills*, which was her first published work and is still considered her finest, Rebecca Harding Davis focused primarily on a class issue, rather than one of gender. In the works that followed, however, such as "The Wife's Story," she turned to the situation of women, especially those with artistic aspirations. Told by their society that they could find fulfillment only in being wives and mothers, women were not sure that they had any right to lives of their own; however, if they suppressed their creative urges, they were unhappy and made their families miserable.

In the female protagonists of her later stories and novels, Davis seems to have fused the salient characteristics of Hugh Wolfe and Deborah. Like Hugh, these characters have a need to create, but like Deborah, because they are women they are expected to sacrifice themselves gladly for the men they love. Thus they are faced with external pressures, with internal conflicts, and, if they do pursue their dreams, with a sense of guilt no less real than that of Hugh. Rather than money, however, they are stealing time and attention from their husbands and children.

By the end of the nineteenth century, writers such as Charlotte Perkins Gilman would assert that women do have the right to put themselves first. Rebecca Harding Davis was not yet ready to make such a radical statement. Instead, she took refuge in ambivalent conclusions or in happy endings which affirm that only in self-abnegation can women find themselves. Yet, even in the sentimental fiction that Davis wrote in order to support her own family, there is evidence that this early realist saw the deplorable predicament of nineteenth century women far more clearly than she was willing to admit to her readers, or perhaps, to herself.

Sources for Further Study

Boudreau, Kristin. " 'The Woman's Flesh of Me': Rebecca Harding Davis's Response to Self-Reliance." *American Transcendental Quarterly* n.s. 6 (June, 1992): 132-140. Argues that "The Wife's Story" is an indictment of Emersonian ideas. Davis sees women as not only trapped in a patriarchal society but also blocked by their own bodies from attaining intellectual independence.

Davis, Rebecca Harding. *Life in the Iron Mills and Other Stories*. Edited by Tillie Olsen. New York: Feminist Press, 1985. An expanded edition which also includes "The Wife's Story" and "Anne." Tillie Olsen's well-documented and perceptive "Biographical Interpretation" provides an excellent overview of Davis' life and works.

Harris, Sharon M. *Rebecca Harding Davis and American Realism*. Philadelphia: University of Pennsylvania Press, 1991. A major study of the author, placing her within the larger context of intellectual history. Also contains useful biographical materials.

Molyneaux, Maribel W. "Sculpture in the Iron Mills: Rebecca Harding Davis's Korl Woman." *Woman's Studies* 17 (January, 1990): 157-177. Assuming that the narrator in *Life in the Iron Mills* is female, Molyneaux sees her as the primary character of the story. As a woman artist and a reformer, the narrator defies custom and enters the province of men. The korl woman thus represents both the woman worker, demanding a better life, and the woman writer, insisting on a place in literary history.

Rose, Jane Atteridge. "Images of Self: The Example of Rebecca Harding Davis and Charlotte Perkins Gilman." *English Language Notes* 29 (June, 1992): 70-78. Uses Davis' "The Wife's Story" and Gilman's *The Yellow Wallpaper* (1899) to indicate a "change in female self-perception" between the 1860's and the 1890's. Although both women writers felt the tension between their domestic duties and their art, Davis was influenced by the ideal of feminine "self-abnegation," while Gilman rejected it, maintaining that each woman has the right to an independent identity.

———. *Rebecca Harding Davis*. New York: Twayne, 1993. A much-needed book-length biographical and critical study. Rose's interpretations of the various works are based on careful readings of the texts.

Contains a chronology, voluminous notes, and an annotated bibliography.

Shurr, William H. "*Life in the Iron Mills*: A Nineteenth-Century Conversion Narrative." *American Transcendental Quarterly* 5 (December, 1991): 245-257. In this interesting essay, Shurr attempts to prove that the mysterious narrator is the dilettante Mitchell, whose religious conversion may have been modeled on that of the British reformer John Ruskin.

Rosemary M. Canfield Reisman

A LITERATURE OF THEIR OWN

Author: Elaine Showalter (1941-)
Type of work: Literary criticism
First published: 1977

Form and Content

In *A Literature of Their Own*, Elaine Showalter traces a tradition of women's literature in England by examining the works and lives of women novelists from 1840 to the present. Her analysis, which includes both great and minor novelists, juxtaposes these writers' lives and work against the social, political, and cultural realities of the lives of "ordinary" women of their time, while tracing the similarities of this female literary subculture to other literary subcultures.

Showalter asserts that she is not concerned with delineating a female imagination, which runs the risk of being defined in stereotypes, but is looking for repeated themes, patterns, and images in literature by women. Therefore, her study considers only women who write for pay and publication.

The author divides women's literary subculture into three stages—the feminine, the feminist, and the female—and traces shifts in perspective toward literature and women's place in it across these stages as women writers struggle to form and maintain a sense of identity in a male-controlled profession. In the feminine stage (1840-1880), women imitate the dominant culture and internalize its ideas about art and society. In the feminist state (1880-1920), women protest against these ideas and advocate their own thoughts about society and art. In the female stage (1920 onward), women search for self-identity by looking inside themselves and away from the dominant culture.

Showalter's study is notable for its balance and generosity as it illuminates the lives and art of such well-known women writers as Charlotte Brontë, George Eliot, and Virginia Woolf by considering them in relation to their relatively unknown literary sisters. Such an agenda allows the author to challenge, or demystify, prevailing interpretations of these women's lives and work. For example, she sees George Eliot as more traditional than radical, and she questions positive assumptions generally associated with Virginia Woolf's concept of androgyny. Throughout the work, Showalter traces women writers' efforts to accommodate, question, or move outside traditional notions of women's domestic nature at the same time that they question the suitability of women's experience as a preparation and basis for writing fiction.

This is a scholarly but highly readable work that not only sheds new light on familiar women writers but also introduces the reader to some of their contemporaries, who, although less well known, share the same artistic and social challenges and concerns. All the women studied take part in a dialogue that spans the nineteenth and twentieth centuries and that shapes their fiction and their self-awareness.

The text includes a biographical appendix and a selected bibliography. The appendix, which contains information on two hundred women writers born in England after 1800, is organized chronologically in order to highlight generational changes and to show shared professional concerns. The bibliography contains publishing information on selected bibliographies, books, and articles relevant to the study of nineteenth and twentieth century women novelists.

Analysis

Showalter asserts that women in England shared a subculture through the physical experience of the sexual life cycle, which could not be openly discussed. This situation created a close sisterly bond among women writers and between women writers and their female audiences. Although women wrote fiction before 1840, Showalter begins her study with this date because women who wrote during and after that time wrote professionally, for publication.

The feminine novelists are divided into three groups: the great innovators, such as the Brontës, Elizabeth Gaskell, Elizabeth Barrett Browning, and George Eliot, who became role models for later women writers; their imitators, such as Charlotte Yonge, Margaret Oliphant, and Elizabeth Lynn Linton; and the sensation novelists and children's book writers who more easily consolidated domestic and professional roles.

The feminine novelists were caught in a double bind: They wanted to achieve, but they did not want to appear unwomanly in doing so. This dilemma was brought about by traditional Victorian gender roles that separated men into public life and women into domesticity. Writing was a self-centered, public act; woman's duty was supposed to be private and other-centered. Victorian women were also denied a language with which to express themselves; traditional gender roles undermined their ability to write about sexuality or strong feelings.

The feminine novelists were predominantly upper-middle-class, were less well educated than their male counterparts, and wrote to support themselves. Feminine novelists often used pseudonyms to circumvent objections by their families and to prevent gender-biased criticism of their work. They took their domestic roles seriously and tried to integrate their personal and professional lives.

No matter how professional they tried to be, however, feminine novelists had to deal with the Victorian double critical standard that judged them as women rather than artists; women's literature was deemed inferior to men's literature because women were supposedly physically and biologically subordinate to men and because women's experience, the basis for their fiction, was limited. It was believed that women's writing was compensatory; they wrote because they could not fulfill their "natural" destinies as wives and mothers. This double critical standard caused Charlotte Brontë to publish *Jane Eyre* (1847) and George Eliot to publish *Adam Bede* (1857) pseudonymously.

Showalter argues that the heroines and heroes of the feminine novelists tended to reflect the writers' desire for a merging of Victorian gender roles. Feminine novelists such as Brontë and Eliot created heroines who combined male qualities of strength and intelligence with female qualities of domesticity and sensitivity. Their heroes, who tended to be either impossibly good or improbably monstrous, projected their authors' desire for male power and freedom.

The feminine novel was subverted by the sensation novelists, who had a better understanding of the business of publishing than their predecessors had had. In the 1860's, for example, presses and magazines owned by women successfully competed in the male-dominated publishing industry. Sensation novels expressed their authors' anger and desire for autonomy more overtly than did the domestic novels. They are typified by Mary E. Braddon's *Lady Audley's Secret* (1862), in which the heroine deserts her child, assumes a false identity, commits bigamy, tries to commit murder, and is ultimately incarcerated for insanity.

Showalter describes the feminist novelists as soberly and seriously assuming the duty of sisterhood. These women appropriated the Victorian myth of female influence and took their assumed spiritual superiority as a mandate for moral leadership. Yet feminist authors did not have specific goals and produced little literature. Showalter sees both their personal lives and their fictional heroines as characterized by unfulfilled promises and a turning inward. Even though the women writers of the suffrage movement produced few novels, Showalter contends that they provided an important bridge between the feminist novelists and the postwar female aesthetic.

The female novelists exchanged the militancy of the feminists for retreat. Their literature is characterized by self-hatred, self-annihilation, and evasion. Showalter examines the life and literature of one of the most famous female novelists, Virginia Woolf, to show how these characteristics emerge. Showalter calls Woolf's solution to the problem of female identity "the flight into androgyny." Whereas feminist critics tend to see Woolf's ideas about androgyny as a viable response to the problem of gender, Showalter contends that it represents a denial of experience and feeling which can only lead to death. She argues that Woolf projects the negative and troubling female qualities of anger, aggression, and sexuality (qualities with which Woolf struggled in her own life) onto her male characters rather than dealing with their presence in women's lives.

In the final chapters of the book, Showalter looks beyond the female aesthetic to contemporary British women writers who are combining feminine realism, feminist protest, and female self-analysis with political and social awareness. She looks at the impact of the women's liberation movement on these novelists and concludes that they must find a balance between an art that links them solely to women's emancipation and a cultural denigration of women's experience as limited and stunting. The room of one's own for contemporary women novelists, she believes, must be a place from which they can move out into the world of action.

Context

A Literature of Their Own is Showalter's response to Virginia Woolf's call for a history of women writers in Woolf's *A Room of One's Own* (1929). Showalter's analysis of a woman's tradition in fiction is an important contribution to the field of feminist literary criticism because it gives a sense of solidity and continuity to the content of women's literature in the nineteenth and twentieth centuries at the same time that it verifies relationships among these women as models and influences. These relationships and continuity are frequently lacking in traditional canonical literary studies, in which women writers tend to be isolated, although some critics contend that placing women writers into a separate literary tradition further isolates them from a literary culture in which they are already marginalized because of their gender. Nevertheless, Showalter's focus on both famous and less-than-famous women novelists introduces the reader to unfamiliar but important women writers, particularly of the nineteenth century, whose work bears reinspection and, in some cases, reevaluation. This focus also allows her to challenge the myths associated with some of these authors and their lives, myths that have arisen in part because of the women's critical isolation from their contemporaries.

Showalter's study is also notable for its emphasis on the social and cultural conditions under which the women she discusses wrote; this concentration allows her to avoid the charge of ahistoricity that has been leveled at some American feminist critics and demonstrates the complexity and direction of the feminine literary tradition in England. Some critics contend that Showalter's text is typical of American feminists' tendency to gloss over class differences; the women writers she studies are mostly middle class, because more of the book is devoted to the nineteenth than to the twentieth century, but Showalter does express the hope that the contemporary feminist movement in England will eventually allow the voices of working-class women to be heard.

Showalter has also written *The Female Malady: Women Madness, and English Culture, 1830-1980* (1985) and *Sexual Anarchy: Gender and Culture at the Fin De Siècle* (1990), and she has edited two collections of feminist literary criticism, *The New Feminist Criticism* (1985) and *Speaking of Gender* (1989).

Sources for Further Study

Gilbert, Sandra M., and Susan Gubar. *The Madwoman in the Attic: The Woman Writer and the Nineteenth-Century Literary Imagination*. New Haven, Conn.: Yale University Press, 1979. This important work of feminist literary criticism examines the responses of nineteenth century women writers in England and America to the male-dominated literary tradition. The readings of the texts are original and provocative, but the study is psychologically rather than socially oriented.

Newton, Judith Lowder. *Women, Power, and Subversion: Social Strategies in British Fiction, 1778-1860*. Athens: University of Georgia Press, 1981. This study combines Marxist criticism and feminist analysis to argue that the novels discussed demonstrate women's response to the ideology of female power as defined by self-sacrifice and influence.

Russ, Joanna. *How to Suppress Women's Writing*. Austin: University of Texas Press, 1983. In this humorous but important study, Russ investigates the ways in which women's writing of the nineteenth and twentieth centuries in England and America has been suppressed, discouraged, and marginalized. Like Showalter's work, its focus is primarily social and cultural.

Spender, Dale, ed. *Living by the Pen: Early British Women Writers*. New York: Teachers College Press, 1992. This collection of essays on eighteenth and early nineteenth century women writers attempts to correct the idea that they were literary dilettantes and argues that they wrote for publication in order to support themselves and their families.

Woolf, Virginia. *A Room of One's Own*. New York: Harcourt Brace, 1929. In this text, Woolf initiates the idea of a woman's tradition in literature to which Showalter's work responds. Like Showalter, Woolf calls attention to forgotten women writers while arguing their importance as literary models for future women artists.

Karen Volland Waters

LITTLE WOMEN

Author: Louisa May Alcott (1832-1888)
Type of work: Novel
Type of plot: Domestic realism
Time of plot: The 1860's
Locale: The northeastern United States
First published: 1868-1869

Principal Characters

Jo March, the second oldest of the four March daughters, a tomboyish and spirited young woman

Meg March, the oldest daughter

Beth March, the quietest of the four and a musically gifted young woman

Amy March, the youngest and the artist of the family

Mrs. March ("Marmee"), their mother

Mr. March, their father

Theodore Laurence, the young man who lives next door with his grandfather, often called Laurie or Teddy

Mr. Laurence, Laurie's grandfather

Aunt March, the girls' elderly and ill-tempered aunt

Friedrich Bhaer, a professor in his native Berlin who works as a German tutor

John Brooke, Laurie's tutor

Form and Content

Written in response to a publisher's request for a "girls' book," *Little Women* is an enduring classic of domestic realism, tracing the lives of four sisters from adolescence through early adulthood. The narrator is omniscient and intrusive, frequently interrupting the narrative to provide moral commentary. Often didactic and sentimental, the novel nevertheless realistically portrays family life in the mid-nineteenth century United States. Like female counterparts of John Bunyan's Christian from *Pilgrim's Progress*, the four "little women" of the March family journey into womanhood, learning difficult lessons of poverty, obedience, charity, and hard work along the way.

The novel is arranged in two parts; Alcott wrote and published part 1 first, gauging its reception before continuing with part 2. Part 1 covers approximately one year in the life of the March family, during which time the father is away, serving his country as a chaplain during the Civil War. "Marmee" and her daughters learn to live with meager resources; the two older girls work outside the home to help support the family, and all four girls keep busy with sewing, housekeeping, and helping the one family servant, Hannah, with the household chores.

Their experience of poverty, hardship, and their father's absence is counterbalanced by many occasions of fun and good humor. The sisters put on plays for the neighborhood, have picnics with their friends, and set up the "Pickwick Club," where they create a literary newspaper and soon include their neighbor, Laurie, among the group.

Each sister has her particular identity, including an artistic talent, character flaws, and positive traits. Meg, the oldest, bears the responsibility for her younger sisters but longs for a rich life full of beautiful things and free from material want and hardship. Jo is the literary genius, spending much of her free time in the attic, scribbling away at the stories she writes first for her family's amusement and later for publication and for money. She is courageous, strong, and active, but she has to learn to control her temper and her rebellious nature. Beth is cheerful and good but suffers from ill health and shyness. She learns to overcome her timidity when she begins to visit the Laurences, after receiving permission to play their piano. Amy develops a wide range of artistic talents (drawing, painting, sculpture) and insists upon social correctness, sometimes to the point of prissiness, but her polite and charming ways offset this flaw.

Part 1 ends with Mr. March's homecoming and Beth's successful recovery from scarlet fever. Part 2 continues the little women's lives three years later, when Meg marries John Brooke and the other sisters continue with their artistic endeavors and outside occupations.

The family has become more diffuse, with Meg in a house of her own, Jo working as a governess in New York, and Amy on her grand tour of Europe with Aunt March. Laurie is away at college and later in Europe; his boyhood friendship with Jo has developed into infatuation. She rejects his marriage proposal, despite her deep affection for him, for she knows that they are too much alike to have a successful marriage.

By the end of the novel, the "little women" have grown up. Despite the sadness of Beth's death, the novel ends happily, with the remaining three sisters all married and with families of their own; all of them live nearby and continue to share in one another's lives.

Analysis

Little Women is a study in contrasts and juxtapositions: At times seriously didactic and moralistic, the novel's tone can also be playful and humorous, even satirical at times. Genuine in its appreciation of motherhood, marriage, and domesticity, it also calls these traditional values into question, most often through the character of Jo March. These artistic and thematic tensions are often attributed to Louisa May Alcott's own ambivalence about her conflicting roles of dutiful daughter and aspiring author. *Little Women* is predominantly autobiographical, especially in part 1, and it reveals the disappointments as well as the triumphs of Alcott's life.

The characteristics typical of domestic fiction's heroines—piousness, obedience, charity, industriousness, self-control—are reflected in the four "little women" of the March family. Jo struggles the most to acquire these traits, especially because of her quick temper and her rebellion against social prescription. In time, however, she learns to channel her energy and spirit into her art and her work, as she fulfills her lifelong dream of being a "mother" to boys when she establishes her school at Plumfield.

Throughout the novel, female community—here, the March family itself—is presented as one of the most important social institutions. Women educate and support one another, they form bonds of friendship and sisterhood, and they struggle against hardship together, often sacrificing their own needs and wants for those of others. The March sisters learn to overcome their own selfishness and self-centeredness through hard-won lessons: the absence and nearly fatal illness of their father, Beth's ongoing illness and death, the callous gossip of acquaintances (which is often concerned with the family's lack of wealth and social standing), the loss of suitors, and the hard compromises that must be made in marriage.

The novel is episodic in form, focusing on specific events in the lives of the March and Laurence families. These episodes end with moral lessons but also reveal more about the character of each sister and of Laurie. Realistic portrayals of nineteenth century social customs (making calls, society balls, touring the European continent) extend the setting of the novel outside its primary focus of the March family home.

Although the novel's primary focus is domestic, concerned with family education and acculturation, it also expresses some feminist views. Jo rejects Laurie's proposal—even through he is an outstanding "catch"—and with it, the idea of marriage. Jo has difficulty in accepting Meg's marriage to John Brooke, for it begins the process of separating the close-knit community of sisters. The nineteenth century feminist ideal of equality in marriage is one that Jo herself strives toward and finally achieves in her own marriage to professor Bhaer: He is a willing partner in her Plumfield school, an experienced surrogate parent (to his orphaned nephews), and secure in his own identity, as evidenced by his adaptation from renowned professor in Berlin to successful immigrant in America.

Long viewed as a moralistic and even superficial children's novel, *Little Women* is far more complex than earlier generations of critics have acknowledged. Issues central to sociocultural debates of Victorian America—partnership in marriage, the positive aspects of spinsterhood, female community, and male-female friendship—are all treated with sensitivity and depth. Through the character of Jo March, Alcott was able to criticize social norms and mores while still appealing to her audience's expectations of morality and social propriety through portrayals of the other characters.

The two most interesting characters in the novel, Jo and Laurie, form an androgynous pair, as their names suggest. Their friendship in the first part of the novel reveals that Jo's development as a woman owes much to her "romps" with Laurie, for in them she learns independence, assertiveness, and courage. Likewise, through his acquaintance with the March family, and especially his close association with Jo, Laurie learns the concern for others, charity, and industriousness that are crucial to his development as a proper young gentleman. Though they do not mary (as Alcott's readers wished they would, before the publication of part 2), they maintain a lifelong friendship, a testimony to the enduring bond they formed as adolescents.

Context

Little Women is a classic of children's literature and of domestic realism. Read even today by young girls, it is perhaps the most successful girls' book ever written. Since its publication, *Little Women* has never been out of print; it has been translated into more than two dozen languages, has been made into several film versions, and has inspired generations of young women who, like Jo March, went on to become famous writers.

The ongoing appeal of *Little Women* stems from its realistic portrayal of the struggles of adolescents to become women, a process that is never presented as easy or unequivocally acceptable. Even Marmee, who seems saint-like in her placidity, charity, and generosity, has had to learn to control her temper and develop as an equal partner in her marriage to a man who, because of his work, must often leave her with the primary responsibility for their children. The fully drawn and very different "little women" of the March family appeal to a wide range of tastes, for they range from romantic to rebel, sentimental to socialite.

The character of Jo, modeled after Alcott herself, is most often cited as the reason for the novel's enduring popularity: She rebels against conformity but succeeds in both her professional work as a writer and in her personal life as a wife and mother. Despite the conflicted feminist message inherent in Jo's eventual marriage—for even though she disparages marriage throughout the novel, she willingly acquiesces to Friedrich Bhaer—she remains a model of assertiveness and independence.

Little Women is both part of the tradition of girls' literature and an example of the emergent realism that addressed women's concerns and issues after the Civil War. Like other popular women writers who created series of books around a set of characters (Martha Finley is one example), Alcott wrote several series on the March family and other characters. Yet her work also belongs in the tradition of Fanny Fern (Sarah Payson Willis Parton), whose *Ruth Hall* (1855) is a fictional autobiography of a woman who makes her living by writing, and Elizabeth Stuart Phelps, who wrote of strong, independent women in *The Silent Partner* (1871) and *Doctor Zay* (1882).

Alcott's other works, especially the novels she wrote for adults and her pseudonymously published sensation stories, are early classics of feminist literature: They portray women who succeed in creating independent careers for themselves outside the home and who also form lasting emotional attachments, often but not exclusively as wives and mothers.

Sources for Further Study

Elbert, Sarah. *A Hunger for Home: Louisa May Alcott's Place in American Culture*. New Brunswick, N.J.: Rutgers University Press, 1987. Elbert provides both biographical background and critical coverage, tracing the two predominant themes in *Little Women* and in Alcott's work generally: domesticity and feminism. The chapters "Writing *Little Women*" and "Reading *Little Women*" are particularly useful.

Kaledin, Eugenia. "Louisa May Alcott: Success and the Sorrow of Self-Denial." *Women's Studies* 5 (1978): 251-263. Kaledin argues that Alcott's need to succeed financially prevented her from becoming a true literary success. Kaledin offers several persuasive biographical interpretations of *Little Women*, showing the similarities between the fictional Jo March and Louisa May Alcott.

MacDonald, Ruth K. *Louisa May Alcott*. Boston: Twayne, 1983. MacDonald's critical overview of Alcott's works includes a chapter on "The March Family Stories," which covers not only *Little Women* but also its sequels: *Good Wives* (which is part 2 of the novel), *Little Men*, and *Jo's Boys*. While acknowledging the autobiographical basis of *Little Women*, MacDonald also shows how the work departs from factual details of Alcott family life.

Payne, Alma J. *Louisa May Alcott: A Reference Guide*. Boston: G. K. Hall, 1980. The most complete bibliography of works by and about Alcott; entries are arranged chronologically and contain descriptive annotations. Includes an index.

Saxton, Martha. *Louisa May: A Modern Biography*

of Louisa May Alcott. Boston: Houghton Mifflin, 1977. Saxton's biography gives full coverage of Alcott's life and the range of her writing. Saxton tends to favor Alcott's novels for adults over those for children, but her discussion of *Little Women* is valuable, especially in the light of the thorough biographical treatment. Contains an extensive bibliography and an index.

Stern, Madeleine. *Louisa May Alcott*. Norman: University of Oklahoma Press, 1950. Stern is one of the first scholars to give serious consideration to Alcott's juvenile fiction and to recover her more sensationalist works. Stern traces the development of *Little Women* not only biographically but also in its publication history. Includes a full bibliography and an index.

Strickland, Charles. *Victorian Domesticity: Families in the Life and Art of Louisa May Alcott*. University: University of Alabama Press, 1985. A historical account of sentimentality, family life, and the education of young women in nineteenth century America. Strickland's critical discussion of Alcott's life and work provides very useful background to the issues that concerned Alcott, and it discusses the sociocultural milieu in which she wrote.

Ann A. Merrill

THE LOVER

Author: Marguerite Duras (1914-   )
Type of work: Novel
Type of plot: Psychological realism
Time of plot: 1929-1960
Locale: Sadec and Saigon, Vietnam; and Paris, France
First published: *L'Amant*, 1984 (English translation, 1985)

Principal characters:

The narrator, a French teenager who takes a Chinese lover

The Chinese lover, the son of a wealthy, opium-addicted businessman

The mother, the director of the French school, widowed with two sons and a daughter

The elder brother, a thief and an opium smoker who terrorizes his brother and sister

The younger brother, the playtime companion for the narrator, who is also frightened of the elder brother

Form and Content

The Lover is apparently titled after the wealthy young Chinese man who is the teenage narrator's lover. The title, however, also suggests the narrator, her mother, and her younger brother. The narrator loves sensually and physically, seeking caresses and consummation from her Chinese lover. The mother loves her older son destructively, sheltering him and enabling him to remain immature, dependent on her. The younger brother, during the voyage to France when the narrator is seventeen, becomes the lover of a married woman on shipboard. The French title, in its masculine form (*L'Amant*), refers to the wealthy young Chinese man with the limousine. The lover himself raises what is a central issue in the writing of women: defining the self as subject (actor) or object (acted upon).

The short novel is framed by the present for the narrator, beginning with a comment by a friend about the narrator's old and "ravaged" face and ending with the Chinese lover's admission (as an old man on a visit to France) that he still loves her. Within this framework, Marguerite Duras—in associative rather than chronological order—provides glimpses of different time periods, never specifying a sequence. Although many of the narrator's reminiscences match Duras' biography (the death of her father when she was very young, the mother's work, the destruction by flood of family property in Vietnam, two older brothers, having a son, and, of course, being a writer, to list a few of the parallels), telling a story is not the central function of the novel; re-creating experience is. Her method of associating bits of memory and describing them sensually affects a reader viscerally as well as hypnotically. The novel is palpable.

The defining moment in the narrator's reminiscences is her image of herself, at fifteen and a half, crossing the Mekong River on a ferry. The precision of the image carries through to the precision of the teenager's assertion of age, a realistic detail of adolescent perception. This moment on the ferry, when she is first seen by her lover, contains the seeds of the narrator's self-discovery as well as of her destruction. Her image of herself at this time becomes her obsession. The young woman's adolescent thinness and mannish hat are complemented by the shoes she wears: high heels of gold lamé. She realizes that she looks like a prostitute, which is arguably her role with the Chinese lover.

The narrative voice appears to shift from the first to the third person, but in fact this apparent shift serves to exemplify the narrator's separateness. Not a technical flaw, the shift exemplifies the narrator as subject and object within this text. Duras objectifies the narrator, for example, in a passage describing the narrator as she watches her lover, believing that he acted "in accordance with my body's destiny." The beginnings of the narrator's sense of separation from herself are evident in her recollection of a destiny for her body, not her. The narrator, however, becomes a third-person object as this scene progresses:

> I had become his child. It was with his own child he made love every evening. And sometimes he takes fright, suddenly he's worried about her health, as if he suddenly realized she was mortal and it suddenly struck him he might lose her. Her being so thin strikes him, and sometimes this makes him suddenly afraid.

The remainder of the passage describing the two lovers is told in the third person; no longer is the narrator "I." The shift to the third person implies distance, a separate presence observing. Such separateness underlies the expression of female experience in the novel.

Analysis

The Lover succeeds as an intensely visual book. The sweep of the water, the expression on the face of the crazed woman who chases the eight-year-old narrator, and the indelible image of the narrator on the ferry all satisfy a reader's need to visualize. Duras' prose offers a series of brief pictures, with breaks in the narrative sheltering the reader from seeing a painful scene too long and too clearly.

One recurring theme of *The Lover* is detachment. The narrator, for example, explains her response to aging by saying, "I watched this process with the same sort of interest I might have taken in the reading of a book." The same implied visual distance controls a further evidence of detachment as the narrator remembers her ferry ride across the Mekong River: "I think it was during this journey that the image became detached, removed from all the rest." The narrator's perspective becomes a lens for the reader as the separation of image from subject continues: "Suddenly I see myself as another, as another would be seen, outside myself, available to all, available to all eyes, in circulation for cities, journeys, desire." In such passages, Duras suggests that desire and passion force the narrator to become an observable object, intensity of perception requiring separation.

A reader could also identify memory and desire as central to the novel. The narrator remembers scenes and people, juxtaposing scenes from her childhood with scenes with her lover, memories themselves almost invariably connected with desire. One relationship in particular exemplifies the connection between memory and desire: the narrator's friendship with Helene Lagonelle. The narrator never heard from Helene after leaving the boarding school; therefore, the young woman is memory, no part of the living present. An innocent and unaware young woman, unselfconscious to the point that she walked naked through the dormitory, Helene was clearly an object of the narrator's passion. The narrator explains herself to be "worn out with desire for Helene Lagonelle," describing the young woman's great physical beauty and her own intense attraction—the memory of desire.

Perhaps the most compelling theme in *The Lover* is its nearly overpowering connection between desire and death. A part of the mother's past illustrates the connection. Duras recounts an affair that the mother had with a young man who killed himself when the family moved away—evidence of destructive desire. Further connection is evident in the narrator's wish to take Helene Lagonelle to the Chinese lover: "via Helene Lagonelle's body, through it . . . the ultimate pleasure would pass from him to me. A pleasure unto death." Images also reinforce the connection. The river is described at the beginning of the novel as carrying dead animals and dead people out to sea, all swept away in an overpowering current. The current becomes the vehicle of desire with her lover: "And then the pain is possessed in its turn, changed, slowly drawn away, borne toward pleasure, clasped to it. The sea, formless, simply beyond compare." Duras fuses desire and death in circumstance, imagination, and image.

Context

When it was published in France, *The Lover* won the Prix Goncourt, an honor that assured its rapid publication in English as well as significant attention from reviewers in the American press. The immediate translation of *The Lover* from French into English underscores the importance of the book to the current of discussion on women's writing and women's representations of truths of self. The novel does reflect one direction taken by French feminists. Feminism in France may be characterized as being divided between belief in activism intended to create social structures in which women have equal access to power and belief in the philosophical recognition of the feminine at a deeper level of difference, a psychic difference that is clearly represented in women's language. *The Lover* explores women's language, with its associative structure and silences, never suggesting a social agenda, but instead emphasizing individual perception and acceptance of desire. The description of female passion and experience in the novel places it in the tradition of Virginia Woolf, the early twentieth century English writer who argued that women should write honestly about their own experiences, not allowing themselves to be censored by fear of male judgment. Paradoxically, Duras' novel also reflects the advice of Emily Dickinson in the nineteenth century: "Tell all the Truth/ But tell it Slant/ Success in circuit lies." The narrator of *The Lover* shifts away from her intense descriptions of sexual response to provide character sketches of acquaintances and friends as well as recollections of events in the lives of her family. The circuitous route to truth of desire, then, touches women as well as men, others as well as family. Duras' book describes lesbian desire for Helene Lagonelle and hints of incestuous love between brother and sister, mother and son.

The despair inherent in the desires of the narrator parallels the tone of Duras' plays and film scripts. Released in 1992, the film *The Lover*, for example, achieves on the screen much of the mood and message of the novel. The film's unifying device is the image of the young narrator on the ferry, crossing the Mekong. The room to which the lover takes the narrator, with its sepia tones and dust motes in muted sunbeams, fulfills the dark intention of those scenes in the novel. Duras' work, then, identifies her as a writer of scene and dialogue who relinquishes much of plot and narrative.

Duras influences other writers with her impressionistic treatment of destructive, obsessive love, an influence evident in, for example, the writing of Annie Ernaux, a French writer whose novel *Simple Passion* (1993) recounts a narrator's affair with a married man. Ernaux's works are also autobiographical and are more unified by image and tone than by narration. As writers look honestly at love and passion, the style and content of the work of Marguerite Duras will continue to influence their work.

Sources for Further Study

Cusset, Catherine, et al. "Marguerite Duras." *Yale French Studies*, Fall, 1988, 61-64. Beginning with a useful and brief biography of Duras, Cusset notes the reception of *L'Amant* as a determining factor in increasing Duras' reading audience. Cusset identifies the autobiographical basis of surging waters as a central image in Duras' works (the dam that was destroyed by the Pacific Ocean allowed the family's land in Vietnam to be flooded and useless). Cusset briefly discusses silence and loss of identity in the works.

Duras, Marguerite, and Xaviere Gauthier. *Woman to Woman*. Translated by Katharine A. Jensen. Lincoln: University of Nebraska Press, 1987. These interviews were begun as an assignment in *Le Monde* (a French magazine) in 1974. In five different interviews, Gauthier and Duras discuss writing and feminism, among many other related topics. Duras' discussion of syntax will be especially interesting to readers of her novels. Especially useful is the afterword that discusses the cultural context within which Duras writes.

Hill, Leslie. "Marguerite Duras: Sexual Difference and Tales of Apocalypse." *Modern Language Review* 84 (July, 1989): 601-614. Hill explores Duras' use of repetition as a structuring device both as a writer and as a filmmaker. Noting the similarity between music and Duras' fiction, Hill asserts that Duras repeats with variations, much as Beethoven does. Hill's treatment of Duras' *Moderato Cantabile* (1958), with its dominant scene and repetitive reworking of that scene, suggests a valid approach to structure in *The Lover*. Hill's discussion of apocalypse and sexuality also apply to *The Lover*.

Solomon, Barbara Probst. "Marguerite Duras: The Politics of Passion." *Partisan Review* 54 (Summer, 1987): 415-422. In an essay originally presented at a spring colloquium held in 1986 by the New York University Department of French in conjunction with the French government and the Alliance Française, Solomon recounts her initial meeting with Duras in 1964 in New York, where she accompanied the author to art galleries, neighborhoods, and shops. Solomon's analysis of *The Lover* focuses on its political symbolism and its theme of incest. Solomon interprets the Chinese lover's return to the narrator at the end of the book in Paris as Indochina's return to the French colonial fold. Solomon argues that the lover is in fact the younger brother.

Janet Taylor Palmer

THE MADWOMAN IN THE ATTIC: The Woman Writer and the Nineteenth-Century Literary Imagination

Authors: Sandra M. Gilbert (1936-) and Susan Gubar (1944-)
Type of work: Literary criticism
First published: 1979

Form and Content

The Madwoman in the Attic: The Woman Writer and the Nineteenth-Century Literary Imagination began as a course on British and American women writers team-taught by Sandra M. Gilbert and Susan Gubar at Indiana University in 1974. These two feminist scholars found, in teaching such writers as Jane Austen, Charlotte Brontë, George Eliot, and Emily Dickinson, that the works of these authors shared, to a great extent, themes and images, despite the fact that they were created in different places at different times. Based on this revelation, they developed a definition of a female literary tradition, the existence of which had often been intuited by readers but which had never been thoroughly researched. The central image of this definition proved to be confinement, both literal and literary, and the authors in the tradition shared an impulse to seek freedom by subverting patriarchal definitions of self, art, and society. Using close readings and many secondary sources, Gilbert and Gubar implemented the methodology of Harold Bloom's *Anxiety of Influence*, a study of male authors based on the premise that literary history involves strong action and inevitable reaction. They also applied the techniques of critics such as J. Hillis Miller in showing the intersection of experience and metaphor.

The text, which is as collaborative as the teaching that produced it, is divided into six jointly or individually written parts: "Towards a Feminist Poetics," "Inside the House of Fiction: Jane Austen's Tenants of Possibility," "How Are We Fal'n? Milton's Daughters," "The Spectral Selves of Charlotte Brontë," "Captivity and Consciousness in George Eliot's Fiction," and "Strength in Agony: Nineteenth-Century Poetry by Women." The first part focuses on a central Western concept of author/authority, one that equates the penis and the pen and makes the "man of letters" the father and owner of the text. The effect of this metaphorical and practical control of text is the "penning up" and "sentencing" of women in images of angels and monsters, making their entrance into authorship complex and stressful. "Infection in the Sentence: The Woman Writer and the Anxiety of Authorship" shifts from the male literary construct to female efforts to escape it. Inverting Bloom's partriarchal notion that the history of literature is driven by oedipal warfare between literary fathers and sons, Gilbert and Gubar show that for the woman writer it is not influence that is feared but authorship itself, because the woman is excluded from it. Indeed, the woman writer looks for female precursors to show that revolt against such exclusion is possible. The effort is monumental, requiring exorcism of male definitions, male plots, male images. Often the effort produces illness, madness, and despair and their literary counterparts, doubleness, secrecy, and duplicity.

Having built this persuasively argued and documented framework with classical, contemporary, and modern sources, the authors then move into close analyses of particular writers, beginning with Jane Austen and moving in roughly chronological order to Mary Shelley, Emily Brontë, Charlotte Brontë, George Eliot, and, finally, Emily Dickinson. Throughout, the individual writers and texts are contextualized by means of the use of a wide range of secondary material, as the forty pages of notes at the back of the book attest.

Analysis

The first chapter of the discussion of Jane Austen—"Shut Up in Prose: Gender and Genre in Jane Austen's Juvenilia"—begins by showing how the reception of the author shows both her double bind as a woman writer and her analysis of the situations in which her heroines find themselves. In *Northanger Abbey*, for example,

Austen plays with the conventions of the gothic novel to show Catherine Morland's maturation process and to critique a society that gives no room in which a woman can write her own story. The "evil" that Catherine must overcome is thus both her failure to submit to reality and the reality itself. "Jane Austen's Cover Story (and Its Secret Agents)" shows how the adult novels expand this double bind of growing up female. Austen's heroines surrender self-definition to achieve self-knowledge, because what they come to know is their vulnerability.

To lay the groundwork for their discussion of Mary Shelley's *Frankenstein*, Gilbert and Gubar show the influence of Milton's misogynistic mythology on women writers, especially when Milton comes in the guise of the wise father. The influence takes one of two forms: The writer either accepts and rewrites the myth or rewrites it to make it a more accurate reflection of female experience. Shelley chose the first alternative. As the daughter of Mary Wollstonecraft and the wife of Percy Bysshe Shelley, she is consciously literary in writing *Frankenstein*, replaying Miltonic themes and images to show her place in the literary tradition. As Eve's daughter, however, she cannot escape identification with the monster: Both are motherless, fallen before they are conceived, judged by their otherness, and excluded from a direct relationship with God.

Emily Brontë chose the rebellious alternative to Milton's influence in *Wuthering Heights* and thus created a romance of metaphysical passion instead of a fantasy of metaphysical horror. In both approaches, however, Gilbert and Gubar find a shared authorial fascination with origins, abandonment, and exile. In both, the authors seek to solve the problem of good and evil, heaven and hell, in a world where nothing is as it seems to be. Finally, the monster of both—female in situation—is a victim rather than a victimizer of "civilization."

Charlotte Brontë tried to bury her early fascination with Miltonic themes, elaborately disguising her rebellion against misogynistic myths in "realistic" stories. From *The Professor* through *Villette*, she oscillated between nightmare and parable, Byron and Goethe. Her heroines seem to be passionless, proper, and submissive, but they harbor monstrous ambition and a desperate hunger for freedom. In the chapter "A Dialogue of Self and Soul: Plain Jane's Progress," Gilbert and Gubar look at this doubleness in *Jane Eyre*, a novel whose rage at female confinement, orphanhood, and starvation shocked the Victorians. Bertha Mason, the "madwoman in the attic," represents the rebellious Jane—imprisoned by passion and society. While Jane escapes this extreme, she must also reject the submissive extreme before she can be united with Rochester, her reward for achieving wholeness.

The wish fulfillment of *Jane Eyre* disguises itself in *Shirley*, a novel about the real tribulation of women: economic dependence on men. The myths justify this inequity, but seeing through them does not enable one to end the exploitation. Repudiating the fairytale, Brontë is left with no alternative, because the problem of female strength and survival is not subject to change.

Villette is, according to Gilbert and Gubar, Brontë's most overtly and despairingly feminist work. The protagonist, Lucy Snowe, is, from beginning to end, outside society, without parents or friends, lacking physical or mental attractiveness, without wealth or confidence or health. Lucy creates a self against overwhelming odds and, as author of her self, mirrors Brontë's creation of a literary self that subverts patriarchal art by sheer will. Lucy/Brontë moves from being a victim of objectification to imagining herself as subject, inviting the reader to experience the interiority of the other. For these reasons, Brontë is a powerful precursor (to use Bloom's word) for women writers.

In part 5, which is dedicated to the life and fiction of George Eliot, the authors trace Eliot's development of Charlotte Brontë's double consciousness into a concern for female internalization of male values and the problematic role of women in a male-dominated culture. She is also, like Brontë, fascinated by the gothic, an element that is visible especially in "The Lifted Veil," an early story that shows the curse of vision when no one will heed it. The veil is another attic, a wall of secrecy and imprisonment that confines and enrages the monster. Later works, including *The Mill on the Floss* and *Middlemarch*, expand on these themes by creating female monsters of goodness, women who use their unavoidable suffering to "torpedo" the male plot.

The sixth and final section weaves the images from earlier parts into an analysis of Emily Dickinson's poetry, particularly her use of sewing and weaving metaphors. Gilbert and Gubar argue that Dickinson's life in the attic was her way of enacting female entrapment without being maddened by it. They also point to biographical and literary moments, however, to suggest that the choice of isolation enraged as well as freed the poet.

Context

Since its publication in 1979, *The Madwoman in the Attic* has given critics new strategies and issues to consider in reading women writers. Their encyclopedic array of primary and secondary material gives Gilbert and Gubar's argument great authority. While the texts they analyze do not receive equal attention, the writers' tracing of parallel images and themes creates an impressively coherent argument, especially given the length of the book (719 pages). Some critics have noted that the same images and themes can be traced in male authors, but no one has yet pursued the research necessary to make that case. The fact that *The Madwoman in the Attic* is scholarship begun in the classroom and based on female conversation is evident in its readability and its practical use of literary theory.

Sources for Further Study

Abel, Elizabeth, Marianne Hirsch, and Elizabeth Langland, eds. *The Voyage In: Fictions of Female Development.* Hanover, N.H.: University Press of New England, 1983. A collection of essays on the female *Bildungsroman*, or novel of development. Interesting considerations of the relationship between gender and development in nineteenth and twentieth century British women writers.

Auerbach, Nina. *Romantic Imprisonment: Women and Other Glorified Outcasts.* New York: Columbia University Press, 1985. A collection of essays that examine many of the same authors and issues analyzed in *The Madwoman in the Attic.* Auerbach's interpretations are characteristically provocative.

Homans, Margaret. *Bearing the Word.* Chicago: University of Chicago Press, 1986. An analysis of nineteenth century women writers that uses psychology to draw relationships between the maternal and language.

Pratt, Annis. *Archetypal Patterns in Women's Fiction.* Bloomington: Indiana University Press, 1981. Pratt argues that women's fiction should be read as an interrelated field of texts reflecting feminine archetypes in conflict with patriarchal culture.

Showalter, Elaine. *A Literature of Their Own: British Women Novelists from Brontë to Lessing.* Princeton, N.J.: Princeton University Press, 1977. Cited in *The Madwoman in the Attic*, Showalter's work is a source of information on the female literary tradition, breaking down that tradition into three stages: 1840-1880 (the feminine stage of imitation of the dominant male discourse), 1880-1920 (the feminist stage of protest against that dominance), and 1920 onward (the female stage of searching for a new identity).

Carol E. Burr

MALE AND FEMALE: A Study of the Sexes in a Changing World

Author: Margaret Mead (1901-1978)
Type of work: Social criticism
First published: 1949

Form and Content

In *Male and Female: A Study of the Sexes in a Changing World*, drawing upon data she had gathered during field trips in Oceania among seven diverse cultures, anthropologist Margaret Mead explored the formation of gender roles among human beings. In every known culture, humans have emphasized differences in gender and have valued male and female roles unequally. Whereas in previous studies, such as *Coming of Age in Samoa* (1938) and *Sex and Temperament in Three Primitive Societies* (1935), Mead had sought cultural determinants in gender formation, in *Male and Female* she searched for universal biological constants. She did so by applying Freudian psychoanalytic theory.

Male and Female is divided into four sections. In part 1, Mead described the nature of her inquiry and the methods by which she, as an anthropologist, observed and analyzed cultures. In part 2, adapting Freudian theory, which credits the management of biological milestones such as suckling, weaning, and control of bodily eliminations with determining adult character, Mead evaluated the process by which individuals define their gender identity. In part 3, she investigated the variant biological rhythms of males and females and the means by which societies balance their needs. She also described the forms of the family in which children are nurtured and inculcated in the values of their culture and through which they learn to assume their gender roles.

Whereas the previous sections were concerned with primitive cultures, in part 4, Mead scrutinized American society, identifying common denominators found in American life. Furthermore, she recorded her concerns about the future of American families, a subject she addressed throughout her life.

Although the subject of *Male and Female* is of scholarly concern, Mead wrote for an intelligent popular audience. To that end, she avoided technical language and included few footnotes. Her arguments are clear, and for the ease of the reader, she included a brief description of each culture at the beginning of the book. There are difficulties, however, for the general reader. Because Mead uses a psychoanalytical approach to human culture, although with her own variations—womb envy, rather than penis envy, for example—the reader must possess a fundamental knowledge of psychoanalytical theory. In addition, although biological determinants are the underlying theme of *Male and Female*, there is an apparent lack of connectedness between individual sections, which is particularly evident in part 4, where Mead abandons psychoanalytic theory in her scrutiny of American society. In spite of these difficulties, however, *Male and Female* contributes to the ongoing scholarly and public dialogue regarding the nature of gender.

Analysis

In Male and Female, Mead identifies universal biological constants among human beings. Principal among these is the female imperative for bearing and nurturing children, which, according to Mead, is universally expressed unless a culture actively conditions against it. Among the hostile, cannibalistic Mundugumor, for example, both men and women are taught to detest children. Through the imposition of taboos, men are penalized for impregnating a wife, and women are condemned and punished by their husbands for conceiving a child. Infant mortality caused by neglect and infanticide accordingly is high. The Mundugumor culture, however, is deviant, and at the time of Mead's study it was in danger of self-destruction. At the other extreme are the mountain Arapesh, among whom both sexes are equally nurturing and there is little, if any, sexual differentiation in child rearing. Most commonly, however, child rearing is a female role, and women willingly bear and nurture children.

A second biological constant that Mead specifies is the essential dissimilarity in male and female life rhythms. For women, there is a "biological career line" along which there are sharp discontinuous levels, such as menarche, pregnancy, and the menopause. Because there are no parallels to these events in men's lives, cultures artificially create markers or rights of passage. In a reversal of Freudian penis envy, in which girls are envious because they view themselves as castrated boys and therefore deficient, Mead identifies womb envy among primitive Pacific peoples. Among scantily clad members of Pacific cultures, boys and girls observe male and female anatomy and view women at various stages of pregnancy. In these cultures, a girl learns that she only has to wait, travel through her life-steps, and become a mother. For a boy, however, the sex act appears at best to be tenuously linked to procreation. The little boy, meantime, finding himself unable to conceive and gestate a child and uncertain of his future paternal role, must repeatedly prove his masculinity. This, in turn, leads him toward external creative acts. Thus, according to Mead, there exists a "natural basis for the little girl's emphasis on being rather than on doing." While a little girl is awaiting the fulfillment of her biological function, a boy is learning his future constructive role.

An issue to which Mead returns, after having discussed it in previous works—notably *Sex and Temperament in Three Primitive Societies*—is that of the inculcation of gender roles. In *Male and Female*, Mead analyzed the relative success of girls and boys in terms of their ability to resolve the Oedipus complex, the critical period in which boys and girls must give up their attachment to their opposite-sex parent and learn to view their same-sex parent as a role model. Nevertheless, successful resolution of the Oedipus complex does not fully explain the variation of gender roles within a culture. For that reason, Mead described continuums along which ideals of masculine and feminine roles as well as deviance lie. When comparing continuums within a culture, Mead suggests that there are gender traits that can be attributed to biology. The most aggressive female in a society that values aggressiveness only in its males, for example, may seem aggressive next to the meekest male but submissive next to its most aggressive male.

In the last section of *Male and Female*, Mead abandoned Freudian constructs in analyzing contemporary (1940's) American culture. Her description is taken from her observation of the United States through techniques she developed during World War II for determining the "national characters" of rival nations. In order to aid the war effort, Mead, along with anthropologist Ruth Benedict and others, proposed a means of studying "culture at a distance," for identifying cultural characteristics among members of diverse nations such as Japan and Germany. Because war made fieldwork impossible, they analyzed a vast range of sources, including art, fiction, film, and personal interviews, which then became the bases for national character studies.

Through national character analysis, Mead identified constants within the heterogeneous United States—notably, the ideal of progress and a belief in a fluid social system. She found that children were expected to eclipse their parents' lifetime achievements. The ideal breaks down for women, however, who by their high school years find themselves increasingly excluded from paths that lead to worldly success.

In her prescriptions for the future of American society and in particular for the American family, Mead urges that the innate capacities and talents of men and women be utilized equally for the benefit of the future. According to Mead, only when a society speaks not of limitations but of potentialities can it achieve full growth.

Context

Throughout her professional career, Mead was concerned with the impact of culture on personality. Prior to *Male and Female*, she viewed character formation, including gender, as culturally determined and culturally defined, apparently not recognizing biological bases for masculinity or femininity. In *Sex and Temperament in Three Primitive Societies*, for example, she depicted the range of behaviors found in three Oceania cultures to illustrate the culturally determined basis for gender. *Male and Female*, however, marked a departure for Mead, for in it she explored the biological underpinnings of masculinity and femininity. In addition, she analyzed cultures from a Freudian perspective.

Reflecting the infusion of Freudian psychologists into the United States in the 1930's and 1940's and the adoption of psychoanalytic theory by American social scientists, Mead for the first time employed psychoanalytic theory in examining the pertinency of childhood experiences to adult character formation. In searching for biological constants among human beings, she glorified the female role of child bearing. Contrary to her previous attribution of male and female behavior to the cultural environment, Mead in *Male and Female* found individuals, particularly women, mired in biology. "If women are to be restless and questing, even in the face of child-bearing," wrote Mead, "they must be made so through education." She described motherhood as a woman's most fulfilling role. Furthermore, Mead wrote, men and women have their special "superiorities," and it benefits neither sex if women enter fields defined as male, for it "frightens the males" and "unsexes women." She even accepted, apparently uncritically, the notion of male superiority in mathematics, science, and instrumental music, with concomitant female superiority in human sciences requiring "intuition."

Mead's influence on American women was profound; she was a role model for intelligent, aspiring young women, providing the example of a woman whose education, professional accomplishments, and intellectual achievements rivaled those of any of her colleagues, male or female. Yet her post-World War II espousal of the primacy of the biological role of motherhood was a primary influence in the development of restrictive societal roles for women in the 1950's.

Feminist response to Margaret Mead has been predictably mixed. Many post-1960's feminists have focused on Mead's early cultural analysis of gender, seemingly ignoring her later and more problematic emphasis on female biology. Others, particularly Betty Friedan, have criticized Mead's glorification of women's biological role at the expense of female creativity and intellection. Indeed, Friedan considered *Male and Female* a cornerstone of the "feminine mystique," or the idealized image of woman as suburban mother, subordinating all private desires, goals, or prior accomplishments to her husband and children.

By describing the vast range of behavioral characteristics attributed to individuals by virtue of their sex, Mead's lifetime corpus of work illustrated the culturally as well as biologically specific nature of gender. Mead's legacy in *Male and Female*, however, contributed to the restriction of women to the exclusively domestic, child-bearing roles of the suburban housewife of the 1950's and beyond.

Sources for Further Study

Cassidy, Robert. *Margaret Mead: A Voice for the Century*. New York: Universe Books, 1982. Although Cassidy's analysis tends to be simplistic, his work provides a useful overview of Mead's varied achievements, including a chapter on her views and her impact on feminism. His book is arranged topically, with only a brief paragraph following each chapter describing the sources he used.

Friedan, Betty. *The Feminine Mystique*. New York: W. W. Norton, 1963. In her seminal work, Friedan devotes chapters to Freudian psychoanalysis and to Margaret Mead as primary influences on the "feminine mystique."

Mead, Margaret. *And Keep Your Powder Dry: An Anthropologist Looks at America*. New York: William Morrow, 1942. Mead provides a rationale for the implementation of national character studies and develops many of the ideas and explanations that she uses in describing American culture in *Male and Female*.

______________. *Blackberry Winter: My Earlier Years*. Gloucester, Mass.: Peter Smith, 1989. Mead's autobiography provides insight into her early influences, philosophies, and personal relationships and discusses her professional work. Illustrated and indexed.

Metraux, Rhoda. "Margaret Mead: A Biographical Sketch." *American Anthropologist* 82 (June, 1980): 262-269. Metraux, Mead's friend and collaborator from the American Museum of Natural History, offers a concise but detailed biography of Mead that provides a description of her early life and influences as well as information on her professional career.

Tong, Rosemarie. *Feminist Thought: A Comprehensive Introduction*. Boulder, Colo.: Westview Press, 1989. Tong provides an excellent introduction to feminist theory and theorists by analyzing a variety of women, including many who operate from the premise that gender is culturally specific. Organized topically, the book has sections on liberal, Marxist, radical, psychoanalytic, socialist, existential, and postmodernist feminism. Includes an extensive bibliography.

Yans-McLaughlin, Virginia. "Margaret Mead." In *Women Anthropologists: A Biographical Dictionary*, edited by Ute Gacs et al. New York: Greenwood Press, 1988. A concise biographical essay on Margaret Mead that helps to place *Male and Female* within the context of her prolific career. Provides a selected bibliography of work about and by Margaret Mead.

Mary E. Virginia

MAUD MARTHA

Author: Gwendolyn Brooks (1917-)
Type of work: Novel
Type of plot: Psychological realism
Time of plot: The 1930's and the 1940's
Locale: The South Side of Chicago
First published: 1953

Principal characters:

Maud Martha Brown Phillips, the protagonist
Paul Phillips, Maud's insensitive husband
Belva Brown, Maud's domineering mother
Helen, Maud's older and prettier sister
Abraham, Maud's father, a janitor
David McKemster, Maud's old boyfriend
Paulette, Maud's daughter

Form and Content

Maud Martha is a collection of thirty-four short episodes from a young woman's life. Beginning when she is seven years old, the loosely structured novel traces her childhood, youthful aspirations, dating, and eventual marriage and motherhood. With each chapter, Gwendolyn Brooks creates a poetic description of Maud's interior and exterior worlds, weaving the details of her South Side Chicago neighborhood skillfully into each vignette. Maud's youth is spent feeling second rate, thanks to her sister's self-absorption and the obvious favoritism her parents and brother show for Helen. Weary of the competition, Maud decides that her best contribution to the world is to be a "good Maud Martha," thereafter a characteristic she hones. She never forgets the slights, however, thinking back in adult years to the injustices she suffered as a girl. Brooks uses flashbacks to illustrate this abiding and painful memory.

The novel covers a number of years, during which Maud grows up and leaves home to make a life with Paul Phillips in their roach-infested apartment. After she is married, her days are spent reading and watching the fascinating individuals who live in her building. Eventually, she has a baby whom they name Paulette. Soon Maud finds herself changing diapers, making baking-powder biscuits, and ironing aprons. Longing for intellectual stimulation, she attends lectures at the university; occasionally, she convinces Paul to go with her to a motion picture or musical production. Life, she thinks, can be disappointing, a series of unfulfilled cravings.

Maud Martha believes that people must have something to lean on, which is, in itself, a difficult job. She speculates upon the experiences in life that could provide the "post" for this leaning. Considering marriage, love, and nature as possibilities, she rejects each and comes to the conclusion that life is indeed one long search for something to lean on; the novel ends without a resolution to her search. On life's quest, one post for Maud is the Christmas tradition, which she wants to create for Paulette as her parents did for her. Instead, she finds herself pandering to Paul's preference for pretzels and beer, a far cry from the gold and silver decorations stored so lovingly and securely in the basement, and in her memory.

To enliven the everyday routine, Maud begins people watching. Brooks's chapter "Kitchenette Folks" describes a number of fascinating characters, including Oberto, whose marital situation seems to amuse Maud. Oberto's wife, Marie, is a woman of leisure, rising each day at ten or after, unlike the rest of the apartment dwellers, who go to work early. Rumor has it that Marie is unfaithful and that now and then "she was obliged to make quiet calls of business on a certain Madame Lomiss, of Thirty-fourth and Calumet." Among the other heart-wrenching residents of the neighborhood is Clement Levy, a little boy who comes home to an empty apartment every day after school, letting himself in with his key and keeping a lookout for his mother, who usually arrives around seven.

Escape from the kitchenette seems unlikely. In addition to other problems, Maud endures a painful encounter with an old beau, David McKemster, and even worse humiliation in her efforts to find part-time employment as a housekeeper for Mrs. Burns-Cooper in Winnetka. The worst indignity occurs, however, when she takes Paulette to see Santa Claus. Silent in the first two encounters, she finally speaks out against racist violence when she explains to her daughter that Santa Claus loves her as much as he does any white child. In the final chapter, Maud does not know whether to laugh or cry. Her brother is home alive from the war, one of the survivors in another of humanity's ridiculous efforts to destroy the world, and she is pregnant.

Analysis

Brooks's primary intention in *Maud Martha* is to provide an extraordinary look into an ordinary woman's life. She has crafted a tale of an African American female trapped by very real and very common restraints of family, husband, neighborhood, and society. True to the author's purpose, the final chapter, with its paradoxical and open-ended structure, posits a questionable future, as Maud reads "in the Negro press" the stories of the ongoing lynchings in Georgia and Mississippi and contemplates the new life growing within her body. Brooks's novel shows how one woman survives life's injustices and disappointments with little personal, political, or economic power. To give her character more than a sense of humor and goodness would be a lie.

Brooks illustrates how African Americans held on to their humanity in spite of deplorable treatment by whites. When Paul is laid off, Maud goes to work for a bigoted society woman who asks her to use the back entrance and to refrain from using a mop, saying, "You can do a better job on your knees." The final indignity comes when Mrs. Burns-Cooper sets out to prove that she is not a snob by coming into the kitchen and "talking at" Maud about her debut, the imported lace on her lingerie, and the charm of the Nile. Maud listens in silence and assures herself when she hangs up her apron that she will never go back. As she endures the racist stupidity and cruelty for one afternoon, she understands what Paul endures daily: "As his boss looked at Paul, so these people looked at her. As though she were a child, a ridiculous one, and one that ought to be given a little shaking, except that shaking was—not quite the thing, would not quite do." By the early 1950's, African American men had served in two world wars; in fact, the final chapter shows Maud's brother returning home from the war. In spite of this, those men were still not being treated as human beings. Brooks is equally concerned about the damaging effects of racism on women and children in the black community.

The society portrayed in *Maud Martha* is certainly racially oppressive, but Brooks makes it clear that other oppressions can be just as deadly. For women, the experience of growing up in a world dominated by male power and privilege can be devastating. Maud is an ordinary girl who becomes an ordinary woman. Much of her life is spent trying to find a place in a patriarchal society that denies her very existence. Her father makes clear his preference for pretty, not smart, women. He discourages her intellectual pursuits, instead worrying incessantly about Helen and her boyfriends. After her repressive childhood, men stifle and silence Maud later in life. When she goes to hear the newest young black author speak on the university campus, she runs into an old boyfriend, David McKemster. She decides to talk with him even though she suspects he will be cold. After all, she is in his world, his element, the university. She is right; only moments later he yawns, "I'll put you on a streetcar. God, I'm tired." Maud's embarrassment is not over; in fact, her disillusionment with the academic community is just beginning. David spies some white friends and proceeds to regale them with comments about Aristotle, subjecting her not only to his egotistical diatribe but also to the condescending stares of his intellectual friends.

Although Brooks's novel seems simple, it contains a number of complex issues and presents them in an equally complex narrative structure. One of the major themes is identity-shaping within a hostile environment. The chapter "Kitchenette Folks" interrupts the narrative with a series of social and political issues: abortion, latchkey children, discrimination, poverty, and insanity. Many of the vignettes explore women's choices or lack thereof. Maud is constantly aware that she is being judged, as are all women of her race. Brooks tries to address this issue through language. One of Maud's quirky neighbors is Maryginia Washington, a gnarled old woman who claims to be a descendant of the first president of the United States. Because Maryginia loathes the darker members of her race, she encourages them to apply lightening creams, "because they ain't no sense in lookin' any worser'n you have to, is they, dearie?" Her comment in dialect brings up issues of pigmentocracy, for language and color, particularly for women, either support or challenge existing stereotypes. Brooks's novel encourages the defiant acceptance of one's own identity rather than the goal of assimilation that Maryginia suggests.

Maud Martha can be read as a modernist transition from the Harlem Renaissance works by Zora Neale Hurston and Nella Larson to the contemporary African American novels of Alice Walker, Toni Morrison, or Gloria Naylor. Although Brooks's Maud is not as sassy, perhaps, as some of Naylor's self-affirming characters, she is a woman who persists and survives despite being trapped in an environment defined by poverty and discrimination.

Context

Prior to the publication of *Maud Martha*, modern white American writers, in an effort to challenge artistic complacency and cultural institutions, broke spatial wholeness into fragments and disrupted the traditional temporal sequence of the novel. Yet, for all their literary innovation, modernist writers were deeply conservative in one important respect: They failed to challenge white male power and privilege. While Brooks's novel clearly fits the new fragmented framework, it breaks ground in its challenges to the patriarchal structure. Brooks uses modernist devices to explore women's assigned role as the second sex, their lives fragmented by a society that cannot even imagine them. Her work is both radical and hopeful. It engages and enrages readers through its examination of a woman's humiliation at being stereotyped in a racist, misogynist America.

Brooks includes men as both subjects and objects, but she reserves the role of wise and resilient knower for Maud, whose silence, therefore, should not be misread as naïveté or acceptance of society. Brooks has said that *Maud Martha* is an autobiographical novel. Maud is as wise as Brooks herself, yet unlike Brooks she lacks the power of words. The short chapters mirror Maud's own aborted attempts to communicate verbally, while the text illustrates Maud's insight into the miseries of life, her unflinching honesty, and her writer's memory for detail.

Since its publication in 1953, *Maud Martha* has not received the critical attention it deserves. Although critics frequently comment on Brooks's Pulitzer Prize-winning poetry, they virtually ignore her novel. Clearly, the work fills a literary gap and offers a woman's perspective on the racial discrimination addressed by other writers of the time, such as Richard Wright and Ralph Ellison. Brooks's novel is not peopled with tragic heroes. As Maud says, "The truth was, if you got a good Tragedy out of a lifetime, one good, ripping tragedy, . . . you were doing well." Instead, the book challenges readers to understand how one woman maintains her dignity in the daily struggles within a destructive society.

Sources for Further Study

Christian, Barbara. "Nuance and the Novella: A Study of Gwendolyn Brooks' *Maud Martha*." In *A Life Distilled: Gwendolyn Brooks, Her Poetry and Fiction*, edited by Maria K. Mootry and Gary Smith. Urbana: University of Illinois Press, 1987. A look at the critical reception of *Maud Martha* and an analysis of why it received less attention and favor than the works of Baldwin, Wright, or Ellison. This essay presents a useful commentary on why the ordinary rituals of daily life must be made into art.

Shaw, Harry B. "The War with Beauty." In *A Life Distilled: Gwendolyn Brooks, Her Poetry and Fiction*, edited by Maria K. Mootry and Gary Smith. Urbana: University of Illinois Press, 1987. A discussion of how *Maud Martha* reveals society's rejection of individuals based on color differences, within both the African American community and society as a whole. Explores Maud's relationships with her sister, her husband, her employer, and her daughter.

Washington, Mary Helen. " 'Taming All That Anger Down': Rage and Silence in Gwendolyn Brooks' *Maud Martha*." *The Massachusetts Review* 24 (Summer, 1983): 453-466. Examines the autobiographical novel as a work about silences. This essay reads the gaps within the text, exploring Maud's reasons for muteness and, ultimately, her rage.

Carol F. Bender

THE MEMBER OF THE WEDDING

Author: Carson McCullers (1917-1967)
Type of work: Novel
Type of plot: Social realism
Time of plot: The summer of 1944
Locale: A small town in Georgia
First published: 1946

Principal characters:

Frankie Addams, a boyish, highly imaginative, and lonely twelve-year-old girl
Berenice Sadie Brown, the Addams family cook
John Henry West, Frankie's six-year-old cousin and constant companion
Royal Quincy Addams, Frankie's father, a widower
Jarvis Addams, Frankie's brother, a corporal in the Army
Janice Williams, Jarvis' fiancée
Ludie Freeman, Berenice's favorite of her four husbands
Honey, the young black man who lives with Berenice, T. T. Williams, and Big Mama
Uncle Charles, John Henry's great-uncle
Aunt Pet and **Uncle Ustace,** John Henry's parents
The red-haired soldier, a young man who meets Frankie in a bar and invites her to his room upstairs
Mary Littlejohn, Frankie's new friend

Form and Content

This female initiation story is told in three parts and focuses on the changes that take place within the maturing twelve-year-old who has called herself Frankie until she decides to become a member of the wedding. In part 2, she is F. Jasmine and believes that she is destined for an exciting life with Jarvis and Janice. By part 3, she has left her childish self behind and is referring to herself as Frances.

All of the events of part 1 as well as much of the past take place in the kitchen of the Addams home. Berenice's domain has become a precious and private sanctuary where Berenice, Frankie, and John Henry have spent most of the summer prior to the wedding. After Jarvis and Janice come for lunch on the last Friday of August, Frankie's thoughts and conversation are totally centered on the wedding; Berenice accuses her of actually being in love with the wedding. That evening, after Frankie decides that she is a member of the wedding and that she will begin her new life by going with the couple on their honeymoon, she is a different, more confident person and changes her name to F. Jasmine.

Part 2 describes this new F. Jasmine, who spends the entire next day sharing her good news and looking at the town and at her former life as if she has already left them behind. For the first time in her life, she enters the Blue Moon, a place that has always fascinated her because it is forbidden to children but is enjoyed by soldiers on holiday and the grown and the free. In the bar, F. Jasmine sees for the first time the red-headed stranger with whom she exchanges an immediate look of recognition.

As the clock at the Baptist Church strikes twelve, she hears the sound of the organ and sets out to find the monkey-man. The now-drunk red-haired soldier is trying to buy the monkey. F. Jasmine attempts polite conversation with the soldier, who forgets the monkey, invites her to have a beer with him at the Blue Moon, and asks for a date with her at nine that evening.

Back home, she learns that because of the death of Uncle Charles, Berenice and John Henry are to attend the wedding with her and her father. F. Jasmine shares a beautiful last evening with Berenice and John Henry; the conversation is of love, death, separation, and loss. They end up with F. Jasmine in Berenice's lap and John Henry's arms around both of them, and all three share a good cry.

Her evening ends in a very frightening way when she meets the soldier at the Blue Moon; he takes her to his room, pushes her onto his bed, and sticks his tongue in her mouth. She promptly bites his tongue and runs away after hitting him on the head with the water pitcher. She is not certain but is afraid that she has killed him. She finally gets into her own bed, even more thankful that she will be going to Winter Hill the next morning for the wedding and will never return.

Part 3 begins with a short account of the bitter disappointment of the wedding day. The wedding was like a dream; she was left out of everything, never even had a chance to tell the bride and groom of her plans, and disgraced herself as the couple drove away by flinging herself into the dust and crying, "Take me! Take me!" Back at home, she is still determined to go into the world by herself. She types her father a goodbye note, signs it "Frances Addams," and leaves homes. The train station is closed and the streets are lonesome; she cannot find even the monkey and the monkey-man; so she returns to the Blue Moon, where she expects to be arrested for the murder of the soldier. Instead, her father comes to take her home.

The last section in part 3 is a quick summary of the very real changes that have taken place over the next few weeks. The story ends in late November with a brief look at Frances and Berenice on their last evening in the old kitchen. The next day, Frances and her father will move to a new house in the suburbs; her new friend, Mary Littlejohn, is coming to spend the night. Frances is leaving Berenice behind, along with her Frankie and F. Jasmine selves.

Analysis

The actual circumstances described in *The Member of the Wedding* take place on the last Friday, Saturday, and Sunday of August, 1944, but the narrative shifts in time to include the past along with the present and a brief glimpse of the future. Even though the narrator appears to be omniscient, the perspective from which the story is told is always Frankie's, F. Jasmine's, or Frances'. The tone and language appropriately reveal the active and vivid mind of a young adolescent who has written and produced plays and intends to become a famous poet. She is very intelligent but knows less about the adult world than she thinks she does. During the course of the narrative, her entire emotional world is upset and transformed by her reaction to the wedding. The disappointments she suffers help her to reevaluate her perspective of the world, to grow in knowledge and understanding of life and death, and to become better prepared for losing John Henry, entering the seventh grade, moving to a new house, and leaving Berenice behind. Even though Frances is far from being an adult, she is at least no longer a child, and she has learned something of the importance of being connected through love and feeling a sense of solidarity.

As the story progresses, F. Jasmine undergoes several major losses that prepare for and demonstrate her loss of childhood innocence. One of these is the death of Uncle Charles, which prompts F. Jasmine to review the other seven dead people she has known. She has not felt close to any of them, but Berenice's vivid accounting of the death of Ludie Freeman, her beloved and cherished husband, actually brings the idea of death into the kitchen, the realm of childish things. The fact that Ludie died on November 1, 1931, the very day that she was born, compels F. Jasmine to feel a closeness and connectedness with him. These experiences help to prepare her for the death of John Henry.

She needs even more preparation for the separation from Berenice's lap and the womblike security of her kitchen; she cannot deal directly with the thought that Berenice would leave her, so she makes elaborate plans for her own departure. She rejects Berenice in words by deliberately saying things that will hurt her and even throws a kitchen knife at her in a symbolic attempt to sever the tie between them. Ironically, she accuses Berenice of not being able to understand, although the ability to know, to love, and to understand is Berenice's greatest skill. Finding it much easier to ignore Berenice's pain than to acknowledge it, Frances attempts to alienate the person whom she loves more than any other. In an imitation of adult behavior, she copes with the pain of leaving her childhood home by focusing on her future plans with Mary Littlejohn instead of attempting to tell Berenice goodbye.

In direct contrast to the intimacy of the kitchen, which represents the innocent security of childhood, is the harsh adult world of the Blue Moon. Frankie had frequently stood outside the door looking in, but F. Jasmine dares to enter this realm of adult mysteries and significantly finds that she has a language barrier that is symbolized by her telling the story of the wedding to the Portuguese owner, who literally speaks another language. Her being a "foreigner" is also vividly demonstrated by her confusion and inability to understand the language of adult sexuality, which is spoken to her by the red-haired soldier. In spite of her false sophistication, her knowledge of adult sexuality is extremely limited.

The insinuations of the soldier simply puzzle her. The sensation of the soldier's tongue in her mouth shocks her into an awareness that is quite alien to the world of the "nice little white beau" that Berenice has prescribed for her and all of Berenice's other familiar and reassuring "candy opinions." Berenice recognizes even though F. Jasmine does not, the sexual connotations of her confusion as well as her fascination with the aura of happiness that surrounds Janice and Jarvis and that she wants to share.

Before the wedding entered her life, Frankie had been like the organ-grinder's monkey—forced to dance to music that she did not make. By becoming a member of the wedding, F. Jasmine tries to turn off the rhythms and music of her childhood, which in the kitchen are represented by the constant presence of the radio, which has not been turned off all summer. The radio has provided for Frankie the only link between the world of the kitchen and the war and other elements of reality. Significantly, Jarvis turns off the radio as he enters the house; his coming forces Frankie to readjust and redefine her entire imaginative conception of the world and of the adult relationships within the world. She attempts to make her own music; throughout Saturday, memories of the past and plans for the future are mingled with the snatches of forgotten music that spring to her mind as her telling of the wedding takes on a shape like that of a song. She is at least closer to being able to create art on her own. By the time the Addams house has been sold, the kitchen walls have been repainted; all the pictures that John Henry and Frankie have painted there have been obscured from view. Frances is forming a new set of imaginative pictures of the world, which is symbolized by her studying the paintings of Michaelangelo and planning to become a poet.

Context

Frankie, in this coming-of-age story published in 1946, still serves as an effective role model for young postmodern women; McCullers' handling of gender identity and racial differences deserves particular attention.

Like her contemporaries Flannery O'Connor and Eudora Welty, McCullers is fascinated with freaks and other "grotesque" aspects of Southern life. Frankie is concerned that she is or will become a freak; a favorite topic of conversation for her and John Henry is the half-man, half-woman in the freak show at the county fair. The androgynous name Frankie wears is borne out of her attire, her boy's haircut, all of her favorite activities, and her conception of the ideal world in which everyone could change from boy to girl and back to boy at will—just as her cat changes from Charlie to Charlina. Having grown four inches in the past year, she calculates that she will be nine feet tall by the time she is eighteen. Her fears that she will be a physical freak are enforced by her fascination with knives and her worries about the "criminal deed" that she has committed in stealing a knife at Sears. All of her fears are compounded in her fear that she has killed the soldier who has attempted to treat her body as that of an adult woman. These issues, along with her father's indifference and rejection, are perfect for feminist psychoanalysts.

McCullers' loving portrayal of Berenice provides a significant commentary on racial issues. Berenice has been both mother and father to Frankie and has nourished and cherished her from birth, yet she knows the vast social differences between herself and the Addams family. When Berenice, John Henry, and Frankie discuss the ways in which they would improve God's creation, "The Holy God Berenice Sadie Brown" envisions a single race of light brown human beings with blue eyes and black hair in one loving family. Yet she is very much aware that this ideal does not exist; when Frankie asks Berenice to describe Jarvis, she says he is "a nice looking white boy," and when Berenice comments on personal identity, she explains that everyone is "caught" by the circumstances of birth, but, she goes on, she is more caught than white people just in having been born colored. The colored have all been squeezed off in a corner where they cannot breathe any more. She says that every one must find a way "to widen free" and that a boy like Honey believes that he has to break something or break himself. The Army refused to accept Honey, and his inability to do something constructive is making him feel desperate. Berenice's fears for him are realistic; by the end of the story, he is in prison with a sentence of eight years, and Berenice has been as powerless to save him as she was to save John Henry. In the final scene, Berenice is holding the little pinched fox fur that Ludie had given her many years ago; this is the symbol of her own hope and indomitable courage to continue to attempt to break free. Although she knows that she will always be squeezed off simply because she has been born black, Berenice will survive.

Sources for Further Study

Box, Patricia S. "Androgyny and the Musical Vision: A Study of Two Novels by Carson McCullers." *Southern Quarterly* 16 (1978): 117-123. This article provides insight into Frankie and her concern with gender issues.

Carr, Virginia S. *The Lonely Hunter: A Biography of Carson McCullers*. Garden City, N.Y.: Doubleday, 1975. Written from a feminist perspective, this biography provides photographs as well as many useful insights into McCullers as a person and the writing of the novel.

Chamlee, Kenneth D. "Cafés and Community in Three McCullers Novels." *Studies in American Fiction* 18 (Autumn, 1990): 233-240. The bar at the Blue Moon, like the café in *The Ballad of the Sad Café*, is a place where personal encounters bring about personal insights that lead to growth.

McCullers, Carson. *The Mortgaged Heart*. Edited by Margarita G. Smith. Boston: Houghton Mifflin, 1971. This collection of short stories and personal essays by McCullers is an important primary source for information on her life as well as her motives and practices in writing.

Constance M. Fulmer

MEMOIRS OF A DUTIFUL DAUGHTER

Author: Simone de Beauvoir (1908-1986)
Type of work: Autobiography
Time of work: 1908-1929
Locale: Paris, France
First published: *Mémoires d'une jeune fille rangée*, 1958 (English translation, 1959)

Principal personages:

Simone de Beauvoir, the narrator and protagonist
Georges and **Françoise de Beauvoir,** her parents
Elizabeth Le Coin, her best friend, called Elizabeth Mabille or "Zaza"
Hélène, her younger sister, called "Poupette"
Jacques Champigneulle, her cousin, mentioned only as "Jacques"
Jean-Paul Sartre, a philosopher

Form and Content

Memoirs of a Dutiful Daughter is the first and best-known volume of Simone de Beauvoir's four-volume autobiography, and as such it covers her life from birth to age twenty-one. The title, in English as in French, resonates with irony: What the reader will find in the book is the opposite of a portrait of a docile, traditional, family-oriented girl; instead Beauvoir depicts the story of her childhood, adolescence, and young adulthood as a gradual rebellion against and finally a total rejection of her conventional family and her conservative milieu, in favor of a life of autonomy, scholarship, and literary creativity.

Chronologically organized, and interspersed with portraits of the important people at different stages of her life, the book begins with Beauvoir's birth and her early upbringing in an upper-middle-class Catholic Parisian family. Hers is a happy, cosseted childhood, but even as a preadolescent, the girl begins to question many of the certainties of her familial milieu, as well as the dictates of her class and religion. When she reaches adolescence, with all of its turmoil and upheavals, she grows increasingly critical of her society, and she ends up breaking away from its stifling limitations, by shedding her belief in God and by taking refuge in what will become the enduring components of her existence: study, reading, and writing. She sees the latter as a way to fulfill herself and to formulate and impose her own vision and values. When she becomes a philosophy student at the Sorbonne and meets her fellow student Jean-Paul Sartre, she is living the life she imagined, while, in sad contrast, her friend Zaza succumbs and dies in the struggle against what Beauvoir calls "the revolting fate that had lain ahead of us . . ."—that is, the traditional life of a dutiful daughter of the bourgeoisie.

In the preface to the second volume of her autobiography, Beauvoir justifies her autobiographical project by saying that readers want to know why and how a particular author comes to writing. By 1958, when the *Memoirs* were published, Beauvoir was an established, even a notorious writer, especially since the publication of *The Second Sex* in 1949, a book that launched post-World War II feminism onto not only the French but also the international scene. She had a large readership, especially among women, and it is for them that she intends her memoirs.

Beauvoir constructs a paradigm of a typically female trajectory and of a recognizable female experience: the upbringing in an environment perceived to be increasingly alienating; the yearning for and the eventual discovery of other, more challenging, more enlivening possibilities; the struggle to escape from intellectual and emotional imprisonment and to gain self-realization and personal freedom. The issues Beauvoir had to confront when growing up remain of concern to women: issues of independence, of access to self-fulfillment, and of relationships with others, both hostile and supportive. Women readers may thus find in these memoirs ways of understanding and interpreting their own lives.

Analysis

In this first volume of her autobiography, Beauvoir intends to depict the genesis of her vocation as a writer and to establish, in the re-creation of her childhood and adolescence, a coherent basis for understanding the woman she will be throughout her life. Critics have objected that such a recovery of the past, from the standpoint of a fifty-year-old woman, is necessarily flawed, since it is impossible not to interpret the past in the light of one's later beliefs and convictions. The problem is an epistemological one that is inherent, to a certain extent, in all autobiography: how to know, accurately, a past self. Beauvoir addresses the problem by evoking her younger self as the necessary foundation of her older self and by implying the coherent persistence of a unified, indestructible self. She depicts this self as a figure of great strength and determination. A network of images evoking giantlike appetites and endeavors underlies the autobiographical narrative. Like a giant, the young Simone wants to conquer and devour the world—in her case, a world of books, knowledge, and experience. Her vigor and her vitality are impetuous and immoderate, and they explain her need to escape from the narrow confines of her milieu. A certain ruthlessness is inseparable from her relentless drive toward freedom and self-expression, and conflicts necessarily arise with the warm, protective figures of the past: family, teachers, friends. The drive is, however, both motivated and justified by a strong sense of vocation: Very early on, Beauvoir decides that she wants to be an author—that is, someone who is endowed with autonomy, authority, and uniqueness. She wants to become a writer because she admires writers above all and is "convinced of their supremacy."

The voice adopted by Beauvoir to depict her younger self is sometimes an ironic one; she sees the child Simone as being influenced by the prejudices and the snobberies of her milieu. More often, however, the voice is one of sympathy and compassion as Beauvoir paints the insights of the young Simone, her struggles, efforts, and aspirations, her difficulties and her yearnings, not as the slightly ridiculous antics of an overambitious child, but as the necessary travails of giving birth to an independent girl and woman. Similarly, when she speaks of those who surround her, the authorial voice is in turn imbued with a profound irony when she addresses the pretensions, the pettiness, and the mediocrity of her milieu and with sympathy when she remembers the innocent joys, occupations, and affections of her protected childhood.

Memoirs of a Dutiful Daughter also offers an interesting perspective on Beauvoir's convictions and theories concerning women's roles and destinies as she had expressed and analyzed them in *Le Deuxième sexe* (1949; *The Second Sex*, 1953). While that treatise is informed by the existentialist philosophy proposed by Jean-Paul Sartre, it also reflects some of the realities of women's lives that Beauvoir had observed as a child and as a young woman. Female figures of oppression and suppression are to be found throughout the *Memoirs*, and, although Beauvoir never presents herself as a victim, as a conquered being, she makes it clear that she has suffered from her father's treatment of her: He appreciates her intelligence and her accomplishments, but he also wants her to be a conventionally alluring girl, destined for a traditional "good marriage." His expectations, as well as those of her mother, who wants her to be a pious person above all, make her believe that "I was an object, not a woman," and one may see here the origin in her own experience of what she theorizes in *The Second Sex* in existentialist terms as the reification of women in a bourgeois society. Her hatred for her class, her dislike of the family structure, her mistrust of motherhood, her deep conviction that women's economic independence is crucial for their freedom, all repeatedly expressed in *The Second Sex*, spring from her own experiences as recalled in the *Memoirs of a Dutiful Daughter*.

Finally, the book offers an instructive view of life in France during the period between the two world wars. Many of the intellectual, literary, sociopolitical and economic realities of the time are either evoked or suggested, and they provide the reader with a vivid context for an understanding of the young Beauvoir and her contemporaries.

Context

The Second Sex, Beauvoir's pioneering work on the female condition, had been a resounding success in France and elsewhere, and readers found in the *Memoirs of a Dutiful Daughter* many of the same ideas, now embodied in women of flesh and blood. What had been abstract issues are here embedded in a lived experience, told by an urgent and daring voice, the voice of a "real" woman rather than that of an erudite but distant scholar. The impact of *The Second Sex*, especially on American feminists, has thus been prolonged and reinforced in the autobiographical work, since the memoirs seem to offer a case study of female liberation. In that sense, the memoirs go beyond *The Second Sex*, which tends to describe women primarily as caught in states of passivity and inferiority.

Women readers have reacted to Beauvoir's openness about her early years with enthusiasm, interest, and emulation, since Beauvoir's book seems to have opened the way for many self-writings by women. Of course, there exist earlier autobiographies by women authors, but hers is one of the first to demonstrate the possibility of deliberately seizing control of one's future and the direction of one's existence. The *Memoirs of a Dutiful Daughter* are an enactment of one woman's persistent striving toward goals of self-determination and creativity, and as such they offer an encouraging example to women setting out to attain similar goals.

Although Beauvoir's autobiographical enterprise has been criticized for remaining within the parameters of the male autobiographical tradition, going back in France to the eighteenth century Jean-Jacques Rousseau, scholars have recognized that, by evoking the fears and hopes of her young self, Beauvoir shows that a female autobiography—and therefore a woman's life—may be a story not of defeat and submission, but of accomplishments and triumphs.

The subsequent volumes of Beauvoir's autobiography, all of which reveal the pervading and dominant presence and force of Beauvoir's personality, offer amply documented insights into her adult life and into the political, social, and intellectual evolution of post-World War II France, but none has quite the same absorbing urgency, stemming from Beauvoir's description of her own hard-won genesis as a writer and a free person, as this first volume.

Sources for Further Study

Bair, Deirdre. *Simone de Beauvoir: A Biography.* New York: Summit Books, 1990. An informative biography based on extensive interviews with Simone de Beauvoir and with many of her contemporaries. Carefully documented, with great attention to detail, the book offers an indispensable background and a comprehensive context for a reading of Beauvoir's work. Excellent notes, a useful index, and sixteen pages of photographs.

Brosman, Catharine Savage. *Simone de Beauvoir Revisited.* Boston: Twayne, 1991. An introduction to Simone de Beauvoir's thought and an assessment of her lasting contributions to philosophy and literature. The book is an update of Konrad Bieber's *Simone de Beauvoir* (1979) in the light of more recent work done on Beauvoir. A selected bibliography concentrates on studies published since 1975.

Cottrell, Robert D. *Simone de Beauvoir.* New York: Frederick Ungar, 1975. Starting with a chapter on *Memoirs of a Dutiful Daughter*, this concise work examines Beauvoir's philosophical and ethical positions and their evolution in the context of her writing career. A bibliography of the earlier work done on Beauvoir is included.

Hewitt, Leah D. *Autobiographical Tightropes.* Lincoln: University of Nebraska Press, 1990. This book has a chapter on Beauvoir's autobiography as a problematic female autobiography, and juxtaposes it with the autobiographical writings of Nathalie Sarraute, Marguerite Duras, Monique Wittig, and Maryse Condé.

Marks, Elaine. *Critical Essays on Simone de Beauvoir.* Boston: G. K. Hall, 1987. Twenty-seven essays on Beauvoir, some by French authors (translated into English) and others by well-known American writers and scholars such as Mary McCarthy, Elizabeth Hardwick, Kate Millett, Gerda Lerner, and Alice Jardin, discuss various aspects of Beauvoir's life, work, and influence.

Patterson, Yolanda Astarita. *Simone de Beauvoir and the Demystification of Motherhood.* Ann Arbor, Mich.: UMI Research Press, 1989. In her introduction, Patterson considers American and French views of motherhood and then goes on to explore the treatment of the theme in Beauvoir's works as well as Beauvoir's presentation of her own mother. Includes interviews with Beauvoir and her sister Hélène. Has a good bibliography and a useful index.

Tilde Sankovitch

THE MERMAID AND THE MINOTAUR: Sexual Arrangements and Human Malaise

Author: Dorothy Dinnerstein
Type of work: Social criticism
First published: 1976

Form and Content

An emotionally charged work intended to enrage the reader, *The Mermaid and the Minotaur: Sexual Arrangements and Human Malaise* analyzes the way in which female-dominated child-rearing arrangements lie at the roots of masculinity and femininity. Dorothy Dinnerstein argues that the "human malaise," the deeply pathological and fundamentally life-threatening attitude that the species has toward itself and nature, arises from the same sexual arrangements that are intended to alleviate the pain of that malaise. The division of labor into male and female spheres, responsibilities, and privileges, in other words, is both the symptom and the cause of the sickness of humanity. More frightening, perhaps, is the idea that men and women accept this division. Explaining why they do so is Dinnerstein's primary goal. From the outset, then, her book is profoundly feminist: It begins with the assumption that current gender arrangements must be changed and that without such a change the human species will succeed in committing collective suicide.

The book's title captures these primary assumptions. The mermaid symbolizes a treacherous femininity, the lure of a deadly, underwater darkness. The masculine minotaur represents unnatural lust in all of its mindless, greedy power. Together, the two images evoke the ambiguous position of humanity as a species in the animal kingdom, while signifying Dinnerstein's more specific focus on the cancer of gender. She claims that "until we grow strong enough to renounce the pernicious prevailing forms of collaboration between the sexes, both man and woman will remain semi-human, monstrous." Furthermore, as semi-humans, men and women will continue to deny the life-affirming aspects of existence, instead placing their hopes in the cold machinery of a rationalized, commercialized technology that rejects that which is bodily and organic.

Beginning with a speculative history of the gendered evolution of the species, an account that draws attention to the apparently natural causes of primary female child care in early humans, Dinnerstein asks why contemporary women continue to be confined to their prehistoric role. Technological innovations have eliminated whatever original need there was for women to confine themselves to the domestic sphere. Although in the past childbearing and lactation may have taken up the bulk of a woman's adult life, increases in the life span and the availability of contraception have eliminated this requirement. Additionally, although survival needs probably made a certain degree of aggressiveness a valuable trait in prehistoric men, neither this nor strength is necessary for success in most areas of modern society. The two answers that Dinnerstein provides to the question of the continuation of prehistoric sexual arrangements in contemporary understandings of gender form the structure of the book.

Briefly stated, the reasons that people continue to accept the gendered division of society involve, first, the emotional impact of primary female child care—that is, the way in which men and women develop a particular psychological structure because of their ties to their mothers—and, second, the species' ambivalent relationship to technology—the attempt to control an uncontrollable environment. In analyzing both the relationship between mother and infant and that between humanity and environment, Dinnerstein concludes that the survival of the species requires a fundamental change in child-rearing arrangements. If humans are to develop as fully formed men and women, both sexes must participate in child care.

Although Dinnerstein intends to enrage her readers by challenging the sacredness of motherhood, and despite the fact that she claims not to have written an academic book, *The Mermaid and the Minotaur* is systematically and coherently argued. Dinnerstein engages a number of prominent thinkers, including Sigmund Freud, Simone de Beauvoir, Erich Fromm, Melanie Klein, and Herbert Marcuse. Additionally, she provides numerous examples, arguments, and commentaries in boxed paragraphs that remain separate from the text. These engage the reader without interrupting the flow of her argument. Skillfully interweaving passion and commitment with reason and erudition, Dinnerstein provides a disturbing and compelling analysis of the ramifications of the duality of masculinity and femininity.

Analysis

Dinnerstein's analysis of the problematic structure of gender begins with the assumptions of the universality of the practice and meaning of women's mothering. For Dinnerstein, the significance of women's mothering lies primarily in its emotional impact on children. She argues that the dependence of the infant on the mother underlies many of the contradictions of the human situation. Indeed, the tie between infant and mother is the prototype of the human relationship to life: The child experiences both pain and pleasure from the mother, both the fear of being cut off from her and the desire for independence. Children are not fully aware of these experiences. Instead, they become influential components of the unconscious. Thus, they affect people's fantasy lives, emerging as images such as those of minotaurs and mermaids. They also come into play in sexual relations, impelling people toward others with whom they can reenact the experiences of pleasure and remedy those of pain that they underwent in their early years.

First, female-dominated child care guarantees the double standard of sexual behavior upon which men insist and with which women comply. The man seeks to repeat the exclusive relationship he had as an infant with his mother in his relationship with women. Similarly, the woman seeks to be for the man what her mother was to her: a stable source of love and affection. Simply put, the sexual double standard is the result of the emotional connection between mother and baby.

Second, women's mothering has the consequence of making women into quasi-human creatures. For the infant, the mother is omnipotent, the representative of nature, which provides nurturance but which may also be capricious and uncertain. This equation of the mother with nature secures a wide variety of antagonisms within human relations: the fear of female subjectivity, the conviction of women's inferiority and untrustworthiness, and the assumption that women exist as resources to be owned and harvested, with little regard for their sustenance and replenishment. As Dinnerstein explains, women, too, accept the derogation of femininity. Because infant girls experience the same helplessness and dependence that boys do, women can grapple with the all-encompassing power of the mother by submitting to the authority of the less-powerful father. Patriarchy is thus a response to the infant's experience of its mother; it provides the reassurance of autonomy in the face of complete dependency.

Turning to humanity's uncertainty regarding the spirit of mastery and inventiveness which motivates human activity, Dinnerstein argues that male rule is an aspect of the species' efforts to come to grips with the problems arising from human's long period of infant dependency. On the one hand, humans have a deep desire to escape the all-encompassing mother and achieve independence. Dominating nature and other persons, gaining control of the forces around them, is a way of realizing this desire. On the other hand, however, this desire can never be fully realized. Although humans are responsible for their fates, they can never achieve total control. Additionally, while they may crave freedom and creativity, they often fear the accompanying responsibility. Humans have coped with these tensions by making men responsible for world-creation, for technological innovation and mastery. Women become both the witnesses to men's achievements and the scapegoats for humanity's fleshly fragility. (Because women are a link to the physical world, they remain tied to nature.) Yet, as Dinnerstein explains, such a split enables humanity to avoid taking responsibility for itself and the world around it. Each sex presumes that the other is accountable. Whereas women assume that men will continue the historical task of world-making, men assume that women will provide never-ending nurturance and support. Unfortunately, neither recognizes the other as an equal participant in a communal effort to find nondestructive forms of living and working together. The species as a whole fails to come to grips with the more existential dilemma of its collective fate or the fact of its mortality.

Dinnerstein interprets the changes in American society since World War II as the beginning of an effort to face up to the problems occasioned by gender. After the power of technology was made clear in Hiroshima and Nagasaki, many people started to reevaluate the public and private aspects of their lives. The public sphere of science and work seemed dangerous and overrated; private concerns of face-to-face relations, nature, and the everyday offered more meaning. Yet many of the men and women of the Left who came to endorse change were unwilling to take the ultimate step of challenging the basic notions of gender. In writing *The Mermaid and the Minotaur*, Dinnerstein takes this step.

Context

Along with Nancy Chodorow's *The Reproduction of Mothering* (1978) and Juliet Mitchell's *Psychoanalysis and Feminism* (1974), *The Mermaid and the Minotaur* helped to shift American feminist thought toward an analysis of the psychological roots of gender. Previously, repelled by Freud's negative attitude toward women and his discussion of penis envy, a number of feminists had rejected psychoanalysis altogether. Thanks to Dinnerstein and others, feminists have begun to look more closely at the importance of sexuality and desire. Furthermore, whereas earlier feminists had focused on the material and institutional dimensions of women's subordination, psychoanalytically informed works such as *The Mermaid and the Minotaur* challenged women to consider the impact of family arrangements and child-rearing practices on human mental and emotional development.

A key aspect of Dinnerstein's contribution is the attention she gives to early childhood relationships. Unlike Freud, who stressed the role of the father, her focus on the mother's role provides deep insights into the psychological effects of child-rearing arrangements long accepted as natural and necessary. To be sure, some critics have suggested that Dinnerstein overstates her case, in effect "blaming the mother." Other critics have questioned her emphasis on biology, arguing that the meaning of motherhood is culturally variable. These critics question the decisive split between nature and culture which underlies Dinnerstein's argument. Finally, given the depth of the pathology Dinnerstein describes, some have wondered if having men participate in child rearing is enough of a solution. Perhaps this idea reasserts the idea of men as heroes, urging them to come to the rescue of humanity. Despite these criticisms, however, *The Mermaid and the Minotaur* provides a provocative discussion of the destructive potential of gender and a compelling argument for the transformation of existing sexual arrangements.

Sources for Further Study

Benjamin, Jessica. *The Bonds of Love*. New York: Pantheon Books, 1988. A further investigation of the role of primary female child care in gender identity and personality development.

Brennan, Teresa, ed. *Between Feminism and Psychoanalysis*. London: Routledge, 1989. A collection of essays that may help the reader situate Dinnerstein within a larger context of feminism and psychoanalysis.

Chodorow, Nancy. *The Reproduction of Mothering: Psychoanalysis and the Sociology of Gender*. Berkeley: University of California Press, 1978. Provides an analysis of gender similar to Dinnerstein's, although less bleak.

Flax, Jane. *Thinking Fragments: Psychoanalysis, Feminism, and Postmodernism in the Contemporary West*. Berkeley: University of California Press, 1990. A consideration of major developments in recent critical thought with a discussion of Dinnerstein's contribution to feminism and psychoanalysis.

Gilligan, Carol. *In a Different Voice: Psychological Theory and Women's Development*. Cambridge, Mass.: Harvard University Press, 1982. Draws on Dinnerstein's work to consider the effects of women's mothering, but it has a more positive appraisal of motherhood and the virtues associated with it.

Jodi Dean

A MIDWIFE'S TALE: The Life of Martha Ballard, Based on Her Diary, 1785-1812

Author: Laurel Thatcher Ulrich (1938-)
Type of work: History
Time of work: 1785-1812
Locale: Maine
First published: 1990

Principal personages:

Martha Ballard, a midwife
Ephraim Ballard, Martha's husband
Jonathan Ballard, Martha's son
Sally Pierce, Jonathan's wife
Dr. Benjamin Page, a young doctor determined to make midwifery a part of his practice
Mehettable Pierce, Sally's younger sister
John Vassall Davis, Jr., a prominent local man who fathered a child by Mehettable
Henry Sewall, the town clerk of Hallowell and a diarist
Isaac and **Rebecca Foster,** a local minister and his wife who alienated the people in Hallowell
Judge North, a man who is accused of raping Rebecca Foster and at whose trial Martha is a witness
Captain James Purrinton, the murderer of all but one member of his family

Form and Content

Laurel Thatcher Ulrich's interest in writing *A Midwife's Tale: The Life of Martha Ballard, Based on Her Diary, 1785-1812* was the result of a visit to the state library in Augusta, Maine, to look at two diaries she had seen in a bibliography of women's history. Realizing the treasure trove that Martha Ballard's extensive diary was, Ulrich began to work on Martha's story. While the major focus of the book is on Martha Ballard's work as a midwife, the work provides insight into the social history of the 1785-1812 era: medical practices—birth, delivery practices, obstetric mortality, diseases; the female economy; sexual and matrimonial mores; debtor prisons; class and generational conflicts. Because there are few women's diaries for this period, Ulrich's work is an important contribution to the understanding of the day-to-day life of a woman who was a working professional, a mother, and a wife.

Ulrich's previous work on *Good Wives: Image and Reality in the Lives of Women in Northern New England, 1650-1750* (1982) gave her the perfect background for understanding Martha's diary, since it enabled her to see things in the diary entries that others might have missed. She supplemented the Ballard diary with an examination of the diaries of her contemporaries, Henry Sewall and William Howard, the wealthiest man in Hallowell, as well as court and other public records, medical treatises, novels, religious tracts, and records of Maine physicians. By using supplementary sources, Ulrich was able to flesh out the stories that Martha had recorded.

Martha's diary describes the world of women, a world unmentioned in other sources for the history of this period. It exposes the importance of the female-managed economy for the sustenance of the community. With the aid of Ulrich, the reader can see that Martha's work as a midwife involved a system of early health care, a mechanism of social control, a strategy for family support, and a deeply personal calling. In short, it opens a small and often cloudy window on women's lives in late eighteenth and early nineteenth century America.

Analysis

Ulrich's organization of the material provides an introduction to the work followed by ten chapters in chronological order. Each chapter is introduced by a short passage from Martha's diary, and is followed by

Ulrich's narrative essay, which expands on the diary entries. At times, the reader can become lost in the plethora of names that are mentioned and that do not often seem to be closely enough related to the main theme to require their identification.

In chapters 1 and 5, Ulrich deals with Martha's work as a midwife, which included being a nurse, physician, mortician, and pharmacist. Her diary also made her a chronicler of the medical history of the area. Martha's chief concern was to give her patients what she called "ease." Although Martha at times worked under the direction of a doctor, she most often worked alone. In the eighteenth century, the work of doctors was beginning to include delivering babies. Working with other women, Martha cared not only for the pregnant and newly delivered but also for those who had had accidents or who were suffering from a multitude of diseases. In chapter 5, Ulrich records that by 1793 Martha was experiencing more competition from physician Benjamin Page, who seemed bent on making midwifery a part of his full-time practice. Martha was not reticent in reporting Page's errors in the Sally Cock case, whereby Sally was delivered of a dead daughter with dislocated legs. Despite his inexperience but because of his gender, Dr. Page was paid $6.00 for a delivery; Martha was paid $2.00. Despite this competition, by the end of the century, Martha was delivering two-thirds of the babies born in Hallowell. During the second stage of labor, other women were called in to witness the birth. This was important both to certify that the midwife did all that was possible to ensure a safe delivery and to take testimony in the case of illegitimacy. Although midwifery paid well for females, it was an arduous occupation, as Martha's many trips across the Kennebec River in all sorts of weather proved.

Chapter 2 centers on the female-managed economy and the importance of weaving, which was both a family and a community activity. From this chapter, it becomes obvious that in the Ballard household there were two family economies: one managed by Martha's husband Ephraim and one managed by Martha herself. Part of Martha's economy was the money she made from her midwifery work.

Martha was not one to record scandals, but there is enough in the diary for Ulrich to find the rest of the story in other records. In chapter 3, it is the rape of the fired minister's wife, Rebecca Foster. Here Martha's diary provides some insight into the sexual mores of the era. The Reverend Mr. Isaac Foster was dismissed because he was too liberal in his theology and given to complaints and lawsuits against his neighbors. About a year after his dismissal but before the Fosters left town, Rebecca Foster accused Judge North and others of rape. Martha was called to testify at the trial based on what Rebecca had confided to her ten days after the assault and before her resulting pregnancy was confirmed. Whoever was responsible for the deed, then, as often is still true, it was a case of "he said, she said"; Judge North was acquitted. Martha offered her opinion in one sentence: "North acquitted to the great surprise of all that I heard speak of it." The second scandal is the James Purrinton mass killing in chapter 9. Purrinton went mad and killed himself and every member of his family save one. Martha was at the scene and helped to lay out the bodies, one of her duties as a midwife.

The incidence of premarital sex was a theme in chapters 4 and 7. Martha's own son Jonathan was named in a paternity suit by Sally Pierce, whom he eventually married. Although not all instances of premarital sex resulted in suits, there was plenty of evidence that many first children were born "early." If a child was born to a single mother, the midwife played an important role in determining the identity of the father. Testimony was taken at the time of birth and reported to the authorities to ensure that the father would support his child. Since death was always a possibility when delivering, it was generally thought that a woman would not lie while in the throes of labor. Premarital sex knew no class lines; 87 percent of the men who married their pregnant lovers were sons of established families, as the case of John Vassall Davis shows. Davis had seduced Mehettable Pierce, sister to Martha's daughter-in-law Sally. Martha's diary is the only surviving record of Davis' dalliance with Pierce and the only confirming evidence that he gloried in the shame of his illegitimate son, whom he did support. Chapter 7 tells the story of the birth and then that of the child's death from burns. It also includes the record of Martha's attendance at the autopsy of the child, which was merely one of many that she attended.

Whereas the South had slaves and the Middle Atlantic states had indentured servants, New England had only family labor. Once the children were grown and on their own, the parents were left to find the help they needed. Generational problems of this type are covered in chapters 6 and 8. While Ephraim was out surveying, Martha was left to tend both to his work and her own, seeking help from whomever she could find. Despite having children in the area, Martha was often left to fend for herself. By 1804, Martha and Ephraim, now elderly though active, were living in semidependence on their son Jonathan's farm. Ephraim was imprisoned for debt; as tax collector, he had failed to collect enough taxes for the town. Even though the younger members of the family could have discharged the debt, they did not. This made Martha even more dependent on Jonathan, who soon moved his family into the house where Martha was living. Finally, Ephraim was released and Jonathan built a new house, but for months Martha was a virtual prisoner in her own home.

The tenth chapter centers on the last years of Martha and the changes occurring in Maine. By 1809, Ephraim was eighty-four years old and Martha was seventy-four. Both were still active, with Martha continuing to deliver babies, work in her garden, and record the activities of the Indians who were in revolt against the proprietors who owned most of the land. Despite her age, Martha delivered as many babies in the last four months of her life as she did in the first year of her diary. One reason for this was that she and Ephraim needed the money for necessities. Martha died in 1812 at age seventy-seven, a gentle, courageous, and practical woman.

Context

Ulrich's book, which won the prestigious Bancroft Prize in American history in 1991, constitutes an important addition to women's history on several levels. It shows the importance of midwifery and women's eventual replacement by male physicians; it gives detail on rape trials, illegitimacy, relationships between generations, imprisonment for debt, women's economic contributions, and generational problems. Ulrich's other works include *Good Wives* and "Of Pins and Needles: Sources in Early American Women's History," in the *Journal of American History* (1990).

Sources for Further Study

Donegan, Jane B. *Women and Men Midwives*. Westport, Conn.: Greenwood Press, 1978. Connects the rise of male-dominated obstetrics with the rise of middle-class morality, reform movements, and emerging feminism. Chapter 3, " 'Churgeons,' Midwives and Physicians in English America," provides good background for understanding Ballard's role in Maine. Excellent bibliography and good illustrations.

Donnison, Jean. *Midwives and Medical Men: A History of Inter-Professional Rivalries and Women's Rights*. New York: Schocken Books, 1977. Although primarily a book about English midwives, it has two good chapters that relate to midwives in the eighteenth century: "Office of Midwife" and "The Decline of the Midwife." Donnison believes that the decline of midwives was related to three things: the continuing professionalization of medicine, the invention of midwife forceps in 1720, and the attempt of the middle class to imitate the upper class, who used doctors rather than midwives. Good bibliography, footnotes, and illustrations.

Litoff, Judy Barrett. *American Midwives, 1860 to the Present*. Westport, Conn.: Greenwood Press, 1978. Chapter 1, "The Midwife Throughout History: A Brief Overview to 1860," mentions Ballard and her diary. Excellent for tracing the fall of midwives and the rise of male doctors delivering babies. Excellent bibliography of primary and secondary sources, including theses and dissertations.

Towler, Jean, and Joan Bramall. *Midwives in History and Society*. London: Croom Helm, 1986. This history traces midwives from prehistoric times and includes the issue of witches and midwives. Good for English background on midwifery. Mentions three books on midwifery written by women in the seventeenth and eighteenth centuries. Includes illustrations, footnotes, and suggestions for further reading.

Ulrich, Laurel Thatcher. "Document: Martha's Diary and Mine." *Journal of Women's History* 4 (Fall, 1992): 157-160. Ulrich's acceptance speech for the Bancroft Prize offers insights on how she was able to interpret and squeeze the most historical meaning out of Ballard's diary.

Anne Kearney

MRS. DALLOWAY

Author: Virginia Woolf (1882-1941)
Type of work: Novel
Type of plot: Psychological realism
Time of plot: The 1920's
Locale: London and the countryside
First published: 1925

Principal characters:

Mrs. Clarissa Dalloway, a middle-aged matron who is famous for her parties

Septimus Warren Smith, a young veteran of World War I who suffers from "shell shock"

Peter Walsh, Clarissa's former lover

Richard Dalloway, Clarissa's husband, a rich businessman

Elizabeth Dalloway, Clarissa and Richard's teenaged daughter

Miss Kilman, a religious and political fanatic and Elizabeth's mentor

Lucrezia (Rezia) Smith, Septimus' Italian wife

Sally Seton, Clarissa's girlfriend from the past

Form and Content

Mrs. Dalloway follows the title character on a typical day, as she plans a party, shops, meets old friends, and makes her grand entrance at the party, all the while rethinking her life, her choices, her problems with identity, her sense of self, and the conflicting demands of love. Like Irish writer James Joyce's *Ulysses* (1922), this is a "stream-of-consciousness" novel, but the book really illustrates Virginia Woolf's notion of the webs of humanity, love, hate, and even apathy that connect all people. The book also clearly focuses on the metaphor of "the bubbles of selfhood" that surround people and that even those who love them have difficulty penetrating.

Like Joyce's, Woolf's style is impressionistic in the sense that she uses interior monologue (characters' thoughts and feelings) and individual glimpses that illuminate the hearts and souls of her characters while the pace of the plot pauses. To Virginia Woolf, time, selfhood, existence, and the soul or psyche are interrelated and thus must be dealt with intrinsically, each a component or crucial facet of the other.

By presenting apparently unrelated bits and pieces of characters, their actions and choices, and their interactions with others, Virginia Woolf forged an unforgettable and wonderful new writing style that has changed the direction and focus of much twentieth century literature.

Thus, Mrs. Dalloway's character may be symbolic of purity, sensitivity, and reason, all of which lead her to accept her life without question, while her double, Septimus Warren Smith, poignantly represents destruction, apathy, and a passionate rejection of the fraud of civilization, the needs of love, and the despair of life itself. Their juxtaposition is at the heart of Woolf's attempt to reveal Clarissa Dalloway's true character as a woman in search of her self, threatened by the demands of love and apathy, passion and reason. Whereas Smith commits suicide by leaping out of his apartment window, Clarissa's is an emotional suicide that allows her a chance to believe that she is in control of her self, her nature, her identity.

Clarissa and Septimus never meet but are connected by the streets and activities of London and by the much-repeated Shakespearean line " 'Fear no more the heat o' the sun/ Nor the furious winter's rages,' " which clarifies Woolf's focus on love, hate, apathy, and fear. The phrase is from *Cymbeline* (c. 1610), a play about deceit and marital infidelity which ends in love and reconciliation. Its recurrence in *Mrs. Dalloway* may suggest the author's ironic view of love as a threat to one's sense of self. For Woolf, erotic love is much too demanding of one's identity, particularly if one is female. In her own life, she helplessly watched as her emotionally demanding father killed first his wife and then Woolf's older sister with his incessant need for totally unconditional acceptance and support. Her own marriage to Leonard Woolf was often too much for her, since his sexual demands were unwelcome and frightening, despite his otherwise kind behavior. For Mrs. Dalloway, too, erotic love requires too much of one's heart and soul; it was far better to marry the undemanding Richard, who did not care whether she loved him or not, than to risk her fragile sense of self with the passion of Peter or the purity of Sally.

Analysis

Those critics who complain that *Mrs. Dalloway* has no plot and only minimal characterization are right in the sense that the events of a day in the life of a London society matron have no point or significance in the grand scheme of life. Similarly, except for Clarissa and Septimus, Woolf's characters are seemingly mere skeletons, stereotypical images of the spurned lover, the dull husband, the ruthless, power-mad doctor, and so forth. Yet Woolf deliberately creates a world in which the consciousness and searches for identity of two strangers can be seen as metaphors for all human existence, for who does not seek identity, love, and purpose? It is this flowing stream of images, thoughts, and feelings that engulfs the reader, who shares a conscious awareness of each individual's connections to all people over all time, as well as a recognition of the individual's delicate sense of self, which is threatened by those very people and experiences.

In her introduction to the 1928 Modern Library edition of *Mrs. Dalloway*, Woolf admitted that originally Clarissa was to commit suicide at the end of her party, but later Woolf created the suicidal Septimus Warren Smith as Clarissa's double when her focus changed from a picture of a loveless woman bent on self-destruction to a portrait of the conflicting demands of selfhood and love for others.

For many critics, Clarissa is a woman who is in love with life, one who accepts her secure, passionless life even while she begins to recognize, sadly, that she has missed something—perhaps the ecstasy of erotic love?—and so her character has become hard, almost brittle. For Clarissa, love destroys one by threatening the self, one's individuality, one's psyche, complicating one's life and making one vulnerable to someone who may disappoint or disillusion one.

Like Septimus, whose friends died in the war, Mrs. Dalloway is lonely for her loved ones who have also left, rejected by her—Peter to an adventure in India, Sally to the country as a wife and mother, Elizabeth taken over as Miss Kilman's "disciple." Everyone else is merely a "party friend," with a party face and party manners. She means no more to them than does Septimus, a stranger, a madman, a suicide.

Some critics of the 1930's and 1950's have dismissed Woolf as "extremely insignificant" compared to writers such as James Joyce and British author H. G. Wells, and some have even accused her of being a poor, childish imitation of Joyce (Wyndham Lewis, 1934) or have claimed that her novels are merely "tenuous, amorphous and vague" (D. S. Savage, 1950). Most critics, however, agree with scholars such as Reuben Arthur Brower, who says that Woolf has a "Shakespearean imagination" and a wealth of visual and auditory images and symbols that recur throughout *Mrs. Dalloway* to reveal the "terror" and the joy of life and the fear of interruptions of that joy.

For Mrs. Dalloway, as for Woolf, people are connected by "tenuous" threads to the web of life, love, experience, and one another. For them, the joy of life comes from being part of the wave-like process, but also, standing apart from it, they take joy in the moment while fearing the suspense of "interruptions" of that calm, that peace—life itself. Characters such as Clarissa's former lover, Peter Walsh, and her daughter Elizabeth likewise experience her love of precious moments, unlike Clarissa's double, who cannot connect because he is alienated and alone, outside the world, outside life itself.

It is Clarissa alone who recognizes Smith's suicide as a means of communication, a way of maintaining his rightful independence of spirit, of defying those who would control him—even his wife Rezia, who loves him. Clarissa also has rejected the passionate but controlling love offered by Peter and the purity of feeling offered by Sally, instead choosing the unfeeling and undemanding Richard. Although she has compromised some of her purity, Clarissa has also given back some joy in the moment to those whom she meets and entertains.

By repeating images, symbols, and metaphors such as those of the sea—waves of feeling, of joy, of life—sewing, building, mirroring, Big Ben, "Fear no more the heat o' the sun," and solemnity versus love, Woolf connects the fragmented bits of characters, choices, and the day itself with fluidity, kinetic energy, and imagination to suggest her vision of the postwar English life of the contented but loveless Mrs. Dalloway.

A central metaphor here is that of vision, sight, insight, windows, and mirrors: Smith is a mirror image of Clarissa; if she is without passion in her life, having rejected love twice (with Sally and then Peter) in order to maintain her tentative sense of self, Smith thinks he feels nothing while he is overwhelmingly passionate in his survivor guilt and his love of life and notions of goodness, distorted by the war. She dreams of love while gazing into her mirror and looking out her window to connect with all life, while he sees the world from the outside and only rejoins humanity by killing himself to preserve the integrity of his soul.

Ironically, throughout the novel, the reader senses Clarissa's fear of death, which occasions her reassessment of her peaceful life, given significance by Smith's act of throwing his own life away. His suicide leads to Clarissa's recognition of her own love of life and its momentary treasures. It is the mirroring of passion and life that unifies this impressionistic vision of the falsity of clock time—single lives, as opposed to the true, intuitive, flowing consciousness that connects all humanity. Thus, Mrs. Dalloway identifies with Smith at the precise moment of his annihilation and is inspired to accept the ebb and flow of being, the profusion of hopes and fears, the joys and terrors of life.

Context

Mrs. Dalloway is the first of Virginia Woolf's successful, mature, experimental novels, one that uses impressionistic techniques and interior monologues like those of James Joyce or European writer Marcel Proust to reveal the personalities of her characters, Mrs. Dalloway, Peter Walsh, and Septimus Smith. For Woolf, the human psyche, one's sense of self (existence), and time are interrelated. For her, the past and present exist simultaneously in the human mind, and the self is not a precise point, as Mrs. Dalloway would hope, but rather a series of ongoing processes. At any given moment, one is the total of one's experiences, thoughts, choices, hopes, fears, and fantasies.

Virginia Woolf has emerged as the grande dame of feminist writers. Her essays, such as *A Room of One's Own* (1929) and *Three Guineas* (1938), have always had a major influence on twentieth century feminist philosophy, but in *Mrs. Dalloway* she manages to make a great artistic contribution to literature and to reveal the destructive nature of erotic love to the individual, particularly the female. To Woolf, love is dangerous because it threatens to engulf and even submerge the individual self, who must sacrifice its identity to keep the love object happy and fulfilled. For Mrs. Dalloway, then, passion is rejected so that she may remain her own inexorable, psychically virginal self.

Woolf's success indicates the clarity, purity, and sensitivity that are the unique characteristics of feminist literature. The conflicting demands of love and individuality, madness and sanity, passion and reason find their way into Clarissa Dalloway's life at a time when she feels compelled to reassess her life of passionless (yet apparently selfless) wifely and motherly duty. Her double, Septimus Warren Smith, is realized symbolically as the person she might have been: If she cares too little, Smith cares far too much, for his friend Evans (killed in the war), for his young bride, for Shakespearean England, and for all the abstract terms that mean something only to those willing to die to preserve them—love, honor, integrity, justice, and so forth.

Septimus' suicide compares with Clarissa's "emotional suicide" as a way of maintaining one's freedom from subversion and preserving one's integrity, even against those whom one loves. It is this contradictory vision, coupled with the psychological realism of the novel and the lyrically woven strings of thought, time, experience, personalities, identities, love, and madness, that has made *Mrs. Dalloway* one of the most significant books of the twentieth century. Feminists and antifeminists alike find this work a monumental achievement. Other works by Woolf include *Jacob's Room* (1922), *To the Lighthouse* (1927), *The Waves* (1931), *Orlando* (1928), *Flush: A Biography* (1933), *The Years* (1937), and *Between the Acts* (1941).

Sources for Further Study

Abel, Elizabeth. "Narrative Structure(s) and Female Development: The Case of *Mrs. Dalloway*." In *Virginia Woolf: A Collection of Critical Essays*, edited by Margaret Homans. Englewood Cliffs, N.J.: Prentice Hall, 1993. Analysis of *Mrs. Dalloway* as a "typically female text" that hides its "subversive impulses," which resist the typical narrative structure. Points out that Clarissa's real passion was not for Peter but for Sally, whose kiss gave Clarissa "a moment of unparalleled radiance and intensity."

Blackstone, Bernard. *Virginia Woolf: A Commentary.* London: Hogarth Press, 1949. Blackstone was one of the first scholars to evaluate *Mrs. Dalloway* in terms of excellent characterization and recurrent images of time, which connect the friends, lovers, and strangers here.

Brower, Reuben Arthur. "Something Central Which Permeated: Virginia Woolf and *Mrs. Dalloway.*" In *The Fields of Light: An Experiment in Critical Reading.* New York: Oxford University Press, 1951. Analyzes the recurring images of time, Shakespeare's "Fear no more," "wave," "sea," "plunge," "solemn," and so forth to suggest Woolf's use of symbols to reveal the central metaphor of life's joy and the terror of "interruptions" of life.

Daiches, David. "Virginia Woolf." In *The Novel and the Modern World.* Rev. ed. Chicago: University of Chicago Press, 1960. Revels in the rhythms of Woolf's style, with repetitions and qualifications of impressionistic "patterns of meaning" that are almost "hypnotic." Focuses on time, death, and personality as key themes and compares Woolf favorably to James Joyce in her stream-of-consciousness technique, which limits space and time to reveal individual consciousness and memory.

Harper, Howard. "*Mrs. Dalloway.*" In *Between Language and Silence: The Novels of Virginia Woolf.* Baton Rouge: Louisiana State University Press, 1982. Harper reveals the genesis of *Mrs. Dalloway* and its characters, who are based on Woolf's own friends and family members. Discusses the absence of a mother, Clarissa's own ambivalence about her life, the imagery of sea and wind, and the work's parallels in *Night and Day* (1919), *The Voyage Out* (1915), and *To the Lighthouse.*

Henke, Suzette A. "*Mrs. Dalloway*: The Communion of Saints." In *New Feminist Essays on Virginia Woolf,* edited by Jane Marcus. Lincoln: University of Nebraska Press, 1981. Discusses *Mrs. Dalloway* as a "scathing indictment of the British class system and . . . patriarchy," focusing on her use of Greek tragedy and Christian doctrine to create a symbolic story of good vs. evil, art vs. war, privacy vs. passion, homosexuality vs. heterosexuality, sacrifice vs. revelation.

Minow-Pinkney, Makiko. *Virginia Woolf and the Problem of the Subject.* New Brunswick, N.J.: Rutgers University Press, 1987. An examination of five of Woolf's novels in terms of her "feminist subversion of conventions." The chapter on *Mrs. Dalloway* explains how Woolf deliberately confuses past and present thoughts and actions to diminish the "linear progress" of the narrative to blur the identity of the subject, thus producing a feeling of fluidity, spontaneity, and sensibility.

Linda L. Labin

MY ÁNTONIA

Author: Willa Cather (1873-1947)
Type of work: Novel
Type of plot: Romance
Time of plot: The 1880's to the 1910's
Locale: Rural Nebraska
First published: 1918

Principal characters:

Ántonia Shimerda, an immigrant from Bohemia who comes with her family to farm in frontier Nebraska

Jim Burden, Ántonia's neighbor and special friend

Lena Lingard, Ántonia's close friend, a Norwegian immigrant

Tiny Soderball, a Swedish immigrant and another of Ántonia's companions

Mr. Shimerda, Ántonia's father, a gentle and cultured man

Mrs. Shimerda, Ántonia's mother, who is greedy and selfish

Ambrosch Shimerda, Ántonia's repulsive older brother and their mother's favorite

Cuzak, Ántonia's husband

Form and Content

Jim Burden, a middle-aged, successful New York railway lawyer with a sterile marriage and a host of nostalgic memories, writes his reminiscences about his rural Nebraska youth. These reminiscences are *My Ántonia*, a coming-of-age story, but not primarily the story of Burden's coming-of-age. His early life provides the plot's framework. After three years on his grandparents' farm, he moves with them to the prairie town of Black Hawk. From there he will go to college, law school, and his career in New York. Burden's memories, however, center more on Ántonia than on himself. He remembers her early years as she struggled to overcome her father's death and bore too much of the burden of her family's hardscrabble fight to survive. He recalls his fears that Ántonia might be so coarsened by her experiences that she might become like her mother and her brother Ambrosch. After he moves to town and enters his teens, his feelings about Ántonia change. Ántonia also comes to Black Hawk as a hired girl in a neighboring home. Before, she had been a childhood playmate; now, she was a beautiful young woman. Ántonia will always respect and treasure Jim like a beloved younger brother. Jim's feelings toward her grow more complex. He will come to love her, but his is love with little sexual desire. It will be more spiritual. She will embody all elements of woman—wife, mother, sister, sweetheart—and become a part of himself.

There were other immigrant farm daughters who came to work in Black Hawk. Free-spirited, they labored diligently, played hard, and saved their money. They particularly loved dancing and mingling with the boys. Black Hawk's old stock citizens were scandalized, especially the women. Young females did not dance; indeed, exercise was seen as unladylike and possibly scandalous. These country girls seemingly threatened the prevailing morality, but they would not be intimidated. Ántonia and her friends Lena and Tiny Soderball were the leaders of these exuberant young women. Jim Burden thought that they brought vitality to the town's barren social life. He also later realized that most of these girls would be extremely successful, either in their own careers, like Lena and Tiny, or as dominant heads of successful farm families.

Jim leaves for college and loses contact with Ántonia. After graduation, he returns home briefly to learn she had fallen in love with a young railroad conductor who had promised to marry her and then deserted her, unmarried and pregnant. Jim journeys out to visit the Shimerdas. Ántonia once more is working in the fields. Determined to make a good life for her baby, she will not despair. In an emotional scene, they assure each other that whatever else happens in life, spiritually they will always be close.

Burden goes to law school and will not see Ántonia

for twenty years. Although his business for the railroad often involves western travel, he avoids her, afraid he will find her aged and broken. Finally he seeks her out, discovering that she has flourished. Happily married, she has a home full of children and is the undisputed mistress of a prosperous farm. Although she is older in looks, her irrepressible vitality is undiminished. Awash in memories and believing that Ántonia has achieved true fulfillment, he is determined never to be so far away again. He will take some of her sons on hunting trips, befriend her husband, and maintain vital connections with Ántonia and her own.

Analysis

Willa Cather spent much of her youth in rural Nebraska. *My Ántonia* contains much that was taken from those years. She knew a Bohemian girl who is the prototype for Ántonia. The area was being farmed by immigrants. Many of the book's characters and incidents are drawn from life. Black Hawk is actually her home of Red Cloud. To some extent, the book is history, and much of it is autobiography. Cather reveals this aspect not only through factual elements but also through the pervasive nostalgic mood in which she wraps the story. Above all, however, *My Ántonia* is fiction. Cather has transmuted her past into a romantic story, one that goes beneath experience to deeper significance.

Woman is the key theme of this complex work: her roles, her ultimate meaning. Strong female figures dominate *My Ántonia*; the men are either basically nice but docile, like Jim and Cuzak, or repellent, like Ambrosch. Most of the women, with the exception of Mrs. Shimerda and some of the crabbed Black Hawk ladies, are admirable. The immigrant women are the real heroines who defy the male-dominated Victorian culture of respectability that posited women as sheltered, fragile, inferior beings. Through these girls, Cather says that women should be allowed to live the way they wish, have the same chance for pleasure as men, and be able to compete equally. Lena and Tiny show that women can break free. Escaping Black Hawk, which stands for the stultifying older America, they have established themselves in the more exciting urban scene. Although they are better off than the trapped women of Black Hawk, they seem to be hardened, lonely. There remains a void in their lives. At the time she wrote this book, Cather was living on her own in the urban East as a professional writer. She was a Lena, a Tiny who now perhaps looked back with envy at the pioneer girls who returned to the land. It is these women, patterned after ones Cather had known, who in *My Ántonia* most realize their potential. Producing large families and taking charge of their own farms, they prove to be the best models, the most complete women. Ántonia is their representative, their symbol. Cather gives her mythic stature. By the end of the book, she is the mother of a new stalwart race and the shaper of destiny. She also stands for the land's goodness and fertility. Ántonia becomes an earth goddess.

Cather invests the land in *My Ántonia* with great meaning. This book is also about the prairie, about the vast environment that awaited those who sought to farm it. Although the prairie is presented as sometimes harsh and dangerous, especially in the winter, Cather, through Burden's eyes, conjures up a basically beneficent land that is almost magical in its beauty during the growing seasons. When she lived in Nebraska, she was not enamored of the prairie; now she imparts to it Edenic qualities, especially after it has been farmed. It was magnificent before the coming of the pioneers, but the plow has made it sublime. This is a pastoral story, with the land as garden and farming as the ideal existence. It is an old theme leading back through American and European literature to classical times. It is significant, however, that it had almost always been a masculine story, told by men with males as protagonists. Willa Cather is the first American author to claim it for women and, through Ántonia as both pioneer and earth goddess, offer a female vision of the taming of the land.

That Ántonia and her female friends are immigrants is also critical. Cather was writing at a time when many native-born Americans demanded that immigrants should conform to their culture or be excluded from the country. Cather believed, however, that their heritages were important, that they brought energy and enrichment to the United States, to a society too much like Black Hawk. Ántonia and the other immigrants, while opening up new territories, were reinvigorating the older lands.

Although Cather celebrates Ántonia's world at the book's conclusion, there is nevertheless a growing elegiac tone. She sees signs that the next immigrant generation is becoming Americanized, losing its special qualities. Cather also knew that by 1918 there were really no significant farming frontiers left and that family agriculture was probably in terminal decline. She may well have thought that the Nebraska of Ántonia and of Willa Cather was disappearing.

Cather fashioned the novel in an unusual way. People emerge, disappear from the story for some time, and then reappear. Seemingly minor characters often have more real importance than do others with larger roles. The narrative continually stops for stories, some relating to the plot, others irrelevant. Yet everything eventually comes together. The stories are particularly effective. When the novel begins to become too sentimental, Cather provides a short tale of violence, and she has some extremely nasty ones: a tramp jumping into a threshing machine, a domestic murder-suicide, an attempted rape. Such episodes bring the reader back to reality quickly. When events become grim, however, softer incidents or lyrical descriptions of the environment appear to restore the more romantic mood. Cather utilizes archetypes, realistic details, metaphors, and symbols. Sometimes her prose is plain and direct, and sometimes it is supple or lush. She seems to be concerned primarily with using whatever will help her elicit feelings, an emotional rather than an intellectual response from the reader.

Context

My Ántonia is Willa Cather's most important contribution to American women's literature. Appearing at a time when old Victorian standards were crumbling and debate raged over women's rights and responsibilities, Cather argued for women's freedom to choose their own lifestyles. She also clearly suggested that females were superior to men. Willa Cather will be known by feminists for her creation of strong, dominant women. By 1918, Cather had already published two novels, *O Pioneers!* (1913) and *The Song of the Lark* (1915), with powerful female figures, but the mythic Ántonia stands as Cather's most complete, transcendent heroine.

My Ántonia received favorable critical reviews, eventually becoming an American classic. Its position on women's concerns was not the only reason for its success. Cather's eulogizing of the land clearly struck a chord. This theme had also been present in *O Pioneers!* and *The Song of the Lark*, but as was the heroine motif, it was most fully realized in *My Ántonia*. Many Americans, unhappy about the spread of industrialism, with its blighting of the landscape and destruction of the rural heritage, would be drawn to Cather's romantic evocation of the prairie and its pioneers.

Cather continued to write after *My Ántonia*, but her concerns changed. There was less autobiography. Increasingly, she became more interested in a remoter past, and the prairie gave way to a fascination with the arid Southwest. Her focus on women diminished, became blurred. The females became weaker, while the males gained somewhat in stature. One should look to her earlier works for Cather's true impact on the discussion of women's issues. These works, such as *My Ántonia*, made Willa Cather one of the major American women writers.

Sources for Further Study

Brown, Edward Killoran. *Willa Cather: A Critical Biography*. New York: Alfred A. Knopf, 1953. Brown was Cather's first biographer. A gracefully written book that still provides insights into Cather's writings, this work is penetrating in its discussion of Cather's use of feelings and nostalgic memories in *My Ántonia*. Brown died before he could finish the biography, and Leon Edel completed the work.

Jessup, Josephine Lurie. *The Faith of Our Feminists*. New York: Richard R. Smith, 1950. An early feminist scholar, Jessup compares Cather favorably with Edith Wharton and Ellen Glasgow, particularly in her development of strong female characters. This is a short but important book.

Lee, Hermione. *Willa Cather: Double Lives*. New York: Pantheon Books, 1989. In this major biography of Cather, Lee presents a sweeping, multilayered examination of her life and art. Utilizing the most recent scholarship and finely honed critical skills, she assays all the writings, often producing original and controversial interpretations. Her discussion of the pastoral is a significant contribution to understanding Cather's use of the land motif. The book contains a valuable short bibliography.

Stouck, David. *Willa Cather's Imagination*. Lincoln: University of Nebraska Press, 1975. Although Stouck is primarily interested in an appreciation of all Cather's writings, he does offer some valuable observations about memory and the pastoral in *My Ántonia*. His book also has a helpful selected bibliography.

Woodress, James. *Willa Cather: Her Life and Art*. Lincoln: University of Nebraska Press, 1982. Woodress, an established Cather expert, provides a clear, enthusiastic treatment of Cather's accomplishments. He argues that *My Ántonia* is her finest novel and one of the best written by an American.

Clarke Wilhelm

MY BRILLIANT CAREER

Author: Miles Franklin (1879-1954)
Type of work: Novel
Type of plot: Social criticism
Time of plot: The late 1880's to 1899
Locale: New South Wales
First published: 1901

Principal characters:

Sybylla Melvyn, the sixteen-year-old protagonist
Lucy Melvyn, Sybylla's mother
Dick Melvyn, Sybylla's father, an alcoholic
Mrs. Bossier, Sybylla's kindly and well-off grandmother
Helen Bell, Mrs. Bossier's daughter and Sybylla's aunt
Harold Beecham, a wealthy young farmer who is rejected by Sybylla
Gertie Melvyn, Sybylla's beautiful younger sister

Form and Content

My Brilliant Career is an ironic title, for this first-person fictional autobiography makes the point that there were no brilliant careers possible for the vast majority of young women in Australia at the end of the nineteenth century. By focusing on the romantic and life adventures of its sixteen-year-old heroine, Sybylla Melvyn, the novel shows how grindingly oppressive life was on this recent frontier in the Southern Hemisphere, and how doubly oppressive it was for women. Stella Maria Sarah Miles Franklin, which she shortened to the male-sounding name Miles Franklin, wrote the novel when she was herself sixteen, and the work has all the passion and verve of late adolescence, along with some youthful faults as well. The general plot follows the outline of Franklin's own experiences, though the book is also fictional in its details.

Sybylla, like Franklin, begins life as a "little bush-girl," a child surrounded by horses, stock, drovers, jackeroos (cowboys), and other inhabitants of the Australian Outback. She receives very little formal education, and only her love of reading and the arts makes her different from the other bush inhabitants, whose reading runs to farm price reports. Initially, life on a "station," or ranch, is pleasant and interesting; however, Sybylla's youthful existence declines in quality as her alcoholic and inept father drags her family into rural poverty in a dairy-farming area. The novel moves from this desperate life to the idyllic days Sybylla spends with her grandmother at Caddagat, then returns to grim (though sometimes darkly comic) pictures of life on a sheep station, and once again moves to a dairy farm. Along the way, readers are shown a wide variety of Australian social types and learn much about farming and stock raising during a drought.

The dairy-farming episodes take place in Possum Gully, a flat, arid area quite unlike the beautiful high country of Sybylla's early childhood. This part of the novel is noteworthy for its excellent portraits of the appalling difficulties of dairying during extended drought. In addition to milking dozens of cows twice a day and taking care of all the normal chores involved in farming, the Melvyns and their neighbors have to lift cows who have collapsed from hunger; the struggle to put the animals on their feet is a group enterprise, involving even younger girls such as Sybylla, who must also cook, wash, garden, chop wood, and keep the household running. A brief set-piece entitled "A Drought Idyll" introduces the theme of the "brilliant career" available to Outback girls such as Sybylla: "Weariness! Weariness!" in fifteen-year-olds working sixteen hours and more a day in temperatures well above a hundred degrees in the shade.

In contrast to the grim realism of Possum Gully are the Caddagat episodes, which constitute the bulk of the novel. Mrs. Bossier, Sybylla's grandmother, is a country "swell" living very comfortably in a true idyll, that of the pastoral life untouched by drought, poverty, or meanness. These sections no doubt reflect Franklin's own childhood memories of the high country area—a place, at least in the imagination, of endlessly proliferating flowers, of perfumed and gentle summer nights, of fruit in wide variety available for the picking. Caddagat is well watered and seemingly untouched by the economic troubles surrounding it; even the failure of a neighboring farm seems sudden and unprepared for. The glorious environment transforms the people who live in it: Sybylla's grandmother, aunt, uncle, and the various jackeroos and neighbors spar gently with one another but generally behave with unimpeachable middle-class propriety. Even Sybylla's complaints and insecurities are moderated; under the tutelage of Aunt Helen, she begins to recognize her own attractiveness, and she begins a romance with Harold Beecham, the idealized neighbor at Five Bob Downs. Sybylla is still frustrated with the role that females must play and with the limited artistic activities available, but these objections begin to seem carping, given the strength and authority of her female relatives at Caddagat and the isolation that is part of the area's beauty.

It is only when she is forced to become a governess on an isolated sheep station called Barney's Gap that Sybylla truly appreciates Caddagat's virtues. The grim realism of the beginning of the book is ameliorated here by some comedy, as Sybylla tries to instruct Australian "peasants" who have only a dim idea that Jesus had "something to do with God." The chickens and pigs have a regular run of this household, and here the thermometer goes above one hundred and twenty degrees. When conditions become too much for Sybylla, she returns to Possum Gully and her "brilliant career" there as an Australian peon.

Analysis

My Brilliant Career was widely hailed as the first truly Australian novel, Australian in the sense that it was clearly written by a resident of the country and not by a visitor or tourist seeing it from the outside. There is no doubt about Sybylla and Miles Franklin's "Australianness," as readers are treated to, and sometimes puzzled by, a steady stream of Australian names, words for people and trades, names of flora and fauna, and general expressions heard only "down under." Though context makes most of the language clear, the book is obviously directed to an Aussie, rather than a British or American, audience: Little formal explanation is provided.

In addition to local culture, Sybylla is also full of an unremitting Australian nationalism, a pride in the equality with which people treat one another—or at least in its potential. The book is unmarred by egregious comparisons with the British class system; instead, it is only the struggle against nature that demeans and impoverishes the rural classes, not a struggle against fellow men and women. Even the swinish M'Swat family, which lets its pigs eat leftovers under the dinner table, is consistently described as "good-hearted" and morally upright. In fact, Sybylla's flirtations with socialist doctrine seem rather empty given the lack of true class struggle; throughout, Australians at all levels are shown to be decent and generous to a fault, with wrong-headedness confined to a few misguided souls. The novel only hints at the violence against women and men around the low pubs that Sybylla's father patronizes. The yearning throughout this book is for a society arranged on the model of Caddagat: rural, egalitarian, prosperous, and pacific. Departures from this ideal tend to be ascribed to the natural disaster of the drought, to personal failings such as Dick Melvyn's alcoholism, but mostly to the bitter effects of isolation and ignorance in a huge, empty country.

Sybylla's two main charges against Australia are the vulgarity and philistinism of its "peasantry" and the exploitation of women, especially in the Outback. Both charges are somewhat undercut by the strengths of the novel, the fervent nationalism and the sympathetic understanding given to the plight of the rural peasantry, isolated and self-dependent.

Sybylla's terrible experiences with dairy farming and as governess to the M'Swat sheep station make the reader sympathetic to her desire for culture, and even for some reading matter of any kind. Yet the vivid portraits of travel by coach, train, and then horse cart for two or three days make one cognizant of the immensity of Australia, and of its newness as a European culture. No reader can fail to respond to the heroine's feelings of being alone, yet one could expect little else in the middle of this vast frontier. Also, the reading matter provided at Caddagat, the literate letters sent back and forth, and the regular musical evenings throughout show a spirited response to isolation which makes Sybylla's criticisms seem those of a young girl bored by any rural environment. The final refutation to her complaint is provided, ironically, by the very novel itself: Miles Franklin was reared under isolated circumstances very similar to Sybylla's, yet she was able at the age of sixteen to produce a literate, witty, and at times sophisticated novel, one in which the main character quotes Australian writers with confident familiarity. The primitive loneliness of the Outback must have been an oppressive burden on the literate and artistic, but the novel shows how thoroughly the obstacle could be overcome. Sybylla's language, though often regional, is as archly convoluted and formal as that of any Victorian heroine; she may be a bushgirl, but the outside world of literature and culture not only has intruded but also has been assimilated.

Sybylla and Franklin's feminism has given *My Brilliant Career* a second "career" as an early feminist masterwork, as the introduction to the 1980 edition by Carmen Callil shows. Sybylla's refusal to marry a virtually perfect suitor even when she is under circumstances of voluntary slavery to an alcoholic father and an unappreciative mother is seen by Callil as a desirable feminine response to the limits imposed by marriage: " 'Yes, you're right,' " say Callil's "million female voices, 'Sybylla is me.' " Putting aside Sybylla's resulting condemnation of her family to lifelong poverty, and ignoring what Eileen Kennedy calls her obvious sadomasochism (and, one might add, her sibling rivalry with Gertie), it is difficult to take Sybylla's "petulant idealism and perpetual complaint" as "political insight," in the words of Phyllis Rose. The mature reader is likely to see Sybylla using the "perfect" to argue against the "possible," to perceive in her tormenting of an ideal possible husband a revenge fantasy indulged in by a writer enamored of deep personal feelings rather than with feelings for others.

Context

For all the artistic and intellectual limitations that have troubled critics, *My Brilliant Career* remains a remarkable novel, a wonderful read, a superb picture of Australian life, and most important, an excellent window into the thinking of a young, intelligent feminist surrounded by hostile country and hostile people. The brilliance of Franklin's achievement is not in her indictment of Australian provincialism (which her own work tends to belie) or in the feminist philosophy expressed throughout (which suffers when put into the vocabulary and psychology of a girl with limited experience) but rather in the portrait of Sybylla herself—protean, contradictory, smart as a whip, irritating, amusing, odd. Sybylla is certainly a great achievement, not for the value of her philosophy but for the sharpness and wit of the psychological portrait. It is patronizing to Franklin to harp on her tender age at the time of composition, yet that must figure in the evaluation of her achievement. Sybylla's self-knowledge and awareness of others is simply remarkable given one's knowledge of the author's limited experience of the world, for even in a much older writer such insight would be admirable. One can forgive Sybylla's petulant and immature behavior and focus instead on what she does have to reveal: the grinding millstone of passing days in the Australian wilderness.

Franklin's contribution is not to feminist thought—whatever the advantages and disadvantages of marriage, few would advocate behaving as self-destructively as Sybylla does—but in its presentation of a voice not previously heard, that of a youthful, intelligent, witty young woman in circumstances that would seem to destroy all these qualities.

Sources for Further Study

Callil, Carmen. Introduction to *My Brilliant Career*. New York: St. Martin's Press, 1980. The essay establishes the initial modern perspective on the novel, a perspective debated since this reprinting.

Davis, Beatrice. "Tribute to Miles Franklin: A True Australian." *Southerly* 16, no. 2 (1955): 83-85. Impressed by Franklin's character, talent, and devotion to Australia, Davis provides a tribute and a chronicle in which she praises Franklin's lyrical depiction of the Australian countryside, its pageants and traditions, and sympathizes with her criticism of the social order—in particular of the dull, drab, "hennishness" of women's lives.

Ewers, John K. *Creative Writing in Australia: A Selective Survey*. Rev. ed. Melbourne, Australia: Georgian House, 1966. Ewers compares the works of Joseph Furphy and Miles Franklin. He finds Franklin's *My Brilliant Career* true to Australia, with a clear vision of reality and a scorn of pretense, and advises reading it together with its sequel, *My Career Goes Bung* (1946) for a clear picture of an "extraordinary mind."

Hadgraft, Cecil. "The New Century: First Harvest of

Fiction." In *Australian Literature: A Critical Account to 1955*. London: Heinemann, 1960. Although Hadgraft finds *My Brilliant Career*'s literary value to be unequal to its human interest and the dominating personality to be odd, he praises its setting, vocabulary, and circumstances as convincingly Australian, and a "remarkable" achievement.

Kennedy, Eileen. "*My Brilliant Career*." *Best Sellers* 40, no. 11 (February, 1981): 389. Despite her criticism of plot devices reminiscent of Charlotte Brontë's *Jane Eyre* (1847) and uneven stylistics that move from "clean honest" description of land and character to "stilted" pomposities, Kennedy praises Franklin's complicated, finely drawn, self-destructive heroine and the tension between point of view and reader assessment of it.

Rose, Phyllis. "Her So-So Career." *The New York Times Book Review* 86 (January 4, 1981): 8, 21. Rose criticizes the novel's "stilted" language and "Byronic" romanticism, concluding that Sybylla's feminism offers only a "silly" choice between an emotional life and a brilliant career.

Andrew F. Macdonald

'NIGHT, MOTHER

Author: Marsha Norman (1947-)
Type of work: Drama
Type of plot: Social realism
Time of plot: A Saturday night in the present
Locale: A comfortable house in the country
First produced: 1982 at American Repertory Theatre, Cambridge, Massachusetts
First published: 1983

Principal characters:

Jessie Cates, a sad and lonely woman who plans to commit suicide
Thelma Cates (Mama), Jessie's mother, who is accustomed to being in control
Dawson Cates, Jessie's brother, who does not appear
Cecil, the husband that Mama picked for Jessie, who has left her
Ricky, Jessie and Cecil's son, a troubled teenager
Agnes Fletcher, Mama's friend, who comes up in conversation

Form and Content

The entire drama of *'night, Mother* is a conversation between mother and daughter which begins about 8:15 on a Saturday evening. There is no intermission. Clocks are visible onstage in the kitchen and the living room and run throughout the play; Jessie, her mother, and the audience are clearly aware of the time passing moment by moment, and during one tense moment Jessie winds the small clock on the table. The house is relatively new and is on a country road. Jessie spends the evening preparing for her suicide and attempting to explain her reason for shooting herself to her mother.

Mama has never understood Jessie, and her comment following the fatal shot indicates that at the end of the play she still does not realize that Jessie is a mature woman with a mind and a will of her own. She says, "Jessie, Jessie, child . . . Forgive me. I thought you were mine." In taking her own life, Jessie has at last asserted her own individuality, declared her independence, and taken over her own existence.

Mama has never realized that Jessie has always been so alone and so lonely. She has also been under the impression that she simply "allows" Jessie to think that she is taking care of her to give Jessie an excuse to share her house; Mama now comes to the painful realization that she is truly dependent on Jessie. In a sense, the drama centers on Mama's changing sense of herself, shifting perceptions of reality, and growing realization that Jessie means what she says about her life and her death; as the evening progresses, Mama attempts to think of "reasons" for Jessie to live as she comes to terms with the reality that she will surely die.

When the play opens, Jessie is busily making preparations to shoot herself. She then breaks the news to her mother that she intends to bid her goodnight for the last time in a couple of hours. She briskly answers her mother's questions and responds to her mother's objections. Then she begins her own explanation of why she plans to end her life. She says that she is not having a good time, that she is tired, hurt, sad, and feels used. She uses an example that she thinks Mama will understand; she says that her life is like an unpleasant bus ride and that she sees no reason to continue the ride for fifty more blocks when she can get off right then. She finally says that she might want to live if there was at least one thing she really liked—even cornflakes or rice pudding. In response, Thelma desperately tries to think of things that might interest Jessie. She suggests that they get a dog, that they take a taxi to the grocery store, that Jessie take a job, that she might try to get a driver's license. Jessie patiently makes clear why it is too late for any of these suggestions to work; her bus ride ends at the next stop.

Then Jessie asks her mother a series of questions. Thelma becomes deeply and genuinely upset; as she attempts to give honest answers, the lack of communication and absence of understanding between them becomes painfully apparent. Thelma never has told Jessie that she has had "fits" all of her life, that her father also had "fits," what she is like while she is having a seizure, or how she has been ashamed of her, has never loved her father, has been jealous of Jessie's love for her father, and has blamed herself for Jessie's "fits." Jessie mentions looking at a baby picture of herself and seeing that she was somebody else. She points out that she is not really her mother's child. She realizes that her "own self" is not going to show up and sees no reason to keep waiting for it to come.

Thelma finally faces the fact that she is afraid for Jessie to die because she is afraid to die herself; Jessie once again patiently explains to Mama that the uncertainty is the scary part and that she is certain that her own time has come and that she is not afraid. The turning point in the emotional drama comes as Mama then says that she cannot just sit there and tell her that it is acceptable to kill herself. Jessie replies that she just did.

After this, Jessie helps her mother think about the funeral plans, what she will wear, and what she will say to each person. Then she drills her mother on the specific steps she is to take that evening after she hears the shot. In the final minutes, Jessie takes her mother's mind off what is going to happen by going through a box of her own belongings and telling her what to do with them. Then she says that it is time to go, and she goes.

Analysis

This intense drama, Marsha Norman's first play, opened on Broadway in March, 1983. It was awarded the 1983 Pulitzer Prize for drama. The long conversation between mother and daughter demonstrates the fact that a mother can live in the same house with her daughter and think she knows her quite well while she actually knows very little about her. Jessie understands herself quite well; on this last evening of her life, she talks more than she ever has and demonstrates for the first time a sense of determination and purpose, a peaceful energy, her newly discovered self-confidence, and a "quirky" sense of humor that has never amused anyone except herself. She firmly believes that her decision to commit suicide is the best one she has ever made and that it is right for her. She also seems to be confident that her mother is capable of taking care of herself and that she will be better off doing so.

The previous lack of communication between the two is perhaps the major theme of the play. It is ironic that a woman who talks as much as Thelma has neglected to say so many truly meaningful things. Jessie has never asked questions, shared her opinions, or chosen to talk to anyone except her father. When Thelma asks what the two of them whispered about, Jessie replies that they were discussing important things such as why black socks are warmer than blue socks. Jessie has been very secure with her father's habit of just sitting, of being quiet, and of not doing anything; Thelma has never understood it. In making strings of paper "boyfriends" and animals for Jessie, her father has given her the only memory of her childhood that she seems to value.

Thelma has a deep lack of self-confidence that becomes apparent for the first time after Jessie questions her about her lack of love for her husband. She says that Jessie's father married her because he wanted a plain country woman and that is what she was and continues to be, yet she always thought he expected and wanted her to change. Like Jessie, she has been lonely and has felt misunderstood and unappreciated.

Jessie insists that she must use her father's gun to kill herself and has to have her mother tell her where it is. She also has her former husband's gun, however, just in case she cannot find her father's. Her brother Dawson has told her how to get the bullets. The gun is obviously a phallic symbol indicating her assuming for the occasion an unaccustomed sense of masculine assertiveness. Until now, she has been virtually sexless as well as selfless.

In order to save face with her family, Jessie had written a note and pretended that Cecil had left it for her; she explains that she had never expected to go with him, knowing that a person rarely takes his garbage with him when he moves. Jessie knows that Cecil tried to make a success of their marriage; he tried to interest her in horseback riding and other things he enjoyed. He took pride in his skill as a carpenter and worked to help Jessie find herself and find a medical way to deal with her epilepsy, just as he worked so long building a crib for Ricky.

Each of the items in the box Jessie gives to Thelma to deliver to family members and to keep for herself has inherent symbolic significance. She leaves her grandmother's ring to Thelma and sees no more value in the heritage she has received from the past than she does in the house slippers Dawson gives her each year. She has never worn any of them; he has bought them to fit Loretta rather than her, and she wants her mother to tell him this. Her genuine thoughtfulness and her understanding of her mother's appreciation of the little pleasure in life are demonstrated in the little gifts she wants her mother to open one at a time as she feels the need. She also knows that Thelma needs something to look forward to and tells her that she has made out lists of gifts for Dawson to buy for her for several birthdays to come.

Context

It is very difficult to face the possibility that there are women who have as little self-respect or reason to live as Jessie has, yet there are many lonely women who have no control over their lives or their bodies and who seem to have lost even the desire to assert themselves. The play causes one to ask whether suicide is valid in such situations. When Thelma points out to Jessie that suicide is a sin, Jessie immediately replies that, in a sense, Jesus committed suicide. Neither woman appears to have any real spiritual dimension; their concern with the funeral is social rather than religious—Jessie wants to help Thelma keep up appearances because she knows that this is important to her mother.

The play powerfully affirms how essential it is to value conventional rituals and to take pleasure in small things—even trivial things. The weekly manicure that Jessie usually gives to Thelma is the only thing they seem to share and to enjoy together. Jessie says that she has been looking forward to holding hands with her mother one last time. On this last Saturday evening, the manicure is pushed aside and overlooked; when Thelma says she is ready, Jessie says that it is now too late. They have waited too long to see the value in this shared activity.

The fact that Thelma does value seemingly insignificant and small pleasures (traditionally feminine ones) such as her cupcakes and candy treats, her weekly crossword puzzle, and her knitting, and that she looks forward to birthdays and visits from Dawson becomes her salvation. She will be able to go on and take care of herself because she sees meaning in what Jessie considers meaningless. The play compels the reader to take a serious look at the meaning and significance of small pleasures and to realize that they are the stuff from which existence is made.

Sources for Further Study

Browder, Sally. " 'I Thought You Were Mine': Marsha Norman's *'night, Mother*." In *Mother Puzzles: Daughters and Mothers in Contemporary American Literature*, edited by Mickey Pearlman. New York: Greenwood Press, 1989. This article looks at Jessie's reliance on her mother, Thelma's reliance on her daughter, and what impact these relationships have on the self-concept of each woman.

Burkman, Katherine H. "The Demeter Myth and Doubling in Marsha Norman's *'night, Mother*." In *Modern American Drama: The Female Canon*, edited by June Schlueter. Rutherford, N.J.: Fairleigh Dickinson University Press, 1990. This feminist look at the mother-daughter relationship focuses on images of death and rebirth in the play.

Demastes, William W. "Jessie and Thelma Revisited: Marsha Norman's Conceptual Challenge in *'night, Mother*." *Modern Drama* 36, no. 1 (1993): 109-120. Demastes suggests that, although it is a realistic social drama, the play attacks the established order and denies understanding.

Grieff, Louis K. "Fathers, Daughters, and Spiritual Sisters: Marsha Norman's *'night, Mother* and Tennessee Williams's *The Glass Menagerie*." *Text and Performance Quarterly* 9, no. 3 (1989): 224-228. The focus of this study is the relationship of the emotionally crippled daughter with her long-absent father.

Kane, Leslie. "The Way Out, the Way In: Paths to Self in the Plays of Marsha Norman." In *Feminine Focus: The New Women Playwrights*, edited by Enoch Brater. Oxford, England: Oxford University Press, 1989. This article compares the mother-child relationships and the development of self in *'night, Mother* to similar concepts examined in Norman's other plays.

Morrow, Laura. "Orality and Identity in *'night, Mother* and *Crimes of the Heart*." *Studies in American Drama* 3 (1988): 23-39. This study examines the relationship of orality in the development of female identity in Norman's play and compares it to Beth Henley's play.

Porter, Laurin R. "Woman Re-Conceived: Changing Perceptions of Women in Contemporary American Drama." *Conference of College Teachers of English Studies* 54 (1989): 53-59. This journal article provides a comparison of the play to *Crimes of the Heart* and *Agnes of God*.

Smith, Raynette Halvorsen. "'night, Mother and *True*

West: Mirror Images of Violence and Gender." In *Violence in Drama*, edited by James Redmond. Cambridge, England: Cambridge University Press, 1991. Smith compares Norman's and Sam Shepard's treatment of violence in relationship to gender.

Spencer, Jenny S. "Norman's *'night, Mother*: Psycho-Drama of Female Identity." *Modern Drama* 30, no. 3 (1987): 364-375. Takes a psychological approach in comparing the audience response of men to the play with the audience response of women.

Constance M. Fulmer

NO MAN'S LAND: The Place of the Woman Writer in the Twentieth Century

Authors: Sandra M. Gilbert (1936-) and Susan Gubar (1944-)
Type of work: Literary criticism
First published: 1988-1994

Form and Content

With the publication of their critically acclaimed study *The Madwoman in the Attic: The Woman Writer and the Nineteenth-Century Literary Imagination* (1979), Sandra M. Gilbert and Susan Gubar began what they envisioned as a sequel that would bring the discussion into the twentieth century. They soon realized that in order to understand the period, they needed to immerse themselves in men's as well as women's writing, in social as well as literary history. A single volume could not contain so vast an undertaking. Thus was born a three-part study under the general heading *No Man's Land: The Place of the Woman Writer in the Twentieth Century*.

Volume 1, subtitled *The War of the Words*, explores the idea that the pen is "a metaphorical pistol" and words "the weapons with which the sexes have fought over territory and authority." Gilbert and Gubar's re-reading and reinterpretations of standard literary texts show that, however subtly, the written word tends to maintain and reinforce man's dominance and power.

When societal changes in the mid-nineteenth century gave greater voice to women and their concerns, a kind of locking of horns resulted. The authors note that many men of the late nineteenth and early twentieth century saw women as alien forces, summoning trouble, while women viewed men as guardians of an outdated order. They add that the increased visibility of women in the public sphere led men and women of letters into a battle of the sexes.

Volume 1 surveys the major changes from the mid-nineteenth century to the late twentieth century in literary influences, in the social status of women, and in the ways in which language that preserves the old order is evolving to reflect the new. It details the conflict that resulted when Victorian concepts of femininity were challenged by the rise of feminism.

This volume is divided into five segments. The first explores male fears of emerging feminism. The second details the female struggle for social and literary independence. The third discusses the sociocultural redefinitions of gender. The fourth shows how eventually having a female literary tradition upon which to draw affected women writers. The fifth shows how language can be used to include and exclude. The authors under discussion include Nathaniel Hawthorne, Henry James, Algernon Charles Swinburne, Oscar Wilde, Henry Adams, T. S. Eliot, Ezra Pound, D. H. Lawrence, James Joyce, F. Scott Fitzgerald, William Faulkner, Ernest Hemingway, Nathanael West, and Henry Miller.

Volume 2, subtitled *Sexchanges*, deals with the evolution of sex and sex roles, from the rejection of Victorian concepts of femininity to the adoption of nearly as stultifying codes of conduct (sometimes called the feminization of women) and then to a dramatic shift in earlier perceptions caused, in part, by World War I and the emergence of a "visible lesbian community." The emphasis, in this volume, though outwardly on men and women of letters, is largely on matters of social history.

Many of the issues and critical works discussed in the earlier volume are given in-depth treatment, with whole segments devoted to Kate Chopin, Edith Wharton, Willa Cather, and Gertrude Stein. The second volume also provides a more comprehensive discussion of changes in sex roles, in modes of dress for women, and in the very language used by each gender to exclude the other.

The third book, subtitled *Letters from the Front*, explores the works and lives of such writers as Virginia Woolf, Zora Neale Hurston, Edna St. Vincent Millay, Marianne Moore, and H. D. (Hilda Doolittle). The authors hope that the series will

> help to illuminate the radical transformations of culture that we must all continue to face, transformations that have made not just the territory of literature but the institutions of marriage and the family, of education and the professions, into a no man's land—a vexed terrain—in which scattered armies of men and women all too often clash by day and by night.

Analysis

The first section of volume 1 begins with an admonition by D. H. Lawrence: "Fight for your life, men. Fight your wife out of her own self-conscious preoccupation with herself. Batter her out of it till she's stunned." The authors then turn to standard texts to cull other battle imagery and evidence of gender antagonism. While mid-Victorian stories by writers of both sexes show women in defeat, turn-of-the-century tales of what would happen if women gained power abound: Hordes of Amazons and Titans make men into sex slaves or eradicate them altogether. These tales of killing, of humiliation, of societies ruled by women who revel in the destruction of men, are balanced by more traditional ones of men pillaging and raping.

Gilbert and Gubar explain that as more women entered the world of literature, a field formerly dominated by men, they met with resistance from those who thought that they might be taking away work rightfully belonging to men. Sometimes their successes were discounted as being spawned by a readership mainly consisting of inconsequential women of leisure. Nathaniel Hawthorne called them a "damned mob of scribbl[ers]." Later, twentieth century misogyny may have grown from the position in which many male writers found themselves. Some were dependent upon women patrons who subsidized their work or female editors who evaluated their work, exercising the power to cut or reject.

This increasingly hostile climate was intensified by fears engendered by the suffrage movement. To many men of letters, the emancipation of women heralded a feminine takeover. Text upon text in this period dealt with "the Woman Question." Victorian moralist Nicholas Francis Cooke observed in 1870 that "this matter of 'Women's Rights' " will result in woman becoming "rapidly unsexed and degraded . . . ; she will cease to be the gentle mother, and become the Amazonian brawler." In *Geschlecht und Charakter* (1903; *Sex and Character*, 1906), Otto Weininger noted that "Women have no existence and no essence; they are not, they are nothing. . . . Woman has no share in ontological reality."

These assumptions were most widely challenged at the beginning of the twentieth century, a period marked by upheaval and change. Women, initially excluded from higher education, now founded their own colleges and eventually gained access to male institutions and to greater intellectual autonomy. Advances in birth control methods gave them a freedom they had not known before. Then, with the advent of World War I in 1914, opportunities for meaningful employment expanded.

Large numbers of women entered a workforce vacated by men called to battle. For these men, who had gone to war with visions of a swift conflict followed by a victorious return, the grim realities of trench warfare, the protracted horror of death and decay, created resentment—of the older generation that had created the war and the women who had replaced them so easily in the factories. The women did flourish, to the point that some treated the prospect of the end of the war and return to domestic life as a sad occasion.

The war, a liberating experience for women, served to enslave many men who were unable to forget what they had seen, to forgive what they had endured. Some experienced severe shell shock, one doctor noting that combat survivors on occasion displayed symptoms formerly thought of as female maladies.

In the postwar period, a literature of impotency, of emasculation emerged. Male characters were literally or figuratively castrated, made weak by war or women or circumstances. Citing an Emily Dickinson poem, "I rose—because He sank—," Gilbert and Gubar note that women writers of this period seem curiously strengthened, as though they were free to rise only if their men "sank." Their female characters, however, often turned guilt at being empowered into a kind of punishment. They enjoyed a moment of power but suffered sad consequences. Emancipation and equality did not come easily.

The volumes of *No Man's Land* are interlaced with humor, at times a punning and wordplay that some critics find annoying and forced. Nevertheless, Gilbert and Gubar's conversational tone helps to make their work readable and accessible to both scholar and layperson. Their discussions of the early masters of the canon will change the reading of these artists henceforth.

Context

Some critics have charged Gilbert and Gubar with raising more questions than they have answered, with offering unsubstantiated claims, and with virtually ignoring contemporary feminist thinking and returning to the politics of the 1960's. Others, however, credit them with identifying the questions that should be asked, with providing a foundation upon which to base further research, and with stirring the waters enough to attract attention and inspire debate. In their forays from the familiar territory of literature to spheres of social history, an area of self-admitted uncertainty, they falter, but not disastrously so. In seeing with the eyes of nonspecialists, they allow the casual reader to explore with them. Even the critics who quarrel with their scholarship, their assumptions, their inclusions of some writers to the exclusion of others, their purported concentration of the works of women but tendency to afford greater coverage to ones by men, and their inability to pass by a chance for a pun or a bon mot do recognize that Gilbert and Gubar have set a standard from which all future scholarship will grow and upon which it will be based.

Their works have given readers a new way of looking at old texts, new ways to assess patriarchal concerns, new methods to detect gender bias, and a new view of underlying causes of tensions that result in battling between the sexes. Though at times bias predominates and scholarship is suited to serve the purpose, these feminist scholars have produced a body of work of seminal importance. Their overstatement and slanting does not negate the existence of troublesome images in literature and the biased language of the creators of that literature. *No Man's Land* provides a whole new approach to looking at the period, and, as Carolyn Heilbrun, a feminist writer, critic, and teacher observes, "The study of modernism will never be the same."

Sandra Gilbert and Susan Gubar have coedited *The Norton Anthology of Literature by Women: The Tradition in English* (1985) and *Shakespeare's Sisters: Feminist Essays on Women Poets* (1979), and they coauthored *The Female Imagination and the Modernist Aesthetic* (1986) and *The Madwoman in the Attic*.

Sources for Further Study

Ammons, Elizabeth. *Conflicting Stories: American Women Writers at the Turn into the Twentieth Century*. New York: Oxford University Press, 1991. Deals with seventeen women writers from diverse ethnic and racial backgrounds. Ammons finds underlying themes of unity as these writers, in a wide range of narrative forms, strove to give voice to women's concerns.

Armstrong, Nancy. *Desire and Domestic Fiction: A Political History of the Novel*. New York: Oxford University Press, 1987. Armstrong explores the role of women in shaping modern literary and social institutions. Her detailed historical discussion leads to implicit criticism of Gilbert and Gubar's stress on victimization.

Gilbert, Sandra M., and Susan Gubar. *The Madwoman in the Attic: The Woman Writer and the Nineteenth-Century Literary Imagination*. New Haven, Conn.: Yale University Press, 1979. An excellent study of major women writers in nineteenth century England, this precursor to *No Man's Land* received wide critical acclaim.

Moi, Toril. *Sexual/Textual Politics: Feminist Literary Theory*. London: Routledge, 1985. A useful guide to key issues in feminist literary analysis, this small volume contains a detailed critique of Gilbert and Gubar's approach.

Showalter, Elaine, ed. *Speaking of Gender*. New York: Routledge, 1989. These essays by leading scholars and critics offer detailed insights on a wide range of texts. They provide discussion of many of the issues raised in more general fashion by the work of Gilbert and Gubar.

Gay Zieger

O PIONEERS!

Author: Willa Cather (1873-1947)
Type of work: Novel
Type of plot: Naturalism
Time of plot; The late nineteenth and early twentieth centuries
Locale: The Nebraska prairie near Hanover
First published: 1913

Principal characters:

Alexandra Bergson, a young woman struggling to keep her family together
Carl Linstrum, the son of a neighboring homesteader
Emil Bergson, Alexandra's youngest brother
Marie Tovesky, a young, spirited, Bohemian woman
Frank Shabata, a Bohemian farmer who is blindly possessive about his pretty young wife, Marie
Lou and **Oscar Bergson,** Alexandra's older brothers
Crazy Ivar, a pious old Swedish hermit

Form and Content

O Pioneers! presents one woman's experiences as she struggles to keep her family together in harsh conditions on the Nebraska prairie, called "the divide" in the book, in the late nineteenth and early twentieth centuries. The book is divided into five parts. Part 1, called "The Wild Land," introduces the teenaged Alexandra Bergson, her young brother Emil, her friend Carl Linstrum (who is slightly younger than herself), and an already captivating girl, Marie Tovesky, who is visiting her uncle. Even in this first section, it is clear that Alexandra is in charge of her family's farm now, since her father is bedridden. It is she whom he trusts with the care of the farm, especially since he knows that he will die soon. John Bergson recognizes in Alexandra strength of will and a direct way of thinking things out, but he would rather have seen these traits in one of his sons, believing that it is a man's place to lead. John Bergson's prejudice against his most able child because of her gender prepares readers for the other biases that Alexandra will encounter.

Part 2, "Neighboring Fields," takes place sixteen years after John Bergson's death. The prairie has given up its struggle against the farmers and now yields abundant crops. Amid all the abundance is Emil, scything the grass in the old Norwegian cemetery, and Marie, who has come to give him a ride home. This scene foreshadows many others to come. Two future events are of special importance. After the death of his best friend, Amedee, Emil decides that he cannot waste his life because death can come at any moment; at Amedee's grave he decides that he will have Marie, his beloved, who is already married to Frank Shabata. The cemetery also foretells a scene that the reader is not shown but which must happen after Emil and Marie are found making love in the Shabata orchard.

The neighboring fields are Marie and Frank's, but they are not the only neighbors with whom Alexandra must deal. Her own brothers, Lou and Oscar, have now taken their shares of the much-expanded farmstead. Their jealousy of Alexandra's continued success without them makes them unfriendly when Carl Linstrum returns from Missouri to visit. When they realize that Alexandra is seriously considering marrying Carl, the brothers accost her, telling her that she cannot hand over her land to a man because it still belongs to them, the men of the family. Alexandra points out legalities to them and reminds them of her contributions to and literal salvation of the homestead. To Lou and Oscar, the idea that Alexandra, who is nearing forty, would want to get married is ludicrous.

It is only Emil who supports Alexandra's love for Carl. Even Carl has doubts: He calls himself a failure and is unable to marry into comfort—believing, like most men of his time, that he has to prove himself successful in order to claim that he is fully a man. Thus Alexandra is denied by the American belief of rugged individualism the happiness that she had been denying herself all those years. Emil, meanwhile, declares his love to Marie. Because of her devout Catholicism, she warns him that they have to pretend that they are not in love, or they would not be able to continue to be friends.

In part 3, "Winter Memories," Emil is in Mexico trying to forget Marie, and Carl has gone to Alaska to try to make his fortune. Alexandra and Marie while away the winter days visiting. It is during one of these visits that Alexandra first learns that Marie is unhappy as Frank's wife. Such a candid disclosure makes Alexandra uncomfortable, however, and as most people do in uncomfortable situations, she chooses to ignore Marie's troubles.

Alexandra is not immune from such human foibles. In part 4, "The White Mulberry Tree," Alexandra is blind to Emil and Marie's love for each other. Their passion is accentuated by the birth of Amedee's first child and his sudden death from appendicitis. Unable to keep away from Marie any longer, Emil rushes to her. It is in the orchard, the description of which bears many symbolic references to the garden of Eden, that Frank finds Emil and Marie making love. In his fury, he shoots them both.

Part 5, "Alexandra," shows how much the patriarchal culture is ingrained in Alexandra despite her independent nature. Even though she acknowledges that Marie was more than simply a married woman, she still blames Marie for Emil's death and Frank's imprisonment. Despite Alexandra's own desire to live her life as she sees fit, she is still part of the culture that condemns women for seeming to entice young men to grievous ends. Like many who value men more than women, Alexandra can only see the loss of the two men's lives, not Marie's.

Analysis

The second of Willa Cather's novels, *O Pioneers!* began as two separate stories, one about Alexandra and one about the lovers Emil and Marie, called "The White Mulberry Tree." Combining the two came naturally for Cather, who said that writing the book was like revisiting familiar places.

Cather intertwines folklore and Christian values to create a vibrant view of life on the plains at the beginning of the twentieth century. The most religious people in *O Pioneers!*, the hermit Crazy Ivar and Marie, are also the two who have effectively combined the mythic elements of folklore and Christianity to create a religion of their own—a religion replete with concerns for the nature around them. Crazy Ivar does not allow guns on his property and only wants to heal animals, choosing to live with them instead of humans. Marie loves her orchard, where, as she tells Emil, she would worship if she did not have the Catholic church.

As in much literature dealing with wayward lovers, Cather uses the garden of Eden symbolism in the orchard scenes between Emil and Marie to heighten readers' sensibilities to the tension between the two lovers. Marie teases Emil, while he uses a scythe to cut the grass, to watch out for snakes. Other fateful imagery includes a duck hunting scene. Keen on hunting together, Marie is remorseful when she actually sees the pair of dead ducks that Emil dumps in her apron. She laments having ended the ducks' happiness and makes Emil promise not to hunt anymore. Both the reader and Carl, who witnessed the affection between the two, clearly get a sense of a similar doom for the two young people.

The problems that women faced on the prairie are especially brought to the foreground as Alexandra struggles with her brothers over ownership of the land; as she tries to persuade Carl to marry her for love and companionship, to forget his male pride for their mutual happiness; as she emblazons Emil with the status of the favored son; and as she herself condemns Marie—who, the reader knows, is less guilty than Emil because she tries her best to discourage his advances—for Emil's death and Frank's imprisonment. Marie also expresses envy for Emil's ability to wander about the world anywhere and anytime that he pleases.

While one learns that divorce was becoming more common at this time, a fact that infuriates possessive Frank when he reads the newspaper, women are still expected to lead traditional wifely roles. It is only because she remained single that Alexandra was able to influence her brothers and run her own farm as she did.

Context

Three motifs have traditionally been examined in *O Pioneers!*: the Old World versus the New World, the struggling American pioneer, and the maternal as seen in both Alexandra and nature. Much has been made of

Cather's attempts to capture the essence and the effects of immigrants and their cultures on the settlement of the plains. Similarly, the novel has been heralded for its obvious homage to those pioneering farmers who struggled to homestead the land because of the book's elaborate descriptions of the place and people. Cather's traditional use of nature as the feminine to be controlled into a source of nurturance accentuated many critics' view of Alexandra as the patient and wise mother of generations. What had been ignored, until more recently, was the fact that Alexandra is not a mother, but an independent, intelligent woman who—no matter how hard she tries to be her own person—still succumbs to the traditional patriarchal point of view sermonized in so many stories written about pioneers.

Feminist critics have begun to examine Alexandra more closely, as they compare her with two of Cather's other strong female protagonists: Thea Kronborg in *The Song of the Lark* (1915) and Ántonia Shimerda in *My Ántonia* (1918). All three women are immigrants or children of immigrants and seem to draw their strengths from being different from other American women—stronger, more headstrong, and more independent.

As Cather had been influenced by Henry James and Sarah Orne Jewett, she seems to have had an encouraging effect on regional writers, lending respect to regional fiction by such authors as Wallace Stegner and William Kittredge. The ambiance of Cather's descriptions of a particular place and nature in general also comes across in several works by Gretel Ehrlich and in Kathleen Norris' *Dakota* (1993).

Sources for Further Study

Motley, Warren. "The Unfinished Self: Willa Cather's *O Pioneers!* and the Psychic Cost of a Woman's Success." *Women's Studies: An Interdisciplinary Journal* 12, no. 2 (1986): 149-165. Discusses the conflicts between many women's desire for independence in the early twentieth century and their repression by society, especially in discussing Alexandra's isolation.

Murphy, John J., ed. *Critical Essays on Willa Cather*. Boston: G. K. Hall, 1984. This collection of essays deals with various themes and ideas, such as sexuality and childhood, encountered in Cather's novels.

____________, ed. *Willa Cather: Family, Community, and History*. Provo, Utah: Brigham Young University, 1990. This collection of critical essays examines recurrent motifs in Cather's novels, such as how socialized concepts affect individual ideas about one's place in the family, community, and history.

O'Brien, Sharon. *Willa Cather: The Emerging Voice*. New York: Oxford University Press, 1987. This biography examines Cather's life before 1915, when she was becoming more famous for her novels, and speculates on her search for both a gender identity and a personal narrative voice.

Rosowski, Susan J. "Willa Cather and the Fatality of Place: *O Pioneers!*, *My Ántonia*, and *A Lost Lady*." In *Geography and Literature: A Meeting of the Disciplines*, edited by William E. Mallory and Paul Simpson-Housley. Syracuse, N.Y.: Syracuse University Press, 1987. Explores gender differences based on interactions with nature: Men attempt to create order in nature, and women attempt to place themselves within nature.

Slote, Bernice. "Willa Cather and the Sense of History." In *Women, Women Writers, and the West*, edited by L. L. Lee and Merrill Lewis. Troy, N.Y.: Whitston, 1979. Examines the historical and mythical qualities of Cather's novels that are used to connect the Old World with the New World.

Slote, Bernice, and Virginia Faulkner, eds. *The Art of Willa Cather*. Lincoln: University of Nebraska Press, 1974. A collection of essays by noted Cather scholars discussing various aspects of her style of fiction.

Wiesenthal, C. Susan. "Female Sexuality in Willa Cather's *O Pioneers!* and the Era of Scientific Sexology: A Dialogue Between Frontiers." *Ariel: A Review of International English Literature* 21, no. 1 (1990): 41-63. Provides insights into the use of science to explain and to examine women's sexuality in the early twentieth century and how such science applies to *O Pioneers!*.

Woodress, James. *Willa Cather: Her Life and Art*. New York: Egasus, 1970. A critical biography, this work examines the connections between Cather's personal life and her writing.

Ruth J. Heflin

OF WOMAN BORN: Motherhood as Experience and Institution

Author: Adrienne Rich (1929-)
Type of work: Social criticism
First published: 1976

Form and Content

Already established as a powerful feminist poet, Adrienne Rich ventured into the field of social criticism with the publication of *Of Woman Born: Motherhood as Experience and Institution.* A self-identified feminist/lesbian/socialist, Rich made the transition to a new genre of writing with a carefully annotated scholarly work which departs from traditional impersonal research by combining a comprehensive feminist analysis of the institution of motherhood (objective research) with Rich's personal experience of struggle as a mother and a poet (subjective experience). Written as a collection of essays with a common theme, *Of Woman Born* explores the dark and disturbing side of motherhood in discourse that counters popular romanticized views of maternity.

Rich's life and emotions are laid bare as *Of Woman Born* weaves scholarly analysis with anecdotes and insights from her experiences of motherhood, as both a parent of three sons and as a daughter herself. Anger, tenderness, loneliness, and guilt contribute to the experience of alienation in the modern reality of motherhood. Alienation, or the separation of the institution of motherhood from the authentic experience of mothering, is the driving force of Rich's analysis throughout the book. History, anthropology, mythology, literature, sociology, and psychology provide *Of Woman Born* with key resources for describing and explaining the alienation experienced by women. Rich does not believe, however, that maternal alienation is an inevitable fact of motherhood; it is a creation of the social institutions that have an impact on the relationships of men and women (hence the dichotomy in the subtitle). Rich begins by exploring the experience of motherhood in the 1950's and 1960's, a period that roughly corresponds to her own motherhood, but her search becomes transhistorical as she searches for the roots of the modern understanding of motherhood. *Of Woman Born* does not offer a chronological development of motherhood. Instead, in advancing Rich's presentation of alienation, *Of Woman Born* contains analyses of various historical periods that are held together by strands of feminist social criticism.

Rich uses examples from the history of women in the United States—from the British colonies through the Industrial Revolution—to demonstrate the "sacred calling" of motherhood. Historically, while women could hardly afford to concentrate only on child rearing, nevertheless this role became identified as the primary function of women in society. Motherhood became an institution of patriarchy (which Rich describes as "the power of the fathers") that further advanced the oppression of women. *Of Woman Born* applies this theme of patriarchal motherhood to the economic institutions of capitalism and socialism, to the religious institution of Christianity, to the medical institution in the United States, and to the social institution of personal relationships. The latter analysis is an extended challenge to the modern social norm of what Rich refers to as "compulsory heterosexuality." Rich argues that these institutions perpetuate patriarchy while shaping the alienating institution of motherhood.

In the final chapters of *Of Woman Born*, Rich analyzes one of the results of historical institutional alienation—the potential for maternal violence against children. In particular, the phenomenon and history of infanticide is explored. Rich draws upon feminist psychoanalysis to describe the interpersonal dynamics that can lead to this taboo act. Yet *Of Woman Born* does not indict mothers. According to Rich, such feelings of violence are the result of the maternal alienation created by powerful social institutions which attempt to define and control motherhood. For Rich, alienation is a product of external control.

Analysis

The fundamental point of analysis in *Of Woman Born* is a rejection of the belief that the experience of motherhood is universally positive and should be normative for all women. Rich presents a significant challenge to the romanticized notion of maternal bliss. *Of Woman Born* takes the reader on a difficult and disturbing journey through feminist analysis of motherhood. Rich also challenges traditional male scholarship by valuing her own diaries and journal entries equally with her formal research.

Rich's social criticism authentically reflects the feminist theme that "the personal is political." Women's experience is essential to the arguments developed in *Of Woman Born*. Rich explicitly attempts to overcome the mind/body split, or dualism, that permeates patriarchal language. In this dualism, matters of thought or the mind are considered superior to matters of the body or sensual experience. Historically, men have been associated with the former and women have been associated with the latter. *Of Woman Born* draws the two realms together as Rich's eloquent prose relates her bodily experience of motherhood. This "theory of the body" is ultimately concerned with control. Motherhood as experience is controlled by women, while motherhood as institution is controlled by men.

Of Woman Born is highly critical of patriarchy without making generalizations about men. In fact, the relationship between men and women is not the central focus of this book. On several occasions, Rich calls for a change in patterns toward equality in parenting relationships and responsibility. Rich is more concerned, however, with the relationship of mothers to their children, and in particular to daughters. While Rich is critical of men for creating and maintaining sexist institutions, she is also critical of women for perpetuating dependency upon men by participating in the patriarchal institution of motherhood. This participation comes through child rearing, which replicates the tradition of alienated motherhood in daughters. Yet Rich's analysis recognizes the power of social and political forces in shaping child-rearing practices and therefore ultimately exonerates mothers as she discusses her attempts to recapture appreciation for her own mother.

The analysis in *Of Woman Born* represents a deconstruction of traditional motherhood in its alienating form, but the book also represents hope for women in the form of female power. While the distortions of patriarchal society extend to mother-daughter relationships, Rich believes that motherhood does not have to be alienating. Like many feminist theories, Rich's analysis breaks down women's oppression to find its origin and resources, but her analysis also finds sources of autonomous female strength. One such strength can be derived from sisterhood. Rich calls for women to find strength in female bonding in communities that value diversity. The creative power of motherhood can also be a source of empowerment and hope for women. History and mythology provide themes of female power from which modern women can draw. *Of Woman Born* demonstrates that female power historically has been suppressed and misdirected, resulting in alienation. With male experience as normative, social institutions transform mothers into "others," resulting in anger, fear, and depression—the dark side of motherhood.

Her analysis makes the connection between this alienation and violence that mothers sometimes commit against their children. In the personalist approach found in *Of Woman Born*, Rich, while never having committed any act of violence against her children, explains her identification with the emotions that make such acts possible. *Of Woman Born* gives voice to the feelings that mothers have had but dared not speak. In Rich's cathartic analysis, she participates in the feminist process of identifying and naming the previously unnamed.

Because *Of Woman Born* draws upon so many diverse disciplines in the process of creating an overarching theory of motherhood, it has been criticized for lacking appropriate depth in any particular field of analysis. The use of various historical examples of patriarchically determined motherhood has resulted in concerns that the context of these phenomena were not fully developed. While Rich focuses upon mother-daughter relationships, other social factors contributing to the creation of the institution of motherhood are ignored. In this manner, Rich has been criticized for portraying mothers as more powerful than perhaps they are: Mothers cannot control all the factors that contribute to their children's socialization. This narrow focus also makes possible a related criticism of utopianism, because Rich's solution ultimately rests with altering the child-rearing patterns of mothers.

Context

Of Woman Born is a principal work in a larger debate within feminism over the complex relationship between reproductive issues, motherhood, and women's oppression. For example, in Shulamith Firestone's *The Dialectic of Sex: The Case for Feminist Revolution* (1970) the argument is made that biological inequality between the sexes is the cause of social inequality. Firestone's solution is a mandate to overcome biological differences through technology. Rich agrees with Firestone's analysis when it is limited to institutional motherhood as it is constructed by society. In accord with Rich's analysis of alienation, if women were in control of the experience of motherhood, there would be no need to "overcome" biological differences. This debate is indicative of the plurality of positions within feminism.

The mixed reviews that met the publication of *Of Woman Born* demonstrate how this work identified a previously undiscussed topic. Many of these reviews reflected gender bias. Because the forum for mothers expressing the negative side of their parenting experience was limited, many were shocked by Rich's revelations. Some attempted to dismiss Rich's analysis as an aberration and therefore not indicative of the feelings of a majority of mothers. Other women writers and scholars, however, while not always in agreement with her argumentation, would subsequently reinforce and vindicate the themes in *Of Woman Born*. For example, Nancy Chodorow discusses the creation of the institution of motherhood and the need for dual parenting from a psychoanalytic perspective in *The Reproduction of Mothering: Psychoanalysis and the Sociology of Gender* (1978). In 1986, the popularity and significance of *Of Woman Born* was marked with a tenth anniversary edition which included a new forword by the author.

While continuing to produce critically acclaimed and prize-winning poetry, Rich has compiled an impressive collection of works on cultural criticism, including *On Lies, Secrets, and Silences: Selected Prose 1966-1978* (1979), *Blood, Bread, and Poetry: Selected Prose 1979-1985* (1986), and *What Is Found There: Notebooks on Poetry and Politics* (1993). Among her essays, "Compulsory Heterosexuality and Lesbian Experience: The Meaning of Our Love for Women Is What We Have Constantly to Expand" (1980) is considered a watershed critique of homophobia in modern culture.

Sources for Further Study

Cooper, Jane Roberta, ed. *Reading Adrienne Rich: Reviews and Re-Visions, 1951-81*. Ann Arbor: University of Michigan Press, 1984. A balanced collection of essays and reviews of Rich's poetry and prose. Five entries focus upon *Of Woman Born* including a negative review typical of the mainstream assessment of this work.

Erkkila, Betsy. *The Wicked Sisters: Women Poets, Literary History, and Discord*. New York: Oxford University Press, 1992. Chapter 5, "Adrienne Rich, Emily Dickinson, and the Limits of Sisterhood," contextualizes the writings of these two poets within their historical settings. The life of each woman is plumbed for its impact on her writings and politics.

Gelpi, Barbara Charlesworth, and Albert Gelpi. *Adrienne Rich's Poetry and Prose*. New York: W. W Norton, 1993. A comprehensive treatment of Rich's writings, including selections of her poetry and prose. An extensive selection of reviews is provided, as well as a chronology of Rich's life and a bibliography of her work.

Keyes, Claire. *The Aesthetics of Power: The Poetry of Adrienne Rich*. Athens: University of Georgia Press, 1986. While this book only deals with *Of Woman Born* in passing, it offers a useful chronological approach to the emergence of Rich's analytical themes. Her transformation into a leader in the feminist literary movement is carefully traced. A brief biography is included.

Martin, Wendy. *An American Triptych: Anne Bradstreet, Emily Dickinson, Adrienne Rich*. Chapel Hill: University of North Carolina Press, 1984. A thematic approach to the works of three American poets. The lives and works of these women are juxtaposed against one another in a revealing analysis of the rise of feminist consciousness. Instead of a work-by-work analysis, the breadth of Rich's writings is considered for their development of various themes.

Tong, Rosemarie. *Feminist Thought: A Comprehensive Introduction* . Boulder, Colo.: Westview Press, 1989. Although this text does not focus primarily on *Of Woman Born*, it does place the social criticism of Rich in the proper context within the sweep of feminist writing. An excellent primer to the various strands of feminism, providing an extensive bibliographical listing by category of feminist thought.

Werner, Craig. *Adrienne Rich: The Poet and Her Critics*. Chicago: American Library Association, 1988. Rich's writings are placed in the context of critical debates in culture, politics, and theory. Significant attention is paid to the evolution of her thought, including its lesbian, feminist, and radical dimensions.

Maurice Hamington

ON LIES, SECRETS, AND SILENCE: Selected Prose 1966-1978

Author: Adrienne Rich (1929-　　)
Type of work: Essays
First published: 1979

Form and Content

Adrienne Rich's *On Lies, Secrets, and Silence: Selected Prose 1966-1978* is a collection of twenty-two essays, some of which appeared earlier in such journals as *Chrysalis: A Magazine of Women's Culture*, *Parnassus: Poetry in Review*, and *Heresies: A Feminist Magazine of Art and Politics*. Others have served as introductions to books, and a few are previously unpublished talks. In a 1979 review of the work, literary critic Ellen Moers noted a misleading title, given its hint of "whining and whimpering," believing that "Feminism, Pedagogy, and Literature" would have more aptly described the content.

The essays deal with such matters as child care, consciousness-raising, tokenism, women's studies programs, male psychiatrists, motherhood, lesbianism, black feminism, abortion, sexual harassment on the job, woman beating, equal pay, pornography, and the rights of lesbian mothers. Rich makes a strong argument for a woman-centered university where female teachers would not need to seek male mentor approval, or the female student teacher/father approval. She devotes whole segments to Charlotte Brontë's novel *Jane Eyre* (1847); writers Anne Bradstreet, Emily Dickinson, Anne Sexton, and Eleanor Ross Taylor; and the war in Vietnam.

In these essays, Rich associates women with victimhood, men with violence, and heterosexuality with rape. She tends toward a romantic vision of a female-dominated society and mythologizes the forebears of current feminist literature. She challenges traditional female roles, contending that "middle class marriages and factory labor enslaved women." Says Rich: "We have been expected to lie with our bodies: to bleach, redden, unkink or curl our hair, pluck eyebrows, shave armpits, wear padding in various places or lace ourselves, take little steps, glaze finger and toe nails, wear clothes that emphasized our helplessness." She further notes that women have been called upon for

> world-protection, world-preservation, world-repair [with] the million tiny stitches, the friction of the scrubbing brush, the scouring cloth, the iron across the shirt, the rubbing of cloth against itself to exorcise the stain, the renewal of the scorched pot, the rusted knifeblade, the invisible weaving of a frayed and threadbare family, the cleaning up of soil and waste left behind by men and children

for love, rather than pay. She prefaces many of her essays with explanations of the factors that led her to feel as she did at the time of each writing. She charts how her views have changed or have been reinforced, and what responses they have met. On occasion, she offers an apology for hasty judgments.

Adrienne Rich's most notable work is her poetry, but her prose speaks eloquently to issues of womanhood and of the challenges that feminists, and more specifically lesbians, face in a male-dominated culture. More recent works reflect a modification of particular arguments, an emending of others, and a total rejection of some earlier views, but her anger with the power structure remains constant.

Analysis

Adrienne Rich was very much the product of her times. In 1951, she graduated Phi Beta Kappa from Radcliffe College. In the same year, with the encouragement and guidance of noted literary figure W. H. Auden, she published her first collection of poems, *A Change of World*. As Auden observed in a patronizing foreword, "The poems a reader will encounter in this book are neatly and modestly dressed, speak quietly but do not mumble, respect their elders but are not cowed by them, and do not tell fibs."

Rich's early poetry is markedly different from her later works. She feels that in the beginning she was writing for men, particularly her father, which could explain the orderliness noted by Auden. It was only later, during the frustration of trying to fulfill the obligations of wife (she married in 1953) and mother (by the time she was twenty-nine, she had three sons) that her poetry began to reflect her rage and she began to express her true feelings.

Though not a man-hater by any means, Rich does present, claim many critics, a biased account of the power structure and who is to blame for the subjugation of women. She recognizes that, at times, women are their own worst enemies but does not fault them for their suspicions of or aversions to radical feminism, seeing them as victims of their social environment. Her central contention is that all women everywhere are socialized, victimized, and indoctrinated. Her arguments to support this thesis are often convincing.

Misogyny in all its subtle and insidious forms abounds in all cultures. Western society is based upon a principle of patriarchy in which men make most major decisions. Discrimination determines even the way in which women view one another, resulting in part from the fact that most written portraits of women were conceived by men. Hence, in fiction there are lovely young ladies who often die at the height of their powers. It is the concept of the woman as appendage that offends Rich: Woman as "the painter's model and the poet's muse . . . comforter, nurse, cook, bearer of his seed, secretarial assistant, and copyist of manuscripts. . . ." Seldom are woman reflected as living and thinking, having the same basic requirements as man for spiritual and intellectual fulfillment.

Rich's belief that, historically, women often have been trivialized is clearly valid. Some critics charge, however, that *On Lies, Secrets, and Silence* indulges in polemics. The evils of society affect men as well as women. Expectations for men are as unrealistic and ultimately numbing as the lack of them for women. All people are victims of faceless oppression.

Critics also wonder about her view that women's creative energies originate from their inherent lesbian qualities, that "the dutiful daughter of the fathers within us is only a hack." (Rich later amended this argument, saying that perhaps the term "lesbian" was too "charged" and could possibly be changed to the "self-chosen woman," the one who "refuses to obey" and says " 'no' to the fathers.") They question, too, the idea of heterosexuality being fostered by the "white male dominated capitalist culture to keep women enchained, lest they lapse into more threatening lifestyles."

Rich's assertion that a woman's self-knowledge and solace come only through intense relationships with other women unnerved some critics, as did the idea that "much male fear of feminism is the fear that, in becoming whole human beings, women will cease to mother men, to provide the breast, the lullaby, the continuous attention associated by the infant with the mother."

It was after her third child that Rich began to feel that she was either a "failed woman" or a "failed poet." She was frightened by what appeared to be her destiny, by her loss of being in touch with herself. She says she was "writing very little, partly from fatigue, that female fatigue of suppressed anger and loss of contact with my own being; partly from the discontinuity of female life with its attention to small chores, errands, work that others constantly undo, small children's constant needs." She most missed having time for uninterrupted, quiet contemplation. She longed for a certain "freedom of the mind . . . freedom to press on, to enter the currents of your thought like a glider pilot, knowing that your motion can be sustained, that the buoyancy of your attention will not be suddenly snatched away." She experienced a conflict between traditional female functions and creative ones, finding it hard to put aside "imaginative activity." As she noted, "Biological motherhood has long been used as a reason for condemning women to a role of powerlessness and subservience in the social order."

In one of the strongest essays in the collection, on the Vietnam War, she equates maleness with killing, seeing the ravaging of that small country as a rape, brought on by a male desire to dominate and destroy. She sees the bombings as "so wholly sadistic, gratuitous and demonic that they can finally be seen . . . [as] acts of concrete sexual violence, an expression of the congruence of violence and sex in the masculine psyche." Rich's observations in 1983 in the essay "Blood, Bread, and Poetry: The Location of the Poet" on her past and what brought her to lesbian feminism help to clarify the views that she espoused in *On Lies, Secrets, and Silence*:

> Even before I named myself a feminist, or a lesbian, I felt impelled to bring together, in my understanding and in my poems, the political world "out there"—the world of children dynamited or napalmed, of the urban ghetto and militarist violence, and the supposedly private, lyrical world of sex and of male/female relationships.

Context

Adrienne Rich has had considerable impact on the women's movement. She is a prolific writer, and hers was the first forceful voice of lesbian-feminism. Critics agree that, though her biases sometimes deflect her message, she deserves serious attention. She raises questions, poses dilemmas, and enlightens. She forces both a looking inward and a looking outward. She addresses problems that affect all people.

Rich has received widespread literary recognition. She won the Ridgely Torrence Memorial Award of the Poetry Society of America in 1955, the Grace Thayer Bradley Award of Friends of Literature in 1956, the National Institute of Arts and Letters award for poetry in 1961, the Bess Hokin Prize of *Poetry* magazine in 1963, the Eunice Teitjens Memorial Prize of *Poetry* magazine in 1968, a National Endowment for the Arts grant in 1970, the Shelley Memorial Award of the Poetry Society of America in 1971, and in 1974 the coveted National Book Award for her poetry collection *Diving into the Wreck* (1973). She refused to accept this last award as an individual, in protest of the token role to which women of the time were relegated, taking it instead in honor of all women. Her other prose works include *Of Woman Born: Motherhood as Experience and Institution* (1976) and *Blood, Bread, and Poetry: Selected Prose 1979-1985* (1986). Critics have noted that, though some of her themes are derivative, having been well covered in other feminist tracts, she conveys the message with the grace of a poet.

Sources for Further Study

Erkkila, Betsy. *The Wicked Sisters: Women Poets, Literary History, and Discord*. New York: Oxford University Press, 1992. A chapter entitled "Adrienne Rich, Emily Dickinson, and the Limits of Sisterhood" provides an astute analysis of the place of Rich in the feminist movement from the 1960's to the 1990's.

Hooks, Bell. *Feminist Theory from Margin to Center*. Boston: South End Press, 1984. A work that further defines and expands feminism, reflecting the outcome of the split in the late 1970's into particular agendas. As Hooks says, "The vision of Sisterhood evoked by women's liberationists was based on the idea of common oppression [but that] was a false and corrupt platform. . . . Women are divided by sexist attitudes, racism, class privilege, and a host of other prejudices."

Michie, Helena. *The Flesh Made Word: Female Figures and Women's Bodies*. New York: Oxford University Press, 1987. An examination of the Victorian portrayal of female bodies in art, poems, novels, and popular publications, such as sex manuals and etiquette books. This short volume also provides a new reading of the works of Adrienne Rich, Charlotte and Emily Brontë, George Eliot, Thomas Hardy, Audre Lorde, and many others.

Moers, Ellen. *Literary Women*. Garden City, N.Y.: Doubleday, 1976. Considered a classic, this is a good place to start a serious study of feminist criticism. Includes discussions of Jane Austen, George Sand, Colette, Simone Weil, and Virginia Woolf.

Rich, Adrienne. *Blood, Bread, and Poetry: Selected Prose 1979-1985*. New York: W. W. Norton, 1986. Rich's writings reflect her growth as she defines and redefines herself. She is always evolving, and these later writings sometimes negate or undo earlier ones.

Gay Zieger

ORLANDO: A Biography

Author: Virginia Woolf (1882-1941)
Type of work: Novel
Type of plot: Fantasy
Time of plot: The sixteenth to the twentieth centuries
Locale: London and its environs and Constantinople
First published: 1928

Principal characters:

Orlando, the handsome, long-lived protagonist, who changes from a man to a woman over four centuries

Queen Elizabeth I, Orlando's mentor, mother figure, and lover

Sasha (Princess Marousha Stanislovska Dagmar Matasha Iliana Romanovitch), Orlando's love from the court of czarist Russia

Nicholas Greene, a bilious Jacobean poet admired by Orlando

Archduchess Harriet Griselda, Orlando's suitor from Finster-Aarhorn and Scandop-Boom in the Romanian Territory

Marmaduke Bonthrop Shelmerdine, a gallant ship owner and captain who marries Orlando

Form and Content

The genesis for Virginia Woolf's *Orlando: A Biography* came about in an hour. The author recalls wanting to create a historical work outlining all of her friends in a single work. The idea of writing a biography appealed to her. It follows the title character over four centuries, touching on the social, political, and literary tastes of each. Woolf is able to poke fun at the foibles of passing generations, reflect on time, and comment on the schism between men and women.

Orlando is introduced as a sixteen-year-old English lad during the reign of Queen Elizabeth I, around 1586. He is a handsome youth, given to literary ambitions as a poet and dramatist, a love of nature, and a deep respect for queen and country. In short, he is a true English gentleman. Elizabeth notices his noble qualities, his youthful enthusiasm, and his gorgeous legs, thinking him the proper English courtier. He becomes her surrogate son, lover, and appointed treasurer and steward of Elizabeth's court.

Orlando's life takes a turn during the reign of the succeeding monarch, King James I. Although engaged, Orlando falls in love with Russian Princess Sasha. She breaks his heart, leaving him while he waits in vain to elope with her. (Orlando would never trust women again, though he always remembered Sasha over the centuries.) Disgraced at court, he returns to his ancestral home. While there, he falls into a week-long trance, the first of several. Upon awakening, he buries himself in his work, taking greater pleasure in his vast estate. He becomes seriously interested again in literature, finding time to write plays, histories, romances, and poems, particularly his major opus, "The Oak Tree."

Orlando's comfortable literary pretensions collapse when he invites the poet Nicholas Greene to visit for six weeks. Greene, a marvelous wordsmith, but a foul-mouthed, rapacious character, accepts Orlando's generosity and his yearly pension but scurrilously attacks his work. Orlando is further dismayed by the ardent wooing efforts of the Romanian Archduchess Harriet. Orlando decides to leave England and is appointed Ambassador Extraordinary to Constantinople, where he performs good service for King Charles II and his successors and is rewarded for his efforts. During his stay, he secretly marries a gypsy woman, becomes involved in a revolution, and falls into another trance. This time when he awakens, he has been visited by the three Graces of Purity, Chastity, and Modesty and is metamorphosed into a woman.

When Orlando returns to England during the eighteenth century, her life becomes a social whirl of parties and intellectual hobnobbing with famous literary and philosophical figures. Woolf is at her critical best describing Orlando's feelings about becoming a woman. Because a woman cannot hold property by English law,

Orlando must litigate in court to hold onto her estates and wealth, a battle that takes more than a century to fight. Orlando's psychological and emotional change into a woman, played out over many decades, is also skillfully realized by the writer.

Time passes, and it is the dawning of the Victorian age. She meets, and is willingly seduced by, Marmaduke Shelmerdine, a wealthy gentleman and a ship's captain. They marry, he leaves, and she has a baby. Orlando meets Nicholas Greene, who is still very much alive. The now much-honored poet takes her work "The Oak Tree" and has it published to great critical acclaim. The heroine lives into the age of King Edward II in the twentieth century. The novel ends on October 11, 1928, with Orlando, looking no more than thirty-six, eagerly awaiting the arrival of her husband after a long sea voyage.

Analysis

Virginia Woolf's *Orlando* is really a literary hybrid, easy to read but difficult to define. The writer called it a mock-biography because it allowed her greater expression of comic fantasy and showcased her ornate style of writing. The novel, however, is more than a biography because it blends the genre with fantasy, fiction, poetry, and allegory. It can also be viewed as an satire, a feminist tract, or a pleasant comic examination of English literature through metaphor. Despite its lightness of tone, Woolf intended the novel as an examination of the creative process, sexual identity and inequality, and the experience of psychological time.

No analysis of *Orlando* is considered complete or definitive without an understanding of her complex relationship with fellow writer Victoria (Vita) Sackville-West. Woolf and Sackville-West, an acknowledged bisexual, were intimate friends and lovers. They first met at a dinner party in December, 1922, but the affair was slow in developing and did not flourish until the years between 1925 and 1929. Initially, the much older Woolf was shy and both repelled and fascinated by Sackville-West's nature. For Sackville-West, it was one of numerous lesbian affairs carried out in the 1920's, but for the married Woolf, it was her first. In fact, the affair became Woolf's grand passion and the inspiration for her writings, particularly *Orlando*, which reached a creative peak during this same period.

Orlando is dedicated to Sackville-West, the title character patterned closely after her. Orlando's long-lived history is modeled after her four-centuries-old aristocratic heritage. Woolf's information came from Sackville-West's own published book, *Knole and the Sackvilles* (1922), a biography of her grand country estate. The author used her lover's Elizabethan ancestor, Lord Thomas Brockhurst, as her model for the young Orlando. The male character's feelings, attitudes, and literary inclinations belong to Sackville-West, however, and intensify when the gender transformation takes place.

Throughout the novel, Orlando is depicted as a sexually ambiguous figure, as though the character possesses both feminine and masculine attributes. Both Sackville-West and Orlando, for example, exhibit public transvestism. Other parallels between them abound, including personal details, exquisite legs, love of nature and animals, and attachment to heritage and home. Even Orlando's struggle to retain her ancestral estates, to be taken away, solely because she is a woman, can be found in Sackville-West's similar, but unsuccessful, attempt to keep her property. The names and personalities of several of the book's characters can also be found in her ancestry.

The connection goes further. In the original 1928 edition, the book has a series of illustrations featuring Orlando, posed by Sackville-West. Yet Woolf's portrait is not always flattering. Orlando is depicted as an inferior writer—after all, it takes the character more than four hundred years to get published—but Sackville-West was definitely a good one. Also, Orlando's fickle nature probably serves as a reprimand. Still, in all, Woolf viewed the work as a public reconciliation of her own sexual duality and, more important, as a lover's gift.

In *Orlando*, Woolf cleverly uses the biographical third-person narrator throughout. The stylistic technique allows for a detached perspective, freeing her "biographer" to comment fully with flights of fanciful description. Two such passages, frequently anthologized, are the Great Frost (adapted into an animated cartoon) during the Jacobean period, and the narrative at the inception of the Victorian age. Woolf speaks openly on the complexities found in the human personality, touching on creativity, androgyny, and immortality. At other times, her biographer is at odds with the artist, a struggle that the latter always wins. Woolf's narrator, therefore, is a mask that can be dropped as the occasion warrants. The biographer-persona allows her to mock established evidence from biography, history, and eyewitness account. Woolf also attacks official biography as a genre even as she employs the device. The novel, for example, begins in mid-action and is focused on Orlando's private thoughts and feelings. Woolf's work did little to revitalize biography but did much to break ground for imaginative writing.

Context

Virginia Woolf's *Orlando* has had a positive impact on women's literature. As in her other eight novels, Woolf is concerned with creating a feminine perspective, employing female characters as the focal point of her work. *Orlando* appears to be an exception because the title character is male, but he is so androgynous that when the gender change takes place the character can easily be viewed as female. Woolf's aim was to deny basic differences between male and female. (In 1993, English director Sally Potter released *Orlando* as a feminist feature film and cast actress Tilda Swinton to play the main character throughout the centuries.) She shows continuity with her other novels by revealing victory over time and death.

Orlando allows Woolf to give free rein to a host of women's concerns. First, and foremost, through the creation of a physically desirable hero suddenly turned ravishing heroine, Woolf is able to reveal differing aspects of masculinity and femininity within one being. Women's secondary status in society is closely examined, particularly after Orlando's transformation. The privilege of enjoying certain male prerogatives is denied the same female character, as is the right to inherit her estate. Woolf's feminist thesis is given sharper expression in the eighteenth century when Orlando sadly realizes that even the most liberal-thinking males consider women inferior. In one interesting passage, the feminine Orlando curses "himself" for once insisting that women remain demure, ornate, and exquisitely dressed.

Virginia Woolf is considered one of the most renowned English women of literature. Her literary accomplishments have almost always been admired. She is hailed as one of the first, and most influential, of the modernist writers. Her novels, once neglected, are now in print again, with effusive introductions by various editors. Her writings have been translated into more than fifty languages. Critical studies on Woolf abound, and her novels, short stories, essays, letters, diaries, and fragmented manuscripts have been carefully examined. In short, Woolf became one of the most discussed authors of the twentieth century. *Orlando* remains a dazzling, multifaceted, witty, and original piece of feminist writing.

Sources for Further Study

Apter, T. E. *Virginia Woolf: A Study of Her Novels*. New York: New York University Press, 1979. A broad overview of Woolf's novels, focusing on the epistemological and psychological ramifications of her vision, sensibility, and symbolism. *Orlando* is examined in a short, separate chapter.

Booth, Alison. *Greatness Engendered*. Ithaca, N.Y.: Cornell University Press, 1992. Presented from a feminist perspective, this study compares Woolf and George Eliot, specifically their depiction of women characters. The author originally had a more favorable opinion of Eliot as an activist and feminist, but reversed herself on closer examination of Woolf's work. Her chapter "Trespassing in Cultural History: The Heroines of *Romola* and *Orlando*" offers insight into Orlando's changing sexuality.

Brewster, Dorothy. *Virginia Woolf*. New York: New York University Press, 1962. Brewster provides lengthy summaries of Woolf's biography, critical essays, and attitudes while commenting on her novels. She examines *Orlando* briefly and praises the work for encouraging Woolf to write direct sentences and teaching her continuity and narrative.

Gorsky, Susan Rubinow. *Virginia Woolf*. Rev. ed. Boston: Twayne, 1989. A solid and competent study of Woolf's literary career. Gorsky examines *Orlando* in a separate section and finds much to admire. Important parallels between Orlando and Woolf's close friend and lover Vita Sackville-West are clearly drawn. Recommended as a good overall guide to Woolf. A valuable chronology and bibliography are included.

Johnson, Manly. *Virginia Woolf*. New York: Frederick Ungar, 1973. Offers a good, short introduction to Woolf's work. Johnson includes a useful chronology and a preface outlining her life, essays, and biographies before examining her novels and short stories. The chapter on *Orlando* is brief but enjoyable and to the point.

Lee, Hermione. *The Novels of Virginia Woolf.* New York: Holmes & Meier, 1977. A sensible examination of Woolf the writer. Lee dismisses the Bloomsburyans', feminists', and dichotomists' approach to her work. Woolf is examined and depicted as an admirable writer, but not foremost in the modernist movement. Contains a good chapter on *Orlando*, which Lee asserts is different from Woolf's other novels.

Terry Theodore

OUT OF AFRICA

Author: Isak Dinesen (Baroness Karen Blixen-Finecke, 1885-1962)
Type of work: Memoir
Time of work: The 1920's
Locale: Kenya, Africa
First published: *Den afrikanske Farm*, 1937 (English translation, 1937)

Principal personages:

Karen Blixen, a farm owner in Africa
Denys Finch-Hatton, Karen's lover
Berkely Cole, an English aristocrat
Farah, Karen's majordomo
Kamante, one of Karen's servants
Kinanjui, the Kikuyu chief

Form and Content

Out of Africa, the mythical autobiography of Karen Blixen (who wrote under the name Isak Dinesen), offers an idyll in which humans recover the original unity among themselves, society, and nature. This paradise collapses because of natural and historical interventions. The work is divided into five parts—four acts of idyll, then a fifth describing a swift, unaccountable fall. The dreamlike structure becomes progressively more tangible in its description of the farm's loss. Parts 1 and 2 represent what Dinesen calls Africa's "music."

Part 1, "Kamante and Lulu," tells of a wounded native, Kamante, and of a tiny gazelle, Lulu. Dinesen expresses African music by describing the civilized and wild qualities in each. Kamante's culinary genius makes Dinesen reconsider her own civilization. Elegant Lulu has the air of a wellborn lady. Karen's discovery of civilized traits in nature implies that civilized accomplishments can be judged by their congruence with nature.

"A Shooting Incident on the Farm," the second part, demonstrates the farm's social operation and contrasts European and African justice systems. Because of an accidental shooting, a Kyama (local court) is formed to settle the matter according to native laws. Karen is appointed judge because of her importance to the natives, but because she does not know local laws, she summons Kinanjui, the chief of the Kikuyu, to judge the Kyama.

Part 3, "Visitors to the Farm," describes her European guests and shows that those who frequented the farm were "outcasts," aristocrats such as Denys Finch-Hatton and Berkely Cole who should have lived before the Industrial Revolution or characters with aristocratic viewpoints, such as Knudsen and Emmanuelson. These people get along with Africans because of the orderliness of African society. Although Karen helps Emmanuelson and works with Knudsen, she forms a selective society with Berkely and Denys. When Berkely sulks at having to drink wine from coarse glasses in the jungle, Karen acknowledges his aristocracy by bringing him fine crystal. Denys teaches her how to read Latin and Greek and how to hunt lions. He takes her in his airplane to oversee the land and its animals, a flight so exhilarating that Karen compares Denys to the Archangel Gabriel.

Part 4, "From an Immigrant's Notebook," contains only observations, fables, and reflections. Although it breaks the narrative, it reiterates the book's themes and serves as a transition between idyll and fall. This section contains several animal fables, two about oxen. The first is about a wild ox who eludes capture through a leopard's mutilation, illustrating aristocratic spirit through the animal's energy and pride. The second, about a domesticated ox, illustrates that same pride broken. These animal stories have counterparts in tales about similar human beings. A meditation, "I Will Not Let Thee Go Except Thou Bless Me," implies that in relinquishment of both good and bad experience, people are blessed. This meditation prepares the reader for part 5, "Farewell to the Farm."

"Farewell to the Farm" presents Dinesen's loss of paradise in a series of catastrophes. The first is the collapse of the farm's economy because of grasshoppers and rising coffee prices. The next is Dinesen's failure to grant Chief Kinanjui's deathbed wish. Another betrayal follows when at Chief Kinanjui's funeral, rites are taken over by Christians, who bury the pagan chief in an undersized coffin. Then Denys Finch-Hatton dies in a plane crash. After these disasters, Karen asks for a sign, recognizing it when she sees a white cock biting out the tongue of a chameleon; she concludes that the "Great Powers" are laughing at her.

Analysis

Dinesen's pastoral mourns the loss of the old order of Africa and the similar old order of preindustrial Europe. The story has the structure of the fall of humanity. Its moral is the Lord's answer to Job. Karen's belief that the Great Powers are laughing at her is similar to the answer that Job received from God, that Job had neither the power nor the right to question Him. Karen concludes from her answer that the proper response to life is to experience joy both in beauty and in horror. Having experienced the unbearable, Karen passes through a kind of death, transcends her experiences, and weaves them into a pastoral fable about a paradise lost. This loss is not through choice, but through the outside forces of the modern world and nature.

Out of Africa conveys a common personal experience, the moral growth that occurs after a world is smashed and the resulting adaptation. The book restates this message on a cultural level. It retells, in an African setting, European myths about otherness and a past Golden Age. In order to convey myth, Dinesen is vague. She rarely mentions her name, Karen Blixen. The reader knows only that she is adored by both black and white and that Denys Finch-Hatton is her very close friend. This vagueness sustains the dreamlike nature of the memoir, both as a realized personal dream and as the Golden Age of psychic and cultural childhoods. The mythologizing process achieves the aim of romantic autobiography, illustrating the ideal in the real through individual personal experience.

Dinesen's implicit question, the one answered by the Great Powers is whether life is significant. Emmanuelson, part charlatan and part actor, points to life's significance (although he is not sure what it is) through its grandeur as perceived through the imagination. That Emmanuelson expresses this opinion is apt, for Dinesen considers transcendence to have an element of fakery, since it cannot be justified by facts.

In writing about the rhythms of African life, Dinesen also reconstructs the world of the European romantic past. The coffee plantation's loss to creditors represents the destruction of old European society based on mutual responsibility and affection. The tragedy of the old order's breakup is illustrated by the tribes' desire to stay on the land even after the farm is sold. In a traditional example of noblesse oblige, Karen pesters government offices until she secures the tribes a large reservation. Because of their attachment to nature, the natives' sense of morality is stoic. Their passive strength and endurance of hardships reflect, in their simplicity, the point to which the highest morality returns, at a complete acceptance of God's will.

In the same sense, the natives' primitive Ngomas, or dancing parties, while reminiscent of prehistoric times, also suggest the highest civilization. Karen's description of the people dancing in their appointed places, with intense care for one another's well-being, suggests the essence of social principle. Her description of Ngomas, landscapes, or animals as glorious, primitive, but timeless sights best expresses the message of *Out of Africa*. The glorious sight is Dinesen's perception of otherness, of life apart from human perception, a view articulated by the showman's answer to Count Schimmelmann's question of whether wild animals exist if humans do not see them: The showman answers that God sees them.

This glorious, timeless sight includes recognition that the primitive and the civilized contain elements of each other. If the elements of civilization can be found in primitive nature, then these accomplishments acquire absolute value. Thus a civilization can be judged as to how well it conforms to these absolutes in nature. The central vision of *Out of Africa* is one in which the old order is lauded and the modern one condemned. The right kind of civilization involves recovering those virtues lost in the Fall.

Karen's belief that the Great Powers are laughing at her aids her in her transcendent embrace of all experience. Life, she intimates, is not happy or easy, but sublime. With the right attitude, it can be received with joy. The sublime overview is symbolized in her last airplane flight with Denys. Karen's experience and survival of the lost paradise gives readers the hope that they too can survive such traumas and can even reconstruct through the imagination what has been lost in fact.

Context

Isak Dinesen blazed new trails for women. She farmed an African plantation, hunted lions, doctored native peoples, and judged their Kyamas. Dinesen was also a pioneer in the male province of adventure memoirs, a fact that she acknowledged by assuming a masculine pen name.

Ironically, Dinesen's gender and failure as a farmer began her writing career. Brought up in a privileged family, she was taught only to marry well. When she returned to Denmark, penniless and divorced, her brother Thomas said that her suggested careers were positions always reserved for men. When Dinesen tentatively suggested writing, Thomas enthusiastically supported her.

Two years later, Dinesen had a short-story collection in manuscript form and several rejection slips. Determined to find a publisher, she wrangled an invitation to a London luncheon where the head of a publishing house was a guest. She broached the subject of her manuscript, but when Mr. Huntington learned that her book contained short stories, he refused to read them—short stories were difficult to sell. Later, Thomas handed the manuscript to writer Dorothy Canfield, who passed it on to publisher Robert Haas. He published the work with no expectation of commercial success, but although criticized for lacking a man's wisdom, *Seven Gothic Tales* was a great American success. As Baroness Blixen, she had gotten nowhere with Huntington, but Huntington wrote a letter full of praise to Isak Dinesen and asked for "his" address. Yet the book was not received well in Denmark. When the public discovered that Isak Dinesen was not a man, criticism of the erotic decadence of *Seven Gothic Tales* increased. One critic accused her of coquetry, shallowness, caprice, and most of all, perversity.

During her first book's success, *Out of Africa* was taking shape. As she wrote, years of subconscious ideas emerged. The work was published in the United States, England, and Denmark. It was well received in America and Denmark, but Huntington reported that only intellectuals liked the book in England. Although she was now lionized and financially independent, Blixen nevertheless received criticism from those dear to her. An old family member believed it almost scandalous for a lady to make money writing books.

Out of Africa places a woman in the center of adventure, instead of as a spectator or supporting figure. Like Job, to whom all was eventually restored, Blixen restored Africa to herself through her imagination.

Sources for Further Study

Gilead, Sarah. "Emigrant Selves: Narrative Strategies in Three Women's Autobiographies." *Criticism* 30, no. 1 (Winter, 1988): 43-62. Perceptively comments on Dinesen's escape into art when her coffee plantation fails. Gilead points out that the self that narrates *Out of Africa* is stable, not changing, as it narrates its chronicle of a lost paradise, and that this stable voice adds to *Out of Africa*'s mythic quality.

Langbaum, Robert. *The Gayety of Vision*. New York: Random House, 1965. Contains an excellent chapter on *Out of Africa* in which its mythical nature is analyzed. Also shows Dinesen's central theme of the unfortunate decay of an old, humane social order. The book also examines Dinesen's claim that the myth-making tradition of Africans is similar to that of Danes centuries ago.

Migel, Parmenia. *Titania*. London: Josef, 1967. A fascinating official biography, notable for its illustrations and quotations. The last chapters chronicle Dinesen's successful lecture tours; her interactions with such famous people as Marilyn Monroe, Marianne Moore, and Pearl Buck; and her poignant death.

Pelensky, Olga Anastasia. *Isak Dinesen: The Life and Imagination of a Seducer*. Athens: Ohio University Press, 1991. This biography contains previously unpublished information about the influence of Dinesen's father and of Charles Darwin's and Friedrich Nietzsche's works on her imagination. A chapter on *Out of Africa* examines the book as a thematic extension of *Seven Gothic Tales*.

Thurman, Judith. *Isak Dinesen*. New York: St. Martin's Press, 1982. This biography, which stresses Dinesen's literary career, was the first to include letters and family documents. Provides detailed descriptions of important events in Dinesen's life, such as lion hunts, that were later incorporated into *Out of Africa*. Also touches on Dinesen's religious faith.

Mary Hanford Bruce

OUTRAGEOUS ACTS AND EVERYDAY REBELLIONS

Author: Gloria Steinem (1934-)
Type of work: Essays
First published: 1983

Form and Content

Gloria Steinem, feminist activist and founder of *Ms.* magazine, has been a writer throughout her career. Most of her works have been essay-length magazine articles, and this book is a compendium of selections of those writings. It is a volume of essays that give, in various ways, insights into the experience and character of the author. Some of the essays are comic ("If Men Could Menstruate"), some are sad ("Ruth's Song"), and others evoke horror ("The International Crime of Genital Mutilation"). Some are autobiographical ("I Was a Playboy Bunny") and others are about public figures ("Marilyn Monroe: The Woman Who Died Too Soon"). All are told from a feminist perspective; that is, they flow out of Steinem's conviction that women matter and that women's needs are important. These essays are widely varied in content and focus. What they have in common is that each illustrates an aspect of Steinem's view of the world and her commitment to women's concerns.

The volume begins with an introduction that tells the reader something about Steinem's feminist activism, including her work in founding *Ms.* magazine in 1972, at that time the only magazine editorially controlled solely by women. More than an introduction, however, this initial portion of the book is an essay in itself, whose purpose is to explain the experiences and observations that shaped the author of all the essays that follow.

The narrator of these essays is an unqualified "I." Steinem notes in the introduction that as a young journalist she was taught always to take the "objective" point of view. In these works, however, she unabashedly writes from her own. The essays are personal, self-disclosing, and authoritative. The reader learns what the author thinks and what she has learned.

Steinem divides her offerings into four sections. In the first, "Learning from Experience," the reader learns about some of the events that shaped the author, from growing up with a mentally ill mother during the Depression to going undercover as a Playboy bunny in her years as a reporter. The next section, "Other Basic Discoveries," covers perhaps the widest range of topics, including, for example, insights into the beauty of women's bodies of all shapes and sizes, a discussion of differing male and female styles of communication, and an analysis of the difference between pornography and erotica.

The third section gives Steinem's thoughts about five well-known women. In five separate essays, the reader learns what Steinem has to say about such diverse individuals as Marilyn Monroe, Patricia Nixon, Linda Lovelace, Jackie Onassis, and Alice Walker. The final section is called "Transforming Politics," and true to the feminist adage that "the personal is political," it takes the reader from a fantasy on the ramifications of male menstruation to a report from the 1977 National Women's Conference in Houston, Texas.

The unifying factor in this collection is the mind of Gloria Steinem. The whole book is both personal, her perspective on life as she knows it, and political, relating to the world at large and the way it treats women.

Analysis

The title *Outrageous Acts and Everyday Rebellions* deserves analysis. Gloria Steinem means to tell the reader that outrageousness and rebelliousness are positive characteristics for women, who have been trained for many generations to be polite, quiet, and obedient. Although she is not as outrageous and rebellious as some feminist authors, such as Mary Daly, Steinem nevertheless claims the words as the title for her collection of essays.

Steinem grew up in a lower-middle-class home in Toledo, Ohio, during the Depression, and in "Ruth's Song (Because She Could Not Sing It)," Steinem explores her experience living in a fragmented family with a mentally ill mother. The reader learns how it felt for the young girl, who from age ten to age seventeen lived alone with her mother and took on all the adult responsibilities. Steinem writes of her ambivalence about her mother at that time. Yet this essay is not merely a sharing of childhood pain; it takes the reader with Gloria Steinem as she begins to understand her mother's life from her mother's own perspective, to find the person within the woman with whom she had grown up. She finds out about the facts of her mother's life before her illness, the pressures placed on her to conform to societal expectations of womanhood, and the self-limiting choices that eventually led to her mental breakdown. She shares Ruth with the reader so that the reader too can begin to know and appreciate this woman.

"In Praise of Women's Bodies" takes the reader to a women's health spa with the author, to watch with her as her fellow clients slowly come to accept their own bodies in their varieties of shapes, sizes, and types. At first embarrassed because they are not perfect, these women gradually open up, at least in this all-woman environment, becoming willing to appear before one another despite scars, stretch marks, protruding stomachs, wrinkled skin, and other human physical characteristics that women have learned to think of as ugly. As in "Ruth's Song," Steinem offers a feminist analysis of an ordinary event. She asks why it is that men's scars, signs of battle and violence, are emblems of pride, whereas the scars and stretch marks that women earn in the process of giving birth are signs of shame and embarrassment and ugliness. This point of view makes it possible for Steinem and her readers to look at women's scars in a whole new light.

Marilyn Monroe has been analyzed and reanalyzed in the years since her death in 1962, but Gloria Steinem gives the reader a feminist analysis of this woman who epitomizes the very opposite of a feminist role model. Many of the essays in this book explore the subject that would be the topic of Steinem's second book, *Revolution from Within: A Book of Self-Esteem* (1992), and this essay is no exception. Steinem wonders whether Monroe's life might have been different if she had lived long enough to benefit from the women's movement that began only a few years after her death. Specifically, she wonders whether she might have learned to resist the dependency on sexual attractiveness as her only measure of self-worth, her need to define herself totally based on approval and recognition from men. What, Steinem wonders, would have happened if Marilyn Monroe had known the love and friendship of other women?

The book ends with "Far from the Opposite Shore," a look back at the previous ten years or so of the women's movement and a look ahead. In this closing essay, Steinem shares strategies for feminists, including what she calls survival lessons. For example, facing the backlash of the late 1970's and early 1980's, she reminds the reader that serious opposition to feminism is a sign not of failure but of success. It is only because a specter of real equality has faced those who profit from inequality that the backlash has occurred. She ends her book by confessing that she had planned to involve herself in feminist activism for only a few years and then go back to her "real life." Now she knows that there is no turning back, that feminists are in it for life.

Context

Outrageous Acts and Everyday Rebellions is not a self-important, scholarly analysis of women's issues, but instead is simply a volume of essays about very ordinary topics. This book has value precisely because it is about topics everyone can relate to, as thought about by a woman who, though famous, sees herself as ordinary, as only one of many feminists in a wide and diverse community.

The humor and warmth of the essays make them easy to read, yet each packs a punch that stops the reader in her or his tracks with moments of insight—or, in *Ms.*'s language, "clicks." The light goes on—something new must be thought about or something old must be viewed in a new way.

The book is pro-women without being anti-men. It analyzes each subject from an unqualified female perspective, from inside a woman's experience. It looks at women and women's experiences with gentleness, love, and immense understanding. Reading this book could help women accept and love themselves as women, and it could help men see what few men have had the opportunity or have taken the time to see: what things look like from inside a woman's mind.

More even than her later book, *Revolution from Within*, which is more self-consciously introspective and autobiographical, this book helps the reader see who Gloria Steinem is. In the process of writing about a great variety of topics, she discloses herself, and the reader can see inside the mind of a woman who has been influential in the second wave of the women's movement.

Sources for Further Study

Davis, Flora. *Moving the Mountain: The Women's Movement in America Since 1960*. New York: Simon & Schuster, 1991. This history of thirty years of the feminist movement will help the reader understand the events and issues in which Gloria Steinem has been deeply involved. Steinem is mentioned several times in the book, allowing the reader to see how her journalistic and political work has been woven in with the efforts of others.

Freeman, Jo. *The Politic of Women's Liberation*. New York: David McKay, 1975. This early analysis of the women's movement helps the reader understand how it got started, and the various factions and their emphases. Steinem's work in founding *Ms.* and the National Women's Political Caucus is described.

Henry, Sondra, and Emily Taitz. *One Woman's Power: A Biography of Gloria Steinem*. Minneapolis: Dillon Press, 1987. Written for younger readers, this highly readable biography includes an afterword by Steinem herself. The book takes the reader from Steinem's childhood through her years as a young journalist, the founding of *Ms.*, and her political activism to the publication of *Outrageous Acts and Everyday Rebellions*.

Steinem, Gloria. *Revolution from Within: A Book of Self-Esteem*. Boston: Little, Brown, 1992. Steinem's second book is an examination of the importance of self-esteem in women's lives. Using the language and concepts of the self-help movements of the 1980's and 1990's, this book is self-revealing as well as analytical.

Wandersee, Winifred D. *On the Move: American Women in the 1970's*. Boston: Twayne, 1988. An analysis of the feminist movement in the 1970's from the perspective of a later time. It discusses the controversies between liberal and radical feminists, and the political strategies and events of the seventies, including Steinem's contributions.

Eleanor B. Amico

PALE HORSE, PALE RIDER: Three Short Novels

Author: Katherine Anne Porter (1890-1980)
Type of work: Novellas
First published: 1939

Form and Content

These short novels—"Old Mortality," "Noon Wine," and "Pale Horse, Pale Rider"—vary considerably in form, but all are realistic and are concerned primarily with death and its effects on the living. "Old Mortality" is a kind of family chronicle in which two motherless girls, Miranda and Maria, grow up surrounded by a family which romanticizes some of its members. The chief subject of romantic memory is Aunt Amy, a beautiful and wild young woman who consistently rejected the advances of Gabriel, her chief suitor, and refused to allow illness to limit her activities. Amy finally gave in to Gabriel and died not long after marrying him. In the course of the narrative, the girls grow up. The most important episode in their maturation is an encounter with Gabriel at a racetrack near New Orleans and a subsequent meeting with the grim woman who is his second wife. Gabriel, present in family legend as slender and handsome, is grossly fat and obsequious, and not even the fact that each girl has won a hundred dollars betting on one of his horses can counteract his unromantic presence. Miranda eventually tries to escape the family by eloping, but an encounter with a relative on a train trip back home for a family funeral shows her that although she will keep rebelling, she will never truly escape the family.

"Noon Wine" deals with another social level. Royal Earl Thompson and his family farm a run-down place in South Texas. His wife is sickly, his sons are unthinking dullards, and he is lazy and selfish. Into their lives comes Olaf Helton, a handyman who sets everything straight on the farm, tames the boys, and through his labor, makes the farm prosper for the first time. This paradise is destroyed when Mr. Hatch arrives, a bounty hunter who brings the news that Helton is in fact an escaped murderer who killed his brother and was committed to an insane asylum. In the minutes that follow, Thompson tries to prevent Hatch from seizing Helton and in doing so somehow kills the bounty hunter with a knife. A posse tracks down Helton and manhandles him so roughly that he dies soon after being put in jail. Thompson is cleared of any wrongdoing, but he cannot come to terms with what has happened to him. He takes his wife with him on increasingly desperate visits to all of his neighbors, trying to explain to them what had happened and why he should not be blamed. The neighbors become increasingly tired of his rationalizing and more and more skeptical about what really happened. Eventually, unable to live with himself and his belief that people think he was guilty of murder, he writes an incoherent note trying once more to justify himself, and commits suicide.

"Pale Horse, Pale Rider" returns Miranda to the center of attention. During World War I, she is a reporter on a newspaper in an unnamed city which resembles Denver, Colorado. Her main job is reporting on bond drives and other war-related activities in the community, and in the course of her work, she meets a handsome young officer named Adam. About to be sent overseas, he has military duties that are almost certain to get him killed. They are beginning to fall in love when Miranda falls ill with the influenza that has become a national epidemic. Adam looks after her, as she becomes more and more delirious, until she can be taken to a hospital. In the next few days, Miranda becomes increasingly subject to hallucinations in which she sees Death as a figure on horseback. She is tended by a doctor named Hildesheim, and his German name evokes in her all the images of anti-German propaganda she has absorbed in her work; she fears and hates him, but he helps her through a near-death experience and she begins to recover. When she is finally able to read her mail, she comes across a note from a buddy of Adam, telling her that Adam had died of influenza. In the end, she is ready to return to the world, but it has become flat, dull, and empty.

Analysis

The manner of "Old Mortality" and "Pale Horse, Pale Rider" is intimate, as if the narrator were almost inside the character of Miranda, which is not surprising in view of the fact that Porter uses the character to present a version of her own experiences. The action of "Old Mortality" is seen in terms of its effect on the two sisters, but chiefly Miranda. The sisters are not at the center of the action until the latter part of the story, but the behavior of Aunt Amy, Gabriel, and the other figures is seen in terms of its impact on them.

In "Pale Horse, Pale Rider," Miranda is the central character, the focus of all the narration, and in several places the narration becomes an internal monologue which conveys the delirium that accompanies her illness. This is especially important because it is in those passages that Miranda imagines death, in terms of a song remembered from her childhood, as a pale rider coming for her on horseback. It is also in one of those passages that the fevered imagery based on wartime hatred of Germans comes to be focused on the doctor in Miranda's own fever. The tragic mood of the ending of the story is made especially moving by the contrast between Miranda's deep depression and the elation of the other characters at the ending of the war.

"Noon Wine," in contrast to the other stories, is told by an omniscient narrator who has no emotional commitment to any of the characters. Helton is in some ways the most sympathetic figure, but that is because he is a helpless victim of the despicable Hatch. On the other hand, he is clearly abnormal, playing the "Noon Wine" tune over and over on the harmonica, which is the only thing he seems to value. Moreover, he has killed his own brother and his handling of the Thompson's sons is harsh, if not brutal. Thompson is feckless and stupid, his wife a weakling, his sons crude and in other ways much like their father. Thompson's suicide, like his fruitless attempts to justify himself to his neighbors, is more an act of weakness than one of remorse or sorrow.

The power of all three novellas is in Porter's use of detail and her depiction of character. The members of Miranda's family are very much individuals, defined by traits of character or dress. In "Pale Horse, Pale Rider," the people Miranda meets in the course of her work are highly individualized, while Adam, a kind of dream lover, is deliberately made a stock romantic figure, too good to be real in the sense that the other characters are real. The wartime atmosphere is especially convincing in its ugly fervor, which is made to seem an infection like the influenza that is rampant in the community and in the country. The details of farm life provide a firmly realistic backdrop for the violent action in "Noon Wine."

Context

Of these three short novels, "Noon Wine" is the least concerned with women's issues. Mrs. Thompson is a slight character, weak physically and personally, unable to control her sons, unable to do anything either to control or to comfort her husband. She is a type character, representing the image of farm wives as a beaten-down group, worn out by childbearing and by the hard physical labor of running a farm, especially if the husband is lazy and improvident.

In the stories about Miranda, however, Porter is presenting female figures who are struggling for independence against the forces of family and society. What happens to Aunt Amy in "Old Mortality" makes her a romantic figure to the young girls, but it is also a warning to Miranda of how strong the bonds of family can be; Miranda's elopement into an unsuccessful marriage is still preferable to allowing herself to be buried in the family's mythology. Whatever becomes of her, she will not be another Amy. Her meeting on the train with Cousin Eva, despised because of her unattractiveness, reinforces her determination. Eva has made a life for herself as a crusader for women's suffrage, and Miranda promises herself that she will be equally independent. She is naïve in her self-confidence, but she will learn.

What she learns in "Pale Horse, Pale Rider" is that life is indeed hard and precarious. As a reporter, she fights to avoid being assigned only to women's interest stories, and she is attacked verbally in the newsroom by a hack performer resentful of one of her reviews. She struggles to avoid the fate of her friend Towney, condemned always to write the women's page. As a person, she finds the beginning of love with the handsome soldier, only to be stricken by influenza and to learn that her lover is dead of the disease. She has gained the independence she wished for in "Old Mortality," but her naïveté is destroyed by the iron facts of life and death.

Sources for Further Study

DeMouy, Jane Krause. *Katherine Anne Porter's Women: The Eye of Her Fiction*. Austin: University of Texas Press, 1983. A feminist reading of Porter's fiction, this book argues that Porter is a precursor of later feminism in her concentration on female characters trying to live independently in a world dominated by men.

Givner, Joan. *Katherine Anne Porter: A Life*. New York: Simon & Schuster, 1982. A detailed and somewhat unsympathetic biography which shows how Porter made use of her experiences, transforming them into fictions that made her early life seem more glamorous and more prosperous than it actually was.

Hilt, Kathryn. *Katherine Anne Porter: An Annotated Bibliography*. New York: Garland, 1990. A listing of all Porter's works and the books and essays written about her through the mid-1980's.

Lopez, Enrique Hank. *Conversations with Katherine Anne Porter: Refugee from Indian Creek*. Boston: Little, Brown, 1981. Stories about Porter's life as she told them to the man who was her companion during the last years of her life.

Unrue, Darlene Harbour. *Truth and Vision in Katherine Anne Porter's Fiction*. Athens: University of Georgia Press, 1985. The best extended critical work on Porter's fiction, this study is distinguished by its focus on an overriding theme in that fiction: the insistence on artistic order in a chaotic world. Also includes close readings of the works.

Warren, Robert Penn, ed. *Katherine Anne Porter*. Englewood Cliffs, N.J.: Prentice Hall, 1979. A collection of essays about Porter's work, by a variety of critics.

John M. Muste

PARALLEL LIVES: Five Victorian Marriages

Author: Phyllis Rose (1942-)
Type of work: History
Time of work: The nineteenth century
Locale: Great Britain
First published: 1983

Principal personages:

Jane Welsh, a brilliant salon hostess and correspondent
Thomas Carlyle, a social philosopher
Effie Gray, the model for several Pre-Raphaelite paintings
John Ruskin, an art critic who championed the Pre-Raphaelite Brotherhood
John Everett Millais, a Pre-Raphaelite painter
Harriet Taylor, the coauthor of *The Subjection of Women* (1869)
John Stuart Mill, a utilitarian and feminist and the official author of *The Subjection of Women*
Catherine Hogarth, a Scotswoman who married Charles Dickens
Charles Dickens, a prolific and hugely popular novelist
Marian Evans, a novelist who used the pen name George Eliot
George Henry Lewes, a literary journalist and Evans' unofficial manager

Form and Content

Inspired by *The Mausoleum Book*—Sir Leslie Stephen's marital memoir prompted by James Anthony Froude's biographical portrait of Thomas Carlyle as insensitive husband—*Parallel Lives* explores the relationships of five Victorian writers to their mates. Through these marriages, or parallel lives, Phyllis Rose examines not only the power dynamics between romantic partners but also the way in which each union "seems . . . a subjectivist fiction with two points of view often deeply in conflict, sometimes fortuitously congruent." Her political and literary perspectives fuse into a feminist study of the imaginative patterns shaping Victorian couplehood, and to some extent modern marriages as well.

Rose focuses on a particular period or issue for each couple and arranges the vignettes so as to suggest the progressive stages in a relationship. Opening the book with the courtship of Jane Welsh and Thomas Carlyle, she next explores Effie Gray and John Ruskin's honeymoon and their eventual triangle with John Everett Millais; Harriet Taylor and John Stuart Mill's two-decade companionship during her marriage to another man, the father of her three children; Catherine Hogarth and Charles Dickens' growing alienation, then publicized separation, in middle age; and Marian Evans and George Henry Lewes' backstreet happiness until his death. Rose distinguishes the Carlyles as the couple who impelled her study by using them as a framing device for the entire text. Thus each of the other narratives follows a Carlylean "prelude"—a brief anecdote thematically linking Jane and Thomas to their contemporaries—while the final pages revisit the pair decades after their courtship, when the balance of power had begun to shift from husband to wife. After two likewise Carlylean postludes that lead into a broader consideration of sexual politics, the book provides a selected bibliography following a chronology of Victorian relationships—in which Charles Darwin and his wife Emma Wedgwood figure prominently as a conventionally happy couple.

The manner in which Rose combines sound scholarship—attested by twenty-one pages of footnotes—with an informal, lively style is consistent with her suggestion that gossip about others' private affairs can be "the beginning of moral inquiry." In pursuing this inquiry, she draws on such diverse cultural critics as Sigmund Freud, Christopher Lasch, Simone de Beauvoir, Leo Tolstoy, Steven Marcus, and Maggie Scarf for fuller interpretation of her couples' interactions, which she describes vividly. As her prologue acknowledges, Victorian scholars will discover no new material in her pages, but Rose's emphasis on the selected marriages as clichéd or innovative constructs within nineteenth century patriarchal conventions of matrimony is original. Similarly new is her respect for the inventiveness and flexibility with which some of her couples accommodated themselves to their age's insistence on the permanence of marriage.

By considering the expectations and failings of both individuals in each couple, Rose avoids a simplistic denunciation of male dominance. Instead, with psychological and political insight, she explores the liabilities incurred by both men and women who allow narrowly traditional marriage plots to define their life partnerships. It is no surprise, therefore, that she regards Marian Evans and George Henry Lewes, who forged their exemplary happiness outside social conventions, as the "heroine and hero of the book."

Analysis

In covering the five years between Jane Welsh and Thomas Carlyle's first meeting and their wedding, Rose investigates female resistance to wifehood as a prescribed role and to marital intimacy with a man who does not inspire passion. Welsh, a young, spunky heiress reminiscent of Jane Austen's Emma and aspiring to be a Scottish Madame de Staël, steadily rebuffed Carlyle's attempts to turn their correspondence into something less platonic: "By a judicious wielding of anger, mockery, and coolness, she . . . won the initial struggle for power between them." Eventually, however, when her need for his intellectual validation combined with her distaste for remaining an unmarried woman in her widowed mother's house, Welsh ignored clues that her poor, lowborn schoolteacher suitor expected a helpmate devoted not to her studies but to "housewife duties." Thus, according to Rose, Carlyle's major achievement as a tutor had been to mold Welsh into a woman who wanted him as her husband.

The theme of sexual disinclination recurs in the story of newlyweds Effie Gray and John Ruskin, but on the husband's side. If the couple's failure to consummate their union in their entire first year together seems peculiar, evidently their honeymoon anxiety and inexperience were only too typical for the age. In recounting the notorious episode of John's "wedding-night trauma," Rose emphasizes Victorian culture's failure to educate its women and to prepare couples for shifting from prenuptial denial of sexual needs to compulsory intimacy. As noteworthy as their virginity, Rose suggests, was the Ruskins' difficulty with the universal newlywed task of cutting apron strings to forge a new identity as a couple. Still attached to his parents, John spared little time and energy for Effie, while demanding greater submission and solicitude from her; she resisted her in-laws' authority and retreated from domestic strife to her parental home. When Effie eventually sued for annulment of the marriage on grounds of nonconsummation, won her case, and wed the Pre-Raphaelite painter John Everett Millais—originally the couple's protégé—John Ruskin felt far more bitter about losing his fellow-artist's company than his wife's.

Whereas John Ruskin clearly undervalued women's worth, John Stuart Mill often seemed painfully uxorious—even before he married his platonic companion of two decades—the bold, passionate Mrs. Harriet Taylor. Impressively, Harriet exerted enough power after four years of marriage to John Taylor, who disappointed her intellectually and imposed on her sexually, to convince him both to tolerate her intimacy with Mill and to give up his conjugal rights. For his part, Mill respected her so much that he made her his collaborator in all he wrote after 1843 and prepared for their wedding (after her husband's death) by renouncing his future legal rights over her property and person. Given Harriet Taylor's dominance on all fronts, what Mill considered a marriage of equals strikes Rose as being more a "domestic case of affirmative action."

By contrast, a far more conventional inequality marked the marriage of Charles Dickens to Catherine Hogarth, whom he initially appreciated as "that dignifying satellite, a wife" only to become disillusioned after her twenty-odd years of subordination, childbirth, and poor housekeeping. Restless at forty-five, Charles denied their early happiness together, concocting a melodramatic fiction of Catherine as a monstrously inadequate wife and mother, and of himself as her victim. When he eventually maneuvered her into requesting a separation, he justified himself to a public steeped in his novelistic images of domestic bliss by publishing a letter in *The Times* to explain their incompatibility—and to deny the accurate rumors about his interest in the young actress Ellen Ternan. Manipulating for power and popularity, deceiving himself and others, Charles Dickens exemplifies the way in which Rose believes one should not end a marriage.

From the frustrations of the traditional Dickens' union, the book moves to the "joint life of exceptional richness" led by Marian Evans and George Henry Lewes, "literary London's most celebrated illicit couple." Faced with unreasonable laws that prevented his divorce from a faithless wife, Lewes committed himself to Evans in an unofficial relationship that lasted twenty-four years and challenged Victorian norms for life partnership. From her fulfillment in this union came her discovery of her creative talents: Thus, the offspring of their union was George Eliot.

To round out the series of marital portraits, Rose returns to the Carlyles, with Thomas as widower agonizing over the diary in which Jane had bitterly chronicled his neglect of her. He chose to expiate his guilt by editing her letters for publication and writing the remorseful *Reminiscences* (1881). If Jane haunted his conscience, however, perhaps he had the last word by shaping her image for posterity.

Context

Parallel Lives is a feminist milestone in a number of ways. First, Rose challenges prevailing misogynist versions of these five relationships. For example, she explores criticism's resistance to Mill's own claim that Harriet Taylor was his collaborator, its emphasis on Marian Evans as a neurotically needy spinster rather than a woman who pursued love assertively, and its assumption that Catherine Hogarth indeed failed Dickens through her middle-aged frumpiness. Second, Rose argues the need to go beyond assigning blame for "bad" behavior in individuals to confronting the deep problems "generated inevitably by the peculiar privileges and stresses of traditional marriage." In fact, merely by introducing the women of the couples first, before their change of status and name, Rose emphasizes the female equality that she considers exceptional, even impossible, in patriarchy's domestic paradigms. With the exception of Catherine Hogarth, her women are clearly role models of female strength in adversity, especially Rose's favorite, the feisty Jane Welsh.

Rose also challenges the facile equation of "Victorian" with "prudish" or "repressed" by re-visioning some of the unusual asexual arrangements in her narratives as innovative and inspired. Moreover, she argues convincingly that such irregular pre-Freudian unions as the Carlyles' and the Ruskins' might teach important lessons in flexibility—and that redefining couplehood is still relevant in the late twentieth century, with easy divorce doing little to undermine the monopoly of the marriage plot on people's life choices. Finally, Rose underlines the frequent consistency between familial and national tyranny, by tracing Thomas Carlyle's, John Ruskin's, and Charles Dickens' authoritarianism on the one hand and John Stuart Mill's and George Henry Lewes' liberalism on the other, from their marriages to their political stands on slavery, class, and imperialism.

Parallel Lives found favor with critics as an original, provocative, and witty book. Even Nina Auerbach, whose review in *The New York Times Book Review* faulted Rose for giving her male protagonists the usual lion's share of attention, conceded that the familiar episodes unfold so "compellingly here, they spring to life all over again." Rose's 1978 study *Woman of Letters: A Life of Virginia Woolf* had the same feminist biographical underpinnings.

Sources for Further Study

Basch, Françoise. *Relative Creatures: Victorian Women in Society and the Novel.* Translated by Rudolf Anthony. New York: Schocken, 1974. Basch opens this impressively documented book with the daily life of actual Victorian women, then considers their fictional counterparts in the works of such writers as Dickens, Eliot, William Makepeace Thackeray and the Brontës. Like Rose, Basch suggests that fulfillment came to Eliot and Lewes, Taylor and Mill—and even Dickens and Ellen Ternan—because they defied Victorian conventions.

Harrison, Fraser. *The Dark Angel: Aspects of Victorian Sexuality.* New York: Universe Books, 1978. Harrison examines social constructions of marriage in the Victorian era, drawing on the ideas and imagery of Ruskin, Dickens, Mill, and Millais, among others, for his first section on "Middle-Class Sexuality." Harrison sensitively explores some of the same issues as Rose: courtship stress, wifely submission, and female education.

Longford, Elizabeth. *Eminent Victorian Women.* New York: Alfred A. Knopf, 1981. Longford introduces her study of family influences and career-romance conflicts in eleven female lives, with a section on Queen Victoria's and John Stuart Mill's dissimilar views on women's rights. Although her only subject in common with Rose is George Eliot, the book—with a wealth of photographs, illustrations, and *Punch* cartoons—resembles *Parallel Lives* in its readability, its feminist perspective, and its period detail.

Lutyens, Mary. *Millais and the Ruskins*. London: John Murray, 1967. A detailed account of the disintegration of the Ruskins' marriage during their friendship with John Everett Millais. Lutyens' chief sources are original letters, on which she draws generously in order to let the principals speak for themselves.

Wohl, Anthony S., ed. *The Victorian Family: Structure and Stresses*. New York: St. Martin's Press, 1978. This book of nine essays explores the Victorian family as a microcosm of its culture, with special attention to the subordination of women and children. The issue of power so central to Rose's study is particularly prominent in David Roberts' "The Paterfamilias of the Victorian Governing Classes" and Michael Brooks's "Love and Possession in a Victorian Household: The Example of the Ruskins."

Margaret Bozenna Goscilo

PASSING

Author: Nella Larsen (1891-1964)
Type of work: Novel
Type of plot: Social realism
Time of plot: 1927
Locale: New York City
First published: 1929

Principal characters:

Irene Redfield, a light-skinned, upper-middle-class, African American woman

Clare Kendry, Irene's childhood friend, a light-skinned African American woman who is "passing" as white

Brian Redfield, Irene's husband, a doctor with a lucrative Harlem practice

John (Jack) Bellew, Clare's wealthy, bigoted white husband, who does not know that she is black and who affectionately calls her "Nig"

Gertrude Martin, a light-skinned African American woman happily married to a white man from whom she has no secrets

Hugh Wentworth, a white intellectual who often attends Irene's parties

Form and Content

Passing is a conventionally structured novel in which the tale is told from the controlled omniscient perspective. It is a story whose tension emanates from the three main characters and which concludes in a web of ambiguity and mystery. The unmistakable purpose lies in the psychological-social problem area, for the racial dilemmas illuminate intricate personal relationships, all of them possibly doomed.

Nella Larsen, an African American writer and prominent participant in the Harlem Renaissance, explores the consequences of "passing" (a phenomenon sometimes, in social science, called "crossing"; both terms are used to describe a light-skinned African American's choice to live in society as white without revealing his or her true racial history). She also studies potential marital problems precipitated by jealousy and suspicion, dilemmas of child rearing and infidelity, and financial security versus personal fulfillment. There is no doubt, however, that the catalyst propelling the narrative, initiating examination into personal values, and forcing a confrontation with individual racial identity is Clare Kendry, the woman who is, indeed, passing, and whose characterization embodies the theme noted in literary history as "the tragic mulatta."

Larsen's challenging novel focuses on two African American women whose lives have taken radically different paths, it would seem, and who meet after years of separation. In passing, Clare has deliberately distanced herself from the past, but Irene quickly remembers, with more than a touch of uneasiness, her old friend as unpredictable, an aggressive, risk-taking woman who delights in living dangerously. Irene Redfield, proud of her black identity and disapproving of Clare's way of life, instinctively fears the imminent intrusion into her own safe and secure home. Yet, fascinated with the possibilities, she allows it, even encourages it, to happen. The persistent Clare, aided and abetted, however reluctantly, by Irene, makes herself part of the Redfield circle. When her husband, the racist Bellew, goes off on his frequent business trips, Clare and the Redfields are together, for at these moments the passing woman feels that, in a sense, she is openly validating her own identity, reaching out to relate to the people and that part of herself that she had rejected—and that she continues to reject in her life as a white wife. Irene Redfield tolerates the imposition of her old friend, and, in fact, introduces Clare into the sophisticated group of friends, black and white, who gather regularly for art shows, discussions, or parties. It appears that Clare's identity problems and her daily life, poised over the abyss between two disparate worlds, create a riveting, hypnotic aura around Irene. She is repulsed by Clare's passing but must admire her willingness to take the risk that is involved, a risk similar to that of starting a new life, which she is unwilling to take with her husband Brian. A clearly ambivalent Irene feels the palpable invasion of a new spirit into her home. The bickerings and sometimes harsh arguments between her and her husband are soon exacerbated.

Irene Redfield's understandable contentment with her luxurious home and handsome, articulate children has seemingly created in her a fetish of economic security and marital safety, leading her to oppose Brian's desire that they leave the United States. At the same time, she recognizes that Clare's passing is similarly motivated by the desire for economic survival, safety, and security. The two are, actually, not so different in their overall perception of what is important in life. Thus, suddenly, as if struck by a lightning bolt, Irene, irritated at the domestic turbulence with her husband, realizes that Clare Kendry is a direct threat to her own home and marriage. In response to a question about what she would do if her secret of passing were discovered, Clare asserts that she would move to Harlem to be with her people. Recalling this, Irene becomes suspicious and fearful. If Clare cannot be made to vanish from the earth, at least her secret must be kept and protected at all costs—to keep the Redfields together.

Through an accidental meeting with Irene in the company of a black friend, Bellew is alerted to the possibility that his "Nig" is indeed, passing. Driven by the fury of his hatred, he sets out to discover the truth, first going to the Redfield home and then directly to a sixth-floor apartment where a black cultural soirée is in progress, with Clare in attendance. Unabashed, the racist bolts angrily onto the scene, furiously denouncing his wife as a "nigger." Larsen has set her finale in mystery, one that, nevertheless, dooms all the crucial relationships depicted in her narrative. On Bellew's frantically charged entrance, the frightened Irene rushes to Clare's side, for her passing friend had been calmly standing by an open window. Little of what follows is made perfectly clear, but two things are evident: Clare goes tumbling out the window to her death; her husband did not push her. Many questions, however, remain. Why did Irene rush to Clare? Because the revelation of Clare's passing to Bellew would have ended the union and would have driven her to Harlem, a fear of Irene's, did Irene push Clare out the window? Accidentally or intentionally, driven by fear, propelled by her psychological desire to have Clare "disappear," did she commit murder? Did Clare, terrified by her husband's fury, accidentally fall? Perhaps Clare committed suicide, realizing that her passing days were over and that her "white" daughter would be lost to her? Amid these questions and possibilities the narrative concludes, leaving evidence for all the interpretations suggested.

Analysis

In *Passing*, Nella Larsen has composed a novel that simultaneously engages several levels of the human experience and, through insightful psychological portraiture, illuminates the often subtle and complex passions roiling about a society whose dilemmas are compounded by racism. She brings about consideration of challenging issues through her penetrating treatment of characters whose emotional dilemmas are highlighted by an intricate series of personal interrelationships.

One valid critical approach is to insist that the major theme in *Passing* is not race at all, but marriage and security. Although Irene Redfield is not passing as white, she is passing as an upper-middle-class American with full access to the opportunities and privileges of any wealthy citizen. Feeling safe and secure, she is even waited on by black servants. Indeed, though Irene does not deny her negritude—as Clare does—she is still, in a sense, passing, all the while trying to ignore her husband's dissatisfaction with life in the United States for a black family. Although Irene Redfield is active in the Negro Welfare League (NWL), she remains apart from her struggling brothers and sisters in the ghetto and in no way wishes to endanger her safety. Irene enjoys material comfort; she will not risk starting a new life in Brazil, although her refusal means sacrificing her husband's happiness.

Thus it is that Irene subconsciously appreciates—though she does not outwardly condone—her friend Clare Kendry's passing, for Kendry, aggressive and impetuous, has taken a risk that has brought her complete access to the upper-middle-class American Dream. From this vantage point, Irene's psychological reaction becomes clear: Her ambivalent attraction toward and repulsion from Clare stems from what she perceives as shortcomings within herself; namely, her inability to take risks, rationalized in the need for safety and security, and her own distancing from less-fortunate black people in Harlem's ghetto. With the dangerous Clare hovering about her secure home, Irene is unable to eliminate her friend's presence even though she begins to live in fear that this "mysterious stranger" will take away her husband and destroy the safety that is her life. It is no wonder, too, that subconsciously Irene wants Clare to disappear, to vanish, to die. Although there is no evidence of an affair between Clare and Dr. Redfield, Irene has become emotionally distraught at the possibility, a turbulent package of nerves fixated on the possible loss of her much-loved material life of leisure, opulence, and exciting friends. Psychologically, if not legally, she is guilty of "eliminating" Clare. Whether she took an active role when the sudden opportunity came will be a matter of conjecture. Nella Larsen's text, concluding in deliberate literary ambiguity, suggests this as a possibility.

Clare Kendry demonstrates the psychological consequences inherent in passing, for in choosing the economic and social safety of the white world, she has repudiated the blood of her ancestors and has destroyed her own identity. Clare must live in a schizophrenic world where her life of deceit now forces the unhappy woman to oscillate between her role as white matron and that of temporary black sojourner. Her days are filled with an atavistic desire to reengage her essential self by associating with negroes, members of the race so bitterly detested by her husband. Clare's sense of isolation and loneliness is compounded by her realization that, should the dark and menacing secret of her passing be revealed, her daughter, who has no knowledge of her mother's true past, will be forever lost to her. Yet it is a subconscious need to be discovered, perhaps, that helps to precipitate Clare's perilous risk-taking adventures with the Redfields, jeopardizing her position each time her husband leaves town. This possible desire to be discovered would then quite naturally deliver her back to her people, without the need to feel that she had abandoned her child. Over the years, Clare Kendry has distorted the essential part of herself and has assumed a disguise that is now odious to her. Yet it is too late for truth; there is too much to be lost. The "passing" woman's consciousness of her emotionally intimidating situation thwarts her ability to make the choice for which her psyche is screaming. The results would be disastrous either way. In the end, does she commit suicide? Does she passively allow herself to be thrown from the window? Has Nella Larsen killed her as punishment for denying her identity or as a possible means to preserve the Redfields' marriage? Curiously enough, at Clare's death scene it is Irene Redfield who is alone and apart, feeling strangely guilty in an all-black group of people.

Dr. Brian Redfield is the third person in this triangle, and although the reader is never privy to Clare's thoughts about him, his own attitudes toward her move from rejection to attention. After a time, it becomes clear that Redfield sees and admires in her the chief virtue that he believes is lacking in his wife: a fearless, risk-taking personality that leads her to choose a means, however onerous, to escape the sting of racism in America. He, too, feels a kinship with Clare Kendry. Although he does not condone passing, Redfield grudgingly recognizes the impulse that prompts it: the desire to escape from the prejudices of racism in everyday American life. He, too, would like to escape these continual pressures by running away—as, in a sense, Kendry has done.

This trio of complicated psychological entities, then, carries Larsen's straightforward fictional narrative. The author fully explores the choices and decisions made by her protagonists: She understands but does not excuse Clare's passing and orchestrates the woman's mysterious death; she empathizes with Dr. Redfield's feelings about racism but leaves him tangled in his conventional, unhappy marriage and superficially fulfilling career; most of all, however, Nella Larsen concentrates on Irene Redfield, who, motivated by traditional concerns for safety and security, makes what she believes are the ethically and appropriately weighed choices for herself and her family, even choosing to remain a black woman in the United States, but who at the end feels isolated, morally ambiguous, and even criminal.

Context

Dedicated to Carl Van Vechten and his actress wife Fania Marinoff, both prominent patrons of black artists during the Harlem Renaissance of the 1920's, *Passing* established Nella Larsen as one of the most promising writers to come from that important aesthetic movement. With this novel, her achievement as an African American woman author is especially notable, for the book examines the psychological divisions and challenges in modern middle-class marriage, emphasizing the women's perspective. The book further explores the limits that society of the mid-1920's imposed on all women, with, naturally, the additional restrictions put upon women of color. *Passing* deals, too, in subtle fashion with female sexuality and its role in the context of racism as well as its power within the emotional drama acted out among Irene, Clare, and Brian, for much of the tension in their unhappy confluence appears to be unleashed by overtones of a suggestive sensual energy. While Larsen has studied the chaotic emotional ambience surrounding the woman who passes, and while her treatment of the tragic mulatta theme is possibly the best in American writing, the social burdens of both women are also demonstrated, with suffering and death finally epitomizing their individual struggles.

Nella Larsen does not sentimentalize women's plight; she approaches the depiction of her women with realism. The limits to a woman's actual freedom in the 1920's were stringent; economic security meant dependence on a husband for support. The freedom of Clare Kendry and Irene Redfield is tied directly to their marriages, Clare's complicated by her "passing" and Irene's threatened by her husband's unhappiness. Here, then, is a portrait of woman as prisoner, a person whose very identity is suspect without acknowledged attachment to a man. Thus, while *Passing* derives its materials profoundly from the experience of the African American woman, it also addresses areas of concern for all women.

Although she was neither a crusader for women's rights nor a modern feminist, Larsen created a quietly powerful portrait of the forces and pressures exerted upon women in America in her time. Perhaps her most important contribution to women's literature lies in her having written *Passing*, a book whose social realism and psychological insight herald an achievement in American letters by a black woman writer whose artistry delineated two vital themes of enduring critical concern: the quest for identity and the struggle of women—both within the context of racism.

Sources for Further Study

Davis, Arthur P. *From the Dark Tower: Afro-American Writers, 1900-1960*. Washington, D.C.: Howard University Press, 1981. Takes a historical perspective, focusing on Larsen's fiction and its place in the larger aesthetic ambience of black American writing of the twentieth century.

Fuller, Hoyt. Introduction to *Passing*. New York: Collier Books, 1971. A valuable introduction to Larsen's novel that emphasizes the aesthetic structure of the book and the social dilemmas portrayed through the phenomenon of passing.

Kramer, Victor A., ed. *The Harlem Renaissance Reexamined*. New York: AMS Press, 1987. Especially important in this collection of contemporary background essays updating the critical views on Nella Larsen and her literary associates is Lillie P. Howard's study of the novelist's employment of the themes of crossing and materialism.

Larsen, Nella. *An Intimation of Things Distant: The Collected Fiction of Nella Larsen*. Edited by Charles Larsen. New York: Anchor Books, 1992. A perceptive introduction emphasizing the major motifs and themes embodying the creative energy in *Passing* and, at the same time, relating these themes to the author's life.

Robinson, William H. Introduction to *Passing*. New York: Arno Press, 1969. Introductory remarks focus on the theme of the mulatto as well as on Larsen's expression of the materials within black culture.

Singh, Amritjit. *The Novels of the Harlem Renaissance: Twelve Black Writers, 1923-1933*. University Park: Pennsylvania State University Press, 1976. An analytical survey of prominent contributors to the Harlem Renaissance that includes a study of the psychological and social pressures depicted by Larsen in her text.

Washington, Mary Helen. "Nella Larsen: Mystery Woman of the Harlem Renaissance." *Ms.* 9 (December, 1980): 44-50. This article details the personal saga of Nella Larsen and the concomitant pressures stemming therefrom, all contributing significantly to the materials and the resolution of her novel.

Abe C. Ravitz

PATRIARCHAL ATTITUDES

Author: Eva Figes (1932-   )
Type of work: Social criticism
First published: 1970

Form and Content

Eva Figes's 1970 publication *Patriarchal Attitudes* was one of a group of three books that came out that year explicating the history and root causes of women's oppression by men. It was a banner year for women; as Figes's book hit the stores, along with Kate Millett's *Sexual Politics* and Germaine Greer's *The Female Eunuch* the next year, the women's liberation movement was born into a world already at a fever-pitch of political excitement over the Vietnam War and the Civil Rights movement. Women who had learned how to organize working for other issues were ready to challenge the basic tenets that ruled their own lives and enforced their oppression.

Figes offered the analysis women needed in their quest for equality. Taking up the age-old question "What makes a woman a woman?" she reviewed centuries of teaching, economics, and social science. Figes concludes that the way in which people are nurtured, not their innate nature, determines their values and actions. People become what culture teaches them to be, and the mainstream cultural works that Figes had just reviewed were extraordinarily hostile to women.

Figes uses the words of some of Western civilization's most renowned speakers to show the widespread fear of women that permeates Western society. She quotes Moses, Giovanni Boccaccio, Jean-Jacques Rousseau, Sigmund Freud, and others, marching through the canon of written works that contain Western culture's most revered ideas. Ancient Hebrew myth, John Milton, and the poetic tradition all add their voices to the cultural chorus. Figes unearths a society that idealizes woman when she identifies completely with a man's desires and demonizes her whenever she opposes him.

Chapter by chapter, Figes shows that Westerners live in a world in which man controls woman to elevate himself. In Western religion, in economics, in philosophy, science, and psychology, male needs are presumed to be universal human needs, while women are forced into a mold that denies their most basic personal goals and aspirations.

It is the breadth of Figes's analysis that makes her position difficult to dispute. By allowing her argument to grow out of the words of culture's most revered icons, she uses their presumptive brilliance to prove her points. The work is short, not quite two hundred pages including notes, bibliography, and index, but it presents a comprehensive view of Western society and women's lives within it. *Patriarchal Attitudes* provides readers a context within which to place current pronouncements upon the nature of women, along with enough information to deconstruct the assumptions underlying contemporary culture.

Analysis

Figes phrases her arguments in universal terms, speaking categorically of "A Man's World" and "A Man's God," but it is important for the careful reader to note that she examines only Western culture, Judeo-Christian religion, and literature that was written in or translated into English. Thus, while she makes no note of the cultural biases of her study, some generalizations may not apply to cultures that are based in different texts and traditions.

Figes begins her examination of the question, "What makes a woman a woman?" by acknowledging the basic biological differences between the sexes. Most women can bear children; men categorically cannot. Women tend to live longer than men, their blood carries a different mixture of hormones, and generally their muscles are less well developed. The first two differences appear to be unalterable; the last depends very much upon the activity in which the individual engages, as Figes proves by quoting anthropologists who have studied many cultures. If musculature is alterable by usage and custom, what other supposedly innate characteristics can be similarly affected? Boys and girls enjoy largely the same hormone balance prior to puberty, yet behavioral differences emerge far earlier in their lives. Education is responsible for these differences, Figes demonstrates; in fact, it is responsible for virtually all human responses—physical, emotional, and intellectual—to the world of stimuli.

In her chapter "A Man's World," Figes asserts that the cultural environment has been defined by male eyes. Language, mathematics, music, and art have all been delineated by male scholars. The world they have mapped excludes women's perceptions. In fact, woman's identity is entirely a male construct; women are taught to want and to be the things man wants in a woman, not the things that would fill their own lives with meaning. Through art, history, and literature, men perpetuate the image of themselves as the doers of all heroic deeds, as the embodiment of all greatness, as the face of God, and as the defenders of a self-created moral code. They impose this worldview by sheer physical power, by economic exclusion, and by granting themselves unequal rights under the law.

The concept of God may once have included women, Figes notes in "A Man's God," but if people once believed it was Eurynome who laid the world egg, they have now converted to a religion that is almost exclusively male in both its icons and its aims. Childbirth appeared to ancient humanity, she argues, as an incontrovertible sign of women's divinity. Once man realized the connection between sex and childbirth, however, he understood how to co-opt woman's power for himself. By claiming ownership of a woman and ensuring that the only man who touched her was himself, he could guarantee the legitimacy of his offspring. Man then began to construct his own immortality based on long lines of descendants; the endless genealogies of the Old Testament give witness to this preoccupation.

Man's religion proclaimed his control over women essential. Men fear being manipulated by sexuality, a fear that Figes finds throughout literature. They fear being emasculated, as Samson was, and they fear women's supposedly endless sexual appetite, which threatens to suck men dry. Therefore, religion portrayed woman as responsible for humankind's fall from grace. Celibacy was promoted, and woman was depicted as an evil temptress who would lure man into sin, but lust repressed does not disappear, it merely changes form. Figes cites the witch burnings of the fourteenth and fifteenth centuries, which annihilated up to one-quarter of the population in certain areas, as an example of male lust projected onto women. Just as God controls man, so man must control woman, even if that control takes the form of mass murder.

It has been a slower process for men to dominate women's economic status, yet Figes claims that here, too, women have gradually lost their equality. Until recent decades, mere survival depended upon the labor of both sexes. In sixteenth century England, there was very little division between the worlds of home and work. Marriage was a partnership in which a woman's work truly mattered; as a result, not only were women permitted to inherit their husbands' businesses but also they were admitted to guilds and allowed to engage in independent trade. With the rise of capitalism, the consolidation of capital, and the separation of home and work, however, women were increasingly excluded from the economic world. By Victorian times, upper-class women were forbidden to work by strict social mores. In addition, because industry and thrift were considered prime virtues in a capitalistic society, man's role as the sole breadwinner bolstered his convictions of superiority and simultaneously gave him complete control over his household's every need.

This autocratic rule was oddly incongruent in a world whose political climate focused more and more clearly upon the inalienable rights of man. Eighteenth century philosophers proclaimed that man was born free; revolutions were fought to achieve that freedom. Yet woman was not liberated. Figes points to the Romantic movement as the intellectual sleight-of-hand that allowed men to exclude women from the rights of mankind. Woman was both idealized and marginalized, regarded as morally superior but intellectually incapable. Thus, woman, with her tender sympathy, was given the job of taming man's aggressions, of being the ideal mother whose power lay in her complete selflessness.

Nineteenth century scientists also tried to prove the fundamental rightness of man's domination. Charles Darwin's theory of survival of the fittest was said to demonstrate that man's rule was a matter of scientific law. Philosophers used intricate logic to demonstrate that man was spirit and woman was material; he was reason and she was emotion. Figes proposes that precisely such divisive, bipolar thinking allowed Nazi Germany to annihilate millions of Jews in the gas chamber. If one pole represents perfection, the other must embody all that is loathsome and must therefore be dominated or destroyed.

Women did not always accept their subordination meekly. Toward the end of the nineteenth century, many women actively sought greater equality and participation in the exclusively male professional world. Religion, economics, and philosophy alone were not enough to stall their drive toward productive lives. Into this threatening situation stepped Sigmund Freud, whose theories of psychoanalysis had a profound effect upon modern thinking. Women, Freud pronounced, were inherently inimical to the aims of civilization. Their innate drives were too strong for them to fully repress; therefore, men must exert control in the interests of preserving all that is of value in an orderly world. Women who objected to this control were merely demonstrating their neurotic desire to possess what they could never have: a penis. Ambition in women was a sickness, a reason for pity and sympathy, but not a desire that should ever be gratified.

Even women who have realized their own ambitions have discriminated against other women throughout history. Frequently, successful women look at their sisters and find them despicable. Powerful women must understand that their own success does not disprove the oppression of millions or demonstrate that the oppressed deserve their condition.

Finally, Figes offers some suggestions for human evolution. They seem thin in the light of the weight of custom she has laid before the reader so convincingly, but perhaps the changes in family law, the easing of divorce laws, the provision of state support for children that she suggests would make some practical difference. Economic independence, she admits, is not a guarantee of emotional independence, but it is a necessary condition.

Context

Eva Figes is only one in a long line of women philosophers who have attempted to delineate the causes and history of female oppression. Mary Wollestonecraft first posited the notion that women's upbringing rather than their inherent nature was responsible for their seeming inferiority. Simone de Beauvoir, Virginia Woolf, and countless other theorists have made the same arguments that Figes worked out. Even in the face of such history, Figes believed that she worked in isolation. Perhaps that feeling of isolation is the key to the significance of her work, for while the ideas that she outlines are not new, they are ideas that are continually being forgotten. Figes's work marks the beginning of a great period of female scholarship that took as its primary task the rediscovery of women's cultural heritage. *Patriarchal Attitudes* demonstrates the great need for women to seek their image and identity in the words and works of their sisters. It teaches that male perceptions exclude much that women find valuable in the world.

Figes's subsequent works are largely fictional and seek to provide precisely that feminist viewpoint that she taught her readers to value. Highly experimental both stylistically and philosophically, they examine issues of identity and history through the eyes and interests of women.

Sources for Further Study

Beauvoir, Simone de. *The Second Sex*. Translated by H. M. Parshley. New York: Alfred A. Knopf, 1953. Figes read this classic volume of feminist theory, and although in various articles she claims it offered too little analysis of women as sexual beings, many arguments made by Beauvoir appear in Figes's work.

Friedan, Betty. *The Feminine Mystique*. New York: W. W. Norton, 1963. Friedan attacks cultural views of women that keep them in the home. In doing so, she takes on Freud and a host of anthropologists, including Margaret Mead.

Tomalin, Claire. "What Does a Woman Want?" *New Statesman* 26 (June, 1970): 917-918. Tomalin agrees with much of Figes's analysis but argues that the importance of family was not given enough weight.

Vidal, Gore. "In Another Country." *New York Review of Books* 22 (July, 1971): 8-10. Vidal points out the similarities between *Patriarchal Attitudes*, Kate Millett's *Sexual Politics*, and Germaine Greer's *The Female Eunuch*. He elevates Figes's work above the others, especially endorsing her argument that social conditioning produces human behavior. This is true not only for women, Vidal notes, but also for men.

Woolf, Virginia. *The Three Guineas*. London: Harcourt, Brace, 1938. Woolf was the first to suggest the connection between sexual oppression and political oppression, a connection that Figes stresses even more strongly in regard to Nazi Germany.

Susan E. Keegan

PILGRIM AT TINKER CREEK

Author: Annie Dillard (1945-)
Type of work: Essays
First published: 1974

Form and Content

The fifteen interconnected yet surprisingly independent chapters of *Pilgrim at Tinker Creek* chronicle the cycle of seasons in and around the place the author identifies as "a creek, Tinker Creek, in a valley in Virginia's Blue Ridge." This place will not be found on any map, yet no reader would accuse the writer of creating an imaginary stream. Tinker Creek is real and holy to the writer, and Dillard aims to leave the reader believing in Tinker Creek's existence, continuance, and, ultimately, its importance.

In chronicling the year, *Pilgrim at Tinker Creek* presents the reader early on with "one of those excellent January partly cloudies." The book ends at a similar point approximately twelve months later when, in the last chapter, the reader learns, "Today is the winter solstice," and "Another year has twined away, unrolled and dropped across nowhere."

In taking the reader through the seasons of this sacred spot, the "pilgrim" narrator reveals little about herself. The reader learns that she smokes, that she reads astonishingly widely, and that she has a cat who jumps in through the bedroom window at night and leaves her covered in bloody paw prints. Except for these few incidental personal details, the reader's gaze is rarely fixed on the viewer, focusing instead on the viewer's world, on what is seen. Dillard would have the reader see not herself, but what she sees. Perhaps the most important thing that the reader learns about Dillard is that she has an infinite capacity for wonder and surprise—twin capacities that she uses to reawaken the same responses in her readers.

Dillard initially set her book in Maine and made the narrator a young man, but her editors eventually convinced her to do otherwise. In a taped interview with Kay Bonetti in 1989, she recounts living in a tent one fall in Maine and doing little else but reading. Among the books she was reading was one in which the writer referred to lightning bugs and to his ignorance of how they worked. Realizing that she knew how lightning bugs worked and that she knew much more about the natural world and writing than this writer did, Dillard concluded, "I should be writing this book."

Dillard wrote *Pilgrim at Tinker Creek* while she was in her late twenties. She completed the book in less than a year, working from her collection of about nineteen journals. She wrote from December to August, and she recalls of that time, "I was not living then, I was just writing. I would never do it again. It was like fighting a war."

The book has been labeled a collection of essays, a designation that displeases Dillard. She insists that *Pilgrim at Tinker Creek* is a sustained narrative. Another designation that Dillard finds particularly distasteful is meditation. She believes that the term "meditation" suggests randomness and passiveness and ignores *Pilgrim at Tinker Creek*'s muscularity.

Throughout her book, which is inscribed simply "For Richard," Dillard offers an account of what she sees, and she presents the reader with an eye and a voice that, while never mistaken for masculine, resist overtly proclaiming themselves feminine. It is perhaps in its uncompromising validation of personal vision—anyone's vision—that the book makes its greatest contribution.

Dillard refuses to present a sanitized, airbrushed view of nature to the reader. In addition to the beauties of a mockingbird's free fall and the tree with the lights in it, the reader also witnesses the giant water beetle that sucks the life from its victim and the praying mantis that beheads and devours its partner during the act of mating. "It's rough out there," Dillard reminds the reader repeatedly.

Dillard writes seemingly with no set agenda. She frankly admits, "We don't know what's going on here." She adds that

> Our life is a faint tracing on the surface of mystery. . . . We must somehow take a wider view, look at the whole landscape, really see it, and describe what's going on here. Then we can at least wail the right question into the swaddling band of darkness, or, if it comes to that, choir the proper praise.

Analysis

Dillard never lets the reader lose track of the season under consideration, but it is much more than a calendar year that binds *Pilgrim at Tinker Creek* together. The book presents the reader with a view of the outer world as it is reconstructed indoors—filtered, sorted, and sifted through the writer's own inner world. "I bloom indoors in the winter like a forced forsythia; I come in to come out. At night I read and write, and things I have never understood become clear; I reap the harvest of the rest of the year's planting," Dillard writes. At one point, Dillard calls her book "a mental ramble" and refers to her mind as a "trivia machine." "Like the bear who went over the mountain," she says, I wanted to "see what I could see."

What Dillard sees and records includes what she has read. Her book includes references to philosophy, religion, insects, Arctic exploration, medicine, poetry, and various other subjects. She devotes several pages to a summary of a book about newly sighted persons and their experience of the world. The pattern of the entire text could perhaps best be described as following the formula "I went here, I saw this, it made me think of this, I saw something else, and then I came home."

In many ways, Dillard's text reads like a travelogue. One finds many of that genre's typical markers: "I set out," "I go," "I sit," "I cross," "West of the house," and "north of me." Yet the book is no more a travelogue than it is a psalm, a field book, a reflection, a diary, a poem, an eyewitness account. The book defies classification in any of the traditional genres. Dillard's voyage is at once physical and spiritual. The sense of self and the sense of place are inextricably intertwined. Speaking of the creek, Dillard says, "I come to it as to an oracle; I return to it as a man years later will seek out the battlefield where he lost a leg or an arm."

Dillard has been compared with a number of writers, including Emily Dickinson, William Wordsworth, Gerard Manley Hopkins, W. B. Yeats, Rainer Maria Rilke, and Paul Valéry. It is to the Jesuit poet-priest Hopkins that Dillard pays most homage in her work. One hears echoes of "God's Grandeur" when Dillard maintains that "the whole world sparks and flames." Dillard evokes "The Windhover" when she speaks of "the most beautiful day of the year," which leaves her with "a dizzying, drawn sensation." She quotes several lines from one of Hopkins' lesser-known works, "As Kingfishers Catch Fire." Her closing lines of the book also evoke Hopkins as she returns to the opening image of her book—the cat that makes the bloody paw prints. The encounter leaves her, as does her encounter with the larger world, "bloodied and mauled, wrung, dazzled, drawn." *Pilgrim at Tinker Creek* also contains references to Andrew Marvell, William Blake, Robert Burns, and Dylan Thomas.

Dillard's tonal ranges include the sober, the philosophical, the flippant, and the celebratory. She can be exacting in her observations, yet she can also be carefree, as can be seen in this early statement: "I was walking along the edge of the island to see what I could see in the water, and mainly to scare frogs." She frequently uses a light-hearted tone to offset her serious and, at times, terrifying subject matter. This lighter tone can be heard in such statements as "Fish gotta swim and bird gotta fly; insects, it seems, gotta do one horrible thing after another."

Dillard sees around her both the horrible and the humorous. She chooses to share both in *Pilgrim at Tinker Creek*. At times the reader gets both in one breath. Speaking of the endless variety in nature, she observes, "No form is too gruesome, no behavior too grotesque," and she counters with, "you ain't so handsome yourself."

Context

Dillard is often likened to Henry David Thoreau, to whom she refers frequently in her book. Her experience at Tinker Creek is often compared with Thoreau's self-imposed isolation at Walden Pond. Dillard has resisted seeing herself as a feminist writer, and she said in an interview, "I want to divorce myself from the notion of the female writer right away and then not elaborate." Despite any protests or disclaimers by the author, *Pilgrim at Tinker Creek* continues to be considered a feminist text by many readers. It refuses to confine woman to home and hearth, to an inner world. It refuses to define woman in terms of relationships with others. The book also staunchly refuses to privilege one sex as designated explorers of the natural world. Although Dillard's femaleness, her femininity, are not in the foreground in the text, *Pilgrim at Tinker Creek* can be seen, on the one hand, as transcending issues of gender, and, on the other hand, as inscribing a place for the solitary woman in the unbounded out-of-doors.

Sources for Further Study

Chénetier, Marc. "Tinkering, Extravagance: Thoreau, Melville, and Annie Dillard." *Critique* 31, no. 3 (Spring, 1990): 157-172. Chénetier stresses that "Dillard's work amply feeds upon classical texts" and notes that Dillard's readers engage "in a sort of symphonic reading" inasmuch as hearing Dillard's voice, unmistakable and distinctive as it is, involves hearing numerous other voices.

Clark, Suzanne. "The Woman in Nature and the Subject of Nonfiction." In *Literary Nonfiction: Theory, Criticism, Pedagogy*, edited by Chris Anderson. Carbondale: Southern Illinois University Press, 1989. Clark explores the apparent "lack of self" in Dillard's prose, the writer's refusal to emphasize her female identity, and the overlapping voices of "woman, poet, madman and mystic."

Dillard, Annie. "A Face Aflame: An Interview with Annie Dillard." Interview by Philip Yancey. *Christianity Today* 22 (May 5, 1978): 14-19. Dillard identifies her audience as "the unbeliever" yet acknowledges a large readership among people of many religious persuasions. She discusses readers' reactions to her work and describes herself as someone "grounded strongly in art and weakly in theology."

____________. *Teaching a Stone to Talk: Expeditions and Encounters*. New York: Harper & Row, 1982. In fourteen essays, many of which have been anthologized, Dillard explores themes introduced earlier in *Pilgrim at Tinker Creek.*

Dunn, Robert Paul. "The Artist as Nun: Theme, Tone, and Vision in the Writings of Annie Dillard." *Studia Mystica* 1, no. 4 (1978): 17-31. Dunn suggests that Dillard's works "are important because they suggest the possibility and value of recapturing in our materialistic age the beauty and pain of mystical vision." He explores Dillard's remarkable ability to speak convincingly to agnostics and believers alike, and her adoption of the dual role of artist and nun.

McIlroy, Gary. "*Pilgrim at Tinker Creek* and the Social Legacy of *Walden*." *The South Atlantic Quarterly* 85, no. 2 (Spring, 1986): 111-122. McIlroy describes the immediate environment around Tinker Creek and demonstrates that the boundaries between nature and society are anything but fixed. He addresses Dillard's detachment or "social isolation" and the critics who fault Dillard for not writing a political text. He finds in Dillard a "detachment from society as well as [an] acknowledgement of the common bond of all living things." He notes, "Like a prophet, she travels alone."

Maddocks, Melvin. "Terror and Celebration." *Time* 117 (March 18, 1974): 78. Maddocks warns: "Reader, beware of this deceptive girl, mouthing her piety. . . . Here is no gentle romantic twirling a buttercup." He adds that "Miss Dillard is stalking the reader as surely as any predator stalks its game." Maddocks concludes that what Dillard achieves in *Pilgrim at Tinker Creek* is "a remarkable psalm of terror and celebration."

Scheick, William J. "Annie Dillard: Narrative Fringe." In *Contemporary American Women Writers: Narrative Strategies*, edited by Catherine Rainwater and William J. Scheick. Lexington: University Press of Kentucky, 1985. Scheick proposes that Dillard's statement "We wake, if we ever wake at all, to mystery" forms the thesis of *Pilgrim at Tinker Creek* and other of her works. Includes a bibliography of Dillard's writings.

Beverly J. Matiko

POEMS AND FRAGMENTS

Author: Sappho (c. 615 B.C. -c. 550 B.C.)
Type of work: Poetry
First published: Written third century B.C.; published 1560 (English translation, 1735)

Form and Content

In classical antiquity, the standard edition of Sappho appears to have been arranged into nine books. The first book included 330 Sapphic stanzas, a total of 1,320 lines in the meter invented by her and named for her. The length of a book averaged 1,000 to 1,500 lines; the extent of Sappho's lost works can be gauged by the fact that only about 1,700 lines have survived, most of which are fragmentary and some amounting to no more than a letter. Books 2 and 3 consisted, respectively, of poems in dactylic hexameters and poems in the Asclepiadean meter. The fourth book seems also to have been metrically consistent. Books 4 through 8 were apparently compiled on bases other than meter, although there is scant mention of any of them by ancient commentators, and on the sixth book there is no information of any kind. The ninth book, the only one given a title instead of a number, was called "Epithalamia" (wedding songs). The classical scholar Denys Page summarizes this editorial information and elucidates the contents of Sappho's poetry as "Epithalamians," "Aphrodite," "Divine and Heroic Legend," and "Political and Domestic Allusions."

Some translators arrange Sappho's poems and fragments in thematic groups. Paul Roche, for example, entitles his groupings "Overtures of Loving," "Petitions and Observations," "Converse," "Epithalamia," "The Taut Tongue," and "Memory-and-Malediction." Josephine Balmer has nine groupings: "Love," "Desire," "Despair," "Marriage," "Mother-and-Daughter," "The Goddess of Love," "Religion," "Poetry-and-the-Muses," and "Nature-and-Wisdom." The two representative lists have in common only the themes of love and marriage, but all the titles are variously descriptive of the content of the poetry.

The formal character of Sappho's poetry is to be discerned in its intricate metrical compositions and in the Aeolic dialect of Lesbos, neither of which can be more than distantly reflected in English translations of her works. Sappho and her contemporary compatriot Alcaeus, with whom an invalid tradition links her in romance, shared the Aeolic dialect, which is free of aspirated consonants, that is, of the equivalent of the letter *h*. It is consequently smooth in sound and conducive to melodious phrasing. Aeolian poetry is generally intended for solo performance as opposed to choral rendition; that is, it is monodic as opposed to choric. Smooth consonance (*psilosis*) and monodicism both lend themselves effectively to the intimacy and subjectivity that Sappho's poetry generates.

The formal content of Sappho's poetry can be illustrated by brief passages from her severely fragmented canon. An example of her mastery of pure lyric is the following stanza: "and through the branches of the trees there is/ a rustling sound of cool water; roses lend/ their shadows to the grove, and sleep pours down from/ whispering tree leaves." Translation can suggest, but not reproduce, the Sapphic meter and the fluid soughing of softly guttural and sustained sibilant music. An example of her dedication to love as the preeminent human value is the following opening of a poem: "According to some, the best thing on this/ dark earth is the cavalry, to others/ the infantry, to others the navy, to me it/ is one's beloved." Another feature of her poetry is her preoccupation with the divine personifications of human impulsions, notably the goddess of love, whom she invokes, in the one poem of all her works that has survived in virtual entirety, as "Colorfully-throned Aphrodite." Finally, her sense of her worth as a poet is frankly and prophetically expressed in these lines: "The golden Muses have truly blessed me;/ I shall not be forgotten after death."

Analysis

Discussion of Sappho's poetry necessarily entails what has come to be identified as her primary motif; namely, female homoeroticism. The term "lesbian" in its late nineteenth and twentieth century English usage is referentially derived from the reputation of Sappho of Lesbos. The grounds for diagnosing Sappho as homosexual involve two assumptions: that Sappho's expressions of emotion are subjectively her own and that her use of her own name in homoerotic context is self-identical and not generic. In most studies of Sappho, these assumptions are both unstated and understood.

That not all Sappho's poems express homoeroticism and that Sappho, even in self-identical context, is not exclusively homosexual are suppositions that any reader of her work in translations published during the latter half of the twentieth century will recognize. Earlier translations, commentaries, and scholarly articles presented a Sappho varying from an almost deranged homosexual to a paragon of heterosexual chastity or moral purity. In her hymn to Aphrodite, the single poem that has been preserved in full, Sappho presents herself, or her generic namesake, as being addressed by name by Aphrodite, to whom she has prayed for the renewed affection of her beloved and by whom she is told that the now indifferent beloved will soon be courting Sappho's favor. A single letter, missing from some codices but included in others, is the determinant that the indifferent beloved is a woman. In the absence of that letter (an *alpha*, denoting feminine gender), Sappho's, or her namesake's, beloved may be either male or female. A translation published in 1902 by John Philip Merivale makes the beloved a male; but almost all later translations, even those by scholars who prefer a chaste Sappho and consider homosexuality, in Denys Page's word, a "perversion," adhere to the supposition of a female beloved.

Sappho's attention to heterosexuality is attested in lines such as "svelte Aphrodite has melted my will away/ and filled me with longing for a boy," as well as in the epithalamia, which celebrate the formalizing of conjugal heterosexual love. Sappho's own conjugal heterosexuality is made explicit in two fragments in which she refers to her daughter Kleis.

There is nothing in Sappho's poetry to support the legend that she loved a man named Phaon; there is no historical evidence that she, having abandoned her homosexuality in his interests, leaped to her death from a cliff when he subsequently deserted her. The legend was propagated by the Greek dramatist Menander (second century B.C.) in a line from one of his plays that is quoted by Strabo (c. 64 B.C.-A.D. 24); it is also the subject of a long Latin poem questionably ascribed to Ovid (43 B.C.-A.D. 18).]

Legend and biographical fictions inhibit the analysis of Sappho's work, likewise the conjectures of editors and translators that add to her extant text words and passages. For example, the fragment ". . . ēr' a . . . dērat . . . Gongyla . . . " appears in Paul Roche's translation as "Then Gongyla spoke." In Josephine Balmer's translation, it is "[I tell you I am miserable,] /Gongyla. . . ." Most translators settle for "Gongyla . . . to retain the only intelligible word in the sequence. Some translators, and for that matter some editors, expunge the entire sequence in preference to interpolation or emendation. Guy Davenport offers as his translation "Spring/ Too long/ Gongyla," insisting that "the misreading, if misreading it be, is by this time too resonant to change." He is perhaps referring to the popularity of Ezra Pound's poem "Papyrus," published in *Lustra* (1916) and reading "Spring . . ./ Too long . . ./ Gongula . . ."

The most cogent analysis of Sappho's lyricism is found in the essay on sublimity written, according to most estimates, in the first century A.D. by a critic called "Longinus." The author exemplifies sublimity by quoting, and thereby preserving for posterity, four stanzas of a poem in the meter named for Sappho. The stanzas describe an observer, presumably Sappho, reacting to the sight of a man seated next to a woman whom the observer adores. The man impresses the observer as virtually godlike both because he is favored by the woman's presence and because he can retain his equanimity when the very sight of the woman sends the observer into emotional excess. Longinus writes that Sappho always selects the precise, the greatest, and the most intense symptoms of love and combines them into an illustrious whole. The symptoms in the poem include loss of voice, sight, and hearing; fever, with cold sweat and spasms; pallor; and a sense of death. Longinus explains that the paradox of being both hot and cold and both rational and unhinged is expressed as a synthesized emotional integer. Sappho's rationality, or *noesis*, is found in her observer's logical diagnosis as she simultaneously suffers emotion and disciplines her rendition of the event with precise metric.

Context

The opening lines of the poem preserved by Longinus achieved key status in one area of twentieth century feminist criticism. In literal translation they read: "He seems to me to be on a par with the gods, that man who sits facing you." A feminist preference is to eliminate an actual male presence in favor of a hypothetical one; this is done by changing "that man who" to "whatever man" or "whoever." Although K. J. Dover rightly pointed out, in *Greek Homosexuality* (1978), that Greek grammar precludes such a reading, the change was effected in many later twentieth century English translations, attesting the success with which Sappho's canon was enlisted in the support of women's issues.

Two factors in Sappho's verse that gained new emphasis during the twentieth century, and in turn helped to determine the direction of modern feminism, are Sappho's independence as an artistic genius and the frank sexuality to which her art gives unabashed expression. As the feminist movement gained momentum, Sappho received proportionately more attention. Every decade of the twentieth century had its Sappho publications: translations, editions, or articles. The preoccupation with Sappho's "moral purity" or with the minimalizing of her homoeroticism, carried over from the nineteenth century into the beginning of the twentieth, gradually gave way to the picture of Sappho as a consummate lyricist forthright in her projection of sexuality, whatever its turn; Sappho became a picture of a feminist for feminists.

It is significant that in the twentieth century Sappho received attention from more women translators, scholars, editors, and hermeneucists than in virtually all previous centuries combined. Eva-Maria Voigt's masterly edition of Sappho and Alcaeus in 1971 superseded the standard edition by Edgar Lobel and Denys Page in 1955. Translations by women became commonplace: Olga Marx in 1945, Mary Barnard in 1958, Suzy Q. Groden in 1966, Anne Pippin Burnett in 1983, Sherri Williams in 1990, Diane Rayor in 1991, Josephine Balmer in 1992, and Sasha Newborn in 1993. The renditions by Barnard, Groden, Burnett, and Balmer set new standards for reliability. In addition, the feminist scholar Mary R. Lefkowitz reeducated the modern reader by repudiating the tradition that Sappho's erotic lyrics were self-referential and by cautioning against deriving from the poetry autobiographical elements that would then become the means of interpreting it.

Sources for Further Study

Bowra, C. M. *Greek Lyric Poetry: From Alcman to Simonides*. 2d ed. London: Oxford University Press, 1961. Chapter 5 remains the prime introduction to the poetry of Sappho in its temporal setting. All but a few quotations in the original Greek are translated or paraphrased.

Burnett, Anne Pippin. *Three Archaic Poets: Archilochus, Alcaeus, Sappho*. Cambridge, Mass.: Harvard University Press, 1983. "Part Three: Sappho" is a searching and informative essay on the poet and includes accurate translations of the poems and fragments, with occasional rhyme that is both efficacious and unobtrusive.

Campbell, David A. ed and trans. *Sappho, Alcaeus*. Vol. 1 in *Greek Lyric*. Loeb Classical Library 142. Cambridge, Mass.: Harvard University Press, 1982. Superbly supersedes the 1928 Loeb Library edition by J. M. Edmonds; incorporates a half century of valuable scholarship. Campbell's prose translations adhere meticulously to the Greek text, which is included on facing pages.

DeJean, Joan. *Fictions of Sappho, 1546-1937*. Chicago: University of Chicago Press, 1989. Exceptionally informative scholarship. DeJean makes it clear that translations of Sappho and speculation regarding her sexuality reflect the mores of the times and countries in which her work is published.

Duban, Jeffrey M., ed. *Ancient and Modern Images of Sappho: Translations and Studies in Archaic Greek Love Lyric*. Lanham, Md.: University Press of America, 1983. Contains the first-rate summary "Sappho in Recent Criticism," as well as a less satisfactory comparison of various translations of Sappho's poems and fragments favoring Duban's own thirty-eight rhymed translations.

Lefkowitz, Mary R. "Critical Stereotypes and the Poetry of Sappho." *Greek, Roman, and Byzantine Studies* 14 (1973): 113-123. Cogently questions the validity of Sappho's work as inherently self-referential.

Page, Denys. *Sappho and Alcaeus: An Introduction to the Study of Ancient Lesbian Poetry*. London: Oxford University Press, 1955. Staid but requisite orientation in the study of Sappho. Page claims that while Sappho was not averse to homoeroticism, there is no evidence in her extant work of her taking part in it.

Rayor, Diane. *Sappho's Lyre: Archaic Lyric and Women Poets of Ancient Greece*. Berkeley: University of California Press, 1991. Information about and translations of seven male lyric poets and (including Sappho) ten female lyric poets. With helpful notes and bibliographical references.

Roy Arthur Swanson

POEMS ON VARIOUS SUBJECTS, RELIGIOUS AND MORAL

Author: Phillis Wheatley (1753?-1784)
Type of work: Poetry
First published: 1773

Form and Content

Poems on Various Subjects, Religious and Moral is the collection of poems produced by a nineteen-year-old Colonial American slave, Phillis Wheatley, the first African American woman ever to be published. The significance of this publication can be understood best in terms of the author's identity and social position, and less by the poetry itself, which is largely imitative of the style and material that were popular at the time. Wheatley was brought as a captive from Senegambia (now Senegal and Gambia) to New England when she was approximately seven years old and was educated by the family who bought her. She was considered a prodigy, since she learned the English language within less than two years of her arrival and successfully studied Latin, the Bible, and English poetry—especially the work of Alexander Pope and John Milton. At age thirteen, she wrote her first religious verse, which was published. Her work became widely known after her elegy on the death of the popular preacher George Whitefield was published in 1770.

Wheatley's collection is written almost entirely in the popular neoclassical form. Neoclassicism is an emulation of what the English believed to have been the Greek ideals of reason and restraint in art. Most of the thirty-nine poems are elegies, which are formal poems wherein the author meditates on a solemn occasion or theme, such as death. Wheatley is best known for her elegies, and she was often commissioned to write them. Her subjects include widows, widowers, parents who had lost children, and numerous popular male figures who were usually respected members of the clergy. Besides elegies, Wheatley's collection contains two stories from the Bible transformed into couplets (pairs of rhyming lines), one Latin translation, several patriotic praises (one to George Washington), and tributes to morning, evening, the imagination, and African American Bostonian artist Scipio Moorhead.

Wheatley lived in an age when there was a great debate among the white slave-owning population over the humanity of African Americans. Her education and poetry demonstrated that African Americans were indeed intellectually capable of engaging in the "arts and sciences," even if her work was limited and was censored by her audience, which acted as both patron and oppressor. Before her poems could be published, Wheatley had to be "examined" by eighteen of Boston's most prestigious male minds, who signed a document attesting the authenticity of her work. This document was appended to the book before it was published, since the work otherwise would not have been believed to be hers. Wheatley's membership in the church, even though it, too, was segregated into black and white, provided the only possibility for freedom and equality in her life and in her art, and the theme of spiritual salvation is prevalent throughout her writing.

Analysis

As neoclassicism demands, Wheatley's poetry recognizes the human being as a limited, imperfect creature in need of instruction, order, and harmony; imagination is highly regarded, but it is never an alternative to the harsh realities of life. Neoclassical poems were valued for their instruction, and they avoided both the adverse and the highly imaginative aspects of nature. This restrictive form suited Wheatley's social status as a slave and conformed to the Christian idea of an individual as an imperfect being whose only hope of salvation rests in the figure of Christ.

Wheatley's poems often begin with the neoclassical appeal to the Muses and often employ Greek deities and legends, remaining mindful of the structured Greek universe; in her poetry, however, God is the highest deity. Wheatley's focus is on salvation and resurrection, as is apparent in her numerous elegies, in which the idea of the well-ordered universe extends to human suffering; even the death of an infant is the will of God and should be looked on as such. Wheatley constructs her elegies (which frequently resemble one another and which were often written in only a few days) of several components that do not always occur in the same order. First, she stresses that death itself comes from the hand of God: "His fatal sceptre rules the spacious whole" ("To a Lady on the Death of Three Relations"). Second, she graciously acknowledges and pictures the mourners' suffering: "Thy sisters, too, fair mourner, feel the dart/ Of death, and with fresh torture rend thine heart." Third, she includes an appeal to mourners to transform their sorrow to joy: "Smile on the tomb, and soothe the raging pain." Often, the dead themselves speak to the mourners from above. (In some elegies to male figures who were prominent in the church, Wheatley emphasizes their earthly deeds, as if petitioning for their entry into the state of bliss.) Finally, a new vision of the deceased is offered to the onlooker: "From bondage freed, the exulting spirit flies."

With few exceptions, the lines of Wheatley's poems are predictably structured in iambic pentameter, each line consisting of ten syllables, five of which are stressed. Wheatley often contracts words, such as "watery" to "wat'ry" in order to conform to the required pattern, using the customary neoclassical rhymed couplet, or pair of rhyming lines. She was skilled in the use of metaphor (identifying one object with another), as the young biblical hero David demonstrates in "Goliath of Gath": "Jehovah's name—no other arms I bear." Her transformative images are also memorable, such as the trees that turn into ships in "To a Gentleman in the Navy": "Where willing forests leave their native plain,/ Descend, and instant, plough the wat'ry main."

Wheatley often uses personification, attributing human qualities to objects or ideas. "On Imagination" is an example of personification, celebrating that faculty (imagination) and its marvelous transforming power; sadly, but true to the neoclassic tenets, the poem ends by acknowledging the limits of the imagination, conceding that the reality of "winter" and "northern tempests" must win over the mind in the end: "They chill the tides of Fancy's flowing sea,/ Cease then, my song, cease the unequal lay."

Wheatley's poems abound in skillfully rendered alliteration, the repetition of consonant or vowel sounds in lines, as in the opening of her elegy for the Reverend George Whitefield: "Hail, happy saint, on thine immortal throne,/ Possest of glory, life and bliss unknown." She also effectively employed the technique of repeating the same word at the start of sentences or clauses (anaphora).

Some critics see Wheatley as having waged an invisible war against slavery in her poetry, mostly in biblical allusions that ultimately admonish Christian slaveholders. Her poem "On Being Brought from Africa to America" is an example of this. In it, she refers to her "benighted soul," acknowledging the widely held theory of her time that equated dark skin with sinfulness, and quotes Christians who would say of African Americans, " 'Their color is a diabolic die.' " At the same time, Wheatley refutes the connection between skin color and sinfulness, since the reference is to her "soul" before she knew the "light of Christ" and not to her skin color. She also reminds Christians in the same poem that even Cain, who was "black," could be assured of the salvation of Christ.

Wheatley consistently refers to the dark skin of the African American as "sable" in her poems, and she often alludes to Africa as "Eden," a reminder to Christian audiences that Eden was thought to have been located in Africa. Additionally, Wheatley also uses the term "Ethiope" to designate African Americans, connecting her race with ancient Ethiopians who are mentioned throughout the Bible, thus elevating the status of the African American through the perspective of Christianity. Many of Wheatley's poems are didactic and at the same time signal her racial identity, such as "To the University of Cambridge, in New England": ". . . Ye blooming planets of human race divine,/An Ethiop tells you 'tis [sin] your greatest foe." Other poems tell of her pride in her African heritage and of her love and admiration for fellow African Americans; "An Ode/On the Birthday of Pompey Stockenridge" praises a fellow African American Christian man, and the poem to Scipio Moorhead is a tribute to African American artists.

Context

Wheatley's poetry was well received as an example of superior African intellect. Her work was used as an evangelical tool among slave-holders who wished to convert their slaves to Christianity. Her poems were also held up by the abolitionists as proof of the humanity of African Americans. In other words, she was well received to the extent that she served the purpose of others, as her role as an African American, woman, slave, and Christian patriot in Colonial America dictated.

Wheatley was censored by her audience, and she was

unable to publish without approval and verification; her situation was comparable to that of black writers in South Africa under the system of apartheid, which was rendered untenable by the laws of censorship, banning, and exile. Wheatley was further censored by her obligation to the Wheatley family for her privileged position in their household. It must be recognized that even her skill as a writer was "owned" by someone else, and that it was the only survival skill available to Wheatley.

Critics have complained about, ignored, and indicted Wheatley's poetry on the ground that it lacks feeling, racial identity, and warmth. One must consider what she was allowed, however, and that her privileged status did not make her any less a slave or any less censored—perhaps it made her even more so, judging by the poetry of the more outspoken (and less privileged) George Moses Horton, which was published with hers by abolitionists in 1838. Wheatley can also be viewed as more isolated than other African Americans because she was cut off from other slaves. Her greatest friend and lifelong correspondent, Obour Tanner, mirrored rather than ameliorated this isolation, since she, too, was a domestic slave who was literate and was a member of the church.

There is much irony in the fact that the material produced by the first published African American woman does not make explicit her achievement or reveal the significance of that achievement to African American and female writers who followed her. Perhaps proving the fundamental fact that African Americans were human and literate was the only public achievement that could have been allowed Wheatley during her lifetime; she was forced to imitate the white culture in order to gain ground and hold a place for the more diverse and authentic African American expression that was to follow.

Wheatley's life after her publication demonstrates further irony; her own attempts to continue selling her work in America were cut short by the Boston Tea Party in 1773 (in one of her poems, Wheatley admonishes England as a harsh mother, unduly taxing her overburdened son), and then made impossible by her unexpected acquisition of freedom in 1778 (two years after the United States declared its independence) when the elder Mr. Wheatley died, at which time she married, cutting herself off from the remaining Wheatley family. Wheatley spent the end of her short life working with her hands; she and her three infants died soon after she gained her freedom, in poverty and obscurity.

Sources for Further Study

O'Neale, Sondra. "A Slave's Subtle War: Phillis Wheatley's Use of Biblical Myth and Symbol." *Early American Literature* 21 (Fall, 1986): 144-165. In this article, O'Neale examines Wheatley's careful use of words to describe color and her use of words to describe sin, arguing that Wheatley both admonished Christians and attempted to change their perceptions of African Americans through her word choice. She also shows how Wheatley used biblical allusions to elevate the status of the African American in the eyes of white Christians.

Richmond, M. A. *Bid the Vassal Soar: Interpretive Essays on the Life and Poetry of Phillis Wheatley and George Moses Horton*. Washington, D.C.: Howard University Press, 1974. This book examines the poetry of two African American slaves in order to discover what impact the institution of slavery has had on African American identity; what is left unsaid in their poetry is more important to this discovery than what remains in print.

Robinson, William H. *Phillis Wheatley and Her Writings*. New York: Garland, 1984. This book is so far the most complete collection of Phillis Wheatley's writings, including extant poems and letters, a facsimile of her published volume, annotations, a sketch of her life and of Boston during her times, and an examination of her poetry. A selected bibliography is included.

__________. *Phillis Wheatley in the Black American Beginnings*. Detroit: Broadside Press, 1975. This book offers a new perspective of Wheatley's poetry, considering it from the social, religious, and literary standpoints of Colonial America. It argues that Wheatley was conscientiously aware of her racial identity and African roots.

Wheatley, Phillis. *Life and Works of Phillis Wheatley*, edited by G. Herbert Renfro. Freeport, N.Y.: Books for Libraries Press, 1970. Written in the late 1800's, this book is significant in that it provides the contemporary reader with an account of Wheatley's life written by a sympathetic and well-educated man who lived just after her times. It is both interesting and ironic in that it is a positive account of her life yet is laced with inherent sexism. For example, Renfro claims: "Nature had designed Phillis for a queen, not for a slave."

Jennifer McLeod

POPCORN VENUS: Women, Movies, and the American Dream

Author: Marjorie Rosen (1944-)
Type of work: Social criticism
First published: 1973

Form and Content

Films came into existence in the closing years of the nineteenth century and were thus born in an atmosphere of Victorian morality, but Marjorie Rosen points out that their birth also coincided with, and hastened, the genesis of the modern woman. In *Popcorn Venus: Women, Movies, and the American Dream*, the question Rosen explores is: To what extent has the modern woman found adequate images of herself on the screen? The answer, Rosen suggests, is less than encouraging.

The first two decades of the century constitute the formative years of the cinema. Those years saw the rise of a new phenomenon: the film star. Women stars were not all cut from the same cloth. Theda Bara's vamp figure was a grotesque variation on the venerable theme of the woman as temptress and destroyer. Mary Pickford, "America's Sweetheart," specialized in playing children and adolescent girls whose combination of pluck and innocence won the hearts of audiences. Bara's vogue was shortlived, however, and audiences refused to let their sweetheart Mary grow up. She was still playing little girls well into her thirties. What both Bara and Pickford may represent, then, is the early cinema's reluctance to deal honestly with the experience of women. Even the greatest filmmaker of that era, D. W. Griffith, saw women largely in terms of Victorian conventions of sentimentality and idealization.

The 1920's and the 1940's represent for Rosen periods of relative, though finally compromised, liberation. The flapper of the 1920's, most eloquently captured in the performances of Clara Bow, spoke for a woman's right to enjoy freedoms comparable to those taken for granted by men. Yet the films assured their audiences that the flapper would ultimately find fulfillment in marriage to the right man, who might turn out to be the flapper's millionaire employer. One value the flapper surely symbolized was social mobility; she might finally respect moral boundaries, but she was undaunted by the boundaries of class.

The relative emancipation of the 1940's arose largely out of the necessities of wartime. Women were required to step out of their stereotypical roles and to assume responsibilities long regarded as masculine. While this period saw the emergence of the pinup girl (Betty Grable, Rita Hayworth) and the bobby soxer, it also paid significant attention to the theme of women living without men. Love might remain the central point of conflict, but the films of stars such as Rosalind Russell and Katharine Hepburn, especially when Hepburn teamed with Spencer Tracy, suggest that self-awareness and professional élan may exist side by side with romance.

The 1930's and 1950's, however, were periods of relative regression and repression. Women suffered disproportionately from the effects of the Great Depression of the 1930's, but neither the reality of their lives nor the generosity of their aspirations found more than intermittent expression on the screen. The period had its share of powerful female stars. Greta Garbo and Marlene Dietrich found new complexity and depth in the figure of the mysterious woman, and Jean Harlow and Mae West embodied in their different ways the woman as subject, rather than object, of desire. Too often, however, the women of Depression-era films appear as sacrificial lambs, willingly denying their own needs for the sake of their men, or as profligate socialites in the social fantasies that were among Hollywood's favorite strategies of denial.

By the 1950's, women had become the numerical majority in American society, but the films of the era reveal a shift away from the relatively autonomous heroine of the 1940's. Whereas in the real world the national divorce rate was climbing precipitately, films were asserting the value of marriage over a career. The woes of the "woman alone" became a common subject, and not even Katharine Hepburn, in such "spinster films" as *The African Queen* and *Summertime*, managed to depart from the premise that the middle-aged unmarried female was merely half a person. One of the great stars of the period was Marilyn Monroe, who is viewed with sympathy by Rosen but is ultimately classified with her many imitators under the heading of "Mammary Madness."

From the perspective of 1973, Rosen's view of what

the 1960's and after represent, while not without hope, remains tentative at best. She can, in speaking of this period, use words such as "revolution" and "renaissance," but she follows them with a question mark. Finally, she is uncertain whether the future holds the promise of breakthrough or the threat of backlash.

Analysis

Proceeding for the most part in chronological order, and organizing her book decade by decade, Rosen tells the story of the changing images of women projected by motion pictures over the years. She works from two assumptions. The first is that art reflects life. To some extent, then, films function as a mirror held up to the face of society. They reflect society's changing images of women over the years under consideration. According to her second assumption, however, life also reflects art. Specifically, people derive from motion pictures perceptions, values, and attitudes that they apply to everyday life. No one should be surprised, she argues, that American women have often been expected, and have themselves often aspired, to live up to the glittering images of women projected on the motion-picture screen.

From one point of view, *Popcorn Venus* is a history of those images, but it is a critical history, not a mere chronicle. The story involves the constant conflict of repression and emancipation. What one sees on the screen also forms complex patterns of interaction with the world beyond the cinema. Rosen juxtaposes her observations about the films of each decade with a sociological and historical analysis of the situation of women. This material is too closely interwoven with her analysis of films to be dismissed as "background." The films and the sociohistorical conditions are meant to be mutually illuminating and, together, to realize the author's purpose: to define woman's position in the decade being examined and to explore the ways in which films reflect and reinforce that position.

The actual content of the book, however, is only in part determined by the author's dominant purpose. Rosen seems compelled to provide, as far as possible, an exhaustive account of the images of women and the careers of important actresses in each of the decades she considers. It is thus not advisable to read the book as a systematic development of organizing ideas. Such ideas serve Rosen primarily as points of departure. If a film or film artist interests her, she will pursue that interest, even if to do so compromises the formal integrity of her argument.

The organization by decades presents problems of its own. It may seem arbitrary, for example, to chop a long and impressive career such as that of Katharine Hepburn up into ten-year segments; one result is that little sense of the continuity of the career, and of what the career in its continuity might suggest about the portrayal of women in the cinema, can emerge. Rosen could certainly reply that some principle of organization is necessary, and all have their limitations. Still, a greater flexibility might have been attempted.

It is always possible to argue with an author's approach to her material, and often the argument is in essence the wish that the author had written a different book. There are different books to be written on the subject of *Popcorn Venus*. In fact, some of those books have already been written. Rosen's is perhaps best understood as an informal critical history of its subject, covering a range of material that others will examine more selectively and developing in broad terms themes that others will refine. When it appeared in 1973, *Popcorn Venus* was a pioneer study. It remains a lively introduction to its subject, and that is perhaps its most important function.

Context

Marjorie Rosen's subject in *Popcorn Venus* is the portrayal of women in motion pictures from the beginnings to early in the 1970's. The subject had not received extended consideration before 1973. Ironically, in that same year, Molly Haskell's *From Reverence to Rape: The Treatment of Women in the Movies*, which covered much of the same material, also appeared.

It is not surprising—although it must have surprised both authors—that these two books appeared in 1973. The women's liberation movement, which had emerged in the 1960's, had reached by 1973 a point of maturity and influence that made it inevitable that attention would turn to the treatment of women in popular culture and in art, and films belong to both categories.

In its exploration of images of women, including such topics as film characters as role models for women in society, *Popcorn Venus* represents a relatively early stage of feminist criticism. Some later feminist critics would look more closely at how masculine values are embedded in basic film structures and strategies. The emergence of a number of woman directors in the years following the publication of *Popcorn Venus* has provided others with their subject, leading to attempts to define what a woman's cinema might be. In addition, some feminist critics have found in the very films Rosen considers more liberating qualities than she acknowledges. Rosen herself has been criticized by some feminists for letting ideological categories narrow her perceptions.

Yet Rosen's belief that life imitates art remains justified. As long as films continue to affect how people perceive reality and how they process their perceptions, what Marjorie Rosen has to say will remain relevant.

Sources for Further Study

Basinger, Jeanine. *A Woman's View: How Hollywood Spoke to Women 1930-1960.* New York: Alfred A. Knopf, 1993. In the "woman's film" the author locates a dialectic of repressions and hidden liberations. Basinger places in a later perspective many of the materials examined by Rosen.

Byars, Jackie. *All That Hollywood Allows: Reading Gender in 1950s Melodrama.* Chapel Hill: University of North Carolina Press, 1991. Byars, like Brandon French, finds in the American films of the 1950's more complexity than Rosen does; many films of the period, Byars argues, challenged sacrosanct gender roles.

Doane, Mary Ann. *The Desire to Desire: The Woman's Film of the 1940s.* Bloomington: Indiana University Press, 1987. Focusing on one of the three decades covered by Basinger, this is an academic, theory-driven, difficult book. It may provide a useful and suggestive alternative to the more empirical approaches of Basinger and Rosen.

French, Brandon. *On the Verge of Revolt: Women in American Films of the Fifties.* New York: Frederick Ungar, 1978. Examining the films of a decade that was, for Rosen, especially depressing from a feminist point of view, French sees things differently: Many films of the decade explore critically the malaise of domesticity and the untenably narrow boundaries of the female role, foreshadowing the feminism of the 1960's.

Haskell, Molly. *From Reverence to Rape: The Treatment of Women in the Movies.* 2d ed. Chicago: University of Chicago Press, 1987. Published almost simultaneously with *Popcorn Venus*, Haskell's book was perceived by a majority of critics as the more psychologically astute and critically sensitive of the two, although some later critics have been disturbed by what they regard as Haskell's cultural conservatism. The second edition brings the story forward to 1987, finding evidence of progress and of unfinished business.

Lesser, Wendy. *His Other Half: Men Looking at Women Through Art.* Cambridge, Mass.: Harvard University Press, 1991. Several essays in this stimulating collection discuss cinema. Lesser challenges what she regards as the "orthodox feminist" treatment of filmmakers such as Alfred Hitchcock and film stars such as Marilyn Monroe and Barbara Stanwyck. Her interests intersect provocatively with those of Rosen.

McCreadie, Marsha. "The Feminists." In *Women on Film: The Critical Eye.* New York: Praeger, 1983. Compares Rosen's work to that of Molly Haskell, who is, in McCreadie's view, more stylistically and referentially sophisticated. Rosen, says McCreadie, has absorbed the standards of the women's liberation movement uncritically and has applied them mechanically.

Modleski, Tania. *The Women Who Knew Too Much: Hitchcock and Feminist Theory.* New York: Methuen, 1988. A close feminist analysis of the work of one of the major filmmakers discussed by Rosen. Modleski's flexible and sophisticated approach illuminates nuances invisible to Rosen.

W. P. Kenney

PORNOGRAPHY AND SILENCE: Culture's Revenge Against Nature

Author: Susan Griffin (1943-)
Type of work: Social criticism
First published: 1981

Form and Content

Susan Griffin's *Pornography and Silence: Culture's Revenge Against Nature* is a provocative and poetic study of the chauvinist mind. The author argues that "the other," whether woman, black, or Jew, has been excluded from society by the split between nature and culture. Pornography is the mythology of this chauvinist mind, which sees in opposites. Through her focus on six lives damaged by pornographic culture, Griffin examines the results of misogyny and racism. The historical figures she spotlights are the American novelist Kate Chopin; Franz Marc, a German painter; the Marquis de Sade, a French pornographer; actress Marilyn Monroe; convicted rapist Laurence Singleton; and Holocaust victim and diarist Anne Frank.

Griffin uses each of these lives as an "emblem" to illustrate some aspect of the chauvinist mind. In "Sacred Images," her first chapter, she examines the lives of Marc and Chopin—two artists who censored themselves because of society's outraged reactions to their honest depictions of sensuality. She regards the female body and sensuality as victims in both pornography and religion, which demand a deadening of feeling. The necessity for exerting control over feeling is explained further in "The Death of the Heart," in which Griffin examines ancient mythology, popular culture, and modern novels that focus on women's death as the price paid for male vitality and freedom. Men's fear that women will trap them, Griffin argues, leads to attempts to silence women through rape, violence, and murder (as she demonstrates through her analysis of the Singleton case).

"The Sacrificial Lamb," which focuses generally on racism and specifically on anti-Semitism, analyzes the ways in which hateful racial caricatures (such as those of evil, materialistic Jews and ignorant, sexually powerful blacks) parallel sexist caricatures. To Griffin, the racist mind and the pornographic mind are identical. Both separate "the other" (nonwhites, women) from prevalent culture and assign them secondary status as part of nature. Although nature is relegated to inferior status, the chauvinist mind fears its power and presence in every human being. Such hatred and fear is woven into every aspect of life, from pornographic images to racist jokes. In "Silence," the necessity of altering one's self so as to be "seen and not heard" for the sake of social, economic, or physical survival is graphically illustrated through stories about fashion models, actresses, and concentration camp victims.

Through her exploration of images from the pornographic mind, Griffin shows how the severe split between male and female, eros and pornography, "the other" and the chauvinist dominate culture in history, film, religion, literature, and art. Her vision is not, however, entirely negative. In her epilogue, she offers hope that those such as Franz Marc and Kate Chopin—those who tried to heal the split self and reconcile nature with culture—will leave records for the world to emulate.

Analysis

Griffin's book is a fine example of a trend in recent feminist writing: She combines academic research with personal reaction and passionate feeling for her subject, as does Rachel Blau DuPlessis in *The Pink Guitar* (1990). Her examples are far-reaching and eclectic. Compassionate analysis of six lives damaged by pornographic culture illustrates her points; she also studies the chauvinist mind in examples as diverse as the classics, films from the Hollywood mainstream and underground, mythology, religion, high fashion, punk rock, and traditional writers such as Alfred, Lord Tennyson, Algernon Swinburne, William Faulkner, and Edgar Allan Poe. Here she relates the victimization of the subject and of the pornographer, examining the psychological and social—as well as sexual—dynamics of the situation. An important aspect of these dynamics is the degradation of innocence: Through cynicism and "the death of the heart," pornography turns a human being with a soul into an object.

Griffin acknowledges the immense power that pornographic images and thinking have in Western culture, but she does not pose her work as an argument for censorship. Instead, she challenges the basic assumptions people make about erotica, about sexism, and about racism. She equates pornography not with any one legalistic definition, but with a fear of bodily knowledge and the desire to silence eros. Pornography is not about erotic desire or the life of the body, but about fear and control of that fear. Her definition of pornography draws considerably from sexual psychology and from close analysis of actual pornographic writings and films. Griffin's approach is broadly interdisciplinary, crossing boundaries between traditional divisions of "academic" and "popular." She uses not only the analyses of psychologists such as Sigmund Freud, Carl Gustav Jung and R. D. Laing but also first-person accounts and quotations from Holocaust survivors, pornographic actors, and commentary on excerpts from Adolf Hitler's *Mein Kampf.*

This work does not fit neatly into a particular category; it balances research with powerful poetic writing and commentary. As a poet, Griffin discusses the fact that women's bodies in pornography are used as symbols, analyzing the "madonna/whore" dichotomy demanded of women by religion as one example. She finds symbols of her own to represent her major categories of discussion: the heart (love and desire), the triangle (Judaism), the circle (inclusiveness), and the rose (beauty).

"Sacred Images" delineates the difference between the erotic and the pornographic. Marc's early paintings and Chopin's *The Awakening* (1899) show the influence of two strains of the Romantic movement. The former refuses to acknowledge the existence of eros and the importance of nature; nature becomes feared (as in Lord Byron and Friedrich von Schiller) as "darkness" or "the other." The other strain of Romanticism desired political and sexual freedom and a celebration of nature (as in William Blake and Elizabeth Barrett Browning). Griffin shows how women came to be equated with nature and to be seen as threatening to their "opposite"—culture.

Women's sexuality affords only the negative power of seductively destroying a man's soul (particularly in Griffin's reading of biblical and mythological themes). Sexual knowledge brings men down to earth; they are made aware of and vulnerable to the true inseparability of culture and nature, spirit and matter. Control of emotion and impulse—represented by nature—has become increasingly important. Such falsity is expressed, Griffin writes, in the designs of high fashion, in punk rock's nihilism, in stereotypical religious images, and in pornography itself. Like many feminist texts, such as Margaret Atwood's *Surfacing* (1972) and Marilyn French's *The Women's Room* (1977), Griffin's work shows how both sexes have been terribly damaged by the elevation of culture over nature.

In "The Death of the Heart," Griffin uses Euripides' *Iphigenia* and the Marquis de Sade's *Justine* to show the difference between a great tragedy and pornography: feeling. Each work focuses on the sacrifice of a young woman, yet *Justine* kills emotion and numbs the reader to brutality. Pornography, Griffin writes, is essentially cruel and lacking in soul. Culture outside pornography has demanded "tough" heroes such as Norman Mailer and Marlon Brando. She discusses how arguments defending pornography are merely a reflection of the pornographic mind, decrying the idea that males' need for catharsis must be met because violence is a "natural" instinct.

Griffin examines the power of images, arguing that because pornography's link to violence has not been indisputably proved, it still cannot be discounted. She points out that pornography is a sadistic art, an act of degradation, using graphic accounts from former pornographic actress Linda Lovelace's autobiography as examples of female submissiveness taken one step further. The last section in this chapter examines the transformative power of illusion on culture, and its role in creating the violence and fear felt by many women and children: schoolyard humiliation, sexist jokes, sexual harassment, battering.

The Third Reich's official racism and sexism is described in "The Sacrificial Lamb." Racism and pornographic sensibility are equated as similar "mass delusional forms." These delusions force the chauvinist to be trapped inside his fears. Such fears about "the other"—in this case, the Jew—leads to dehumanization of both victor and victim. The fascist persona demands "hardness" and brutality, a more extreme manifestation of the "toughness" required of men in dominant culture.

Griffin notes, in "Silence," that a terrible danger lies in women's belief in the pornographer's message. She shows the self's split between the false, socially acceptable one and the lost true one. The schism leads to a numbness, a sleepwalking quality shown by damaged women such as Marilyn Monroe. The horrific and pornographic *The Story of O* is used to show a woman's transformation into first a symbol of conquered nature and then a symbol of nothingness.

The twisted fruits of oppositional thinking—racism, sexism, pornography, and violence—are brilliantly and passionately depicted in this book. Although it analyzes and criticizes aspects of society and the literature it produces, *Pornography and Silence* is deeply personal. Its style is passionate and poetic, sometimes repeating a word or phrase as an incantation. Griffin's vision is of a world in which people choose beauty over silence, in which knowledge of eros gives back to people their capacity for culture, for expression, and for joy.

Context

Pornography and Silence is unusual in its treatment of a subject long debated by women's rights advocates. Feminists disagree on the question of censoring pornography because of its negative effects on women and because of the idea of freedom of speech. Griffin puts these questions in a larger context, believing that if people work for a more egalitarian society, pornography will no longer be seen as a necessary evil by so many people.

The work's unique style is one of its most important strengths. It is an early example of feminist criticism that links poetic writing and personal approach with academic research. Although it conveys a protest against the horrific price paid for "culture's revenge against nature," Griffin's tone is elegiac rather than angry or bitter. She attempts to get inside the mind of the chauvinist and to see his fears and humiliations with compassion and understanding. Griffin also calls readers to rethink their most basic assumptions about beauty, fashion, classic literature, and film. Seeing these genres as productions of a pornographic and deeply fearful society explains the hateful messages against women that they spread.

The book is sometimes difficult to read—not because of its style, which is deeply poetic and moving—but because of the graphic descriptions of dehumanizing pornographic images. Griffin ends with a hopeful image of a "seventh life," a life that transcends narrow and hurtful stereotypes and lives forever. Her breadth of vision and originality make *Pornography and Silence* essential reading for those who are interested in feminist analyses of pornography.

Sources for Further Study

Faludi, Susan. *Backlash: The Undeclared War Against American Women*. New York: Crown, 1991. A thorough and readable study of how feminism came to be seen as a scapegoat for a broad spectrum of problems in American society. Faludi examines popular culture, including fashion, film, magazines, television, and the men's movement, to trace the backlash against the movement for women's equality.

Greer, Germaine. *The Female Eunuch*. London: Paladin Books, 1971. Greer examines ways in which women can find motives and causes for political and social action through reassessing themselves and through questioning basic elements of education and socialization. The provocative quotations inserted into the main text and the thorough footnotes are helpful.

Griffin, Susan. *Woman and Nature: The Roaring Inside Her*. New York: Harper & Row, 1980. Written in a style similar to that of *Pornography and Silence*, this "long prose poem" focuses on the oppression of women. Griffin links the exploitation of women with the victimization of the earth; both are sustaining forces and are often victims of male revenge.

Showalter, Elaine, ed. *The New Feminist Criticism: Essays on Women, Literature, and Theory*. New York: Pantheon Books, 1985. Sections on feminism and the academy, feminist criticism of literature and society, and women's writing make this essential reading for those interested in understanding feminism and its influence on reading and writing. Very thorough bibliography.

Steinem, Gloria. *Revolution from Within: A Book of Self-Esteem*. Boston: Little, Brown, 1992. Research on factors that affect self-esteem, combined with personal stories from Steinem and other women. Steinem examines education, the family, the body, and ways of working for positive change.

Michelle L. Jones

POSSESSING THE SECRET OF JOY

Author: Alice Walker (1944-)
Type of work: Novel
Type of plot: Social realism
Time of plot: The last half of the twentieth century
Locale: California and a village in Africa
First published: 1992

Principal characters:

Tashi, an Olinkan woman who undergoes the genital and facial mutilation traditional to her people
Adam, Tashi's American husband
Olivia, Adam's sister
Lisette, a refined French woman who becomes Adam's lover
Benny (Bentu Moraga), Tashi's partially retarded son
Pierre, Lisette and Adam's son
M'Lissa, the old woman who brought Tashi into the world
Mbati, a young woman who becomes Tashi's spiritual daughter
Raya, an American therapist
Mzee (Old Man), Lisette's uncle, a therapist
Dura, Tashi's older sister

Form and Content

Possessing the Secret of Joy, which Alice Walker dedicates "with tenderness and respect to the blameless Vulva," is divided into twenty-one parts; each is the reflection of one of the characters. The story is prefaced by a quote from Walker's novel *The Color Purple* (1982), and the last section is told by Tashi's soul after she has been shot by the firing squad. The sections are not in chronological order, and many relate African legends and myths that the characters are learning and that help them to explain genital mutilation and the ancient, ancestral tribal practices that are the heritage of the Olinkans. Tashi finally understands and identifies with her people, who are simple and natural and actually possess the secret of joy, which enables them to survive the suffering and humiliation inflicted upon them.

Although the story is told by Tashi, Adam, and Olivia when they are well-advanced in middle age and are quite white-headed, the narrative goes back to the time when the missionaries arrived from America. When Adam and Olivia first see Tashi, she is still crying inwardly and outwardly because of the death that morning of her sister Dura, who has bled to death following the female initiation ceremony. The implications and circumstances of Dura's death and Tashi's own circumcision are gradually remembered by Tashi with the help of Olivia, who remains the sister of her heart; Adam; and her therapists.

As a young adult, Tashi has run away to go to M'Lissa and submit herself to the cutting of tribal marks on her face and to the female initiation ceremony, which is usually done at age eleven. In spite of the protests of the missionaries, Tashi wants to demonstrate her loyalty to the practices of the Olinkan people. Adam, who is in love with her, follows her to the distant Mbele camp and brings her home to the Olinkan village. He demonstrates his support by having his own face cut with tribal marks on the day before their wedding and return to America for the reunion with Celie and Shug, which takes place in the final scenes of *The Color Purple*.

Prior to this, Tashi and Adam have defied the Olinkan customs and have made love in the fields, loving in the way that is the greatest taboo of all—but that brings the most pleasure—in which Adam caresses her clitoris with his tongue. Tashi receives as much pleasure as Adam does and thus experiences the secret joy of total but forbidden sexual pleasure.

Living in California, Tashi frequently checks herself into the Waverly Psychiatric Hospital. She suffers from the odor of her mutilation, the difficulty of urination and menstruation, and the impossibility of sexual intercourse. She has undergone the removal of her entire genital area; the remaining sides of her vulva have been stitched together, leaving only a very small opening. The tendons in her upper legs have also been harmed, so she walks with a shuffle, as do the other Olinkan women. Because of her humiliation and suffering, Tashi constantly wants to mutilate herself, and once she cuts rings about her own ankles.

Her first breakthrough in therapy comes when she and Adam are in Switzerland visiting Lisette's uncle. In the security of his villa, she responds to this old man's love and sympathy. One day, Tashi passes out while watching some films of his trips to Africa. The scene that disturbs her shows young girls lying on the ground waiting to be circumcised while a large fighting cock walks proudly about. For hours after she is revived, Tashi paints a large rooster again and again until she is able to recall that at Dura's death M'Lissa had thrown her severed clitoris to the chickens. For the first time, Tashi is able to acknowledge to herself that Dura was, in effect, murdered as she finally remembers the circumstances that she observed as a young child hiding in the grass outside the hut where the mutilation took place.

Back in California, Tashi is able to express to her therapist, Raya, her new understanding of Dura's death and of what has been done to her. Raya relates to Tashi's pain, and she attempts to show her sympathy by having her gums mutilated to help her understand pain and by coming to Olinka to be present at her execution.

Lisette's presence in Adam's life also causes her pain, yet after Lisette has died of stomach cancer, Tashi begins to recognize that she had been sincere in wanting to understand and to help Tashi as well as Adam. Lisette and Adam met in the Olinkan village in the hut of an old man who was refused care by everyone in the village because he lost control of his young wife, who ran away and drowned herself after he cut her open with a hunting knife so that they could have intercourse. His act was acceptable behavior, and her rebellion threatened the web of society, of life itself. Lisette has grown up in a different culture and is profoundly affected by this story. Much later, she confesses to her son Pierre that her refusal to marry is the result of having actually known a young woman who ran away from her husband and was forced to return.

When Pierre first attempts to visit Tashi, she stones him and he runs away. His gentle persistence and his extensive knowledge of the history of genital mutilation and of the ancient traditions of her people finally convince Tashi to accept his love and support.

Tashi goes to the Olinkan village in order to confront M'Lissa, the woman who has killed her sister. She finds the old woman, now greatly revered by the Olinkan people, in bed. Tashi bathes her body and listens to her tell of her life and of her own suffering; Tashi actually learns to relate to her suffering and to realize that she can forgive even this woman whom she has hated and resented for so long. M'Lissa tells her that it is traditional for a well-appreciated *tsunga* to be murdered and then burned by someone whom she has circumcised. In placing a pillow over her face, Tashi is simply carrying out what the old woman expects of her.

The penultimate section of the novel is a letter signed "Tashi Evelyn Johnson, Reborn soon to be Deceased," to Lisette. In it, Tashi explains that she is now ready to face the firing squad and looks forward to being Lisette's friend in heaven. She explains that she has already come to be her friend through knowing her son.

In the last section, Tashi's spirit recalls the moment when she was shot and the fact that Adam, Olivia, Benny, Pierre, Raya, and Mbati were all holding a huge banner that said *RESISTANCE* IS THE SECRET OF JOY!

Analysis

Walker's novel is about love, forgiveness, and self-acceptance. Tashi experiences physical and emotional pain so intense that it is almost inconceivable, yet she resists self-destruction and finds inner peace.

Tashi explains in her letter to Lisette that even though he was more progressive than most preachers of color, Adam's sermons always focused on the suffering of Jesus and thus tended to exclude the suffering of others. She wanted her own suffering to be recognized and acknowledged. Ironically, it is Pierre, the son of Adam and Lisette, who has submerged himself into the mystery of her suffering and whose life is dedicated to destroying the suffering caused by torture. He has helped her to understand herself, her mother, M'Lissa, and all the women who have been crucified as well as those who are still cringing before the might and weapons of torturers. In having found this self-knowledge, she is able to recognize and acknowledge suffering and to accept death without anxiety.

Pierre also has been kind enough to befriend and patient enough to teach Benny, his retarded half brother. With his help, Benny will be able to survive in a cruel and indifferent world. He is also able to help Benny find a way to deal with what is happening to his mother on a level that he can understand in his own simple terms.

Both boys work with Adam in caring for the many AIDS patients who are crowded into one floor of the Olinkan prison where Tashi has been held throughout her trial. Working with these suffering men, women, and children who patiently wait for death with animal-like acceptance helps Adam to understand Tashi's suffering and his own. One young man thinks Adam is a priest and, as he dies a miserable and painful death, confesses to Adam that he has killed the monkeys whose kidneys were to be used to grow the cultures that had produced the vaccines that spread the AIDS virus. Adam learns from his suffering, the suffering of the girls whose infection was spread by the unclean knife when they were circumcised, and Tashi's suffering that there is no greater hell for humans to fear than the one on Earth. He accepts himself as a man of God and as a human man who has been a loving friend to Tashi. At last, he also realizes that he has always depended on his sister Olivia to be his feeling side and that he is now able to feel and to suffer as himself.

Context

In an interview with Pratibha Parmar, the coauthor of her book *Warrior Marks: Female Genital Mutilation and the Sexual Blinding of Women* (1993), Alice Walker makes it very clear that *Possessing the Secret of Joy* is a protest novel. She wants to enlighten women to ways in which women in all parts of the world are rather routinely mutilated and to the fact that pain that is done to women is often overlooked because women can accept pain. Walker uses as an example her own visual mutilation, which occurred when she was eight. She was blinded in one eye when her brother shot her, causing her pain, humiliation, and serious medical problems. Yet her parents always dismissed the incident and referred to it as "Alice's accident."

Alice Walker uses a portion of the proceeds from her novel to support projects designed to educate women about various types of mutilation, and she travels to all parts of the world to encourage women to take a political and moral stand against such practices.

In the novel, Pierre is a sensitive, well-informed, and dedicated feminist who possesses the secret of joy in making his life's work the resistance of such harmful practices. He studies the traditional patriarchal attitudes that have created the practices and have kept them alive, and even more important, he lovingly shares the lessons he learns with Tashi and intends to continue to share them with other women.

The novel also makes an important statement about the spread of AIDS and the suffering that AIDS brings to women and children as well as to men. The compassionate care that Adam, Pierre, Benny, and Olivia give to those who are dying from AIDS also encourages women to take a political and moral stand.

The bonding between women and the mutual support and encouragement that women provide for one another is clearly shown not only between Tashi and Olivia but also in the relationships that Raya, Mbati, and Lisette have with Tashi.

Lisette is a wonderful example of a strong and independent woman who values sexual pleasure even in childbirth and who follows the example of her grandmother in refusing to be intimidated by traditional social expectations. She educates her son by precept and example to be strong in his resistance against traditional masculine beliefs and practices that do not value and respect women and women's right to education, information, and independence.

Sources for Further Study

Barker-Benfield, G. J. *The Horrors of the Half-Known Life: Male Attitudes Toward Women and Sexuality in Nineteenth-Century America*. New York: Harper & Row, 1976. Explains the practice of female circumcision in the United States and the circumstances that allowed it to occur.

El Dareer, Asma. *Woman, Why Do You Weep?* London: Zed Press, 1982. The author is one of the women Alice Walker quotes frequently in *Warrior Marks*, and this work is recommended at the end of *Possessing the Secret of Joy*.

Kemp, Yakini. Review of *Warrior Marks*, by Alice Walker and Pratibha Parmar. *Belles Lettres* 8 (Fall, 1992): 57. This insightful review describes the novel as a poetic and powerful condemnation of the practice of female genital mutilation.

Lightfoot-Klein, Hanny. *Prisoners of Ritual: An Odyssey into Female Genital Circumcision in Africa*. New York: Haworth Press, 1989. This book explains that those who practice female genital circumcision are, generally speaking, kept ignorant of its real dangers, which include the breakdown of the spirit and the body as well as the spread of disease.

Walker, Alice. *In Search of Our Mothers' Gardens: Womanist Prose*. San Diego: Harcourt Brace Jovanovich, 1983.

______________. *Living By the Word: Selected Writings, 1973-1987*. San Diego: Harcourt Brace Jovanovich, 1988. These essays enable the reader to get to know Alice Walker as a person, to learn more about her own visual mutilation, and to follow her interest in fighting all practices that undervalue women.

Walker, Alice, and Pratibha Parmar. *Warrior Marks: Female Genital Mutilation and the Sexual Blinding of Women*. New York: Harcourt Brace, 1993. Records the story of Walker and Parmar's collaboration in making a film about female genital mutilation and about women they interviewed in Africa who have been circumcised, who have had their daughters circumcised, and who actually perform the circumcisions. Contains many photographs and an excellent bibliography.

Constance M. Fulmer

PRAISESONG FOR THE WIDOW

Author: Paule Marshall (1929-   )
Type of work: Novel
Type of plot: Psychological realism
Time of plot: 1976
Locale: The Caribbean islands of Grenada and Carriacou, Tatem Island (off the South Carolina coast), and Brooklyn
First published: 1983

Principal characters:

Avatara (Avey) Johnson, a sixty-four-year-old widow who has lost touch with her African cultural roots

Great-Aunt Cuney, an old woman who rejects institutions that enslave black people with empty standards of behavior and expression

Lebert Joseph, the proprietor of a rum shop in Grenada

Marion Johnson, Avey's youngest daughter

Form and Content

When Avey was a girl, her Aunt Cuney called her to pass the cultural heritage from one generation to the next. Aunt Cuney would take Avey to the Landing and tell the story about the arrival of a shipload of Ibo slaves. At first, Avey answered her calling and told her brothers, but once her trips to Tatem Island stopped and after her adult attention shifted to achieving the American Dream, Avey sublimated what she had learned. The breach between Avey and her cultural heritage widened, and Avey stopped identifying with the struggles and concerns of other African Americans. She, along with her husband Jay, focused attention on material possessions and social status. Avey wrapped herself in her mink stole, attended social functions with her husband, and after his fatal stroke took Caribbean cruises with her friends. Voyages on a luxury liner and then on a flimsy schooner finally take Avey on a difficult yet successful journey back to her cultural origins.

During one voyage, aboard the *Bianca Pride*, Avey begins having troubling dreams about Aunt Cuney, and she remembers the early years of her marriage when she and her husband, though poor, were happy. She cannot recognize her image in mirrors, and the rich foods that are served, especially a peach parfait à la Versailles, are nauseating. Avey tries to regain her composure by seeking solitude. Despite her efforts, she cannot escape the crass materialism of the shipboard environment, which becomes overwhelmingly repulsive. She is horrified and outraged by one symbol of American society, a skeletal old man wearing red and white striped trunks and a blue visor who tugs at her skirt and invites her to have a seat beside him. Neither her friends' protests nor the loss of the $1,500 fare for the cruise are enough to dissuade Avey from her decision to leave the ship and return to New York.

Avey thinks that she will be able to return to the comfort and familiarity of life in North White Plains. Her return is delayed because she arrives in Grenada too late to catch a plane that leaves once a day for New York City. While determining where she will spend the night, Avey notices a crowd of people along a wharf waiting for boats to take them to a place about which she knows nothing. Avey does not want to be among these strangers, who speak a patois she cannot understand. Although Avey feels out of place, a man mistakes her for a woman named Ida. She is like these people even though she does not recognize her relationship to them. The people are Carriacou out-islanders who are participating in the annual Carriacou Excursion. This tradition foreshadows Avey's communal and personal journey back to her cultural origins.

Avey spends a restless night in a hotel dreaming about her husband's preoccupation with working long hours to make enough money to provide for his family and her suspicions that he was having affairs with the white women who worked with him. The next day, Avey awakes feeling as though her mind has become a tabula rasa. After showering, she puts on a wrinkled dress, half combs her hair, does not wear makeup, and leaves her watch in the bathroom. Gradually, Avey is shedding her concern about possessions and outward appearances.

Avey leaves the hotel and walks aimlessly until she enters a seedy but pleasant rum shop, where she meets the shop's ancient proprietor, Lebert Joseph. Initially, he is uncomfortable with Avey's strangeness; however, after some faltering attempts at communication, his attitude softens, and Lebert shares his family history with Avey. He tells her that people participate in the excursion because they need to relax, celebrate, and, most important, give remembrance to the "Long-time People." Avey tries to leave, but she is tired from her long walk and her troubling dreams. She begins to tell Lebert about her recent experiences, but she cannot tell him everything. The pain is too recent. Somehow, Lebert understands her unspoken words, and he invites Avey to accompany him to Carriacou that day.

The boat ride makes Avey ill. The vessel is not sturdy; people are packed on board, and the motion of the sea makes Avey lean with her head over the railing so that she can disgorge whatever is making her nauseated. Old women soothe Avey. At Carriacou, other women bathe and feed Avey until she senses physical renewal. When she witnesses the dancing, the songs, and the rituals of the Big Drum and the Beg Pardon, Avey remembers her cultural past. She recognizes the lamentations of the sorrow songs whose "source had to be the heart, the bruised still-bleeding innermost chamber of the collective heart."

Avey returns to America, but not to New York. She goes back to Tatem Island. She has been called to remember her past that had been lost in a quest for material possessions and social status. After her trip to Carriacou, Avey determines that "at least twice a week . . . she would lead them, grandchildren and visitors alike, in a troop over to the Landing," and she would tell them about the Ibos who came in slave ships.

Analysis

Avatara is the name Avey's Aunt Cuney chose for her. Avatara has been called to pass along the culture from one generation to the next by Cuney, who has performed that role. Cuney appears in Avatara's dreams to call her back to a remembrance of her ancestors. Marshall writes the story of Avatara's movement away from and back to her cultural roots by using several techniques. She divides the novel into four parts to describe the stages of Avatara's journey, and she uses images and symbols that are peculiar to the feminine creative experience. While Avatara progresses from one stage to the next, Marshall recounts Avatara's dreams, which are often detailed memories of past experiences that may have been either personal or communal. These memories have relevance to the present when Avatara notices the resemblances between the ceremonial rituals she witnessed as a child and those she observes at Carriacou. Marshall's references to literary selections written by black writers from the United States are apt expressions of black experiences that occurred on slave ships in the Caribbean and in the collective consciousness of black people regardless of their geographical location.

In the first section, "Runagate," Avatara is escaping her bondage to the materialism represented by the luxury liner, the *Bianca Pride* (*bianca* is Italian for "white"). She has been dreaming of her trips to the Landing with Cuney. There was a serious ceremonial air about the journeys past the woods, the church, and the homes that held the histories of black people in America, and Cuney would take Avatara to the place where the stories begins. Cuney wore two belts, as the other old women did when they went out. One belt cinched the waist of their skirts, and the other belt was "strapped low around the hips like the belt for a sword or a gun holster." People believed that this belt gave the women strength.

"Sleeper's Awake" and "Lave Tete" are the second and third sections of the novel. The Ibos knew that black people would suffer in America, so they returned to Africa. For thirty years, Avatara has avoided thinking about the connections between her life and those of black people who suffered during civil rights demonstrations or those of women who endured abusive marital relationships. Avatara's acceptance of middle-class American life has separated her from her people, and that separation has manifested itself in psychological discomfiture and physical illness. She must awaken from an anesthetized existence, but before she can be reborn, Avatara's body, soul, and mind must be cleansed.

The voyage to Carriacou upsets Avatara, and she begins vomiting. More than a reaction to the schooner's movements, Avatara is suffering from the pains of her new self's birth. Avatara's body is racked with waves of nausea. "She might have fallen overboard were it not for the old women. They tried cushioning her as much as possible from the repeated shocks of the turbulence." After a while, Avatara is left alone in the schooner's small deckhouse, where she is reminded of the accommodations slaves had during the Middle Passage. Her suffering pales by comparison.

The setting in this novel is dominated by an image of water that functions in several ways. Water is the vehicle for Avatara's journey aboard the cruise ship and later on the schooner that takes her to Carriacou. Water and boat transportation are central to the experiences of black people. Ibos came to America on a slave ship. Out-islanders traveled to Carriacou on boats. Blacks in New York took an annual excursion up the Hudson River. Water is also the symbol of spiritual renewal. The Ibos walked the water to return to their homeland, and Avatara's experience on the schooner is the sign that a new life is coming into the world.

The fourth section of the novel, "The Beg Pardon," brings Avatara to an understanding of how the past and the present relate to each other. Just as she remembered going on the excursion up the Hudson River when she was a girl, Avatara recognizes furniture and table settings that remind her of ceremonial rituals that defined her past. The Carriacou Tramp reminded her of the Ring Shout that took place in the black church on Tatem Island. Furnishings, food, physical movement, and the act of remembering form a link between past and present that completes Avatara's sense of self and brings her into a community that is complex in its relationships between past and present and different geographical locations but simple in the symbol of a circle that encompasses all.

Marshall's story is about the creative process of birth, renewal, and remembrance. Black women are singularly significant in this process because they fulfill the role of passing the cultural heritage from one generation to another. Although men such as Lebert Joseph influence this process, the strength to perform this task is generated in a community of women. Even though Lebert invites Avatara on the excursion, when she begins to suffer agonizing and massive contractions, he can only wait anxiously by the door while the old women make her comfortable. Marshall's emphasis on Avatara's calling and on the help she gets from black women points to the importance of black women to the black cultural heritage.

Context

The feminist movement of the 1970's and its demands for social equality increased an awareness of and interest in novels written by women. Coming after the civil rights and black power movements, this increased feminism led to the publication of novels that focused on the experiences of African American women. In the 1980's, several novels written by black women demonstrated that islands of black feminine existence were not separate from an understanding of the communal African American experience. Female-centered novels such as Alice Walker's *The Color Purple* (1982), Gloria Naylor's *The Women of Brewster Place* (1982), and Toni Morrison's *Beloved* (1987) underscore the significance of women to the black community. These novels also show that there is a community of women who understand one another, who protect one another, and who, like Avey, assume the responsibility of teaching black children about their cultural heritage. These authors are models for other African American women, such as Bebe Moore Campbell (*Your Blues Ain't Like Mine*, 1992), Thulani Davis (*1959*, 1992), and Rita Dove (*Through the Ivory Gate*, 1992).

Sources for Further Study

Christian, Barbara T. "Ritualistic Process and the Structure of Paule Marshall's *Praisesong for the Widow*." *Callaloo* 6 (Spring/Summer, 1983): 74-84. The article focuses on the rituals of naming and "tribal" ceremonies that recall Avey Johnson to reaffirm the essential connection between the individual and the community.

Pettis, Joyce. "Self Definition and Redefinition in Paule Marshall's *Praisesong for the Widow*." In *Perspectives of Black Popular Culture*, edited by Harry B. Shaw. Bowling Green, Ohio: Bowling Green State University Popular Press, 1990. Through a literal and a metaphorical journey, Avey Johnson becomes a "new woman" in the canon of African American literature, who rejects materialistic values and replaces them with a renewed sense of her connection to her African past.

Scarpa, Giulia. " 'Couldn't They Have Done Differently?' Caught in the Web of Race, Gender, and Class: Paule Marshall's *Praisesong for the Widow*." *World Literature Written in English* 29 (Fall, 1989): 94-104. Points out that reminiscences allow Avey Johnson to revive a past that had been overshadowed by cultural and personal sacrifices she had made while imitating the living standards of a homogenized American society.

Waxman, Barbara Frey. "The Widow's Journey to Self and Roots: Aging and Society in Paule Marshall's *Praisesong for the Widow*." *Frontiers* 9, no. 3 (1987): 94-99. A "young-old" widow completes a self-purification ritual through which she integrates body and soul and identifies with her ethnic heritage.

Wilentz, Gay. "Towards a Spiritual Middle Passage Back: Paule Marshall's Diasporic Vision in *Praisesong for the Widow*." *Obsidian II* 5, no. 3 (Winter, 1990): 1-21. A varied treatment of the effect of females, particularly female ancestors, who motivate Avey Johnson to reconcile her African and American selves and assume the woman's role of passing on stories and cultural traditions to her daughter and a wide community of African American children.

Judith E. B. Harmon

PRIDE AND PREJUDICE

Author: Jane Austen (1775-1817)
Type of work: Novel
Type of plot: Domestic realism
Time of plot: The early nineteenth century
Locale: Hertfordshire, Derbyshire, Kent, and London, England
First published: 1813

Principal characters:

Elizabeth Bennet, the protagonist
Fitzwilliam Darcy, an aristocrat and one of the most eligible men in English society
Mr. Bennet, Elizabeth's father
Mrs. Bennet, his wife, who embarrasses the more intelligent members of her family
Jane Bennet, Elizabeth's older sister
Charles Bingley, Darcy's friend
Charlotte Lucas, Elizabeth's best friend
William Collins, a clergyman who marries Charlotte Lucas
George Wickham, a military officer who runs away with Elizabeth's youngest sister, Lydia

Form and Content

Pride and Prejudice is a novel about marriage. The author's purpose is to make it possible for her two most interesting characters, Elizabeth Bennet and Fitzwilliam Darcy, to be united. In order to accomplish the author's purpose, they must overcome both external obstacles and the personal flaws suggested in the title of the book. Although he is attracted to Elizabeth, the proud aristocrat Darcy is prejudiced against her family because of their social inferiority, which is evident to him in the folly of Mrs. Bennet and her younger daughters, as well as in the fact that the family has a kinsman in trade. Elizabeth's own pride is injured when she overhears Darcy's slighting comment about her; her resulting prejudice is confirmed by George Wickham's lies and by her own discovery that Darcy had advised Charles Bingley not to proceed with his courtship of Jane Bennet. If the lovers are finally to come together, not only must Wickham be exposed and Jane be reunited with Bingley, but also both Elizabeth and Darcy must become wiser, so that in the future their judgments will be based not on pride or on prejudice, but on reason.

In form, it has been noted, *Pride and Prejudice* is highly dramatic. Each character is introduced with a short summary much like those found in playscripts. The story proceeds through dialogue, with Austen herself functioning as an onstage commentator, summing up what has happened since the last scene or adding stage directions; for example, exits, entrances, or displays of grief or anger. *Pride and Prejudice* even falls into five segments, or acts, as do the witty comedies of manners by William Congreve, Oliver Goldsmith, and Richard Brinsley Sheridan on which it is probably modeled.

The first dozen or so chapters of the work, like the first act of a play, are devoted to exposition. The Bennets are introduced; it is established that the five girls of the family, as well as their friend Charlotte Lucas, need husbands; and two eligible single men, Darcy and Bingley, appear on the scene.

In the second segment of the novel, two more unmarried men, William Collins and George Wickham, enter the lives of the Bennets. Wickham tells Elizabeth that Darcy has behaved villainously toward him. Collins, who would have married either of the two older Bennet girls, finds himself a wife in the person of Charlotte Lucas.

In the third act, while visiting Charlotte at her new home, Elizabeth once again encounters Darcy, whose aunt is Collins' patron. To Elizabeth's surprise, Darcy proposes; after she has haughtily turned him down, Elizabeth discovers that she has wronged her suitor and admits to herself that she does indeed love him.

The proof of Darcy's character comes in the final two sections of the novel. When Lydia Bennet elopes with Wickham, Darcy chooses to help the Bennet family avoid disgrace. He finds the couple and forces Wickham to marry Lydia. In the process, he befriend's Elizabeth's tradesman uncle and revises his assumption that merit can be found only in the landed gentry. Like all traditional comedies, the novel ends with appropriate marriages. Jane weds Bingley, and Elizabeth is at last united with Darcy.

Analysis

It has often been pointed out that Jane Austen's novels deal only with the world of which she had first-hand knowledge. They are set in the ballrooms, the drawing rooms, the bedrooms, and the gardens where, like the ladies in her books, she spent her life. Her books do not reflect the political turmoil of her time, revolution and conquest on the Continent, fears of revolution in Great Britain. If her works are limited in scope, however, they are not without serious import. Austen's methods are those of the satirist, her subject is society, and her preoccupation is the creation of an effective family unit through marriage.

As Austen shows so clearly in *Pride and Prejudice*, unsuitable marriages lead only to unhappiness and social instability. After discovering that his wife is incapable of comprehending anything he says, Mr. Bennet has stopped trying to communicate with her. A man of his reserved and scholarly nature can adjust easily to isolation from his family, and Mrs. Bennet is too scatter-brained to suspect that something may be missing from her relationship with her husband. It is the Bennet children who suffer most from the ill-conceived marriage of their parents. Three of the five Bennet daughters turn out badly. Mary Bennet is a pedant without intellectual gifts; Kitty Bennet, a flirtatious fool; and Lydia, a girl so unthinking that she runs off with the first plausible man who comes along, thereby disgracing her family and destroying the possibility of any other marriage or even, if she remains unmarried, her acceptance in respectable society. As Mr. Bennet admits, Lydia's actions are in part the consequence of his paternal neglect, but that in turn is the result of his marrying unwisely, without regard for his future wife's suitability in temperament, character, and intelligence.

Austen supports her argument that a bad marriage is worse than no marriage at all with two additional examples. Collins marries Charlotte only because, as a clergyman, he needs a respectable wife; she marries him because, at twenty-seven, she is becoming desperate. The result is not surprising. When Elizabeth goes to visit the newlyweds, she finds that Charlotte has developed a daily routine that places her as far away from her husband as possible. If Charlotte's situation proves how miserable a marriage of convenience can be, what happens to Lydia and Wickham shows the folly of allowing mere sexual attraction to govern one's decision about a partner for life. Forced to marry Lydia, Wickham soon tires of her, and before long her affection for him has also died. Moreover, since neither of them is capable of planning for the future, Lydia and Wickham live unsettled lives, frequently moving, constantly plagued by financial difficulties, surviving only through the aid of their prosperous relatives.

Thus, the author shows the unhappy consequences of unwise marriages. Nevertheless, what Austen sees as essential for a happy union is not equality of either fortune or caste. Although they live comfortably, the Bennets do not have the wealth that both Bingley and Darcy possess, and while Mr. Bennet is a member of the gentry, he ranks well below the aristocracy. Jane and Bingley are both easy-going and tolerant people, however, while Elizabeth and Darcy share the same incisive intelligence and strength of will. What Austen seems to be saying is surprisingly modern: that the best basis for marriage is a love based on mutual respect and shown in an easy, comfortable companionship.

Context

Jane Austen's heroines have long been admired. Like Elizabeth, they are all intelligent, independent, and strong-willed. Nevertheless, all of them have flaws. The imaginative young Catherine Morland of *Northanger Abbey* (1817) tries to make a Gothic novel out of ordinary life, while in *Emma* (1815), the forceful title character, Emma Woodhouse, is so determined to do good that she ignores the wishes of others, with unfortunate results. The deficiencies of Austen's heroines, however, are defects not of character, but of judgment. When, in the course of the novels, they come to know themselves better and to see others more clearly, their inherent virtues are strengthened by wisdom.

With the growth of feminist criticism, however, have come new questions about Austen's intentions, especially where her heroines are concerned. While there is still general agreement that Elizabeth Bennet is the most admirable, as well as the most appealing, of her female characters, some critics argue that Elizabeth's marriage to Darcy represents a sacrifice of her selfhood. Even in a patriarchal society such as Austen's, a girl whose father is as passive as Mr. Bennet can rule her own life unless, like Lydia, she blatantly defies society. Darcy, however, is quite a different kind of person from Mr. Bennet. It is questioned whether Elizabeth can maintain her independence as the wife of a man who is her equal in will and intellect and her superior in rank and wealth, especially since she will be moving in his social circle.

Since Austen wrote no sequel to *Pride and Prejudice* which could settle the issue, however, most critics continue to believe that the novel ends happily. They see Elizabeth as a woman who will assert herself, no matter what her situation, and Darcy as a man who would never attempt to destroy the very qualities in Elizabeth that initially elicited his admiration. Perhaps the significance of these questions is not merely that they emphasize how repressive Jane Austen's environment actually was, but also that they underline her amazing achievement. In a society dominated by males, she managed to bring to life a number of strong-willed female characters and to produce some of the finest literary works of her era.

Sources for Further Study

Gillie, Christopher. *A Preface to Jane Austen*. London: Longman, 1974. An invaluable guide that includes useful background material and brief discussions of Austen's novels. A reference section contains notes on people and places of importance, maps, and explanations of numerous words used in the works. Amply illustrated. Annotated bibliography.

Halperin, John, ed. *Jane Austen: Bicentenary Essays*. New York: Cambridge University Press, 1975. A collection of essays on various aspects of Austen's work. An excellent chapter by Robert B. Heilman explains how the title *Pride and Prejudice* defines the theme and the structure of the novel. In another essay, Karl Kroeber suggests some reasons for the work's lasting popularity.

__________. *The Life of Jane Austen*. Baltimore: The Johns Hopkins University Press, 1984. A thorough and highly readable critical biography, written with the stated purpose of making Jane Austen "come alive." Argues that neither Elizabeth Bennet nor any other character in the novels should be taken as representing so complex a person as Austen. Has perhaps the best summary available of the theories about the genesis of *Pride and Prejudice*.

Howe, Florence, ed. *Tradition and the Talents of Women*. Urbana: University of Illinois Press, 1991. Feminist criticism of various writers. An essay by Jen Ferguson Carr notes that although both Mrs. Bennet and Elizabeth are excluded from power in a male-dominated society, only the daughter is intelligent enough to use language to "dissociate herself from her devalued position."

Kirkham, Margaret. *Jane Austen, Feminism, and Fiction*. Brighton, Sussex, England: Harvester Press, 1983. Although Elizabeth Bennet is the most appealing of Austen's heroines, the novelist herself had misgivings about *Pride and Prejudice*, probably because its lighthearted ending depends upon Elizabeth's losing her integrity. Concludes with a helpful summary of the critical tradition.

McMaster, Juliet, ed. *Jane Austen's Achievement*. New York: Barnes & Noble, 1976. A collection of six papers delivered at the Jane Austen Bicentennial Conference at the University of Alberta. Lloyd W. Brown's chapter "The Business of Marrying and Mothering" and A. Walton Litz's " 'A Development of Self': Character and Personality in Jane Austen's Fiction" both deal with *Pride and Prejudice*.

Moler, Kenneth L. *Pride and Prejudice: A Study in Artistic Economy*. Boston: Twayne, 1989. Places the novel in its historical and critical context and then proceeds to comment on theme, symbolism, style, and literary allusions. Includes also a chronology and an annotated bibliography. Well-organized and lucid.

Smith, LeRoy W. *Jane Austen and the Drama of Woman*. New York: St. Martin's Press, 1983. In *Pride and Prejudice*, Austen shows the ideal marriage as depending upon overcoming the institution's "threat to selfhood." Unlike most women of her period, Elizabeth Bennet insists both on choosing her husband and on retaining her intellectual and emotional independence.

Sulloway, Alison G. *Jane Austen and the Province of Womanhood*. Philadelphia: University of Pennsylvania Press, 1989. Pointing out that in nineteenth century society men had "rights" and women had "duties," this author examines the various areas in which women function in Austen's novels, including the "Ballroom," the "Drawing Room," and the "Garden." Sulloway's approach is original and perceptive.

Yaeger, Patricia, and Beth Kowaleski-Wallace, eds. *Refiguring the Father: New Feminist Readings of Patriarchy*. Carbondale: Southern Illinois University Press, 1989. A collection of essays on various writers. In "The Humiliation of Elizabeth Bennet," Susan Fraiman argues that when Elizabeth Bennet marries Darcy, she is exchanging a passive, permissive father for a father figure who, as a strong-willed male of lofty social status, may give her ease but will certainly take away her independence.

Rosemary M. Canfield Reisman

THE PRINCESS OF CLÈVES

Author: Madame de La Fayette (Marie-Madeleine Pioche de la Vergne, 1634-1693)
Type of work: Novel
Type of plot: Psychological realism
Time of plot: 1558-1559
Locale: Paris, France
First published: *La Princesse de Clèves*, 1678 (English translation, 1679)

Principal characters:

The Princess of Clèves, a beautiful heiress from one of the most important families in France
Jacques de Savoie, the Duc de Nemours, an eligible bachelor who falls in love with the Princess of Clèves
The Prince of Clèves, the husband of the Princess
Madame de Chartres, the mother of the Princess
King Henry II, the reigning king of France and the son of the notable king François I
Diane de Poitiers, the Duchesse de Valentinois and the mistress of both François I and Henry II
Catherine de Mèdicis, the queen of France as the wife of Henry II
Mary Stuart, Queen of Scots and the "Queen Dauphine" as the wife of the king's oldest son

Form and Content

The Princess of Clèves presents a new twist on an age-old dilemma, the conflict between love and duty. As the title of the novel suggests, the main focus is on the Princess of Clèves and her predicament. On the one hand, she has a duty toward her husband, but on the other, she seeks gratification through her love for Nemours. The novel explores the competing demands of duty toward others and toward oneself; it does this by presenting a sympathetic and complex heroine, one of the first such female characters in literature and one with enduring importance. The psychology of other characters is important insofar as it contributes to this dilemma, but otherwise remains undeveloped.

The core of the drama is whether the Princess should follow love or duty. When she marries, she is honest with her husband—an honesty consistent with her open disposition—and tells him that although she respects and honors him, she does not love him. At the time, the Prince of Clèves is satisfied with unrequited love, hoping that someday their affection will be mutual, but as he becomes aware of his wife's feelings for Nemours, the challenge of keeping his word becomes increasingly difficult. His death leaves the Princess free to fulfill her desire and remarry, this time to her true love, the bachelor Nemours, but her controversial decision at the end of the novel to remain a widow and retire from society appears to place duty before love.

The novel is set principally during the reign of Henry II, particularly in the years 1558 and 1559, and it draws considerably on historical events. Thus, when the novel opens, Elizabeth of England has just succeeded to the throne of England and Mary Stuart has just married the heir to the throne of France, the dauphine, events that took place in 1558. Toward the end of the novel, Henry II is killed in a tournament and peace for France is achieved through a series of arranged marriages alluded to in the novel, events that took place in 1559.

The author, Madame de La Fayette, scrupulously observes the historical record for the most part, but within this framework she invents the conversations and details of intrigue that occupy her novel. The major departure from history is the character of the Princess herself. This is not to say that the character of the Princess is without historical basis: She may have been modeled on Anne d'Este, who married first the Duke of Guise (who also figures in Madame de La Fayette's novel) and then the Duc de Nemours.

The novel is divided into four "books" of approximately equal length. Each book leads the reader up to a new crisis in the plot, increasing the tension until the final resolution. Thus, the first book ends with the death of Madame de Chartres, the Princess' mother. This leaves the Princess vulnerable and without an ally, for Madame de Chartres had been her confidante and counselor. Madame de Chartres recognized the difficulty of the ordeal that her daughter faced and in her dying words encouraged her to do her duty and to leave the court to avoid temptation.

When the Princess tries to do the right thing, circumstances thwart her good intentions. Thus, she attempts to follow her mother's advice to leave court, but ironically it is her husband's wish that she remain, and in obeying him she is exposed to greater temptation. Such psychological twists add to the dramatic irony of the novel by making the Prince complicit in his own eventual unhappiness.

At other times, the Princess is betrayed by her own feelings in spite of her attempt to control and conceal them. She also learns that love does not bring only happiness; when she believes she has a rival for Nemours' affection, she experiences the pain of jealousy, a factor that will be important in her final decision.

The Prince of Clèves is also trapped in a similar dilemma. He cannot reproach his wife with dishonesty, but his emotions get the better of him at times. Thus, he proclaims that, because of the value he places on sincerity, he would not react bitterly if his wife confessed she loved another, but when the Princess heeds his words, he finds that he is unable to maintain his equanimity. Although the Princess achieves some peace of mind through her confession (another important factor in her final decision), the shared knowledge drives a wedge between the couple. The Prince is increasingly tormented by jealousy, and he sends spies to watch his wife. As further evidence of his tragically flawed nature, he erroneously concludes from these reports that his wife has been unfaithful, and he falls fatally ill.

The court setting of the novel offers several advantages. Court life constantly combines love and politics, showing at every turn how love and power are interrelated. This background highlights the value of the pure disinterested love felt by the Princess. The contrast between the hypocritical life at court and her sincerity adds to the interest of the main character. The court setting also means that the Princess is constantly exposed to scrutiny and that virtually no action can remain private or secret, which heightens the psychological pressure.

Analysis

The Princess of Clèves is generally considered to be the first psychological novel in French and one of the best examples of the emerging novel genre in any language. Although many of the secondary characters are not developed, the behavior and decisions of the Princess of Clèves are given thorough psychological underpinning and treatment.

This is not to say that everyone agrees on the degree of realism; indeed, this very problem of "verisimilitude" has been much discussed. In particular, Madame de La Fayette's contemporaries cited two scenes they found especially unbelievable: the confession scene (when the Princess tells her husband that she loves another) and the renunciation (when the Princess decides not to marry Nemours even though she is free to do so). Close attention to the text shows that Madame de La Fayette prepares and defends these choices on the part of her heroine. The Prince practically invites such a confession, and when the Princess makes it, she reiterates that she is aware of how unusual it is. In addition, the "frank and open disposition" of the character is stressed. In the case of her decision not to marry Nemours, this is prepared carefully in the text (by the emphasis on duty, by the moral weight of death-bed promises, by the Princess' experiences of the pain of jealousy and the value she places on peace of mind).

An important formal aspect of the novel is the use of embedded narratives (subplots or secondary stories narrated or "nested" within the framework of the main story). There are four of these in the novel. Although they have sometimes been viewed as digressions that distract the reader from the main plot, a comparison between the themes of the main plot and the embedded narratives reveals that they are closely linked. The four embedded narratives occur in the first two books and at the beginning of book 3. Occasionally, they serve to form a bridge between one chapter and the next. Each of the four narratives concerns the love life of a female character and contains a lesson for either the Princess of Clèves or Nemours. The first narrative, told by Madame de Chartres, answers the question (posed by the Princess) of what attracts Henry II to his older mistress, Diane de Poitiers, by telling the story of Diane's political triumph. It illustrates the point frequently articulated by Madame de Chartres that anyone who judges people at court by appearances will be deceived. The second embedded narrative concerns the deception of Madame de Tournon, the mistress of one of the Prince's friends. This story also illustrates the deceptiveness of appearances, but its main importance is that it provides the occasion for the

Prince to tell his wife that he would be sympathetic if she were in love with someone else. The third narrative concerns Anne Boleyn, the wife of Henry VIII of England. It suggests that love does not survive marriage: In the story, Anne Boleyn is Henry's mistress for nine years, but after they are married, he suddenly becomes jealous and has her executed. One of the factors that the Princess weighs when she decides not to marry Nemours is her belief that he will not remain faithful once she marries him. The final narrative tells the story of the Vidame's friendship with Queen Catherine and highlights the dangers of deception.

From an examination of the psychological motivations of the characters and the structural composition of the novel, *The Princess of Clèves* appears to be a carefully composed and expertly written novel.

Context

The significance of this novel for women's literature is twofold. It provides an unusual example of a woman writer whose eminent place in the canon has never been questioned. Although *The Princess of Clèves* was first published anonymously, the identity of the author was quickly discovered. Because she was the author of the first psychological novel, Madame de La Fayette's name has not been forgotten. (It is true, however, that her authorship of the novel has been questioned.) There has been a tendency to consider Madame de La Fayette as an exception to the generalization that women of her period did not write, but the trend in contemporary scholarship (in the work of Joan DeJean, for example) is to see her as part of a larger movement of women writers rather than as the token exception.

The second point of significance concerns the central character and the theme of the novel. *The Princess of Clèves* features a central female character who may be viewed as a role model and focuses on issues of concern to women—love and marriage, and the circumstances in which a woman might reject them. Although the ending has been read as traditional female sacrifice and renunciation, some critics (such as Nancy K. Miller) have also argued that the Princess offers an example of female empowerment by depicting a woman who refuses the traditional marriage plot in favor of less tangible but more important advantages.

Sources for Further Study

Danahy, Michael. *The Feminization of the Novel*. Gainesville: University of Florida Press, 1991. A long chapter on *The Princess of Clèves* in this book focuses on gendered spatial archetypes and patterns of communication.

DeJean, Joan. *Tender Geographies: Women and the Origins of the Novel in France*. New York: Columbia University Press, 1991. The extensive chapter "Lafayette and the Generation of 1660-1689" places *The Princess of Clèves* in a broad historical context and situates it with regard to politics and to other French women writers of the period.

Kamuf, Peggy. *Fictions of Feminine Desire: Disclosures of Heloise*. Lincoln: University of Nebraska Press, 1982. Analyzes a number of novels, including *The Princess of Clèves*, in which the author focuses on the role of Madame de Chartres in "constructing" her daughter.

Lyons, John D. "1678: The Emergence of the Novel." In *A New History of French Literature*, edited by Denis Hollier et al. Cambridge, Mass.: Harvard University Press, 1989. A brief but useful article that situates the novel in its historical literary context.

Miller, Nancy K. *Subject to Change: Reading Feminist Writing*. New York: Columbia University Press, 1988. This book reprints Miller's seminal article "Emphasis Added: Plots and Plausibilities in Women's Fiction." Miller takes up the question of verisimilitude ("plausibility") to offer a new interpretation of the Princess' choice as an act of desire rather than renunciation.

Stanton, Domna C. "The Ideal of 'Repos' in Seventeenth-Century French Literature." *L'Esprit Créateur* 15 (Spring/Summer, 1975): 79-104. Stanton traces the origins and meaning of the term "repos," one of the key values in the Princess' moral code.

Melanie C. Hawthorne

REBECCA

Author: Daphne du Maurier (1907-1989)
Type of work: Novel
Type of plot: Romance
Time of plot: The 1930's
Locale: Rural Cornwall, England
First published: 1938

Principal characters:

The narrator, a woman who becomes obsessed with her husband's first wife, Rebecca

Maxim (Max) de Winter, her husband, the owner of Manderley

Mrs. Danvers, the housekeeper at Manderley

Jack Favell, Rebecca's cousin

Frank Crawley, Max's agent and the narrator's confidant

Colonel Julwin, the magistrate for Kerrith

Form and Content

Rebecca is a gothic romance of the kind that has been popular since the genre was invented in the late eighteenth century. The plot is conventional: The protagonist, a young woman, finds herself in an unfamiliar and sinister setting, where she must solve a mystery and win the heart of a handsome man. This novel, which is considered one of the finest of its type, continues to be popular in the late twentieth century, despite the fact that the central character accepts a subservient role in society and in marriage.

Rebecca begins, "Last night I dreamt I went to Manderley again." This often-quoted line sets the story in motion, not only establishing the narrative voice but also indicating that what follows will be an account of past events, ending sadly. In the pages that follow, however, the narrator explains that although they must live far from home, she and her husband are devoted to each other. After further arousing the curiosity of her readers with tantalizing references to the title character and to a Mrs. Danvers, Daphne du Maurier begins her story.

Although from this point on the novel moves chronologically, the narrator frequently uses similar hints to foreshadow future events, thus maintaining a high level of suspense. For example, in chapter 3 she muses, "I wonder what my life would be today, if Mrs. Van Hopper had not been a snob." It soon becomes clear that the social aspirations of this rich American woman vacationing in Monte Carlo have resulted in the introduction of the narrator, who is Mrs. Van Hopper's hired companion, to the aristocratic Maxim de Winter, and eventually in their marriage. When Mrs. Van Hopper decides to leave immediately for New York, the recently widowed Max does not want to lose his young companion, and to the older woman's astonishment, he proposes. The result of Mrs. Van Hopper's snobbery is now clear; what is still to be explained is the rest of the sentence, which recalls the narrator's statements about suffering in the introductory chapters. For those answers, one must read on.

After this brief beginning, the novel moves to England and Manderley, Max's country house by the sea. From the moment she sees the staff waiting for her, the narrator feels insecure. Ill at ease in British upper-class society, the shy, inexperienced girl fears that she cannot live up to the standards set by Max's late wife Rebecca, a woman of great sophistication and legendary beauty. The narrator's sense of inadequacy is carefully nurtured by the housekeeper Mrs. Danvers, who adored Rebecca and who takes every opportunity to make her successor feel like an intruder. Unfortunately, Max goes on with his own life, minimizing his wife's concerns and refusing to talk about Rebecca. Thus isolated, the narrator is sustained only by the kindness of Max's sister Beatrice Lacy and by the evident approval of his agent Frank Crawley.

Without any facts at her disposal, the protagonist proceeds blindly, with no way of knowing what will please or displease her husband. When she breaks a valuable ornament, horrifying Mrs. Danvers, Max treats the matter as trivial. Yet he disapproves of his wife's going into a boathouse used by Rebecca, and he becomes livid after learning that Rebecca's cousin Jack Favell has put in an appearance. The protagonist does not feel Max's full fury, however, until the ball. When he sees her in the costume that Mrs. Danvers had suggested, he becomes enraged. Without explaining that Rebecca had previously worn an identical costume, he simply tells his wife to change and throughout the evening treats her like a stranger. Taking advantage of this breach between husband and wife, Mrs. Danvers has begun hypnotizing the broken-hearted girl into jumping to her death when, providentially, the explosion of rockets, signaling a shipwreck, shocks the narrator into sanity.

Ironically, it is the shipwreck that reunites the couple, even though it also results in Max's having to defend himself against a suspicion of murder. When he hears that divers have found Rebecca's body on her sunken boat, Max finally takes the narrator into his confidence. Throughout their marriage, he says, Rebecca had been malicious and promiscuous; when she indicated that she was to have a bastard child, who would inherit Manderley, Max shot her, put her body in the boat, and sank it. Now, he says, Rebecca has won. When the narrator assures him that she has no intention of deserting him, however, it is evident that, in fact, Rebecca has lost. Whatever follows, love has triumphed.

The final segment of the book describes the inquest and its aftermath. Despite the efforts of Jack Favell and Mrs. Danvers, Max is officially cleared of suspicion. Even though he has guessed the truth, the magistrate, Colonel Julwin, is so sympathetic with Max's sufferings and so repelled by Favell's attempts at blackmail that when he discovers Rebecca had been terminally ill, he chooses to call the drowning a suicide. On their way back from London, however, Max and his wife see a glow in the sky and realize that Rebecca's two friends have taken revenge by setting Manderley on fire.

Analysis

Even though she is writing in the well-worn gothic pattern, Daphne du Maurier incorporates elements from other literary traditions into her novels. Both thematically and symbolically, her works are much richer than most others of their kind.

For example, *Rebecca* reflects one of the central motifs in literature: the expulsion from paradise. Significantly, when in the first chapters of the novel the protagonist mentions her grief, the focus is not on Manderley, the house, but instead on that area of the grounds called the Happy Valley. The house was a showplace, created by Rebecca and imbued with her evil spirit. Her presence dominated the west wing, overlooking the ocean, and it was almost as evident in the east wing, where the newly wedded couple had been placed, for their rooms had been prepared by Rebecca's second self, Mrs. Danvers. Rebecca seemed to haunt the oceanside cottage, where she had met her lovers, and the ocean itself, whose deceptive beauty and destructive force mirrored her own being.

While in her dream the narrator does return briefly to the library at Manderley, where she and Max had some companionable moments, it is the Happy Valley that must be seen as their paradise. At Monte Carlo, when he first describes his home to his future wife, Max dwells not on the house, but on that particular area of the grounds. Even without his comments, however, the protagonist would have recognized the importance of the Happy Valley. When Max takes her there, she sees his joy, she finds herself freed from the oppression that grips her elsewhere on the estate, and somehow she knows that the Happy Valley is the heart, the central reality, of Manderley.

The fact that the Happy Valley still exists after the house has been destroyed represents the triumph of good over evil, which is central to du Maurier's story. Although Max, and the protagonist along with him, must pay the price of murder by being expelled from Manderley and turned away from the paradise at the heart of it, in their love for each other, which the forces of evil could not destroy, the pair carry with them into exile the goodness that they sensed resided in the Happy Valley.

Closely associated with the theme of the lost paradise in *Rebecca* is that of the loss of innocence. In her choice of a female protagonist as the character who moves from innocence to experience during the course of the story, du Maurier is merely following a convention of gothic romance. By having her narrator play the role of her earlier self as she relates the story, however, the author can show how closely innocence is allied with ignorance and even with potentially deadly error. Admittedly, initially Max finds the protagonist appealing because, unlike Rebecca, she is so innocent. Admittedly, he does send her into danger by evading her questions about the past. It is as much her own imagination as Max's silence, however, which very nearly results in the protagonist's suicide. In a sense, while she lives at Manderley, the narrator is writing her own novel. She busies herself inventing scenes in which the gentry criticize her and pity Max—scenes in which she is unfavorably compared to Rebecca. At one point, to Max's horror, she even acts the part of the Rebecca she imagines. After Max confides in her, it becomes clear how erroneous all the narrator's assumptions have been. The world she has created does not exist except in her imagination. What du Maurier seems to be suggesting is that in the real world, innocence can be dangerous, even fatal. It is experience, not innocence, knowledge, not ignorance, which enable the narrator to survive.

Context

When *Rebecca* appeared in 1938, it was dismissed as a romance written to fit a familiar formula, designed purely for entertainment. Critics admired du Maurier's technical skill, but they did not look in the novel for thematic or symbolic subtleties. The fact that since its publication *Rebecca* has continually remained in print, selling steadily over the years, must be attributed primarily to its still holding the same appeal for readers which made it such a commercial success a half century ago. The book is exciting and suspenseful, it has the kind of setting that lends itself to ghost stories, and it is essentially a love story with a happy ending.

Although many women readers evidently can still identify with heroines as subservient as the protagonist of *Rebecca*, contemporary critics are taking a new look at the novel. It is difficult to reconcile its seeming acceptance of a patriarchal system of male dominance with what, in her authorized biography, Margaret Forster has shown about the author herself. Not only was du Maurier convinced from childhood that she was a male in a female body, but, though a wife and mother, she felt free to have affairs with other people of both sexes. In other words, although she was not selfish and spiteful, in many ways du Maurier resembled Rebecca more than she did the virtuous protagonist of her novel.

Evidently, *Rebecca* is a more complex work than it was once thought to be. While it can hardly be argued that Rebecca is a sympathetic character or that her minions, Favell and Mrs. Danvers, are anything but revolting, du Maurier does show how dangerous not only innocence but also a system based on female subservience can be for both partners in a relationship. As she finally realizes, the narrator is of little use either to herself or to Max until she has developed an identity of her own. It is not the shy and helpless girl, but a woman—strong, self-confident, and independent—who chooses to support her husband in his ordeal and, in their exile, to make his life worth living.

Sources for Further Study

Bakerman, Jane S., ed. *And Then There Were Nine . . . More Women of Mystery*. Bowling Green, Ohio: Bowling Green State University Popular Press, 1985. A collection of essays. Bakerman's chapter on Daphne du Maurier argues that in her six "romantic suspense novels," including *Rebecca*, can be seen not only new uses of the gothic "formula" but also reflections of other literary traditions. Sees du Maurier as preeminent in her genre.

Beauman, Sally. "Rereading Rebecca." *The New Yorker* 69, no. 37 (November 8, 1993): 127-138. Points out that the publication in 1993 of Forster's biography of du Maurier and of Susan Hill's *Mrs. de Winter*, a sequel to the novel, indicate the lasting importance of *Rebecca* in literary history. Beauman voices her surprise that feminist critics have not turned their attention to a work in which the narrator so clearly equates love with submission. A balanced and perceptive analysis.

Conroy, Sarah Booth. "Daphne du Maurier's Legacy of Dreams." *The Washington Post*, April 23, 1989, pp. F1, F8. Accounts for du Maurier's continuing appeal by placing her in the oral tradition. The deep-seated "universal fears" that are experienced by her characters and the rhythms of her prose are reminiscent of fireside storytelling. Of all of her well-developed characters, the most convincing is Manderley itself.

Forster, Margaret. *Daphne du Maurier: The Secret Life of the Renowned Storyteller*. New York: Doubleday, 1993. The first authorized biography of du Maurier. With the aid of previously unavailable source materials, Forster reveals du Maurier's lifelong ambivalence as to her sexual identity. She concludes that the novels permitted du Maurier to be psychologically, as well as financially, independent. Although it contains little critical analysis of the works, the volume is a useful addition to du Maurier scholarship.

"Novel of the Week: Survival." *The Times Literary Supplement*, August 6, 1938, 517. A contemporary review of *Rebecca*, "a low-brow story with a middle-brow finish." Of the characters, only the narrator is believable; however, the work is well crafted and readable, one of the few in its genre which can be considered an unqualified success.

Rosemary M. Canfield Reisman

REVOLUTION FROM WITHIN: A Book of Self-Esteem

Author: Gloria Steinem (1934-)
Type of work: Social criticism
First published: 1991

Form and Content

Gloria Steinem's *Revolution from Within* locates the possibility for revolution in the psyche rather than in the ability to act decisively and independently in the world. Wherever she traveled, Steinem found that although women were acting in courageous, ambitious, and committed ways, they did not see that they were doing so. Steinem began to admit to her own feelings of self-doubt and emptiness. Through her personal experience and the personal experiences of others, Steinem located a crucial problem for contemporary women that accompanies the great expectations they hold for themselves: As they try to succeed in many roles, their self-esteem can be damaged by the ongoing expectations that they should fill those roles. After Steinem had written 250 dry, unsuccessful pages, Steinem's friend, a family therapist, read the manuscript and commented that Steinem had a self-esteem problem. Yet Steinem had been named one of the ten most confident women in the United States. The irony made her even more convinced that women were in serious trouble.

To rewrite her book, Steinem added autobiographical elements and invited her readers to connect her stories with their own. Her approach reflects feminist consciousness: the movement back and forth between the personal and the political. Steinem has a political purpose for addressing self-esteem; she sees it as the basis of any real democracy. By locating strength in the self-belief, she draws connections between self-esteem and the ability to demand fairness and to change the hierarchical paradigms of the family, the nation, and even the world.

Steinem structures the book by first giving a detailed account of self-esteem. She relates not only her own parable (by this she means a personal anecdote from which more far-reaching generalizations can be made) but also a history of the notion of self-esteem that goes beyond Western culture to Egypt in 2,500 B.C.E., Hinduism, and the Upanishads. She introduces early on what will be a recurring theme throughout the book: the belief that there is a crucial core self that is a powerful part of human identity, one that needs to be recognized and liberated.

Because she locates this core identity in the child, one must, as a step toward self-healing, rediscover that unique child—a waiting true self. Hence, one must journey back to what one has lost, recover what that child experienced, and re-parent oneself in order to reclaim one's most true, creative core. In the appendix is a "Meditation Guide" that can assist one in making the journey inward.

She follows with chapters that discuss education and the ways in which it undermines intellectual and interpersonal self-esteem. She advocates not only a change in institutional structures but also the revision of the very norms against which people judge experience. By giving a brief history of scientific "facts" that have been used to bolster social prejudices, she seriously calls into question modern measuring techniques that still rank individuals based on mainstream (white, male, middle-class, heterosexual) knowledge.

The book goes on to address issues such as women's bodies, love, romance, and animal rights. Throughout, Steinem returns to the theme of authenticity. Beauty is the ability to decide what is beautiful within oneself, not how well one measures up to what is considered beautiful. Pleasure and creativity are expressions of the true self. Love exists when one is loved for an authentic self. Her message finally is that there is one true inner voice, and that by trusting it, one can stretch one's abilities without sacrificing self-esteem.

Analysis

Steinem's most central issue is that of self-esteem, particularly—though not exclusively—as it concerns women. Under this umbrella term "self-esteem," however, she is able to address the range of challenges that face contemporary women. Her style is fluid, ranging from that of an informed academic, to that of an articulate social critic, to that of a close personal friend. Although she certainly believes that she knows how women might better themselves in many settings, she does not relate her knowledge or advice with either a patronizing or a condescending attitude. Her voice is consistently supportive, even consoling at times, as she encourages her readers to reconsider how they might see themselves in more positive ways. Because of this tone, the book occasionally takes on the tenor of popular psychology, but because Steinem balances this tenor with that of the scholar who has done good research on her topic, the book cannot be dismissed as formulaic self-help jargon.

Ironically, Steinem did not receive her strongest criticism because of her dubious move into pop psychology. As she herself points out in her final chapter, "One Year Later," the majority of her critics focused on the personal revelations she makes throughout the book, especially the ones that involve her love life in the chapter on romance. Because of the emphasis on the personal within the book, Steinem was accused of abandoning feminism and the politics that have driven her career. Clearly, however, Steinem was doing something quite different in bringing into her book so much personal revelation; each personal anecdote is told as a means to build toward a generalization that takes on political significance.

For example, in the chapter on romance, she does tell about a fairly recent love affair in which she herself reenacted a common fantasy within romance mythology—that of rescue. She relates this experience, however, for a political purpose—to demonstrate to her readers how romance mythology works to disempower rather than empower women. From her own particular experience, she can extrapolate about the dissembling that women do in relationships in order to secure them, the feminine disease she refers to as empathy sickness (knowing the feelings of others better than one's own), and the tendency women have to fall in love with powerful men by way of mourning for the power they need and rarely have. She also provides a thorough and convincing analysis of Emily Brontë's star-crossed lovers, Catherine and Heathcliff, and the patriarchal, gender-polarized culture in which women yearn, like Catherine, to be whole but become enmeshed instead in the addictive cycle of romance. Steinem's attention to the personal fits with the feminist view that even women's intimate lives are affected by the political.

What is more problematic, however, is her unyielding belief in the possibility of retrieving a true, authentic self. It is here that she takes a very different path from those of contemporary feminist critical theorists, who see the possibility of such a true self as suspect or simply nonexistent. Feminist theory is diverse, but an overwhelming number of feminists have long been wary of any notion of an essential self that could too easily be linked with biology. Steinem tries to avoid such essentialism by locating the true self in girlhood, before a woman meets the powerful enculturating pressures of adolescence. She wants to get back to the wild child, who is untamed, spontaneous, outspoken, and sure of herself before she is culturally trained to be nice, to be a good listener, and to defer to male authority and discourse. This may be one version of the self that it would be beneficial to reenvision, but to hypothesize that such a wild child is there waiting within all women and that she is the most authentic self one has is a troubling concept, particularly for the intellectual, because it is striking in its naïveté and oversimplification.

Nevertheless, Steinem's book contains valuable material that women can consider and put to use in their own lives. She speaks to those issues that challenge women most deeply and gives women real things that they can do to better meet those challenges without sacrificing their sense of well-being and their potential.

Context

Revolution from Within appeared during a crucial year for feminism. Susan Faludi's *Backlash*, Elizabeth Fox-Genovese's *Feminism Without Illusions*, and Naomi Wolf's *The Beauty Myth* had also recently appeared in print. Women were talking again about what it means to be a feminist and what it means to be part of the feminist community. Because it came from one of the recognized leaders of the feminist movement, Steinem's book caused a certain amount of consternation for feminist social critics. Nowhere in the title is the label "feminism" or "feminist" used. Instead, it purports to be "A Book of Self-Esteem," and the revolution described involves an interior, psychic revolution, not the overthrow of oppressive sexism. It made feminists wonder whether this was a book of social criticism or a self-help book for the victim in all women.

There continues to be a division within the feminist ranks that is now even more clearly delineated by the publication of Katie Roiphe's *The Morning After*. Some people believe that feminists dwell too much on the victimization of women and, therefore, encourage women to identify themselves as passive and helpless against the far-reaching hegemony of patriarchal ideology. Others believe that, by studying and articulating ways in which women become the victims of patriarchal hierarchies, women become empowered, because they are then more conscious of those hierarchies and self-conscious of their willingness to respect them rather than question them. Steinem would certainly be disappointed by the charge that her book encourages women to identify themselves as victims. Her aim was to write both a social critique and a self-help book, and in that sense the book is a success. It increases women's awareness while it provides ways and means to resist oppression.

Furthermore, although the book's title does suggest that its focus will be on the individual, Steinem makes it clear throughout that women realize their power only by interacting with other women, that a revolution from within is not feasible without a community that can support that revolution. Steinem ends the book with "A Proposal for the Future" (written one year after the book's initial publication), in which she calls for "A national honeycomb of diverse, small, personal/political groups that are committed to each member's welfare through both inner and outer change, self-realization and social justice." Steinem realizes that dwelling on the needs of the individual and inner change at the expense of the needs of the community and outer change will have little effect in terms of remedying social injustice. Her call for action is sensible and inspirational and provides a necessary conclusion to a book that works to further women's understanding that the personal and political are so inextricably intertwined, that women must address both in order to bring about worthwhile social change.

Sources for Further Study

Estes, Clarissa Pinkola. *Women Who Run with the Wolves: Myths and Stories of the Wild Woman Archetype*. New York: Ballantine, 1992. Estes' project, like Steinem's, is to empower women, but she goes about it by privileging feminine instinctive nature and the restoration of women's vitality by means of the Wild Woman archetype.

Fox-Genovese, Elizabeth. *Feminism Without Illusions: A Critique of Individualism*. Chapel Hill: University of North Carolina Press, 1991. Fox-Genovese addresses the important discrepancy between the commitment of women to their own personal successes as individuals and their commitment to collective communities of women that seek power in hierarchical institutions.

Gilligan, Carol, Nona P. Lyons, and Trudy J. Hanmer, eds. *Making Connections: The Relational Worlds of Adolescent Girls at Emma Willard School*. Cambridge, Mass.: Harvard University Press, 1990. Gilligan and her colleagues studied pre-adolescent girls over a period of crucial years, noting the ways in which the girls came to lose confidence in their ability to know and came to denigrate their own clear-sightedness.

Roiphe, Katie. *The Morning After: Sex, Fear, and Feminism on Campus*. Boston: Little, Brown, 1993. Roiphe's controversial book critiques feminists' focus on rape and sexual harassment because it reinscribes women's need to be protected and collapses their personal, social, and psychological possibilities. She is also critical of the rigid orthodoxy that feminists around her have created.

Wolf, Naomi. *The Beauty Myth: How Images of Beauty Are Used Against Women*. New York: Doubleday, 1991. Wolf draws an important connection between female liberation and female beauty, arguing that images of beauty are used as political weapons against women's advancement because they, in fact, prescribe behavior, not appearance.

Janet Mason Ellerby

RICH IN LOVE

Author: Josephine Humphreys (1945-   )
Type of work: Novel
Type of plot: Domestic realism
Time of plot: The mid-1980's
Locale: Mount Pleasant and Charleston, South Carolina
First published: 1987

Principal characters:

Lucille Odom, a seventeen-year-old high school senior
Warren Odom, Lucille's father, a sixty-year-old retired demolition expert
Helen Odom, Lucille's mother, who leaves suddenly
Rae, Lucille's sister
Billy McQueen, Rae's husband
Rhody Poole, Rae's black friend
Vera Oxendine, Warren Odom's hair stylist

Form and Content

Rich in Love is a coming-of-age novel about a young woman growing to adulthood in the American South toward the end of the twentieth century. Rich in the sense of place—generally, the United States, and specifically, the environs of Charleston, South Carolina—the novel interweaves and expands the family relationships of the Odoms. The precipitating action of the novel is one woman's liberation of herself from marriage.

Lucille's mother, Helen, disappears abruptly on May 10, leaving behind her Volkswagen van with the door open and ice cream melting on the seat. Lucille finds a note that her mother has left for her father, saying that she has left to start a new life. Troubled by the note's cool tone, she rewrites it before her father comes home. For days, she and her father drive all over Mount Pleasant and Charleston, searching for her mother frantically but unsuccessfully.

Trying desperately to keep the family together, Lucille fails to take the exams that would enable her to complete her senior year of high school. Eventually, Helen calls Warren and Lucille on the telephone so that they know she is all right, but she refuses to come home. As Warren grows accustomed to Helen's absence, he begins dating Vera Oxendine.

Summoned by Lucille, Rae shows up with Billy McQueen, a man she had met in Washington and married in Myrtle Beach, South Carolina, on the way to Mount Pleasant. Their marriage is at least in part the result of the fact that Rae is pregnant with a child she is not sure she wants. From Rae, Lucille learns that Helen had tried to have an abortion when she was pregnant with Lucille. The abortion had been only partly successful, and one of the twins—Lucille—survived. The truth about Lucille's past unfolds just as her present is changing.

As Warren Odom and Vera Oxendine become more involved with each other and Rae and Billy pull farther apart, Lucille becomes more desperate to keep the family together. Rae's pregnancy makes her despondent, and she withdraws from Billy. Lucille, believing that she is responsible for keeping the family together, spends more and more time with Billy, who helps her study for her makeup exams. On Halloween night, dressed in costumes (although Lucille has removed her mask), Billy and Lucille make love in the study, where for weeks Billy has been working on his doctorate and Lucille has been studying for her high school makeup exams.

Eventually, Rhody leads Lucille to Helen, who has been living in the shell of a house built by Rhody's father "on a piece of no-man's land." She has been taking the bus to a job at a gift shop not far from the Odom household. Lucille and her mother have a tearful reunion, but Helen has no intention of returning to live with Warren. "Marriage was killing me," she says.

Meanwhile, Rae's pregnancy comes to term, and she gives birth to a daughter, Phoebe. The novel ends with a rearrangement of the family into new families, all of which are connected with the old. Rae, Billy, and Phoebe now live together in Charleston. Warren has moved into Vera's bungalow. Rhody has taken an apartment with her daughter Evelyn, and Lucille has joined her mother.

Analysis

The events of the plot of *Rich in Love* suggest a much grimmer story than the one Lucille tells. Describing the plot—a seventeen-year-old whose mother leaves, who is the survivor of an attempted abortion, who has two sex relationships, whose unhappily pregnant sister considers an abortion and gives birth to her baby in a toilet—may make the book sound depressing. It is, however, not depressing at all, but life-affirming.

In fact, the book is rich in sensuous details and comic effects. Lucille's narrative voice often sounds like that of a mature and poetic adult. Humphreys' central intention is celebratory as she develops Lucille's character in a situation "rich in love." Lucille is experiencing a chaotic time in her own life at a chaotic time in history—domestic history, rather than the traditional history of wars and political upheavals.

The novel as a whole is structured around parallels: The black Poole family parallels the white Odoms. Rhody Poole, who left her daughter to be reared by her mother, parallels Rae Odom McQueen, whose mother is unlikely to rear her child. Rae's pregnancy and her not wanting the baby parallels Helen's situation when she was pregnant with Lucille. These parallels reinforce the connections among the characters' lives and put their individual decisions in perspective.

During most of *Rich in Love*, Lucille is a neglected child who is looking out for her parents, but what appears to be chaos in the Odoms' lives is the result of changing mores, including changing sex-role expectations. Lucille is therefore also growing up and learning about the varieties of love in a place she loves, a place rich not only in love but also in varieties of history.

The setting of the novel is an area that is rich in history. At one point, Lucille and Billy collect Indian pottery shards from the river bank. Lucille finds a shard and gives it to Billy, who identifies it precisely as an artifact from 500 B.C.E. Fishbone Johnson's club, where Rae goes to sing, is in an old AME (African Methodist Episcopal) Church built in 1866. At nearby Fort Moultrie, bees have made a nest in a statue of Osceola. Lucille imagines that the bees have filled the statue with honey. The honey-filled statue suggests the sweetness of Lucille's view of history.

Lucille's love for the Charleston area makes her love history as it is normally defined, but she also loves history defined a little differently. "I also felt that history was a category comprising not only famous men of bygone eras, but *me, yesterday,*" she says. Lucille's own "yesterday" takes on a complicated significance for her when Rae explains that Lucille is a twin whose sibling was aborted. She begins to distrust the past.

Lucille loves her hometown and the people closest to her. To be rich in love is to be sensitive to the things of this world. *Rich in Love* is therefore rich in comic and sensuous details. One example will show how details reflect the larger patterns of the novel. In a tender love scene, Billy and Lucille explore each other's scars, emotional and physical. Under his hair Billy hides a scar on his forehead that he got after falling off bleachers at a baseball game. Lucille pretends that she cannot see the scar, even when he points it out. Similarly, Billy claims not to be able to see the thin scar that was left when Lucille's harelip was repaired. This parallel brings the characters together emotionally; being sympathetically attentive to physical details is an aspect of the intimacy of love.

Lucille tries to hold on to the past, as does Warren when he tries to remember his life before Helen. That remembering, that history, gives Warren a firm enough sense of his own identity to go on developing. Something similar happens to Lucille, who learns how to face the future by understanding her own past.

In the jargon of social psychology, the Odoms are a dysfunctional or, as Lucille says, a "defunct" family, but *Rich in Love* affirms that there is more than one way for a family to function. In the end, all of the Odoms find new ways to get the security and assurance that the traditional family of four (as Lucille says) used to provide.

Context

When Helen telephones after she has left, Lucille wants to know, ". . . is it something feminist . . . or is it something real?" The light-hearted tone of the question captures the spirit of Humphreys' treatment of women's issues, which is not to say that the novel is antifeminist. Lucille's voice *is* a woman's point of view.

The major events in the novel are precipitated by changes in women's roles: Helen can no longer define herself as a wife and mother. Rae is not prepared to be defined that way either. Lucille can no longer rely on her mother as a nurturer. All of the women in the novel are unwilling to submerge their identities in their husbands' identities or in marriage. The "traditional family," as represented by the Odoms before Helen's departure, is replaced quite satisfactorily in *Rich in Love* by a new and more flexible definition of family.

Many incidents reflect changing attitudes toward sexuality and gender. No one in the novel, male or female, has to do anything. No one is bound by gender stereotypes. Neither the males nor the females are expected to be self-sacrificing. Lucille is learning a lesson in independence from her mother. Helen Odom loves Warren, Rae, and Lucille, but she must also love herself.

Lucille has sexual intercourse with two different males without becoming a victim or an outcast. *Rich in Love* deals openly and unaffectedly with birth control. Women in the novel assume responsibility for contraception. As practiced by Lucille (and less effectively by Rae), it is a matter-of-fact choice. By the same token, Humphreys recognizes the complexity of human interaction. Finally, contraception allows Lucille to experiment with sex and learn about love in the process.

A generation ago in a typical novel, a character similar to Lucille might have gotten pregnant and married Wayne. Rae and Billy's marriage might have been melodramatically destroyed by Lucille's flirtation with Billy. Humphreys' novel, however, has a happy and at the same time "realistic" ending—which may, ironically, distress some readers who disapprove of Lucille's behavior. Rather than propose one answer for all women, *Rich in Love* portrays a variety of legitimate options. Rae, Billy, and Phoebe stay together, but their lives will be different from the Odoms' family life.

Changes in women's roles also mean changes in men's roles. Billy's love for Rae and his tenderness toward Lucille are presented appealingly. Humphreys has Lucille portray both Rae and Billy sympathetically, each struggling with the desire for freedom and the desire to embrace marriage as the natural outcome of love between a man and a woman.

Sources for Further Study

Henley, Ann. " 'Space for Herself': Nadine Gordimer's *A Sport of Nature* and Josephine Humphreys' *Rich in Love*." *Frontiers: A Journal of Women's Studies* 13, no. 1 (1992): 81-89. Henley argues that "for a woman, 'being' is made possible not by belonging to but by being freed from place." Lucille, like Helen, must be freed from the Odom household to find her own identity.

Humphreys, Josephine. "Continuity and Separation: An Interview with Josephine Humphreys." Interview by Rosemary Magee. *Southern Review* 27, no. 4 (Autumn, 1991): 792-802. In this interview conducted in May, 1990, Humphreys talks about her approach to writing. She refers several times to *Rich in Love* as well as to her other novels.

______________. "My Real Invisible Self." In *A World Unsuspected: Portraits of Southern Childhood*, edited by Alex Harris. Chapel Hill: University of North Carolina Press, 1987. Humphreys contributes a section to this anthology of childhood reminiscences by eleven Southern writers.

Malone, Michael. "Rich in Words." *The Nation*, October 10, 1987, 388-389. Reviewing *Rich in Love*, Malone compares the novel at some length with Humphreys' earlier novel, *Dreams of Sleep*, and praises *Rich in Love* for Lucille's "wry wit, and fine comic timing."

Seaquist, Carla. "Someone Who Cares." *Belles Lettres: A Review of Books by Women* 3, no. 5 (May/June, 1988): 5. This review, written in a slangy style for a feminist audience, describes Lucille's narration as a "feisty female voice."

Wickenden, Dorothy. "What Lucille Knew." *The New Republic* (October 19, 1987): 45-46. This review praises Humphreys' handling of her characters' inner lives "with subtlety, originality and deadpan humor," but balances that praise with criticism of the "mannered sentimentality and . . . pat psychology" of the ending of the novel.

Thomas Lisk

A ROOM OF ONE'S OWN

Author: Virginia Woolf (1882-1941)
Type of work: Essays
First published: 1929

Form and Content

What is now known as *A Room of One's Own* began as two essays, parts of which were read to the Arts Society at Newnham and to the Odtaa at Girton in October of 1928. These essays were later revised and extended by Woolf into a short book of six chapters which mixes fact and fiction to analyze the roles and relationships of money and gender in regard to the production of art, specifically fiction by women.

Woolf composed the original essays to deliver as speeches to groups of young college women—women who were at that time forbidden to enter England's university system because of their gender. The topic of "women and fiction" forms the continuing motif of the book, as Woolf attempts different compositions of the question before attempting to answer them: What are women like? What is fiction written by women like? What is fiction written about women like? These questions led her to connect gender and fiction with economics at a time when women had just recently received the right to vote and the right to own property. She thus further asks such questions as "Why did men drink wine and women water?" and "What effect has poverty on fiction?"

Woolf begins to answer the questions about women and fiction by inventing a fictional college called Fernham. She refers to herself as a fictional character—"I"—and stresses that she speaks as a kind of Everywoman. She finds not only that she is barred from the library because of her gender but also that women have historically been barred from writing fiction for the same reason.

By comparing the furnishings and the food served at Fernham to those of men's universities, she suggests a correlation between women's fiction and money. The necessity of money to produce art, specifically fiction, leads Woolf to the formulaic answer of the title: What a woman needs to write fiction is money (five hundred British pounds annually) and a room of her own.

The six chapters explore the connections of gender, money, and fiction through an imagined visit to the British Museum, an examination of George Trevelyan's *History of England*, a review of nineteenth century British women novelists, a comparison of the representations of women in historical works with their representation by men in literature (including a speculation about what would have happened to William Shakespeare had he been born a woman), and a final call for an androgynous approach to the production of art.

Analysis

Adopting the tone and style of a speech, Woolf's persona addresses an imagined audience of young women in college. She describes an imagined visit to a fictional women's college (Fernham) in which she is entertained at dinner by a woman whom she calls Mary Seton and is given a history of the origin of the college. Woolf's persona details the dinner in a subtly sarcastic manner: The soup is described as a weak broth, "a plain gravy soup"; the main course as a "homely trinity" of beef, greens, and potatoes; the dessert as prunes and custard, the prunes "stringy as a miser's heart."

Woolf first asks why one gender has been allowed access to the universities while the other has not. She asks repeatedly why women have been given few resources to provide for their education, while men have been funded in a comparatively lavish manner. She draws no conclusions in the text, but she implies that the difference is not based on anything except gender.

In the second chapter, Woolf imagines a visit to the British Museum, not having found a sufficient answer to her questions regarding women and fiction. This question now has reformed itself as the question regarding women and money and fiction. Woolf looks up the category "women and fiction" and expresses surprise at the tremendous number of men who have written on the topic. Some of these men had academic qualifications, but many had "no apparent qualification save that they are not women." Noting that women have not historically written books about men, she lists the numerous subject areas in which men have written about women.

She suggests that most of these writings are useless, having been written "in the red light of emotion and not in the white light of truth." This distinction of emotional writing versus "incandescent" writing foreshadows the later discussions of Shakespeare's abilities and her call for an androgynous attitude in writing. She offers a sarcastic Freudian interpretation of the misogynistic attitude she discovers in male writings throughout history, especially in her fictitious example of Professor von X's *The Mental, Moral, and Physical Inferiority of the Female Sex.* Once again, however, Woolf suggests that equality of the sexes—for example, in occupational areas—will not change the perceived differences in gender. She reformulates the question of women, money, and fiction once again, and she heads to the shelves of history books to search for a suitable answer.

In the third chapter, Woolf consults Professor Trevelyan's *History of England.* She finds that women have little recorded history in this volume. The first reference occurs about 1470 and details the socially accepted practice of wife-beating. The next reference, about two hundred years later, confirms the status of women as property of men. Woolf contrasts these images with those of the female characters in fiction written by men, from Clytemnestra, Antigone, and Cleopatra to Clarissa, Becky Sharp, and Emma Bovary. While women in history were abused and without individual rights, she observes that women in fiction were never lacking in personality and character. Furthermore, the subject matter of the entire history of England concerns the social and public realms of male influence rather than the personal or family concerns that she suggests the female writer would have recorded.

She acknowledges that a woman of Shakespeare's time could not have written the works of Shakespeare, but she argues that it would have been a matter not of gender but of opportunity. She then imagines what Shakespeare's sister—a fictitious entity Woolf dubs Judith—would have encountered had she been as talented as her brother William. "Judith" Shakespeare follows her aspirations for the theater and fiction writing in a manner similar to that of William, yet her life and art are stifled by the men she encounters. She ultimately kills herself out of frustration. Woolf further admires the writing of nineteenth century women in the light of their limited experiences and their lack of money even to buy paper or to have a room of their own.

In chapter 4, she expands on the difficulties faced by women writers. The profession was considered improper for women, and women such as Aphra Behn, who made a living by writing, were considered immoral. She notes that many women chose to write under a pseudonym, and she notes that these women had to write under adverse conditions. She praises the forerunners of modern novelists, such as Jane Austen, the Brontës, and George Eliot, although in Charlotte Brontë she finds that gender affects the integrity of her writing. The others show little anger or emotion in their writing, more closely approximating the unemotional, incandescent quality of Shakespeare's writing. She says that these women writers are necessary to future women writers in the same way that Shakespeare, Christopher Marlowe, Geoffrey Chaucer, and earlier poets were necessary to subsequent male writers.

Chapter 5 examines how literature written by men portrays women only through the eyes of men. Similarly, the world in literature written by men is portrayed only through male eyes, focusing only on what is important to men, such as war, sports, and so forth. All writers, however, must move beyond a gender-specific focus in order to achieve the unemotional tone she admires.

Chapter 6 broadens the discussion from gender and literature to gender and philosophy. Not only in writing but also in life in general, both women and men should try to achieve an androgynous attitude, to stop thinking of the genders as distinct from each other. If one achieves this unity of the mind, one can also achieve that incandescent quality of mind evidenced by the greatest of writers, exemplified by Shakespeare.

Context

Of all the artists and writers who were part of the Bloomsbury circle of intellectuals in early twentieth century England, Virginia Woolf has proved to be the most influential and enduring, except perhaps for Maynard Keynes and his effects on economic theory. *A Room of One's Own* has become an icon of feminism, although its content often was distorted by critics as its influence grew.

The many works alluding to Woolf's title have made the work a symbolic statement of feminist philosophy.

After its first publication, however, reaction was muted. Some saw it as a harsh complaint with unrealistic expectations (for example, five hundred British pounds in 1929 was roughly equivalent to an annual income of fifty thousand dollars, a fortune for that time). Others saw it as an accurate portrayal of social conventions in regard to gender. The time in history of its publication, the period between two world wars, diminished its initial impact; in fact, Woolf reiterated much of the argument in her 1938 *Three Guineas*, mixing women's equality into the context of the masculine institutions of war and government. Indisputably, the central image of *A Room of One's Own* has contributed to the understanding that gender equality has more to do with economic power than with biology.

Woolf's work is usually considered to be ardently feminist and a product of her repression based on gender. Yet Woolf was a privileged woman with access to education other than the university, and her financial status allowed her not only to publish her own works but also to publish other writers at her and her husband Leonard's Hogarth Press. The book criticizes discrimination based on wealth; it criticizes the subjugation of any group because of economic repression, whether that group is defined by gender or any other criterion.

Woolf, like Edgar Allan Poe, was much maligned following her death by suicide in 1941; her mental instabilities were emphasized far more than her insightful social and political analysis. In more recent criticism, her artistic temperament and her gender are less the focus of study than her straightforward and innovative analysis of literature and economic power.

Sources for Further Study

Bell, Quentin. *Virginia Woolf: A Biography*. London: Hogarth Press, 1972. Written by Virginia Woolf's nephew, this first complete biography of Woolf was first published in England in two volumes (here combined). It includes numerous photographs, a detailed chronology, references, and a bibliography. Bell drew on Virginia's letters and diaries; however, his work was completed before all of Woolf's letters and diaries were compiled.

DeSalvo, Louise A. *The Impact of Childhood Sexual Abuse on Her Life and Work*. Boston: Beacon Press, 1989. A detailed study of Woolf's life and personality based on her diaries, letters, and biographical sources. Although the abuse is predicated on vague diary entries about her half brother George Duckworth, this work provides a feminist analysis of Woolf's lesbianism.

Gilbert, Sandra M., and Susan Gubar. *The Madwoman in the Attic: The Woman Writer and the Nineteenth-Century Literary Imagination*. New Haven, Conn.: Yale University Press, 1979. Perhaps the most influential feminist criticism of its time, *The Madwoman in the Attic* reevaluates nineteenth century literature by women from a feminist perspective, citing Woolf as writer, feminist, and critic.

Showalter, Elaine. *A Literature of Their Own: British Women Novelists from Brontë to Lessing*. Princeton, N.J.: Princeton University Press, 1977. Alluding to Woolf's work in its title, this analysis of women writers categorizes them into female, feminine, and feminist, which are somewhat useful but arbitrary definitions. The survey of women novelists is an early example of influential feminist revision.

Woolf, Virginia. *The Diaries of Virginia Woolf*. Edited by Anne Olivier Bell. Vols. 1-5. New York: Harcourt Brace Jovanovich, 1977-1985. Though vast, these five volumes are well indexed and provide the most authoritative source for any study of Woolf or her politics and philosophy. Includes an introduction by Quentin Bell.

__________. *Women and Fiction: The Manuscript Versions of A Room of One's Own*. Edited by S. P. Rosenbaum. Cambridge, Mass.: Oxford University Press, 1992. For any detailed study of Woolf's thoughts and the composing process of *A Room of One's Own*, this work is mandatory.

Bradley R. Bowers

RUBYFRUIT JUNGLE

Author: Rita Mae Brown (1944-)
Type of work: Novel
Type of plot: Picaresque
Time of plot: 1950-1968
Locale: Coffee Hollow, Pennsylvania; Ft. Lauderdale and Gainesville, Florida; and New York City
First published: 1973

Principal characters:

Molly Bolt, the protagonist, who grows up poor, smart, and lesbian in small-town Pennsylvania
Leroy Denman, Molly's cousin, ally, admirer, and first male sexual partner
Carolyn Simpson and **Connie Pen,** Molly's high school friends
Carrie Bolt, Molly's adoptive mother
Carl Bolt, Molly's adoptive father
Faye Raider, Molly's roommate and lover at the University of Florida
Holly, Molly's coworker in New York City
Polina Bellantoni, a scholar whose bizarre sexual fantasies interfere with her and Molly's affair

Form and Content

Rubyfruit Jungle, Rita Mae Brown's first novel, is semiautobiographical. Its heroine, Molly Bolt, is described with considerable admiration and sympathy by her creator. Molly grows from a rebellious child into a "self-actualizing lesbian"—an unprecedented validation of lesbian existence.

Born illegitimate and adopted in infancy, Molly learns at an early age the meaning of the word "bastard." Her sense of not belonging serves as a catalyst for her subsequent determination to carve out an identity for herself independent of class, gender, and family. Young Molly defies many small-town social expectations: She fights like a boy, locks her mother in the cellar, and engages in sex play without inhibitions. By the time Molly's family moves to Florida, where she attends high school, Molly has formulated a clear goal: to escape. She has also learned that one must "play the game" in order to accomplish the goal. For this reason, she makes high grades, excels at sports, joins the right clubs, dates the right boys (and a girl or two), generally keeps her nose clean, and earns the all-important full scholarship to college. Although Molly gets off to a promising start socially and academically, the University of Florida does not turn out to be her ticket to independence and success. She and her roommate fall in love, and both are expelled when their affair becomes known. Rejected by Carrie when she tries to return home, Molly heads to New York, where she has heard "there are so many queers . . . that one more wouldn't rock the boat."

In New York, Molly does not immediately "rock the boat," but she does need to learn who the other passengers are. She meets many people, most of whom appear to want something from her—sex, love, obedience, commitment. The lesbians she encounters are either snobbish (Chryssa), role-bound (Mighty Mo), insecure (Holly), or only temporarily on leave from heterosexuality (Polina). The straight women, however, are far worse—obsessed with men and makeup to the exclusion of all else. The men, oddly enough, are nicer. Some of them—Ralph the college student, gay, sweet Calvin, James the editor—can be counted on for help, friendship, or collegiality. Older men on the make, however, such as Mr. Cohen at work, Paul the poetry scholar ("a living study in human debris"), and Professor Walgren at New York University (a "fake-hippie, middle-aged wash-out"), are silly or repulsive or both.

By the end of *Rubyfruit Jungle*, Molly explicitly understands what she has known intuitively all along—that she must make her way alone. In 1968, even her summa cum laude film degree opens no doors; she is offered secretarial jobs, while less-talented male classmates enter big studios on the fast track. She has little in common with her "downwardly mobile" contemporaries in the antiwar movement. Even the newly formed women's groups suffer from middle-class bias, conformism, and homophobia, and Molly suspects that they would "trash me just the same." The novel closes with Molly—still alone, still copyediting for Mr. Cohen—vowing to make her movies even if she has to "fight until I'm fifty."

Analysis

Rubyfruit Jungle was originally published in 1973 by the feminist press Daughters, Inc. It quickly became an underground bestseller, gaining a wide alternative readership. In 1977, Bantam reissued it as a mass-market paperback; it sold an astonishing one million copies. For mainstream readers, *Rubyfruit Jungle* represented an upbeat and amusing glimpse of contemporary lesbian life, but for lesbian readers it meant far more. Molly Bolt was a psychologically healthy, outspoken, and empowered woman—a huge contrast to most earlier fictional portrayals of lesbians. For example, a lesbian reader before 1973 would probably have read Radclyffe Hall's *The Well of Loneliness* (1928), the story of unhappy Stephen Gordon, who internalizes male psychologists' labeling of lesbians as "inverts." She might have read or seen Lillian Hellman's play *The Children's Hour* (1934), which ends with a lesbian schoolmistress declaring her love and then shooting herself. If she was lucky, she had come upon Claire Morgan's *The Price of Salt* (1952), which equivocally validated its lesbian characters. Yet a lesbian was more likely to find her reading material in "adult" bookstores or bus terminals, which sold soft-porn pulp novels about lesbians, often written by men for men. Given this limited literary background, *Rubyfruit Jungle* ("a novel about being different and loving it") had an amazing positive impact. It counteracted the "dying fall" lesbian novel, in which the heroine, lonely and ostracized, is attracted only to other psychologically unstable individuals. Instead, *Rubyfruit Jungle* describes Molly Bolt's "enabling escape" and her "rebellion against social stigma and self-contempt." Indeed, Molly's name may symbolize her desire for flight and freedom.

Nevertheless, it would be an oversimplification to assume that *Rubyfruit Jungle* is only about escape. Molly's name evokes a second meaning as well; a molly-bolt, available in any hardware store, is a fastener that, when inserted through wood into empty space beyond, opens and anchors itself to the away side. Similarly, the fictional Molly Bolt seeks a place in the world where, through her own grit and talent, she can feel secure—"anchored." *Rubyfruit Jungle* is at root a picaresque novel, the story of a marginalized outsider who is seeking acceptance and success. Because its *picaro* is female and gay, it has often been read as a radical work. Certainly, the striking commercial profitability of *Rubyfruit Jungle* was largely the result of the risky novelty of its subject matter. The picaresque is, however, fundamentally a conservative genre; it neither questions society's basic values nor threatens to overturn its power structure. Molly may graduate summa cum laude and Phi Beta Kappa, but she is still an outsider at the novel's end. Molly "succeeds" in remaining true to her (marginalized) self, but she fails to squeeze past the powerful male gatekeepers who control access to the realm of "corporate" prosperity.

At the same time that one recognizes how *Rubyfruit Jungle* reinforces Molly Bolt's marginality and assumes an essentially conservative view of the world, one must not underestimate the degree of Molly's nonconformism. Throughout the novel, Molly repeatedly rejects society's heterosexist assumptions, especially when they are based on artificial gender roles. As a woman, she knows that traditional marriage is an inherently unequal institution in which wives are economically, politically, and socially powerless. She has seen its stultifying effect on Carrie, on Mrs. Cohen, and on her sixth-grade friend Leota. Molly also knows that men—specifically, Carl and Leroy—suffer as marriage limits their options and even their humanity. She lays blame on the institution of marriage, based as it is on artificially constructed male and female roles and on the romantic fiction of "now and forever." An important part of Molly's education in *Rubyfruit Jungle*, however, is her realization that role-playing relationships are just as bad outside marriage as in it. She sees lesbian butch-femme role-playing as nothing more than a pathetic copying of heterosexual roles: "What's the point of being a lesbian," she asks, "if a woman is going to look and act like an imitation man?" Finally, Molly also rejects fantasy role-playing. She is disgusted to learn that Polina and her lover Paul cannot experience sexual satisfaction with each other unless they go through an elaborate transgender fantasy; Polina imagines herself in a men's room while other men admire her "big juicy cock," and Paul imagines other women fondling his "voluptuous breasts." Molly's rejection of all these roles represents an extreme position, for it includes not only marriage but also gender limitations and even monogamy. She wishes only to be herself; her vision of women's sexuality as a "rubyfruit jungle" is her closest approach to a fantasy.

In short, *Rubyfruit Jungle* sends both a conservative and a radical message. Its picaresque dimension reinforces the exclusion, even the punishment, of the gender outlaw. At the same time, although Molly Bolt does not "develop" as much as does the typical *Bildungsroman* protagonist, her education leads her to an increasingly extreme rejection of heterosexual institutions.

Sources for Further Study

Abel, Elizabeth, Marianne Hirsch, and Elizabeth Langland, eds. *The Voyage In: Fictions of Female Development*. Hanover, N.H.: University Press of New England, 1983. This valuable collection of essays examines developmental novels by women writers. Rita Mae Brown and *Rubyfruit Jungle* are discussed at length in Bonnie Zimmerman's "Exiting from the Patriarchy: The Lesbian Novel of Development." Zimmerman's 1990 book *The Safe Sea of Women* expands many ideas from this essay.

Boyle, Sharon D. "Rita Mae Brown." In *Contemporary Lesbian Writers of the United States: A Bio-Bibliographical Critical Sourcebook*, edited by Sandra Pollack and Denise D. Knight. Westport, Conn.: Greenwood Press, 1993. Boyle's article profiles Rita Mae Brown's life and work, including an extended discussion of *Rubyfruit Jungle* and a useful bibliography.

Chew, Martha. "Rita Mae Brown: Feminist Theorist and Southern Novelist." *Southern Quarterly* 22 (1983): 61-80. Chew shows how Rita Mae Brown's early novels (including *Rubyfruit Jungle*) are informed by a specifically "lesbian feminist political vision," whereas her later works are "increasingly directed toward a mainstream audience."

Farwell, Marilyn R. "Toward a Definition of the Lesbian Literary Imagination." *Signs: Journal of Women in Culture and Society* 14 (Autumn, 1988): 100-118. Although Farwell's article does not refer explicitly to *Rubyfruit Jungle*, it is an extremely useful exploration of recurring themes in lesbian literature. Farwell suggests that feminist literary critics use "lesbian" as a metaphor, a "positive, utopian image of woman's creativity."

Mandrell, James. "Questions of Genre and Gender: Contemporary American Versions of the Feminine Picaresque." *Novel: A Forum on Fiction* 20, no. 2 (Winter, 1987): 149-170. Using *Rubyfruit Jungle* and two other novels as illustrations, Mandrell explores how genre can influence a woman author's "viewpoint and the ideological slant of her work." He focuses on Rita Mae Brown's use of the picaresque genre, pointing out that Molly Bolt's story "changes nothing, . . . but, rather, *acquiesces* to and *confirms* the marginality experienced by those who are not straight, white middle-class males."

Palmer, Paulina. "Contemporary Lesbian Feminist Fiction: Texts for Everywoman." In *Plotting Change: Contemporary Women's Fiction*, edited by Linda Anderson. London: Edward Arnold, 1990. Palmer sees *Rubyfruit Jungle* as representative of early lesbian feminist fiction, which "generally utilized the form of the *bildungsroman* and concentrated, somewhat narrowly, on the theme of Coming Out."

Stimpson, Catharine R. "Zero Degree Deviancy: The Lesbian Novel in English." In *Writing and Sexual Difference*, edited by Elizabeth Abel. Chicago: University of Chicago Press, 1982. This groundbreaking article describes and distinguishes between the "dying fall" and "enabling escape" patterns of lesbian narrative, using *Rubyfruit Jungle* as a prime example of the second category.

Zimmerman, Bonnie. *The Safe Sea of Women: Lesbian Fiction, 1969-1989*. Boston: Beacon Press, 1990. This insightful book-length study of contemporary lesbian prose literature explores the interaction between fiction and community—specifically, how lesbian novels and short stories have both reflected and shaped the lesbian community. Zimmerman describes *Rubyfruit Jungle* as the quintessential "coming-out" novel.

Deborah T. Meem

THE SECOND SEX

Author: Simone de Beauvoir (1908-1986)
Type of work: Social criticism
First published: *Le Deuxième sexe*, 1949 (English translation, 1953)

Form and Content

The "serious, all-inclusive, and uninhibited work on woman," as its translator, Howard M. Parshley, calls *The Second Sex*, consists of 1,071 pages in the Gallimard/Folio edition of the original and comprises two separate volumes.

The first volume, *Facts and Myths*, comprises three parts. The first part, "Destiny," is given over to biological data, psychoanalytic perspective, and the perspective of historical materialism (Marxist socialism): Biology does not answer the question "Why is woman the Other, the second?"; psychoanalytic research also does not, but defines woman in the context of sexuality instead of that of existential consciousness; Marxism properly stresses woman's economic instead of her physiological situation but does not provide the existentialist infrastructure that discloses the unity of *human life* (*une vie*, a life, male or female).

Part 2 traces woman's situation in "History" from primitive to modern society, from nomadic existence to the women's suffrage movement. Part 3, "Myths," establishes the unilaterally male primacy of sexual myths and the manifestation of myths that develop male fears and ideals relative to woman, as exemplified in the writings of Henri de Montherlant, for whom woman is "the bread of disgust"; D. H. Lawrence, who asserts "phallic pride"; Paul Claudel, whose Catholicism views woman as fulfilling herself through subservience, ultimately as the "servant of the Lord"; and André Breton, who idealizes woman, as Dante idealized Beatrice and as Petrarch idealized Laura, and identifies woman abstractly as "Poetry." Stendhal is appended as an exemplar of one for whom woman is human; he is a "Romanticist of reality" whose sensual love of women is always informed by his experience of women as subjects, not objects, and who berated those women who looked upon themselves as objects.

The second volume, *Woman's Life Today*, consists of four parts dealing, respectively, with "The Formative Years," "Situation," "Justifications," and, under the heading "Toward Liberation," the independent woman.

"The Formative Years" traces the restraints and demands that are imposed upon woman in childhood and girlhood, the "anatomic destiny" of woman after sexual initiation, and, along with the misunderstanding that lesbianism is an inauthentic attitude, the traditional misinformation that sets it apart as unnatural.

"Situation" investigates the placement of woman as wife, as mother, in family and social life, as prostitute and hetaira, and in maturity and old age. At every turn woman, according to Beauvoir, is enlaced in repetition that results in her clinging to routine and is disempowered by male authority to the end that she herself participates in her alienation from lucidity and develops her unfamiliarity with plausibility.

"Justifications" recounts the ways in which woman compensates for her Otherness, for her being relegated to inferiority in a world of male primacy or male orientation. The categories of compensation are narcissism; self-surrender in love, which amounts to accepting her enslavement to a man as an expression of freedom to do so and to attempting transcendence of her situation as "inessential object" by total acceptance of it; and mysticism, a turning toward God.

"Toward Liberation" summarizes in graphic detail the modes of independence open to woman—abjuration of femininity through chastity, homosexuality, or viragoism, in opposition to the emphasis of femininity in coquetry, flirtation, and masochistic or aggressive love. Beauvoir insists that man is a sexual human being and that woman, as a total individual, can be equal to the male only if she too is a sexual human being, retaining her femaleness and having the same access as the male to personal satisfaction. If woman is to know the same freedom as man, her economic independence must be achieved through Marxist socialism and her sexual independence must be provided by man's willingness to yield his traditional primacy and its concomitant control of the situation of woman.

Analysis

The French Revolution's ideal of "Liberty, Equality, and Fraternity" is the standard against which Beauvoir measures the status, or situation, of woman both during and before the twentieth century. At almost every juncture, she finds that the revolutionary ideal refers to men, not to women. She concludes that the reference can best be extended to women in a world that adheres to the principles of Marxist socialism and to the tenets of existentialist freedom. It is in the context of existentialism that she analyzes the Otherness, the secondness, of woman. To her concept of woman as the Other she gives the name "alterity" (*alterité*), derived from the Latin word *alter*, which means both "other" and "second."

In the existentialism propounded by Beauvoir and Jean-Paul Sartre, the self is subject (I exist, I feel) and anyone or anything exterior to the self is object (someone or something that I may use or that I find to stand in my way). All objects constitute the Other. Beauvoir's thesis is that man sees himself collectively as subject and that woman, historically seen by man as object, must first recognize that she has been conditioned to see herself as the Other and then strive, as a free individual, both to assert herself as subject and to win recognition as subject from man. Those subjects existing in freedom (*liberté*) who see each other as subjects (as equals) live in confraternity. The very last statement of *The Second Sex* is this: ". . . it is necessary . . . that, beyond their natural differentiations, men and women affirm their brotherhood (*fraternité*) unequivocally."

The obstacle to fraternal affirmation is alterity, a persistent form of prejudicial objectification. The concept is explained in chapter 9, "Dreams, Fears, Idols," which is the last chapter of part 3, "Myths." Beauvoir claims that men see themselves as subject-heroes and define woman only in her relation to man. This renders the categories of male and female asymmetrical, as the unilateralism of sexual myths makes clear. Woman is elevated as a divine presence (Athena, the Virgin Mary, and so forth) and yet degraded as a power of evil (Eve, Pandora, Delilah). In neither case is she seen for what, in fact, she is—a free individual on an existential par with man. It is as though men justify their contempt for women by simultaneously idealizing them. Man thereby sustains his need of woman as servant and scapegoat by projecting his self-idealization onto woman as ideal being, the source of life, the healing presence, mother.

The applicability of this concept to other forms of prejudice can be readily inferred. Ethnic prejudice, for example, will justify scornful objectification of a race by conceding a very positive trait as characteristic of that race. Whites, for example, would insist that, while blacks were inferior in intelligence, they were superior in athletics; anti-Semites would, like Adolf Hitler, concede the superior intelligence of Jews as long as the Jews' alleged pecuniary bent were acknowledged. Woman, accordingly, is alternately placed upon a pedestal and consigned to a pit, but is never accorded the same level of human activity as man.

Man is not painted in *The Second Sex* as a tyrannic villain, and woman is not depicted as an inherently helpless victim. The cogency of the essay comes from its fairness and its even-tempered observations. Woman is shown as being a participant in her own subordination by reason of her acquiescence and her inauthentic acceptance of secondary status. Authenticity, the quality that Beauvoir finds Stendhal to have admired in women and reflected in his female characters, is responsible freedom. It is the awareness that, as an existent, one is free to choose and determine the course of one's existence, and it entails one's acceptance of full responsibility for one's choice. Beauvoir says matter-of-factly that women have not been in the habit of cultivating existential awareness and are consequently frustrated by discontents that they cannot fathom but from which they seek indirect and inconclusive escape. In effect, Beauvoir discloses to women their situation as secondary human beings and urges upon them, as prerequisite to authentic choice, an honest awareness of their alterity. Even if a woman chooses to remain the passive Other in relation to men, her choice, made in awareness, is an authentic action for which she accepts active responsibility. A commitment to oppose alterity is not more authentic, since any choice made in awareness is authentic, but it is the better part of action and more in keeping with Beauvoir's existentialist notions about the nature of human life.

Context

The Second Sex was received with shock in Catholic France but had no lack of buyers. Margaret Crosland notes in her biography of Simone de Beauvoir that twenty thousand copies of the first volume were sold within a week of its publication. She adds that the Catholic church banned the book and that writers such as Albert Camus and François Mauriac belittled it. The English-speaking world received it more approvingly in the Parshley translation. Beauvoir was likened in England to Mary Wollstonecraft; still, she received harsh criticism from women who were unwilling to participate in the feminist movement. Beauvoir was surprised at the shock her book had generated and bemused at being identified as a feminist. Her aim in using the abstraction "woman" was not universal feminist protest or demand but each woman's relation of "her self" to the abstraction as a point of departure toward individual self-determination.

Julia Kristeva, in "Le Temps des femmes" (1979; "Women's Time," 1981), identifies the first phase of the twentieth century women's movement as "the struggle of suffragists and of existential feminists." Beauvoir would belong to this phase, not as a suffragist but as an existentialist. According to Kristeva, two post-1968 phases reject and supersede the directions of the early movement. Jane Heath, in her essay on Beauvoir, suggests that "Simone de Beauvoir spoke predominantly the discourse of repression" and "allowed the man in her to speak." Toril Moi takes the measure of later twentieth century rejections and disfavorings of Beauvoir's writings by the feminist whose essays appear in Elaine Marks's collection *Critical Essays on Simone de Beauvoir* (1987); Moi believes that the hostility toward Beauvoir is the outgrowth of a sense of critical superiority to a predecessor whose sense of equality with the male should have developed into militant opposition to the male and whose writing is insufficiently complex.

In the history of the twentieth century feminist movement, Beauvoir's place in the vanguard is assured, even by hostile latter-day critics: The sheer quantity of books and articles about her since the 1970's ensures that attention will be paid to this important pioneer, whose conclusions relative to the "second sex" are given substance in her fiction, definition in other of her existentialist essays, and self-examination in her volumes of autobiography.

Sources for Further Study

Appignanesi, Lisa. *Simone de Beauvoir*. New York: Penguin Books, 1988. Chapter 4, "The Ethics of Existentialism," and chapter 5, "Being a Woman," constitute an essay that is pertinently ancillary to a reading of *The Second Sex*. The emphasis is on Beauvoir's "portrayal of the independent woman."

Bair, Deirdre. *Simone de Beauvoir: A Biography*. New York: Summit Books, 1990. The most informative of the biographies of Beauvoir. Chapters 26 and 28, "The High Priestess of Existentialism" and "A Book About Women," respectively, are essential to a study of *The Second Sex*.

Bieber, Konrad. *Simone de Beauvoir*. Boston: Twayne, 1979. Scorned by feminists of the 1980's and 1990's for its male obtuseness, this introductory study nevertheless contains much valuable information and includes a nineteen-page outline of *The Second Sex*. Bieber's attention to Beauvoir's slips and errors is undercut by his presenting the time setting of her short story "Monologue" as "Christmas night" when it is actually New Year's Eve.

Crosland, Margaret. *Simone de Beauvoir: The Woman and Her Work*. London: Heinemann, 1992. A searching retrospective of Beauvoir's life and career. Crosland shows how Beauvoir's commitment to feminism in the late 1960's and early 1970's had developed in coincidence with feminism's catching up to *The Second Sex*.

Evans, Mary. *Simone de Beauvoir: A Feminist Mandarin*. New York: Tavistock, 1985. Places Beauvoir securely within the context of feminism and appraises *The Second Sex* as an exceptionally influential feminist text.

Heath, Jane. *Simone de Beauvoir*. New York: Harvester Wheatsheaf, 1989. Focuses "not on 'Simone de Beauvoir—Feminist', but on the feminine in her texts." Heath uses *The Second Sex* as a point of departure for studying Beauvoir's fictional and autobiographical works.

Moi, Toril. *Feminist Theory and Simone de Beauvoir*. Oxford, England: Basil Blackwell, 1990. A concise investigation into the critical reception and critical implications of Beauvoir's work.

Winegarten, Renée. *Simone de Beauvoir: A Critical View*. Oxford, England: Berg, 1988. A rather severe rightist assessment of Beauvoir as shrewish, domineering, naïve, and irrational in her personal and political positions. Toril Moi offers a fair corrective to Winegarten, whose anti-Marxist reading of the Marxist Beauvoir offers a challenging approach to an understanding of Beauvoir's ideological arena.

Roy Arthur Swanson

SEDUCTION AND BETRAYAL: Women and Literature

Author: Elizabeth Hardwick (1916-)
Type of work: Literary criticism
First published: 1974

Form and Content

A collection of essays that originally appeared in the influential *New York Review of Books*, a journal that Hardwick helped to found in 1963, *Seduction and Betrayal: Women and Literature* focuses on both women's lives in literature and literature in the lives of women. As a woman critic writing about other women, both real and fictional, Hardwick provides interesting pieces of literary, biographical, and social criticism from a viewpoint that, at the time of their original appearance, was clearly in the minority.

Beginning with an extended discussion of the role of literature in the lives of the three Brontë sisters, Anne, Charlotte, and Emily, Hardwick makes her main foray into the lives of fictional women with substantial essays on three plays by the Norwegian dramatist Henrik Ibsen: *A Doll's House* (1879), *Hedda Gabler* (1890), and *Rosmersholm* (1886). This section is followed by a series of essays on three twentieth century women—Zelda Fitzgerald, Sylvia Plath, and Virginia Woolf—after which Hardwick turns to the Romantic period and the early nineteenth century. Her discussions of Dorothy Wordsworth (the sister of the poet William Wordsworth) and Jane Carlyle (the wife of the great man of letters Thomas Carlyle), which together constitute a section of her book that has been entitled "Amateurs," is followed by the volume's title essay, which is the most wide-ranging and speculative piece in the book. About the essay "Seduction and Betrayal" Hardwick tells the reader, in a prefatory note, that it was presented as a lecture at Vassar College in 1972, and the setting of its original presentation (a college audience consisting, presumably, mostly of women) may account for the rather pointed formulation of its thesis, which is that although seduction may be very damaging to the victim, the seducer's activity is fundamentally comic. The female perspective is clearly present here, since most men would be likely to regard their efforts at seduction as serious business indeed.

Hardwick shows much empathy toward the subjects of her essays, especially those women who had to overcome great obstacles in order to become published writers. There is a particular appreciation for the situation of the woman writer whose husband is also a literary artist. This sympathetic understanding no doubt has its roots in Hardwick's own situation as the wife of the poet Robert Lowell, whose stature often seemed to eclipse her work. Hardwick, who in addition to two volumes of essays and numerous short stories also produced three novels, clearly knew by experience how difficult it can be for a woman to find time and space in which to do her intellectual work.

There is also, however, clear evidence of Hardwick's ability to be truly critical of the subjects of her essays, be they men or women. There is no glossing over the fact that Thomas Carlyle's domestic behavior bordered on abuse or that William Wordsworth took advantage of his sister's work. Her censure is at its strongest, however, when she speaks about such Ibsen characters as Hedda Gabler, in whom she finds no redeeming qualities, and Rebecca West, the female protagonist of *Rosmersholm*. Hardwick is able to admire many of Ibsen's women without finding it necessary to admire those traits in them which lead to the destruction of both themselves and others.

Analysis

Hardwick's interest in the public and private lives of women manifests itself throughout *Seduction and Betrayal*, as does her special understanding of the many difficulties that have to be overcome by the successful woman writer. Most of these difficulties have to do with the position of women in the family and in society under the rule of patriarchy. In her first essay, "The Brontës," Hardwick discusses how Anne, Charlotte, and Emily

Brontë developed their literary talents and careers in the face of particular challenges: poverty, illness, and lack of love.

The lives of Ibsen's women figures are of interest to Hardwick, much as if these characters had been creatures of flesh and blood. Willingly suspending her knowledge that Ibsen's women are not real human beings, she submits them to the kind of careful psychological analysis that might have been appropriate in a biographical essay. Hardwick also goes beyond the Ibsen characters themselves to the real people who inspired them, noting, for example, the connection between Ibsen's young German friend Emilie Bardach and the siren Hilde Wangel in *The Master Builder* (1892).

Hardwick's discussion of the character Nora Helmer in *A Doll's House* is an excellent example of how a consideration of both the literary figure and the human model behind her can be helpful. After offering a close, clear, concise, and insightful reading of the play, Hardwick poses the question of how the impressions of Nora which are given in the first act can be reconciled with the picture of Nora which is presented in the final act of the drama. The problem is, says Hardwick, that Nora seems to have developed too far and too fast. Hardwick points out, however, that the woman who served as the model for Nora in real life was well known to Ibsen as a resourceful and intelligent person, and she holds that Nora Helmer should therefore be regarded as someone who, from the very beginning, is a highly capable person. When the interpreter shifts the accent from Nora's development to the way in which she is forced to hide her true abilities, both Nora's character and Ibsen's drama come across as being highly unified.

Hardwick's reading of *Hedda Gabler* rivals that of *A Doll's House* in importance. Hardwick feels a need to censure Hedda, but she is also aware of the role that this bored and unmotivated protagonist has played in the cultural development that has taken place since the publication of the drama. Hedda, says Hardwick, is much more of a cultural prophecy than is Nora, because numerous literary characters created after Ibsen created her are her spiritual descendants.

The third and final section on Ibsen is devoted to a discussion of the love triangle in the play *Rosmersholm*. Its female protagonist, Rebecca West, is a strong woman who, unfortunately, is lacking in scruples. In the end, however, her destructive bent turns self-destructive, and her suicide, says Hardwick, is a logical consequence of the way she has chosen to live.

Hardwick continues her meditations on the theme of self-destruction in the next segment of her book, "Victims and Victors." Zelda Fitzgerald, Sylvia Plath, and Virginia Woolf were all tormented human beings whose sufferings, it seems, were prerequisites to their work. These are heroic women, and their defeats add to their heroism. In her discussion of Virginia Woolf, Hardwick also devotes considerable attention to the sexual experimentation of the members of the Bloomsbury group, the group of intellectuals among whom Woolf lived and worked.

As a contrast to the specifically modern tribulations of Fitzgerald, Plath, and Woolf, Hardwick details the life situations of Dorothy Wordsworth and Jane Carlyle, who essentially sacrificed their lives and possible careers for, respectively, a brother and a husband. Hardwick regards Dorothy Wordsworth as utterly dependent on others because there was no other way open to her, whereas Jane Carlyle's ironic and ambivalent bent makes her a very interesting representative of the Victorian wife.

Hardwick rounds off her volume with her essay "Seduction and Betrayal," which is largely a study of illicit sex in literature. She concludes that since innocence no longer has any social value, seduction has lost its tragic potential and sex has become useless as literary material.

Context

Seduction and Betrayal was Hardwick's second volume of essays. The first, *A View of My Own: Essays in Literature and Society* (1962), whose title alluded to Virginia Woolf's well-known feminist statement *A Room of One's Own* (1929), signaled that Hardwick was consciously placing her work in a feminist tradition of writing. Many of the essays that were collected in *Seduction and Betrayal*, particularly those that discuss Ibsen's women characters, touch on the image of women which is presented in literature. They are thus in line with much other feminist criticism that came forth in the 1960's and the early 1970's, although Hardwick is not as critical of Ibsen as some of her sister feminists were of the male authors about whom they were writing. Other essays in the volume, which are exercises in literary biography and social criticism at least as much as they are specifically *literary* criticism, show a much more acute awareness of the way women have suffered in patriarchal society. These essays are representative of a trend in women's studies which gathered momentum around the year 1975, when feminist scholars and critics developed a perspective that was centered on women, focusing their writing almost exclusively on women's literature and women's experiences in life. Hardwick's work is clearly in the vanguard of this movement and may even have had a hand in shaping it.

Hardwick has received high praise for her polished style of writing, her sensibility, and her wit. Addressing such women's concerns as how women have had to balance their relationships with men against their concern for their own work, how women, owing to their biology, have been vulnerable, and how they have had to cope with a socially limited set of options in life, she touches on themes of universal interest. Because these essays originally appeared in the pages of *The New York Review of Books*, a journal that Hardwick helped to found and edit, they reached an important segment of the American public and affected the cultural and political climate in the country.

Elizabeth Hardwick's other works include the novels *The Ghostly Lover* (1945), *The Simple Truth* (1955), and *Sleepless Nights* (1979), as well as many short stories and essays. A third volume of essays is *Bartleby in Manhattan and Other Essays* (1983).

Sources for Further Study

Friedan, Betty. *The Feminine Mystique*. New York: W. W. Norton, 1963. An exploration of the ways in which women's behavior is controlled through social norms, Friedan's book was a harbinger of the American women's movement in the latter part of the twentieth century. A classic of its kind.

Gilbert, Sandra M., and Susan Gubar. *The Madwoman in the Attic: The Woman Writer and the Nineteenth-Century Literary Imagination*. New Haven, Conn.: Yale University Press, 1979. A collection of readings of major woman writers of the nineteenth century, the volume also presents a controversial theory of female creativity. The authors maintain that male writers have traditionally looked to their sexuality as a source of imagery for explanations of their creativity, and they propose that this has put women literary artists at a disadvantage. Therefore, Gilbert and Gubar claim, women writers should explain their own creativity with reference to the female body. The scope of *The Madwoman in the Attic* is formidable. The book is, however, also highly readable.

Millett, Kate. *Sexual Politics*. Garden City, N.Y.: Doubleday, 1970. A pioneering work in feminist literary criticism, Millett's book first defines the nature of the power relationship between the sexes and then demonstrates how this relationship is enacted in works by such male authors as D. H. Lawrence, Henry Miller, Norman Mailer, and Jean Genet. A highly political work, Millett's book has been criticized for being one sided. It is, however, both powerfully argued and readable. It has a good index.

Moi, Toril. *Sexual-Textual Politics: Feminist Literary Theory*. London: Methuen, 1985. Emphasizing the Anglo-American and French traditions of feminist literary theory, Moi offers a brief and readable introduction to the field from a leftist perspective. Of particular value is Moi's discussion of the French feminist theorists Hélène Cixous, Luce Irigaray, and Julia Kristeva. Her section on Anglo-American feminist criticism gives useful summaries of the work of Betty Friedan, Kate Millett, Sandra Gilbert, and Susan Gubar, as well as Elaine Showalter. *Sexual-Textual Politics* contains an index, a bibliography, and suggestions for further reading.

Showalter, Elaine. *A Literature of Their Own: British Women Novelists from Brontë to Lessing*. Princeton, N.J.: Princeton University Press, 1977. Although some feminists believe that Showalter is not sufficiently critical of patriarchal power, Showalter's book is useful. It contains both an index and a useful bibliography

Jan Sjåvik

SEXING THE CHERRY

Author: Jeanette Winterson (1959-)
Type of work: Novel
Type of plot: Fable
Time of plot: 1630-1666 and the late twentieth century
Locale: England
First published: 1989

Principal characters:

Jordan, a young man in Renaissance England
The Dog-Woman, the independent giantess who adopted Jordan as an infant
John Tradescant, the Royal Gardener to the king and an explorer
Fortunata, the youngest of the Twelve Dancing Princesses and the object of Jordan's affections
Nicolas Jordan, a modern counterpart to Jordan, who gives up his career in the Navy to join an ecological protest
A chemist, the unnamed modern recipient of Dog-Woman's prodigious outrage and Fortunata's charisma
Dog-Woman's neighbor, a filthy woman with occult powers
Preacher Scroggs and **Neighbor Firebrace,** opportunists who join the Puritan uprising

Form and Content

The title *Sexing the Cherry* refers to determining the gender of a grafted cherry tree. New to the seventeenth century, the art of grafting fruit trees is practiced by the protagonist, Jordan, during his apprenticeship to the Renaissance figure John Tradescant. Metaphorically minded, Jordan seeks to fuse himself with spirits of self-possessed women to form a hardier, more complete self. The form of the novel is itself a graft of perspectives, with its alternating narrations of a mother and her adopted son, which in turn contain the fabulous tales of others, especially women, who overcome obstacles by living fearlessly in new ways.

Indeed, Jordan, in his journey to find himself, becomes a collector of exotic experiments in living, as well as the man who brings the first pineapple to England. On one occasion, disguising himself as a woman in hopes of finding the elusive dancer Fortunata, Jordan lives among kept prostitutes who escape their fortress nightly on an underground river. On another occasion, he accompanies a word cleaner as she mops up, from her balloon, the clusters of spent phrases hovering above the town. He dreams of a town of cunning debtors who tear down and move their homes nightly to escape their creditors. He is struck by the power and melancholy of the myth of Artemis, who reminds him of his mother, and he causes a riot in a city attempting to recover from plagues of love. He is most enamored of the drifting city whose inhabitants have given up gravity. The unmoored town, beloved by the Twelve Dancing Princesses, glides by several times, embodying Jordan's sense of shifting time and space.

The Dog-Woman, in contrast, never goes far from London and keeps a linear sense of time. Through her, the reader watches Jordan grow from the infant found among the bulrushes to the young man she knows must leave her. Through her, the reader witnesses the swelling uprising of Cromwell and the Puritans. She attends the trial of King Charles I and his subsequent beheading but lives to see Cromwell's corpse unearthed and his followers dismembered, and she wreaks her own Old Testament vengeance on enough Puritans to obtain 119 eyeballs and 2,000 teeth. A revealing narrator but a protective mother, the Dog-Woman does not want to hold her son back with the knowledge of her own humiliating experience of romantic love or by letting him know how much she will miss him, and he is hurt by this.

After the climax of Jordan's own story, after he has found Fortunata and she has sent him on with a kiss, the narration takes a leap of three hundred years and is taken up by clearly recognizable descendants of the original narrators. The young Nicolas Jordan has the same boat-building obsession that his namesake possesses, and he is inspired by a painting of the first pineapple being presented to Charles II. The young, unnamed descendent of the Dog-Woman outgrows her prepubescent girth, however, and takes on the more svelte but no less avenging profile of Artemis, and Nicolas is as taken by a glimpse of her as Jordan was with Fortunata. In both centuries, the women fight alone against the pollution and greed of their times as the men who would be heroes look to them for love.

Analysis

Like the journeys concealing journeys Jordan wishes to record, the narratives contain narratives and the meditations meditations in *Sexing the Cherry*, and, in the tradition of all fables, their true meanings seem viscerally obvious while remaining literally elusive. In outline a kind of picaresque search for an idealized, heterosexual love, the novel ultimately questions the possibility of such a union and seems to posit instead self-realization as a rather melancholy bonding with a community of self-made, parentless individuals.

Nowhere in its many tales is there an example of a happy traditional marriage. It is as if by this time in human history it is already too late for men and women to be together. By the time Jordan finds Fortunata on her island, she is past hoping to belong to someone else; she has learned to dance alone, and she recounts for him the myth of Artemis as if to argue that this has always been the way for strong women. The stories of the Twelve Dancing Princesses reiterate this point. In this feminist revision of the traditional fairy tale, the princesses create their own happy endings by escaping marriage to live alone or with other women. Their tales read like a catalog of the ways in which men are unworthy; men are unloving, unfaithful, untrusting, unattractive, distracted, depressed, intolerant, and simply pale in comparison to the women with whom three of the princesses are in love. When the novel leaps to the late twentieth century, the strong female is still unmarried and alone, passionately involved in her own work, not hating men, just wishing they would try harder.

Against this emerging litany of bad male behavior, which includes the antics of Puritans Preacher Scroggs and Neighbour Firebrace, the god Orion, and the polluting captains of industry, stands the sweet, poetic soul of the male protagonist. Jordan, who loves his Rabelaisian freak of a mother, employs great compassion and a philosophic diction in his consideration of all things and exhibits an especially high regard for women. From his earliest memory of slowly being engulfed in a fog to his finally running into himself in the smoke of burning London, Jordan is a guileless seeker of the sense of existence, whose narration captures the sympathy of the reader and helps exonerate his gender. He only wants the women he loves to ask him to stay; that they never do lends the story a tragic cast.

Educated and metaphysically minded, Jordan tests the accepted notions of his time against his gathered experiences. Discussing the nature of time itself, he notes the difference between an outward perception of linear progression and the inward sense of moving freely between memory and precognition. Indeed, Jordan himself seems to move beyond his time when he describes matter as empty space and light, and when he uses peculiarly modern phrases such as "out-of-body"' and "superconductivity." For all his precocious understanding, however, by novel's end he is more certain about the shifting nature of reality than he is about the proper stance toward love.

Inside his story is that of his mother. Uneducated and of limited experience, the Dog-Woman reaches more pragmatic and more definitive conclusions. Her language is more medieval and is infused with biblical allusion. Describing being in love as "that cruelty which takes us straight to the gates of Paradise only to remind us they are closed for ever," she resigns herself to knowing only the loyal love of her dogs and her boy. She intuitively rejects the inflexibility and narrowness of the Puritan doctrine, but she considers grafting an unnatural practice that goes against the Bible, and she refuses to believe that the earth is anything but flat. Her practicality and self-acceptance efface her fantastic girth, but it is her exceptional dimension that ultimately makes her the model of the self-sufficient woman. Men persecute her at their peril; their muskets are impotent against her.

Throughout the novel, women are granted special powers that level the playing field for them in their dealings with societies defined by men. The size of the Dog-Woman, the sorcery of the crone, the hunting skills of Artemis, the intellectual prowess of the chemist, the lightness of Fortunata, and the individual cunning of each of Fortunata's sisters give these women the edge that allows them to make their own decisions. Given the chance to live as they will, they seem to be smarting from the ways men act and not ready at novel's end to let them do more than help them achieve their goals.

Context

Given her huge proportions and seventeenth century lifetime, Jeanette Winterson's Dog-Woman is clearly following in Gargantua's footsteps. Unlike the sixteenth century French satirist Rabelais' King in *Gargantua and Pantagruel*, she has the more modest appetite of a peasant woman, and she uses her girth to fight for social justice as she personalizes it. Hers is a caricature informed by a twentieth century sensibility that empowers the woman who is scorned because her figure fails to conform to the standards of attractiveness set by male society. Although she can wreak havoc on those who cross her, she cannot make them love her romantically, so she still suffers in the ways that women conventionally have in literature. After all, it is her son who does the adventuring after love, while she stays at home, the abandoned mother, longing for his return.

It is in the revision of the fairy tale in the stories of the Twelve Dancing Princesses that Winterson's women defy their restricted choices and refuse to accept the marriages that have been arranged for them. She also has Fortunata give Artemis' side of the story regarding the death of Orion; to hear her retell it, it was a tale not of love and accidental death but of rape and revenge. In choosing to alter the archetypes, Winterson, like Angela Carter in *Strangers and Saints* and *The Company of Wolves*, has targeted the very source of the fearsome instruction that is aimed at clipping female wings. It is a testament to these writers' literary skill that the new versions of old stories read like recast emotional truths rather than rhetorical diatribes.

Winterson's first book, *Oranges Are Not the Only Fruit*, was an autobiographical lesbian coming-out story in the tradition of Rita Mae Brown's *Rubyfruit Jungle*, tinged with a macabre religiosity reminiscent of Flannery O'Connor. Having established her sexual preference in the first person, Winterson began using the device of switching back and forth between male and female narrators, first in *The Passion* and then in *Sexing the Cherry*, as if these were two sides of herself. Virginia Woolf used a similar technique in *Orlando*, where the hero/heroine changes gender as he/she lives across centuries. Both women use gender juxtaposition to point out the inequities that women suffer solely because of their sex and use the gender switch to consider women sexually, although Winterson is not shy about having women pursue women. Hers is an inclusive vision, more focused on the nature of love and self-fulfillment than on political realities, and although it is gender-blended, ultimately, like the titular cherry, it is female.

Sources for Further Study

Brown, Rosellen. Review of *Sexing the Cherry*. *Women's Review of Books* 12 (September, 1990): 9. A critical review of *Sexing the Cherry* from a feminist perspective. Thorough and accessible, it both praises Winterson and takes her to task.

Gerrard, Nicci. *Into the Mainstream: How Feminism Has Changed Women's Writing*. London: Pandora Press, 1989. An overview of the milieu of women's writing that brings in the opinions of women writers, literary agents, and editors and puts Jeanette Winterson's early work into a comprehensible context.

Gorra, Michael. Review of *Sexing the Cherry*. *The New York Times Book Review*, April 29, 1990, p. 24. A somewhat defensive but nevertheless insightfully critical review that considers *Sexing the Cherry* a fashionable historical pastiche with a unique emotional intensity.

Hunt, Sally, ed. *New Lesbian Criticism, Literary and Cultural Readings*. London: Simon & Schuster, 1992. The essay on Jeanette Winterson discusses *Oranges Are Not the Only Fruit* as a "cross-over" text into the dominant culture that lost its radical lesbian content when it was made into a television movie.

Innes, Charlotte. Review of *Sexing the Cherry*. *The Nation* 251, no. 2 (July 9, 1990): 64-65. A substantive review of *Sexing the Cherry*, locating the work within the genre of lesbian fiction and clearly elucidating its complex reality.

Krist, Gary. Review of *Sexing the Cherry*. *Hudson Review* 43, no. 4 (Winter, 1991): 695-707. An in-depth review of *Sexing the Cherry* from a male perspective. While judging the work to be unfair to men, Krist finds much in it to admire.

Susan Chainey

SEXUAL POLITICS

Author: Kate Millett (1934-   )
Type of work: Social criticism
First published: 1970

Form and Content

Sexual Politics is a study of the political aspects of sex. It is divided into three parts: "Sexual Politics," "Historical Background," and "The Literary Reflection." In part 1, Millett gives examples of the ways in which power and domination are defined in contemporary literary descriptions of sexual activity. She analyzes the work of Henry Miller, Norman Mailer, and Jean Genet. A good example of Millett's style and point of view in this section is her treatment of Norman Mailer's novel *An American Dream*, in which "female sexuality is depersonalized to the point of being a matter of class or a matter of nature." Mailer's hero, Stephen Rojack, has anal intercourse with a German maid, Ruta, who has the "invaluable 'knowledge of a city rat.' " The word "invaluable" is Millett's, and she uses it to emphasize the ideology of sex that she finds deplorable in Mailer's writing. To combat Mailer's domination of women through his use of language, she responds with a dismissive and sarcastic style: "How evil resides in [Ruta's] bowels or why Ruta has a greater share of it than her master may appear difficult to explain, but many uncanny things are possible with our author." Mailer is only one example that proves that "sex is a status category"—as Millett puts it in "Theory of Sexual Politics," the second chapter of part 1.

In part 2, Millett describes the development of sex roles in the nineteenth and twentieth centuries, the efforts of women to achieve equal status with men, and the male "patriarchal" reaction aimed at thwarting revolutionary change and women's liberation. Mary Wollstonecraft's *A Vindication of the Rights of Woman* (1792) is discussed as the "first document asserting the full humanity of women and insisting upon its recognition." The book was written in the milieu of the French Revolution, and its ideas were taken up by men and women who focused on educational reform and the establishment of schools in the 1830's, which mark the proper beginning of "The Woman's Movement." Millett surveys the political organizations, the suffrage movement, and the nature of employment in this period of the "sexual revolution." She also analyzes the polemical writings for and against women's rights, focusing on the debate between John Stuart Mill (1806-1873) and John Ruskin (1819-1900), and on the writings of Karl Marx (1818-1883) and Friedrich Engels (1820-1895)—the latter providing the "most comprehensive account of patriarchal history and economy." These philosophers and social critics are compared with literary figures such as Thomas Hardy, whose novel *Jude the Obscure* (1894) is about the trials of two male and female figures rebelling against the patriarchal institutions of their times. The last chapter of part 2, "The Counterrevolution," attempts to explain why many of the advances in women's rights were reversed or undermined. Her theory is essentially intellectual and psychological: "Only the outer surface of society has been changed; underneath the essential system was preserved undisturbed. Should it receive new sources of support, new ratification, new ideological justifications, it could be mobilized anew." Hence, she concentrates on Sigmund Freud (1856-1939), whose theories of female sexuality were used to sponsor conservative and antifeminist arguments and actions.

In part 3, Millett conducts a spirited analysis of the content of literary works by D. H. Lawrence, Henry Miller, Norman Mailer, and Jean Genet. Each of these authors—all were thought to be daring and revolutionary—is severely chastised for promulgating a climate of opinion hostile to feminism and female liberation. She discovers that their characters, themes, and plots frustrate the possibility of revolutionary change in sexual roles and assure the continuation of a patriarchal way of life.

Analysis

Millett began writing *Sexual Politics* as a doctoral dissertation under the guidance of Steven Marcus, a distinguished critic and professor at Columbia University. In books such as *The Other Victorians: A Study of*

Sexuality and Pornography in Mid-Nineteenth Century England, Marcus combines a sensitive understanding of historical trends and literary works to create a highly nuanced and sophisticated brand of cultural criticism. The structure of *Sexual Politics* shows that Millett employs Marcus' method to write a polemical and political form of history and criticism. She is not merely concerned with political and literary arguments in their historical context; she is determined to advance the argument for sexual revolution and the liberation of women. Her critique is radical in that she is calling for change and measuring the writers she studies against her criteria regarding what constitutes positive reform. She is, in other words, avowedly ideological. She is asking whether a specific work has the right politics—does it demean or honor women's rights?

By adopting an ideological position and pursuing it with verve, Millett is able to write with extraordinary energy and humor. She is not awed by the august writers she analyzes, because it is not their greatness per se that she confronts but rather their positions on the sexual issues that interest her and that she has defined to her satisfaction. She is thus her own authority on the subject, and as such she can face her formidable male subjects on the same level. It is an unusual stance for a historian or literary critic to assume, especially one who has been academically trained. Usually it is the creative writer turned critic who adopts such a commanding voice.

A good example of Millett's stance is her treatment of D. H. Lawrence's novel *The Rainbow*. Lawrence has often been admired for creating strong women, but Millett sees in his creation of Ursula a stereotype of the castrating female: "Her vehicle of destruction is moonlight, for Lawrence is addicted to the notion of the moon as a female symbol, once beneficent, but lately malefic and a considerable public danger." This is classic Millett, deflating with humor what she regards as Lawrence's pretentious symbolism and his factitious use of women to support it. To say "Lawrence is addicted" is to reduce his literary work to the level of a personal compulsion, a neurosis, and to deprive him of his authority. By calling attention to such characters and scenes, Millett is probing the peculiarity of male creations; she is implicitly asking why women have to be presented in this way. Her criticism is disconcerting because it will not take the author's creation as a given; instead, she investigates the roots of such scenes in the author's own attitudes toward women, thus making the author's literature seem tendentious.

No part of *Sexual Politics* created a greater stir when it was first published than the section on Henry Miller. Miller had been regarded as the apostle of sexual liberation, a heroic figure because he had been censored and banned in the United States. In one sentence, Millett stands the heretofore conventional view of Miller on its head: "Actually, Miller is a compendium of American sexual neuroses, and his value lies not in freeing us from such afflictions, but in having had the honesty to express and dramatize them." He is given a tribute of sorts, but hardly the kind he had been accorded by others, who hailed his freedom from bourgeois restraints and the leftover Victorianism inhibiting his contemporaries from treating sexual matters as frankly and as robustly as he did. Millett does not deny his appeal: "There is a culturally cathartic release in Miller's writing, but it is really a result of the fact that he first gave voice to the unutterable." The women in Miller's fiction are barely seen as human beings, Millett argues: "Miller confronts nothing more challenging than the undifferentiated genital that exists in masturbatory reverie."

Millett reserves some of her angriest and funniest prose for Norman Mailer— perhaps because he is closer to her generation (he was born in 1923) and has been so outspoken about male prerogatives. As she puts it, "his critical and political prose is based on a set of values so blatantly and comically chauvinist, as to constitute a new aesthetic." His theory, says Millett, is that "men have 'more rights and more powers' because life takes more out of them, leaves them 'used more.' " One passage in her chapter on Mailer constitutes the apotheosis of her attack on the male author's infantile quest for power and domination:

> As he settles into patriarchal middle age, Mailer's obsession with machismo brings to mind a certain curio sold in Coney Island and called a Peter Meter; a quaint bit of folk art, stamped out in the shape of a ruler with printed inches and appropriate epithets to equate excellence with size. Mailer operates on this scale on an abstract or metaphoric plane. His characters, male and female, labor under simpler delusions. Guinevere [in *Barbary Shore*] is indefatigable on the subject of her lover's "whangs"; D. J. [in *Why Are We in Vietnam?*] is paralyzed with the usual fear that someone else has a bigger one.

By situating Mailer so snugly in the context of popular, pornographic culture, she deprives him of his claims to literary and male superiority. She comes close to saying that in Mailer's "new aesthetic," literature is male—no matter how ridiculous that notion seems.

Jean Genet, the last major male literary figure Millett engages, seems to represent the antithesis of Mailer, because Genet's homosexuality is something that Mailer cannot abide. Yet Millett finds the same disturbing pattern in Genet: "Masculine is superior strength, feminine is inferior weakness." The only exception to this generalization is the intelligence and moral courage he reserves for his homosexual queens and for himself.

It is hard not to conclude from Millett's relentless polemic that male authors are virtually incapable of creating full-fledged and free female characters. Why this is so, she argues, can be understood by examining the springs of their own psychology and the society that has produced them.

Context

It is difficult to exaggerate the impact of *Sexual Politics* on literary and cultural criticism, and on the women's movement in the 1970's and afterward. It was a best-seller, a controversial work both praised and attacked, and a text used in many college courses in literature and women's studies. Although female critics before Millett raised similar issues, none of them were as bold, as inflammatory, or amusing. Even readers who opposed her ideas could no longer regard writers such as Miller and Mailer in the old way. Woman as a category in literature deserving special attention was given new meaning, and exhilarated students and scholars took up the polemics of *Sexual Politics*, refining the book's conclusions and modifying and expanding its theses. The phrase "sexual politics" became part of the vocabulary of the time.

Sexual Politics has maintained its special place in women's studies. It is universally acknowledged as a pioneering work. Feminist scholars have serious reservations about Millett's book and have deplored the crudeness of some of its techniques—chiefly a penchant for ignoring the style and structure of literary works in favor of a content analysis that implies that a writer's work is merely the sum of his or her ideas and opinions. Millett lacks subtlety, these scholars conclude, and she exaggerates the originality of her own position by ignoring the foundations in women's literature and criticism on which her own work is built. Even Millett's harshest critics, however, pay tribute to her vivid style, which continues to energize readers and to pose important questions. She set an agenda for women's studies which has by no means been exhausted.

Sources for Further Study

Belsey, Catherine, and Jane Moore, eds. *The Feminist Reader: Essays in Gender and the Politics of Literary Criticism.* New York: Basil Blackwell, 1989. The introduction links Millett's work with Germaine Greer's *The Female Eunuch* and Eva Figes' *Patriarchal Attitudes*, witty, eloquent, and wide-ranging polemics reflective of the 1960's, when the existing authorities were challenged by the politics of liberation.

Gornick, Vivian. *Essays in Feminism.* New York: Harper & Row, 1978. In "Why Do These Men Hate Women," Gornick discusses Mailer's response in *The Prisoner of Sex* to *Sexual Politics*. While praising his eloquent defense of Miller and Lawrence against Millett's "distorting polemic," she finds that other aspects of his argument confirm Millett's conclusions.

Humm, Maggie. *Feminist Criticism: Women as Contemporary Critics.* New York: St. Martin's Press, 1986. Discusses Millett as a pioneer in feminist criticism and her indebtedness to Simone de Beauvoir. Provides a close reading of *Sexual Politics*.

Mailer, Norman. *The Prisoner of Sex.* Boston: Little, Brown, 1971. Mailer's rebuttal to Millett, which takes the form of a keen literary analysis of two of Millett's targets: D. H. Lawrence and Henry Miller. Mailer demonstrates that Millett rips quotations out of context and literally rewrites many of the scenes she purports to describe.

Miller, Nancy K. *Getting Personal: Feminist Occasions and the Other Autobiographical Acts.* New York: Routledge, 1991. Recognizes Millett as a pioneering feminist scholar who takes on the "massively male precincts of literary history."

Moi, Toril. *Sexual/Textual Politics: Feminist Literary Theory.* New York: Methuen, 1985. Contains a chapter on *Sexual Politics* as a feminist classic. Discusses the response of feminist critics to the book, particularly their rehabilitation of Freud and their reservations about Millett's treatment of him.

Carl Rollyson

SILENT SPRING

Author: Rachel Carson (1907-1964)
Type of work: Social criticism
First published: 1962

Form and Content

Citing a letter written by Olga Owens Huckins in 1958 as her inspiration for writing, Rachel Carson begins *Silent Spring* with a warning: If humans do not stop their greed and carelessness, they will destroy the earth. Huckins told Carson of her own bitter experience of a small world made lifeless; Carson then goes on to reveal how her findings as a trained scientist led her to speak out against the reckless male-dominated society that poisons the world.

To lay the groundwork for her book and to explain the title *Silent Spring*, pioneer ecofeminist Carson begins with what she calls "a fable for tomorrow." She sketches a bountiful American community that is destroyed by a strange blight that moves like a shadow of death across the land, eventually creating a spring without bees or birds—a silent spring. This mythical community has countless counterparts around the world thanks to what Carson calls the "impetuous and heedless pace of man."

Continuing with a history of life on earth to show the natural interaction between living things, *Silent Spring* meticulously exposes the lethal contamination of air, earth, rivers, and seas. Carson draws on her research into the way in which chemicals pass from one organism to another through all the links in the food chain to illustrate the need to control products she calls not "insecticides" but "biocides." She reminds citizens of their rights to protect themselves against lethal poisons that have increased alarmingly in the twentieth century.

Each chapter addresses one aspect of the deadly contamination process, explaining in scientific terms the chemical structure and then exposing the resulting effects on the natural habitat. Carson illustrates the cost of this negligence by examining regions, cities, and individuals across America that have suffered from the dangerous interaction of chemicals with the environment. These illustrations are carefully selected to extend the work beyond a strictly scientific observation into the realm of social criticism. For example, Carson describes housewives in Michigan sweeping granules of poisonous insecticide from their porches and sidewalks, where they are reported to have looked like snow. Within a few days after the insecticide-spraying operation that caused this deadly rain, Detroiters began to report large numbers of dead and dying birds to the local Audubon Society. Throughout the book, Carson's actual scenarios parallel in a frightening fashion the mythical fable that begins the book.

Horrifyingly beautiful is a way one might describe Carson's writing. Aesthetically pleasing in its sensitive descriptions of earth and its inhabitants, this 262-page work is at the same time scientifically well-documented, listing thirty pages of notes and scholarly research. While Carson remains a critical and scrupulous scientist, she makes her most persuasive appeal through her emphasis on the value and beauty of the natural world. Her criticism of a number of entities responsible for the assaults upon the environment—the narrowly specialized scientific community, the dollar-driven chemical industry, and weak government agencies—constitutes a landmark challenge to a social system in need of a warning cry. The work paves the way for extended analysis and commentary by later twentieth century ecologists and eco-feminists.

Analysis

In her desire to put an end to the false assurances that the public is asked to accept about the safety of the environment, Carson puts forth a full complement of facts, noting that the obligation to endure gives people the right to know. In the chapter "Surface Waters and Underground Seas," the author's discussion of the amazing history of Clear Lake, California, for example, exposes the results of anglers' efforts to control a small gnat, *Chaoborus astictopus*. Carson explains that their chemical of choice, DDD, a close relative of DDT, apparently offered fewer threats to fish life. Gnat control was fairly good but needed follow-up applications to be truly successful. Eventually, the biocide also wiped out the grebe population and created massive concentrations of the poison in the lake's fish, which were caught and eaten by anglers. Research proved that DDD has a strong cell-destroying capacity, especially of the cells that make up the human adrenal cortex.

In "Indiscriminately from the Skies," Carson shows what extensive damage was done when irresponsible large-scale treatment was undertaken to eradicate the gypsy moth. The Waller farm in northern Westchester County, New York, was sprayed twice although its owners specifically requested agriculture officials not to proceed. Milk samples taken from the Wallers' cows contained large amounts of DDT. Although the county Health Organization was notified, the milk was still marketed. Nearby truck farms also suffered contamination. Peas tested at fourteen to twenty parts per million of DDT; the legal minimum is seven parts per million. Nevertheless, growers, fearing heavy losses, sold produce containing illegal residues. Carson strongly criticizes this "rain of death," noting that modern poisons, though more dangerous than any known before, are used more indiscriminately.

To illustrate nature's reply to society's chemical assault, the author includes the chapter "Nature Fights Back." Sometimes, chemical application has created an increase in the very problem the spraying was designed to eliminate. In Ontario, for example, blackflies became seventeen times more abundant following spraying. In the Midwest, farmers who attempted to eradicate the Japanese beetle did so successfully, only to find that the much more destructive corn borer was unleashed following the elimination of its natural predator. Nature, it seems, is not easily molded. Yet both nature and humans are considerably weakened by the assault.

Citing society's failure to foresee potential hazards, Carson cautions that even researchers are accustomed to look for the gross and immediate effect and to ignore all else. Thus, the population must be more concerned with the cumulative and delayed effects of absorbing small amounts of chemicals over a lifetime of exposure. The author explains that there is "an ecology of the world within our bodies." A change in even one molecule may initiate changes in seemingly unrelated organs and tissues. In a prophetic statement, for Carson herself was soon to die from cancer, she says, "The most determined effort should be made to eliminate those carcinogens that now contaminate our food, our water supplies, and our atmosphere, because these provide the most dangerous type of contact—minute exposures repeated over and over throughout the years."

To demonstrate that society must make a conscious choice to slow and eventually eliminate the chemical poisoning of the world, in her final chapter, "The Other Road," Carson reminds the reader of Robert Frost's familiar poem "The Road Not Taken." The smooth superhighway that people are on is deceptively easy and clearly disastrous. Other roads lie before modern humans, including opportunities for biological solutions to environmental problems. Some of the most fascinating of the new techniques include those that turn the strength of a species against itself. Yet Carson scorns the very premise upon which many of these biological and chemical controls rest. She says the control of nature is a phrase "conceived in arrogance, born of the Neanderthal age of biology and philosophy, when it was supposed that nature exists for the convenience of man." It is a shame that society uses its most sophisticated technology for such a primitive goal.

The final chapter, which is perhaps the most valuable, deals with the future. In it, Carson argues for humility and an intelligent approach to human interaction with all creatures. Many of the battles with nature that she describes throughout the book have been fought and lost. Unless people revere the miracle of life instead of struggling against it, they are doomed to lose again.

Context

Winner of eight awards, *Silent Spring* is a monumental book that shocked the world with its frightening revelations about the earth's contamination. Not surprisingly, Carson's profound sense of urgency awakened and angered the traditionally male-dominated scientific community, business world, and government agencies. Some critics dismissed her as a hysterical woman and a pseudoscientist, although her work shows her to be neither. Others said that she was merely a recluse interested in preserving the wildflowers along the country's roadsides. Clearly, she had a greater goal in mind. In her book, Carson calls on readers to question the masculinist philosophy and methods of controlling nature. In its boldness, her work has served as an example for ecologists and ecofeminists the world over.

Carson accepts the responsibility for the accuracy

and validity of the voluminous amount of scientific research the book represents, graciously acknowledging four women who were vital to the success of the work: her three research assistants, Jeanne Davis, Dorothy Algire, and Bette Haney Duff; and her housekeeper, Ida Sprow. *Silent Spring* artfully translates Carson's scientific expertise into general readers' terms, a feat that comes as no surprise to many critics following her earlier beautifully written book *The Sea Around Us* (1951). The publication of *Silent Spring* was greeted with waves of fear by men who knew she spoke the truth, men who stood to lose power, prestige, or money through the disclosures and warnings the work contained. Carson, ironically, battled cancer herself in the final stages of writing the book, but she did not permit her personal struggle to get in the way of her goal of presenting the facts and letting the public decide.

Aside from being a concerned woman who awakened the world to the dangers in the air, earth, and water, Rachel Carson was a gifted writer who created memorable images and finely crafted sentences. She says, "deliberately poisoning our food, then policing the result—is too reminiscent of Lewis Carroll's White Knight who thought of 'a plan to dye one's whiskers green, and always use so large a fan that they could not be seen.' " Her pioneering exposé of humanity's foolish behavior strips away those equally foolish efforts to cover up the results. The silence that humanity tried to impose upon nature was broken by this brave woman's voice.

Sources for Further Study

Anderson, Lorraine, ed. *Sisters of the Earth*. New York: Vintage Books, 1991. A collection of women's works of prose and poetry about nature that reflect many of the same issues Rachel Carson raised in *Silent Spring*. The women's voices in this volume express a caring rather than a controlling relationship with nature. Contains a thirty-seven-page annotated bibliography of selected works by women about nature.

Hynes, H. Patricia. *The Recurring Silent Spring*. New York: Pergamon Press, 1989. A work that explores the struggles Carson faced and examines the social and political ramifications of her work. This book examines the new hazards of technology that Carson alluded to in her final chapter.

Inter Press Service, comp. *Story Earth: Native Voices on the Environment*. San Francisco: Mercury House, 1993. This collection of essays gives voice to non-Western cultures and their relationship between humankind and nature. Unlike Western culture, which has sought to subdue nature, the traditional societies examined in this book view it as sacred.

Wallace, Aubrey. *Eco-Heroes: Twelve Tales of Environmental Victory*. Edited by David Gancher. San Francisco: Mercury House, 1993. A series of twelve portraits of environmental activists from around the globe. Thinking globally but acting locally, these eco-heroes have received the Goldman Environmental Prize, considered the Nobel Prize for environmentalists. The essays in this collection explore the stories behind their victories.

Carol F. Bender

SLOUCHING TOWARDS BETHLEHEM

Author: Joan Didion (1934-)
Type of work: Essays
First published: 1968

Form and Content

The first of Joan Didion's collections of essays, *Slouching Towards Bethlehem* takes its title from the last line of "The Second Coming" (1924) by Irish poet William Butler Yeats. The apocalyptic images of that poem had been, Didion says, her "points of reference" at the time she wrote the title essay in 1967. Faced with what she called a "conviction . . . that the world as I had understood it no longer existed," she went to San Francisco to learn about the emerging hippie culture in the Haight-Ashbury district: It was necessary, she wrote, "to come to terms with disorder." Most of the reviewers of this volume have read the collection as a whole in the light of the themes of social upheaval and moral decay that were raised first in this piece.

A preface to the volume contains an explanation of the genesis of the title and the motivation for several of the essays, Didion's reflections on her state of mind during the time she was writing, and descriptions of her habits as a writer during those years. The twenty essays were originally written for magazines—among them *Vogue*, *The Saturday Evening Post*, *The New York Times Magazine*, and *The American Scholar*—during the years 1965 through 1967.

The book is organized into three sections. "Life Styles in the Golden Land" contains eight essays focused on California, which are typically read either as pieces of journalism or as evidence of Didion's regionalism. The five pieces in the section titled "Personals" are often anthologized as "personal essays" in college readers and collections of modern essayists. Of the works in this volume, these are the most explicitly centered in the "I," or persona, of the writer. "Seven Places of the Mind" brings together seven essays, each centered on a geographical location: four on California; one each on Hawaii, Mexico, and Newport, Rhode Island. Neither travel pieces nor distinctly personal, these are perhaps best explained by Didion in her preface: "Since I am neither a camera eye nor much given to writing pieces which do not interest me, whatever I do write reflects, sometimes gratuitously, how I feel."

The essays in this collection represent a range of types of literary nonfiction. Some are intensely personal, offering the details of Didion's own self-doubting under titles such as "On Self-Respect" or "On Keeping a Notebook"; others address subjects such as John Wayne, Las Vegas wedding chapels, and folk singer Joan Baez's school in Carmel. Didion has published in many of the most respected literary periodicals, and she has become a highly respected voice in American letters.

Analysis

By the time *Slouching Towards Bethlehem* appeared, Didion had already won acclaim for her piece by the same title, published in *The Saturday Evening Post*. She was one of the most talented among what had come to be known as the New Journalists. They were practitioners of a kind of "maverick" journalism, and their work was characterized by a focus on subjects considered marginal to mainstream culture, a personal involvement by the writer in the subject, unconventional form often suggested by the subject itself, and a style that violated or transcended (depending upon the point of view) the strict laws of "objectivity" in traditional journalism by placing in the foreground the presence and perspective of the writer. Critical response to Didion's nonfiction has continued to address many of those features so highly touted in "Slouching Towards Bethlehem": her social commentary, her eye for detail, the quality of her voice, and the character or persona inhabited by her essays.

The first sentence of "Slouching Towards Bethlehem"—"The center was not holding"—takes from Yeats's poem the defining metaphor for Didion's social analysis. Danger, cataclysm, and disintegration are evoked in the opening section by an apocalyptic vision of the cultural, social, and moral conditions of the country, drawn with the broad strokes of an epic and haunting cadences in past tense. Haight-Ashbury, with its hippies, drugs, and runaways, was "where the social hemorrhaging was showing up."

Many of the stylistic devices for which Didion is best known are evident here, such as her use of anaphora in the way the sentences begin and clauses are joined, piling images in a tightening spiral of language and vision. Like a number of her other essays, "Slouching Towards Bethlehem" is constructed as a collage: bits of narrative, dialogue, and found texts organized in segments that sometimes break off abruptly and are separated only by white space, without traditional transitions, explicit connectors, or clear chronology. Some readers see the structure of "Slouching Towards Bethlehem" as disjointed, a mirror of the atomization about which Didion writes. Others see its shape as a referent more for her investigative method—accumulating experiences and impressions—than for the social chaos she encountered.

While the subjects of her essays may suggest that she is drawn to themes of social and moral disintegration, an equally important concern for Didion is an exploration of the dissonance between public stories and dreams and individual realities, often illuminated by her relentless focus on the details that do not fit the story. In "7000 Romaine, Los Angeles 38"—an essay ostensibly about the reclusive millionaire Howard Hughes—she calls this dissonance "the apparently bottomless gulf . . . between what we officially admire and secretly desire." Another essay, "Some Dreamers of the Golden Dream," is about Lucille Miller, who was accused and convicted of murdering her husband. In the details of Miller's life and trial, Didion finds a woman who seemed to have imbibed all the myths about upward mobility and the "golden dream" of suburban Southern California, and a lack of moral center that Didion suggests is somehow revealed in the geographical and cultural landscape. In "John Wayne: A Love Song," Didion explores the actor in the light of the cultural myth that had grown up around him, a myth that left no room for a man who could be defeated by a disease such as cancer.

Many of the pieces in this collection have come to be called personal essays, rooted in the strong presence of the first person at the center of the piece and in often uncomfortable revelations about Didion's life, fears, and desires. This is not to say that her other essays do not make use of the personal or the first person. "John Wayne: A Love Song" opens, for example, with memories of watching Wayne's films during the summer of 1943 and reflections on the ways in which lines from those movies have continued to have meaning for her ever since. Didion's personal revelation is not itself the focal point of this essay; it serves, instead, to illustrate a point around which the rest of the essay will develop, about the internal landscape of a generation of women and a figure who "determined forever certain of our dreams."

Differing understandings of the function of the personal in an essay have led to varying interpretations of Didion's literary nonfiction. For some, the personal voice invites analysis of her character and personality. She has been called neurotic, over sensitive, whiny, a woman of brittle nerves, extremely fragile, and consumed by a sense of loss. Indeed, much of the critical response to Didion's nonfiction labels it as autobiography, or as a means to understand the characters in her novels.

While most of the essays in *Slouching Towards Bethlehem* have to do in one way or another with California subjects, they are also about "something else," as Didion almost always asserts somewhere in each piece, and they are not comfortably categorized. "Notes from a Native Daughter," for example, has been read as a description of the particular flavor and character of Sacramento and the Central Valley of California, and as a nostalgic longing for the pastoral and privileged world of Didion's childhood among the landed descendants of original settlers.

Above all, in this collection Didion is a superb stylist. In the haunting rhythms of her sentences, in her startling juxtapositions, her precise effort to get the right word and the right articulation of an idea or an image, her prose is distinctive. Her voice is lyrical and intense, sometimes witty, sometimes pained. Her eye for detail creates what have been called verbal snapshots. Her driving interest in the seemingly irrelevant or marginal, the unreported detail, is one of the most remarkable features of her essays.

Context

At the time that *Slouching Towards Bethlehem* was published, Didion was usually the only woman mentioned among the New Journalists. She is now one of the most recognized essayists in American letters, especially because the attention paid to the essay in college classrooms and literary magazines has grown.

The essays collected in *Slouching Towards Bethlehem*, whether personal or reportage, present a woman's point of view inasmuch as Didion writes out of the particularities of what is repeatedly noted by readers and reviewers as very personal experience. Grounded in the first person, they present the voice of a woman who is not afraid to make her doubts, fears, and longings the subjects of her public musings or to include them in her investigations. Didion does not, in this volume, identify herself as being explicitly concerned with women or women's issues. Her nonfiction is rarely spoken of in terms of feminist concerns; perhaps for this reason, few reviewers and scholars have analyzed it from that critical perspective. This is less true of her fiction, largely because her main characters are all women.

In a 1970 interview, when asked specifically about the women's movement, she responded that social action "does not much engage my imagination"; in a 1979 interview she was described as "skeptical" of it. Her essay "The Women's Movement," published first in *The New York Times Book Review* (1972) and later collected in *The White Album* (1979), is an unsympathetic analysis of what was a relatively young movement at the time of her writing. Response to it by feminist critics—Catharine Stimpson most prominent among them—has taken Didion to task for, among other things, what they claim to be a superficial and inaccurate understanding of the history of the women's movement and of feminism.

Nonfiction by Didion includes the collections of essays *The White Album* (1979) and *After Henry* (1992) and the book-length works *Salvador* (1983) and *Miami* (1987). She remains foremost among American essayists, male or female, recognized for the elegance and distinctness of her style, the precision of her social critique, and the insistently strong presence of the first person in her work.

Sources for Further Study

Anderson, Chris. *Style as Argument: Contemporary American Nonfiction*. Carbondale: Southern Illinois University Press, 1987. Anderson closely examines the literary nonfiction of Tom Wolfe, Truman Capote, Norman Mailer, and Didion, attending particularly to the relationship between style and theme. Relying on classical and contemporary rhetorical and literary theory, Anderson claims that, despite the unique stylistic and rhetorical features of each, what these writers have in common is a self-consciousness about the limits of language. Anderson's is the only major study that engages Didion's nonfiction on its own terms rather than using it as an aid in reading her fiction or telling her biography.

Carton, Evan. "Joan Didion's Dreampolitics of the Self." *Western Humanities Review* 40 (Winter, 1986): 307-328. Carton reads the personal element in *Slouching Towards Bethlehem* as an assertion of self against the seeming disintegration of the cultural landscape which Didion appears to document. He makes his argument through an analysis of the theme and structure of the individual essays. He sees Didion's project as paradoxically related to Marxist and feminist critiques of the "natural, autonomous, decontextualized self."

Didion, Joan. "Cautionary Tales." Interview by Susan Stamberg. In *Joan Didion: Essays and Conversations*, edited by Ellen G. Friedman. Princeton, N.J.: Ontario Review Press, 1984. In an interview originally aired by National Public Radio in 1977, Didion talks about her habits and style as a writer of both fiction and nonfiction.

Felton, Sharon, ed. *The Critical Response to Joan Didion*. Westport, Conn.: Greenwood Press, 1994. Felton's introduction to this collection is the most up-to-date and far-ranging survey of the full scope of Didion's work, making thematic connections among her screenplays, fiction, and nonfiction. The volume contains reviews, selected critical response to Didion's entire canon, a chronology, and an extensive bibliography.

Henderson, Katherine Usher. *Joan Didion*. New York: Frederick Ungar, 1981. This short volume aimed at college students and the general reader, which is among the most frequently cited works of Didion criticism, devotes one chapter to each of Didion's volumes. Henderson reads Didion's fiction and nonfiction as explorations of the moral dilemmas created in the explosion of traditional American myths. She summarizes and provides publication history for each essay in *Slouching Towards Bethlehem*, but she also draws loose and misleading inferences about Didion's life from the essays.

Kazin, Alfred. "Joan Didion: Portrait of a Professional." *Harper's Magazine* 243 (December, 1971): 112-122. This chatty article blends stylistic analysis of Didion's sentences and her moral vision. Although Kazin is one of the most respected American literary and cultural critics, his analysis of Didion's personality may now be read as dated and patronizing.

Stimpson, Catharine. "The Case of Miss Joan Didion." *Ms.* 7 (January, 1973): 36-41. This article is useful in its description and analysis of what Stimpson calls "Didion Woman," who is either child or victim, and with whom Stimpson has lost patience. Among other things, she takes Didion to task for her ignorance about feminism in "The Women's Movement."

Laura Julier

SONNETS FROM THE PORTUGUESE

Author: Elizabeth Barrett Browning (1806-1861)
Type of work: Poetry
First published: 1850, in *Poems*

Form and Content

Sonnets from the Portuguese chronicles the stages in the romance of poet Elizabeth Barrett Browning and her husband, poet Robert Browning. The theme of the entire sequence is announced in the first sonnet. Reading Theocritus, the speaker muses on her own life and its melancholy. While in the midst of her dismal thoughts, she is pulled from behind by the hair. She thinks it is death, but she is corrected: " 'Not Death, but Love.' " This phrase resounds throughout this entire work, which tells how love entered her life and how the beloved, as if he were truly heaven sent, turned her from darkness and the contemplation of the grave to light, love, and life.

The first stage of the relationship runs from Sonnet 1 through Sonnet 9, in which the speaker says she is not worthy to be loved. She portrays herself as old, confined, solitary, and on the verge of death, and she compares this image of herself to the beloved, who is by contrast young, vibrant, sociable, and full of the world of which he is a part. In this stage, she repeatedly asks him to leave her, although ultimately she acknowledges that they are part of each other. She knows that if he does go, she will never be the same. When God sees her tears, the beloved's tears will have blended with them.

Sonnet 10 marks the change to her acceptance of his love and her transformation. She has become aware that love dispels the darkness; she shines radiantly, with a kind of holiness. Nevertheless, her doubts continue; she asks him to love her only for the sake of love. In Sonnet 16, though, she makes the pronouncement that her "strife" is ended, saying that if he entreats her to enter into a loving relationship, she will "rise" to it, and, in Sonnet 20, she affirms life. The next five sonnets portray the union of their souls and show her as being reborn through their union. She becomes safe and happy. Sonnets 28 and 29 are breathlessly passionate love poems.

Yet the new security and confidence in love is held in balance by the insecurity of giving one's self and life over to it (Sonnets 30 to 36). In Sonnet 30, she doubts that love is real, and in the next, she asks that the beloved calm her fears. Whereas Sonnet 33 sounds a note of complete confidence in the relationship, in Sonnet 35 doubts return.

Sonnets 38 through 42 show that love has won. Homage is paid to the beloved, and the speaker now unqualifiedly opts for love and life. By the time she reaches Sonnet 42, she resolves not to let her past life impinge on her future with her beloved, who is better than she could have dreamed anyone to be. One of the most famous poems in the English language crowns the sequence—Sonnet 43, which begins, "How do I love thee?" After this most complete statement of eternal love, Sonnet 44 offers the sonnets to the beloved, just as he has given her many flowers.

Analysis

Disguised on its publication as a translation from the work of the Portuguese poet Luis Vas de Camoëns, *Sonnets from the Portuguese* consists of forty-four sonnets—fourteen-line poems of rhymed iambic pentameter. The first four lines of an Italian, or Petrarchan, sonnet make a statement that the next four lines prove. These eight lines are the "octave." There follows a "turn" in thought. The next six lines, the "sestet," prove further and conclude the statement. The Petrarchan rhyme scheme is *abba, abba, cde, cde*. Browning often writes her sestets, however, with a rhyme scheme of *cdcdcd*. She has been criticized for not adhering strictly to tradition and for not making her rhymes exact.

Nevertheless, her experiments in slant rhyme, which were previously considered technical faults, show Browning to have a more modern ear, for in the twentieth century, exact rhyme rings more and more false as the century wears on. She has been criticized also for not stopping at the ends of each quatrain or at the end of the octave, and for running the lines on past their traditional stopping points. This technique, however, which is called enjambment, delivers her sonnets from what to a modern ear is the sing-song sound of end-stopped rhyme and allows her greater fluidity of thought.

Browning has been criticized also for writing extremely personal and intense love poetry, with no mask either to protect the writer's emotions or to shield the reader from getting too close. Yet it is in this aspect that the sonnets are brilliant. This first-person point of view is actually that of the poet (the progress of the poems can be read along with the same story in Elizabeth and Robert's letters); it is also the voice of a specific woman speaking to a specific listener, and for a century and a half, readers have known who these people are: an ailing and middle-aged woman poet who has seen in her future only the same feebleness of body and spirit that she experienced earlier, and a younger man, also a poet. They tell a story that contains as much reality as romance. The romance is that her beloved has come to rescue her. The reality is that she sees herself as unrescuable. The story of the *Sonnets from the Portuguese* is the story of that middle-aged, unrescuable, and therefore unlovable (according to her) woman poet who is overwhelmed by love and by life. This is not a series of idealizing love poems, but a cycle of very real expressions of a woman who has suffered not only ill health and disappointment but also disillusionment and loss of hope.

Although the *Sonnets* are autobiographical, they are at the same time consciously crafted works written in one of the most difficult poetic forms by a major artistic voice of her time and place. The controlling idea for the entire sequence is that love is, in fact, stronger than death. She expresses this theme through certain aesthetic moves. After she has established her own melancholy, by mentioning tears and weeping, heavy-heartedness and grief, she shows that the beloved has come between her and her grave (Sonnet 7). She continues, however, to use images of grief to characterize herself, and it is in her grief and world-weariness more than anything that she claims she is unworthy of his love (Sonnet 8). She contrasts herself to him, usually using royal images to portray him, but never portraying him as concretely as she portrays herself. She shows herself to be an agent of decay: "I will not soil thy purple with my dust,/ Nor breathe my poison on thy Venice-glass" (Sonnet 9). Venetian glass was believed to shatter when it came in contact with poisoned liquids.

When she speaks of the union of souls, however, the poet uses images of light and fire, flashing flames, a "golden throne" (Sonnet 12), "wings" that "break into fire" (Sonnet 22). These images gain even more brilliance because much of the imagery of the sonnets is dark, of dust and of enclosure. Yet images of light and life prevail, since love has created them. Whereas she has characterized her earlier despondency as a life that is colorless because tears have faded it, in the last sonnet she asks the beloved to "keep the colors [of the flowers] true."

Just as she compares herself to her beloved, darkness to light, and death to life, she compares past to future. She repeatedly shows that before she met him, she had lost her faith in living; she looked to God for strength to go on, but she lived in a kind of bleak despair that had no vision of a future. His love changes the entire direction of her life. She is uplifted to the point of being able to see that ever so much as the human heart thinks it wants, God gives more than one can imagine; and her beloved is more than she ever thought to pray for. She had reconciled herself to seek her future in heaven, but his love draws her back from the grave.

In Sonnet 43, many of the themes of the sequence come together. This is Browning's most famous work and one of the most famous poems in the English language. "How do I love thee? Let me count the ways" has captured the hearts of readers for almost 150 years. It is written in much more abstract terms than is the rest of the sequence, but the poems that have come before it have in a sense already defined what one reads here. For example, she has already written of souls in connections with light and ascent, so when she writes here of "the depth and breadth and height/ My soul can reach," one has already read of the expansiveness of the soul in love. She has also written over and over again about her grief and how she has thought herself destined for only the grave, so the reader should already understand about "the passions put to use/ In my old griefs." The last two lines of this sonnet pull the entire sequence together: "and, if God choose,/ I shall but love thee better after death." In the first instance, the beloved has turned her away from death to life in this world. In doing so, he has turned her away from a contemplation of heaven in an afterlife. It becomes this very love that inspires her back toward God, toward a desire for eternity. Here, however, it is not an eternity that is longed for only for the sake of its being something better than this life. It is an eternity in which temporal love has itself become eternal.

Sonnets from the Portuguese is an enduring record of the love of one individual for another and, through that love, of the restoration of hope and the enhancement of the will to live. The sequence is captivating because in it, a real female voice writes about her most private feelings of love. At first, one thinks one is hearing Shakespeare or Petrarch, but then one realizes that Browning has dropped the conventional metaphors and masks. In fact, she goes so far as hardly to create an image of the beloved at all. One hears the first-person "I," and, as much as one thinks one ought to say that it is her poetic persona, one knows that it is the voice of Elizabeth Barrett Browning.

Context

Like her female predecessors of the French and Italian Renaissance, and like Mary Wroth in the English Renaissance, in her pastoral sonnet cycle *Pamphilia to Amphilanthus* (1621), in *Sonnets from the Portuguese*, Browning inserts the female voice into the Petrarchan sonnet tradition. She assumes the stance of the silent Laura hearing Petrarch, the silent Catarina hearing Camoës, but she herself speaks of ideal love. This voice is her own, and the idealized beloved is her very real husband. Even though one hears only her voice, one can imagine the listener. In this way, Browning's sonnets border on crossing with the form her husband perfected in such poems as "My Last Duchess": the dramatic monologue, in which a specific speaker speaks to a specific listener in a specific situation. Moreover, the speaker does not stylize herself as the male Petrarchan voice stylizes himself and his beloved. She changes the tradition also by expressing concerns about her family connections.

Sonnets from the Portuguese marks Browning's breaking off from the Romantic tradition upon which her poetics rests, the style of her predecessors L. E. L. and Felicia Hemans. The masks drop away, the literary conventions transform, and Browning writes in a bold "I." Influenced by Shakespeare, John Milton, and William Wordsworth in their use of the sonnet form, she was most likely also aware of Charlotte Smith's *Elegiac Sonnets* (1787) as well as the work of the numerous other women poets of the Romantic and early Victorian eras.

In the nineteenth century, she was held in higher repute than was her husband. She had been considered, in fact, for the laureateship. Not until the twentieth century was she taken less seriously. After the widespread popularity of the play *The Barretts of Wimpole Street*, she came to be seen solely as the invalid poetess who had been perishing in her enclosed room, where she had been locked by her tyrannical father until she was rescued by the dashing Robert. She became known only for her love poetry throughout most of the twentieth century. In the 1970's, feminist critics brought back to light her social and political works, such as the verse narrative *Aurora Leigh* and "The Cry of the Children." Her poetic achievement is currently being reassessed in accord with new ways of reading women poets and in accord with contemporary assessments of writers. Her aesthetic accomplishments and her social and political themes give her a significant place in Victorian poetry.

Sources for Further Study

Cooper, Helen. *Elizabeth Barrett Browning: Woman and Artist*. Chapel Hill: University of North Carolina Press, 1988. Valuable for close readings of Browning's poems.

Falk, Alice. "Elizabeth Barrett Browning and Her Prometheuses: Self-Will and a Woman Poet." *Tulsa Studies in Women's Literature* 7, no. 1 (Spring, 1988): 69-85. Discusses Browning's translations of Aeschylus and her familiarity with and use of classical images.

Forster, Margaret. *Elizabeth Barrett Browning: A Biography*. New York: Doubleday, 1989. Shows Mary Barrett, Elizabeth's mother, to have been the shaping influence in her education. Revises the myth of Elizabeth's father as the tyrant of Wimpole Street.

Leighton, Angela. *Elizabeth Barrett Browning*. Bloomington: Indiana University Press, 1986. A feminist reevaluation of Browning's life and works that also examines the Browning myth. Discusses the poet in relation to her male predecessors.

Mermin, Dorothy. *Elizabeth Barrett Browning: The Origins of a New Poetry*. Chicago: University of Chicago Press, 1989. Mermin claims that Browning originated a female tradition in Victorian poetry. She draws heavily on Browning's earlier diary and numerous letters. Extensive notes and bibliography.

______________. "The Female Poet and the Embarrassed Reader: Elizabeth Barrett Browning's *Sonnets from the Portuguese*." *ELH* 48, no. 2 (Summer, 1981): 351-367. Mermin makes the case for the "embarrassed reader" who is forced to be an eavesdropper; who, aware of the voice in the male sonnet tradition, hears Browning's "awkward, mawkish, and indecently personal" voice and is embarrassed.

Paul, Sarah. "Strategic Self-Centering and the Female Narrator: Elizabeth Barrett Browning's *Sonnets from the Portuguese*." *Browning Institute Studies* 17 (1989): 75-91. Sees the speaker in the *Sonnets* as covertly empowering herself. Includes an interesting discussion of reversals of gender roles.

Radley, Virginia L. *Elizabeth Barrett Browning*. New York: Twayne, 1972. Gives a short biography and studies each stage of Browning's work, including a chapter on the *Sonnets from the Portuguese*. Includes a good but dated annotated bibliography.

Stephenson, Glennis. *Elizabeth Barrett Browning and the Poetry of Love*. Ann Arbor, Mich.: UMI Research Press, 1989. Begins by discussing Browning's immediate predecessors, then examines her early ballads and lyrics, *Lady Geraldine's Courtship*, *Sonnets from the Portuguese*, *Aurora Leigh*, and *Last Poems*. Discussion of the sonnets considers how the female poet enters into a male poetic tradition, specifically examining the role of distance in the sonnet tradition and Browning's use of it as well as the replacement by Browning of predominantly visual images with predominantly "tactual" images.

Taplin, Gardner. *The Life of Elizabeth Barrett Browning*. Hamden, Conn.: Archon Books, 1970. Includes discussion of *Sonnets from the Portuguese*.

Donna G. Berliner

A SOR JUANA ANTHOLOGY

Author: Sor Juana Inés de la Cruz (1651?-1695)
Type of work: Essays and poetry
First published: 1988

Form and Content

A Sor Juana Anthology is a collection of some of the best poetry of Sor Juana Inés de la Cruz, along with a sample of her poetic drama and prose, selected by Mexican poet and essayist Octavio Paz and translator Alan S. Trueblood. Since her poetry is the heart of her achievement, it forms the major part of the anthology, divided to indicate general themes and type of verse: convent and court, vicarious love, music, divine love, self and the world, lighter pieces, and festive worship (*villancicos*). Sor Juana's work clearly places her among Spanish poets of the Baroque in the tradition of Luis de Góngora and Pedro Calderón de la Barca. Her lyrical poetry was praised for its ingenious use of conventional forms: decorative and exotic imagery, symbolism, hyperbole, antithesis, paradox, and references to philosophy, science, and other areas of learning. The modern reader, however, may occasionally sense an individual voice behind the conventions and appreciate glimpses of Sor Juana's struggles to express herself artistically under the constraints of being a woman in seventeenth century Mexico.

Sor Juana's poetic drama is exemplified by excerpts from *El divino Narciso* (c. 1680; *The Divine Narcissus*, 1945), a series of allegorical tableaux in which human nature reveals her quest of Christ in the form of Narcissus. As an *auto sacramental* (one-act play celebrating the Eucharist), it is considered a masterpiece.

"First Dream" (1692), Sor Juana's longest and most important poem, is included in its entirety and expresses the search for knowledge that ultimately ends in disillusionment. Using the account of a dream remembered during waking hours, Sor Juana focuses on the question of human aspiration for knowledge and understanding of the world. She demonstrates a wide range of scholarship herself, including philosophical and literary illusions, and incorporates the various images of sleep that would have been well known by her audience: contrast of night and day, sleep as death and as having dominion over human beings, and the deceptiveness of dreams.

At the end of the anthology, Sor Juana's famous justification of her pursuit of knowledge, "The Reply to Sor Philothea" (1691), is included. Upon this famous manuscript rests much of Sor Juana's reputation as a feminist. After recognizing her own overpowering desire to know and indicating how she learns not only from books but also from everyday life, she argues the case for allowing women to study. The form shows, first of all, the conventions of her time, including formulas of humility and Latin citations as well as references to Scripture. She uses scholastic argumentation and demonstrates her ability to reveal the interrelated character of fields of study. Taking information from various sources, Sor Juana compiles her argument with skill and astuteness, justifying her studies as a means of understanding Scripture better. To the criticism that she should study more sacred works, she readily agrees—although her letter reveals that she already knows much about the Bible and religious writers. Her questioning, searching mind is apparent in her careful and well-formulated argument. It is clear that she was often misunderstood—and opposed—within her convent community because of her need to study and her belief that women, like men, should be allowed full intellectual development.

Analysis

This anthology illustrates the range of poetry that Sor Juana cultivated, including occasional verse (for special occasions and poetry contests), love poetry, religious verses (especially *villancicos*), and humorous poetry. Critics have found it impossible to date most of this work since the originals have been lost and her style does not evolve. From the beginning, Sor Juana's verse shows the wit, polish, and learning expected in the Baroque period. Her work demonstrates a sense of form and proportion as well as a control of classical references and the metaphorical imagery of her time: exotic material, gems, fragrances, and creatures, often with symbolic meaning. The Baroque use of paradox, hyperbole, antithesis, repetition, and scholarly logic and argument characterize her work. In accordance with the conventions of the time, her poems are not personal revelations but rather a demonstration of poetic skill. With the forms dictated by convention, her individual talent emerges through the ingenious use of well-known images or in her particular tone or emphasis.

A number of her poems touch on conventional aspects of love, including the idealization of the beloved, the pain of separation and rejection, the feelings of distant and pure love, and the irrational effects of love. Some critics have observed that Sor Juana's perspective at times seems more masculine than feminine, that poetry addressed to a woman is often more intense than that addressed to shadowy male figures named Silvio or Fabio. One explanation notes that Sor Juana's early life lacked strong male figures; however, a more probable explanation is that the poetic tradition she was following was exclusively masculine—there was no appropriate feminine language to celebrate love. As an intellectual, she availed herself of the conventional forms.

In describing her world, Sor Juana shows great skill in portraiture with well-crafted variations to present the interplay between portrait and subject. One poem disavows a portrait of herself as flattery, reflecting the Baroque attitude toward the vanity and illusion of life. The poem ends with a conventional idea: "all efforts fail and in the end/ a body goes to dust, to shade, to nought."

Writing was a central part of Sor Juana's life and identity, and this fact is reflected in poems that identify her with her pen. Her pen expresses the pain of separation with sad, black-colored pen strokes, and words of mourning become "black tears." A frequent wordplay, made possible by the fact that *pluma* in Spanish is both pen and feather, is noted in the introductory materials, "Pluma" is a synecdoche for wing, contributing an extra dimension to the image of bold flight so important to Sor Juana. "First Dream," for example, focuses on intellectual striving, or what translator Trueblood calls "unrepentant boldness," associated with the Greek myth of Phaëthon and his failed flight in Helios' chariot.

Baroque poetry is characterized by its exoticism and its opulence in description. In Sor Juana's poetry, one finds references to her own land, exotic to the Europeans. One poem refers to a sorcerer's brew of "the herb-doctors of my country." In a *villancico* for the feast of the Assumption, she introduces the tocotín, a lively Aztec dance, with accompanying Nahuatl words. In others, she focuses on Africa, incorporating rhythmic African words in a refrain or presenting "two Guinean queens/ with faces of jet." The pride of her country-women shines forth in verses such as these: "Black is the Bride,/ the Sun scorches her face./ Though she calls herself black,/ her blackness, she shall say,/ makes her the more comely."

In other poems, Sor Juana addresses her personal situation through a direct confrontation with the price of her intellectual distinction. The most famous poses this question: "World, in hounding me what do you gain?/ How can it harm you if I choose, astutely,/ rather to stock my mind with things of beauty,/ than waste its stock on every beauty's claim?" She is also acutely aware of the role that her gender plays in the praise of her work, as well as in its criticism. In an unfinished poem, she writes of her aspirations and failures. Rationally considering the situation, she wonders if being a woman has not made European readers too quick to praise her: "Might it be the surprise of my sex/ that explains why you are willing/ to allow an unusual case/ to pass itself off as perfection?" Praised or criticized, she found herself in the position of being an anomaly.

Context

Although Sor Juana is recognized today as an outstanding poet of Mexico's colonial period, her work reflects the life of an intelligent woman who was not nurtured in this endeavor by her seventeenth century environment. Not allowed to attend the university, she was essentially self-taught, and her work is the product of a searching mind which enjoyed scholarly activity. The very existence of this work is a great accomplishment.

In conflict with society's expectations of a woman of her time, Sor Juana nevertheless found a way to develop her talent. Since education was a prerogative of the Catholic church, she entered the convent of Santa Paula, of the Hieronymite Order, in 1669. Her religious duties seem to have been compatible with a very active scholastic life. Sometimes celebrated as an early feminist, Sor Juana gave voice to the idea that women did not need to remain ignorant. A *villancico* for the Saint's Day of Catherine of Alexandria (1691) uses the humorous tone of the common people in telling the story of Catherine, who "knew a lot, so they say,/ though she *was* female." Fortunately, this did not present a problem: "The makings of sainthood/ was in her, they say;/ even knowing so much/ didn't get in her way." Humor was used again in her famous poem on the double standard ("Silly, you men—so very adept/ at wrongly faulting womankind"), in which she points out that men criticize women regardless of how they act: If they spurn men, they are ungrateful; if they succumb to their advances, they are lewd.

Sor Juana's decision regarding marriage may have been influenced by the fact that she was illegitimate and had no dowry. It is clear, however, that her greatest passion was intellectual, and her choice of the convent can be seen in that light. As she argues in "The Reply to Sor Philothea," she had a vocation which could not be denied. Her explanation and defense of learning are written all the more frankly as she did not expect the letter to be published. Continued opposition within her community and as the loss of the protective support of a patron in Mexico made Sor Juana's life more difficult after the publication of "The Reply to Sor Philothea." In 1692, with the pressures of hunger riots and the resulting demands for penitential acts, she was increasingly isolated and in 1693 wrote a document of repentance herself. In the last two years of her life, she wrote nothing. Nevertheless, readers discovering her work today find a body of lyric poetry that confirms her stature as an important poet of the seventeenth century, as well as writings, including "The Reply to Sor Philothea," which are testament to a strong woman's need to understand her world and give expression to her discoveries.

Sources for Further Study

Flynn, Gerard. *Sor Juana Inés de la Cruz.* Boston: Twayne, 1971. A readable introduction to the life of Sor Juana and her work. Selections of her poetry and both secular and religious drama are reviewed, with quotations from the texts. (English translations are provided.) Includes helpful explanatory notes to each chapter and a bibliography with mainly Spanish-language sources.

Merrim, Stephanie, ed. *Feminist Perspectives on Sor Juana Inés de la Cruz.* Detroit: Wayne State University Press, 1991. Eight articles explore from a feminist perspective each of the genres in which Sor Juana wrote, also discussing her cultural climate and personal pressures. Of particular interest are the introductory essay on key issues in Sor Juana criticism and readings of "First Dream," "The Reply to Sor Philothea," and selected love poetry. Offers a brief bibliography, including English editions of her work, and a chronology.

Montross, Constance M. *Virtue or Vice? Sor Juana's Use of Thomistic Thought.* Washington, D.C.: University Press of America, 1981. Examines Sor Juana's use of Scholastic doctrine and methodology, specifically the ideas of Saint Thomas Aquinas. The author analyzes the combination of belief and questioning in "First Dream" and "The Reply to Sor Philothea." An extensive bibliography is provided, as well as the full Spanish text of "First Dream."

Paz, Octavio, ed. *Mexican Poetry: An Anthology.* Translated by Samuel Beckett. Reprint. New York: Grove Press, 1985. Complements Paz's *Sor Juana: Or, The Traps of Faith* with a discussion in the introduction of Sor Juana's place in the history of Mexican poetry. The anthology includes translations of twelve of her poems.

______________. *Sor Juana: Or, The Traps of Faith.* Translated by Margaret Sayers Peden. Cambridge, Mass.: Harvard University Press, 1988. An important biography of Sor Juana emphasizing her uniqueness as a poet and her struggle for an intellectual and creative life. Particular focus is on the key questions of why she entered a convent and why she renounced learning at the end of her life. Considers historical settings and traditions in some detail, with illustrations including portraits of Sor Juana. A helpful listing of Spanish literary terms is provided.

Royer, Fanchón. *The Tenth Muse: Sor Juana Inés de la Cruz.* Paterson, N.J.: St. Anthony Guild Press, 1952. A good introductory source. Each chapter begins with a translated quote from Sor Juana's work and presents the basic biographical facts along with interpretive commentary. The appendix contains selected poems in Spanish, as well as a short bibliography of Spanish-language sources.

Susan L. Piepke

A SPY IN THE HOUSE OF LOVE

Author: Anaïs Nin (1903-1977)
Type of work: Novel
Type of plot: Psychological realism
Time of plot: The 1940's, during World War II
Locale: New York City
First published: 1954

Principal characters:

Sabina, a passionate woman who has sexual relationships with a variety of men
The lie detector, a surreal father figure who represents Sabina's guilty conscience
Alan, Sabina's husband, who seems oblivious to her affairs
Philip, one of Sabina's lovers, a handsome opera star
Mambo, a drummer at a small jazz club and another of Sabina's lovers
John, a grounded aviator and another of Sabina's lovers
Donald, Sabina's final lover before she breaks down
Jay, an artist and Sabina's former lover
Djuna, Sabina's friend and confidante

Form and Content

The best known of Anaïs Nin's novels, *A Spy in the House of Love* is a surreal journey through one woman's mind as she attempts to satisfy her sexual desire and to understand love. Like all Nin's fiction, the narrative form of the text is experimental. Poetic impressions reflecting the complicated nature of Sabina's personality are linked by semichronological events; supporting characters are minimally described, and only in reference to Sabina. Dialogue is restricted to the most relevant exchanges; setting and action are included only when their symbolic weight provides insight to Sabina's frame of mind. The result is a novel that explores the various layers of a single personality, undermining the notion that a woman's identity can be categorized or limited to a single facet.

A telephone awakens the lie detector at the beginning of the novel. Sabina has placed a call at random, seeking comfort from a strange voice in the middle of the night. The lie detector tells her that she needs to confess or she would not have called a stranger, since "Guilt is the one burden human beings can't bear alone." He has the call traced and finds Sabina in a bar, where he observes and analyzes her voyeuristically. At dawn, he follows her.

The point of view shifts to Sabina, where it remains for most of the rest of the work. She awakens anxiously, then hides her chaotic expression with makeup. She dresses in a black cape for its protectiveness, its masculinity, as though dressed for battle. Outside on the streets of New York City, however, she is panicked by enormous trucks that block the sun with their rolling wheels; she feels insignificant and threatened. At such moments of insecurity, Sabina visualizes her husband, Alan. She returns to the hotel, checks out, then walks two blocks home where she finds Alan and the fleeting happiness of safety.

As after all of her affairs, Sabina is worried about hurting her husband—or worse, losing him and the stability that he provides. So she lies to him, describing her week-long acting role as Madame Bovary. Later, beside him in bed, she silently recalls her affair with Philip, a handsome opera star who discovered her lying naked on the beach. Philip is used to noncommittal sexual relationships and is easily satisfied by their lovemaking. Sabina, however, does not climax and feels angry, defeated, and jealous of Philip's casual ability to possess a stranger.

Attempting to mimic Philip's sexual freedom, she enters an affair with Mambo, a drum player at a local jazz club. This time it is Mambo who is disappointed, because he realizes that Sabina desires him sexually but is unwilling to form a commitment. Though Sabina achieves her goal of physical fulfillment with relational freedom, she is increasingly afraid of seeing Alan while with Mambo. Her inability to experience both love and passion in a single relationship makes her feel that she is a spy in the house of love.

Her next affair is with John, a grounded aviator who completely satisfies Sabina physically but refuses to see her more than once. He cannot love the kind of woman who would have sex so easily, and he leaves her filled with guilt. Seeking atonement for his curse, she seeks a relationship with someone resembling John and finds Donald, the least adequate of her lovers. Donald worships Sabina as a mother and is therefore afraid of having sex with her. She mothers him until she finds her own passion fading.

Fragmented from playing so many roles, she seeks advice from her friend Djuna. The lie detector reappears; he and Djuna help Sabina realize that negative self- judgment and unrealistic expectations of others have prevented her from experiencing love.

Analysis

A Spy in the House of Love is the fourth in a series of five works that Nin wrote as a continuous novel called *Cities of the Interior*. The novels can be read in any order, with the overall meaning preserved. The theme of the entire collection is female psychology: Each book examines a different aspect of female identity, and though a number of women are depicted in the series, the characters can ultimately be read as overlapping aspects of one persona. The series is a thorough reworking and expanding of the female ideal depicted in traditional literature, and it is most remembered for expressing previously unfashionable or forbidden subjects in a lyrical, accurate, and analytical manner.

Sabina is a recurring figure throughout Nin's fiction, always appearing as a sensual, sexually assertive woman. Like all Nin's female characters, Sabina is torn between her sense of responsibility and her desire to experience pleasure. Developed most fully in *A Spy in the House of Love*, Sabina enjoys sex but finds herself emotionally fragmented by attempting to satisfy and be satisfied by so many lovers. Sabina's quest is to emulate Philip's, or any man's ability to enjoy sex with a stranger. She assumes that she will find emotional gratification this way, but she learns otherwise in her relationships with Philip, Mambo, and John. When she does make commitments, she limits her identity in order to please her partners. She tries to be the child she thinks Alan wants and the mother Donald needs, and in both cases she is physically unsatisfied.

Nin makes it clear that Sabina is at fault not for having affairs but for failing to confront her own subconscious, with its simmering confusion of passion and guilt. This is particularly true of Sabina's affair with John, whose seed is described as poison. His own shame for surviving the war is taken out on Sabina: "He had mingled poison with every drop of pleasure, . . . every thrust of sensual pleasure the thrust of a knife killing what he desired, killing with guilt." Sabina unconsciously soaks up John's attitude: Because he thinks she is bad, she thinks so too. She attempts to cleanse her spirit by nurturing Donald, but her plan fails. After Sabina becomes the mother Donald desires, she compares herself to a caged bird with faded plumage.

In yielding to her lovers' needs, Sabina is depleted, her spirit broken and dismembered. Jay's portraits of her, which she had not understood years before while they were lovers, finally make sense when she sees them hanging at the jazz club:

> His figures exploded and constellated into fragments, like spilled puzzles, each piece having flown far enough away to seem irretrievable and yet not far enough to be disassociated. . . . By one effort of contraction at the core they might still amalgamate to form the body of a woman.

What Sabina sought in her affairs was solace, a synthesis of emotional and physical pleasure. Instead, she has been pulled apart by separating her roles as seductress, lover, mother, and child. The aspects of her identity are still connected, however, suggesting their validity. If she can locate the core, she might realize stability by accepting her own multifaceted nature.

Alone, tired, and emotionally lost, Sabina finally understands Marcel Duchamp's famous painting *Nude Descending a Staircase*, which outlines the same woman in numerous positions, "like many multiple exposures of a woman's personality, neatly divided into many layers, walking down the stairs in unison." An actress, a wearer of many disguises, Sabina no longer senses a single inner identity. Afraid that she can no longer portray an isolated aspect of her personality, that of the innocent child, she fears going home to Alan for the first time and seeks forgiveness and atonement from a confessor. The lie detector, her own guilty conscience, must be confronted.

It is Djuna who points out that Alan's paternal attitude

is nurtured by Sabina's refusal to display her maturing selves. Because Sabina acts like a child with Alan, he acts like a parent. This is a revelation for Sabina, who has looked to others for personal fulfillment. Literature is filled with stories about women finding complete satisfaction in relationships with men who know what is best for them; in this case, such attempts repeatedly fail. Rather than mimicking her lovers, or molding herself to their needs, Sabina must accept the components of her own identity and relate to people wholly, honestly. Instead of feeling guilty about her desires, she must confront them if she is to experience anything besides vicarious happiness in the house of love.

Nin's narrative style has been praised for its ability to portray a psychological journey metaphorically. Unchronological, imagistic passages are layered expressionistically, depicting the essence of characters rather than their physical exteriors. Information traditionally considered vital to plot development is discarded in favor of poetic analysis, encouraging the reader to identify with how a character thinks. In this way, the text becomes personal: The voice of the narrative is not the lie detector, or Alan, or any male trying to understand a woman, but Sabina representing Nin, woman explaining woman. The result is a novel that encourages affirming rather than judgmental forms of self-discovery.

Context

Before Nin, few authors writing in English had explicitly addressed the subject of women's sexuality, and none had so thoroughly examined the topic from a woman's point of view. Her work was considered scandalous, and *A Spy in the House of Love* was turned down by 127 publishers before Nin had it printed at her own expense. Many critics ignored Nin, or condemned her fiction for its erotic content, until the publication of her diaries in the 1960's and 1970's. Then, when thousands of women saw themselves reflected in Nin's journals and crowded to her lectures, elevating her to celebrity status, book reviewers joined in by enthusiastically praising her work. Nin herself felt that the diaries were sketch pads next to her fiction, that she had accomplished her best work in *Cities of the Interior*. Even so, the majority of analysis available on Nin focuses on her diaries and her personal life.

Her views about relationships were, and still are in some circles, daringly radical. Like her literary predecessor Colette, Nin lived by the philosophies described in her books. She vehemently defended a woman's right to experience multiple relationships, as men have for centuries. She believed that psychological and erotic liberation can only be achieved by dispensing with guilt, the single factor responsible for Sabina's fragmentation of spirit. Moreover, as Sabina discovers, eroticism itself must be seen as multifaceted if all the aspects of human identity are to find satisfaction.

In *A Spy in the House of Love*, Nin examines topics previously untouched in literature: the female Don Juan figure; the exploitation of a black man by a white woman; and the frustration and anger experienced by the aroused woman who fails to achieve orgasm. In other works, Nin explored homosexuality, adultery, fantasized incest, and masturbation. She is recognized as the first to describe such aspects of human sexuality openly and is celebrated for doing so from a distinctly female perspective, without misanthropy and without violence.

Sources for Further Study

Franklin, Benjamin V., and Duane Schneider. *Anaïs Nin: An Introduction*. Athens: Ohio University Press, 1979. Provides concise, thorough summaries and insightful accompanying interpretations of Nin's works, including *A Spy in the House of Love*.

Knapp, Bettina L. *Anaïs Nin*. New York: Frederick Ungar, 1978. Discusses Nin's works as personal quests, literary self-explorations affirming the multiplicity of identities contained within one woman and, by extension, every person. Discusses the impact of the New Novel movement on Nin and the use of surreal narrative forms in *Cities of the Interior*.

Molyneux, Maxine, and Julia Casterton. "Looking Again at Anaïs Nin." *The Minnesota Review* 18 (Spring, 1982): 86-101. Includes a previously unpublished interview with Nin from 1970 and subsequent commentary by the authors examining Nin's embrace of feminine characteristics typically condemned as stereotypical. Parallels Sabina's need to confess with Nin's process of self-examination in her diaries.

Scholar, Nancy. *Anaïs Nin*. Boston: Twayne, 1984. Explicates Nin's works, pointing out similarities between her diaries and *Cities of the Interior*, as well as Nin's goal to understand herself better in producing the continuous novel. The interpretations assume familiarity with Nin's works.

Spencer, Sharon. *Collage of Dreams: The Writings of Anaïs Nin*. Chicago: Swallow Press, 1981. An excellent critical introduction to Nin's life, perspectives on sexuality and gender, influential relationships, and literary work. Discusses Nin's use of symbolism to develop a literary female psyche.

Mary Pierce Frost

THE STORY OF MY LIFE

Author: Helen Keller (1880-1968)
Type of work: Autobiography
Time of work: 1880-1903
Locale: Alabama, Massachusetts, and New York
First published: 1903, rev. ed. 1966

Principal personages:

Helen Keller, the author, a blind and deaf young woman

Anne Sullivan, Keller's first teacher, who helped her communicate with the outside world

Form and Content

The Story of My Life is an account of the early years of a woman who overcame incredible problems to become an accomplished, literate adult. The book does not give a complete account of the author's life, as it was written when she was still a college student. It is, however, a unique account of one young woman's passage from almost total despair to success in a world mostly populated by hearing and seeing people. This book is relatively short, but the modern editions also include letters written by and to Helen Keller and an analysis of her education from a later standpoint.

The Story of My Life begins with Keller's vague memories of early childhood. She was born in 1880 in Alabama, an apparently normal child. According to her recollections, she began to speak before she was a year old. The early chapters recount the little girl's love of the natural world, a theme that is repeated many times throughout the work, and her generally happy home life, with loving and nurturing parents.

At the age of nineteen months, however, Keller was stricken with an unexplained disease—certainly unexplained in the nineteenth century, with no suggestion in the book of any later diagnosis—which left her both blind and deaf. She became a domineering child, with behavior that was totally unacceptable. Keller mainly lays the blame for this behavior upon her frustration at the futility of trying to communicate her thoughts and feelings without any ability to speak, read, or write.

The breakthrough came when the Kellers visited noted inventor Alexander Graham Bell in Washington, D.C., who referred them to the Perkins Institution, a school for blind children in Boston. The school sent a woman named Anne Sullivan to teach young Helen to behave properly and, if possible, to teach her to be a "normal" child. Most of the book deals with Sullivan's training of Keller, showing her how to behave decently, to use the manual alphabet to communicate her thoughts, and to read books in raised letters and later in braille. In the last chapters, there is much emphasis on Keller's higher education.

According to her own recollections, young Helen Keller's greatest love, apart from the natural world, was language. She learned to read not only English but also French, German, Latin, and Greek. She began writing in her early teens. There is also considerable discussion of her examinations and preparation for admission into Radcliffe College, the sister college to Harvard, and her eventual acceptance.

Keller writes about her attempts to use speech as a means of communication, but she largely considers these attempts to be failures: She never really learned to speak well. Keller demonstrates that the process of learning to speak is difficult for any person who is either blind or deaf and virtually impossible for someone who lacks both senses. Instead, Keller became a great lover of books, which became her only real way of relating to the world outside. The book ends on this note, with a list of favorite authors and a wish to be counted among them.

Analysis

The Story of My Life is the story of one young woman's emergence from the most extreme isolation possible. It is not a story of an "emerging woman" in the usual sense of the term; there is no discussion of sexuality, of women's place in society, or of societal attitudes. Rather, young Helen was an emerging human being. This is a story of a young woman learning to reach out to the world.

Apart from a few short opening chapters relating to Keller's vague memories of her early childhood, the tone of this book is largely one of joy. Every new word, every new concept, is a major revelation. A long passage describes her discovery that all objects are associated with words, and a special emphasis is placed on water, the first concept that the young Helen learned to refer to with both speech and sign.

Above all, there is a focus on the essential importance of language. Keller clearly believes that abstract thought is impossible without language, that language is the single most important factor that sets human beings apart from other animals. More than anything else, the author recounts her efforts to use human languages and her emergence as a "real person" as a result of this newfound ability.

There is more than one way to interpret this emphasis. Most people take language for granted. Children who have normal senses of sight and hearing and adequate intelligence do not have to be taught to speak. They learn by listening and watching, by imitation. This path was closed to the little girl trapped in a dark and silent world. It is natural that she should focus on her process of learning to communicate with the outside world.

Keller learned to read and write several foreign languages. At the end of the book, there are references to her emerging love of the works of William Shakespeare, the Greek classics, and other great works of literature. There is a long discussion about her early attempts at becoming a writer herself, at the age of twelve. In later life, Keller would indeed become a successful writer, among other things. At the time that *The Story of My Life* was written, however, she was still in the process of learning to communicate, and there is very little said about what she would later wish to communicate to the outside world. Language, in itself, is the essential theme of the book.

In this regard, it is necessary to consider *The Story of My Life* in context. When she wrote this book, Keller was a student in one of the greatest centers of learning in the world. Being graduated from Radcliffe College with honors is far from an easy task, even for someone with a normal sensory system. There is a sense of Keller's fierce determination, but it is always tempered with love and understanding and with great praise for the various people who helped her, especially Anne Sullivan, her teacher in childhood and her helper in later life.

Keller uses language in two quite different ways in *The Story of My Life*. She makes the reader very much aware of how the world appears to someone who passes through life deaf and blind. On the other hand, she also makes use of visual and auditory images that she could not have experienced, doing so quite convincingly. These two uses of language underscore the reality of the author's roles as a person who experienced the world in a unique way and as a successful author who could relate to the way in which other people experience life.

Context

When *The Story of My Life* was written in 1902, many female authors were still using male pseudonyms in an attempt to give their work some credence in a literary world dominated by men. It would be almost twenty years before women were given the right to vote and a much longer period before they made any real impact on the political and literary scenes.

Decades later, Helen Keller would be considered one of the great social leaders of the time, and her earlier works would be considered inspirational to women and to society in general. Keller's social work was primarily aimed at helping people with assorted disabilities, but not necessarily physical ones. She took upon herself the task of improving society in general, regardless of sex, race, nationality, or social standing. *The Story of My Life* cannot be considered "feminist" in any real sense, as the author at that time of her life had problems considerably more difficult to overcome than merely being a woman in a male-dominated society. In a broader context, however, this book has been inspirational to people faced with difficulties that must be overcome—physical, emotional, or societal.

Sources for Further Study

Boylan, Esther, ed. *Women and Disability*. Atlantic Highlands, N.J.: Zed Books, 1991. A series of articles on the situation of disabled women in the world. This book places emphasis on the concept that women have a "double handicap" by being female as well as disabled.

Brooks, Van Wyck. *Helen Keller: Sketch for a Portrait*. New York: E. P. Dutton, 1956. A biography of Keller covering her early years, her later development as an adult author and activist, and her continuing relationship with Anne Sullivan Macy, her teacher from early childhood.

Hillyer, Barbara. *Feminism and Disability*. Norman: University of Oklahoma Press, 1993. The story of a woman bringing up a disabled little girl. The stress in this book is on the feminist movement and the movement for the rights of disabled people of both sexes, and on how the two issues may come into conflict.

Keller, Helen. *Midstream: My Later Life*. Westport, Conn.: Greenwood Press, 1968. A reprint of an autobiography of Keller originally published in 1929. This book continues where *The Story of My Life* left off. It offers insights into the author's later development, after she was graduated from college and entered the mainstream of American society.

______________. *Teacher: Anne Sullivan Macy*. Garden City, N.Y.: Doubleday, 1955. A biography of Helen Keller's early teacher and longtime companion and helper. Explores Keller's training from a later point of view, as well as providing insight into the life of Anne Sullivan and the long-standing relationship between the two women.

Lash, Joseph P. *Helen and Teacher: The Story of Helen Keller and Anne Sullivan Macy*. New York: Delacorte Press, 1980. The story of Keller's training and the relationship between Keller and her teacher. Traces the development of both women from Sullivan's childhood in the 1860's through Keller's death in 1968.

McInnes, J. M., and J. A. Treffry. *Deaf-Blind Infants and Children: A Developmental Guide*. Toronto: University of Toronto Press, 1982. A modern guide to the teaching of children with Helen Keller's problems. This book provides a discussion of modern methods used in treating such children, which have changed greatly since the days of Keller's childhood.

Marc Goldstein

STORYTELLER

Author: Leslie Marmon Silko (1948-)
Type of work: Folklore, memoir, poetry, and short stories
First published: 1981

Form and Content

Although it includes materials from many different literary genres—poetry, short story, myth, memoir, and biography—*Storyteller* viewed in its entirety is essentially an autobiography, a portrait, as its title makes explicit, of the artist as a young storyteller. In addition to the literary materials, interspersed throughout are photographs of Leslie Marmon Silko and her family and of various scenes in and around her childhood home, Laguna Pueblo in New Mexico. What unifies these diverse materials is the pervasive focus on Silko's development as an artist, on the familial and cultural factors that shaped her conception of herself as a writer—or, as she prefers to think of herself, a storyteller—working in the tradition of oral storytelling as it was practiced from the earliest times among the Laguna people and concentrating, though not exclusively, on female experience in both the autobiographical and the fictional parts of the book.

The biographical sections, mostly concerning relatives who told Silko stories when she was a child, and the autobiographical sections, mostly concerning experiences related to the stories, are scattered throughout the book and function as introductions to and links between the stories, poems, and Laguna myths that make up the bulk of the book. Some critics have been troubled by what they have seen as a lack of originality in *Storyteller* since much of this material had already been published elsewhere: many of the poems in *Laguna Woman* (1974), many of the short stories in a collection edited by Kenneth Rosen entitled *The Man to Send Rain Clouds* (1974), and many of the Laguna myths in Silko's novel *Ceremony* (1977). Silko's defenders have pointed out, however, that this "retelling" is perfectly consistent with and indeed necessary to Silko's concept of storytelling. In the oral tradition, which Silko is attempting to adapt to the circumstances of a literate culture, storytellers have a repertoire of tales that they tell over and over again. Indeed, Silko believes that one of the beauties of the oral tradition is that every time a story is retold, even if repeated word for word by the same teller sitting in the same chair, it becomes a new and unique story. Silko's intention is to help readers get a sense of how a story would sound if they were hearing it.

In keeping with this desire to approximate the oral tradition, *Storyteller* begins by explaining the importance of storytelling in Laguna culture and in Silko's own life through a brief biography of her father's Aunt Susie, a member of the last generation of Laguna people who maintained the oral tradition whereby the entire culture and the people's sense of identity were passed on from one generation to the next. From her, Silko heard several of the traditional stories that are included in *Storyteller*, among them two which appear early in the book and which Silko has said derive from the matriarchal nature of Laguna culture in which the mother is the real authority figure. The first is about a little girl, Waithea, who wants corn mush to eat and drowns herself when her mother refuses to give her any, and the second is about a little girl and her baby sister who are left behind by their mother when the people flee to a mesa to escape a flood. Other stories taken from the Laguna oral tradition include the story of the evil magician who persuaded the Lagunas to abandon the care of the Mother Corn altar and to rely on his magic instead; the story of the quarrel between Reed Woman and Corn Woman; the story of Kaup'a'ta, the Gambler, who shut up the storm clouds until they were rescued by the Sun; and the story of how Arrowboy, a hero figure prominent in Laguna myth, escaped from the power of his witch-wife. If Aunt Susie is the last of the traditional Laguna storytellers, Silko is the first of the new generation of storytellers, and she accepts the responsibility although hers is a literate rather than an oral tradition.

Just what accepting this responsibility entails is the subject of the first of the original short stories in the book. It is also entitled "Storyteller," and its plot deals with two Inuit storytellers, an old man and the young girl who lives with him. The old man, who represents the traditional storyteller, is compelled to tell in endless detail over a long period of time a story about a hunter and a giant white bear which will ultimately kill him at the same time that the old storyteller dies. The young girl represents the storyteller in the modern world. She is compelled to tell the story of her revenge on the white man who sold her parents the contaminated alcohol that killed them. It is a story of the dishonesty, prejudice, and sexual depravity of the white men, and of their exploitation of the Inuits, the Inuit land, and especially the Inuit women. In *Storyteller*, Silko assumes the functions both of the traditional storyteller, who must preserve the legacy of the past, and of the new generation storyteller, who must tell the truth about the present. The materials in the rest of the book fit into one or the other of these categories, or else deal with the cultural, biographical, and autobiographical information needed to understand them.

Analysis

In addition to generating Silko's sense of identity, the theme of the storyteller and storytelling gives unity to the diverse materials collected in *Storyteller*. Growing up as a person of mixed blood, Silko was not fully accepted in Laguna culture or in white culture. As a storyteller who both preserves the oral tradition and functions in the tradition of literate authorship, however, she can establish a bridge between the two cultures and find an identity worthy of respect in both. Moreover, one of the major themes in this book, as it is in her novel *Ceremony*, is that the traditional stories are not merely relics of the past but are relevant to the very different world of today. As Silko says in the selection entitled "Storytelling," it is important for people to understand, through stories, how things were in the past, not only to have an accurate knowledge of history but also because history repeats itself and "it is the same/ even now." This theme is developed further in the short story "Yellow Woman," which is often anthologized and is perhaps Silko's best-known work. Yellow Woman, known to the Lagunas as Kochininako, is the subject of many stories in the oral tradition. In Silko's story, a young Laguna wife has a sexual encounter with a stranger. She remembers and identifies with the story of Yellow Woman's encounter with a spirit from the north with whom she went away and lived. The story emphasizes Silko's cyclical view of history and her belief in the importance of stories in providing a sense of identity.

The exploitation of American Indians by whites is another major theme in *Storyteller*, not only in the short story "Storyteller" but also in three other stories. In "Lullaby," the white rancher for whom the Navajo Chato has worked loyally for many years heartlessly evicts him and his old wife from their shack when Chato gets too old to work. In "Tony's Story," a sadistic state policeman harasses two young pueblo men. In "A Geronimo Story," Laguna scouts who are forced to help the white men track down Apaches are not allowed to sleep in the house with the white soldiers and must sleep outside with the horses. In addition, many of the biographical and autobiographical sections deal with the bigotry that Silko and her family encountered in their dealings with whites.

The natural world, the environment, and animals also constitute important interests in *Storyteller*, as they do in all of Silko's works. Silko's love of the mountains and the desert surrounding Laguna is apparent. Hiking and hunting are activities that she enjoyed as she was growing up, and the stories and poems are filled with careful observations of nature and of animal behavior. Deer, bears, goats, roosters, horses, coyotes, badgers, and sheep all figure prominently in them.

The most striking and pervasive theme to emerge from *Storyteller*, however, is the theme of the value of family. Silko speaks of her family—her great-aunts and great-uncles, great-grandparents, grandparents, aunts and uncles, father, and sisters—with unfailing love and respect. They are important parts of her story and important influences on her as a storyteller. (References to her mother, however, are notably absent.) Through the biographical and autobiographical segments and the photographs, readers are introduced to the members of the Stagner and Marmon families who played such an important role in Silko's development as an author and who continue to play an important role in her affections.

Context

Silko is one of the best-known and most highly acclaimed American Indian writers. She has received many awards for her work, including the so-called genius prize, a MacArthur Foundation Fellowship, in 1981. One of her greatest strengths as a writer is her ability to portray not only female but also male experience realistically and convincingly. She believes that at the deepest levels of human consciousness, men and women are the same, and she has attributed her success in portraying male experience to the fact that in the Laguna culture boys and girls are not segregated as they are in white American society. Consequently, when growing up she was able to observe both male and female experience equally.

As Silko has also pointed out, however, traditional Laguna society is matriarchal, and she grew up in the midst of a group of strong-minded, intelligent, and hard-working women—such as her Aunt Susie, her Grandma A'mooh (Marie Anaya Marmon), and her Grandma Lillie (Francesca Stagner)—and in a community in which the homes are considered the property of the women and in which the women do much of what white American society would consider man's work. The matriarchal nature of Laguna culture is reflected in its concept of the deities, the most important of which are female. Corn Woman and Spider Woman figure prominently in the traditional stories that are incorporated in *Storyteller*. Thus, Silko is important in the history of women's literature not only because she is the first American Indian woman to achieve considerable recognition as a writer but also because her work embodies the matriarchal consciousness of Laguna culture and presents with great accuracy, realism, and psychological insight the experiences of both genders within that culture.

Sources for Further Study

Graulich, Melody, ed. *"Yellow Woman": Leslie Marmon Silko*. New Brunswick, N.J.: Rutgers University Press, 1993. Includes an excellent introduction by Graulich setting *Storyteller* in its cultural, biographical, and critical contexts. Also includes essays dealing with *Storyteller* by Linda Danielson, Patricia Jones, Bernard Hirsch, and Arnold Krupat.

Seyersted, Per. *Leslie Marmon Silko*. Boise, Idaho: Boise State University, 1980. A good introduction to Laguna culture and to Silko's early work up to and including *Storyteller*, which was in press and available to Seyersted when he published his analysis.

Silko, Leslie Marmon, and James Wright. *The Delicacy and Strength of Lace: Letters Between Leslie Marmon Silko and James Wright*. Edited by Anne Wright. St. Paul, Minn.: Graywolf Press, 1986. Correspondence between Silko and poet James Wright from 1978 to 1980, in which Silko discusses *Storyteller*: its genesis and structure, the decision to include photos, and several of the people, stories, and poems that appear. The best source for biographical information on Silko up to 1980.

Studies in American Indian Literatures 5, no. 1 (Spring, 1993). A special edition devoted to *Storyteller*. Linda Danielson summarizes its critical reception to 1993. Toby C. S. Langen discusses it as a treatise on literature at the same time that it is a work of literature. Robert M. Nelson compares Silko's tellings of traditional Laguna stories to the tellings of John Gunn, which were published in 1917. Helen Jaskoski discusses five writing assignments related to *Storyteller* that provide insight into American Indian literatures and to literature in general. Also included are several photographs taken by Silko's father that are relevant to *Storyteller*.

Wiget, Andrew. *Native American Literature*. Boston: Twayne, 1985. Discusses Silko's achievement in terms of her realization of the possibilities of American Indian myths and storytelling as a principle for plot construction and characterization.

Dennis Hoilman

THE STREET

Author: Ann Petry (1911-)
Type of work: Novel
Type of plot: Naturalism
Time of plot: 1944
Locale: Harlem, in New York City
First published: 1946

Principal characters:

Lutie Mae Johnson, a hardworking, African American single mother with middle-class aspirations
Boots, a musician and pimp
Mrs. Hedges, a tenant in Lutie's building who runs a house of prostitution for Junto
Junto, the Jewish owner of the nightclub where Boots works and the brothel that Mrs. Hedges operates
The "Supe," the demented superintendent of the apartment building
Min, the superintendent's common-law wife

Form and Content

Ann Lane Petry was the first African American woman writer to record book sales of more than one million copies. She reworked her experiences as a reporter for two Harlem newspapers, *The Amsterdam News* and *The People's News*, into her novel *The Street*. Organized into eighteen chapters and set in 1944, *The Street* introduces Lutie Mae Johnson, who has moved to 116th Street in Harlem following the dissolution of her marriage. Lutie was forced into an early marriage because of the security that it would provide, but the marriage failed primarily because of the inability of her husband, Jim, to find work. His continual unemployment required Lutie to accept work as a live-in domestic for a wealthy white family in Connecticut. While working for the Chandlers, Lutie became imbued with white American cultural values, which emphasize the belief that success (seemingly equated with money) is possible if one works hard enough.

Lutie adopted this work ethic, choosing Benjamin Franklin as her hero. She accepted the American myth that Franklin had arrived in Philadelphia with only two loaves of bread and prospered. Although she learned from the Chandlers' experiences that the mere possession of money does not bring happiness, she now uncritically pursues the American Dream.

Lutie has been exposed to the American Dream not only through her work for the "filthy rich" Chandlers but also through her education and her friendship with the Prizzinis, an Italian immigrant couple who operate the local grocery store. Following these models, Lutie continually strives to achieve her dream of upward mobility. During the day, she works in a laundry, and at night, she studies to pass a civil service exam. No matter how much Lutie tries, however, she cannot progress economically. She is unable to accumulate the extra money that she needs for her and her son to move from their dingy apartment. She believes that she will obtain success somehow if only she works hard enough.

The door opens a crack when she meets Boots, a musician who tells her that she can become a singer in his band. To prepare for this career change, Lutie decides to take singing lessons. Mr. Cross, the teacher, offers her lessons in exchange for her body. Lutie refuses to use her sexuality to advance her career, although it seems to be the only way that she can attain the financial security she seeks.

Boots must renege on the job offer when Junto, the Jewish owner of the Casino nightclub, tells Boots that he wants Lutie for himself. Lutie refuses both Boots and Junto, recalling bits of conversation that she overheard while working for the Chandlers about the immorality of African American women. Lutie understood perfectly this type of thinking that automatically evoked cultural stereotypes of African American women. She knew that her race and her gender made her immediately suspect and available. Lutie's grandmother had frequently cautioned her about the indecent intentions of white men.

Her grandmother forgot to warn Lutie, however,

about African American men. The urban North produced little contact between white men and African American women, and the white man was not always the enemy, as Lutie discovers. In desperate need of money to obtain the release of her eight-year-old son, who has been arrested, Lutie goes to Boots. Boots tells her that she can have the money but that she must submit sexually to both him and Junto. Boots's slap after she spurns his sexual advances triggers the release of a lifetime of suppressed anger and frustration. Her subsequent killing of Boots is the culmination of years of disappointment.

Analysis

Petry's stated purpose in writing *The Street* was "to show how simply and easily the environment can change the course of a person's life." The wind symbolically represents the environment in the opening paragraph. It portends the life that awaits Lutie Johnson and her son, Bub. Like the wind that scatters litter and people alike, Lutie's life will be buffeted by social, economic, and cultural forces that will assault her sense of self and dignity, never allowing her to meet her goals. She is ultimately defeated because she yearns for more than the choices allowed African American women within a tripartite system of oppression: racism, sexism, and classism.

Unlike Richard Wright's Bigger Thomas, in *Native Son* (1940), Lutie neither fears nor hates whites. She is naïve, however, in her opinion of their system: She does not understand that as an African American woman in the 1940's she is excluded from the American Dream. Lutie believes that she has as much chance for success as a white person or an immigrant because she has accepted the myths of American culture. From her education to her observation of the Chandlers to the machinations of Madison Avenue, she has unthinkingly accepted these myths. She knows from personal observation that money does not equate contentment, but she disregards the unhappiness that permeates the Chandler family. When a suicide committed on Christmas Day in the Chandlers' home is treated as an accident in order to avoid social difficulty, Lutie only notes the power of money to change perceptions.

She not only accepts the myth of Benjamin Franklin but also embraces the idea of a "woman's place." Lutie assumes that her place is in the home and consequently feels guilt because she must work. She does not understand that the system is not designed for her aspirations. Although she indiscriminately accepts white social values, she uncritically rejects the surrounding African American community. She considers herself and her son superior to the other blacks on "the street" by virtue of her education and exposure to the white elite. By isolating herself from the community, she lacks the support that would have sustained her and challenged her ideas for realizing the American Dream. By attempting to achieve autonomy without the support of the African American community and by being too judgmental of other African American women, she sabotages herself.

Yet Petry does not naïvely blame the African American men in *The Street* for the problems in the black community. Boots, Jim, and the "Supe" are as much victims as Lutie. The source of the problems plaguing the African American community are people like Junto and the Chandlers. These white representatives of an oppressive system gain their privilege and power through the racial and economic exploitation of African Americans.

Lutie seemingly is unaware of how white patriarchal power functions and of her inability to change the system or to work within it. She—like many other women—blames herself for the failures in her life. Even so, Lutie never loses her dignity as a woman. The stereotypical images of African American women held by the dominant society were never the images that she had of herself.

Context

The Street was the first work by an African American woman in which a woman faced the challenges of a hostile environment in the same manner as a man. As a result of the inequities inherent in the American social system, Lutie's outward behavior resembles that of Bigger Thomas or of Bob Jones in Chester Himes's *If He Hollers Let Him Go* (1945). She murders out of frustration that comes from her inability to achieve material success in accordance with the precepts of the American Dream.

The Street conforms to the naturalistic mode of writing that was prevalent in African American literature of the 1940's. Naturalism stresses the power of external forces, the environment or the social system, to block human freedom. It may also emphasize the power of internal forces, irrational beliefs or the subconscious, to limit human rationality and responsibility. A standard characteristic of naturalism is that life for the protagonist is a downhill struggle ending in acceptance of the oppressive forces or in death. Lutie's naturalistic flaw seems to be her inability to understand or intellectually accept that black life and the American Dream of material success are diametrically opposed.

As she was writing in the naturalistic mode at the same time as Richard Wright and Chester Himes, Petry's novel was dismissed as an ineffectual imitation of her contemporaries, probably because of her focus on a woman. Although the novel has received much critical attention, until quite recently it had received little literary acclaim. The limited reception of the novel by literary critics did not prevent it from becoming a best-seller. Although the first few chapters won the Houghton Mifflin Literary Fellowship of $2,400 in 1943, many critics missed a crucial difference between Petry's novel and those of her contemporaries: gender.

Although African American men and African American women share a common history, the women have faced and continue to face triple oppression: race, class, and gender. Lutie is female, and her reality is distinct from that of Bigger Thomas or Bob Jones. In *The Street*, Petry chronicles the consequences of racial, sexual, and economic oppression on the psyche of an African American woman. Because of the societal conventions to which Lutie is subjected, particularly sexual exploitation, an extra dimension is added to her experiences that would be missing in a man's. The stereotyping of Lutie as an immoral African American woman denies her certain privileges within society. In addition, she is battered not only spiritually and economically by society but also physically and mentally by African American men.

The Street, published in 1946, was a forerunner of the women's movement of the 1960's and 1970's. By illustrating the abusive and controlling nature of some African American men as well as of white men, Petry allowed African American women to question the assumption that race was their only obstacle to full participation in American society.

Sources for Further Study

Bell, Bernard W. "Ann Petry's Demythologizing of American Culture and Afro-American Character." In *Conjuring: Black Women, Fiction, and Literary Tradition*, edited by Marjorie Pryse and Hortense J. Spillers. Bloomington: Indiana University Press, 1985. Through an examination of Petry's three major novels—*The Street*, *Country Place* (1947), and *The Narrows* (1953)—Bell concludes that Petry's characters have been shaped differently by their environment than those of her contemporaries, Wright and Himes. Petry's more complex delineation of black personality allows for women characters who are more varied and complex.

Clark, Keith. "A Distaff Dream Deferred? Ann Petry and the Art of Subversion." *African-American Review* 26, no. 3 (Fall, 1992): 495-505. Clark suggests that Petry offers alternative methods of achieving the American Dream of success through two minor female characters, Mrs. Hedges and Min.

Dempsey, David. "Uncle Tom's Ghost and the Literary Abolitionists." *Antioch Review* 6 (September, 1946): 442-448. Petry is one of several literary "abolitionists" writing during the 1940's who do not include a lynching.

Gayle, Addison. *The Way of the New World*. Garden City, N.Y.: Doubleday, 1975. Claims that Petry is more concerned with the effects of the environment on her characters than with the characters themselves.

Ivey, James. "Ann Petry Talks About Her First Novel." In *Sturdy Black Bridges: Visions of Black Women in Literature*, edited by Roseann P. Bell, Bettye J. Parker, and Beverly Guy-Sheftall. Garden City, N.Y.: Anchor Press, 1979. The source of Petry's statement that her purpose "is to show how simply and easily the environment can change the course of a person's life."

Pryse, Marjorie. " 'Patterns Against the Sky': Deism and Motherhood in Ann Petry's *The Street*." In *Conjuring: Black Women, Fiction, and Literary Tradition*, edited by Pryse and Hortense J. Spillers. Bloomington: Indiana University Press, 1985. Besides exploring and expanding references to Benjamin Franklin in the text, Pryse analyzes two other female characters, Min and Mrs. Hedges.

Shinn, Thelma J. "Women in the Novels of Ann Petry." *Critique: Studies in Modern Fiction* 16, no. 1 (1974): 110-120. Shinn argues that women, both African American and white, must conform to society's notions of feminine behavior or be ostracized.

Yarborough, Richard. "The Quest for the American Dream in Three Afro-American Novels: *If He Hollers Let Him Go, The Street, Invisible Man.*" *MELUS* 8 (1981): 33-59. Yarborough argues that according to these three novels, the American Dream is not possible for African Americans.

Mary Young

SULA

Author: Toni Morrison (Chloe Anthony Wofford, 1931-)
Type of work: Novel
Type of plot: *Bildungsroman*
Time of plot: 1919-1965
Locale: "The Bottom," a community in Medallion, Ohio
First published: 1973

Principal characters:

Sula Peace, a resident of "the Bottom," an African American community, who rebels against tradition
Nel Wright, Sula's best friend and foil
Hannah Peace, Sula's mother
Eva Peace, Sula's grandmother
Helene Wright, Nel's mother
Shadrack, a shell-shocked soldier who starts his own holiday called National Suicide Day
Albert Jacks (Ajax), Sula's lover

Form and Content

In *Sula*, Toni Morrison explores a community's role in the individual's search for wholeness. The story begins at the end, after the African American community known as "the Bottom" has been destroyed and replaced with a golf course. The narrator reveals the history of "the Bottom" forty years before it was destroyed, in chapters titled simply by the year of focus, beginning with 1919 and ending with 1965.

The community gained its name from a joke played on a slave by a white farmer. After promising his slave freedom and land upon the completion of some difficult chores, the farmer did not want to part with his choice land. So he told the slave that the hilly land—difficult to plant and plagued by high winds and sliding soil—was the bottom of heaven, the "best land there is." Consequently, the slave accepted the land, and "the Bottom" is where Sula Peace and Nel Wright are born.

Nel, her mother Helene, and her father live in a home Nel considers to be oppressively neat. Carefully groomed by her mother, who is admired in the community for her beauty and grace, Nel prefers the disorder that she finds in Sula's home, where "something was always cooking on the stove, . . . the mother, Hannah, never scolded or gave directions" and "all sorts of people dropped in." During her only trip outside Medallion, ten-year-old Nel meets Helene's estranged mother and sees her own mother's usual grace disturbed by Southern remnants of racist oppression. Nel and Helene must sit in the "colored only" car of the train, and because there were no "colored only" restrooms past Birmingham, they urinate in the woods when the train stops. Helene is pleased to return home. After Nel insists, Helene welcomes the young Sula into her home, in spite of Hannah Peace's reputation for being "sooty."

Sula and Nel's development into adults follows some predictable and some unpredictable patterns. Nel becomes a carbon copy of her mother. She marries, has children, and bases her entire identity on the roles of mother and wife, an identity disrupted by her best friend. After attending college and traveling to some major American cities, Sula returns to Medallion, where she continues her mother's legacy of promiscuity and has her mean-spirited grandmother placed, against her will, in a home for the elderly.

To Nel's dismay, Sula has sex with Nel's husband, Jude. Feeling betrayed by her husband and her best friend, Nel says that her life and her "thighs . . . [are] truly empty and dead." After nearly three years of not speaking to each other, Nel visits Sula after hearing that she is sick. Nel leaves unsatisfied with Sula's shallow reason for having sex with Jude. Sula dies of an unnamed illness at the age of thirty.

On January 3, 1941, the National Suicide Day after Sula's death, Shadrack continues his tradition, although with less passion since he misses Sula. This year, many town members participate in his parade. They march gayly to "the white part of town," distinguished by the tunnel excavation and beginnings of remodeling for the city. Angered by not being permitted to work on the renovations, many citizens of "the Bottom" crowd into the tunnel as an action of self-assertion and protest. Tragically, the tunnel collapses, killing an unspecified number of the protesters (approximately twelve to fifteen).

By 1965, the hills of "the Bottom" are largely populated by whites, and the narrator laments the lack of cohesion among the African Americans who have moved to the valley. As the narrator notes, there were not as many spontaneous visits and everyone had his or her own television and telephone. After Nel visits Eva in the home for the elderly, Nel remembers calling the hospital, mortuary, and police after Sula's body was found—eyes open and mouth open—in Eva's bed. Only after Nel leaves the cemetery does she discover that all the pain and loneliness that she had been feeling was from missing having Sula in her life, not Jude.

Analysis

In *Sula*, the concept of class and its relation to sex and race occupies much of Morrison's attention as she chronicles the development of Sula and Nel. A few fundamental concepts shape Morrison's vision of the human condition—particularly, as critic Dorothy Lee points out, her preoccupation with how a community affects the individual's achievement and retention of an acceptable self.

The African American citizens of "the Bottom" were victims of a cruel joke begun by the white farmer who gave the hilly land its ironic name by refusing to surrender to the slave the land that he deserved. Although African Americans work hard and serve their country in war, their rewards are few. Morrison's presentation provides a bleak look at a community suffering from oppression and the denial of rewards or even acknowledgment. The men are limited to menial jobs that do not even give them the pleasure of muscle-fatiguing labor; they cannot work on the tunnel. The women are placed in the positions of mothers, wives, or whores; there is no in-between. Though victims, they all victimize one another, maintaining a status quo that they did not set.

Sula Peace is a significant part of this community's history. As her name suggests, she seeks inner peace, a personal wholeness that the restrictions of life deny her. These restrictions are largely a result of limited traditional roles designated for women and racial prejudice aimed at African Americans. Determined to face life truthfully, Sula rebels against nearly all tradition and endures the wrath and scorn of her community. She embodies much of the frustration and pain of her community members.

Nel and Sula represent conformity and rebellion, respectively, to their community's expectations. Nel marries a man from "the Bottom" and performs her duties, including sex, as a mother and wife. After her husband's infidelity with Sula, Nel describes her thighs—a metaphor for her sexuality and her self—as "empty and dead." Jude leaves Nel, and without the role as wife condoned by society, Nel becomes unsure of her identity.

Sula chooses to stand outside society, to define herself as a revolt against it. Unlike Nel, she ignores traditional roles and society's expectations: "She went to bed with men as frequently as possible." Consequently, Sula functions as pariah for her community: "She was pariah, then, and knew it. Knew that they despised her and believed that they framed their hatred as disgust for the easy way she lay with men." Sula's promiscuous behavior makes her the chaos and evil against which the community must define and protect itself.

Helene Wright attempts to transcend the boundaries set by race by denying her New Orleans roots, cleaning incessantly, and wearing nice clothes. Shadrack tries to cope with his pain by dedicating a special day to it. Eva copes with her pain by inflicting pain on herself and others.

The lack of a happy ending, the deaths of many community members near the end of the work, and the lack of cohesion in the 1965 community as emphasized by the narrator in the final chapter all indicate the power that Morrison perceives in communal energy. She seems to imply that without the strength and support that a healthy community provides—that is, a community made up of strong, supportive, loving individuals who are not oppressed and subjugated by society—the development of people into productive, content, spiritually whole individuals is stifled or, at worst, impossible.

Context

Morrison's exploration of friendship between African American women makes *Sula* a major link between Zora Neale Hurston's *Their Eyes Were Watching God* (1937) and Alice Walker's *The Color Purple* (1982). Furthermore, the friendship between Sula and Nel does not depend on or revolve around men. Morrison explores this friendship, its maturity and its eventual dissolution.

Nel and Sula's relationship blossoms out of mutual admiration, for Sula appreciates the quiet orderliness of Nel's home. In stark contrast, and in addition to Hannah's sexual liaisons, the Peace home is characterized by Eva's unpredictability. Sula's grandmother has one leg, and the town rumor is that she either placed the other on a railroad track or sold it to a hospital. In either case, Eva provides food and shelter for her family. Yet Eva is not simply a provider; she is also a sacrificer. When her son, Plum, returns from the war in a questionable mental and physical condition, she burns him to death as he sleeps in his room.

Helene, Nel, Sula, Eva, and Hannah continually challenge stereotypes as the narrator reveals these women's thoughts, fears, and concerns. Morrison's depictions stress the fact that women cannot be limited to select roles; they are too wonderfully diverse. Not unlike Hurston, Walker, and a host of other female writers, Morrison gives voices to the many women who remained silent when required to choose between severely limited life options.

Although the possibilities for women in American society have expanded since the publication of *Sula* in 1973, the novel reminds its readers of a time that should be remembered. In the late 1960's, the women's liberation movement was in full force to combat sexual discrimination and gain legal, economic, vocational, educational, and social rights and opportunities for women that were equal to those of men. It is important to women, and clearly important to Morrison, that the history of this struggle and the stories of these women not be forgotten.

Sources for Further Study

Carby, Hazel V., ed. *Reconstructing Womanhood.* New York: Oxford University Press, 1987. This collection of essays includes a thorough study of the female characters found in African American literature. The authors explore the works of African American women writers from Harriet Jacobs, the author of *Incidents in the Life of a Slave Girl* (1861), to Toni Morrison.

Christian, Barbara, ed. *Black Feminist Criticism: Perspectives on Black Women Writers.* New York: Pergamon Press, 1985. This compilation of criticism and commentary on literature by African American women addresses literature by Toni Morrison, Alice Walker, Gloria Naylor, and Gwendolyn Brooks. The book is composed of essays that include extensive analyses of individual works, as well as examinations of common traits found in literature by African American women. Each essay contains many explanatory notes and lists of sources.

Gates, Henry L., Jr., ed. *Reading Black, Reading Feminist: A Critical Anthology.* New York: Meridian/New American Library, 1990. This collection of critical essays explores the effects that African American female writers have had on literature. Includes the work of May Helen Washington, Barbara Christian, Hazel V. Carby, Mae Gwendolyn Henderson, and many other leaders in the field of African American literary studies. Their critical analyses go far beyond the surface as they examine the characters (mostly female) from the novels of Morrison and other African American female authors.

Lee, Robert A. *Black Fiction: New Studies in the Afro-American Novel Since 1945.* London: Vision Press, 1980. These insightful essays explore the African American novel in order to identify recurring themes and techniques. One particular essay, by Faith Pullin, addresses *Sula* and Morrison's creation of women in this text who do not fit common stereotypes.

Morrison, Toni. "Toni Morrison's Black Magic." Interview by Jean Strouse. *Newsweek* 97 (March 30, 1981): 52-56. Morrison appeared on the cover of this issue of *Newsweek*, and she was the first African American woman to do so. It is one of the most revealing interviews she has given. Provides valuable biographical information, starting from her childhood, and she discusses her writing as a reflection of her perception of life.

Jeryl J. Prescott

SURFACING

Author: Margaret Atwood (1939-   )
Type of work: Novel
Type of plot: Social criticism
Time of plot: About 1970
Locale: An island in northern Quebec
First published: 1972

Principal characters:

The narrator, an unnamed woman in her late twenties who works as a commercial artist
Joe, the narrator's boyfriend, an artist who makes pots
Anna, the narrator's closest female friend
David, Anna's husband of nine years
The narrator's father, a retired botanist who is missing
The narrator's mother, who died of cancer
The narrator's brother, a prospector in Australia

Form and Content

The story of *Surfacing* covers nine days that the four younger people—the narrator, Joe, Anna, and David—spend on the island that had been the narrator's childhood home and several more days when she is there alone. Though the unnamed narrator is attempting to find explanations for her father's mysterious disappearance, the others treat it more as a vacation, filming quaint Quebec oddities during the trip and their own outdoorsy exploits on the island. They expect the narrator to entertain them by taking them fishing and blueberry picking.

The detective-novel feel of the early part of the novel is emphasized as the group hunts for traces of the narrator's father on the island and as the narrator searches the cabin for something that might indicate his whereabouts. The past gradually comes into sharper focus for the narrator as she finds things in the cabin that trigger memories of her childhood and her young adult years. Memories of her wedding and her child are juxtaposed with memories of her school years and images from drawings she produced as a child that her mother kept in scrapbooks.

After finding childlike drawings of strange animals and figures among her father's papers, the narrator concludes that he must have gone crazy as he spent another winter alone in the isolated cabin. She fears that he is alive on the island and a danger to her friends. The forced intimacy on the island is also proving dangerous, as David and Anna bicker and insult each other while Joe broods silently.

Digging further into her father's papers, while the others try to amuse themselves with reading old paperbacks from the cabin or working on a film called "Random Samples," the narrator comes across letters from an archaeologist to her father. Apparently, the odd drawings were not indications of her father's madness but sketches of ancient Indian rock paintings from around the area. She does not share her theories with the others but feels compelled to prove to herself that her father is not crazy, but dead. Realizing that the water level would have risen and covered the rock paintings when the timber company dammed the lake decades ago, the narrator plans a solitary trip to a nearby site, where she will be able to dive underwater and search for the paintings.

Diving in search of not only the paintings but some sort of answer about her father's fate as well, the narrator is also forced to confront her own past and repressed memories. She does not see any paintings, but as her breath is running out, she sights a body below her in the murky lake. Bursting out of the water, she has surfaced to the knowledge that her father is indeed dead and that she can no longer lie to herself about her past. The former husband and abandoned child assume their real forms as an art professor with whom she had an affair and their child, which was aborted. Her father's death is confirmed the next day as some men stop by the island to tell her that his body was hooked by a fisherman.

Her cleared vision causes the narrator to realize that she needs to stop fighting nature with her modern Americanized life and redeem her past by producing a child. The night before they are to leave the island, she knows that she is fertile and leads Joe outside to have sex on the ground. The narrator continues her revolt against civilization as she destroys the men's film and refuses to leave with the others when the boat comes to pick them up. Hiding in the woods, she knows that she must find answers about her parents, her past, and who she is.

Over the next few days, she becomes increasingly like an animal, as she somehow knows that it is taboo for her to enter the cabin, wear clothes, or eat prepared food. She believes that she must destroy man-made things and breaks, ruins, or burns much of the cabin's contents. She knows that there is a child growing inside her, and she does not want it tainted by modern life. The narrator is physically weakened by several days with little food, but she becomes more powerful spiritually. She finds her answers as visions of her parents appear to her—her mother feeding the birds with outstretched arms and her father as a half-human, half-animal figure resembling the cliff drawings. This mystical experience transforms her, and she is again able to enter the cabin, eat, wear clothes, and perhaps return to civilization. The novel ends ambiguously as Joe returns to the island and calls for her.

Analysis

Atwood's unstable and less-than-trustworthy narrator undermines the security of the plot but causes readers to focus instead on her mental state and interpretations. The events that she reports are not as important as how she sees them. Because of her scrambled and deliberately evasive memories, the narrator provides an example of a mind unable to accept modern civilization and a psychological study of a woman attempting to cope.

Atwood's didacticism and moral message are especially evident in the conflict between civilization and nature. She questions whether the so-called progress of culture is only an illusion. Canadian nationalism also figures in the story, as David and the narrator rail against Americans or people with Americanized attitudes who kill animals for fun and pollute the environment. The narrator becomes increasingly alienated from civilization, yet David and Anna are securely anchored in modern technological society. Joe remains on the border—his silence shows that he has not been completely coopted by modern existence. At the end of the story, he is described as an ambassador or mediator between civilization and wilderness.

After she has surfaced to the knowledge about her delusions and past lies, the narrator needs to reject the trappings of modern life. Her destruction of the film is one aspect of this, as is her abandonment of her clothing in the lake—a baptism or ritual cleansing. She is attempting to become part of nature because her years of trying to become civilized were unsuccessful. When searchers return to the island for her, she is afraid that the natural woman she is becoming will be treated like an animal—brutally killed or put on display.

The question "What is natural?" is also raised in the love relationships in *Surfacing*. The narrator feels incapable of love and feels trapped when Joe, instead of asking the expected "Do you love me?" asks her to marry him. She is unable to commit, fearfully remembering past relationships, while Joe wants a yes-or-no answer. For him, there is no middle ground. By contrast, Anna claims that she and David have remained married because they have an emotional bond. After observing their warped interaction, the narrator begins to wonder if that emotion is hate rather than love.

Parent-child relationships are also questioned. While the others have cast off their parents, the narrator is equivocal toward her family and her past. She distanced herself from them because of her own failure to become a parent: She felt too guilty to face them after her abortion. Achieving harmony with her parents' spirits is the climax of her period of heightened sensory awareness. She realizes that she can learn from her parents, even after their deaths. The narrator's vision of what her father has become functions as a warning about trying to get too close to ancient gods and meanings without proper reverence. Her vision of her mother feeding the birds somehow satisfies her need to explain this mysterious woman's significance. Her confrontation with their spirits is prefigured by the token that she believes her mother has left for her in one of the scrapbooks: a drawing that the narrator had made as a child showing a pregnant woman confronting a horned god, while her baby watches from inside her stomach.

The novel's title indicates the complex theme and image pattern involving birth and abortion. The narrator's constructed memories about her child have double meanings when reread with the knowledge that she actually had an abortion. Images of body and blood fit both situations. Linked to this is her "memory" (though the event happened before she was born) of her brother's near drowning and images of the frogs and other animals that he kept in jars in his secret laboratory. She remembers his anger when she released the animals that had not already died, while she is haunted with her own created memories of dead babies in jars like lab specimens.

The death images are contrasted with those of rebirth: the narrator's surfacing to life and knowledge after she sees her father's body in the water and her symbolic baptism as she is cleansed by the lake after the others have left. Her sunny childhood drawings of rabbits and eggs suggest fertility and reinforce her powerful pregnant condition at the novel's close. The themes of drowning and surfacing also resonate with the narrator's descent into her unconscious, nonrational mind to seek explanations for questions about her parents and her life.

Context

Atwood's novel raises many issues about women and about modern society. The narrator's need to control her destiny at the end of the novel arises out of the drifting young adult years when she let others—such as the married professor with whom she had the affair—make choices for her. Atwood explores how women react when they cannot live as they desire. The narrator responded to her abortion by building more socially acceptable fantasies to hide her behavior from herself and others. Anna responds by playing the victim role: She loves David and defines herself as his wife, so she endures his cruel jokes and his infidelity.

Likewise, the narrator's namelessness can be seen to signify the role of women in a society where they are not valued as individuals. Her lack of a title emphasizes her lack of secure role or position. Her namelessness also suggests that the search that she undertakes is something all women must do—she is Everywoman. Many critics see the novel as exemplifying a female quest. The characters and events can be viewed as archetypal patterns that resonate with mythology and folklore about heroic women.

Because of the recognition gained by Atwood's poetry and her first novel, *The Edible Woman* (1969), *Surfacing* was not released in obscurity. Critics recognized in it Atwood's previously established patterns of feminism, Canadian nationalism, and ecological issues. *Surfacing*, however, is the novel after which Atwood began to be considered as a public voice for women. Some critics made the link between the victimization of female characters and a postcolonial Canadian attitude of victimization.

Sources for Further Study

Davey, Frank. *Margaret Atwood: A Feminist Poetics*. Vancouver: Talonbooks, 1984. Provides a useful biography of Atwood which is interspersed with quotes from interviews. Also examines her poetry, novels, short fiction, and criticism.

Davidson, Arnold E., and Cathy N. Davidson, eds. *The Art of Margaret Atwood*. Toronto: Anansi, 1981. Thirteen essays dealing with Atwood as a poet, novelist, and critic. Two fairly contrasting views of *Surfacing* are presented, one a feminist archetypal view and the other a psychological comparison with Atwood's first and third novels.

Grace, Sherrill E., and Lorraine Weir, eds. *Margaret Atwood: Language, Text, and System*. Vancouver: University of British Columbia Press, 1983. A varied collection of essays by Canadian scholars. Those addressing *Surfacing* deal with shamanism and syntax.

Rigney, Barbara Hill. *Margaret Atwood*. Totowa, N.J.: Barnes & Noble Books, 1987. A chronological exploration of Atwood's work with a feminist interpretation. The examination of *Surfacing* deals especially with thematic patterns and symbols and connections with Atwood's poetry.

Van Spanckeren, Kathryn, and Jan Garden Castro, eds. *Margaret Atwood: Vision and Forms*. Carbondale: Southern Illinois University Press, 1988. Presents fifteen essays on Atwood's poetry and prose, with two specifically on *Surfacing*. An interview with Atwood and a foreword written by the author provide insight into her writings.

Woodcock, George. *Introducing Margaret Atwood's "Surfacing."* Ontario: ECW Press, 1990. Woodcock provides background information on Atwood, discusses the reception of *Surfacing* in Canada and the United States, and explores at length its style, structure, and themes.

Rebecca L. Wheeler

TELL ME A RIDDLE

Author: Tillie Olsen (1913-)
Type of work: Novella and short stories
First published: 1961

Form and Content

The title story of this collection, "Tell Me a Riddle," is a novella in which Tillie Olsen depicts the inevitably destructive dynamic in a dysfunctional marriage that has endured for almost half a century when both elderly members are forced to confront their regrets. Divided into four parts, it portrays the current anguish and past tribulations of a dying woman, Eva, the knowledge of whose terminal illness, like so much that she deserved and desired to know, has been kept from her. Part 1 opens with the first of many riddles that haunt the novella. The adult children of the couple married forty-seven years are puzzled that their parents cannot get along. Eva and Dave literally and figuratively tune each other out during part 1: he, by turning up the television volume; she, by turning off her hearing aid. The major conflict that their relentless banter surrounds is David's desire to move to the Haven, a comfortable and "carefree" retirement community for the aged, and Eva's refusal to sell the house and do so, since she has finally realized a "reconciled peace" in her own space.

Determined to preserve her hard-won ability "at last to live within and not move to the rhythms of others," she ignores her husband's various derogatory and dismissive names for her (Mrs. Live Alone and Like It), though she cannot ignore her physical pain. She agrees to see doctor and son-in-law Phil after her first doctor could not determine the cause of her discomfort. Part 1 ends with son Paul's silencing of his wife Nancy's cruel allegation that it was merely psychosomatic, for Phil has reported that the gall bladder operation revealed cancer.

Part 2 includes subsequent visits to her children (Hannah and Vivi) which exacerbate Eva's frustration in wishing to be alone and to forget; she cannot do so when daughter Vivi's guilt, gratitude, and sorrow pour forth in a deluge of memories. Part 2 brings them to Los Angeles, where granddaughter Jeannie, a nurse, takes care of them both. When they meet Mrs. Mayes, an old friend whose life has gone from eight children to aloneness in a coffin-like room, Eva realizes the extent of her own suffocation. At the end of part 3, upon seeing for the first time David's concern for her, Eva solves the riddle of the incessant travel: She understands now that she is dying. Part 3, then, involves Eva and David's gradual acceptance not only of her swiftly consuming death but also of the truth of their lives. Eva struggles to remember and articulate the trauma of her Siberian imprisonment during the revolution and the tragic forfeiture of her and David's ideals as their lives became determined by familial needs.

In his own last efforts to reconstruct the past as worthwhile and happy, David resents Eva's stream-of-consciousness focus on the hardships that permeated her existence, children's quarrels and endless demands, her humiliation in poverty, and so forth. Yet the revolutionary songs she utters exact his own confrontation with reality. Jeannie assuages this blow and becomes very close to both of them. Indeed, her art of healing captures the love that is still inherent in their embrace; she is at once able to help David redeem his grief at Eva's loss and ease his remorse. Tillie Olsen has rendered in this moving work of fiction the reality of her own mother's difficult life as a struggling social activist, wife, and caretaker who, in parallel fashion, lost a battle with cancer.

Analysis

Olsen's novella within this collection breathlessly illustrates the mental, emotional, spiritual, and physical agony that results from the disintegration of love and idealism. David and Eva are no longer able to grant each other true peace, so they must settle for the ironic and fraudulent quiet of willfully not listening to each other. Eva holds her lifetime investment in futile housewifely duties against David, because these continual obligations make her family the enemy of her own aching wants and needs: to be a social activist, to read, to listen to music, to discuss philosophy. One important riddle, in fact, is that now that she has the time and space to pursue these passions (the children are grown), her degenerating health cruelly limits her. Her eyesight and hearing are failing.

Eva's all-consuming love for her children had suffocated all of her other desires. These maternal capacities all used up, she cannot bear to be near Vivi's newborn baby, who reminds her of her personal history of deprivation. The literal and figurative drain of maternity had drowned her beyond the ability to risk reopening wounds by touching any other baby.

In a sense, she is recovering from the "lovely drunkenness" that has usurped her passion; she would not dare to endanger her "reconciled peace" by submitting to the temptation of another drink. Thus do grudges and manipulation now preoccupy Eva and David's interaction; for example, David's constant badgering about the Haven forces Eva to relive old grievances in spite of their children's meager efforts to make them compromise on the basis of their years invested, as son Lenny—who, saddened by what in his mother and himself never lived and who learned at an early age to mother himself—argues they should.

For Eva, her investment has exacted an extraordinary intensity and anxiety, and thus she welcomes the poetic justice inherent in David's finally having to worry about how they are going to make do. This justified revenge stems from Eva's disdain for the way David has always opted to run from life rather than face it. As she tells her granddaughter, she can no longer tell riddles, perhaps because she has endured too many riddles in her life, which has been replete with contradictions and unresolvable dilemmas: She cannot bear her husband, yet they still love each other.

Eva's life as wife and mother has become a riddle. Clara, her oldest daughter, regrets that she and her mother have lost each other in harshness, silence, and withdrawal. She wants Eva to repay the affection she lost because she had so many younger siblings and laments that she and Eva never knew each other. Further, Eva's obligation to attend to Vivi's children's interests (Richard's rock collections, Ann's autumn leaves) tires Eva, for the weight of the trust is too burdensome, the agonizing self-effacing past it calls up, too oppressive. The screaming of the children, for example, reminds her of Lisa, her beloved friend and cellmate in a Siberian prison, whose rage and anguish at their betrayal by their traitorous friend compelled Lisa to murder the traitor in heinous fashion, by attacking her and biting her jugular vein—a savage act that Eva witnessed fifty years ago and cannot forget.

Again one senses the disparity between Eva and David, for he runs from the pain and the past. He recalls not the suffering but rather their ideals and dreams, and Eva's elegance in expressing those hopes during the revolution. Amazed by the profundity of Eva's convictions, David nevertheless regrets how much he has lost, finally confronting the bereavement he had repressed through the century. Eva's reminiscence—in their final days, she focuses on the negative only—David takes as her betrayal of them both. He wonders if their beliefs were false, for his self-pity and egocentric perception distort the realities of the past. He can no longer accept Eva's brutal honesty about the multiple imprisonments—including wifehood and motherhood—which have constituted her life.

One such incarceration from which she has liberated herself is religion, which she deems a farce that has perpetuated and sanctioned, even glorified, women's subordination. By exempting herself from the tidy and conventional classifications society imposes to confine, define, and divide people—race and religion—Eva defies conventional categories that have made sacrosanct the dual persecution she has endured as a Jewish woman. She declares that her "race" is "human," her "religion," "none."

Stream-of-consciousness technique—noted in the graphics of the text as italics—literally and figuratively casts a particular slant on these major themes. Reinforced by the power of words to wound, verbal and nonverbal sounds evoke inescapable images and memories, unifying the intense novel through associative prose and prominent motifs, including noise and other pollution, singing as a catalyst for memory, paper dolls, riddles rooted in oxymoron (Eva's "swollen thinness"), the importance of women's own self-cultivated, maintained, and desired space, and human regression to infant or animal-like status (Eva's clasping hands become clawlike as she reverts inward to a fetal position).

Stream of consciousness also prevails in other stories in this collection. For example, in "Hey Sailor, What Ship?"—the second story—Whitey is a drunken sailor who tries to buy the affection and reluctant acceptance of his former shipmate Lennie's family. After their rebellious teenager, Jeannie, rejects his misguided generosity, he turns more solidly to his bottle, his only constant and solace. A biting commentary on the likely destructiveness of life in the service, this classic is painfully realistic.

Context

Olsen's novella has had an inexhaustible impact upon and relevance to women's literature. Even in one of the mother-daughter conflicts surrounding Eva's disgust with institutionalized religion, the reader witnesses the intergenerational gap between social activist Eva and religious conformist daughter Hannah, who lost her childhood in the premature responsibilities of helping to rear younger siblings and now duplicates her mother's selfless exhaustion. When Hannah was growing up, Eva had neither the luxury of excess time nor the desire to pass on what she deemed to be "superstition" (the lighting of Sabbath candles). Indeed, she resented others' blind obeisance to such traditions in times of severe poverty: using potatoes as candle holders when there was nothing to eat, buying candles when there was no money for soap. She sees Hannah invoking these submissive gestures to appease her husband and his family and to fill in the emptiness and darkness that Hannah has yet to admit also fills her traditional life. Eva is angry that Hannah would opt to teach her offspring these practices rather than the pragmatic and realistic ways in which social activism could improve the world.

Nevertheless, the cyclic repetition of women's lives pains Eva. She sees that Hannah, too, is run ragged by her children's and her husband's needs and has no time left for herself. Similarly, Vivi's wornness worries Eva. Vivi's own empathy with her mother's past self-sacrifice gushes forth in her gratitude over the catalog of humiliations and grief that Eva suffered for their sake: sewing all their clothes; taking them to the train station when they had no heat; begging for bones, allegedly for their dog in the winter. No wonder, then, that the paper dolls Ann makes for Eva assume disproportionate significance. Like Eva's and Vivi's, their eyes are fatigue-ringed, their one-dimensional bodies flattened, aproned, and flowery in their ancient pliability.

Eva wishes that the new generation would break this merciless repetition of women's lives: She wishes that granddaughter Dody, like her brother Richard, would climb trees and hang freely from them. With her oldest granddaughter and ultimate caretaker, Jeannie, as well, Eva bears witness to the hope that this second generation of women has the potential to offer and cultivate. Eva tells Jeannie that by the time she was her age, both her own mother and her grandmother had already buried children, as Eva had buried Davy; significantly, Jeannie is tied to neither husband nor children. Eva fantasizes that, by extension, Jeannie will not have to sacrifice her youthful vigor and generous capacity to give, and that she will not have to beg a self-absorbed man to honor her dying request to return to her home and hard-won "reconciled peace." Perhaps Jeannie will not fall prey to doctors who, assuming that women's ailments are psychological, contribute to the abbreviation of their lives by not diagnosing soon enough a problem as grave as cancer.

Olsen, as the second of seven children of Jewish immigrant parents who fled Russia after the 1905 rebellion, knew at firsthand the poverty and political activism she portrayed. A member of the Young Communist League, she wrote a proletarian novel, *Yonnondio*, after serving a jail term for union organizing. Because she supported four daughters through a series of blue-collar jobs, she was not able to finish it until forty years later. She began work on *Tell Me a Riddle* in 1955, when a Stanford University fellowship gave her the economic freedom to focus on her writing. Typical of many struggling working-class women writers, Olsen was not able to complete the novella until a Ford Foundation grant in 1959 again offered her the wherewithal to do so.

The novella's universal themes of race, class, and gender obstacles and implications won for it an enthusiastic reception as well as the O. Henry Award for the best short story of 1961, the same year in which she published "I Stand Here Ironing," the second most well-known of the stories in this collection. This confessional narrative is a remorseful retrospective of Olsen's oldest daughter Emily's problematic childhood with a single working mother whose husband left them and of her troubled adolescence as a helping "mother, housekeeper, and shopper" of four smaller children by Olsen's second marriage.

Like those of Clara, Hannah, and Vivi, Emily's youth was short-lived because of the expectations of the need for assistance with childrearing. Like Eva, the autobiographical "I" in "I Stand Here Ironing" is still haunted by her daughter's unmet needs and the consequent rivalry between them. This story exemplifies the difficult, distracting lives of working-class mothers and explains in part why recognition by Radclyffe Institute and National Endowment of the Arts fellowships, a MacDowell Colony grant, and teaching at three universities made it possible for Olsen to complete *Yonnondio* forty years after she had begun it (1974).

Olsen again addresses the interstices of race, class, and—to a lesser degree—gender in the third story of this collection, "O Yes." Here, she dramatizes the differences in religious expression across race lines when twelve-year-old, white Carol attends the baptismal service of her black friend Parialee. The revivalistic hype of this service overwhelms the unprepared Carol, who—as a result of the trauma—comes to realize the emotional cost of caring. Her mother simultaneously recognizes the blessing that these "negroes" have in their loving, supportive, and understanding acceptance of and strength in one another's woe.

Olsen's interest in women's writing was rekindled by the 1960's, and she has been instrumental in retrieving such works as Rebecca Harding Davis' *Life in the Iron Mills*, which the Feminist Press published in 1972 and for which Olsen wrote an afterword that was longer than the poignant novel itself. *Silences* (1978), Olsen's third book, describes how circumstances of the disenfranchised (poor Jewish women) preclude the resources and space necessary to create, since wives and mothers place others' needs before their own—a theme that resurfaces in each of the other works of this collection as well, including "Hey Sailor, What Ship?" and "O Yes." The recipient of several honorary degrees, Olsen continues to encourage women to develop the potential of their own creative powers and transformative imaginations and to offer a voice to the inarticulate and silent.

Sources for Further Study

Culver, Sara. "Extending the Boundaries of the Ego: Eva in 'Tell Me a Riddle.' " *Midwestern Miscellany* 10 (1982): 38-49. Culver suggests the waste that results from using women as servants and breeders. Suppressing their intellect, artistic ability, courage, and idealism causes women bitterness and is a blight on their children as well, in part because those children learn to assume a mother's self-sacrifice as their due. Eva is thus betrayed by the cultural confinement of motherhood.

Jacobs, Naomi. "Earth, Air, Fire, and Water in *Tell Me a Riddle*." *Studies in Short Fiction* 23, no. 4 (1986): 401-406. Jacobs contends that earth, air, fire, and water are metaphors for Eva's various spiritual states on the continuum between isolation and union, quarrel and embrace, silence and song, life and death.

Kamel, Rose. "Literary Foremothers and Writers' Silences: Tillie Olsen's Autobiographical Fiction." *MELUS* 12, no. 3 (Fall, 1985): 55-72. Kamel discusses each of Olsen's works, including her postscript to Rebecca Harding Davis' *Life in the Iron Mills*, which blend critical analysis and self-scrutiny. Davis and Olsen both experienced working-class hardship, observed human misery, and suffered sexism's demands on women, which Kamel discovers in such stylistic features as inverted syntax, run-on sentences, fragments, repetitions, alliterative parallels, and incantatory rhythms that reflect the chaos and drudgery of working women's lives.

Nilsen, Helge Normann. "Tillie Olsen's *Tell Me a Riddle*: The Political Theme." *Etudes Anglaises* 37, no. 2 (April-June, 1984): 163-169. Nilsen suggests the essentially political identity that Eva needs to cultivate once her children are grown, in order to offset the stunted development of her talents and faculties incurred by stifling motherhood. With a radicalism that Nilsen argues is rooted in American transcendentalism, Eva sees that love transcends personal, familial boundaries to include a commitment to better the world.

Olsen, Tillie. *Silences*. New York: Delta Press, 1978. The self-referential voice of the extended wail in *Tell Me a Riddle* offers an apologia or lamentation for Olsen's own sparse literary output and for the waste of creative potential in working-class women's lives. Olsen cites the ongoing tension between artists who crave a voice and an audience, and societally imposed, psychically internalized silence.

Trensky, Anne. "The Unnatural Silences of Tillie Olsen." *Studies in Short Fiction* 27, no. 4 (Fall, 1990): 509-516. Trensky studies silence as a theory and metaphor that give form and definition to women's lives in *Tell Me a Riddle*.

Roseanne L. Hoefel

THE TENTH MUSE LATELY SPRUNG UP IN AMERICA

Author: Anne Bradstreet (1612-1672)
Type of work: Poetry
First published: 1650

Form and Content

The Tenth Muse Lately Sprung Up in America is a collection of poems by Anne Bradstreet (née Dudley) which was published in London by an admiring brother-in-law. The volume begins with a number of short poems honoring Bradstreet by various New England worthies, followed by a respectful poem dedicated to her father Thomas Dudley, after which appear longer scholarly poems ("quaternions") on the four elements (fire, earth, water, and air); the four humors (or bodily fluids); the four ages of life; the four seasons; and the four "monarchies" (a truncated world history up to the Romans). Following these come shorter verses such as "A Dialogue Between Old and New England: An elegy Upon Sir Philip Sidney" (the courtier and poet the Dudleys claimed as kinsman); a poem in praise of the French poet Guillaume Du Bartas (1544-1590), whom the Puritans held in high esteem; and poems, many of them dedicatory, on a variety of other subjects. Before her death, Bradstreet made emendations and added still more poems for a projected revised edition; some of these added poems are regarded as her finest. This new book, known as *Several Poems*, was published in Boston, Massachusetts, in 1678.

The Tenth Muse (the full title runs more than two dozen lines) is certainly not a title that Anne Bradstreet chose herself, for while she was realistically aware of her talent, she would have considered it pretentious to call herself "the tenth muse," a latter-day addition to the nine immortal sisters whom the ancient Greeks saw as inspiring artists of every sort. Yet *The Tenth Muse* and *Several Poems* constitute one of the two most remarkable poetic achievements in English of the colonial period—the other being the work of Edward Taylor (1644-1729). Although her keen and scholarly mind roamed in many directions, even to "the most important political and ecclesiastical problems of her day," it is often when she writes of *Kinder*, *Küche*, and *Kirche*—children, the kitchen (domestic activity), and the church (the devout life)—that she most delights the reader. Wife, mother of eight, and formidable intellect, she was loved as well as admired.

Anne Bradstreet left Boston, England, as a teenage wife in June of 1630 with her husband Simon, her parents, and her brother and sisters. She sailed aboard the *Arbella*, flagship of a fleet of eleven ships and seven hundred colonists under the leadership of John Winthrop (1588-1649). The Great Migration, though not so widely remembered as the journey of the Pilgrims, who landed at Plymouth, Massachusetts, some ten years earlier, was a much better organized and financed project guided by essentially the same purpose: to establish a religious freedom that seemed impossible in the mother country.

Although Bradstreet's family was of considerable ability and means—both her father and her husband became governors—life in the new land proved to be difficult and fraught with dangers. The *Arbella* took sixty days to cross an Atlantic rife with early spring storms and another three to make its way down the northeast coast to the tiny settlement of Salem, Massachusetts, which was only two years old and had fewer than twenty houses.

There the settlers unloaded their ships and built makeshift shelters, some modeled after the huts of the Indians or partially dug into hillsides. The Dudleys and Bradstreets, however, did not stay long. In another month, they left Salem for Charlestown, about twenty-five rugged miles south across the Charles River from Shawmut (Boston), then moved to Cambridge, later to Ipswich, and finally north to Andover.

Analysis

The bulk of Bradstreet's work is perhaps of most interest to the scholar. John Berryman's long biographical ode "Homage to Mistress Bradstreet" (1956), however, served to reawaken a general interest in her poetry, an interest that has been sustained by the poetry's own merits. Sometimes unjustly called "imitative," Bradstreet works within carefully established traditions in which modern notions of originality have less meaning.

In her elegy "In Honor of Du Bartas," an early poem in praise of the "pearl of France," written in the rhymed iambic couplets she found in Joshua Sylvester's translation, "the tenth muse" calls her own muse only a "child" but reverently brings her "daisy" to the religious poet's hearse, using the same conventions that the English poet John Milton (1608-1674) did in "Lycidas" (1637). Although her funeral offering is humble, she hopes someday to do more; in other words, she intends to establish herself as a poet, a goal she would pursue with total dedication.

While Bradstreet is generally subservient to men ("Men do best, and women know it well"), recent feminist scholars have begun to show in her an independence that "subverts biblical patriarchy." In her poem "In Honor of Queen Elizabeth," to mention only one place, she takes issue bluntly with men in general, stating wittily: "Let such as say our sex is void of reason,/ Know 'tis slander now but once was treason."

Her long poems written in Ipswich about 1642 on the four elements and the four humors reflect the poet's wide reading. Bradstreet had before her the example of her respected father Thomas Dudley, who had composed a poem—no longer extant—on the four parts of the world, each represented by a sister. His approbation may have encouraged his daughter further; she composed two more quaternions, one on the ages of man and a second on the four seasons. All these poems are loosely linked to show "how divers natures, make one unity." "The Four Monarchies," the last of the quaternions, is unrelated to the others and is indebted to Sir Walter Raleigh's *History of the World*.

It is a second group of poems, however, found mostly in *Several Poems*, about her life, her family, and her husband that attracts modern readers to Bradstreet. In "Before the Birth of One of Her Children," she refers to herself charmingly as her husband's "friend" and worries that soon she might die and her children might fall into the hands of a "stepdame" (stepmother). The thought of parting from her husband plays a role in several of her "marriage poems." "To My Dear and Loving Husband" expresses the notion that the couple should live such lives that they both will achieve eternal life: "Then while we live, in love let's so persevere/ That when we live no more, we may live ever." This concluding couplet ("persevere" rhymed with "ever" in the seventeenth century) provides the familiar paradox that only in dying does the Christian attain life everlasting. "A Letter to Her Husband Absent Upon Public Employment" states her desire that Simon should quickly return to her as the sun returns to the earth in summer. "Another (Letter to Her Husband)" again identifies her husband with the sun (Phoebus) and makes use of what the English metaphysical poet John Donne (1572-1631) calls "tear-floods" and "sigh-tempests." This poem is entirely secular, however, a rarity for her, as is the following one in *Several Poems*, which is also called "Another (Letter to Her Husband)." It, too, relies on contemporary conventions, especially on puns, as when the poet calls herself "hartless," meaning both that her heart left when her husband had to go away and that she is a "hind" (or doe) whose "hart" (or buck) has gone.

"In Reference to Her Children" identifies each child with a bird, her four boys ("four cocks") and four girls ("four hens"). Children are the subjects of many of Bradstreet's poems, such as one called "In Memory of My Dear Grandchild Elizabeth," in which the poet points out that fruits and vegetables in time mature and die, but that a baby not yet two years old should die can only be evidence of a special Providence. The same theme of unquestioning faith appears in "Upon the Burning of Our House," in which she identifies her house as "His." It is, however, her realistic depiction of fire in the night, the destruction of her library and papers, and the wistful lingering over lost possessions that move the reader most.

Context

Undoubtedly, too much has been made of Nathaniel Ward's (1578-1652) dismissal of Bradstreet as a "girl" in his introductory poem in *The Tenth Muse*. Forgotten are the facts that this eccentric curmudgeon is not speaking in his own voice here, that he was decades older than Anne Bradstreet, and that he personally did as much as he could to further her career.

It seems likely that, while Bradstreet had to contend with prejudice against her sex, she enjoyed loyal support from her family and a wide circle of friends. It is also possible that Puritan society was less repressive toward women—or at least some women—than has been thought. Although she enjoyed praise and assistance from some men, however, she bristles in her "Prologue" at those who will denigrate her accomplishments, believing that "a needle better fits a woman's hand."

It must be remembered that *The Tenth Muse Lately Sprung Up in America* was extremely popular, going through five reprintings in its first year. Indeed, a British bookman later mentions it in a list of best-sellers. *The Tenth Muse* was the only poetry collection in Edward Taylor's personal library, and the famous Boston minister Cotton Mather (1663-1728) enthusiastically includes Anne Bradstreet—admittedly, his great-aunt—in the list of famous women poets of the world.

Anne Bradstreet wrote poetry because she wanted to, for no one writes as much and as skillfully for any other reason. If she wrote chiefly for family members, they could never have been the only audience she envisioned; indeed, before her death, she saw that she had an international one. It has been asserted often that she composed poetry to escape the harsh life of early New England, but the long hours she needed at her desk must certainly have represented a sacrifice rather than escape. In the midst of sickness, births, and myriad household duties in a harsh new land, she found the time to compose both the poems that her contemporaries admired and those that the modern age has found appealing.

Sources for Further Study

Bradstreet, Anne. *The Complete Works of Anne Bradstreet.* Edited by Joseph R. McElrath and Allan P. Robb. Boston: Twayne, 1981. This volume makes accessible to beginning and advanced students all the discovered poetry and writings of Bradstreet. Moreover, it offers a very brief summary of the various views taken toward the poet that have emerged over the years, finally taking its own balanced, moderately feminist position. A publishing history of the poetry and an account of all Bradstreet's work is provided along with discussion of textual variations.

Piercy, Josephine K. *Anne Bradstreet.* New York: Twayne, 1965. Two prominent aspects of this older but widely available book are open to some questions: that Anne Bradstreet underwent a struggle of faith with orthodoxy and that she serves as a sort of pre-Romantic English poet. Neither of these readings detracts from the value of the study, which is sensitive and helpful to the general reader.

Rosenmeier, Rosamond. *Anne Bradstreet Revisited.* Boston: Twayne, 1991. This revisionist and feminist study offers an Anne Bradstreet for the modern time, an intellectual and theologian committed to an impelling and progressive *Weltanschauung*. Rosenmeier makes the too-often-ignored point that Puritanism was a house of many mansions.

Stanford, Ann. "Anne Bradstreet." In *Major Writers of Early American Literature*, edited by Everett Emerson. Madison: University of Wisconsin Press, 1972. Although much work has been done on Bradstreet since this essay appeared, this work remains a valuable introduction. Stanford provides an overview of the author's life, era, and poetry, emphasizing the meditational systems of devotion long popular in Europe among Catholics and Protestants alike that inform Bradstreet's thought.

White, Elizabeth Wade. *Anne Bradstreet: "The Tenth Muse."* New York: Oxford University Press, 1971. Solid scholarship in the fine tradition of historical criticism. White has deep knowledge of both the Old and New World in which Anne Bradstreet lived. An indispensable work with a splendid bibliography and a fine index.

James E. Devlin

THEIR EYES WERE WATCHING GOD

Author: Zora Neale Hurston (1891-1960)
Type of work: Novel
Type of plot: Social criticism
Time of plot: The 1930's
Locale: Eatonville, Florida
First published: 1937

Principal characters:

Janie Crawford Killicks Starks Woods, the protagonist and initial narrator
Nanny, Janie's grandmother
Joe Starks, Janie's second husband
Verigible "Teacake" Woods, Janie's third husband
Pheoby, Janie's best friend

Form and Content

Zora Neale Hurston wrote most of *Their Eyes Were Watching God* in 1937 during a seven-week period she spent in Haiti. Hurston, the recipient of a Guggenheim fellowship, spent her days gathering anthropological data about life in Haiti, but she spent her evenings working on what was to become her greatest novel. The impetus for such an outpouring of words was a love affair with Albert Price III, a young graduate student of West Indian descent whom she had left in New York. Hurston undoubtedly realized that her relationship with Price was doomed, and thus she invested much of her own emotional life in the creation of her protagonist, Janie Crawford Killicks Starks Woods. The reader witnesses the internal maturation of Janie as she embarks on a journey for self-knowledge.

Janie tells the story of her life to Pheoby, her best friend, a woman who sympathizes with her and who is eager to hear Janie's story. Although Janie's brief narration is introduced by and then taken over by a third-person, or "public," narrator, the narrative voices that speak throughout the text always move toward convergence with Janie's voice. Janie's conscious life begins in her grandmother's backyard, where she first experiences sexual ecstasy. When Nanny sees Janie kissing Johnny Taylor, she insists that Janie marry Logan Killicks. Nanny tells Janie that the white man gives his workload to the black man, and the black man gives his workload to the black woman; therefore, the "nigger" woman is the mule of the world. After her marriage to Killicks, Janie quickly discovers that marriage does not equal love, and when the opportunity presents itself, Janie simply walks away and never looks back.

Janie's opportunity to leave Killicks presents itself in the form of Joe Starks. Starks is on his way to a town in Florida that has been established by and for African Americans. He is a man of the world and plans to be a "big voice" in the town of Eatonville. Janie marries Joe and moves with him to Eatonville. She is soon disappointed in her marriage, however, because Joe Starks places Janie on a pedestal, far above the common riffraff of the town, and thus effectively silences her. Janie ceases to love Joe, and their marriage moves from the bedroom into the parlor. During the years of her marriage to Joe, Janie's self-awareness grows. She discovers that she has a "jewel" inside her. Janie discovers that she understands Joe's motives, that she can see a man's head "naked of its skull." Finally, after twenty years of marriage, Joe dies. Janie, rejoicing in her newfound freedom, rejects the community's efforts to marry her to another man.

Janie is unwilling to allow the community of Eatonville to find her another husband; however, she finds a new mate when Teacake Woods enters her store. Although he is much younger than Janie, Teacake teaches her to laugh and to play again, and together they leave Eatonville to work in the Everglades as farm laborers. In the Everglades, or the Muck, their relationship is challenged by the community of laborers, a community whose attitudes and activities present a microcosm of African American society. Janie and Teacake are also challenged by god, or nature, in the form of a hurricane. During their struggle to survive the hurricane, Teacake is bitten by a rabid dog and becomes rabid himself; Janie is forced to shoot him. Janie is brought to trial and acquitted by a white jury. The circularity of the novel is completed as Janie returns to Eatonville. The narrative ends as Janie pulls her life in about her and drapes it over her shoulders like a great fishnet.

Analysis

Although *Their Eyes Were Watching God* is a work of fiction, it is autobiographical as well. Hurston reveals her personality through the narrative events and through the interplay of the author's, narrator's, and protagonist's voices. This novel not only tells the reader about Hurston's emotional life but also "signifies" upon (revises) feminine images in nineteenth century narratives written by African American women. Therefore, it provides an important link between those earlier narratives and novels written by African American women in the last quarter of twentieth century. Unlike literary foremothers such as Jessie Fauset, Frances E. W. Harper, and Pauline Hopkins, Hurston refused either to stereotype her protagonist or to conform to earlier plot lines established by white predecessors. Hurston moved Janie far beyond the boundaries that restrained the "true woman" of the nineteenth century, and in doing so, she provided the model of a heroic African American woman that was to profoundly influence twentieth century writers such as Alice Walker.

Their Eyes Were Watching God is the first self-conscious effort by an American ethnic writer both to subvert patriarchal discourse and to give voice to women of color. Hurston's protagonist moves from object to subject, from a passive woman with no voice who is dominated by her husband to a woman who can think and act for herself. Janie's change in status begins when she realizes that she is as important and knowledgeable as her husband. Soon after this realization Janie begins to find her voice. The casual conversation of the men on the porch of Joe Starks's store reveals the extent of their sexism. The favorite topics of these men are the stupidity or meanness of mules and women, and the heroics of folk heroes such as Big John de Conquer.

On the day that Janie "thrust" herself into the conversation, the men are all in agreement that if the nagging Mrs. Tony were married to any of them, they would kill her. Janie suddenly realizes that female obedience and chatteldom are in themselves a metaphorical death, that they place woman in the position of "the mule." Janie informs the men that they do not know half as much about women as they think they do, that God speaks to women as well as to men, and that men have no idea how much women know about them.

Hurston's use of language is an important and somewhat revolutionary aspect of her narrative. Her characters use African American dialect, a form of speech that is also often adopted by the narrator. The use of dialect with free indirect discourse (dialogue without quotes or direct indication of speaker) serves to move the narrative voice toward convergence with a given character's speech. Hurston uses free indirect discourse most often and most empathetically when Janie speaks.

The use of language is presented in terms of power throughout the narrative. Joe Starks uses his "big voice" to silence Janie. Janie, in turn, uses her voice to rob Joe Starks of his illusion of irresistible maleness and to some extent destroys the authority that Joe has established in the town of Eatonville. The use of language in Janie's discourse with Teacake Woods is quite different. Janie tells her friend Pheoby that Teacake taught her a new language, with new thoughts and new words. Hurston's sentence structure demonstrates the equality that exists in the early phase of Janie and Teacake's' relationship. Hurston uses compound subjects with single active verbs to describe the two lovers at play, two lovers who together are thinking new thoughts and creating a new language that could possibly bridge the communicative chasm that separates male from female.

Unfortunately, Janie and Teacake are unable to complete the creation of their new language. Janie's relationship with Teacake does not survive the challenges posed by society and nature. Hurston was undoubtedly describing her emotional relationship with Albert Price as she wrote about Jane and Teacake. Although Janie returns to Eatonville alone, she returns as a strong, self-actualized woman; in a sense, she is a new woman. Hurston's narrative advocates both freedom from sexist and racist oppression and the rejection of community and cultural values that enforce such oppression. Hurston also presents an imaginative consciousness that speaks of wandering and independence in a time when women were somewhat restricted. Ultimately, Janie, like Hurston and many African American women of the twentieth century, becomes a woman who can think and act for herself, who can make her own world.

Context

Their Eyes Were Watching God is a groundbreaking narrative. Hurston's protagonist, Janie Woods, is a new kind of African American woman. Hurston revised the images of women presented in earlier African American narratives in which African American women were modeled upon white protagonists or were dedicated to the notion of "uplifting" the entire race. Through Janie, Hurston calls attention to the silencing of women and to their exclusion as storytellers within the African American community. She also demonstrates how the men of Eatonville, the "porch talkers," set the boundaries of discourse for the entire community. The language of the men, unlike the language used by Janie, is a game, a competition; it reveals no internal development. Although Hurston is somewhat ambivalent toward Janie and allows her husband, Teacake, to beat her, she nevertheless depicts her as a questing hero, as a woman who moves from object to subject. *Their Eyes Were Watching God* is a feminist novel, and it may be considered the first such novel in the African American tradition.

Hurston's life and work provided a model for later African American writers. Alice Walker has stated that *Their Eyes Were Watching God* had a profound effect upon her writing and that if she were marooned on a desert island with only ten books, Hurston's masterpiece would be among those she would choose to take with her. Literary critics believe that one of Walker's protagonists, Shug, of *The Color Purple*, is a re-creation of Hurston herself. Hurston has become a literary "foremother" not only for Walker but also for other African American women writers, including Gayl Jones, Gloria Naylor, Toni Cade Bambara, and Toni Morrison. Although Hurston failed to define new parameters for discourse between men and women, she gave her protagonist a voice that allowed her to speak for herself. *Their Eyes Were Watching God* offers a point of departure for a new generation of African American women writers who are attempting to bridge the communicative chasm that exists between men and women.

Sources for Further Study

Awkward, Michael. *Inspiriting Influences: Tradition, Revision, and Afro-American Women's Novels*. New York: Harper Perennial, 1990. Awkward's chapter on Hurston focuses on the importance of community and communal voice in Hurston's novel. He argues that Janie's voice becomes one with the African American community and reflects the emphasis on oral tradition within that community.

Dixon, Melvin. *Ride Out the Wilderness: Geography and Identity in Afro-American Literature*. Chicago: University of Chicago Press, 1987. Dixon's chapter on Hurston's novel includes an analysis of Janie's search for identity as she moves from one geographical location to another, from the porch to the Muck, and back to Eatonville at the end of the narrative.

Gates, Henry Louis, Jr. *The Signifying Monkey: A Theory of African-American Literary Criticism*. New York: Oxford University Press, 1988. This analysis of the African American literary canon includes a chapter on the structure and content of *Their Eyes Were Watching God*. Gates argues that Hurston's combination of African American dialect with free indirect discourse revises, or "signifies" upon, earlier African American texts.

Hemenway, Robert E. *Zora Neale Hurston: A Literary Biography*. Chicago: University of Chicago Press, 1977. In this historical analysis of Hurston's life and writing, the chapter on *Their Eyes Were Watching God* describes how Hurston came to write her most famous novel. Hemenway underestimates the autobiographical content of the novel.

Hurston, Zora Neale. *Dust Tracks on a Road*. 1942. Reprint. New York: Harper Perennial, 1991. Hurston's "official" autobiography, this volume contains both the story of her life and her account of the circumstances surrounding the creation of *Their Eyes Were Watching God*. This book provides insights into the real and fictional worlds created by Hurston.

______________. *Mules and Men*. 1935. Reprint. New York: Harper & Row, 1990. This account of Hurston's anthropological research offers insight into the folktales contained in *Their Eyes Were Watching God*. The text contains many of the same metaphors that appear in Hurston's other autobiographical books.

Yvonne Johnson

THIS SEX WHICH IS NOT ONE

Author: Luce Irigaray (1930-)
Type of work: Essays
First published: *Ce Sexe qui n'en est pas un*, 1979 (English translation, 1985)

Form and Content

Based on Luce Irigaray's work as a psychoanalyst, linguist, and philosopher, the eleven essays collected in *This Sex Which Is Not One* critically analyze Western culture's descriptions of female identity and the many ways in which these representations influence women's psychic, social, and economic development. Irigaray explores a number of related issues, including the restrictive nature of masculinist language systems and the subsequent limitations in male-defined images of female sexuality, women's absence in Western philosophical tradition, and the importance of developing exclusively feminine modes of communication. The nonlinear, poetic writing styles she employs in many of these essays make it difficult to arrive at definitive statements concerning her theories of the feminine, yet this elusiveness is an important part of her undertaking. By unsettling readers' expectations, she challenges them to rethink conventional definitions of masculinity and femininity.

Although many of the essays in *This Sex Which Is Not One* were previously published in various journals and can be read separately, the arguments presented in each chapter are interconnected and mutually dependent. The title essay offers a useful entry into Irigaray's work, for it provides readers with an overview of her theory of the feminine. In addition to arguing that women's pleasure and female sexuality cannot be adequately described in Western culture's patriarchal language systems, Irigaray contrasts women's autoeroticism with men's and offers an alternative perspective on the feminine, which she describes as plural, nonunitary, and fluid.

Irigaray expands her analysis of Western culture's restrictive notions of female sexuality in other chapters and includes more explicit analyses of how psychoanalytic theory's unacknowledged masculine bias prevents the development of autonomous definitions of the feminine. In "Psychoanalytic Theory: Another Look," she begins by summarizing Sigmund Freud's theory of femininity and briefly examines how later psychoanalysts, including Karen Horney, Melanie Klein, Ernest Jones, Helene Deutsch, and Marie Bonaparte, reject, revise, or support Freudian views. "The Power of Discourse and the Subordination of the Feminine" and "Questions" are transcripts of interviews containing Irigaray's comments on her groundbreaking 1974 text *Speculum de l'autre femme* (*Speculum of the Other Woman*, 1985) and her replies to commonly asked questions about her theories and methods. These chapters provide readers with accessible discussions of Irigaray's views on conventional psychoanalytic theory, women's liberation movements, mother/daughter relationships, "sexual indifference," the existence of a feminine unconscious, women's lack of agency, and the economic exploitation of women. In "Cosí Fan Tutte," a witty, sophisticated essay critiquing Jacques Lacan, Freud's major twentieth century proponent and Irigaray's former teacher, Irigaray used Lacan's own words to illustrate the hidden biases in his theory of femininity. In the following essay, "The 'Mechanics' of Fluids," she again indirectly challenges Lacanian descriptions of the feminine and exposes the inadequacies in masculinist language systems. In later chapters, such as "Women on the Market," "Commodities Among Themselves," and " 'Frenchwomen,' Stop Trying," Irigaray explores how Western culture's limited definitions of women and femininity reinforce hierarchical male/female social and economic relations.

Irigaray's writing style is highly original. Although she draws on her own extensive knowledge of classic Western philosophy, she does so primarily to demonstrate that traditional knowledge systems have erased women's presence. She rejects the linear reasoning and the conventional forms of argument found in canonical texts and employs a number of subversive strategies, including puns, paradoxical statements, rhetorical questions, parenthetical comments, and quotation marks around problematic terms. The volume's title illustrates one form that Irigaray's playful technique assumes, for the phrase "This Sex Which Is Not One" refers both to the absence of a specifically female sexuality and to the feminine's plural, nonunitary nature. This ambiguous, subversive style—which Irigaray describes as "jamming the theoretical machinery"—serves two interrelated purposes. First, it enables her to critique patriarchal language systems; and second, it allows her to begin inventing an alternative discourse capable of representing and expressing the feminine. The opening and closing essays, "The Looking Glass, from the Other Side" and "When Our Lips Speak Together," provide the most extensive demonstrations of Irigaray's unique style.

Analysis

Throughout the essays collected in *This Sex Which Is Not One*, Irigaray engages in a twofold movement: She simultaneously critiques the hidden male bias in Western philosophical systems and attempts to develop new forms of writing and speaking that reflect women's specificity. Central to this undertaking is her call for a theory of sexual difference in which femininity and masculinity would indicate autonomous, qualitatively different models of subjectivity, or consciousness. Drawing primarily on psychoanalytic insights developed by Freud and Lacan, Irigaray maintains that Western linguistic and philosophical traditions are based on what she calls "sexual indifference," or an unacknowledged conflation of two independent sexes into a single, pseudo-universal model of personhood that subordinates the feminine. In this representational system, which she and other theorists describe as "phallocentric," woman or the feminine is defined as being quantitatively, rather than qualitatively, different from the masculine. Thus, for example, Freud describes the girl's clitoris as a little penis, not as a specifically female organ.

Irigaray argues that by denying women an independent, sexually specific identity, this phallocentric model reduces the feminine to "the inverse, indeed the underside, of the masculine." Woman, for example, is defined only as man's "other." In "The Power of Discourse" and "Questions," she attributes Freud's restrictive account of femininity to this hierarchical binary system. She explains that because sexuality assumes a single, masculine form in Freudian theory, women's sexual pleasure and women's unconscious have meaning only in relation to the masculine: "The feminine is defined as the necessary complement to the operation of male sexuality, and, more often, as a negative image that provides male sexuality with an unfailingly phallic self-representation."

According to Irigaray, this absence of sexually specific representations of the feminine has significant implications for women in Western cultures. Without a language capable of reflecting their specific needs, they lack an autonomous identity and remain silenced, unable to express, or even to recognize, their desires. In "Women on the Market" and "Commodities Among Themselves," she associates this lack of sexually specific representations of the feminine with what she describes as the "ho(m)mo-sexual monopoly," or the homosocial bonding between men that provides the foundation for patriarchal social orders and the heterosexual contract. Basing her arguments on Claude Lévi-Strauss's anthropological study of kinship structures, in which the exchange of women is used to establish social relations among men from different groups, she explains that phallocentric systems prevent women from actively participating in the creation of culture. Because the feminine has value solely in relation to the masculine, women function only as commodities whose circulation between men maintains the existing social order. In other words, women are products whose use-value is derived solely from their mediational role: Men from nonrelated social groups solidify their relationships with one another by exchanging women in marriage. Irigaray further argues that women's restrictive social roles establish a system of rivalry that prevents them from establishing mutually supportive relationships with one another.

Irigaray combines her critique of phallocentric linguistic and social systems with suggestions for the development of an exclusively feminine discourse, or new ways of speaking and writing that are capable of reflecting women's sexually specific needs. Significantly, she does not simply attempt to overturn existing conditions by elevating the feminine over the masculine; as she explains in "Questions," strategies of reversal remain locked in hierarchical binary systems. Instead, she calls for the creation of a specifically feminine language that would exist in addition to, rather than in replacement of, the masculine. The final essay, "When Our Lips Speak Together," illustrates one form that this exclusively feminine writing might take. Irigaray uses poetic language and the figure of lips both to subvert unitary, phallic models of sexuality and to provide alternative representations of female identity which emphasize autonomy and self-sufficiency, while also acknowledging women's interrelatedness. This description of female sexuality provides a significant alternative to the currently existing social system in which women function only as objects of exchange.

Context

Like traditional psychoanalysts, Irigaray explores the ways in which language constructs gendered identities; however, by using her psychoanalytic training to analyze psychoanalysis itself, she exposes its unacknowledged masculine bias. As in *Speculum of the Other Woman* and her later writings, she attempts in *This Sex Which Is Not One* to develop a theory and practice of sexual difference that demonstrates the secularized nature of all Western philosophical and representational systems. This undertaking has important political implications, for Irigaray maintains that the pseudo-neutrality of rational thought and objective knowledge has led to the development of patriarchal social systems that oppress women economically, socially, and psychically. She suggests that the creation of specifically feminine ways of writing and speaking offers the possibility of developing alternate epistemologies and new forms of society.

Irigaray's theory of sexual difference makes a significant contribution to feminist analyses of twentieth century knowledge systems. With the rise in gender studies in the 1980's, increasing attention has been paid to her analysis of the sexualized nature of all linguistic systems and social structures. By exposing the phallocentric foundations of Western culture's reliance on logical rational thought and the subsequent bias in all supposedly neutral accounts of objective knowledge, Irigaray provides theorists with important tools in their attempts to develop alternatives to analytical forms of thinking.

Yet Irigaray's elusive, ambiguous style; her many references to an extensive body of male-authored texts; her descriptions of the feminine as fluid, nonunitary, and plural; and her poetic allusions to women's anatomical parts have led to many debates concerning her work, especially among European American feminists. A number of theorists argue that Irigaray's attempt to develop sexually specific forms of writing and speaking inadvertently supports stereotypical views of the feminine. They maintain that her Lacanian-influenced belief in an all-encompassing phallocentric representational system denies women's agency, thus reinforcing their subordinate status in Western knowledge systems. Others, however, argue that Irigaray's emphasis on an irreducible difference between the masculine and the feminine and her attempts to establish openly sexualized bodies of knowledge indicate radical breaks from the relational masculine/feminine binary oppositions structuring Western thought systems. The confusion concerning Irigaray's theories is made even more problematic by the inaccurate assumptions that Julia Kristeva, Hélène Cixous, and Irigaray represent a single school of "French feminist" thought. There are, however, significant theoretical, stylistic, and political differences between them. Moreover, all three theorists distance themselves in various degrees from twentieth century feminist movements.

Sources for Further Study

Burke, Carolyn. "Irigaray Through the Looking Glass." *Feminist Studies* 7 (Summer, 1981): 288-306. This essay provides a useful overview of Irigaray's career, including her break with Lacan, the role that Jacques Derrida's deconstructive philosophy plays in her theory of feminine writing, and her impact on feminist studies. It offers a highly sympathetic reading of Irigaray's elusive style and insightful summaries of several essays in *This Sex Which Is Not One*, including "The Looking Glass, from the Other Side" and "When Our Lips Speak Together."

Fuss Diana. *Essentially Speaking: Feminism, Nature, and Difference*. New York: Routledge, 1989. Chapter 4, "Luce Irigaray's Language of Essence," summarizes European American debates concerning Irigaray's use of female anatomy to describe feminine writing. In addition to exploring how literal readings of Irigaray's references to lips lead to misinterpretations, this chapter briefly discusses her theory of sexual difference.

Grosz, Elizabeth. *Sexual Subversions: Three French Feminists*. Sydney: Allen & Unwin, 1989. This examination of recent theories of sexual difference situates Irigaray's work in the context of Kristeva's and Michele Montreley's theories of the feminine. In addition to exploring Irigaray's use of Lacanian psychoanalysis and Derridean deconstruction, the two chapters on Irigaray summarize key concepts, including her analysis of phallocentric language systems, her attempt to develop autonomous representations of the feminine, and her call for alternative descriptions of mother/daughter relationships.

Moi, Toril. *Sexual/Textual Politics: Feminist Literary Theory*. New York: Routledge, 1983. A comparative analysis of European American feminism and French theories of the feminine developed by Cixous, Irigaray, and Kristeva. The chapter on Irigaray discusses *Specu-*

lum of the Other Woman, This Sex Which Is Not One, and Irigaray's reception in the United States.

Whitford, Margaret. *Luce Irigaray: Philosophy in the Feminine*. New York: Routledge, 1991. This book provides an extremely comprehensive account of Irigaray's theories and an analysis of her contributions to twentieth century psychoanalytic and philosophic traditions. It includes extensive primary and secondary bibliographies of French and English texts.

AnnLouise Keating

THREE LIVES

Author: Gertrude Stein (1874-1946)
Type of work: Novel
Type of plot: Psychological realism
Time of plot: The early twentieth century
Locale: The fictional town of Bridgepoint
First published: 1909

Principal characters:

Anna Federner, a forty-year-old German American domestic servant
Miss Mathilda, Anna's employer
Mrs. Lehntman, a widow, Anna's closest friend
Melanctha Herbert, an eighteen-year-old mulatta
Jane Harden, Melanctha's footloose friend with a yearning for men
Rose Johnson, Melanctha's married friend
Dr. Jeff Campbell, physician to Melanctha's mother
Jem Richards, a gambler
Lena Mainz, a young German American girl
Mrs. Haydon, Lena's overbearing aunt
Herman Kreder, a German American tailor
Mrs. Kreder, Herman's mother

Form and Content

Three Lives consists of three episodes, the novella-length "Melanctha" and two short pieces, "The Good Anna" and "The Gentle Lena." The work is generally called a novel because of its thematic unity, although it is not a novel in the conventional sense of the word. Stein set out to portray "the bottom nature," as she called it, of three lower-middle-class women employed as domestic servants. In all three episodes, Stein pushes language to its extremes, using her rhetoric to reflect salient elements in the three women about whom she writes.

Each of the women—Anna Federner, Melanctha Herbert, and Lena Mainz—represents a generalized type of character, although Melanctha rises above the stereotypical and becomes the best realized character of the three. "Melanctha" is among the first works by a white writer to depict a black character in depth.

The episodes, told in the present with ramblings into the past, are not overtly connected to one another, nor do characters from one episode recur in either of the other two. A major connecting thread from one episode to another is love: Stein uses each episode to speculate on a different kind of love.

Stein, shortly before she wrote *Three Lives*, was herself working through a triangular love affair with May Bookstaver and Mabel Haynes and had, for some time, been Bookstaver's lover. Much of this book is Stein's attempt to work out her own feelings and organize her own thoughts about love.

The good Anna idolizes her employer, Miss Mary Wadsmith, as she had her previous employers, Dr. Shonjen and Miss Mathilda. Generous to a fault, Anna can always be depended upon—and this is precisely what she wants in her relationships with people. She is fulfilled when others depend upon her. Anna loves her dogs, Peter and Rags, almost as much as she loves her employers, but in her love of both dogs and people, Anna must have control.

Melanctha Herbert's love is quite different from Anna's. Melanctha is a sensuous kind of woman who loves erotically more than spiritually. Her friend Jane Harden has helped to make Melanctha streetwise. She has felt no real emotional attachment to any man, but when Jeff Campbell, a physician, comes to treat her mother, she finds him attractive, and they fall into a relationship in which neither has very deep emotional involvement. Melanctha throws Jeff over for Jem Richards, whose life as a gambler offers little hope of stability. He tells Melanctha that he does not love her at about the same time that her friend Rose Johnson tells Melanctha that she never wants to see her again. Melanctha contracts tuberculosis and, as this segment of *Three Lives* ends, she is alone and confined to a home for "consumptives." She dies there.

Lena Mainz represents antilove more than she does

any positive form of love. She lacks the emotional depth to feel any profound emotions, and her husband, Herman Kreder, is as emotionally bankrupt as Lena. Herman, who is twenty-eight years old, lives with his parents, who dominate him completely. When it is arranged that Herman and Lena will marry, Herman runs away, delaying the nuptials for a week, but his father brings him back and the wedding takes place.

The main implication in this bleak story seems to be that human beings are meant to reproduce, to continue the species. Herman does this. Lena, having borne four children, is expendable. Her death is not mourned by those who knew her or, indeed, by many who read about her in *Three Lives*.

Analysis

Three Lives, an extensive literary experiment in language and psychology, is generally called a novel, as noted above, because of the unifying thematic threads that run through it. The book is more than three disparate episodes gathered together in a single volume. Much influenced by Gustave Flaubert's *Trois Contes* (1877; *Three Tales*, 1903), *Three Lives* is as realistic in its recording of the speech patterns of commonplace people as Stein can make it. Stein's medical research took her into lower-middle-class neighborhoods in Baltimore, where she became fascinated by the way people spoke. The characters in her books speak in the same repetitive, stream-of-consciousness constructions that Stein heard from the working-class people of Baltimore with whom she came into contact.

Stein is unfailingly interested in the psychological underpinnings of the characters of the three servant women she has chosen to portray. She reveals each in her relationships with other people, and in so doing, she develops with considerable insight and sensitivity three distinctly different personalities, each with a unique view of love and life.

Lena (whose name suggests that she is a "leaner") is best summed up in her response when her aunt, Mrs. Haydon, presses her to marry Herman Kreder, whom she has no desire to marry. Lena merely tells her aunt that she will do whatever she (Mrs. Haydon) tells her is right to do. She agrees to marry Herman because Mrs. Haydon wants her to.

Juxtaposed with Lena in this episode is Herman, who is as weak and spineless as his bride-to-be. When his parents decide that he will marry Lena, they tell Mrs. Haydon not to discuss the matter with their son. Mrs. Kreder tells Herman that Lena is thrifty, a good worker, and never wants her own way. Herman's response is a grunt that is taken for assent.

Unlike Lena, both Anna and Melanctha have considerable backbone. Anna is more resolute than Melanctha, but she is also more than twice Melanctha's age and appears to have gained self-confidence over the years. Anna's pattern in life has been to seek out bungling, dependent people who need her, then to run their lives for them.

Anna is unswerving in her notions of decency, as a result of which she occasionally suffers grave disappointments, as she did when she discovered that Mrs. Lehntman, whom Stein describes as the "romance in Anna's life," has been involved in something shady with the doctor with whom she is working. Having once made a judgment of this sort, Anna is intractable.

Melanctha's development depends on Stein's showing her in relation to her two close female friends, Rose Johnson and Jane Harden, as well as in relation to the three men who are important in her life: her father, Jeff Campbell, and Jem Richards. As it turns out, Melanctha loses everyone she cares about, but she has never really cared deeply about anyone. Her death is sad but falls far short of being tragic because of Stein's portrayal of Melanctha as insensitive. Stein exposes her readers neither to Melanctha's eventual physical decline nor to her death throes. Instead, she reports Melanctha's death almost incidentally at the end of this longest section of *Three Lives*.

As Stein portrays them, both Anna and Lena, despite the great differences in their personalities, are mundane characters whose intellectual and emotional compasses are limited. Stein captures their banality well, particularly in her faithful depiction of their speech patterns. The endless repetition in their dialogue reinforces the lack of drama and the constant recurrences in their lives.

Melanctha, however, is a far more romantic character than is either Anna or Lena. As a mulatta, she has a foot in the black world and one in the white, even though the milieu in which Stein presents her is black. Jeff Campbell, a professional who represents the rising black upper middle class, displays many of the characteristics and values of whites.

Melanctha, however, rejects Jeff in favor of Jem, a man who fits Stein's conceptions of the black men of her day, only to be discarded by him. Melanctha is the most fully realized character in *Three Lives*, although each of Stein's three major characters is memorable.

The components of *Three Lives* reflect the personal problems with which Stein was dealing when she wrote the book: moral uncertainty, fear of rejection, mixed emotions about her relationship with May Bookstaver, and sexual desire without a stable object toward which she might direct it. Alice B. Toklas was not yet in Stein's life when *Three Lives* was being conceived, although the two were living together by the time it was published. This book, in a sense, is a cry by a highly intelligent woman who had not yet found what she was seeking for herself.

Context

For Gertrude Stein, *Three Lives* was a quite personal book. In writing it, Stein did not consciously aim to write a feminist tract, and the book did not turn into one. It is a penetrating psychological study of three distinctly different women and of the three faces of love that they represent. As women's issues have become a prominent concern in assessing and analyzing literature, however, *Three Lives* has emerged as an important book in that regard.

The world of *Three Lives* is one of male dominance. The three women whom Stein portrays are locked by their social class into a setting that definitely limits their possibilities in life. Anna Federner, who shows definite signs of having lesbian tendencies, lived a life of willing self-sacrifice, inviting—indeed, needing—people to take advantage of her good will and generosity. Perhaps this is Anna's means of expiation for essentially having desires of which she, as staunchly moral as she is and living in the age in which she lived, can hardly approve and possibly cannot admit even to herself. If she has lesbian tendencies, as seems quite probable, it is unthinkable that she has ever acted on them or has even considered doing so.

Lena has the sexuality of a slug. She seems to be living life just to get it over with. She has no enthusiasms, no *joie de vivre*. She is in a class with Frank Norris's McTeague (*McTeague*, 1899), a fictional character with whom Stein may have been familiar. McTeague has a bit more gumption than does Lena, who seems totally lacking in that characteristic.

The news that Lena has died leaves some readers thinking, "Thank heaven. What a terrible mother she would have made!" Then, however, one remembers that her children will be left with Herman Kreder, and the scenario darkens. Naturally, someone—his parents or Mrs. Haydon—will probably tell Herman to remarry, and he will accommodate that wish.

Lena might be viewed as a woman who has been beaten down by a male-dominated society, but more accurately, she is a person so lacking in personality and potential that, brought up in nearly any other environment, she probably would have been no different. Indeed, viewing Lena in medical terms, one might wonder whether she suffered from a deficiency in her body chemistry. So lacking is she in emotion and personality that she cannot even be viewed as depressive.

Only Melanctha emerges from *Three Lives* as someone who finds a degree of normal joy in life—or, at least, has the potential to do so. Melanctha, however, is young and undeveloped. Emotionally, she is still sending out trial balloons. Her selfhood is tied to the personalities of the men in her life, and they treat her only as an object. The women in her life certainly provide her with no role models.

Sources for Further Study

Bloom, Harold, ed. *Gertrude Stein*. New York: Chelsea House, 1986. Part of the Modern Critical Views Series, this work includes fifteen essays on Stein, a chronology, and a bibliography. Donald Sutherland's essay on *Three Lives* and Richard Bridgman's on *Things as They Are* and *Three Lives* are instructive.

Hobhouse, Janet. *Everyone Who Was Anybody: A Biography of Gertrude Stein*. New York: G. P. Putnam's Sons, 1989. This book gives a good run-down of the significant people who frequented 27 rue de Fleurus. Well illustrated.

Mellow, James R. *Charmed Circle: Gertrude Stein and Company*. New York: Praeger, 1974. The well-illustrated book captures the vibrant spirit of the circle of painters, sculptors, writers, and fascinating passersby that came within the Stein-Toklas social orbit.

Souhami, Diana. *Gertrude and Alice*. New York: HarperCollins, 1991. The most thorough account of

Gertrude Stein's long lesbian relationship with Alice B. Toklas, this book shows how strong Toklas was and how she dominated many aspects of her forty-year association with Stein.

______________. Introduction to *Three Lives*. New York: Bantam Books, 1992. In her thirteen-page introduction, Souhami provides a strong feminist reading of *Three Lives*.

Sprigge, Elizabeth. *Gertrude Stein: Her Life and Work*. New York: Harper Brothers, 1957. Like Mellow's book, this well-written biography is replete with excellent illustrations. Tells much about the genesis of *Three Lives*.

R. Baird Shuman

TO KILL A MOCKINGBIRD

Author: Harper Lee (1926-)
Type of work: Novel
Type of plot: Social criticism
Time of plot: The 1930's
Locale: Maycomb, Alabama
First published: 1960

Principal characters:

Scout Finch, a six-year-old girl living in a small Southern town
Jem Finch, Scout's older brother
Atticus Finch, the father of Scout and Jem, an honorable lawyer
Tom Robinson, a young black man wrongly accused of raping Mayella Ewell
Bob Ewell, the shiftless father of Mayella Ewell
Boo Radley, the recluse of the town

Form and Content

To Kill a Mockingbird is narrated by Jean Louise Finch, nicknamed Scout, who recalls her childhood spent in the sleepy Southern town of Maycomb, Alabama. Set in the Great Depression of the 1930's, part 1 of the novel mainly consists of Scout's everyday trials and tribulations with her father, Atticus; her older brother, Jem; their black housekeeper, Calpurnia; and their neighbors. Scout and Jem are becoming more aware of the adult world around them. Atticus Finch desires his children to be more tolerant in a town that has certain deep-rooted prejudices. Scout and Jem begin this struggle for understanding when Dill, a precocious nephew of their neighbor Stephanie Crawford, visits one summer. Dill proposes that they try to make Boo Radley come out of his house. Fascinated by the town's rumors that Boo is insane, the children make several attempts to lure the mysterious recluse out into the open.

When Dill leaves in the fall, the children's ideas concerning Boo fade. Scout encounters the school system for the first time. On the first day of school, she gets in trouble with her new teacher because Atticus has been teaching Scout to read; the teacher insists that Scout learn to read "properly"—that is, in school. From this encounter, Atticus teaches Scout about compromise—they will continue to read together every night, but Scout must learn her teacher's reading methods as well— and about the value of seeing things from another person's perspective.

Later in the school year, Jem discovers gifts left in the knot hole of a tree on the Radley place. The children realize that Boo Radley may have left these gifts for them. The children's pondering over Boo Radley's existence is overtaken, however, by Atticus' involvement with the trial of Tom Robinson, a black man wrongfully accused of raping a white woman. Atticus tries his best to prepared his children for the months ahead. At Christmas, Atticus gives the children their first air rifles but cautions that it is a sin to kill a mockingbird because mockingbirds only bring pleasure. Later, Scout connects this comment about the innocent mockingbird to Boo Radley.

Part 2 is the more serious section of the novel, moving from the happy memories of Scout's childhood to Tom Robinson's trial and its long-reaching effects on Atticus and the children. On the night before the hearing, a lynch party is narrowly diverted when Scout, having followed Atticus to the jail along with Jem and Dill, recognizes a classmate's father. Her innocent remarks to the man cause him to disband the lynch mob.

The trial brings the whole county of Maycomb to hear the testimony of Mayella Ewell, a white girl who lives in extreme poverty with her shiftless father, Bob Ewell. During cross-examination, Atticus proves that the Ewells are lying about Tom, but unfortunately, as Jem and Scout learn, the jury upholds Ewell's word, and Tom is convicted of rape. The children and their father barely get over the pain of this conviction before word comes that Tom has been killed while trying to escape from prison.

By the fall of Scout's eighth year, the controversy has

died down, but Bob Ewell continues to threaten members of the court who he feels discredited him. He publicly spits on Atticus. Later, Ewell attacks Jem and Scout on their way home from the town's Halloween pageant. Scout survives the attack unscathed, but Jem is badly hurt. Reunited with a frightened Atticus, she learns that it was their reclusive neighbor, Boo Radley, who killed Ewell and saved the children's lives. Atticus and the town sheriff decide not to tell the town of Boo's deed, and Scout agrees, reminding Atticus that it would be "like shootin' a mockingbird." After walking Boo home, Scout stands on his front porch and finally understands her father's words about seeing things from another's point of view.

Analysis

Most critics agree that the strength of *To Kill a Mockingbird* lies in Harper Lee's use of the point of view of Scout. This point of view works in two ways: It is the voice of a perceptive, independent six-year-old girl and at the same time it is the mature voice of a woman telling about her childhood in retrospect. Lee skillfully blends these voices so that the reader recognizes that both are working at the same time but that neither detracts from the story. Through the voice of the child and the mature reflection of the adult, Lee is able to relate freshly the two powerful events in the novel: Atticus Finch's doomed defense of Tom Robinson and the appearance of the town recluse, Boo Radley. The child's voice gives a fresh approach to looking at the racism issue in the novel. Both Scout and Jem struggle with confusion over why some people are acceptable in the social strata of their community and others are not. As Scout wisely answers Jem, "There's just folks." The mature adult voice serves to give the reader reflections on the events that a child could not yet see.

Regarding the plights of Tom Robinson and Boo Radley, Lee draws on the symbol of the mockingbird. Both Tom and Boo are victims of the prejudices of their community. Tom, who is an innocent black man accused of rape, is convicted by a white jury even though Atticus Finch proves that the evidence against Tom is false. Boo is another victim—first, of his father's harsh religious views, and second, of the town's ignorance and gossip. Both men are closely related to the symbol of the mockingbird. Atticus and Miss Maudie, their wise neighbor, tell the children it is a sin to kill a mockingbird because the bird brings only pleasure to humans. When Tom is killed trying to escape, the editor of Maycomb's newspaper likens Tom's death to the senseless killing of songbirds by hunters and children. Later, after Atticus and the sheriff decide not to tell anyone that Boo Radley killed Ewell in defense of the Finch children, Scout agrees and equates exposing Boo Radley to the curious town to killing a mockingbird.

Two major themes dominate the novel: that of growing from ignorance to knowledge and that of determining what is cowardice and what is heroism. The "ignorance-to-knowledge" theme is developed through the characterization of the maturing children. Scout and Jem both develop understanding and an awareness of the adult world as they grow through their experiences. Lee represents children as having a fairer sense of justice than adults. Thus, when Robinson is convicted, the children are the ones who cannot accept it. Atticus' insistence that his children learn to be tolerant and not judge people only on appearances becomes one of the moral lessons of the book.

The other theme regards the children's growing awareness of what is cowardice and what is true heroism. The central figure and model for them here is their father, Atticus. In part 1, the children do not consider their father much of a hero because he will not play football with the Baptists. Only when Atticus shoots a rabid dog do the children learn that their humble father is "the deadest shot in Maycomb county." Atticus tries to redefine heroism for the children when he has Jem and Scout read to the hated Mrs. Dubose. He tells them after her death that she was a morphine addict trying to free herself of her addiction before dying. Atticus comments that true heroism is "when you're licked before you begin but you begin anyway." In part 2 of the novel, Atticus lives up to this definition of heroism by his courageous defense of Tom Robinson.

Context

Published in 1960, *To Kill a Mockingbird* has become an American literary classic. It won the Pulitzer Prize in 1961 and was made into an Academy Award-winning film in 1962, with Gregory Peck playing Atticus Finch.

The novel also won the Brotherhood Award of the National Conference of Christians and Jews in 1961 and was *Best Sellers* magazine "Paperback of the Year" in 1961.

Although Harper Lee has not published a major work since *To Kill a Mockingbird*, the book retains its place in American literature for its telling of a regional story with a universal message. Also, although it is not a main issue, the novel features a feminist struggle. Even though the main focus of the novel remains Scout's growing recognition of the prejudices of her surroundings, Scout struggles for an understanding of womanhood. Through the strong, lyrical voice of this independent tomboy, the reader sees a young girl unsure of her place in Southern femininity. Scout struggles with how to fit into the world of "ladies," as exemplified by her Aunt Alexandria, and how to retain the independence that she has had as a child. Men still hold the main arena, and their world seems much more interesting to Scout than the world of caretaking that her aunt enjoys. Only Miss Maudie, Scout's outspoken neighbor, offers a good model for Scout. Maudis is independent and speaks her mind, yet she enjoys her baking and tending her garden.

Lee has been linked to other Southern writers who emerged in American literature after World War II, such as Truman Capote (who was the model for Dill in the novel), Carson McCullers, William Styron, and Eudora Welty. Along with these writers, Lee celebrates the Southern tradition of looking back on the past as did her predecessor William Faulkner. The new Southern writers, however, wrote about a "new South," a region that looked not only to its past but also to its future. Critics praised Lee for her portrayal of the new Southern liberal in the character of Atticus Finch. They also praise her technical use of point of view and her strong evocation of place as the strengths of *To Kill a Mockingbird*.

Sources for Further Study

Dave, R. A. "*To Kill a Mockingbird*: Harper Lee's Tragic Vision." In *Indian Studies in American Literature*, edited by M. K. Naik et al. Dharwar, India: Karnatak University, 1974. Dave provides an interesting discussion of the history of the mockingbird as a symbol of innocence and joy in American literature. He draws parallels between *To Kill a Mockingbird* and Walt Whitman's poem "Out of the Cradle Endlessly Rocking." Dave also explores how Lee, like Jane Austen, evokes a regional place yet makes it a macrocosm describing a range of human behavior.

Erisman, Fred. "The Romantic Regionalism of Harper Lee." *Alabama Review* 26 (April, 1973): 123-136. Erisman's article discusses in depth Lee's evocation of the "new South," one that looks back on its past but is beginning to look forward and not dwell on pre-Civil War glories. Also contains a good discussion of Atticus Finch as Lee's strong portrayal of the new Southern liberal trying to come to terms with the old traditions and prejudices of the South.

Going, William T. "Store and Mockingbird: Two Pulitzer Novels About Alabama." In *Essays on Alabama Literature*. University: University of Alabama Press, 1975. Contains a good discussion on Lee's use of point of view to relate the story's themes in a fresh manner. Going also discusses Lee's ties to the other new Southern writers who emerged in the late 1950's and early 1960's.

Johnson, Claudia. "Secret Courts of Men's Hearts: Code and Law in Harper Lee's *To Kill a Mockingbird*." *Studies in Fiction* 19, no. 2 (1991): 129-139. Johnson gives an excellent overview of the history of racial conflicts in Alabama during the 1930's, when the novel is set, and conflicts in the late 1950's, when the novel was being written, that Harper Lee drew upon for the trial of Tom Robinson.

Rubin, Louis D., Jr., ed. *The History of Southern Literature*. Baton Rouge: Louisiana State University Press, 1985. A brief history of Harper Lee's place among the new Southern writers such as Capote, Welty, Styron, and McCullers. Rubin discusses how the new writers reflect on the past yet look toward the future, explore the plight of the black man in the South, and focus on portrayals of the new type of Southerner—the liberal who is in conflict with his or her environment because of an awareness of racism.

Shelley Burkhalter

TOP GIRLS

Author: Caryl Churchill (1938-)
Type of work: Drama
Type of plot: Psychological realism
Time of plot: The early 1980's
Locale: England
First produced: 1982, at Royal Court Theatre, London, England
First published: 1982

Principal characters:

Marlene, the managing director of the Top Girls employment agency
Joyce, Marlene's sister, a housewife separated from her husband
Angie, Joyce's sixteen-year-old daughter
Win and **Nell,** employment counselors at Top Girls
Jeanine, a Top Girls applicant, a secretary wanting a better job
Louise, a Top Girls applicant whose career has stagnated in middle management
Shona, a Top Girls applicant, a gifted charlatan with no actual business experience

Form and Content

Top Girls is the story of one woman's rise to success and of the other women in her life (as well as those in history) whose experiences call hers into question. Its all-female cast speaks from a wide variety of cultural and political positions in dialogue that is orchestrated on the page almost like musical lines and themes, with numerous interruptions, dual conversations, and simultaneous speeches which undercut or highlight one another. The cast must also be prepared to perform multiple roles, particularly in the long opening scene, which may be Marlene's dream or a fantasia outside the plot serving as a prologue.

The play opens in a stylish restaurant as Marlene prepares for the celebration of her promotion at Top Girls. As the guests arrive, the dinner party takes on the nature of a celebration of "top girls" from history and legend who fought and achieved: Isabella Bird, a nineteenth century Scottish woman who became a noted world traveler after the age of forty; Lady Nijo, a medieval courtesan forsaken by her lover, the Japanese emperor, to wander as a Buddhist nun; Dull Gret, a figure in a Hans Brueghel painting who leads a band of peasant women into hell to fight the devils; Pope Joan, who is fabled to have ruled as pope in the ninth century, disguised as a man; and Patient Griselda, an exemplary, long-suffering wife in Geoffrey Chaucer's *Canterbury Tales*. The women's lively conversation veers into anguish as each woman reveals the high toll that her success exacted: exhaustion, neglect, abuse, loneliness, even murder. Much of this came at the hands of men or from the societal expectations against which these women struggled. The dinner party dissolves into a cacophony of broken dishes, tears, and outbursts of rage.

The rest of act 1 begins in the offices of the Top Girls agency the first day of Marlene's new position, then moves to Joyce's house the day before; likewise, the two scenes of act 2 begin by continuing the day at Top Girls, then shifting a year earlier, to Joyce's house. In the first scene at the agency, Marlene interviews Jeanine; Marlene's energy and drive are shown in counterpoint to Jeanine's uncertainty. Following this, Angie is seen playing with Kit, a younger playmate; Angie seems not to relate to children her own age. Kit, who is good in school, both admires the older girl and finds her strange and threatening. Joyce and Angie argue, while Joyce worries about Angie's chances in life. The tension escalates between them, and Angie confides to Kit that she wants to kill Joyce.

In act 2, between job interviews Win and Nell discuss their own prospects in love and careers, none of which seem promising. Angie turns up at the office, surprising Marlene, who is fond of Angie but does not know what to do with her, particularly as Angie hints that she wants to stay and become a success as well. Angie watches as

Marlene is confronted by the wife of the runner-up for Marlene's new position, who accuses Marlene of taking away jobs meant for men, even of betraying other women who support their husbands' careers. Marlene angrily defends her success and her life. Later, Win relates a similar but less happy story to Angie, involving burnout from having to outwork and prove herself to men. The scene closes with Marlene, Nell, and Win discussing Angie, who has fallen asleep; Marlene concedes ultimately that Angie is "not going to make it."

The final scene is a flashback to Marlene's visit to Joyce and Angie the previous year after many years away. The center of the scene is an angry discussion between the sisters over their lives, their agreement that Joyce would rear Angie (who is actually Marlene's child), and the political philosophies that divide them. The argument goes unresolved, as does the sisters' attempt to relate as family despite their differences. Finally, a shaken, tipsy Marlene tries to comfort herself and Angie, who cannot sleep. Marlene tries to persuade Angie that things will be fine, but Angie only repeats one word: "Frightening."

Analysis

Caryl Churchill has commented that *Top Girls* grew from two particular initial ideas: that of women from the past appearing to and speaking with present-day women, and the idea of the variety of jobs that women fill, both in the economy and in culture. Though her work is strongly influenced by Churchill's feminism—she wrote *Vinegar Tom* (1976) in collaboration with a feminist theater group—the scenarios she presents here open up the question of what feminism is for different women, how they define the concept not only in theory but also through their actions and choices.

The solidarity of women becomes both a theme and a problem. The historical figures of the dinner party in act 1 can be seen as a context for Marlene's success, a tradition of women who took risks and made their presences felt. Yet each is also presented as isolated in her historical moment, unsupported by a larger society of women and actively discouraged or attacked by men or institutions created by men. Similarly, in the ensuing modern scenes, Marlene and the other Top Girls are shown to have paid high prices in the attempt to succeed in a "man's world" not established with their ascent or their needs in mind.

Perhaps gender equity has improved if a woman such as Marlene can rise into management or Margaret Thatcher can be named prime minister; these advances form the basis for Marlene's claim that women do not need a movement or feminist politics to move forward. This seeming rise is potentially damaging to women; Joyce and Angie's scenes show that, in Churchill's view, most women face disadvantages and lack of opportunity and that the career track of Marlene is a rare exception, not a prototype that all women can follow. For every Lady Nijo or Isabella Bird, there have been uncounted women restricted in their options, left to obscurity and poverty.

For every Marlene, there are many women like the three job applicants: underqualified, unconfident, and lacking the rare combination of intelligence, beauty, drive, and style that have propelled Marlene. Marlene offers to help them, and companies pay her well to do so, but the women must play by her rules—for example, keeping quiet about plans to marry someday. Remaking women in her own image is the key to Marlene's success, and supposedly to theirs. Aggressive confidence and the power to persuade employers and sales clients are methods recognized by the men with whom such women must work and against whom they must compete. Yet even the women who manage to "beat" the patriarchal system are merely outwitting it, not reforming it to make the field more fair to all women.

The connection between economics and feminism is continually at issue in *Top Girls*. Women have traditionally been relegated to the private sphere of homemaking and parenting, and a woman such as Marlene, who dares not only to enter but also to insist on advancement in the public sphere of economic activity, necessarily embodies a larger, inherent cultural tension. Giving up her daughter, beating out other women, and living without a partner are Marlene's particular instances of the larger disjunctions between women's rights and the rules of capitalist society, as Churchill sees it.

The problem is not simple: The issue is not whether successful businesswomen are paragons of feminist victory or bloodthirsty man-haters (though characters in the play express both these notions) but whether these women, like all beneficiaries of capitalism, have lost much in the quality of their lives, even as they appear to reject economic subservience to men. Such women, like their male counterparts, have acquiesced to a system of domination and profit refined over centuries by men in power, and even if they benefit from it as individuals, they ultimately are complicit in the oppression of their own gender. Marlene works at eradicating the signs of inequality between women and men in public life, but she does not pay attention to the larger patterns of dominance. This can take the form of Marlene's competing subtly with her friends Win and Nell, her apparent neglect of her sister and daughter, or even the spiritual emptiness and despair behind her bright demeanor, glimpses of which Churchill allows at moments throughout the play.

Context

Perhaps the most immediate impact of *Top Girls* is visual as well as structural: Its audience sees a play where every actor on stage is a woman. Churchill's casting strategy is striking seen against a dramatic tradition in which the great majority of characters are male, with perhaps a handful of female characters at most, usually in stock roles such as romantic interest, villain, or servant. The historical figures in the dinner scene serve as a reminder that, regardless of whether they were acknowledged by dramatists, women have played a number of "dramatic" roles in lived experience, as full of adventure and conflict as the male-centered stories of most traditional dramas. The action of the contemporary story points out that many of the lives and experiences of women have not been encompassed by traditional dramatic narrative.

Churchill has often relied on writing practices that also go against traditional notions of authorship. Several of her plays, including *Owners* (1972), *Cloud Nine* (1979), and *A Mouthful of Birds* (1986), were developed in a group process. Playwright, actors, and staff discuss ideas in an open workshop and do collective research; then Churchill works with the collected material in a writing period, after which the group moves into rehearsals. Though this process was not in effect for *Top Girls*, other elements of the play show Churchill's interest in changing traditional forms. Her interlaced conversational lines and transformations of the linear narrative time frame combine with her casting and thematic choices to show that there are stories not yet heard that women can tell, both on stage and as authors, and that there may be new ways to communicate them dramatically.

Churchill's impact is felt widely in the theater, as she has become one of the most widely produced women playwrights in English, writing for British radio and television as well as the stage. *Serious Money* (1987) was a success in London's West End, as well as at the influential producer Joseph Papp's Public Theater in New York; her other works have been performed in many regional and university theaters in the United States and the United Kingdom.

Sources for Further Study

Cousin, Geraldine. *Churchill the Playwright*. London: Methuen Drama, 1989. This study views Churchill's plays in the context of her experimentations with collaborative productions, in which the author, actors, and director research, write, and develop a play together through a prerehearsal workshop period. Cousin examines *Top Girls* for the way in which it manipulates traditional time schemes and questions notions of achievement, success, and what Churchill considers "joy."

Fitzsimmons, Linda, comp. *File on Churchill*. London: Methuen Drama, 1989. A useful compilation of materials on Churchill's plays, their contexts and critical reactions. The volume includes a chronology of her career, brief synopses of the plays, comments from reviews and interviews, a select bibliography, and statements from the writer on her work.

Kritzer, Amelia Howe. *The Plays of Caryl Churchill: Theatre of Empowerment*. New York: St. Martin's Press, 1991. A wide-ranging study of Churchill's plays for radio, television, and the stage, as they move from traditional to more alternative forms of writing and staging. Kritzer focuses on Churchill's use of theater to give voice to formerly silenced groups, and she argues that *Top Girls* rejects ideas of feminist progress without their connection to socialist politics.

Randall, Phyllis, ed. *Caryl Churchill: A Casebook*. New York: Garland, 1989. The first book-length collection of essays on Churchill. The essay on *Top Girls* discusses it in the light of the "second wave" of feminism, which moves from individual struggles for rights to envisioning a transformation of society as a whole. Includes primary and secondary bibliographies.

Keith Todd

TOWARD A NEW PSYCHOLOGY OF WOMEN

Author: Jean Baker Miller (1927-)
Type of work: Social criticism
First published: 1976

Form and Content

Created by one of a group of women who were struggling to formulate a theory and practice of feminist therapy in the early 1970's, Jean Baker Miller's *Toward a New Psychology of Women* affirms a distinctly female psychology. Because men dominate in society, Miller contends that a woman's way of being has been forced underground and, if it is seen at all, has been highly suspect. She claims that psychoanalysis, in its attempt to probe the depths of the human mind, has unearthed this domain of suppressed qualities that are, essentially, the feminine psyche.

Toward a New Psychology of Women is composed of three sections. In part 1, Miller argues that the male-female relationship is predicated on inequality. This fundamental inequality between men and women is not unlike the sociological imbalances of power found between races, religions, nationalities, and classes. The dynamic of domination-subordination demands that the subordinate group's identity be constructed around the dominant group's perceptions and needs. The male-dominated culture has deemed certain human potentials more valuable than others and has shunted the "less desirable" qualities onto women.

Part 2 develops the theme that these very characteristics relegated to women which seem to be weaknesses are, in fact, strengths that hold the potential for an advanced way of living. Qualities such as vulnerability, weakness, caretaking, dependency, and cooperation fuel the drive to be connected in relationships. The problem for women is that these propensities become subsumed into the male-centered system and that the female identity, apart from who a woman is in relation to others, is eclipsed.

Part 3 addresses the direction in which women are headed. Miller contends that the future holds a more authentic female identity for women who, grounded in the understanding that the organizing principle for women's selfhood is affiliation, embrace cooperation, their own creativity and personal power, and constructive conflict.

Throughout the book, Miller illustrates her ideas with vignettes of women who struggle with these issues. One example is Anne, an artist with two children and a husband who feels free to paint only when she has done everything possible to meet her family's needs. When her husband dies at a young age, she is overwhelmed by a sense of purposelessness. Her children and the need to support them keep her going, however, and she is able to embrace her art with deep concentration because it is now essential to her family's livelihood. In doing so, Anne comes to feel a greater sense of herself than she ever had when her life centered solely on her husband's and children's needs. When she remarries and her work is not essential financially, she struggles once again with her commitment to her work. "She felt that she did not have the right to devote herself to something 'just for me.' " Anne's dilemma typifies that of many of the women Miller portrays. A woman's tendency, Miller believes, is to derive meaning and satisfaction from her work "when it takes place in the context of relationships to other human beings—and even more so when it leads to the enhancement of others."

Analysis

Toward a New Psychology of Women emerged out of Miller's therapeutic work with women. Through observing the problems that women confront in their lives, Miller became convinced that there is a distinction between male and female psychological development. Miller believes that traditional psychoanalytic theory's organizing principle for personality development, autonomous selfhood, is descriptive of male experience. The goal of autonomy is separateness and self- direction. Women's selfhood, is predicated on the opposite principle of affiliation, or the need to be in relationships.

Miller contends that the culture sets up a double bind

for women. On the one hand, the male-dominated society relegates the very qualities it fears to women. Women are conditioned to develop passivity, dependency, cooperation, emotion, and nurturing of others. On the other hand, women are seen as psychologically immature for making relationships central to their lives and are thus punished for having the very qualities that have been assigned to them by the culture. Miller concedes that there are women who have chosen to follow self-directed paths of growth but holds that the woman who does so violates "a dominant system of values that says she is not worthy . . . that there must be something wrong with her for even wanting alternatives."

In the context of a dominant-subordinate culture, truly mutual affiliation is impossible. In this relationship of unequals, women relinquish their own personal power. Conditioned from an early age to attend to the needs of others, women experience difficulty establishing an identity apart from what others expect of them. Miller has found this often to be the root of women's psychological problems.

The answer to the dilemma lies in abandoning the model of domination-subordination without abandoning the drive toward affiliation and reclaiming one's personal power. A woman must attend to herself, focusing on her own needs and desires, even if it means displeasing others. This is no small task. A woman is so conditioned to think of others' needs before her own that she often has difficulty ascertaining what she wants. Moreover, the perceived risk of abandonment or condemnation for self-care can be terrifying and can seem to be utterly contrary to the need for affiliation. Miller maintains, however, that it is a necessary risk.

Miller views the dominant male culture as a "low-level, primitive organization built on an exceedingly restricted conception of the total human potential. It holds up narrow and ultimately destructive goals for the dominant group and attempts to deny vast areas of life." Psychoanalysis has revealed that those denied areas, embodied in the female psyche, have to do with the desire for relationship. Miller believes that as women attend to themselves in the context of their affiliations, they will challenge their partners into adopting new ways of living more creatively and cooperatively. Conflict, which was either denied or played out destructively under the old model, will be embraced as good and as a pathway to growth.

Context

Miller's small volume has become a classic in circles concerned with women's issues. In the years since *Toward a New Psychology of Women*'s publication, the frequency of its citation in journal articles has only increased. In 1979, there were twelve references to this work in professional articles; in 1992, there were sixty-three. Miller's book has broad implications, since it is cited in fields as diverse as women's issues, health and medicine, psychology, sociology, education, and the law.

Toward a New Psychology of Women was seminal in suggesting that female psychological development is distinctive, thus challenging a cultural icon, the psychoanalytic tradition. Refuting the notion that a woman must either defer to expected roles or feel guilty for not doing so, Miller maintained that a woman's impulse toward personal growth is good. She links one of the most common psychological problems women face, depression, directly to the suppression of the impulse toward personal growth.

Sources for Further Study

Chernin, Kim. *Reinventing Eve: Modern Woman in Search of Herself.* New York: Harper & Row, 1987. Chernin offers her own journey of self-discovery and an interpretation of modern culture's limitations on women's lives. She uses religion, myth, literature, and psychoanalysis to suggest transformative images for women.

Chodorow, Nancy. *The Reproduction of Mothering: Psychoanalysis and the Sociology of Gender.* Berkeley: University of California Press, 1978. Chodorow provides extensive psychoanalytic grounding for her argument that parenting should be shared equally by both men and women.

Gilligan, Carol. *In a Different Voice: Psychological Theory and Women's Development.* Cambridge, Mass.: Harvard University Press, 1982. Gilligan argues that developmental theories in psychology have been built on the observations of men. Grounded in research, her study illuminates the distinctiveness of female identity and moral development as rooted primarily in connectedness with others.

Gilligan, Carol, Annie G. Rogers, and Deborah L. Tolman, eds. *Women, Girls, and Psychotherapy: Reframing Resistance*. New York: Haworth Press, 1991. This collection of essays focuses on the psychological development of adolescent girls. Highlighting the unique problems they face, how they cope through the teenage years, and how teenage experiences affect their adult lives, the essays also reveal the social pressures placed on girls to submit and "be nice," and illuminate their resistance to accepting the limits of socially defined femininity.

Schaef, Anne Wilson. *Women's Reality: An Emerging System in White Male Society*. 3d ed. San Francisco: Harper San Francisco, 1992. Schaef elucidates the psychosexual differences between men and women. Based on her experiences as a psychotherapist, she writes an accessible analysis of women's experience and reality vis-à-vis those of men.

Kim Dickson Rogers

TOWARD A RECOGNITION OF ANDROGYNY

Author: Carolyn G. Heilbrun (1926-)
Type of work: Literary criticism
First published: 1973

Form and Content

Written during the height of the women's movement, at a time when women were questioning society's rigid definitions of what it meant to be a woman or man, *Toward a Recognition of Androgyny* suggests that the salvation of the human race depends upon the ability to transcend gender stereotyping and allow individuals a full range of human behaviors. This ideal state of understanding is "androgyny," a term derived from the Greek *andro* ("male") and *gyn* ("female"), meaning "a condition under which the characteristics of the sexes, and the human impulses expressed by men and women, are not rigidly assigned." Turning to literature for examples of this androgynous vision, Carolyn G. Heilbrun, then professor of English literature at Columbia University, finds them in writers as diverse as Sophocles, William Shakespeare, Emily Brontë, and Virginia Woolf in this ambitious reexamination of some of the major texts of Western literature.

The book is divided into three separate but interrelated sections. The first traces "The Hidden River of Androgyny" embodied in Greek mythology and literature and continuing through the Renaissance, finding its fullest expression in Shakespeare's complex heroines. Proceeding chronologically and shifting, for the most part, to fiction, "The Woman as Hero" section is the longest. This section examines mostly female characters from some of the most important novels written in English from the eighteenth through the twentieth centuries who embody both "female" and "male" characteristics. In novels by writers including Samuel Richardson, Emily Brontë, William Makepeace Thackeray, Nathaniel Hawthorne, Henry James, and E. M. Forster, it identifies vibrant, atypical heroines who rebel, in their various ways, against their societies' gender constraints. The last section, "The Bloomsbury Group," moves from fiction to fact by examining Virginia Woolf, Lytton Strachey, Clive Bell, and their circle, the group of writers and artists who met in Bloomsbury Square in London from 1904 to the 1930's, as the first example of the androgynous life in practice.

Heilbrun's work includes references to philosophers and literary critics, to Greek mythology, the Bible, and writers as disparate as Sophocles and George Bernard Shaw. A literary critic, Heilbrun is primarily concerned with reading the various texts, often in startling new ways, and understanding them in their historical context. Although the reader who has read the works to which she alludes will benefit most from this ambitious study, Heilbrun provides enough examples so that most readers can understand her main point: that in great literature, particularly novels, there has been, consistently, a recognition, whether conscious or not, of the limitations placed on the individual by gender expectations. As a result, such literature has imagined other, sometimes freer but always more complex, possibilities for women and men.

Toward a Recognition of Androgyny is both scholarly and accessible. Heilbrun includes the mandatory notes and index, but both are kept to a minimum. Moreover, the writing style is direct and clear, without the inflated rhetoric that is typical of much academic prose.

Analysis

Claiming in her introduction that "androgyny seeks to liberate the individual from the confines of the appropriate," Heilbrun sets out to find examples of this liberating impulse in Western thought and literature. Moving freely between cultures and through time, she hones in on specific examples that prove her point, often contrasting them with works expressing an opposing (and she would say more limited) vision.

In Greek literature, Heilbrun finds a "hidden" tradition of androgyny embodied in such plays as *Antigone* (c. 441 B.C.) by Sophocles and *Medea* (431 B.C.) by Euripides. She argues that in the former, for example, by reversing the expected gender roles played by Antigone and Haemon, Sophocles makes his female protagonist play the "male" part: a woman acts to avenge her brother's death. Haemon, Antigone's lover, sacrifices himself for his beloved in proper "female" fashion. To further underscore the theme, Heilbrun adds that Sophocles provides Ismene, Antigone's sister, as an ineffectual woman following a prescribed gender role, and the blind prophet Teiresias, who is both male and female, as the true visionary.

Although the Judeo-Christian tradition and that of Islam emphasized patriarchy almost exclusively, feminine, civilizing principles reenter in the medieval period, according to Heilbrun, with the rise of romance and the growth of popular adoration of the Virgin Mary. By the Renaissance, and particularly in Shakespeare's women, Heilbrun argues that the androgynous impulse emerged in full flower. Citing several examples—Hamlet's sacrificing of Ophelia as an example of his killing his "feminine" self in *Hamlet* (1603); the recognition of the daughter as her father's true inheritor in *King Lear* (1608) and the late romances; the vitality and moral force of the comic heroines disguised as men, such as Rosalind in *As You Like It* (1623)—she argues convincingly for Shakespeare's androgynous vision.

In part 2 of the work, "The Woman as Hero," Heilbrun turns to fiction to trace the continuation of the androgynous impulse in literature written in English from the eighteenth century through the early twentieth century. Beginning with Samuel Richardson's *Clarissa* (1747-1748), which she calls the first androgynous novel, Heilbrun goes on to discuss others, including William Makepeace Thackeray's *Vanity Fair* (1847-1848), Emily Brontë's *Wuthering Heights* (1847), and Nathaniel Hawthorne's *The Scarlet Letter* (1850). Each contains an example of the androgynous female hero, who is, according to Heilbrun, a dominant figure that is unlike the traditional, more passive heroine. By juxtaposing these novels, Heilbrun uncovers startling similarities: For example, in their sense of themselves, their wasted talents, and their qualities of martyrdom and sainthood, Richardson's Clarissa and Hawthorne's Hester Prynne achieve a similar kind of mythic grandeur and moral authority in their respective novels.

Examining the work of the great women writers of the nineteenth century—Jane Austen, Charlotte and Emily Brontë, and George Eliot (Mary Ann Evans)—Heilbrun demonstrates the ways in which all but one demonstrate the androgynous vision in their fiction. Although she is "no more a feminist than Dickens," Jane Austen is also not the "feminine" writer whom critics for years have been patronizing, according to Heilbrun. Austen's genius, instead, is her ability to imagine a society in which women and men are equally responsible for their actions and equally able to imagine their own selfhood. Therein lies her claim to androgyny.

To Heilbrun, Emily Brontë's *Wuthering Heights* reveals the androgynous ideal in the love between Catherine and Heathcliff, which represents an unattainable merging of male and female principles. Abandoning Heathcliff, her "masculine" self, Catherine succumbs to the limited "female" role that society has prescribed for her: the protection and "respect" of marriage. Unlike Jane Austen, George Eliot was not able to envision androgynous characters, Heilbrun explains. She also did not suggest a way in which a talented woman could discover a destiny equal to her talents. Yet Eliot's androgynous vision emerges in her suggestion in the novel *Middlemarch* (1871-1872), for example, that "the separation of the sexes is somehow fundamentally connected with the impotence of society to hasten human progress." It is Charlotte Brontë whose vision is not androgynous, according to Heilbrun, perhaps because she was so passionately aware of the disabilities under which gifted women struggle.

Heilbrun claims that it was not until the late nineteenth century that "the woman as hero" appeared. Unlike earlier women in fiction, the woman hero, Heilbrun explains, "is sustained by some sense of her own autonomy as she contemplates and searches for a destiny; she does not wait to be swept up by life as a girl is swept up in a waltz." This character is thus more like the traditional male hero in her awareness of her own individuality and selfhood. Perhaps ironically, she was also exclusively the creation of male writers. As Heilbrun explains, she was invented by Norwegian playwright Henrik Ibsen and American-born novelist Henry James. Nora Helmer in *A Doll's House* (1879) and Isabel Archer in *The Portrait of a Lady* (1881) are her earliest manifestations.

In characters such as Margaret Schlegel in E. M. Forster's *Howard's End* (1910) and Ursula Brangwen in D. H. Lawrence's *The Rainbow* (1915), Heilbrun finds independent women who are literary ancestors of these earlier heroes. Demonstrating that androgyny is not limited to female characters, she examines James Joyce's "womanly" hero, Leopold Bloom, from *Ulysses* (1922). In the post-World War II worlds created by American writers such as Philip Roth, Bernard Malamud, Norman Mailer, and Saul Bellow, Heilbrun finds the death of the woman as hero as their male characters exploit, demean, or escape women.

Finally, in "The Bloomsbury Group," Heilbrun discusses the writers who met in Bloomsbury Square in London from 1904 to the 1930's as the first example of the androgynous way of life in practice. Contending that in their lives and works masculinity and femininity were mixed, reason and passion holding equal sway, Heilbrun examines at some length the works of Clive Bell and Lytton Strachey. In the novels of Virginia Woolf, she finds the fullest expression of a synthesis between female and male vision, rereading *To the Lighthouse* (1927) as a search for balance between the individually limited ideas of Mr. and Mrs. Ramsay, not as a celebration of femininity, as it has been read more commonly.

In her afterword, Heilbrun calls for writers to create, once again, androgynous works in which characters are conceived in all their human complexity. Convinced that women writers should not only write about their victimization, she hopes that they will eventually discover a literary form in which to represent their autonomy.

Context

Toward a Recognition of Androgyny elicited strong responses from its supporters and detractors. The former, many of them women, found it liberating: For the first time, someone had articulated what (among other things) made some writers great and others not so great. The giants, women and men, possessed a certain vision that enabled them to see beyond rigid gender boundaries. The book's detractors, many of them men, wanted a more precise definition of androgyny and failed to recognize the difference between the androgynous writer and the feminist, a distinction that Heilbrun makes a few times in the text. Some critics questioned individual interpretations.

The book's position in the history of literary criticism, and feminist literary criticism in particular, is secure. Only three years after the publication of Kate Millett's *Sexual Politics* (1970), in which Millett exposed the misogyny in authors such as Norman Mailer and Henry Miller, Heilbrun's book contributed a different perspective. By examining the idea of androgyny, a notion that had been introduced into literary criticism by Samuel Taylor Coleridge and had been discussed by Virginia Woolf, Heilbrun not only reread the literature of the past but also offered a blueprint for writers of the future.

In later works, including *Reinventing Womanhood* (1978), *Writing a Woman's Life* (1988), and *Hamlet's Mother and Other Women* (1990), Carolyn Heilbrun has continued to examine women's lives, in fiction and in fact, in order to make sense of them.

Sources for Further Study

Diamond, Arlyn, and Lee Edwards, eds. *The Authority of Experience: Essays in Feminist Criticism*. Amherst: University of Massachusetts Press, 1977. An early collection of excellent feminist essays on writers including Shakespeare, Richardson, Charlotte Brontë, and Virginia Woolf.

Edwards, Lee R. *Psyche as Hero: Female Heroism and Fictional Form*. Middletown, Conn.: Wesleyan University Press, 1984. A study of the fulfillment or frustration of heroic possibilities in a variety of English and American novels from the mid-eighteenth century to the present. Edwards examines many of the same novels that Heilbrun does.

Gilbert, Sandra M., and Susan Gubar. *The Madwoman in the Attic: The Woman Writer and the Nineteenth-Century Literary Imagination*. New Haven, Conn.: Yale University Press, 1979. A bold interpretation of the major women writers of the nineteenth century that traces in their works a distinctly female literary tradition.

Heilbrun, Carolyn G., and Margaret R. Higonnet, eds. *The Representation of Women in Fiction*. Series: Selected Papers from the English Institute, 1981. Baltimore: The Johns Hopkins University Press, 1983. Six important essays from the English Institute's first session on feminist criticism. Relevant are Jane Marcus on Virginia Woolf and Mary Poovey on Jane Austen. Heilbrun contributes a brief introduction.

Springer, Marlene, ed. *What Manner of Woman: Essays on English and American Life and Literature*. New York: New York University Press, 1977. A superb collection of essays on women in literature from the medieval period to the present which deals with many of the authors in Heilbrun's study. Includes an essay by Heilbrun on marriage in English literature from 1873 to 1941.

Donna Perry

TWENTY YEARS AT HULL-HOUSE

Author: Jane Addams (1860-1935)
Type of work: Autobiography
Time of work: 1860-1910
Locale: The United States and Europe
First published: 1910

Principal personages:

John H. Addams, Jane's father and the primary influence on her
Louise de Koven Bowen, president of the Juvenile Protective Association
Dr. Alice Hamilton, a specialist in industrial medicine
Julia C. Lathrop, the organizer of the Cook County Juvenile Court and the first head of the Children's Bureau
Florence Kelley, a socialist resident who transformed Addams from a philanthropist to a reformer
Johnny Powers, a corrupt alderman
Mary Rozet Smith, a trustee of Hull-House
Ellen Gates Starr, a cofounder of Hull-House
Alzina Stevens, a textile worker active in unions and the first probation officer in Cook County
Leo Tolstoy, a Russian novelist who sought peace by undertaking to do his daily share of the physical labor of the world

Form and Content

Jane Addams wrote *Twenty Years at Hull-House* for two main reasons: to present a record of the founding and first years of the Hull-House settlement in Chicago, and to stop the publication of two biographies of herself. The first four chapters trace Addams' life from her childhood through college and tours of Europe to her decision to begin Hull-House. The primary influence in these years was Addams' wealthy abolitionist father, who stressed morality and sensitivity to the poor. The second important influence was Abraham Lincoln. John H. Addams was both a supporter and a personal friend of Lincoln, and although Jane Addams was only a small child when Lincoln was assassinated, she had heard many stories of him from her father. Addams saw Lincoln as the best role model for the new immigrants, since Lincoln too had emerged from humble surroundings without ever forgetting his past and the lessons that he had learned from his experiences. These two men helped to form Jane Addams' character and influenced the direction that her life took.

It is in these early chapters that Addams makes clear the problem that the first generation of college-educated women faced: what to do with their lives. As happened to other women of this generation, Addams suffered psychological conflict that resulted in physical distress. One result of her ailment was a physician's recommendation to visit Europe for two years. Had she been male, a tour of Europe would have been part of her maturing experiences. Addams and Ellen Gates Starr, her college friend, visited not only museums and art galleries but also the wretched poor in the East End of London. Although Addams had spent a year in medical school before illness resulted in her tour, she now realized that there might be other ways to help the poor besides practicing medicine.

Addams' experiences in Europe brought into focus the problem that she and other women faced. As she described it herself, they were smothered with advantages and had lost the ability to react to human suffering. The assumption of society was that an educated "girl" could have nothing to do with the poverty that was particularly acute in the large cities. Addams' trip did not cure her physical ailments, but a second trip with Starr, when she attended a meeting of the striking London match girls, began the crystallization of her plans for renting a house in Chicago where she might live and work among those mired in poverty.

The other fourteen chapters deal with Addams' life work at Hull-House, which involved a wide variety of activities and an amazing array of exceptionally talented women who were nurtured, trained, and readied there to do social battle on larger fronts than that of the neighborhood of Halsted Street. The activities at Hull-House involved almost every important person of the late nineteenth and early twentieth centuries, from John Dewey and Henry George to Prince Peter Kropotkin.

Although these later chapters begin with a chronological chapter telling of the first days at Hull-House, Addams soon switches to a topical approach, discussing poverty, economics, labor problems, immigrants, ideas from European settlements and experiments, local political campaigns, social clubs, and the arts at Hull-House and ending with the story of revolutionaries from Russia. These chapters are filled with engaging stories that illustrate what Hull-House was attempting on these various fronts.

Analysis

The central issue in Hull-House is that the various socioeconomic classes have a reciprocal dependency and can therefore learn from one another. As Addams saw it, a settlement house would provide a place where "young women who had been given over too exclusively to study, might restore a balance of activity along traditional lines and learn of life from life itself." Here was the crux of the matter: maintaining traditional lines while at the same time doing things that were very nontraditional. A few examples of Hull-House residents will demonstrate this mode of operation. Julia Lathrop, a lawyer, moved to Hull-House in 1890 and soon became a member of the State Board of Charities and organized the first juvenile court. Florence Kelley was the first factory inspector for the State of Illinois, and one of her deputies, Alzina Stevens, became the first president of the Working Woman's Union and later the first probation officer of the Cook County Juvenile Court. Alice Hamilton identified flies as the carriers of disease and later wrote *Hamilton and Hardy's Industrial Toxicology*, which was printed in its fourth edition in 1983. At one point, Addams herself was named garbage inspector for her ward, which shocked her neighbors, because that was "unwomanly work." Addams replied that if it was a womanly task to nurse the sick, then it certainly was a womanly task to prevent those conditions that caused the illness. As one biography opined: "She revolted against the stereotype of woman as submissive, gentle and intuitive but did not publicly challenge the stereotype."

Addams had considerable skill as a writer, and in *Twenty Years at Hull-House*, she captures the reader's attention with engaging anecdotes that proved her points. These range from a cooking class that enabled a young woman to keep the husband who had threatened to leave her if he did not get a decent meal to the tale of a young Italian boy who died at seventeen because of his use of legally available cocaine. Because of her writing skill, Addams became one of the best known and most revered settlement leaders of the early twentieth century.

In her autobiography, Addams followed the typical format of a heroine's life story: a weak and handicapped ugly child who had a childhood dream of helping the poor and being sensitive to their needs. This is illustrated by the story of Addams' father advising her not to wear her new and beautiful coat because those who did not have one might feel badly at seeing hers.

The second part of the format is a conversion experience, or epiphany, in which the heroine changes her life's path. According to Addams, this took place at a bullfight in Madrid in 1888. Here Addams realized that she had been deluding herself with travel and study as a preparation for some promise of future action. Putting aside further procrastination, Addams began speaking about her plans to move into the city and live with the poor. The next January she and Starr sought a place in Chicago. That place was Hull-House. At last, the heroine had found her life's task.

Addams' biography defined and consolidated her position as a social reformer and identified and presented her as a symbol of Americanism. Addams, taking her cue from Lincoln, wanted to ensure that democracy would endure, and the only way that could happen with the influx of immigrants from southern and eastern Europe was for the settlements to socialize democracy by means of educational, philanthropic, civil, and social undertakings. It was in this way that the finer and freer aspects of living would be incorporated into the common life of the country, providing mobility for all.

Context

Addams' effect on women's issues was a result of her activities rather than of any specific writings. Addams supported the suffrage movement and worked to secure the vote in municipal elections, but her feminism saw women as morally superior. To such feminists, suffrage was not only a right but also something that would result in a moral uplifting of the political world. It was not Addams' role in suffrage, however, that had the most long-lasting effect; it was her life, which served as a role model. In addition to working at Hull-House, she was an academic who taught college extension courses, published in professional journals, and at times referred to herself as a sociologist.

Addams' effect as a role model is best seen in the life of Hilda Polacheck, who wrote of her experiences in *I Came a Stranger: The Story of a Hull-House Girl* (1989). After her marriage, she moved to Milwaukee, where she supported Addams' feminist activities and invited her to inaugurate Milwaukee's chapter of the Women's International League for Peace and Freedom. When she later worked on the Work Projects Administration's Writer's Project, she wrote on Hull-House. She gave full credit to Jane Addams for the effect she had had on her life.

Among Addams' other writings are *Hull-House Maps and Papers* (1895), *Democracy and Social Ethics* (1902), *Newer Ideals of Peace* (1906), *Spirit of Youth and the City Streets* (1909), *A New Conscience and an Ancient Evil* (1912), *Women at the Hague* (1915), *The Long Road of Woman's Memory* (1916), *Peace and Bread in Time of War* (1922), *Second Twenty Years at Hull-House* (1930), and *My Friend Julia Lathrop* (1935).

Sources for Further Study

Brieland, Donald. "The Hull-House Tradition and the Contemporary Social Worker: Was Jane Addams Really a Social Worker?" *Social Work 35* (March, 1990): 134-138. Based on six objectives from the mission and purpose statement of social workers, Brieland concludes that the answer to the question posed in the article's title is yes.

Carson, Mina. *Settlement Folk: Social Thought and the American Settlement Movement, 1885-1930*. Chicago: University of Chicago Press, 1990. Emphasizes how well Jane Addams exemplified the Victorian cult of personality. Sees her as a master at publicizing her causes. Describes settlement houses as agents of social control and claims that their promotion of industrial education was to keep the immigrants in the working class.

Davis, Allen F. *American Heroine: The Life and Legend of Jane Addams*. New York: Oxford University Press, 1973. A critical yet sympathetic treatment of Addams which explores her self-created legend, relates it to the facts of her life, and shows how the two became intertwined. Includes a good bibliography.

Davis, Allen F., and Mary Lynn McCree. *Eighty Years at Hull-House*. Chicago: Quadrangle Books, 1969. Contains reprinted articles by Starr, Mary Kenney (O'Sullivan), Kelley, Hamilton, Bowen, Dr. Dorothea Moore, and Edith Abbott as well as by men who lived in or visited Hull-House in its first twenty years. Shows Hull-House through the eyes of its residents and those most closely involved in its work.

Farrell, John C. *Beloved Lady: A History of Jane Addams' Ideas on Reform and Peace*. Baltimore: The Johns Hopkins University Press, 1967. Contains a superior annotated bibliography and a complete listing of Addams' writings. Places Addams in the context of the Progressive Era and examines her views on education and urban recreation as well as peace.

Levine, Daniel. *Jane Addams and the Liberal Tradition*. Madison: State Historical Society of Wisconsin, 1971. Places Jane Addams and her work in the liberal tradition of alleviating suffering by reforming society. Part 1 ("Jane Addams and Hull-House") and part 2 ("Rousing the New Conscience") most closely parallel her work from 1889 to 1909.

Linn, James Weber. *Jane Addams: A Biography*. New York: D. Appleton-Century, 1935. The author, Jane Addams' nephew, provides insights into Addams' personality. "Six Women" is a good discussion of Starr, Lathrop, Kelley, Bowen, Hamilton, and Smith.

Lissak, Rivka Shpak. *Pluralism and Progressives: Hull House and the New Immigrants, 1890-1919*. Chicago: University of Chicago Press, 1989. Like Carson, Lissak sees Hull-House as an instrument of social control, pushing assimilation to keep the immigrants in their place for the benefit of the middle class. The work's focus is on eastern European Jewish immigrants, but some attention is devoted to Italian and Greek immigrants in the Hull-House neighborhood.

Polacheck, Hilda Satt. *I Came a Stranger: The Story of a Hull-House Girl*. Edited by Dena J. Polacheck Epstein. Chicago: University of Illinois Press, 1989. A view of Hull-House from the neighborhood. Part 3, "Growing Up with Hull-House," is particularly valuable. A good counterbalance to Carson and Lissak.

Anne Kearney

UNCLE TOM'S CABIN: Or, Life Among the Lowly

Author: Harriet Beecher Stowe (1811-1896)
Type of work: Novel
Type of plot: Social criticism
Time of plot: 1850
Locale: Kentucky and the swamps of Louisiana
First published: 1851-1852 (serial), 1852 (book)

Principal characters:

Tom, a loyal, virtuous Christian slave
Eliza Harris, a beautiful slave woman
George Harris, Eliza's husband and Harry's father
Mr. Augustine St. Clare, Tom's second, kind owner
Topsy, the wayward St. Clare family slave girl
Evangeline, or **Little Eva,** the angelic daughter of the St. Clare family
Miss Ophelia, the old-fashioned Calvinist aunt of the St. Clare family
Simon Legree, Tom's jealous and vicious owner

Form and Content

Uncle Tom's Cabin: Or, Life Among the Lowly is the most powerful and enduring work of art ever written about American slavery. It was the greatest fiction success of the nineteenth century. Uncle Tom, Simon Legree, and Little Eva became symbols known to most people. Although the book was out of print in the middle of the twentieth century, in the 1960's, with the renewed struggle over civil rights in the South, the book became available again and there was a new interest in the book.

The purpose of *Uncle Tom's Cabin* is to provide powerful propaganda against slavery. The theme of the novel is the idea that slavery and Christianity cannot exist together. Stowe believed that the owning, buying, and selling of slaves was inhumane and un-Christian. The widest opposition to slavery, Stowe believed and demonstrated, stemmed from an individual's—usually a woman's—outraged feeling. She gave constant examples, presented emotionally, from the world she knew, the world of home and family, of incidents she had seen herself or of stories she had heard that dealt with atrocities to individuals or to family units.

Stowe felt that to describe the process of so harshly tearing child from mother, husband from wife, was to expose the heartlessness and cruelty of slavery. The audience to which she appealed consisted largely of women such as herself who could comprehend the horror of families being separated, churchgoing women whom she made to see the inhumane and un-Christian aspects of slavery. She showed her readers how slavery violated the home and went against the religion of her readers. She wrote *Uncle Tom's Cabin* out of religious inspiration.

The passage of the Fugitive Slave Act of 1850, which not only gave slave owners the right to pursue their escaped slaves even into free states but also forced the people of these free states to assist the slave owners in retrieving their "property" led to Stowe's decision to write *Uncle Tom's Cabin*. She wrote the book in serial format, to be published in the *National Era*, an abolitionist paper in Washington, D.C. The first chapter was published on June 5, 1851, the last on April 1, 1852.

One learns much about how *Uncle Tom's Cabin* was written through anecdotes in the biographies of Harriet Beecher Stowe written by Annie Fields, a fellow author and close friend, and compiled by the son of Harriet, the Reverend Charles Edward Stowe.

According to an account of the creation of *Uncle Tom's Cabin*, certain scenes flashed before the eyes of Stowe and she included them in the book. One account said that the dramatic scene of the death of Uncle Tom came to her in church. She finally suggested that she had not written *Uncle Tom's Cabin* herself but had taken it in dictation from God.

Analysis

During her life, Harriet Beecher Stowe had been personally disturbed by slavery but socially and publicly uncommitted to action until the passage of the Fugitive Slave Act. The passage of this cruel, inhumane, un-Christian act caused her to write *Uncle Tom's Cabin*. Stowe brought a moral passion to her indictment of slavery which was impossible for Americans to forget. Harriet Beecher Stowe had great dramatic instincts as a novelist. She saw everything in terms of polarities: slavery as sin versus Christian love; men active in the cruel social process of buying and selling slaves versus women as redeemers, by virtue of their feelings for family values. She depicts the glory of family life in Uncle Tom's cabin—glory that is contrasted with Tom's separation from his family and his unhappy end at the Legree plantation.

Undoubtedly, many events in the novel were taken from Stowe's life. While her husband Calvin Stowe, a biblical scholar, was a teacher at Lane Theological Seminary, she had lived in Cincinnati, Ohio, where slavery was a prominent issue because Cincinnati was a location where many slaves tried to escape North. She understood slavery as an economic system and had also heard many details and anecdotes about slavery from family members. Her brother Charles had worked in Louisiana, and her brother Edward had lived through riots over slavery in Illinois. Harriet Beecher Stowe knew Josiah Henson, an escaped slave, who was the model for Uncle Tom. Eliza Harris was drawn from life. She may have been a fugitive who was helped by Calvin Stowe and Henry Ward Beecher. The original of Eva was the dead daughter of Stowe herself. The original of Topsy was a slave named Celeste, who was known to the Stowe family in Cincinnati. The character Simon Legree, although sketched by Charles Stowe, owes much to writers of melodrama and gothic novelists as well as the imagination of Harriet Beecher Stowe herself.

The novel is divided into three sections. The first section takes place on the Shelby estate. It is an accurate description of the scene, since Stowe had been as far South as Kentucky. The second section, which introduces Topsy, Evangeline, and St. Clare, enriches the novel with wit and humor. This section, containing descriptions of the efforts of Miss Ophelia to discipline Topsy, points to the true moral of the tale—that love is above the law. After the efforts of Miss Ophelia are unsuccessful, it is the superhuman love of Little Eva that starts Topsy on the path toward decency and honesty. The third section, containing Simon Legree, introduces terror into the novel. In the wild flight of Eliza at the beginning of the novel, one sees a similar terror, which is a dramatic foreboding of the powerful conclusion of the novel. The secluded wilderness plantation of Legree, with its grotesque and cruel inhabitants, its pitiable victims, and the intervention of supernatural powers, could be material for a gothic novelist such as Ann Radcliffe.

The last few chapters of the novel, which are reflections on slavery, are anticlimactic. The true end of the story comes with the end of Tom in chapter 40, when "Legree, foaming with rage, smote his victim to the ground." Tom nobly suffered martyrdom, lingering long enough to bid farewell to his young master from Kentucky, who had reached him too late to buy his freedom. George Harris was a new man once he regarded himself as "free," but Uncle Tom had an outlook that was different from that of George Harris and his creator, Harriet Beecher Stowe. Tom was a true Christian among the heathen, and for him, slavery was only one added indignity. His reading of the New Testament, an "unfashionable old book," separated him more completely from his fellows than did either his race or his status as a slave. Tom wanted his freedom as ardently as Stowe wanted it for him, but he preferred slavery and martyrdom to dishonorable flight. He was a black Christ who was shaming a Yankee Satan. The conviction of Stowe against slavery was so strong that she had "religious" visions, such as that of the killing of Uncle Tom—visions that she included as scenes in the novel.

Context

Harriet Beecher Stowe visited the White House in 1863 to urge President Abraham Lincoln to do something positive about the thousands of slaves who had fled to Washington, D.C. The often-quoted statement by Abraham Lincoln on that occasion, that Mrs. Stowe was "the little woman who wrote the book that made this great war," points to the role of *Uncle Tom's Cabin* in the history of women's literature, not only because of its impact on the history of women's literature but also because of its impact on American literature and American history in general. Because of her religious background, Stowe strongly opposed slavery because it was un-Christian. The buying and selling of slaves violated Christian regard for human rights, for the rights of other human beings.

The strongest objection to slavery expressed by Stowe as a woman was that slavery broke up slave families. In Mark Twain's *The Adventures of Huckleberry Finn*, the strongest, most emotional feelings expressed by the slave Jim were that he missed his family. Stowe stressed the dangers of capitalism to family values. She saw the slave trade as a masculine, unfeeling occupation and appealed to her female readers to end slavery because it destroyed the family. She never viewed women as abolitionists; that was a masculine pursuit. She believed that by writing her novels and appealing to her female reading audience, she could effect a change and abolish slavery. She reflected on the suffering that she herself felt when she lost a child and compared it to what a slave mother must feel when her child is sold away from her.

The enactment of the Fugitive Slave Act led Stowe to write *Uncle Tom's Cabin*. From the beginning, Stowe had unequivocally advocated absolute legal freedom for all slaves. She shows in the novel the difference that being free makes on the former slaves. George Harris, once he regarded himself as "free," held his head up higher and spoke and moved like a different man, even though he was unsure of his safety. Slavery, in its criminal disregard for human souls, in its treatment of human beings as property, was different from and worse than any other atrocity in life.

Sources for Further Study

Adams, John R. *Harriet Beecher Stowe*. Rev. ed. Boston: G. K. Hall, 1989. This work expands Adam's earlier study, the first and only comprehensive analysis of the life and works of Stowe. Adams discusses recently disclosed biographical information about the Beecher family and numerous critical examinations of Stowe written in the twenty-five years since the early study was published. The author connects *Uncle Tom's Cabin* to the religious ideas and personal experiences of Stowe. The volume includes an up-to-date bibliography and chronology.

Beach, Seth Curtis. *Daughters of the Puritans: A Group of Brief Biographies*. 1905. Reprint. Freeport, N.Y.: Books for Libraries Press, 1967. This book contains a forty-page introductory biography of Harriet Beecher Stowe, a background against which to study *Uncle Tom's Cabin*. The object of the study is to show the influences that molded Stowe, to present the salient features of her career and her characteristic qualities. The selection is interesting and informative and provides background material for all readers. It can be read by high school students as well as college undergraduates.

Fields, Annie. *Life and Letters of Harriet Beecher Stowe*. Boston: Houghton Mifflin, 1898. The second definitive biography of Harriet Beecher Stowe after the book by her son Charles, this sympathetic portrait was written by her personal friend and professional associate who was also a celebrity in her own right. This readable biography contains many now-famous anecdotes about Harriet Beecher Stowe.

Gossett, Thomas F. *Uncle Tom's Cabin and American Culture*. Dallas: Southern Methodist University Press, 1985. This excellent, detailed book shows why *Uncle Tom's Cabin* was the most widely read American novel of its time. The first section, about eighty pages long, describes the conditions that led to the creation of the book. The second section, another eighty pages, is an analysis of the book as fiction and social criticism. The remaining two hundred and fifty pages recount the reception of the book in the North, the South, and Europe; the replies; the dramatic versions; and adverse criticism. Contains extensive notes and a comprehensive bibliography.

Stowe, Charles Edward. *The Life of Harriet Beecher Stowe*. Boston: Houghton Mifflin, 1889. This excellent biography of Harriet Beecher Stowe was compiled by her son, the Reverend Charles Edward Stowe, from her letters and journals. The authorized family biography, it contains the first printing of indispensable letters and other documents and is the foundation of all later biographies. It tells the story of the life of Harriet Beecher Stowe as she had wished and had hoped to tell it herself in her autobiography. Two later books by members of the Stowe family add additional material: Charles Edward Stowe and Lyman Beecher Stowe's *Harriet Beecher Stowe: The Story of Her Life* (1941) and Lyman Beecher Stowe's *Saints, Sinners, and Beechers* (1934).

Wangenknecht, Edward. *Harriet Beecher Stowe: The Known and the Unknown*. New York: Oxford University Press, 1965. A combination of biography and literary criticism, this book contains a description of the literary and personal character of Harriet Beecher Stowe. The details are arranged topically, with chapters on Stowe as writer, reader, and reformer as well as daughter, wife, and mother.

Linda Silverstein Gordon

A VINDICATION OF THE RIGHTS OF WOMAN

Author: Mary Wollstonecraft (1759-1797)
Type of work: Social criticism
First published: 1792

Form and Content

First published in London in 1792, in the wake of the American and French revolutions, Mary Wollstonecraft's *A Vindication of the Rights of Woman* was itself a revolutionary book—a powerful argument for the establishment of legal, political, and social equality between men and women. Though by no means the first "feminist" writing in English (that honor should properly go to Mary Astell, who wrote approximately a hundred years before Wollstonecraft), Wollstonecraft spoke with uncommon force and vigor about the institutionalized, culturally sponsored oppression of women. Wollstonecraft's governing premise in *A Vindication of the Rights of Woman* can be traced back through Thomas Jefferson and the American Declaration of Independence to the English philosopher John Locke: She claims that men and women are moral and intellectual (if not physical) equals, and are thus equally entitled to the same "natural rights." Her first steps in presenting her case are to set forth the problem and to establish her authority—the grounds on which she will argue against the oppression of women.

The problem, simply put, is that women have traditionally been relegated to a secondary, subordinate place in society—assigned a role, as a modern feminist put it, as the "second sex." Wollstonecraft recognizes that this is hardly a phenomenon of her time alone. Throughout history, women have been represented as intellectually and morally inferior to men, and this supposed inferiority has been used as the excuse to keep them in a subordinate position, without the power to act—or even to think—freely. Society has further conspired to institutionalize sexual oppression, reinforcing and perpetuating this subordination by denying women access to the same "rational" education as men and by insisting instead that they concern themselves only with finding ways to make themselves more attractive to men. The result, as Wollstonecraft trenchantly puts it, is that women have been kept in a state of "perpetual childhood," a state that inhibits moral and intellectual growth and only increases their dependence on men. Independence, which Wollstonecraft sees as the necessary basis for true equality, can only come about through a "revolution in female manners" built on the recognition that women are as capable of moral and intellectual improvement as men are.

Wollstonecraft's authority in making such claims is fundamentally religious. She argues that men and women alike have been created in the image of the "Supreme Being" and have thus been equally endowed with reason, which she sees as the attribute that defines what it means to be human and thus sets humankind above "brute creation." Reason is not, however, simply a proof of humanity or of humankind's superiority over the rest of creation; it is the divine gift by means of which human beings can attain knowledge, acquire virtue, and ultimately perfect themselves spiritually and morally. That "spiritual" equality guarantees both moral and intellectual equality is the basic principle upon which Wollstonecraft constructs her argument for women's rights. For her, the fact that fully half of humankind has been forced into a position "below the standard of rational creatures" is not merely wrong; it is an affront against God. The only way to remedy this situation, as Wollstonecraft points out time and again, is to abandon the idea of essential sexual difference and to provide women with the educational opportunities that will allow them to think and act as full moral beings.

Wollstonecraft's argument most frequently proceeds by way of analogy. As she moves through her discussion, considering the specific problem of female oppression within the context of society as a whole, she repeatedly discovers similar examples of oppression, some of them involving men as the subjects of the oppression. The behavior of military officers toward their men, of monarchs toward their subjects, of parents toward their children, of bishops toward their curates—all serve to illustrate Wollstonecraft's proposition that the subordination of one group to another through the exercise of arbitrary power will nearly always result in the abuse of that power; in other words, in oppression—and oppression of any kind degrades men and women alike and presents nearly insuperable barriers to social progress.

Analysis

In *A Vindication of the Rights of Woman*, Wollstonecraft sets an enormous task for herself—nothing less than a wide-reaching critique of human society—and she meets the challenge head on. Her aim, she says early on, is to be "useful," and from the first page the reader senses her determination to shun "delicacy" and to pursue the truth wherever it leads her. In order to appreciate the full extent of Wollstonecraft's vision, it is important to note precisely where and how far the truth does lead her. Her critique does not stop at the issue of female oppression but reaches out further to examine the ways in which society functions to oppress and enslave whole classes of people across the social spectrum. What finally makes *A Vindication of the Rights of Woman* so important and "relevant" a document is Wollstonecraft's tacit recognition that the establishment of women's rights can only be accomplished through a radical, sweeping transformation of society as a whole that abolishes all oppression.

Although Wollstonecraft's political and social views were without doubt radical and even revolutionary, she was in other ways—especially in terms of her intellectual heritage—a child of her age. As was the case with many of her contemporaries, two of the chief influences on her thought were the English philosopher John Locke (1632-1704) and the French writer-philosopher Jean-Jacques Rousseau (1712-1778). By the 1790's, Locke's ideas about education and government, in particular, had long been incorporated into mainstream thought, as had his "sensationalist" theory of how people learn. If the mind at birth is, as Locke held, a *tabula rasa* (clean slate), and humans acquire knowledge only through experience, by way of the senses, then both men and women begin life with equal intellectual potential, and the importance of environment and education—so vigorously argued by Wollstonecraft—is supreme. Rousseau's more current ideas influenced an entire generation of thinkers and writers, and were formative in the early stages of what is now called the "Romantic" age of English literature. Wollstonecraft repeatedly refers to Rousseau, both in her text and in extensive footnotes, most often to take issue with him on his view of women as weak and passive creatures born only to please men.

Another important influence on Wollstonecraft was Catharine Macaulay, whose *Letters on Education* (1790) was enthusiastically reviewed by Wollstonecraft in the *Analytical Review*, an important liberal journal. Like Wollstonecraft after her, Macaulay was interested not only in reforming female manners through physical exercise and education but also in challenging the traditional idea that women were intrinsically inferior to men. Equally influential, though in a negative sense, were such writers of female "conduct" literature as James Fordyce and John Gregory, whose popular books advised young women to avoid all physical and intellectual endeavors and to concentrate instead on making themselves more attractive and pleasing to men. Wollstonecraft clearly recognized such texts as lying near the heart of the problem: Men who instructed young women to behave as meek and passive objects of desire, as though such behavior were "natural" to their sex, were in essence preparing them for a life of subordination and oppression. To Wollstonecraft, such instruction was itself a form of enslavement, aimed at fashioning creatures fit only for life in a "seraglio."

In any discussion of *A Vindication of the Rights of Woman*, it is also important to recognize—as her critics often have not—the limits of Wollstonecraft's radicalism. Although the work may rightly be called a "feminist manifesto," and although Wollstonecraft's program for social reform may have required fundamental changes across the sociopolitical spectrum, it most certainly did not call for or entail an essential reconfiguration either of the family or of woman's role in the family. Nothing in *A Vindication of the Rights of Woman* even remotely suggests that women should abandon the idea of motherhood. If anything, Wollstonecraft's theoretical "model" for the enlightened society was the middle-class household seen as an independent social-economic unit managed by the middle-class woman. Wollstonecraft would never have agreed with the idea that a woman's only place is in the home, but she did see the "domestic sphere"—where, in her capacity as wife and mother, a woman functions as primary educator and caregiver—as the place where the progress of civilization can most effectively be advanced.

Context

History did not treat Wollstonecraft kindly—or at all fairly. The initial reception of *A Vindication of the Rights of Woman* was largely positive (although it can be argued that the early reviewers of Wollstonecraft's work, most of whom regarded it as a treatise on "female education," either missed or overlooked its more radical implications). Shortly after her death in 1797 (of complications following the birth of her second child—a daughter, Mary, who was later to marry the poet Percy Shelley and write her own story of power and oppression, *Frankenstein*), however, the press began to vilify Wollstonecraft. As reactionary forces gathered in the wake of the failure of the French Revolution to produce the kind of apocalyptic social change its adherents had thought certain, Wollstonecraft's work came to be ridiculed and her life treated as scandal: In time, she became an object lesson, a cautionary example of the dangers of female education and emancipation. As late as the 1940's, it was still fashionable to ignore the sweeping, humanitarian vision of her work and to focus instead on her life and personality, portraying her as a shrill, man-hating neurotic whose vision was based on a contempt for all traditional values. Following the advent of the women's movement in the 1960's, however, feminist writers turned to Wollstonecraft for direction and inspiration, in the process demanding that she be judged for what she really was: a powerful force in the struggle for human freedom.

Sources for Further Study

Ferguson, Moira, and Janet M. Todd. *Mary Wollstonecraft*. Boston: Twayne, 1984. An excellent introduction to Wollstonecraft and her work. Particularly good on the intellectual background of *A Vindication of the Rights of Woman*.

Flexner, Eleanor. *Mary Wollstonecraft*. New York: Coward-McCann, 1972. A sound biography with a thorough discussion of Wollstonecraft's writings.

George, Margaret. *One Woman's "Situation": A Study of Mary Wollstonecraft*. Urbana: University of Illinois Press, 1970. Though much has been written about Wollstonecraft since 1970, this remains a sensitive discussion of her life and work.

Poovey, Mary. *The Proper Lady and the Woman Writer*. Chicago: University of Chicago Press, 1984. An important study of the emergence of the woman writer. Poovey's psychoanalytic reading of Wollstonecraft's work is fascinating and revealing.

Posten, Carol H., ed. *A Vindication of the Rights of Woman*, by Mary Wollstonecraft. 2d ed. New York: W. W. Norton, 1988. Perhaps the best place to begin a detailed study of Wollstonecraft's work. A fully annotated text, together with a bibliography, selected modern criticism and background material, and a section outlining the "Wollstonecraft debate."

Todd, Janet. *A Wollstonecraft Anthology*. New York: Columbia University Press, 1990. Selections from all Wollstonecraft's works together with a very useful introduction and bibliography.

Michael Stuprich

THE WAR BETWEEN THE TATES

Author: Alison Lurie (1926-)
Type of work: Novel
Type of plot: Social criticism
Time of plot: 1969-1970
Locale: Upstate New York and New York City
First published: 1974

Principal characters:

Brian Tate, a forty-six-year-old political science professor at Corinth University

Erica Tate, Brian's wife

Wendy Gahaghan, the graduate student with whom Brian becomes entangled

Danielle Zimmern, Erica's best friend and a divorcée who teaches French at Brian's university

Sanford Finkelstein ("Zed"), owner of the Krishna Bookshop

Muffy and **Jeffo,** the Tates' teenagers, formally christened Matilda and Jeffrey

Form and Content

The War Between the Tates is told from the omniscient point of view, allowing Alison Lurie to alternate between camps in reporting from the front. Along with their private war, the Tates wage a joint campaign against the generation of the late 1960's. As Erica and Brian face off over the marital disruption introduced by Wendy Gahaghan, they are both adjusting to a world that threatens their established values. Moreover, both have private battles with themselves that cloud their perceptions of their situations. The all-knowing narrator keeps up with all this strife in a series of well-observed and sometimes quite comic scenes that move rapidly toward the Tates' armistice day.

Brian's career at Corinth University has been safe, conventional, and dull. At forty-six, he yearns for more—not only more from the academy but also something more from Erica in terms of conjugal excitement, something raging and Faustian. He is always conscious of being only five feet five, and he has an unhappy sense of a stunted life.

Erica has grown up safe, too. Conservative in her social, sexual, and cultural values, she now finds her traditionalism sorely tested. She has always worshipped the children, whose boorish adolescence has her on the brink of apostasy. A shopping center is about to blot her pastoral landscape, a gut-blow from the industrial-commercial bogeyman that troubles the dreams of liberals like the Tates. Brian has not become the mighty scholar she had hoped he would be, leaving her as the woman behind less of a man than she had fantasized.

Wendy Gahaghan, then, can be seen as the Tates' salvation in that she rejuvenates their lives. Wendy has a raffish flower-child sexiness, and when she presents herself to Brian as an offering to his solid goodness, the war is on. The sequence is an old one: adulterous liaisons, wifely rage on discovery, a bristly truce, pregnancy of the mistress, and the husband's removal to an apartment. Much of Brian's estrangement not only pains him in every way but also bores him. A serious student of George Kennan is hardly suited to camping out with dope-smoking counterculture guerrillas. Yet he fights on.

Erica, meanwhile, consults her friend Danielle Zimmern, who is already divorced from her husband, Leonard, an English-professor. Encouraged, perhaps, by Danielle's happy affair with a robust, easygoing veterinarian, Bernie Kotelchuk, Erica timidly accepts the futile love of Zed Finkelstein. When Erica knew Zed at Radcliffe and Harvard, he was Sanford, but "Zed" suits the higher purpose evident in one who runs an establishment called the Krishna Bookstore and serves as guru to the socially alienated. Unfortunately, Erica does not have the luck of her worldly friend Danielle, and the spiritual Zed fumbles where the carnal Bernie moves with swift purpose.

During this domestic turmoil, Brian facetiously suggests to Wendy's feminist collaborators that they take hostage the much-despised target of their rage, Don Dibble, a conservative colleague of Brian's whom he much dislikes. To Brian's shock, they do precisely that, and it then falls to Brian to rescue the victim by smuggling a rope into Dibble's office. The furious women get revenge by beating Brian in a ridiculous denouement.

This slapstick virtually concludes Brian's tour of duty with the psychedelic underground, but Wendy, after having had one abortion, announces that she is pregnant again. The *deus ex machina* for Brian is a foreign one—a Pakistani graduate student in engineering who may be the father. The new friend with whom Wendy leaves for a "far-out commune" in Northern California is Ralph, who "really digs kids" and is eager to work out "a total relationship" with Wendy. With Zed's departure from Corinth at the same time, the Tates are left to survey the battle damage and begin postwar reconstruction. Such a finale is an inkblot that readers are left to interpret to her or his satisfaction, but the gentleness with which Lurie puts her characters through their paces suggests that life will not be more than usually intolerable for the Tates if they remain under their creator's care.

Analysis

The main characters in *The War Between the Tates* are set in motion by acts of adultery. In their reactions to the marital betrayals of the two husbands, Brian Tate and Leonard Zimmern, the two couples reveal totally different visions of life. They define themselves by means of their sexual behavior.

The Tates are social and political liberals but cultural conservatives. Deep down—and not always so deep—they prize bourgeois family life and see themselves as upholders of a tradition. They are religious people without a church, heirs of rationalism and believers in progress. Thus, their self-images suffer a great shock as they entangle themselves with people whose values and orientations they cannot share. After the erotic regeneration that Brian enjoys with Wendy begins to wear off, he does not really want to endure her trivial chitchat any longer simply to have her young body at his disposal, and he does not want to move on to ever fresher Wendys. What he really wants to do is to go home to Erica and burrow back into the security of the middle-class life for which he has worked. Certainly, that is also what Erica wants.

The Zimmerns are another case. Leonard Zimmern is unique among Lurie's characters in that he appears in four other of her novels. In *Real People* (1969), Leonard Zimmern is a scholar at a writers' colony, a ruthless critic and an intent marauder among vulnerable women. *Only Children* (1979) goes back in time to show the fourteen-year-old Lennie, already disgruntled with life and living with his detested father and stepmother while taking out his malign urges in teasing and cruel jokes. Later on, in the early 1980's, the setting of *Foreign Affairs* (1984), L. D. Zimmern surfaces as the sixtyish critic who attacks Vinnie Miner's scholarship; his daughter, Ruth Zimmern Turner, is married to Fred Turner, Vinnie Miner's coprotagonist. In *The Truth About Lorin Jones* (1988), Leonard Zimmern pops up as the half brother of the title character.

Leonard Zimmern is what Brian Tate could never be: a man apparently driven to seek out sexual alliances without regard for consequences. Moreover, he must be an accomplished seducer of a kind that Brian would not even aspire to be. His former wife, Danielle, although obviously hurt by Leonard's adulteries, is tougher than Erica. After all, Danielle teaches French literature as little more than a series of studies in the vicissitudes of passion, whereas Erica writes children's books about an ostrich named Sanford. Danielle rebounds quickly, too. It is a fair inference that what drew Leonard and Danielle together in the first place was a mutual excellence in sex, and when Danielle accepts another man it is not a sexual incompetent (such as Erica's Zed) to whom she turns, but a man who is at home with all of life's challenges—Bernie Kotelchuk, a veterinarian who feels no urge to be a Don Juan. Danielle does not need another intellectual; the self-confident Bernie comforts her spirit.

If adultery occupies the foreground of *The War Between the Tates* in a sort of Shakespearean comic do-si-do of shifting partners, then it is the raucous social scene of the late 1960's that fills up the background. Social chaos and change recapitulate domestic chaos and change. The peace march at the end of the novel is a perfect vignette of the 1960's and includes all of what Brian calls "freakish, violent, and socially disruptive elements": guerrilla theater players, Maoist troublemakers, Gay Power advocates, and a delegation from WHEN. The good liberal Brian, however, would probably agree that despite their scruffiness and the many opportunities they presented for satire when caught in ludicrous postures, the various civil rights campaigners evolved better lives for their subjects. Who would not choose as companions the campus protesters over the pharisee Dibble?

Lurie has a sharp eye for social satire, but only self-oriented manipulators such as the ubiquitous Leonard Zimmern seem to be without salvation in her world. Herself an academic—an English professor at Cornell University, an authority on children's literature, and a student of changing habits of dress—she is well positioned to survey the social anthropology of university families and departmental clan structures. She adopts a policy of justice tempered by mercy—and a warning to keep a sharp eye out for the Lennie Zimmerns of the world.

Context

Alison Lurie is a teacher, a scholar, and a writer of fiction about upper-middle-class professors and creative people in the arts, and she usually depicts the struggles and crises of women in this mixed milieu. Many of these struggles—*most* of them—are, by the nature of things, with men, and these contests between the sexes are seen predominantly from the woman's point of view and imply a special sympathy for her ordeal but without caricaturing all men as demons.

Lurie's own career should be a testimony to the possibilities of achievement open to women. While still an undergraduate at Radcliffe, she published poems in *Poetry* and stories in *Commentary* and *Woman's Press*, but after eight years of rejections, she quit writing. During this dry period, she married Jonathan Peale Bishop, son of the poet John Peale Bishop, and moved with him to western Massachusetts, where he taught English at Amherst College. Before their separation in 1975, they had three sons.

Lurie was jolted out of the barrenness in her creative life by two significant events. First was the death in 1956 of a close friend, the poet, playwright, and actress V. R. (Bunny) Lang; the writing *V. R. Lang: A Memoir* (privately printed, 1959) changed Lurie's life irrevocably. In studying the career of a talented woman who overcame many obstacles, Lurie escaped the frustrating round of domestic duties that preoccupied her and further educated herself about the lifestyle she would soon depict in her novels of manners.

The second important change in Lurie's life was moving with her family in 1957 to Los Angeles, where her husband was to teach at the University of California. She soon freed her mind of Amherst by writing her first published novel, *Love and Friendship* (1962), followed by a novel treating the culture shock of a New England girl transplanted to California, *The Nowhere City* (1965). Two other novels came next, *Imaginary Friends* (1967) and *Real People* (1969), before the critical and popular success of *The War Between the Tates* established Lurie as a major figure in American fiction. Official honors came with the Pulitzer Prize for *Foreign Affairs* (1984).

Sources for Further Study

Ackroyd, Peter. "Miss American Pie." *Spectator* 232 (June 29, 1974): 807. Praise for *The War Between the Tates* from a British critic. Ackroyd plays down the significance of the novel's background in the troubled Vietnam years and emphasizes its comic elements in the vein of James Thurber.

Aldridge, John W. "How Good Is Alison Lurie?" *Commentary* 59 (January, 1975): 79-81. Aldridge faults Lurie for what he sees as a trivial approach to academic life. This article is one of the more authoritative negative judgments on Lurie's work.

Costa, Richard Hauer. *Alison Lurie*. New York: Macmillan, 1992. An indispensable source for biographical information. The perceptive commentary includes a whole chapter on *The War Between the Tates*, and the bibliography is excellent.

Cowen, Rachel B. "The Bore Between the Tates." *Ms.* 4 (January, 1975): 41-42. This is a strong feminist reading. Cowen argues that Erica Tate should have aligned herself with the women revolutionaries and used the whole episode of Brian's affair as an occasion to grow as a woman.

Helfand, Michael S. "The Dialectic of Self and Community in Alison Lurie's *The War Between the Tates*." *Perspectives on Contemporary Literature* 3 (November, 1977): 65-70. Helfand's major interest in *The War Between the Tates* is the political commentary that he identifies. Brian Tate's interest in the foreign policy doctrines of George Kennan helps Helfand to understand some of the problems of modern liberalism.

Rogers, Katharine M. "Alison Lurie: The Uses of Adultery." In *American Women Writing Fiction: Memory, Identity, Family, Space*, edited by Mickey Pearlman. Lexington: University Press of Kentucky, 1989. An excellent broad treatment of adultery and its significance in women's lives. All of Lurie's novels through *Foreign Affairs* are analyzed.

Frank Day

THE WELL OF LONELINESS

Author: Radclyffe Hall (1880-1943)
Type of work: Novel
Type of plot: Tragedy
Time of plot: World War I
Locale: England and France
First published: 1928

Principal characters:

Stephen Gordon, the only child of English gentry

Sir Philip Gordon, Stephen's father, who waited ten years for a son only to have a daughter

Lady Anna Gordon, Stephen's mother, the "archetype of the very perfect woman"

Miss Puddleton, known as "Puddle," Stephen's schoolmistress at Morton and her later companion

Martin Hallam, Stephen's friend and rival

Angela Crossby, the neighbor with whom Stephen falls in love

Mary Llewellyn, a woman with whom Stephen falls in love

Form and Content

The Well of Loneliness examines the lonely life of Stephen Gordon. The only child of English country gentry, she is reared as the son her parents never had. Boyish and awkward, Stephen is close to her father, sharing his interests in riding, hunting, and learning. Yet her mother never finds a way to love this odd and ungraceful child. Stephen's isolation is rather acute: She is educated at home by governesses.

In one of her first attempts at finding love, the young Stephen forms an intense crush on a family maid, becoming enraged upon discovering the woman embracing the footman. After he learns of his daughter's heartache, Sir Philip involves himself even more in Stephen's upbringing, although he never tells Stephen or his wife of his suspicions. Neither does the schoolmistress, Puddle, although the author heavily implies that this woman's own oddness gives her special insight into her young charge.

Once Martin Hallam enters the picture, it appears that Stephen may not be as strange or different as her father has suspected. Yet, after Stephen is insulted and enraged by Martin's proposal, it is clear that she will never marry. Soon after, Stephen's father dies, and Stephen turns to Angela Crossby for emotional consolation. Angela uses Stephen, however, returning the girl's love with betrayal: Although she had spent much time in Stephen's arms, talking of love and accepting expensive gifts, Angela shows her husband one of Stephen's passionate letters. Angela's attempt to end the relationship with Stephen results in her husband's exposing Stephen to her mother. Lady Anna condemns her daughter, banishing her from Morton, the family estate.

Stephen and Puddle move to London, where Stephen becomes a successful novelist. At the urging of a homosexual acquaintance, Jonathan Brockett, they move to Paris, where Stephen has her first glimpse of lesbian culture. With the outbreak of World War I, Stephen becomes an ambulance driver, receiving both a medal and a scar of honor and becoming acquainted with Mary Llewellyn. Although the relationship proceeds rather slowly, Mary's love for Stephen overcomes Stephen's reservations, and they finally set up housekeeping back in Paris.

Yet their relationship is not an easy one. Stephen is forbidden to bring Mary to Morton. The only acquaintances they make in respectable society cancel invitations and refuse to associate with them. Stephen is busy with her writing, and Mary has little to do. With no place else to turn, they venture into the lesbian subculture, finding friends among "their own kind." Yet many of the women they meet lead tragic lives, drowning in alcohol, poverty, and self-loathing.

At this point, Martin Hallam reappears. Although his friendship with Mary begins innocently enough, providing a welcome reentry to mainstream society, he falls in love with her. He and Stephen begin a battle of the heart and will. Mary clings to Stephen devotedly, although she does have feelings for Martin. Determined to save Mary from the pain and isolation of lesbian life, Stephen feigns an affair with another woman, deliberately pushing Mary into Martin's waiting arms.

Analysis

As it depicts "the love that dare not speak its name," *The Well of Loneliness* clearly portrays the isolation, condemnation, and struggle of lesbian life as it was in the recent past and unfortunately remains in some pockets of contemporary society. In so doing, however, it gives a dignity to lesbian relationships, showing the suffering and sacrifices made in the effort to find and give love. Although the writing has the tenor of other late Victorian novels, with its detailed pastoral scenes, attribution of human insights and emotions to animals, and vagueness and delicacy with regard to sex, its controversial subject matter marks it as on the cusp of modernity. The pain and angst of its heroine has an existential quality that resonates with the struggle for meaning and identity that is often thematized in the modern novel.

Not once in the novel does Radclyffe Hall use the word "lesbian," and rarely does she use the medical term often employed by early sexologists: "invert." Instead, through her descriptions of the young Stephen's oddness, boyishness, and disdain for traditionally feminine clothing and pursuits, the writer evokes her heroine's lesbianism. While Stephen's strong sense of honor, her religious faith, and her respect for the land and traditions of Morton establish her as a strong and sympathetic character, the author's reluctance to name Stephen's "condition," to say "what" she is, creates the dramatic tension that enables the reader to identify Stephen. More specifically, both Sir Philip and Puddle refuse to tell Stephen what she is. This refusal replays within the novel the tension between naming and suspicion which marks the reader's relationship to the author. Like Stephen, the reader suspects that a certain difference and abnormality is afoot, but is left to pull the pieces together.

Just as the avoidance of naming signifies Stephen's separateness from the world of accepted societal norms and definitions, so is her isolation rendered explicit by the tension between her own sense of the worthiness and naturalness of her love and the condemnation of the world around her. At one point, as she speaks the language of love to Angela Crossby, describing how they could run away together, Angela asks, "Could you marry me, Stephen?" Knowing all too well the answer to this question, Stephen faces the loneliness of her position: "She could only debase what she longed to exalt, defile what she longed to keep pure."

To be sure, as some critics have pointed out, Hall's own sense of purity and endorsement of social conventions tend to lead her to depict lesbian life ambiguously. On the one hand, the lesbian subculture in Paris provides Stephen and Mary with a circle of accepting friends. Yet, on the other, many of those in this subculture are haunted and tormented, a decadent, miserable army of society's outcasts. Forced either to live a lie or to remain in the darkness of bars and nightclubs, they are bereft of social dignity. Although their situation is ultimately blamed on society's failure to accept difference, such a melancholy portrayal of homosexuality has been said to undermine Hall's general defense of same-sex love.

In one of the book's most memorable scenes, the depth of Stephen's pain and isolation comes out with particular poignancy. Her mother has read the letter describing Stephen's love for Angela Crossby and has found this love shameful, unnatural, and unworthy. Tormented by her mother's rejection and condemnation, Stephen refuses to be ashamed. She attempts to defend her love as the best part of her, comparing it to the bond between her parents. Despite the eloquence of her appeal to this sacred tie, Lady Anna cannot accept her daughter and, indeed, finds the comparison an abomination, thus damning herself and forever cutting her daughter off from the familial tie that is so important to her.

Similarly, Stephen cuts herself off from the relationship that she and Mary have built together for the sake of allowing Mary to live in the type of family that is legitimized by society. The book thus culminates with a tragic lament that nevertheless contains within it the possibility of hope. As she watches Mary leave in Martin's arms, she hears the cries of other men and women who are similarly cut off from love by societal dictates. Their call is both to her and to God to acknowledge their right to existence. As a writer, then, Stephen is uniquely placed to describe and defend homosexual love. Ultimately, her sacrifice of Mary becomes the cost to be paid for fighting this lonely battle and earning the right to happiness.

Context

The significance of *The Well of Loneliness* cannot be overestimated. It was banned in England shortly after its publication as obscene, and the publicity surrounding its trial helped to establish the book as an heroic defense of homosexuality. Additionally, as the press at the time and many critics since have noted, Radclyffe Hall's own public life as a lesbian added to the book's success, although the book is not autobiographical. Since 1928, *The Well of Loneliness* has been translated and reissued numerous times and remains the best-known lesbian novel.

For many women, this novel proved to them that they were neither alone nor unnatural in their love for other women. Heterosexual readers, moreover, often responded to its dignified account of lesbianism. To be sure, because it is one of the few lesbian novels, the impact of the book has been mixed. Its stereotypic equation of lesbianism with masculinity, with the concomitant disavowal of femininity, seemed to confirm restrictive prejudices regarding lesbian identity. This led some women into "butch" styles that were foreign to their own identities and desires. Additionally, its strict adherence to early theories of the "cause" and "symptoms" of lesbianism adds to the view of lesbianism as pathology: Few lesbians want to be men, and fewer still can be said to have "become" lesbians because their fathers wanted sons. Despite these drawbacks, however, *The Well of Loneliness* and the courage of Radclyffe Hall helped to increase the visibility of lesbians and pave the way for further writers.

The Well of Loneliness is Hall's only novel to take up specifically lesbian themes. Her other writings include a collection of poetry, *A Sheaf of Verses* (1908); *The Unlit Lamp* (1924); *Miss Ogilvy Finds Herself* (1934); and *The Sixth Beatitude* (1936).

Sources for Further Study

Baker, Michael. *Our Three Selves: The Life of Radclyffe Hall*. New York: William Morrow, 1985. A comprehensive biography of Radclyffe Hall which examines the publication and reception of *The Well of Loneliness*. Several chapters deal with the trial and publicity surrounding the banning of the book in England. Includes photographs of Radclyffe Hall, her family, and lovers. The discussion connecting *The Well of Loneliness* to Hall's other novels is also helpful.

Faderman, Lillian. *Odd Girls and Twilight Lovers*. New York: Penguin Books, 1991. This history of lesbianism in twentieth century America provides a historical framework for understanding the experiences of women who love women and includes a discussion of the role of *The Well of Loneliness* in providing women with knowledge of lesbianism.

Franks, Claudia Stillman. *Beyond "The Well of Loneliness."* Aldershot, Hampshire, England: Avebury, 1984. One of the most thorough critical treatments of the novel.

Jay, Karla, and Joanne Glasgow, eds. *Lesbian Texts and Contexts: Radical Revisions*. New York: New York University Press, 1990. A collection of critical essays on lesbian fiction and literature, a number of which discuss Radclyffe Hall and her work. A selective bibliography lists numerous fiction, nonfiction, and critical works by and about lesbians.

O'Rourke, Rebecca. *Reflecting on "The Well of Loneliness."* London: Routledge, 1989. A critical examination of *The Well of Loneliness* with a selected bibliography of books and articles by and about Radclyffe Hall. Especially interesting is the author's discussion of the reactions of lesbian and heterosexual readers of the book.

Troubridge, Una Vincenzo, Lady. *The Life and Death of Radclyffe Hall*. London: Hammond & Hammond, 1961. A biography of Hall by her longtime companion.

Jodi Dean

WEST WITH THE NIGHT

Author: Beryl Markham (1902-1986)
Type of work: Autobiography
Time of work: 1906-1936
Locale: Africa, Australia, and Europe
First published: 1942

Principal personages:

Lord and **Lady Delamere,** Kenyan colonialists who owned the Equator Ranch
Tom Black, a pioneer aviator
Baron Bror Blixen-Finecke, a Kenyan big game hunter and the husband of Karen Blixen-Finecke (Isak Dinesen)
Denys Finch-Hatton, a Kenyan big-game hunter and pioneer aviator

Form and Content

Beryl Markham wrote her autobiography in four sections she called books, which she subdivided into twenty-four chapters. Of those chapters, twenty take place in East Africa. Yet the title of the book, *West with the Night*, refers to her record solo flight across the Atlantic in September, 1936. She flew from Gravesend, England, to Cape Breton Island, Newfoundland. Other pilots had flown solo from West to East, most notably Charles Lindbergh and Amelia Earhart, but Markham was the first pilot, male or female, to fly solo across the Atlantic against the prevailing winds. When the book was originally published in 1942, her international fame and reputation was built on that flight.

The title is also symbolic of Markham's life. Her twenty-one-hour, twenty-five-minute flight in a Vega Gull plane culminated a life spent breaking stereotypes and records. The material she selected for the autobiography illustrates how her life shaped her into a person who flew alone across the Atlantic under adverse circumstances. By extension, her life, and, perhaps, every woman's life is seen as the process of soloing a small plane across the Atlantic in adverse circumstances.

Book 1 is composed of four chapters describing a flight in 1935 to deliver medicine to a dying miner in a remote area of Kenya. Book 1 ends with the flight back to Nairobi; en route, Markham rescues a friend whose plane has crashed.

Book 2 is composed of chapters 5 through 10. These cover Markham's childhood years from the age of four on her father's farm at Njoro, Kenya, to the age of seventeen, when she leaves the farm. Prophetically, in the last chapter, she helps to birth a colt she names Pegasus. On Pegasus, she rides away to a neighboring farm when her father emigrates to South America.

Book 3 relates Markham's successes at a farm in Molo, Kenya. As result of her skill with horses, she wins the prestigious Kenya Derby. She also meets Tom Black in an encounter she describes as destiny. Black, a pioneer aviator and the 1934 winner of the International Air Race from England to Australia, becomes her flight instructor and mentor.

The chapters dealing with the period from the beginning of her flying lessons to the transatlantic crossing are contained in book 4. With Black as her instructor and a DeHavilland Gipsy Moth for a plane, Markham earns her commercial license in eighteen months by virtue of hundreds of hours of study and more than a thousand hours of flying time. She also tells of her experiences with Denys Finch-Hatton. Finch-Hatton was an early aviator, an Eton-educated big-game hunter, and Markham's lover. This last fact is not discussed in the autobiography. Finch-Hatton teaches her to scout elephants from a plane for European safaris, and she states that this was her most lucrative freelance flying job. Markham describes Finch-Hatton's death in a plane crash.

She frequently flies for one of her best friends, Baron Bror Blixen-Finecke, who is better known as the husband of Isak Dinesen, author of *Out of Africa*. Dinesen, too, was a close friend of Markham. With Bror Blixen-Finecke as a passenger, Markham tells how she pilots a plane from Kenya to London in March of 1936. In London, she meets the people who finance her Atlantic solo flight. Chapter 23 is the title chapter, and, in it, she describes her flight.

Analysis

Beryl Markham's autobiography can be analyzed on the basis of details she included and details she excluded. Those that are included illustrate what she believes is required of a person who breaks stereotypes and records. Those that are excluded are details that might detract, because of their controversial nature, from the case she attempts to build about herself. The details that she included present a woman who lived an unorthodox life and loved it. The three passions of her unorthodox life were Africa, horses, and flying.

Markham's love of Africa is clear. Brought to Kenya at the age of four, she chose to live most of her adult life there, and she died there. Her early years provided her with rigorous training. Of particular importance are the descriptions of her childhood, when she lived close to the Nandi and Masai tribes. She writes of being attacked by lion and leopard, of being left alone at night on the plains after a hunt with her Nandi friends, and of being left to fend for herself at the age of seventeen.

Horses provided her opportunities early in life to break stereotypes, and they, like Africa, remained a lifelong love. The triumph of her horse Wise Child at the Kenya Derby gives Markham her first taste of fame and fortune in the predominantly male world of horse racing. Her success in horse racing foreshadows her success in flying. In both cases, she credits her success to prodigious labor and reading. She writes frequently about the hours of work she logged with her horses, even sleeping in their stalls, and she read volumes about horses. Markham left nothing to chance, and this same attitude applied later to flying.

Some particularly revealing lines about how Markham perceived herself are found in one of the chapters dealing with horses. In them, she incorporates one of her numerous literary allusions. She compares Pegasus to a knight's beautiful steed and identifies herself with Don Quixote. Ultimately, Markham died in 1986 as the result of injuries suffered when she fell from a horse. She was eighty-four years old and still riding.

Moving from the male-dominated worlds of rural Kenya and horse racing to the new, dangerous world of flying was natural for the adventurous Markham. By detailing her pilot's lessons, elephant tracking by plane, and white-knuckle-flying rescue missions, Markham shows that she is prepared to fly the Atlantic alone.

An event not related to Africa, horses, or flying reveals Markham's one fear: orthodoxy. The event described is her meeting with a prostitute in Benghazi, Libya, in 1936. It is noteworthy because almost as much space is devoted to this woman as to the transatlantic flight. Markham learns that the woman had been sold into white slavery as a child and describes her as helpless and trapped. For Markham, there is little difference between the prostitute's life and that of the ordinary housewife.

Markham carefully selected for inclusion events in her life which ultimately led to her successful solo flight. Of equal importance are the details of her life which she omitted. They reveal a person who did what was necessary to achieve, and what she did and achieved was highly unconventional for a woman in the early twentieth century.

The exclusion of other women is surely deliberate. There is no mention of Markham's mother, Clara, who returned to London and left Beryl, at age four, in Kenya with her father. No mention is made of her stepmother, Ada. Lady Delamere is given one line. No reference is made to her friend Isak Dinesen. The importance of her relationship with Baron Blixen-Finecke is discussed at length, but not her relationship with his wife.

She also does not mention any of her three husbands: Jock Purves, Mansfield Markham, and Raoul Schumacher. Schumacher is thanked on the dedication page of the book, but the book is dedicated to her father. Her only child, a son, Gervaise Markham, born in 1929, is omitted. In a move reminiscent of her own mother's, she left him in London to be reared by his grandmother, and she returned to Kenya. She rarely saw him again. When he died, she could not afford to fly from Kenya to Europe for the funeral.

She discusses none of her lovers, yet she is reputed to have had many. A mystery surrounds the birth of her son, whom some believe to be the child of one of her most famous paramours, Prince Henry, Duke of Gloucester, who was third in line to the British throne. Her divorce from Mansfield Markham was occasioned by her public affair with Prince Henry. For fear of scandal, the prince was not named in the divorce proceedings, and Beryl left the palace. From 1929, the year of her son's birth, until her death in 1986, an annuity was paid to her from a trust in Prince Henry's name. Neither this affair nor any other is even hinted at in the autobiography.

Another omission is the source of her name. She used her second husband's surname, yet her maiden name was Clutterbuck. Perhaps Beryl Clutterbuck did not have the lyrical ring necessary for a woman who could ride winged horses.

Context

Houghton-Mifflin was the first publisher of *West with the Night*. The book should have been a success, but in 1942, the world's attention was fixed on World War II. Small royalties were generated for about two years, but then the book disappeared and did not emerge again until 1983. Despite its lack of commercial success in 1942, the book was universally acclaimed by critics from *The New York Times*, *Boston Globe*, and *Saturday Review of Books*. The positive reviews mentioned the fascinating content of the story and the lyrical quality of the writing. Critics believed that Markham had contributed to the literature of Africa, flying, and the philosophy of the human spirit.

Some reviewers saw in her lyrical writing the influence of her friend Antoine de Saint-Éxupéry, another writer and aviator. Indeed, isolated passages bear a resemblance to his published works. Nevertheless, the consensus seems to be that he helped her to discover her literary style.

A significant controversy surrounding the original publication was based on rumors that Markham's third husband, Raoul Schumacher, had ghostwritten the book. The history of events surrounding the book's publication, however, seems to belie this theory. In March of 1941, Markham met with representatives of Houghton Mifflin. On the basis of four sets of typewritten manuscripts submitted by June 26, 1941, the company accepted her book, and she signed a contract in mid-July of 1941. Markham was introduced to Schumacher in California in August of 1941. It is true that the last six chapters of the book were written after she began living with Schumacher, but her biographer sees no change in writing style. Schumacher at various times made claims that he had been the writer, but chronology and style are cited as the salient arguments against him. He is credited with some editing.

The autobiography's republication in 1983 continues to bear out the view that Markham added to the literature of the early colonial period of East Africa, to the early history of avionics, and to the literature that speaks about the unyielding spirit of humans to fly, literally and metaphorically. Such bold adventure stories are often the province of men, and this fact may account for the book's disappearance until 1983. Social attitudes regarding what is proper and acceptable for women have changed substantially since 1942. It is likely that this fact accounts for the continuing revival of Markham's story.

Sources for Further Study

Bull, Bartle. *Safari: A Chronicle of Adventure*. New York: Viking Press, 1988. Bull chronicles the history of safaris in Africa from 1836. He provides detailed descriptions and photographs of Markham, her friends, and their lifestyles in the British colony of Kenya.

Lomax, Judy. *Women of the Air*. New York: Dodd, Mead, 1987. Lomax examines women's contributions in the field of aviation. The chapter on Markham contains anecdotes about her entire life and specific details about her transatlantic solo flight.

Lovell, Mary S. *Straight On Till Morning*. New York: St. Martin's Press, 1987. This definitive biography was written after Lovell conducted extensive interviews with Markham. Included is information on her family's English background and the controversial material that Markham kept out of her autobiography. Numerous pictures of Markham, her family, and friends are presented. Lovell uses for her title one of the titles originally considered by Markham for her autobiography.

Judith L. Steininger

WIDE SARGASSO SEA

Author: Jean Rhys (Ella Gwendolen Rees Williams, 1894-1979)
Type of work: Novel
Type of plot: Psychological realism
Time of plot: The mid-nineteenth century
Locale: Spanish Town, Jamaica; Massacre, a village on the Windward Islands; and Great Britain
First published: 1966

Principal characters:

Antoinette Cosway, a girl who is rejected by her emotionally disturbed mother and the townspeople, who look down on decadent white landowners

Rochester, an Englishman who comes to Spanish Town and receives thirty thousand pounds for his marriage to Antoinette

Annette Mason, Antoinette's mother

Christophine, the Martinique-born housekeeper who possesses the knowledge of voodoo

Daniel Cosway, Antoinette's half-brother

Amelie, the "little half-caste servant" of Antoinette

Form and Content

In *Wide Sargasso Sea*, Jean Rhys's characters fall into mental instability as a result of the rejection and isolation that dominate their lives. Rhys does not give a sentimental version of her characters' declines but offers a detached journalistic account from two perspectives. The novel is divided into three sections. Section 1 is narrated by Antoinette, who describes the rejection that penetrates her early childhood. She also narrates section 3, which further depicts isolation as she is placed in an alien environment in England. Section 2 is narrated by her husband, Rochester, who offers his perspective on the peculiarities of life in the islands and of life with Antoinette. This shift in narrators is effective because it allows readers to understand each character's dilemma.

To set the atmosphere of rejection, Rhys opens the novel with Antoinette describing the attitudes of the Spanish Town residents toward her mother, Annette. Many factors contribute to Annette's nonacceptance by the local residents, who believe that Annette is out of place because she was born in Martinique rather than Jamaica. They believe that she is far too young for her husband, so they question her motives for marrying him. They also talk about Pierre, her son, who was born with a mental disability. In addition, because the wounds of slavery have not healed, enmity exists between former slaves and landholders. Annette had been accustomed to social status when her husband's plantation had been prosperous, so the isolation drives her to madness.

The impact of the rejection goes beyond Annette. Her daughter, Antoinette, is also ostracized by the community. As the narrator of section 1, she describes the relationships of the community toward her mother and herself as well as the relationship between mother and daughter. After the loss of Coulibri, the family estate, and of Pierre, Annette completely rejects her daughter. Antoinette is sent to a convent, where she experiences a life that is totally unlike the one she knew at Coulibri. Catholicism contrasts sharply with the superstition and magic she had learned from Christophine, her family's housekeeper. Antoinette feels confusion, another factor contributing to her isolation. Section 1 ends after Antoinette attends her mother's funeral. Throughout the narration of this opening segment, Rhys depicts a childhood in which rejection and isolation are the dominant factors. The result is that Antoinette is unable to communicate; she does not know how to give of herself to others.

Antoinette seeks companionship and an end to her isolation by "buying" a husband from Britain. Rhys has this gentleman narrate the second section of *Wide Sargasso Sea*. Rochester's narration reveals his struggle to maintain his identity in this new environment, which initially entrances him but which also clashes with the values of his upbringing. Rhys establishes characters who contribute to their own undoing; blame is not assigned to others. Antoinette's inability to communicate leads her to use extreme methods in an effort to overcome her isolation. Rochester's inability to be flexible in adapting to a new way of life creates a further barrier to communication.

Section 3 is narrated by Antoinette, who describes her isolation in her husband's British estate. Instead of Rochester being the alien in her island environment, she is now the alien in his homeland. Her madness becomes complete in these final years of isolation.

In *Wide Sargasso Sea*, Jean Rhys speculates about the history that evolved the characters in Charlotte Brontë's *Jane Eyre*. Brontë's Rochester is a neurotic, embittered man who keeps his unstable wife closeted in the attic. *Wide Sargasso Sea* ends where *Jane Eyre* begins.

Analysis

Jean Rhys's *Wide Sargasso Sea* is a study of individuals who are entangled and finally consumed by their obsessions, just as divers are ensnared by the thick sargasso seaweed that surrounds the Windward Islands. Rhys's characters are similar to the grotesques described in Sherwood Anderson's "The Book of the Grotesque." He describes characters who cling to singular ideas, adapting them as personal truths. Their limited perspectives act as barriers to communication that cause the sea between individuals to widen. Isolation results as characters reside within their own psychological islands. Because the memories of slavery are so fresh in their minds, the townspeople cannot let go of their hatred of white landholders. Annette cannot release either her desire for social acceptance or her fear of the blacks. Antoinette is obsessed with the need to be loved, while Christophine cannot release her faith in obeah. Finally, Rochester cannot relinquish his civilized social decorum. All these characters have become entangled in their own truths. The tighter they hold on to their particular perspectives, the more isolated and grotesque they become. Rhys demonstrates that isolation leads to psychological demise.

Isolation is not necessarily self-inflicted. At times, historical factors influence relationships. This is seen in the rejection by the blacks in Spanish Town of Annette. The Coulibri estate had been a flourishing plantation during the days of slavery, but when slavery was abolished, workers' wages became too costly and many white "aristocrats" watched their lands decay. As property deteriorated, the respect that went along with land ownership also dwindled. The townspeople could not forget the history of slavery, and Annette could not ignore the hatred she felt directed toward her by the blacks. No communication took place, so the sea between Annette and the townspeople grew wider. After the burning of Coulibri, Annette went into complete isolation, even from her family members.

Wide Sargasso Sea is also a story of cultural clashes and the isolation that results from the inability to communicate. This is best demonstrated in the character Rochester, who has been reared according to British social decorum. When he first comes into contact with the wildness of the island's vegetation and running water, he is excited. Excitement is also revealed in the early sexual play of the newlyweds. As time passes, however, the sensuality, spontaneity, and superstition of Jamaican culture appear as aggressive abandon, which conflicts with Rochester's disciplined background. Viewing his wife through the eyes of European civilization, Rochester begins to doubt her. He lets his British rationalization dominate his feelings. He chooses to maintain his cultural identity at the expense of his marriage. He returns to Britain with Antoinette, and she lives in isolation in an alien environment.

Some critics claim that *Wide Sargasso Sea* is a story of male domination. They refer to Rochester's locking his wife up in the attic of his English estate, in the environment in which he could best assert his strength. Even in the village of Massacre, however, Antoinette had isolated herself from everyone but Christophine and the bottle. Antoinette's love for Rochester was so great that she wanted to possess him. After all, she had bought him for thirty thousand pounds. Yet the free environment of the islands would not permit anyone to be owned. Antoinette's desire for Rochester led her to summon Christophine to use obeah to instill desire in her husband. Antoinette's obsession to have her husband's love drove him away from her. Rather than be possessed by his wife, Rochester took control. He gained this control in England, where he knew the rules of domination.

Antoinette does not know how to communicate. Having lived with rejection since childhood, she has never learned how to share herself with others. She believes that she can buy a husband, but this results in further loneliness. A marriage without love offers no communication, no companionship. Her obsession to possess someone, to fill the rejection she had known all of her life, is too powerful. Antoinette's obsession for love brings about her demise.

Context

Jean Rhys's works are known for depicting females as spontaneous and fragile and males as cold and destructive. In *Wide Sargasso Sea*, however, to distinguish between the oppressors and the victims is difficult. Both genders seem to be at the mercy of their environments. Annette is the victim of historical prejudices resulting from the abolition of slavery. Antoinette is the victim of growing up in a family that was filled with rejection, leaving her unable to communicate with others. Rochester is the victim of being reared in European society and then being transported to a new environment where he is surrounded by the freedom of island culture. Each character must struggle to survive in difficult or unfamiliar conditions.

Rhys avoids sentimentality for her victims and reports journalistically. In isolation, the female characters struggle to form some sense of self-identity, but they seem always to be grasping for smoke. Rhys seems to suggest that women too often base their identities on their ties with others. Women pursue dependent roles and seem to lack identity in isolation. With an absence of self, women are continually grasping and often slide into mental instability.

Some critics claim that Rhys writes of cold-hearted men who take advantage of weak, dependent women. In *Wide Sargasso Sea*, Rochester takes Antoinette's dowry and shares a passionate beginning with her before turning away from her, leaving her in a state of imbalance. Rhys, however, does not paint Rochester as a cold, heartless character. She places Rochester in an alien environment and then depicts his state of loss. He is continually investigating his new environment, continually questioning his emotions in regard to Antoinette, continually trying to explain himself in letters to his father. The struggle to maintain his European culture in the free island atmosphere is not easy for him. Rhys, however, gives him the strength to recognize the problem. He realizes that he is out of place in the island environment and returns to England. His strength is in recognizing the cause of his confusion and in having the independence to return. Women, who are dependent on others, seem to lack the ability to step out of confusion.

Antoinette lacks any sense of self, which requires years of communication with others to develop. She has never learned to communicate. She relies on money to acquire a husband, rather than relying on her own personality or character. She relies on an aphrodisiac to seduce her husband rather than believing she can accomplish the seduction herself. Each of these decisions reflects Antoinette's lack of self-esteem. Rejection has made her unknown to herself. The irony in the story is that self-identity is acquired from interaction with others, yet that same interaction often results in loss of identity. To maintain balance is difficult for everyone, regardless of gender.

In *Wide Sargasso Sea*, Rhys does not place the blame for women's passivity, lack of identity, or disorientation on men. She instead creates characters who are responsible for their own fates. In showing the negative consequences of depending on others for identity, Rhys encourages the development of a strong sense of self. She punctuates that personal goal with doubt, however, by emphasizing that people are products of their environments.

Sources for Further Study

Anderson, Sherwood. "The Book of the Grotesque." In *Winesburg, Ohio*. New York: Penguin Books, 1992. This first chapter gives a thorough explanation of "grotesqueness," the inability to communicate with others. The rejection that results further strengthens the barriers against communication. Anderson's explanation facilitates an understanding of the characters in *Wide Sargasso Sea*.

Angier, Carole. *Jean Rhys: Life and Work*. Boston: Little, Brown, 1991. These seven hundred pages give a thorough discussion of Rhys's early life, her schooling, her clash of cultural backgrounds, her chorus line experience, her self-inflicted isolation, and her relationships. Angier connects Rhys's life with those of the characters in her books.

Hulbert, Ann. "Jean Rhys: Life and Work." *The New Republic* 206 (February 17, 1992): 38-41. This lengthy article reviews the biography of the same name by

Carole Angier. Much information is given about Rhys's life and about the characters in her novels. Rhys claims, "I have only ever written about myself."

Rhys, Jean. *After Leaving Mr. Mackenzie*. New York: Harper & Row, 1931. This second novel by Rhys is the story of Julia, who marries in order to escape Britain and to go to the Continent. After the collapse of her marriage, Julia goes from man to man and takes up drinking. Julia tries to grasp the essence of herself but finds her hands empty. Other novels by Rhys include *Quartet* (1928), *Voyage in the Dark* (1934), and *Good Morning, Midnight* (1939).

Linda J. Meyers

WITCHES, MIDWIVES, AND NURSES: A History of Women Healers

Authors: Barbara Ehrenreich (1941-) and Deirdre English (1948-)
Type of work: Social criticism
First published: 1973

Form and Content

Considering that women have always been healers, Barbara Ehrenreich and Deirdre English set out to recover that tradition in *Witches, Midwives, and Nurses: A History of Women Healers*. Their book encourages women employed in health care, especially nurses, to work out the struggles that they face in a profession which became the bailiwick of male professionals. The authors approach their task by devoting half their book to the history of witchcraft and medicine in the Middle Ages and half to the history of women and the rise of the medical profession in the United States. In each case, they show women as both humane and empirical with respect to their attitudes toward healing. How then, they ask, were women suppressed as health workers in the development of a male-dominated profession?

In uncovering the political, religious, and economic reasons for medieval witch-hunts, Ehrenreich and English present a picture of witches as peasant women healers. With the rise of the European medical profession and the exclusion of women from universities, both by rule and by economics, independent women healers could be seen as witches. Precisely as women—seen as seductive, lusty, and the reason for man's fall from grace; and not educated in university-based medical study, thereby healing by the power of evil—female healers were accused, tried, and burned at the stake.

In the early nineteenth century United States, midwives and folk healers as well as other practitioners held sway. Women's place in medicine centered on a people's medicine. They employed primarily mild herbal medications, dietary suggestions, and personal support for their patients, while the "regulars" in medicine preferred "heroic" measures, such as bloodletting and surgery. Religious arguments concerning the "nature of woman," economic considerations with regard to paying clientele, and political considerations linked to power were bolstered by arguments about biological destiny and the technical superiority of males. With the rise of medical schools, women, barred from medical study, formed their own schools. Upon graduation, they were still barred from internships and from membership in medical associations. By the early part of the twentieth century, midwives were eventually outlawed, most of the women's medical schools were closed, and the loss in the percentage of female physicians was not to be regained until the 1950's and 1960's. The nurse was the role left to women, an ancillary role for the woman healer.

The beauty of this book lies not only in its content but also in its form. Its clarity and pointedness in presenting the similarities between the witch burnings and the exclusion of women from medicine in the nineteenth and early twentieth century allow the reader to see the differences in approach and argumentation between the two eras. These differences tend to point up the double binds in which numbers of women in the healing professions still find themselves. While the work is a concise forty-seven pages, it is sweeping in approach and eminently readable; it is also interspersed with illustrations that lend to the overall feel, scope, and meaning of the text. While the book is scholarly in its conclusions, it is not so overly documented as to break the reader's attention and sense of flow. It provides a two-page bibliography indicating some of the classic works from which the authors draw their conclusions, such as *The Malleus Maleficarum* (1486) and what has been called *The Flexner Report* (1910). The gift of this book lies in its balance among scholarship, women's experience, and a call to action.

Analysis

In keeping with their sense that women's knowledge of their own history is the beginning of their opportunity to take up the struggle again, Ehrenreich and English provide two clear, readable, historic foci of women's story as health workers and uncover a history long suppressed. Written in 1973, this history not only recovered women's story as unlicensed doctors, midwives, anatomists, pharmacists, nurses, and counselors but also provided some explanation for women's contemporary experiences of facelessness and subservience in the healing professions. It pointed to women's situation as a majority of numbers with a minority of power in the health fields.

The book places this subservience within the context of a male takeover of the previously female leadership of health care, a takeover tied to larger sex and class struggles. Ehrenreich and English see the four centuries of witch-hunting as an ongoing movement by church and state to drive the "wise women" from the realm of healing. To the church, the witches' understanding of herbs, drugs, and anatomy and their use of their senses for information threatened doctrinal, misogynist, and antisexual teachings. To the state, the "wise women" may have represented organized communication networks of peasant women who were dissidents as well as healers. The medieval university-trained doctors, male and upper class, were the main beneficiaries of the witch-hunting purges that drove women out of medicine. The authors place the burning of witches in classist and sexist categories, giving fragmentary evidence that some of the women were involved in the peasant rebellions of the time.

In the nineteenth century United States, where medical practice had been traditionally open to anyone who could demonstrate healing skills, the male takeover started later but ultimately went much further. Although an early attempt by formally trained doctors to monopolize medicine by posing professionalism as an alternative to lay practice was met with indignation in the form of a popular health movement, the "regulars" eventually won the day. The popular health movement converged with the feminist movement in the 1830's and 1840's. The "irregulars," mostly lay practitioners and midwives, were seen as unscientific at a time when healing had little or no scientific foundation. By the beginning of the twentieth century, the "regulars" had European science and American ruling class power and money available to help them monopolize the medical profession. Medicine, now requiring lengthy and expensive higher education and training, became the preserve of wealthy white males. Nursing, invented by upper-class women reformers for improving hospital conditions, evolved into an elaborate set of subservient caring roles based on the Victorian notion of femininity.

In their historical approach and social critique, Ehrenreich and English uncover some of the mystique of "science" by lifting some of its disguises of power. They also lift the veil that had fallen over women's place in healing, providing an opportunity for women to reexperience pride in their contributions to curing and caring and providing an opportunity for women to learn from history.

The authors provide the seeds of a sociological analysis of the class systems that support male power and have been institutionalized in the male-dominated practice of medicine. They find that the deep-rooted nature of sexism is older than medical science itself but that it redrew its arguments in terms of biology and medicine. They point out the inconsistencies, both in terms of scientific logic and in terms of theories of "women's innate nature," in the arguments for excluding women from healing roles and relegating them to subservient ones by clarifying the shift in stereotypes used for making the same exclusionary arguments. They make a clear connection between the rise of the medical profession in the United States as part of the nineteenth century struggles around power vis-à-vis class and sex and the peak of the popular health movement coinciding with the beginnings of the feminist movement.

Drawing a clear set of distinctions between professionalism and expertise, Ehrenreich and English encourage women to challenge science rather than to be mystified by it. They encourage an open-eyed approach to the monopoly of scientific knowledge with a goal of opening medicine to all women, rather than merely opening the medical profession to women. They accomplish this by breaking down the distinctions between women as health care workers and women as health care consumers.

Context

The material in *Witches, Midwives, and Nurses* came from the authors' research and ideas for their course on women and health at State University of New York, Old Westbury. Published in 1973 by the Feminist Press, *Witches, Midwives, and Nurses* and its companion piece, *Complaints and Disorders: The Sexual Politics of Sickness* (1973), made ties between previous research and new possibilities. The authors' approach to women's history in healing opened the way for a significant amount of detailed research to come, beginning in the late 1970's. Their books provided scholarly conclusions in a style which invited a wide variety of readers to grasp, enjoy, and be moved by the recovered history and the logical and sociological critique.

Neither professional historians nor social scientists, Ehrenreich and English presented a fresh view at a time when a women's health movement in the United States was gathering and growing as a precisely feminist phenomenon. Both pieces received diverse responses from varying types of groups. The books became not only the bases for discussion in grass-roots and consciousness-raising groups but also texts on reading lists in nursing schools and women's studies programs. By 1974, when Ehrenreich and English began their book *For Her Own Good: One Hundred Fifty Years of the Experts' Advice to Women* (1979), there had been an amazing growth in women's studies programs. The women's health movement was moving toward self-help, lay midwifery, and expanded networking.

These first two pamphlets from the Feminist Press encouraged the movement for women's health and provided a mirror in which female health care workers could see themselves. They evoked a new moral force growing in consciousness-raising groups and led to women seeking increased knowledge concerning questions of their own health care (such as the pill, IUDs, hysterectomies, cesarean sections, and hormonal treatments), eventually giving rise to women's clinics and health care centers. By 1976, the Boston Health Collective's *Our Bodies, Ourselves* (2d ed., 1976) was published, as well as Adrienne Rich's *Of Woman Born: Motherhood as Experience and Institution* (1976). Feminist critiques of medical practices, as well as feminist social analysis and feminist alternatives, were on a path of growth.

Sources for Further Study

Abram, Ruth J., ed. *"Send Us a Lady Physician": Women Doctors in America, 1835-1920.* New York: W. W. Norton, 1985. A collection of essays that explore in greater detail some of the ideas presented by Ehrenreich and English. The essays present the professionalization of medicine in nineteenth century United States, women's entrance into the medical profession, and the reason for the decline in the percentage of women physicians at the end of the nineteenth century.

Achterberg, Jeanne. *Woman as Healer.* Boston: Shambala, 1990. A survey of women's healing activities from prehistory to 1990. The chapters "Fate of the Wise Women" and "Professionalization of the Healing Arts" are particularly pertinent.

Hubbard, Ruth. *The Politics of Women's Biology.* New Brunswick, N.J.: Rutgers University Press, 1990. An exploration of the relationship between science and political decision making. Hubbard finds "women's biology" to be a social construct and a political concept rather than a scientific one. She mentions pertinent nineteenth century data with regard to women's attempts at access to higher education.

Sherwin, Susan. *No Longer Patient.* Philadelphia: Temple University Press, 1992. A feminist approach to bioethics. The author shows that a feminist ethics of health care must ask its questions regarding health care practices with attention to the overall power structures of dominance and subordination. Chapter 9 considers how the construction of a medicalized view of women's experience assumes proprietorship over women's lives.

Todd, Alexandra Dundas. *Intimate Adversaries: Cultural Conflict Between Doctors and Women Patients.* Philadelphia: University of Pennsylvania Press, 1989. Based on a two-and-a-half-year study of audiotaped and observed conversations between gynecologists and women patients. Todd examines doctor-patient relationships with a focus on the woman patient.

Frances R. Belmonte

WOMAN AND NATURE: The Roaring Inside Her

Author: Susan Griffin (1943-)
Type of work: Social criticism
First published: 1978

Form and Content

Susan Griffin's *Woman and Nature: The Roaring Inside Her* is the result of a lecture that Griffin was asked to deliver on women and ecology, and is, in its author's words, "an unconventional book." Juxtaposing the objective, authoritative, and detached voice of patriarchy with the emotional, initially tentative, and collective voices of women, Griffin posits a dialogue between these voices that reveals the significance of cultural and gender-based points of view regarding nature. By refusing to be limited by literary conventions commonly associated with prose, Griffin manages to blend the genres of prose and poetry in a critique of the relationships between Western civilization and nature, between men and women, and between objectivity and emotion.

Woman and Nature explores the traditional Western identification of woman with Earth and, in this sense, is a cultural anthropology chronicling the attitudes surrounding this identification. Griffin's extensive research ranges from philosopher Plato to psychologist Sigmund Freud, from novelist Charlotte Perkins Gilman to poet Adrienne Rich, and the illustrations that she provides from her research result in the inclusion of many voices. The two predominating voices in the book—that of patriarchy and that of the "other," notably woman—are indicated by different type-styles both to represent the dialogue between the two voices visually and to allow the reader to see how differences in language result in profound differences in relationships with nature. Pairing these disparate viewpoints lets Griffin display and describe a completely different way of seeing the natural world that she believes is largely associated with the feminine and is, finally, incontrovertible.

Griffin begins *Woman and Nature* by tracing the history of patriarchal ideas about the nature of matter and arranges these ideas and judgments alongside patriarchal comments about the nature of woman. In "Matter," the first of four "books," Griffin discusses the land, timber, cows, and other bodies (including the female body), as well as the very nature of matter itself. The analogies drawn here between woman and nature extend throughout the other books ("Separation," "Passage," and "Her Vision") as well as in the section entitled "Matter Revisited." Griffin initially thought of the form of the book as being that of a mirror which would reflect, in reverse order, the differences in describing and seeing as ascribed to the patriarchal and to the female. Yet as Griffin notes in her preface, " 'Her Vision' would not be so constricted." Written associatively rather than narratively, *Woman and Nature* utilizes insightful associations to mirror cultural attitudes about woman, history, literature, agriculture, and nature. Griffin's expansive notes and bibliography at the end of the book disclose how widely the issues that she raises range—from gynecology textbooks to office manuals—and are provocative in and of themselves.

Analysis

In *Woman and Nature*, Griffin catalogs how Western patriarchal attitudes are embodied in the language that science, commerce, and the arts generally use to describe and comprehend the natural world. This language is not neutral or value-free. The section that begins *Woman and Nature* is entitled "Matter" and immediately adopts a distanced, authoritative, and judgmental tone that is a "parody of a voice with such presumptions." One of the two voices that dominate the entire text, this voice implies that it alone is in possession of absolute truths and "recognized opinion." The voice of patriarchy is realized by Griffin's use of impersonal pronouns and declarative sentence structure ("It is said") as well as by passionless descriptions of very personal and passionate events, such as a breast operation or a clitoral excision: "The mass is exorcised. Tissue posterior to it is sectioned. Deep sutures are tied as the pins are removed." Additionally, the voice of patriarchy is represented in a standard typeface, unlike the words of woman, which are represented in italic and intervene in the spaces left by patriarchal language. As Griffin's text develops, the language of woman appears more and more frequently as well as more forcefully, eventually appropriating the text itself.

"Matter" is the longest section and sets up the dichotomies between the voices and the content of those voices that pervade the entire work. Among the analogies that Griffin offers to the reader are the comparisons of the selection of trees for timber and the perfect office worker or of women's bodies and those of horses or cows. For example, Griffin links such seemingly dissimilar "animals" as women and mules when she writes: "*And we know we are not logical.* The mule balks for no apparent reason. For no rhyme or reason. *We remember weeping suddenly for no good reason*." As a result, both women and mules need to be controlled by the more objective and rational males, who apparently do not "balk" without an "apparent" or "good" reason.

After exploring the development of the patriarchal viewpoint regarding "matter," Griffin's next section, entitled "Separation," considers the implications of the many kinds of separation developing from and required by patriarchy. Like the other sections that make up *Woman and Nature*, book 2 begins with a citation from a woman, in this case Emily Dickinson's "I felt a Cleaving in my Mind—." All that follows chronicles the separations of body from mind, from distance, from time, from soul. "Separation" begins with a hysterectomy and moves on to enumerate and protest these separations from self and the world, separations that Griffin declares are required to survive in patriarchy. The dire consequences of such separation provide one of Griffin's major themes, and according to the evidence that Griffin has marshaled, these consequences have had a calamitous impact on Western culture. An example of this can be observed in the dividing up of time and space into increments that can be measured and thus controlled in an attempt to "keep watch" over chaos. Book 2 ends with a section called "Terror," which attests that what is known through patriarchy is really not certain and thus leads to terror and to the unknown.

Book 3, named "Passages," is the shortest section of *Woman and Nature*. Only seven pages in length, this book is subtitled "Her Journey Through the Labyrinth to the Cave Where She Has Her Vision." In essence, this section of the work is a leap—although a painful one—from the distanced language and isolated point of view of the patriarchy to the personalized, collective language of woman. In this section, for the first time, Griffin has the italicized language of woman supersede and replace the language of received thought, of separation, of patriarchy. This book is where the vision of nature shifts from one of control and fear to one of identification and re-vision. Instead of the labyrinth provoking fear as in the Greek myth, it invokes possibility: *"The rectangular shape of his book of knowledge, bending."* Ironically, perhaps, book 3 separates the slowly evolving feminine consciousness from the rigid, fearful patriarchal consciousness.

Book 4 is "Her" vision, and woman's vision prevails in this section; the world is no longer "his." This portion of *Woman and Nature* revises the world vision to embrace such ideas as "Mystery," "Our Dreams," and "Transformation." Subtitled "The Separate Rejoined," this book scrutinizes what Griffin calls a "New Space" and a "New Time" (as well as "Flying," "Deviling," "Dancing," and "Animals Familiar") and reunites the parts of the soul and mind that were divided by the male-dominated view of the world. She becomes "The Lion in the Den of the Prophets," and "devours them." As Griffin notes in her preface, however, "Her Vision" will not be constrained, and the response to the patriarchy spills over into another section entitled "Matter Revisited." Griffin rewrites "The Anatomy Lesson" from an earlier section of "Separation" and reveals the female body to be a witness to personal strength while tracing the history of female desire, intelligence, and possibility: *"we know what we know."*

Throughout *Woman and Nature*, Griffin resists a purely linear development of her themes of separation, isolation, patriarchal oppression, female silence, and the collective nature of woman's voice. Instead, she is recursive, layered, and complex in the ways in which she unfolds her critiques. Additionally, Griffin is very careful to let the language of the patriarchy speak for itself, and it is only when the reader reconsiders received and conventionally accepted language in the light of the more reticent language of woman as represented in *Woman and Nature* that the conflicts in perception become clear. By mixing genres—the section called "Dancing," for example, is written as a poem—and using the cumulative effects of the varying typefaces, quotations, and "official" and personal languages, Griffin manages to build a sense of discomfort with notions of things as they are—or as readers have been told that they are by Western culture. It is ultimately this discomfort that Griffin channels into an alternative viewpoint based on women's ways of seeing and knowing.

Context

Although *Woman and Nature* was hailed as "extraordinary" (*Publishers Weekly*), "stirring" (*Library Journal*), and "visionary prediction" (*Ms.*), it is not poet Susan Griffin's best-known work. Griffin—who has won such awards as the Ina Coolbrith Award for Poetry, an Emmy Award, a National Endowment for the Arts (NEA) grant, and a Kentucky Foundation for Women grant—is perhaps best known for another work of social criticism, *Pornography and Silence: Culture's Revolt Against Nature* (1981). Griffin's scholarly interests also include the narrative techniques of Henry James and the nature of authorship. Much of Griffin's later thinking and writing, however, can be traced to many of the themes and the blendings of genre evident in *Woman and Nature*.

Like Mary Daly, whom Griffin acknowledges as an influence in her writing of *Woman and Nature*, Griffin seeks to rethink and reinvent the manner and the very words women use to name their own experiences. The resulting book is not conventional in its form or scope, but it is certainly a powerful statement and an indictment of the silencing of woman and of nature throughout Western thought. Griffin deliberately limits the scope of *Woman and Nature* to Western civilization, and she cites expansively from the traditional canons across centuries and national boundaries. By challenging literary conventions as well as received histories and interpretations, Griffin enables the reader of *Woman and Nature* to participate in a feminist revision of the Western worldview as she encourages female scholarship.

Sources for Further Study

Charney, Diane Joy. Review of *Woman and Nature: The Roaring Inside Her. Library Journal* 104 (February 1, 1979): 414. Charney gives a brief review of the book under the heading of "Social Science," summing up the main theme as being one of discoveries about the nature of matter in conjunction with man's opinions about the nature of woman.

Miner, Valerie. Review of *Woman and Nature: The Roaring Inside Her. Ms.* 7 (April, 1979): 85-86. In an extensive review of *Woman and Nature*, Miner discusses the "new words, tones and rhythm" of the book. Named an encouraging and helpful critic by Griffin in the "Acknowledgments" section of her book, Miner is a sensitive reader of the text who considers it to be a tour de force in places.

Spayde, Jon. Review of *A Chorus of Stones*, by Susan Griffin. *Utne Reader*, May/June, 1993, 120-121. Spayde reviews Griffin's *A Chorus of Stones: The Private Life of War* (1992), referring to *Woman and Nature* as "her harrowing history of Western ideas of womanhood."

Willis, Ellen. "Nature's Revenge." *The New York Times Book Review*, July 12, 1981, 9. While reviewing Griffin's *Pornography and Silence* and Andrea Dworkin's *Pornography: Men Possessing Women* (1981), Willis notes many of the techniques—the juxtaposition of conflicting viewpoints and the blending of genres—that Griffin made use of in her earlier work, *Woman and Nature*.

Virginia Dumont-Poston

WOMAN AS FORCE IN HISTORY: A Study in Traditions and Realities

Author: Mary Ritter Beard (1876-1958)
Type of work: History
Time of work: From ancient times to the twentieth century
Locale: Greece, Rome, Europe, and the United States
First published: 1946

Principal personages:

Sir William Blackstone, an eighteenth century authority on English common law and its effects on women

Pearl Buck, an author who compared the roles of Chinese and American women

Elizabeth Cady Stanton, an early advocate of suffrage and equal rights for women

Joseph Story, an authority on equity jurisprudence

Mary Wollstonecraft, an advocate of women's rights in England

Form and Content

As a result of many years of historical research and writing with her husband, Charles A. Beard, Mary Ritter Beard cultivated a deep desire to examine the role of women in history; *Woman as Force in History: A Study in Traditions and Realities* is the fulfillment of that desire. Although the author assumed that a difference existed between the traditions and realities of women's role in history, she made no attempt to reach definite conclusions.

Throughout the book, Beard analyzes the impact of Anglo-American common law and its major exponent, Sir William Blackstone, on the position of women in a male-dominated society. The basic starting point for Beard was to see if women had been in absolute subjection to men in reality or only in tradition. She reviewed the century after the first women's rights assembly in America, the Seneca Falls Convention organized by Elizabeth Cady Stanton and Lucretia Mott in 1848. Beard's goal was to see if subjection was real, and if it was, to see if total equality based on equity jurisprudence was the answer.

Woman as Force in History traces the attitudes of both men and women concerning woman's role in history. The author reveals the sins of omission as well as the sins of commission regarding the recognition of women's impact on the history of the world. Beard looks at various types of writers, such as sociologists, anthropologists, and psychologists, as well as historians, in search of their attitudes toward women. Being a historian herself, she criticizes that group for not giving proper recognition to the accomplishments of women. As an example, Beard uses the American History series volume *The Middle Period, 1817-1858* (1897), by John W. Burgess. Beard believes that the rare references to women by Burgess do not give an accurate picture of the influence of women in that critical period of American history. Burgess refers to a law in Virginia that severely penalized white women who cohabited with African American slaves, and the only women whom he mentions are a slaveowner named Mary Brown and a fugitive slave named Ellen Crafts. Yet he makes no mention of Harriet Beecher Stowe and other women who had an impact on that period.

Beard's long experience as a historian led her back to the Greco-Roman world as the beginning of the historical analysis of her work. She refers to such documents as Rome's *Twelve Tables*, written in the fifth century B.C., and the *Corpus Juris Civilis*, under the Byzantine emperor Justinian in the sixth century A.D. Beard then proceeds to a detailed look at women's role in the economic, social, educational, and intellectual life of medieval Europe. She uses her last chapter to analyze how women have affected history, as well as how that effect has been perceived by most male writers.

Woman as Force in History offers a good balance between fact and theory. Unsupported speculation is kept to a minimum, and Beard quotes freely from many sources to substantiate her text. She gives the reader of this work the opportunity to see the totality of the force that women have exerted throughout history.

Analysis

Throughout *Woman as Force in History*, Mary Beard seems to project the idea that if women had always been the victims of a masculine plot to hold them in a slavery of subjection, they would not have exerted the force in history that she believes they have. Although she sympathizes with the intent of the Declaration of Sentiments adopted at the Seneca Falls Convention in 1848, Beard does not fully accept its unqualified assertion that the masculine goal throughout history had been to maintain absolute tyranny over women. After rejecting the idea of a forced subjection, Beard proceeds to trace how the idea developed and how it was perceived by women in the nineteenth century such as Elizabeth Cady Stanton. The author then discusses how the concept of equality was developed and advocated as a cure for the perceived subjection.

Beard begins her work by describing the relationship between men and women as one of the most visible revolutionary movements of modern times. The book is better understood and much more significant when one considers that it was written with the shadows of such men as Adolph Hitler, Benito Mussolini, and Joseph Stalin looming in the background. Beard discusses the influence of women on the momentous events of that time.

The author first covers the force exerted on Russia by Nadejda Krupskaya, the wife of Vladimir Lenin, whose marriage to Lenin created a revolutionary partnership. Krupskaya is credited with being the driving force to include women's rights as a vital part of the Bolshevik agenda in 1917. The idealistic nature of Marxist communism made it impossible for Lenin to ignore that force, which Beard credits with much of the success of the Bolshevik revolution. Beard continues by describing the same impact of women on the success of Fascism in Italy under Mussolini, in Germany under Hitler, and in Spain under Francisco Franco. Beard specifically reveals how Hitler used the concept of women's rights to persuade women to support the Nazi Party, and how that support led to his initial success. The author then reveals how Hitler used the blind support of women to produce the army of soldiers that ignited a worldwide military conflagration in 1939.

In her chapters surveying various men and women writers, Beard gives the reader a broad overview of the perceived subjection of women. She reveals certain errors that perpetuated themselves to the point that even women writers such as Dr. Elizabeth Adams accepted them. One error was that since there are few records of women's education in Ancient Greece and Rome, such education was almost nonexistent. Beard accurately points out that a lack of historical record is not proof that something did not occur. Later in the book, she cites the example of Theano, the wife of the sixth century B.C. Greek philosopher Pythagoras, who was herself a highly educated and highly respected philosopher. Beard does not adequately recognize, however, that Theano was the exception and not the rule.

Beard is critical of historians as a group for not recognizing the force that women have been in history. Even when later social historians such as Arthur Schlesinger tried to correct this problem, they were uncertain, because of a lack of precedent, of how to do so. In support of women's role in shaping early American democracy, Beard quotes the French visitor Alexis de Tocqueville. In his book *Democracy in America* (1835), Tocqueville declared that if he were asked to name the one thing most responsible for the success of American democracy, his answer would be the superiority of American women.

Woman as Force in History gives the reader an excellent evaluation of Blackstone's *Commentaries on the Laws of England* (1765), the recognized authority on common law. Beard does not accept Blackstone's belief that English common law pronounced "civil death" on women when they married; by this, he meant that all of a woman's property became the property of her husband. Beard is equally critical of Blackstone's belief that common law judges could rule statutory laws null and void if they violated common reason. Beard appreciates the good intentions of Mary Wollstonecraft and her book *A Vindication of the Rights of Woman* (1792), but she is disappointed that Wollstonecraft accepted so much of Blackstone's work. Wollstonecraft recognized the power of women to move men, but Beard believes that she described and defended that power in a way that was degrading to women as a whole.

Much of *Woman as Force in History* is devoted to the improvement of American law over its English foundation. Most American colonies and later states modified unacceptable parts of English common law, including provisions relating to women, by statutory law. Unlike Blackstone, American leaders such as Thomas Jefferson declared that statutory law must always have precedence over common law. Throughout her book, Beard traces and partially rejects the argument that the answer to women's rights is equity jurisprudence. She recognizes that this jurisprudence through chancery courts can remedy much injustice to women, but she does not see it as a solution to every problem. Instead of seeking an overall solution, Beard continually returns to her basic belief that, in spite of centuries of neglect, women have exerted a major force in the history of the world.

Context

Woman as Force in History was one of the earliest attempts, particularly by a well-known historian, to study the impact of women throughout history. By its very nature, the book immediately became a controversial topic of conversation and literary criticism. Although advocates of women's rights applauded Beard's attempt to correct historical injustice to women, many did not accept her belief that female historical subjection was only a myth. They were also critical of Beard's rejection of legal equality as a means of correcting that subjection.

Professional historians greeted *Woman as Force in History* with varying degrees of skepticism and criticism. Most of their criticism was based on Beard's style of writing rather than on the content of the book. They believed that the work was too repetitious and included too many long quotations. Some thought that Beard should have made a greater effort to reach a conclusion in her study and to offer solutions. A few historians criticized what they perceived as Beard's errors in historical research. Predictions by the more optimistic that, in the future, major historical works would include more of the impact of women failed to materialize. More than twenty years later, *A World History* (1967), by William McNeill, listed only one woman in the index.

An earlier book by Beard, *On Understanding Women* (1931), covered many of the same points as *Woman as Force in History*, but with fewer historical illustrations. The two books are much more easily understood and have a greater impact when taken together. The books coauthored by Mary Beard and her husband, Charles A. Beard, also contribute to a better understanding of their combined denial of female subjection; these books include *The Rise of American Civilization* (1927) and *The American Spirit* (1942).

Like many controversial books, *Woman as Force in History*, after several years of neglect, experienced a revival of interest. A paperbound reissue in 1962 coincided with an increase of interest in women's rights. It enjoyed significant popularity well into the 1970's, and it has had a profound impact on the liberation of women in general.

Sources for Further Study

Beard, Mary Ritter, ed. *America Through Women's Eyes*. New York: Macmillan, 1933. This volume is a collection of writings by women covering various aspects of American history. Presents viewpoints on frontier life, the Civil War, industrialization, World War I, and other significant periods not found in most sources.

______________. *On Understanding Women*. Westport, Conn.: Greenwood Press, 1931. This earlier book by Beard is more philosophical in nature than *Woman as Force in History*. Nevertheless, it does include several illustrations of how women's role in life has been misunderstood over the centuries. Includes a good bibliography of other attempts to study the subject.

______________. *A Woman Making History: Mary Ritter Beard Through Her Letters*. Edited by Nancy F. Cott. New Haven, Conn.: Yale University Press, 1991. An anthology of some of the letters of Mary Beard. Beard did not want her letters published and therefore destroyed most before she died, but Cott secured enough to reveal much of what motivated Beard. Examines how Beard arrived at the title for *Woman as Force in History*.

Carroll, Berenice A., ed. *Liberating Women's History: Theoretical and Critical Essays*. Chicago: University of Illinois Press, 1976. An interesting source of writings evaluating historiography concerning women. Includes a critique of *Woman as Force in History* and other writings, some covering different time periods, including the medieval period.

Christie, Jane Johnstone. *The Advance of Women: From the Earliest Times to the Present*. Philadelphia: J. B. Lippincott, 1912. This interesting study was one of the first attempts in modern times to study the role of women in history. Christie is clear and strong in her criticism of the injustice committed by men against women over the centuries, but she offers few suggestions for improving conditions in the future.

Glenn L. Swygart

WOMAN ON THE EDGE OF TIME

Author: Marge Piercy (1936-)
Type of work: Novel
Type of plot: Science fiction
Time of plot: The late twentieth century, interspersed with visits to 2137
Locale: Several mental institutions in New York City and Mattapoisett, a village in Massachusetts
First published: 1976

Principal characters:

Connie (Consuelo Camacho Ramos), a Mexican American woman unfairly institutionalized as violent

Luciente, an androgynous visitor from the future, whose lovers include Jackrabbit and Bee

Dolly, Connie's niece, a prostitute

Gildina, an alternate version of either Connie or Dolly existing in a dystopian future

Sibyl, Connie's closest friend on the violent ward

Skip, another friend on the ward

Form and Content

Woman on the Edge of Time tells the story of Connie Ramos who, incarcerated in a mental institution, travels into a possible utopian future. Structurally, the novel alternates Connie's experiences on several mental wards with a series of visits to the future world of Mattapoisett, Massachusetts, in 2137. Moving from a false spring to a permanent winter, Connie enacts an ironic version of the hero's journey outlined by Joseph Campbell in *The Hero with a Thousand Faces* (1949). Luciente, Connie's guide, is the bright shadow of Connie's despair; Connie notes that Luciente's name in Spanish means "shining, brilliant, full of light." She provides the call to adventure, contacting Connie just before Connie wallops her niece's pimp, an act which takes her across the threshold of Bellevue hospital and into the "belly of the iron beast" to Rockover State.

During this time, Connie's trips to the future often mirror or compensate for aspects of her past or events on the ward. Her anguish at losing her daughter to adoption and her desire to once again live in a family are answered by her inclusion in Luciente's family and her contact with Luciente's daughter, Dawn. When an old woman on the ward dies, Connie attends the honored death of Sappho, a storyteller in the future. When her niece Dolly fails to show up for a visit, Connie attends a festival, sees one of Jackrabbit's holographs ("holis"), and has sex with Bee, a large, gentle black man who reminds her of Claud, her deceased lover.

At Rockover, Connie and her friends Sybil and Skip are selected for operations to experiment with chemical control of emotions; simultaneously, Connie learns that Luciente and her society are at war with the remnants of a multinational powerbase whose use of "robots or cybernauts" as fighters links them to Connie's doctors, who are trying to master the technology of brain control. After seeing how the implants depersonalize another patient, Alice, Connie plans and executes an escape. Caught and returned to custody, Connie watches as the surgery finally enables Skip to commit suicide. In the parallel universe of the future, Jackrabbit is killed while serving on defense.

Once Connie herself has the operation, her contacts with Luciente's world become increasingly muddled. An attempt to reach Mattapoisett catapults her into a negative version of the future, where she meets Gildina, the debased opposite of Luciente, who like Dolly is a prostitute. After a visit to attend Jackrabbit's wake, Connie decides to enlist as a fighter in the war against the mechanistic future, at one point flying in what she thinks is a battle against the soldiers of the future and finally deciding to carry the war into her own time by poisoning the hospital staff with the parathion that she steals from her brother's greenhouse. The novel ends with a series of excerpts from Connie's official files, revealing that she was permanently incarcerated at Rockover. By killing her doctors, however, she may have helped Luciente's future come into existence.

Analysis

An extended, feminist revision of Ken Kesey's *One Flew over the Cuckoo's Nest* (1962), *Woman on the Edge of Time* combines a critique of authoritarian institutions with one of the most fully realized feminist utopias. Connie's visits to Luciente's world map out systematic alternatives to the abuses of power that she suffers as a patient and as a middle-aged, poor, Chicana single mother. These visits explore three interrelated categories of concern shared by all Piercy's work: a Marxist critique of economically based power hierarchies; a feminist critique of sex roles, gender inequities, and child-rearing practices; and a humanist critique of scientific ignorance of and disregard for the ecological unity of the human mind and the natural environment. As one of Luciente's family members explains, "the original division of labor" between men and women enabled "later divvies into have and have-nots, powerful and powerless, enjoyers and workers, rapists and victims. The patriarchal mind/body split turned the body to machine and the rest of the universe into booty on which the will could run rampant."

Luciente's world functions as a classless utopia whose equal distribution of labor and wealth emphasizes the importance of productive, meaningful work and indicts excessive consumption. Rejecting capitalism, they no longer buy or sell anything; they have "dumped the jobs telling people what to do, counting money and moving it about." Concentration of wealth and power in the hands of a privileged few is a central evil in every reality of the book. Luciente explains that "the force that destroyed so many races of beings, human and animal . . . was profit-oriented greed." It is the remnants of these greedy profiteers whom Luciente and her friends are battling; the misogynistic alternate reality of Gildina is run by "the richies" whom she names as "the Rockemellons, the Morganfords, the Duke-Ponts."

Luciente's future lacks not only classes but also gender hierarchies. Sex roles as Connie suffers under them are nonexistent, eliminated along with motherhood. Children are no longer born by women. Incubated in a "brooder," each child has three genetically unrelated "comothers," at least two of whom, regardless of sex, take hormone treatments that allow them to nurse. Initially repulsed by the sexual arrangements of the future, Connie hates the brooder, seeing the whole process as mechanistic reduction of children to animals. Yet despite her rage at the sight of a man breast-feeding, she finally concludes that this future fulfills her fantasy of "a better world for the children," wishing passionately that her daughter Angelina could grow up as strong, proud, and unafraid as Luciente's children.

Children in Luciente's world are allowed to explore the full range of their human potential. Nurturing mind in body, the culture educates "the senses, the imagination, the social being, the muscles, the nervous system, the intuition, the sense of beauty—as well as memory and intellect." Jackrabbit lists their priorities: They have tried to learn from "cultures that dealt well with handling conflict, promoting cooperation, coming of age, growing a sense of community, getting sick, aging, going mad, dying." Educational practices and initiation and healing rituals to deal with each of these life tasks are drawn with rich pragmatic detail during Connie's visits.

The future's holistic attitude toward the individual parallels their sense of connection to the natural world. Following the heritage of the American Indians, they "put a lot of work into feeding everybody without destroying the soil." Although they can automate whole factories, they use technology mainly for inhumanly mindless tasks. An Earth Advocate and an Animal Advocate sit on all planning councils, making sure human needs are balanced with those of the biosphere.

Life in Mattapoisett is thus a point-by-point refutation of the power structure of Connie's world where "the whole social-pigeonholing establishment" routinely reduces individuals to a category of disease, subjecting them to the absolute whim of doctors who try to manipulate the human mind while knowing almost nothing about it. Instead, Piercy crafts a culture which can accept idiosyncracy and conflict, a place where individual differences and emotions are understood and honored, where the care and nurturing of children is the central task of families supported by a unified community, and where everyone lives in a balance of useful work and creative play. Even if Connie's trips to the future are all hallucinations, the reality that she creates is saner than the world that her doctors control.

Context

Written after Piercy's two most explicitly feminist works, *Small Changes* and *To Be of Use*, both published in 1973, *Woman on the Edge of Time* details many of the same women's issues: the trauma of illegal abortion and rape, the self-abasement required by conventional gender roles, the pain and anger of mother-daughter relationships, the need to extend the nuclear family, the difficult loyalties of female friendships, and the humane recognition of alternatives to heterosexuality. Its most important contributions to feminism, however, lie in its status as a heterosexual feminist utopia, its invention of a richly nonsexist language for describing human emotions, and its imaginative embodiment of alternative motherhood.

Piercy's theoretical foundation in Marxism and practical experience in community activism makes hers one of the most rigorously conceived of all feminist utopias. Luciente's wry acknowledgement that governing by consensus means spending endless time in meetings, as well as the finely dramatized details of the "worming" process by which the community helps her resolve her conflicts with one of Jackrabbit's other lovers, are renditions of the politics of consciousness-raising groups. Another index of the novel's realism is its genial inclusion of men. Most of the works to which the novel is usually compared—Charlotte Perkins Gilman's *Herland* (1915), Joanna Russ's *The Female Man* (1975), Suzy Charnas' *Motherlines* (1978), and Sally Gearheart's *The Wanderground* (1979)—posit separatist worlds where men have ceased to exist or appear only occasionally for necessary breeding.

Piercy's poetic ear also enriches feminist dimensions of the novel. While the invention of the gender-neutral pronoun "per" is one obvious answer to linguistic sexism, a more subtle corrective is supplied by the metaphorical richness of Luciente's language, particularly its strong, kinetic verbs such as "inknow," (to sense body-mind connections), "graze" (to contact mentally), "paint the bones" (to use euphemisms), "bottom" (to feel depressed), "grasp" (to understand), and "sling" (to criticize).

The most revolutionary of Piercy's innovations, however, is the elimination of motherhood, a literal extrapolation of Shulamith Firestone's call in *The Dialectic of Sex: The Case for Feminist Revolution* (1970) for women to socialize the technologies of biological reproduction so that they will no longer be physically or psychologically responsible for child care. Also incorporating Juliet Mitchell's emphasis in *Woman's Estate* (1971) on the need for corollary revolutions in women's work, sexual freedom, and child-rearing practices, Piercy confronts the dilemmas of mothering contemporaneously outlined in Adrienne Rich's *Of Woman Born: Motherhood as Experience and Institution* (1976) and Dorothy Dinnerstein's *The Mermaid and the Minotaur: Sexual Arrangements and Human Malaise* (1977). The solution of Luciente's world—"So we all became mothers"—anticipates Nancy Chodorow's *The Reproduction of Mothering: Psychoanalysis and the Sociology of Gender* (1978) in suggesting that women will not achieve sexual equality until men are "humanized to be loving and tender" by fully participating in child rearing.

Sources for Further Study

Adams, Karen C. "The Utopian Vision of Marge Piercy in *Woman on the Edge of Time*." In *Ways of Knowing: Essays on Marge Piercy*, edited by Sue Walker and Eugenie Hamner. Mobile, Ala.: Negative Capability, 1991. A good general introduction, this essay summarizes the novel as a feminist utopia, comparing its central concerns with those in Charlotte Perkins Gilman's *Herland*.

Bartkowski, Frances. *Feminist Utopias*. Lincoln: University of Nebraska Press, 1989. Chapter 2, "The Kinship Web," compares Piercy's novel to Joanna Russ's *The Female Man*, discussing utopian conventions and placing the novel in the context of feminist and Marxist critiques. Good on the use of language and the role of the artist.

Gygax, Franziska. "Demur—You're Straightway Dangerous: *Woman on the Edge of Time*." In *Ways of Knowing: Essays on Marge Piercy*, edited by Sue Walker and Eugenie Hamner. Mobile, Ala.: Negative Capability, 1991. Emphasizes psychiatric critique, mentioning Piercy's involvement with the Mental Patients Liberation Front and her familiarity with the work of Phyllis Chessler. A psychological analysis of androgyny in the novel compares it to works by Adrienne Rich and Doris Lessing.

Kessler, Carol Farley. "*Woman on the Edge of Time*: A Novel 'To Be of Use.' " *Extrapolation* 28, no. 4 (Winter, 1987): 310-318. Stressing the didactic function of Piercy's novel, examines communal, ecological, and spiritual values, arguing that the violent conclusion of the novel is a call for reader involvement.

Pearson, Carol. "Coming Home: Four Feminist Utopias and Patriarchal Experience." In *Future Females*, edited by Marleen S. Barr. Bowling Green, Ohio: Bowling Green State University Popular Press, 1981. A revision of "Women's Fantasies and Feminist Utopias" in

Frontiers 2, no. 3 (Fall, 1977): 50-61. The original article places Piercy's *Woman on the Edge of Time* in the tradition of feminist utopias such as those by Joanna Russ, Ursula Le Guin, James Tiptree, Mary Bradley Lane, Charlotte Perkins Gilman, Dorothy Bryant, and Mary Staton (only the last four are discussed in the revision), systematically discussing their similar treatments of women's work, violence against women, sex roles, and the need to revolutionize economic structures, the nuclear family, and societal attitudes toward nature.

Rosinsky, Natalie. *Feminist Futures: Contemporary Women's Speculative Fiction*. Ann Arbor, Mich.: UMI Research Press, 1984. Chapter 3, "Battle of the Sexes," contrasts Piercy and Joanna Russ's advocation of androgyny with Sally Gearheart's separatism in *The Wanderground*. Noting the humorous, ironic elements of Piercy's novel, Rosinsky analyzes the flexibility of Piercy's feminist solutions.

Elisa Kay Sparks

THE WOMAN WARRIOR: Memoirs of a Girlhood Among Ghosts

Author: Maxine Hong Kingston (1940-)
Type of work: Memoir
Time of work: The mythic past and the twentieth century
Locale: China, New York, and California
First published: 1976

Principal personages:

Maxine Hong Kingston, the American daughter of Chinese immigrants who tries to make sense of her dual heritage
Brave Orchid, her mother, a doctor and a ghost fighter in China
Moon Orchid, Brave Orchid's sister
No Name Woman, Maxine's father's sister, who kills herself and her illegitimate child
Fa Mu Lan, the legendary Chinese woman warrior
Ts'ai Yen, a Chinese woman who was scholar, poet, and musician

Form and Content

In *The Woman Warrior: Memoirs of a Girlhood Among Ghosts*, Maxine Hong Kingston presents a series of mythic and autobiographic stories that illuminate the way in which the author must deal with the sexism and racism in her world. As a young Chinese American girl, who is called such racist names as "gook" and who is repeatedly told such misogynist Chinese sayings as "girls are maggots in the rice" by her own parents, Kingston feels alienated both from the dominant American culture and from the male-dominated Chinese culture. In her memoirs, Kingston tells of her search for women role models, interweaving imaginative stories concerning such characters as Fa Mu Lan, a Chinese woman warrior, with memories of her own relationship with her strong-willed mother, Brave Orchid. Through these various stories, the narrator searches to affirm her Chinese American female identity in the context of her bicultural world.

The narrator begins her autobiography with her mother telling her a cautionary tale about her Chinese aunt, whom Kingston calls the No Name Woman. Her married aunt, who became pregnant from an illicit affair, incurs the wrath of the Chinese villagers, who attack her family's house. Her aunt gives birth to her child and drowns both herself and the child in the family well. Kingston calls her aunt "No Name Woman" because her family, blaming the aunt for the shame that she brought to them, deliberately attempts to erase her from the family's memory. Although Brave Orchid warns Maxine not to repeat her aunt's story, Maxine uses the story as a catalyst for her creative imagination. Maxine attempts to imagine her aunt's reason for adultery: Was she in love? Was she raped? Most important, she tries to transform her aunt from a mere object lesson—of misguided passion punished by communal wrath—into a human being who should not be forgotten by the family.

Yet Brave Orchid tells Maxine stories not only of women who have been ostracized by a punitive feudal community but also of powerful women such as Fa Mu Lan, a Chinese woman warrior who saves her community. Fa Mu Lan serves as a central inspiration for Maxine who, in her imagination, becomes the woman warrior fighting battles to right the wrongs perpetrated against her people. Although she fantasizes that she is like the woman warrior who fights tyrants, Maxine acknowledges her own limitations in her everyday life; when she attempts to challenge her boss's racist comments, he simply ignores her "bad, small-person's voice."

In the latter part of her autobiography, Kingston turns her attention to the life of Brave Orchid, who acts as both an adversary and a role model for her. She depicts two ostensibly conflicting pictures of her mother. On the one hand, her mother, who married her husband right before he left for the United States, lives an independent life in China, going to medical school and becoming a doctor. On the other hand, when she goes to the United States years later to be with her husband, she reverts back to the traditional role of wife. Nevertheless, Kingston's strong-willed mother stands in stark contrast to Brave Orchid's sister, Moon Orchid, who comes to the United States after being separated from her husband for three decades. Brave Orchid commands Moon Orchid to insist that her husband, who has taken another wife, recognize her role as "first wife." Instead, Moon Orchid's husband, now a successful American doctor, rejects her with a hostile stare. Unable to endure her husband's rejection or to adapt to her new country, Moon Orchid becomes paranoid and eventually insane.

Although Brave Orchid is a powerful matriarchal figure, she ostensibly attempts to pass on patriarchal values to Maxine. Thus, in a key scene, Maxine verbally "battles" with her mother, in order to assert her own identity and autonomy. In the end, however, Maxine realizes that she and her mother—both born in the year of the dragon—have much in common; both are fighters and storytellers.

Analysis

In this work, Kingston explores the ways in which women can find their voices in patriarchal cultures that seek to silence them. Although Kingston begins her autobiography with her mother's injunction "not to tell," she breaks her silence in order to relate the story of No Name Woman and to begin a search for self-expression, finding ways to challenge sexist and racist oppression.

Kingston uses the stories of her two aunts—No Name Woman and Moon Orchid—to highlight the danger of silence, which Maxine associates with victimization and the loss of identity. Because of her illicit affair, No Name Woman's family blames her for the community's punitive actions and after her death attempts to forget her existence; they attempt to "silence" her by eradicating her very memory. When Moon Orchid confronts her unfaithful husband, he turns upon her and effectively silences her. Soon after, Moon Orchid becomes insane. Later, Maxine observes, "I thought talking and not talking made the difference between sanity and insanity. Insane people were the ones who couldn't explain themselves."

As an antidote to these "silenced" women, Maxine imagines the stories of powerful women such as Fa Mu Lan and Brave Orchid. While Fa Mu Lan is a woman warrior who fights to "right the wrongs" carved on her back by her parents, her independent mother Brave Orchid is a strong-willed matriarch, a "champion talker." There are ways, however, that both Fa Mu Lan and Brave Orchid perpetuate the values of patriarchal cultures. Fa Mu Lan is able to be a leader precisely because her followers assume that she is a man; when she finishes her fighting, she resumes the duties of the traditional Chinese wife and daughter. Although Brave Orchid lived an independent life as a doctor—a nontraditional role for a woman—in China, when she is reunited with her husband in America she resumes her traditional role as wife, bearing her husband six children and working long hours in a laundry. It is most significant, however, that she enculturates her daughter by passing on the misogynist sayings and antifemale cultural prejudices. Moreover, she cuts her daughter's frenulum, the membrane fold under the tongue—which Maxine interprets as an act of violation and repression. Although Brave Orchid later insists that she cut Maxine's frenulum precisely so that she would not be tongue-tied, Maxine, who believes that this act made her mute in school, accuses her mother of attempting to silence her.

Kingston believes that it is critical to claim her own voice, her own autonomy. In a climactic scene, the young Maxine challenges her mother in a shouting match, enacting a forbidden tirade against her mother, refusing to be a victim of silence. Yet she feels strangely dissatisfied with her verbal battle with her mother. She realizes that speech can also be used as an oppressive force—an agent of patriarchal rhetoric—to silence another. Kingston learns, in the end, not to privilege speech for its own sake. Although she sees the importance of speech as a means of self-expression, she also recognizes how speech can be used as a means of oppression.

In ending her autobiography with the story of Ts'ai Yen, Kingston is presenting a hopeful vision for the possibility of interethnic harmony and positive roles for women. Symbolically, Kingston is also relating a story of reconciliation, between her mother and herself, between the different cultures of America and China. Kingston learns of this story from her mother, but as she states, "The beginning is hers, the ending, mine." When the poet Ts'ai Yen was twenty, she was stolen by a barbarian chieftain from her people; while in captivity, she bore two children and created songs. After twelve years, she was ransomed from the barbarians, and she returned to China with her songs. Like Ts'ai Yen, Kingston learns to channel her anger against oppression into artistic acts—which, in Kingston's case, speak of the hope for racial and gender harmony. Like Ts'ai Yen's bicultural songs, Kingston's narrative crosses national boundaries; moreover, her work also crosses generic boundaries, those of autobiography, myth, history, fantasy, and folklore. Through her multiple stories, Kingston demonstrates that truth itself can be multiple; as she transcribes the Chinese oral tradition into written English, she believes that "it translates well."

Context

Although other Asian American women writers preceded her, Kingston was one of the first to garner national recognition, winning the National Book Critics Circle Award in 1976 for *The Woman Warrior*. Thus, she has been seen as a pioneer for other Asian American women writers who have succeeded her. Politically, Kingston's *The Woman Warrior* has excited interest not only because the work provides a feminist vision from a Chinese American woman's perspective but also because of the negative reaction that it has produced in such Chinese American men as Frank Chin.

On the one hand, Kingston provides a critique of a patriarchal and misogynist feudal China that can trap women in demeaning, slavelike roles, subject to such cultural practices as foot-binding. On the other hand, Kingston points out that the Chinese culture itself provides her with such powerful women role models as Fa Mu Lan and Ts'ai Yen. Out of this complex tradition, Kingston forges a bicultural self that will allow her to enact her own "woman warrior" identity in an American society with its own racist and patriarchal legacy.

Nevertheless, Chinese American playwright Frank Chin has criticized Kingston's work on the grounds that it propagates racist views of Chinese Americans. Interested in championing a Chinese heroic tradition to combat the often-emasculating vision that the dominant American culture has of Asian American men, Chin believes that Kingston's feminist views distort an authentic picture of China and Chinese Americans. Certainly, however, one can argue that Kingston's work is an autobiographic, not an ethnographic, study; Kingston is conveying her understanding of her mother's talk-stories, which reflect a living immigrant oral culture, not a series of static, "authentic" tales. Moreover, Kingston has reformulated male heroic traditions, highlighting the contributions of women to that tradition. Thus, Kingston's work broadens the concept of a Chinese mythos precisely because she embeds her hybrid American and feminist views within that tradition, claiming her own "woman warrior's" voice.

Sources for Further Study

Chan, Jeffrey Paul, Frank Chin, Lawson Fusao Inada, and Shawn Wong, eds. *The Big Aiiieeeee! An Anthology of Asian American Writers*. New York: New American Library/Meridian, 1991. Chin has accused *The Woman Warrior*, shaped by its feminist vision, of being a "fake book," providing an inauthentic picture of Chinese American history and catering to a racist American culture.

Cheung, King-Kok. *Articulate Silences: Hisaye Yamamoto, Maxine Hong Kingston, Joy Kogawa*. Ithaca, N.Y.: Cornell University Press, 1993. In her chapter on Kingston, Cheung notes the way in which historical and parental silence provokes the author to use her imagination to create possible versions of stories that her taciturn parents refuse to convey.

Johnson, Diane. *Terrorists and Novelists*. New York: Alfred A. Knopf, 1982. Comparing Kingston to Carobeth Laird and N. Scott Momaday, Johnson writes that *The Woman Warrior* is an "antiautobiography," a work which blurs the boundaries between fiction and autobiography. Johnson argues that Kingston, in challenging the "female condition," resists her culture in order to triumph over it.

Lim, Shirley Geok-lin, ed. *Approaches to Teaching Kingston's "The Woman Warrior."* New York: Modern Language Association, 1991. This collection of essays is an excellent source for cultural background and close readings of the text. Includes a helpful bibliographic essay, a personal statement from Kingston on *The Woman Warrior*, a section providing sociohistorical information to help readers better understand references to the Chinese American culture contained in the work, and close analyses of the text. Also highlights different approaches to the text, including feminist, postmodernist, and thematic approaches.

Ling, Amy. *Between Worlds: Women Writers of Chinese Ancestry*. New York: Pergamon, 1990. Ling locates Kingston's work within a historical tradition of Chinese

American writers. She highlights Kingston's need for "writing wrongs" by "writing about the wrongs."

Smith, Sidonie. *A Poetics of Women's Autobiography: Marginality and the Fictions of Self-Representation*. Bloomington: Indiana University Press, 1987. Smith notes the ways in which Kingston uses autobiography as a means of creating identity and breaking out of the silence that her culture imposes on her. She also states that *The Woman Warrior* is "an autobiography about women's autobiographical storytelling," emphasizing the relationship between genre and gender.

Sandra K. Stanley

THE WOMAN'S BIBLE

Author: Elizabeth Cady Stanton (1815-1902)
Type of work: Literary criticism
First published: 1895-1898

Form and Content

Struggling for women's rights in the nineteenth century, the early feminists were constantly told that the Bible ordains woman's sphere as helper to man and woman's status as inferior to man. Having heard this throughout her decades of labor in the women's rights movement, Elizabeth Cady Stanton determined in 1895 to investigate the Bible and what it really says about women. She attempted to obtain the assistance of a number of female scholars of Hebrew and Greek, but several turned her down, fearing that their reputations would be compromised. Other women were afraid to critique the Bible for religious reasons. Still others, Stanton notes in her introduction, did not want to bother with a book they felt was antiquated and of little importance.

She finally chose a committee of women she believed would make a valuable contribution, primarily based on her perception of their liberal ideas and ability to make sense out of what they read. This was the "Revising Committee" that shared billing with Stanton for the work. Stanton herself, however, wrote most of the commentary, and it contains her own beliefs and values.

When women struggling for their rights in the nineteenth century were referred to the Bible with the explanation that God ordained their inferior position, Stanton notes that there were a variety of responses. Some glossed over the most antiwoman aspects of the Bible and interpreted the rest liberally, thus maintaining their belief in its divine inspiration. Others noticed that biblical law, church law, and the English common law that was the basis of American jurisprudence in the nineteenth century all had a common theme and dismissed them all as human in origin. Still others simply accepted traditional interpretations and the belief that women's equality would be antireligious and dangerous to the home, the nation, and the church.

For herself, Stanton accepted that the Bible is a mixture of valuable principles of love, liberty, justice, and equality (as, she says, are the holy books of all religions) which at the same time includes passages that degrade women and make their emancipation impossible. One cannot, she says, accept or reject the Bible as a whole since, although it includes some divine, spiritual truths, it is a human book full of human error. Therefore, her goal was to analyze in detail the 10 percent of the book that she believed relevant to women.

The Woman's Bible is divided into two volumes. The first deals with the five books of the Pentateuch and the second all the other parts of the Bible upon which Stanton and her committee chose to comment. There are commentaries in the first part on Genesis, Exodus, Leviticus, Numbers, and Deuteronomy and in the second part on Joshua, Judges, Ruth, Samuel, Kings, Esther, Job, Psalms, Proverbs, Ecclesiastes, the Song of Solomon, Isaiah, Daniel, Micah, Malachi, and even the Kabbalah, a medieval Jewish mystical writing. This section also includes commentary on the New Testament books of Matthew, Mark, Luke, John, Acts, Romans, Corinthians, Timothy, Peter, the letters of John, and Revelation. All of the book is written by women, much of it by Elizabeth Cady Stanton herself.

Analysis

Stanton's own comments on the first chapter of Genesis provide an example of her radical understanding of the Scripture. Noting that in this Creation story there is divine consultation, and therefore seemingly a plurality of divine beings, and that the man and woman were both created in the image of God, Stanton concurs with other scholars that the Trinity is represented here. Rather than three male beings, however, it is more logically made up of divine Father, Mother, and Son. She then suggests that women's lot in life would be improved if prayers were offered to the Heavenly Mother as well as to the Heavenly Father.

The next author introduces the reader to what at the time was the height of scholarly biblical criticism: the division of the Pentateuch into several original sources that were later put together by an editor. Although her understanding of biblical sources is naïve and overly simplistic by modern standards, Ellen Batelle Dietrick's explanation that Genesis holds two separate stories of the Creation is accepted biblical scholarship today.

Finally for this passage, Lillie Devereux Blake presents another bit of logic by pointing out that one cannot assert that woman's creation after man in the second story signifies her inferiority without at the same time admitting that man is inferior to creeping things, since he was created after them in the first story.

Later in Genesis, Stanton finds one verse (36:18) on which to comment, and one sees here not only the kinds of insights that she had and questions that she raised but also an explanation of her approach to the biblical text. The verse simply names the three sons of Esau's wife Aholibamah. Stanton's first thought is to wonder who this woman was and why one does not learn any more of her. Stanton would like to know what she thought, what she said, what she did.

Then noting that some biblical interpreters try to find deep symbolic meanings in what she reads as simple records of a people, she admits that she herself is not versed in theories of biblical interpretation. If the Bible, she says, is meant to point the way to salvation, it does not make sense for it to require great symbolic interpretations in order to understand it, any more than road signs should require complicated symbolic interpretation. She therefore gives the reader fair warning that she intends to base her comments on the Bible as she reads it in plain English.

Stanton's comments frequently do not stick to the passage under discussion. Quite often, the passage merely serves as a spark to the exposition of an idea on the author's mind. For example, in her commentary on Exodus 32, wherein the jewelry of the Israelites (which Stanton assumes belonged mostly to the women) is melted down to make a golden calf, the primary lesson she draws is one about self-sacrifice. It is a virtue highly valued in women, she notes. She would rather teach women that self-development is a higher ideal. This was one of Stanton's primary themes throughout her life, and she finds several places to repeat it in this book, including here, even though it has very little to do with the story of the golden calf.

Stanton was also not above imaginative leaps into the ludicrous. In a discussion of Elijah's ascent into Heaven in a fiery chariot in I Kings 17, in all seriousness she conjectures that he rode a balloon. The perplexed widow who witnessed the ascent, she suggests, had no idea that he did not ascend all the way to Heaven but probably landed in some farmer's cornfield.

Stanton's dictum about the virtue of self-development is repeated in her discussion of the New Testament story of the widow's mite in Mark 12. To this woman who gave all she had to the temple, Stanton would like to say that sacrificing everything to a religious organization, neglecting her own self-development, is wrong.

These are only a few of the topics addressed by Stanton and the Revising Committee. The book ends with a selection of letters from still other women, responding to the questions of whether the Bible has advanced or retarded the emancipation of women, whether it has dignified or degraded them.

Context

After the publication of the first volume, one clergyman opined that "It is the work of women, and the devil." Stanton replied: "This is a grave mistake. His Satanic Majesty was not invited to join the Revising Committee, which consists of women alone." Stanton's stand in questioning the religious authority of the Bible and the beliefs about women which were based on it led to ridicule, vitriolic attacks by the clergy, and even a move by her fellow feminists in the suffrage movement. In 1896, against the impassioned advice of Stanton's friend Susan B. Anthony, even the National American Woman Suffrage Association repudiated any connection with *The Woman's Bible*, the official reason being the nonsectarian nature of the association.

The book was controversial by its very nature, since it attacked not only the Bible's use as an authority on which to base women's subordination but also its divine inspiration. For many years, Stanton's work was all but forgotten, existing chiefly in the attics of a few remaining supporters in the early twentieth century. With the revival of feminism in the late 1960's, however, interest in the book as a historical document was revived. It was reprinted in 1972 by Arno Press and also in 1974 by the Coalition Task Force on Women and Religion.

Although full of inaccuracies and quaint interpretations, the questions that Stanton raised were still important, and the arguments from the Bible for women's subordination could still be heard. Therefore, Stanton's interest in the portrayal of women in the Bible was also revived along with the twentieth century feminist movement. *The Woman's Bible* presaged a large number of scholarly works. Because more women have had the opportunity to become learned in biblical studies, these works are highly sophisticated and professional biblical scholarship when compared with Stanton's largely amateurish work. The names of Phyllis Trible, Phyllis Bird, Elizabeth Schussler Fiorenza, Alice Laffey, and Carol Meyers represent only a tiny sampling of the most well known of these biblical scholars. Their work stems from a similar concern about what the Bible really says about women.

Sources for Further Study

Banner, Lois W. *Elizabeth Cady Stanton: A Radical for Woman's Rights*. Boston: Little, Brown, 1980. This biography of Stanton covers the reformer's long and productive life, from her childhood through her marriage and years as a mother of seven, her organization of the first Women's Rights Convention of 1848, her association with Susan B. Anthony, and her continuing activism until her death in 1902.

Laffey, Alice L. *An Introduction to the Old Testament: A Feminist Perspective*. Philadelphia: Fortress Press, 1988. An example of modern biblical study. Laffey takes readers through the Old Testament/Hebrew Bible with analyses from a feminist point of view of both the texts and the cultural factors behind them. Although this work deals only with the Old Testament, it illustrates the kind of feminist biblical scholarship being done.

Oakley, Mary Ann B. *Elizabeth Cady Stanton*. Old Westbury, N.Y.: Feminist Press, 1972. Another biography of Stanton, this one is somewhat shorter than Lois Banner's (above). Written in a narrative style, including many conversational quotations. Takes the reader from Stanton's childhood in New York through her older years.

Stanton, Elizabeth Cady. *Elizabeth Cady Stanton*. Edited by Theodore Stanton and Harriet Stanton Blatch. 2 vols. New York: Arno Press, 1969. This set, compiled by two of her children, is the most complete work about Stanton's life. The first volume is a revision of her autobiography, published in 1898 under the title *Eighty Years and More*. The second volume begins with selections of her letters from 1839 to 1850 and ends with her diary from 1880 to her death in 1902.

Stanton, Elizabeth Cady, Susan B. Anthony, Matilda Jocelyn Gage, and Ida H. Harper, eds. *History of Woman Suffrage*. 6 vols. New York: Fowler and Wells, 1881-1922. Reprint. New York: Source Book Press, 1970. Originally a three-volume set which was later expanded by other editors to make a total of six. Offers a complete documentation of the struggle for women's suffrage, from the 1848 Women's Rights Convention to the final ratification of the Nineteenth Amendment granting women the vote in 1920. Speeches, reports, newspaper articles, letters, and other archival information, linked together with a running narrative by the authors.

Waggenspack, Beth Marie. *The Search for Self-Sovereignty: The Oratory of Elizabeth Cady Stanton*. New York: Greenwood Press, 1989. Part of a series on Great American Orators, this book takes readers directly into the work of Stanton as a public speaker. Although her career as an orator for women's rights was complicated both by the demands of her work in the home as a mother and by the opposition to women as public speakers, she nevertheless made many important speeches. The first part of this book discusses Stanton's life and work, and the second part reprints seven of her speeches. Complete with notes and an annotated bibliography.

Eleanor B. Amico

WOMEN AND MADNESS

Author: Phyllis Chesler (1940-)
Type of work: Social criticism
First published: 1972

Form and Content

Phyllis Chesler's *Women and Madness* is a feminist indictment of the male-dominated psycho-medical establishment. Chesler examines the gender-based power relations in psychology and psychiatry from many perspectives and uses many tools: statistical studies, transcripts of interviews, quotations from many sources, personal reminiscences, charts and graphs, illustrations, extensive (almost chatty) footnotes, tales from classical mythology, and free speculation. Throughout her investigation, she consistently finds that women have been oppressed by the power of male definitions of mental health and mental illness, of treatment and cure.

Chesler divides her book into two sections, "Madness" and "Women." In the first section, she considers the role of "madness" in the lives of four famous female mental patients: Elizabeth Packard (1816-c.1890), Ellen West (c.1890-1926), Zelda Fitzgerald (1900-1948), and Sylvia Plath (1932-1963). In trying to live authentically—faithful to her own light in terms of religion, artistic creativity, or simple physical energy and adventurousness—each of these women ran afoul of gender-based societal expectations and consequently found herself in the power of men in the psychiatric industry. Once identified as "patients," the women were then coached, coaxed, and coerced to mend their ways and return to the path of compliant wifedom. Chesler finds mental asylums, and most psychotherapy, to be bureaucratized extensions of the patriarchal family, carrying out the will of husbands of mostly female patient populations. Using epidemiological studies done by others, she demonstrates that the standard for mental health in Western society is not the same for men and women and that it is unfair to women.

In her first section, Chesler not only offers statistics and actual life stories of historical figures but also introduces Jungian tools: She recruits mythic presences into her discussion. She examines the figures of Demeter and her daughters, the Virgin Mary, and Joan of Arc for the ways in which they embody certain constellations of typical female experiences.

The second section of the book is dominated by the results of Chesler's informal interviews with sixty women. Her interview subjects were selected to represent five distinct groups: women who have sex with their therapists, who are confined to mental hospitals, who are lesbians, who are members of ethnic minority groups, and who are feminists in therapy. In each chapter concerning these issues, Chesler briefly describes the demographics of her interview group, gives transcripts from her interviews, and presents some general discussion of her results. She is careful to point out that her study population was not randomized, and she makes no claim that her interviews describe anything except the subjective experience of the group of women that she interviewed. From her eclectic, personal, and openly adversarial feminist perspective, Chesler raises many questions and advances many conclusions about the psychiatric establishment. In general, she finds that in a male-dominated society, treatment of the forms of deviance that are termed "mental illness" is necessarily patriarchal. In other words, male-dominated psychiatry and psychology stand to serve the tense and oppressive power relations that exist between men and women. Sex-role stereotypes exist for both men and women, but Chesler finds that women are allowed a much narrower margin of deviation from role than men before society labels them "mad." "Madness," according to Chesler, may consist in either going too far in acting out the devalued female role (passivity, indecisiveness, frigidity, or depression) or in rejecting one's sex-role stereotype altogether and venturing to show traits that are considered appropriate for the other gender.

Analysis

Women and Madness is organized around the central observation of the numerical gender imbalance in psychiatry: Most patients are women, but psychotherapy is in the control of men. Chesler documents both sides of this imbalance with statistics and considers why the field is so slanted in this particular direction. One possible explanation that she considers is the "help-seeking nature of the female role." Women, who are socialized to value connectedness and interdependence, may simply be more comfortable initiating relationships where they ask for and receive help and advice than are men, who are socialized to value independence, autonomy, and competitive victory. This greater comfort with "help-seeking" may manifest as a greater frequency of doctor visits.

Similarly, the parallels between psychiatric institutions and the nuclear family may make it easier for women than for men to switch from one to the other. Chesler suggests that the typical mental hospital is, dynamically speaking, a "family," with doctor-daddies, nurse-mommies, and female patients who return to the role of the "biologically owned child." In this role, the female patient is expected to be childlike in obedience and trust of her "elders." She is also expected to be childlike in another way: virginal in regard to her own needs but sexually exploitable by her therapist. The female mental patient's hospital role is congruent with her outside role (daughter and/or wife) in a way that the male patient's role is not.

Among Chesler's other plausible reasons for the preponderance of female mental patients is the objective, real-world oppression of women. Women's role as an oppressed caste may cause them to suffer greater stress, provoking greater numbers of psychiatric symptoms. Also, she notes that there has been a differentiation between the social response to extreme acting out of the male social role versus the female role. Male-style acting out—aggression and violence—is largely dealt with by the criminal justice system and not the mental health system. This leaves psychiatric hospitals full of people whose mode of acting out involves extremes of the female passive, dependent role—primarily women.

Perhaps the most significant factor in the overrepresentation of women in psychopathology statistics is the possibility that, in Western society, "mentally healthy" is defined to mean "male." To support this claim, Chesler cites a 1970 study in which a group of mental health professionals of both sexes were asked to complete personality profiles describing a healthy male, a healthy female, and a healthy adult of unspecified gender. It was discovered that the personality profile of an ideal healthy male was very similar to that of a healthy adult of unspecified gender, while the ideal of the healthy female was significantly different: more submissive, less adventurous, and less independent. This suggests that there is no way for a female to be socially defined as mentally healthy: If she fits the ideal of a healthy adult, then she deviates from the ideal of a healthy woman; if she fits the ideal of a healthy woman, then she must be less than fully adult. If this study truly represents the social norm of mental health, it would seem there is no way for women to win. Therefore, women must overwhelmingly outnumber men in psychiatric treatment; womanhood is deviance, by definition.

It should be noted that Chesler's consideration of the high rates of mental illness in women focuses purely on social factors. Never does she consider physiological factors. Biochemical imbalances, genetic predispositions, hormonal disturbances, neurological lesions, allergies, toxins, enlargements of the ventricles in the brain—many of the most active areas of neuropsychiatric research in the last quarter of the twentieth century—are not discussed.

Context

In the early 1970's, when Chesler's book appeared, there was a tremendous popularization of psychotherapy. The most significant impact of *Women and Madness* was to open this territory of psychiatry and psychotherapy for feminist exploration. By 1972, a number of biographical and autobiographical works had already appeared to detail individual women's struggles with insanity and the label of "insanity," notably Nancy Milford's *Zelda* (1970) and Sylvia Plath's *The Bell Jar* (1971). What was still lacking, however, was a broader discussion that would identify common patterns in these personal stories and situate them in a general social context. It was this gap that Chesler sought to fill with *Women and Madness*.

The book's publication was greeted with extremely mixed reviews, and it was not only opponents of feminism who quarreled with its stance. Chesler's exhortation that women take power was seen by some as a call to adopt the ways of the oppressor, instead of doing away with oppression—to simply substitute male madness for female. Some claimed that she romanticized madness itself and failed to distinguish between being identified as mad by others, feeling oneself to be mad, and truly being mad in some objective sense. Others criticized the book's emphatic attack stance, which failed to address the idea of reforming the field of psychiatry. The patchwork nature of the text—with epidemiological data loosely stitched to personal narrative and mythology to polemic—seemed to some critics poorly edited. Some accused her of misinterpretations and frank errors in her statistics. In addition, as was almost obligatory with feminist writers of the period, her tone was called "strident."

In spite of such criticism, *Women and Madness* was an influential book. Turning a feminist eye on the psychiatric industry was a productive move, even if the fruit that it bore may have been more polished in later hands. Chesler's idiosyncratic and personal style in the book, while striking some readers at the time as slapdash, actually became part of a new trend of relinquishing the pretense of impersonal objectivity, the pose of standing apart and separate from the subject of study. Quite apart from its place in general historical trends is the role that this book has played in the lives of many individual women who have found it a comfort and a catalyst in their own struggles with mental health institutions in the United States.

Sources for Further Study

Bolen, Jean Shinoda. *Goddesses in Everywoman: A New Psychology of Women*. San Francisco: Harper & Row, 1984. The exploration of goddess archetypes as patterns of female personality, with which Chesler opens and closes *Women and Madness*, is more fully developed here. With this book, Bolen became one of the luminaries of the resurgent popularization of Jungian psychology in the 1980's and 1990's.

Castillejo, Irene Claremont de. *Knowing Woman: A Feminine Psychology*. 1973. Reprint. Boston: Shambhala, 1990. An attempt to map the psychic terrain of women. This work is closer to classical Jungian theory than Jean Shinoda Bolen's or Chesler's, especially in its view of the differentiation of personality into masculine and feminine.

Formanek, Ruth, and Anita Gurian, eds. *Women and Depression: A Lifespan Perspective*. New York: Springer, 1987. A collection of essays from a variety of theoretical perspectives about female depression in childhood, adolescence, adulthood, and old age. Depression is recognized by Chesler and others as being the primary psychiatric symptom of women in contemporary urban society.

Gilligan, Carol. *In a Different Voice: Psychological Theory and Women's Development*. Cambridge, Mass.: Harvard University Press, 1982. Contrasts women's imperative to nurture and protect relationships with men's imperative to achieve status and advancement.

Heilbrun, Carolyn G. *Reinventing Womanhood*. New York: W. W. Norton, 1979. Using literary, personal, psychological, historical, and mythological material, Heilbrun challenges women to create imaginatively a new, autonomous identity for themselves.

Jack, Dana Crowley. *Silencing the Self: Women and Depression*. Cambridge, Mass.: Harvard University Press, 1991. Many writers have analyzed depression in women as a response to loss. In this work, Jack, following Carol Gilligan, considers depression as a response not to an external loss but to a loss of self. Attention is given to women's sacrifice of self in primary relationships and to the impact on daughters of maternal self-sacrifice.

Milford, Nancy. *Zelda: A Biography*. New York: Harper & Row, 1970. A carefully documented biography of Zelda Fitzgerald which became a model for other women's biographies. This highly respected work was one of Chesler's sources for the much briefer account in *Women and Madness* of Fitzgerald's life as typical of the way in which women's identification as mentally ill is used to deprive them of power and freedom.

Rich, Adrienne. Review of *Women and Madness*. *The New York Times Book Review*, December 31, 1972, 1, 20-21. One of feminism's leading thinkers reviews the strengths and weaknesses of Chesler's work.

Donna Glee Williams

WOMEN IN MODERN AMERICA: A Brief History

Author: Lois W. Banner (1939-)
Type of work: History
Time of work: The late nineteenth century to the 1970's
Locale: The United States
First published: 1974

Principal personages:

Jane Addams, a settlement house worker and social reformer
Susan B. Anthony, a woman suffrage advocate
Carrie Chapman Catt, a suffragist leader
Betty Friedan, a feminist writer of the 1960's
Alice Paul, an advocate of the Equal Rights Amendment
Eleanor Roosevelt, a First Lady and reformer
Elizabeth Cady Stanton, a woman suffrage leader

Form and Content

Designed as a supplementary text for courses in twentieth century United States history and women's history, *Women in Modern America: A Brief History* offers an analytic narrative of the actions of women from the end of the nineteenth century to the mid-1970's. Lois W. Banner's goal is to acquaint the reader with the women, both famous and obscure, who shaped the story of females in the United States and to "provide a corrective to the traditional histories from which women are absent." She wrote her book at a time when the modern interest in women's history was just getting under way, and her account became an influential contribution to the literature in the field during the 1970's.

Banner divides the time span of the book into three distinct periods: 1890 to 1920, when women pursued suffrage and other reforms; 1920 to 1960, an era of "greater complacency about women's problems"; and 1960 to 1974, when a more radical feminism emerged. Within these three broad eras, Banner considers a wide range of women, including African Americans, immigrants, the poor, and the middle class. Her goal is to portray how these groups of women responded to social changes while giving appropriate attention to the women who fought for greater rights for all females.

The years covered in the book were a time of rapid change that subjected women at all levels of society to new pressures and strains. Throughout the period, however, Banner believes that contrasting images of women as the embodiment of virtue and a source of temptation and evil have influenced society's attitude toward women and their place in the social order.

Banner also deals with the complex issue of feminism and the shifting definitions of the term during the years that her book covers. She examines the development of feminism after 1900 and tracks its varied manifestations throughout the first three-quarters of the century. Banner distinguishes among four types of followers: radical feminists, militants, social feminists, and domestic feminists. These explanatory categories help trace the occasions when divisions within feminism as a movement worked against the furtherance of the cause of women generally.

To facilitate further research, Banner provides extensive bibliographies for each chapter. There are also reference notes for the quoted materials and the sources that she used. This apparatus makes the book particularly useful as a guideline for scholarship on women and accounted in part for the impact that the book had on other scholars writing about women during the 1970's and 1980's. Banner also sought to achieve a measured and balanced tone toward the events and people she was describing, achieving a high degree of success in that regard. The book also contains an abundance of drawings and contemporary photographs that illustrate Banner's text in a very effective way.

Analysis

From the outset of her narrative, Banner stresses that progress for American women occurred when pressure from women compelled changes in male attitudes. Men sometimes yielded portions of their privileged status, but the surest course to meaningful change was for women to assert themselves in politics, in the professions, and at home. Banner's assessment of the record for women during the 1890's indicates the mixed results that came from a reliance on male willingness to move in the direction of greater gender equality.

In dealing with the turbulent years between 1900 and 1920 that brought so many important changes for women, Banner first draws a historical profile of the condition of females in the United States during these two decades. This strategy enables her to examine the diversity of women's experiences in a chapter that blends equal parts of economic and social history. The section on prostitutes is notable for its sympathetic treatment of these women and for its dispassionate analysis of the forces that led them into that profession. Banner both anticipated and stimulated the growing body of feminist scholarship that treats prostitution and society's response to it as a means of understanding more general attitudes toward women.

The suffrage movement of the Progressive Era presents Banner with an occasion when women made up a significant element in the mainstream of national reform. While discussing suffrage activities in detail, she also shows how women became involved in myriad other social justice campaigns. Organized women, especially club women, sparked efforts to beautify cities, to create better conditions in schools, and to improve the quality of municipal government. Banner devotes particular attention to the importance of settlement houses such as Hull-House, operated by Jane Addams, in this reform process.

Amid this ferment, radical feminist ideas received a hearing. Banner examines the whole spectrum of opinion among the most advanced feminist thinkers, including Margaret Sanger, Emma Goldman, and Charlotte Perkins Gilman. In the end, woman suffrage provided a rallying point for many female reformers. Banner argues that the cause of suffrage required both the middle-class tactics of Carrie Chapman Catt of the National American Woman Suffrage Association and the more confrontational approach of Alice Paul and the Woman's Party. The text also explores how the promise of the suffrage campaign did not lead to the gains for women that its more enthusiastic advocates had anticipated.

After the tumult of winning suffrage, the thirty years that followed brought setbacks and difficulties for American women. Banner traces the breakup of political unity among women after 1920 and the fragmented response of many female groups to the challenges of the new decades. The greater emphasis on home, family, and female beauty indicated to Banner a return of antifeminist attitudes to a place of dominance in society. The "flaming youth" of the 1920's expressed more interest in pleasure than social causes. For Banner, the whole decade represented a series of missed opportunities for women.

The Great Depression and World War II brought new forces that changed the situation of American women without disturbing the society's underlying assumptions about masculine superiority. The New Deal addressed some concerns about the conditions of women in the workplace during the 1930's, but not as part of any feminist agenda. Similarly, World War II produced opportunities for women to enter the labor force, but only while men were away fighting. Banner's exploration of the effects of the Depression and world conflict in this book contributed to an enhanced awareness among historians of the importance of the period between 1920 and 1945. *Women in Modern America* thus proved to be a stimulus to other historians to explore more fully this previously neglected phase of women's history in the United States.

The rise of modern feminism began during the period after the end of World War II, and this significant change in the attitudes of women in the United States forms the natural climax of Banner's narrative. The process of militancy began slowly in the late 1940's and into the 1950's because traditional values toward men had reasserted themselves after the end of the war. In the postwar decade, American society emphasized home life and domesticity; feminist issues accordingly receded for a time.

The more reformist social climate of the 1960's provided a context for a reawakening of feminist ideas. Betty Friedan's *The Feminine Mystique* (1963) alerted its readers to the discrimination that women still faced and delivered a powerful challenge to Freudian ideas about a woman's proper role. Meanwhile, the Civil Rights movement and the protests against the war in Vietnam fostered a new generation of feminist activism among women who had marched and worked in these other causes. New groups such as the Women's Political Caucus and the National Organization for Women

(NOW) appeared. Banner concludes with a survey of feminism and its achievements during the 1970's. She found it encouraging that feminism had not faded away in a single generation, as it had during the Progressive Era, but she could not forecast where the struggle for female equality and opportunity would lead during the remainder of the twentieth century.

Context

Textbooks do not usually have a large effect on the direction of scholarship in their subject field. That is not the case, however, with Lois Banner's volume. Her ability to summarize the state of existing knowledge about women in the twentieth century in clear prose with relevant examples made the book a favorite with instructors in women's history courses. Banner's suggestions about further research and opportunities for new inquiries also encouraged graduate students to mine her text for potential dissertations and articles.

Decades after its publication, *Women in Modern America* also stands out for its prescience in identifying broad areas where historians would do constructive work. Banner's section on prostitution in the Progressive Era was a harbinger of numerous monographs and articles on this controversial topic. Banner also pointed the way toward the intense interest about the activities of women during the 1920's and 1930's that has characterized writing about women's history since the mid-1970's. Textbooks often become dated soon after they are published, but Banner's book remains as fresh, thoughtful, and provocative as when it first appeared. It repays reading for the beginning student of women's history and the expert alike.

After *Women in Modern America*, her first book, Banner published a biography of Elizabeth Cady Stanton in 1979, an exploration of the importance of appearance in *American Beauty* (1983), and a book on women and aging called *In Full Flower: Aging Women, Power, and Sexuality* (1992).

Sources for Further Study

Banner, Lois W. *In Full Flower: Aging Women, Power, and Sexuality*. New York: Alfred A. Knopf, 1992. Banner's more recent work offers an opportunity to see how her thinking about women and feminist issues has evolved since the publication of *Women in Modern America* in 1974.

Chafe, William. *The Paradox of Change: American Women in the Twentieth Century*. Rev. ed. New York: Oxford University Press, 1991. Chafe first published his history of American women in the twentieth century in 1972. This revised and updated volume can be used to contrast how two scholars approach what are essentially the same type of historical issues.

Evans, Sara. *Born for Liberty: A History of Women in America*. New York: Free Press, 1989. This overview of the whole history of women in the United States offers a good basis for comparison with Banner's treatment of the period between 1890 and the 1970's.

Hartmann, Susan. *From Margin to Mainstream: American Women and Politics Since 1960*. New York: Alfred A. Knopf, 1989. One of a series of brief narratives on key decades during the twentieth century, Hartmann's book offers a more detailed examination of the period covered in the last chapters of Banner's text.

Kerber, Linda K., and Jane De Hart Mathews, eds. *Women's America: Refocusing the Past*. 3d ed. New York: Oxford University Press, 1991. A collection of documents and essays about women in American history, this text provides an indication of the direction that more recent scholarship on women has taken.

Kessler-Harris, Alice. *Out to Work: A History of Wage-Earning Women in the United States*. New York: Oxford University Press, 1982. This book indicates how the study of women in the workforce evolved during the decade after Banner's book was first published.

Rosenberg, Rosalind. *Divided Lives: American Women in the Twentieth Century*. New York: Hill and Wang, 1992. Rosenberg deals with the same issues as Banner does, but her interpretations reflect the impact of feminist scholarship in the two decades since Banner's work first appeared.

Sklar, Kathryn Kish, and Thomas Dublin, eds. *Women and Power in American History: A Reader*. Vol 2. Englewood Cliffs, N.J.: Prentice Hall, 1991. This volume, which begins with 1870, is a useful collection of scholarly essays that illuminates many of the issues that Banner treated.

Lewis L. Gould

THE WOMEN OF BREWSTER PLACE

Author: Gloria Naylor (1950-)
Type of work: Novel
Type of plot: Social realism
Time of plot: The 1960's, with flashbacks to the 1930's
Locale: Brewster Place, an African American inner-city neighborhood
First published: 1982

Principal characters:

Mattie Michael, a middle-aged woman from Tennessee who is like a mother to the residents of Brewster Place

Etta Mae Johnson, Mattie's best friend, who has pursued worthless men

Kiswana Browne, an activist college dropout, the daughter of a wealthy suburban family

Lucielia ("Ciel") Louise Turner, a sort of foster daughter to Mattie

Cora Lee, a woman who loves babies, but not children

Lorraine and **Theresa ("Tee"),** a lesbian couple

Ben, the old, alcoholic janitor who drinks to forget his faithless wife and lame daughter

Form and Content

Like modernist author Sherwood Anderson's *Winesburg, Ohio* (1919), *The Women of Brewster Place* is unified by locale (an inner city in the North), and Gloria Naylor uses individual chapters to focus on the lives and affairs of one or two characters. The themes of love and loss, trust and betrayal, hope and despair all help to unify the plot and characterization in a visually appealing portrait of the hard lives and gentle strength of seven black women in the 1960's.

Each character sketch begins with the present circumstances in which the woman finds herself, and then flashbacks of a few weeks, years, or even decades reveal each character's story of love and loss. Mattie, the matriarchal figure of Brewster Place, was the darling of her old father, who wished to protect her from men but who beat her savagely with a broom handle when she refused to reveal the man who impregnated her. Like the other women in this book, Mattie's only fault is loving too much, trusting the lies of the man she loves. In almost every case, erotic love between men and women leads inevitably to illegitimate children, poverty, abuse, abandonment, and despair. Men are shown as lazy, cowardly, and brutal characters whose only joys are hard liquor or drugs, sex and violence. The women are shown in a slightly more sympathetic light, but some of them, too, are revealed as equally culpable and willing victims of their abusive men. Even the lesbian couple, Lorraine and Tee, who have no interest in men, seek some tolerance from the other black women who themselves are victims of racism and sexism. They, too, become the victims of prejudice and brutality.

Although each woman has a different story to tell, like the people of *Winesburg, Ohio* they are all alienated from God, nature, one another, and themselves. Their only hope is the love that each woman has for the others. Ultimately, Naylor claims, it is women who are victimized by ignorance, violence, and prejudice, and even love. Together, however, women can reject the first three and hold out for appropriate objects of love. It is only when people's little world is shaken by the dark evil of violence that they care enough to take back what is theirs. Change can only come from within.

Yet one should not ignore the positive images that also appear in *The Women of Brewster Place*. Every woman has at least one other person whom she loves selflessly and unconditionally, and when faced with the horrors of modern life, such as the death of a child or the loss of a lover, the women come together with kindness, generosity, and the strong spirit of African American women. There is a gentle yet unshakable will that refuses to be destroyed by betrayal, loss, and violence.

Analysis

Brewster Place is a dead-end street in fact and in symbol, for the women who move there are trapped by their hopes and fears. For them, Brewster Place is both the birth and the death of their dreams. The brick wall that separates Brewster Place from the nicer neighborhoods represents the wall of prejudice and shame, racism and sexism that must be smashed by the residents. They alone can effect change in this climate of hostility and mistrust. The garbage in the alley symbolizes the character of the street toughs who run drugs, rape, and kill here. No one can stop them until the women on Brewster Place join forces and souls to fight back courageously against the human trash terrorizing their neighborhood.

Despite the violence in these women's lives, the language that Naylor uses is as potent and engaging as poetry—colorful and provocative, realistic but not bitter. Thus critics praise Naylor's style, even as some suggest that hers is not a new story. Her characters are as archetypal as the characters of Porgy and Bess in George Gershwin's 1935 black opera, as William Bradley Hooper claims, but they are also convincing and vivid, according to Anne Gottlieb.

Some suggest that Naylor's characters are too stereotypical or flat. For example, many male critics have complained about the totally negative images of black men in *The Women of Brewster Place*, the same complaint made about Alice Walker's *The Color Purple* (1982). Still others comment that Kiswana, the young activist, and the two lesbians, Lorraine and Tee, are undeveloped characters. Since early in the novel these are the only women who have not been the victims of heterosexual affairs, Naylor has been accused of failing to present black women in successful love relationships. The climactic gang rape of Lorraine reflects Naylor's theme of male violence directed at women, and the women's response—their togetherness in tearing down the wall of Brewster Place (in Mattie's dream, anyway)—underscores the difference between the sexes in terms of reactions to their environment. It is this remarkable, hope-filled ending that impresses the majority of scholars.

The book is to a certain extent a political treatise on the effects of poverty, ignorance, and violence, but it is also a love story. Yet it is not a love story in the traditional sense: There is no romance between men and women except that which ends in disappointment or tragedy, such as Ciel's love for her husband and the needless death of their only child. Maternal love is also thwarted. Mattie's sacrifice for her son, her thirty years of drudgery to give him a decent home and the opportunity that she was denied, means no more to him than a quick drink or a senseless bar fight. In Cora Lee, one sees the other end of despair, for she deserts her children emotionally, which is as devastating as Ciel's or Mattie's losses.

Yet despite poverty, fatigue, desperation, and suspicion, the women of Brewster Place hold one another in heartfelt love and care. It is not *eros* (romantic love) but the selfless *philia* (friendship love), described by fifth century B.C. Greek philosopher Plato and recommended by feminist writers Mary Wollstonecraft and Charlotte Perkins Gilman, that these women experience and in which they revel. Their friendship teaches them to survive. One cannot live without loss; it is the human condition. Naylor shows, however, that for women—and black women in particular—survival comes from the courage and support of those who share pain and anguish and yet also share the triumph of the human spirit, from families created not by genes and blood and law but by the heart and soul.

Context

As Naylor's first novel, the award-winning *The Women of Brewster Place* brought her into the realm of serious critical interest. She went on to publish *Linden Hills* (1985) and *Mama Day* (1987), which deal with black men and women struggling with the American Dream or being torn between black mysticism and the lure of the big city. Neither of these books met with as much praise as *The Women of Brewster Place*, although most critics commended Naylor's talent.

Naylor is accepted as a major contemporary writer, and scholars agree that her language is clear but gritty, like the people whom she portrays, and that her imagery is evocative and her vision consistent and believable. Some say that she is in accord with the realism of her contemporaries, black women authors Alice Walker and Toni Morrison, but that the extent of her talent has yet to be proven.

In interviews and speeches on college campuses, Naylor has repeated the story of her "traditional" schooling, of her love of reading, of coming-of-age in the revolutionary 1960's and being unaware that blacks wrote novels until she was twenty-six, when she was first introduced to literature written by and about African Americans. To those who take for granted the presence of multicultural emphases in the classroom, Naylor's story seems as unbelievable as the tales of separate drinking fountains, restrooms, and restaurants for whites and blacks that existed until the Civil Rights movement and Supreme Court decisions revolutionized race relations in the United States. It is important to recall these realities when considering the impact of *The Women of Brewster Place* on Americans, regardless of race, gender, age, or sexual orientation.

The fact that *The Women of Brewster Place* was translated to a television film in 1989 starring Oprah Winfrey, who was also executive producer and who ensured that the film was a clear, accurate depiction of the book, suggests the popularity of the novel. More important, however, it reveals the significant impact Naylor's portrait of black urban women has had on the reading and viewing public. The favorable reception given the motion picture helped increase sales of the book to the general public, and Naylor's works have joined those of other black writers in college literature courses.

In many ways, *The Women of Brewster Place* may prove to be as significant in its way as Southern writer William Faulkner's mythic Yoknapatawpha County or Sherwood Anderson's *Winesburg, Ohio*. It provides a realistic vision of black urban women's lives and inspires readers with the courage and spirit of black women in America.

Sources for Further Study

Branzburg, Judith V. "Seven Women and a Wall." *Callaloo* 7, no. 2 (Spring/Summer, 1984): 116-119. Branzburg broaches the politically explosive topic of black women who write negatively, although truthfully, about black men and places Naylor in the company of such serious writers as Toni Morrison and Toni Cade Bambara. She praises the "rich, sensuous, rhythmic language" and "sense of reality" in *The Women of Brewster Place* and its effort to show the importance of individual responsibility to women who seek independent lives.

Gomez, Jewelle. "Naylor's Inferno." *The Women's Review of Books* 2, no. 11 (August, 1985): 7-8. An analysis of Naylor's second novel, *Linden Hills*, which concerns blacks who have achieved the financial and political success only dreamt of by the residents of Brewster Place. Linden Hills is the middle-class suburb from which Kiswana, the young activist of *The Women of Brewster Place*, came. Comparing the two novels, Gomez discusses Naylor's use of Italian Renaissance poet Dante Alighieri's *Inferno* as symbolic of the evils of greed, power, madness, and racism (even among blacks, some of whom favor lighter skin). The writer criticizes Naylor's confusion of time periods in both novels but praises her talent.

Hooper, William Bradley. Review of *The Women of Brewster Place*. *Booklist* 78, no. 19 (June 1, 1982): 1300. A review that praises Naylor's conviction, beautiful style, and characterization, which Hooper finds believable and without bitterness.

Jones, Robert. "A Place in the Suburbs." *Commonweal* 112, no. 9 (May 3, 1985): 283-285. Compares *Linden Hills* to *The Women of Brewster Place* in terms of Naylor's recognition of the symbolic foundation and effects of geography on the human heart and mind, as well as the corruption that results from loss of memory. Both works are connected in terms of the strength of spirit and belief in invincibility so common to Americans, black or white. Yet for Naylor, it is family, not land or culture, that is the psychic center for African Americans.

Wickenden, Dorothy. Review of *The Women of Brewster Place*. *The New Republic* 187, no. 10 (September 6, 1982): 37-38. Compares the novel to Alice Walker's *The Color Purple*, in terms of both books' negative images of black men. Wickenden claims that Naylor goes beyond a mere celebration of "female solidarity" to focus on the importance of redemption and maternal love.

Linda L. Labin

THE WOMEN'S ROOM

Author: Marilyn French (1929-)
Type of work: Novel
Type of plot: *Bildungsroman*
Time of plot: The 1950's to the 1960's
Locale: New Jersey; Cambridge, Massachusetts; and the coast of Maine
First published: 1977

Principal characters:

Mira, a woman disillusioned with wifehood, motherhood, and suburbia who searches for friendships among women

Norm, Mira's former husband, known as the Great God Norm

Natalie, one of Mira's suburban friends, married to Hamp, a boyish man

Adele, one of Mira's suburban friends, unhappily married to Paul

Samantha, one of Mira's suburban friends, married to the unemployed Simp

Lily, one of Mira's suburban friends, married to Carl, who abuses her

Ben Voler, Mira's lover

Martha, one of Mira's suburban friends, in an "open" marriage

Valerie, one of Mira's Harvard friends, with a liberated sexual identity

Ava, one of Mira's Harvard friends, a frustrated ballet dancer

Clarissa, one of Mira's Harvard friends, unhappily married to Duke

Kyla, one of Mira's Harvard friends, unhappy with Harley

Iso or **Isolde,** one of Mira's Harvard friends, a lesbian

Form and Content

The Women's Room features a cover in which the word "Ladies' " is crossed out, renaming the "Ladies' Room" toilet at Harvard University and, symbolically, challenging the rigid gender roles assigned to females in modern America. The title also comically evokes the title of one of Marilyn French's feminist mentors, Virginia Woolf, whose earlier masterpiece *A Room of One's Own* (1929) proclaimed women's androgynous right to economic independence. Like Woolf, French creates an autobiographical voice that takes the reader on a mental journey that inquires into the theme "what women want."

This mid-twentieth century *Bildungsroman* is a long novel which has been called shapeless and unplotted, but in fact its contents are carefully structured. In form, the novel consists of six units. The opening describes thirty-eight-year-old Mira hiding in the toilet and her new Harvard milieu, introducing the themes of gender relations, personal freedom, and men problems. The second section flashes back to her earlier life, motherhood, and frustrating friendships with suburban women. The third unit traces the vicissitudes of Mira's marriage to Norm, ending with his request for a divorce. The fourth is a meditation on sin and civil rights that leads away from her suicide attempt and toward the "ideal" lover, Ben Voler. The fifth section follows the decline of her Harvard relationships, which are pried away from Mira. In the concluding epilogue, Mira reveals herself to be the autobiographical narrator of her life's story and identifies herself as a solitary beach walker in Maine.

Another way of viewing the novel's form is to see it as a comparison and contrast between two sociologically different American environments: the suburban enclave, whether for struggling young couples or middle-class success stories; and the academic environs of Cambridge, Massachusetts, near Harvard University. However disparate on the surface, underneath these two distinctive "cultures" turn out to be the same place, one in which men and women are incompatible. The novel's narrator and her friends passionately debate why this should be so. Why are women conditioned to be dependent upon men? How is it that women, in fact, grow away from men and become mothers whose lives revolve around their children? *The Women's Room* explores women's innocent disbelief in these problems, as well as men's possessive power. Yet the interactions between the sexes, regardless of age or marital status, turn out in the novel to be as enervating for women at Harvard as they are in America's gray suburbs.

French chose these themes and organizing devices partly from the validation that they receive from her own life experiences. French was divorced in 1957 and attended Hofstra College in the 1960's and Harvard University in the 1970's, experiences drawn upon for this novel. Its content has often been called polemical, but readers have widely accepted the contemporary validity of French's characterizations of two cultures and her criticism of men's androcentric worldview. Fiercely full of life, and refusing to compromise, Mira's story is brilliantly accurate with its dialogue, characterizations, and knowledge of changing relationships between men and women over three decades and two generations.

This novel of ideas focuses on the grinding details of a woman's daily life. Its complexity is drawn from a diverse number of characters; French's experience as a Shakespeare scholar has taught her how to pattern an elaborated narrative with character clusters that reinforce thematic patterns. The novelist works to speak candidly to the reader, avoiding a sense of the narrator's superiority over a reader but nevertheless challenging the reader to think about the philosophical issues involved in choosing selfhood rather than servitude. Thus the novel's rhetorical strategy is to address the reader as an adult friend, in effect a member of the women's gatherings—a participant in the community of women, its sufferings and celebrations.

Analysis

Marilyn French's central intention is the stretching of readers' moral sense by making them think about and examine the unpleasant aspects of men's and women's relationships. Her portrait of the enculturation of a typical American girl in the 1950's is startling in terms of its protagonist's ordinariness. Mira, the girl who thinks the world will give her a beautiful view, is presented as an Everywoman who, like her many friends, suffers from America's gender dynamics. As in such earlier protesting tales as Sylvia Plath's *The Bell Jar* (1963), French propels an anguished girl into an unhappy adulthood. French widens and deepens the theme, however, by her insistence on a broad span of time and a wide panorama that replicates the pattern of female suffering. Called mad, oversexed, undersexed, boring, or stupid, such women either refuse to submit and be destroyed by insensitive men or are driven "over the line."

Yet French's first novel is not written as an antimale polemic; the narrator repeatedly pauses in her narrative to mull over questions about men's motivation and perceptions, how life must appear to them and hence the inevitability of their viewpoint. Mira herself is a producer of male "childflesh," the mother of sons whom she cherishes and hopes to make into androgynous gentlemen. Unlike their father, who cannot "equate the act" of sex with feeling, Mira tries to teach her boys that it is possible to grow into more than their father, her friends' husbands, or Barbie's Ken, "clean-cut and polite and blank." In fact, Mira is no reverse misogynist; she "distrusts generalized hatred" and faults Val for saying that "all men are the enemy" after she has been maddened by grief over her daughter's rape, both literally and then by the patriarchal system. Mira's more reasonable view is that men need emotional education; her long narrative insists that the American Dream must not "eradicate" women in order for them to become men's possessions. It is the unquestioned political and economic gender system which must be changed so that men will cease being the thoughtlessly superior group automatically deferred to by subordinate women.

French's novel galvanized readers in 1977 when the book was published. *The Women's Room* has been called as fictionally influential as *The Feminine Mystique* (1963), Betty Friedan's study of domestic discontent. Against the background of a chaotic period in American history—the Civil Rights movement, assassinations, the Vietnam War, the peace movement, the Kent State shootings—French goes beyond other tales of women's suffering. She draws readers because of her creation of a visionary women's community, laid out against a philosophically argued background, that appeals to thoughtful analysis and humane justice. Rebutting the wide and common assumption that American women dislike one another, she presents a different reality: They need and enjoy one another's support, but they often fail to live up to its ideal. Their "jiggling moments" of intense and complete human harmony may not be sustainable, but they are real. This is French's vision of community within the novel—maintained inadequately in suburbia, sustained temporarily in the graduate school enclave, and meditated upon in the author's seaside retreat at the novel's conclusion. Nevertheless, the narrator's commitment to "the dancing moments that were a person" is cultivated within a human community. Her learned mind assures the careful reader that much about men's and women's relationships fails because of historically shaped facts that have led the two sexes in America to become two incompatible cultures.

Though she never captures the secret of two human beings sharing "togetherness and separateness," Mira's refusal to meet men's goal of "adjustment" to their role's expectations leads her to analyze the problem in terms of women's training to be fairy-tale princesses. Her *Bildungsroman* rejects the beautiful "but not true" fairyland of suburban married life and offers the Maine coastline as a better "symbol of what life is all about." Women in the novel, such as Clarissa, dream of being Sleeping Beauty, Mummy and Daddy's "little princess" for whom whatever is wanted will be whisked in by the "good fairy's" wand. This character marries a Duke and is surely kissed, but it does not save her from the consequences of disempowerment. Mira learns that she and her various friends aren't "happy children playing ring-around-the-rosy."

As a corrective, the narrator cleverly suggests a re-writing of Virginia Woolf's tale of Shakespeare's sister in *A Room of One's Own*; this revision would show the creative Renaissance woman not being destroyed but marrying, becoming a mother, and surviving through the controls available in language. This is exactly what Mira herself does. She refuses to live by her mirror like the "queen in *Snow White*" and makes a commitment to "let the voices out," to "write it all down" and make sense out of it. Thus the narrator demythicizes women's lives, rejecting men's savior role. Mira adds, "What prince is going to cut through brambles to reach me? Besides they are mostly spurious princes." Mira still believes in the potential for a "corporation of the heart." Having survived fifteen years of marriage, a soap-opera life of suburban loneliness, and even the role of being the "Old Wise Woman of Cambridge" at the end of the novel, the protagonist's adult identity is based upon a recognition that no man—indeed, no person—can create one's mental health, which must be a consequence "of lowered expectations."

Context

Marilyn French calls *The Women's Room* a "collective biography" of a large group of American citizens. Her goal was to break the mold of conventional women's novels by presenting a pattern that weaves together and emphasizes the ordinariness of her suffering women characters. Her thesis is that women must accept life as a lonely chaos in which there is no foreseeable complementarity between men and women. In fact, French believes that women are more intimately bonded to their children than to men, that romance and lust are temporary conditions, and that candor on these issues is freeing.

Called a feminist classic, *The Women's Room* draws upon French's admiration for Simone de Beauvoir's *Le Deuxième sexe* (1949; *The Second Sex*, 1953). Her first novel provides a feminine perspective that rejects the positioning of women as the "other" or object in a world determined and controlled by men. Its explosive best-seller status is probably a consequence of its verisimilitude. The phenomenal popular success of *The Women's Room* in 1977 was dependent on American women's recognition of its central theme that women inadequately oppose men's possessive power; they innately value nonjudgmental nurturance.

Many ardent feminists may have been puzzled by a polemical novel that criticizes not only men but women as well; they have not treated the book as a marching banner. Its endorsement of motherhood left it standing alone, neither a conventionally conservative nor a radical text. Later women writers, such as Alice Walker in *The Color Purple* (1982) or Margaret Atwood in *The Handmaid's Tale* (1986), borrowed French's technique of developing a microcosm of American society and using it to illustrate gender disparities in power and their damning consequences for women. Sex segregation and the oppression of women have consequently become popular themes for women writers.

Preceded by such feminist thinkers as Woolf and Beauvoir, French is an anomaly, a distinguished academic scholar whose breakthrough best-seller brilliantly engages the reader who eagerly accepts her characters' reactions to life. Brimming with energy, this novel fiercely refuses to compromise. Perhaps it straddles the ideologies of middle-American women and feminists because French's depiction of women's plight is universalized by her diverse examples and because she shows women's problems with intimacy to be universal human experiences. There is no idealized woman-to-man bond or woman-to-woman bond in *The Women's Room*; rather, French proposes that women's dominant commitment is to rearing their children, a role that is the center of their lives. This is why Valerie's abandonment of her daughter Chris is treated as a tragedy in the novel. It also illustrates how French proposes to use her fiction to clarify human values of the past such as motherhood, working within accepted moral traditions to stretch readers' moral sense by reminding them about how the past continues to shape modern lives.

Sources for Further Study

Clarke, Betsy. *The Turmoils of Gender: Marilyn French and Mary Gordon*. Rockford, Ill.: Rockford Institute, 1982. An interesting discussion by two modern feminist writers about their respective literary treatments of what some have called "the longest war."

French, Marilyn. "The Emancipation of Betty Friedan." In *Fifty Who Made the Difference*. New York: Villard Books, 1984. Praises a feminist predecessor who opened the public dialogue about middle-class housewives' discontent in America during the 1960's.

—————. "The Masculine Mystique." *Literary Review* 36 (Fall, 1992): 17-27. Complementing Betty Friedan's analysis of women's ambivalent power base in a female mystique, French considers the background of men's power base. She addresses the question of why she does not focus her fiction upon male characters and explains why men's unselfconscious, phallocentric worldview has its dangers.

—————. "Self-Respect: A Female Perspective." *The Humanist* 46 (November/December, 1986): 18-23. A serious philosophical consideration of gender-based class superiority. French draws upon classical thinkers such as Aristotle to provide a background for her feminist analysis of self-respect. Feminism privileges pleasure for women, not power, she argues, and balances selfhood against the external world. Adults examine options and accept the consequences, including suffering. The essay concludes that adults know virtue is its own reward.

Homans, Margaret. " 'Her Very Own Howl': The Ambiguities of Representation in Recent Women's Fiction." *Signs* 9 (Winter, 1983): 186-205. Explores French's relationship to language in the context of other contemporary women novelists.

Wagner, Linda W. "The French Definition." *Arizona Quarterly* 38 (Winter, 1982): 293-302. Discusses how French's narrative voice in *The Women's Room* and *The Bleeding Heart* (1980) defines contemporary women's ideas concerning the societally induced role of women as sufferers who exempt men from the burden of suffering.

Sandra Parker

WUTHERING HEIGHTS

Author: Emily Brontë (1818-1848)
Type of work: Novel
Type of plot: Romance
Time of plot: The late eighteenth century
Locale: The West Yorkshire moors
First published: 1847

Principal characters:

Catherine Earnshaw, Heathcliff's soulmate, who marries Edgar Linton
Heathcliff, a foundling brought into the Earnshaw home, a passionate man
Mr. Lockwood, a gentleman of private means who becomes Heathcliff's tenant at Thrushcross Grange
Nelly Dean, the housekeeper of Thrushcross Grange
Hindley Earnshaw, Catherine's older brother, who is brutal in his treatment of Heathcliff
Edgar Linton, a somewhat spoiled, wealthy inhabitant of Thrushcross Grange
Isabella Linton, Edgar's sister, who marries Heathcliff
Catherine Linton, the daughter of Edgar Linton and Catherine Earnshaw
Linton Heathcliff, the son of Heathcliff and Isabella Linton
Hareton Earnshaw, the son of Hindley Earnshaw, who is in love with Catherine Linton
Joseph, the servant of the Earnshaws at Wuthering Heights

Form and Content

Wuthering Heights is a story of passionate love that encompasses two generations of two families, the Earnshaws and the Lintons. It is a framed tale narrated by two different characters, one with intimate knowledge of the families (Nelly Dean) and one unacquainted with their history. The first narrator is the stranger, Mr. Lockwood. A wealthy, educated man, Lockwood has chosen to rent a house in the isolated moors, saying that he has wearied of society. Yet his actions belie his words: He pursues a friendship with Heathcliff despite the latter's objections and seeks information about all the citizens of the neighborhood. Lockwood is steeped in the conventions of his class, and he consistently misjudges the people he meets at Wuthering Heights. He assumes that Hareton Earnshaw, the rightful owner of Wuthering Heights, is a servant and that Catherine Linton is a demure wife to Heathcliff. His statements, even about himself, are untrustworthy, requiring the corrective of Nelly Dean's narrative.

Lockwood cultivates Nelly Dean's friendship when a long illness, brought on by his foolish attempt to visit Heathcliff during a snowstorm, keeps him bedridden for weeks. Nelly has been reared with the Earnshaws and has been a servant in both households. She has observed much of the central drama between the two families, but her statements, too, are colored by prejudice. Nelly dislikes Catherine Earnshaw, who behaved selfishly and treated the servants badly at times, and she supports Edgar Linton because he was a gentleman.

Through these two unreliable lenses are filtered the love stories of Catherine and Heathcliff, Catherine and Edgar, and in the second generation, Catherine Linton and Hareton Earnshaw. The antithesis of character—Heathcliff's past is a blank, Edgar is a gentleman's son; Heathcliff is dark and brooding, Edgar is fair and cannot conceal his feelings—is echoed with other oppositions. Wuthering Heights is an exposed, cold farmhouse; Thrushcross Grange is an orderly gentleman's home with plush furnishings, warm fires, and an enclosed park. The houses, instead of places of safety, become literal prisons for the female characters, while the wild moors (which nearly kill Lockwood) represent freedom and naturalness of behavior.

Patterns of dualism and opposition are played out between the first and second generations as well. Heathcliff, the physically strongest father, has the weakest child, Linton Heathcliff. By dying young, Linton dissolves the triangular relationship that has so plagued the older generation, undermining Heathcliff's influence. Hareton Earnshaw, abused like Heathcliff and demonstrating surprising similarities of character, nevertheless retains some sense of moral behavior and is not motivated by revenge. Catherine Earnshaw's daughter, as willful and spirited as her mother, does not have to make the same difficult choice between passionate love and socially sanctioned marriage. Instead, Catherine Linton and Hareton Earnshaw are left to help each other and inherit the positive legacies of the past, enjoying both the social amenities of Thrushcross Grange and the natural environment of Wuthering Heights.

Analysis

An essential element of *Wuthering Heights* is the exploration and extension of the meaning of romance. By contrasting the passionate, natural love of Catherine and Heathcliff with the socially constructed forms of courtship and marriage, Emily Brontë makes an argument in favor of individual choice. Catherine and Heathcliff both assert that they know the other as themselves, that they are an integral part of each other, and that one's death will diminish the other immeasurably. This communion, however, is doomed to failure while they live because of social constraints. Heathcliff's unknown parentage, his poverty, and his lack of education make him an unsuitable partner for a gentlewoman, no matter how liberated her expressions of independence. Brontë suggests the possibility of reunion after death when local residents believe they see the ghosts of Heathcliff and Catherine together, but this notion is explicitly denied by Lockwood's last assertion in the novel, that the dead slumber quietly.

The profound influence of Romantic poetry on Brontë's literary imagination is evident in her development of Heathcliff as a Byronic hero. This characterization contributes to the impossibility of any happy union of Catherine and Heathcliff while they live. Heathcliff looms larger than life, subject to violent extremes of emotion, amenable to neither education nor nurturing. Like Frankenstein's monster, he craves love and considers revenge the only fit justice when he is rejected by others. Catherine, self-involved and prone to emotional storms, has just enough sense of self-preservation to recognize Heathcliff's faults, including his amorality. Choosing to marry Edgar Linton is to choose psychic fragmentation and separation from her other self, but she sees no way to reconcile her psychological need for wholeness with the physical support and emotional stability that she requires. Unable to earn a living, dependent on a brother who is squandering the family fortune, she is impelled to accept the social privileges and luxuries that Edgar offers.

Yet conventional forms of romance provide no clear guide to successful marriage either; both Edgar and his sister, Isabella, suffer by acting on stereotypical notions of love. Edgar does not know Catherine in any true sense, and his attempts to control her force her subversive self-destruction. Isabella, fascinated by the Byronic qualities with which Heathcliff is so richly endowed, believes that she really loves him and becomes a willing victim in his scheme of revenge. What remains is a paradoxical statement about the nature and value of love and a question about whether any love can transcend social and natural barriers.

Another theme that Brontë examines is the effect of abuse and brutality on human nature. The novel contains minimal examples of nurturing, and most instruction to children is of the negative kind that Joseph provides with his lectures threatening damnation. Children demonstrably suffer from a lack of love from their parents, whose attention alternates between total neglect and physical threats. The novel is full of violence, exemplified by the dreams that Lockwood has when he stays in Wuthering Heights. After being weakened by a nosebleed which occurs when Heathcliff's dogs attack him, Lockwood spends the night in Catherine Earnshaw's old room. He dreams first of being accused of an unpardonable sin and being beaten by a congregation in church, then of a small girl, presumably Catherine, who is trying to enter the chamber's window. Terrified, he rubs her wrist back and forth on a broken windowpane until he is covered in blood. These dreams anticipate further violence: Hindley's drunken assaults on his son and animals, Catherine's bloody capture by the Lintons' bulldog, Edgar's blow to Heathcliff's neck, and Heathcliff's mad headbanging when he learns of Catherine's death. Heathcliff never recovers from the neglect and abuse that he has experienced as a child; all that motivates him in adulthood is revenge and a philosophy that the weak deserve to be crushed. Hareton presents the possibility that degraded character can be redeemed and improved through the twin forces of education and love, yet this argument seems little more than a way of acknowledging the popular cultural stereotype and lacks the conviction that Brontë reveals when she focuses on the negative effects of brutality.

A third significant theme of *Wuthering Heights* is the power of the natural setting. Emily Brontë loved the wildness of the moors and incorporated much of her affection into her novel. Catherine and Heathcliff are most at one with each other when they are outdoors. The freedom that they experience is profound; not only have they escaped Hindley's anger, but they are free from social restraints and expectations as well. When Catherine's mind wanders before her death, she insists on opening the windows to breathe the wind off the moors, and she believes herself to be under Penistone Crag with Heathcliff. Her fondest memories are of the times on the moors; the enclosed environment of Thrushcross Grange seems a petty prison. In contrast to Catherine and Heathcliff, other characters prefer the indoors and crave the protection that the houses afford. Lockwood is dependent on the comforts of home and hearth, and the Lintons are portrayed as weaklings because of their upbringing in a sheltered setting. This method of delineating character by identifying with nature is another aspect of Emily Brontë's inheritance from the Romantic poets.

Context

When it was first published, *Wuthering Heights* received almost no attention from critics, and what little there was proved to be negative. Critical opinion deemed the book immoral, and Charlotte Brontë felt moved to apologize for it after Emily's death by saying that her sister wrote during the feverish stages of tuberculosis. To publish at all, the Brontë sisters chose to submit their works using male pseudonyms because they believed that it would be impossible to market their poems and novels otherwise. They experienced many rejections and were never recompensed fairly for the value of their work. When their identity was revealed, many critics expressed surprise (that the novels could be written by inexperienced women who lived in isolated circumstances) and shock (that the violence and passion of *Wuthering Heights* could be conceived by a woman at all). There has even been a serious attempt made to prove that Emily's brother, Branwell, was the true author of *Wuthering Heights*.

This reaction suggests the reluctance of the Victorian public to accept challenges to the dominant belief that women were beneficent moral influences whose primary function was to provide a pure environment for men who, of necessity, sullied themselves in the world of work. *Wuthering Heights* provides no overt rebellion against this view, but the depiction of female characters who display anger, passion, and a desire for independence demonstrates Emily Brontë's judgment that women were suited to a wider sphere of action.

Contemporary feminist critics have seen Catherine Earnshaw as a character for whom no meaningful choices are possible. Her self-starvation and periods of madness can be read as signs of female powerlessness and rage. Even her death can be seen as the last resort of the oppressed, a kind of willed suicide which she announces is her only form of revenge against both Edgar Linton and Heathcliff for thwarting her true nature. The second half of the novel, focusing on Catherine Linton, is an assertion of Victorian society's values countering Catherine Earnshaw's desire to be self-determining. Catherine Linton is beautiful in a conventional way, and she dutifully serves as daughter, wife, nurse, and teacher. Yet, compared to her mother's, her story has much less drama and fails to persuade the reader of its truth. In fact, it best serves to highlight the unique and deeply felt nature of her mother's subjugation.

Sources for Further Study

Craik, W. A. *The Brontë Novels*. London: Methuen, 1968. An early attempt to separate the biographical material from the artistic skill of the writers. Craik focuses on the development of character in *Wuthering Heights*.

Eagleton, Terence. *Myths of Power*. London: Macmillan, 1975. A Marxist approach to works by the Brontë sisters which places *Wuthering Heights* in a broad historical and political context.

Ewbank, Inga-Stina. *Their Proper Sphere: A Study of the Brontë Sisters as Early-Victorian Female Novelists*. Cambridge, Mass.: Harvard University Press, 1966. Addresses the contained world of *Wuthering Heights*, which despite its isolation, functions as a microcosm of the human condition.

Gérin, Winifred. *Emily Brontë*. New York: Oxford

University Press, 1971. A comprehensive biography of Emily Brontë, informed by Gérin's research on other members of the Brontë family and her intimate knowledge of Haworth and the surrounding moors of West Yorkshire.

Gilbert, Sandra M., and Susan Gubar. *The Madwoman in the Attic: The Woman Writer and the Nineteenth-Century Literary Imagination*. New Haven, Conn.: Yale University Press, 1979. An important feminist reading of nineteenth century women writers, including an insightful chapter on Emily Brontë.

Ratchford, Fannie. *The Brontës' Web of Childhood*. New York: Columbia University Press, 1941. The first book to examine the relationship of the childhood writings to the adult novels of the Brontë sisters. Ratchford outlines the children's collaboration on the stories about Verdopolis, and she explains how Emily and Anne created the world of Gondal.

Weissman, Judith. *Half Savage and Hardy and Free: Women and Rural Radicalism in the Nineteenth-Century Novel*. Middletown, Conn.: Weslayan University Press, 1987. Contains an examination of the Romantic influence and radical politics of *Wuthering Heights*.

Williams, Raymond. *The English Novel*. New York: Oxford University Press, 1973. Presents a Marxist reading of *Wuthering Heights* as a novel which challenges repressive structures and achieves emotional directness.

Gweneth A. Dunleavy

THE YELLOW WALLPAPER

Author: Charlotte Perkins Gilman (1860-1935)
Type of work: Novella
Type of plot: Social criticism
Time of plot: The late nineteenth century
Locale: New England
First published: 1892

Principal characters:

The narrator, an imaginative, creative woman apparently suffering from postpartum depression
John, the narrator's husband, a physician
Jennie, John's sister, who serves as housekeeper
Weir Mitchell, the real-life doctor who popularized the "rest cure" prescribed to the narrator (and the author as well)

Form and Content

The structure of *The Yellow Wallpaper* creates a sense of immediacy and intimacy. The story is written in a journal-style, first-person narrative which includes nine short entries, each entry indicated by a small space between it and the last. The journal entries span three months during which John attempts to cure his wife's "nervous condition" through the rest cure of Weir Mitchell, which assumes that intellectual stimulation damages a woman physically and psychologically. In the beginning of the story, the narrator appears sane and believable, but as the story continues, the reader realizes that she is unreliable because she withholds and confuses information. By the end, the structure—short paragraphs, fragmented and disjointed thought patterns—reflects the narrator's mental disorder. Through the revelations contained in the journal, the reader is allowed an intimate view of the narrator's gradual mental breakdown.

The journal begins when John and the narrator move into a temporary home John has procured to provide the narrator the break from routine that he believes necessary for her rest and recovery. She, on the other hand, doubts the necessity of such a move and wonders if the mysterious house is haunted. John reveals his superior attitude toward his wife by laughing at her "fancies," a response which the narrator finds quite natural because, as she explains, one must expect such treatment in marriage. She even suggests that his indifference to her opinions on the house and her illness keeps her from getting well faster. Her suggestion turns out to be a fateful prediction.

Against her wishes, John decides that he and his wife will sleep in the attic room of the house, which at one point may have been a nursery. Actually, the room seems to be more of a prison than a place for children to play. The windows have bars on them, and the bed is nailed to the floor. There is even a gate at the top of the stairs. Even more disturbing to the narrator, however, is the yellow wallpaper, peeling or pulled off the walls in strips. In the beginning, the paper's pattern jolts and annoys the narrator's sensibilities, but later her attitude has a bizarre change.

The narrator's morbid fascination with the yellow wallpaper is the first clue of her degenerating sanity. She begins to attribute lifelike characteristics to the paper, saying that it knows how it affects her and that its eyes stare at her. She even begins to believe that the paper has two levels, a front pattern and a shadowy figure trapped behind its bars. The narrator betrays the progression of her illness when she begins to believe that the figure behind the wallpaper is a woman, trapped like herself.

The woman behind the wallpaper becomes an obsession. The narrator begins to crawl, like the woman behind the paper, around the edge of the room, making a groove or "smooch" on the wall. The narrator begins to catch glimpses of the woman out the windows, creeping around the garden on her hands and knees. She also starts peeling off the wallpaper in an effort to completely free the woman (or women, as she soon believes) trapped in that second layer. John and his sister, Jennie, begin to suspect that something is terribly wrong, and yet they are pleased with her apparent progress. She appears more normal to them at times because she is saving her energy for nighttime, when the woman behind the paper is most active. Her apparent normality is a façade.

The story's climactic scene occurs as their stay in the rented house is coming to a close. On their last night, John is once again in town attending to a patient, and the narrator asks Jennie not to disturb her. Left alone, the narrator locks herself in the nursery to allow uninterrupted time for peeling wallpaper and thus freeing the shadowy woman. As the narrator works, she identifies more closely and intensely with the trapped woman until, ultimately, she loses her sense of individual identity and merges with the woman behind the wallpaper. John breaks down the nursery door to find his wife crawling amid the torn paper, proclaiming that she is free at last, and no one can put her back behind the wallpaper. John faints, and his wife continues her creeping over his fallen body.

Analysis

Charlotte Perkins Gilman used her personal bout with postpartum depression to create a powerful fictional narrative which has broad implications for women. When the narrator recognizes that there is more than one trapped, creeping woman, Gilman indicates that the meaning of her story extends beyond an isolated, individual situation. Gilman's main purpose in writing *The Yellow Wallpaper* is to condemn not only a specific medical treatment but also the misogynistic principles and resulting sexual politics that make such a treatment possible.

The unequal relationship between the narrator and John is a microcosm of the larger gender inequity in society. Gilman makes it clear that much of John's condescending and paternal behavior toward his wife has little to do with her illness. He dismisses her well-thought-out opinions and her "flights of fancy" with equal disdain, while he belittles her creative impulses. He speaks of her as he would a child, calling her his "little girl" and saying of her, "Bless her little heart." He overrides her judgments on the best course of treatment for herself as he would on any issue, making her live in a house she does not like, in a room she detests, and in an isolated environment which makes her unhappy and lonely. John's solicitous "care" shows that he believes the prevailing scientific theories which claim that women's innate inferiority leaves them, childlike, in a state of infantile dependence.

Gilman makes John the window through which readers can view the negative images of women in her society. In Gilman's lifetime, women's right to become full citizens and to vote became one of the primary issues debated in the home, the media, and the political arena. As women's reform movements gained the strength that would eventually win the vote in 1920, the backlash became more vicious and dangerous. Noted psychologists detailed theories that "proved" women's developmental immaturity, low cognitive skills, and emotional instability. Physicians, who actually had little knowledge of the inner workings of the female body, presented complex theories arguing that the womb created hysteria and madness, that it was the source of women's inferiority. Ministers urged women to fulfill their duty to God and their husbands with equal submission and piety. In indicting John's patronizing treatment of his wife, Gilman indicts the system as a whole, in which many women were trapped behind damaging social definitions of the female.

One can see the negative effects of John's (and society's) treatment of the narrator in her response to the rest cure. At first, she tries to fight against the growing lethargy that controls her. She even challenges John's treatment of her. Yet, while one part of her may believe John wrong, another part that has internalized the negative definitions of womanhood believes that since he is the man, the doctor, and therefore the authority, then he may be right. Because they hold unequal power positions in the relationship and in society, she lacks the courage and self-esteem to assert her will over his even though she knows that his "treatment" is harming her. Deprived of meaningful activity, purpose, and self-definition, the narrator's mind becomes confused and, predictably, childlike in its fascination with the shadows in the wallpaper.

In the end, the narrator triumphs over John—she literally crawls over him—but escapes from him only into madness. As a leading feminist lecturer and writer, Gilman found other options than madness to end her confinement in traditional definitions of womanhood. Eventually, Gilman divorced her husband, who married her best friend, and her husband and her best friend reared her child. The public, friends, and family so sharply censured Gilman for her actions that she knew many women would stay in unhealthy situations rather than risk such condemnation. By having the story end with the narrator's descent into insanity, Gilman laments the reality that few viable options exist for creative, intellectual women to escape the damaging social definitions of womanhood represented by John. In her horrifying depiction of a housewife gone mad, Gilman attempts to warn her readership that denying women full humanity is dangerous to women, family, and society as a whole.

Context

The publication of *The Yellow Wallpaper* had both immediate and long-term effects on women's issues. Gilman writes in her essay "Why I Wrote *The Yellow Wallpaper*" that the story was meant to save women from further suffering under the rest cure, and that her plan was successful. She says that after her former physician, Weir Mitchell, read a copy of the story that she had sent to him, he altered his treatment of women with nervous disorders. Therefore, the novella served an immediate purpose in the real, everyday lives of late nineteenth and early twentieth century women.

Originally viewed as a gothic horror story in the tradition of Edgar Allan Poe, *The Yellow Wallpaper* also helped to establish Gilman as an important woman writer in this genre. While few other critics gave it much attention, William Dean Howells praised the novella for its ability to "freeze the blood" and included it in his 1920 collection of *The Great Modern American Stories*. The novella became well known among such later horror writers as H. P. Lovecraft, who included it in *Supernatural Horror in Literature* (1945).

It was not until the 1970's and the advent of feminist scholarship, however, that critics began to explore the social, political, and cultural implications of *The Yellow Wallpaper*. Since then, feminist scholars have identified the novella as an indictment of a social structure which deters women's intellectual, psychological, and creative growth in an effort to keep women childlike and submissive. The work is now often included in American literature anthologies and feminist resources as a fine early example of fiction that criticizes social restrictions placed on women.

Feminist scholars have also found that the destructive impact of social definitions of womanhood on women of the late nineteenth and early twentieth centuries illustrated in this novella appear in other women's fiction of the time. For example, the central protagonist of Kate Chopin's *The Awakening* (1899) faces similar damaging social definitions of womanhood and, not finding a place for herself among them, commits suicide (not madness, but a similar escape). In another example, Mary E. Wilkins Freeman writes of a woman, "Old Woman Magoun," who allows her beloved granddaughter to die rather than be traded in a card deal; she then goes mad. Gilman was not alone in showing how misogynistic attitudes destroy women.

Sources for Further Study

Gilbert, Sandra M., and Susan Gubar. *The Madwoman in the Attic: The Woman Writer and the Nineteenth-Century Literary Imagination*. New Haven, Conn.: Yale University Press, 1979. One of the premier critical works on nineteenth century women writers. Includes a discussion of *The Yellow Wallpaper* linking the pattern in the wallpaper to patriarchal text patterns that women writers had to escape.

Gilman, Charlotte Perkins. "Why I Wrote *The Yellow Wallpaper*." *Forerunner* 4 (1913): 271. A one-page article in which Gilman explains that her main reason for writing *The Yellow Wallpaper* was to save other women from fates similar to her own under the rest cure.

Golden, Catherine. *The Captive Imagination: A Casebook on "The Yellow Wallpaper."* New York: Feminist Press, 1992. This indispensable compilation includes the text of *The Yellow Wallpaper* with the original illustrations, useful biographical and background information, well-selected critical essays, and a solid introduction.

Kolodny, Annette. "A Map for Rereading: Or, Gender and the Interpretation of Literary Texts." *New Literary History* 11, no. 3 (1980): 451-467. In this article, Kolodny argues that Gilman's contemporaries did not understand the implications of *The Yellow Wallpaper* because they did not have the context to understand her point.

Meyering, Sheryl L., ed. *Charlotte Perkins Gilman: The Woman and Her Work*. Ann Arbor, Mich.: UMI Research Press, 1989. An important collection of critical essays on Gilman and her works, including one by Linda Wagner-Martin focusing on *The Yellow Wallpaper*.

Amy E. Hudock

YONNONDIO: From the Thirties

Author: Tillie Olsen (1913-)
Type of work: Novel
Type of plot: Social realism
Time of plot: The early 1920's
Locale: Wyoming, South Dakota, and Nebraska
First published: 1974

Principal characters:

Anna Holbrook, a woman of the working class
Jim Holbrook, her husband, who loses much of his humanity through hardship
Mazie Holbrook, their child, who must face adversity
Will, Ben, Jim, and **Bess,** Mazie's siblings
Anna Mae, Gertrude ("Jinella") Skolnick, Erina, Ellie, Katie, and **Char,** Mazie's friends and playmates
Elias ("Old Man") Caldwell, a dying man who takes an interest in Mazie's life
Sheen McEvoy, Jim's coworker in the mine

Form and Content

Through the Holbrook family, *Yonnondio: From the Thirties* tells the stories of working people in three states and at least as many forms of employment. In particular, the novel shows Mazie Holbrook approaching her teen years and simultaneously developing a consciousness of the injustices and perplexities of the world, ranging from violence to avarice. Mazie stands on the developmental threshold between childhood and young adulthood, the emotional threshold between hope and despair, and the artistic threshold between creating beauty and yielding to the forces that would preempt or corrupt such beauty.

Yonnondio, Tillie Olsen's first novel, was published for the first time in 1974, but its writing was begun as early as 1932. At that time, Olsen hoped to unite her commitments as an artist and an activist by generating this socially conscious text. The novel's opening chapter, "The Iron Throat," originally appeared in *Partisan Review* in 1934. It is the only portion of the novel published when first written. Olsen completed the rest of the text in two stages spanning the intervening years. Therefore, the novel that she published in 1974 represents a painstaking reconstruction of text.

During the 1970's, Olsen received a grant from the MacDowell Colony, an artists' community, to attempt completion of her as yet unpublished novel. She resolved to assemble the novel entirely from extant manuscript pages, adding no new writing to the published text. Olsen spent five months there, weaving together remaining fragments of the earlier manuscript. Of the novel she first envisioned, Olsen laments in her epilogue to the 1974 book, "These pages you have read are all that is deemed publishable of it. Only fragments, rough drafts, outlines, scraps remain—to tell what might have been, and never will be now." This reclaiming of a Depression era story helps explain the work's subtitle, *From the Thirties*. The slender volume has an eight-chapter structure.

The novel's allusion in both title and epigram to poet Walt Whitman's "Yonnondio" underscores this issue of lost or vanishing speech. Indeed, narrative strategies employed throughout the novel recall the struggle to be heard. *Yonnondio* is a multivocal text, switching perspectives and forms of address frequently. At times, the narration reflects the awareness of young Mazie Holbrook. At other points, the narrative foregrounds the concerns of Mazie's mother, Anna Holbrook. Still other passages address the reader directly with commentary concerning matters of social, economic, and political injustice. Elements of dialogue provide acoustic detail through the speech patterns of individual characters. The shifting narrative voices of *Yonnondio* bring texture and dimension to the unfolding of its events and relationships. In keeping with this chorus of narrative voices, settings used within the novel—from mines to slaughterhouses—have one feature in common: a dense screen of industrial, agricultural, and human sound, over which characters must strain to make themselves heard. Contemplation and reflection, whether in overcrowded homes or mechanized work sites, seem nothing short of impossible within this environment.

Analysis

Olsen began *Yonnondio* as a novel of protest, which may explain why many literary critics have tended to discuss the novel chiefly in terms of the genre of 1930's proletarian fiction. This characterization of Olsen's text seems fitting from a thematic standpoint, because the story concerns a working-class family grappling with unemployment, workplace hazards, industrial strikes, illness, and poverty. It chronicles the plight of the working poor whose circumstances constantly threaten survival. In service of this objective, the novel documents even the smallest details of life for the Holbrooks, both inside and outside the home. Olsen suggests the spirit of ordinary citizens by demonstrating the full extent of the hardships that they endure. Therefore, without idealizing characters, Olsen furnishes the reader with ways to understand their actions and responses, even their acts of cruelty and desperation.

Yonnondio is not easily classified as exclusively a proletarian novel, however, because it has other important textual dimensions. Even if viewed as a work of proletarian fiction, Olsen's novel remains somewhat atypical of that genre of writing in the United States. Although *Yonnondio* registers Olsen's rejection of the prevailing orders of industrial capitalism and agribusiness, the novel declines to offer hope (to characters or to readers) in the form of a revolution or radical transformation of those orders. Apart from the implicit suggestions that existing gender roles constrain familial relations and that unorganized and nonunion workers become subject to endless indignities, relocations, and risks, Olsen's principled dissent stops short of establishing a specific position of political advocacy. Furthermore, although Olsen was once a member of the Young Communist League, her characters undergo no conversions to revolutionary consciousness.

Because Olsen writes *Yonnondio* from the perspective of a working woman and about the perspective of working women, she also helps address a rather large gap in the body of 1930's proletarian fiction, which concentrated chiefly on the plight of male workers. As a woman-centered text attentive to the working class, *Yonnondio* proves unusual among political fiction of the day, with the exception of the rediscovered texts of a few of Olsen's contemporaries, such as Fielding Burke, Agnes Smedley, Meridel Le Sueur, Tess Slesinger, and Josephine Herbst.

Olsen has asserted that her writings forgo the familiar preoccupation in fiction with heroic quests for identity. Forsaking such literary conventions as too much of a luxury for the people who populate *Yonnondio*, she calls attention to the more basic issue of human survival—social, economic, physical, and spiritual. Identity and self-determination, the ultimate attainments of heroic quest in literature, are far from sufficient to address the inequalities of conditions at work in this class- stratified world. Consequently, Olsen does not develop her characters as fully as is traditional within fiction. Instead, she sketches figures who are representative of a larger group or situation. Anna, for example, stands as the embattled familiar center. In efforts to sustain her family, Anna maintains some hope for her children, although she no longer hopes much for herself. Anna's dreams seem to have receded with her youth. Therefore, although a significant portion of the novel chronicles the experiences and perspective of Anna, she is not engaged in a heroic voyage of discovery. If anything, she has discovered more than she cares to of what this world has to offer her.

As published, *Yonnondio* concludes with a scene of the Holbrook family feverish in the heat of a summer night, a situation offset in some measure (and underlined in another) by the contrasting exuberance of young Bess at play. Anna's is the last voice heard in the text, uttering a modest hope for the day to come. Of that coming day, nothing is said and little more implied. Based upon the writer's early outlines for *Yonnondio*, however, Olsen anticipated a labor strike, Jim's abandonment of the family, and Anna's recurrent fate of pregnancy, this time faced alone. Left to support a large family on her own, Anna subsequently tries to secure an abortion. As the 1934 outline continues, Anna and Ben Holbrook both meet untimely deaths. The Holbrook children are then distributed to friends, other family members, and—in the case of Bess—an orphanage. In time, a homeless Mazie and Will venture to California, where Will becomes a political organizer for the American Communist Party.

Context

Through her poems, essays, and fictions, Tillie Olsen has devised and demonstrated a theory of women's writing as it is variously silenced in an androcentric culture. This novel, published belatedly and rescued from textual fragments written decades earlier, represents a case study in women's literary silence. It is the novel readers nearly did not see; it is a reconstituted work through which Olsen attempted "to tell what might have been, and never will be now." Even the women who appear in *Yonnondio*, most notably Mazie and Anna, find themselves restrained from artistic expression or fulfillment by the oppressive contexts in which they must operate. Therefore, Olsen calls attention not only to those silences that customarily punctuate cycles of writing activity but also to "unnatural" silences that, through circumstance, thwart otherwise productive writers or condemn them to obscurity.

With her concern for reconstructing narratives of the literary and cultural past, and her examples of how that objective might be approached (through both fiction and nonfiction), Olsen inspires readers and writers alike to take note of such silencing forces as gender roles limiting women's authority to engage writing with "totality of self" and notions of excellence that tend to render women's perspectives minor, marginal, or invisible. Among other factors, Olsen notes that the demands of marriage and motherhood compete with women's time and energy for written expression. Drawing from the lives of many of the most famous figures of women's literature written in English, Olsen observes that many such women never married: Louisa May Alcott, Jane Austen, Emily Brontë, Willa Cather, Emily Dickinson, Ellen Glasgow, Sarah Orne Jewett, Marianne Moore, Christina Rossetti, Gertrude Stein, and Eudora Welty. Other women writers did not marry until their thirties: Charlotte Brontë, Elizabeth Barrett Browning, George Eliot, and Olive Schreiner. Many writers, though married, were childless: Lillian Hellman, Katherine Mansfield, Dorothy Parker, Katherine Anne Porter, Dorothy Richardson, Edith Wharton, and Virginia Woolf.

Through her vivid reenvisioning of literary history, of voices both heard and unheard, Tillie Olsen has helped to initiate a praxis of feminist criticism, scholarship, and fiction directing itself toward a collective consciousness of women's journey into speech and struggle toward empowerment. Olsen's influence on both feminists and writers of the New Left can be discerned in the work of such women writers as Adrienne Rich and Susan Griffin.

Sources for Further Study

Duncan, Erika. *Unless Soul Clap Its Hands: Portraits and Passages*. New York: Schocken, 1984. Duncan's chapter on Tillie Olsen's life and work, based in part on her own interviews with Olsen, makes frequent reference to *Yonnondio*. Of particular interest is a rather detailed description of the original outline for elements not incorporated in the published text.

Olsen, Tillie. *Silences*. New York: Delacorte Press/Sarah Lawrence, 1978. Within this volume, Olsen has collected a number of her writings directly relating to women's struggle for a literary voice. Especially notable among these are two critical pieces, "Silences in Literature" and "One Out of Twelve: Writers Who Are Women in Our Century," in which Olsen renders the loss to literary history because of prohibitive economic and social restraints to women's writing.

Orr, Elaine Nell. *Tillie Olsen and a Feminist Spiritual Vision*. Jackson: University Press of Mississippi, 1987. Orr maintains that while Olsen's novel incorporates motifs associated with working-class literature, its writing is more aptly considered as an act of women's political and spiritual consciousness.

Pearlman, Mickey, and Abby H. P. Werlock. *Tille Olsen*. Boston: Twayne, 1991. This volume devotes a fifteen-page chapter to *Yonnondio*. Pearlman and Werlock characterize the novel in terms of its portrayal of themes such as disillusionment and loss, offset by Olsen's representations of moments marked by a transcendent human will.

Rosenfelt, Deborah. "From the Thirties: Tillie Olsen and the Radical Tradition." *Feminist Studies* 7, no. 3 (Fall, 1981): 389-394. This rich source of historical information situates Olsen in the context of radical literature associated with the 1930's Old Left. In this way, Olsen's work becomes linked to that of Edna St. Vincent Millay, Katherine Anne Porter, Mary McCarthy, and Dorothy Parker.

Stimpson, Catharine. *Where the Meanings Are*. New York: Methuen, 1988. In her sixth chapter, "Tillie Olsen: Witness as Servant (1977)," Stimpson explores the responsibilities of the writer as citizen as well as artist. She sees Olsen's novel as bearing witness to the lives of those often belittled or denied by previous literature, and she praises Olsen's ability to represent the interlocking oppressions of gender and class.

Yalom, Marilyn, Ed. *Women Writers of the West Coast: Speaking of Their Lives and Careers*. Santa Barbara, Calif.: Capra Press, 1983. The essay on Olsen included here has its origins in a dialogue between Olsen and Yalom. These conversations yielded a discussion of the experience of marginality. Also discusses the effect that Olsen achieves when she reads her works aloud.

Linda S. Watts

TITLE INDEX

AUTHOR INDEX